# THE COLLECTED SHORT STORIES OF EDITH WHARTON

A Digireads.com Book
Digireads.com Publishing

The Collected Short Stories of Edith Wharton
By Edith Wharton
ISBN 10: 1-4209-4152-6
ISBN 13: 978-1-4209-4152-4

Please visit *www.digireads.com*

# CONTENTS

4

# MRS. MANSTEY'S VIEW

As first published in *Scribner's Magazine*, July, 1891

THE VIEW from Mrs. Manstey's window was not a striking one, but to her at least it was full of interest and beauty. Mrs. Manstey occupied the back room on the third floor of a New York boarding-house, in a street where the ash-barrels lingered late on the sidewalk and the gaps in the pavement would have staggered a Quintus Curtius. She was the widow of a clerk in a large wholesale house, and his death had left her alone, for her only daughter had married in California, and could not afford the long journey to New York to see her mother. Mrs. Manstey, perhaps, might have joined her daughter in the West, but they had now been so many years apart that they had ceased to feel any need of each other's society, and their intercourse had long been limited to the exchange of a few perfunctory letters, written with indifference by the daughter, and with difficulty by Mrs. Manstey, whose right hand was growing stiff with gout. Even had she felt a stronger desire for her daughter's companionship, Mrs. Manstey's increasing infirmity, which caused her to dread the three flights of stairs between her room and the street, would have given her pause on the eve of undertaking so long a journey; and without perhaps, formulating these reasons she had long since accepted as a matter of course her solitary life in New York.

She was, indeed, not quite lonely, for a few friends still toiled up now and then to her room; but their visits grew rare as the years went by. Mrs. Manstey had never been a sociable woman, and during her husband's lifetime his companionship had been all-sufficient to her. For many years she had cherished a desire to live in the country, to have a hen-house and a garden; but this longing had faded with age, leaving only in the breast of the uncommunicative old woman a vague tenderness for plants and animals. It was, perhaps, this tenderness which made her cling so fervently to her view from her window, a view in which the most optimistic eye would at first have failed to discover anything admirable.

Mrs. Manstey, from her coign of vantage (a slightly projecting bow-window where she nursed an ivy and a succession of unwholesome-looking bulbs), looked out first upon the yard of her own dwelling, of which, however, she could get but a restricted glimpse. Still, her gaze took in the topmost boughs of the ailanthus below her window, and she knew how early each year the clump of dicentra strung its bending stalk with hearts of pink.

But of greater interest were the yards beyond. Being for the most part attached to boarding-houses they were in a state of chronic untidiness and fluttering, on certain days of the week, with miscellaneous garments and frayed table-cloths. In spite of this Mrs. Manstey found much to admire in the long vista which she commanded. Some of the yards were, indeed, but stony wastes, with grass in the cracks of the pavement and no shade in spring save that afforded by the intermittent leafage of the clothes-lines. These yards Mrs. Manstey disapproved of, but the others, the green ones, she loved. She had grown used to their disorder; the broken barrels, the empty bottles and paths unswept no longer annoyed her; hers was the happy faculty of dwelling on the pleasanter side of the prospect before her.

In the very next enclosure did not a magnolia open its hard white flowers against the watery blue of April? And was there not, a little way down the line, a fence foamed over every May be lilac waves of wisteria? Farther still, a horse-chestnut lifted its candelabra of buff and pink blossoms above broad fans of foliage; while in the opposite yard June was sweet with the breath of a neglected syringa, which persisted in growing in spite of the countless obstacles opposed to its welfare.

But if nature occupied the front rank in Mrs. Manstey's view, there was much of a more personal character to interest her in the aspect of the houses and their inmates. She deeply disapproved of the mustard-colored curtains which had lately been hung in the doctor's window opposite; but she glowed with pleasure when the house farther down had its old bricks washed with a coat of paint. The occupants of the houses did not often show themselves at the back windows, but the servants were always in sight. Noisy slatterns, Mrs. Manstey pronounced the greater number; she knew their ways and hated them. But to the quiet cook in the newly painted house, whose mistress bullied her, and who secretly fed the stray cats at nightfall, Mrs. Manstey's warmest sympathies were given. On one occasion her feelings were racked by the neglect of a housemaid, who for two days forgot to feed the parrot committed to her care. On the third day, Mrs. Manstey, in spite of her gouty hand, had just penned a letter, beginning: "Madam, it is now three days since your parrot has been fed," when the forgetful maid appeared at the window with a cup of seed in her hand.

But in Mrs. Manstey's more meditative moods it was the narrowing perspective of far-off yards which pleased her best. She loved, at twilight, when the distant brown-stone spire seemed melting in the fluid yellow of the west, to lose herself in vague memories of a trip to Europe, made years ago, and now reduced in her mind's eye to a pale phantasmagoria of indistinct steeples and dreamy skies. Perhaps at heart Mrs. Manstey was an artist; at all events she was sensible of many changes of color unnoticed by the average eye, and dear to her as the green of early spring was the black lattice of branches against a cold sulphur sky at the close of a snowy day. She enjoyed, also, the sunny thaws of March, when patches of earth showed through the snow, like ink-spots spreading on a sheet of white blotting-paper; and, better still, the haze of boughs, leafless but swollen, which replaced the clear-cut tracery of winter. She even watched with a certain interest the trail of smoke from a far-off factory chimney, and missed a detail in the landscape when the factory was closed and the smoke disappeared.

Mrs. Manstey, in the long hours which she spent at her window, was not idle. She read a little, and knitted numberless stockings; but the view surrounded and shaped her life as the sea does a lonely island. When her rare callers came it was difficult for her to detach herself from the contemplation of the opposite window-washing, or the scrutiny of certain green points in a neighboring flower-bed which might, or might not, turn into hyacinths, while she feigned an interest in her visitor's anecdotes about some unknown grandchild. Mrs. Manstey's real friends were the denizens of the yards, the hyacinths, the magnolia, the green parrot, the maid who fed the cats, the doctor who studied late behind his mustard-colored curtains; and the confidant of her tenderer musings was the church-spire floating in the sunset.

One April day, as she sat in her usual place, with knitting cast aside and eyes fixed on the blue sky mottled with round clouds, a knock at the door announced the entrance of her landlady. Mrs. Manstey did not care for her landlady, but she submitted to her visits with ladylike resignation. To-day, however, it seemed harder than usual to turn from the blue sky and the blossoming magnolia to Mrs. Sampson's unsuggestive face, and Mrs. Manstey was conscious of a distinct effort as she did so.

"The magnolia is out earlier than usual this year, Mrs. Sampson," she remarked, yielding to a rare impulse, for she seldom alluded to the absorbing interest of her life. In the first place it was a topic not likely to appeal to her visitors and, besides, she lacked the power of expression and could not have given utterance to her feelings had she wished to.

"The what, Mrs. Manstey?" inquired the landlady, glancing about the room as if to find there the explanation of Mrs. Manstey's statement.

"The magnolia in the next yard—in Mrs. Black's yard," Mrs. Manstey repeated.

"Is it, indeed? I didn't know there was a magnolia there," said Mrs. Sampson, carelessly. Mrs. Manstey looked at her; she did not know that there was a magnolia in the next yard!

"By the way," Mrs. Sampson continued, "speaking of Mrs. Black reminds me that the work on the extension is to begin next week."

"The what?" it was Mrs. Manstey's turn to ask.

"The extension," said Mrs. Sampson, nodding her head in the direction of the ignored magnolia. "You knew, of course, that Mrs. Black was going to build an extension to her house? Yes, ma'am. I hear it is to run right back to the end of the yard. How she can afford to build an extension in these hard times I don't see; but she always was crazy about building. She used to keep a boarding-house in Seventeenth Street, and she nearly ruined herself then by sticking out bow-windows and what not; I should have thought that would have cured her of building, but I guess it's a disease, like drink. Anyhow, the work is to begin on Monday."

Mrs. Manstey had grown pale. She always spoke slowly, so the landlady did not heed the long pause which followed. At last Mrs. Manstey said: "Do you know how high the extension will be?"

"That's the most absurd part of it. The extension is to be built right up to the roof of the main building; now, did you ever?"

Mrs. Manstey paused again. "Won't it be a great annoyance to you, Mrs. Sampson?" she asked.

"I should say it would. But there's no help for it; if people have got a mind to build extensions there's no law to prevent 'em, that I'm aware of." Mrs. Manstey, knowing this, was silent. "There is no help for it," Mrs. Sampson repeated, "but if I AM a church member, I wouldn't be so sorry if it ruined Eliza Black. Well, good-day, Mrs. Manstey; I'm glad to find you so comfortable."

So comfortable—so comfortable! Left to herself the old woman turned once more to the window. How lovely the view was that day! The blue sky with its round clouds shed a brightness over everything; the ailanthus had put on a tinge of yellow-green, the hyacinths were budding, the magnolia flowers looked more than ever like rosettes carved in alabaster. Soon the wisteria would bloom, then the horse-chestnut; but not for her. Between her eyes and them a barrier of brick and mortar would swiftly rise; presently even the spire would disappear, and all her radiant world be blotted out. Mrs. Manstey sent away untouched the dinner-tray brought to her that evening. She lingered in the window until the windy sunset died in bat-colored dusk; then, going to bed, she lay sleepless all night.

Early the next day she was up and at the window. It was raining, but even through the slanting gray gauze the scene had its charm—and then the rain was so good for the trees. She had noticed the day before that the ailanthus was growing dusty.

"Of course I might move," said Mrs. Manstey aloud, and turning from the window she looked about her room. She might move, of course; so might she be flayed alive; but she was not likely to survive either operation. The room, though far less important to her happiness than the view, was as much a part of her existence. She had lived in it seventeen years. She knew every stain on the wall-paper, every rent in the carpet; the light fell in a certain way on her engravings, her books had grown shabby on their shelves, her bulbs and ivy were used to their window and knew which way to lean to the sun. "We are all too old to move," she said.

That afternoon it cleared. Wet and radiant the blue reappeared through torn rags of cloud; the ailanthus sparkled; the earth in the flower-borders looked rich and warm. It was Thursday, and on Monday the building of the extension was to begin.

On Sunday afternoon a card was brought to Mrs. Black, as she was engaged in gathering up the fragments of the boarders' dinner in the basement. The card, black-edged, bore Mrs. Manstey's name.

"One of Mrs. Sampson's boarders; wants to move, I suppose. Well, I can give her a room next year in the extension. Dinah," said Mrs. Black, "tell the lady I'll be upstairs in a minute."

Mrs. Black found Mrs. Manstey standing in the long parlor garnished with statuettes and antimacassars; in that house she could not sit down.

Stooping hurriedly to open the register, which let out a cloud of dust, Mrs. Black advanced on her visitor.

"I'm happy to meet you, Mrs. Manstey; take a seat, please," the landlady remarked in her prosperous voice, the voice of a woman who can afford to build extensions. There was no help for it; Mrs. Manstey sat down.

"Is there anything I can do for you, ma'am?" Mrs. Black continued. "My house is full at present, but I am going to build an extension, and—"

"It is about the extension that I wish to speak," said Mrs. Manstey, suddenly. "I am a poor woman, Mrs. Black, and I have never been a happy one. I shall have to talk about myself first to—to make you understand."

Mrs. Black, astonished but imperturbable, bowed at this parenthesis.

"I never had what I wanted," Mrs. Manstey continued. "It was always one disappointment after another. For years I wanted to live in the country. I dreamed and dreamed about it; but we never could manage it. There was no sunny window in our house, and so all my plants died. My daughter married years ago and went away— besides, she never cared for the same things. Then my husband died and I was left alone. That was seventeen years ago. I went to live at Mrs. Sampson's, and I have been there ever since. I have grown a little infirm, as you see, and I don't get out often; only on fine days, if I am feeling very well. So you can understand my sitting a great deal in my window—the back window on the third floor—"

"Well, Mrs. Manstey," said Mrs. Black, liberally, "I could give you a back room, I dare say; one of the new rooms in the ex—"

"But I don't want to move; I can't move," said Mrs. Manstey, almost with a scream. "And I came to tell you that if you build that extension I shall have no view from my window—no view! Do you understand?"

Mrs. Black thought herself face to face with a lunatic, and she had always heard that lunatics must be humored.

"Dear me, dear me," she remarked, pushing her chair back a little way, "that is too bad, isn't it? Why, I never thought of that. To be sure, the extension *will* interfere with your view, Mrs. Manstey."

"You do understand?" Mrs. Manstey gasped.

"Of course I do. And I'm real sorry about it, too. But there, don't you worry, Mrs.

Manstey. I guess we can fix that all right."

Mrs. Manstey rose from her seat, and Mrs. Black slipped toward the door.

"What do you mean by fixing it? Do you mean that I can induce you to change your mind about the extension? Oh, Mrs. Black, listen to me. I have two thousand dollars in the bank and I could manage, I know I could manage, to give you a thousand if—" Mrs. Manstey paused; the tears were rolling down her cheeks.

"There, there, Mrs. Manstey, don't you worry," repeated Mrs. Black, soothingly. "I am sure we can settle it. I am sorry that I can't stay and talk about it any longer, but this is such a busy time of day, with supper to get—"

Her hand was on the door-knob, but with sudden vigor Mrs. Manstey seized her wrist.

"You are not giving me a definite answer. Do you mean to say that you accept my proposition?"

"Why, I'll think it over, Mrs. Manstey, certainly I will. I wouldn't annoy you for the world—"

"But the work is to begin tomorrow, I am told," Mrs. Manstey persisted.

Mrs. Black hesitated. "It shan't begin, I promise you that; I'll send word to the builder this very night." Mrs. Manstey tightened her hold.

"You are not deceiving me, are you?" she said.

"No—no," stammered Mrs. Black. "How can you think such a thing of me, Mrs. Manstey?"

Slowly Mrs. Manstey's clutch relaxed, and she passed through the open door. "One thousand dollars," she repeated, pausing in the hall; then she let herself out of the house and hobbled down the steps, supporting herself on the cast-iron railing.

"My goodness," exclaimed Mrs. Black, shutting and bolting the hall-door, "I never knew the old woman was crazy! And she looks so quiet and ladylike, too."

Mrs. Manstey slept well that night, but early the next morning she was awakened by a sound of hammering. She got to her window with what haste she might and, looking out saw that Mrs. Black's yard was full of workmen. Some were carrying loads of brick from the kitchen to the yard, others beginning to demolish the old-fashioned wooden balcony which adorned each story of Mrs. Black's house. Mrs. Manstey saw that she had been deceived. At first she thought of confiding her trouble to Mrs. Sampson, but a settled discouragement soon took possession of her and she went back to bed, not caring to see what was going on.

Toward afternoon, however, feeling that she must know the worst, she rose and dressed herself. It was a laborious task, for her hands were stiffer than usual, and the hooks and buttons seemed to evade her.

When she seated herself in the window, she saw that the workmen had removed the upper part of the balcony, and that the bricks had multiplied since morning. One of the men, a coarse fellow with a bloated face, picked a magnolia blossom and, after smelling it, threw it to the ground; the next man, carrying a load of bricks, trod on the flower in passing.

"Look out, Jim," called one of the men to another who was smoking a pipe, "if you throw matches around near those barrels of paper you'll have the old tinder-box burning down before you know it." And Mrs. Manstey, leaning forward, perceived that there were several barrels of paper and rubbish under the wooden balcony.

At length the work ceased and twilight fell. The sunset was perfect and a roseate light, transfiguring the distant spire, lingered late in the west. When it grew dark Mrs.

Manstey drew down the shades and proceeded, in her usual methodical manner, to light her lamp. She always filled and lit it with her own hands, keeping a kettle of kerosene on a zinc-covered shelf in a closet. As the lamp-light filled the room it assumed its usual peaceful aspect. The books and pictures and plants seemed, like their mistress, to settle themselves down for another quiet evening, and Mrs. Manstey, as was her wont, drew up her armchair to the table and began to knit.

That night she could not sleep. The weather had changed and a wild wind was abroad, blotting the stars with close-driven clouds. Mrs. Manstey rose once or twice and looked out of the window; but of the view nothing was discernible save a tardy light or two in the opposite windows. These lights at last went out, and Mrs. Manstey, who had watched for their extinction, began to dress herself. She was in evident haste, for she merely flung a thin dressing-gown over her night-dress and wrapped her head in a scarf; then she opened her closet and cautiously took out the kettle of kerosene. Having slipped a bundle of wooden matches into her pocket she proceeded, with increasing precautions, to unlock her door, and a few moments later she was feeling her way down the dark staircase, led by a glimmer of gas from the lower hall. At length she reached the bottom of the stairs and began the more difficult descent into the utter darkness of the basement. Here, however, she could move more freely, as there was less danger of being overheard; and without much delay she contrived to unlock the iron door leading into the yard. A gust of cold wind smote her as she stepped out and groped shiveringly under the clothes-lines.

That morning at three o'clock an alarm of fire brought the engines to Mrs. Black's door, and also brought Mrs. Sampson's startled boarders to their windows. The wooden balcony at the back of Mrs. Black's house was ablaze, and among those who watched the progress of the flames was Mrs. Manstey, leaning in her thin dressing-gown from the open window.

The fire, however, was soon put out, and the frightened occupants of the house, who had fled in scant attire, reassembled at dawn to find that little mischief had been done beyond the cracking of window panes and smoking of ceilings. In fact, the chief sufferer by the fire was Mrs. Manstey, who was found in the morning gasping with pneumonia, a not unnatural result, as everyone remarked, of her having hung out of an open window at her age in a dressing-gown. It was easy to see that she was very ill, but no one had guessed how grave the doctor's verdict would be, and the faces gathered that evening about Mrs. Sampson's table were awestruck and disturbed. Not that any of the boarders knew Mrs. Manstey well; she "kept to herself," as they said, and seemed to fancy herself too good for them; but then it is always disagreeable to have anyone dying in the house and, as one lady observed to another: "It might just as well have been you or me, my dear."

But it was only Mrs. Manstey; and she was dying, as she had lived, lonely if not alone. The doctor had sent a trained nurse, and Mrs. Sampson, with muffled step, came in from time to time; but both, to Mrs. Manstey, seemed remote and unsubstantial as the figures in a dream. All day she said nothing; but when she was asked for her daughter's address she shook her head. At times the nurse noticed that she seemed to be listening attentively for some sound which did not come; then again she dozed.

The next morning at daylight she was very low. The nurse called Mrs. Sampson and as the two bent over the old woman they saw her lips move.

"Lift me up—out of bed," she whispered.

They raised her in their arms, and with her stiff hand she pointed to the window.

"Oh, the window—she wants to sit in the window. She used to sit there all day," Mrs. Sampson explained. "It can do her no harm, I suppose?"

"Nothing matters now," said the nurse.

They carried Mrs. Manstey to the window and placed her in her chair. The dawn was abroad, a jubilant spring dawn; the spire had already caught a golden ray, though the magnolia and horse-chestnut still slumbered in shadow. In Mrs. Black's yard all was quiet. The charred timbers of the balcony lay where they had fallen. It was evident that since the fire the builders had not returned to their work. The magnolia had unfolded a few more sculptural flowers; the view was undisturbed.

It was hard for Mrs. Manstey to breathe; each moment it grew more difficult. She tried to make them open the window, but they would not understand. If she could have tasted the air, sweet with the penetrating ailanthus savor, it would have eased her; but the view at least was there—the spire was golden now, the heavens had warmed from pearl to blue, day was alight from east to west, even the magnolia had caught the sun.

Mrs. Manstey's head fell back and smiling she died.

That day the building of the extension was resumed.

## THE FULLNESS OF LIFE

As first published in *Scribner's Magazine*, December, 1893

FOR HOURS she had lain in a kind of gentle torpor, not unlike that sweet lassitude which masters one in the hush of a midsummer noon, when the heat seems to have silenced the very birds and insects, and, lying sunk in the tasseled meadow grasses, one looks up through a level roofing of maple-leaves at the vast shadowless, and unsuggestive blue. Now and then, at ever-lengthening intervals, a flash of pain darted through her, like the ripple of sheet-lightning across such a midsummer sky; but it was too transitory to shake her stupor, that calm, delicious, bottomless stupor into which she felt herself sinking more and more deeply, without a disturbing impulse of resistance, an effort of reattachment to the vanishing edges of consciousness.

The resistance, the effort, had known their hour of violence; but now they were at an end. Through her mind, long harried by grotesque visions, fragmentary images of the life that she was leaving, tormenting lines of verse, obstinate presentments of pictures once beheld, indistinct impressions of rivers, towers, and cupolas, gathered in the length of journeys half forgotten—through her mind there now only moved a few primal sensations of colorless well-being; a vague satisfaction in the thought that she had swallowed her noxious last draught of medicine . . . and that she should never again hear the creaking of her husband's boots—those horrible boots—and that no one would come to bother her about the next day's dinner . . . or the butcher's book. . . .

At last even these dim sensations spent themselves in the thickening obscurity which enveloped her; a dusk now filled with pale geometric roses, circling softly, interminably before her, now darkened to a uniform blue-blackness, the hue of a summer night without stars. And into this darkness she felt herself sinking, sinking, with the gentle sense of security of one upheld from beneath. Like a tepid tide it rose around her, gliding ever higher and higher, folding in its velvety embrace her relaxed and tired body, now submerging her breast and shoulders, now creeping gradually, with soft inexorableness, over her throat to her chin, to her ears, to her mouth. . . . Ah, now it was rising too high; the impulse to struggle was renewed . . . her mouth was full . . . she was choking. . . .

Help!

"It is all over," said the nurse, drawing down the eyelids with official composure.

The clock struck three. They remembered it afterward. Someone opened the window and let in a blast of that strange, neutral air which walks the earth between darkness and dawn; someone else led the husband into another room. He walked vaguely, like a blind man, on his creaking boots.

## II

SHE stood, as it seemed, on a threshold, yet no tangible gateway was in front of her. Only a wide vista of light, mild yet penetrating as the gathered glimmer of innumerable stars, expanded gradually before her eyes, in blissful contrast to the cavernous darkness from which she had of late emerged.

She stepped forward, not frightened, but hesitating, and as her eyes began to grow more familiar with the melting depths of light about her, she distinguished the outlines of a landscape, at first swimming in the opaline uncertainty of Shelley's vaporous creations, then gradually resolved into distincter shape—the vast unrolling of a sunlit plain, aerial forms of mountains, and presently the silver crescent of a river in the valley, and a blue stenciling of trees along its curve—something suggestive in its ineffable hue of an azure background of Leonardo's, strange, enchanting, mysterious, leading on the eye and the imagination into regions of fabulous delight. As she gazed, her heart beat with a soft and rapturous surprise; so exquisite a promise she read in the summons of that hyaline distance.

"And so death is not the end after all," in sheer gladness she heard herself exclaiming aloud. "I always knew that it couldn't be. I believed in Darwin, of course. I do still; but then Darwin himself said that he wasn't sure about the soul—at least, I think he did—and Wallace was a spiritualist; and then there was St. George Mivart—"

Her gaze lost itself in the ethereal remoteness of the mountains.

"How beautiful! How satisfying!" she murmured. "Perhaps now I shall really know what it is to live."

As she spoke she felt a sudden thickening of her heart-beats, and looking up she was aware that before her stood the Spirit of Life.

"Have you never really known what it is to live?" the Spirit of Life asked her.

"I have never known," she replied, "that fullness of life which we all feel ourselves capable of knowing; though my life has not been without scattered hints of it, like the scent of earth which comes to one sometimes far out at sea."

"And what do you call the fullness of life?" the Spirit asked again.

"Oh, I can't tell you, if you don't know," she said, almost reproachfully. "Many words are supposed to define it—love and sympathy are those in commonest use, but I am not even sure that they are the right ones, and so few people really know what they mean."

"You were married," said the Spirit, "yet you did not find the fullness of life in your marriage?"

"Oh, dear, no," she replied, with an indulgent scorn, "my marriage was a very incomplete affair."

"And yet you were fond of your husband?"

"You have hit upon the exact word; I was fond of him, yes, just as I was fond of my grandmother, and the house that I was born in, and my old nurse. Oh, I was fond of him, and we were counted a very happy couple. But I have sometimes thought that a woman's nature is like a great house full of rooms: there is the hall, through which everyone passes in going in and out; the drawing room, where one receives formal visits; the sitting-room, where the members of the family come and go as they list; but beyond that, far beyond, are other rooms, the handles of whose doors perhaps are never turned; no one knows the way to them, no one knows whither they lead; and in the innermost room, the holy of holies, the soul sits alone and waits for a footstep that never comes."

"And your husband," asked the Spirit, after a pause, "never got beyond the family sitting-room?"

"Never," she returned, impatiently; "and the worst of it was that he was quite content to remain there. He thought it perfectly beautiful, and sometimes, when he was admiring its commonplace furniture, insignificant as the chairs and tables of a hotel parlor, I felt like crying out to him: 'Fool, will you never guess that close at hand are rooms full of treasures and wonders, such as the eye of man hath not seen, rooms that no step has crossed, but that might be yours to live in, could you but find the handle of the door?'"

"Then," the Spirit continued, "those moments of which you lately spoke, which seemed to come to you like scattered hints of the fullness of life, were not shared with your husband?"

"Oh, no—never. He was different. His boots creaked, and he always slammed the door when he went out, and he never read anything but railway novels and the sporting advertisements in the papers—and—and, in short, we never understood each other in the least."

"To what influence, then, did you owe those exquisite sensations?"

"I can hardly tell. Sometimes to the perfume of a flower; sometimes to a verse of Dante or of Shakespeare; sometimes to a picture or a sunset, or to one of those calm days at sea, when one seems to be lying in the hollow of a blue pearl; sometimes, but rarely, to a word spoken by someone who chanced to give utterance, at the right moment, to what I felt but could not express."

"Someone whom you loved?" asked the Spirit.

"I never loved anyone, in that way," she said, rather sadly, "nor was I thinking of any one person when I spoke, but of two or three who, by touching for an instant upon a certain chord of my being, had called forth a single note of that strange melody which seemed sleeping in my soul. It has seldom happened, however, that I have owed such feelings to people; and no one ever gave me a moment of such happiness as it was my lot to feel one evening in the Church of Or San Michele, in Florence."

"Tell me about it," said the Spirit.

"It was near sunset on a rainy spring afternoon in Easter week. The clouds had vanished, dispersed by a sudden wind, and as we entered the church the fiery panes of the high windows shone out like lamps through the dusk. A priest was at the high altar, his white cope a livid spot in the incense-laden obscurity, the light of the candles flickering up and down like fireflies about his head; a few people knelt near by. We stole behind them and sat down on a bench close to the tabernacle of Orcagna.

"Strange to say, though Florence was not new to me, I had never been in the church before; and in that magical light I saw for the first time the inlaid steps, the fluted columns, the sculptured bas-reliefs and canopy of the marvelous shrine. The marble, worn and mellowed by the subtle hand of time, took on an unspeakable rosy hue, suggestive in some remote way of the honey-colored columns of the Parthenon, but more mystic, more complex, a color not born of the sun's inveterate kiss, but made up of cryptal twilight, and the flame of candles upon martyrs' tombs, and gleams of sunset through symbolic panes of chrysoprase and ruby; such a light as illumines the missiles in the library of Siena, or burns like a hidden fire through the Madonna of Gian Bellini in the Church of the Redeemer, at Venice; the light of the Middle Ages, richer, more solemn, more significant than the limpid sunshine of Greece.

"The church was silent, but for the wail of the priest and the occasional scraping of a chair against the floor, and as I sat there, bathed in that light, absorbed in rapt contemplation of the marble miracle which rose before me, cunningly wrought as a casket of ivory and enriched with jewel-like incrustations and tarnished gleams of gold, I felt myself borne onward along a mighty current, whose source seemed to be in the very beginning of things, and whose tremendous waters gathered as they went all the mingled streams of human passion and endeavor. Life in all its varied manifestations of beauty and strangeness seemed weaving a rhythmical dance around me as I moved, and wherever the spirit of man had passed I knew that my foot had once been familiar.

"As I gazed the mediaeval bosses of the tabernacle of Orcagna seemed to melt and flow into their primal forms so that the folded lotus of the Nile and the Greek acanthus were braided with the runic knots and fish-tailed monsters of the North, and all the plastic terror and beauty born of man's hand from the Ganges to the Baltic quivered and mingled in Orcagna's apotheosis of Mary. And so the river bore me on, past the alien face of antique civilizations and the familiar wonders of Greece, till I swam upon the fiercely rushing tide of the Middle Ages, with its swirling eddies of passion, its heaven-reflecting pools of poetry and art; I heard the rhythmic blow of the craftsmen's hammers in the goldsmiths' workshops and on the walls of churches, the party-cries of armed factions in the narrow streets, the organ roll of Dante's verse, the crackle of the fagots around Arnold of Brescia, the twitter of the swallows to which St. Francis preached, the laughter of the ladies listening on the hillside to the quips of the Decameron, while plague-struck Florence howled beneath them—all this and much more I heard, joined in strange unison with voices earlier and more remote, fierce, passionate, or tender, yet subdued to such awful harmony that I thought of the song that the morning stars sang together and felt as though it were sounding in my ears. My heart beat to suffocation, the tears burned my lids, the joy, the mystery of it seemed too intolerable to be borne. I could not understand even then the words of the song; but I knew that if there had been someone at my side who could have heard it with me, we might have found the key to it together.

"I turned to my husband, who was sitting beside me in an attitude of patient dejection, gazing into the bottom of his hat; but at that moment he rose, and stretching his stiffened legs, said, mildly: 'Hadn't we better be going? There doesn't seem to be much to see here, and you know the table d'hôte dinner is at half-past six o'clock.'"

Her recital ended, there was an interval of silence; then the Spirit of Life said: "There is a compensation in store for such needs as you have expressed."

"Oh, then you *do* understand?" she exclaimed. "Tell me what compensation, I entreat you!"

"It is ordained," the Spirit answered, "that every soul which seeks in vain on earth for a kindred soul to whom it can lay bare its inmost being shall find that soul here and be united to it for eternity."

A glad cry broke from her lips. "Ah, shall I find him at last?" she cried, exultant.

"He is here," said the Spirit of Life.

She looked up and saw that a man stood near whose soul (for in that unwonted light she seemed to see his soul more clearly than his face) drew her toward him with an invincible force.

"Are you really he?" she murmured.

"I am he," he answered.

She laid her hand in his and drew him toward the parapet which overhung the valley.

"Shall we go down together," she asked him, "into that marvelous country; shall we see it together, as if with the self-same eyes, and tell each other in the same words all that we think and feel?"

"So," he replied, "have I hoped and dreamed."

"What?" she asked, with rising joy. "Then you, too, have looked for me?"

"All my life."

"How wonderful! And did you never, never find anyone in the other world who understood you?"

"Not wholly—not as you and I understand each other."

"Then you feel it, too? Oh, I am happy," she sighed.

They stood, hand in hand, looking down over the parapet upon the shimmering landscape which stretched forth beneath them into sapphirine space, and the Spirit of Life, who kept watch near the threshold, heard now and then a floating fragment of their talk blown backward like the stray swallows which the wind sometimes separates from their migratory tribe.

"Did you never feel at sunset—"

"Ah, yes; but I never heard anyone else say so. Did you?"

"Do you remember that line in the third canto of the *Inferno*?"

"Ah, that line—my favorite always. Is it possible—"

"You know the stooping 'Victory' in the frieze of the 'Nike Apteros'?"

"You mean the one who is tying her sandal? Then you have noticed, too, that all Botticelli and Mantegna are dormant in those flying folds of her drapery?"

"After a storm in autumn have you never seen—"

"Yes, it is curious how certain flowers suggest certain painters-the perfume of the incarnation, Leonardo; that of the rose, Titian; the tuberose, Crivelli—"

"I never supposed that anyone else had noticed it."

"Have you never thought—"

"Oh, yes, often and often; but I never dreamed that anyone else had."

"But surely you must have felt—"

"Oh, yes, yes; and you, too—"

"How beautiful! How strange—"

Their voices rose and fell, like the murmur of two fountains answering each other across a garden full of flowers. At length, with a certain tender impatience, he turned to her and said: "Love, why should we linger here? All eternity lies before us. Let us go down into that beautiful country together and make a home for ourselves on some blue hill above the shining river."

As he spoke, the hand she had forgotten in his was suddenly withdrawn, and he felt that a cloud was passing over the radiance of her soul.

"A home," she repeated, slowly, "a home for you and me to live in for all eternity?"

"Why not, love? Am I not the soul that yours has sought?"

"Y-yes—yes, I know—but, don't you see, home would not be like home to me, unless—"

"Unless?" he wonderingly repeated.

She did not answer, but she thought to herself, with an impulse of whimsical inconsistency, "Unless you slammed the door and wore creaking boots."

But he had recovered his hold upon her hand, and by imperceptible degrees was leading her toward the shining steps which descended to the valley.

"Come, O my soul's soul," he passionately implored; "why delay a moment? Surely you feel, as I do, that eternity itself is too short to hold such bliss as ours. It seems to me that I can see our home already. Have I not always seem it in my dreams? It is white, love, is it not, with polished columns, and a sculptured cornice against the blue? Groves of laurel and oleander and thickets of roses surround it; but from the terrace where we walk at sunset, the eye looks out over woodlands and cool meadows where, deep-bowered under ancient boughs, a stream goes delicately toward the river. Indoors our favorite pictures hang upon the walls and the rooms are lined with books. Think, dear, at last we shall have time to read them all. With which shall we begin? Come, help me to choose. Shall it be *Faust* or the *Vita Nuova*, *The Tempest* or *Les Caprices de Marianne*, or the thirty-first canto of the *Paradise*, or *Epipsychidion* or *Lycidas*? Tell me, dear, which one?"

As he spoke he saw the answer trembling joyously upon her lips; but it died in the ensuing silence, and she stood motionless, resisting the persuasion of his hand.

"What is it?" he entreated.

"Wait a moment," she said, with a strange hesitation in her voice. "Tell me first, are you quite sure of yourself? Is there no one on earth whom you sometimes remember?"

"Not since I have seen you," he replied; for, being a man, he had indeed forgotten.

Still she stood motionless, and he saw that the shadow deepened on her soul.

"Surely, love," he rebuked her, "it was not that which troubled you? For my part I have walked through Lethe. The past has melted like a cloud before the moon. I never lived until I saw you."

She made no answer to his pleadings, but at length, rousing herself with a visible effort, she turned away from him and moved toward the Spirit of Life, who still stood near the threshold.

"I want to ask you a question," she said, in a troubled voice.

"Ask," said the Spirit.

"A little while ago," she began, slowly, "you told me that every soul which has not found a kindred soul on earth is destined to find one here."

"And have you not found one?" asked the Spirit.

"Yes; but will it be so with my husband's soul also?"

"No," answered the Spirit of Life, "for your husband imagined that he had found his soul's mate on earth in you; and for such delusions eternity itself contains no cure."

She gave a little cry. Was it of disappointment or triumph?

"Then—then what will happen to him when he comes here?"

"That I cannot tell you. Some field of activity and happiness he will doubtless find, in due measure to his capacity for being active and happy."

She interrupted, almost angrily: "He will never be happy without me."

"Do not be too sure of that," said the Spirit.

She took no notice of this, and the Spirit continued: "He will not understand you here any better than he did on earth."

"No matter," she said; "I shall be the only sufferer, for he always thought that he understood me."

"His boots will creak just as much as ever—"

"No matter."

"And he will slam the door—"

"Very likely."

"And continue to read railway novels—"

She interposed, impatiently: "Many men do worse than that."

"But you said just now," said the Spirit, "that you did not love him."

"True," she answered, simply; "but don't you understand that I shouldn't feel at home without him? It is all very well for a week or two—but for eternity! After all, I never minded the creaking of his boots, except when my head ached, and I don't suppose it will ache *here*; and he was always so sorry when he had slammed the door, only he never *could* remember not to. Besides, no one else would know how to look after him, he is so helpless. His inkstand would never be filled, and he would always be out of stamps and visiting-cards. He would never remember to have his umbrella re-covered, or to ask the price of anything before he bought it. Why, he wouldn't even know what novels to read. I always had to choose the kind he liked, with a murder or a forgery and a successful detective."

She turned abruptly to her kindred soul, who stood listening with a mien of wonder and dismay.

"Don't you see," she said, "that I can't possibly go with you?"

"But what do you intend to do?" asked the Spirit of Life.

"What do I intend to do?" she returned, indignantly. "Why, I mean to wait for my husband, of course. If he had come here first he would have waited for me for years and years; and it would break his heart not to find me here when he comes." She pointed with a contemptuous gesture to the magic vision of hill and vale sloping away to the translucent mountains. "He wouldn't give a fig for all that," she said, "if he didn't find me here."

"But consider," warned the Spirit, "that you are now choosing for eternity. It is a solemn moment."

"Choosing!" she said, with a half-sad smile. "Do you still keep up here that old fiction about choosing? I should have thought that you knew better than that. How can I help myself? He will expect to find me here when he comes, and he would never believe you if you told him that I had gone away with someone else—never, never."

"So be it," said the Spirit. "Here, as on earth, each one must decide for himself."

She turned to her kindred soul and looked at him gently, almost wistfully. "I am sorry," she said. "I should have liked to talk with you again; but you will understand, I know, and I dare say you will find someone else a great deal cleverer—"

And without pausing to hear his answer she waved him a swift farewell and turned back toward the threshold.

"Will my husband come soon?" she asked the Spirit of Life.

"That you are not destined to know," the Spirit replied.

"No matter," she said, cheerfully; "I have all eternity to wait in."

And still seated alone on the threshold, she listens for the creaking of his boots.

# THAT GOOD MAY COME

As first published in *Scribner's Magazine*, May, 1894

"OH, it's the same old story," said Birkton, impatiently. "They've all come home to roost, as usual."

He glanced at a heap of type-written pages which lay on the shabby desk at his elbow; then, pushing back his chair, he began to stride up and down the length of the little bedroom in which he and Helfenridge sat.

"What magazines have you tried?"

"All the good ones—every one. Nobody wants poetry nowadays. One of the editors told me the other day that it 'was going out.'"

Helfenridge picked up the sheet which lay nearest him and began to read, half to himself, half aloud, with a warmth of undertoned emphasis which made the lines glow.

Neither of the men was far beyond twenty-five. Birkton, the younger of the two, had the musing, irresolute profile of the dreamer of dreams; while his friend, stouter, squarer, of more clayey make, was nevertheless too much like him to prove a useful counterpoise.

"I always liked 'The Old Odysseus,'" Helfenridge murmured. "There's something tremendously suggestive in that fancy of yours, that tradition has misrepresented the real feelings of all the great heroes and heroines; or rather, has only handed down to us the official statement of their sentiments, as an epitaph records the obligatory virtues which the defunct ought to have had, if he hadn't. That theory, now, that Odysseus never really forgot Circe; and that Esther was in love with Haman, and decoyed him to the banquet with Ahasuerus just for the sake of once having him near her and hearing him speak; and that Dante, perhaps, if he could have been brought to book, would have had to confess for caring a great deal more for the *pietosa donna* of the window than for the mummified memory of a long-dead Beatrice—well, you know, it tallies wonderfully with the inconsequences and surprises that one is always discovering under the superficial fitnesses of life."

"Ah," said Birkton, "I meant to get a cycle of poems out of that idea—but what's the use, when I can't even get the first one into print?"

"You've tried sending 'The Old Odysseus'?"

Birkton nodded.

"To *Scribner's* and *The Century*?"

"And all the rest."

"Queer!" protested Helfenridge. "If I were an editor—now this, for instance, is so fine:

> *'Circe, Circe, the sharp anguish of that last long speechless night*
> *With the flame of tears unfallen scorches still mine aching sight;*
> *Still I feel the thunderous blackness of the hot sky overhead,*
> *While we two with close-locked fingers through thy pillared porches strayed,*
> *And athwart the sullen darkness, from the shadow-muffled shore,*
> *Heard aghast the savage summons of the sea's incoming roar,*
> *Shouting like a voice from Ilium, wailing like a voice from home,*
> *Shrieking through the pillared porches, Up, Odysseus, wake and come!'*

"Devil take it, why isn't there an audience for that sort of thing? And this line too—

*'Where Persephone remembers the Trinacrian buds and bees—'*

what a light, allegretto movement it has, following on all that gloom and horror! Ah—and here's that delicious little nocturne from 'The New and the Old.'

> *'Before the yellow dawn is up,*
>   *With pomp of shield and shaft,*
> *Drink we of night's fast ebbing cup*
>   *One last delicious draught.*

> *'The shadowy wine of night is sweet,*
>   *With subtle, slumberous fumes*
> *Pressed by the Hours' melodious feet*
>   *From bloodless elder-blooms.'*

"There—isn't that just like a little bacchanalian scene on a Greek gem?"

"Oh, don't go on," said Birkton sharply, "I'm sick of them."

"Don't say that," Helfenridge rebuked him. "It's like disowning one's own children. But if they say that mythology and classicism and *plastik* are played out—if they want Manet in place of David, or Cazin instead of Claude—why don't they like 'Boulterby Ridge,' with its grim mystery intensified by a setting of such modern realism? What lines there are in that!

> *'It was dark on Boulterby Ridge, with an ultimate darkness like death,*
> *And the weak wind flagged and gasped like a sick man straining for breath,*
> *And one star's ineffectual flicker shot pale through a gap in the gloom,*
> *As faint as the taper that struggles with night in the sick man's room.'*

"There's something about that beginning that makes me feel quietly cold from head to foot. And how charming the description of the girl is:

> *'She walked with a springing step, as if to some inner tune,*
> *And her cheeks had the lucent pink of maple wings in June.'*

"There's Millet and nature for you! And then when he meets her ghost on Boulterby Ridge—

> *'White in the palpable black as a lily moored on a moat—'*

what a contrast, eh? And the deadly hopeless chill of the last line, too—

> *'For the grave is deeper than grief, and longer than life is death.'*

"By Jove, I don't see how that could be improved!"

"Neither do I," said Birkton, bitterly, "more's the pity."

"And what comes next? Ah, that strange sonnet on the Cinque Cento. Did you ever carry out your scheme of writing a series of sonnets embodying all the great epochs of art?"

"No," said Birkton, indifferently.

"It seems a pity, after such a fine beginning. Now just listen to this—listen to it as if it had been written by somebody else:

> *'Strange hour of art's august ascendency*
> *When Sin and Beauty, the old lovers, met*
> *In a new paradise, still sword-beset*
> *With monkish terrors, but wherein the tree*
> *Of knowledge held its golden apples free*
> *To lips unstayed by hell's familiar threat;*
> *And men, grown mad upon the fruit they ate,*
> *Dreamed a wild dream of lust and liberty;*
> *Strange hour, when the dead gods arose in Rome*
> *From altars where the mass was sacrificed,*
> *When Phryne flaunted on the tiaraed tomb*
> *Of him who dearly sold the grace unpriced.*
> *And, twixt old shames and infamies to come,*
> *Cellini in his prison talked with Christ!'*

"There now, don't you call that a very happy definition of the most magical moment the world has ever known?"

"Don't," said Birkton, with an impatient gesture. "You're very good, old man, but don't go on."

Helfenridge, with a sigh, replaced the loose sheets on the desk.

"Well," he repeated, "I can't understand it. But the tide's got to turn, Maurice—it's got to. Don't forget that."

Birkton laughed drearily.

"Haven't you had a single opening—not one since I saw you?"

"Not one; at least nothing to speak of," said Birkton, reddening. "I've had one offer, but what do you suppose it was? Do you remember that idiotic squib that I wrote the other day about Mrs. Tolquitt's being seen alone with Dick Blason at Koster & Bial's? The thing I read that night in Bradley's rooms after supper?"

Helfenridge nodded.

"Well, I'm sorry I read it now. Somebody must have betrayed me (of course, though no names are mentioned, they all knew who was meant), for who should turn up yesterday but Baker Buley, the editor of the *Social Kite*, with an offer of a hundred and fifty dollars for my poem."

"You didn't, Maurice—?"

"Hang you, Helfenridge, what do you take me for? I told him to go to the devil."

There was a long pause, during which Helfenridge relit his pipe. Then he said, "But the book reviews in the *Symbolic* keep you going, don't they?"

"After a fashion," said Birkton, with a shrug. "Luckily my mother has had a tremendous lot of visiting-lists to make up lately, and she has written the invitations for half the balls that have been given this winter, so that between us we manage to keep Annette and ourselves alive; but God knows what would happen if one of us fell ill."

"Something else will happen before that. You'll be offered a hundred and fifty dollars for one of *those*," said Helfenridge, pointing to the pile of verses.

"I wish you were an editor!" Birkton retorted.

Helfenridge rose, picking up his battered gray hat, and slipping his pipe into his pocket. "I'm not an editor and I'm no good at all," he said, mournfully.

"Don't say that, old man. It's been the saving of me to be believed in by somebody."

Their hands met closely, and with a quick nod and inarticulate grunt Helfenridge turned from the room.

Maurice, left alone, dropped the smile which he had assumed to speed his friend, and sank into the nearest chair. His eyes, the sensitive eyes of the seer whom Beauty has anointed with her mysterious unguent, travelled painfully about the little room. Not a detail of it but was stamped upon his mind with a morbid accuracy—the yellowish-brown paper which had peeled off here and there, revealing the discolored plaster beneath; the ink-stained desk at which all his poems had been written; the rickety wash-stand of ash, with a strip of marbled oil-cloth nailed over it, and a cracked pitcher and basin; the gas-stove in which a low flame glimmered, the blurred looking-glass, and the book-case which held his thirty or forty worn volumes; yet he never took note of his sordid surroundings without a fresh movement of disgust.

"And this is our best room," he muttered to himself.

His mother and sister slept in the next room, which opened on an air-shaft in the center of the house, and beyond that was the kitchen, drawing its ventilation from the same shaft, and sending its smells with corresponding facility into the room occupied by the two women.

The apartment in which they lived, by courtesy called a flat, was in reality a thinly disguised tenement in one of those ignoble quarters of New York where the shabby has lapsed into the degraded. They had moved there a year earlier, leaving reluctantly, under pressure of a diminished purse, the pleasant little flat up-town, with its three bedrooms and sunny parlor, which had been their former home. Maurice winced when he remembered that he had made the change imperative by resigning his clerkship in a wholesale warehouse in order to give more leisure to the writing of the literary criticisms with which he supplied the *Symbolic Weekly Review*. His mother had approved, had even urged his course; but in the unsparing light of poverty it showed as less inevitable than he had imagined. And then, somehow, the great novel, which he had planned to write as soon as he should be released from his clerical task, was still in embryo. He had time and to spare, but his pen persisted in turning to sonnets, and only the opening chapters of the romance had been summarily blocked out. All this was not very satisfactory, and Maurice was glad to be called from the contemplation of facts so unamiable by the sound of his mother's voice in the adjoining room.

"Maurice, dear, has your friend gone?" Mrs. Birkton asked, advancing timidly across the threshold. She had the step and gesture of one who has spent her best energies in a vain endeavor to propitiate fate, and her small, pale face was like a palimpsest on which the record of suffering had been so deeply written that its original lines were concealed beyond recovery.

"If you are not writing, Maurice," she continued, "I might come and finish Mrs. Rushingham's list and save the gas for an hour longer. The light is so good at your window."

"Come," said Maurice, sweeping the poems into his desk and pushing a chair forward for his mother.

Mrs. Birkton, as she seated herself and opened her neat blank-book, glanced up almost furtively into her son's face.

"No news, dear?" she asked, in a low tone.

"None," said Maurice, briefly. "I tried the editor of the *Inter Oceanic* when I was out just now, and he likes 'The Old Odysseus' and 'Boulterby Ridge' very much, but they aren't exactly suited to his purpose. That's their formula, you know."

Mrs. Birkton dipped her fine steel pen into the inkstand, and began to write, in a delicate copperplate hand:

*Mrs. Albert Lowbridge, 14 East Seventy-fifth Street.*
*Mrs. Charles M. McManus, 910 Fifth Avenue.*
*The Misses McManus, 910 Fifth Avenue.*
*Mr. & Mrs. Hugh Lovermore, 30 East Ninety-sixth Street.*

She wrote on in silence, but Maurice, who had seated himself near her, saw a glimmer of tears on her thin lashes as her head moved mechanically to and fro with the motion of the pen.

"Well," he said, trying for a more cheerful note, "*your* literary productions are always in demand, at all events. Mrs. Stapleton's ball ought to bring you in a very tidy little sum. Some one told me the other day that she was going to send out two thousand invitations."

"Oh, Maurice—the Stapleton ball! Haven't you heard?"

"What about it?"

"Mr. Seymour Carbridge, Mrs. Stapleton's uncle, died yesterday, and the ball is given up."

Maurice rose from his seat with a movement of dismay.

"The stars in their courses fight against us!" he exclaimed. "I'm afraid this will make a great difference to you, won't it, mother?"

"It does make a difference," she assented, writing on uninterruptedly. "You see I was to have rewritten her whole visiting-list, besides doing the invitations to the ball. And Lent comes so early this year."

Maurice was silent, and for some twenty minutes Mrs. Birkton's pen continued to move steadily forward over the ruled sheets of the visiting-book. The short January afternoon was fast darkening into a snowy twilight, and Maurice presently stretched out his hand toward the match-box which lay on the desk.

"Oh, Maurice, don't light the gas yet. I can see quite well, and you had better keep the stove going a little longer. It's so cold."

"Why not have both?"

"You extravagant boy! When it gets really dark I shall take my writing into the kitchen, but meanwhile it is so much pleasanter here; and I don't believe Annette has lit the kitchen stove yet. I haven't heard her come in."

"Where has she been this afternoon?"

"At her confirmation class. Father Thurifer holds a class every afternoon this week in the chantry. You know Annette is to be confirmed next Sunday."

"Is she? No—I had forgotten."

"But she must have come in by this time," Mrs. Birkton continued, with a glance at the darkening window. "Go and see, dear, will you?"

Maurice obediently stepped out into the narrow passage-way which led from his bedroom to the kitchen. The kitchen door was shut, and as he opened it he came abruptly upon the figure of a young girl, seated in an attitude of tragic self-abandonment at the deal table in the middle of the room. She had evidently just come in, for her shabby hat and jacket and two or three devotional-looking little volumes lay on a chair at her side. Her arms were flung out across the table, with her face hidden between, so that the bluish glimmer of the gas-jet overhead, vaguely outlining her figure, seemed to concentrate all its light upon the mass of her wheat-colored braids. At the sound of the opening door she sprang up suddenly, turning upon Maurice a small disordered face, with red lids and struggling mouth. She was evidently not more than fifteen years old and her undeveloped figure and little round face, in its setting of pale hair, presented that curious mixture of maturity and childishness often seen in girls of her age who have been carefully watched over at home, yet inevitably exposed to the grim diurnal spectacle of poverty and degradation.

"Annette!" Maurice said, catching the hand with which she tried to hide her face.

"Oh, Maurice, don't—don't please!" she entreated, "I wasn't crying—I wasn't! I was only a little tired; and it was so cold walking home from church."

"If you are cold, why haven't you lit the stove?" he asked, giving her time to regain her composure.

"I will—I was going to."

"Carry your things to your room, and I'll light it for you."

"As he spoke his eye fell on the slim little volumes at her side, and he picked up one, which was emblazoned with a cross, surmounted by the title: *Passion Flowers*.

"And so you are going to be confirmed very soon, Annette?" he asked, his glance wandering over the wide-margined pages with their reiterated invocations in delicate italics:

> *O Jesu Christ! Eternal sweetness of them that love Thee,*
> *O Jesu, Paradise of delights and very glory of the Angels,*
> *O Jesu, mirror of everlasting love,*
> *O King most lovely, and Loving One most dear,*
> *impress I pray Thee, O Lord Jesus,*
> *all Thy wounds upon my heart!*

Annette's face was smoothed into instant serenity. "Next Sunday—just think, Maurice, only three days more to wait! It will be Sexagesima Sunday, you know."

"Will it? And are you glad to be confirmed?"

"Oh, Maurice! I have waited so long—some girls are confirmed at thirteen."

"Are they? And why did you have to wait?"

"Because Father Thurifer thought it best," she answered, humbly. "You see I am very young for my age, and very stupid in some ways. He was afraid that I might not understand all the holy mysteries."

"And do you now?"

"Oh, yes—as well as a girl can presume to. At least Father Thurifer says so."

"That is very nice," said Maurice. "Now run away and I'll light the fire. Mother will be coming soon to sit here."

He went back to his bedroom, where Mrs. Birkton's pen, in the thickening obscurity, still travelled unremittingly over the smooth pages.

"Mother, what's the matter with Annette? When I went into the kitchen I found her crying."

Mrs. Birkton pushed her work aside with a vexed exclamation.

"Poor child!" she said. "After all, Maurice, she is only a child; one can't be too hard on her."

"Hard on her? But why? What's the matter?"

"You see," continued Mrs. Birkton, who invariably put her apologies before her explanations, "she would never have allowed herself to think of it if we hadn't been so sure of the Stapleton ball."

"To think of what?"

"Her white dress, Maurice, her confirmation dress. At the Church of the Precious Blood all the girls are confirmed in white muslin dresses, with tulle veils and moire sashes. Father Thurifer makes a point of it."

"And you promised Annette such a dress?"

"I thought I might, dear, when Mrs. Stapleton decided to give her ball. You see there is a very large class of candidates for confirmation, and I knew it would be very trying for Annette to be the only one not dressed in white—and at such a solemn time, too. But now, of course, she will have to give it up."

"Yes," said Maurice, absently. He stood with his hands in his pockets, his unseeing eyes fixed upon the yellow gleam of the gas-stove, which was now the only point of light in the room.

"And that is what Annette is crying about?" he asked at length.

"Poor child," murmured his mother, deprecatingly; "it is such a solemn moment, Maurice."

"Yes, yes—I know. That's just it. That's why I don't understand—Annette is a very religious girl, isn't she?"

"Father Thurifer tells me that he has never seen a more religious nature. He said that it was as natural to her to believe as to breathe. Isn't that such a beautiful expression?"

"And yet—yet—at such a solemn moment, as you say, it is the color of her dress that is uppermost in her mind?"

"Oh, Maurice, don't you see that it is just because she has so much devotional feeling, poor child, that she suffers at the thought of not appearing worthily at such a time?"

"As if Mrs. Stapleton should ask me to lead the cotillion at her ball when my dress coat is in pawn?"

"Maurice!" said his mother.

"I beg your pardon, mother; I didn't mean that; forgive me. But it all seems so queer—I don't understand."

"I wish you went oftener to church, Maurice," said Mrs. Birkton, sadly.

"I wish I understood Annette better," he returned in a musing tone.

"Annette is a very good girl," said Mrs. Birkton, gathering up her pen and papers. "After the first shock is over she will bear her disappointment bravely; but don't tell her that I have spoken to you about it, for she would never forgive me."

"Poor little thing," Maurice sighed, as his mother groped her way to the door.

He sat still in the darkness after she had left, companioned by the dismal brood of his disappointments, until half an hour later Annette's knock told him that their slender supper was ready.

When he re-entered the kitchen his sister's face had grown as smooth and serene as that of some young seraph of Van Eyck's. She had tied a white apron over her dress and was busy carrying the hot toast and fried eggs from the stove to the table, which had meanwhile been covered with a white cloth and neatly set for the evening meal.

Maurice sat down between her and his mother, listening in silence to their talk, which fell like the trickle of a cool stream upon his aching nerves. They were speaking as usual of church matters, in which the daughter took an eager and precocious, the mother a somewhat ex-official interest; it seemed to Maurice as though Mrs. Birkton, who had resigned herself to getting on without so many things, had even surrendered her direct share in the scheme of redemption, or rather tacitly passed it on to her child. But what more especially struck him was the force of will displayed in Annette's demeanor. Her disappointment, which he felt to be very real, was impenetrably masked behind a mien of gay activity; and Maurice, knowing his own facile tendency to be swayed by the emotion of the moment, marveled at the child's self-control.

The next morning he went out earlier than usual. As he opened the hall-door he turned back and called to his mother, who was washing the breakfast dishes in the kitchen:

"Mother, if Helfenridge comes you can say that you don't know when I shall be back. Say that I may not be in all day."

"Very well, dear," she replied, with some surprise; but her son's face forbade questioning, and she went on silently with her work.

Maurice, as it happened, returned in time for their one o'clock dinner. His mother thought that he looked pale and spiritless, and feared that he had endured another defeat at the hands of some unenlightened editor.

"Has Helfenridge been here?" he inquired.

"Yes," Mrs. Birkton answered. "He stopped on his way down town just after you had gone out. He was very sorry not to find you, and said that he would come again tomorrow evening."

"Has Annette got back from school?" Maurice asked, irrelevantly.

"I think I hear her step now," Mrs. Birkton replied, and at the same moment the kitchen-door opened, admitting the young girl, whose small face was touched with a frosty pink by the cold.

As she entered Maurice went up to her, extending something in his hand with an awkward gesture.

"Look here—will that buy you a white dress like the rest of the girls?" he said, abruptly.

Annette grew red and then pale; her lips parted, but she made no motion to take the roll of bills which he held out to her.

"Maurice!" his mother gasped. "Have they accepted something? What is it? What is it to appear in?"

Her small features, flattened into life-long submission to failure, seemed almost convulsed by the unwonted expression of a less negative emotion.

Maurice made no answer; he was still looking at Annette.

"Why don't you take it, Annette?" he said, a tinge of impatience in his voice.

"Annette! Annette! why do you stand there? Can't you speak? Why don't you thank your brother?" Mrs. Birkton cried, in a storm of exultation.

Annette held out her hand, but as she took the bills her face again grew crimson.

"Maurice, how did you know about the dress? Mother, you promised not to tell him!" Then, glancing at the roll of money, "But what have you given me, Maurice? A hundred dollars—a hundred and fifty dollars? Mother, what does he mean?"

"Maurice!" Mrs. Birkton almost shrieked.

"Well," said Maurice with a laugh, "isn't it enough to buy your dress?"

Annette stood, trembling, between sobs and laughter; but her mother's tears overflowed.

"Oh, my boy, my son, I'm so happy! I knew it would come. I knew it must—Mr. Helfenridge said so only this morning. But I didn't dream it would be so soon!" She lifted her poor, joy-distorted face to his averted kiss. "Oh, it's too beautiful, Maurice, it's too beautiful! But you haven't told us yet which poem it is."

Maurice turned sharply away, his hand on the door.

"Not yet—not now. I've forgotten something. I'm going out," he stammered.

"Why, Maurice! Without your dinner? You're not well, my son!"

"Nonsense, mother. I shall be back presently. Annette, keep some dinner for me."

"But, Maurice," the girl cried, springing forward, "you mustn't leave all this money with me."

"I've told you it's yours," he said, with a violence which made the women's startled eyes meet.

"Why, Maurice, you must be joking! A hundred and fifty dollars? I oughtn't to keep a penny of it, with all the things that you and mother need."

"Nonsense, keep it all. If it's too much for your dress, mother can take the rest for herself. I don't want it. But mind you spend it all on yourselves; don't use any of it for the household. And remember I won't touch a penny of it."

"But, Maurice," said Mrs. Birkton, "the dress won't cost twenty dollars."

"So much the worse," he retorted; and the door shut on him with a crash that was conclusive.

Helfenridge, whose work (he was a clerk in the same establishment which had been the scene of Maurice's brief commercial experience) often delayed him down town long after his dinner-hour, did not reach his friend's house until eight o'clock on the following evening. As he started on his long ascent of the steep tenement-stairs some one ran against him on the first landing, and he drew back in surprise, recognizing Maurice in the flare of the gas-jet against the whitewashed wall.

"Hullo, Maurice! Didn't Mrs. Birkton tell you that I was coming this evening?"

"I—yes—the fact is, I was just going out," Birkton said, confusedly.

Helfenridge glanced at him, marking his evasive eye.

"Oh, very well. If you're going out I'll try again."

"No—no. You'd better come up after all. I'd rather see you now. I've got something to say to you."

"Are you sure?" said Helfenridge. "I'd rather not be taken on sufferance."

"I want to see you," Birkton repeated, with sudden force; and the two men climbed the stairs together in silence.

"Come this way," said Maurice, leading Helfenridge into his bedroom.

He put a match to the gas-burner, and another to the stove, and pushed his only easy-chair forward within the radius of the dry, yellow heat, while Helfenridge threw aside his hat and overcoat, which were fringed with frozen snow.

"You don't look well, Maurice," he said, taking the seat proffered by his friend.

"It's because I'm new at it, I suppose," the other returned, dryly.

"New at what? What do you mean?"

"Wait a minute," said Maurice; "I want to show you something first."

He opened the door as he spoke, and Helfenridge heard him walk along the narrow passage-way to the kitchen; then came the opening of another door, which launched a confusion of soft, gay tones upon the intervening obscurity. "Oh, no, no," Helfenridge heard a young voice half laughingly protest; then an older tone interposed, gently urgent, mingled with an odd unfamiliar laugh from Maurice; lastly the door of the bedroom was suddenly thrown wide, and Maurice reappeared, pushing before him his sister, clad from head to foot in white muslin, her flat, childish waist defined by a wide white sash, even her little feet shod in immaculate ivory kid.

Above all this whiteness her flushed face emerged like a pink crocus from a snow-drift; her lips were parted in tremulous, inarticulate apologies, but no explanatory word reached Helfenridge.

"Why, Miss Annette, how lovely!" he exclaimed at random, questioning Maurice with his eyes.

"There—doesn't she look nice?" the brother asked, retaining his grasp of her white shoulders. "That's her confirmation dress, if you please! She's going to be confirmed next Sunday at the Church of the Precious Blood, and you've got to be there to see it."

"Oh, Maurice," murmured Annette.

"Of course I shall be there," said Helfenridge, warmly. "But what a beautiful dress! Are all confirmation dresses as beautiful as that?"

"Oh, no, Mr. Helfenridge; but Maurice—"

"Father Thurifer likes all the girls in the class to be dressed like that," Maurice quickly interposed. "And now off before your finery gets tumbled," he added, pushing her out of the room with a smile which softened the abruptness of the gesture.

He shut the door and the two men stood looking at each other.

"She's lovely," said Helfenridge, gently.

"Poor little girl," said Maurice. "Isn't it a pretty fancy to dress them all in white?"

"Yes—I suppose it's a High Church idea?"

"I suppose so. I never knew anything about it until the other day—until two days ago, in fact. Then I found that Father Thurifer had requested all the girls who are to be confirmed to dress in white muslin; and we hadn't a penny between us to buy her a dress with."

"Yes?" said Helfenridge, tentatively.

"Annette's a very good little girl, you know—immensely religious. Father Thurifer says he never saw a more religious nature. And it nearly killed her not to have a white dress—not to appear worthy of the day. She regards it as the most solemn day of her life. Can you understand how she must have felt? I couldn't at first, but I think I do now. After all, she's only a child."

"I understand," said Helfenridge.

"Well, neither my mother nor I had a copper left. There was no way of getting the dress—and it seemed to me she had to have it."

"Yes?"

"I said the other day that I didn't know what would happen if one of us fell ill; but in a way it would have been simpler than this. Annette, now—if Annette had been ill we could have sent her to the hospital. My mother is too sensible to have any prejudice against hospitals. But this is different—there was no other way of getting the dress; and it had to be got somehow. I don't believe her wedding-dress will seem half so important to her—there's so little perspective at fifteen."

"Well?" said Helfenridge after a pause.

"Well, so I—good God, Helfenridge, won't you understand?"

Both men were silent; Helfenridge sat with his hands clenched on the arms of his chair.

Suddenly he said, as if in a flash of remembrance: "You sent that thing to Baker

Buley—the thing about Mrs. Tolquitt?"

"Yes," said Maurice.

A long pause followed, in which the thoughts of the two men cried aloud to each other.

At length Maurice exclaimed, "I wish you'd speak out—say what you think."

"I don't know," said Helfenridge, in a low tone.

"You don't know? You mean you don't know what to say?"

"What to think."

"What to think of a man who's sold his soul?"

"I'm not sure if you have. It seems to me that I'm not sure of anything," Helfenridge said.

"I am—I'm sure that Annette had to have her dress," said Maurice, with a defiant laugh.

"When does it come out?"

"It's out already—it came out this morning. It's all over town by this time."

"Do they know?" asked Helfenridge, suddenly.

"My mother and Annette? God forbid. Do you suppose they would have touched the money?"

"How did you account to them for having it?"

"I told them that was my secret—that they shouldn't know for the present. Of course the—the thing in the Kite is not signed; and later, if one of my poems ever finds its way into print, they'll think it's that—but they'll have to wait."

Helfenridge rose. "I must be going," he said.

"Why do you go? Because you're afraid to tell me what you think? You may say what you please—it can't make any difference. Annette had to have the dress. I've been trying to avoid you for two days because I was afraid to tell you, but now I'd rather talk about it—that is if you care to have anything more to do with me. Because, after all, I'm no better than a blackguard now, you know—there's no getting around that fact. You've a perfect right to cut me."

Helfenridge was mechanically pulling on his overcoat.

"At what time does the confirmation take place?" he asked. "Tell Miss Annette that I shall certainly be there."

On the ensuing Sunday morning, punctually at half-past ten o'clock, a closed carriage from the nearest livery-stable drew up before the house occupied by the Birktons. It was snowing hard, and Annette's spotless draperies and flowing veil were concealed under an old cloak of her mother's as, sheltered by Maurice's umbrella, she stepped across the sidewalk, clasping her prayer-book in one tremulous, white-gloved hand. Mrs. Birkton followed, her shabby bonnet refurbished with fresh velvet strings, and a glow of excitement on her small effaced features. She and her son placed themselves on the front seat, leaving Annette to expand her crisp robe over the width of the opposite cushions; and the carriage rolled off heavily through the deepening snow.

All three sat silent during their slow, noiseless drive. Maurice was looking out of the window, so that the women saw only his uncommunicative profile. Mrs. Birkton sat wiping away the tears from her flushed face. They were pleasant tears, and she let them roll gently down her cheeks before she dried them. As for Annette, her face was pale, with the candid pallor of an intense but scarce-comprehended emotion. She sat bolt upright, in a kind of pre-Raphaelite rigidity which accorded with the primitive inexpressiveness of her rapt young features and the shadowless chalk-like mass of her dress and veil.

At length the carriage paused behind a train of others; and after some moments of delay, which seemed to lend a preparatory solemnity to their approach, Maurice, in the wake of his mother and sister, passed from the snowy crudeness of the outer world into the rich and complex atmosphere of the Church of the Precious Blood.

The raw, sunless daylight, mellowed by the jeweled opacity of stained-glass windows, fell with a caressing brilliance across the aisles, streaking the clustered shafts with heraldic emblazonments of gules and azure and leaving the intervening spaces swathed in a velvety dusk. On the altar, with its embroidered hanging, the candle-flames hovered like yellow moths over the white lilies rigidly disposed in tall silver vases; while in their midst, relieved against the sculptured intricacies of the reredos of grayish stone, rose the outstretched arms of the great golden crucifix.

The church was already crowded; but a ribbon, latitudinally dividing the central aisle, indicated that the foremost rows of chairs (there were no pews in the Church of the Precious Blood) had been reserved for the candidates for confirmation and their relations. Thither Maurice followed his mother and Annette, passing through a dove-like subsidence of feathery white and a double row of innocent young faces to the seats assigned to them by the verger. Glancing about as he moved up the aisle he had caught a glimpse of Helfenridge seated far back, with his head against a pillar; and the sight lent him some momentary comfort.

Maurice cast down his eyes while Mrs. Birkton and Annette knelt to pray; and when he looked up the long white procession of choristers, preceded by the crucifer, was winding toward the chancel, while the first notes of the hymn

> *How bright these glorious spirits shine!*
> *Whence all their white array?*

leapt jubilantly out of the expectant hush.

Maurice, observing his sister, saw the gravity of her vague young profile intensified to awe as the procession swept past their seats, closed by the sumptuous grouping of the ample-sleeved bishop with his attendant clergy in their embroidered vestments, and seen through the mauve mist of drifting incense fumes. To him it was like fingering the leaves of a missal in some Umbrian sacristy, speculating idly, as he looked, upon the meaning of the delicate miniatures, wherein serene-visaged personages, saintly or seraphic, enacted their mysterious drama in a setting of fanciful white architecture or against a blue background starred with gold. But to Annette, he perceived, it was something real, as real as physical birth or death. Through the symbolic phantasmagoria, which she perhaps understood still less than he, ran a thread of actuality, linking her timid being to the occult significance of the whole splendid scene; and Maurice saw her tremble with the sense of that august alliance. Perhaps, after all, he reflected, it was the white dress which formed the actual point of contact. At least he was glad to think that it made her a part of the pageant, a conscious factor in the gorgeous sacrifice of praise and prayer.

As he mused thus his unquiet eyes again began to wander; and suddenly they fell upon a lady who sat near by with a little girl in white muslin at her side. The lady's face was very familiar to him, though he had never before seen it composed into its present expression of devotional repose. It was a pretty face, crowned by abrupt waves of reddish hair just dashed here and there with a streak of gray, and lit by an insinuating, agate-colored glance; but the sight of it burned Maurice's eyeballs like vitriol, for it was the face of Mrs. Tolquitt.

He had never seen her thus before, with sober lips and modestly meditative lids; nor had he ever seen the small, solemn replica of herself now seated beside her in billows of clear white muslin. The sight was an intolerable rebuke, and he would have given the world to hear her familiar laugh rattle derisively through the high quietude of the aisles. As he gazed she turned her head, fixing upon him an absent look which gradually melted into a subdued smile of recognition. Then she made a slight sideward motion of her eyes, which plainly said, "This is my little girl."

Maurice noticed that she showed no surprise at seeing him there; she seemed to consider his presence as much a matter of course as her own, and with a shudder he said to himself, "Good heavens, perhaps she thinks I have come to see her daughter confirmed!"

The service rolled on, with its bursts of music and interludes of prayer, its mystical moving of brilliant figures and flitting of lights about the altar; and at length Maurice was aware of a pause, followed by a stirring of the white dovecote in whose midst he sat. He saw Mrs. Birkton glance tearfully at Annette. The girl's lips and eyelids were trembling, and for a moment she seemed unable to move. At length she looked up, fixing her eyes on the golden crucifix above the altar; then, as if hypnotized by the sight, she rose and glided into the aisle, mingling with the fluctuant mass of white-veiled figures which had begun to move slowly toward the apse.

Presently they were all kneeling together on the chancel step, settling their dresses with the quick motions of a flock of birds; and above them, whitely hovering, Maurice saw the pontifical head and voluminous sleeves of the bishop. Annette knelt so that he could just see her between the intervening piers; but Mrs. Tolquitt's daughter was hidden from him, lost in the impersonal array of white veils and bowed heads.

The organ murmured a soft accompaniment above which rose the monotonous cadence of the episcopal supplication, "Defend, O Lord, this thy child. . . . Defend, O Lord, this thy child . . ." reiterated like an incantation, as the invoking hands passed slowly down the line of motionless young heads.

Maurice saw the hands sway above Annette's pale braids, which shone like winter sunshine through her veil; then they moved on, and his eyes turned involuntarily to Mrs. Tolquitt. But she did not see him now; she was crying, not daintily, for the gallery, but in genuine self-surrender, her shoulders shaking, her handkerchief pressed against her face.

There came over Maurice an uncontrollable longing to escape; the smoke of the incense and the strong fragrance of the lilies sickened him, and Mrs. Tolquitt's sobs seemed to be choking in his own throat.

At length the white line about the chancel swayed, broke, and dissolved itself; the choir burst into another victorious hymn, and the little veiled figures came fluttering back to their seats. In the ensuing disturbance, Maurice rose with a quick whisper to his mother—"Let me pass—I'm going out. I can't stand the incense"—and while Mrs. Birkton made way for him, startled and disappointed, his glance fell for a moment on Annette's illuminated face, as she moved toward her seat with fixed eyes and folded hands. Her whole gaze was bent upon the inner vision; she did not even see him as he brushed her dress in passing out.

It was like a new birth to get out into the snow again, and Maurice, after a sharp breath or two, stepped forth rapidly against the wind, courting the tingle of the barbed flakes upon his face.

He did not go home until late that evening, and when he entered the kitchen, he was met by the festal spectacle of the supper-table adorned with a cluster of white lilies and a delicate array of fruit and angel-cake. Annette, in her habitual dress of dark stuff, looked more familiar and less supernal than before, and though her face still shone, it now seemed to Maurice that he could discern the mingling of a gratified childish vanity with the mystical emotions of the morning.

"I'm so glad you have come, dear," Mrs. Birkton exclaimed, her countenance still dewy with a pleasant agitation. "Annette, is the chicken ready? We have a broiled chicken for you, Maurice, dear, and a little mayonnaise of tomatoes."

As she spoke her eye turned toward the supper-table, dumbly challenging his praise.

"How nice it looks," he murmured, obediently.

"It is all owing to you, dear," his mother replied. "We asked Mr. Helfenridge to come to supper, too; we thought you would like to have him."

"Is he coming?" Maurice asked, abruptly.

"No, he couldn't unfortunately. He said he had promised to go to his sister's."

They sat down, Annette mutely radiant at the head of the table, with her mother and Maurice at the sides; but to the dismay of the two women Maurice refused to partake of the delicacies which they had prepared. He had a headache, he said; but he sat watching them eat, in spite of his mother's entreaties that he should go and lie down in his own room.

When supper was over, however, he rose and bade them good-night; Annette's kiss was mingled with an inarticulate whisper of gratitude, but he pushed her gently aside, and the women heard him cross the passage-way and shut himself into his own room.

In a few moments, however, he was aroused by a timorous knock, which he recognized as his mother's.

"Come in," he called, and Mrs. Birkton stepped apologetically across the threshold.

"Maurice, is your head very bad?"

"No, no—it's not bad at all. I only want to be quiet."

"I know, dear, and I'm very sorry to disturb you. But here is the rest of this money—I can't keep it, you know, Maurice. Annette's dress and shoes and veil, and the carriage and supper, and the new strings for my bonnet, only cost twenty-seven dollars and a half, and I can't possibly keep the rest unless you will let me use it for the household expenses, as usual."

Maurice sprang up, white to the lips.

"For God's sake, mother, understand me. I don't want the money—I won't touch it. I can provide plenty for the household; I haven't let you starve yet. And this is Annette's; yours and hers. If you won't spend it for yourself let Annette put it in the savings-bank; or let her throw it into the street; I don't care what becomes of it—but don't speak to me of it again. I'm sick to death of hearing about it!"

Mrs. Birkton shrank back, trembling at his unwonted tone. She was afraid that he was going to be really ill, and her one thought was to withdraw without increasing his agitation.

"Very well, dear—just as you please," she said, deprecatingly. "It was foolish of me to trouble you. Don't think of it again, but go to bed and try to sleep. I ought not to have disturbed you."

And she slipped back into the passage-way, stealthily closing the door.

Maurice had no thought of going to bed. He sank into his arm-chair, which he had pushed close to the gas-stove, and sat staring at the hard yellow brilliance of the polished radiator.

Helfenridge had gone to see Annette confirmed, but he had not been willing to come to supper; and Maurice knew him too well not to penetrate the shallow excuse which had satisfied Mrs. Birkton. Well, Helfenridge was right; no man can handle pitch without being defiled. And once a man's hand is soiled, why should his friends care to touch it?

After all, no cheap condonation of Helfenridge's would have helped Maurice now; rather did he feel a tonic force in his friend's disapproval. It showed Helfenridge to be the better and stronger man; and there was a kind of dispassionate consolation in that. If one had to fail it was better that the other should hold fast than be dragged down with him; and Helfenridge had always been the firmer-footed of the two.

So Maurice mused, letting the desolate hours travel on unregarded; till suddenly his vigil was disturbed by a knock, sharp and resolute this time, which made him start to his feet.

"Helfenridge!" he exclaimed, and there on the threshold stood his friend.

Maurice, on seeing him enter, had felt an involuntary thrill of relief, as though he were regaining his moral footing, but the illusion was transient and left him to sink back into profounder depths of self-accusal.

"I thought you weren't coming. You would have been quite right not to come," he said, without asking his friend to sit down.

"I didn't mean to come," Helfenridge answered, taking off his coat. "Your mother asked me to supper, but I refused. I couldn't see my way clear at first—even in church that little white seraph didn't seem to justify it for a moment; but I have been thinking hard all day—and now I've come."

He held out his hand, but Maurice made no motion to take it.

"It's no use," he said, heavily. "No amount of thinking will make it right. What's that in the Bible about doing evil that good may come? That's what I've done. I've done evil that good might come—but it hasn't come—it can't. The fellow in the Bible was right. You think Annette's dress was white? I tell you it was black—black as pitch."

"No, no," said Helfenridge, taking the chair which Maurice had not offered him. "The whole business is horribly mixed up, like most human affairs, but there's a germ of right in it somewhere, and the best thing we can do now is to nurse that and get it to flower."

"To flower?—bah—a poison-ivy—"

"Some poisons are valuable medicines," said Helfenridge.

"Oh, stop—drop that inane metaphor. I tell you there's no excuse for what I did; and what's worse there's no reparation. I'd give myself up, I'd go and proclaim the whole thing—but what good would that do? Smother everybody in mud—Annette, and my mother, and that poor woman! Helfenridge—"

"Well?"

"That woman—Mrs. Tolquitt—was in church with her little girl, who was confirmed. Think of it, will you! Her little girl was confirmed with Annette! And they sat next to us—only a few seats off. Helfenridge, I never knew she had a little girl."

"I don't suppose we any of us know much about anybody else," said Helfenridge.

"And there she sat crying—crying, I tell you. Just such tears as my mother's—glad and proud and sorry all at once!"

"Yes, I saw her."

"You saw her—and you're here now?"

"I'm here, Maurice, because I know what you're suffering."

They were both silent, Helfenridge seated with bowed head, Birkton stirring uneasily about the room with the thwarted movements of a caged animal.

At length he flung himself down in the chair in front of his desk and hid his face against his arms. Helfenridge heard his sobs.

It seemed a long time before either of them spoke; but finally Helfenridge rose and touched his friend's shoulder.

"My eyes are clearer than yours just now," he said, "and I shouldn't be here if I didn't see a way out of it."

"A way out of it?"

"Yes, only it's no empirical remedy: *geschehen ist geschehen*. But you spoke just now of the biblical axiom that good can't come out of evil; well, no generalization of that sort is final. It seems to me, on the contrary, that this good can come out of evil; that having done evil once it may become impossible to do it again. One ill act may become the strongest rampart one can build against further ill-doing. It divides things, it classifies them. It may be the means of lifting one forever out of the region of quibbles and compromises and moral subtleties, in which we who are curious in emotions are apt to loiter till we get a shaking up of some sort. It's horrible to make a stepping-stone out of a poor woman's anguish and humiliation; but the anguish and humiliation can't be prevented now; and who knows? in the occult economy of things they may be of some use to her if they help somebody else."

Maurice flung off his hand with a passionate gesture. "Quibbles and compromises and moral subtleties! What else is your reasoning made up of, I should like to know? It's nothing but the basest Liguorianism. The plain fact is that I'm a damned blackguard, not fit to look decent people in the face again."

His head sank once more upon his outstretched arms, and Helfenridge drew back.

"Shall I go then, Maurice?"

"Yes, go; it's worse when you're here."

Helfenridge for a few moments stood irresolute, as if waiting for his friend to recall him; but Maurice still sat without moving, bowed beneath the immensity of his shame.

"Well, I'm going," Helfenridge reluctantly declared.

Maurice made no reply; his shoulders still shook, although his grief had grown noiseless.

"Remember, Maurice," his friend conjured him, "that whatever you do your mother and sister mustn't find out about this business. That's your first duty now, to hide the whole thing from them."

Still there came no answer. Helfenridge turned to the door and slowly opened it, glancing back as he did so at Maurice's downcast head; then he stepped out into the passage-way. But as the door closed behind him a new impulse, uncontrollable in its suddenness, made him turn back abruptly and re-enter the room.

"Look here, Maurice, listen to me," he exclaimed. "I didn't mean to tell you—but, hang it all, there's no use in your taking it like this. Blason was waiting for Mrs. Tolquitt outside the church, and I saw them drive away together in her brougham, with the little girl between them."

# THE LAMP OF PSYCHE

As first published in *Scribner's Magazine*, October, 1895

DELIA CORBETT was too happy; her happiness frightened her. Not on theological grounds, however; she was sure that people had a right to be happy; but she was equally sure that it was a right seldom recognized by destiny. And her happiness almost touched the confines of pain—it bordered on that sharp ecstasy which she had known, through one sleepless night after another, when what had now become a reality had haunted her as an unattainable longing.

Delia Corbett was not in the habit of using what the French call *gros mots* in the rendering of her own emotions; she took herself, as a rule, rather flippantly, with a dash of contemptuous pity. But she felt that she had now entered upon a phase of existence wherein it became her to pay herself an almost reverential regard. Love had set his golden crown upon her forehead, and the awe of the office allotted to her subdued her doubting heart. To her had been given the one portion denied to all other women on earth, the immense, the unapproachable privilege of becoming Laurence Corbett's wife.

Here she burst out laughing at the sound of her own thoughts, and rising from her seat walked across the drawing-room and looked at herself in the mirror above the mantel-piece. She was past thirty and had never been very pretty; but she knew herself to be capable of loving her husband better and pleasing him longer than any other woman in the world. She was not afraid of rivals; he and she had seen each other's souls.

She turned away, smiling carelessly at her insignificant reflection, and went back to her arm-chair near the balcony. The room in which she sat was very beautiful; it pleased Corbett to make all his surroundings beautiful. It was the drawing-room of his hotel in Paris, and the balcony near which his wife sat overlooked a small bosky garden framed in ivied walls, with a moldering terra-cotta statue in the center of its cup-shaped lawn. They had now been married some two months, and, after travelling for several weeks, had both desired to return to Paris; Corbett because he was really happier there than elsewhere, Delia because she passionately longed to enter as a wife the house where she had so often come and gone as a guest. How she used to find herself dreaming in the midst of one of Corbett's delightful dinners (to which she and her husband were continually being summoned) of a day when she might sit at the same table, but facing its master, a day when no carriage should wait to whirl her away from the brightly lit porte-cochere, and when, after the guests had gone, he and she should be left alone in his library, and she might sit down beside him and put her hand in his! The high-minded reader may infer from this that I am presenting him, in the person of Delia Corbett, with a heroine whom he would not like his wife to meet; but how many of us could face each other in the calm consciousness of moral rectitude if our inmost desire were not hidden under a convenient garb of lawful observance?

Delia Corbett, as Delia Benson, had been a very good wife to her first husband; some people (Corbett among them) had even thought her laxly tolerant of "poor Benson's" weaknesses. But then she knew her own; and it is admitted that nothing goes so far toward making us blink the foibles of others as the wish to have them extend a like mercy to ourselves. Not that Delia's foibles were of a tangible nature; they belonged to the order which escapes analysis by the coarse process of our social standards. Perhaps their very immateriality, the consciousness that she could never be brought to book for them before any human tribunal, made her the more restive under their weight; for she was of a nature to prefer buying her happiness to stealing it. But her rising scruples were perpetually being allayed by some fresh indiscretion of Benson's, to which she submitted with an undeviating amiability which flung her into the opposite extreme of wondering if she didn't really influence him to do wrong—if she mightn't help him to do better. All these psychological subtleties exerted, however, no influence over her conduct which, since the day of her marriage, had been a model of delicate circumspection. It was only necessary to look at Benson to see that the most eager reformer could have done little to improve him. In the first place he must have encountered the initial difficulty, most disheartening to reformers, of making his neophyte distinguish between right and wrong. Undoubtedly it was within the measure even of Benson's primitive perceptions to recognize that some actions were permissible and others were not; but his sole means of classifying them was to try both, and then deny having committed those of which his wife disapproved. Delia had once owned a poodle who greatly desired to sleep on a white fur rug which she destined to other uses. She and the poodle disagreed on the subject, and the later, though submitting to her authority (when reinforced by a whip), could never be made to see the justice of her demand, and consequently (as the rug frequently revealed) never missed an opportunity of evading it when her back was turned. Her husband often reminded her of the poodle, and, not having a whip or its moral equivalent to control him with, she had long since resigned herself to seeing him smudge the whiteness of her early illusions. The worst of it was that her resignation was such a cheap virtue. She had to be perpetually rousing herself to a sense of Benson's enormities; through the ever-lengthening perspective of her indifference they looked as small as the details of a landscape seen through the wrong end of a telescope. Now and then she tried to remind herself that she had married him for love; but she was well aware that the sentiment she had once entertained for him had nothing in common with the state of mind which the words now represented to her; and this naturally diminished the force of the argument. She had married him at nineteen, because he had beautiful blue eyes and always wore a gardenia in his coat; really, as far as she could remember, these considerations had been the determining factors in her choice. Delia as a child (her parents were since dead) had been a much-indulged daughter, with a liberal allowance of pocket-money, and permission to spend it unquestioned and unadvised. Subsequently, she used sometimes to look, in a critical humor, at the various articles which she had purchased in her teens; futile chains and lockets, valueless china knick-knacks, and poor engravings of sentimental pictures. These, as a chastisement to her taste, she religiously preserved; and they often made her think of Benson. No one, she could not but reflect, would have blamed her if, with the acquirement of a fuller discrimination, she had thrown them all out of the window and replaced them by some object of permanent merit; but she was expected not only to keep Benson for life, but to conceal the fact that her taste had long since discarded him.

It could hardly be expected that a woman who reasoned so dispassionately about her mistakes should attempt to deceive herself about her preferences. Corbett personified all those finer amenities of mind and manners which may convert the mere act of being into a beneficent career; to Delia he seemed the most admirable man she had ever met, and she would have thought it disloyal to her best aspirations not to admire him. But she did not attempt to palliate her warmer feeling under the mask of a plausible esteem; she knew that she loved him, and scorned to disavow that also. So well, however, did she keep her secret that Corbett himself never suspected it, until her husband's death freed her from the obligation of concealment. Then, indeed, she gloried in its confession; and after two years of widowhood, and more than two months of marriage, she was still under the spell of that moment of exquisite avowal.

She was reliving it now, as she often did in the rare hours which separated her from her husband; when presently she heard his step on the stairs, and started up with the blush of eighteen. As she walked across the room to meet him she asked herself perversely (she was given to such obliqueness of self-scrutiny) if to a dispassionate eye he would appear as complete, as supremely well-equipped as she beheld him, or if she walked in a cloud of delusion, dense as the god-concealing mist of Homer. But whenever she put this question to herself, Corbett's appearance instantly relegated it to the limbo of solved enigmas; he was so obviously admirable that she wondered that people didn't stop her in the street to attest her good fortune.

As he came forward now, this renewal of satisfaction was so strong in her that she felt an impulse to seize him and assure herself of his reality; he was so perilously like the phantasms of joy which had mocked her dissatisfied past. But his coat-sleeve was convincingly tangible; and, pinching it, she felt the muscles beneath.

"What—all alone?" he said, smiling back her welcome.

"No, I wasn't—I was with you!" she exclaimed; then fearing to appear fatuous, added, with a slight shrug, "Don't be alarmed—it won't last."

"That's what frightens me," he answered, gravely.

"Precisely," she laughed; "and I shall take good care not to reassure you!"

They stood face to face for a moment, reading in each other's eyes the completeness of their communion; then he broke the silence by saying, "By the way, I'd forgotten; here's a letter for you."

She took it unregardingly, her eyes still deep in his; but as her glance turned to the envelope she uttered a note of pleasure.

"Oh, how nice—it's from your only rival!"

"Your Aunt Mary?"

She nodded. "I haven't heard from her in a month—and I'm afraid I haven't written to her either. You don't know how many beneficent intentions of mine you divert from their proper channels."

"But your Aunt Mary has had you all your life—I've only had you two months," he objected.

Delia was still contemplating the letter with a smile. "Dear thing!" she murmured. "I wonder when I shall see her?"

"Write and ask her to come and spend the winter with us."

"What—and leave Boston, and her kindergartens, and associated charities, and symphony concerts, and debating clubs? You don't know Aunt Mary!"

"No, I don't. It seems so incongruous that you should adore such a bundle of pedantries."

"I forgive that, because you've never seen her. How I wish you could!"

He stood looking down at her with the all-promising smile of the happy lover. "Well, if she won't come to us we'll go to her."

"Laurence—and leave this!"

"It will keep—we'll come back to it. My dear girl, don't beam so; you make me feel as if you hadn't been happy until now."

"No—but it's your thinking of it!"

"I'll do more than think; I'll act; I'll take you to Boston to see your Aunt Mary."

"Oh, Laurence, you'd hate doing it."

"Not doing it together."

She laid her hand for a moment on his. "What a difference that does make in things!" she said, as she broke the seal of the letter.

"Well, I'll leave you to commune with Aunt Mary. When you've done, come and find me in the library."

Delia sat down joyfully to the perusal of her letter, but as her eye travelled over the closely written pages her gratified expression turned to one of growing concern; and presently, thrusting it back into the envelope, she followed her husband to the library. It was a charming room and singularly indicative, to her fancy, of its occupant's character; the expanse of harmonious bindings, the fruity bloom of Renaissance bronzes, and the imprisoned sunlight of two or three old pictures fitly epitomizing the delicate ramifications of her husband's taste. But now her glance lingered less appreciatively than usual on the warm tones and fine lines which formed so expressive a background for Corbett's fastidious figure.

"Aunt Mary has been ill—I'm afraid she's been seriously ill," she announced as he rose to receive her. "She fell in coming downstairs from one of her tenement-house inspections, and it brought on water on the knee. She's been laid up ever since—some three or four weeks now. I'm afraid it's rather bad at her age; and I don't know how she will resign herself to keeping quiet."

"I'm very sorry," said Corbett, sympathetically; "but water on the knee isn't dangerous, you know."

"No—but the doctor says she mustn't go out for weeks and weeks; and that will drive her mad. She'll think the universe has come to a standstill."

"She'll find it hasn't," suggested Corbett, with a smile which took the edge from his comment.

"Ah, but such discoveries hurt—especially if one makes them late in life!"

Corbett stood looking affectionately at his wife.

"How long is it," he asked, "since you have seen your Aunt Mary?"

"I think it must be two years. Yes, just two years; you know I went home on business after—" She stopped; they never alluded to her first marriage.

Corbett took her hand. "Well," he declared, glancing rather wistfully at the Paris Bordone above the mantel-piece, "we'll sail next month and pay her a little visit."

## II

CORBETT was really making an immense concession in going to America at that season; he disliked the prospect at all times, but just as his hotel in Paris had reopened its luxurious arms to him for the winter, the thought of departure was peculiarly distasteful. Delia knew it, and winced under the enormity of the sacrifice which he had imposed upon himself; but he bore the burden so lightly, and so smilingly derided her impulse to magnify the heroism of his conduct, that she gradually yielded to the undisturbed enjoyment of her anticipations. She was really very glad to be returning to Boston as Corbett's wife; her occasional appearances there as Mrs. Benson had been so eminently unsatisfactory to herself and her relatives that she naturally desired to efface them by so triumphal a re-entry. She had passed so great a part of her own life in Europe that she viewed with a secret leniency Corbett's indifference to his native land; but though she did not mind his not caring for his country she was intensely anxious that his country should care for him. He was a New Yorker, and entirely unknown, save by name, to her little circle of friends and relatives in Boston; but she reflected, with tranquil satisfaction, that, if he were cosmopolitan enough for Fifth Avenue, he was also cultured enough for Beacon Street. She was not so confident of his being altruistic enough for Aunt Mary; but Aunt Mary's appreciations covered so wide a range that there seemed small doubt of his coming under the head of one of her manifold enthusiasms.

Altogether Delia's anticipations grew steadily rosier with the approach to Sandy Hook; and to her confident eye the Statue of Liberty, as they passed under it in the red brilliance of a winter sunrise, seemed to look down upon Corbett with her Aunt Mary's most approving smile.

Delia's Aunt Mary—known from the Back Bay to the South End as Mrs. Mason Hayne—had been the chief formative influence of her niece's youth. Delia, after the death of her parents, had even spent two years under Mrs. Hayne's roof, in direct contact with all her apostolic ardors, her inflammatory zeal for righteousness in everything from baking-powder to municipal government; and though the girl never felt any inclination to interpret her aunt's influence in action, it was potent in modifying her judgment of herself and others. Her parents had been incurably frivolous, Mrs. Hayne was incurably serious, and Delia, by some unconscious powers of selection, tended to frivolity of conduct, corrected by seriousness of thought. She would have shrunk from the life of unadorned activity, the unsmiling pursuit of Purposes with a capital letter, to which Mrs. Hayne's energies were dedicated; but it lent relief to her enjoyment of the purposeless to measure her own conduct by her aunt's utilitarian standards. This curious sympathy with aims so at variance with her own ideals would hardly have been possible to Delia had Mrs. Hayne been a narrow enthusiast without visual range beyond the blinders of her own vocation; it was the consciousness that her aunt's perceptions included even such obvious inutility as hers which made her so tolerant of her aunt's usefulness. All this she had tried, on the way across the Atlantic, to put vividly before Corbett; but she was conscious of a vague inability on his part to adjust his conception of Mrs. Hayne to his wife's view of her; and Delia could only count on her aunt's abounding personality to correct the one-sidedness of his impression.

Mrs. Hayne lived in a wide brick house on Mount Vernon Street, which had belonged to her parents and grandparents, and from which she had never thought of moving. Thither, on the evening of their arrival in Boston, the Corbetts were driven from the Providence Station. Mrs. Hayne had written to her niece that Cyrus would meet them with a "hack;" Cyrus was a sable factotum designated in Mrs. Hayne's vocabulary as a "chore-man." When the train entered the station he was, in fact, conspicuous on the platform, his smile shining like an open piano, while he proclaimed with abundant gesture the proximity of "de hack," and Delia, descending from the train into his dusky embrace, found herself guiltily wishing that he could have been omitted from the function of their arrival. She could not help wondering what her husband's valet would think of him. The valet was to be lodged at a hotel: Corbett himself had suggested that his presence might disturb the routine of Mrs. Hayne's household, a view in which Delia had eagerly acquiesced. There was, however, no possibility of dissembling Cyrus, and under the valet's depreciatory eye the Corbetts suffered him to precede them to the livery-stable landau, with blue shades and a confidentially disposed driver, which awaited them outside the station.

During the drive to Mount Vernon Street Delia was silent; but as they approached her aunt's swell-fronted domicile she said, hurriedly, "You won't like the house."

Corbett laughed. "It's the inmate I've come to see," he commented.

"Oh, I'm not afraid of her," Delia almost too confidently rejoined.

The parlor-maid who admitted them to the hall (a discouraging hall, with a large-patterned oil-cloth and buff walls stenciled with a Greek border) informed them that Mrs. Hayne was above; and ascending to the next floor they found her genial figure, supported on crutches, awaiting them at the drawing-room door. Mrs. Hayne was a tall, stoutish woman, whose bland expanse of feature was accentuated by a pair of gray eyes of such surpassing penetration that Delia often accused her of answering people's thoughts before they had finished thinking them. These eyes, through the close fold of Delia's embrace, pierced instantly to Corbett, and never had that accomplished gentleman been more conscious of being called upon to present his credentials. But there was no reservation in the uncritical warmth of Mrs. Hayne's welcome, and it was obvious that she was unaffectedly happy in their coming.

She led them into the drawing-room, still clinging to Delia, and Corbett, as he followed, understood why his wife had said that he would not like the house. One saw at a glance that Mrs. Hayne had never had time to think of her house or her dress. Both were scrupulously neat, but her gown might have been an unaltered one of her mother's, and her drawing-room wore the same appearance of contented archaism. There was a sufficient number of arm-chairs, and the tables (mostly marble-topped) were redeemed from monotony by their freight of books; but it had not occurred to Mrs. Hayne to substitute logs for hard coal in her fireplace, nor to replace by more personal works of art the smoky expanses of canvas "after" Raphael and Murillo which lurched heavily forward from the walls. She had even preserved the knotty antimacassars on her high-backed armchairs, and Corbett, who was growing bald, resignedly reflected that during his stay in Mount Vernon Street he should not be able to indulge in any lounging.

## III

DELIA held back for three days the question which burned her lip; then, following her husband upstairs after an evening during which Mrs. Hayne had proved herself especially comprehensive (even questioning Corbett upon the tendencies of modern French art), she let escape the imminent "Well?"

"She's charming," Corbett returned, with the fine smile which always seemed like a delicate criticism.

"Really?"

"Really, Delia. Do you think me so narrow that I can't value such a character as your aunt's simply because it's cast in different lines from mine? I once told you that she must be a bundle of pedantries, and you prophesied that my first sight of her would correct that impression. You were right; she's a bundle of extraordinary vitalities. I never saw a woman more thoroughly alive; and that's the great secret of living—to be thoroughly alive."

"I knew it; I knew it!" his wife exclaimed. "Two such people couldn't help liking each other."

"Oh, I should think she might very well help liking me."

"She doesn't; she admires you immensely; but why?"

"Well, I don't precisely fit into any of her ideals, and the worst part of having ideals is that the people who don't fit into them have to be discarded."

"Aunt Mary doesn't discard anybody," Delia interpolated.

"Her heart may not, but I fancy her judgment does."

"But she doesn't exactly fit into any of your ideals, and yet you like her," his wife persisted.

"I haven't any ideals," Corbett lightly responded. "*Je prends mon bien où je le trouve*; and I find a great deal in your Aunt Mary."

Delia did not ask Mrs. Hayne what she thought of her husband; she was sure that, in due time, her aunt would deliver her verdict; it was impossible for her to leave any one unclassified. Perhaps, too, there was a latent cowardice in Delia's reticence; an unacknowledged dread lest Mrs. Hayne should range Corbett among the intermediate types.

After a day or two of mutual inspection and adjustment the three lives under Mrs. Hayne's roof lapsed into their separate routines. Mrs. Hayne once more set in motion the complicated machinery of her own existence (rendered more intricate by the accident of her lameness), and Corbett and his wife began to dine out and return the visits of their friends. There were, however, some hours which Corbett devoted to the club or to the frequentation of the public libraries, and these Delia gave to her aunt, driving with Mrs. Hayne from one committee meeting to another, writing business letters at her dictation, or reading aloud to her the reports of the various philanthropic, educational, or political institutions in which she was interested. She had been conscious on her arrival of a certain aloofness from her aunt's militant activities; but within a week she was swept back into the strong current of Mrs. Hayne's existence. It was like stepping from a gondola to an ocean steamer; at first she was dazed by the throb of the screw and the rush of the parting waters, but gradually she felt herself infected by the exhilaration of getting to a fixed place in the shortest possible time. She could make sufficient allowance for the versatility of her moods to know that, a few weeks after her return to Paris, all that seemed most strenuous in Mrs. Hayne's occupations would fade to unreality; but that did not defend her from the strong spell of the moment. In its light her own life seemed vacuous, her husband's aims trivial as the subtleties of Chinese ivory carving; and she wondered if he walked in the same revealing flash.

Some three weeks after the arrival of the Corbetts in Mount Vernon Street it became manifest that Mrs. Hayne had overtaxed her strength and must return for an undetermined period to her lounge. The life of restricted activity to which this necessity condemned her left her an occasional hour of leisure when there seemed no more letters to be dictated, no more reports to be read; and Corbett, always sure to do the right thing, was at hand to speed such unoccupied moments with the ready charm of his talk.

One day when, after sitting with her for some time, he departed to the club, Mrs. Hayne, turning to Delia, who came in to replace him, said, emphatically, "My dear, he's delightful."

"Oh, Aunt Mary, so are you!" burst gratefully from Mrs. Corbett.

Mrs. Hayne smiled. "Have you suspended your judgment of me until now?" she asked.

"No; but your liking each other seems to complete you both."

"Really, Delia, your husband couldn't have put that more gracefully. But sit down and tell me about him."

"Tell you about him?" repeated Delia, thinking of the voluminous letters in which she had enumerated to Mrs. Hayne the sum of her husband's merits.

"Yes," Mrs. Hayne continued, cutting, as she talked, the pages of a report on state lunatic asylums; "for instance, you've never told me why so charming an American has condemned America to the hard fate of being obliged to get on without him."

"You and he will never agree on that point, Aunt Mary," said Mrs. Corbett, coloring.

"Never mind; I rather like listening to reasons that I know beforehand I'm bound to disagree with; it saves so much mental effort. And besides, how can you tell? I'm very uncertain."

"You are very broad-minded, but you'll never understand his just having drifted into it. Any definite reason would seem to you better than that."

"Ah—he drifted into it?"

"Well, yes. You know his sister, who married the Comte de Vitrey and went to live in Paris, was very unhappy after her marriage; and when Laurence's mother died there was no one left to look after her; and so Laurence went abroad in order to be near her. After a few years Monsieur de Vitrey died too; but by that time Laurence didn't care to come back."

"Well," said Mrs. Hayne, "I see nothing so shocking in that. Your husband can gratify his tastes much more easily in Europe than in America; and, after all, that is what we're all secretly striving to do. I'm sure if there were more lunatic asylums and poor-houses and hospitals in Europe than there are here I should be very much inclined to go and live there myself."

Delia laughed. "I knew you would like Laurence," she said, with a wisdom bred of the event.

"Of course I like him; he's a liberal education. It's very interesting to study the determining motives in such a man's career. How old is your husband, Delia?"

"Laurence is fifty-two."

"And when did he go abroad to look after his sister?"

"Let me see—when he was about twenty-eight; it was in 1867, I think."

"And before that he had lived in America?"

"Yes, the greater part of the time."

"Then of course he was in the war?" Mrs. Hayne continued, laying down her pamphlet. "You've never told me about that. Did he see any active service?"

As she spoke Delia grew pale; for a moment she sat looking blankly at her aunt.

"I don't think he was in the war at all," she said at length, in a low tone.

Mrs. Hayne stared at her. "Oh, you must be mistaken," she said, decidedly. "Why shouldn't he have been in the war? What else could he have been doing?"

Mrs. Corbett was silent. All the men of her family, all the men of her friends' families, had fought in the war; Mrs. Hayne's husband had been killed at Bull Run, and one of Delia's cousins at Gettysburg. Ever since she could remember it had been regarded as a matter of course by those about her that every man of her husband's generation who was neither lame, halt, nor blind should have fought in the war. Husbands had left their wives, fathers their children, young men their sweethearts, in answer to that summons; and those who had been deaf to it she had never heard designated by any name but one.

But all that had happened long ago; for years it had ceased to be a part of her consciousness. She had forgotten about the war; about her uncle who fell at Bull Run, and her cousin who was killed at Gettysburg. Now, of a sudden, it all came back to her, and she asked herself the question which her aunt had just put to her—why had her husband not been in the war? What else could he have been doing?

But the very word, as she repeated it, struck her as incongruous; Corbett was a man who never did anything. His elaborate intellectual processes bore no flower of result; he simply was—but had she not hitherto found that sufficient? She rose from her seat, turning away from Mrs. Hayne.

"I really don't know," she said, coldly. "I never asked him."

IV

TWO weeks later the Corbetts returned to Europe. Corbett had really been charmed with his visit, and had in fact shown a marked inclination to outstay the date originally fixed for their departure. But Delia was firm; she did not wish to remain in Boston. She acknowledged that she was sorry to leave her Aunt Mary; but she wanted to get home.

"You turncoat!" Corbett said, laughing. "Two months ago you reserved that sacred designation for Boston."

"One can't tell where it is until one tries," she answered, vaguely.

"You mean that you don't want to come back and live in Boston?"

"Oh, no—no!"

"Very well. But pray take note of the fact that I'm very sorry to leave. Under your Aunt Mary's tutelage I'm becoming a passionate patriot."

Delia turned away in silence. She was counting the moments which led to their departure. She longed with an unreasoning intensity to get away from it all; from the dreary house in Mount Vernon Street, with its stenciled hall and hideous drawing-room, its monotonous food served in unappetizing profusion; from the rarefied atmosphere of philanthropy and reform which she had once found so invigorating; and most of all from the reproval of her aunt's altruistic activities. The recollection of her husband's delightful house in Paris, so framed for a noble leisure, seemed to mock the aesthetic barrenness of Mrs. Hayne's environment. Delia thought tenderly of the mellow bindings, the deep-piled rugs, the pictures, bronzes, and tapestries; of the "first nights" at the Français, the eagerly discussed *conférences* on art or literature, the dreaming hours in galleries and museums, and all the delicate enjoyments of the life to which she was returning. It would be like passing from a hospital-ward to a flower-filled drawing-room; how could her husband linger on the threshold?

Corbett, who observed her attentively, noticed that a change had come over her during the last two weeks of their stay in Mount Vernon Street. He wondered uneasily if she were capricious; a man who has formed his own habits upon principles of the finest selection does not care to think that he has married a capricious woman. Then he reflected that the love of Paris is an insidious disease, breaking out when its victim least looks for it, and concluded that Delia was suffering from some such unexpected attack.

Delia certainly was suffering. Ever since Mrs. Hayne had asked her that innocent question—"Why shouldn't your husband have been in the war?"—she had been repeating it to herself day and night with the monotonous iteration of a monomaniac. Whenever Corbett came into the room, with that air of giving the simplest act its due value which made episodes of his entrances she was tempted to cry out to him—"Why weren't you in the war?" When she heard him, at a dinner, point one of his polished epigrams, or smilingly demolish the syllogism of an antagonist, her pride in his achievement was chilled by the question—"Why wasn't he in the war?" When she saw him, in the street, give a coin to a crossing-sweeper, or lift his hat ceremoniously to one of Mrs. Hayne's maid-servants (he was always considerate of poor people and servants) her approval winced under the reminder—"Why wasn't he in the war?" And when they were alone together, all through the spell of his talk and the exquisite pervasion of his presence ran the embittering undercurrent, "Why wasn't he in the war?"

At times she hated herself for the thought; it seemed a disloyalty to life's best gift.

After all, what did it matter now? The war was over and forgotten; it was what the newspapers call "a dead issue." And why should any act of her husband's youth affect their present happiness together? Whatever he might once have been, he was perfect now; admirable in every relation of life; kind, generous, upright; a loyal friend, an accomplished gentleman, and, above all, the man she loved. Yes—but why had he not been in the war? And so began again the reiterant torment of the question. It rose up and lay down with her; it watched with her through sleepless nights, and followed her into the street; it mocked her from the eyes of strangers, and she dreaded lest her husband should read it in her own. In her saner moments she told herself that she was under the influence of a passing mood, which would vanish at the contact of her wonted life in Paris. She had become over-strung in the high air of Mrs. Hayne's moral enthusiasms; all she needed was to descend again to regions of more temperate virtue. This thought increased her impatience to be gone; and the days seemed interminable which divided her from departure.

The return to Paris, however, did not yield the hoped-for alleviation. The question was still with her, clamoring for a reply, and reinforced, with separation, by the increasing fear of her aunt's unspoken verdict. That shrewd woman had never again alluded to the subject of her brief colloquy with Delia; up to the moment of his farewell she had been unreservedly cordial to Corbett; but she was not the woman to palter with her convictions.

Delia knew what she must think; she knew what name, in the old days, Corbett would have gone by in her aunt's uncompromising circle.

Then came a flash of resistance—the heart's instinct of self-preservation. After all, what did she herself know of her husband's reasons for not being in the war? What right had she to set down to cowardice a course which might have been enforced by necessity, or dictated by unimpeachable motives? Why should she not put to him the question which she was perpetually asking herself? And not having done so, how dared she condemn him unheard?

A month or more passed in this torturing indecision. Corbett had returned with fresh zest to his accustomed way of life, weaned, by his first glimpse of the Champs Élysées, from his factitious enthusiasm for Boston. He and his wife entertained their friends delightfully, and frequented all the "first nights" and "private views" of the season, and Corbett continued to bring back knowing "bits" from the Hotel Drouot, and rare books from the quays; never had he appeared more cultivated, more decorative and enviable; people agreed that Delia Benson had been uncommonly clever to catch him.

One afternoon he returned later than usual from the club, and, finding his wife alone in the drawing-room, begged her for a cup of tea. Delia reflected, in complying, that she had never seen him look better; his fifty-two years sat upon him like a finish which made youth appear crude, and his voice, as he recounted his afternoon's doings, had the intimate inflections reserved for her ear.

"By the way," he said presently, as he set down his tea-cup, "I had almost forgotten that I've brought you a present—something I picked up in a little shop in the Rue Bonaparte. Oh, don't look too expectant; it's not a *chef-d'oeuvre;* on the contrary, it's about as bad as it can be. But you'll see presently why I bought it."

As he spoke he drew a small flat parcel from the breast-pocket of his impeccable frock-coat and handed it to his wife.

Delia, loosening the paper which wrapped it, discovered within an oval frame studded with pearls and containing the crudely executed miniature of an unknown young man in the uniform of a United States cavalry officer. She glanced inquiringly at Corbett.

"Turn it over," he said.

She did so, and on the back, beneath two unfamiliar initials, read the brief inscription:

"Fell at Chancellorsville, May 3, 1863."

The blood rushed to her face as she stood gazing at the words.

"You see now why I bought it?" Corbett continued. "All the pieties of one's youth seemed to protest against leaving it in the clutches of a Jew pawnbroker in the Rue Bonaparte. It's awfully bad, isn't it?—but some poor soul might be glad to think that it had passed again into the possession of fellow-countrymen." He took it back from her, bending to examine it critically. "What a daub!" he murmured. "I wonder who he was? Do you suppose that by taking a little trouble one might find out and restore it to his people?"

"I don't know—I dare say," she murmured, absently.

He looked up at the sound of her voice. "What's the matter, Delia? Don't you feel well?" he asked.

"Oh, yes. I was only thinking"—she took the miniature from his hand. "It was kind of you, Laurence, to buy this—it was like you."

"Thanks for the latter clause," he returned, smiling.

Delia stood staring at the vivid flesh-tints of the young man who had fallen at Chancellorsville.

"You weren't very strong at his age, were you, Laurence? Weren't you often ill?" she asked.

Corbett gave her a surprised glance. "Not that I'm aware of," he said; "I had the measles at twelve, but since then I've been unromantically robust."

"And you—you were in America until you came abroad to be with your sister?"

"Yes—barring a trip of a few weeks in Europe."

Delia looked again at the miniature; then she fixed her eyes upon her husband's.

"Then why weren't you in the war?" she said.

Corbett answered her gaze for a moment; then his lids dropped, and he shifted his position slightly.

"Really," he said, with a smile, "I don't think I know."

They were the very words which she had used in answering her aunt.

"You don't know?" she repeated, the question leaping out like an electric shock. "What do you mean when you say that you don't know?"

"Well—it all happened some time ago," he answered, still smiling, "and the truth is that I've completely forgotten the excellent reasons that I doubtless had at the time for remaining at home."

"Reasons for remaining at home? But there were none; every man of your age went to the war; no one stayed at home who wasn't lame, or blind, or deaf, or ill, or—" Her face blazed, her voice broke passionately.

Corbett looked at her with rising amazement.

"Or—?" he said.

"Or a coward," she flashed out. The miniature dropped from her hands, falling loudly on the polished floor.

The two confronted each other in silence; Corbett was very pale.

"I've told you," he said, at length, "that I was neither lame, deaf, blind, nor ill. Your classification is so simple that it will be easy for you to draw your own conclusion."

And very quietly, with that admirable air which always put him in the right, he walked out of the room. Delia, left alone, bent down and picked up the miniature; its protecting crystal had been broken by the fall. She pressed it close to her and burst into tears.

An hour later, of course, she went to ask her husband's forgiveness. As a woman of sense she could do no less; and her conduct had been so absurd that it was the more obviously pardonable. Corbett, as he kissed her hand, assured her that he had known it was only nervousness; and after dinner, during which he made himself exceptionally agreeable, he proposed their ending the evening at the Palais Royal, where a new play was being given.

Delia had undoubtedly behaved like a fool, and was prepared to do meet penance for her folly by submitting to the gentle sarcasm of her husband's pardon; but when the episode was over, and she realized that she had asked her question and received her answer, she knew that she had passed a milestone in her existence. Corbett was perfectly charming; it was inevitable that he should go on being charming to the end of the chapter. It was equally inevitable that she should go on being in love with him; but her love had undergone a modification which the years were not to efface.

Formerly he had been to her like an unexplored country, full of bewitching surprises and recurrent revelations of wonder and beauty; now she had measured and mapped him, and knew beforehand the direction of every path she trod. His answer to her question had given her the clue to the labyrinth; knowing what he had once done, it seemed quite simple to forecast his future conduct. For that long-past action was still a part of his actual being; he had not outlived or disowned it; he had not even seen that it needed defending.

Her ideal of him was shivered like the crystal above the miniature of the warrior of Chancellorsville. She had the crystal replaced by a piece of clear glass which (as the jeweler pointed out to her) cost much less and looked equally well; and for the passionate worship which she had paid her husband she substituted a tolerant affection which possessed precisely the same advantages.

## THE VALLEY OF CHILDISH THINGS, AND OTHER EMBLEMS

### As first published in *The Century Magazine*, July, 1896

ONCE UPON A TIME a number of children lived together in the Valley of Childish Things, playing all manner of delightful games, and studying the same lesson-books. But one day a little girl, one of their number, decided that it was time to see something of the world about which the lesson-books had taught her; and as none of the other children cared to leave their games, she set out alone to climb the pass which led out of the valley.

It was a hard climb, but at length she reached a cold, bleak table-land beyond the mountains. Here she saw cities and men, and learned many useful arts, and in so doing grew to be a woman. But the table-land was bleak and cold, and when she had served her apprenticeship she decided to return to her old companions in the Valley of Childish Things, and work with them instead of with strangers.

It was a weary way back, and her feet were bruised by the stones, and her face was beaten by the weather; but half way down the pass she met a man, who kindly helped her over the roughest places. Like herself, he was lame and weather-beaten; but as soon as he spoke she recognized him as one of her old playmates. He too had been out in the world, and was going back to the valley; and on the way they talked together of the work they meant to do there. He had been a dull boy, and she had never taken much notice of him; but as she listened to his plans for building bridges and draining swamps and cutting roads through the jungle, she thought to herself, "Since he has grown into such a fine fellow, what splendid men and women my other playmates must have become!"

But what was her surprise to find, on reaching the valley, that her former companions, instead of growing into men and women, had all remained little children. Most of them were playing the same old games, and the few who affected to be working were engaged in such strenuous occupations as building mud-pies and sailing paper boats in basins. As for the lad who had been the favorite companion of her studies, he was playing marbles with all the youngest boys in the valley.

At first, the children seemed glad to have her back, but soon she saw that her presence interfered with their games; and when she tried to tell them of the great things that were being done on the table-land beyond the mountains, they picked up their toys and went farther down the valley to play.

Then she turned to her fellow-traveler, who was the only grown man in the valley; but he was on his knees before a dear little girl with blue eyes and a coral necklace, for whom he was making a garden out of cockle-shells and bits of glass, and broken flowers stuck in sand.

The little girl was clapping her hands and crowing (she was too young to speak articulately); and when she who had grown to be a woman laid her hand on the man's shoulder, and asked him if he did not want to set to work with her building bridges, draining swamps, and cutting roads through the jungle, he replied that at that particular moment he was too busy.

And as she turned away, he added in the kindest possible way, "Really, my dear, you ought to have taken better care of your complexion."

II

THERE was once a maiden lady who lived alone in a commodious brick house facing north and south. The lady was very fond of warmth and sunshine, but unfortunately her room was on the north side of the house, so that in winter she had no sun at all.

This distressed her so much that, after long deliberation, she sent for an architect, and asked him if it would be possible to turn the house around so that her room should face the south. The architect replied that anything could be done for money; but the estimated cost of turning the house around was so high that the lady, who enjoyed a handsome income, was obliged to reduce her way of living and sell her securities at a sacrifice to raise money enough for the purpose. At length, however, the house was turned around, and she felt almost consoled for her impoverishment by the first ray of sunlight which stole through her shutters the next morning.

That very day she received a visit from an old friend who had been absent a year; and this friend, finding her seated at her window in a flood of sunlight, immediately exclaimed:

"My dear, how sensible of you to have moved into a south room! I never could understand why you persisted so long in living on the north side of the house."

And the following day the architect sent in his bill.

## III

THERE was once a little girl who was so very intelligent that her parents feared that she would die.

But an aged aunt, who had crossed the Atlantic in a sailing-vessel, said, "My dears, let her marry the first man she falls in love with, and she will make such a fool of herself that it will probably save her life."

## IV

A THINLY clad man, who was trudging afoot through a wintry and shelterless region, met another wrapped in a big black cloak. The cloak hung heavily on its wearer, and seemed to drag him back, but at least it kept off the cold.

"That's a fine warm cloak you've got," said the first man through his chattering teeth.

"Oh," said the other, "it's none of my choosing, I promise you. It's only my old happiness dyed black and made over into a sorrow; but in this weather a man must wear what he's got."

"To think of some people's luck!" muttered the first man, as the other passed on. "Now I never had enough happiness to make a sorrow out of."

## V

THERE was once a man who married a sweet little wife; but when he set out with her from her father's house, he found that she had never been taught to walk. They had a long way to go, and there was nothing for him to do but to carry her; and as he carried her she grew heavier and heavier.

Then they came to a wide, deep river, and he found that she had never been taught to swim. So he told her to hold fast to his shoulder, and started to swim with her across the river. And as he swam she grew frightened, and dragged him down in her struggles. And the river was deep and wide, and the current ran fast; and once or twice she nearly had him under. But he fought his way through, and landed her safely on the other side; and behold, he found himself in a strange country, beyond all imagining delightful. And as he looked about him and gave thanks, he said to himself:

"Perhaps if I hadn't had to carry her over, I shouldn't have kept up long enough to get here myself."

## VI

A SOUL once cowered in a gray waste, and a mighty shape came by. Then the soul cried out for help, saying, "Shall I be left to perish alone in this desert of Unsatisfied Desires?"

"But you are mistaken," the shape replied; "this is the land of Gratified Longings. And, moreover, you are not alone, for the country is full of people; but whoever tarries here grows blind."

## VII

THERE was once a very successful architect who made a great name for himself. At length he built a magnificent temple, to which he devoted more time and thought than to any of the other buildings he had erected; and the world pronounced it his masterpiece. Shortly afterward he died, and when he came before the judgment angel he was not asked how many sins he had committed, but how many houses he had built.

He hung his head and said, more than he could count.

The judgment angel asked what they were like, and the architect said that he was afraid they were pretty bad.

"And are you sorry?" asked the angel.

"Very sorry," said the architect, with honest contrition.

"And how about that famous temple that you built just before you died?" the angel continued. "Are you satisfied with that?"

"Oh, no," the architect exclaimed. "I really think it has some good points about it,—I did try my best, you know,—but there's one dreadful mistake that I'd give my soul to go back and rectify."

"Well," said the angel, "you can't go back and rectify it, but you can take your choice of the following alternatives: either we can let the world go on thinking your temple a masterpiece and you the greatest architect that ever lived, or we can send to earth a young fellow we've got here who will discover your mistake at a glance, and point it out so clearly to posterity that you'll be the laughing-stock of all succeeding generations of architects. Which do you choose?"

"Oh, well," said the architect, "if it comes to that, you know—as long as it suits my clients as it is, I really don't see the use of making such a fuss."

## VIII

A MAN once married a charming young person who agreed with him on every question. At first they were very happy, for the man thought his wife the most interesting companion he had ever met, and they spent their days telling each other what wonderful people they were. But by and by the man began to find his wife rather tiresome. Wherever he went she insisted upon going; whatever he did, she was sure to tell him that it would have been better to do the opposite; and moreover, it gradually dawned upon him that his friends had never thought so highly of her as he did. Having made this discovery, he naturally felt justified in regarding himself as the aggrieved party; she took the same view of her situation, and their life was one of incessant recrimination.

Finally, after years spent in violent quarrels and short-lived reconciliations, the man grew weary, and decided to divorce his wife.

He engaged an able lawyer, who assured him that he would have no difficulty in obtaining a divorce; but to his surprise, the judge refused to grant it.

"But—" said the man, and he began to recapitulate his injuries.

"That's all very true," said the judge, "and nothing would be easier than for you to obtain a divorce if you had only married another person."

"What do you mean by another person?" asked the man in astonishment.

"Well," replied the judge, "it appears that you inadvertently married yourself; that is a union no court has the power to dissolve."

"Oh, said the man; and he was secretly glad, for in his heart he was already longing to make it up again with his wife.

## IX

THERE was once a gentleman who greatly disliked to assume any responsibility. Being possessed of ample means and numerous poor relatives, he might have indulged a variety of tastes and even a few virtues; but since there is no occupation that does not bring a few cares in its train, this gentleman resolutely refrained from doing anything.

He ceased to visit his old mother, who lived in the country, because it made him nervous to catch the train; he subscribed to no charities because it was a bother to write the checks; he received no visits because he did not wish to be under the obligation of returning them; he invited no guests to stay with him, for fear of being bored before they left; he gave no presents because it was so troublesome to choose them; finally, he even gave up asking his friends to dine because it was such a nuisance to tell the cook that they were coming.

This gentleman took an honest pride in his complete detachment from the trivial importunities of life, and was never tired of ridiculing those who complained of the weight of their responsibilities, justly remarking that if they really wished to be their own masters they had only to follow his example.

One day, however, one of his servants carelessly left the front door open, and Death walked in unannounced, and begged the gentleman to come along as quickly as possible, as there were a good many more people to be called for that afternoon.

"But I can't," cried the gentleman, in dismay. "I really can't, you know. I—why, I've asked some people to dine with me this evening."

"That's a little too much," said Death. And the devil carried the gentleman off in a big black bag.

## X

THERE was once a man who had seen the Parthenon, and he wished to build his god a temple like it.

But he was not a skillful man, and, try as he would, he could produce only a mud hut thatched with straw; and he sat down and wept because he could not build a temple for his god.

But one who passed by said to him:

"There are two worse plights than yours. One is to have no god; the other is to build a mud hut and mistake it for the Parthenon."

# THE GREATER INCLINATION (1899)

## THE MUSE'S TRAGEDY

DANYERS AFTERWARDS liked to fancy that he had recognized Mrs. Anerton at once; but that, of course, was absurd, since he had seen no portrait of her—she affected a strict anonymity, refusing even her photograph to the most privileged—and from Mrs. Memorall, whom he revered and cultivated as her friend, he had extracted but the one impressionist phrase: "Oh, well, she's like one of those old prints where the lines have the value of color."

He was almost certain, at all events, that he had been thinking of Mrs. Anerton as he sat over his breakfast in the empty hotel restaurant, and that, looking up on the approach of the lady who seated herself at the table near the window, he had said to himself, "*That might be she.*"

Ever since his Harvard days—he was still young enough to think of them as immensely remote—Danyers had dreamed of Mrs. Anerton, the Silvia of Vincent Rendle's immortal sonnet-cycle, the Mrs. A. of the *Life and Letters*. Her name was enshrined in some of the noblest English verse of the nineteenth century—and of all past or future centuries, as Danyers, from the stand-point of a maturer judgment, still believed. The first reading of certain poems—of the *Antinous*, the *Pia Tolomei*, the *Sonnets to Silvia*—had been epochs in Danyers' growth, and the verse seemed to gain in mellowness, in amplitude, in meaning as one brought to its interpretation more experience of life, a finer emotional sense. Where, in his boyhood, he had felt only the perfect, the almost austere beauty of form, the subtle interplay of vowel-sounds, the rush and fullness of lyric emotion, he now thrilled to the close-packed significance of each line, the allusiveness of each word—his imagination lured hither and thither on fresh trails of thought, and perpetually spurred by the sense that, beyond what he had already discovered, more marvelous regions lay waiting to be explored. Danyers had written, at college, the prize essay on Rendle's poetry (it chanced to be the moment of the great man's death); he had fashioned the fugitive verse of his own storm-and-stress period on the forms which Rendle had first given to English meter; and when two years later the *Life and Letters* appeared, and the Silvia of the sonnets took substance as Mrs. A., he had included in his worship of Rendle the woman who had inspired not only such divine verse but such playful, tender, incomparable prose.

Danyers never forgot the day when Mrs. Memorall happened to mention that she knew Mrs. Anerton. He had known Mrs. Memorall for a year or more, and had somewhat contemptuously classified her as the kind of woman who runs cheap excursions to celebrities; when one afternoon she remarked, as she put a second lump of sugar in his tea:

"Is it right this time? You're almost as particular as Mary Anerton."

"Mary Anerton?"

"Yes, I never *can* remember how she likes her tea. Either it's lemon *with* sugar, or lemon without sugar, or cream without either, and whichever it is must be put into the cup before the tea is poured in; and if one hasn't remembered, one must begin all over again. I suppose it was Vincent Rendle's way of taking his tea and has become a sacred rite."

"Do you *know* Mrs. Anerton?" cried Danyers, disturbed by this careless familiarity with the habits of his divinity.

"'And did I once see Shelley plain?' Mercy, yes! She and I were at school together—she's an American, you know. We were at a *pension* near Tours for nearly a year; then she went back to New York, and I didn't see her again till after her marriage. She and Anerton spent a winter in Rome while my husband was attached to our Legation there, and she used to be with us a great deal." Mrs. Memorall smiled reminiscently. "It was *the* winter."

"The winter they first met?"

"Precisely—but unluckily I left Rome just before the meeting took place. Wasn't it too bad? I might have been in the *Life and Letters*. You know he mentions that stupid Madame Vodki, at whose house he first saw her."

"And did you see much of her after that?"

"Not during Rendle's life. You know she has lived in Europe almost entirely, and though I used to see her off and on when I went abroad, she was always so engrossed, so preoccupied, that one felt one wasn't wanted. The fact is, she cared only about his friends—she separated herself gradually from all her own people. Now, of course, it's different; she's desperately lonely; she's taken to writing to me now and then; and last year, when she heard I was going abroad, she asked me to meet her in Venice, and I spent a week with her there."

"And Rendle?"

Mrs. Memorall smiled and shook her head. "Oh, I never was allowed a peep at *him*; none of her old friends met him, except by accident. Ill-natured people say that was the reason she kept him so long. If one happened in while he was there, he was hustled into Anerton's study, and the husband mounted guard till the inopportune visitor had departed. Anerton, you know, was really much more ridiculous about it than his wife. Mary was too clever to lose her head, or at least to show she'd lost it—but Anerton couldn't conceal his pride in the conquest. I've seen Mary shiver when he spoke of Rendle as *our poet*. Rendle always had to have a certain seat at the dinner-table, away from the draught and not too near the fire, and a box of cigars that no one else was allowed to touch, and a writing-table of his own in Mary's sitting-room—and Anerton was always telling one of the great man's idiosyncrasies: how he never would cut the ends of his cigars, though Anerton himself had given him a gold cutter set with a star-sapphire, and how untidy his writing-table was, and how the house- maid had orders always to bring the waste-paper basket to her mistress before emptying it, lest some immortal verse should be thrown into the dust-bin."

"The Anertons never separated, did they?"

"Separated? Bless you, no. He never would have left Rendle! And besides, he was very fond of his wife."

"And she?"

"Oh, she saw he was the kind of man who was fated to make himself ridiculous, and she never interfered with his natural tendencies."

From Mrs. Memorall, Danyers further learned that Mrs. Anerton, whose husband had died some years before her poet, now divided her life between Rome, where she had a small apartment, and England, where she occasionally went to stay with those of her friends who had been Rendle's. She had been engaged, for some time after his death, in editing some juvenilia which he had bequeathed to her care; but that task being accomplished, she had been left without definite occupation, and Mrs. Memorall, on the occasion of their last meeting, had found her listless and out of spirits.

"She misses him too much—her life is too empty. I told her so—I told her she ought to marry."

"Oh!"

"Why not, pray? She's a young woman still—what many people would call young," Mrs. Memorall interjected, with a parenthetic glance at the mirror. "Why not accept the inevitable and begin over again? All the King's horses and all the King's men won't bring Rendle to life-and besides, she didn't marry *him* when she had the chance."

Danyers winced slightly at this rude fingering of his idol. Was it possible that Mrs. Memorall did not see what an anti-climax such a marriage would have been? Fancy Rendle "making an honest woman" of Silvia; for so society would have viewed it! How such a reparation would have vulgarized their past—it would have been like "restoring" a masterpiece; and how exquisite must have been the perceptions of the woman who, in defiance of appearances, and perhaps of her own secret inclination, chose to go down to posterity as Silvia rather than as Mrs. Vincent Rendle!

Mrs. Memorall, from this day forth, acquired an interest in Danyers' eyes. She was like a volume of unindexed and discursive memoirs, through which he patiently plodded in the hope of finding embedded amid layers of dusty twaddle some precious allusion to the subject of his thought. When, some months later, he brought out his first slim volume, in which the remodeled college essay on Rendle figured among a dozen, somewhat overstudied "appreciations," he offered a copy to Mrs. Memorall; who surprised him, the next time they met, with the announcement that she had sent the book to Mrs. Anerton.

Mrs. Anerton in due time wrote to thank her friend. Danyers was privileged to read the few lines in which, in terms that suggested the habit of "acknowledging" similar tributes, she spoke of the author's "feeling and insight," and was "so glad of the opportunity," etc. He went away disappointed, without clearly knowing what else he had expected.

The following spring, when he went abroad, Mrs. Memorall offered him letters to everybody, from the Archbishop of Canterbury to Louise Michel. She did not include Mrs. Anerton, however, and Danyers knew, from a previous conversation, that Silvia objected to people who "brought letters." He knew also that she travelled during the summer, and was unlikely to return to Rome before the term of his holiday should be reached, and the hope of meeting her was not included among his anticipations.

The lady whose entrance broke upon his solitary repast in the restaurant of the Hotel Villa d'Este had seated herself in such a way that her profile was detached against the window; and thus viewed, her domed forehead, small arched nose, and fastidious lip suggested a silhouette of Marie Antoinette. In the lady's dress and movements—in the very turn of her wrist as she poured out her coffee—Danyers thought he detected the same fastidiousness, the same air of tacitly excluding the obvious and unexceptional. Here was a woman who had been much bored and keenly interested. The waiter brought her a *Secolo*, and as she bent above it Danyers noticed that the hair rolled back from her forehead was turning gray; but her figure was straight and slender, and she had the invaluable gift of a girlish back.

The rush of Anglo-Saxon travel had not set toward the lakes, and with the exception of an Italian family or two, and a hump-backed youth with an *abbé*, Danyers and the lady had the marble halls of the Villa d'Este to themselves.

When he returned from his morning ramble among the hills he saw her sitting at one of the little tables at the edge of the lake. She was writing, and a heap of books and newspapers lay on the table at her side. That evening they met again in the garden. He had strolled out to smoke a last cigarette before dinner, and under the black vaulting of ilexes, near the steps leading down to the boat-landing, he found her leaning on the parapet above the lake. At the sound of his approach she turned and looked at him. She had thrown a black lace scarf over her head, and in this somber setting her face seemed thin and unhappy. He remembered afterwards that her eyes, as they met his, expressed not so much sorrow as profound discontent.

To his surprise she stepped toward him with a detaining gesture.

"Mr. Lewis Danyers, I believe?"

He bowed.

"I am Mrs. Anerton. I saw your name on the visitors' list and wished to thank you for an essay on Mr. Rendle's poetry—or rather to tell you how much I appreciated it. The book was sent to me last winter by Mrs. Memorall."

She spoke in even melancholy tones, as though the habit of perfunctory utterance had robbed her voice of more spontaneous accents; but her smile was charming. They sat down on a stone bench under the ilexes, and she told him how much pleasure his essay had given her. She thought it the best in the book—she was sure he had put more of himself into it than into any other; was she not right in conjecturing that he had been very deeply influenced by Mr. Rendle's poetry? *Pour comprendre il faut aimer*, and it seemed to her that, in some ways, he had penetrated the poet's inner meaning more completely than any other critic. There were certain problems, of course, that he had left untouched; certain aspects of that many-sided mind that he had perhaps failed to seize—

"But then you are young," she concluded gently, "and one could not wish you, as yet, the experience that a fuller understanding would imply."

II

SHE stayed a month at Villa d'Este, and Danyers was with her daily. She showed an unaffected pleasure in his society; a pleasure so obviously founded on their common veneration of Rendle, that the young man could enjoy it without fear of fatuity. At first he was merely one more grain of frankincense on the altar of her insatiable divinity; but gradually a more personal note crept into their intercourse. If she still liked him only because he appreciated Rendle, she at least perceptibly distinguished him from the herd of Rendle's appreciators.

Her attitude toward the great man's memory struck Danyers as perfect. She neither proclaimed nor disavowed her identity. She was frankly Silvia to those who knew and cared; but there was no trace of the Egeria in her pose. She spoke often of Rendle's books, but seldom of himself; there was no posthumous conjugality, no use of the possessive tense, in her abounding reminiscences. Of the master's intellectual life, of his habits of thought and work, she never wearied of talking. She knew the history of each poem; by what scene or episode each image had been evoked; how many times the words in a certain line had been transposed; how long a certain adjective had been sought, and what had at last suggested it; she could even explain that one impenetrable line, the torment of critics, the joy of detractors, the last line of *The Old Odysseus*.

Danyers felt that in talking of these things she was no mere echo of Rendle's thought. If her identity had appeared to be merged in his it was because they thought alike, not because he had thought for her. Posterity is apt to regard the women whom poets have sung as chance pegs on which they hung their garlands; but Mrs. Anerton's mind was like some fertile garden wherein, inevitably, Rendle's imagination had rooted itself and flowered. Danyers began to see how many threads of his complex mental tissue the poet had owed to the blending of her temperament with his; in a certain sense Silvia had herself created the *Sonnets to Silvia*.

To be the custodian of Rendle's inner self, the door, as it were, to the sanctuary, had at first seemed to Danyers so comprehensive a privilege that he had the sense, as his friendship with Mrs. Anerton advanced, of forcing his way into a life already crowded. What room was there, among such towering memories, for so small an actuality as his? Quite suddenly, after this, he discovered that Mrs. Memorall knew better: his fortunate friend was bored as well as lonely.

"You have had more than any other woman!" he had exclaimed to her one day; and her smile flashed a derisive light on his blunder. Fool that he was, not to have seen that she had not had enough! That she was young still—do years count?—tender, human, a woman; that the living have need of the living.

After that, when they climbed the alleys of the hanging park, resting in one of the little ruined temples, or watching, through a ripple of foliage, the remote blue flash of the lake, they did not always talk of Rendle or of literature. She encouraged Danyers to speak of himself; to confide his ambitions to her; she asked him the questions which are the wise woman's substitute for advice.

"You must write," she said, administering the most exquisite flattery that human lips could give.

Of course he meant to write—why not to do something great in his turn? His best, at least; with the resolve, at the outset, that his best should be *the* best. Nothing less seemed possible with that mandate in his ears. How she had divined him; lifted and disentangled his groping ambitions; laid the awakening touch on his spirit with her creative *Let there be light!*

It was his last day with her, and he was feeling very hopeless and happy.

"You ought to write a book about *him*," she went on gently.

Danyers started; he was beginning to dislike Rendle's way of walking in unannounced.

"You ought to do it," she insisted. "A complete interpretation—a summing-up of his style, his purpose, his theory of life and art. No one else could do it as well."

He sat looking at her perplexedly. Suddenly—dared he guess?

"I couldn't do it without you," he faltered.

"I could help you—I would help you, of course."

They sat silent, both looking at the lake.

It was agreed, when they parted, that he should rejoin her six weeks later in Venice. There they were to talk about the book.

### III

*Lago d'Iseo, August 14th.*

WHEN I said good-by to you yesterday I promised to come back to Venice in a week: I was to give you your answer then. I was not honest in saying that; I didn't mean to go back to Venice or to see you again. I was running away from you—and I mean to keep on running! If *you* won't, *I* must. Somebody must save you from marrying a disappointed woman of—well, you say years don't count, and why should they, after all, since you are not to marry me?

That is what I dare not go back to say. *You are not to marry me.* We have had our month together in Venice (such a good month, was it not?) and now you are to go home and write a book—any book but the one we—didn't talk of!—and I am to stay here, attitudinizing among my memories like a sort of female Tithonus. The dreariness of this enforced immortality!

But you shall know the truth. I care for you, or at least for your love, enough to owe you that.

You thought it was because Vincent Rendle had loved me that there was so little hope for you. I had had what I wanted to the full; wasn't that what you said? It is just when a man begins to think he understands a woman that he may be sure he doesn't! It is because Vincent Rendle *didn't love me* that there is no hope for you. I never had what I wanted, and never, never, never will I stoop to wanting anything else.

Do you begin to understand? It was all a sham then, you say? No, it was all real as far as it went. You are young—you haven't learned, as you will later, the thousand imperceptible signs by which one gropes one's way through the labyrinth of human nature; but didn't it strike you, sometimes, that I never told you any foolish little anecdotes about him? His trick, for instance, of twirling a paper-knife round and round between his thumb and forefinger while he talked; his mania for saving the backs of notes; his greediness for wild strawberries, the little pungent Alpine ones; his childish delight in acrobats and jugglers; his way of always calling me *you—dear you*, every letter began—I never told you a word of all that, did I? Do you suppose I could have helped telling you, if he had loved me? These little things would have been mine, then, a part of my life—of our life—they would have slipped out in spite of me (it's only your unhappy woman who is always reticent and dignified). But there never was any "our life;" it was always "our lives" to the end....

If you knew what a relief it is to tell some one at last, you would bear with me, you would let me hurt you! I shall never be quite so lonely again, now that some one knows.

Let me begin at the beginning. When I first met Vincent Rendle I was not twenty-five. That was twenty years ago. From that time until his death, five years ago, we were fast friends. He gave me fifteen years, perhaps the best fifteen years, of his life. The world, as you know, thinks that his greatest poems were written during those years; I am supposed to have "inspired" them, and in a sense I did. From the first, the intellectual sympathy between us was almost complete; my mind must have been to him (I fancy) like some perfectly tuned instrument on which he was never tired of playing. Some one told me of his once saying of me that I "always understood;" it is the only praise I ever heard of his giving me. I don't even know if he thought me pretty, though I hardly think my appearance could have been disagreeable to him, for he hated to be with ugly people. At all events he fell into the way of spending more and more of his time with me. He liked our house; our ways suited him. He was nervous, irritable; people bored him and yet he disliked solitude. He took sanctuary with us. When we travelled he went with us; in the winter he took rooms near us in Rome. In England or on the continent he was always with us for a good part of the year. In small ways I was able to help him in his work; he grew dependent on me. When we were apart he wrote to me continually—he liked to have me share in all he was doing or thinking; he was impatient for my criticism of every new book that interested him; I was a part of his intellectual life. The pity of it was that I wanted to be something more. I was a young woman and I was in love with him—not because he was Vincent Rendle, but just because he was himself!

People began to talk, of course—I was Vincent Rendle's Mrs. Anerton; when the

*Sonnets to Silvia* appeared, it was whispered that I was Silvia. Wherever he went, I was invited; people made up to me in the hope of getting to know him; when I was in London my doorbell never stopped ringing. Elderly peeresses, aspiring hostesses, love-sick girls and struggling authors overwhelmed me with their assiduities. I hugged my success, for I knew what it meant—they thought that Rendle was in love with me! Do you know, at times, they almost made me think so too? Oh, there was no phase of folly I didn't go through. You can't imagine the excuses a woman will invent for a man's not telling her that he loves her— pitiable arguments that she would see through at a glance if any other woman used them! But all the while, deep down, I knew he had never cared. I should have known it if he had made love to me every day of his life. I could never guess whether he knew what people said about us—he listened so little to what people said; and cared still less, when he heard. He was always quite honest and straightforward with me; he treated me as one man treats another; and yet at times I felt he *must* see that with me it was different. If he did see, he made no sign. Perhaps he never noticed—I am sure he never meant to be cruel. He had never made love to me; it was no fault of his if I wanted more than he could give me. The *Sonnets to Silvia*, you say? But what are they? A cosmic philosophy, not a love-poem; addressed to Woman, not to a woman!

But then, the letters? Ah, the letters! Well, I'll make a clean breast of it. You have noticed the breaks in the letters here and there, just as they seem to be on the point of growing a little—warmer? The critics, you may remember, praised the editor for his commendable delicacy and good taste (so rare in these days!) in omitting from the correspondence all personal allusions, all those *détails intimes* which should be kept sacred from the public gaze. They referred, of course, to the asterisks in the letters to Mrs. A. Those letters I myself prepared for publication; that is to say, I copied them out for the editor, and every now and then I put in a line of asterisks to make it appear that something had been left out. You understand? The asterisks were a sham—*there was nothing to leave out.*

No one but a woman could understand what I went through during those years—the moments of revolt, when I felt I must break away from it all, fling the truth in his face and never see him again; the inevitable reaction, when not to see him seemed the one unendurable thing, and I trembled lest a look or word of mine should disturb the poise of our friendship; the silly days when I hugged the delusion that he *must* love me, since everybody thought he did; the long periods of numbness, when I didn't seem to care whether he loved me or not. Between these wretched days came others when our intellectual accord was so perfect that I forgot everything else in the joy of feeling myself lifted up on the wings of his thought. Sometimes, then, the heavens seemed to be opened....

All this time he was so dear a friend! He had the genius of friendship, and he spent it all on me. Yes, you were right when you said that I have had more than any other woman. *Il faut de l'adresse pour aimer*, Pascal says; and I was so quiet, so cheerful, so frankly affectionate with him, that in all those years I am almost sure I never bored him. Could I have hoped as much if he had loved me?

You mustn't think of him, though, as having been tied to my skirts. He came and went as he pleased, and so did his fancies. There was a girl once (I am telling you everything), a lovely being who called his poetry "deep" and gave him *Lucile* on his birthday. He followed her to Switzerland one summer, and all the time that he was dangling after her (a little too conspicuously, I always thought, for a Great Man), he was writing to *me* about his theory of vowel-combinations—or was it his experiments in English hexameter? The letters were dated from the very places where I knew they went and sat by waterfalls together and he thought out adjectives for her hair. He talked to me about it quite frankly afterwards. She was perfectly beautiful and it had been a pure delight to watch her; but she *would* talk, and her mind, he said, was "all elbows." And yet, the next year, when her marriage was announced, he went away alone, quite suddenly … and it was just afterwards that he published *Love's Viaticum*. Men are queer!

After my husband died—I am putting things crudely, you see—I had a return of hope. It was because he loved me, I argued, that he had never spoken; because he had always hoped some day to make me his wife; because he wanted to spare me the "reproach." Rubbish! I knew well enough, in my heart of hearts, that my one chance lay in the force of habit. He had grown used to me; he was no longer young; he dreaded new people and new ways; *il avait pris son pli.* Would it not be easier to marry me?

I don't believe he ever thought of it. He wrote me what people call "a beautiful letter;" he was kind; considerate, decently commiserating; then, after a few weeks, he slipped into his old way of coming in every afternoon, and our interminable talks began again just where they had left off. I heard later that people thought I had shown "such good taste" in not marrying him.

So we jogged on for five years longer. Perhaps they were the best years, for I had given up hoping. Then he died.

After his death—this is curious—there came to me a kind of mirage of love. All the books and articles written about him, all the reviews of the *Life*, were full of discreet allusions to Silvia. I became again the Mrs. Anerton of the glorious days. Sentimental girls and dear lads like you turned pink when somebody whispered, "that was Silvia you were talking to." Idiots begged for my autograph—publishers urged me to write my reminiscences of him—critics consulted me about the reading of doubtful lines. And I knew that, to all these people, I was the woman Vincent Rendle had loved.

After a while that fire went out too and I was left alone with my past. Alone—quite alone; for he had never really been with me. The intellectual union counted for nothing now. It had been soul to soul, but never hand in hand, and there were no little things to remember him by.

Then there set in a kind of Arctic winter. I crawled into myself as into a snow-hut. I hated my solitude and yet dreaded any one who disturbed it. That phase, of course, passed like the others. I took up life again, and began to read the papers and consider the cut of my gowns. But there was one question that I could not be rid of, that haunted me night and day. Why had he never loved me? Why had I been so much to him, and no more? Was I so ugly, so essentially unlovable, that though a man might cherish me as his mind's comrade, he could not care for me as a woman? I can't tell you how that question tortured me. It became an obsession.

My poor friend, do you begin to see? I had to find out what some other man thought of me. Don't be too hard on me! Listen first—consider. When I first met Vincent Rendle I was a young woman, who had married early and led the quietest kind of life; I had had no "experiences." From the hour of our first meeting to the day of his death I never looked at any other man, and never noticed whether any other man looked at me. When he died, five years ago, I knew the extent of my powers no more than a baby. Was it too late to find out? Should I never know *why*?

Forgive me—forgive me. You are so young; it will be an episode, a mere "document," to you so soon! And, besides, it wasn't as deliberate, as cold-blooded as these disjointed lines have made it appear. I didn't plan it, like a woman in a book. Life is so much more complex than any rendering of it can be. I liked you from the first—I was drawn to you (you must have seen that)—I wanted you to like me; it was not a mere psychological experiment. And yet in a sense it was that, too—I must be honest. I had to have an answer to that question; it was a ghost that had to be laid.

At first I was afraid—oh, so much afraid—that you cared for me only because I was Silvia, that you loved me because you thought Rendle had loved me. I began to think there was no escaping my destiny.

How happy I was when I discovered that you were growing jealous of my past; that you actually hated Rendle! My heart beat like a girl's when you told me you meant to follow me to Venice.

After our parting at Villa d'Este my old doubts reasserted themselves. What did I know of your feeling for me, after all? Were you capable of analyzing it yourself? Was it not likely to be two-thirds vanity and curiosity, and one-third literary sentimentality? You might easily fancy that you cared for Mary Anerton when you were really in love with Silvia— the heart is such a hypocrite! Or you might be more calculating than I had supposed. Perhaps it was you who had been flattering *my* vanity in the hope (the pardonable hope!) of turning me, after a decent interval, into a pretty little essay with a margin.

When you arrived in Venice and we met again—do you remember the music on the lagoon, that evening, from my balcony?—I was so afraid you would begin to talk about the book—the book, you remember, was your ostensible reason for coming. You never spoke of it, and I soon saw your one fear was I might do so—might remind you of your object in being with me. Then I knew you cared for me! yes, at that moment really cared! We never mentioned the book once, did we, during that month in Venice?

I have read my letter over; and now I wish that I had said this to you instead of writing it. I could have felt my way then, watching your face and seeing if you understood. But, no, I could not go back to Venice; and I could not tell you (though I tried) while we were there together. I couldn't spoil that month—my one month. It was so good, for once in my life, to get away from literature.

You will be angry with me at first—but, alas! not for long. What I have done would have been cruel if I had been a younger woman; as it is, the experiment will hurt no one but myself. And it will hurt me horribly (as much as, in your first anger, you may perhaps wish), because it has shown me, for the first time, all that I have missed.

## A JOURNEY

AS SHE LAY in her berth, staring at the shadows overhead, the rush of the wheels was in her brain, driving her deeper and deeper into circles of wakeful lucidity. The sleeping-car had sunk into its night-silence. Through the wet window-pane she watched the sudden lights, the long stretches of hurrying blackness. Now and then she turned her head and looked through the opening in the hangings at her husband's curtains across the aisle....

She wondered restlessly if he wanted anything and if she could hear him if he called. His voice had grown very weak within the last months and it irritated him when she did not hear. This irritability, this increasing childish petulance seemed to give expression to their imperceptible estrangement. Like two faces looking at one another through a sheet of glass they were close together, almost touching, but they could not hear or feel each other: the conductivity between them was broken. She, at least, had this sense of separation, and she fancied sometimes that she saw it reflected in the look with which he supplemented his failing words. Doubtless the fault was hers. She was too impenetrably healthy to be touched by the irrelevancies of disease. Her self-reproachful tenderness was tinged with the sense of his irrationality: she had a vague feeling that there was a purpose in his helpless tyrannies. The suddenness of the change had found her so unprepared. A year ago their pulses had beat to one robust measure; both had the same prodigal confidence in an exhaustless future. Now their energies no longer kept step: hers still bounded ahead of life, preempting unclaimed regions of hope and activity, while his lagged behind, vainly struggling to overtake her.

When they married, she had such arrears of living to make up: her days had been as bare as the whitewashed school-room where she forced innutritious facts upon reluctant children. His coming had broken in on the slumber of circumstance, widening the present till it became the encloser of remotest chances. But imperceptibly the horizon narrowed. Life had a grudge against her: she was never to be allowed to spread her wings.

At first the doctors had said that six weeks of mild air would set him right; but when he came back this assurance was explained as having of course included a winter in a dry climate. They gave up their pretty house, storing the wedding presents and new furniture, and went to Colorado. She had hated it there from the first. Nobody knew her or cared about her; there was no one to wonder at the good match she had made, or to envy her the new dresses and the visiting-cards which were still a surprise to her. And he kept growing worse. She felt herself beset with difficulties too evasive to be fought by so direct a temperament. She still loved him, of course; but he was gradually, undefinably ceasing to be himself. The man she had married had been strong, active, gently masterful: the male whose pleasure it is to clear a way through the material obstructions of life; but now it was she who was the protector, he who must be shielded from importunities and given his drops or his beef-juice though the skies were falling. The routine of the sick-room bewildered her; this punctual administering of medicine seemed as idle as some uncomprehended religious mummery.

There were moments, indeed, when warm gushes of pity swept away her instinctive resentment of his condition, when she still found his old self in his eyes as they groped for each other through the dense medium of his weakness. But these moments had grown rare. Sometimes he frightened her: his sunken expressionless face seemed that of a stranger; his voice was weak and hoarse; his thin-lipped smile a mere muscular contraction. Her hand avoided his damp soft skin, which had lost the familiar roughness of health: she caught herself furtively watching him as she might have watched a strange animal. It frightened her to feel that this was the man she loved; there were hours when to tell him what she suffered seemed the one escape from her fears. But in general she judged herself more leniently, reflecting that she had perhaps been too long alone with him, and that she would feel differently when they were at home again, surrounded by her robust and buoyant family. How she had rejoiced when the doctors at last gave their consent to his going home! She knew, of course, what the decision meant; they both knew. It meant that he was to die; but they dressed the truth in hopeful euphuisms, and at times, in the joy of preparation, she really forgot the purpose of their journey, and slipped into an eager allusion to next year's plans.

At last the day of leaving came. She had a dreadful fear that they would never get away; that somehow at the last moment he would fail her; that the doctors held one of their accustomed treacheries in reserve; but nothing happened. They drove to the station, he was installed in a seat with a rug over his knees and a cushion at his back, and she hung out of the window waving unregretful farewells to the acquaintances she had really never liked till then.

The first twenty-four hours had passed off well. He revived a little and it amused him to look out of the window and to observe the humors of the car. The second day he began to grow weary and to chafe under the dispassionate stare of the freckled child with the lump of chewing-gum. She had to explain to the child's mother that her husband was too ill to be disturbed: a statement received by that lady with a resentment visibly supported by the maternal sentiment of the whole car. . . .

That night he slept badly and the next morning his temperature frightened her: she was sure he was growing worse. The day passed slowly, punctuated by the small irritations of travel. Watching his tired face, she traced in its contractions every rattle and jolt of the tram, till her own body vibrated with sympathetic fatigue. She felt the others observing him too, and hovered restlessly between him and the line of interrogative eyes. The freckled child hung about him like a fly; offers of candy and picture- books failed to dislodge her: she twisted one leg around the other and watched him imperturbably. The porter, as he passed, lingered with vague proffers of help, probably inspired by philanthropic passengers swelling with the sense that "something ought to be done;" and one nervous man in a skull-cap was audibly concerned as to the possible effect on his wife's health.

The hours dragged on in a dreary inoccupation. Towards dusk she sat down beside him and he laid his hand on hers. The touch startled her. He seemed to be calling her from far off. She looked at him helplessly and his smile went through her like a physical pang.

"Are you very tired?" she asked.

"No, not very."

"We'll be there soon now."

"Yes, very soon."

"This time tomorrow—"

He nodded and they sat silent. When she had put him to bed and crawled into her own berth she tried to cheer herself with the thought that in less than twenty-four hours they would be in New York. Her people would all be at the station to meet her—she pictured their round unanxious faces pressing through the crowd. She only hoped they would not tell him too loudly that he was looking splendidly and would be all right in no time: the subtler sympathies developed by long contact with suffering were making her aware of a certain coarseness of texture in the family sensibilities.

Suddenly she thought she heard him call. She parted the curtains and listened. No, it was only a man snoring at the other end of the car. His snores had a greasy sound, as though they passed through tallow. She lay down and tried to sleep . . . Had she not heard him move? She started up trembling . . . The silence frightened her more than any sound. He might not be able to make her hear—he might be calling her now . . . What made her think of such things? It was merely the familiar tendency of an over-tired mind to fasten itself on the most intolerable chance within the range of its forebodings. . . . Putting her head out, she listened; but she could not distinguish his breathing from that of the other pairs of lungs about her. She longed to get up and look at him, but she knew the impulse was a mere vent for her restlessness, and the fear of disturbing him restrained her. . . . The regular movement of his curtain reassured her, she knew not why; she remembered that he had wished her a cheerful good-night; and the sheer inability to endure her fears a moment longer made her put them from her with an effort of her whole sound tired body.

She turned on her side and slept.

She sat up stiffly, staring out at the dawn. The train was rushing through a region of bare hillocks huddled against a lifeless sky. It looked like the first day of creation. The air of the car was close, and she pushed up her window to let in the keen wind. Then she looked at her watch: it was seven o'clock, and soon the people about her would be stirring. She slipped into her clothes, smoothed her disheveled hair and crept to the dressing-room. When she had washed her face and adjusted her dress she felt more hopeful. It was always a struggle for her not to be cheerful in the morning. Her cheeks burned deliciously under the coarse towel and the wet hair about her temples broke into strong upward tendrils. Every inch of her was full of life and elasticity. And in ten hours they would be at home!

She stepped to her husband's berth: it was time for him to take his early glass of milk. The window-shade was down, and in the dusk of the curtained enclosure she could just see that he lay sideways, with his face away from her. She leaned over him and drew up the shade. As she did so she touched one of his hands. It felt cold. . . .

She bent closer, laying her hand on his arm and calling him by name. He did not move. She spoke again more loudly; she grasped his shoulder and gently shook it. He lay motionless. She caught hold of his hand again: it slipped from her limply, like a dead thing. A dead thing?

Her breath caught. She must see his face. She leaned forward, and hurriedly, shrinkingly, with a sickening reluctance of the flesh, laid her hands on his shoulders and turned him over. His head fell back; his face looked small and smooth; he gazed at her with steady eyes.

She remained motionless for a long time, holding him thus; and they looked at each other. Suddenly she shrank back: the longing to scream, to call out, to fly from him, had almost overpowered her. But a strong hand arrested her. Good God! If it were known that he was dead they would be put off the train at the next station—

In a terrifying flash of remembrance there arose before her a scene she had once witnessed in travelling, when a husband and wife, whose child had died in the train, had been thrust out at some chance station. She saw them standing on the platform with the child's body between them; she had never forgotten the dazed look with which they followed the receding train. And this was what would happen to her. Within the next hour she might find herself on the platform of some strange station, alone with her husband's body. . . . Anything but that! It was too horrible—She quivered like a creature at bay.

As she cowered there, she felt the train moving more slowly. It was coming then—they were approaching a station! She saw again the husband and wife standing on the lonely platform; and with a violent gesture she drew down the shade to hide her husband's face.

Feeling dizzy, she sank down on the edge of the berth, keeping away from his outstretched body, and pulling the curtains close, so that he and she were shut into a kind of sepulchral twilight. She tried to think. At all costs she must conceal the fact that he was dead. But how? Her mind refused to act: she could not plan, combine. She could think of no way but to sit there, clutching the curtains, all day long. . . .

She heard the porter making up her bed; people were beginning to move about the car; the dressing-room door was being opened and shut. She tried to rouse herself. At length with a supreme effort she rose to her feet, stepping into the aisle of the car and drawing the curtains tight behind her. She noticed that they still parted slightly with the motion of the car, and finding a pin in her dress she fastened them together. Now she was safe. She looked round and saw the porter. She fancied he was watching her.

"Ain't he awake yet?" he enquired.

"No," she faltered.

"I got his milk all ready when he wants it. You know you told me to have it for him by seven."

She nodded silently and crept into her seat.

At half-past eight the train reached Buffalo. By this time the other passengers were dressed and the berths had been folded back for the day. The porter, moving to and fro under his burden of sheets and pillows, glanced at her as he passed. At length he said: "Ain't he going to get up? You know we're ordered to make up the berths as early as we can."

She turned cold with fear. They were just entering the station.

"Oh, not yet," she stammered. "Not till he's had his milk. Won't you get it, please?"

"All right. Soon as we start again."

When the train moved on he reappeared with the milk. She took it from him and sat vaguely looking at it: her brain moved slowly from one idea to another, as though they were stepping-stones set far apart across a whirling flood. At length she became aware that the porter still hovered expectantly.

"Will I give it to him?" he suggested.

"Oh, no," she cried, rising. "He—he's asleep yet, I think—"

She waited till the porter had passed on; then she unpinned the curtains and slipped behind them. In the semi-obscurity her husband's face stared up at her like a marble mask with agate eyes. The eyes were dreadful. She put out her hand and drew down the lids. Then she remembered the glass of milk in her other hand: what was she to do with it? She thought of raising the window and throwing it out; but to do so she would have to lean across his body and bring her face close to his. She decided to drink the milk.

She returned to her seat with the empty glass and after a while the porter came back to get it.

"When'll I fold up his bed?" he asked.

"Oh, not now—not yet; he's ill—he's very ill. Can't you let him stay as he is? The doctor wants him to lie down as much as possible."

He scratched his head. "Well, if he's *really* sick—"

He took the empty glass and walked away, explaining to the passengers that the party behind the curtains was too sick to get up just yet.

She found herself the center of sympathetic eyes. A motherly woman with an intimate smile sat down beside her.

"I'm real sorry to hear your husband's sick. I've had a remarkable amount of sickness in my family and maybe I could assist you. Can I take a look at him?"

"Oh, no—no, please! He mustn't be disturbed."

The lady accepted the rebuff indulgently.

"Well, it's just as you say, of course, but you don't look to me as if you'd had much experience in sickness and I'd have been glad to assist you. What do you generally do when your husband's taken this way?"

"I—I let him sleep."

"Too much sleep ain't any too healthful either. Don't you give him any medicine?"

"Y—yes."

"Don't you wake him to take it?"

"Yes."

"When does he take the next dose?"

"Not for—two hours—"

The lady looked disappointed. "Well, if I was you I'd try giving it oftener. That's what I do with my folks."

After that many faces seemed to press upon her. The passengers were on their way to the dining-car, and she was conscious that as they passed down the aisle they glanced curiously at the closed curtains. One lantern- jawed man with prominent eyes stood still and tried to shoot his projecting glance through the division between the folds. The freckled child, returning from breakfast, waylaid the passers with a buttery clutch, saying in a loud whisper, "He's sick;" and once the conductor came by, asking for tickets. She shrank into her corner and looked out of the window at the flying trees and houses, meaningless hieroglyphs of an endlessly unrolled papyrus.

Now and then the train stopped, and the newcomers on entering the car stared in turn at the closed curtains. More and more people seemed to pass—their faces began to blend fantastically with the images surging in her brain. . . .

Later in the day a fat man detached himself from the mist of faces. He had a creased stomach and soft pale lips. As he pressed himself into the seat facing her she noticed that he was dressed in black broadcloth, with a soiled white tie.

"Husband's pretty bad this morning, is he?"

"Yes."

"Dear, dear! Now that's terribly distressing, ain't it?" An apostolic smile revealed his gold-filled teeth. "Of course you know there's no sech thing as sickness. Ain't that a lovely thought? Death itself is but a deloosion of our grosser senses. On'y lay yourself open to the influx of the sperrit, submit yourself passively to the action of the divine force, and disease and dissolution will cease to exist for you. If you could indooce your husband to read this little pamphlet—"

The faces about her again grew indistinct. She had a vague recollection of hearing the motherly lady and the parent of the freckled child ardently disputing the relative advantages of trying several medicines at once, or of taking each in turn; the motherly lady maintaining that the competitive system saved time; the other objecting that you couldn't tell which remedy had effected the cure; their voices went on and on, like bell-buoys droning through a fog. . . . The porter came up now and then with questions that she did not understand, but that somehow she must have answered since he went away again without repeating them; every two hours the motherly lady reminded her that her husband ought to have his drops; people left the car and others replaced them . . .

Her head was spinning and she tried to steady herself by clutching at her thoughts as they swept by, but they slipped away from her like bushes on the side of a sheer precipice down which she seemed to be falling. Suddenly her mind grew clear again and she found herself vividly picturing what would happen when the train reached New York. She shuddered as it occurred to her that he would be quite cold and that some one might perceive he had been dead since morning.

She thought hurriedly:—"If they see I am not surprised they will suspect something. They will ask questions, and if I tell them the truth they won't believe me—no one would believe me! It will be terrible"—and she kept repeating to herself:—"I must pretend I don't know. I must pretend I don't know. When they open the curtains I must go up to him quite naturally—and then I must scream.". . . She had an idea that the scream would be very hard to do.

Gradually new thoughts crowded upon her, vivid and urgent: she tried to separate and restrain them, but they beset her clamorously, like her school-children at the end of a hot day, when she was too tired to silence them. Her head grew confused, and she felt a sick fear of forgetting her part, of betraying herself by some unguarded word or look.

"I must pretend I don't know," she went on murmuring. The words had lost their significance, but she repeated them mechanically, as though they had been a magic formula, until suddenly she heard herself saying: "I can't remember, I can't remember!"

Her voice sounded very loud, and she looked about her in terror; but no one seemed to notice that she had spoken.

As she glanced down the car her eye caught the curtains of her husband's berth, and she began to examine the monotonous arabesques woven through their heavy folds. The pattern was intricate and difficult to trace; she gazed fixedly at the curtains and as she did so the thick stuff grew transparent and through it she saw her husband's face—his dead face. She struggled to avert her look, but her eyes refused to move and her head seemed to be held in a vice. At last, with an effort that left her weak and shaking, she turned away; but it was of no use; close in front of her, small and smooth, was her husband's face. It seemed to be suspended in the air between her and the false braids of the woman who sat in front of her. With an uncontrollable gesture she stretched out her hand to push the face away, and suddenly she felt the touch of his smooth skin. She repressed a cry and half started from her seat. The woman with the false braids looked around, and feeling that she must justify her movement in some way she rose and lifted her travelling-bag from the opposite seat. She unlocked the bag and looked into it; but the first object her hand met was a small flask of her husband's, thrust there at the last moment, in the haste of departure. She locked the bag and closed her eyes . . . his face was there again, hanging between her eye-balls and lids like a waxen mask against a red curtain. . . .

She roused herself with a shiver. Had she fainted or slept? Hours seemed to have elapsed; but it was still broad day, and the people about her were sitting in the same attitudes as before.

A sudden sense of hunger made her aware that she had eaten nothing since morning. The thought of food filled her with disgust, but she dreaded a return of faintness, and remembering that she had some biscuits in her bag she took one out and ate it. The dry crumbs choked her, and she hastily swallowed a little brandy from her husband's flask. The burning sensation in her throat acted as a counter-irritant, momentarily relieving the dull ache of her nerves. Then she felt a gently-stealing warmth, as though a soft air fanned her, and the swarming fears relaxed their clutch, receding through the stillness that enclosed her, a stillness soothing as the spacious quietude of a summer day. She slept.

Through her sleep she felt the impetuous rush of the train. It seemed to be life itself that was sweeping her on with headlong inexorable force— sweeping her into darkness and terror, and the awe of unknown days.—Now all at once everything was still—not a sound, not a pulsation . . . She was dead in her turn, and lay beside him with smooth upstaring face. How quiet it was!—and yet she heard feet coming, the feet of the men who were to carry them away. . . . She could feel too—she felt a sudden prolonged vibration, a series of hard shocks, and then another plunge into darkness: the darkness of death this time—a black whirlwind on which they were both spinning like leaves, in wild uncoiling spirals, with millions and millions of the dead. . . .

She sprang up in terror. Her sleep must have lasted a long time, for the winter day had paled and the lights had been lit. The car was in confusion, and as she regained her self-possession she saw that the passengers were gathering up their wraps and bags. The woman with the false braids had brought from the dressing-room a sickly ivy-plant in a bottle, and the Christian Scientist was reversing his cuffs. The porter passed down the aisle with his impartial brush. An impersonal figure with a gold-banded cap asked for her husband's ticket. A voice shouted "Baig-gage *express!*" and she heard the clicking of metal as the passengers handed over their checks.

Presently her window was blocked by an expanse of sooty wall, and the train passed into the Harlem tunnel. The journey was over; in a few minutes she would see her family pushing their joyous way through the throng at the station. Her heart dilated. The worst terror was past. . . .

"We'd better get him up now, hadn't we?" asked the porter, touching her arm.

He had her husband's hat in his hand and was meditatively revolving it under his brush.

She looked at the hat and tried to speak; but suddenly the car grew dark. She flung up her arms, struggling to catch at something, and fell face downward, striking her head against the dead man's berth.

## THE PELICAN

SHE WAS very pretty when I first knew her, with the sweet straight nose and short upper lip of the cameo-brooch divinity, humanized by a dimple that flowered in her cheek whenever anything was said possessing the outward attributes of humor without its intrinsic quality. For the dear lady was providentially deficient in humor: the least hint of the real thing clouded her lovely eye like the hovering shadow of an algebraic problem.

I don't think nature had meant her to be "intellectual;" but what can a poor thing do, whose husband has died of drink when her baby is hardly six months old, and who finds her coral necklace and her grandfather's edition of the British Dramatists inadequate to the demands of the creditors?

Her mother, the celebrated Irene Astarte Pratt, had written a poem in blank verse on "The Fall of Man;" one of her aunts was dean of a girls' college; another had translated Euripides—with such a family, the poor child's fate was sealed in advance. The only way of paying her husband's debts and keeping the baby clothed was to be intellectual; and, after some hesitation as to the form her mental activity was to take, it was unanimously decided that she was to give lectures.

They began by being drawing-room lectures. The first time I saw her she was standing by the piano, against a flippant background of Dresden china and photographs, telling a roomful of women preoccupied with their spring bonnets all she thought she knew about Greek art. The ladies assembled to hear her had given me to understand that she was "doing it for the baby," and this fact, together with the shortness of her upper lip and the bewildering co-operation of her dimple, disposed me to listen leniently to her dissertation. Happily, at that time Greek art was still, if I may use the phrase, easily handled: it was as simple as walking down a museum- gallery lined with pleasant familiar Venuses and Apollos. All the later complications—the archaic and archaistic conundrums; the influences of Assyria and Asia Minor; the conflicting attributions and the wrangles of the erudite—still slumbered in the bosom of the future "scientific critic." Greek art in those days began with Phidias and ended with the Apollo Belvedere; and a child could travel from one to the other without danger of losing his way.

Mrs. Amyot had two fatal gifts: a capacious but inaccurate memory, and an extraordinary fluency of speech. There was nothing she did not remember— wrongly; but her halting facts were swathed in so many layers of rhetoric that their infirmities were imperceptible to her friendly critics. Besides, she had been taught Greek by the aunt who had translated Euripides; and the mere sound of the αις and οις that she now and then not unskillfully let slip (correcting herself, of course, with a start, and indulgently mistranslating the phrase), struck awe to the hearts of ladies whose only "accomplishment" was French—if you didn't speak too quickly.

I had then but a momentary glimpse of Mrs. Amyot, but a few months later I came upon her again in the New England university town where the celebrated Irene Astarte Pratt lived on the summit of a local Parnassus, with lesser muses and college professors respectfully grouped on the lower ledges of the sacred declivity. Mrs. Amyot, who, after her husband's death, had returned to the maternal roof (even during her father's lifetime the roof had been distinctively maternal), Mrs. Amyot, thanks to her upper lip, her dimple and her Greek, was already ensconced in a snug hollow of the Parnassian slope.

After the lecture was over it happened that I walked home with Mrs. Amyot. From the incensed glances of two or three learned gentlemen who were hovering on the door-step when we emerged, I inferred that Mrs. Amyot, at that period, did not often walk home alone; but I doubt whether any of my discomfited rivals, whatever his claims to favor, was ever treated to so ravishing a mixture of shyness and self-abandonment, of sham erudition and real teeth and hair, as it was my privilege to enjoy. Even at the opening of her public career Mrs. Amyot had a tender eye for strangers, as possible links with successive centers of culture to which in due course the torch of Greek art might be handed on.

She began by telling me that she had never been so frightened in her life. She knew, of course, how dreadfully learned I was, and when, just as she was going to begin, her hostess had whispered to her that I was in the room, she had felt ready to sink through the floor. Then (with a flying dimple) she had remembered Emerson's line—wasn't it Emerson's?—that beauty is its own excuse for *seeing*, and that had made her feel a little more confident, since she was sure that no one *saw* beauty more vividly than she—as a child she used to sit for hours gazing at an Etruscan vase on the bookcase in the library, while her sisters played with their dolls—and if *seeing* beauty was the only excuse one needed for talking about it, why, she was sure I would make allowances and not be *too* critical and sarcastic, especially if, as she thought probable, I had heard of her having lost her poor husband, and how she had to do it for the baby.

Being abundantly assured of my sympathy on these points, she went on to say that she had always wanted so much to consult me about her lectures. Of course, one subject wasn't enough (this view of the limitations of Greek art as a "subject" gave me a startling idea of the rate at which a successful lecturer might exhaust the universe); she must find others; she had not ventured on any as yet, but she had thought of Tennyson—didn't I *love* Tennyson? She *worshipped* him so that she was sure she could help others to understand him; or what did I think of a "course" on Raphael or Michelangelo—or on the heroines of Shakespeare? There were some fine steel-engravings of Raphael's Madonnas and of the Sistine ceiling in her mother's library, and she had seen Miss Cushman in several Shakespearian roles, so that on these subjects also she felt qualified to speak with authority.

When we reached her mother's door she begged me to come in and talk the matter over; she wanted me to see the baby—she felt as though I should understand her better if I saw the baby—and the dimple flashed through a tear.

The fear of encountering the author of "The Fall of Man," combined with the opportune recollection of a dinner engagement, made me evade this appeal with the promise of returning on the morrow. On the morrow, I left too early to redeem my promise; and for several years afterwards I saw no more of Mrs. Amyot.

My calling at that time took me at irregular intervals from one to another of our larger cities, and as Mrs. Amyot was also peripatetic it was inevitable that sooner or later we should cross each other's path. It was therefore without surprise that, one snowy afternoon in Boston, I learned from the lady with whom I chanced to be lunching that, as soon as the meal was over, I was to be taken to hear Mrs. Amyot lecture.

"On Greek art?" I suggested.

"Oh, you've heard her then? No, this is one of the series called 'Homes and Haunts of the Poets.' Last week we had Wordsworth and the Lake Poets, to-day we are to have Goethe and Weimar. She is a wonderful creature—all the women of her family are geniuses. You know, of course, that her mother was Irene Astarte Pratt, who wrote a poem on 'The Fall of Man'; N.P. Willis called her the female Milton of America. One of Mrs. Amyot's aunts has translated Eurip—"

"And is she as pretty as ever?" I irrelevantly interposed.

My hostess looked shocked. "She is excessively modest and retiring. She says it is actual suffering for her to speak in public. You know she only does it for the baby."

Punctually at the hour appointed, we took our seats in a lecture-hall full of strenuous females in ulsters. Mrs. Amyot was evidently a favorite with these austere sisters, for every corner was crowded, and as we entered a pale usher with an educated mispronunciation was setting forth to several dejected applicants the impossibility of supplying them with seats.

Our own were happily so near the front that when the curtains at the back of the platform parted, and Mrs. Amyot appeared, I was at once able to establish a comparison between the lady placidly dimpling to the applause of her public and the shrinking drawing-room orator of my earlier recollections.

Mrs. Amyot was as pretty as ever, and there was the same curious discrepancy between the freshness of her aspect and the staleness of her theme, but something was gone of the blushing unsteadiness with which she had fired her first random shots at Greek art. It was not that the shots were less uncertain, but that she now had an air of assuming that, for her purpose, the bull's-eye was everywhere, so that there was no need to be flustered in taking aim. This assurance had so facilitated the flow of her eloquence that she seemed to be performing a trick analogous to that of the conjuror who pulls hundreds of yards of white paper out of his mouth. From a large assortment of stock adjectives she chose, with unerring deftness and rapidity, the one that taste and discrimination would most surely have rejected, fitting out her subject with a whole wardrobe of slop-shop epithets irrelevant in cut and size. To the invaluable knack of not disturbing the association of ideas in her audience, she added the gift of what may be called a confidential manner—so that her fluent generalizations about Goethe and his place in literature (the lecture was, of course, manufactured out of Lewes's book) had the flavor of personal experience, of views sympathetically exchanged with her audience on the best way of knitting children's socks, or of putting up preserves for the winter. It was, I am sure, to this personal accent—the moral equivalent of her dimple—that Mrs. Amyot owed her prodigious, her irrational success. It was her art of transposing second-hand ideas into first-hand emotions that so endeared her to her feminine listeners.

To any one not in search of "documents" Mrs. Amyot's success was hardly of a kind to make her more interesting, and my curiosity flagged with the growing conviction that the "suffering" entailed on her by public speaking was at most a retrospective pang. I was sure that she had reached the point of measuring and enjoying her effects, of deliberately manipulating her public; and there must indeed have been a certain exhilaration in attaining results so considerable by means involving so little conscious effort. Mrs. Amyot's art was simply an extension of coquetry: she flirted with her audience.

In this mood of enlightened skepticism I responded but languidly to my hostess's suggestion that I should go with her that evening to see Mrs. Amyot. The aunt who had translated Euripides was at home on Saturday evenings, and one met "thoughtful" people there, my hostess explained: it was one of the intellectual centers of Boston. My mood remained distinctly resentful of any connection between Mrs. Amyot and intellectuality, and I declined to go; but the next day I met Mrs. Amyot in the street.

She stopped me reproachfully. She had heard I was in Boston; why had I not come last night? She had been told that I was at her lecture, and it had frightened her—yes, really, almost as much as years ago in Hillbridge. She never *could* get over that stupid shyness, and the whole business was as distasteful to her as ever; but what could she do? There was the baby— he was a big boy now, and boys were so expensive! But did I really think she had improved the least little bit? And why wouldn't I come home with her now, and see the boy, and tell her frankly what I had thought of the lecture? She had plenty of flattery—people were so kind, and everyone knew that she did it for the baby— but what she felt the need of was criticism, severe, discriminating criticism like mine— oh, she knew that I was dreadfully discriminating!

I went home with her and saw the boy. In the early heat of her Tennyson- worship Mrs. Amyot had christened him Lancelot, and he looked it. Perhaps, however, it was his black velvet dress and the exasperating length of his yellow curls, together with the fact of his having been taught to recite Browning to visitors, that raised to fever-heat the itching of my palms in his Infant-Samuel-like presence. I have since had reason to think that he would have preferred to be called Billy, and to hunt cats with the other boys in the block: his curls and his poetry were simply another outlet for Mrs. Amyot's irrepressible coquetry.

But if Lancelot was not genuine, his mother's love for him was. It justified everything—the lectures *were* for the baby, after all. I had not been ten minutes in the room before I was pledged to help Mrs. Amyot carry out her triumphant fraud. If she wanted to lecture on Plato she should—Plato must take his chance like the rest of us! There was no use, of course, in being "discriminating." I preserved sufficient reason to avoid that pitfall, but I suggested "subjects" and made lists of books for her with a fatuity that became more obvious as time attenuated the remembrance of her smile; I even remember thinking that some men might have cut the knot by marrying her, but I handed over Plato as a hostage and escaped by the afternoon train.

The next time I saw her was in New York, when she had become so fashionable that it was a part of the whole duty of woman to be seen at her lectures. The lady who suggested that of course I ought to go and hear Mrs. Amyot, was not very clear about anything except that she was perfectly lovely, and had had a horrid husband, and was doing it to support her boy. The subject of the discourse (I think it was on Ruskin) was clearly of minor importance, not only to my friend, but to the throng of well-dressed and absent-minded ladies who rustled in late, dropped their muffs and pocket-books, and undisguisedly lost themselves in the study of each other's apparel. They received Mrs. Amyot with warmth, but she evidently represented a social obligation like going to church, rather than any more personal interest; in fact, I suspect that every one of the ladies would have remained away, had they been sure that none of the others were coming.

Whether Mrs. Amyot was disheartened by the lack of sympathy between herself and her hearers, or whether the sport of arousing it had become a task, she certainly imparted her platitudes with less convincing warmth than of old. Her voice had the same confidential inflections, but it was like a voice reproduced by a gramophone: the real woman seemed far away. She had grown stouter without losing her dewy freshness, and her smart gown might have been taken to show either the potentialities of a settled income, or a politic concession to the taste of her hearers. As I listened I reproached myself for ever having suspected her of self-deception in saying that she took no pleasure in her work. I was sure now that she did it only for Lancelot, and judging from the size of her audience and the price of the tickets I concluded that Lancelot must be receiving a liberal education.

I was living in New York that winter, and in the rotation of dinners I found myself one evening at Mrs. Amyot's side. The dimple came out at my greeting as punctually as a cuckoo in a Swiss clock, and I detected the same automatic quality in the tone in which she made her usual pretty demand for advice. She was like a musical-box charged with popular airs. They succeeded one another with breathless rapidity, but there was a moment after each when the cylinders scraped and whizzed.

Mrs. Amyot, as I found when I called on her, was living in a sunny flat, with a sitting-room full of flowers and a tea-table that had the air of expecting visitors. She owned that she had been ridiculously successful. It was delightful, of course, on Lancelot's account. Lancelot had been sent to the best school in the country, and if things went well and people didn't tire of his silly mother he was to go to Harvard afterwards. During the next two or three years Mrs. Amyot kept her flat in New York, and radiated art and literature upon the suburbs. I saw her now and then, always stouter, better dressed, more successful and more automatic: she had become a lecturing-machine.

I went abroad for a year or two and when I came back she had disappeared. I asked several people about her, but life had closed over her. She had been last heard of as lecturing—still lecturing—but no one seemed to know when or where.

It was in Boston that I found her at last, forlornly swaying to the oscillations of an overhead strap in a crowded trolley-car. Her face had so changed that I lost myself in a startled reckoning of the time that had elapsed since our parting. She spoke to me shyly, as though aware of my hurried calculation, and conscious that in five years she ought not to have altered so much as to upset my notion of time. Then she seemed to set it down to her dress, for she nervously gathered her cloak over a gown that asked only to be concealed, and shrank into a seat behind the line of prehensile bipeds blocking the aisle of the car.

It was perhaps because she so obviously avoided me that I felt for the first time that I might be of use to her; and when she left the car I made no excuse for following her.

She said nothing of needing advice and did not ask me to walk home with her, concealing, as we talked, her transparent preoccupations under the guise of a sudden interest in all I had been doing since she had last seen me. Of what concerned her, I learned only that Lancelot was well and that for the present she was not lecturing—she was tired and her doctor had ordered her to rest. On the doorstep of a shabby house she paused and held out her hand. She had been so glad to see me and perhaps if I were in Boston again—the tired dimple, as it were, bowed me out and closed the door on the conclusion of the phrase.

Two or three weeks later, at my club in New York, I found a letter from her. In it she owned that she was troubled, that of late she had been unsuccessful, and that, if I chanced to be coming back to Boston, and could spare her a little of that invaluable advice which—. A few days later the advice was at her disposal. She told me frankly what had happened. Her public had grown tired of her. She had seen it coming on for some time, and was shrewd enough in detecting the causes. She had more rivals than formerly— younger women, she admitted, with a smile that could still afford to be generous—and then her audiences had grown more critical and consequently more exacting. Lecturing— as she understood it— used to be simple enough. You chose your topic—Raphael, Shakespeare, Gothic Architecture, or some such big familiar "subject"—and read up about it for a week or so at the Athenaeum or the Astor Library, and then told your audience what you had read. Now, it appeared, that simple process was no longer adequate. People had tired of familiar "subjects"; it was the fashion to be interested in things that one hadn't always known about—natural selection, animal magnetism, sociology and comparative folk-lore; while, in literature, the demand had become equally difficult to meet, since Matthew Arnold had introduced the habit of studying the "influence" of one author on another. She had tried lecturing on influences, and had done very well as long as the public was satisfied with the tracing of such obvious influences as that of Turner on Ruskin, of Schiller on Goethe, of Shakespeare on English literature; but such investigations had soon lost all charm for her too-sophisticated audiences, who now demanded either that the influence or the influenced should be quite unknown, or that there should be no perceptible connection between the two. The zest of the performance lay in the measure of ingenuity with which the lecturer established a relation between two people who had probably never heard of each other, much less read each other's works. A pretty Miss Williams with red hair had, for instance, been lecturing with great success on the influence of the Rosicrucians upon the poetry of Keats, while somebody else had given a "course" on the influence of St. Thomas Aquinas upon Professor Huxley.

Mrs. Amyot, warmed by my participation in her distress, went on to say that the growing demand for evolution was what most troubled her. Her grandfather had been a pillar of the Presbyterian ministry, and the idea of her lecturing on Darwin or Herbert Spencer was deeply shocking to her mother and aunts. In one sense the family had staked its literary as well as its spiritual hopes on the literal inspiration of Genesis: what became of "The Fall of Man" in the light of modern exegesis?

The upshot of it was that she had ceased to lecture because she could no longer sell tickets enough to pay for the hire of a lecture-hall; and as for the managers, they wouldn't look at her. She had tried her luck all through the Eastern States and as far south as Washington; but it was of no use, and unless she could get hold of some new subjects— or, better still, of some new audiences—she must simply go out of the business. That would mean the failure of all she had worked for, since Lancelot would have to leave Harvard. She paused, and wept some of the unbecoming tears that spring from real grief. Lancelot, it appeared, was to be a genius. He had passed his opening examinations brilliantly; he had "literary gifts"; he had written beautiful poetry, much of which his mother had copied out, in reverentially slanting characters, in a velvet-bound volume which she drew from a locked drawer.

Lancelot's verse struck me as nothing more alarming than growing-pains; but it was not to learn this that she had summoned me. What she wanted was to be assured that he was worth working for, an assurance which I managed to convey by the simple stratagem of remarking that the poems reminded me of Swinburne—and so they did, as well as of Browning, Tennyson, Rossetti, and all the other poets who supply young authors with original inspirations.

This point being established, it remained to be decided by what means his mother was, in the French phrase, to pay herself the luxury of a poet. It was clear that this indulgence could be bought only with counterfeit coin, and that the one way of helping Mrs. Amyot was to become a party to the circulation of such currency. My fetish of intellectual integrity went down like a ninepin before the appeal of a woman no longer young and distinctly foolish, but full of those dear contradictions and irrelevancies that will always make flesh and blood prevail against a syllogism. When I took leave of Mrs. Amyot I had promised her a dozen letters to Western universities and had half pledged myself to sketch out a lecture on the reconciliation of science and religion.

In the West she achieved a success which for a year or more embittered my perusal of the morning papers. The fascination that lures the murderer back to the scene of his crime drew my eye to every paragraph celebrating Mrs. Amyot's last brilliant lecture on the influence of something upon somebody; and her own letters—she overwhelmed me with them—spared me no detail of the entertainment given in her honor by the Palimpsest Club of Omaha or of her reception at the University of Leadville. The college professors were especially kind: she assured me that she had never before met with such discriminating sympathy. I winced at the adjective, which cast a sudden light on the vast machinery of fraud that I had set in motion. All over my native land, men of hitherto unblemished integrity were conniving with me in urging their friends to go and hear Mrs. Amyot lecture on the reconciliation of science and religion! My only hope was that, somewhere among the number of my accomplices, Mrs. Amyot might find one who would marry her in the defense of his convictions.

None, apparently, resorted to such heroic measures; for about two years later I was startled by the announcement that Mrs. Amyot was lecturing in Trenton, New Jersey, on modern theosophy in the light of the Vedas. The following week she was at Newark, discussing Schopenhauer in the light of recent psychology. The week after that I was on the deck of an ocean steamer, reconsidering my share in Mrs. Amyot's triumphs with the impartiality with which one views an episode that is being left behind at the rate of twenty knots an hour. After all, I had been helping a mother to educate her son.

The next ten years of my life were spent in Europe, and when I came home the recollection of Mrs. Amyot had become as inoffensive as one of those pathetic ghosts who are said to strive in vain to make themselves visible to the living. I did not even notice the fact that I no longer heard her spoken of; she had dropped like a dead leaf from the bough of memory.

A year or two after my return I was condemned to one of the worst punishments a worker can undergo—an enforced holiday. The doctors who pronounced the inhuman sentence decreed that it should be worked out in the South, and for a whole winter I carried my cough, my thermometer and my idleness from one fashionable orange-grove to another. In the vast and melancholy sea of my disoccupation I clutched like a drowning man at any human driftwood within reach. I took a critical and depreciatory interest in the coughs, the thermometers and the idleness of my fellow-sufferers; but to the healthy, the occupied, the transient I clung with undiscriminating enthusiasm.

In no other way can I explain, as I look back on it, the importance I attached to the leisurely confidences of a new arrival with a brown beard who, tilted back at my side on a hotel veranda hung with roses, imparted to me one afternoon the simple annals of his past. There was nothing in the tale to kindle the most inflammable imagination, and though the man had a pleasant frank face and a voice differing agreeably from the shrill inflections of our fellow-lodgers, it is probable that under different conditions his discursive history of successful business ventures in a Western city would have affected me somewhat in the manner of a lullaby.

Even at the tune I was not sure I liked his agreeable voice: it had a self-importance out of keeping with the humdrum nature of his story, as though a breeze engaged in shaking out a table-cloth should have fancied itself inflating a banner. But this criticism may have been a mere mark of my own fastidiousness, for the man seemed a simple fellow, satisfied with his middling fortunes, and already (he was not much past thirty) deep-sunk in conjugal content.

He had just started on an anecdote connected with the cutting of his eldest boy's teeth, when a lady I knew, returning from her late drive, paused before us for a moment in the twilight, with the smile which is the feminine equivalent of beads to savages.

"Won't you take a ticket?" she said sweetly.

Of course I would take a ticket—but for what? I ventured to inquire.

"Oh, that's *so* good of you—for the lecture this evening. You needn't go, you know; we're none of us going; most of us have been through it already at Aiken and at Saint Augustine and at Palm Beach. I've given away my tickets to some new people who've just come from the North, and some of us are going to send our maids, just to fill up the room."

"And may I ask to whom you are going to pay this delicate attention?"

"Oh, I thought you knew—to poor Mrs. Amyot. She's been lecturing all over the South this winter; she's simply *haunted* me ever since I left New York—and we had six weeks of her at Bar Harbor last summer! One has to take tickets, you know, because she's a widow and does it for her son—to pay for his education. She's so plucky and nice about it, and talks about him in such a touching unaffected way, that everybody is sorry for her, and we all simply ruin ourselves in tickets. I do hope that boy's nearly educated!"

"Mrs. Amyot? Mrs. Amyot?" I repeated. "Is she *still* educating her son?"

"Oh, do you know about her? Has she been at it long? There's some comfort in that, for I suppose when the boy's provided for the poor thing will be able to take a rest—and give us one!"

She laughed and held out her hand.

"Here's your ticket. Did you say *tickets*—two? Oh, thanks. Of course you needn't go."

"But I mean to go. Mrs. Amyot is an old friend of mine."

"Do you really? That's awfully good of you. Perhaps I'll go too if I can persuade Charlie and the others to come. And I wonder"—in a well-directed aside—"if your friend—?"

I telegraphed her under cover of the dusk that my friend was of too recent standing to be drawn into her charitable toils, and she masked her mistake under a rattle of friendly adjurations not to be late, and to be sure to keep a seat for her, as she had quite made up her mind to go even if Charlie and the others wouldn't.

The flutter of her skirts subsided in the distance, and my neighbor, who had half turned away to light a cigar, made no effort to reopen the conversation. At length, fearing he might have overheard the allusion to himself, I ventured to ask if he were going to the lecture that evening.

"Much obliged—I have a ticket," he said abruptly.

This struck me as in such bad taste that I made no answer; and it was he who spoke next.

"Did I understand you to say that you were an old friend of Mrs. Amyot's?"

"I think I may claim to be, if it is the same Mrs. Amyot I had the pleasure of knowing many years ago. My Mrs. Amyot used to lecture too—"

"To pay for her son's education?"

"I believe so."

"Well—see you later."

He got up and walked into the house.

In the hotel drawing-room that evening there was but a meager sprinkling of guests, among whom I saw my brown-bearded friend sitting alone on a sofa, with his head against the wall. It could not have been curiosity to see Mrs. Amyot that had impelled him to attend the performance, for it would have been impossible for him, without changing his place, to command the improvised platform at the end of the room. When I looked at him he seemed lost in contemplation of the chandelier.

The lady from whom I had bought my tickets fluttered in late, unattended by Charlie and the others, and assuring me that she would *scream* if we had the lecture on Ibsen— she had heard it three times already that winter. A glance at the program reassured her: it informed us (in the lecturer's own slanting hand) that Mrs. Amyot was to lecture on the Cosmogony.

After a long pause, during which the small audience coughed and moved its chairs and showed signs of regretting that it had come, the door opened, and Mrs. Amyot stepped upon the platform. Ah, poor lady!

Some one said "Hush!" The coughing and chair-shifting subsided, and she began.

It was like looking at one's self early in the morning in a cracked mirror. I had no idea I had grown so old. As for Lancelot, he must have a beard. A beard? The word struck me, and without knowing why I glanced across the room at my bearded friend on the sofa. Oddly enough he was looking at me, with a half-defiant, half-sullen expression; and as our glances crossed, and his fell, the conviction came to me that *he was Lancelot*.

I don't remember a word of the lecture; and yet there were enough of them to have filled a good-sized dictionary. The stream of Mrs. Amyot's eloquence had become a flood: one had the despairing sense that she had sprung a leak, and that until the plumber came there was nothing to be done about it.

The plumber came at length, in the shape of a clock striking ten; my companion, with a sigh of relief, drifted away in search of Charlie and the others; the audience scattered with the precipitation of people who had discharged a duty; and, without surprise, I found the brown-bearded stranger at my elbow.

We stood alone in the bare-floored room, under the flaring chandelier.

"I think you told me this afternoon that you were an old friend of Mrs. Amyot's?" he began awkwardly.

I assented.

"Will you come in and see her?"

"Now? I shall be very glad to, if—"

"She's ready; she's expecting you," he interposed.

He offered no further explanation, and I followed him in silence. He led me down the long corridor, and pushed open the door of a sitting-room.

"Mother," he said, closing the door after we had entered, "here's the gentleman who says he used to know you."

Mrs. Amyot, who sat in an easy-chair stirring a cup of bouillon, looked up with a start. She had evidently not seen me in the audience, and her son's description had failed to convey my identity. I saw a frightened look in her eyes; then, like a frost flower on a window-pane, the dimple expanded on her wrinkled cheek, and she held out her hand.

"I'm so glad," she said, "so glad!"

She turned to her son, who stood watching us. "You must have told Lancelot all about me—you've known me so long!"

"I haven't had time to talk to your son—since I knew he was your son," I explained.

Her brow cleared. "Then you haven't had time to say anything very dreadful?" she said with a laugh.

"It is he who has been saying dreadful things," I returned, trying to fall in with her tone.

I saw my mistake. "What things?" she faltered.

"Making me feel how old I am by telling me about his children."

"My grandchildren!" she exclaimed with a blush.

"Well, if you choose to put it so."

She laughed again, vaguely, and was silent. I hesitated a moment and then put out my hand.

"I see you are tired. I shouldn't have ventured to come in at this hour if your son—"

The son stepped between us. "Yes, I asked him to come," he said to his mother, in his clear self-assertive voice. "I haven't told him anything yet; but you've got to—now. That's what I brought him for."

His mother straightened herself, but I saw her eye waver.

"Lancelot—" she began.

"Mr. Amyot," I said, turning to the young man, "if your mother will let me come back tomorrow, I shall be very glad—"

He struck his hand hard against the table on which he was leaning.

"No, sir! It won't take long, but it's got to be said now."

He moved nearer to his mother, and I saw his lip twitch under his beard. After all, he was younger and less sure of himself than I had fancied.

"See here, mother," he went on, "there's something here that's got to be cleared up, and as you say this gentleman is an old friend of yours it had better be cleared up in his presence. Maybe he can help explain it—and if he can't, it's got to be explained to *him*."

Mrs. Amyot's lips moved, but she made no sound. She glanced at me helplessly and sat down. My early inclination to thrash Lancelot was beginning to reassert itself. I took up my hat and moved toward the door.

"Mrs. Amyot is under no obligation to explain anything whatever to me," I said curtly.

"Well! She's under an obligation to me, then—to explain something in your presence." He turned to her again. "Do you know what the people in this hotel are saying? Do you know what he thinks—what they all think? That you're doing this lecturing to support me—to pay for my education! They say you go round telling them so. That's what they buy the tickets for— they do it out of charity. Ask him if it isn't what they say—ask him if they weren't joking about it on the piazza before dinner. The others think I'm a little boy, but he's known you for years, and he must have known how old I was. *He* must have known it wasn't to pay for my education!"

He stood before her with his hands clenched, the veins beating in his temples. She had grown very pale, and her cheeks looked hollow. When she spoke her voice had an odd click in it.

"If—if these ladies and gentlemen have been coming to my lectures out of charity, I see nothing to be ashamed of in that—" she faltered.

"If they've been coming out of charity to *me*," he retorted, "don't you see you've been making me a party to a fraud? Isn't there any shame in that?" His forehead reddened. "Mother! Can't you see the shame of letting people think I was a d—beat, who sponged on you for my keep? Let alone making us both the laughing-stock of every place you go to!"

"I never did that, Lancelot!"

"Did what?"

"Made you a laughing-stock—"

He stepped close to her and caught her wrist.

"Will you look me in the face and swear you never told people you were doing this lecturing business to support me?"

There was a long silence. He dropped her wrist and she lifted a limp handkerchief to her frightened eyes. "I did do it—to support you—to educate you"—she sobbed.

"We're not talking about what you did when I was a boy. Everybody who knows me knows I've been a grateful son. Have I ever taken a penny from you since I left college ten years ago?"

"I never said you had! How can you accuse your mother of such wickedness, Lancelot?"

"Have you never told anybody in this hotel—or anywhere else in the last ten years— that you were lecturing to support me? Answer me that!"

"How can you," she wept, "before a stranger?"

"Haven't you said such things about *me* to strangers?" he retorted.

"Lancelot!"

"Well—answer me, then. Say you haven't, mother!" His voice broke unexpectedly and he took her hand with a gentler touch. "I'll believe anything you tell me," he said almost humbly.

She mistook his tone and raised her head with a rash clutch at dignity.

"I think you'd better ask this gentleman to excuse you first."

"No, by God, I won't!" he cried. "This gentleman says he knows all about you and I mean him to know all about me too. I don't mean that he or anybody else under this roof shall go on thinking for another twenty-four hours that a cent of their money has ever gone into my pockets since I was old enough to shift for myself. And he shan't leave this room till you've made that clear to him."

He stepped back as he spoke and put his shoulders against the door.

"My dear young gentleman," I said politely, "I shall leave this room exactly when I see fit to do so—and that is now. I have already told you that Mrs. Amyot owes me no explanation of her conduct."

"But I owe you an explanation of mine—you and every one who has bought a single one of her lecture tickets. Do you suppose a man who's been through what I went through while that woman was talking to you in the porch before dinner is going to hold his tongue, and not attempt to justify himself? No decent man is going to sit down under that sort of thing. It's enough to ruin his character. If you're my mother's friend, you owe it to me to hear what I've got to say."

He pulled out his handkerchief and wiped his forehead.

"Good God, mother!" he burst out suddenly, "what did you do it for? Haven't you had everything you wanted ever since I was able to pay for it? Haven't I paid you back every cent you spent on me when I was in college? Have I ever gone back on you since I was big enough to work?" He turned to me with a laugh. "I thought she did it to amuse herself—and because there was such a demand for her lectures. *Such a demand!* That's what she always told me. When we asked her to come out and spend this winter with us in Minneapolis, she wrote back that she couldn't because she had engagements all through the south, and her manager wouldn't let her off. That's the reason why I came all the way on here to see her. We thought she was the most popular lecturer in the United States, my wife and I did! We were awfully proud of it too, I can tell you." He dropped into a chair, still laughing.

"How can you, Lancelot, how can you!" His mother, forgetful of my presence, was clinging to him with tentative caresses. "When you didn't need the money any longer I spent it all on the children—you know I did."

"Yes, on lace christening dresses and life-size rocking-horses with real manes! The kind of thing children can't do without."

"Oh, Lancelot, Lancelot—I loved them so! How can you believe such falsehoods about me?"

"What falsehoods about you?"

"That I ever told anybody such dreadful things?"

He put her back gently, keeping his eyes on hers. "Did you never tell anybody in this house that you were lecturing to support your son?"

Her hands dropped from his shoulders and she flashed round on me in sudden anger.

"I know what I think of people who call themselves friends and who come between a mother and her son!"

"Oh, mother, mother!" he groaned.

I went up to him and laid my hand on his shoulder.

"My dear man," I said, "don't you see the uselessness of prolonging this?"

"Yes, I do," he answered abruptly; and before I could forestall his movement he rose and walked out of the room.

There was a long silence, measured by the lessening reverberations of his footsteps down the wooden floor of the corridor.

When they ceased I approached Mrs. Amyot, who had sunk into her chair. I held out my hand and she took it without a trace of resentment on her ravaged face.

"I sent his wife a seal-skin jacket at Christmas!" she said, with the tears running down her cheeks.

## SOULS BELATED

THEIR RAILWAY carriage had been full when the train left Bologna; but at the first station beyond Milan their only remaining companion—a courtly person who ate garlic out of a carpet-bag—had left his crumb-strewn seat with a bow.

Lydia's eye regretfully followed the shiny broadcloth of his retreating back till it lost itself in the cloud of touts and cab-drivers hanging about the station; then she glanced across at Gannett and caught the same regret in his look. They were both sorry to be alone.

"*Par-ten-za!*" shouted the guard. The train vibrated to a sudden slamming of doors; a waiter ran along the platform with a tray of fossilized sandwiches; a belated porter flung a bundle of shawls and band-boxes into a third-class carriage; the guard snapped out a brief *Partenza!* which indicated the purely ornamental nature of his first shout; and the train swung out of the station.

The direction of the road had changed, and a shaft of sunlight struck across the dusty red velvet seats into Lydia's corner. Gannett did not notice it. He had returned to his *Revue de Paris*, and she had to rise and lower the shade of the farther window. Against the vast horizon of their leisure such incidents stood out sharply.

Having lowered the shade, Lydia sat down, leaving the length of the carriage between herself and Gannett. At length he missed her and looked up.

"I moved out of the sun," she hastily explained.

He looked at her curiously: the sun was beating on her through the shade.

"Very well," he said pleasantly; adding, "You don't mind?" as he drew a cigarette-case from his pocket.

It was a refreshing touch, relieving the tension of her spirit with the suggestion that, after all, if he could *smoke—!* The relief was only momentary. Her experience of smokers was limited (her husband had disapproved of the use of tobacco) but she knew from hearsay that men sometimes smoked to get away from things; that a cigar might be the masculine equivalent of darkened windows and a headache. Gannett, after a puff or two, returned to his review.

It was just as she had foreseen; he feared to speak as much as she did. It was one of the misfortunes of their situation that they were never busy enough to necessitate, or even to justify, the postponement of unpleasant discussions. If they avoided a question it was obviously, unconcealably because the question was disagreeable. They had unlimited leisure and an accumulation of mental energy to devote to any subject that presented itself; new topics were in fact at a premium. Lydia sometimes had premonitions of a famine-stricken period when there would he nothing left to talk about, and she had already caught herself doling out piecemeal what, in the first prodigality of their confidences, she would have flung to him in a breath. Their silence therefore might simply mean that they had nothing to say; but it was another disadvantage of their position that it allowed infinite opportunity for the classification of minute differences. Lydia had learned to distinguish between real and factitious silences; and under Gannett's she now detected a hum of speech to which her own thoughts made breathless answer.

How could it be otherwise, with that thing between them? She glanced up at the rack overhead. The *thing* was there, in her dressing-bag, symbolically suspended over her head and his. He was thinking of it now, just as she was; they had been thinking of it in unison ever since they had entered the train. While the carriage had held other travellers they had screened her from his thoughts; but now that he and she were alone she knew exactly what was passing through his mind; she could almost hear him asking himself what he should say to her. . . .

The thing had come that morning, brought up to her in an innocent-looking envelope with the rest of their letters, as they were leaving the hotel at Bologna. As she tore it open, she and Gannett were laughing over some ineptitude of the local guide-book—they had been driven, of late, to make the most of such incidental humors of travel. Even when she had unfolded the document she took it for some unimportant business paper sent abroad for her signature, and her eye travelled inattentively over the curly *Whereases* of the preamble until a word arrested her:—Divorce. There it stood, an impassable barrier, between her husband's name and hers.

She had been prepared for it, of course, as healthy people are said to be prepared for death, in the sense of knowing it must come without in the least expecting that it will. She had known from the first that Tillotson meant to divorce her—but what did it matter? Nothing mattered, in those first days of supreme deliverance, but the fact that she was free; and not so much (she had begun to be aware) that freedom had released her from Tillotson as that it had given her to Gannett. This discovery had not been agreeable to her self-esteem. She had preferred to think that Tillotson had himself embodied all her reasons for leaving him; and those he represented had seemed cogent enough to stand in no need of reinforcement. Yet she had not left him till she met Gannett. It was her love for Gannett that had made life with Tillotson so poor and incomplete a business. If she had never, from the first, regarded her marriage as a full cancelling of her claims upon life, she had at least, for a number of years, accepted it as a provisional compensation,—she had made it "do." Existence in the commodious Tillotson mansion in Fifth Avenue—with Mrs. Tillotson senior commanding the approaches from the second-story front windows—had been reduced to a series of purely automatic acts. The moral atmosphere of the Tillotson interior was as carefully screened and curtained as the house itself: Mrs. Tillotson senior dreaded ideas as much as a draught in her back. Prudent people liked an even temperature; and to do anything unexpected was as foolish as going out in the rain. One of the chief advantages of being rich was that one need not be exposed to unforeseen contingencies: by the use of ordinary firmness and common sense one could make sure of doing exactly the same thing every day at the same hour. These doctrines, reverentially imbibed with his mother's milk, Tillotson (a model son who had never given his parents an hour's anxiety) complacently expounded to his wife, testifying to his sense of their importance by the regularity with which he wore galoshes on damp days, his punctuality at meals, and his elaborate precautions against burglars and contagious diseases. Lydia, coming from a smaller town, and entering New York life through the portals of the Tillotson mansion, had mechanically accepted this point of view as inseparable from having a front pew in church and a parterre box at the opera. All the people who came to the house revolved in the same small circle of prejudices. It was the kind of society in which, after dinner, the ladies compared the exorbitant charges of their children's teachers, and agreed that, even with the new duties on French clothes, it was cheaper in the end to get everything from Worth; while the husbands, over their cigars, lamented municipal corruption, and decided that the men to start a reform were those who had no private interests at stake.

To Lydia this view of life had become a matter of course, just as lumbering about in her mother-in-law's landau had come to seem the only possible means of locomotion, and listening every Sunday to a fashionable Presbyterian divine the inevitable atonement for having thought oneself bored on the other six days of the week. Before she met Gannett her life had seemed merely dull: his coming made it appear like one of those dismal Cruikshank prints in which the people are all ugly and all engaged in occupations that are either vulgar or stupid.

It was natural that Tillotson should be the chief sufferer from this readjustment of focus. Gannett's nearness had made her husband ridiculous, and a part of the ridicule had been reflected on herself. Her tolerance laid her open to a suspicion of obtuseness from which she must, at all costs, clear herself in Gannett's eyes.

She did not understand this until afterwards. At the time she fancied that she had merely reached the limits of endurance. In so large a charter of liberties as the mere act of leaving Tillotson seemed to confer, the small question of divorce or no divorce did not count. It was when she saw that she had left her husband only to be with Gannett that she perceived the significance of anything affecting their relations. Her husband, in casting her off, had virtually flung her at Gannett: it was thus that the world viewed it. The measure of alacrity with which Gannett would receive her would be the subject of curious speculation over afternoon-tea tables and in club corners. She knew what would be said—she had heard it so often of others! The recollection bathed her in misery. The men would probably back Gannett to "do the decent thing"; but the ladies' eye-brows would emphasize the worthlessness of such enforced fidelity; and after all, they would be right. She had put herself in a position where Gannett "owed" her something; where, as a gentleman, he was bound to "stand the damage." The idea of accepting such compensation had never crossed her mind; the so-called rehabilitation of such a marriage had always seemed to her the only real disgrace. What she dreaded was the necessity of having to explain herself; of having to combat his arguments; of calculating, in spite of herself, the exact measure of insistence with which he pressed them. She knew not whether she most shrank from his insisting too much or too little. In such a case the nicest sense of proportion might be at fault; and how easy to fall into the error of taking her resistance for a test of his sincerity! Whichever way she turned, an ironical implication confronted her: she had the exasperated sense of having walked into the trap of some stupid practical joke.

Beneath all these preoccupations lurked the dread of what he was thinking. Sooner or later, of course, he would have to speak; but that, in the meantime, he should think, even for a moment, that there was any use in speaking, seemed to her simply unendurable. Her sensitiveness on this point was aggravated by another fear, as yet barely on the level of consciousness; the fear of unwillingly involving Gannett in the trammels of her dependence. To look upon him as the instrument of her liberation; to resist in herself the least tendency to a wifely taking possession of his future; had seemed to Lydia the one way of maintaining the dignity of their relation. Her view had not changed, but she was aware of a growing inability to keep her thoughts fixed on the essential point—the point of parting with Gannett. It was easy to face as long as she kept it sufficiently far off: but what was this act of mental postponement but a gradual encroachment on his future? What was needful was the courage to recognize the moment when, by some word or look, their voluntary fellowship should be transformed into a bondage the more wearing that it was based on none of those common obligations which make the most imperfect marriage in some sort a center of gravity.

When the porter, at the next station, threw the door open, Lydia drew back, making way for the hoped-for intruder; but none came, and the train took up its leisurely progress through the spring wheat-fields and budding copses. She now began to hope that Gannett would speak before the next station. She watched him furtively, half-disposed to return to the seat opposite his, but there was an artificiality about his absorption that restrained her. She had never before seen him read with so conspicuous an air of warding off interruption. What could he be thinking of? Why should he be afraid to speak? Or was it her answer that he dreaded?

The train paused for the passing of an express, and he put down his book and leaned out of the window. Presently he turned to her with a smile. "There's a jolly old villa out here," he said.

His easy tone relieved her, and she smiled back at him as she crossed over to his corner.

Beyond the embankment, through the opening in a mossy wall, she caught sight of the villa, with its broken balustrades, its stagnant fountains, and the stone satyr closing the perspective of a dusky grass-walk.

"How should you like to live there?" he asked as the train moved on.

"There?"

"In some such place, I mean. One might do worse, don't you think so? There must be at least two centuries of solitude under those yew-trees. Shouldn't you like it?"

"I—I don't know," she faltered. She knew now that he meant to speak.

He lit another cigarette. "We shall have to live somewhere, you know," he said as he bent above the match.

Lydia tried to speak carelessly. "*Je n'en vois pas la nécessité!* Why not live everywhere, as we have been doing?"

"But we can't travel forever, can we?"

"Oh, forever's a long word," she objected, picking up the review he had thrown aside.

"For the rest of our lives then," he said, moving nearer.

She made a slight gesture which caused his hand to slip from hers.

"Why should we make plans? I thought you agreed with me that it's pleasanter to drift."

He looked at her hesitatingly. "It's been pleasant, certainly; but I suppose I shall have to get at my work again some day. You know I haven't written a line since—all this time," he hastily emended.

She flamed with sympathy and self-reproach. "Oh, if you mean *that*—if you want to write—of course we must settle down. How stupid of me not to have thought of it sooner! Where shall we go? Where do you think you could work best? We oughtn't to lose any more time."

He hesitated again. "I had thought of a villa in these parts. It's quiet; we shouldn't be bothered. Should you like it?"

"Of course I should like it." She paused and looked away. "But I thought— I remember your telling me once that your best work had been done in a crowd—in big cities. Why should you shut yourself up in a desert?"

Gannett, for a moment, made no reply. At length he said, avoiding her eye as carefully as she avoided his: "It might be different now; I can't tell, of course, till I try. A writer ought not to be dependent on his milieu; it's a mistake to humor oneself in that way; and I thought that just at first you might prefer to be—"

She faced him. "To be what?"

"Well—quiet. I mean—"

"What do you mean by 'at first'?" she interrupted.

He paused again. "I mean after we are married."

She thrust up her chin and turned toward the window. "Thank you!" she tossed back at him.

"Lydia!" he exclaimed blankly; and she felt in every fiber of her averted person that he had made the inconceivable, the unpardonable mistake of anticipating her acquiescence.

The train rattled on and he groped for a third cigarette. Lydia remained silent.

"I haven't offended you?" he ventured at length, in the tone of a man who feels his way.

She shook her head with a sigh. "I thought you understood," she moaned. Their eyes met and she moved back to his side.

"Do you want to know how not to offend me? By taking it for granted, once for all, that you've said your say on this odious question and that I've said mine, and that we stand just where we did this morning before that— that hateful paper came to spoil everything between us!"

"To spoil everything between us? What on earth do you mean? Aren't you glad to be free?"

"I was free before."

"Not to marry me," he suggested.

"But I don't *want* to marry you!" she cried.

She saw that he turned pale. "I'm obtuse, I suppose," he said slowly. "I confess I don't see what you're driving at. Are you tired of the whole business? Or was I simply a—an excuse for getting away? Perhaps you didn't care to travel alone? Was that it? And now you want to chuck me?" His voice had grown harsh. "You owe me a straight answer, you know; don't be tenderhearted!"

Her eyes swam as she leaned to him. "Don't you see it's because I care— because I care so much? Oh, Ralph! Can't you see how it would humiliate me? Try to feel it as a woman would! Don't you see the misery of being made your wife in this way? If I'd known you as a girl—that would have been a real marriage! But now—this vulgar fraud upon society—and upon a society we despised and laughed at—this sneaking back into a position that we've voluntarily forfeited: don't you see what a cheap compromise it is? We neither of us believe in the abstract 'sacredness' of marriage; we both know that no ceremony is needed to consecrate our love for each other; what object can we have in marrying, except the secret fear of each that the other may escape, or the secret longing to work our way back gradually—oh, very gradually—into the esteem of the people whose conventional morality we have always ridiculed and hated? And the very fact that, after a decent interval, these same people would come and dine with us—the women who talk about the indissolubility of marriage, and who would let me die in a gutter to-day because I am 'leading a life of sin'— doesn't that disgust you more than their turning their backs on us now? I can stand being cut by them, but I couldn't stand their coming to call and asking what I meant to do about visiting that unfortunate Mrs. So-and-so!"

She paused, and Gannett maintained a perplexed silence.

"You judge things too theoretically," he said at length, slowly. "Life is made up of compromises."

"The life we ran away from—yes! If we had been willing to accept them"— she flushed—"we might have gone on meeting each other at Mrs. Tillotson's dinners."

He smiled slightly. "I didn't know that we ran away to found a new system of ethics. I supposed it was because we loved each other."

"Life is complex, of course; isn't it the very recognition of that fact that separates us from the people who see it *tout d'une pièce*? If *they* are right—if marriage is sacred in itself and the individual must always be sacrificed to the family—then there can be no real marriage between us, since our—our being together is a protest against the sacrifice of the individual to the family." She interrupted herself with a laugh. "You'll say now that I'm giving you a lecture on sociology! Of course one acts as one can—as one must, perhaps—pulled by all sorts of invisible threads; but at least one needn't pretend, for social advantages, to subscribe to a creed that ignores the complexity of human motives—that classifies people by arbitrary signs, and puts it in everybody's reach to be on Mrs. Tillotson's visiting-list. It may be necessary that the world should be ruled by conventions—but if we believed in them, why did we break through them? And if we don't believe in them, is it honest to take advantage of the protection they afford?"

Gannett hesitated. "One may believe in them or not; but as long as they do rule the world it is only by taking advantage of their protection that one can find a *modus vivendi.*"

"Do outlaws need a *modus vivendi*?"

He looked at her hopelessly. Nothing is more perplexing to man than the mental process of a woman who reasons her emotions.

She thought she had scored a point and followed it up passionately. "You do understand, don't you? You see how the very thought of the thing humiliates me! We are together to-day because we choose to be—don't let us look any farther than that!" She caught his hands. "*Promise* me you'll never speak of it again; promise me you'll never *think* of it even," she implored, with a tearful prodigality of italics.

Through what followed—his protests, his arguments, his final unconvinced submission to her wishes—she had a sense of his but half-discerning all that, for her, had made the moment so tumultuous. They had reached that memorable point in every heart-history when, for the first time, the man seems obtuse and the woman irrational. It was the abundance of his intentions that consoled her, on reflection, for what they lacked in quality. After all, it would have been worse, incalculably worse, to have detected any over-readiness to understand her.

II

WHEN the train at night-fall brought them to their journey's end at the edge of one of the lakes, Lydia was glad that they were not, as usual, to pass from one solitude to another. Their wanderings during the year had indeed been like the flight of outlaws: through Sicily, Dalmatia, Transylvania and Southern Italy they had persisted in their tacit avoidance of their kind. Isolation, at first, had deepened the flavor of their happiness, as night intensifies the scent of certain flowers; but in the new phase on which they were entering, Lydia's chief wish was that they should be less abnormally exposed to the action of each other's thoughts.

She shrank, nevertheless, as the brightly-looming bulk of the fashionable Anglo-American hotel on the water's brink began to radiate toward their advancing boat its vivid suggestion of social order, visitors' lists, Church services, and the bland inquisition of the *table d'hôte*. The mere fact that in a moment or two she must take her place on the hotel register as Mrs. Gannett seemed to weaken the springs of her resistance.

They had meant to stay for a night only, on their way to a lofty village among the glaciers of Monte Rosa; but after the first plunge into publicity, when they entered the dining-room, Lydia felt the relief of being lost in a crowd, of ceasing for a moment to be the center of Gannett's scrutiny; and in his face she caught the reflection of her feeling. After dinner, when she went upstairs, he strolled into the smoking-room, and an hour or two later, sitting in the darkness of her window, she heard his voice below and saw him walking up and down the terrace with a companion cigar at his side. When he came up he told her he had been talking to the hotel chaplain—a very good sort of fellow.

"Queer little microcosms, these hotels! Most of these people live here all summer and then migrate to Italy or the Riviera. The English are the only people who can lead that kind of life with dignity—those soft-voiced old ladies in Shetland shawls somehow carry the British Empire under their caps. *Civis Romanus sum.* It's a curious study—there might be some good things to work up here."

He stood before her with the vivid preoccupied stare of the novelist on the trail of a "subject." With a relief that was half painful she noticed that, for the first time since they had been together, he was hardly aware of her presence.

"Do you think you could write here?"

"Here? I don't know." His stare dropped. "After being out of things so long one's first impressions are bound to be tremendously vivid, you know. I see a dozen threads already that one might follow—"

He broke off with a touch of embarrassment.

"Then follow them. We'll stay," she said with sudden decision.

"Stay here?" He glanced at her in surprise, and then, walking to the window, looked out upon the dusky slumber of the garden.

"Why not?" she said at length, in a tone of veiled irritation.

"The place is full of old cats in caps who gossip with the chaplain. Shall you like—I mean, it would be different if—"

She flamed up.

"Do you suppose I care? It's none of their business."

"Of course not; but you won't get them to think so."

"They may think what they please."

He looked at her doubtfully.

"It's for you to decide."

"We'll stay," she repeated.

Gannett, before they met, had made himself known as a successful writer of short stories and of a novel which had achieved the distinction of being widely discussed. The reviewers called him "promising," and Lydia now accused herself of having too long interfered with the fulfilment of his promise. There was a special irony in the fact, since his passionate assurances that only the stimulus of her companionship could bring out his latent faculty had almost given the dignity of a "vocation" to her course: there had been moments when she had felt unable to assume, before posterity, the responsibility of thwarting his career. And, after all, he had not written a line since they had been together: his first desire to write had come from renewed contact with the world! Was it all a mistake then? Must the most intelligent choice work more disastrously than the blundering combinations of chance? Or was there a still more humiliating answer to her perplexities? His sudden impulse of activity so exactly coincided with her own wish to withdraw, for a time, from the range of his observation, that she wondered if he too were not seeking sanctuary from intolerable problems.

"You must begin tomorrow!" she cried, hiding a tremor under the laugh with which she added, "I wonder if there's any ink in the inkstand?"

Whatever else they had at the Hotel Bellosguardo, they had, as Miss Pinsent said, "a certain tone." It was to Lady Susan Condit that they owed this inestimable benefit; an advantage ranking in Miss Pinsent's opinion above even the lawn tennis courts and the resident chaplain. It was the fact of Lady Susan's annual visit that made the hotel what it was. Miss Pinsent was certainly the last to underrate such a privilege:—"It's so important, my dear, forming as we do a little family, that there should be some one to give *the tone*; and no one could do it better than Lady Susan—an earl's daughter and a person of such determination. Dear Mrs. Ainger now—who really *ought*, you know, when Lady Susan's away— absolutely refuses to assert herself." Miss Pinsent sniffed derisively. "A bishop's niece!—my dear, I saw her once actually give in to some South Americans—and before us all. She gave up her seat at table to oblige them—such a lack of dignity! Lady Susan spoke to her very plainly about it afterwards."

Miss Pinsent glanced across the lake and adjusted her auburn front.

"But of course I don't deny that the stand Lady Susan takes is not always easy to live up to—for the rest of us, I mean. Monsieur Grossart, our good proprietor, finds it trying at times, I know—he has said as much, privately, to Mrs. Ainger and me. After all, the poor man is not to blame for wanting to fill his hotel, is he? And Lady Susan is so difficult—so very difficult—about new people. One might almost say that she disapproves of them beforehand, on principle. And yet she's had warnings— she very nearly made a dreadful mistake once with the Duchess of Levens, who dyed her hair and—well, swore and smoked. One would have thought that might have been a lesson to Lady Susan." Miss Pinsent resumed her knitting with a sigh. "There are exceptions, of course. She took at once to you and Mr. Gannett—it was quite remarkable, really. Oh, I don't mean that either—of course not! It was perfectly natural—we *all* thought you so charming and interesting from the first day—we knew at once that Mr. Gannett was intellectual, by the magazines you took in; but you know what I mean. Lady Susan is so very—well, I won't say prejudiced, as Mrs. Ainger does—but so prepared not to like new people, that her taking to you in that way was a surprise to us all, I confess."

Miss Pinsent sent a significant glance down the long laurustinus alley from the other end of which two people—a lady and gentleman—were strolling toward them through the smiling neglect of the garden.

"In this case, of course, it's very different; that I'm willing to admit. Their looks are against them; but, as Mrs. Ainger says, one can't exactly tell them so."

"She's very handsome," Lydia ventured, with her eyes on the lady, who showed, under the dome of a vivid sunshade, the hour-glass figure and superlative coloring of a Christmas chromo.

"That's the worst of it. She's too handsome."

"Well, after all, she can't help that."

"Other people manage to," said Miss Pinsent skeptically.

"But isn't it rather unfair of Lady Susan—considering that nothing is known about them?"

"But, my dear, that's the very thing that's against them. It's infinitely worse than any actual knowledge."

Lydia mentally agreed that, in the case of Mrs. Linton, it possibly might be.

"I wonder why they came here?" she mused.

"That's against them too. It's always a bad sign when loud people come to a quiet place. And they've brought van-loads of boxes—her maid told Mrs. Ainger's that they meant to stop indefinitely."

"And Lady Susan actually turned her back on her in the salon?"

"My dear, she said it was for our sakes: that makes it so unanswerable! But poor Grossart is in a way! The Lintons have taken his most expensive suite, you know—the yellow damask drawing-room above the portico—and they have champagne with every meal!"

They were silent as Mr. and Mrs. Linton sauntered by; the lady with tempestuous brows and challenging chin; the gentleman, a blond stripling, trailing after her, head downward, like a reluctant child dragged by his nurse.

"What does your husband think of them, my dear?" Miss Pinsent whispered as they passed out of earshot.

Lydia stooped to pick a violet in the border.

"He hasn't told me."

"Of your speaking to them, I mean. Would he approve of that? I know how very particular nice Americans are. I think your action might make a difference; it would certainly carry weight with Lady Susan."

"Dear Miss Pinsent, you flatter me!"

Lydia rose and gathered up her book and sunshade.

"Well, if you're asked for an opinion—if Lady Susan asks you for one—I think you ought to be prepared," Miss Pinsent admonished her as she moved away.

### III

LADY SUSAN held her own. She ignored the Lintons, and her little family, as Miss Pinsent phrased it, followed suit. Even Mrs. Ainger agreed that it was obligatory. If Lady Susan owed it to the others not to speak to the Lintons, the others clearly owed it to Lady Susan to back her up. It was generally found expedient, at the Hotel Bellosguardo, to adopt this form of reasoning.

Whatever effect this combined action may have had upon the Lintons, it did not at least have that of driving them away. Monsieur Grossart, after a few days of suspense, had the satisfaction of seeing them settle down in his yellow damask *premier* with what looked like a permanent installation of palm-trees and silk sofa-cushions, and a gratifying continuance in the consumption of champagne. Mrs. Linton trailed her Doucet draperies up and down the garden with the same challenging air, while her husband, smoking innumerable cigarettes, dragged himself dejectedly in her wake; but neither of them, after the first encounter with Lady Susan, made any attempt to extend their acquaintance. They simply ignored their ignorers. As Miss Pinsent resentfully observed, they behaved exactly as though the hotel were empty.

It was therefore a matter of surprise, as well as of displeasure, to Lydia, to find, on glancing up one day from her seat in the garden, that the shadow which had fallen across her book was that of the enigmatic Mrs. Linton.

"I want to speak to you," that lady said, in a rich hard voice that seemed the audible expression of her gown and her complexion.

Lydia started. She certainly did not want to speak to Mrs. Linton.

"Shall I sit down here?" the latter continued, fixing her intensely-shaded eyes on Lydia's face, "or are you afraid of being seen with me?"

"Afraid?" Lydia colored. "Sit down, please. What is it that you wish to say?"

Mrs. Linton, with a smile, drew up a garden-chair and crossed one open-work ankle above the other.

"I want you to tell me what my husband said to your husband last night."

Lydia turned pale.

"My husband—to yours?" she faltered, staring at the other.

"Didn't you know they were closeted together for hours in the smoking-room after you went upstairs? My man didn't get to bed until nearly two o'clock and when he did I couldn't get a word out of him. When he wants to be aggravating I'll back him against anybody living!" Her teeth and eyes flashed persuasively upon Lydia. "But you'll tell me what they were talking about, won't you? I know I can trust you—you look so awfully kind. And it's for his own good. He's such a precious donkey and I'm so afraid he's got into some beastly scrape or other. If he'd only trust his own old woman! But they're always writing to him and setting him against me. And I've got nobody to turn to." She laid her hand on Lydia's with a rattle of bracelets. "You'll help me, won't you?"

Lydia drew back from the smiling fierceness of her brows.

"I'm sorry—but I don't think I understand. My husband has said nothing to me of—of yours."

The great black crescents above Mrs. Linton's eyes met angrily.

"I say—is that true?" she demanded.

Lydia rose from her seat.

"Oh, look here, I didn't mean that, you know—you mustn't take one up so! Can't you see how rattled I am?"

Lydia saw that, in fact, her beautiful mouth was quivering beneath softened eyes.

"I'm beside myself!" the splendid creature wailed, dropping into her seat.

"I'm so sorry," Lydia repeated, forcing herself to speak kindly; "but how can I help you?"

Mrs. Linton raised her head sharply.

"By finding out—there's a darling!"

"Finding what out?"

"What Trevenna told him."

"Trevenna—?" Lydia echoed in bewilderment.

Mrs. Linton clapped her hand to her mouth.

"Oh, Lord—there, it's out! What a fool I am! But I supposed of course you knew; I supposed everybody knew." She dried her eyes and bridled. "Didn't you know that he's Lord Trevenna? I'm Mrs. Cope."

Lydia recognized the names. They had figured in a flamboyant elopement which had thrilled fashionable London some six months earlier.

"Now you see how it is—you understand, don't you?" Mrs. Cope continued on a note of appeal. "I knew you would—that's the reason I came to you. I suppose *he* felt the same thing about your husband; he's not spoken to another soul in the place." Her face grew anxious again. "He's awfully sensitive, generally—he feels our position, he says—as if it wasn't my place to feel that! But when he does get talking there's no knowing what he'll say. I know he's been brooding over something lately, and I *must* find out what it is—it's to his interest that I should. I always tell him that I think only of his interest; if he'd only trust me! But he's been so odd lately—I can't think what he's plotting. You will help me, dear?"

Lydia, who had remained standing, looked away uncomfortably.

"If you mean by finding out what Lord Trevenna has told my husband, I'm afraid it's impossible."

"Why impossible?"

"Because I infer that it was told in confidence."

Mrs. Cope stared incredulously.

"Well, what of that? Your husband looks such a dear—any one can see he's awfully gone on you. What's to prevent your getting it out of him?"

Lydia flushed.

"I'm not a spy!" she exclaimed.

"A spy—a spy? How dare you?" Mrs. Cope flamed out. "Oh, I don't mean that either! Don't be angry with me—I'm so miserable." She essayed a softer note. "Do you call that spying—for one woman to help out another? I do need help so dreadfully! I'm at my wits' end with Trevenna, I am indeed. He's such a boy—a mere baby, you know; he's only two-and-twenty." She dropped her orbed lids. "He's younger than me—only fancy! a few months younger. I tell him he ought to listen to me as if I was his mother; oughtn't he now? But he won't, he won't! All his people are at him, you see—oh, I know *their* little game! Trying to get him away from me before I can get my divorce—that's what they're up to. At first he wouldn't listen to them; he used to toss their letters over to me to read; but now he reads them himself, and answers 'em too, I fancy; he's always shut up in his room, writing. If I only knew what his plan is I could stop him fast enough—he's such a simpleton. But he's dreadfully deep too—at times I can't make him out. But I know he's told your husband everything—I knew that last night the minute I laid eyes on him. And I *must* find out—you must help me—I've got no one else to turn to!"

She caught Lydia's fingers in a stormy pressure.

"Say you'll help me—you and your husband."

Lydia tried to free herself.

"What you ask is impossible; you must see that it is. No one could interfere in—in the way you ask."

Mrs. Cope's clutch tightened.

"You won't, then? You won't?"

"Certainly not. Let me go, please."

Mrs. Cope released her with a laugh.

"Oh, go by all means—pray don't let me detain you! Shall you go and tell Lady Susan Condit that there's a pair of us—or shall I save you the trouble of enlightening her?"

Lydia stood still in the middle of the path, seeing her antagonist through a mist of terror. Mrs. Cope was still laughing.

"Oh, I'm not spiteful by nature, my dear; but you're a little more than flesh and blood can stand! It's impossible, is it? Let you go, indeed! You're too good to be mixed up in my affairs, are you? Why, you little fool, the first day I laid eyes on you I saw that you and I were both in the same box—that's the reason I spoke to you."

She stepped nearer, her smile dilating on Lydia like a lamp through a fog.

"You can take your choice, you know; I always play fair. If you'll tell I'll promise not to. Now then, which is it to be?"

Lydia, involuntarily, had begun to move away from the pelting storm of words; but at this she turned and sat down again.

"You may go," she said simply. "I shall stay here."

IV

SHE stayed there for a long time, in the hypnotized contemplation, not of Mrs. Cope's present, but of her own past. Gannett, early that morning, had gone off on a long walk—he had fallen into the habit of taking these mountain-tramps with various fellow-lodgers; but even had he been within reach she could not have gone to him just then. She had to deal with herself first. She was surprised to find how, in the last months, she had lost the habit of introspection. Since their coming to the Hotel Bellosguardo she and Gannett had tacitly avoided themselves and each other.

She was aroused by the whistle of the three o'clock steamboat as it neared the landing just beyond the hotel gates. Three o'clock! Then Gannett would soon be back—he had told her to expect him before four. She rose hurriedly, her face averted from the inquisitorial facade of the hotel. She could not see him just yet; she could not go indoors.

She slipped through one of the overgrown garden-alleys and climbed a steep path to the hills.

It was dark when she opened their sitting-room door. Gannett was sitting on the window-ledge smoking a cigarette. Cigarettes were now his chief resource: he had not written a line during the two months they had spent at the Hotel Bellosguardo. In that respect, it had turned out not to be the right *milieu* after all.

He started up at Lydia's entrance.

"Where have you been? I was getting anxious."

She sat down in a chair near the door.

"Up the mountain," she said wearily.

"Alone?"

"Yes."

Gannett threw away his cigarette: the sound of her voice made him want to see her face.

"Shall we have a little light?" he suggested.

She made no answer and he lifted the globe from the lamp and put a match to the wick. Then he looked at her.

"Anything wrong? You look done up."

She sat glancing vaguely about the little sitting-room, dimly lit by the pallid-globed lamp, which left in twilight the outlines of the furniture, of his writing-table heaped with books and papers, of the tea-roses and jasmine drooping on the mantel-piece. How like home it had all grown—how like home!

"Lydia, what is wrong?" he repeated.

She moved away from him, feeling for her hatpins and turning to lay her hat and sunshade on the table.

Suddenly she said: "That woman has been talking to me."

Gannett stared.

"That woman? What woman?"

"Mrs. Linton—Mrs. Cope."

He gave a start of annoyance, still, as she perceived, not grasping the full import of her words.

"The deuce! She told you—?"

"She told me everything."

Gannett looked at her anxiously.

"What impudence! I'm so sorry that you should have been exposed to this, dear."

"Exposed!" Lydia laughed.

Gannett's brow clouded and they looked away from each other.

"Do you know *why* she told me? She had the best of reasons. The first time she laid eyes on me she saw that we were both in the same box."

"Lydia!"

"So it was natural, of course, that she should turn to me in a difficulty."

"What difficulty?"

"It seems she has reason to think that Lord Trevenna's people are trying to get him away from her before she gets her divorce—"

"Well?"

"And she fancied he had been consulting with you last night as to—as to the best way of escaping from her."

Gannett stood up with an angry forehead.

"Well—what concern of yours was all this dirty business? Why should she go to you?"

"Don't you see? It's so simple. I was to wheedle his secret out of you."

"To oblige that woman?"

"Yes; or, if I was unwilling to oblige her, then to protect myself."

"To protect yourself? Against whom?"

"Against her telling every one in the hotel that she and I are in the same box."

"She threatened that?"

"She left me the choice of telling it myself or of doing it for me."

"The beast!"

There was a long silence. Lydia had seated herself on the sofa, beyond the radius of the lamp, and he leaned against the window. His next question surprised her.

"When did this happen? At what time, I mean?"

She looked at him vaguely.

"I don't know—after luncheon, I think. Yes, I remember; it must have been at about three o'clock."

He stepped into the middle of the room and as he approached the light she saw that his brow had cleared.

"Why do you ask?" she said.

"Because when I came in, at about half-past three, the mail was just being distributed, and Mrs. Cope was waiting as usual to pounce on her letters; you know she was always watching for the postman. She was standing so close to me that I couldn't help seeing a big official-looking envelope that was handed to her. She tore it open, gave one look at the inside, and rushed off upstairs like a whirlwind, with the director shouting after her that she had left all her other letters behind. I don't believe she ever thought of you again after that paper was put into her hand."

"Why?"

"Because she was too busy. I was sitting in the window, watching for you, when the five o'clock boat left, and who should go on board, bag and baggage, valet and maid, dressing-bags and poodle, but Mrs. Cope and Trevenna. Just an hour and a half to pack up in! And you should have seen her when they started. She was radiant—shaking hands with everybody— waving her handkerchief from the deck—distributing bows and smiles like an empress. If ever a woman got what she wanted just in the nick of time that woman did. She'll be Lady Trevenna within a week, I'll wager."

"You think she has her divorce?"

"I'm sure of it. And she must have got it just after her talk with you."

Lydia was silent.

At length she said, with a kind of reluctance, "She was horribly angry when she left me. It wouldn't have taken long to tell Lady Susan Condit."

"Lady Susan Condit has not been told."

"How do you know?"

"Because when I went downstairs half an hour ago I met Lady Susan on the way—"

He stopped, half smiling.

"Well?"

"And she stopped to ask if I thought you would act as patroness to a charity concert she is getting up."

In spite of themselves they both broke into a laugh. Lydia's ended in sobs and she sank down with her face hidden. Gannett bent over her, seeking her hands.

"That vile woman—I ought to have warned you to keep away from her; I can't forgive myself! But he spoke to me in confidence; and I never dreamed—well, it's all over now."

Lydia lifted her head.

"Not for me. It's only just beginning."

"What do you mean?"

She put him gently aside and moved in her turn to the window. Then she went on, with her face turned toward the shimmering blackness of the lake, "You see of course that it might happen again at any moment."

"What?"

"This—this risk of being found out. And we could hardly count again on such a lucky combination of chances, could we?"

He sat down with a groan.

Still keeping her face toward the darkness, she said, "I want you to go and tell Lady Susan—and the others."

Gannett, who had moved towards her, paused a few feet off.

"Why do you wish me to do this?" he said at length, with less surprise in his voice than she had been prepared for.

"Because I've behaved basely, abominably, since we came here: letting these people believe we were married—lying with every breath I drew—"

"Yes, I've felt that too," Gannett exclaimed with sudden energy.

The words shook her like a tempest: all her thoughts seemed to fall about her in ruins.

"You—you've felt so?"

"Of course I have." He spoke with low-voiced vehemence. "Do you suppose I like playing the sneak any better than you do? It's damnable."

He had dropped on the arm of a chair, and they stared at each other like blind people who suddenly see.

"But you have liked it here," she faltered.

"Oh, I've liked it—I've liked it." He moved impatiently. "Haven't you?"

"Yes," she burst out; "that's the worst of it—that's what I can't bear. I fancied it was for your sake that I insisted on staying—because you thought you could write here; and perhaps just at first that really was the reason. But afterwards I wanted to stay myself—I loved it." She broke into a laugh. "Oh, do you see the full derision of it? These people—the very prototypes of the bores you took me away from, with the same fenced— in view of life, the same keep-off-the-grass morality, the same little cautious virtues and the same little frightened vices—well, I've clung to them, I've delighted in them, I've done my best to please them. I've toadied Lady Susan, I've gossiped with Miss Pinsent, I've pretended to be shocked with Mrs. Ainger. Respectability! It was the one thing in life that I was sure I didn't care about, and it's grown so precious to me that I've stolen it because I couldn't get it in any other way."

She moved across the room and returned to his side with another laugh.

"I who used to fancy myself unconventional! I must have been born with a card-case in my hand. You should have seen me with that poor woman in the garden. She came to me for help, poor creature, because she fancied that, having 'sinned,' as they call it, I might feel some pity for others who had been tempted in the same way. Not I! She didn't know me. Lady Susan would have been kinder, because Lady Susan wouldn't have been afraid. I hated the woman—my one thought was not to be seen with her—I could have killed her for guessing my secret. The one thing that mattered to me at that moment was my standing with Lady Susan!"

Gannett did not speak.

"And you—you've felt it too!" she broke out accusingly. "You've enjoyed being with these people as much as I have; you've let the chaplain talk to you by the hour about 'The Reign of Law' and Professor Drummond. When they asked you to hand the plate in church I was watching you—*you wanted to accept*."

She stepped close, laying her hand on his arm.

"Do you know, I begin to see what marriage is for. It's to keep people away from each other. Sometimes I think that two people who love each other can be saved from madness only by the things that come between them—children, duties, visits, bores, relations—the things that protect married people from each other. We've been too close together—that has been our sin. We've seen the nakedness of each other's souls."

She sank again on the sofa, hiding her face in her hands.

Gannett stood above her perplexedly: he felt as though she were being swept away by some implacable current while he stood helpless on its bank.

At length he said, "Lydia, don't think me a brute—but don't you see yourself that it won't do?"

"Yes, I see it won't do," she said without raising her head.

His face cleared.

"Then we'll go tomorrow."

"Go—where?"

"To Paris; to be married."

For a long time she made no answer; then she asked slowly, "Would they have us here if we were married?"

"Have us here?"

"I mean Lady Susan—and the others."

"Have us here? Of course they would."

"Not if they knew—at least, not unless they could pretend not to know."

He made an impatient gesture.

"We shouldn't come back here, of course; and other people needn't know—no one need know."

She sighed. "Then it's only another form of deception and a meaner one. Don't you see that?"

"I see that we're not accountable to any Lady Susans on earth!"

"Then why are you ashamed of what we are doing here?"

"Because I'm sick of pretending that you're my wife when you're not—when you won't be."

She looked at him sadly.

"If I were your wife you'd have to go on pretending. You'd have to pretend that I'd never been—anything else. And our friends would have to pretend that they believed what you pretended."

Gannett pulled off the sofa-tassel and flung it away.

"You're impossible," he groaned.

"It's not I—it's our being together that's impossible. I only want you to see that marriage won't help it."

"What will help it then?"

She raised her head.

"My leaving you."

"Your leaving me?" He sat motionless, staring at the tassel which lay at the other end of the room. At length some impulse of retaliation for the pain she was inflicting made him say deliberately:

"And where would you go if you left me?"

"Oh!" she cried.

He was at her side in an instant.

"Lydia—Lydia—you know I didn't mean it; I couldn't mean it! But you've driven me out of my senses; I don't know what I'm saying. Can't you get out of this labyrinth of self-torture? It's destroying us both."

"That's why I must leave you."

"How easily you say it!" He drew her hands down and made her face him. "You're very scrupulous about yourself—and others. But have you thought of me? You have no right to leave me unless you've ceased to care—"

"It's because I care—"

"Then I have a right to be heard. If you love me you can't leave me."

Her eyes defied him.

"Why not?"

He dropped her hands and rose from her side.

"Can you?" he said sadly.

The hour was late and the lamp flickered and sank. She stood up with a shiver and turned toward the door of her room.

## V

AT daylight a sound in Lydia's room woke Gannett from a troubled sleep. He sat up and listened. She was moving about softly, as though fearful of disturbing him. He heard her push back one of the creaking shutters; then there was a moment's silence, which seemed to indicate that she was waiting to see if the noise had roused him.

Presently she began to move again. She had spent a sleepless night, probably, and was dressing to go down to the garden for a breath of air. Gannett rose also; but some undefinable instinct made his movements as cautious as hers. He stole to his window and looked out through the slats of the shutter.

It had rained in the night and the dawn was gray and lifeless. The cloud-muffled hills across the lake were reflected in its surface as in a tarnished mirror. In the garden, the birds were beginning to shake the drops from the motionless laurustinus boughs.

An immense pity for Lydia filled Gannett's soul. Her seeming intellectual independence had blinded him for a time to the feminine cast of her mind. He had never thought of her as a woman who wept and clung: there was a lucidity in her intuitions that made them appear to be the result of reasoning. Now he saw the cruelty he had committed in detaching her from the normal conditions of life; he felt, too, the insight with which she had hit upon the real cause of their suffering. Their life was "impossible," as she had said—and its worst penalty was that it had made any other life impossible for them. Even had his love lessened, he was bound to her now by a hundred ties of pity and self-reproach; and she, poor child! must turn back to him as Latude returned to his cell.

A new sound startled him: it was the stealthy closing of Lydia's door. He crept to his own and heard her footsteps passing down the corridor. Then he went back to the window and looked out.

A minute or two later he saw her go down the steps of the porch and enter the garden. From his post of observation her face was invisible, but something about her appearance struck him. She wore a long travelling cloak and under its folds he detected the outline of a bag or bundle. He drew a deep breath and stood watching her.

She walked quickly down the laurustinus alley toward the gate; there she paused a moment, glancing about the little shady square. The stone benches under the trees were empty, and she seemed to gather resolution from the solitude about her, for she crossed the square to the steam-boat landing, and he saw her pause before the ticket-office at the head of the wharf. Now she was buying her ticket. Gannett turned his head a moment to look at the clock: the boat was due in five minutes. He had time to jump into his clothes and overtake her—

He made no attempt to move; an obscure reluctance restrained him. If any thought emerged from the tumult of his sensations, it was that he must let her go if she wished it. He had spoken last night of his rights: what were they? At the last issue, he and she were two separate beings, not made one by the miracle of common forbearances, duties, abnegations, but bound together in a *noyade* of passion that left them resisting yet clinging as they went down.

After buying her ticket, Lydia had stood for a moment looking out across the lake; then he saw her seat herself on one of the benches near the landing. He and she, at that moment, were both listening for the same sound: the whistle of the boat as it rounded the nearest promontory. Gannett turned again to glance at the clock: the boat was due now.

Where would she go? What would her life be when she had left him? She had no near relations and few friends. There was money enough . . . but she asked so much of life, in ways so complex and immaterial. He thought of her as walking bare-footed through a stony waste. No one would understand her—no one would pity her—and he, who did both, was powerless to come to her aid. . . .

He saw that she had risen from the bench and walked toward the edge of the lake. She stood looking in the direction from which the steamboat was to come; then she turned to the ticket-office, doubtless to ask the cause of the delay. After that she went back to the bench and sat down with bent head. What was she thinking of?

The whistle sounded; she started up, and Gannett involuntarily made a movement toward the door. But he turned back and continued to watch her. She stood motionless, her eyes on the trail of smoke that preceded the appearance of the boat. Then the little craft rounded the point, a dead- white object on the leaden water: a minute later it was puffing and backing at the wharf.

The few passengers who were waiting—two or three peasants and a snuffy priest— were clustered near the ticket-office. Lydia stood apart under the trees.

The boat lay alongside now; the gangplank was run out and the peasants went on board with their baskets of vegetables, followed by the priest. Still Lydia did not move. A bell began to ring querulously; there was a shriek of steam, and some one must have called to her that she would be late, for she started forward, as though in answer to a summons. She moved waveringly, and at the edge of the wharf she paused. Gannett saw a sailor beckon to her; the bell rang again and she stepped upon the gangplank.

Halfway down the short incline to the deck she stopped again; then she turned and ran back to the land. The gang-plank was drawn in, the bell ceased to ring, and the boat backed out into the lake. Lydia, with slow steps, was walking toward the garden.

As she approached the hotel she looked up furtively and Gannett drew back into the room. He sat down beside a table; a Bradshaw lay at his elbow, and mechanically, without knowing what he did, he began looking out the trains to Paris.

## A COWARD

"MY DAUGHTER Irene," said Mrs. Carstyle (she made it rhyme with *tureen*), "has had no social advantages; but if Mr. Carstyle had chosen—" she paused significantly and looked at the shabby sofa on the opposite side of the fire-place as though it had been Mr. Carstyle. Vibart was glad that it was not.

Mrs. Carstyle was one of the women who make refinement vulgar. She invariably spoke of her husband as *Mr. Carstyle* and, though she had but one daughter, was always careful to designate the young lady by name. At luncheon she had talked a great deal of elevating influences and ideals, and had fluctuated between apologies for the overdone mutton and affected surprise that the bewildered maid-servant should have forgotten to serve the coffee and liqueurs *as usual*.

Vibart was almost sorry that he had come. Miss Carstyle was still beautiful—almost as beautiful as when, two days earlier, against the leafy background of a June garden-party, he had seen her for the first time—but her mother's expositions and elucidations cheapened her beauty as sign-posts vulgarize a woodland solitude. Mrs. Carstyle's eye was perpetually plying between her daughter and Vibart, like an empty cab in quest of a fare. Miss Carstyle, the young man decided, was the kind of girl whose surroundings rub off on her; or was it rather that Mrs. Carstyle's idiosyncrasies were of a nature to color every one within reach? Vibart, looking across the table as this consolatory alternative occurred to him, was sure that they had not colored Mr. Carstyle; but that, perhaps, was only because they had bleached him instead. Mr. Carstyle was quite colorless; it would have been impossible to guess his native tint. His wife's qualities, if they had affected him at all, had acted negatively. He did not apologize for the mutton, and he wandered off after luncheon without pretending to wait for the diurnal coffee and liqueurs; while the few remarks that he had contributed to the conversation during the meal had not been in the direction of abstract conceptions of life. As he strayed away, with his vague oblique step, and the stoop that suggested the habit of dodging missiles, Vibart, who was still in the age of formulas, found himself wondering what life could be worth to a man who had evidently resigned himself to travelling with his back to the wind; so that Mrs. Carstyle's allusion to her daughter's lack of advantages (imparted while Irene searched the house for an undiscoverable cigarette) had an appositeness unintended by the speaker.

"If Mr. Carstyle had chosen," that lady repeated, "we might have had our city home" (she never used so small a word as town) "and Irene could have mixed in the society to which I myself was accustomed at her age." Her sigh pointed unmistakably to a past when young men had come to luncheon to see *her*.

The sigh led Vibart to look at her, and the look led him to the unwelcome conclusion that Irene "took after" her mother. It was certainly not from the sapless paternal stock that the girl had drawn her warm bloom: Mrs. Carstyle had contributed the high lights to the picture.

Mrs. Carstyle caught his look and appropriated it with the complacency of a vicarious beauty. She was quite aware of the value of her appearance as guaranteeing Irene's development into a fine woman.

"But perhaps," she continued, taking up the thread of her explanation, "you have heard of Mr. Carstyle's extraordinary hallucination. Mr. Carstyle knows that I call it so— as I tell him, it is the most charitable view to take."

She looked coldly at the threadbare sofa and indulgently at the young man who filled a corner of it.

"You may think it odd, Mr. Vibart, that I should take you into my confidence in this way after so short an acquaintance, but somehow I can't help regarding you as a friend already. I believe in those intuitive sympathies, don't you? They have never misled me—" her lids drooped retrospectively—"and besides, I always tell Mr. Carstyle that on this point I will have no false pretenses. Where truth is concerned I am inexorable, and I consider it my duty to let our friends know that our restricted way of living is due entirely to choice—to Mr. Carstyle's choice. When I married Mr. Carstyle it was with the expectation of living in New York and of keeping my carriage; and there is no reason for our not doing so—there is no reason, Mr. Vibart, why my daughter Ireen should have been denied the intellectual advantages of foreign travel. I wish that to be understood. It is owing to her father's deliberate choice that Ireen and I have been imprisoned in the narrow limits of Millbrook society. For myself I do not complain. If Mr. Carstyle chooses to place others before his wife it is not for his wife to repine. His course may be noble—Quixotic; I do not allow myself to pronounce judgment on it, though others have thought that in sacrificing his own family to strangers he was violating the most sacred obligations of domestic life. This is the opinion of my pastor and of other valued friends; but, as I have always told them, for myself I make no claims. Where my daughter Ireen is concerned it is different—"

It was a relief to Vibart when, at this point, Mrs. Carstyle's discharge of her duty was cut short by her daughter's reappearance. Irene had been unable to find a cigarette for Mr. Vibart, and her mother, with beaming irrelevance, suggested that in that case she had better show him the garden.

The Carstyle house stood but a few yards back from the brick-paved Millbrook street, and the garden was a very small place, unless measured, as Mrs. Carstyle probably intended that it should be, by the extent of her daughter's charms. These were so considerable that Vibart walked back and forward half a dozen times between the porch and the gate, before he discovered the limitations of the Carstyle domain. It was not till Irene had accused him of being sarcastic and had confided in him that "the girls" were furious with her for letting him talk to her so long at his aunt's garden-party, that he awoke to the exiguity of his surroundings; and then it was with a touch of irritation that he noticed Mr. Carstyle's inconspicuous profile bent above a newspaper in one of the lower windows. Vibart had an idea that Mr. Carstyle, while ostensibly reading the paper, had kept count of the number of times that his daughter had led her companion up and down between the syringa-bushes; and for some undefinable reason he resented Mr. Carstyle's unperturbed observation more than his wife's zealous self-effacement. To a man who is trying to please a pretty girl there are moments when the proximity of an impartial spectator is more disconcerting than the most obvious connivance; and something about Mr. Carstyle's expression conveyed his good-humored indifference to Irene's processes.

When the garden-gate closed behind Vibart he had become aware that his preoccupation with the Carstyles had shifted its center from the daughter to the father; but he was accustomed to such emotional surprises, and skilled in seizing any compensations they might offer.

## II

THE Carstyles belonged to the all-the-year-round Millbrook of paper-mills, cable-cars, brick pavements and church sociables, while Mrs. Vance, the aunt with whom Vibart lived, was an ornament of the summer colony whose big country-houses dotted the surrounding hills. Mrs. Vance had, however, no difficulty in appeasing the curiosity which Mrs. Carstyle's enigmatic utterances had aroused in the young man. Mrs. Carstyle's relentless veracity vented itself mainly on the "summer people," as they were called: she did not propose that any one within ten miles of Millbrook should keep a carriage without knowing that she was entitled to keep one too. Mrs. Vance remarked with a sigh that Mrs. Carstyle's annual demand to have her position understood came in as punctually as the taxes and the water rates.

"My dear, it's simply this: when Andrew Carstyle married her years ago— Heaven knows why he did; he's one of the Albany Carstyles, you know, and she was a daughter of old Deacon Ash of South Millbrook—well, when he married her he had a tidy little income, and I suppose the bride expected to set up an establishment in New York and be hand-in-glove with the whole Carstyle clan. But whether he was ashamed of her from the first, or for some other unexplained reason, he bought a country-place and settled down here for life. For a few years they lived comfortably enough, and she had plenty of smart clothes, and drove about in a victoria calling on the summer people. Then, when the beautiful Irene was about ten years old, Mr. Carstyle's only brother died, and it turned out that he had made away with a lot of trust-property. It was a horrid business: over three hundred thousand dollars were gone, and of course most of it had belonged to widows and orphans. As soon as the facts were made known, Andrew Carstyle announced that he would pay back what his brother had stolen. He sold his country-place and his wife's carriage, and they moved to the little house they live in now. Mr. Carstyle's income is probably not as large as his wife would like to have it thought, and though I'm told he puts aside, a good part of it every year to pay off his brother's obligations, I fancy the debt won't be discharged for some time to come. To help things along he opened a law office—he had studied law in his youth—but though he is said to be clever I hear that he has very little to do. People are afraid of him: he's too dry and quiet. Nobody believes in a man who doesn't believe in himself, and Mr. Carstyle always seems to be winking at you through a slit in his professional manner. People don't like it—his wife doesn't like it. I believe she would have accepted the sacrifice of the country-place and the carriage if he had struck an attitude and talked about doing his duty. It was his regarding the whole thing as a matter of course that exasperated her. What is the use of doing something difficult in a way that makes it look perfectly easy? I feel sorry for Mrs. Carstyle. She's lost her house and her carriage, and she hasn't been allowed to be heroic."

Vibart had listened attentively.

"I wonder what Miss Carstyle thinks of it?" he mused.

Mrs. Vance looked at him with a tentative smile. "I wonder what *you* think of Miss Carstyle?" she returned,

His answer reassured her.

"I think she takes after her mother," he said.

"Ah," cried his aunt cheerfully, "then I needn't write to your mother, and I can have Irene at all my parties!"

Miss Carstyle was an important factor in the restricted social combinations of a

Millbrook hostess. A local beauty is always a useful addition to a Saturday-to-Monday house-party, and the beautiful Irene was served up as a perennial novelty to the jaded guests of the summer colony. As Vibart's aunt remarked, she was perfect till she became playful, and she never became playful till the third day.

Under these conditions, it was natural that Vibart should see a good deal of the young lady, and before he was aware of it he had drifted into the anomalous position of paying court to the daughter in order to ingratiate himself with the father. Miss Carstyle was beautiful, Vibart was young, and the days were long in his aunt's spacious and distinguished house; but it was really the desire to know something more of Mr. Carstyle that led the young man to partake so often of that gentleman's overdone mutton. Vibart's imagination had been touched by the discovery that this little huddled-up man, instead of travelling with the wind, was persistently facing a domestic gale of considerable velocity. That he should have paid off his brother's debt at one stroke was to the young man a conceivable feat; but that he should go on methodically and uninterruptedly accumulating the needed amount, under the perpetual accusation of Irene's inadequate frocks and Mrs. Carstyle's apologies for the mutton, seemed to Vibart proof of unexampled heroism. Mr. Carstyle was as inaccessible as the average American parent, and led a life so detached from the preoccupations of his womankind that Vibart had some difficulty in fixing his attention. To Mr. Carstyle, Vibart was simply the inevitable young man who had been hanging about the house ever since Irene had left school; and Vibart's efforts to differentiate himself from this enamored abstraction were hampered by Mrs. Carstyle's cheerful assumption that he was the young man, and by Irene's frank appropriation of his visits.

In this extremity he suddenly observed a slight but significant change in the manner of the two ladies. Irene, instead of charging him with being sarcastic and horrid, and declaring herself unable to believe a word he said, began to receive his remarks with the impersonal smile which he had seen her accord to the married men of his aunt's house-parties; while Mrs. Carstyle, talking over his head to an invisible but evidently sympathetic and intelligent listener, debated the propriety of Irene's accepting an invitation to spend the month of August at Narragansett. When Vibart, rashly trespassing on the rights of this unseen oracle, remarked that a few weeks at the seashore would make a delightful change for Miss Carstyle, the ladies looked at him and then laughed.

It was at this point that Vibart, for the first time, found himself observed by Mr. Carstyle. They were grouped about the debris of a luncheon which had ended precipitously with veal stew (Mrs. Carstyle explaining that poor cooks *always* failed with their sweet dish when there was company) and Mr. Carstyle, his hands thrust in his pockets, his lean baggy-coated shoulders pressed against his chair-back, sat contemplating his guest with a smile of unmistakable approval. When Vibart caught his eye the smile vanished, and Mr. Carstyle, dropping his glasses from the bridge of his thin nose, looked out of the window with the expression of a man determined to prove an alibi. But Vibart was sure of the smile: it had established, between his host and himself, a complicity which Mr. Carstyle's attempted evasion served only to confirm.

On the strength of this incident Vibart, a few days later, called at Mr. Carstyle's office. Ostensibly, the young man had come to ask, on his aunt's behalf, some question on a point at issue between herself and the Millbrook telephone company; but his purpose in offering to perform the errand had been the hope of taking up his intercourse with Mr. Carstyle where that gentleman's smile had left it. Vibart was not disappointed. In a dingy office, with a single window looking out on a blank wall, he found Mr. Carstyle, in an alpaca coat, reading Montaigne.

It evidently did not occur to him that Vibart had come on business, and the warmth of his welcome gave the young man a sense of furnishing the last word in a conjugal argument in which, for once, Mr. Carstyle had come off triumphant.

The legal question disposed of, Vibart reverted to Montaigne: had Mr. Carstyle seen young So-and-so's volume of essays? There was one on Montaigne that had a decided flavor: the point of view was curious. Vibart was surprised to find that Mr. Carstyle had heard of young So-and-so. Clever young men are given to thinking that their elders have never got beyond Macaulay; but Mr. Carstyle seemed sufficiently familiar with recent literature not to take it too seriously. He accepted Vibart's offer of young So-and-so's volume, admitting that his own library was not exactly up-to-date.

Vibart went away musing. The next day he came back with the volume of essays. It seemed to be tacitly understood that he was to call at the office when he wished to see Mr. Carstyle, whose legal engagements did not seriously interfere with the pursuit of literature.

For a week or ten days Mrs. Carstyle, in Vibart's presence, continued to take counsel with her unseen adviser on the subject of her daughter's visit to Narragansett. Once or twice Irene dropped her impersonal smile to tax Vibart with not caring whether she went or not; and Mrs. Carstyle seized a moment of *tête-à-tête* to confide in him that the dear child hated the idea of leaving, and was going only because her friend Mrs. Higby would not let her off. Of course, if it had not been for Mr. Carstyle's peculiarities they would have had their own seaside home—at Newport, probably: Mrs. Carstyle preferred the tone of Newport—and Irene would not have been dependent on the *charity* of her friends; but as it was, they must be thankful for small mercies, and Mrs. Higby was certainly very kind in her way, and had a charming social position—for Narragansett.

These confidences, however, were soon superseded by an exchange, between mother and daughter, of increasingly frequent allusions to the delights of Narragansett, the popularity of Mrs. Higby, and the jolliness of her house; with an occasional reference on Mrs. Carstyle's part to the probability of Hewlett Bain's being there as usual—hadn't Irene heard from Mrs. Higby that he was to be there? Upon this note Miss Carstyle at length departed, leaving Vibart to the undisputed enjoyment of her father's company.

Vibart had at no time a keen taste for the summer joys of Millbrook, and the family obligation which, for several months of the year, kept him at his aunt's side (Mrs. Vance was a childless widow and he filled the onerous post of favorite nephew) gave a sense of compulsion to the light occupations that checkered his leisure. Mrs. Vance, who fancied herself lonely when he was away, was too much engaged with notes, telegrams and arriving and departing guests, to do more than breathlessly smile upon his presence, or implore him to take the dullest girl of the party for a drive (and would he go by way of Millbrook, like a dear, and stop at the market to ask why the lobsters hadn't come?); and the house itself, and the guests who came and went in it like people rushing through a railway- station, offered no points of repose to his thoughts. Some houses are companions in themselves: the walls, the book-shelves, the very chairs and tables, have the qualities of a sympathetic mind; but Mrs. Vance's interior was as impersonal as the setting of a classic drama.

These conditions made Vibart cultivate an assiduous exchange of books between himself and Mr. Carstyle. The young man went down almost daily to the little house in the town, where Mrs. Carstyle, who had now an air of receiving him in curl-papers, and of not always immediately distinguishing him from the piano-tuner, made no effort to detain him on his way to her husband's study.

## III

NOW and then, at the close of one of Vibart's visits, Mr. Carstyle put on a mildewed Panama hat and accompanied the young man for a mile or two on his way home. The road to Mrs. Vance's lay through one of the most amiable suburbs of Millbrook, and Mr. Carstyle, walking with his slow uneager step, his hat pushed back, and his stick dragging behind him, seemed to take a philosophic pleasure in the aspect of the trim lawns and opulent gardens.

Vibart could never induce his companion to prolong his walk as far as Mrs. Vance's drawing-room; but one afternoon, when the distant hills lay blue beyond the twilight of overarching elms, the two men strolled on into the country past that lady's hospitable gateposts.

It was a still day, the road was deserted, and every sound came sharply through the air. Mr. Carstyle was in the midst of a disquisition on Diderot, when he raised his head and stood still.

"What's that?" he said. "Listen!"

Vibart listened and heard a distant storm of hoof-beats. A moment later, a buggy drawn by a pair of trotters swung round the turn of the road. It was about thirty yards off, coming toward them at full speed. The man who drove was leaning forward with outstretched arms; beside him sat a girl.

Suddenly Vibart saw Mr. Carstyle jump into the middle of the road, in front of the buggy. He stood there immovable, his arms extended, his legs apart, in an attitude of indomitable resistance. Almost at the same moment Vibart realized that the man in the buggy had his horses in hand.

"They're not running!" Vibart shouted, springing into the road and catching Mr. Carstyle's alpaca sleeve. The older man looked around vaguely: he seemed dazed.

"Come away, sir, come away!" cried Vibart, gripping his arm. The buggy swept past them, and Mr. Carstyle stood in the dust gazing after it.

At length he drew out his handkerchief and wiped his forehead. He was very pale and Vibart noticed that his hand shook.

"That was a close call, sir, wasn't it? I suppose you thought they were running."

"Yes," said Mr. Carstyle slowly, "I thought they were running."

"It certainly looked like it for a minute. Let's sit down, shall we? I feel rather breathless myself."

Vibart saw that his friend could hardly stand. They seated themselves on a tree-trunk by the roadside, and Mr. Carstyle continued to wipe his forehead in silence.

At length he turned to Vibart and said abruptly:

"I made straight for the middle of the road, didn't I? If there *had* been a runaway I should have stopped it?"

Vibart looked at him in surprise.

"You would have tried to, undoubtedly, unless I'd had time to drag you away."

Mr. Carstyle straightened his narrow shoulders.

"There was no hesitation, at all events? I—I showed no signs of—avoiding it?"

"I should say not, sir; it was I who funked it for you."

Mr. Carstyle was silent: his head had dropped forward and he looked like an old man.

"It was just my cursed luck again!" he exclaimed suddenly in a loud voice.

For a moment Vibart thought that he was wandering; but he raised his head and went on speaking in more natural tones.

"I daresay I appeared ridiculous enough to you just now, eh? Perhaps you saw all along that the horses weren't running? Your eyes are younger than mine; and then you're not always looking out for runaways, as I am. Do you know that in thirty years I've never seen a runaway?"

"You're fortunate," said Vibart, still bewildered.

"Fortunate? Good God, man, I've *prayed* to see one: not a runaway especially, but any bad accident; anything that endangered people's lives. There are accidents happening all the time all over the world; why shouldn't I ever come across one? It's not for want of trying! At one time I used to haunt the theatres in the hope of a fire: fires in theatres are so apt to be fatal. Well, will you believe it? I was in the Brooklyn theatre the night before it burned down; I left the old Madison Square Garden half an hour before the walls fell in. And it's the same way with street accidents—I always miss them; I'm always just too late. Last year there was a boy knocked down by a cable-car at our corner; I got to my gate just as they were carrying him off on a stretcher. And so it goes. If anybody else had been walking along this road, those horses would have been running away. And there was a girl in the buggy, too—a mere child!"

Mr. Carstyle's head sank again.

"You're wondering what this means," he began after another pause. "I was a little confused for a moment—must have seemed incoherent." His voice cleared and he made an effort to straighten himself. "Well, I was a damned coward once and I've been trying to live it down ever since."

Vibart looked at him incredulously and Mr. Carstyle caught the look with a smile.

"Why not? Do I look like a Hercules?" He held up his loose-skinned hand and shrunken wrist. "Not built for the part, certainly; but that doesn't count, of course. Man's unconquerable soul, and all the rest of it . . . well, I was a coward every inch of me, body and soul."

He paused and glanced up and down the road. There was no one in sight.

"It happened when I was a young chap just out of college. I was travelling round the world with another youngster of my own age and an older man— Charles Meriton—who has since made a name for himself. You may have heard of him."

"Meriton, the archaeologist? The man who discovered those ruined African cities the other day?"

"That's the man. He was a college tutor then, and my father, who had known him since he was a boy, and who had a very high opinion of him, had asked him to make the tour with us. We both—my friend Collis and I—had an immense admiration for Meriton. He was just the fellow to excite a boy's enthusiasm: cool, quick, imperturbable—the kind of man whose hand is always on the hilt of action. His explorations had led him into all sorts of tight places, and he'd shown an extraordinary combination of calculating patience and reckless courage. He never talked about his doings; we picked them up from various people on our journey. He'd been everywhere, he knew everybody, and everybody had something stirring to tell about him. I daresay this account of the man sounds exaggerated; perhaps it is; I've never seen him since; but at that time he seemed to me a tremendous fellow—a kind of scientific Ajax. He was a capital travelling-companion, at any rate: good-tempered, cheerful, easily amused, with none of the been-there-before superiority so irritating to youngsters. He made us feel as though it were all as new to him as to us: he never chilled our enthusiasms or took the bloom off our surprises. There was nobody else whose good opinion I cared as much about: he was the biggest thing in sight.

"On the way home Collis broke down with diphtheria. We were in the Mediterranean, cruising about the Sporades in a felucca. He was taken ill at Chios. The attack came on suddenly and we were afraid to run the risk of taking him back to Athens in the felucca. We established ourselves in the inn at Chios and there the poor fellow lay for weeks. Luckily there was a fairly good doctor on the island and we sent to Athens for a sister to help with the nursing. Poor Collis was desperately bad: the diphtheria was followed by partial paralysis. The doctor assured us that the danger was past; he would gradually regain the use of his limbs; but his recovery would be slow. The sister encouraged us too—she had seen such cases before; and he certainly did improve a shade each day. Meriton and I had taken turns with the sister in nursing him, but after the paralysis had set in there wasn't much to do, and there was nothing to prevent Meriton's leaving us for a day or two. He had received word from some place on the coast of Asia Minor that a remarkable tomb had been discovered somewhere in the interior; he had not been willing to take us there, as the journey was not a particularly safe one; but now that we were tied up at Chios there seemed no reason why he shouldn't go and take a look at the place. The expedition would not take more than three days; Collis was convalescent; the doctor and nurse assured us that there was no cause for uneasiness; and so Meriton started off one evening at sunset. I walked down to the quay with him and saw him rowed off to the felucca. I would have given a good deal to be going with him; the prospect of danger allured me.

"'You'll see that Collis is never left alone, won't you?' he shouted back to me as the boat pulled out into the harbor; I remembered I rather resented the suggestion.

"I walked back to the inn and went to bed: the nurse sat up with Collis at night. The next morning I relieved her at the usual hour. It was a sultry day with a queer coppery-looking sky; the air was stifling. In the middle of the day the nurse came to take my place while I dined; when I went back to Collis's room she said she would go out for a breath of air.

"I sat down by Collis's bed and began to fan him with the fan the sister had been using. The heat made him uneasy and I turned him over in bed, for he was still helpless: the whole of his right side was numb. Presently he fell asleep and I went to the window and sat looking down on the hot deserted square, with a bunch of donkeys and their drivers asleep in the shade of the convent-wall across the way. I remember noticing the blue beads about the donkeys' necks. . . . Were you ever in an earthquake? No? I'd never been in one either. It's an indescribable sensation . . . there's a Day of Judgment feeling in the air. It began with the donkeys waking up and trembling; I noticed that and thought it queer. Then the drivers jumped up—I saw the terror in their faces. Then a roar. . . . I remember noticing a big black crack in the convent-wall opposite—a zigzag crack, like a flash of lightning in a wood-cut. . . . I thought of that, too, at the time; then all the bells in the place began to ring—it made a fearful discord.... I saw people rushing across the square . . . the air was full of crashing noises. The floor went down under me in a sickening way and then jumped back and pitched me to the ceiling . . . but where was the ceiling? And the door? I said to myself: *We're two stories up—the stairs are just wide enough for one.* . . . I gave one glance at Collis: he was lying in bed, wide awake, looking straight at me. I ran. Something struck me on the head as I bolted downstairs—I kept on running. I suppose the knock I got dazed me, for I don't remember much of anything till I found myself in a vineyard a mile from the town. I was roused by the warm blood running down my nose and heard myself explaining to Meriton exactly how it had happened. . . .

"When I crawled back to the town they told me that all the houses near the inn were in ruins and that a dozen people had been killed. Collis was among them, of course. The ceiling had come down on him."

Mr. Carstyle wiped his forehead. Vibart sat looking away from him.

"Two days later Meriton came back. I began to tell him the story, but he interrupted me.

"'There was no one with him at the time, then? You'd left him alone?'

"'No, he wasn't alone.'

"'Who was with him? You said the sister was out.'

"'I was with him.'

"'*You were with him?*'

"I shall never forget Meriton's look. I believe I had meant to explain, to accuse myself, to shout out my agony of soul; but I saw the uselessness of it. A door had been shut between us. Neither of us spoke another word. He was very kind to me on the way home; he looked after me in a motherly way that was a good deal harder to stand than his open contempt. I saw the man was honestly trying to pity me; but it was no good—he simply couldn't."

Mr. Carstyle rose slowly, with a certain stiffness.

"Shall we turn toward home? Perhaps I'm keeping you."

They walked on a few steps in silence; then he spoke again.

"That business altered my whole life. Of course I oughtn't to have allowed it to—that was another form of cowardice. But I saw myself only with Meriton's eyes—it is one of the worst miseries of youth that one is always trying to be somebody else. I had meant to be a Meriton—I saw I'd better go home and study law.

"It's a childish fancy, a survival of the primitive savage, if you like; but from that hour to this I've hankered day and night for a chance to retrieve myself, to set myself right with the man I meant to be. I want to prove to that man that it was all an accident— an unaccountable deviation from my normal instincts; that having once been a coward doesn't mean that a man's cowardly . . . and I can't, I can't!"

Mr. Carstyle's tone had passed insensibly from agitation to irony. He had got back to his usual objective standpoint.

"Why, I'm a perfect olive branch," he concluded, with his dry indulgent laugh; "the very babies stop crying at my approach—I carry a sort of millennium about with me—I'd make my fortune as an agent of the Peace Society. I shall go to the grave leaving that other man unconvinced!"

Vibart walked back with him to Millbrook. On her doorstep they met Mrs. Carstyle, flushed and feathered, with a card-case and dusty boots.

"I don't ask you in," she said plaintively, to Vibart, "because I can't answer for the food this evening. My maid-of-all-work tells me that she's going to a ball—which is more than I've done in years! And besides, it would be cruel to ask you to spend such a hot evening in our stuffy little house—the air is so much cooler at Mrs. Vance's. Remember me to Mrs. Vance, please, and tell her how sorry I am that I can no longer include her in my round of visits. When I had my carriage I saw the people I liked, but now that I have to walk, my social opportunities are more limited. I was not obliged to do my visiting on foot when I was younger, and my doctor tells me that to persons accustomed to a carriage no exercise is more injurious than walking."

She glanced at her husband with a smile of unforgiving sweetness. "Fortunately," she concluded, "it agrees with Mr. Carstyle."

## THE TWILIGHT OF THE GOD

*A Newport drawing-room. Tapestries, flowers, bric-a-brac. Through the windows, a geranium-edged lawn, the cliffs and the sea.* ISABEL WARLAND *sits reading.* LUCIUS WARLAND *enters in flannels and a yachting-cap.*

ISABEL. Back already?

WARLAND. The wind dropped—it turned into a drifting race. Langham took me off the yacht on his launch. What time is it? Two o'clock? Where's Mrs. Raynor?

ISABEL. On her way to New York.

WARLAND. To New York?

ISABEL. Precisely. The boat must be just leaving; she started an hour ago and took Laura with her. In fact I'm alone in the house—that is, until this evening. Some people are coming then.

WARLAND. But what in the world—

ISABEL. Her aunt, Mrs. Griscom, has had a fit. She has them constantly. They're not serious—at least they wouldn't be, if Mrs. Griscom were not so rich—and childless. Naturally, under the circumstances, Marian feels a peculiar sympathy for her; her position is such a sad one; there's positively no one to care whether she lives or dies—except her heirs. Of course they all rush to Newburgh whenever she has a fit. It's hard on Marian, for she lives the farthest away; but she has come to an understanding with the housekeeper, who always telegraphs her first, so that she gets a start of several hours. She will be at Newburgh to-night at ten, and she has calculated that the others can't possibly arrive before midnight.

WARLAND. You have a delightful way of putting things. I suppose you'd talk of me like that.

ISABEL. Oh, no. It's too humiliating to doubt one's husband's disinterestedness.

WARLAND. I wish I had a rich aunt who had fits.

ISABEL. If I were wishing I should choose heart disease.

WARLAND. There's no doing anything without money or influence.

ISABEL (*picking up her book*). Have you heard from Washington?

WARLAND. Yes. That's what I was going to speak of when I asked for Mrs. Raynor. I wanted to bid her good-bye.

ISABEL. You're going?

WARLAND. By the five train. Fagott has just wired me that the Ambassador will be in Washington on Monday. He hasn't named his secretaries yet, but there isn't much hope for me. He has a nephew—

ISABEL. They always have. Like the Popes.

WARLAND. Well, I'm going all the same. You'll explain to Mrs. Raynor if she gets back before I do? Are there to be people at dinner? I don't suppose it matters. You can always pick up an extra man on a Saturday.

ISABEL. By the way, that reminds me that Marian left me a list of the people who are arriving this afternoon. My novel is so absorbing that I forgot to look at it. Where can it be? Ah, here—Let me see: the Jack Merringtons, Adelaide Clinton, Ned Lender—all from New York, by seven P.M. train. Lewis Darley to-night, by Fall River boat. John

Oberville, from Boston at five P.M. Why, I didn't know—

WARLAND (*excitedly*). John Oberville? John Oberville? Here? To-day at five o'clock? Let me see—let me look at the list. Are you sure you're not mistaken? Why, she never said a word! Why the deuce didn't you tell me?

ISABEL. I didn't know.

WARLAND. Oberville—Oberville—!

ISABEL. Why, what difference does it make?

WARLAND. What difference? What difference? Don't look at me as if you didn't understand English! Why, if Oberville's coming—(*a pause*) Look here, Isabel, didn't you know him very well at one time?

ISABEL. Very well—yes.

WARLAND. I thought so—of course—I remember now; I heard all about it before I met you. Let me see—didn't you and your mother spend a winter in Washington when he was Undersecretary of State?

ISABEL. That was before the deluge.

WARLAND. I remember—it all comes back to me. I used to hear it said that he admired you tremendously; there was a report that you were engaged. Don't you remember? Why, it was in all the papers. By Jove, Isabel, what a match that would have been!

ISABEL. You *are* disinterested!

WARLAND. Well, I can't help thinking—

ISABEL. That I paid you a handsome compliment?

WARLAND (*preoccupied*). Eh?—Ah, yes—exactly. What was I saying? Oh—about the report of your engagement. (*Playfully.*) He was awfully gone on you, wasn't he?

ISABEL. It's not for me to diminish your triumph.

WARLAND. By Jove, I can't think why Mrs. Raynor didn't tell me he was coming. A man like that—one doesn't take him for granted, like the piano- tuner! I wonder I didn't see it in the papers.

ISABEL. Is he grown such a great man?

WARLAND. Oberville? Great? John Oberville? I'll tell you what he is—the power behind the throne, the black Pope, the King-maker and all the rest of it. Don't you read the papers? Of course I'll never get on if you won't interest yourself in politics. And to think you might have married that man!

ISABEL. And got you your Secretaryship!

WARLAND. Oberville has them all in the hollow of his hand.

ISABEL. Well, you'll see him at five o'clock.

WARLAND. I don't suppose he's ever heard of *me*, worse luck! (*A silence.*) Isabel, look here. I never ask questions, do I? But it was so long ago—and Oberville almost belongs to history—he will one of these days at any rate. Just tell me—did he want to marry you?

ISABEL. Since you answer for his immortality—(*after a pause*) I was very much in love with him.

WARLAND. Then of course he did. (*Another pause.*) But what in the world—

ISABEL (*musing*). As you say, it was so long ago; I don't see why I shouldn't tell you. There was a married woman who had—what is the correct expression?—made sacrifices for him. There was only one sacrifice she objected to making—and he didn't consider himself free. It sounds rather *rococo*, doesn't it? It was odd that she died the year after we were married.

WARLAND. Whew!

ISABEL (*following her own thoughts*). I've never seen him since; it must be ten years ago. I'm certainly thirty-two, and I was just twenty-two then. It's curious to talk of it. I had put it away so carefully. How it smells of camphor! And what an old-fashioned cut it has! (*Rising.*) Where's the list, Lucius? You wanted to know if there were to be people at dinner tonight—

WARLAND. Here it is—but never mind. Isabel—(*silence*) Isabel—

ISABEL. Well?

WARLAND. It's odd he never married.

ISABEL. The comparison is to my disadvantage. But then I met you.

WARLAND. Don't be so confoundedly sarcastic. I wonder how he'll feel about seeing you. Oh, I don't mean any sentimental rot, of course . . . but you're an uncommonly agreeable woman. I daresay he'll be pleased to see you again; you're fifty times more attractive than when I married you.

ISABEL. I wish your other investments had appreciated at the same rate. Unfortunately my charms won't pay the butcher.

WARLAND. Damn the butcher!

ISABEL. I happened to mention him because he's just written again; but I might as well have said the baker or the candlestick-maker. The candlestick-maker—I wonder what he is, by the way? He must have more faith in human nature than the others, for I haven't heard from him yet. I wonder if there is a Creditor's Polite Letter-writer which they all consult; their style is so exactly alike. I advise you to pass through New York incognito on your way to Washington; their attentions might be oppressive.

WARLAND. Confoundedly oppressive. What a dog's life it is! My poor Isabel—

ISABEL. Don't pity me. I didn't marry yon for a home.

WARLAND (*after a pause*). What *did* you marry me for, if you cared for Oberville? (*Another pause.*) Eh?

ISABEL. Don't make me regret my confidence.

WARLAND. I beg your pardon.

ISABEL. Oh, it was only a subterfuge to conceal the fact that I have no distinct recollection of my reasons. The fact is, a girl's motives in marrying are like a passport— apt to get mislaid. One is so seldom asked for either. But mine certainly couldn't have been mercenary: I never heard a mother praise you to her daughters.

WARLAND. No, I never was much of a match.

ISABEL. You impugn my judgment.

WARLAND. If I only had a head for business, now, I might have done something by this time. But I'd sooner break stones in the road.

ISABEL. It must be very hard to get an opening in that profession. So many of my friends have aspired to it, and yet I never knew any one who actually did it.

WARLAND. If I could only get the Secretaryship. How that kind of life would suit you! It's as much for you that I want it—

ISABEL. And almost as much for the butcher. Don't belittle the circle of your benevolence. (*She walks across the room.*) Three o'clock already— and Marian asked me to give orders about the carriages. Let me see—Mr. Oberville is the first arrival; if you'll ring I will send word to the stable. I suppose you'll stay now?

WARLAND. Stay?

ISABEL. Not go to Washington. I thought you spoke as if he could help you.

WARLAND. He could settle the whole thing in five minutes. The President can't refuse him anything. But he doesn't know me; he may have a candidate of his own. It's a pity you haven't seen him for so long—and yet I don't know; perhaps it's just as well. The others don't arrive till seven? It seems as if—How long is he going to be here? Till tomorrow night, I suppose? I wonder what he's come for. The Merringtons will bore him to death, and Adelaide, of course, will be philandering with Lender. I wonder (*a pause*) if Darley likes boating. (*Rings the bell.*)

ISABEL. Boating?

WARLAND. Oh, I was only thinking—Where are the matches? One may smoke here, I suppose? (*He looks at his wife.*) If I were you I'd put on that black gown of yours to-night—the one with the spangles.—It's only that Fred Langham asked me to go over to Narragansett in his launch tomorrow morning, and I was thinking that I might take Darley; I always liked Darley.

ISABEL (*to the footman who enters*). Mrs. Raynor wishes the dog-cart sent to the station at five o'clock to meet Mr. Oberville.

FOOTMAN. Very good, m'm. Shall I serve tea at the usual time, m'm?

ISABEL. Yes. That is, when Mr. Oberville arrives.

FOOTMAN (*going out*). Very good, m'm.

WARLAND (*to Isabel, who is moving toward the door*). Where are you going?

ISABEL. To my room now—for a walk later.

WARLAND. Later? It's past three already.

ISABEL. I've no engagement this afternoon.

WARLAND. Oh, I didn't know. (*As she reaches the door.*) You'll be back, I suppose?

ISABEL. I have no intention of eloping.

WARLAND. For tea, I mean?

ISABEL. I never take tea. (*Warland shrugs his shoulders.*)

## II

*The same drawing room.* ISABEL *enters from the lawn in hat and gloves. The tea table is set out, and the footman just lighting the lamp under the kettle.*

ISABEL. You may take the tea things away. I never take tea.

FOOTMAN. Very good, m'm. (*He hesitates.*) I understood, m'm, that Mr. Oberville was to have tea?

ISABEL. Mr. Oberville? But he was to arrive long ago! What time is it?

FOOTMAN. Only a quarter past five, m'm.

ISABEL. A quarter past five? (*She goes up to the clock.*) Surely you're mistaken? I thought it was long after six. (*To herself.*) I walked and walked—I must have walked too fast . . . (*To the Footman.*) I'm going out again. When Mr. Oberville arrives please give him his tea without waiting for me. I shall not be back till dinner-time.

FOOTMAN. Very good, m'm. Here are some letters, m'm.

ISABEL (*glancing at them with a movement of disgust*). You may send them up to my room.

FOOTMAN. I beg pardon, m'm, but one is a note from Mme. Fanfreluche, and the man who brought it is waiting for an answer.

ISABEL. Didn't you tell him I was out?

FOOTMAN. Yes, m'm. But he said he had orders to wait till you came in.

ISABEL. Ah—let me see. (*She opens the note.*) Ah, yes. (*A pause.*) Please say that I am on my way now to Mme Fanfreluche's to give her the answer in person. You may tell the man that I have already started. Do you understand? Already started.

FOOTMAN. Yes, m'm.

ISABEL. And—wait. (*With an effort.*) You may tell me when the man has started. I shall wait here till then. Be sure you let me know.

FOOTMAN. Yes, m'm. (*He goes out.*)

ISABEL (*sinking into a chair and hiding her face*). Ah! (*After a moment she rises, taking up her gloves and sunshade, and walks toward the window which opens on the lawn.*) I'm so tired. (*She hesitates and turns back into the room.*) Where can I go to? (*She sits down again by the tea- table, and bends over the kettle. The clock strikes half-past five.*)

ISABEL (*picking up her sunshade, walks back to the window*). If I must meet one of them…

OBERVILLE (*speaking in the hall*). Thanks. I'll take tea first. (*He enters the room, and pauses doubtfully on seeing Isabel.*)

ISABEL (*stepping towards him with a smile*). It's not that I've changed, of course, but only that I happened to have my back to the light. Isn't that what you are going to say?

OBERVILLE. Mrs. Warland!

ISABELLE. So you really *have* become a great man! They always remember people's names.

OBERVILLE. Were you afraid I was going to call you Isabel?

ISABEL. Bravo! *Crescendo!*

OBERVILLE. But you have changed, all the same.

ISABEL. You must indeed have reached a dizzy eminence, since you can indulge yourself by speaking the truth!

OBERVILLE. It's your voice. I knew it at once, and yet it's different.

ISABEL. I hope it can still convey the pleasure I feel in seeing an old friend. (*She holds out her hand. He takes it.*) You know, I suppose, that Mrs. Raynor is not here to receive you? She was called away this morning very suddenly by her aunt's illness.

OBERVILLE. Yes. She left a note for me. (*Absently.*) I'm sorry to hear of Mrs. Griscom's illness.

ISABEL. Oh, Mrs. Griscom's illnesses are less alarming than her recoveries. But I am forgetting to offer you any tea. (*She hands him a cup.*) I remember you liked it very strong.

OBERVILLE. What else do you remember?

ISABEL. A number of equally useless things. My mind is a store-room of obsolete information.

OBERVILLE. Why obsolete, since I am providing you with a use for it?

ISABEL. At any rate, it's open to question whether it was worth storing for that length of time. Especially as there must have been others more fitted—by opportunity—to undertake the duty.

OBERVILLE. The duty?

ISABEL. Of remembering how you like your tea.

OBERVILLE (*with a change of tone*). Since you call it a duty—I may remind you that it's one I have never asked any one else to perform.

ISABEL. As a duty! But as a pleasure?

OBERVILLE. Do you really want to know?

ISABEL. Oh, I don't require and charge you.

OBERVILLE. You dislike as much as ever having the *i*'s dotted?

ISABEL. With a handwriting I know as well as yours!

OBERVILLE (*recovering his lightness of manner*). Accomplished woman! (*He examines her approvingly.*) I'd no idea that you were here. I never was more surprised.

ISABEL. I hope you like being surprised. To my mind it's an overrated pleasure.

OBERVILLE. Is it? I'm sorry to hear that.

ISABEL. Why? Have you a surprise to dispose of?

OBERVILLE. I'm not sure that I haven't.

ISABEL. Don't part with it too hastily. It may improve by being kept.

OBERVILLE (*tentatively*). Does that mean that you don't want it?

ISABEL. Heaven forbid! I want everything I can get.

OBERVILLE. And you get everything you want. At least you used to.

ISABEL. Let us talk of your surprise.

OBERVILLE. It's to be yours, you know. (*A pause. He speaks gravely.*) I find that I've never got over having lost you.

ISABEL (*also gravely*). And is that a surprise—to you too?

OBERVILLE. Honestly—yes. I thought I'd crammed my life full. I didn't know there was a cranny left anywhere. At first, you know, I stuffed in everything I could lay my hands on—there was such a big void to fill. And after all I haven't filled it. I felt that the moment I saw you. (*A pause.*) I'm talking stupidly.

ISABEL. It would be odious if you were eloquent.

OBERVILLE. What do you mean?

ISABEL. That's a question you never used to ask me.

OBERVILLE. Be merciful. Remember how little practice I've had lately.

ISABEL. In what?

Oberville. Never mind! (*He rises and walks away; then comes back and stands in front of her.*) What a fool I was to give you up!

ISABEL. Oh, don't say that! I've lived on it!

OBERVILLE. On my letting you go?

ISABEL. On your letting everything go—but the right.

OBERVILLE. Oh, hang the right! What is truth? We had the right to be happy!

ISABEL (*with rising emotion*). I used to think so sometimes.

OBERVILLE. Did you? Triple fool that I was!

ISABEL. But you showed me—

OBERVILLE. Why, good God, we belonged to each other—and I let you go! It's fabulous. I've fought for things since that weren't worth a crooked sixpence; fought as well as other men. And you—you—I lost you because I couldn't face a scene! Hang it, suppose there'd been a dozen scenes—I might have survived them. Men have been known to. They're not necessarily fatal.

ISABEL. A scene?

OBERVILLE. It's a form of fear that women don't understand. How you must have despised me!

ISABEL. You were—afraid—of a scene?

OBERVILLE. I was a damned coward, Isabel. That's about the size of it.

ISABEL. Ah—I had thought it so much larger!

OBERVILLE. What did you say?

ISABEL. I said that you have forgotten to drink your tea. It must be quite cold.

OBERVILLE. Ah—

ISABEL. Let me give you another cup.

OBERVILLE (*collecting himself*). No—no. This is perfect.

ISABEL. You haven't tasted it.

OBERVILLE (*falling into her mood*) . You always made it to perfection. Only you never gave me enough sugar.

ISABEL. I know better now. (*She puts another lump in his cup.*)

OBERVILLE (*drinks his tea, and then says, with an air of reproach*). Isn't all this chaff rather a waste of time between two old friends who haven't met for so many years?

ISABEL (*lightly*). Oh, it's only a hors d'oeuvre—the tuning of the instruments. I'm out of practice too.

OBERVILLE. Let us come to the grand air, then. (*Sits down near her.*) Tell me about yourself. What are you doing?

ISABEL. At this moment? You'll never guess. I'm trying to remember you.

OBERVILLE. To remember me?

Isabel. Until you came into the room just now my recollection of you was so vivid; you were a living whole in my thoughts. Now I am engaged in gathering up the fragments—in laboriously reconstructing you. . . .

OBERVILLE. I have changed so much, then?

ISABEL. No, I don't believe that you've changed. It's only that I see you differently. Don't you know how hard it is to convince elderly people that the type of the evening paper is no smaller than when they were young?

OBERVILLE. I've shrunk then?

ISABEL. You couldn't have grown bigger. Oh, I'm serious now; you needn't prepare a smile. For years you were the tallest object on my horizon. I used to climb to the thought of you, as people who live in a flat country mount the church steeple for a view. It's wonderful how much I used to see from there! And the air was so strong and pure!

OBERVILLE. And now?

ISABEL. Now I can fancy how delightful it must be to sit next to you at dinner.

OBERVILLE. You're unmerciful. Have I said anything to offend you?

ISABEL. Of course not. How absurd!

OOBERVILLE. I lost my head a little—I forgot how long it is since we have met. When I saw you I forgot everything except what you had once been to me. (*She is silent.*) I thought you too generous to resent that. Perhaps I have overtaxed your generosity. (*A pause.*) Shall I confess it? When I first saw you I thought for a moment that you had remembered—as I had. You see I can only excuse myself by saying something inexcusable.

ISABEL (*deliberately*). Not inexcusable.

OBERVILLE. Not—?

ISABEL. I had remembered.

Oberville. Isabel!

ISABEL. But now—

OBERVILLE. Ah, give me a moment before you unsay it!

ISABEL. I don't mean to unsay it. There's no use in repealing an obsolete law. That's the pity of it! You say you lost me ten years ago. (*A pause.*) I never lost you till now.

OBERVILLE. Now?

ISABEL. Only this morning you were my supreme court of justice; there was no appeal from your verdict. Not an hour ago you decided a case for me—against myself! And now—. And the worst of it is that it's not because you've changed. How do I know if you've changed? You haven't said a hundred words to me. You haven't been an hour in the room. And the years must have enriched you—I daresay you've doubled your capital. You've been in the thick of life, and the metal you're made of brightens with use. Success on some men looks like a borrowed coat; it sits on you as though it had been made to order. I see all this; I know it; but I don't *feel* it. I don't feel anything . . . anywhere . . . I'm numb. (*A pause.*) Don't laugh, but I really don't think I should know now if you came into the room—unless I actually saw you. (*They are both silent.*)

OBERVILLE (*at length*). Then, to put the most merciful interpretation upon your epigrams, your feeling for me was made out of poorer stuff than mine for you.

ISABEL. Perhaps it has had harder wear.

OBERVILLE. Or been less cared for?

ISABEL. If one has only one cloak one must wear it in all weathers.

OBERVILLE. Unless it is so beautiful and precious that one prefers to go cold and keep it under lock and key.

ISABEL. In the cedar-chest of indifference—the key of which is usually lost.

OBERVILLE. Ah, Isabel, you're too pat! How much I preferred your hesitations.

ISABEL. My hesitations? That reminds me how much your coming has simplified things. I feel as if I'd had an auction sale of fallacies.

OBERVILLE. You speak in enigmas, and I have a notion that your riddles are the reverse of the sphinx's—more dangerous to guess than to give up. And yet I used to find your thoughts such good reading.

ISABEL. One cares so little for the style in which one's praises are written.

OBERVILLE. You've been praising me for the last ten minutes and I find your style detestable. I would rather have you find fault with me like a friend than approve me like a dilettante.

ISABEL. A dilettante! The very word I wanted!

OBERVILLE. I am proud to have enriched so full a vocabulary. But I am still waiting for the word I want. (*He grows serious.*) Isabel, look in your heart—give me the first word you find there. You've no idea how much a beggar can buy with a penny!

ISABEL. It's empty, my poor friend, it's empty.

OBERVILLE. Beggars never say that to each other.

ISABEL. No; never, unless it's true.

OBERVILLE (*after another silence*). Why do you look at me so curiously?

ISABEL. I'm—what was it you said? Approving you as a dilettante. Don't be alarmed; you can bear examination; I don't see a crack anywhere. After all, it's a satisfaction to find that one's idol makes a handsome bibelot.

OBERVILLE (*with an attempt at lightness*). I was right then—you're a collector?

ISABEL (*modestly*). One must make a beginning. I think I shall begin with you. (*She smiles at him.*) Positively, I must have you on my mantel- shelf! (*She rises and looks at the clock.*) But it's time to dress for dinner. (*She holds out her hand to him and he kisses it. They look at each other, and it is clear that he does not quite understand, but is watching eagerly for his cue.*)

WARLAND (*coming in*). Hullo, Isabel—you're here after all?

ISABEL. And so is Mr. Oberville. (*She looks straight at Warland.*) I stayed in on purpose to meet him. My husband—(*The two men bow.*)

WARLAND (*effusively*). So glad to meet you. My wife talks of you so often. She's been looking forward tremendously to your visit.

OBERVILLE. It's a long time since I've had the pleasure of seeing Mrs. Warland.

ISABEL. But now we are going to make up for lost time. (*As he goes to the door.*) I claim you tomorrow for the whole day.

*Oberville bows and goes out.*

ISABEL. Lucius . . . I think you'd better go to Washington, after all. (*Musing.*) Narragansett might do for the others, though. . . . Couldn't you get Fred Langham to ask all the rest of the party to go over there with him tomorrow morning? I shall have a headache and stay at home. (*He looks at her doubtfully.*) Mr. Oberville is a bad sailor.

*Warland advances demonstratively.*

ISABEL (*drawing back*). It's time to go and dress. I think you said the black gown with spangles?

## A CUP OF COLD WATER

IT WAS three o'clock in the morning, and the cotillion was at its height, when Woburn left the over-heated splendor of the Gildermere ballroom, and after a delay caused by the determination of the drowsy footman to give him a ready-made overcoat with an imitation astrachan collar in place of his own unimpeachable Poole garment, found himself breasting the icy solitude of the Fifth Avenue. He was still smiling, as he emerged from the awning, at his insistence in claiming his own overcoat: it illustrated, humorously enough, the invincible force of habit. As he faced the wind, however, he discerned a providence in his persistency, for his coat was fur-lined, and he had a cold voyage before him on the morrow.

It had rained hard during the earlier part of the night, and the carriages waiting in triple line before the Gildermeres' door were still domed by shining umbrellas, while the electric lamps extending down the avenue blinked Narcissus-like at their watery images in the hollows of the sidewalk. A dry blast had come out of the north, with pledge of frost before daylight, and to Woburn's shivering fancy the pools in the pavement seemed already stiffening into ice. He turned up his coat-collar and stepped out rapidly, his hands deep in his coat pockets.

As he walked he glanced curiously up at the ladder-like door-steps which may well suggest to the future archaeologist that all the streets of New York were once canals; at the spectral tracery of the trees about St. Luke's, the fretted mass of the Cathedral, and the mean vista of the long side-streets. The knowledge that he was perhaps looking at it all for the last time caused every detail to start out like a challenge to memory, and lit the brown-stone house-fronts with the glamor of sword-barred Edens.

It was an odd impulse that had led him that night to the Gildermere ball; but the same change in his condition which made him stare wonderingly at the houses in the Fifth Avenue gave the thrill of an exploit to the tame business of ball-going. Who would have imagined, Woburn mused, that such a situation as his would possess the priceless quality of sharpening the blunt edge of habit?

It was certainly curious to reflect, as he leaned against the doorway of Mrs. Gildermere's ball-room, enveloped in the warm atmosphere of the accustomed, that twenty-four hours later the people brushing by him with looks of friendly recognition would start at the thought of having seen him and slur over the recollection of having taken his hand!

And the girl he had gone there to see: what would she think of him? He knew well enough that her trenchant classifications of life admitted no overlapping of good and evil, made no allowance for that incalculable interplay of motives that justifies the subtlest casuistry of compassion. Miss Talcott was too young to distinguish the intermediate tints of the moral spectrum; and her judgments were further simplified by a peculiar concreteness of mind. Her bringing-up had fostered this tendency and she was surrounded by people who focused on life in the same way. To the girls in Miss Talcott's set, the attentions of a clever man who had to work for his living had the zest of a forbidden pleasure; but to marry such a man would be as unpardonable as to have one's carriage seen at the door of a cheap dress-maker. Poverty might make a man fascinating; but a settled income was the best evidence of stability of character. If there were anything in heredity, how could a nice girl trust a man whose parents had been careless enough to leave him unprovided for?

Neither Miss Talcott nor any of her friends could be charged with formulating these views; but they were implicit in the slope of every white shoulder and in the ripple of every yard of imported tulle dappling the foreground of Mrs. Gildermere's ball-room. The advantages of line and color in veiling the crudities of a creed are obvious to emotional minds; and besides, Woburn was conscious that it was to the cheerful materialism of their parents that the young girls he admired owed that fine distinction of outline in which their skillfully-rippled hair and skillfully-hung draperies co-operated with the slimness and erectness that came of participating in the most expensive sports, eating the most expensive food and breathing the most expensive air. Since the process which had produced them was so costly, how could they help being costly themselves? Woburn was too logical to expect to give no more for a piece of old Sevres than for a bit of kitchen crockery; he had no faith in wonderful bargains, and believed that one got in life just what one was willing to pay for. He had no mind to dispute the taste of those who preferred the rustic simplicity of the earthen crock; but his own fancy inclined to the piece of *pâte tendre* which must be kept in a glass case and handled as delicately as a flower.

It was not merely by the external grace of these drawing-room ornaments that Woburn's sensibilities were charmed. His imagination was touched by the curious exoticism of view resulting from such conditions; He had always enjoyed listening to Miss Talcott even more than looking at her. Her ideas had the brilliant bloom and audacious irrelevance of those tropical orchids which strike root in air. Miss Talcott's opinions had no connection with the actual; her very materialism had the grace of artificiality. Woburn had been enchanted once by seeing her helpless before a smoking lamp: she had been obliged to ring for a servant because she did not know how to put it out.

Her supreme charm was the simplicity that comes of taking it for granted that people are born with carriages and country-places: it never occurred to her that such congenital attributes could be matter for self- consciousness, and she had none of the nouveau riche prudery which classes poverty with the nude in art and is not sure how to behave in the presence of either.

The conditions of Woburn's own life had made him peculiarly susceptible to those forms of elegance which are the flower of ease. His father had lost a comfortable property through sheer inability to go over his agent's accounts; and this disaster, coming at the outset of Woburn's school-days, had given a new bent to the family temperament. The father characteristically died when the effort of living might have made it possible to retrieve his fortunes; and Woburn's mother and sister, embittered by this final evasion, settled down to a vindictive war with circumstances. They were the kind of women who think that it lightens the burden of life to throw over the amenities, as a reduced housekeeper puts away her knick-knacks to make the dusting easier. They fought mean conditions meanly; but Woburn, in his resentment of their attitude, did not allow for the suffering which had brought it about: his own tendency was to overcome difficulties by conciliation rather than by conflict. Such surroundings threw into vivid relief the charming figure of Miss Talcott. Woburn instinctively associated poverty with bad food, ugly furniture, complaints and recriminations: it was natural that he should be drawn toward the luminous atmosphere where life was a series of peaceful and good-humored acts, unimpeded by petty obstacles. To spend one's time in such society gave one the illusion of unlimited credit; and also, unhappily, created the need for it.

It was here in fact that Woburn's difficulties began. To marry Miss Talcott it was necessary to be a rich man: even to dine out in her set involved certain minor extravagances. Woburn had determined to marry her sooner or later; and in the meanwhile to be with her as much as possible.

As he stood leaning in the doorway of the Gildermere ball-room, watching her pass him in the waltz, he tried to remember how it had begun. First there had been the tailor's bill; the fur-lined overcoat with cuffs and collar of Alaska sable had alone cost more than he had spent on his clothes for two or three years previously. Then there were theatre-tickets; cab-fares; florist's bills; tips to servants at the country- houses where he went because he knew that she was invited; the *Omar Khayyám* bound by Sullivan that he sent her at Christmas; the contributions to her pet charities; the reckless purchases at fairs where she had a stall. His whole way of life had imperceptibly changed and his year's salary was gone before the second quarter was due.

He had invested the few thousand dollars which had been his portion of his father's shrunken estate: when his debts began to pile up, he took a flyer in stocks and after a few months of varying luck his little patrimony disappeared. Meanwhile his courtship was proceeding at an inverse ratio to his financial ventures. Miss Talcott was growing tender and he began to feel that the game was in his hands. The nearness of the goal exasperated him. She was not the girl to wait and he knew that it must be now or never. A friend lent him five thousand dollars on his personal note and he bought railway stocks on margin. They went up and he held them for a higher rise: they fluctuated, dragged, dropped below the level at which he had bought, and slowly continued their uninterrupted descent. His broker called for more margin; he could not respond and was sold out.

What followed came about quite naturally. For several years he had been cashier in a well-known banking-house. When the note he had given his friend became due it was obviously necessary to pay it and he used the firm's money for the purpose. To repay the money thus taken, he increased his debt to his employers and bought more stocks; and on these operations he made a profit of ten thousand dollars. Miss Talcott rode in the Park, and he bought a smart hack for seven hundred, paid off his tradesmen, and went on speculating with the remainder of his profits. He made a little more, but failed to take advantage of the market and lost all that he had staked, including the amount taken from the firm. He increased his over- draft by another ten thousand and lost that; he over-drew a farther sum and lost again. Suddenly he woke to the fact that he owed his employers fifty thousand dollars and that the partners were to make their semi- annual inspection in two days. He realized then that within forty-eight hours what he had called borrowing would become theft.

There was no time to be lost: he must clear out and start life over again somewhere else. The day that he reached this decision he was to have met Miss Talcott at dinner. He went to the dinner, but she did not appear: she had a headache, his hostess explained. Well, he was not to have a last look at her, after all; better so, perhaps. He took leave early and on his way home stopped at a florist's and sent her a bunch of violets. The next morning he got a little note from her: the violets had done her head so much good—she would tell him all about it that evening at the Gildermere ball. Woburn laughed and tossed the note into the fire. That evening he would be on board ship: the examination of the books was to take place the following morning at ten.

Woburn went down to the bank as usual; he did not want to do anything that might excite suspicion as to his plans, and from one or two questions which one of the partners had lately put to him he divined that he was being observed. At the bank the day passed uneventfully. He discharged his business with his accustomed care and went uptown at the usual hour.

In the first flush of his successful speculations he had set up bachelor lodgings, moved by the temptation to get away from the dismal atmosphere of home, from his mother's struggles with the cook and his sister's curiosity about his letters. He had been influenced also by the wish for surroundings more adapted to his tastes. He wanted to be able to give little teas, to which Miss Talcott might come with a married friend. She came once or twice and pronounced it all delightful: she thought it so nice to have only a few Whistler etchings on the walls and the simplest crushed levant for all one's books.

To these rooms Woburn returned on leaving the bank. His plans had taken definite shape. He had engaged passage on a steamer sailing for Halifax early the next morning; and there was nothing for him to do before going on board but to pack his clothes and tear up a few letters. He threw his clothes into a couple of portmanteaux, and when these had been called for by an expressman he emptied his pockets and counted up his ready money. He found that he possessed just fifty dollars and seventy-five cents; but his passage to Halifax was paid, and once there he could pawn his watch and rings. This calculation completed, he unlocked his writing-table drawer and took out a handful of letters. They were notes from Miss Talcott. He read them over and threw them into the fire. On his table stood her photograph. He slipped it out of its frame and tossed it on top of the blazing letters. Having performed this rite, he got into his dress-clothes and went to a small French restaurant to dine.

He had meant to go on board the steamer immediately after dinner; but a sudden vision of introspective hours in a silent cabin made him call for the evening paper and run his eye over the list of theatres. It would be as easy to go on board at midnight as now.

He selected a new vaudeville and listened to it with surprising freshness of interest; but toward eleven o'clock he again began to dread the approaching necessity of going down to the steamer. There was something peculiarly unnerving in the idea of spending the rest of the night in a stifling cabin jammed against the side of a wharf.

He left the theatre and strolled across to the Fifth Avenue. It was now nearly midnight and a stream of carriages poured up town from the opera and the theatres. As he stood on the corner watching the familiar spectacle it occurred to him that many of the people driving by him in smart broughams and C-spring landaus were on their way to the Gildermere ball. He remembered Miss Talcott's note of the morning and wondered if she were in one of the passing carriages; she had spoken so confidently of meeting him at the ball. What if he should go and take a last look at her? There was really nothing to prevent it. He was not likely to run across any member of the firm: in Miss Talcott's set his social standing was good for another ten hours at least. He smiled in anticipation of her surprise at seeing him, and then reflected with a start that she would not be surprised at all.

His meditations were cut short by a fall of sleety rain, and hailing a hansom he gave the driver Mrs. Gildermere's address.

As he drove up the avenue he looked about him like a traveller in a strange city. The buildings which had been so unobtrusively familiar stood out with sudden distinctness: he noticed a hundred details which had escaped his observation. The people on the sidewalks looked like strangers: he wondered where they were going and tried to picture the lives they led; but his own relation to life had been so suddenly reversed that he found it impossible to recover his mental perspective.

At one corner he saw a shabby man lurking in the shadow of the side street; as the hansom passed, a policeman ordered him to move on. Farther on, Woburn noticed a woman crouching on the door-step of a handsome house. She had drawn a shawl over her head and was sunk in the apathy of despair or drink. A well-dressed couple paused to look at her. The electric globe at the corner lit up their faces, and Woburn saw the lady, who was young and pretty, turn away with a little grimace, drawing her companion after her.

The desire to see Miss Talcott had driven Woburn to the Gildermeres'; but once in the ball-room he made no effort to find her. The people about him seemed more like strangers than those he had passed in the street. He stood in the doorway, studying the petty maneuvers of the women and the resigned amenities of their partners. Was it possible that these were his friends? These mincing women, all paint and dye and whalebone, these apathetic men who looked as much alike as the figures that children cut out of a folded sheet of paper? Was it to live among such puppets that he had sold his soul? What had any of these people done that was noble, exceptional, distinguished? Who knew them by name even, except their tradesmen and the society reporters? Who were they, that they should sit in judgment on him?

The bald man with the globular stomach, who stood at Mrs. Gildermere's elbow surveying the dancers, was old Boylston, who had made his pile in wrecking railroads; the smooth chap with glazed eyes, at whom a pretty girl smiled up so confidingly, was Collerton, the political lawyer, who had been mixed up to his own advantage in an ugly lobbying transaction; near him stood Brice Lyndham, whose recent failure had ruined his friends and associates, but had not visibly affected the welfare of his large and expensive family. The slim fellow dancing with Miss Gildermere was Alec Vance, who lived on a salary of five thousand a year, but whose wife was such a good manager that they kept a brougham and victoria and always put in their season at Newport and their spring trip to Europe. The little ferret-faced youth in the corner was Regie Colby, who wrote the "Entre-Nous" paragraphs in the *Social Searchlight:* the women were charming to him and he got all the financial tips he wanted from their husbands and fathers.

And the women? Well, the women knew all about the men, and flattered them and married them and tried to catch them for their daughters. It was a domino-party at which the guests were forbidden to unmask, though they all saw through each other's disguises.

And these were the people who, within twenty-four hours, would be agreeing that they had always felt there was something wrong about Woburn! They would be extremely sorry for him, of course, poor devil; but there are certain standards, after all— what would society be without standards? His new friends, his future associates, were the suspicious-looking man whom the policeman had ordered to move on, and the drunken woman asleep on the door-step. To these he was linked by the freemasonry of failure.

Miss Talcott passed him on Collerton's arm; she was giving him one of the smiles of which Woburn had fancied himself sole owner. Collerton was a sharp fellow; he must have made a lot in that last deal; probably she would marry him. How much did she know about the transaction? She was a shrewd girl and her father was in Wall Street. If Woburn's luck had turned the other way she might have married him instead; and if he had confessed his sin to her one evening, as they drove home from the opera in their new brougham, she would have said that really it was of no use to tell her, for she never *could* understand about business, but that she did entreat him in future to be nicer to Regie Colby. Even now, if he made a big strike somewhere, and came back in ten years with a beard and a steam yacht, they would all deny that anything had been proved against him, and Mrs. Collerton might blush and remind him of their friendship. Well—why not? Was not all morality based on a convention? What was the stanchest code of ethics but a trunk with a series of false bottoms? Now and then one had the illusion of getting down to absolute right or wrong, but it was only a false bottom—a removable hypothesis—with another false bottom underneath. There was no getting beyond the relative.

The cotillion had begun. Miss Talcott sat nearly opposite him: she was dancing with young Boylston and giving him a Woburn-Collerton smile. So young Boylston was in the syndicate too!

Presently Woburn was aware that she had forgotten young Boylston and was glancing absently about the room. She was looking for some one, and meant the some one to know it: he knew that *Lost Chord* look in her eyes.

A new figure was being formed. The partners circled about the room and Miss Talcott's flying tulle drifted close to him as she passed. Then the favors were distributed; white skirts wavered across the floor like thistle-down on summer air; men rose from their seats and fresh couples filled the shining parquet.

Miss Talcott, after taking from the basket a Legion of Honor in red enamel, surveyed the room for a moment; then she made her way through the dancers and held out the favor to Woburn. He fastened it in his coat, and emerging from the crowd of men about the doorway, slipped his arm about her. Their eyes met; hers were serious and a little sad. How fine and slender she was! He noticed the little tendrils of hair about the pink convolution of her ear. Her waist was firm and yet elastic; she breathed calmly and regularly, as though dancing were her natural motion. She did not look at him again and neither of them spoke.

When the music ceased they paused near her chair. Her partner was waiting for her and Woburn left her with a bow.

He made his way downstairs and out of the house. He was glad that he had not spoken to Miss Talcott. There had been a healing power in their silence. All bitterness had gone from him and he thought of her now quite simply, as the girl he loved.

At Thirty-fifth Street he reflected that he had better jump into a car and go down to his steamer. Again there rose before him the repulsive vision of the dark cabin, with creaking noises overhead, and the cold wash of water against the pier: he thought he would stop in a cafe and take a drink. He turned into Broadway and entered a brightly-lit cafe; but when he had taken his whisky and soda there seemed no reason for lingering. He had never been the kind of man who could escape difficulties in that way. Yet he was conscious that his will was weakening; that he did not mean to go down to the steamer just yet. What did he mean to do? He began to feel horribly tired and it occurred to him that a few hours' sleep in a decent bed would make a new man of him. Why not go on board the next morning at daylight?

He could not go back to his rooms, for on leaving the house he had taken the precaution of dropping his latch-key into his letter-box; but he was in a neighborhood of discreet hotels and he wandered on till he came to one which was known to offer a dispassionate hospitality to luggage-less travellers in dress clothes.

II

HE pushed open the swinging door and found himself in a long corridor with a tessellated floor, at the end of which, in a brightly-lit enclosure of plate-glass and mahogany, the night-clerk dozed over a copy of the *Police Gazette*. The air in the corridor was rich in reminiscences of yesterday's dinners, and a bronzed radiator poured a wave of dry heat into Woburn's face.

The night-clerk, roused by the swinging of the door, sat watching Woburn's approach with the unexpectant eye of one who has full confidence in his capacity for digesting surprises. Not that there was anything surprising in Woburn's appearance; but the night-clerk's callers were given to such imaginative flights in explaining their luggageless arrival in the small hours of the morning, that he fared habitually on fictions which would have staggered a less experienced stomach. The night-clerk, whose unwrinkled bloom showed that he throve on this high-seasoned diet, had a fancy for classifying his applicants before they could frame their explanations.

"This one's been locked out," he said to himself as he mustered Woburn.

Having exercised his powers of divination with his accustomed accuracy he listened without stirring an eye-lid to Woburn's statement; merely replying, when the latter asked the price of a room, "Two-fifty."

"Very well," said Woburn, pushing the money under the brass lattice, "I'll go up at once; and I want to be called at seven."

To this the night-clerk proffered no reply, but stretching out his hand to press an electric button, returned apathetically to the perusal of the *Police Gazette*. His summons was answered by the appearance of a man in shirt-sleeves, whose rumpled head indicated that he had recently risen from some kind of makeshift repose; to him the night-clerk tossed a key, with the brief comment, "Ninety-seven;" and the man, after a sleepy glance at Woburn, turned on his heel and lounged toward the staircase at the back of the corridor.

Woburn followed and they climbed three flights in silence. At each landing Woburn glanced down, the long passage-way lit by a lowered gas-jet, with a double line of boots before the doors, waiting, like yesterday's deeds, to carry their owners so many miles farther on the morrow's destined road. On the third landing the man paused, and after examining the number on the key, turned to the left, and slouching past three or four doors, finally unlocked one and preceded Woburn into a room lit only by the upward gleam of the electric globes in the street below.

The man felt in his pockets; then he turned to Woburn. "Got a match?" he asked.

Woburn politely offered him one, and he applied it to the gas-fixture which extended its jointed arm above an ash dressing-table with a blurred mirror fixed between two standards. Having performed this office with an air of detachment designed to make Woburn recognize it as an act of supererogation, he turned without a word and vanished down the passageway.

Woburn, after an indifferent glance about the room, which seemed to afford the amount of luxury generally obtainable for two dollars and a half in a fashionable quarter of New York, locked the door and sat down at the ink- stained writing-table in the window. Far below him lay the pallidly-lit depths of the forsaken thoroughfare. Now and then he heard the jingle of a horsecar and the ring of hoofs on the freezing pavement, or saw the lonely figure of a policeman eclipsing the illumination of the plate-glass windows on the opposite side of the street. He sat thus for a long time, his elbows on the table, his chin between his hands, till at length the contemplation of the abandoned sidewalks, above which the electric globes kept Stylites-like vigil, became intolerable to him, and he drew down the window-shade, and lit the gas-fixture beside the dressing-table. Then he took a cigar from his case, and held it to the flame.

The passage from the stinging freshness of the night to the stale overheated atmosphere of the Haslemere Hotel had checked the preternaturally rapid working of his mind, and he was now scarcely conscious of thinking at all. His head was heavy, and he would have thrown himself on the bed had he not feared to oversleep the hour fixed for his departure. He thought it safest, instead, to seat himself once more by the table, in the most uncomfortable chair that he could find, and smoke one cigar after another till the first sign of dawn should give an excuse for action.

He had laid his watch on the table before him, and was gazing at the hour- hand, and trying to convince himself by so doing that he was still wide awake, when a noise in the adjoining room suddenly straightened him in his chair and banished all fear of sleep.

There was no mistaking the nature of the noise; it was that of a woman's sobs. The sobs were not loud, but the sound reached him distinctly through the frail door between the two rooms; it expressed an utter abandonment to grief; not the cloud-burst of some passing emotion, but the slow down-pour of a whole heaven of sorrow.

Woburn sat listening. There was nothing else to be done; and at least his listening was a mute tribute to the trouble he was powerless to relieve. It roused, too, the drugged pulses of his own grief: he was touched by the chance propinquity of two alien sorrows in a great city throbbing with multifarious passions. It would have been more in keeping with the irony of life had he found himself next to a mother singing her child to sleep: there seemed a mute commiseration in the hand that had led him to such neighborhood.

Gradually the sobs subsided, with pauses betokening an effort at self- control. At last they died off softly, like the intermittent drops that end a day of rain.

"Poor soul," Woburn mused, "she's got the better of it for the time. I wonder what it's all about?"

At the same moment he heard another sound that made him jump to his feet. It was a very low sound, but in that nocturnal silence which gives distinctness to the faintest noises, Woburn knew at once that he had heard the click of a pistol.

"What is she up to now?" he asked himself, with his eye on the door between the two rooms; and the brightly-lit keyhole seemed to reply with a glance of intelligence. He turned out the gas and crept to the door, pressing his eye to the illuminated circle.

After a moment or two of adjustment, during which he seemed to himself to be breathing like a steam-engine, he discerned a room like his own, with the same dressing-table flanked by gas-fixtures, and the same table in the window. This table was directly in his line of vision; and beside it stood a woman with a small revolver in her hands. The lights being behind her, Woburn could only infer her youth from her slender silhouette and the nimbus of fair hair defining her head. Her dress seemed dark and simple, and on a chair under one of the gas-jets lay a jacket edged with cheap fur and a small travelling-bag. He could not see the other end of the room, but something in her manner told him that she was alone. At length she put the revolver down and took up a letter that lay on the table. She drew the letter from its envelope and read it over two or three times; then she put it back, sealing the envelope, and placing it conspicuously against the mirror of the dressing table.

There was so grave a significance in this dumb-show that Woburn felt sure that her next act would be to return to the table and take up the revolver; but he had not reckoned on the vanity of woman. After putting the letter in place she still lingered at the mirror, standing a little sideways, so that he could now see her face, which was distinctly pretty, but of a small and unelastic mold, inadequate to the expression of the larger emotions. For some moments she continued to study herself with the expression of a child looking at a playmate who has been scolded; then she turned to the table and lifted the revolver to her forehead.

A sudden crash made her arm drop, and sent her darting backward to the opposite side of the room. Woburn had broken down the door, and stood torn and breathless in the breach.

"Oh!" she gasped, pressing closer to the wall.

"Don't be frightened," he said; "I saw what you were going to do and I had to stop you."

She looked at him for a moment in silence, and he saw the terrified flutter of her breast; then she said, "No one can stop me for long. And besides, what right have you—"

"Every one has the right to prevent a crime," he returned, the sound of the last word sending the blood to his forehead.

"I deny it," she said passionately. "Every one who has tried to live and failed has the right to die."

"Failed in what?"

"In everything!" she replied. They stood looking at each other in silence.

At length he advanced a few steps.

"You've no right to say you've failed," he said, "while you have breath to try again." He drew the revolver from her hand.

"Try again—try again? I tell you I've tried seventy times seven!"

"What have you tried?"

She looked at him with a certain dignity.

"I don't know," she said, "that you've any right to question me—or to be in this room at all—" and suddenly she burst into tears.

The discrepancy between her words and action struck the chord which, in a man's heart, always responds to the touch of feminine unreason. She dropped into the nearest chair, hiding her face in her hands, while Woburn watched the course of her weeping.

At last she lifted her head, looking up between drenched lashes.

"Please go away," she said in childish entreaty.

"How can I?" he returned. "It's impossible that I should leave you in this state. Trust me—let me help you. Tell me what has gone wrong, and let's see if there's no other way out of it."

Woburn had a voice full of sensitive inflections, and it was now trembling with profoundest pity. Its note seemed to reassure the girl, for she said, with a beginning of confidence in her own tones, "But I don't even know who you are."

Woburn was silent: the words startled him. He moved nearer to her and went on in the same quieting tone.

"I am a man who has suffered enough to want to help others. I don't want to know any more about you than will enable me to do what I can for you. I've probably seen more of life than you have, and if you're willing to tell me your troubles perhaps together we may find a way out of them."

She dried her eyes and glanced at the revolver.

"That's the only way out," she said.

"How do you know? Are you sure you've tried every other?"

"Perfectly sure, I've written and written, and humbled myself like a slave before him, and she won't even let him answer my letters. Oh, but you don't understand"—she broke off with a renewal of weeping.

"I begin to understand—you're sorry for something you've done?"

"Oh, I've never denied that—I've never denied that I was wicked."

"And you want the forgiveness of some one you care about?"

"My husband," she whispered.

"You've done something to displease your husband?"

"To displease him? I ran away with another man!" There was a dismal exultation in her tone, as though she were paying Woburn off for having underrated her offense.

She had certainly surprised him; at worst he had expected a quarrel over a rival, with a possible complication of mother-in-law. He wondered how such helpless little feet could have taken so bold a step; then he remembered that there is no audacity like that of weakness.

He was wondering how to lead her to completer avowal when she added forlornly, "You see there's nothing else to do."

Woburn took a turn in the room. It was certainly a narrower strait than he had foreseen, and he hardly knew how to answer; but the first flow of confession had eased her, and she went on without farther persuasion.

"I don't know how I could ever have done it; I must have been downright crazy. I didn't care much for Joe when I married him—he wasn't exactly handsome, and girls think such a lot of that. But he just laid down and worshipped me, and I *was* getting fond of him in a way; only the life was so dull. I'd been used to a big city—I come from Detroit—and Hinksville is such a poky little place; that's where we lived; Joe is telegraph- operator on the railroad there. He'd have been in a much bigger place now, if he hadn't—well, after all, he behaved perfectly splendidly about *that*.

"I really was getting fond of him, and I believe I should have realized in time how good and noble and unselfish he was, if his mother hadn't been always sitting there and everlastingly telling me so. We learned in school about the Athenians hating some man who was always called just, and that's the way I felt about Joe. Whenever I did anything that wasn't quite right his mother would say how differently Joe would have done it. And she was forever telling me that Joe didn't approve of this and that and the other. When we were alone he approved of everything, but when his mother was round he'd sit quiet and let her say he didn't. I knew he'd let me have my way afterwards, but somehow that didn't prevent my getting mad at the time.

"And then the evenings were so long, with Joe away, and Mrs. Glenn (that's his mother) sitting there like an image knitting socks for the heathen. The only caller we ever had was the Baptist minister, and he never took any more notice of me than if I'd been a piece of furniture. I believe he was afraid to before Mrs. Glenn."

She paused breathlessly, and the tears in her eyes were now of anger.

"Well?" said Woburn gently.

"Well—then Arthur Hackett came along; he was travelling for a big publishing firm in Philadelphia. He was awfully handsome and as clever and sarcastic as anything. He used to lend me lots of novels and magazines, and tell me all about society life in New

York. All the girls were after him, and Alice Sprague, whose father is the richest man in Hinksville, fell desperately in love with him and carried on like a fool; but he wouldn't take any notice of her. He never looked at anybody but me." Her face lit up with a reminiscent smile, and then clouded again. "I hate him now," she exclaimed, with a change of tone that startled Woburn. "I'd like to kill him—but he's killed me instead.

"Well, he bewitched me so I didn't know what I was doing; I was like somebody in a trance. When he wasn't there I didn't want to speak to anybody; I used to lie in bed half the day just to get away from folks; I hated Joe and Hinksville and everything else. When he came back the days went like a flash; we were together nearly all the time. I knew Joe's mother was spying on us, but I didn't care. And at last it seemed as if I couldn't let him go away again without me; so one evening he stopped at the back gate in a buggy, and we drove off together and caught the eastern express at River Bend. He promised to bring me to New York." She paused, and then added scornfully, "He didn't even do that!"

Woburn had returned to his seat and was watching her attentively. It was curious to note how her passion was spending itself in words; he saw that she would never kill herself while she had any one to talk to.

"That was five months ago," she continued, "and we travelled all through the southern states, and stayed a little while near Philadelphia, where his business is. He did things real stylishly at first. Then he was sent to Albany, and we stayed a week at the Delavan House. One afternoon I went out to do some shopping, and when I came back he was gone. He had taken his trunk with him, and hadn't left any address; but in my travelling-bag I found a fifty-dollar bill, with a slip of paper on which he had written, 'No use coming after me; I'm married.' We'd been together less than four months, and I never saw him again.

"At first I couldn't believe it. I stayed on, thinking it was a joke—or that he'd feel sorry for me and come back. But he never came and never wrote me a line. Then I began to hate him, and to see what a wicked fool I'd been to leave Joe. I was so lonesome—I thought I'd go crazy. And I kept thinking how good and patient Joe had been, and how badly I'd used him, and how lovely it would be to be back in the little parlor at Hinksville, even with Mrs. Glenn and the minister talking about free-will and predestination. So at last I wrote to Joe. I wrote him the humblest letters you ever read, one after another; but I never got any answer.

"Finally I found I'd spent all my money, so I sold my watch and my rings— Joe gave me a lovely turquoise ring when we were married—and came to New York. I felt ashamed to stay alone any longer in Albany; I was afraid that some of Arthur's friends, who had met me with him on the road, might come there and recognize me. After I got here I wrote to Susy Price, a great friend of mine who lives at Hinksville, and she answered at once, and told me just what I had expected—that Joe was ready to forgive me and crazy to have me back, but that his mother wouldn't let him stir a step or write me a line, and that she and the minister were at him all day long, telling him how bad I was and what a sin it would be to forgive me. I got Susy's letter two or three days ago, and after that I saw it was no use writing to Joe. He'll never dare go against his mother and she watches him like a cat. I suppose I deserve it—but he might have given me another chance! I know he would if he could only see me."

Her voice had dropped from anger to lamentation, and her tears again overflowed.

Woburn looked at her with the pity one feels for a child who is suddenly confronted with the result of some unpremeditated naughtiness.

"But why not go back to Hinksville," he suggested, "if your husband is ready to forgive you? You could go to your friend's house, and once your husband knows you are there you can easily persuade him to see you."

"Perhaps I could—Susy thinks I could. But I can't go back; I haven't got a cent left."

"But surely you can borrow money? Can't you ask your friend to forward you the amount of your fare?"

She shook her head.

"Susy ain't well off; she couldn't raise five dollars, and it costs twenty-five to get back to Hinksville. And besides, what would become of me while I waited for the money? They'll turn me out of here tomorrow; I haven't paid my last week's board, and I haven't got anything to give them; my bag's empty; I've pawned everything."

"And don't you know any one here who would lend you the money?"

"No; not a soul. At least I do know one gentleman; he's a friend of Arthur's, a Mr. Devine; he was staying at Rochester when we were there. I met him in the street the other day, and I didn't mean to speak to him, but he came up to me, and said he knew all about Arthur and how meanly he had behaved, and he wanted to know if he couldn't help me— I suppose he saw I was in trouble. He tried to persuade me to go and stay with his aunt, who has a lovely house right round here in Twenty-fourth Street; he must be very rich, for he offered to lend me as much money as I wanted."

"You didn't take it?"

"No," she returned; "I daresay he meant to be kind, but I didn't care to be beholden to any friend of Arthur's. He came here again yesterday, but I wouldn't see him, so he left a note giving me his aunt's address and saying she'd have a room ready for me at any time."

There was a long silence; she had dried her tears and sat looking at Woburn with eyes full of helpless reliance.

"Well," he said at length, "you did right not to take that man's money; but this isn't the only alternative," he added, pointing to the revolver.

"I don't know any other," she answered wearily. "I'm not smart enough to get employment; I can't make dresses or do type-writing, or any of the useful things they teach girls now; and besides, even if I could get work I couldn't stand the loneliness. I can never hold my head up again—I can't bear the disgrace. If I can't go back to Joe I'd rather be dead."

"And if you go back to Joe it will be all right?" Woburn suggested with a smile.

"Oh," she cried, her whole face alight, "if I could only go back to Joe!"

They were both silent again; Woburn sat with his hands in his pockets gazing at the floor. At length his silence seemed to rouse her to the unwontedness of the situation, and she rose from her seat, saying in a more constrained tone, "I don't know why I've told you all this."

"Because you believed that I would help you," Woburn answered, rising also; "and you were right; I'm going to send you home."

She colored vividly.

"You told me I was right not to take Mr. Devine's money," she faltered.

"Yes," he answered, "but did Mr. Devine want to send you home?"

"He wanted me to wait at his aunt's a little while first and then write to Joe again."

"I don't—I want you to start tomorrow morning; this morning, I mean. I'll take you to the station and buy your ticket, and your husband can send me back the money."

"Oh, I can't—I can't—you mustn't—" she stammered, reddening and paling. "Besides, they'll never let me leave here without paying."

"How much do you owe?"

"Fourteen dollars."

"Very well; I'll pay that for you; you can leave me your revolver as a pledge. But you must start by the first train; have you any idea at what time it leaves the Grand Central?"

"I think there's one at eight."

He glanced at his watch.

"In less than two hours, then; it's after six now."

She stood before him with fascinated eyes.

"You must have a very strong will," she said. "When you talk like that you make me feel as if I had to do everything you say."

"Well, you must," said Woburn lightly. "Man was made to be obeyed."

"Oh, you're not like other men," she returned; "I never heard a voice like yours; it's so strong and kind. You must be a very good man; you remind me of Joe; I'm sure you've got just such a nature; and Joe is the best man I've ever seen."

Woburn made no reply, and she rambled on, with little pauses and fresh bursts of confidence.

"Joe's a real hero, you know; he did the most splendid thing you ever heard of. I think I began to tell you about it, but I didn't finish. I'll tell you now. It happened just after we were married; I was mad with him at the time, I'm afraid, but now I see how splendid he was. He'd been telegraph operator at Hinksville for four years and was hoping that he'd get promoted to a bigger place; but he was afraid to ask for a raise. Well, I was very sick with a bad attack of pneumonia and one night the doctor said he wasn't sure whether he could pull me through. When they sent word to Joe at the telegraph office he couldn't stand being away from me another minute. There was a poor consumptive boy always hanging round the station; Joe had taught him how to operate, just to help him along; so he left him in the office and tore home for half an hour, knowing he could get back before the eastern express came along.

"He hadn't been gone five minutes when a freight-train ran off the rails about a mile up the track. It was a very still night, and the boy heard the smash and shouting, and knew something had happened. He couldn't tell what it was, but the minute he heard it he sent a message over the wires like a flash, and caught the eastern express just as it was pulling out of the station above Hinksville. If he'd hesitated a second, or made any mistake, the express would have come on, and the loss of life would have been fearful. The next day the Hinksville papers were full of Operator Glenn's presence of mind; they all said he'd be promoted. That was early in November and Joe didn't hear anything from the company till the first of January. Meanwhile the boy had gone home to his father's farm out in the country, and before Christmas he was dead. Well, on New Year's day Joe got a notice from the company saying that his pay was to be raised, and that he was to be promoted to a big junction near Detroit, in recognition of his presence of mind in stopping the eastern express. It was just what we'd both been pining for and I was nearly wild with joy; but I noticed Joe didn't say much. He just telegraphed for leave, and the next day he went right up to Detroit and told the directors there what had really happened. When he came back he told us they'd suspended him; I cried every night for a week, and even his mother said he was a fool. After that we just lived on at Hinksville, and six months later the company took him back; but I don't suppose they'll ever promote him now."

Her voice again trembled with facile emotion.

"Wasn't it beautiful of him? Ain't he a real hero?" she said. "And I'm sure you'd behave just like him; you'd be just as gentle about little things, and you'd never move an inch about big ones. You'd never do a mean action, but you'd be sorry for people who did; I can see it in your face; that's why I trusted you right off."

Woburn's eyes were fixed on the window; he hardly seemed to hear her. At length he walked across the room and pulled up the shade. The electric lights were dissolving in the gray alembic of the dawn. A milk-cart rattled down the street and, like a witch returning late from the Sabbath, a stray cat whisked into an area. So rose the appointed day.

Woburn turned back, drawing from his pocket the roll of bills which he had thrust there with so different a purpose. He counted them out, and handed her fifteen dollars.

"That will pay for your board, including your breakfast this morning," he said. "We'll breakfast together presently if you like; and meanwhile suppose we sit down and watch the sunrise. I haven't seen it for years."

He pushed two chairs toward the window, and they sat down side by side. The light came gradually, with the icy reluctance of winter; at last a red disk pushed itself above the opposite house-tops and a long cold gleam slanted across their window. They did not talk much; there was a silencing awe in the spectacle.

Presently Woburn rose and looked again at his watch.

"I must go and cover up my dress-coat", he said, "and you had better put on your hat and jacket. We shall have to be starting in half an hour."

As he turned away she laid her hand on his arm.

"You haven't even told me your name," she said.

"No," he answered; "but if you get safely back to Joe you can call me Providence."

"But how am I to send you the money?"

"Oh—well, I'll write you a line in a day or two and give you my address; I don't know myself what it will be; I'm a wanderer on the face of the earth."

"But you must have my name if you mean to write to me."

"Well, what is your name?"

"Ruby Glenn. And I think—I almost think you might send the letter right to Joe's—send it to the Hinksville station."

"Very well."

"You promise?"

"Of course I promise."

He went back into his room, thinking how appropriate it was that she should have an absurd name like Ruby. As he re-entered the room, where the gas sickened in the daylight, it seemed to him that he was returning to some forgotten land; he had passed, with the last few hours, into a wholly new phase of consciousness. He put on his fur coat, turning up the collar and crossing the lapels to hide his white tie. Then he put his cigar-case in his pocket, turned out the gas, and, picking up his hat and stick, walked back through the open doorway.

Ruby Glenn had obediently prepared herself for departure and was standing before the mirror, patting her curls into place. Her eyes were still red, but she had the happy look of a child that has outslept its grief. On the floor he noticed the tattered fragments of the letter which, a few hours earlier, he had seen her place before the mirror.

"Shall we go down now?" he asked.

"Very well," she assented; then, with a quick movement, she stepped close to him, and putting her hands on his shoulders lifted her face to his.

"I believe you're the best man I ever knew," she said, "the very best—except Joe."

She drew back blushing deeply, and unlocked the door which led into the passage-way. Woburn picked up her bag, which she had forgotten, and followed her out of the room. They passed a frowzy chambermaid, who stared at them with a yawn. Before the doors the row of boots still waited; there was a faint new aroma of coffee mingling with the smell of vanished dinners, and a fresh blast of heat had begun to tingle through the radiators.

In the unventilated coffee-room they found a waiter who had the melancholy air of being the last survivor of an exterminated race, and who reluctantly brought them some tea made with water which had not boiled, and a supply of stale rolls and staler butter. On this meager diet they fared in silence, Woburn occasionally glancing at his watch; at length he rose, telling his companion to go and pay her bill while he called a hansom. After all, there was no use in economizing his remaining dollars.

In a few moments she joined him under the portico of the hotel. The hansom stood waiting and he sprang in after her, calling to the driver to take them to the Forty-second Street station.

When they reached the station he found a seat for her and went to buy her ticket. There were several people ahead of him at the window, and when he had bought the ticket he found that it was time to put her in the train. She rose in answer to his glance, and together they walked down the long platform in the murky chill of the roofed-in air. He followed her into the railway carriage, making sure that she had her bag, and that the ticket was safe inside it; then he held out his hand, in its pearl-colored evening glove: he felt that the people in the other seats were staring at them.

"Good-bye," he said.

"Good-bye," she answered, flushing gratefully. "I'll never forget—never. And you *will* write, won't you? Promise!"

"Of course, of course," he said, hastening from the carriage.

He retraced his way along the platform, passed through the dismal waiting- room and stepped out into the early sunshine. On the sidewalk outside the station he hesitated awhile; then he strolled slowly down Forty-second Street and, skirting the melancholy flank of the Reservoir, walked across Bryant Park. Finally he sat down on one of the benches near the Sixth Avenue and lit a cigar.

The signs of life were multiplying around him; he watched the cars roll by with their increasing freight of dingy toilers, the shop-girls hurrying to their work, the children trudging schoolward, their small vague noses red with cold, their satchels clasped in woolen-gloved hands. There is nothing very imposing in the first stirring of a great city's activities; it is a slow reluctant process, like the waking of a heavy sleeper; but to Woburn's mood the sight of that obscure renewal of humble duties was more moving than the spectacle of an army with banners.

He sat for a long time, smoking the last cigar in his case, and murmuring to himself a line from Hamlet—the saddest, he thought, in the play—

*For every man hath business and desire.*

Suddenly an unpremeditated movement made him feel the pressure of Ruby Glenn's revolver in his pocket; it was like a devil's touch on his arm, and he sprang up hastily. In his other pocket there were just four dollars and fifty cents; but that didn't matter now. He had no thought of flight.

For a few minutes he loitered vaguely about the park; then the cold drove him on again, and with the rapidity born of a sudden resolve he began to walk down the Fifth Avenue towards his lodgings. He brushed past a maid- servant who was washing the vestibule and ran upstairs to his room. A fire was burning in the grate and his books and photographs greeted him cheerfully from the walls; the tranquil air of the whole room seemed to take it for granted that he meant to have his bath and breakfast and go down town as usual.

He threw off his coat and pulled the revolver out of his pocket; for some moments he held it curiously in his hand, bending over to examine it as Ruby Glenn had done; then he laid it in the top drawer of a small cabinet, and locking the drawer threw the key into the fire.

After that he went quietly about the usual business of his toilet. In taking off his dress-coat he noticed the Legion of Honor which Miss Talcott had given him at the ball. He pulled it out of his buttonhole and tossed it into the fire-place. When he had finished dressing he saw with surprise that it was nearly ten o'clock. Ruby Glenn was already two hours nearer home.

Woburn stood looking about the room of which he had thought to take final leave the night before; among the ashes beneath the grate he caught sight of a little white heap which symbolized to his fancy the remains of his brief correspondence with Miss Talcott. He roused himself from this unseasonable musing and with a final glance at the familiar setting of his past, turned to face the future which the last hours had prepared for him.

He went downstairs and stepped out of doors, hastening down the street towards Broadway as though he were late for an appointment. Every now and then he encountered an acquaintance, whom he greeted with a nod and smile; he carried his head high, and shunned no man's recognition.

At length he reached the doors of a tall granite building honey-combed with windows. He mounted the steps of the portico, and passing through the double doors of plate-glass, crossed a vestibule floored with mosaic to another glass door on which was emblazoned the name of the firm.

This door he also opened, entering a large room with wainscotted subdivisions, behind which appeared the stooping shoulders of a row of clerks.

As Woburn crossed the threshold a gray-haired man emerged from an inner office at the opposite end of the room.

At sight of Woburn he stopped short.

"Mr. Woburn!" he exclaimed; then he stepped nearer and added in a low tone: "I was requested to tell you when you came that the members of the firm are waiting; will you step into the private office?"

## THE PORTRAIT

IT WAS at Mrs. Mellish's, one Sunday afternoon last spring. We were talking over George Lillo's portraits—a collection of them was being shown at Durand-Ruel's—and a pretty woman had emphatically declared:—

"Nothing on earth would induce me to sit to him!"

There was a chorus of interrogations.

"Oh, because—he makes people look so horrid; the way one looks on board ship, or early in the morning, or when one's hair is out of curl and one knows it. I'd so much rather be done by Mr. Cumberton!"

Little Cumberton, the fashionable purveyor of rose-water pastels, stroked his moustache to hide a conscious smile.

"Lillo is a genius—that we must all admit," he said indulgently, as though condoning a friend's weakness; "but he has an unfortunate temperament. He has been denied the gift—so precious to an artist—of perceiving the ideal. He sees only the defects of his sitters; one might almost fancy that he takes a morbid pleasure in exaggerating their weak points, in painting them on their worst days; but I honestly believe he can't help himself. His peculiar limitations prevent his seeing anything but the most prosaic side of human nature—

> *"A primrose by the river's brim*
> *A yellow primrose is to him,*
> *And it is nothing more."*

Cumberton looked round to surprise an order in the eye of the lady whose sentiments he had so deftly interpreted, but poetry always made her uncomfortable, and her nomadic attention had strayed to other topics. His glance was tripped up by Mrs. Mellish.

"Limitations? But, my dear man, it's because he hasn't any limitations, because he doesn't wear the portrait-painter's conventional blinders, that we're all so afraid of being painted by him. It's not because he sees only one aspect of his sitters, it's because he selects the real, the typical one, as instinctively as a detective collars a pick-pocket in a crowd. If there's nothing to paint—no real person—he paints nothing; look at the sumptuous emptiness of his portrait of Mrs. Guy Awdrey"—("Why," the pretty woman perplexedly interjected, "that's the only nice picture he ever did!") "If there's one positive trait in a negative whole he brings it out in spite of himself; if it isn't a nice trait, so much the worse for the sitter; it isn't Lillo's fault: he's no more to blame than a mirror. Your other painters do the surface—he does the depths; they paint the ripples on the pond, he drags the bottom. He makes flesh seem as fortuitous as clothes. When I look at his portraits of fine ladies in pearls and velvet I seem to see a little naked cowering wisp of a soul sitting beside the big splendid body, like a poor relation in the darkest corner of an opera-box. But look at his pictures of really great people— how great *they* are! There's plenty of ideal there. Take his Professor Clyde; how clearly the man's history is written in those broad steady strokes of the brush: the hard work, the endless patience, the fearless imagination of the great savant! Or the picture of Mr. Domfrey—the man who has felt beauty without having the power to create it. The very brush- work expresses the difference between the two; the crowding of nervous tentative lines, the subtler gradations of color, somehow convey a suggestion of dilettantism. You feel what a delicate instrument the man is, how every sense has been tuned to the finest responsiveness." Mrs. Mellish paused, blushing a little at the echo of her own eloquence. "My advice is, don't let George Lillo paint you if you don't want to be found out—or to find yourself out. That's why I've never let him do *me*; I'm waiting for the day of judgment," she ended with a laugh.

Every ne but the pretty woman, whose eyes betrayed a quivering impatience to discuss clothes, had listened attentively to Mrs. Mellish. Lillo's presence in New York— he had come over from Paris for the first time in twelve years, to arrange the exhibition of his pictures—gave to the analysis of his methods as personal a flavor as though one had been furtively dissecting his domestic relations. The analogy, indeed, is not unapt; for in Lillo's curiously detached existence it is difficult to figure any closer tie than that which unites him to his pictures. In this light, Mrs. Mellish's flushed harangue seemed not unfitted to the trivialities of the tea hour, and some one almost at once carried on the argument by saying:—"But according to your theory—that the significance of his work depends on the significance of the sitter—his portrait of Vard ought to be a master-piece; and it's his biggest failure."

Alonzo Vard's suicide—he killed himself, strangely enough, the day that Lillo's pictures were first shown—had made his portrait the chief feature of the exhibition. It had been painted ten or twelve years earlier, when the terrible "Boss" was at the height of his power; and if ever man presented a type to stimulate such insight as Lillo's, that man was Vard; yet the portrait was a failure. It was magnificently composed; the technique was dazzling; but the face had been—well, expurgated. It was Vard as Cumberton might have painted him—a common man trying to look at ease in a good coat. The picture had never before been exhibited, and there was a general outcry of disappointment. It wasn't only the critics and the artists who grumbled. Even the big public, which had gaped and shuddered at Vard, reveling in his genial villainy, and enjoying in his death that succumbing to divine wrath which, as a spectacle, is next best to its successful defiance—even the public felt itself defrauded. What had the painter done with their hero? Where was the big sneering domineering face that figured so convincingly in political cartoons and patent-medicine advertisements, on cigar-boxes and electioneering posters? They had admired the man for looking his part so boldly; for showing the undisguised blackguard in every line of his coarse body and cruel face; the pseudo-gentleman of Lillo's picture was a poor thing compared to the real Vard. It had been vaguely expected that the great boss's portrait would have the zest of an incriminating document, the scandalous attraction of secret memoirs; and instead, it was as insipid as an obituary. It was as though the artist had been in league with his sitter, had pledged himself to oppose to the lust for post-mortem "revelations" an impassable blank wall of negation. The public was resentful, the critics were aggrieved. Even Mrs. Mellish had to lay down her arms.

"Yes, the portrait of Vard *is* a failure," she admitted, "and I've never known why. If he'd been an obscure elusive type of villain, one could understand Lillo's missing the mark for once; but with that face from the pit—!"

She turned at the announcement of a name which our discussion had drowned, and found herself shaking hands with Lillo.

The pretty woman started and put her hands to her curls; Cumberton dropped a condescending eyelid (he never classed himself by recognizing degrees in the profession), and Mrs. Mellish, cheerfully aware that she had been overheard, said, as she made room for Lillo—

"I wish you'd explain it."

Lillo smoothed his beard and waited for a cup of tea. Then, "Would there be any failures," he said, "if one could explain them?"

"Ah, in some cases I can imagine it's impossible to seize the type—or to say why one has missed it. Some people are like daguerreotypes; in certain lights one can't see them at all. But surely Vard was obvious enough. What I want to know is, what became of him? What did you do with him? How did you manage to shuffle him out of sight?"

"It was much easier than you think. I simply missed an opportunity—"

"That a sign-painter would have seen!"

"Very likely. In fighting shy of the obvious one may miss the significant—"

"—And when I got back from Paris," the pretty woman was heard to wail, "I found all the women here were wearing the very models I'd brought home with me!"

Mrs. Mellish, as became a vigilant hostess, got up and shuffled her guests; and the question of Vard's portrait was dropped.

I left the house with Lillo; and on the way down Fifth Avenue, after one of his long silences, he suddenly asked:

"Is that what is generally said of my picture of Vard? I don't mean in the newspapers, but by the fellows who know?"

I said it was.

He drew a deep breath. "Well," he said, "it's good to know that when one tries to fail one can make such a complete success of it."

"Tries to fail?"

"Well, no; that's not quite it, either; I didn't want to make a failure of Vard's picture, but I did so deliberately, with my eyes open, all the same. It was what one might call a lucid failure."

"But why—?"

"The why of it is rather complicated. I'll tell you some time—" He hesitated. "Come and dine with me at the club by and by, and I'll tell you afterwards. It's a nice morsel for a psychologist."

At dinner he said little; but I didn't mind that. I had known him for years, and had always found something soothing and companionable in his long abstentions from speech. His silence was never unsocial; it was bland as a natural hush; one felt one's self included in it, not left out. He stroked his beard and gazed absently at me; and when we had finished our coffee and liqueurs we strolled down to his studio.

At the studio—which was less draped, less posed, less consciously "artistic" than those of the smaller men—he handed me a cigar, and fell to smoking before the fire. When he began to talk it was of indifferent matters, and I had dismissed the hope of hearing more of Vard's portrait, when my eye lit on a photograph of the picture. I walked across the room to look at it, and Lillo presently followed with a light.

"It certainly is a complete disguise," he muttered over my shoulder; then he turned away and stooped to a big portfolio propped against the wall.

"Did you ever know Miss Vard?" he asked, with his head in the portfolio; and without waiting for my answer he handed me a crayon sketch of a girl's profile.

I had never seen a crayon of Lillo's, and I lost sight of the sitter's personality in the interest aroused by this new aspect of the master's complex genius. The few lines—faint, yet how decisive!—flowered out of the rough paper with the lightness of opening petals. It was a mere hint of a picture, but vivid as some word that wakens long reverberations in the memory.

I felt Lillo at my shoulder again.

"You knew her, I suppose?"

I had to stop and think. Why, of course I'd known her: a silent handsome girl, showy yet ineffective, whom I had seen without seeing the winter that society had capitulated to Vard. Still looking at the crayon, I tried to trace some connection between the Miss Vard I recalled and the grave young seraph of Lillo's sketch. Had the Vards bewitched him? By what masterstroke of suggestion had he been beguiled into drawing the terrible father as a barber's block, the commonplace daughter as this memorable creature?

"You don't remember much about her? No, I suppose not. She was a quiet girl and nobody noticed her much, even when—" he paused with a smile— "you were all asking Vard to dine."

I winced. Yes, it was true—we had all asked Vard to dine. It was some comfort to think that fate had made him expiate our weakness.

Lillo put the sketch on the mantel-shelf and drew his arm-chair to the fire.

"It's cold to-night. Take another cigar, old man; and some whiskey? There ought to be a bottle and some glasses in that cupboard behind you. Help yourself."

II

ABOUT Vard's portrait? (He began.) Well, I'll tell you. It's a queer story, and most people wouldn't see anything in it. My enemies might say it was a roundabout way of explaining a failure; but you know better than that. Mrs. Mellish was right. Between me and Vard there could be no question of failure. The man was made for me—I felt that the first time I clapped eyes on him. I could hardly keep from asking him to sit to me on the spot; but somehow one couldn't ask favors of the fellow. I sat still and prayed he'd come to me, though; for I was looking for something big for the next Salon. It was twelve years ago—the last time I was out here—and I was ravenous for an opportunity. I had the feeling—do you writer-fellows have it too?—that there was something tremendous in me if it could only be got out; and I felt Vard was the Moses to strike the rock. There were vulgar reasons, too, that made me hunger for a victim. I'd been grinding on obscurely for a good many years, without gold or glory, and the first thing of mine that had made a noise was my picture of Pepita, exhibited the year before. There'd been a lot of talk about that, orders were beginning to come in, and I wanted to follow it up with a rousing big thing at the next Salon. Then the critics had been insinuating that I could do only Spanish things—I suppose I *had* overdone the castanet business; it's a nursery-disease we all go through—and I wanted to show that I had plenty more shot in my locker. Don't you get up every morning meaning to prove you're equal to Balzac or Thackeray? That's the way I felt then; *only give me a chance*, I wanted to shout out to them; and I saw at once that Vard was my chance.

I had come over from Paris in the autumn to paint Mrs. Clingsborough, and I met Vard and his daughter at one of the first dinners I went to. After that I could think of nothing but that man's head. What a type! I raked up all the details of his scandalous history; and there were enough to fill an encyclopedia. The papers were full of him just then; he was mud from head to foot; it was about the time of the big viaduct steal, and irreproachable citizens were forming ineffectual leagues to put him down. And all the time one kept meeting him at dinners—that was the beauty of it! Once I remember seeing him next to the Bishop's wife; I've got a little sketch of that duet somewhere . . . Well, he was simply magnificent, a born ruler; what a splendid condottiere he would have made, in gold armor, with a griffin grinning on his casque! You remember those drawings of Leonardo's, where the knight's face and the outline of his helmet combine in one monstrous saurian profile? He always reminded me of that. . . .

But how was I to get at him?—One day it occurred to me to try talking to Miss Vard. She was a monosyllabic person, who didn't seem to see an inch beyond the last remark one had made; but suddenly I found myself blurting out, "I wonder if you know how extraordinarily paintable your father is?" and you should have seen the change that came over her. Her eyes lit up and she looked—well, as I've tried to make her look there. (He glanced up at the sketch.) Yes, she said, *wasn't* her father splendid, and didn't I think him one of the handsomest men I'd ever seen?

That rather staggered me, I confess; I couldn't think her capable of joking on such a subject, yet it seemed impossible that she should be speaking seriously. But she was. I knew it by the way she looked at Vard, who was sitting opposite, his wolfish profile thrown back, the shaggy locks tossed off his narrow high white forehead. The girl worshipped him.

She went on to say how glad she was that I saw him as she did. So many artists admired only regular beauty, the stupid Greek type that was made to be done in marble; but she'd always fancied from what she'd seen of my work—she knew everything I'd done, it appeared—that I looked deeper, cared more for the way in which faces are modeled by temperament and circumstance; "and of course in that sense," she concluded, "my father's face *is* beautiful."

This was even more staggering; but one couldn't question her divine sincerity. I'm afraid my one thought was to take advantage of it; and I let her go on, perceiving that if I wanted to paint Vard all I had to do was to listen.

She poured out her heart. It was a glorious thing for a girl, she said, wasn't it, to be associated with such a life as that? She felt it so strongly, sometimes, that it oppressed her, made her shy and stupid. She was so afraid people would expect her to live up to *him*. But that was absurd, of course; brilliant men so seldom had clever children. Still— did I know?—she would have been happier, much happier, if he hadn't been in public life; if he and she could have hidden themselves away somewhere, with their books and music, and she could have had it all to herself: his cleverness, his learning, his immense unbounded goodness. For no one knew how good he was; no one but herself. Everybody recognized his cleverness, his brilliant abilities; even his enemies had to admit his extraordinary intellectual gifts, and hated him the worse, of course, for the admission; but no one, no one could guess what he was at home. She had heard of great men who were always giving gala performances in public, but whose wives and daughters saw only the empty theatre, with the footlights out and the scenery stacked in the wings; but with him it was just the other way: wonderful as he was in public, in society, she sometimes felt he wasn't doing himself justice—he was so much more wonderful at home. It was like carrying a guilty secret about with her: his friends, his admirers, would never forgive her if they found out that he kept all his best things for *her!*

I don't quite know what I felt in listening to her. I was chiefly taken up with leading her on to the point I had in view; but even through my personal preoccupation I remember being struck by the fact that, though she talked foolishly, she didn't talk like a fool. She was not stupid; she was not obtuse; one felt that her impassive surface was alive with delicate points of perception; and this fact, coupled with her crystalline frankness, flung me back on a startled revision of my impressions of her father. He came out of the test more monstrous than ever, as an ugly image reflected in clear water is made uglier by the purity of the medium. Even then I felt a pang at the use to which fate had put the mountain-pool of Miss Vard's spirit, and an uneasy sense that my own reflection there was not one to linger over. It was odd that I should have scrupled to deceive, on one small point, a girl already so hugely cheated; perhaps it was the completeness of her delusion that gave it the sanctity of a religious belief. At any rate, a distinct sense of discomfort tempered the satisfaction with which, a day or two later, I heard from her that her father had consented to give me a few sittings.

I'm afraid my scruples vanished when I got him before my easel. He was immense, and he was unexplored. From my point of view he'd never been done before—I was his Cortez. As he talked the wonder grew. His daughter came with him, and I began to think she was right in saying that he kept his best for her. It wasn't that she drew him out, or guided the conversation; but one had a sense of delicate vigilance, hardly more perceptible than one of those atmospheric influences that give the pulses a happier turn. She was a vivifying climate. I had meant to turn the talk to public affairs, but it slipped toward books and art, and I was faintly aware of its being kept there without undue pressure. Before long I saw the value of the diversion. It was easy enough to get at the political Vard: the other aspect was rarer and more instructive. His daughter had described him as a scholar. He wasn't that, of course, in any intrinsic sense: like most men of his type he had gulped his knowledge standing, as he had snatched his food from lunch-counters; the wonder of it lay in his extraordinary power of assimilation. It was the strangest instance of a mind to which erudition had given force and fluency without culture; his learning had not educated his perceptions: it was an implement serving to slash others rather than to polish himself. I have said that at first sight he was immense; but as I studied him he began to lessen under my scrutiny. His depth was a false perspective painted on a wall.

It was there that my difficulty lay: I had prepared too big a canvas for him. Intellectually his scope was considerable, but it was like the digital reach of a mediocre pianist—it didn't make him a great musician. And morally he wasn't bad enough; his corruption wasn't sufficiently imaginative to be interesting. It was not so much a means to an end as a kind of virtuosity practiced for its own sake, like a highly-developed skill in cannoning billiard balls. After all, the point of view is what gives distinction to either vice or virtue: a morality with ground-glass windows is no duller than a narrow cynicism.

His daughter's presence—she always came with him—gave unintentional emphasis to these conclusions; for where she was richest he was naked. She had a deep-rooted delicacy that drew color and perfume from the very center of her being: his sentiments, good or bad, were as detachable as his cuffs. Thus her nearness, planned, as I guessed, with the tender intention of displaying, elucidating him, of making him accessible in detail to my dazzled perceptions—this pious design in fact defeated itself. She made him appear at his best, but she cheapened that best by her proximity. For the man was vulgar to the core; vulgar in spite of his force and magnitude; thin, hollow, spectacular; a lath-and-plaster bogey.

Did she suspect it? I think not—then. He was wrapped in her impervious faith... The papers? Oh, their charges were set down to political rivalry; and the only people she saw were his hangers-on, or the fashionable set who had taken him up for their amusement. Besides, she would never have found out in that way: at a direct accusation her resentment would have flamed up and smothered her judgment. If the truth came to her, it would come through knowing intimately some one—different; through—how shall I put it?—an imperceptible shifting of her center of gravity. My besetting fear was that I couldn't count on her obtuseness. She wasn't what is called clever; she left that to him; but she was exquisitely good; and now and then she had intuitive felicities that frightened me. Do I make you see her? We fellows can explain better with the brush; I don't know how to mix my words or lay them on. She wasn't clever; but her heart thought— that's all I can say.

If she'd been stupid it would have been easy enough: I could have painted him as he was. Could have? I did—brushed the face in one day from memory; it was the very man! I painted it out before she came: I couldn't bear to have her see it. I had the feeling that I held her faith in him in my hands, carrying it like a brittle object through a jostling mob; a hair's- breadth swerve and it was in splinters.

When she wasn't there I tried to reason myself out of these subtleties. My business was to paint Vard as he was—if his daughter didn't mind his looks, why should I? The opportunity was magnificent—I knew that by the way his face had leapt out of the canvas at my first touch. It would have been a big thing. Before every sitting I swore to myself I'd do it; then she came, and sat near him, and I—didn't.

I knew that before long she'd notice I was shirking the face. Vard himself took little interest in the portrait, but she watched me closely, and one day when the sitting was over she stayed behind and asked me when I meant to begin what she called "the likeness." I guessed from her tone that the embarrassment was all on my side, or that if she felt any it was at having to touch a vulnerable point in my pride. Thus far the only doubt that troubled her was a distrust of my ability. Well, I put her off with any rot you please: told her she must trust me, must let me wait for the inspiration; that some day the face would come; I should see it suddenly— feel it under my brush . . . The poor child believed me: you can make a woman believe almost anything she doesn't quite understand. She was abashed at her philistinism, and begged me not to tell her father—he would make such fun of her!

After that—well, the sittings went on. Not many, of course; Vard was too busy to give me much time. Still, I could have done him ten times over. Never had I found my formula with such ease, such assurance; there were no hesitations, no obstructions—the face was *there*, waiting for me; at times it almost shaped itself on the canvas. Unfortunately Miss Vard was there too...

All this time the papers were busy with the viaduct scandal. The outcry was getting louder. You remember the circumstances? One of Vard's associates—Bardwell, wasn't it?—threatened disclosures. The rival machine got hold of him, the Independents took him to their bosom, and the press shrieked for an investigation. It was not the first storm Vard had weathered, and his face wore just the right shade of cool vigilance; he wasn't the man to fall into the mistake of appearing too easy. His demeanor would have been superb if it had been inspired by a sense of his own strength; but it struck me rather as based on contempt for his antagonists. Success is an inverted telescope through which one's enemies are apt to look too small and too remote. As for Miss Vard, her serenity was undiminished; but I half-detected a defiance in her unruffled sweetness, and during the last sittings I had the factitious vivacity of a hostess who hears her best china crashing.

One day it *did* crash: the head-lines of the morning papers shouted the catastrophe at me:—"The Monster forced to disgorge—Warrant out against Vard—Bardwell the Boss's Boomerang"—you know the kind of thing.

When I had read the papers I threw them down and went out. As it happened, Vard was to have given me a sitting that morning; but there would have been a certain irony in waiting for him. I wished I had finished the picture—I wished I'd never thought of painting it. I wanted to shake off the whole business, to put it out of my mind, if I could: I had the feeling—I don't know if I can describe it—that there was a kind of disloyalty to the poor girl in my even acknowledging to myself that I knew what all the papers were howling from the housetops.

I had walked for an hour when it suddenly occurred to me that Miss Vard might, after all, come to the studio at the appointed hour. Why should she? I could conceive of no reason; but the mere thought of what, if she *did* come, my absence would imply to her, sent me bolting back to Twelfth Street. It was a presentiment, if you like, for she was there.

As she rose to meet me a newspaper slipped from her hand: I'd been fool enough, when I went out, to leave the damned things lying all over the place.

I muttered some apology for being late, and she said reassuringly:

"But my father's not here yet."

"Your father—?" I could have kicked myself for the way I bungled it!

"He went out very early this morning, and left word that he would meet me here at the usual hour."

She faced me, with an eye full of bright courage, across the newspaper lying between us.

"He ought to be here in a moment now—he's always so punctual. But my watch is a little fast, I think."

She held it out to me almost gaily, and I was just pretending to compare it with mine, when there was a smart rap on the door and Vard stalked in. There was always a civic majesty in his gait, an air of having just stepped off his pedestal and of dissembling an oration in his umbrella; and that day he surpassed himself. Miss Vard had turned pale at the knock; but the mere sight of him replenished her veins, and if she now avoided my eye, it was in mere pity for my discomfiture.

I was in fact the only one of the three who didn't instantly "play up"; but such virtuosity was inspiring, and by the time Vard had thrown off his coat and dropped into a senatorial pose, I was ready to pitch into my work. I swore I'd do his face then and there; do it as she saw it; she sat close to him, and I had only to glance at her while I painted.

Vard himself was masterly: his talk rattled through my hesitations and embarrassments like a brisk northwester sweeping the dry leaves from its path. Even his daughter showed the sudden brilliance of a lamp from which the shade has been removed. We were all surprisingly vivid—it felt, somehow, as though we were being photographed by flash-light.

It was the best sitting we'd ever had—but unfortunately it didn't last more than ten minutes.

It was Vard's secretary who interrupted us—a slinking chap called Cornley, who burst in, as white as sweetbread, with the face of a depositor who hears his bank has stopped payment. Miss Vard started up as he entered, but caught herself together and dropped back into her chair. Vard, who had taken out a cigarette, held the tip tranquilly to his fusee.

"You're here, thank God!" Cornley cried. "There's no time to be lost, Mr. Vard. I've got a carriage waiting round the corner in Thirteenth Street—"

Vard looked at the tip of his cigarette.

"A carriage in Thirteenth Street? My good fellow, my own brougham is at the door."

"I know, I know—but *they're* there too, sir; or they will be, inside of a minute. For God's sake, Mr. Vard, don't trifle!—There's a way out by Thirteenth Street, I tell you"—

"Bardwell's myrmidons, eh?" said Vard. "Help me on with my overcoat, Cornley, will you?"

Cornley's teeth chattered.

"Mr. Vard, your best friends . . . Miss Vard, won't you speak to your father?" He turned to me haggardly;—"We can get out by the back way?"

I nodded.

Vard stood towering—in some infernal way he seemed literally to rise to the situation—one hand in the bosom of his coat, in the attitude of patriotism in bronze. I glanced at his daughter: she hung on him with a drowning look. Suddenly she straightened herself; there was something of Vard in the way she faced her fears—a kind of primitive calm we drawing-room folk don't have. She stepped to him and laid her hand on his arm. The pause hadn't lasted ten seconds.

"Father—" she said.

Vard threw back his head and swept the studio with a sovereign eye.

"The back way, Mr. Vard, the back way," Cornley whimpered. "For God's sake, sir, don't lose a minute."

Vard transfixed his abject henchman.

"I have never yet taken the back way," he enunciated; and, with a gesture matching the words, he turned to me and bowed.

"I regret the disturbance"—and he walked to the door. His daughter was at his side, alert, transfigured.

"Stay here, my dear."

"Never!"

They measured each other an instant; then he drew her arm in his. She flung back one look at me—a paean of victory—and they passed out with Cornley at their heels.

I wish I'd finished the face then; I believe I could have caught something of the look she had tried to make me see in him. Unluckily I was too excited to work that day or the next, and within the week the whole business came out. If the indictment wasn't a put-up job—and on that I believe there were two opinions—all that followed was. You remember the farcical trial, the packed jury, the compliant judge, the triumphant acquittal? . . . It's a spectacle that always carries conviction to the voter: Vard was never more popular than after his "exoneration.". . .

I didn't see Miss Vard for weeks. It was she who came to me at length; came to the studio alone, one afternoon at dusk. She had—what shall I say?—a veiled manner; as though she had dropped a fine gauze between us. I waited for her to speak.

She glanced about the room, admiring a hawthorn vase I had picked up at auction. Then, after a pause, she said:

"You haven't finished the picture?"

"Not quite," I said.

She asked to see it, and I wheeled out the easel and threw the drapery back.

"Oh," she murmured, "you haven't gone on with the face?"

I shook my head.

She looked down on her clasped hands and up at the picture; not once at me.

"You—you're going to finish it?"

"Of course," I cried, throwing the revived purpose into my voice. By God, I would finish it!

The merest tinge of relief stole over her face, faint as the first thin chirp before daylight.

"Is it so very difficult?" she asked tentatively.

"Not insuperably, I hope."

She sat silent, her eyes on the picture. At length, with an effort, she brought out: "Shall you want more sittings?"

For a second I blundered between two conflicting conjectures; then the truth came to me with a leap, and I cried out, "No, no more sittings!"

She looked up at me then for the first time; looked too soon, poor child; for in the spreading light of reassurance that made her eyes like a rainy dawn, I saw, with terrible distinctness, the rout of her disbanded hopes. I knew that she knew. . . .

I finished the picture and sent it home within a week. I tried to make it —what you see.—Too late, you say? Yes—for her; but not for me or for the public. If she could be made to feel, for a day longer, for an hour even, that her miserable secret *was* a secret— why, she'd made it seem worth while to me to chuck my own ambitions for that. . . .

Lillo rose, and taking down the sketch stood looking at it in silence.

After a while I ventured, "And Miss Vard—?"

He opened the portfolio and put the sketch back, tying the strings with deliberation. Then, turning to relight his cigar at the lamp, he said: "She died last year, thank God."

## EARLY UNCOLLECTED STORIES (1900)

### APRIL SHOWERS

As first published in *The Youth's Companion*, January 18, 900

"BUT GUY'S HEART slept under the violets on Muriel's grave."

It was a beautiful ending; Theodora had seen girls cry over last chapters that weren't half as pathetic. She laid her pen aside and read the words over, letting her voice linger on the fall of the sentence; then, drawing a deep breath, she wrote across the foot of the page the name by which she had decided to become known in literature—Gladys Glyn.

Downstairs the library clock struck two. Its muffled thump sounded like an admonitory knock against her bedroom floor. Two o'clock! and she had promised her mother to be up early enough to see that the buttons were sewn on Johnny's reefer, and that Kate had her cod-liver oil before starting for school!

Lingeringly, tenderly she gathered up the pages of her novel,—there were five hundred of them,—and tied them with the blue satin ribbon that her Aunt Julia had given her. She had meant to wear the ribbon with her new dotted muslin on Sundays, but this was putting it to a nobler use. She bound it round her manuscript, tying the ends in a pretty bow. Theodora was clever at making bows, and could have trimmed hats beautifully, had not all her spare moments been given to literature. Then, with a last look at the precious pages, she sealed and addressed the package. She meant to send it off next morning to the *Home Circle*. She knew it would be hard to obtain access to a paper which numbered so many popular authors among its contributors, but she had been encouraged to make the venture by something her Uncle James had said the last time he had come down from Boston.

He had been telling his brother, Doctor Dace, about his new house out at Brookline. Uncle James was prosperous, and was always moving into new houses with more "modern improvements." Hygiene was his passion, and he migrated in the wake of sanitary plumbing.

"The bathrooms alone are worth the money," he was saying, cheerfully, "although it is a big rent. But then, when a man's got no children to save up for—" he glanced compassionately round Doctor Dace's crowded table—"and it *is* something to be in a neighborhood where the drainage is A 1. That's what I was telling our neighbor. Who do you suppose she is, by the way?" He smiled at Theodora. "I rather think that young lady knows all about her. Ever hear of Kathleen Kyd?"

Kathleen Kyd! The famous "society novelist," the creator of more "favorite heroines" than all her predecessors put together had ever turned out; the author of *Fashion and Passion, An American Duchess, Rhona's Revolt*. Was there any intelligent girl from Maine to California whose heart would not have beat faster at the mention of that name?

"Why, yes," Uncle James was saying, "Kathleen Kyd lives next door. Frances G. Wollop is her real name, and her husband's a dentist. She's a very pleasant, sociable kind of woman; you'd never think she was a writer. Ever hear how she began to write? She told me the whole story. It seems she was saleswoman in a store, working on starvation wages, with a mother and a consumptive sister to support. Well, she wrote a story one day, just for fun, and sent it to the *Home Circle*. They'd never heard of her, of course, and she never expected to hear from them. She did, though. They took the story and passed their plate for more. She became a regular contributor and eventually was known all over the country. Now she tells me her books bring her in about ten thousand a year. Rather more than you and I can boast of, eh, John? Well, I hope *this* household doesn't contribute to her support." He glanced sharply at Theodora. "I don't believe in feeding youngsters on sentimental trash; it's like sewer-gas—doesn't smell bad, and infects the system without your knowing it."

Theodora listened breathlessly. Kathleen Kyd's first story had been accepted by the *Home Circle*, and they had asked for more! Why should Gladys Glyn be less fortunate? Theodora had done a great deal of novel-reading,—far more than her parents were aware of,—and felt herself competent to pronounce upon the quality of her own work. She was almost sure that "April Showers" was a remarkable book. If it lacked Kathleen Kyd's lightness of touch, it had an emotional intensity never achieved by that brilliant writer. Theodora did not care to amuse her readers; she left that to more frivolous talents. Her aim was to stir the depths of human nature, and she felt she had succeeded. It was a great thing for a girl to be able to feel that about her first novel. Theodora was only seventeen; and she remembered, with a touch of retrospective compassion, that George Eliot had not become famous till she was nearly forty.

No, there was no doubt about the merit of "April Showers." But would not an inferior work have had a better chance of success? Theodora recalled the early struggles of famous authors, the notorious antagonism of publishers and editors to any new writer of exceptional promise. Would it not be wiser to write the book down to the average reader's level, reserving for some later work the great "effects" into which she had thrown all the fervor of her imagination? The thought was sacrilege! Never would she lay hands on the sacred structure she had reared; never would she resort to the inartistic expedient of modifying her work to suit the popular taste. Better obscure failure than a vulgar triumph. The great authors never stooped to such concessions, and Theodora felt herself included in their ranks by the firmness with which she rejected all thought of conciliating an unappreciative public. The manuscript should be sent as it was.

She woke with a start and a heavy sense of apprehension. The *Home Circle* had refused "April Showers!" No, that couldn't be it; there lay the precious manuscript, waiting to be posted. What was it, then? Ah, that ominous thump below stairs—nine o'clock striking! It was Johnny's buttons!

She sprang out of bed in dismay. She had been so determined not to disappoint her mother about Johnny's buttons! Mrs. Dace, helpless from chronic rheumatism, had to entrust the care of the household to her eldest daughter; and Theodora honestly meant to see that Johnny had his full complement of buttons, and that Kate and Bertha went to school tidy. Unfortunately, the writing of a great novel leaves little time or memory for the lesser obligations of life, and Theodora usually found that her good intentions matured too late for practical results.

Her contrition was softened by the thought that literary success would enable her to make up for all the little negligences of which she was guilty. She meant to spend all her money on her family; and already she had visions of a wheeled chair for her mother, a fresh wallpaper for the doctor's shabby office, bicycles for the girls, and Johnny's establishment at a boarding-school where sewing on his buttons would be included in the curriculum. If her parents could have guessed her intentions, they would not have found fault with her as they did: and Doctor Dace, on this particular morning, would not have looked up to say, with his fagged, ironical air:

"I suppose you didn't get home from the ball till morning."

Theodora's sense of being in the right enabled her to take the thrust with a dignity that would have awed the unfeeling parent of fiction.

"I'm sorry to be late, father," she said.

Doctor Dace, who could never be counted on to behave like a father in a book, shrugged his shoulders impatiently.

"Your sentiments do you credit, but they haven't kept your mother's breakfast warm."

"Hasn't mother's tray gone up yet?"

"Who was to take it, I should like to know? The girls came down so late that I had to hustle them off before they'd finished breakfast, and Johnny's hands were so dirty that I sent him back to his room to make himself decent. It's a pretty thing for the doctor's children to be the dirtiest little savages in Norton!"

Theodora had hastily prepared her mother's tray, leaving her own breakfast untouched. As she entered the room up-stairs, Mrs. Dace's patient face turned to her with a smile much harder to bear than her father's reproaches.

"Mother, I'm *so* sorry—"

"No matter, dear. I suppose Johnny's buttons kept you. I can't think what that boy does to his clothes!"

Theodora set the tray down without speaking. It was impossible to own to having forgotten Johnny's buttons without revealing the cause of her forgetfulness. For a few weeks longer she must bear to be misunderstood; then—ah, then if her novel were accepted, how gladly would she forget and forgive! But what if it were refused? She turned aside to hide the dismay that flushed her face. Well, then she would admit the truth—she would ask her parents' pardon, and settle down without a murmur to an obscure existence of mending and combing.

She had said to herself that after the manuscript had been sent, she would have time to look after the children and catch up with the mending; but she had reckoned without the postman. He came three times a day; and for an hour before each ring she was too excited to do anything but wonder if he would bring an answer this time, and for an hour afterward she moved about in a leaden stupor of disappointment. The children had never been so trying. They seemed to be always coming to pieces, like cheap furniture; one would have supposed they had been put together with bad glue. Mrs. Dace worried herself ill over Johnny's tatters, Bertha's bad marks at school, and Kate's open abstention from cod-liver oil; and Doctor Dace, coming back late from a long round of visits to a fireless office with a smoky lamp, called out furiously to know if Theodora would kindly come down and remove the "East, West, home's best" that hung above the empty grate.

In the midst of it all, Miss Sophy Brill called. It was very kind of her to come, for she was the busiest woman in Norton. She made it her duty to look after other people's affairs, and there was not a house in town but had the benefit of her personal supervision. She generally came when things were going wrong, and the sight of her bonnet on the door-step was a surer sign of calamity than a crape bow on the bell. After she left, Mrs. Dace looked very sad, and the doctor punished Johnny for warbling down the entry:

*"Miss Sophy Brill
Is a bitter pill!"*

while Theodora, locking herself in her room, resolved with tears that she would never write another novel.

The week was a long nightmare. Theodora could neither eat nor sleep. She was up early enough, but instead of looking after the children and seeing that breakfast was ready, she wandered down the road to meet the postman, and came back wan and empty-handed, oblivious of her morning duties. She had no idea how long the suspense would last; but she didn't see how authors could live if they were kept waiting more than a week.

Then suddenly, one afternoon—she never quite knew how or when it happened—she found herself with a *Home Circle* envelope in her hands, and her dazzled eyes flashing over a wild dance of words that wouldn't settle down and make sense.

"Dear Madam:" [They called her *Madam!* And then; yes, the words were beginning to fall into line now.] "Your novel, 'April Showers,' has been received, and we are glad to accept it on the usual terms. A serial on which we were counting for immediate publication has been delayed by the author's illness, and the first chapters of 'April Showers' will therefore appear in our midsummer number. Thanking you for favoring us with your manuscript, we remain," and so forth.

Theodora found herself in the wood beyond the schoolhouse. She was kneeling on the ground, brushing aside the dead leaves and pressing her lips to the little bursting green things that pushed up eager tips through last year's decay. It was spring—spring! Everything was crowding toward the light, and in her own heart hundreds of germinating hopes had burst into sudden leaf. She wondered if the thrust of those little green fingers hurt the surface of the earth as her springing raptures hurt—yes, actually hurt!—her hot, constricted breast! She looked up through interlacing boughs at a tender, opaque blue sky full of the coming of a milky moon. She seemed enveloped in an atmosphere of loving comprehension. The brown earth throbbed with her joy, the tree-tops trembled with it, and a sudden star broke through the branches like an audible "I know!"

Theodora, on the whole, behaved very well. Her mother cried, her father whistled and said he supposed he must put up with grounds in his coffee now, and be thankful if he ever got a hot meal again; while the children took the most deafening and harassing advantage of what seemed a sudden suspension of the laws of nature.

Within a week everybody in Norton knew that Theodora had written a novel, and that it was coming out in the *Home Circle*. On Sundays, when she walked up the aisle, her friends dropped their prayer-books and the soprano sang false in her excitement. Girls with more pin-money than Theodora had ever dreamed of copied her hats and imitated her way of speaking. The local paper asked her for a poem; her old school-teachers stopped to shake hands and grew shy over their congratulations; and Miss Sophy Brill came to call. She had put on her Sunday bonnet, and her manner was almost abject. She ventured, very timidly, to ask her young friend how she wrote, whether it "just came to her," and if she had found that the kind of pen she used made any difference; and wound up by begging Theodora to write a sentiment in her album.

Even Uncle James came down from Boston to talk the wonder over. He called Theodora a "sly baggage," and proposed that she should give him her earnings to invest in a new patent grease-trap company. From what Kathleen Kyd had told him, he thought

Theodora would probably get a thousand dollars for her story. He concluded by suggesting that she should base her next romance on the subject of sanitation, making the heroine nearly die of sewer-gas poisoning because her parents won't listen to the handsome young doctor next door, when he warns them that their plumbing is out of order. That was a subject that would interest everybody, and do a lot more good than the sentimental trash most women wrote.

At last the great day came. Theodora had left an order with the bookseller for the midsummer number of the *Home Circle*, and before the shop was open she was waiting on the sidewalk. She clutched the precious paper and ran home without opening it. Her excitement was almost more than she could bear. Not heeding her father's call to breakfast, she rushed up-stairs and locked herself in her room. Her hands trembled so that she could hardly turn the pages. At last—yes, there it was: "April Showers."

The paper dropped from her hands. What name had she read beneath the title? Had her emotion blinded her?

"April Showers, by *Kathleen Kyd*."

Kathleen Kyd! Oh, cruel misprint! Oh, dastardly typographer! Through tears of rage and disappointment Theodora looked again: yes, there was no mistaking the hateful name. Her glance ran on. She found herself reading a first paragraph that she had never seen before. She read farther. All was strange. The horrible truth burst upon her: *It was not her story!*

She never knew how she got back to the station. She struggled through the crowd on the platform, and a gold-banded arm pushed her into the train just starting for Norton. It would be dark when she reached home; but that didn't matter—nothing mattered now. She sank into her seat, closing her eyes in the vain attempt to shut out the vision of the last few hours; but minute by minute memory forced her to relive it; she felt like a rebellious school child dragged forth to repeat the same detested "piece."

Although she did not know Boston well, she had made her way easily enough to the *Home Circle* building; at least, she supposed she had, since she remembered nothing till she found herself ascending the editorial stairs as easily as one does incredible things in dreams. She must have walked very fast, for her heart was beating furiously, and she had barely breath to whisper the editor's name to a young man who looked out at her from a glass case, like a zoological specimen. The young man led her past other glass cases containing similar specimens to an inner enclosure which seemed filled by an enormous presence. Theodora felt herself enveloped in the presence, submerged by it, gasping for air as she sank under its rising surges.

Gradually fragments of speech floated to the surface. "'April Showers?' Mrs. Kyd's new serial? *Your* manuscript, you say? You have a letter from me? The name, please? Evidently some unfortunate misunderstanding. One moment." And then a bell ringing, a zoological specimen ordered to unlock a safe, her name asked for again, the manuscript, her own precious manuscript, tied with Aunt Julia's ribbon, laid on the table before her, and her outcries, her protests, her interrogations, drowned in a flood of bland apology: "An unfortunate accident—Mrs. Kyd's manuscript received the same day—extraordinary coincidence in the choice of a title—duplicate answers sent by mistake—Miss Dace's novel hardly suited to their purpose—should of course have been returned—regrettable oversight—accidents would happen—sure she understood."

The voice went on, like the steady pressure of a surgeon's hand on a shrieking nerve. When it stopped she was in the street. A cab nearly ran her down, and a car-bell jangled furiously in her ears. She clutched her manuscript, carrying it tenderly through the crowd, like a live thing that had been hurt. She could not bear to look at its soiled edges and the ink-stain on Aunt Julia's ribbon.

The train stopped with a jerk, and she opened her eyes. It was dark, and by the windy flare of gas on the platform she saw the Norton passengers getting out. She stood up stiffly and followed them. A warm wind blew into her face the fragrance of the summer woods, and she remembered how, two months earlier, she had knelt among the dead leaves, pressing her lips to the first shoots of green. Then for the first time she thought of home. She had fled away in the morning without a word, and her heart sank at the thought of her mother's fears. And her father—how angry he would be! She bent her head under the coming storm of his derision.

The night was cloudy, and as she stepped into the darkness beyond the station a hand was slipped in hers. She stood still, too weary to feel frightened, and a voice said, quietly: "Don't walk so fast, child. You look tired."

"Father!" Her hand dropped from his, but he recaptured it and drew it through his arm. When she found voice, it was to whisper, "You were at the station?"

"It's such a good night I thought I'd stroll down and meet you."

Her arm trembled against his. She could not see his face in the dimness, but the light of his cigar looked down on her like a friendly eye, and she took courage to falter out: "Then you knew—"

"That you'd gone to Boston? Well, I rather thought you had."

They walked on slowly, and presently he added, "You see, you left the *Home Circle* lying in your room."

How she blessed the darkness and the muffled sky! She could not have borne the scrutiny of the tiniest star.

"Then mother wasn't very much frightened?"

"Why, no, she didn't appear to be. She's been busy all day over some toggery of Bertha's."

Theodora choked. "Father, I'll—" She groped for words, but they eluded her. "I'll do things—differently; I haven't meant—" Suddenly she heard herself bursting out: "It was all a mistake, you know—about my story. They didn't want it; they won't have it!" and she shrank back involuntarily from his impending mirth.

She felt the pressure of his arm, but he didn't speak, and she figured his mute hilarity. They moved on in silence. Presently he said:

"It hurts a bit just at first, doesn't it?"

"O father!"

He stood still, and the gleam of his cigar showed a face of unexpected participation.

"You see I've been through it myself."

"You, father? You?"

"Why, yes. Didn't I ever tell you? I wrote a novel once. I was just out of college, and I didn't want to be a doctor. No; I wanted to be a genius. So I wrote a novel."

The doctor paused, and Theodora clung to him in a mute passion of commiseration. It was as if a drowning creature caught a live hand through the murderous fury of the waves.

"Father—O father!"

"It took me a year—a whole year's hard work; and when I'd finished it the publishers wouldn't have it, either; not at any price. And that's why I came down to meet you, because I remembered my walk home."

# FRIENDS

As first published in *The Youth's Companion*, August 30, 1990

SAILPORT IS an ugly town. It makes, indeed, certain concessions to the eye in one or two streets on the hill, where there are elms, and houses set apart behind clipped hedges; but this favored quarter is a mere incident in the harsh progressiveness of a New England town seated on a capacious harbor and in touch with a widely radiating railway system.

The streets, too narrow for the present needs of the town, run between buildings of discordant character; the new brick warehouse, like a factory chimney with windows in it, looking down from its lean eminence on the low wooden "store" of a past generation, and the ambitious office building, with its astrologer's tower and rustications of sham granite, turning a contemptuous side wall on the recessed door and balustraded roof of the old dwelling house which had been adapted to commercial uses with the least possible outlay.

These streets, through which the electric cars rush with a rapidity dazing to the simple-minded and perilously fascinating to small boys on the way to school, are full of snow and mud in winter, of dust and garbage in summer. At each corner a narrow cross street leads the eye down to a glimpse of wooden wharves and a confusion of masts and smoke-stacks against a quiver of yellowish water. Nowhere is there the least peep of green, the smallest open space that spring may use as a signboard; even in the outlying districts, where cottages and tenements are being "run up" for the increasing population of laboring men and operatives, the patches of ground between the houses are not gardens, but waste spaces strewn with nameless refuse.

The inhabitants of Sailport would doubtless be surprised to hear their "city" (as they are careful to call it) thus characterized. The greater number are probably of the opinion that handsome is as handsome does; and according to the national interpretation of the adage, Sailport is doing very handsomely, increasing in private and civic wealth, and multiplying with astonishing rapidity its telephone poles and electric wires, its car tracks and factory chimneys.

To Penelope Bent, now emerging from the railway station, her traveling bag in hand, Sailport had never appeared ugly; or only with the homely, lovable ugliness of a face that has bent above one's first awakenings; a face that has always been there; that one would not exchange for any Venus of the museums.

She looked at it now, after her long journey, with an unexpected sense of relief, the consciousness of being once more in a place where Penelope Bent had an identity, where twenty friendly hearts would ache for her, if they but knew! She would have died rather than have them know. As she stepped from the station she shrank even from the scrutiny of the sunshine; yet she was not proof against the comfort of feeling that the sympathy she dreaded was within reach; and she almost smiled at the nod of the Irish apple woman who greeted her as she hurried down the steps.

Everything all these last days had been so unreal; she had journeyed far into such a strange world, passing through so endless a nightmare of unknown sights and sounds and names. Here all was peacefully, prosaically familiar; the streets deep in spring mud, the house fronts blotched with signboards, the hoardings with their flamboyant advertisements, the junction of car tracks and the peristyle of the Baptist Church opposite the station all formed a part of her earliest consciousness.

Although she returned to it all so heavily, although the mere fact of her return testified to a disaster too recent to tolerate the touch of thought, yet the spell of association was upon her before she had picked her way through the mud to the opposite sidewalk.

Miss Bent, in her neat traveling dress, her hat still protected from the contamination of the journey by the folds of a thick veil, did not look like a victim of Olympian ire. She had passed well beyond thirty, in appearance if not in years, and her small, spare figure and pale face suggested the flatness and premature discoloration of a pressed flower. There was, however, nothing else about her in accordance with so tender a simile, her air of almost military precision rather implying a past devoted to the punctual accomplishment of didactic duties.

Her whole mien, in fact, savored of the educational. Her small features were as neatly balanced as a sentence of Lindley Murray's and her black hair assumed, in parting on her forehead, the exact curves of a pair of copybook parentheses. The eyes alone played traitor to this well-tutored mask, all that was feminine and inconsequent in their possessor lurking there under a spring of moisture, like Truth at the bottom of her well.

It was a bright April day, and the clock in the Gothic tower, which an unbridled fancy had recently appended to the classic facade of the city hall, struck twelve as Miss Bent passed beneath it. For a moment she paused, glancing down the main street, congested, as usual at that hour, by the pressure of traffic; then she hastened along the narrow sic drawing down her veil, and pressing close to the sides of the houses to escape the contact of hurrying shoulders.

She had washed her face and smoothed her dress in the toilet room of the sleeping car, and there seemed to be no reason why she should not stop and see Mr. Boutwell for a moment on her way home.

She walked on hurriedly without raising her eyes, till at last, reaching a certain side street, she paused to glance at a building which faced her—a large brick building with brownstone angles and a massive porch. It stood by itself at the end of the street, with an air of moral superiority that at once proclaimed it to be one of the public schools of Sailport.

Miss Bent's heart began to beat. There were *her* windows—the three with geraniums on the sill, at the left-hand corner of the second story. Would she be sitting behind them again, in a day or two at her desk on the raised platform, facing the double file of benches? Why not, indeed? Why even raise the question? What possible doubt could there be of the place having been kept for her?

The whole school board had assured her of it when, a month earlier, laughing and crying, she had taken, as she thought, a last leave of them. "Till the next general meeting we shall engage a temporary substitute. One word from you, and we'll put you back—remember that."

How she had smiled then at such idle toying with impossibilities! But she had smiled through tears of gratification. It was so pleasant to feel that they had liked her, that they had valued her services; to know that no teacher had ever left the school amid such a chorus of lamentations, that none had ever been so urgently entreated by the school board to reconsider her determination and come back to them!

"Why not persuade Mr. Dayton to sell out in Louisville and go into business here?" one commissioner had even laughingly suggested; and she, taken by the humor of it, had promised to submit the plan to Mr. Dayton. It seemed all a part then—the tears, the regrets, the little professional jokes—of the general cumulative pleasantness of life; now the wish of the school board remained the one reed she had to cling to, and she told herself how thankful she ought to be that it was so strong a one.

How many women, after resigning such a place as hers, could comfort themselves with the hope of being able to return to it? How many, whom she knew, had spent years in the vain effort to get into one of the schools!

There was her friend, Vexilla Thurber, for instance—poor Vexilla! How hard she had tried for a place in Penelope's school, how long it had been the unattainable ambition of her life! And she had never even had a hope of success. All Miss Bent's efforts had been unavailing; the school board remained obdurate, retiring behind hazy generalities; but Mr. Boutwell, one of their number, confided to Miss Bent that her friend was not "smart enough."

In vain Miss Bent protested that Vexilla's apparent dullness was only timidity; in vain offered to answer for the sufficiency of her knowledge and for her untiring industry. The school board bowed in general acquiescence, but did not find Miss Thurber to their liking. In vain Miss Bent, letting her eyes speak, reminded them of her friend's difficult situation, with a helpless grandmother, a crippled brother and an idle sister to support; the board bowed again, implying that the public schools of Sailport were not asylums for the indigent.

And so, year after year, Miss Bent had to bear the same heavy news to her friend; and year after year Vexilla, smiling down her discomfiture, had to return to the underpaid toil of a few private lessons, combined with odd jobs in the way of bookkeeping and typewriting. At the recollection Miss Bent's eyes melted. Poor Vexilla—hers was the harder lot!

"Perhaps now, if they're very glad to get me back," Miss Bent murmured under her veil, "I may be able to do something for Vexilla." And she remembered with fresh thankfulness that her letter must have reached Mr. Boutwell three days before the meeting of the school board.

This fortifying thought hastened the step with which she sped along Main Street toward a shabby-looking building, with glass doors surmounted by an inscription declaring it to be the People's Library. Nothing in the interior of the library belied its outer shabbiness; the rooms, as she entered, emitted an odor of much-handled books that gave her a qualm after her draught of salt April air. At a desk near the door sat a young woman with a cold-veal complexion and taffy-colored hair who, in the absence of more pressing duties, was engaged in polishing her nails.

"Is Mr. Boutwell in?" Miss Bent asked.

"Guess he's in his office."

Miss Bent walked down the room between the lines of dingy books to a door at the farther end.

A prompt "Come in" answered her knock, and she entered a room almost filled by a large writing table, at which a man sat in an office chair, collating catalogues.

He raised a pale face, elongated in one direction by the baldness of his high forehead, in the other by the vague neutral tints of his beard, and the expression of distress wrinkling his neuralgic-looking brows seemed involuntarily to contradict the smile of welcome that lent a sudden blueness to his spectacled gray eyes.

"Miss Bent!"

She stood before him, fingering her bag in a spasm of nervousness that gripped her throat.

"O Mr. Boutwell," broke from her at last, as she dropped into the seat he pushed forward. It was so unlike her usual mode of address, she was so little given to feminine falterings and incoherencies, that, under the contagion of her emotion, he could only stammer, "I'm afraid you've had a trying time." And at once he doubted if the words were in good taste.

His perturbation increased when she drew from her pocket a neatly folded handkerchief, and pushing back her veil, silently wiped her eyes.

She restored the handkerchief to her pocket and put her bag aside, keeping one wrist slipped through its handle, as, with the caution of the unaccustomed traveler, she had done during all the long hours of the journey. "You must excuse me," she said, "but I've been in the cars since yesterday afternoon, and I came right here from the station."

"You must be very tired!" he murmured.

"Oh no, not very, but I've been through a good deal."

She glanced vaguely about the little room, with its book-lined walls and the window looking out on a blind alley, full of rubbish.

"You didn't expect me back so soon, did you?" she added, with a sigh.

Boutwell had taken off his spectacles and was rubbing them with a bit of chamois skin. He coughed instead of replying.

"Isn't it a mercy I didn't take mother?" she went on in a tone of confidence that contrasted with her usual impersonal manner. "The long journey there and back would have been too awful for her. I've been so thankful ever since. It seemed to keep me from breaking down, and I needed something to do that. I've been through everything."

"I was afraid so," he answered, feeling now that she would not repudiate his sympathy. "I got your letter."

"Oh, my letter!" she exclaimed.

The blood rushed to her forehead. A few minutes ago, in passing the schoolhouse, she had felt very sure of the future; but now—Her hand slipped from the bag, rejoining the other which trembled on her knee. The librarian's brows were a projecting bunch of wrinkles.

"I got your letter, Miss Bent, but only yesterday."

"Only *yesterday!*"

'Yes, you unfortunately addressed it to me personally, instead of sending it to the school board, and—"

'I did that on purpose," she interposed, "to keep my—to keep it private. I didn't want to have everybody talking about my—my having broken off my engagement; mother doesn't even know yet; I couldn't tear to tell anybody but *you!*"

"I know, I know; I gathered that from what you wrote. But it was most unlucky that you wrote to me, for I've been away, up in Maine for the last week with my wife's mother, who's been sick, and I only got back yesterday."

"Only yes-ter-day!" she repeated, dividing the words into syllables as if they belonged to a foreign tongue which she did not perfectly understand. Then, suddenly lifting her head: "But my place—they must have filled my place?"

"It was filled three days ago at the general meeting. There was no help for it. No one could imagine—" "No, no, of course—of course."

He had been afraid that she would cry again, but to his surprise she remained quite calm.

"Who has it?" she asked.

He hesitated a moment; the words seemed hard to say: "Your friend, Miss Thurber."

"Vexilla!"

The room swung round; her lips grew dry; she felt an inconsequent desire to laugh. "But Vexilla—Vexilla! You always said—why, not one of you would *look* at her—not even for the third primary—and now, my class! My class!"

She was bathed in a hot wave of anger. The whole air seemed thick with ingratitude and treachery, as if all these years she had walked in an atmosphere of lies. What did it mean? What could it mean? Perhaps, even while they were urging her to remain, imploring her to come back to them, they had been plotting her removal; possibly keeping Vexilla to fill this very place, while they glossed over with hypocritical excuses their refusal to give her a lesser one! And Vexilla herself—might not she, too, have had a hand in it? Who could tell, in a world that swarmed with such grinning incongruities?

"But Vexilla—Vexilla—" she repeated.

"I don't wonder at your surprise." Mr. Boutwell's familiar voice fell strangely on the tumult of her thoughts. "We've been unwilling to employ Miss Thurber for reasons with which you are perfectly familiar, and which you have often told me you thought inadequate. You remember how much you've talked with me about her; how often you've told me it was only shyness that made her appear so dull and hesitating; that she was really better educated than many of our present teachers." He paused, but Miss Bent made no answer.

"Well," he continued, "there were very few candidates for your place, and among them there was only one who appeared at all satisfactory to the board, and that was Miss Euphemia Staples. We had just decided to appoint her when she was called out West, to keep house for a brother who has lost his wife; and that left us without a single eligible applicant --for of course Miss Thurber was not among the applicants."

A low sound like a laugh escaped Miss Bent.

"At last somebody suggested Miss Thurber. It rather took us aback at first, but we hadn't much time to think the matter over, and there didn't seem to be anybody else. We recalled what you'd said about her—the board always thought a great deal of your opinion—and finally we sent for her. She was considerably overcome—she cried a good deal—and for a time it didn't seem as if we could get her to accept. She said she'd sooner have taken any other place in the school."

Miss Bent moved impatiently in her seat. Vexilla had evidently expressed all the proper sentiments; for once in her life she had not been tongue-tied; she seemed indeed to have surprised Mr. Boutwell by her eloquence. The supplanted teacher rose, feeling for her bag.

"I guess I'd better be going along," she murmured.

"Wait a minute, please; I haven't quite finished. I hope we shall see you back among us all the same, Miss Bent, for Miss Thurber accepted your place only on the condition that if by any chance you—you changed your mind and came back within the next few weeks, she should be permitted to resign. And I know she'll hold us to our agreement."

Miss Bent turned red, then pale. "Changed my mind? Changed my mind? How dare she?" Her anger dropped and she sank back into her chair. "Did she say that? Did she? Poor Vexilla! That she'd only accept on that condition? She made you promise? She made the whole board agree to it? Poor Vexilla—oh, poor Vexilla!"

"And what's more, she means it, too," Mr. Boutwell went on. "She's restless and worried at the idea of being in your place; says she can't get used to it; it don't seem natural to her. She's a devoted friend, Miss Bent."

"I know, I know."

"I met her only this morning on my way here, and she stopped to talk about you and tell me how she missed you. She said she'd give up her place in a minute to have you back here, and I believe she would, though from what I hear it means a good deal to her to be getting a regular salary. She's had a pretty hard time of it up to now, I guess."

"You met Vexilla this morning?" Miss Bent interrupted, without noticing his last words. "You didn't tell her—about me, did you, Mr. Boutwell?"

"I said nothing."

"Thank you—thank you. You always understand. I'm so confused myself; I don't yet know how I mean to act. Even mother doesn't suspect anything. She doesn't know I've come—she doesn't know but what I'm married!" She gave a constrained laugh and rose once more.

The laugh troubled Boutwell; it seemed to conceal some inaccessible disaster.

"Don't you think," he began, for the sake of saying something, "that it would have been wiser to let Mrs. Bent know? Won't she be considerably startled at seeing you?"

"I'm afraid she will; but I couldn't tell her in a letter; she'd have shown it to everybody. You know she just *has* to talk things over."

"I understand."

Miss Bent looked at him hesitatingly. "I guess I'll go now. I'm very grateful to you for not having spoken about my letter."

"Oh, that's all right," said the librarian, taking refuge again in the examination of his spectacles. "But, see here, Miss Bent, what are you going to do?"

"About what?"

"Why—the school."

"Oh, I don't know," she said slowly. "I'm so bewildered I can't think straight yet. I'll have to go home and quiet down a little. Only please don't let Vexilla know I'm here; don't tell anybody you've seen me; I'm so afraid she'll find out about it before I've seen her."

"Don't worry about that, Miss Bent."

"No; I know I can trust you."

Their hands met and she moved away, adding, as she reached the door, "I'll come in tomorrow and tell you what I've decided."

"Very well; but I'm sure Miss Thurber won't keep the place. I guess she's got a will of her own, and I don't believe you could make her stay if you tried."

Miss Bent turned back abruptly.

"O Mr. Boutwell, I don't know what you must think of me! I was perfectly hateful about Vexilla when you first told me—perfectly hateful! I don't see how I could behave so. As if she hadn't as much right to take my class as anybody else! But the fact is, I'm almost crazy. I don't seem to know what I'm doing—" Her eyes clung to Boutwell with a look of shipwrecked terror. "I must tell you—I must tell you! I can't endure it another minute by myself! What I wrote you wasn't true—about having broken off my engagement. There wasn't a word of truth in it. When I got to Louisville Mr. Dayton wasn't there. He'd gone off the day before, and nobody knew where he was. I had to get detectives—his partner helped me. It took us nearly a week to find him. He was away down in Texas—and he'd married another woman!"

Boutwell jumped up with a wrathful exclamation, but before it was out of his mouth the office door had closed on Miss Bent.

## II

LATE that afternoon Miss Bent, having unpacked her few possessions (she looked the other way as she slipped the gray cashmere with lace ruffles into a drawer by itself), sat in her little bedroom trying to think. The sense of familiarity which had soothed the first moments of her return to Sailport had given way to a profounder estrangement. As she glanced about the room, it seemed impossible that four walls which had held so much of her life should assume a look of such chill indifference. Every line of the furniture, every twist in the pattern of the wallpaper, seemed to repeat the same "I know thee not!" No, she was not the Penelope Bent who had lived there through so many happy, monotonous years; she was a stranger who had never been in the room before, and who knew as little of its history as it knew of hers.

The fanciful wanderings of her thoughts frightened her—she was not accustomed to such divagations; she felt herself on the brink of delirium. The interview with her mother had been terrible. She had told Mrs. Bent that her marriage was postponed, taking refuge in this euphuism under the merciless tenderness of the maternal gaze. It would have been so much easier to face indifference! Mrs. Bent's tremulous avoidance of surmises, her abruptly deflected questions, her unwonted acquiescences, seemed to intensify the vividness of the mute insight that lighted up every corner of her daughter's consciousness. The two women lived in that involuntary familiarity from which neither speech nor silence can give sanctuary.

Suddenly the solitude seemed to be full of her mother's eyes, and Miss Bent, starting up, moved toward the window. Twilight was falling, and a few steps in the open air might do her good. She put on her hat and veil, and unlocking her door, stepped into the cheerful sitting room beyond. Ivy and geranium throve on the sunny window sill, and a lump of coal had just been kindled in the grate.

Mrs. Bent, a small, withered woman, rooted to her seat by some obscure ailment, looked up at her daughter with shrinking, inquisitive eyes. Miss Bent drew up the shawl about her mother's knees, and absently broke a yellow leaf from one of the geranium plants.

Seems to me the geraniums have had too much water this last week," she said.

I'm afraid they have, Penelope. Nobody's got your knack with them."

Miss Bent stirred the soil in the pot. "It needs loosening." She drew on her gloves, avoiding her mother's eye.

You're going out a little way, Penelope?"

"Yes, I'll be back soon." She hesitated. "If anybody comes in mother, don't—don't—
"

Mrs. Bent's eyelids trembled; the violence of her protest confessed her weakness. "Penelope Bent, how can you think—"

"Oh, that's all right!" the daughter said, resignedly.

Although it was growing dark indoors, the spring daylight still lingered, and Miss Bent, instinctively seeking for solitude, turned up a quiet side street, disturbed only by the calls of a few children at play. The air brought little ease to her head, and she was conscious of a growing inability to think. Yet she knew that in a few hours she must act; she could not continue to keep her presence in Sailport a secret; had she cherished any such design, her mother's tongue would have frustrated it She must prepare to meet Vexilla Thurber the next day; before they met she must decide on some course of action, and as yet no conclusion had suggested itself.

Try as she might to examine the problem before her, she could see but one point of it—that she had lost her place at the school, that the greater part of her savings had been absorbed by the journey to Louisville and the preparations for her wedding, and that now she was left stranded, with heavy expenses to face and without means of meeting them. Although Miss Bent had only her mother to support, she had found her salary barely sufficient for her needs. Her own tastes were simple-, but Mrs. Bent's ill health taxed her daughter's purse with demands that had every quality of unexpectedness except that of inevitable recurrence.

Under such conditions, the future looked disheartening enough. She remembered Boutwell's words: "Miss Thurber won't keep the place"; but the suggestion they conveyed was intolerable. Of course, if something else could be found for Vexilla—but she smiled at herself for trusting her hopes to this frail hypothesis. Had not she and all Vexilla's friends been searching for years for that delusive something? Yes, but Boutwell had said that Vexilla would insist on resigning, and he was right in thinking that Vexilla had a will of her own. If Vexilla meant to resign, the whole of Sailport could not stop her. And if she resigned, what was to prevent—

Miss Bent pulled herself together. She had a sudden vision of Vexilla's household, with the infirm grandmother, the crippled brother, helpless as a baby, who lay in his chair playing with tin soldiers, the handsome, slatternly sister, who drifted back from every "job" that Vexilla obtained for her into a languid permanence of novel reading and street corner flirtation. Vexilla had three to support; Miss Bent but one. Yes, but if Vexilla insisted on resigning?

Down the empty street a woman's figure was approaching. Even in the failing light there was no mistaking the thick-set figure, the oscillating walk that suggested a ship with her steering gear out of order, or the round face framed in meek drab hair. Miss Bent glanced about in the instinctive attempt to escape; but it was too late.

"Penelope!"

"Vexilla!"

The two women faced each other, Miss Bent silent, Vexilla Thurber emitting her astonishment in a series of soft cries:

"You, Penelope—*you!* Back in Sailport? Gracious mercy! But is it Lou really? I feel as if it might be your ghost. Oh no, there's your cameo brooch! *Penelope*—why don't you say something?"

"You don't give me time, Vexilla; but I'm not a ghost—and I've come back."

"For mercy's sake! What in the world has happened? Penelope Bent, you've had some misfortune! You'd never have come back—has anything happened to *him*? I know something's happened—you look awful! What *is* it?"

Vexilla's agonized italics echoed through the silent street, and a woman on the opposite sidewalk slackened her pace to listen.

"I can't tell you here, Vexilla. Don't be so excited! I'll walk along with you a little way."

Her friend, clutching her arm, watched her with perturbed blue eyes.

"You needn't talk to *me*, Penelope—something has happened, or else you're sick; one or the other! You're as white as a sheet, and I can feel you trembling all over! Penelope—Penelope—you don't want me to go away and leave you? You aren't angry with me for—for meeting you?" Her apple face was wet with tears; they ran down unheeded, dabbling her fawn-colored dress.

"Nonsense, Vexilla! Why should I be angry with you for meeting me? I've only just got home, and I'm a little tired, that's all!"

"Oh, you poor soul, you're *dead* tired! I can see that. But, Penelope—" She drew closer, her voice sinking to a frightened whisper. "I don't quite understand—*are you married?*"

"No, I'm not married." Miss Bent glanced over her friend's shoulder and saw a group of people approaching. "But we can't stand here and talk, and I can't ask you to come and see me just now. Mother's in the parlor, and we couldn't talk before her."

"No, no; I know we couldn't," Miss Thurber emotionally acquiesced. "But why won't you come home with me for a few minutes? Do, Penelope! Lally will be getting supper for grandma and Phil, and we can have my room all to ourselves. Lally's getting real helpful, Penelope. She cares for grandma so nicely when I have to be out!"

Miss Bent hesitated. "Where were you going, Vexilla?"

"Me? I was only going to run down to Main Street for a minute to get some books. It's of no consequence—" She broke off suddenly and her color rose. The books of which she was in quest were probably the textbooks for her new class at the school. "Come with me, Penelope she deprecatingly entreated.

"Very well," said Miss Bent, with sudden resolution; and they began to walk in the direction of Vexilla's home.

Vexilla, eased of her first agitation, respected her friend's reticence and they moved on silently through the dusk, pricked here and there by the yellow points of the street lamps. At length they reached a house divided from the sidewalk by a strip of down-trodden earth enclosed with broken palings. Vexilla opened the door and led her friend through an entry smelling of boiled cabbage, and up a narrow staircase to the top of the house. On the upper landing she paused to say, with visible embarrassment, "You mustn't mind if Lally and Phil seem surprised to see you back. We've been talking so much about—"

"Yes, yes; I understand," Miss Bent hastily interposed.

Vexilla stepped into a low-ceilinged room which was almost in darkness.

"Why, Lally! Haven't you lighted the lamp? Haven't you got supper?"

Vexilla advanced into the room, leaving Miss Bent on the threshold.

"I can't see where I'm going! Where are the matches? Oh, here. It's a mercy I filled the lamp before I went out, anyway!"

She bent over a lamp which stood on the center table, and the room was presently revealed in all its shabby disorder. In an old bath chair near the window lay the paralyzed boy, his drawn face detached like a death's-head against the shawl thrust pillow-wise behind his head. Lally, the sister, dragging herself from the sofa on which she had been stretched, stepped listlessly into the lamplight, which illuminated the beauty of her heavy white face, helmeted with somber hair.

"Goodness!" she exclaimed. "That you, Miss Bent? Have you got married already? Vexilla never told us you were coming back!"

"Vexilla's got your place at school!" piped the paralyzed boy from the window.

Vexilla paid no heed. She had hurried toward her grandmother, a huge ruin of a woman with a face like a broken statue, who sat vaguely smiling in a rocking chair beside the stove.

"Gracious, Lally, you've left the stove door open, and there's a cinder right in grandma's lap!"

'Tally's been asleep!" the boy shrilly interposed. Vexilla smoothed the old woman's hair, straightened the knitted shawl about her shoulders, and closed the door of the stove. Lally had thrown herself back on the sofa, still gazing at Miss Bent under the projecting visor of her hair, while the boy began impatiently: "Vexilla, aren't you going to get supper?"

"No; Lally's going to." Vexilla turned to her friend. "Come this way, Penelope."

Miss Bent followed her down a passageway to a small room with two beds in it. Miss Thurber struck a match and lighted a lamp which stood on a desk piled with schoolbooks.

"Sit down and wait, please, Penelope. I'll be back in a minute."

She turned away, shutting the door after her, while Miss Bent sank into a chair. She longed to fly, to escape from the depressing influences of Vexilla's home to the orderly silence of her own little room. The cracked looking glass and threadbare carpet, the bed in which the helpless grandmother slept, all the evidences of Vexilla's hardships and privations seemed to add their pressure to the weight upon her burdened nerves. Never before had life appeared so meaningless and cruel.

Vexilla returned, demonstrative and breathless, with a cup of steaming tea.

"Please drink it, Penelope, please do—you're regularly worn out. I can see you are. Just take a mouthful—I know it'll do you good!" Her blue eyes had the look of a dog begging to be noticed.

Miss Bent took the cup and leaned back, sipping the tea reluctantly, while Vexilla sat by in an ecstasy of mute contemplation.

"I do feel better," Miss Bent said at last, meeting her friend's gaze. "And now, Vexilla, we must talk."

She paused a moment, as if rallying her forces, and then began again: "I must tell you—"

Vexilla leaned forward. "Wait a minute, Penelope—there's something I must tell *you* first. I can't bear to have you speak a word before you know what's happened."

Miss Bent looked at her, half smiling. "I know," she said.

"You *know!* About the school?"

"Yes. I've seen Mr. Boutwell."

"Oh!" said Vexilla, in a long shudder of comprehension. For a moment or two both women were silent. Then Vexilla began to speak in quick, entreating tones.

"O Penelope, what *must* you have thought? It all happened so strangely! They sent for me, Penelope—of course I never would have dreamed of applying. Even if I'd been smart enough, I never would have applied for *your* place! And I always supposed they thought I was too stupid. You'd tried so often to get me into the schools that I didn't suppose there was any chance for me. When they sent for me I thought it must be a mistake. I couldn't believe it! And even when I found they really wanted me, I couldn't bear the idea, Penelope. I said if it had only been any other place but yours; but they said that was the only one that was vacant. And of course everybody said you'd never come back here— you were so positive you wouldn't, Penelope—" She paused, shrinking back from the unrevealed mystery of her friend's return. "And I've got so many to think of that it didn't seem as if I ought to refuse. But I said I'd. only take it on one condition. I made them solemnly agree to that—that if you changed your mind and—and decided to come back to Sailport—"

"I know that, too," said Miss Bent, slowly. Bending forward, she kissed the wet cheek of her friend. Fresh tears rose to Vexilla's eyes; but the intensity of the resolve which animated her drove them back and subdued the quivering of her lips.

"I'm glad Mr. Boutwell told you, Penelope. I couldn't bear to have had you think, for one minute, even, that I'd have taken the place on any other terms."

"I knew you wouldn't, Vexilla!"

"O Penelope! How like you to say that!" In the rapture of being understood she ventured to lay one large hand on Miss Bent's. "There's nobody like you—nobody! Oh, it's so good to have you back!" Again she faltered, in fear of appearing to touch intentionally upon Penelope's enigmatic course.

Miss Bent did not speak. She sat motionless, her eyes fixed on a plush-framed photograph of herself that hung above Vexilla's desk. It was the only picture in the room.

"And there's another thing I want to tell you right off, Penelope! I know just what you are—always thinking of other people first and yourself last; and I don't want you to think it's any loss to me to—to give up that place. I don't want to keep it, Penelope! It's a relief to me to give it up. I never should have got used to it. I'm not half bright enough, anyway! I don't much believe they'd have kept me more than one term, even if—and it doesn't suit me, somehow! I'd rather go back to my old work. I—I think I'd have resigned, anyway. I'm sure I would, Penelope! The fact is, it ties me down too much—I'm more independent with my other work."

Miss Bent raised her eyes. "Your bookkeeping and typewriting, you mean? Where's your typewriter, by the way? It always used to stand on your desk."

In the faint candlelight she thought she saw Miss Thurber's color change.

"It's not here now."

"Where is it? What's become of it?"

"I—well, the fact is I sold it."

"You sold it? Why? Oh, because-I see." Miss Bent paused, struggling with a resentment that suddenly forced itself through her sympathy for her friend. She repressed the ungenerous impulse. What could be more natural than that Vexilla should sell her typewriter?

Miss Thurber went on precipitately "I guess I shan't have much time for typewriting, anyway. You see, it's going to be a great help to have had that appointment. I don't believe I'll have a bit of trouble getting private pupils now. Fact is, that's the real reason I was always so crazy to get into the schools. I never thought the work would really suit me—but it makes such a lot of difference if you can refer parents to the board! I guess I'll have more work than I can manage."

Miss Bent laughed, and rising from her seat, laid her hand on Vexilla's shoulder. "You're a goose, Vexilla! How do you know I'm going to stay in Sailport?" "Penelope!"

Miss Thurber had also risen, and the two women stood facing each other.

"You don't know yet why I'm here," Miss Bent continued in the same bantering tone. "It seems to me you're taking a good deal for granted, aren't you?"

"O Penelope! I didn't mean—"

Miss Bent, withdrawing her hand, took a few hesitating steps across the room. Vexilla hung back, waiting for her to speak. "I'm going to tell you, Vexilla," she said at last.

"Yes," the other nodded.

There was another silence. Miss Bent seemed to find difficulty in choosing her words.

"My marriage isn't going to take place—just at present—that's all. When I got to Louisville I found—but I can't tell you all that now; it's too long. Perhaps tomorrow. I only got back this morning, and I had to explain it all to mother. Of course my coming back upset her a good deal."

"Don't say another word, Penelope! I can see how tired you are. Only tell me you're not in any trouble—"

Miss Bent met her gaze calmly.

"I'm not in any trouble, Vexilla. My marriage has been put off for reasons that—that are perfectly satisfactory to Mr. Dayton and myself. He's obliged to be away from Louisville a good deal just now—and I didn't want to stay out there alone—with mother here—"

"O Penelope—but couldn't he have let you know?" Vexilla cried, her sympathy outrunning her discretion.

"I'll explain all that another time. I only want to tell you that I've decided to leave Sailport with mother now, instead of waiting till—afterward. You know she was to have joined me in Louisville, and we've given up our rooms here, so we'd have to move on the first of Ma)', anyhow." She now spoke without perceptible hesitation.

"But, Penelope, I don't understand!" Miss Thurber faltered. "Where are you going? You are not going back to Louisville right off?"

Miss Bent's face stiffened. "No; not there." She paused a moment. "I think we shall go to New York," she said at last. "Aunt Sarah Tillman, mother's younger sister, lives there, and I could get plenty to do in a big place like that. It's very easy, if you know some one who lives there. But it's not on my account; it's because of mother. She's a good deal upset by the change in my plans. She'd made up her mind to leave Sailport, and I'm afraid it would be hard for her to settle down again after making all her preparations to go. You know mother's very excitable."

"I know, but—"

"I've had a good many offers of work in New York," Miss Bent continued, ignoring the interruption. "My aunt's always writing to us to come and stay with her. She says she could get me half a dozen pupils right off. Her husband's related to a Presbyterian minister, with a large parish. And I don't know but what I should like the change, too. I feel rather restless myself."

Miss Thurber continued to gaze at her with a tender incredulity. "But New York—you've never been there—"

"Well, I don't know that it's too late to begin."

"No; but it's all so queer! Why, you've hardly ever been away from Sailport, Penelope! I can't think what you want to go to New York for."

Miss Bent rose again. Her lips were compressed and she forced the words through them with a certain precipitation. "New York is nearer to Louisville, for one thing. You hadn't thought of that, I suppose?"

"No," Vexilla faltered.

"You know Mr. Dayton was never able to get as far east as this."

Miss Thurber colored. She felt that it was singularly obtuse of her not to have understood this. "To be sure," she murmured, "I never thought of it! You must excuse me, Penelope. I've asked you so many questions, and I know how tired you are! But I couldn't help it. It's all so sudden! I can't take it in yet—the idea of your going away again, just as I was so glad to have you back!"

Miss Bent was putting on her jacket and adjusting her brown veil. For a moment she did not speak, and some indefinable change in her face made Vexilla suddenly exclaim: "But *is* it true? Are you really going away?"

Miss Bent turned on her almost angrily. "I don't know what you mean! You talk as if

I didn't know my own mind! I'm not in the habit of saying things I don't mean!"

"Oh, I know, but—" Vexilla's words ran into tears.

Miss Bent leaned forward and gently kissed her.

"Mother and I are going way in a few days, that's quite settled. My reason for telling you so at once is that I was arid you might do something foolish about the school."

"O Penelope, Penelope!"

"And I want you to keep the class, Vexilla. I particularly want you to keep i! I was so glad when Mr. Boutwell told me they'd given it to you! I couldn't bear to think of a stranger in my class. You must write me about the girls, Vexilla, and perhaps I can help you sometimes with your work."

"O Penelope! It seems as if I couldn't bear it—*your* class!"

"You're a goose, Vexilla, and now good-bye! Its dark, and mother will be getting worried."

"Let me walk home with you, Penelope. I feel as if I wasn't ever going to see you again."

"You silly child! You'll see me tomorrow, I hope. Come in the afternoon, while mother's taking her nap."

"You won't let me walk back with you now?"

"Not now. I want to be alone."

She opened the door and stepped hurriedly along the passageway ahead of Vexilla, passing, she hardly knew how, among the inmates of the living room, now gathered about an untidy supper table. On the landing Vexilla clung to her with another mute pressure, full of confused doubts and tremors; then she found herself on the staircase, and a moment later she was alone in the dim street.

For a while she stood irresolute, as if awaiting the subsidence of some strong wave of emotion; then, slowly, she began to move forward along the deserted sidewalk.

At the next corner, instead of turning homeward, she bent her steps toward Main Street, unconsciously quickening her pace as he advanced. She was in that curiously detached state when one's body seems like an inert mass, propelled from one point to another without conscious action of its own. In this condition she reached the corner where the blithely-lighted post-office windows projected their oblongs of yellow light across the shadows of Main Street. She pushed open one of the doors, and, going to a small window at the back of the office, asked for a sheet of paper and a stamped envelope.

Having received them, she withdrew to one of the shelves lining the wall, and dipped a ragged pen into the cup of grayish coagulated matter which a paternal government provides for the convenience of the peripatetic letter writer. She wrote a few lines, which she addressed to Mr. Boutwell, and having dropped the envelope into a letter box, she left the post office and turned toward home.

Her step had lost all hesitancy. She seemed to be moving with decision toward a definitely chosen goal. In the course of the past hour her whole relation to life had changed. The experience of the last weeks had flung her out of her orbit, whirling her through dread spaces of moral darkness and bewilderment. She seemed to have lost her connection with the general scheme of things, to have no further part in the fulfillment of the laws that made life comprehensible and duty a joyful impulse. Now the old sense of security had returned. There still loomed before her, in tragic amplitude, the wreck of her individual hope; but she had escaped from the falling ruins and stood safe, outside of herself, in touch once more with the common troubles of her kind, enfranchised forever from the bondage of a lonely grief.

## THE LINE OF LEAST RESISTANCE

As first published in *Lippincott's Magazine*, October, 1900

MILLICENT WAS LATE—as usual. Mr. Mindon, returning unexpectedly from an interrupted yacht-race, reached home with the legitimate hope of finding her at luncheon; but she was still out. "Was she lunching out then?" he asked the butler, who replied, with the air of making an uncalled-for concession to his master's curiosity, that Mrs. Mindon had given no orders about luncheon.

Mr. Mindon, on this negative information (it was the kind from which his knowledge of his wife's movements was mainly drawn), sat down to the grilled cutlet and glass of Vichy that represented his share in the fabulous daily total of the chef's book. Mr. Mindon's annual food-consumption probably amounted to about half of one per cent. on his cook's perquisites, and of the other luxuries of his complicated establishment he enjoyed considerably less than this fraction. Of course, it was nobody's fault but his own. As Millicent pointed out, she couldn't feed her friends on mutton-chops and Vichy because of his digestive difficulty, nor could she return their hospitality by asking them to play croquet with the children because that happened to be Mr. Mindon's chosen pastime. If that was the kind of life he wanted to lead he should have married a dyspeptic governess, not a young confiding girl, who little dreamed what marriage meant when she passed from her father's roof into the clutches of a tyrant with imperfect gastric secretions.

It was his fault, of course, but then Millicent had faults too, as she had been known to concede when she perceived that the contemplation of her merits was beginning to pall; and it did seem unjust to Mr. Mindon that their life should be one long adaptation to Millicent's faults at the expense of his own. Millicent was unpunctual—but that gave a sense of her importance to the people she kept waiting; she had nervous attacks—but they served to excuse her from dull dinners and family visits; she was bad-tempered—but that merely made the servants insolent to Mr. Mindon; she was extravagant—but that simply necessitated Mr. Mindon's curtailing his summer holiday and giving a closer attention to business. If ever a woman had the qualities of her faults, that woman was Millicent. Like the legendary goose, they laid golden eggs for her, and she nurtured them tenderly in return. If Millicent had been a perfect wife and mother, she and Mr. Mindon would probably have spent their summer in the depressing promiscuity of hotel piazzas. Mr. Mindon was shrewd enough to see that he reaped the advantages of his wife's imperfect domesticity, and that if her faults were the making of her, she was the making of him. It was therefore unreasonable to be angry with Millicent, even if she were late for luncheon, and Mr. Mindon, who prided himself on being a reasonable man, usually found some other outlet for his wrath.

On this occasion it was the unpunctuality of the little girls. They came in with their governess some minutes after he was seated: two small Millicents, with all her arts in miniature. They arranged their frocks carefully before seating themselves and turned up their little Greek noses at the food. Already they showed signs of finding fault with as much ease and discrimination as Millicent; and Mr. Mindon knew that this was an accomplishment not to be undervalued. He himself, for example, though Millicent charged him with being a discontented man, had never acquired her proficiency in depreciation; indeed, he sometimes betrayed a mortifying indifference to trifles that afforded opportunity for the display of his wife's fastidiousness. Mr. Mindon, though no biologist, was vaguely impressed by the way in which that accomplished woman had managed to transmit an acquired characteristic to her children: it struck him with wonder that traits of which he had marked the incipience in Millicent should have become intuitions in her offspring. To rebuke such costly replicas of their mother seemed dangerously like scolding Millicent—and Mr. Mindon's hovering resentment prudently settled on the governess.

He pointed out to her that the children were late for luncheon.

The governess was sorry, but Gladys was always unpunctual. Perhaps her papa would speak to her.

Mr. Mindon changed the subject. "What's that at my feet? There's a dog in the room!"

He looked round furiously at the butler, who gazed impartially over his head. Mr. Mindon knew that it was proper for him to ignore his servants, but was not sure to what extent they ought to reciprocate his treatment.

The governess explained that it was Gwendolen's puppy.

"Gwendolen's puppy? Who gave Gwendolen a puppy?"

"Fwank Antwim," said Gwendolen through a mouthful of mushroom soufflé.

"Mr. Antrim," the governess suggested, in a tone that confessed the futility of the correction.

"*We* don't call him Mr. Antrim; we call him Frank; he likes us to," said Gladys icily.

"You'll do no such thing!" her father snapped.

A soft body came in contact with his toe. He kicked out viciously, and the room was full of yelping.

"Take the animal out instantly!" he stormed: dogs were animals to Mr. Mindon. The butler continued to gaze over his head, and the two footmen took their cue from the butler.

"I won't—I won't—I won't let my puppy go!" Gwendolen violently lamented.

But she should have another, her father assured her—a much handsomer and more expensive one; his darling should have a prize dog; he would telegraph to New York on the instant.

"I don't want a pwize dog; I want Fwank's puppy!"

Mr. Mindon laid down his fork and walked out of the room, while the governess, cutting up Gwendolen's nectarine, said, as though pointing out an error in syntax, "You've vexed your papa again."

"I don't mind vexing papa—nothing happens," said Gwendolen, hugging her puppy; while Gladys, disdaining the subject of dispute, contemptuously nibbled caramels. Gladys was two years older than Gwendolen and had outlived the first freshness of her enthusiasm for Frank Antrim, who, with the notorious indiscrimination of the grown-up, always gave the nicest presents to Gwendolen.

Mr. Mindon, crossing his marble hall between goddesses whose dishabille was still slightly disconcerting to his traditions, stepped out on the terrace above the cliffs. The lawn looked as expensive as a velvet carpet woven in one piece; the flower-borders contained only exotics; and the stretch of blue-satin Atlantic had the air of being furrowed only by the keels of pleasure-boats. The scene, to Mr. Mindon's imagination, never lost the keen edge of its costliness; he had yet to learn Millicent's trick of regarding a Newport villa as a mere pied à terre; but he could not help reflecting that, after all, it was to him she owed her fine sense of relativity. There are certain things one must possess in order not to be awed by them, and it was he who had enabled Millicent to take a Newport villa for granted. And still she was not satisfied! She had reached the point where taking the exceptional as a matter of course becomes in itself a matter of course; and Millicent could not live without novelty. That was the worst of it: she discarded her successes as rapidly as her gowns; Mr. Mindon felt a certain breathlessness in retracing her successive manifestations. And yet he had always made allowances: literally and figuratively, he had gone on making larger and larger allowances, till his whole income, as well as his whole point of view, was practically at Millicent's disposal. But, after all, there was a principle of give and take—if only Millicent could have been brought to see it! One of Millicent's chief sources of strength lay in her magnificent obtuseness: there were certain obligations that simply didn't exist for her, because she couldn't be brought to see them, and the principle of give and take (a favorite principle of Mr. Mindon's) was one of them.

There was Frank Antrim, for instance. Mr. Mindon, who had a high sense of propriety, had schooled himself, not without difficulty, into thinking Antrim a charming fellow. No one was more alive than Mr. Mindon to the expediency of calling the Furies the Eumenides. He knew that as long as he chose to think Frank Antrim a charming fellow, everything was as it should be and his home a temple of the virtues. But why on earth did Millicent let the fellow give presents to the children? Mr. Mindon was dimly conscious that Millicent had been guilty of the kind of failure she would least have liked him to detect—a failure in taste,—and a certain exultation tempered his resentment. To anyone who had suffered as Mr. Mindon had from Millicent's keenness in noting such lapses in others, it was not unpleasant to find that she could be "bad form." A sense of unwonted astuteness fortified Mr. Mindon's wrath. He felt that he had every reason to be angry with Millicent, and decided to go and scold the governess; then he remembered that it was bad for him to lose his temper after eating, and, drawing a small phial from his pocket, he took a pepsin tablet instead.

Having vented his wrath in action, he felt calmer, but scarcely more happy. A marble nymph smiled at him from the terrace; but he knew how much nymphs cost, and was not sure that they were worth the price. Beyond the shrubberies he caught a glimpse of domed glass. His green-houses were the finest in Newport; but since he neither ate fruit nor wore orchids, they yielded at best an indirect satisfaction. At length he decided to go and play with the little girls; but on entering the nursery he found them dressing for a party, with the rapt gaze and fevered cheeks with which Millicent would presently perform the same rite. They took no notice of him, and he crept downstairs again.

His study table was heaped with bills, and as it was bad for his digestion to look over them after luncheon, he wandered on into the other rooms. He did not stay long in the drawing-room: it evoked too vividly the evening hours when he delved for platitudes under the inattentive gaze of listeners who obviously resented his not being somebody else. Much of Mr. Mindon's intercourse with ladies was clouded by the sense of this resentment, and he sometimes avenged himself by wondering if they supposed he would talk to them if he could help it. The sight of the dining-room door increased his depression by recalling the long dinners where, with the pantry-draught on his neck, he languished between the dullest women of the evening. He turned away; but the ball-room beyond roused even more disturbing associations: an orchestra playing all night (Mr. Mindon crept to bed at eleven), carriages shouted for under his windows, and a morrow like the day after an earthquake.

In the library he felt less irritated but not more cheerful. Mr. Mindon had never quite known what the library was for: it was like one of those mysterious ruins over which archaeology endlessly disputes. It could not have been intended for reading, since no one in the house ever read, except an under-housemaid charged with having set fire to her bed in her surreptitious zeal for fiction; and smoking was forbidden there, because the hangings held the odor of tobacco. Mr. Mindon felt a natural pride in being rich enough to permit himself a perfectly useless room; but not liking to take the bloom from its inutility by sitting in it, he passed on to Millicent's boudoir.

Here at least was a room of manifold purposes, the center of Millicent's complex social system. Mr. Mindon entered with the awe of the modest investor treading the inner precincts of finance. He was proud of Millicent's social activities and liked to read over her daily list of engagements and the record of the invitations she received in a season. The number was perpetually swelling, like a rising stock. Mr. Mindon had a vague sense that she would soon be declaring an extra dividend. After all, one must be lenient to a woman as hard-working as Millicent. All about him were the evidences of her toil: her writing-table disappeared under an avalanche of notes and cards; the waste-paper basket overflowed with torn correspondence; and, glancing down, Mr. Mindon saw a crumpled letter at his feet. Being a man of neat habits, he was often tried by Millicent's genial disorder; and his customary rebuke was the act of restoring the strayed object to its place.

He stooped to gather the bit of paper from the floor. As he picked it up his eye caught a word; he smoothed the page and read on. . . .

## II

HE seemed to be cowering on the edge of a boiling flood, watching his small thinking faculty spin round out of reach on the tumult of his sensations. Then a fresh wave of emotion swept the tiny object—the quivering imperceptible ego—back to shore, and it began to reach out drowned tentacles in a faint effort after thought.

He sat up and glanced about him. The room looked back at him, coldly, unfamiliarly, as he had seen Millicent look when he asked her to be reasonable. And who are you? the walls seemed to say. Who am I? Mr. Mindon heard himself retorting. I'll tell you, by God! I'm the man that paid for you—paid for every scrap of you: silk hangings, china rubbish, glasses, chandeliers,—every Frenchified rag of you. Why, if it weren't for me and my money you'd be nothing but a brick-and-plaster shell, naked as the day you were built—no better than a garret or a coal-hole. Why, you wouldn't *be* at all if I chose to tear you down. I could tear the whole house down, if I chose.

He paused, suddenly aware that his eyes were on a photograph of Millicent, and that it was his wife he was apostrophizing. Her lips seemed to shape a "hush:" when he said things she didn't like she always told him not to talk so loud. Had he been talking loud? Well, who was to prevent him? Wasn't the house his and everything in it? Who was Millicent, to bid him hush?

Mr. Mindon felt a sudden increase of stature. He strutted across the room. Why, of course, the room belonged to him, the house belonged to him, and he belonged to himself! That was the best of it! For years he had been the man that Millicent thought him, the mere projection of her disdain; and now he was himself.

It was odd how the expression of her photograph changed, melting, as her face did, from contempt to cajolery, in one of those transitions that hung him breathless on the skirts of her mood. She was looking at him gently now, sadly almost, with the little grieved smile that seemed always to anticipate and pardon his obtuseness. Ah, Millicent! The clock struck and Mr. Mindon stood still. Perhaps she was smiling so now—or the other way. He could have told the other fool where each of her smiles led. There was a fierce enjoyment in his sense of lucidity. He saw it all now. Millicent had kept him for years in bewildered subjection to exigencies as inscrutable as the decrees of Providence; but now his comprehension of her seemed a mere incident in his omniscience.

His sudden translation to the absolute gave him a curious sense of spectatorship: he seemed to be looking on at his own thoughts. His brain was like a brightly lit factory, full of flying wheels and shuttles. All the machinery worked with the greatest rapidity and precision. He was planning, reasoning, arguing, with unimagined facility: words flew out like sparks from each revolving thought. But suddenly he felt himself caught in the wheels of his terrific logic, and swept round, red and shrieking, till he was flung off into space.

The acuter thrill of one sobbing nerve detached itself against his consciousness. What was it that hurt so? Someone was speaking: a voice probed to the central pain—

"Any orders for the stable, sir?"

And Mr. Mindon found himself the mere mouth-piece of a roving impulse that replied—

"No; but you may telephone for a cab for me—at once."

### III

HE drove to one of the hotels. He was breathing more easily now, restored to the safe level of conventional sensation. His late ascent to the rarefied heights of the unexpected had left him weak and exhausted; but he gained reassurance from the way in which his thoughts were slipping back of themselves into the old grooves. He was feeling, he was sure, just as a gentleman ought to feel; all the consecrated phrases—"outraged honor," "a father's heart," "the sanctity of home"—were flocking glibly at his call. He had the self-confidence that comes of knowing one has on the right clothes. He had certainly done the proper thing in leaving the house at once; but, too weak and tired to consider the next step, he yielded himself to one of those soothing intervals of abeyance when life seems to wait submissively at the door.

As his cab breasted the current of the afternoon drive he caught the greeting of the lady with whom he and Millicent were to have dined. He was troubled by the vision of that disrupted dinner. He had not yet reached the point of detachment at which offending Mrs. Targe might become immaterial, and again he felt himself jerked out of his grooves. What ought he to do? Millicent, now, could have told him—if only he might have consulted Millicent! He pulled himself together and tried to think of his wrongs.

At the hotel, the astonished clerk led him upstairs, unlocking the door of a room that smelt of cheap soap. The window had been so long shut that it opened with a jerk, sending a shower of dead flies to the carpet. Out along the sea-front, at that hour, the south-wind was hurrying the waters, but the hotel stood in one of the sheltered streets, where in midsummer there is little life in the air. Mr. Mindon sat down in the provisional attitude of a visitor who is kept waiting. Over the fireplace hung a print of the Landing of Columbus; a fly-blown portrait of General Grant faced it from the opposite wall. The smell of soap was insufferable, and hot noises came up irritatingly from the street. He looked at his watch: it was just four o'clock.

He wondered if Millicent had come in yet, and if she had read his letter. The occupation of picturing how she would feel when she read it proved less exhilarating than he had expected, and he got up and wandered about the room. He opened a drawer in the dressing-table, and seeing in it some burnt matches and a fuzz of hair, shut it with disgust; but just as he was ringing to rebuke the house-maid he remembered that he was not in his own house. He sat down again, wondering if the afternoon post were in, and what letters it had brought. It was annoying not to get his letters. What would be done about them? Would they be sent after him? Sent where? It suddenly occurred to him that he didn't in the least know where he was going. He must be going somewhere, of course; he hadn't left home to settle down in that stifling room. He supposed he should go to town, but with the heat at ninety the prospect was not alluring. He might decide on Lenox or Saratoga; but a doubt as to the propriety of such a course set him once more adrift on a chartless sea of perplexities. His head ached horribly and he threw himself on the bed.

When he sat up, worn out with his thoughts, the room was growing dark. Eight o'clock! Millicent must be dressing—but no; to-night at least, he grimly reflected, she was condemned to the hateful necessity of dining alone; unless, indeed, her audacity sent her to Mrs. Targe's in the always-acceptable role of the pretty woman whose husband has been "called away." Perhaps Antrim would be asked to fill his place!

The thought flung him on his feet, but its impetus carried him no farther. He was borne down by the physical apathy of a traveller who has a week's journey in his bones. He sat down and thought of the little girls, who were just going to bed. They would have welcomed him at that hour: he was aware that they cherished him chiefly as a pretext, a sanctuary from bed-time and lessons. He had never in his life been more than an alternative to anyone.

A vague sense of physical apprehension resolved itself into hunger stripped of appetite, and he decided that he ought to urge himself to eat. He opened his door on a rising aroma of stale coffee and fry.

In the dining room, where a waiter offered him undefinable food in thick-lipped saucers, Mr. Mindon decided to go to New York. Retreating from the heavy assault of a wedge of pie, he pushed back his chair and went upstairs. He felt hot and grimy in the yachting-clothes he had worn since morning, and the Fall River boat would at least be cool. Then he remembered the playful throngs that held the deck, the midnight hilarity of the waltz-tunes, the horror of the morning coffee. His stomach was still tremulous from its late adventure into the unknown, and he shrank from further risks. He had never before realized how much he loved his home.

He grew soft at the vision of his vacant chair. What were they doing and saying without him? His little ones were fatherless—and Millicent? Hitherto he had evaded the thought of Millicent, but now he took a doleful pleasure in picturing her in ruins at his feet. Involuntarily he found himself stooping to her despair; but he straightened himself and said aloud, "I'll take the night-train, then." The sound of his voice surprised him, and he started up. Was that a footstep outside?—a message, a note? Had they found out where he was, and was his wretched wife mad enough to sue for mercy? His ironical smile gave the measure of her madness; but the step passed on, and he sat down rather blankly. The impressiveness of his attitude was being gradually sapped by the sense that no one knew where he was. He had reached the point where he could not be sure of remaining inflexible unless someone asked him to relent.

## IV

AT the sound of a knock he clutched his hat and bag.

"Mindon, I say!" a genial voice adjured him; and before he could take counsel with his newly acquired dignity, which did not immediately respond to a first summons, the door opened on the reassuring presence of Laurence Meysy.

Mr. Mindon felt the relief of a sufferer at the approach of the eminent specialist. Laurence Meysy was the past tense of a dangerous man: though time-worn, still a favorite; a circulating-library romance, dog-eared by many a lovely hand, and still perused with pleasure, though, alas! no longer on the sly. He was said to have wrought much havoc in his youth; and it being now his innocent pleasure to repair the damage done by others, he had become the consulting physician of injured husbands and imprudent wives.

Two gentlemen followed him: Mr. Mindon's uncle and senior partner, the eminent Ezra Brownrigg, and the Reverend Doctor Bonifant, rector of the New York church in which Mr. Mindon owned a pew that was almost as expensive as his opera-box.

Mr. Brownrigg entered silently: to get at anything to say he had to sink an artesian well of meditation; but he always left people impressed by what he would have said if he had spoken. He greeted his nephew with the air of a distinguished mourner at a funeral— the mourner who consciously overshadows the corpse; and Doctor Bonifant did justice to the emotional side of the situation by fervently exclaiming, "Thank Heaven, we are not too late!"

Mr. Mindon looked about him with pardonable pride. The scene suggested something between a vestry-meeting and a conference of railway-directors; and the knowledge that he himself was its central figure, that even his uncle was an accessory, an incident, a mere bit of still-life brushed in by the artist Circumstance to throw Mr. Mindon into fuller prominence, gave that gentleman his first sense of equality with his wife. Equality? In another moment he towered above her, picturing her in an attitude of vaguely imagined penance at Doctor Bonifant's feet. Mr. Mindon had always felt about the clergy much as he did about his library: he had never quite known what they were for; but, with the pleased surprise of the pious naturalist, he now saw that they had their uses, like every other object in the economy of nature.

"My dear fellow," Meysy persuasively went on, "we've come to have a little chat with you."

Mr. Brownrigg and the Rector seated themselves. Mr. Mindon mechanically followed their example, and Meysy, asking the others if they minded his cigarette, cheerfully accommodated himself to the edge of the bed.

From the life-long habit of taking the chair, Mr. Brownrigg coughed and looked at Doctor Bonifant. The Rector leaned forward, stroking his cheek with a hand on which a massive intaglio seemed to be rehearsing the part of the episcopal ring; then his deprecating glance transferred the burden of action to Laurence Meysy. Meysy seemed to be surveying the case through the mitigating medium of cigarette-smoke. His view was that of the professional setting to rights the blunders of two amateurs. It was his theory that the art of carrying on a love affair was very nearly extinct; and he had a far greater contempt for Antrim than for Mr. Mindon.

"My dear fellow," he began, "I've seen Mrs. Mindon—she sent for me."

Mr. Brownrigg, peering between guarded lids, here interposed a "Very proper."

Of course Millicent had done the proper thing! Mr. Mindon could not repress a thrill of pride at her efficiency.

"Mrs. Mindon," Meysy continued, "showed me your letter." He paused. "She was perfectly frank—she throws herself on your mercy."

"That should be remembered in her favor," Doctor Bonifant murmured in a voice of absolution.

"It's a wretched business, Mindon—the poor woman's crushed—crushed. Your uncle here has seen her."

Mr. Brownrigg glanced suspiciously at Meysy, as though not certain whether he cared to corroborate an unauthorized assertion; then he said, "Mrs. Brownrigg has *not*."

Doctor Bonifant sighed: Mrs. Brownrigg was one of his most cherished parishioners.

"And the long and short of it is," Meysy summed up, "that we're here as your friends—and as your wife's friends—to ask you what you mean to do."

There was a pause. Mr. Mindon was disturbed by finding the initiative shifted to his shoulders. He had been talking to himself so volubly for the last six hours that he seemed to have nothing left to say.

"To do—to do?" he stammered. "Why, I mean to go away—leave her—"

"Divorce her?"

"Why,—y-yes—yes—"

Doctor Bonifant sighed again, and Mr. Brownrigg's lips stirred like a door being cautiously unbarred.

Meysy knocked the ashes off his cigarette. "You've quite made up your mind, eh?"

Mr. Mindon faltered another assent. Then, annoyed at the uncertain sound of his voice, he repeated loudly, "I mean to divorce her."

The repetition fortified his resolve; and his declaration seemed to himself against entreaty: their mere presence was a pedestal for his wrongs. The words flocked of themselves, building up his conviction like a throng of masons buttressing a weak wall.

Mr. Brownrigg spoke upon his first pause. "There's the publicity—it's the kind of thing that's prejudicial to a man's business interests.

An hour earlier the words would have turned Mr. Mindon cold; now he brushed them aside. His business interests, forsooth! What good had his money ever done him? What chance had he ever had of enjoying it? All his toil hadn't made him a rich man—it had merely made Millicent a rich woman.

Doctor Bonifant murmured, "The children must be considered."

"They've never considered me!" Mr. Mindon retorted—and turned afresh upon his uncle. Mr. Brownrigg listened impassively. He was a very silent man, but his silence was not a receptacle for the speech of others—it was a hard convex surface on which argument found no footing. Mr. Mindon reverted to the Rector. Doctor Bonifant's attitude towards life was full of a benignant receptivity; as though, logically, a man who had accepted the Thirty-nine Articles was justified in accepting anything else that he chose. His attention had therefore an absorbent quality peculiarly encouraging to those who addressed him. He listened affirmatively, as it were.

Mr. Mindon's spirits rose. It was the first time that he had ever had an audience. He dragged his hearers over every stage of his wrongs, losing sight of the vital injury in the enumeration of incidental grievances. He had the excited sense that at last Millicent would know what he had always thought of her.

Mr. Brownrigg looked at his watch, and Doctor Bonifant bent his head as though under the weight of a pulpit peroration. Meysy, from the bed, watched the three men with the air of an expert who holds the solution of the problem.

He slipped to his feet as Mr. Mindon's speech flagged.

"I suppose you've considered, Mindon, that it rests with you to proclaim the fact that you're no longer—well, the chief object of your wife's affection?"

Mr. Mindon raised his head irritably; interrogation impeded the flow of his diatribe.

"That you—er—in short, create the situation by making it known?" Meysy glanced at the Rector. "Am I right, Bonifant?"

The Rector took meditative counsel of his finger-tips; then slowly, as though formulating a dogma, "Under certain conditions," he conceded, "what is unknown may be said to be non-existent."

Mr. Mindon looked from one to the other.

"Damn it, man—before it's too late," Meysy followed up, "can't you see that *you're* the only person who can make you ridiculous?"

Mr. Brownrigg rose, and Mr. Mindon had the desperate sense that the situation was slipping out of his grasp.

"It rests with you," Doctor Bonifant murmured, "to save your children from even the shadow of obloquy."

"You can't stay here, at any rate," said Mr. Brownrigg heavily.

Mr. Mindon, who had risen, dropped weakly into his chair. His three counselors were now all on their feet, taking up their hats with the air of men who have touched the limit of duty. In another moment they would be gone, and with them Mr. Mindon's audience, his support, his confidence in the immutability of his resolve. He felt himself no more than an evocation of their presence; and, in dread of losing the identity they had created, he groped for a detaining word. "I shan't leave for New York till tomorrow."

"Tomorrow everything will be known," said Mr. Brownrigg, with his hand on the door.

Meysy glanced at his watch with a faint smile. "It's tomorrow now," he added.

He fell back, letting the older men pass out; but, turning as though to follow, he felt a drowning clutch upon his arm.

"It's for the children," Mr. Mindon stammered.

CRUCIAL INSTANCES (1901)

THE DUCHESS AT PRAYER

HAVE YOU ever questioned the long shuttered front of an old Italian house, that motionless mask, smooth, mute, equivocal as the face of a priest behind which buzz the secrets of the confessional? Other houses declare the activities they shelter; they are the clear expressive cuticle of a life flowing close to the surface; but the old palace in its narrow street, the villa on its cypress-hooded hill, are as impenetrable as death. The tall windows are like blind eyes, the great door is a shut mouth. Inside there may be sunshine, the scent of myrtles, and a pulse of life through all the arteries of the huge frame; or a mortal solitude, where bats lodge in the disjointed stones and the keys rust in unused doors. . . .

## II

FROM the loggia, with its vanishing frescoes, I looked down an avenue barred by a ladder of cypress-shadows to the ducal escutcheon and mutilated vases of the gate. Flat noon lay on the gardens, on fountains, porticoes and grottoes. Below the terrace, where a chrome-colored lichen had sheeted the balustrade as with fine *laminae* of gold, vineyards stooped to the rich valley clasped in hills. The lower slopes were strewn with white villages like stars spangling a summer dusk; and beyond these, fold on fold of blue mountain, clear as gauze against the sky. The August air was lifeless, but it seemed light and vivifying after the atmosphere of the shrouded rooms through which I had been led. Their chill was on me and I hugged the sunshine.

"The Duchess's apartments are beyond," said the old man.

He was the oldest man I had ever seen; so sucked back into the past that he seemed more like a memory than a living being. The one trait linking him with the actual was the fixity with which his small saurian eye held the pocket that, as I entered, had yielded a *lira* to the gatekeeper's child. He went on, without removing his eye:

"For two hundred years nothing has been changed in the apartments of the Duchess."

"And no one lives here now?"

"No one, sir. The Duke, goes to Como for the summer season."

I had moved to the other end of the loggia. Below me, through hanging groves, white roofs and domes flashed like a smile.

"And that's Vicenza?"

"*Proprio!*" The old man extended fingers as lean as the hands fading from the walls behind us. "You see the palace roof over there, just to the left of the Basilica? The one with the row of statues like birds taking flight? That's the Duke's town palace, built by Palladio."

"And does the Duke come there?"

"Never. In winter he goes to Rome."

"And the palace and the villa are always closed?"

"As you see—always."

"How long has this been?"

"Since I can remember."

I looked into his eyes: they were like tarnished metal mirrors reflecting nothing. "That must be a long time," I said involuntarily.

"A long time," he assented.

I looked down on the gardens. An opulence of dahlias overran the box-borders, between cypresses that cut the sunshine like basalt shafts. Bees hung above the lavender; lizards sunned themselves on the benches and slipped through the cracks of the dry basins. Everywhere were vanishing traces of that fantastic horticulture of which our dull age has lost the art. Down the alleys maimed statues stretched their arms like rows of whining beggars; faun-eared terms grinned in the thickets, and above the laurustinus walls rose the mock ruin of a temple, falling into real ruin in the bright disintegrating air. The glare was blinding.

"Let us go in," I said.

The old man pushed open a heavy door, behind which the cold lurked like a knife.

"The Duchess's apartments," he said.

Overhead and around us the same evanescent frescoes, underfoot the same scagliola volutes, unrolled themselves interminably. Ebony cabinets, with inlay of precious marbles in cunning perspective, alternated down the room with the tarnished efflorescence of gilt consoles supporting Chinese monsters; and from the chimney-panel a gentleman in the Spanish habit haughtily ignored us.

"Duke Ercole II.," the old man explained, "by the Genoese Priest."

It was a narrow-browed face, sallow as a wax effigy, high-nosed and cautious-lidded, as though modeled by priestly hands; the lips weak and vain rather than cruel; a quibbling mouth that would have snapped at verbal errors like a lizard catching flies, but had never learned the shape of a round yes or no. One of the Duke's hands rested on the head of a dwarf, a simian creature with pearl ear-rings and fantastic dress; the other turned the pages of a folio propped on a skull.

"Beyond is the Duchess's bedroom," the old man reminded me.

Here the shutters admitted but two narrow shafts of light, gold bars deepening the subaqueous gloom. On a dais the bedstead, grim, nuptial, official, lifted its baldachin; a yellow Christ agonized between the curtains, and across the room a lady smiled at us from the chimney breast.

The old man unbarred a shutter and the light touched her face. Such a face it was, with a flicker of laughter over it like the wind on a June meadow, and a singular tender pliancy of mien, as though one of Tiepolo's lenient goddesses had been busked into the stiff sheath of a seventeenth century dress!

"No one has slept here," said the old man, "since the Duchess Violante."

"And she was—?"

"The lady there—first Duchess of Duke Ercole II."

He drew a key from his pocket and unlocked a door at the farther end of the room. "The chapel," he said. "This is the Duchess's balcony." As I turned to follow him the Duchess tossed me a sidelong smile.

I stepped into a grated tribune above a chapel festooned with stucco. Pictures of bituminous saints moldered between the pilasters; the artificial roses in the altar-vases were gray with dust and age, and under the cobwebby rosettes of the vaulting a bird's nest clung. Before the altar stood a row of tattered arm-chairs, and I drew back at sight of a figure kneeling near them.

"The Duchess," the old man whispered. "By the Cavaliere Bernini."

It was the image of a woman in furred robes and spreading fraise, her hand lifted, her face addressed to the tabernacle. There was a strangeness in the sight of that immovable presence locked in prayer before an abandoned shrine. Her face was hidden, and I wondered whether it were grief or gratitude that raised her hands and drew her eyes to the altar, where no living prayer joined her marble invocation. I followed my guide down the tribune steps, impatient to see what mystic version of such terrestrial graces the ingenious artist had found—the Cavaliere was master of such arts. The Duchess's attitude was one of transport, as though heavenly airs fluttered her laces and the love-locks escaping from her coif. I saw how admirably the sculptor had caught the poise of her head, the tender slope of the shoulder; then I crossed over and looked into her face—it was a frozen horror. Never have hate, revolt and agony so possessed a human countenance. . . .

The old man crossed himself and shuffled his feet on the marble.

"The Duchess Violante," he repeated.

"The same as in the picture?"

"Eh—the same."

"But the face—what does it mean?"

He shrugged his shoulders and turned deaf eyes on me. Then he shot a glance round the sepulchral place, clutched my sleeve and said, close to my ear: "It was not always so."

"What was not?"

"The face—so terrible."

"The Duchess's face?"

"The statue's. It changed after—"

"After?"

"It was put here."

"The statue's face *changed*—?"

He mistook my bewilderment for incredulity and his confidential finger dropped from my sleeve. "Eh, that's the story. I tell what I've heard. What do I know?" He resumed his senile shuffle across the marble. "This is a bad place to stay in—no one comes here. It's too cold. But the gentleman said, *I must see everything!*"

I let the *lire* sound. "So I must—and hear everything. This story, now—from whom did you have it?"

His hand stole back. "One that saw it, by God!"

"That saw it?"

"My grandmother, then. I'm a very old man."

"Your grandmother? Your grandmother was—?"

"The Duchess's serving girl, with respect to you."

"Your grandmother? Two hundred years ago?"

"Is it too long ago? That's as God pleases. I am a very old man and she was a very old woman when I was born. When she died she was as black as a miraculous Virgin and her breath whistled like the wind in a keyhole. She told me the story when I was a little boy. She told it to me out there in the garden, on a bench by the fish-pond, one summer night of the year she died. It must be true, for I can show you the very bench we sat on...."

### III

NOON lay heavier on the gardens; not our live humming warmth but the stale exhalation of dead summers. The very statues seemed to drowse like watchers by a death-bed. Lizards shot out of the cracked soil like flames and the bench in the laurustinus-niche was strewn with the blue varnished bodies of dead flies. Before us lay the fish-pond, a yellow marble slab above rotting secrets. The villa looked across it, composed as a dead face, with the cypresses flanking it for candles....

### IV

"IMPOSSIBLE, you say, that my mother's mother should have been the Duchess's maid? What do I know? It is so long since anything has happened here that the old things seem nearer, perhaps, than to those who live in cities.... But how else did she know about the statue then? Answer me that, sir! That she saw with her eyes, I can swear to, and never smiled again, so she told me, till they put her first child in her arms... for she was taken to wife by the steward's son, Antonio, the same who had carried the letters.... But where am I? Ah, well... she was a mere slip, you understand, my grandmother, when the

Duchess died, a niece of the upper maid, Nencia, and suffered about the Duchess because of her pranks and the funny songs she knew. It's possible, you think, she may have heard from others what she afterward fancied she had seen herself? How that is, it's not for an unlettered man to say; though indeed I myself seem to have seen many of the things she told me. This is a strange place. No one comes here, nothing changes, and the old memories stand up as distinct as the statues in the garden. . . .

"It began the summer after they came back from the Brenta. Duke Ercole had married the lady from Venice, you must know; it was a gay city, then, I'm told, with laughter and music on the water, and the days slipped by like boats running with the tide. Well, to humor her he took her back the first autumn to the Brenta. Her father, it appears, had a grand palace there, with such gardens, bowling-alleys, grottoes and casinos as never were; gondolas bobbing at the water-gates, a stable full of gilt coaches, a theatre full of players, and kitchens and offices full of cooks and lackeys to serve up chocolate all day long to the fine ladies in masks and furbelows, with their pet dogs and their blackamoors and their *abates*. Eh! I know it all as if I'd been there, for Nencia, you see, my grandmother's aunt, travelled with the Duchess, and came back with her eyes round as platters, and not a word to say for the rest of the year to any of the lads who'd courted her here in Vicenza.

"What happened there I don't know—my grandmother could never get at the rights of it, for Nencia was mute as a fish where her lady was concerned—but when they came back to Vicenza the Duke ordered the villa set in order; and in the spring he brought the Duchess here and left her. She looked happy enough, my grandmother said, and seemed no object for pity. Perhaps, after all, it was better than being shut up in Vicenza, in the tall painted rooms where priests came and went as softly as cats prowling for birds, and the Duke was forever closeted in his library, talking with learned men. The Duke was a scholar; you noticed he was painted with a book? Well, those that can read 'em make out that they're full of wonderful things; as a man that's been to a fair across the mountains will always tell his people at home it was beyond anything *they'll* ever see. As for the Duchess, she was all for music, play-acting and young company. The Duke was a silent man, stepping quietly, with his eyes down, as though he'd just come from confession; when the Duchess's lap-dog yapped at his heels he danced like a man in a swarm of hornets; when the Duchess laughed he winced as if you'd drawn a diamond across a window-pane. And the Duchess was always laughing.

"When she first came to the villa she was very busy laying out the gardens, designing grottoes, planting groves and planning all manner of agreeable surprises in the way of water-jets that drenched you unexpectedly, and hermits in caves, and wild men that jumped at you out of thickets. She had a very pretty taste in such matters, but after a while she tired of it, and there being no one for her to talk to but her maids and the chaplain—a clumsy man deep in his books—why, she would have strolling players out from Vicenza, mountebanks and fortune-tellers from the market-place, travelling doctors and astrologers, and all manner of trained animals. Still it could be seen that the poor lady pined for company, and her waiting women, who loved her, were glad when the Cavaliere Ascanio, the Duke's cousin, came to live at the vineyard across the valley—you see the pinkish house over there in the mulberries, with a red roof and a pigeon cote?

"The Cavaliere Ascanio was a cadet of one of the great Venetian houses, *pezzi grossi* of the Golden Book. He had been' meant for the Church, I believe, but what! he set fighting above praying and cast in his lot with the captain of the Duke of Mantua's *bravi*, himself a Venetian of good standing, but a little at odds with the law. Well, the next I know, the Cavaliere was in Venice again, perhaps not in good odor on account of his connection with the gentleman I speak of. Some say he tried to carry off a nun from the convent of Santa Croce; how that may be I can't say; but my grandmother declared he had enemies there, and the end of it was that on some pretext or other the Ten banished him to Vicenza. There, of course, the Duke, being his kinsman, had to show him a civil face; and that was how he first came to the villa.

"He was a fine young man, beautiful as a Saint Sebastian, a rare musician, who sang his own songs to the lute in a way that used to make my grandmother's heart melt and run through her body like mulled wine. He had a good word for everybody, too, and was always dressed in the French fashion, and smelt as sweet as a bean-field; and every soul about the place welcomed the sight of him.

"Well, the Duchess, it seemed, welcomed it too; youth will have youth, and laughter turns to laughter; and the two matched each other like the candlesticks on an altar. The Duchess—you've seen her portrait—but to hear my grandmother, sir, it no more approached her than a weed comes up to a rose. The Cavaliere, indeed, as became a poet, paragoned her in his song to all the pagan goddesses of antiquity; and doubtless these were finer to look at than mere women; but so, it seemed, was she; for, to believe my grandmother, she made other women look no more than the big French fashion-doll that used to be shown on Ascension days in the Piazza. She was one, at any rate, that needed no outlandish finery to beautify her; whatever dress she wore became her as feathers fit the bird; and her hair didn't get its color by bleaching on the housetop. It glittered of itself like the threads in an Easter chasuble, and her skin was whiter than fine wheaten bread and her mouth as sweet as a ripe fig.

"Well, sir, you could no more keep them apart than the bees and the lavender. They were always together, singing, bowling, playing cup and ball, walking in the gardens, visiting the aviaries and petting her grace's trick-dogs and monkeys. The Duchess was as gay as a foal, always playing pranks and laughing, tricking out her animals like comedians, disguising herself as a peasant or a nun (you should have seen her one day pass herself off to the chaplain as a mendicant sister), or teaching the lads and girls of the vineyards to dance and sing madrigals together. The Cavaliere had a singular ingenuity in planning such entertainments and the days were hardly long enough for their diversions. But toward the end of the summer the Duchess fell quiet and would hear only sad music, and the two sat much together in the gazebo at the end of the garden. It was there the Duke found them one day when he drove out from Vicenza in his gilt coach. He came but once or twice a year to the villa, and it was, as my grandmother said, just a part of her poor lady's ill-luck to be wearing that day the Venetian habit, which uncovered the shoulders in a way the Duke always scowled at, and her curls loose and powdered with gold. Well, the three drank chocolate in the gazebo, and what happened no one knew, except that the Duke, on taking leave, gave his cousin a seat in his carriage; but the Cavaliere never returned.

"Winter approaching, and the poor lady thus finding herself once more alone, it was surmised among her women that she must fall into a deeper depression of spirits. But far from this being the case, she displayed such cheerfulness and equanimity of humor that my grandmother, for one, was half-vexed with her for giving no more thought to the poor young man who, all this time, was eating his heart out in the house across the valley. It is true she quitted her gold-laced gowns and wore a veil over her head; but Nencia would have it she looked the lovelier for the change and so gave the Duke greater displeasure. Certain it is that the Duke drove out oftener to the villa, and though he found his lady always engaged in some innocent pursuit, such as embroidery or music, or playing games with her young women, yet he always went away with a sour look and a whispered word to the chaplain. Now as to the chaplain, my grandmother owned there had been a time when her grace had not handled him over-wisely. For, according to Nencia, it seems that his reverence, who seldom approached the Duchess, being buried in his library like a mouse in a cheese—well, one day he made bold to appeal to her for a sum of money, a large sum, Nencia said, to buy certain tall books, a chest full of them, that a foreign peddler had brought him; whereupon the Duchess, who could never abide a book, breaks out at him with a laugh and a flash of her old spirit—'Holy Mother of God, must I have more books about me? I was nearly smothered with them in the first year of my marriage;' and the chaplain turning red at the affront, she added: 'You may buy them and welcome, my good chaplain, if you can find the money; but as for me, I am yet seeking a way to pay for my turquoise necklace, and the statue of Daphne at the end of the bowling-green, and the Indian parrot that my black boy brought me last Michaelmas from the Bohemians—so you see I've no money to waste on trifles;' and as he backs out awkwardly she tosses at him over her shoulder: 'You should pray to Saint Blandina to open the Duke's pocket!' to which he returned, very quietly, 'Your excellency's suggestion is an admirable one, and I have already entreated that blessed martyr to open the Duke's understanding.'

"Thereat, Nencia said (who was standing by), the Duchess flushed wonderfully red and waved him out of the room; and then 'Quick!' she cried to my grandmother (who was too glad to run on such errands), 'Call me Antonio, the gardener's boy, to the box-garden; I've a word to say to him about the new clove-carnations. . . .'

"Now I may not have told you, sir, that in the crypt under the chapel there has stood, for more generations than a man can count, a stone coffin containing a thighbone of the blessed Saint Blandina of Lyons, a relic offered, I've been told, by some great Duke of France to one of our own dukes when they fought the Turk together; and the object, ever since, of particular veneration in this illustrious family. Now, since the Duchess had been left to herself, it was observed she affected a fervent devotion to this relic, praying often in the chapel and even causing the stone slab that covered the entrance to the crypt to be replaced by a wooden one, that she might at will descend and kneel by the coffin. This was matter of edification to all the household and should have been peculiarly pleasing to the chaplain; but, with respect to you, he was the kind of man who brings a sour mouth to the eating of the sweetest apple.

"However that may be, the Duchess, when she dismissed him, was seen running to the garden, where she talked earnestly with the boy Antonio about the new clove-carnations; and the rest of the day she sat indoors and played sweetly on the virginal. Now Nencia always had it in mind that her grace had made a mistake in refusing that request of the chaplain's; but she said nothing, for to talk reason to the Duchess was of no more use than praying for rain in a drought.

"Winter came early that year, there was snow on the hills by All Souls, the wind stripped the gardens, and the lemon-trees were nipped in the lemon-house. The Duchess kept her room in this black season, sitting over the fire, embroidering, reading books of devotion (which was a thing she had never done) and praying frequently in the chapel. As for the chaplain, it was a place he never set foot in but to say mass in the morning, with the Duchess overhead in the tribune, and the servants aching with rheumatism on the marble floor. The chaplain himself hated the cold, and galloped through the mass like a man with witches after him. The rest of the day he spent in his library, over a brazier, with his eternal books. . . .

"You'll wonder, sir, if I'm ever to get to the gist of the story; and I've gone slowly, I own, for fear of what's coming. Well, the winter was long and hard. When it fell cold the Duke ceased to come out from Vicenza, and not a soul had the Duchess to speak to but her maid-servants and the gardeners about the place. Yet it was wonderful, my grandmother said, how she kept her brave colors and her spirits; only it was remarked that she prayed longer in the chapel, where a brazier was kept burning for her all day. When the young are denied their natural pleasures they turn often enough to religion; and it was a mercy, as my grandmother said, that she, who had scarce a live sinner to speak to, should take such comfort in a dead saint.

"My grandmother seldom saw her that winter, for though she showed a brave front to all she kept more and more to herself, choosing to have only Nencia about her and dismissing even her when she went to pray. For her devotion had that mark of true piety, that she wished it not to be observed; so that Nencia had strict orders, on the chaplain's approach, to warn her mistress if she happened to be in prayer.

"Well, the winter passed, and spring was well forward, when my grandmother one evening had a bad fright. That it was her own fault I won't deny, for she'd been down the lime-walk with Antonio when her aunt fancied her to be stitching in her chamber; and seeing a sudden light in Nencia's window, she took fright lest her disobedience be found out, and ran up quickly through the laurel-grove to the house. Her way lay by the chapel, and as she crept past it, meaning to slip in through the scullery, and groping her way, for the dark had fallen and the moon was scarce up, she heard a crash close behind her, as though someone had dropped from a window of the chapel. The young fool's heart turned over, but she looked round as she ran, and there, sure enough, was a man scuttling across the terrace; and as he doubled the corner of the house my grandmother swore she caught the whisk of the chaplain's skirts. Now that was a strange thing, certainly; for why should the chaplain be getting out of the chapel window when he might have passed through the door? For you may have noticed, sir, there's a door leads from the chapel into the saloon on the ground floor; the only other way out being through the Duchess's tribune.

"Well, my grandmother turned the matter over, and next time she met Antonio in the lime-walk (which, by reason of her fright, was not for some days) she laid before him what had happened; but to her surprise he only laughed and said, 'You little simpleton, he wasn't getting out of the window, he was trying to look in'; and not another word could she get from him.

"So the season moved on to Easter, and news came the Duke had gone to Rome for that holy festivity. His comings and goings made no change at the villa, and yet there was no one there but felt easier to think his yellow face was on the far side of the Apennines, unless perhaps it was the chaplain.

"Well, it was one day in May that the Duchess, who had walked long with Nencia on the terrace, rejoicing at the sweetness of the prospect and the pleasant scent of the gilly-flowers in the stone vases, the Duchess toward midday withdrew to her rooms, giving orders that her dinner should be served in her bed-chamber. My grandmother helped to carry in the dishes, and observed, she said, the singular beauty of the Duchess, who in honor of the fine weather had put on a gown of shot-silver and hung her bare shoulders with pearls, so that she looked fit to dance at court with an emperor. She had ordered, too, a rare repast for a lady that heeded so little what she ate—jellies, game-pasties, fruits in syrup, spiced cakes and a flagon of Greek wine; and she nodded and clapped her hands as the women set it before her, saying again and again, 'I shall eat well today.'

"But presently another mood seized her; she turned from the table, called for her rosary, and said to Nencia: 'The fine weather has made me neglect my devotions. I must say a litany before I dine.'

"She ordered the women out and barred the door, as her custom was; and Nencia and my grandmother went downstairs to work in the linen-room.

"Now the linen room gives on the court-yard, and suddenly my grandmother saw a strange sight approaching. First up the avenue came the Duke's carriage (whom all thought to be in Rome), and after it, drawn by a long string of mules and oxen, a cart carrying what looked like a kneeling figure wrapped in death-clothes. The strangeness of it struck the girl dumb and the Duke's coach was at the door before she had the wit to cry out that it was coming. Nencia, when she saw it, went white and ran out of the room. My grandmother followed, scared by her face, and the two fled along the corridor to the chapel. On the way they met the chaplain, deep in a book, who asked in surprise where they were running, and when they said, to announce the Duke's arrival, he fell into such astonishment and asked them so many questions and uttered such ohs and ahs, that by the time he let them by the Duke was at their heels. Nencia reached the chapel-door first and cried out that the Duke was coming; and before she had a reply he was at her side, with the chaplain following.

"A moment later the door opened and there stood the Duchess. She held her rosary in one hand and had drawn a scarf over her shoulders; but they shone through it like the moon in a mist, and her countenance sparkled with beauty.

"The Duke took her hand with a bow. 'Madam,' he said, 'I could have had no greater happiness than thus to surprise you at your devotions.'

"'My own happiness,' she replied, 'would have been greater had your excellency prolonged it by giving me notice of your arrival.'

"'Had you expected me, Madam,' said he, 'your appearance could scarcely have been more fitted to the occasion. Few ladies of your youth and beauty array themselves to venerate a saint as they would to welcome a lover.'

"'Sir,' she answered, 'having never enjoyed the latter opportunity, I am constrained to make the most of the former.—What's that?' she cried, falling back, and the rosary dropped from her hand.

"There was a loud noise at the other end of the saloon, as of a heavy object being dragged down the passage; and presently a dozen men were seen haling across the threshold the shrouded thing from the oxcart. The Duke waved his hand toward it. 'That,' said he, 'Madam, is a tribute to your extraordinary piety. I have heard with peculiar satisfaction of your devotion to the blessed relics in this chapel, and to commemorate a zeal which neither the rigors of winter nor the sultriness of summer could abate I have ordered a sculptured image of you, marvelously executed by the Cavaliere Bernini, to be placed before the altar over the entrance to the crypt.'

"The Duchess, who had grown pale, nevertheless smiled playfully at this. 'As to commemorating my piety," she said, 'I recognize there one of your excellency's pleasantries—'

"'A pleasantry?' the Duke interrupted; and he made a sign to the men, who had now reached the threshold of the chapel. In an instant the wrappings fell from the figure, and there knelt the Duchess to the life. A cry of wonder rose from all, but the Duchess herself stood whiter than the marble.

"'You will see,' says the Duke, 'this is no pleasantry, but a triumph of the incomparable Bernini's chisel. The likeness was done from your miniature portrait by the divine Elisabetta Sirani, which I sent to the master some six months ago, with what results all must admire.'

"'Six months!' cried the Duchess, and seemed about to fall; but his excellency caught her by the hand.

"'Nothing,' he said, 'could better please me than the excessive emotion you display, for true piety is ever modest, and your thanks could not take a form that better became you. And now,' says he to the men, 'let the image be put in place.'

"By this, life seemed to have returned to the Duchess, and she answered him with a deep reverence. 'That I should be overcome by so unexpected a grace, your excellency admits to be natural; but what honors you accord it is my privilege to accept, and I entreat only that in mercy to my modesty the image be placed in the remotest part of the chapel.'

"At that the Duke darkened. 'What! You would have this masterpiece of a renowned chisel, which, I disguise not, cost me the price of a good vineyard in gold pieces, you would have it thrust out of sight like the work of a village stonecutter?'

"'It is my semblance, not the sculptor's work, I desire to conceal.'

"'It you are fit for my house, Madam, you are fit for God's, and entitled to the place of honor in both. Bring the statue forward, you dawdlers!' he called out to the men.

"The Duchess fell back submissively. 'You are right, sir, as always; but I would at least have the image stand on the left of the altar, that, looking up, it may behold your excellency's seat in the tribune.'

"'A pretty thought, Madam, for which I thank you; but I design before long to put my companion image on the other side of the altar; and the wife's place, as you know, is at her husband's right hand.'

"'True, my lord—but, again, if my poor presentment is to have the unmerited honor of kneeling beside yours, why not place both before the altar, where it is our habit to pray in life?'

"'And where, Madam, should we kneel if they took our places? Besides,' says the Duke, still speaking very blandly, 'I have a more particular purpose in placing your image over the entrance to the crypt; for not only would I thereby mark your special devotion to the blessed saint who rests there, but, by sealing up the opening in the pavement, would assure the perpetual preservation of that holy martyr's bones, which hitherto have been too thoughtlessly exposed to sacrilegious attempts.'

"'What attempts, my lord?' cries the Duchess. 'No one enters this chapel without my leave.'

"'So I have understood, and can well believe from what I have learned of your piety; yet at night a malefactor might break in through a window, Madam, and your excellency not know it.'

"'I'm a light sleeper,' said the Duchess.

"The Duke looked at her gravely. 'Indeed?' said he. 'A bad sign at your age. I must see that you are provided with a sleeping draught.'

"The Duchess's eyes filled. 'You would deprive me, then, of the consolation of visiting those venerable relics?'

"'I would have you keep eternal guard over them, knowing no one to whose care they may more fittingly be entrusted.'

"By this the image was brought close to the wooden slab that covered the entrance to the crypt, when the Duchess, springing forward, placed herself in the way.

"'Sir, let the statue be put in place tomorrow, and suffer me, to-night, to say a last prayer beside those holy bones.'

"The Duke stepped instantly to her side. 'Well thought, Madam; I will go down with you now, and we will pray together.'

"'Sir, your long absences have, alas! given me the habit of solitary devotion, and I confess that any presence is distracting.'

"'Madam, I accept your rebuke. Hitherto, it is true, the duties of my station have constrained me to long absences; but henceforward I remain with you while you live. Shall we go down into the crypt together?"

"'No; for I fear for your excellency's ague. The air there is excessively damp.'

"'The more reason you should no longer be exposed to it; and to prevent the intemperance of your zeal I will at once make the place inaccessible.'

"The Duchess at this fell on her knees on the slab, weeping excessively and lifting her hands to heaven.

"'Oh,' she cried, 'you are cruel, sir, to deprive me of access to the sacred relics that have enabled me to support with resignation the solitude to which your excellency's duties have condemned me; and if prayer and meditation give me any authority to pronounce on such matters, suffer me to warn you, sir, that I fear the blessed Saint Blandina will punish us for thus abandoning her venerable remains!'

"The Duke at this seemed to pause, for he was a pious man, and my grandmother thought she saw him exchange a glance with the chaplain; who, stepping timidly forward, with his eyes on the ground, said, 'There is indeed much wisdom in her excellency's words, but I would suggest, sir, that her pious wish might be met, and the saint more conspicuously honored, by transferring the relics from the crypt to a place beneath the altar.'

"'True!' cried the Duke, 'and it shall be done at once.'

"But threat the Duchess rose to her feet with a terrible look.

"'No,' she cried, 'by the body of God! For it shall not be said that, after your excellency has chosen to deny every request I addressed to him, I owe his consent to the solicitation of another!'

"The chaplain turned red and the Duke yellow, and for a moment neither spoke.

"Then the Duke said, 'Here are words enough, Madam. Do you wish the relics brought up from the crypt?'

"'I wish nothing that I owe to another's intervention!'

"'Put the image in place then,' says the Duke furiously; and handed her grace to a chair.

"She sat there, my grandmother said, straight as an arrow, her hands locked, her head high, her eyes on the Duke, while the statue was dragged to its place; then she stood up and turned away. As she passed by Nencia, 'Call me Antonio,' she whispered; but before the words were out of her mouth the Duke stepped between them.

"'Madam,' says he, all smiles now, 'I have travelled straight from Rome to bring you the sooner this proof of my esteem. I lay last night at Monselice and have been on the road since daybreak. Will you not invite me to supper?'

"'Surely, my lord,' said the Duchess. 'It shall be laid in the dining-parlor within the hour.'

"'Why not in your chamber and at once, Madam? Since I believe it is your custom to sup there.'

"'In my chamber?' says the Duchess, in disorder.

"'Have you anything against it?' he asked.

"'Assuredly not, sir, if you will give me time to prepare myself.'

"'I will wait in your cabinet,' said the Duke.

"At that, said my grandmother, the Duchess gave one look, as the souls in hell may have looked when the gates closed on our Lord; then she called Nencia and passed to her chamber.

"What happened there my grandmother could never learn, but that the Duchess, in great haste, dressed herself with extraordinary splendor, powdering her hair with gold, painting her face and bosom, and covering herself with jewels till she shone like our Lady of Loreto; and hardly were these preparations complete when the Duke entered from the cabinet, followed by the servants carrying supper. Thereupon the Duchess dismissed Nencia, and what follows my grandmother learned from a pantry-lad who brought up the dishes and waited in the cabinet; for only the Duke's body-servant entered the bedchamber.

"Well, according to this boy, sir, who was looking and listening with his whole body, as it were, because he had never before been suffered so near the Duchess, it appears that the noble couple sat down in great good humor, the Duchess playfully reproving her husband for his long absence, while the Duke swore that to look so beautiful was the best way of punishing him. In this tone the talk continued, with such gay sallies on the part of the Duchess, such tender advances on the Duke's, that the lad declared they were for all the world like a pair of lovers courting on a summer's night in the vineyard; and so it went till the servant brought in the mulled wine.

"'Ah,' the Duke was saying at that moment, 'this agreeable evening repays me for the many dull ones I have spent away from you; nor do I remember to have enjoyed such laughter since the afternoon last year when we drank chocolate in the gazebo with my cousin Ascanio. And that reminds me,' he said, 'is my cousin in good health?'

"'I have no reports of it,' says the Duchess. 'But your excellency should taste these figs stewed in malmsey—'

"'I am in the mood to taste whatever you offer,' said he; and as she helped him to the figs he added, 'If my enjoyment were not complete as it is, I could almost wish my cousin Ascanio were with us. The fellow is rare good company at supper. What do you say, Madam? I hear he's still in the country; shall we send for him to join us?'

"'Ah,' said the Duchess, with a sigh and a languishing look, 'I see your excellency wearies of me already.'

"'I, Madam? Ascanio is a capital good fellow, but to my mind his chief merit at this moment is his absence. It inclines me so tenderly to him that, by God, I could empty a glass to his good health.'

"With that the Duke caught up his goblet and signed to the servant to fill the Duchess's.

"'Here's to the cousin,' he cried, standing, 'who has the good taste to stay away when he's not wanted. I drink to his very long life—and you, Madam?'

"At this the Duchess, who had sat staring at him with a changed face, rose also and lifted her glass to her lips.

"'And I to his happy death,' says she in a wild voice; and as she spoke the empty goblet dropped from her hand and she fell face down on the floor.

"The Duke shouted to her women that she had swooned, and they came and lifted her to the bed. . . . She suffered horribly all night, Nencia said, twisting herself like a heretic at the stake, but without a word escaping her. The Duke watched by her, and toward daylight sent for the chaplain; but by this she was unconscious and, her teeth being locked, our Lord's body could not be passed through them.

"The Duke announced to his relations that his lady had died after partaking too freely of spiced wine and an omelet of carp's roe, at a supper she had prepared in honor of his return; and the next year he brought home a new Duchess, who gave him a son and five daughters. . . ."

V

THE sky had turned to a steel gray, against which the villa stood out sallow and inscrutable. A wind strayed through the gardens, loosening here and there a yellow leaf from the sycamores; and the hills across the valley were purple as thunderclouds.

"And the statue—?" I asked.

"Ah, the statue. Well, sir, this is what my grandmother told me, here on this very bench where we're sitting. The poor child, who worshipped the Duchess as a girl of her years will worship a beautiful kind mistress, spent a night of horror, you may fancy, shut out from her lady's room, hearing the cries that came from it, and seeing, as she crouched in her corner, the women rush to and fro with wild looks, the Duke's lean face in the door, and the chaplain skulking in the antechamber with his eyes on his breviary. No one minded her that night or the next morning; and toward dusk, when it became known the Duchess was no more, the poor girl felt the pious wish to say a prayer for her dead mistress. She crept to the chapel and stole in unobserved. The place was empty and dim, but as she advanced she heard a low moaning, and coming in front of the statue she saw that its face, the day before so sweet and smiling, had the look on it that you know—and the moaning seemed to come from its lips. My grandmother turned cold, but something, she said afterward, kept her from calling or shrieking out, and she turned and ran from the place. In the passage she fell in a swoon; and when she came to her senses, in her own chamber, she heard that the Duke had locked the chapel door and forbidden any to set foot there. . . . The place was never opened again till the Duke died, some ten years later; and then it was that the other servants, going in with the new heir, saw for the first time the horror that my grandmother had kept in her bosom. . . ."

"And the crypt?" I asked. "Has it never been opened?"

"Heaven forbid, sir!" cried the old man, crossing himself. "Was it not the Duchess's express wish that the relics should not be disturbed?"

THE ANGEL AT THE GRAVE

THE HOUSE stood a few yards back from the elm-shaded village street, in that semi-publicity sometimes cited as a democratic protest against old-world standards of domestic exclusiveness. This candid exposure to the public eye is more probably a result of the gregariousness which, in the New England bosom, oddly coexists with a shrinking from direct social contact; most of the inmates of such houses preferring that furtive intercourse which is the result of observations through shuttered windows and a categorical acquaintance with the neighboring clothes-lines. The House, however, faced its public with a difference. For sixty years it had written itself with a capital letter, had self-consciously squared itself in the eye of an admiring nation. The most searching inroads of village intimacy hardly counted in a household that opened on the universe; and a lady whose door-bell was at any moment liable to be rung by visitors from London or Vienna was not likely to flutter up-stairs when she observed a neighbor "stepping over."

The solitary inmate of the Anson House owed this induration of the social texture to the most conspicuous accident in her annals: the fact that she was the only granddaughter of the great Orestes Anson. She had been born, as it were, into a museum, and cradled in a glass case with a label; the first foundations of her consciousness being built on the rock of her grandfather's celebrity. To a little girl who acquires her earliest knowledge of literature through a *Reader* embellished with fragments of her ancestor's prose, that personage necessarily fills an heroic space in the foreground of life. To communicate with one's past through the impressive medium of print, to have, as it were, a footing in every library in the country, and an acknowledged kinship with that world-diffused clan, the descendants of the great, was to be pledged to a standard of manners that amazingly simplified the lesser relations of life. The village street on which Paulina Anson's youth looked out led to all the capitals of Europe; and over the roads of intercommunication unseen caravans bore back to the elm-shaded House the tribute of an admiring world.

Fate seemed to have taken a direct share in fitting Paulina for her part as the custodian of this historic dwelling. It had long been secretly regarded as a "visitation" by the great man's family that he had left no son and that his daughters were not "intellectual." The ladies themselves were the first to lament their deficiency, to own that nature had denied them the gift of making the most of their opportunities. A profound veneration for their parent and an unswerving faith in his doctrines had not amended their congenital incapacity to understand what he had written. Laura, who had her moments of mute rebellion against destiny, had sometimes thought how much easier it would have been if their progenitor had been a poet; for she could recite, with feeling, portions of *The Culprit Fay* and of the poems of Mrs. Hemans; and Phoebe, who was more conspicuous for memory than imagination, kept an album filled with "selections." But the great man was a philosopher; and to both daughters respiration was difficult on the cloudy heights of metaphysic. The situation would have been intolerable but for the fact that, while Phoebe and Laura were still at school, their father's fame had passed from the open ground of conjecture to the chill privacy of certitude. Dr. Anson had in fact achieved one of those anticipated immortalities not uncommon at a time when people were apt to base their literary judgments on their emotions, and when to affect plain food and despise England went a long way toward establishing a man's intellectual pre-eminence. Thus, when the daughters were called on to strike a filial attitude about their parent's pedestal, there was little to do but to pose gracefully and point upward; and there are spines to which the immobility of worship is not a strain. A legend had by this time crystallized about the great Orestes, and it was of more immediate interest to the public to hear what brand of tea he drank, and whether he took off his boots in the hall, than to rouse the drowsy echo of his dialectic. A great man never draws so near his public as when it has become unnecessary to read his books and is still interesting to know what he eats for breakfast.

As recorders of their parent's domestic habits, as pious scavengers of his waste-paper basket, the Misses Anson were unexcelled. They always had an interesting anecdote to impart to the literary pilgrim, and the tact with which, in later years, they intervened between the public and the growing inaccessibility of its idol, sent away many an enthusiast satisfied to have touched the veil before the sanctuary. Still it was felt, especially by old Mrs. Anson, who survived her husband for some years, that Phoebe and Laura were not worthy of their privileges. There had been a third daughter so unworthy of hers that she had married a distant cousin, who had taken her to live in a new Western community where the *Works of Orestes Anson* had not yet become a part of the civic consciousness; but of this daughter little was said, and she was tacitly understood to be excluded from the family heritage of fame. In time, however, it appeared that the traditional penny with which she had been cut off had been invested to unexpected advantage; and the interest on it, when she died, returned to the Anson House in the shape of a granddaughter who was at once felt to be what Mrs. Anson called a "compensation." It was Mrs. Anson's firm belief that the remotest operations of nature were governed by the centripetal force of her husband's greatness and that Paulina's exceptional intelligence could be explained only on the ground that she was designed to act as the guardian of the family temple.

The House, by the time Paulina came to live in it, had already acquired the publicity of a place of worship; not the perfumed chapel of a romantic idolatry but the cold clean empty meeting-house of ethical enthusiasms. The ladies lived on its outskirts, as it were, in cells that left the central fane undisturbed. The very position of the furniture had come to have a ritual significance: the sparse ornaments were the offerings of kindred intellects, the steel engravings by Raphael Morghen marked the Via Sacra of a European tour, and the black-walnut desk with its bronze inkstand modeled on the Pantheon was the altar of this bleak temple of thought.

To a child compact of enthusiasms, and accustomed to pasture them on the scanty herbage of a new social soil, the atmosphere of the old house was full of floating nourishment. In the compressed perspective of Paulina's outlook it stood for a monument of ruined civilizations, and its white portico opened on legendary distances. Its very aspect was impressive to eyes that had first surveyed life from the jig-saw "residence" of a raw-edged Western town. The high-ceilinged rooms, with their paneled walls, their polished mahogany, their portraits of triple-stocked ancestors and of ringleted "females" in crayon, furnished the child with the historic scenery against which a young imagination constructs its vision of the past. To other eyes the cold spotless thinly-furnished interior might have suggested the shuttered mind of a maiden-lady who associates fresh air and sunlight with dust and discoloration; but it is the eye which supplies the coloring-matter, and Paulina's brimmed with the richest hues.

Nevertheless, the House did not immediately dominate her. She had her confused outreachings toward other centers of sensation, her vague intuition of a heliocentric system; but the attraction of habit, the steady pressure of example, gradually fixed her roving allegiance and she bent her neck to the yoke. Vanity had a share in her subjugation; for it had early been discovered that she was the only person in the family who could read her grandfather's works. The fact that she had perused them with delight at an age when (even presupposing a metaphysical bias) it was impossible for her to understand them, seemed to her aunts and grandmother sure evidence of predestination. Paulina was to be the interpreter of the oracle, and the philosophic fumes so vertiginous to meaner minds would throw her into the needed condition of clairvoyance. Nothing could have been more genuine than the emotion on which this theory was based. Paulina, in fact, delighted in her grandfather's writings. His sonorous periods, his mystic vocabulary, his bold flights into the rarefied air of the abstract, were thrilling to a fancy unhampered by the need of definitions. This purely verbal pleasure was supplemented later by the excitement of gathering up crumbs of meaning from the rhetorical board. What could have been more stimulating than to construct the theory of a girlish world out of the fragments of this Titanic cosmogony? Before Paulina's opinions had reached the stage when ossification sets in their form was fatally predetermined.

The fact that Dr. Anson had died and that his apotheosis had taken place before his young priestess's induction to the temple, made her ministrations easier and more inspiring. There were no little personal traits—such as the great man's manner of helping himself to salt, or the guttural cluck that started the wheels of speech—to distract the eye of young veneration from the central fact of his divinity. A man whom one knows only through a crayon portrait and a dozen yellowing, tomes on free-will and intuition is at least secure from the belittling effects of intimacy.

Paulina thus grew up in a world readjusted to the fact of her grandfather's greatness; and as each organism draws from its surroundings the kind of nourishment most needful to its growth, so from this somewhat colorless conception she absorbed warmth, brightness and variety. Paulina was the type of woman who transmutes thought into sensation and nurses a theory in her bosom like a child.

In due course Mrs. Anson "passed away"—no one died in the Anson vocabulary— and Paulina became more than ever the foremost figure of the commemorative group. Laura and Phoebe, content to leave their father's glory in more competent hands, placidly lapsed into needlework and fiction, and their niece stepped into immediate prominence as the chief "authority" on the great man. Historians who were "getting up" the period wrote to consult her and to borrow documents; ladies with inexplicable yearnings begged for an interpretation of phrases which had "influenced" them, but which they had not quite understood; critics applied to her to verify some doubtful citation or to decide some disputed point in chronology; and the great tide of thought and investigation kept up a continuous murmur on the quiet shores of her life.

An explorer of another kind disembarked there one day in the shape of a young man to whom Paulina was primarily a kissable girl, with an after-thought in the shape of a grandfather. From the outset it had been impossible to fix Hewlett Winsloe's attention on Dr. Anson. The young man behaved with the innocent profanity of infants sporting on a tomb. His excuse was that he came from New York, a Cimmerian outskirt which survived in Paulina's geography only because Dr. Anson had gone there once or twice to lecture. The curious thing was that she should have thought it worth-while to find excuses for young Winsloe. The fact that she did so had not escaped the attention of the village; but people, after a gasp of awe, said it was the most natural thing in the world that a girl like Paulina Anson should think of marrying. It would certainly seem a little odd to see a man in the House, but young Winsloe would of course understand that the Doctor's books were not to be disturbed, and that he must go down to the orchard to smoke—. The village had barely framed this *modus vivendi* when it was convulsed by the announcement that young Winsloe declined to live in the House on any terms. Hang going down to the orchard to smoke! He meant to take his wife to New York. The village drew its breath and watched.

Did Persephone, snatched from the warm fields of Enna, peer half-consentingly down the abyss that opened at her feet? Paulina, it must be owned, hung a moment over the black gulf of temptation. She would have found it easy to cope with a deliberate disregard of her grandfather's rights; but young Winsloe's unconsciousness of that shadowy claim was as much a natural function as the falling of leaves on a grave. His love was an embodiment of the perpetual renewal which to some tender spirits seems a crueler process than decay.

On women of Paulina's mold this piety toward implicit demands, toward the ghosts of dead duties walking unappeased among usurping passions, has a stronger hold than any tangible bond. People said that she gave up young Winsloe because her aunts disapproved of her leaving them; but such disapproval as reached her was an emanation from the walls of the House, from the bare desk, the faded portraits, the dozen yellowing tomes that no hand but hers ever lifted from the shelf.

## II

AFTER that the House possessed her. As if conscious of its victory, it imposed a conqueror's claims. It had once been suggested that she should write a life of her grandfather, and the task from which she had shrunk as from a too-oppressive privilege now shaped itself into a justification of her course. In a burst of filial pantheism she tried to lose herself in the vast ancestral consciousness. Her one refuge from scepticism was a blind faith in the magnitude and the endurance of the idea to which she had sacrificed her life, and with a passionate instinct of self-preservation she labored to fortify her position.

The preparations for the *Life* led her through by-ways that the most scrupulous of the previous biographers had left unexplored. She accumulated her material with a blind animal patience unconscious of fortuitous risks. The years stretched before her like some vast blank page spread out to receive the record of her toil; and she had a mystic conviction that she would not die till her work was accomplished.

The aunts, sustained by no such high purpose, withdrew in turn to their respective divisions of the Anson "plot," and Paulina remained alone with her task. She was forty when the book was completed. She had travelled little in her life, and it had become more and more difficult to her to leave the House even for a day; but the dread of entrusting her document to a strange hand made her decide to carry it herself to the publisher. On the way to Boston she had a sudden vision of the loneliness to which this last parting condemned her. All her youth, all her dreams, all her renunciations lay in that neat bundle on her knee. It was not so much her grandfather's life as her own that she had written; and the knowledge that it would come back to her in all the glorification of print was of no more help than, to a mother's grief, the assurance that the lad she must part with will return with epaulets.

She had naturally addressed herself to the firm which had published her grandfather's works. Its founder, a personal friend of the philosopher's, had survived the Olympian group of which he had been a subordinate member, long enough to bestow his octogenarian approval on Paulina's pious undertaking. But he had died soon afterward; and Miss Anson found herself confronted by his grandson, a person with a brisk commercial view of his trade, who was said to have put "new blood" into the firm.

This gentleman listened attentively, fingering her manuscript as though literature were a tactile substance; then, with a confidential twist of his revolving chair, he emitted the verdict: "We ought to have had this ten years sooner."

Miss Anson took the words as an allusion to the repressed avidity of her readers. "It has been a long time for the public to wait," she solemnly assented.

The publisher smiled. "They haven't waited," he said.

She looked at him strangely. "Haven't waited?"

"No—they've gone off; taken another train. Literature's like a big railway-station now, you know: there's a train starting every minute. People are not going to hang round the waiting room. If they can't get to a place when they want to they go somewhere else."

The application of this parable cost Miss Anson several minutes of throbbing silence. At length she said: "Then I am to understand that the public is no longer interested in—in my grandfather?" She felt as though heaven must blast the lips that risked such a conjecture.

"Well, it's this way. He's a name still, of course. People don't exactly want to be caught not knowing who he is; but they don't want to spend two dollars finding out, when they can look him up for nothing in any biographical dictionary."

Miss Anson's world reeled. She felt herself adrift among mysterious forces, and no more thought of prolonging the discussion than of opposing an earthquake with argument. She went home carrying the manuscript like a wounded thing. On the return journey she found herself travelling straight toward a fact that had lurked for months in the background of her life, and that now seemed to await her on the very threshold: the fact that fewer visitors came to the House. She owned to herself that for the last four or five years the number had steadily diminished. Engrossed in her work, she had noted the change only to feel thankful that she had fewer interruptions. There had been a time when, at the travelling season, the bell rang continuously, and the ladies of the House lived in a chronic state of "best silks" and expectancy. It would have been impossible then to carry on any consecutive work; and she now saw that the silence which had gathered round her task had been the hush of death.

Not of *his* death! The very walls cried out against the implication. It was the world's enthusiasm, the world's faith, the world's loyalty that had died. A corrupt generation that had turned aside to worship the brazen serpent. Her heart yearned with a prophetic passion over the lost sheep straying in the wilderness. But all great glories had their interlunar period; and in due time her grandfather would once more flash full-orbed upon a darkling world.

The few friends to whom she confided her adventure reminded her with tender indignation that there were other publishers less subject to the fluctuations of the market; but much as she had braved for her grandfather she could not again brave that particular probation. She found herself, in fact, incapable of any immediate effort. She had lost her way in a labyrinth of conjecture where her worst dread was that she might put her hand upon the clue.

She locked up the manuscript and sat down to wait. If a pilgrim had come just then the priestess would have fallen on his neck; but she continued to celebrate her rites alone. It was a double solitude; for she had always thought a great deal more of the people who came to see the House than of the people who came to see her. She fancied that the neighbors kept a keen eye on the path to the House; and there were days when the figure of a stranger strolling past the gate seemed to focus upon her the scorching sympathies of the village. For a time she thought of travelling; of going to Europe, or even to Boston; but to leave the House now would have seemed like deserting her post. Gradually her scattered energies centered themselves in the fierce resolve to understand what had happened. She was not the woman to live long in an unmapped country or to accept as final her private interpretation of phenomena. Like a traveller in unfamiliar regions she began to store for future guidance the minutest natural signs. Unflinchingly she noted the accumulating symptoms of indifference that marked her grandfather's descent toward posterity. She passed from the heights on which he had been grouped with the sages of his day to the lower level where he had come to be "the friend of Emerson," "the correspondent of Hawthorne," or (later still) "the Dr. Anson" mentioned in their letters. The change had taken place as slowly and imperceptibly as a natural process. She could not say that any ruthless hand had stripped the leaves from the tree: it was simply that, among the evergreen glories of his group, her grandfather's had proved deciduous.

She had still to ask herself why. If the decay had been a natural process, was it not the very pledge of renewal? It was easier to find such arguments than to be convinced by them. Again and again she tried to drug her solicitude with analogies; but at last she saw that such expedients were but the expression of a growing incredulity. The best way of proving her faith in her grandfather was not to be afraid of his critics. She had no notion where these shadowy antagonists lurked; for she had never heard of the great man's doctrine being directly combated. Oblique assaults there must have been, however, Parthian shots at the giant that none dared face; and she thirsted to close with such assailants. The difficulty was to find them. She began by re-reading the *Works;* thence she passed to the writers of the same school, those whose rhetoric bloomed perennial in *First Readers* from which her grandfather's prose had long since faded. Amid that clamor of far-off enthusiasms she detected no controversial note. The little knot of Olympians held their views in common with an early-Christian promiscuity. They were continually proclaiming their admiration for each other, the public joining as chorus in this guileless antiphon of praise; and she discovered no traitor in their midst.

What then had happened? Was it simply that the main current of thought had set another way? Then why did the others survive? Why were they still marked down as tributaries to the philosophic stream? This question carried her still farther afield, and she pressed on with the passion of a champion whose reluctance to know the worst might be construed into a doubt of his cause. At length—slowly but inevitably—an explanation shaped itself. Death had overtaken the doctrines about which her grandfather had draped his cloudy rhetoric. They had disintegrated and been re-absorbed, adding their little pile to the dust drifted about the mute lips of the Sphinx. The great man's contemporaries had survived not by reason of what they taught, but of what they were; and he, who had been the mere mask through which they mouthed their lesson, the instrument on which their tune was played, lay buried deep among the obsolete tools of thought.

The discovery came to Paulina suddenly. She looked up one evening from her reading and it stood before her like a ghost. It had entered her life with stealthy steps, creeping close before she was aware of it. She sat in the library, among the carefully-tended books and portraits; and it seemed to her that she had been walled alive into a tomb hung with the effigies of dead ideas. She felt a desperate longing to escape into the outer air, where people toiled and loved, and living sympathies went hand in hand. It was the sense of wasted labor that oppressed her; of two lives consumed in that ruthless process that uses generations of effort to build a single cell. There was a dreary parallel between her grandfather's fruitless toil and her own unprofitable sacrifice. Each in turn had kept vigil by a corpse.

### III

THE bell rang—she remembered it afterward—with a loud thrilling note. It was what they used to call the "visitor's ring"; not the tentative tinkle of a neighbor dropping in to borrow a sauce-pan or discuss parochial incidents, but a decisive summons from the outer world.

Miss Anson put down her knitting and listened. She sat up-stairs now, making her rheumatism an excuse for avoiding the rooms below. Her interests had insensibly adjusted themselves to the perspective of her neighbors' lives, and she wondered—as the bell re-echoed—if it could mean that Mrs. Heminway's baby had come. Conjecture had time to ripen into certainty, and she was limping toward the closet where her cloak and bonnet hung, when her little maid fluttered in with the announcement: "A gentleman to see the house."

"The *House*?"

"Yes, m'm. I don't know what he means," faltered the messenger, whose memory did not embrace the period when such announcements were a daily part of the domestic routine.

Miss Anson glanced at the proffered card. The name it bore—*Mr. George Corby*—was unknown to her, but the blood rose to her languid cheek. "Hand me my Mechlin cap, Katy," she said, trembling a little, as she laid aside her walking stick. She put her cap on before the mirror, with rapid unsteady touches. "Did you draw up the library blinds?" she breathlessly asked.

She had gradually built up a wall of commonplace between herself and her illusions, but at the first summons of the past filial passion swept away the frail barriers of expediency.

She walked downstairs so hurriedly that her stick clicked like a girlish heel; but in the hall she paused, wondering nervously if Katy had put a match to the fire. The autumn air was cold and she had the reproachful vision of a visitor with elderly ailments shivering by her inhospitable hearth. She thought instinctively of the stranger as a survivor of the days when such a visit was a part of the young enthusiast's itinerary.

The fire was unlit and the room forbiddingly cold; but the figure which, as Miss Anson entered, turned from a lingering scrutiny of the book-shelves, was that of a fresh-eyed sanguine youth clearly independent of any artificial caloric. She stood still a moment, feeling herself the victim of some anterior impression that made this robust presence an insubstantial thing; but the young man advanced with an air of genial assurance which rendered him at once more real and more reminiscent.

"Why this, you know," he exclaimed, "is simply immense!"

The words, which did not immediately present themselves as slang to Miss Anson's unaccustomed ear, echoed with an odd familiarity through the academic silence.

"The room, you know, I mean," he explained with a comprehensive gesture. "These jolly portraits, and the books—that's the old gentleman himself over the mantelpiece, I suppose?—and the elms outside, and—and the whole business. I do like a congruous background—don't you?"

His hostess was silent. No one but Hewlett Winsloe had ever spoken of her grandfather as "the old gentleman."

"It's a hundred times better than I could have hoped," her visitor continued, with a cheerful disregard of her silence. "The seclusion, the remoteness, the philosophic atmosphere—there's so little of that kind of flavor left! I should have simply hated to find that he lived over a grocery, you know.—I had the deuce of a time finding out where he *did* live," he began again, after another glance of parenthetical enjoyment. "But finally I got on the trail through some old book on Brook Farm. I was bound I'd get the environment right before I did my article."

Miss Anson, by this time, had recovered sufficient self-possession to seat herself and assign a chair to her visitor.

"Do I understand," she asked slowly, following his rapid eye about the room, "that you intend to write an article about my grandfather?"

"That's what I'm here for," Mr. Corby genially responded; "that is, if you're willing to help me; for I can't get on without your help," he added with a confident smile.

There was another pause, during which Miss Anson noticed a fleck of dust on the faded leather of the writing-table and a fresh spot of discoloration in the right-hand upper corner of Raphael Morghen's "Parnassus."

"Then you believe in him?" she said, looking up. She could not tell what had prompted her; the words rushed out irresistibly.

"Believe in him?" Corby cried, springing to his feet. "Believe in Orestes Anson? Why, I believe he's simply the greatest—the most stupendous—the most phenomenal figure we've got!"

The color rose to Miss Anson's brow. Her heart was beating passionately. She kept her eyes fixed on the young man's face, as though it might vanish if she looked away.

"You—you mean to say this in your article?" she asked.

"Say it? Why, the facts will say it," he exulted. "The baldest kind of a statement would make it clear. When a man is as big as that he doesn't need a pedestal!"

Miss Anson sighed. "People used to say that when I was young," she murmured. "But now—"

Her visitor stared. "When you were young? But how did they know—when the thing hung fire as it did? When the whole edition was thrown back on his hands?"

"The whole edition—what edition?" It was Miss Anson's turn to stare.

"Why, of his pamphlet—*the* pamphlet—the one thing that counts, that survives, that makes him what he is! For heaven's sake," he tragically adjured her, "don't tell me there isn't a copy of it left!"

Miss Anson was trembling slightly. "I don't think I understand what you mean," she faltered, less bewildered by his vehemence than by the strange sense of coming on an unexplored region in the very heart of her dominion.

"Why, his account of the *amphioxus*, of course! You can't mean that his family didn't know about it—that *you* don't know about it? I came across it by the merest accident myself, in a letter of vindication that he wrote in 1830 to an old scientific paper; but I understood there were journals—early journals; there must be references to it somewhere in the 'twenties. He must have been at least ten or twelve years ahead of Yarrell; and he saw the whole significance of it, too—he saw where it led to. As I understand it, he actually anticipated in his pamphlet Saint Hilaire's theory of the universal type, and supported the hypothesis by describing the notochord of the *amphioxus* as a cartilaginous vertebral column. The specialists of the day jeered at him, of course, as the specialists in Goethe's time jeered at the plant-metamorphosis. As far as I can make out, the anatomists and zoologists were down on Dr. Anson to a man; that was why his cowardly publishers went back on their bargain. But the pamphlet must be here somewhere—he writes as though, in his first disappointment, he had destroyed the whole edition; but surely there must be at least one copy left?"

His scientific jargon was as bewildering as his slang; and there were even moments in his discourse when Miss Anson ceased to distinguish between them; but the suspense with which he continued to gaze on her acted as a challenge to her scattered thoughts.

"The *amphioxus*," she murmured, half-rising. "It's an animal, isn't it—a fish? Yes, I think I remember." She sank back with the inward look of one who retraces some lost line of association.

Gradually the distance cleared, the details started into life. In her researches for the biography she had patiently followed every ramification of her subject, and one of these overgrown paths now led her back to the episode in question. The great Orestes's title of "Doctor" had in fact not been merely the spontaneous tribute of a national admiration; he had actually studied medicine in his youth, and his diaries, as his granddaughter now recalled, showed that he had passed through a brief phase of anatomical ardor before his attention was diverted to super-sensual problems. It had indeed seemed to Paulina, as she scanned those early pages, that they revealed a spontaneity, a freshness of feeling somehow absent from his later lucubrations—as though this one emotion had reached him directly, the others through some intervening medium. In the excess of her commemorative zeal she had even struggled through the unintelligible pamphlet to which a few lines in the journal had bitterly directed her. But the subject and the phraseology were alien to her and unconnected with her conception of the great man's genius; and after a hurried perusal she had averted her thoughts from the episode as from a revelation of failure. At length she rose a little unsteadily, supporting herself against the writing-table. She looked hesitatingly about the room; then she drew a key from her old-fashioned reticule and unlocked a drawer beneath one of the book-cases. Young Corby watched her breathlessly. With a tremulous hand she turned over the dusty documents that seemed to fill the drawer. "Is this it?" she said, holding out a thin discolored volume.

He seized it with a gasp. "Oh, by George," he said, dropping into the nearest chair.

She stood observing him strangely as his eye devoured the moldy pages.

"Is this the only copy left?" he asked at length, looking up for a moment as a thirsty man lifts his head from his glass.

"I think it must be. I found it long ago, among some old papers that my aunts were burning up after my grandmother's death. They said it was of no use—that he'd always meant to destroy the whole edition and that I ought to respect his wishes. But it was something he had written; to burn it was like shutting the door against his voice—against something he had once wished to say, and that nobody had listened to. I wanted him to feel that I was always here, ready to listen, even when others hadn't thought it worth-while; and so I kept the pamphlet, meaning to carry out his wish and destroy it before my death."

Her visitor gave a groan of retrospective anguish. "And but for me—but for to-day—you would have?"

"I should have thought it my duty."

"Oh, by George—by George," he repeated, subdued afresh by the inadequacy of speech.

She continued to watch him in silence. At length he jumped up and impulsively caught her by both hands.

"He's bigger and bigger!" he almost shouted. "He simply leads the field! You'll help me go to the bottom of this, won't you? We must turn out all the papers—letters, journals, memoranda. He must have made notes. He must have left some record of what led up to this. We must leave nothing unexplored. By Jove," he cried, looking up at her with his bright convincing smile, "do you know you're the granddaughter of a Great Man?"

Her color flickered like a girl's. "Are you—sure of him?" she whispered, as though putting him on his guard against a possible betrayal of trust.

"Sure! Sure! My dear lady—" he measured her again with his quick confident glance. "Don't *you* believe in him?"

She drew back with a confused murmur. "I—used to." She had left her hands in his: their pressure seemed to send a warm current to her heart. "It ruined my life!" she cried with sudden passion. He looked at her perplexedly.

"I gave up everything," she went on wildly, "to keep *him* alive. I sacrificed myself—others—I nursed his glory in my bosom and it died—and left me—left me here alone." She paused and gathered her courage with a gasp. "Don't make the same mistake!" she warned him.

He shook his head, still smiling. "No danger of that! You're not alone, my dear lady.

He's here with you—he's come back to you to-day. Don't you see what's happened? Don't you see that it's your love that has kept him alive? If you'd abandoned your post for an instant—let things pass into other hands—if your wonderful tenderness hadn't perpetually kept guard—this might have been—must have been—irretrievably lost." He laid his hand on the pamphlet. "And then—then he *would* have been dead!"

"Oh," she said, "don't tell me too suddenly!" And she turned away and sank into a chair.

The young man stood watching her in an awed silence. For a long time she sat motionless, with her face hidden, and he thought she must be weeping.

At length he said, almost shyly: "You'll let me come back, then? You'll help me work this thing out?"

She rose calmly and held out her hand. "I'll help you," she declared.

"I'll come tomorrow, then. Can we get to work early?"

"As early as you please."

"At eight o'clock, then," he said briskly. "You'll have the papers ready?"

"I'll have everything ready." She added with a half-playful hesitancy: "And the fire shall be lit for you."

He went out with his bright nod. She walked to the window and watched his buoyant figure hastening down the elm-shaded street. When she turned back into the empty room she looked as though youth had touched her on the lips.

## THE RECOVERY

TO THE VISITING STRANGER Hillbridge's first question was, "Have you seen Keniston's things?"

Keniston took precedence of the colonial State House, the Gilbert Stuart Washington and the Ethnological Museum; nay, he ran neck and neck with the President of the University, a prehistoric relic who had known Emerson, and who was still sent about the country in cotton-wool to open educational institutions with a toothless oration on Brook Farm.

Keniston was sent about the country too: he opened art exhibitions, laid the foundation of academies, and acted in a general sense as the spokesman and apologist of art. Hillbridge was proud of him in his peripatetic character, but his fellow-townsmen let it be understood that to "know" Keniston one must come to Hillbridge. Never was work more dependent for its effect on "atmosphere," on *milieu*. Hillbridge was Keniston's *milieu*, and there was one lady, a devotee of his art, who went so far as to assert that once, at an exhibition in New York, she had passed a Keniston without recognizing it. "It simply didn't want to be seen in such surroundings; it was hiding itself under an incognito," she declared.

It was a source of special pride to Hillbridge that it contained all the artist's best works. Strangers were told that Hillbridge had discovered him. The discovery had come about in the simplest manner. Professor Driffert, who had a reputation for "collecting," had one day hung a sketch on his drawing-room wall, and thereafter Mrs. Driffert's visitors (always a little flurried by the sense that it was the kind of house in which one might be suddenly called upon to distinguish between a dry-point and an etching, or between Raphael Mengs and Raphael Sanzio) were not infrequently subjected to the Professor's off-hand inquiry, "By-the-way, have you seen my Keniston?" The visitors, perceptibly awed, would retreat to a critical distance and murmur the usual guarded generalities, while they tried to keep the name in mind long enough to look it up in the Encyclopedia. The name was not in the Encyclopedia; but, as a compensating fact, it became known that the man himself was in Hillbridge. Hillbridge, then, owned an artist whose celebrity it was the proper thing to take for granted! Someone else, emboldened by the thought, bought a Keniston; and the next year, on the occasion of the President's golden jubilee, the Faculty, by unanimous consent, presented him with a Keniston. Two years later there was a Keniston exhibition, to which the art-critics came from New York and Boston; and not long afterward a well-known Chicago collector vainly attempted to buy Professor Driffert's sketch, which the art journals cited as a rare example of the painter's first or silvery manner. Thus there gradually grew up a small circle of connoisseurs known in artistic, circles as men who collected Kenistons.

Professor Wildmarsh, of the chair of Fine Arts and Archaeology, was the first critic to publish a detailed analysis of the master's methods and purpose. The article was illustrated by engravings which (though they had cost the magazine a fortune) were declared by Professor Wildmarsh to give but an imperfect suggestion of the esoteric significance of the originals. The Professor, with a tact that contrived to make each reader feel himself included among the exceptions, went on to say that Keniston's work would never appeal to any but exceptional natures; and he closed with the usual assertion that to apprehend the full meaning of the master's "message" it was necessary to see him in the surroundings of his own home at Hillbridge.

Professor Wildmarsh's article was read one spring afternoon by a young lady just speeding eastward on her first visit to Hillbridge, and already flushed with anticipation of the intellectual opportunities awaiting her. In East Onondaigua, where she lived, Hillbridge was looked on as an Oxford. Magazine writers, with the easy American use of the superlative, designated it as "the venerable Alma Mater," the "antique seat of learning," and Claudia Day had been brought up to regard it as the fountain-head of knowledge, and of that mental distinction which is so much rarer than knowledge. An innate passion for all that was thus distinguished and exceptional made her revere Hillbridge as the native soil of those intellectual amenities that were of such difficult growth in the thin air of East Onondaigua. At the first suggestion of a visit to Hillbridge—whither she went at the invitation of a girl friend who (incredible apotheosis!) had married one of the University professors—Claudia's spirit dilated with the sense of new possibilities. The vision of herself walking under the "historic elms" toward the Memorial Library, standing rapt before the Stuart Washington, or drinking in, from some obscure corner of an academic drawing-room, the President's reminiscences of the Concord group—this vividness of self-projection into the emotions awaiting her made her glad of any delay that prolonged so exquisite a moment.

It was in this mood that she opened the article on Keniston. She knew about him, of course; she was wonderfully "well up," even for East Onondaigua. She had read of him in the magazines; she had met, on a visit to New York, a man who collected Kenistons, and a photogravure of a Keniston in an "artistic" frame hung above her writing-table at home. But Professor Wildmarsh's article made her feel how little she really knew of the master; and she trembled to think of the state of relative ignorance in which, but for the timely purchase of the magazine, she might have entered Hillbridge. She had, for instance, been densely unaware that Keniston had already had three "manners," and was showing symptoms of a fourth. She was equally ignorant of the fact that he had founded a school and "created a formula"; and she learned with a thrill that no one could hope to understand him who had not seen him in his studio at Hillbridge, surrounded by his own works. "The man and the art interpret each other," their exponent declared; and Claudia Day, bending a brilliant eye on the future, wondered if she were ever to be admitted to the privilege of that double initiation.

Keniston, to his other claims to distinction, added that of being hard to know. His friends always hastened to announce the fact to strangers—adding after a pause of suspense that they "would see what they could do." Visitors in whose favor he was induced to make an exception were further warned that he never spoke unless he was interested—so that they mustn't mind if he remained silent. It was under these reassuring conditions that, some ten days after her arrival at Hillbridge, Miss Day was introduced to the master's studio. She found him a tall listless-looking man, who appeared middle-aged to her youth, and who stood before his own pictures with a vaguely interrogative gaze, leaving the task of their interpretation to the lady who had courageously contrived the visit. The studio, to Claudia's surprise, was bare and shabby. It formed a rambling addition to the small cheerless house in which the artist lived with his mother and a widowed sister. For Claudia it added the last touch to his distinction to learn that he was poor, and that what he earned was devoted to the maintenance of the two limp women who formed a neutral-tinted background to his impressive outline. His pictures of course fetched high prices; but he worked slowly—"painfully," as his devotees preferred to phrase it—with frequent intervals of ill health and inactivity, and the circle of Keniston connoisseurs was still as small as it was distinguished. The girl's fancy instantly hailed in him that favorite figure of imaginative youth, the artist who would rather starve than paint a pot-boiler. It is known to comparatively few that the production of successful pot-boilers is an art in itself, and that such heroic abstentions as Keniston's are not always purely voluntary.

On the occasion of her first visit the artist said so little that Claudia was able to indulge to the full the harrowing sense of her inadequacy. No wonder she had not been one of the few that he cared to talk to; every word she uttered must so obviously have diminished the inducement! She had been cheap, trivial, conventional; at once gushing and inexpressive, eager and constrained. She could feel him counting the minutes till the visit was over, and as the door finally closed on the scene of her discomfiture she almost shared the hope with which she confidently credited him—that they might never meet again.

## II

MRS. Davant glanced reverentially about the studio. "I have always said," she murmured, "that they ought to be seen in Europe."

Mrs. Davant was young, credulous and emotionally extravagant: she reminded Claudia of her earlier self—the self that, ten years before, had first set an awestruck foot on that very threshold.

"Not for *his* sake," Mrs. Davant continued, "but for Europe's."

Claudia smiled. She was glad that her husband's pictures were to be exhibited in Paris. She concurred in Mrs. Davant's view of the importance of the event; but she thought her visitor's way of putting the case a little overcharged. Ten years spent in an atmosphere of Keniston-worship had insensibly developed in Claudia a preference for moderation of speech. She believed in her husband, of course; to believe in him, with an increasing abandonment and tenacity, had become one of the necessary laws of being; but she did not believe in his admirers. Their faith in him was perhaps as genuine as her own;

but it seemed to her less able to give an account of itself. Some few of his appreciators doubtless measured him by their own standards; but it was difficult not to feel that in the Hillbridge circle, where rapture ran the highest, he was accepted on what was at best but an indirect valuation; and now and then she had a frightened doubt as to the independence of her own convictions. That innate sense of relativity which even East Onondaigua had not been able to check in Claudia Day had been fostered in Mrs. Keniston by the artistic absolutism of Hillbridge, and she often wondered that her husband remained so uncritical of the quality of admiration accorded him. Her husband's uncritical attitude toward himself and his admirers had in fact been one of the surprises of her marriage. That an artist should believe in his potential powers seemed to her at once the incentive and the pledge of excellence: she knew there was no future for a hesitating talent. What perplexed her was Keniston's satisfaction in his achievement. She had always imagined that the true artist must regard himself as the imperfect vehicle of the cosmic emotion—that beneath every difficulty overcome a new one lurked, the vision widening as the scope enlarged. To be initiated into these creative struggles, to shed on the toiler's path the consolatory ray of faith and encouragement, had seemed the chief privilege of her marriage. But there is something supererogatory in believing in a man obviously disposed to perform that service for himself; and Claudia's ardor gradually spent itself against the dense surface of her husband's complacency. She could smile now at her vision of an intellectual communion which should admit her to the inmost precincts of his inspiration. She had learned that the creative processes are seldom self-explanatory, and Keniston's inarticulateness no longer discouraged her; but she could not reconcile her sense of the continuity of all high effort to his unperturbed air of finishing each picture as though he had dispatched a masterpiece to posterity. In the first recoil from her disillusionment she even allowed herself to perceive that, if he worked slowly, it was not because he mistrusted his powers of expression, but because he had really so little to express.

"It's for Europe," Mrs. Davant vaguely repeated; and Claudia noticed that she was blushingly intent on tracing with the tip of her elaborate sunshade the pattern of the shabby carpet.

"It will be a revelation to them," she went on provisionally, as though Claudia had missed her cue and left an awkward interval to fill.

Claudia had in fact a sudden sense of deficient intuition. She felt that her visitor had something to communicate which required, on her own part, an intelligent co-operation; but what it was her insight failed to suggest. She was, in truth, a little tired of Mrs. Davant, who was Keniston's latest worshipper, who ordered pictures recklessly, who paid for them regally in advance, and whose gallery was, figuratively speaking, crowded with the artist's unpainted masterpieces. Claudia's impatience was perhaps complicated by the uneasy sense that Mrs. Davant was too young, too rich, too inexperienced; that somehow she ought to be warned.—Warned of what? That some of the pictures might never be painted? Scarcely that, since Keniston, who was scrupulous in business transactions, might be trusted not to take any material advantage of such evidence of faith. Claudia's impulse remained undefined. She merely felt that she would have liked to help Mrs. Davant, and that she did not know how.

"You'll be there to see them?" she asked, as her visitor lingered.

"In Paris?" Mrs. Davant's blush deepened. "We must all be there together."

Claudia smiled. "My husband and I mean to go abroad some day—but I don't see any chance of it at present."

"But he *ought* to go—you ought both to go this summer!" Mrs. Davant persisted. "I know Professor Wildmarsh and Professor Driffert and all the other critics think that Mr. Keniston's never having been to Europe has given his work much of its wonderful individuality, its peculiar flavor and meaning—but now that his talent is formed, that he has full command of his means of expression," (Claudia recognized one of Professor Driffert's favorite formulas) "they all think he ought to see the work of the *other* great masters—that he ought to visit the home of his ancestors, as Professor Wildmarsh says!" She stretched an impulsive hand to Claudia. "You ought to let him go, Mrs. Keniston!"

Claudia accepted the admonition with the philosophy of the wife who is used to being advised on the management of her husband. "I shan't interfere with him," she declared; and Mrs. Davant instantly caught her up with a cry of, "Oh, it's too lovely of you to say that!" With this exclamation she left Claudia to a silent renewal of wonder.

A moment later Keniston entered: to a mind curious in combinations it might have occurred that he had met Mrs. Davant on the door-step. In one sense he might, for all his wife cared, have met fifty Mrs. Davants on the door-step: it was long since Claudia had enjoyed the solace of resenting such coincidences. Her only thought now was that her husband's first words might not improbably explain Mrs. Davant's last; and she waited for him to speak.

He paused with his hands in his pockets before an unfinished picture on the easel; then, as his habit was, he began to stroll tourist-like from canvas to canvas, standing before each in a musing ecstasy of contemplation that no readjustment of view ever seemed to disturb. Her eye instinctively joined his in its inspection; it was the one point where their natures merged. Thank God, there, was no doubt about the pictures! She was what she had always dreamed of being—the wife of a great artist. Keniston dropped into an armchair and filled his pipe. "How should you like to go to Europe?" he asked.

His wife looked up quickly. "When?"

"Now—this spring, I mean." He paused to light the pipe. "I should like to be over there while these things are being exhibited."

Claudia was silent.

"Well?" he repeated after a moment.

"How can we afford it?" she asked.

Keniston had always scrupulously fulfilled his duty to the mother and sister whom his marriage had dislodged; and Claudia, who had the atoning temperament which seeks to pay for every happiness by making it a source of fresh obligations, had from the outset accepted his ties with an exaggerated devotion. Any disregard of such a claim would have vulgarized her most delicate pleasures; and her husband's sensitiveness to it in great measure extenuated the artistic obtuseness that often seemed to her like a failure of the moral sense. His loyalty to the dull women who depended on him was, after all, compounded of finer tissues than any mere sensibility to ideal demands.

"Oh, I don't see why we shouldn't," he rejoined. "I think we might manage it."

"At Mrs. Davant's expense?" leaped from Claudia. She could not tell why she had said it; some inner barrier seemed to have given way under a confused pressure of emotions.

He looked up at her with frank surprise. "Well, she *has* been very jolly about it—why not? She has a tremendous feeling for art—the keenest I ever knew in a woman." Claudia imperceptibly smiled. "She wants me to let her pay in advance for the four panels she has ordered for the Memorial Library. That would give us plenty of money for the trip, and my having the panels to do is another reason for my wanting to go abroad just now."

"Another reason?"

"Yes; I've never worked on such a big scale. I want to see how those old chaps did the trick; I want to measure myself with the big fellows over there. An artist ought to, once in his life."

She gave him a wondering look. For the first time his words implied a sense of possible limitation; but his easy tone seemed to retract what they conceded. What he really wanted was fresh food for his self-satisfaction: he was like an army that moves on after exhausting the resources of the country.

Womanlike, she abandoned the general survey of the case for the consideration of a minor point.

"Are you sure you can do that kind of thing?" she asked.

"What kind of thing?"

"The panels."

He glanced at her indulgently: his self-confidence was too impenetrable to feel the pinprick of such a doubt.

"Immensely sure," he said with a smile.

"And you don't mind taking so much money from her in advance?"

He stared. "Why should I? She'll get it back—with interest!" He laughed and drew at his pipe. "It will be an uncommonly interesting experience. I shouldn't wonder if it freshened me up a bit."

She looked at him again. This second hint of self-distrust struck her as the sign of a quickened sensibility. What if, after all, he was beginning to be dissatisfied with his work? The thought filled her with a renovating sense of his sufficiency.

## III

THEY stopped in London to see the National Gallery.

It was thus that, in their inexperience, they had narrowly put it; but in reality every stone of the streets, every trick of the atmosphere, had its message of surprise for their virgin sensibilities. The pictures were simply the summing up, the final interpretation, of the cumulative pressure of an unimagined world; and it seemed to Claudia that long before they reached the doors of the gallery she had some intuitive revelation of what awaited them within.

They moved about from room to room without exchanging a word. The vast noiseless spaces seemed full of sound, like the roar of a distant multitude heard only by the inner ear. Had their speech been articulate their language would have been incomprehensible; and even that far-off murmur of meaning pressed intolerably on Claudia's nerves. Keniston took the onset without outward sign of disturbance. Now and then he paused before a canvas, or prolonged from one of the benches his silent communion with some miracle of line or color; but he neither looked at his wife nor spoke to her. He seemed to have forgotten her presence.

Claudia was conscious of keeping a furtive watch on him; but the sum total of her impressions was negative. She remembered thinking when she first met him that his face was rather expressionless; and he had the habit of self-engrossed silences.

All that evening, at the hotel, they talked about London, and he surprised her by an acuteness of observation that she had sometimes inwardly accused him of lacking. He seemed to have seen everything, to have examined, felt, compared, with nerves as finely adjusted as her own; but he said nothing of the pictures. The next day they returned to the National Gallery, and he began to study the paintings in detail, pointing out differences of technique, analyzing and criticizing, but still without summing up his conclusions. He seemed to have a sort of provincial dread of showing himself too much impressed. Claudia's own sensations were too complex, too overwhelming, to be readily classified. Lacking the craftsman's instinct to steady her, she felt herself carried off her feet by the rush of incoherent impressions. One point she consciously avoided, and that was the comparison of her husband's work with what they were daily seeing. Art, she inwardly argued, was too various, too complex, dependent on too many inter-relations of feeling and environment, to allow of its being judged by any provisional standard. Even the subtleties of technique must be modified by the artist's changing purpose, as this in turn is acted on by influences of which he is himself unconscious. How, then, was an unprepared imagination to distinguish between such varied reflections of the elusive vision? She took refuge in a passionate exaggeration of her own ignorance and insufficiency.

After a week in London they went to Paris. The exhibition of Keniston's pictures had been opened a few days earlier; and as they drove through the streets on the way to the station an "impressionist" poster here and there invited them to the display of the American artist's work. Mrs. Davant, who had been in Paris for the opening, had already written rapturously of the impression produced, enclosing commendatory notices from one or two papers. She reported that there had been a great crowd on the first day, and that the critics had been "immensely struck."

The Kenistons arrived in the evening, and the next morning Claudia, as a matter of course, asked her husband at what time he meant to go and see the pictures.

He looked up absently from his guide-book.

"What pictures?"

"Why—yours," she said, surprised.

"Oh, they'll keep," he answered; adding with a slightly embarrassed laugh, "We'll give the other chaps a show first." Presently he laid down his book and proposed that they should go to the Louvre.

They spent the morning there, lunched at a restaurant near by, and returned to the gallery in the afternoon. Keniston had passed from inarticulateness to an eager volubility. It was clear that he was beginning to co-ordinate his impressions, to find his way about in a corner of the great imaginative universe. He seemed extraordinarily ready to impart his discoveries; and Claudia felt that her ignorance served him as a convenient buffer against the terrific impact of new sensations.

On the way home she asked when he meant to see Mrs. Davant.

His answer surprised her. "Does she know we're here?"

"Not unless you've sent her word," said Claudia, with a touch of harmless irony.

"That's all right, then," he returned simply. "I want to wait and look about a day or two longer. She'd want us to go sight-seeing with her; and I'd rather get my impressions alone."

The next two days were hampered by the necessity of eluding Mrs. Davant. Claudia, under different circumstances, would have scrupled to share in this somewhat shabby conspiracy; but she found herself in a state of suspended judgment, wherein her husband's treatment of Mrs. Davant became for the moment merely a clue to larger meanings.

They had been four days in Paris when Claudia, returning one afternoon from a parenthetical excursion to the Rue de la Paix, was confronted on her threshold by the reproachful figure of their benefactress. It was not to her, however, that Mrs. Davant's reproaches were addressed. Keniston, it appeared, had borne the brunt of them; for he stood leaning against the mantelpiece of their modest salon in that attitude of convicted negligence when, if ever, a man is glad to take refuge behind his wife.

Claudia had however no immediate intention of affording him such shelter. She wanted to observe and wait.

"He's too impossible!" cried Mrs. Davant, sweeping her at once into the central current of her grievance.

Claudia looked from one to the other.

"For not going to see you?"

"For not going to see his pictures!" cried the other nobly.

Claudia colored and Keniston shifted his position uneasily.

"I can't make her understand," he said, turning to his wife.

"I don't care about myself!" Mrs. Davant interjected.

"*I* do, then; it's the only thing I do care about," he hurriedly protested. "I meant to go at once—to write—Claudia wanted to go, but I wouldn't let her." He looked helplessly about the pleasant red-curtained room, which was rapidly burning itself into Claudia's consciousness as a visible extension of Mrs. Davant's claims.

"I can't explain," he broke off.

Mrs. Davant in turn addressed herself to Claudia.

"People think it's so odd," she complained. "So many of the artists here are anxious to meet him; they've all been so charming about the pictures; and several of our American friends have come over from London expressly for the exhibition. I told every one that he would be here for the opening—there was a private view, you know—and they were so disappointed—they wanted to give him an ovation; and I didn't know what to say. What *am* I to say?" she abruptly ended.

"There's nothing to say," said Keniston slowly.

"But the exhibition closes the day after tomorrow."

"Well, *I* shan't close—I shall be here," he declared with an effort at playfullness. "If they want to see me—all these people you're kind enough to mention—won't there be other chances?"

"But I wanted them to see you *among* your pictures—to hear you talk about them, explain them in that wonderful way. I wanted you to interpret each other, as Professor Wildmarsh says!"

"Oh, hang Professor Wildmarsh!" said Keniston, softening the commination with a smile. "If my pictures are good for anything they oughtn't to need explaining."

Mrs. Davant stared. "But I thought that was what made them so interesting!" she exclaimed.

Keniston looked down. "Perhaps it was," he murmured.

There was an awkward silence, which Claudia broke by saying, with a glance at her husband: "But if the exhibition is to remain open tomorrow, could we not meet you there? And perhaps you could send word to some of our friends."

Mrs. Davant brightened like a child whose broken toy is glued together. "Oh, *do* make him!" she implored. "I'll ask them to come in the afternoon—we'll make it into a little tea—a five o'clock. I'll send word at once to everybody!" She gathered up her beruffled boa and sunshade, settling her plumage like a reassured bird. "It will be too lovely!" she ended in a self-consoling murmur.

But in the doorway a new doubt assailed her. "You won't fail me?" she said, turning plaintively to Keniston. "You'll make him come, Mrs. Keniston?"

"I'll bring him!" Claudia promised.

## IV

WHEN, the next morning, she appeared equipped for their customary ramble, her husband surprised her by announcing that he meant to stay at home.

"The fact is I'm rather surfeited," he said, smiling. "I suppose my appetite isn't equal to such a plethora. I think I'll write some letters and join you somewhere later."

She detected the wish to be alone and responded to it with her usual readiness.

"I shall sink to my proper level and buy a bonnet, then," she said. "I haven't had time to take the edge off that appetite."

They agreed to meet at the Hotel Cluny at mid-day, and she set out alone with a vague sense of relief. Neither she nor Keniston had made any direct reference to Mrs. Davant's visit; but its effect was implicit in their eagerness to avoid each other.

Claudia accomplished some shopping in the spirit of perfunctoriness that robs even new bonnets of their bloom; and this business dispatched, she turned aimlessly into the wide inviting brightness of the streets. Never had she felt more isolated amid that ordered beauty which gives a social quality to the very stones and mortar of Paris. All about her were evidences of an artistic sensibility pervading every form of life like the nervous structure of the huge frame—a sensibility so delicate, alert and universal that it seemed to leave no room for obtuseness or error. In such a medium the faculty of plastic expression must develop as unconsciously as any organ in its normal surroundings; to be "artistic" must cease to be an attitude and become a natural function. To Claudia the significance of the whole vast revelation was centered in the light it shed on one tiny spot of consciousness—the value of her husband's work. There are moments when to the groping soul the world's accumulated experiences are but stepping-stones across a private difficulty.

She stood hesitating on a street corner. It was barely eleven, and she had an hour to spare before going to the Hotel Cluny. She seemed to be letting her inclination float as it would on the cross-currents of suggestion emanating from the brilliant complex scene before her; but suddenly, in obedience to an impulse that she became aware of only in acting on it, she called a cab and drove to the gallery where her husband's pictures were exhibited.

A magnificent official in gold braid sold her a ticket and pointed the way up the empty crimson-carpeted stairs. His duplicate, on the upper landing, held out a catalogue with an air of recognizing the futility of the offer; and a moment later she found herself in the long noiseless impressive room full of velvet-covered ottomans and exotic plants. It was clear that the public ardor on which Mrs. Davant had expatiated had spent itself earlier in the week; for Claudia had this luxurious apartment to herself. Something about its air of rich privacy, its diffusion of that sympathetic quality in other countries so conspicuously absent from the public show-room, seemed to emphasize its present emptiness. It was as though the flowers, the carpet, the lounges, surrounded their visitor's solitary advance with the mute assurance that they had done all they could toward making the thing "go off," and that if they had failed it was simply for lack of co-operation. She stood still and looked about her. The pictures struck her instantly as odd gaps in the general harmony; it was self-evident that they had not co-operated. They had not been pushing, aggressive, discordant: they had merely effaced themselves. She swept a startled eye from one familiar painting to another. The canvases were all there—and the frames— but the miracle, the mirage of life and meaning, had vanished like some atmospheric illusion. What was it that had happened? And had it happened to *her* or to the pictures? She tried to rally her frightened thoughts; to push or coax them into a semblance of resistance; but argument was swept off its feet by the huge rush of a single conviction— the conviction that the pictures were bad. There was no standing up against that: she felt herself submerged.

The stealthy fear that had been following her all these days had her by the throat now. The great vision of beauty through which she had been moving as one enchanted was turned to a phantasmagoria of evil mocking shapes. She hated the past; she hated its splendor, its power, its wicked magical vitality. . . . She dropped into a seat and continued to stare at the wall before her. Gradually, as she stared, there stole out to her from the dimmed humbled canvases a reminder of what she had once seen in them, a spectral appeal to her faith to call them back to life. What proof had she that her present estimate of them was less subjective than the other? The confused impressions of the last few days were hardly to be pleaded as a valid theory of art. How, after all, did she know that the pictures were bad? On what suddenly acquired technical standard had she thus decided the case against them? It seemed as though it were a standard outside of herself, as though some unheeded inner sense were gradually making her aware of the presence, in that empty room, of a critical intelligence that was giving out a subtle effluence of disapproval. The fancy was so vivid that, to shake it off, she rose and began to move about again. In the middle of the room stood a monumental divan surmounted by a *massif* of palms and azaleas. As Claudia's muffled wanderings carried her around the angle of this seat, she saw that its farther side was occupied by the figure of a man, who sat with his hands resting on his stick and his head bowed upon them. She gave a little cry and her husband rose and faced her.

Instantly the live point of consciousness was shifted, and she became aware that the quality of the pictures no longer mattered. It was what *he* thought of them that counted: her life hung on that.

They looked at each other a moment in silence; such concussions are not apt to flash into immediate speech. At length he said simply, "I didn't know you were coming here."

She colored as though he had charged her with something underhand.

"I didn't mean to," she stammered; "but I was too early for our appointment—"

Her word's cast a revealing glare on the situation. Neither of them looked at the pictures; but to Claudia those unobtruding presences seemed suddenly to press upon them and force them apart.

Keniston glanced at his watch. "It's twelve o'clock," he said. "Shall we go on?"

## V

AT the door he called a cab and put her in it; then, drawing out his watch again, he said abruptly: "I believe I'll let you go alone. I'll join you at the hotel in time for luncheon." She wondered for a moment if he meant to return to the gallery; but, looking back as she drove off, she saw him walk rapidly away in the opposite direction.

The cabman had carried her half-way to the Hotel Cluny before she realized where she was going, and cried out to him to turn home. There was an acute irony in this mechanical prolongation of the quest of beauty. She had had enough of it, too much of it; her one longing was to escape, to hide herself away from its all-suffusing implacable light.

At the hotel, alone in her room, a few tears came to soften her seared vision; but her mood was too tense to be eased by weeping. Her whole being was centered in the longing to know what her husband thought. Their short exchange of words had, after all, told her nothing. She had guessed a faint resentment at her unexpected appearance; but that might merely imply a dawning sense, on his part, of being furtively watched and criticized. She had sometimes wondered if he was never conscious of her observation; there were moments when it seemed to radiate from her in visible waves. Perhaps, after all, he was aware of it, on his guard against it, as a lurking knife behind the thick curtain of his complacency; and to-day he must have caught the gleam of the blade.

Claudia had not reached the age when pity is the first chord to vibrate in contact with any revelation of failure. Her one hope had been that Keniston should be clear-eyed enough to face the truth. Whatever it turned out to be, she wanted him to measure himself with it. But as his image rose before her she felt a sudden half-maternal longing to thrust herself between him and disaster. Her eagerness to see him tested by circumstances seemed now like a cruel scientific curiosity. She saw in a flash of sympathy that he would need her most if he fell beneath his fate.

He did not, after all, return for luncheon; and when she came up-stairs from her solitary meal their salon was still untenanted. She permitted herself no sensational fears; for she could not, at the height of apprehension, figure Keniston as yielding to any tragic impulse; but the lengthening hours brought an uneasiness that was fuel to her pity. Suddenly she heard the clock strike five. It was the hour at which they had promised to meet Mrs. Davant at the gallery—the hour of the "ovation." Claudia rose and went to the window, straining for a glimpse of her husband in the crowded street. Could it be that he had forgotten her, had gone to the gallery without her? Or had something happened—that veiled "something" which, for the last hour, had grimly hovered on the outskirts of her mind?

She heard a hand on the door and Keniston entered. As she turned to meet him her whole being was swept forward on a great wave of pity: she was so sure, now, that he must know.

But he confronted her with a glance of preoccupied brightness; her first impression was that she had never seen him so vividly, so expressively pleased. If he needed her, it was not to bind up his wounds.

He gave her a smile which was clearly the lingering reflection of some inner light. "I didn't mean to be so late," he said, tossing aside his hat and the little red volume that served as a clue to his explorations. "I turned in to the Louvre for a minute after I left you this morning, and the place fairly swallowed me up—I couldn't get away from it. I've been there ever since." He threw himself into a chair and glanced about for his pipe.

"It takes time," he continued musingly, "to get at them, to make out what they're saying—the big fellows, I mean. They're not a communicative lot. At first I couldn't make much out of their lingo—it was too different from mine! But gradually, by picking up a hint here and there, and piecing them together, I've begun to understand; and to-day, by Jove, I got one or two of the old chaps by the throat and fairly turned them inside out—made them deliver up their last drop." He lifted a brilliant eye to her. "Lord, it was tremendous!" he declared.

He had found his pipe and was musingly filling it. Claudia waited in silence.

"At first," he began again, "I was afraid their language was too hard for me—that I should never quite know what they were driving at; they seemed to cold-shoulder me, to be bent on shutting me out. But I was bound I wouldn't be beaten, and now, to-day"—he paused a moment to strike a match—"when I went to look at those things of mine it all came over me in a flash. By Jove! it was as if I'd made them all into a big bonfire to light me on my road!"

His wife was trembling with a kind of sacred terror. She had been afraid to pray for light for him, and here he was joyfully casting his whole past upon the pyre!

"Is there nothing left?" she faltered.

"Nothing left? There's everything!" he exulted. "Why, here I am, not much over forty, and I've found out already—already!" He stood up and began to move excitedly about the room. "My God! Suppose I'd never known! Suppose I'd gone on painting things like that forever! Why, I feel like those chaps at revivalist meetings when they get up and say they're saved! Won't somebody please start a hymn?"

Claudia, with a tremulous joy, was letting herself go on the strong current of his emotion; but it had not yet carried her beyond her depth, and suddenly she felt hard ground underfoot.

"Mrs. Davant—" she exclaimed.

He stared, as though suddenly recalled from a long distance. "Mrs. Davant?"

"We were to have met her—this afternoon—now—"

"At the gallery? Oh, that's all right. I put a stop to that; I went to see her after I left you; I explained it all to her."

"All?"

"I told her I was going to begin all over again."

Claudia's heart gave a forward bound and then sank back hopelessly.

"But the panels—?"

"That's all right too. I told her about the panels," he reassured her.

"You told her—?"

"That I can't paint them now. She doesn't understand, of course; but she's the best little woman and she trusts me."

She could have wept for joy at his exquisite obtuseness. "But that isn't all," she wailed. "It doesn't matter how much you've explained to her. It doesn't do away with the fact that we're living on those panels!"

"Living on them?"

"On the money that she paid you to paint them. Isn't that what brought us here? And—if you mean to do as you say—to begin all over again—how in the world are we ever to pay her back?"

Her husband turned on her an inspired eye. "There's only one way that I know of," he imperturbably declared, "and that's to stay out here till I learn how to paint them."

COPY

A DIALOGUE

MRS. AMBROSE DALE—*forty, slender, still young—sits in her drawing-room at the tea-table. The winter twilight is falling, a lamp has been lit, there is a fire on the hearth, and the room is pleasantly dim and flower-scented. Books are scattered everywhere— mostly with autograph inscriptions "From the Author"—and a large portrait of* Mrs. Dale, *at her desk, with papers strewn about her, takes up one of the wall-panels. Before* MRS. DALE *stands* HILDA, *fair and twenty, her hands full of letters.*

MRS. DALE. Ten more applications for autographs? Isn't it strange that people who'd blush to borrow twenty dollars don't scruple to beg for an autograph?

HILDA. (*reproachfully*). Oh—

MRS. DALE. What's the difference, pray?

HILDA. Only that *your* last autograph sold for fifty—

MRS. DALE. (*not displeased*). Ah?—I sent for you, Hilda, because I'm dining out to-night, and if there's nothing important to attend to among these letters you needn't sit up for me.

HILDA. You don't mean to work?

MRS. DALE. Perhaps; but I shan't need you. You'll see that my cigarettes and coffee-machine are in place, and: that I don't have to crawl about the floor in search of my pen-wiper? That's all. Now about these letters—

HILDA (*impulsively*). Oh, Mrs. Dale—

MRS. DALE. Well?

HILDA. I'd rather sit up for you.

MRS. DALE. Child, I've nothing for you to do. I shall be blocking out the tenth chapter of *Winged Purposes* and it won't be ready for you till next week.

HILDA. It isn't that—but it's so beautiful to sit here, watching and listening, all alone in the night, and to feel that you're in there (*she points to the study-door*) creating— .(*Impulsively.*) What do I care for sleep?

MRS. DALE (*indulgently*). Child—silly child!—Yes, I should have felt so at your age—it would have been an inspiration—

HILDA (*rapt*). It is!

MRS. DALE. But you must go to bed; I must have you fresh in the morning; for you're still at the age when one *is* fresh in the morning! (*She sighs.*) The letters? (*Abruptly.*) Do you take notes of what you feel, Hilda—here, all alone in the night, as you say?

HILDA (*shyly*). I have—

MES. DALE (*smiling*). For the diary?

HILDA (*nods and blushes*).

MRS. DALE (*caressingly*). Goose!—Well, to business. What is there?

HILDA. Nothing important, except a letter from Stroud & Fayerweather to say that the question of the royalty on *Pomegranate Seed* has been settled in your favor. The English publishers of *Immolation* write to consult you about a six-shilling edition; Olafson, the Copenhagen publisher, applies for permission to bring out a Danish translation of *The Idol's Feet*; and the editor of the *Semaphore* wants a new serial—I think that's all; except that *Woman's Sphere* and *The Droplight* ask for interviews—with photographs—

MRS. DALE. The same old story! I'm so tired of it all. (*To herself, in an undertone.*) But how should I feel if it all stopped? (*The servant brings in a card.*)

MRS. DALE (*reading it*). Is it possible? Paul Ventnor? (*To the servant.*) Show Mr. Ventnor up. (*To herself.*) Paul Ventnor!

HILDA (*breathless*). Oh, Mrs. Dale—the Mr. Ventnor?

MRS. DALE (*smiling*). I fancy there's only one.

HILDA. The great, great poet? (*Irresolute.*) No, I don't dare—

MRS. DALE (*with a tinge of impatience*). What?

HILDA (*fervently*). Ask you—if I might—oh, here in this corner, where he can't possibly notice me—stay just a moment? Just to see him come in? To see the meeting between you—the greatest novelist and the greatest poet of the age? Oh, it's too much to ask! It's an historic moment.

MRS. DALE. Why, I suppose it is. I hadn't thought of it in that light. Well (*smiling*), for the diary—

HILDA. Oh, thank you, *thank you!* I'll be off the very instant I've heard him speak.

MRS. DALE. The very instant, mind. (*She rises, looks at herself in the glass, smooths her hair, sits down again, and rattles the tea-caddy.*) Isn't the room very warm?—(*She looks over at her portrait.*) I've grown stouter since that was painted—. You'll make a fortune out of that diary, Hilda—

HILDA (*modestly*). Four publishers have applied to me already—

THE SERVANT (*announces*). Mr. Paul Ventnor.

(*Tall, nearing fifty, with an incipient stoutness buttoned into a masterly frock-coat,* VENTNOR *drops his glass and advances vaguely, with a short-sighted stare.*)

VENTNOR. Mrs. Dale?

MRS. DALE. My dear friend! This is kind. (*She looks over her shoulder at Hilda, mho vanishes through the door to the left.*) The papers announced your arrival, but I hardly hoped—

VENTNOR (*whose shortsighted stare is seen to conceal a deeper embarrassment*). You hadn't forgotten me, then?

MRS. DALE. Delicious! Do *you* forget that you're public property?

VENTNOR. Forgotten, I mean, that we were old friends?

MRS. DALE. Such old friends! May I remind you that it's nearly twenty years since we've met? Or do you find cold reminiscences indigestible?

VENTNOR. On the contrary, I've come to ask you for a dish of them—we'll warm them up together. You're my first visit.

MRS. DALE. How perfect of you! So few men visit their women friends in chronological order; or at least they generally do it the other way round, beginning with the present day and working back—if there's time—to prehistoric woman.

VENTNOR. But when prehistoric woman has become historic woman—?

MRS. DALE. Oh, it's the reflection of my glory that has guided you here, then?

VENTNOR. It's a spirit in my feet that has led me, at the first opportunity, to the most delightful spot I know.

MRS. DALE. Oh, the first opportunity—!

VENTNOR. I might have seen you very often before; but never just in the right way.

MRS. DALE. Is this the right way?

VENTNOR. It depends on you to make it so.

MRS. DALE. What a responsibility! What shall I do?

VENTNOR. Talk to me—make me think you're a little glad to see me; give me some tea and a cigarette; and say you're out to everyone else.

MRS. DALE. Is that all? (*She hands him a cup of tea.*) The cigarettes are at your elbow—. And do you think I shouldn't have been glad to see you before?

VENTNOR. No; I think I should have been too glad to see *you*.

MRS. DALE. Dear me, what precautions! I hope you always wear galoshes when it looks like rain and never by any chance expose yourself to a draught. But I had an idea that poets courted the emotions—

VENTNOR. Do novelists?

MRS. DALE. If you ask *me*—on paper!

VENTNOR. Just so; that's safest. My best things about the sea have been written on shore. (*He looks at her thoughtfully.*) But it wouldn't have suited us in the old days, would it?

MRS. DALE (*sighing*). When we were real people!

VENTNOR. Real people?

MRS. DALE. Are *you*, now? I died years ago. What you see before you is a figment of the reporter's brain—a monster manufactured out of newspaper paragraphs, with ink in its veins. A keen sense of copyright is *my* nearest approach to an emotion.

VENTNOR (*sighing*). Ah, well, yes—as you say, we're public property.

MRS. DALE. If one shared equally with the public! But the last shred of my identity is gone.

VENTNOR. Most people would be glad to part with theirs on such terms. I have followed your work with immense interest. *Immolation* is a masterpiece. I read it last summer when it first came out.

MRS. DALE (*with a shade less warmth*). *Immolation* has been out three years.

VENTNOR. Oh, by Jove—no? Surely not—But one is so overwhelmed—one loses count. (*Reproachfully.*) Why have you never sent me your books?

MRS. DALE. For that very reason.

VENTNOR (*deprecatingly*). You know I didn't mean it for you! And my first book—do you remember—was dedicated to you.

MRS. DALE. *Silver Trumpets*—

VENTNOR (*much interested*). Have you a copy still, by any chance? The first edition, I mean? Mine was stolen years ago. Do you think you could put your hand on it?

MRS. DALE (*taking a small shabby book from the table at her side*). It's here.

VENTNOR (*eagerly*). May I have it? Ah, thanks. This is very interesting. The last copy sold in London for £40, and they tell me the next will fetch twice as much. It's quite *introuvable*.

MRS. DALE. I know that. (*A pause. She takes the book from him, opens it, and reads, half to herself*—)

> How much we two have seen together,
>   Of other eyes unwist,
> Dear as in days of leafless weather
>   The willow's saffron mist,

> *Strange as the hour when Hesper swings*
> *A-sea in beryl green,*
> *While overhead on dalliant wings*
> *The daylight hangs serene,*
>
> *And thrilling as a meteor's fall*
> *Through depths of lonely sky,*
> *When each to each two watchers call:*
> *I saw it!—So did I.*

VENTNOR. Thin, thin—the troubadour tinkle. Odd how little promise there is in first volumes!

MRS. DALE (*with irresistible emphasis*). I thought there was a distinct promise in this!

VENTNOR (*seeing his mistake*). Ah—the one you would never let me fulfill? (*Sentimentally.*) How inexorable you were! You never dedicated a book to me.

MRS. DALE. I hadn't begun to write when we were—dedicating things to each other.

VENTNOR. Not for the public—but you wrote for me; and, wonderful as you are, you've never written anything since that I care for half as much as—

MRS. DALE (*interested*). Well?

VENTNOR. Your letters.

MRS. DALE (*in a changed voice*). My letters—do you remember them?

VENTNOR. When I don't, I reread them.

MRS. DALE (*incredulous*). You have them still?

VENTNOR (*unguardedly*). You haven't mine, then?

MRS. DALE (*playfully*). Oh, you were a celebrity already. Of course I kept them! (*Smiling.*) Think what they are worth now! I always keep them locked up in my safe over there. (*She indicates a cabinet.*)

VENTNOR (*after a pause*). I always carry yours with me.

MRS. DALE (*laughing*). You—

VENTNOR. Wherever I go. (*A longer pause. She looks at him fixedly.*) I have them with me now.

MRS. DALE (*agitated*). You—have them with you—now?

VENTNOR (*embarrassed*). Why not? One never knows—

MRS. DALE. Never knows—?

VENTNOR (*humorously*). Gad—when the bank-examiner may come round. You forget I'm a married man.

MRS. DALE. Ah—yes.

VENTNOR (*sits down beside her*). I speak to you as I couldn't to anyone else—without deserving a kicking. You know how it all came about. (*A pause.*) You'll bear witness that it wasn't till you denied me all hope—

MRS. DALE (*a little breathless*). Yes, yes—

VENTNOR. Till you sent me from you—

MRS. DALE. It's so easy to be heroic when one is young! One doesn't realize how long life is going to last afterward. (*Musing.*) Nor what weary work it is gathering up the fragments.

VENTNOR. But the time comes when one sends for the china-mender, and has the bits riveted together, and turns the cracked side to the wall—

MRS. DALE. And denies that the article was ever damaged?

VENTNOR. Eh? Well, the great thing, you see, is to keep one's self out of reach of the housemaid's brush. (*A pause.*) If you're married you can't—always. (*Smiling.*) Don't you hate to be taken down and dusted?

MRS. DALE (*with intention*). You forget how long ago my husband died. It's fifteen years since I've been an object of interest to anybody but the public.

VENTNOR (*smiling*). The only one of your admirers to whom you've ever given the least encouragement!

MRS. DALE. Say rather the most easily pleased!

VENTNOR. Or the only one you cared to please?

MRS. DALE. Ah, you haven't kept my letters!

VENTNOR (*gravely*). Is that a challenge? Look here, then! (*He drams a packet from his pocket and holds it out to her.*)

MRS. DALE (*taking the packet and looking at him earnestly*). Why have you brought me these?

VENTNOR. I didn't bring them; they came because I came—that's all. (*Tentatively.*) Are we unwelcome?

MRS. DALE (*who has undone the packet and does not appear to hear him*). The very first I ever wrote you—the day after we met at the concert. How on earth did you happen to keep it? (*She glances over it.*) How perfectly absurd! Well, it's not a compromising document.

VENTNOR. I'm afraid none of them are.

MRS. DALE (*quickly*). Is it to that they owe their immunity? Because one could leave them about like safety matches?—Ah, here's another I remember—I wrote that the day after we went skating together for the first time. (*She reads it slowly.*) How odd! How *very* odd!

VENTNOR. What?

MRS. DALE. Why, it's the most curious thing—I had a letter of this kind to do the other day, in the novel I'm at work on now—the letter of a woman who is just—just beginning—

VENTNOR. Yes—just beginning—?

MRS. DALE. And, do you know, I find the best phrase in it, the phrase I somehow regarded as the fruit of—well, of all my subsequent discoveries—is simply plagiarized, word for word, from this!

VENTNOR (*eagerly*). I told you so! You were all there!

MRS. DALE (*critically*). But the rest of it's poorly done—very poorly. (*Reads the letter over.*) H'm—I didn't know how to leave off. It takes me forever to get out of the door.

VENTNOR (*gayly*). Perhaps I was there to prevent you! (After a pause.) I wonder what I said in return?

MRS. DALE (*interested*). Shall we look? (*She rises.*) Shall we—really? I have them all here, you know. (*She goes toward the cabinet.*)

VENTNOR (*following her with repressed eagerness*). Oh—all!

MRS. DALE (*throws open the door of the cabinet, revealing a number of packets*). Don't you believe me now?

VENTNOR. Good heavens! How I must have repeated myself! But then you were so very deaf.

MRS. DALE (*takes out a packet and returns to her seat. Ventnor extends an impatient hand for the letters*). No—no; wait! I want to find your answer to the one I was just reading. (*After a pause.*) Here it is—yes, I thought so!

VENTNOR. What did you think?

MRS. DALE (*triumphantly*). I thought it was the one in which you quoted *Epipsychidion*—

VENTNOR. Mercy! Did I *quote* things? I don't wonder you were cruel.

MRS. DALE. Ah, and here's the other—the one I—the one I didn't answer—for a long time. Do you remember?

VENTNOR (*with emotion*). Do I remember? I wrote it the morning after we heard *Isolde*—

MRS. DALE (*disappointed*). No—no. *That* wasn't the one I didn't answer! Here—this is the one I mean.

VENTNOR (*takes it curiously*). Ah—h'm—this is very like unrolling a mummy—(*he glances at her*)—with a live grain of wheat in it, perhaps?—Oh, by Jove!

MRS. DALE. What?

VENTNOR. Why, this is the one I made a sonnet out of afterward! By Jove, I'd forgotten where that idea came from. You may know the lines perhaps? They're in the fourth volume of my *Complete Edition*—It's the thing beginning

    *Love came to me with unrelenting eyes*—

one of my best, I rather fancy. Of course, here it's very crudely put—the values aren't brought out—ah! this touch is good though—very good. H'm, I daresay there might be other material. (*He glances toward the cabinet.*)

MRS. DALE (*drily*). The live grain of wheat, as you said!

VENTNOR. Ah, well—my first harvest was sown on rocky ground—now I plant for the fowls of the air. (*Rising and walking toward the cabinet.*) When can I come and carry off all this rubbish?

MRS. DALE. Carry it off?

VENTNOR (*embarrassed*). My dear lady, surely between you and me explicitness is a burden. You must see that these letters of ours can't be left to take their chance like an ordinary correspondence—you said yourself we were public property.

MRS. DALE. To take their chance? Do you suppose that, in my keeping, your letters take any chances? (*Suddenly.*) Do mine—in yours?

VENTNOR (*still more embarrassed*). Helen—! (*He takes a turn through the room.*) You force me to remind you that you and I are differently situated—that in a moment of madness I sacrificed the only right you ever gave me—the right to love you better than any other woman in the world. (*A pause. She says nothing and he continues, with increasing difficulty—*) You asked me just now why I carried your letters about with me—kept them, literally, in my own hands. Well, suppose it's to be sure of their not falling into some one else's?

MRS. DALE. Oh!

VENTNOR (*throws himself into a chair*). For God's sake don't pity me!

MRS. DALE (*after a long pause*). Am I dull—or are you trying to say that you want to give me back my letters?

VENTNOR (*starting up*). I? Give you back—? God forbid! Your letters? Not for the world! The only thing I have left! But you can't dream that in my hands—

MRS. DALE (*suddenly*). You want yours, then?

VENTNOR (*repressing his eagerness*). My dear friend, if I'd ever dreamed that you'd kept them—?

MRS. DALE (*accusingly*). You do want them. (*A pause. He makes a deprecatory gesture.*) Why should they be less safe with me than mine with you? I never forfeited the right to keep them.

VENTNOR (*after another pause*). It's compensation enough, almost, to have you reproach me! (*He moves nearer to her, but she makes no response.*) You forget that I've forfeited *all* my rights—even that of letting you keep my letters.

MRS. DALE. You do want them! (*She rises, throws all the letters into the cabinet, locks the door and puts the key in her pocket.*) There's my answer.

VENTNOR. Helen—!

MRS. DALE. Ah, I paid dearly enough for the right to keep them, and I mean to! (*She turns to him passionately.*) Have you ever asked yourself how I paid for it? With what months and years of solitude, what indifference to flattery, what resistance to affection?—Oh, don't smile because I said affection, and not love. Affection's a warm cloak in cold weather; and I have been cold; and I shall keep on growing colder! Don't talk to me about living in the hearts of my readers! We both know what kind of a domicile that is. Why, before long I shall become a classic! Bound in sets and kept on the top book-shelf—brr, doesn't that sound freezing? I foresee the day when I shall be as lonely as an Etruscan museum! (*She breaks into a laugh.*) That's what I've paid for the right to keep your letters. (*She holds out her hand.*) And now give me mine.

VENTNOR. Yours?

MRS. DALE (*haughtily*). Yes; I claim them.

VENTNOR (*in the same tone*). On what ground?

MRS. DALE. Hear the man!—Because I wrote them, of course.

VENTNOR. But it seems to me that—under your inspiration, I admit—I also wrote mine.

MRS. DALE. Oh, I don't dispute their authenticity—it's yours I deny!

VENTNOR. Mine?

MRS. DALE. You voluntarily ceased to be the man who wrote me those letters—you've admitted as much. You traded paper for flesh and blood. I don't dispute your wisdom—only you must hold to your bargain! The letters are *all* mine.

VENTNOR (*groping between two tones*). Your arguments are as convincing as ever. (*He hazards a faint laugh.*) You're a marvelous dialectician—but, if we're going to settle the matter in the spirit of an arbitration treaty, why, there are accepted conventions in such cases. It's an odious way to put it, but since you won't help me, one of them is—

MRS. DALE. One of them is—?

VENTNOR. That it is usual—that technically, I mean, the letter—belongs to its writer—

MRS. DALE (*after a pause*). Such letters as *these*?

VENTNOR. Such letters especially—

MRS. DALE. But you couldn't have written them if I hadn't—been willing to read them. Surely there's more of myself in them than of you.

VENTNOR. Surely there's nothing in which a man puts more of himself than in his love letters!

MRS. DALE (*with emotion*). But a woman's love-letters are like her child. They belong to her more than to anybody else—

VENTNOR. And a man's?

MRS. DALE (*with sudden violence*). Are all he risks!—There, take them. (*She flings the key of the cabinet at his feet and sinks into a chair.*)

VENTNOR (*starts as though to pick up the key; then approaches and bends over her*). Helen—oh, Helen!

MRS. DALE (*she yields her hands to him, murmuring:*) Paul! (*Suddenly she straightens herself and draws back illuminated.*) What a fool I am! I see it all now. You want them for your memoirs!

VENTNOR (*disconcerted*). Helen—

MRS. DALE (*agitated*). Come, come—the rule is to unmask when the signal's given! You want them for your memoirs.

VENTNOR (*with a forced laugh*). What makes you think so?

MRS. DALE (*triumphantly*). Because I want them for mine!

VENTNOR (*in a changed tone*). Ah—. (*He moves away from her and leans against the mantelpiece. She remains seated, with her eyes fixed on him.*)

MRS. DALE. I wonder I didn't see it sooner. Your reasons were lame enough.

VENTNOR (*ironically*). Yours were masterly. You're the more accomplished actor of the two. I was completely deceived.

MRS. DALE. Oh, I'm a novelist. I can keep up that sort of thing for five hundred pages!

VENTNOR. I congratulate you. (*A pause.*)

MRS. DALE (*moving to her seat behind the tea table*). I've never offered you any tea. (*She bends over the kettle.*) Why don't you take your letters?

VENTNOR. Because you've been clever enough to make it impossible for me. (*He picks up the key and hands it to her. Then abruptly*)—Was it all acting—just now?

MRS. DALE. By what right do you ask?

VENTNOR. By right of renouncing my claim to my letters. Keep them—and tell me.

MRS. DALE. I give you back your claim—and I refuse to tell you.

VENTNOR (*sadly*). Ah, Helen, if you deceived me, you deceived yourself also.

MRS. DALE. What does it matter, now that we're both undeceived? I played a losing game, that's all.

VENTNOR. Why losing—since all the letters are yours?

MRS. DALE. The letters? (*Slowly.*) I'd forgotten the letters—

VENTNOR (*exultant*). Ah, I knew you'd end by telling me the truth!

MRS. DALE. The truth? Where is the truth? (*Half to herself.*) I thought I was lying when I began—but the lies turned into truth as I uttered them! (*She looks at Ventnor.*) I did want your letters for my memoirs—I did think I'd kept them for that purpose—and I wanted to get mine back for the same reason—but now (*she puts out her hand and picks up some of her letters, which are lying scattered on the table near her*)—how fresh they seem, and how they take me back to the time when we lived instead of writing about life!

VENTNOR (*smiling*). The time when we didn't prepare our impromptu effects beforehand and copyright our remarks about the weather!

MRS. DALE. Or keep our epigrams in cold storage and our adjectives under lock and key!

VENTNOR. When our emotions weren't worth ten cents a word, and a signature wasn't an autograph. Ah, Helen, after all, there's nothing like the exhilaration of spending one's capital!

MRS. DALE. Of wasting it, you mean. (*She points to the letters.*) Do you suppose we could have written a word of these if we'd known we were putting our dreams out at interest? (*She sits musing, with her eyes on the fire, and he watches her in silence.*) Paul, do you remember the deserted garden we sometimes used to walk in?

VENTNOR. The old garden with the high wall at the end of the village street? The garden with the ruined box-borders and the broken-down arbor? Why, I remember every weed in the paths and every patch of moss on the walls!

MRS. DALE. Well—I went back there the other day. The village is immensely improved. There's a new hotel with gas-fires, and a trolley in the main street; and the garden has been turned into a public park, where excursionists sit on cast-iron benches admiring the statue of an Abolitionist.

VENTNOR. An Abolitionist—how appropriate!

MRS. DALE. And the man who sold the garden has made a fortune that he doesn't know how to spend—

VENTNOR (*rising impulsively*). Helen, (*he approaches and lays his hand on her letters*), let's sacrifice our fortune and keep the excursionists out!

MRS. DALE (*with a responsive movement*). Paul, do you really mean it?

VENTNOR (*gayly*). Mean it? Why, I feel like a landed proprietor already! It's more than a garden—it's a park.

MRS. DALE. It's more than a park, it's a world—as long as we keep it to ourselves!

VENTNOR. Ah, yes—even the pyramids look small when one sees a Cook's tourist on top of them! (*He takes the key from the table, unlocks the cabinet and brings out his letters, which he lays beside hers.*) Shall we burn the key to our garden?

MRS. DALE. Ah, then it will indeed be boundless! (*Watching him while he throws the letters into the fire.*)

VENTNOR (*turning back to her with a half-sad smile*). But not too big for us to find each other in?

MRS. DALE. Since we shall be the only people there! (*He takes both her hands and they look at each other a moment in silence. Then he goes out by the door to the right. As he reaches the door she takes a step toward him, impulsively; then turning back she leans against the chimney-piece, quietly watching the letters burn.*)

## THE REMBRANDT

"YOU'RE *so* artistic," my cousin Eleanor Copt began.

Of all Eleanor's exordiums it is the one I most dread. When she tells me I'm so clever I know this is merely the preamble to inviting me to meet the last literary obscurity of the moment: a trial to be evaded or endured, as circumstances dictate; whereas her calling me artistic fatally connotes the request to visit, in her company, some distressed gentlewoman whose future hangs on my valuation of her old Saxe or of her grandfather's Marc Antonios. Time was when I attempted to resist these compulsions of Eleanor's; but I soon learned that, short of actual flight, there was no refuge from her beneficent despotism. It is not always easy for the curator of a museum to abandon his post on the plea of escaping a pretty cousin's importunities; and Eleanor, aware of my predicament, is none too magnanimous to take advantage of it. Magnanimity is, in fact, not in Eleanor's line. The virtues, she once explained to me, are like bonnets: the very ones that look best on other people may not happen to suit one's own particular style; and she added, with a slight deflection of metaphor, that none of the ready-made virtues ever *had* fitted her: they all pinched somewhere, and she'd given up trying to wear them.

Therefore when she said to me, "You're *so* artistic." emphasizing the conjunction with a tap of her dripping umbrella (Eleanor is out in all weathers: the elements are as powerless against her as man), I merely stipulated, "It's not old Saxe again?"

She shook her head reassuringly. "A picture—a Rembrandt!"

"Good Lord! Why not a Leonardo?"

"Well"—she smiled—"that, of course, depends on *you.*"

"On me?"

"On your attribution. I dare say Mrs. Fontage would consent to the change—though she's very conservative."

A gleam of hope came to me and I pronounced: "One can't judge of a picture in this weather."

"Of course not. I'm coming for you tomorrow."

"I've an engagement tomorrow."

"I'll come before or after your engagement."

The afternoon paper lay at my elbow and I contrived a furtive consultation of the weather-report. It said "Rain tomorrow," and I answered briskly: "All right, then; come at ten"—rapidly calculating that the clouds on which I counted might lift by noon.

My ingenuity failed of its due reward; for the heavens, as if in league with my cousin, emptied themselves before morning, and punctually at ten Eleanor and the sun appeared together in my office.

I hardly listened, as we descended the Museum steps and got into Eleanor's hansom, to her vivid summing-up of the case. I guessed beforehand that the lady we were about to visit had lapsed by the most distressful degrees from opulence to a "hall-bedroom"; that her grandfather, if he had not been Minister to France, had signed the Declaration of Independence; that the Rembrandt was an heirloom, sole remnant of disbanded treasures; that for years its possessor had been unwilling to part with it, and that even now the question of its disposal must be approached with the most diplomatic obliquity.

Previous experience had taught me that all Eleanor's "cases" presented a harrowing similarity of detail. No circumstance tending to excite the spectator's sympathy and involve his action was omitted from the history of her beneficiaries; the lights and shades were indeed so skillfully adjusted that any impartial expression of opinion took on the hue of cruelty. I could have produced closetfuls of "heirlooms" in attestation of this fact; for it is one more mark of Eleanor's competence that her friends usually pay the interest on her philanthropy. My one hope was that in this case the object, being a picture, might reasonably be rated beyond my means; and as our cab drew up before a blistered brown-stone door-step I formed the self-defensive resolve to place an extreme valuation on Mrs. Fontage's Rembrandt. It is Eleanor's fault if she is sometimes fought with her own weapons.

The house stood in one of those shabby provisional-looking New York streets that seem resignedly awaiting demolition. It was the kind of house that, in its high days, must have had a bow-window with a bronze in it. The bow-window had been replaced by a plumber's *devanture*, and one might conceive the bronze to have gravitated to the limbo where Mexican onyx tables and bric-a-brac in buffalo-horn await the first signs of our next aesthetic reaction.

Eleanor swept me through a hall that smelled of poverty, up unlit stairs to a bare slit of a room. "And she must leave this in a month!" she whispered across her knock.

I had prepared myself for the limp widow's weed of a woman that one figures in such a setting; and confronted abruptly with Mrs. Fontage's white-haired erectness I had the disconcerting sense that I was somehow in her presence at my own solicitation. I instinctively charged Eleanor with this reversal of the situation; but a moment later I saw it must be ascribed to a something about Mrs. Fontage that precluded the possibility of her asking any one a favor. It was not that she was of forbidding, or even majestic, demeanor; but that one guessed, under her aquiline prettiness, a dignity nervously on guard against the petty betrayal of her surroundings. The room was unconcealably poor: the little faded "relics," the high-stocked ancestral silhouettes, the steel-engravings after Raphael and Correggio, grouped in a vain attempt to hide the most obvious stains on the wall-paper, served only to accentuate the contrast of a past evidently diversified by foreign travel and the enjoyment of the arts. Even Mrs. Fontage's dress had the air of being a last expedient, the ultimate outcome of a much-taxed ingenuity in darning and turning. One felt that all the poor lady's barriers were falling save that of her impregnable manner.

To this manner I found myself conveying my appreciation of being admitted to a view of the Rembrandt.

Mrs. Fontage's smile took my homage for granted. "It is always," she conceded, "a privilege to be in the presence of the great masters." Her slim wrinkled hand waved me to a dusky canvas near the window.

"It's *so* interesting, dear Mrs. Fontage," I heard Eleanor exclaiming, "and my cousin will be able to tell you exactly—" Eleanor, in my presence, always admits that she knows nothing about art; but she gives the impression that this is merely because she hasn't had time to look into the matter—and has had me to do it for her.

Mrs. Fontage seated herself without speaking, as though fearful that a breath might disturb my communion with the masterpiece. I felt that she thought Eleanor's reassuring ejaculations ill-timed; and in this I was of one mind with her; for the impossibility of telling her exactly what I thought of her Rembrandt had become clear to me at a glance.

My cousin's vivacities began to languish and the silence seemed to shape itself into a receptacle for my verdict. I stepped back, affecting a more distant scrutiny; and as I did so my eye caught Mrs. Fontage's profile. Her lids trembled slightly. I took refuge in the familiar expedient of asking the history of the picture, and she waved me brightly to a seat.

This was indeed a topic on which she could dilate. The Rembrandt, it appeared, had come into Mr. Fontage's possession many years ago, while the young couple were on their wedding-tour, and under circumstances so romantic that she made no excuse for relating them in all their parenthetic fullness. The picture belonged to an old Belgian Countess of redundant quarterings, whom the extravagances of an ungovernable nephew had compelled to part with her possessions (in the most private manner) about the time of the Fontages' arrival. By a really remarkable coincidence, it happened that their courier (an exceptionally intelligent and superior man) was an old servant of the Countess's, and had thus been able to put them in the way of securing the Rembrandt under the very nose of an English Duke, whose agent had been sent to Brussels to negotiate for its purchase. Mrs. Fontage could not recall the Duke's name, but he was a great collector and had a famous Highland castle, where somebody had been murdered, and which she herself had visited (by moonlight) when she had travelled in Scotland as a girl. The episode had in short been one of the most interesting "experiences" of a tour almost chromo-lithographic in vivacity of impression; and they had always meant to go back to Brussels for the sake of reliving so picturesque a moment. Circumstances (of which the narrator's surroundings declared the nature) had persistently interfered with the projected return to Europe, and the picture had grown doubly valuable as representing the high-water mark of their artistic emotions. Mrs. Fontage's moist eye caressed the canvas. "There is only," she added with a perceptible effort, "one slight drawback: the picture is not signed. But for that the Countess, of course, would have sold it to a museum. All the connoisseurs who have seen it pronounce it an undoubted Rembrandt, in the artist's best manner; but the museums"—she arched her brows in smiling recognition of a well-known weakness—"give the preference to signed examples—"

Mrs. Fontage's words evoked so touching a vision of the young tourists of fifty years ago, entrusting to an accomplished and versatile courier the direction of their helpless zeal for art, that I lost sight for a moment of the point at issue. The old Belgian Countess, the wealthy Duke with a feudal castle in Scotland, Mrs. Fontage's own maiden pilgrimage to Arthur's Seat and Holyrood, all the accessories of the naïf transaction, seemed a part of that vanished Europe to which our young race carried its indiscriminate ardors, its tender romantic credulity: the legendary castellated Europe of keepsakes, brigands and old masters, that compensated, by one such "experience" as Mrs. Fontage's, for an after-life of aesthetic privation.

I was restored to the present by Eleanor's looking at her watch. The action mutely conveyed that something was expected of me. I risked the temporizing statement that the picture was very interesting; but Mrs. Fontage's polite assent revealed the poverty of the expedient. Eleanor's impatience overflowed.

"You would like my cousin to give you an idea of its value?" she suggested.

Mrs. Fontage grew more erect. "No one," she corrected with great gentleness, "can know its value quite as well as I, who live with it—"

We murmured our hasty concurrence.

"But it might be interesting to hear"—she addressed herself to me—"as a mere matter of curiosity—what estimate would be put on it from the purely commercial point of view—if such a term may be used in speaking of a work of art."

I sounded a note of deprecation.

"Oh, I understand, of course," she delicately anticipated me, "that that could never be *your* view, your personal view; but since occasions *may* arise—do arise—when it becomes necessary to—to put a price on the priceless, as it were—I have thought—Miss Copt has suggested—"

"Some day," Eleanor encouraged her, "you might feel that the picture ought to belong to someone who has more—more opportunity of showing it—letting it be seen by the public—for educational reasons—"

"I have tried," Mrs. Fontage admitted, "to see it in that light."

The crucial moment was upon me. To escape the challenge of Mrs. Fontage's brilliant composure I turned once more to the picture. If my courage needed reinforcement, the picture amply furnished it. Looking at that lamentable canvas seemed the surest way of gathering strength to denounce it; but behind me, all the while, I felt Mrs. Fontage's shuddering pride drawn up in a final effort of self-defense. I hated myself for my sentimental perversion of the situation. Reason argued that it was more cruel to deceive Mrs. Fontage than to tell her the truth; but that merely proved the inferiority of reason to instinct in situations involving any concession to the emotions. Along with her faith in the Rembrandt I must destroy not only the whole fabric of Mrs. Fontage's past, but even that lifelong habit of acquiescence in untested formulas that makes the best part of the average feminine strength. I guessed the episode of the picture to be inextricably interwoven with the traditions and convictions which served to veil Mrs. Fontage's destitution not only from others but from herself. Viewed in that light the Rembrandt had perhaps been worth its purchase-money; and I regretted that works of art do not commonly sell on the merit of the moral support they may have rendered.

From this unavailing flight I was recalled by the sense that something must be done. To place a fictitious value on the picture was at best a provisional measure; while the brutal alternative of advising Mrs. Fontage to sell it for a hundred dollars at least afforded an opening to the charitably disposed purchaser. I intended, if other resources failed, to put myself forward in that light; but delicacy of course forbade my coupling my unflattering estimate of the Rembrandt with an immediate offer to buy it. All I could do was to inflict the wound: the healing unguent must be withheld for later application.

I turned to Mrs. Fontage, who sat motionless, her finely-lined cheeks touched with an expectant color, her eyes averted from the picture which was so evidently the one object they beheld.

"My dear madam—" I began. Her vivid smile was like a light held up to dazzle me. It shrouded every alternative in darkness and I had the flurried sense of having lost my way among the intricacies of my contention. Of a sudden I felt the hopelessness of finding a crack in her impenetrable conviction. My words slipped from me like broken weapons. "The picture," I faltered, "would of course be worth more if it were signed. As it is, I—I hardly think—on a conservative estimate—it can be valued at—at more—than—a thousand dollars, say—"

My deflected argument ran on somewhat aimlessly till it found itself plunging full tilt against the barrier of Mrs. Fontage's silence. She sat as impassive as though I had not spoken. Eleanor loosed a few fluttering words of congratulation and encouragement, but their flight was suddenly cut short. Mrs. Fontage had risen with a certain solemnity.

"I could never," she said gently—her gentleness was adamantine—"under any circumstances whatever, consider, for a moment even, the possibility of parting with the picture at such a price."

## II

WITHIN three weeks a tremulous note from Mrs. Fontage requested the favor of another visit. If the writing was tremulous, however, the writer's tone was firm. She named her own day and hour, without the conventional reference to her visitor's convenience.

My first impulse was to turn the note over to Eleanor. I had acquitted myself of my share in the ungrateful business of coming to Mrs. Fontage's aid, and if, as her letter denoted, she had now yielded to the closer pressure of need, the business of finding a purchaser for the Rembrandt might well be left to my cousin's ingenuity. But here conscience put in the uncomfortable reminder that it was I who, in putting a price on the picture, had raised the real obstacle in the way of Mrs. Fontage's rescue. No one would give a thousand dollars for the Rembrandt; but to tell Mrs. Fontage so had become as unthinkable as murder. I had, in fact, on returning from my first inspection of the picture, refrained from imparting to Eleanor my opinion of its value. Eleanor is porous, and I knew that sooner or later the unnecessary truth would exude through the loose texture of her dissimulation. Not infrequently she thus creates the misery she alleviates; and I have sometimes suspected her of paining people in order that she might be sorry for them. I had, at all events, cut off retreat in Eleanor's direction; and the remaining alternative carried me straight to Mrs. Fontage.

She received me with the same commanding sweetness. The room was even barer than before—I believe the carpet was gone—but her manner built up about her a palace to which I was welcomed with high state; and it was as a mere incident of the ceremony that I was presently made aware of her decision to sell the Rembrandt. My previous unsuccess in planning how to deal with Mrs. Fontage had warned me to leave my farther course to chance; and I listened to her explanation with complete detachment. She had resolved to travel for her health; her doctor advised it, and as her absence might be indefinitely prolonged she had reluctantly decided to part with the picture in order to avoid the expense of storage and insurance. Her voice drooped at the admission, and she hurried on, detailing the vague itinerary of a journey that was to combine long-promised visits to impatient friends with various "interesting opportunities" less definitely specified. The poor lady's skill in rearing a screen of verbiage about her enforced avowal had distracted me from my own share in the situation, and it was with dismay that I suddenly caught the drift of her assumptions. She expected me to buy the Rembrandt for the Museum; she had taken my previous valuation as a tentative bid, and when I came to my senses she was in the act of accepting my offer.

Had I had a thousand dollars of my own to dispose of, the bargain would have been concluded on the spot; but I was in the impossible position of being materially unable to buy the picture and morally unable to tell her that it was not worth acquiring for the Museum.

I dashed into the first evasion in sight. I had no authority, I explained, to purchase pictures for the Museum without the consent of the committee.

Mrs. Fontage coped for a moment in silence with the incredible fact that I had rejected her offer; then she ventured, with a kind of pale precipitation: "But I understood—Miss Copt tells me that you practically decide such matters for the committee." I could guess what the effort had cost her.

"My cousin is given to generalizations. My opinion may have some weight with the committee—"

"Well, then—" she timidly prompted.

"For that very reason I can't buy the picture."

She said, with a drooping note, "I don't understand."

"Yet you told me," I reminded her, "that you knew museums didn't buy unsigned pictures."

"Not for what they are worth! Everyone knows that. But I—I understood—the price you named—" Her pride shuddered back from the abasement. "It's a misunderstanding then," she faltered.

To avoid looking at her, I glanced desperately at the Rembrandt. Could I—? But reason rejected the possibility. Even if the committee had been blind—and they all *were* but Crozier—I simply shouldn't have dared to do it. I stood up, feeling that to cut the matter short was the only alleviation within reach.

Mrs. Fontage had summoned her indomitable smile; but its brilliancy dropped, as I opened the door, like a candle blown out by a draft.

"If there's any one else—if you knew anyone who would care to see the picture, I should be most happy—" She kept her eyes on me, and I saw that, in her case, it hurt less than to look at the Rembrandt. "I shall have to leave here, you know," she panted, "if nobody cares to have it—"

III

THAT evening at my club I had just succeeded in losing sight of Mrs. Fontage in the fumes of an excellent cigar, when a voice at my elbow evoked her harassing image.

"I want to talk to you," the speaker said, "about Mrs. Fontage's Rembrandt."

"There isn't any," I was about to growl; but looking up I recognized the confiding countenance of Mr. Jefferson Rose.

Mr. Rose was known to me chiefly as a young man suffused with a vague enthusiasm for Virtue and my cousin Eleanor.

One glance at his glossy exterior conveyed the assurance that his morals were as immaculate as his complexion and his linen. Goodness exuded from his moist eye, his liquid voice, the warm damp pressure of his trustful hand. He had always struck me as one of the most uncomplicated organisms I had ever met. His ideas were as simple and inconsecutive as the propositions in a primer, and he spoke slowly, with a kind of uniformity of emphasis that made his words stand out like the raised type for the blind. An obvious incapacity for abstract conceptions made him peculiarly susceptible to the magic of generalization, and one felt he would have been at the mercy of any Cause that spelled itself with a capital letter. It was hard to explain how, with such a superabundance of merit, he managed to be a good fellow: I can only say that he performed the astonishing feat as naturally as he supported an invalid mother and two sisters on the slender salary of a banker's clerk. He sat down beside me with an air of bright expectancy.

"It's a remarkable picture, isn't it?" he said.

"You've seen it?"

"I've been so fortunate. Miss Copt was kind enough to get Mrs. Fontage's permission; we went this afternoon."

I inwardly wished that Eleanor had selected another victim; unless indeed the visit were part of a plan whereby some third person, better equipped for the cultivation of delusions, was to be made to think the Rembrandt remarkable. Knowing the limitations of Mr. Rose's resources I began to wonder if he had any rich aunts.

"And her buying it in that way, too," he went on with his limpid smile, "from that old Countess in Brussels, makes it all the more interesting, doesn't it? Miss Copt tells me it's very seldom old pictures can be traced back for more than a generation. I suppose the fact of Mrs. Fontage's knowing its history must add a good deal to its value?"

Uncertain as to his drift, I said: "In her eyes it certainly appears to."

Implications are lost on Mr. Rose, who glowingly continued: "That's the reason why I wanted to talk to you about it—to consult you. Miss Copt tells me you value it at a thousand dollars."

There was no denying this, and I grunted a reluctant assent.

"Of course," he went on earnestly, "your valuation is based on the fact that the picture isn't signed—Mrs. Fontage explained that; and it does make a difference, certainly. But the thing is—if the picture's really good—ought one to take advantage—? I mean—one can see that Mrs. Fontage is in a tight place, and I wouldn't for the world—"

My astonished stare arrested him.

"*You* wouldn't—?"

"I mean—you see, it's just this way"; he coughed and blushed: "I can't give more than a thousand dollars myself—it's as big a sum as I can manage to scrape together—but before I make the offer I want to be sure I'm not standing in the way of her getting more money."

My astonishment lapsed to dismay. "You're going to buy the picture for a thousand dollars?"

His blush deepened. "Why, yes. It sounds rather absurd, I suppose. It isn't much in my line, of course. I can see the picture's very beautiful, but I'm no judge—it isn't the kind of thing, naturally, that I could afford to go in for; but in this case I'm very glad to do what I can; the circumstances are so distressing; and knowing what you think of the picture I feel it's a pretty safe investment—"

"I don't think!" I blurted out.

"You—?"

"I don't think the picture's worth a thousand dollars; I don't think it's worth ten cents; I simply lied about it, that's all."

Mr. Rose looked as frightened as though I had charged him with the offense.

"Hang it, man, can't you see how it happened? I saw the poor woman's pride and happiness hung on her faith in that picture. I tried to make her understand that it was worthless—but she wouldn't; I tried to tell her so—but I couldn't. I behaved like a maudlin ass, but you shan't pay for my infernal bungling—you mustn't buy the picture!"

Mr. Rose sat silent, tapping one glossy boot-tip with another. Suddenly he turned on me a glance of stored intelligence. "But you know," he said good-humoredly, "I rather think I must."

"You haven't—already?"

"Oh, no; the offer's not made."

"Well, then—"

His look gathered a brighter significance.

"But if the picture's worth nothing, nobody will buy it—"

I groaned.

"Except," he continued, "some fellow like me, who doesn't know anything. *I* think it's lovely, you know; I mean to hang it in my mother's sitting-room." He rose and clasped my hand in his adhesive pressure. "I'm awfully obliged to you for telling me this; but perhaps you won't mind my asking you not to mention our talk to Miss Copt? It might bother her, you know, to think the picture isn't exactly up to the mark; and it won't make a rap of difference to me."

## IV

MR. ROSE left me to a sleepless night. The next morning my resolve was formed, and it carried me straight to Mrs. Fontage's. She answered my knock by stepping out on the landing, and as she shut the door behind her I caught a glimpse of her devastated interior. She mentioned, with a careful avoidance of the note of pathos on which our last conversation had closed, that she was preparing to leave that afternoon; and the trunks obstructing the threshold showed that her preparations were nearly complete. They were, I felt certain, the same trunks that, strapped behind a rattling vettura, had accompanied the bride and groom on that memorable voyage of discovery of which the booty had till recently adorned her walls; and there was a dim consolation in the thought that those early "finds" in coral and Swiss wood-carving, in lava and alabaster, still lay behind the worn locks, in the security of worthlessness.

Mrs. Fontage, on the landing, among her strapped and corded treasures, maintained the same air of stability that made it impossible, even under such conditions, to regard her flight as anything less dignified than a departure. It was the moral support of what she tacitly assumed that enabled me to set forth with proper deliberation the object of my visit; and she received my announcement with an absence of surprise that struck me as the very flower of tact. Under cover of these mutual assumptions the transaction was rapidly concluded; and it was not till the canvas passed into my hands that, as though the physical contact had unnerved her, Mrs. Fontage suddenly faltered. "It's the giving it up—" she stammered, disguising herself to the last; and I hastened away from the collapse of her splendid effrontery.

I need hardly point out that I had acted impulsively, and that reaction from the most honorable impulses is sometimes attended by moral perturbation. My motives had indeed been mixed enough to justify some uneasiness, but this was allayed by the instinctive feeling that it is more venial to defraud an institution than a man. Since Mrs. Fontage had to be kept from starving by means not wholly defensible, it was better that the obligation should be borne by a rich institution than an impecunious youth. I doubt, in fact, if my scruples would have survived a night's sleep, had they not been complicated by some uncertainty as to my own future. It was true that, subject to the purely formal assent of the committee, I had full power to buy for the Museum, and that the one member of the committee likely to dispute my decision was opportunely travelling in Europe; but the picture once in place I must face the risk of any expert criticism to which chance might expose it. I dismissed this contingency for future study, stored the Rembrandt in the cellar of the Museum, and thanked heaven that Crozier was abroad.

Six months later he strolled into my office. I had just concluded, under conditions of exceptional difficulty, and on terms unexpectedly benign, the purchase of the great Bartley Reynolds; and this circumstance, by relegating the matter of the Rembrandt to a lower stratum of consciousness, enabled me to welcome Crozier with unmixed pleasure. My security was enhanced by his appearance. His smile was charged with amiable reminiscences, and I inferred that his trip had put him in the humor to approve of everything, or at least to ignore what fell short of his approval. I had therefore no uneasiness in accepting his invitation to dine that evening. It is always pleasant to dine with Crozier and never more so than when he is just back from Europe. His conversation gives even the food a flavor of the Café Anglais.

The repast was delightful, and it was not till we had finished a Camembert which he must have brought over with him, that my host said, in a tone of after-dinner perfunctoriness: "I see you've picked up a picture or two since I left."

I assented. "The Bartley Reynolds seemed too good an opportunity to miss, especially as the French government was after it. I think we got it cheap—"

"*Connu, connu*" said Crozier pleasantly. "I know all about the Reynolds. It was the biggest kind of a haul and I congratulate you. Best stroke of business we've done yet. But tell me about the other picture—the Rembrandt."

"I never said it was a Rembrandt." I could hardly have said why, but I felt distinctly annoyed with Crozier.

"Of course not. There's 'Rembrandt' on the frame, but I saw you'd modified it to 'Dutch School'; I apologize." He paused, but I offered no explanation. "What about it?" he went on. "Where did you pick it up?" As he leaned to the flame of the cigar-lighter his face seemed ruddy with enjoyment.

"I got it for a song," I said.

"A thousand, I think?"

"Have you seen it?" I asked abruptly.

"Went over the place this afternoon and found it in the cellar. Why hasn't it been hung, by the way?"

I paused a moment. "I'm waiting—"

"To—?"

"To have it varnished."

"Ah!" He leaned back and poured himself a second glass of Chartreuse. The smile he confided to its golden depths provoked me to challenge him with—

"What do you think of it?"

"The Rembrandt?" He lifted his eyes from the glass. "Just what you do."

"It isn't a Rembrandt."

"I apologize again. You call it, I believe, a picture of the same period?"

"I'm uncertain of the period."

"H'm." He glanced appreciatively along his cigar. "What are you certain of?"

"That it's a damned bad picture," I said savagely.

He nodded. "Just so. That's all we wanted to know."

"*We*?"

"We—I—the committee, in short. You see, my dear fellow, if you hadn't been certain it was a damned bad picture our position would have been a little awkward. As it is, my remaining duty—I ought to explain that in this matter I'm acting for the committee—is as simple as it's agreeable."

"I'll be hanged," I burst out, "if I understand one word you're saying!"

He fixed me with a kind of cruel joyousness. "You will—you will," he assured me; "at least you'll begin to, when you hear that I've seen Miss Copt."

"Miss Copt?"

"And that she has told me under what conditions the picture was bought."

"She doesn't know anything about the conditions! That is," I added, hastening to restrict the assertion, "she doesn't know my opinion of the picture." I thirsted for five minutes with Eleanor.

"Are you quite sure?" Crozier took me up. "Mr. Jefferson Rose does."

"Ah—I see."

"I thought you would," he reminded me. "As soon as I'd laid eyes on the Rembrandt—I beg your pardon!—I saw that it—well, required some explanation."

"You might have come to me."

"I meant to; but I happened to meet Miss Copt, whose encyclopedic information has often before been of service to me. I always go to Miss Copt when I want to look up anything; and I found she knew all about the Rembrandt."

"*All?*"

"Precisely. The knowledge was in fact causing her sleepless nights. Mr. Rose, who was suffering from the same form of insomnia, had taken her into his confidence, and she—ultimately—took me into hers."

"Of course!"

"I must ask you to do your cousin justice. She didn't speak till it became evident to her uncommonly quick perceptions that your buying the picture on its merits would have been infinitely worse for—for everybody—than your diverting a small portion of the Museum's funds to philanthropic uses. Then she told me the moving incident of Mr. Rose. Good fellow, Rose. And the old lady's case was desperate. Somebody had to buy that picture." I moved uneasily in my seat "Wait a moment, will you? I haven't finished my cigar. There's a little head of Il Fiammingo's that you haven't seen, by the way; I picked it up the other day in Parma. We'll go in and have a look at it presently. But meanwhile what I want to say is that I've been charged—in the most informal way—to express to you the committee's appreciation of your admirable promptness and energy in capturing the Bartley Reynolds. We shouldn't have got it at all if you hadn't been uncommonly wide-awake, and to get it at such a price is a double triumph. We'd have thought nothing of a few more thousands—"

"I don't see," I impatiently interposed, "that, as far as I'm concerned, that alters the case."

"The case—?"

"Of Mrs. Fontage's Rembrandt. I bought the picture because, as you say, the situation was desperate, and I couldn't raise a thousand myself. What I did was of course indefensible; but the money shall be refunded tomorrow—"

Crozier raised a protesting hand. "Don't interrupt me when I'm talking ex cathedra. The money's been refunded already. The fact is, the Museum has sold the Rembrandt."

I stared at him wildly. "Sold it? To whom?"

"Why—to the committee.—Hold on a bit, please.—Won't you take another cigar? Then perhaps I can finish what I've got to say.—Why, my dear fellow, the committee's under an obligation to you—that's the way we look at it. I've investigated Mrs. Fontage's case, and—well, the picture had to be bought. She's eating meat now, I believe, for the first time in a year. And they'd have turned her out into the street that very day, your cousin tells me. Something had to be done at once, and you've simply given a number of well-to-do and self-indulgent gentlemen the opportunity of performing, at very small individual expense, a meritorious action in the nick of time. That's the first thing I've got to thank you for. And then—you'll remember, please, that I have the floor—that I'm still speaking for the committee—and secondly, as a slight recognition of your services in securing the Bartley Reynolds at a very much lower figure than we were prepared to pay, we beg you—the committee begs you—to accept the gift of Mrs. Fontage's Rembrandt. Now we'll go in and look at that little head...."

## THE MOVING FINGER

THE NEWS of Mrs. Grancy's death came to me with the shock of an immense blunder— one of fate's most irretrievable acts of vandalism. It was as though all sorts of renovating forces had been checked by the clogging of that one wheel. Not that Mrs. Grancy contributed any perceptible momentum to the social machine: her unique distinction was that of filling to perfection her special place in the world. So many people are like badly-composed statues, over-lapping their niches at one point and leaving them vacant at another. Mrs. Grancy's niche was her husband's life; and if it be argued that the space was not large enough for its vacancy to leave a very big gap, I can only say that, at the last resort, such dimensions must be determined by finer instruments than any ready-made standard of utility. Ralph Grancy's was in short a kind of disembodied usefullness: one of those constructive influences that, instead of crystallizing into definite forms, remain as it were a medium for the development of clear thinking and fine feeling. He faithfully irrigated his own dusty patch of life, and the fruitful moisture stole far beyond his boundaries. If, to carry on the metaphor, Grancy's life was a sedulously-cultivated enclosure, his wife was the flower he had planted in its midst—the embowering tree, rather, which gave him rest and shade at its foot and the wind of dreams in its upper branches.

We had all—his small but devoted band of followers—known a moment when it seemed likely that Grancy would fail us. We had watched him pitted against one stupid obstacle after another—ill-health, poverty, misunderstanding and, worst of all for a man of his texture, his first wife's soft insidious egotism. We had seen him sinking under the leaden embrace of her affection like a swimmer in a drowning clutch; but just as we despaired he had always come to the surface again, blinded, panting, but striking out fiercely for the shore. When at last her death released him it became a question as to how much of the man she had carried with her. Left alone, he revealed numb withered patches, like a tree from which a parasite has been stripped. But gradually he began to put out new leaves; and when he met the lady who was to become his second wife—his one *real* wife, as his friends reckoned—the whole man burst into flower.

The second Mrs. Grancy was past thirty when he married her, and it was clear that she had harvested that crop of middle joy which is rooted in young despair. But if she had lost the surface of eighteen she had kept its inner light; if her cheek lacked the gloss of immaturity her eyes were young with the stored youth of half a life-time. Grancy had first known her somewhere in the East—I believe she was the sister of one of our consuls out there—and when he brought her home to New York she came among us as a stranger. The idea of Grancy's remarriage had been a shock to us all. After one such calcining most men would have kept out of the fire; but we agreed that he was predestined to sentimental blunders, and we awaited with resignation the embodiment of his latest mistake. Then Mrs. Grancy came—and we understood. She was the most beautiful and the most complete of explanations. We shuffled our defeated omniscience out of sight and gave it hasty burial under a prodigality of welcome. For the first time in years we had Grancy off our minds. "He'll do something great now!" the least sanguine of us prophesied; and our sentimentalist emended: "He *has* done it—in marrying her!"

It was Claydon, the portrait-painter, who risked this hyperbole; and who soon afterward, at the happy husband's request, prepared to defend it in a portrait of Mrs. Grancy. We were all—even Claydon—ready to concede that Mrs. Grancy's unwontedness was in some degree a matter of environment. Her graces were complementary and it needed the mate's call to reveal the flash of color beneath her neutral-tinted wings. But if she needed Grancy to interpret her, how much greater was the service she rendered him! Claydon professionally described her as the right frame for him; but if she defined she also enlarged, if she threw the whole into perspective she also cleared new ground, opened fresh vistas, reclaimed whole areas of activity that had run to waste under the harsh husbandry of privation. This interaction of sympathies was not without its visible expression. Claydon was not alone in maintaining that Grancy's presence—or indeed the mere mention of his name—had a perceptible effect on his wife's appearance. It was as though a light were shifted, a curtain drawn back, as though, to borrow another of Claydon's metaphors, Love the indefatigable artist were perpetually seeking a happier "pose" for his model. In this interpretative light Mrs. Grancy acquired the charm which makes some women's faces like a book of which the last page is never turned. There was always something new to read in her eyes. What Claydon read there— or at least such scattered hints of the ritual as reached him through the sanctuary doors— his portrait in due course declared to us. When the picture was exhibited it was at once acclaimed as his masterpiece; but the people who knew Mrs. Grancy smiled and said it was flattered. Claydon, however, had not set out to paint their Mrs. Grancy—or ours even—but Ralph's; and Ralph knew his own at a glance. At the first confrontation he saw that Claydon had understood. As for Mrs. Grancy, when the finished picture was shown to her she turned to the painter and said simply: "Ah, you've done me facing the east!"

The picture, then, for all its value, seemed a mere incident in the unfolding of their double destiny, a foot-note to the illuminated text of their lives. It was not till afterward that it acquired the significance of last words spoken on a threshold never to be recrossed. Grancy, a year after his marriage, had given up his town house and carried his bliss an hour's journey away, to a little place among the hills. His various duties and interests brought him frequently to New York but we necessarily saw him less often than when his house had served as the rallying-point of kindred enthusiasms. It seemed a pity that such an influence should be withdrawn, but we all felt that his long arrears of happiness should be paid in whatever coin he chose. The distance from which the fortunate couple radiated warmth on us was not too great for friendship to traverse; and our conception of a glorified leisure took the form of Sundays spent in the Grancys' library, with its sedative rural outlook, and the portrait of Mrs. Grancy illuminating its studious walls. The picture was at its best in that setting; and we used to accuse Claydon of visiting Mrs. Grancy in order to see her portrait. He met this by declaring that the portrait was Mrs. Grancy; and there were moments when the statement seemed unanswerable. One of us, indeed—I think it must have been the novelist—said that Clayton had been saved from falling in love with Mrs. Grancy only by falling in love with his picture of her; and it was noticeable that he, to whom his finished work was no more than the shed husk of future effort, showed a perennial tenderness for this one achievement. We smiled afterward to think how often, when Mrs. Grancy was in the room, her presence reflecting itself in our talk like a gleam of sky in a hurrying current, Claydon, averted from the real woman, would sit as it were listening to the picture. His attitude, at the time, seemed only a part of the unusualness of those picturesque afternoons, when the most familiar combinations of life underwent a magical change. Some human happiness is a landlocked lake; but the Grancys' was an open sea, stretching a buoyant and illimitable surface to the voyaging interests of life. There was room and to spare on those waters for all our separate ventures; and always beyond the sunset, a mirage of the fortunate isles toward which our prows bent.

II

IT was in Rome that, three years later, I heard of her death. The notice said "suddenly"; I was glad of that. I was glad too—basely perhaps—to be away from Grancy at a time when silence must have seemed obtuse and speech derisive.

I was still in Rome when, a few months afterward, he suddenly arrived there. He had been appointed secretary of legation at Constantinople and was on the way to his post. He had taken the place, he said frankly, "to get away." Our relations with the Porte held out a prospect of hard work, and that, he explained, was what he needed. He could never be satisfied to sit down among the ruins. I saw that, like most of us in moments of extreme moral tension, he was playing a part, behaving as he thought it became a man to behave in the eye of disaster. The instinctive posture of grief is a shuffling compromise between defiance and prostration; and pride feels the need of striking a worthier attitude in face of such a foe. Grancy, by nature musing and retrospective, had chosen the role of the man of action, who answers blow for blow and opposes a mailed front to the thrusts of destiny; and the completeness of the equipment testified to his inner weakness. We talked only of what we were not thinking of, and parted, after a few days, with a sense of relief that proved the inadequacy of friendship to perform, in such cases, the office assigned to it by tradition.

Soon afterward my own work called me home, but Grancy remained several years in Europe. International diplomacy kept its promise of giving him work to do, and during the year in which he acted as *chargé d'affaires* he acquitted himself, under trying conditions, with conspicuous zeal and discretion. A political redistribution of matter removed him from office just as he had proved his usefulness to the government; and the following summer I heard that he had come home and was down at his place in the country.

On my return to town I wrote him and his reply came by the next post. He answered as it were in his natural voice, urging me to spend the following Sunday with him, and suggesting that I should bring down any of the old set who could be persuaded to join me. I thought this a good sign, and yet—shall I own it?—I was vaguely disappointed. Perhaps we are apt to feel that our friends' sorrows should be kept like those historic monuments from which the encroaching ivy is periodically removed.

That very evening at the club I ran across Claydon. I told him of Grancy's invitation and proposed that we should go down together; but he pleaded an engagement. I was sorry, for I had always felt that he and I stood nearer Ralph than the others, and if the old Sundays were to be renewed I should have preferred that we two should spend the first alone with him. I said as much to Claydon and offered to fit my time to his; but he met this by a general refusal.

"I don't want to go to Grancy's," he said bluntly. I waited a moment, but he appended no qualifying clause.

"You've seen him since he came back?" I finally ventured.

Claydon nodded.

"And is he so awfully bad?"

"Bad? No: he's all right."

"All right? How can he be, unless he's changed beyond all recognition?"

"Oh, you'll recognize *him*," said Claydon, with a puzzling deflection of emphasis.

His ambiguity was beginning to exasperate me, and I felt myself shut out from some knowledge to which I had as good a right as he.

"You've been down there already, I suppose?"

"Yes; I've been down there."

"And you've done with each other—the partnership is dissolved?"

"Done with each other? I wish to God we had!" He rose nervously and tossed aside the review from which my approach had diverted him. "Look here," he said, standing before me, "Ralph's the best fellow going and there's nothing under heaven I wouldn't do for him—short of going down there again." And with that he walked out of the room.

Claydon was incalculable enough for me to read a dozen different meanings into his words; but none of my interpretations satisfied me. I determined, at any rate, to seek no farther for a companion; and the next Sunday I travelled down to Grancy's alone. He met me at the station and I saw at once that he had changed since our last meeting. Then he had been in fighting array, but now if he and grief still housed together it was no longer as enemies. Physically the transformation was as marked but less reassuring. If the spirit triumphed the body showed its scars. At five-and-forty he was gray and stooping, with the tired gait of an old man. His serenity, however, was not the resignation of age. I saw that he did not mean to drop out of the game. Almost immediately he began to speak of our old interests; not with an effort, as at our former meeting, but simply and naturally, in the tone of a man whose life has flowed back into its normal channels. I remembered, with a touch of self-reproach, how I had distrusted his reconstructive powers; but my admiration for his reserved force was now tinged by the sense that, after all, such happiness as his ought to have been paid with his last coin. The feeling grew as we neared the house and I found how inextricably his wife was interwoven with my remembrance of the place: how the whole scene was but an extension of that vivid presence.

Within doors nothing was changed, and my hand would have dropped without surprise into her welcoming clasp. It was luncheon-time, and Grancy led me at once to the dining-room, where the walls, the furniture, the very plate and porcelain, seemed a mirror in which a moment since her face had been reflected. I wondered whether Grancy, under the recovered tranquillity of his smile, concealed the same sense of her nearness, saw perpetually between himself and the actual her bright unappeasable ghost. He spoke of her once or twice, in an easy incidental way, and her name seemed to hang in the air after he had uttered it, like a chord that continues to vibrate. If he felt her presence it was evidently as an enveloping medium, the moral atmosphere in which he breathed. I had never before known how completely the dead may survive.

After luncheon we went for a long walk through the autumnal fields and woods, and dusk was falling when we re-entered the house. Grancy led the way to the library, where, at this hour, his wife had always welcomed us back to a bright fire and a cup of tea. The room faced the west, and held a clear light of its own after the rest of the house had grown dark. I remembered how young she had looked in this pale gold light, which irradiated her eyes and hair, or silhouetted her girlish outline as she passed before the windows. Of all the rooms the library was most peculiarly hers; and here I felt that her nearness might take visible shape. Then, all in a moment, as Grancy opened the door, the feeling vanished and a kind of resistance met me on the threshold. I looked about me. Was the room changed? Had some desecrating hand effaced the traces of her presence? No; here too the setting was undisturbed. My feet sank into the same deep-piled Daghestan; the bookshelves took the firelight on the same rows of rich subdued bindings; her armchair stood in its old place near the tea-table; and from the opposite wall her face confronted me.

Her face—but *was* it hers? I moved nearer and stood looking up at the portrait. Grancy's glance had followed mine and I heard him move to my side.

"You see a change in it?" he said.

"What does it mean?" I asked.

"It means—that five years have passed."

"Over *her*?"

"Why not?—Look at me!" He pointed to his gray hair and furrowed temples. "What do you think kept *her* so young? It was happiness! But now—" he looked up at her with infinite tenderness. "I like her better so," he said. "It's what she would have wished."

"Have wished?"

"That we should grow old together. Do you think she would have wanted to be left behind?"

I stood speechless, my gaze travelling from his worn grief-beaten features to the painted face above. It was not furrowed like his; but a veil of years seemed to have descended on it. The bright hair had lost its elasticity, the cheek its clearness, the brow its light: the whole woman had waned.

Grancy laid his hand on my arm. "You don't like it?" he said sadly.

"Like it? I—I've lost her!" I burst out.

"And I've found her," he answered.

"In *that*?" I cried with a reproachful gesture.

"Yes; in that." He swung round on me almost defiantly. "The other had become a sham, a lie! This is the way she would have looked—does look, I mean. Claydon ought to know, oughtn't he?"

I turned suddenly. "Did Claydon do this for you?"

Grancy nodded.

"Since your return?"

"Yes. I sent for him after I'd been back a week—." He turned away and gave a thrust to the smoldering fire. I followed, glad to leave the picture behind me. Grancy threw himself into a chair near the hearth, so that the light fell on his sensitive variable face. He leaned his head back, shading his eyes with his hand, and began to speak.

III

"YOU fellows knew enough of my early history to A guess what my second marriage meant to me. I say guess, because no one could understand—really. I've always had a feminine streak in me, I suppose: the need of a pair of eyes that should see with me, of a pulse that should keep time with mine. Life is a big thing, of course; a magnificent spectacle; but I got so tired of looking at it alone! Still, it's always good to live, and I had plenty of happiness—of the evolved kind. What I'd never had a taste of was the simple inconscient sort that one breathes in like the air. . . .

"Well—I met her. It was like finding the climate in which I was meant to live. You know what she was—how indefinitely she multiplied one's points of contact with life, how she lit up the caverns and bridged the abysses! Well, I swear to you (though I suppose the sense of all that was latent in me) that what I used to think of on my way home at the end of the day, was simply that when I opened this door she'd be sitting over there, with the lamp-light falling in a particular way on one little curl in her neck. . . . When Claydon painted her he caught just the look she used to lift to mine when I came in—I've wondered, sometimes, at his knowing how she looked when she and I were alone.—How I rejoiced in that picture! I used to say to her, 'You're my prisoner now—I shall never lose you. If you grew tired of me and left me you'd leave your real self there on the wall!' It was always one of our jokes that she was going to grow tired of me—

"Three years of it—and then she died. It was so sudden that there was no change, no diminution. It was as if she had suddenly become fixed, immovable, like her own portrait: as if Time had ceased at its happiest hour, just as Claydon had thrown down his brush one day and said, 'I can't do better than that.'

"I went away, as you know, and stayed over there five years. I worked as hard as I knew how, and after the first black months a little light stole in on me. From thinking that she would have been interested in what I was doing I came to feel that she *was* interested—that she was there and that she knew. I'm not talking any psychical jargon—I'm simply trying to express the sense I had that an influence so full, so abounding as hers couldn't pass like a spring shower. We had so lived into each other's hearts and minds that the consciousness of what she would have thought and felt illuminated all I did. At first she used to come back shyly, tentatively, as though not sure of finding me; then she stayed longer and longer, till at last she became again the very air I breathed.... There were bad moments, of course, when her nearness mocked me with the loss of the real woman; but gradually the distinction between the two was effaced and the mere thought of her grew warm as flesh and blood.

"Then I came home. I landed in the morning and came straight down here. The thought of seeing her portrait possessed me and my heart beat like a lover's as I opened the library door. It was in the afternoon and the room was full of light. It fell on her picture—the picture of a young and radiant woman. She smiled at me coldly across the distance that divided us. I had the feeling that she didn't even recognize me. And then I caught sight of myself in the mirror over there—a gray-haired broken man whom she had never known!

"For a week we two lived together—the strange woman and the strange man. I used to sit night after night and question her smiling face; but no answer ever came. What did she know of me, after all? We were irrevocably separated by the five years of life that lay between us. At times, as I sat here, I almost grew to hate her; for her presence had driven away my gentle ghost, the real wife who had wept, aged, struggled with me during those awful years. . . . It was the worst loneliness I've ever known. Then, gradually, I began to notice a look of sadness in the picture's eyes; a look that seemed to say: 'Don't you see that I am lonely too?' And all at once it came over me how she would have hated to be left behind! I remembered her comparing life to a heavy book that could not be read with ease unless two people held it together; and I thought how impatiently her hand would have turned the pages that divided us!—So the idea came to me: 'It's the picture that stands between us; the picture that is dead, and not my wife. To sit in this room is to keep watch beside a corpse.' As this feeling grew on me the portrait became like a beautiful mausoleum in which she had been buried alive: I could hear her beating against the painted walls and crying to me faintly for help.

"One day I found I couldn't stand it any longer and I sent for Claydon. He came down and I told him what I'd been through and what I wanted him to do. At first he refused point-blank to touch the picture. The next morning I went off for a long tramp, and when I came home I found him sitting here alone. He looked at me sharply for a moment and then he said: 'I've changed my mind; I'll do it.' I arranged one of the north rooms as a studio and he shut himself up there for a day; then he sent for me. The picture stood there as you see it now—it was as though she'd met me on the threshold and taken me in her arms! I tried to thank him, to tell him what it meant to me, but he cut me short.

"'There's an up train at five, isn't there?' he asked. 'I'm booked for a dinner to-night. I shall just have time to make a bolt for the station and you can send my traps after me.' I haven't seen him since.

"I can guess what it cost him to lay hands on his masterpiece; but, after all, to him it was only a picture lost, to me it was my wife regained!"

IV

AFTER that, for ten years or more, I watched the strange spectacle of a life of hopeful and productive effort based on the structure of a dream. There could be no doubt to those who saw Grancy during this period that he drew his strength and courage from the sense of his wife's mystic participation in his task. When I went back to see him a few months later I found the portrait had been removed from the library and placed in a small study up-stairs, to which he had transferred his desk and a few books. He told me he always sat there when he was alone, keeping the library for his Sunday visitors. Those who missed the portrait of course made no comment on its absence, and the few who were in his secret respected it. Gradually all his old friends had gathered about him and our Sunday afternoons regained something of their former character; but Claydon never reappeared among us.

As I look back now I see that Grancy must have been failing from the time of his return home. His invincible spirit belied and disguised the signs of weakness that afterward asserted themselves in my remembrance of him. He seemed to have an inexhaustible fund of life to draw on, and more than one of us was a pensioner on his superfluity.

Nevertheless, when I came back one summer from my European holiday and heard that he had been at the point of death, I understood at once that we had believed him well only because he wished us to.

I hastened down to the country and found him midway in a slow convalescence. I felt then that he was lost to us and he read my thought at a glance.

"Ah," he said, "I'm an old man now and no mistake. I suppose we shall have to go half-speed after this; but we shan't need towing just yet!"

The plural pronoun struck me, and involuntarily I looked up at Mrs. Grancy's portrait. Line by line I saw my fear reflected in it. It was the face of a woman *who knows that her husband is dying.* My heart stood still at the thought of what Claydon had done.

Grancy had followed my glance. "Yes, it's changed her," he said quietly. "For months, you know, it was touch and go with me—we had a long fight of it, and it was worse for her than for me." After a pause he added: "Claydon has been very kind; he's so busy nowadays that I seldom see him, but when I sent for him the other day he came down at once."

I was silent and we spoke no more of Grancy's illness; but when I took leave it seemed like shutting him in alone with his death-warrant.

The next time I went down to see him he looked much better. It was a Sunday and he received me in the library, so that I did not see the portrait again. He continued to improve and toward spring we began to feel that, as he had said, he might yet travel a long way without being towed.

One evening, on returning to town after a visit which had confirmed my sense of reassurance, I found Claydon dining alone at the club. He asked me to join him and over the coffee our talk turned to his work.

"If you're not too busy," I said at length, "you ought to make time to go down to Grancy's again."

He looked up quickly. "Why?" he asked.

"Because he's quite well again," I returned with a touch of cruelty. "His wife's prognostications were mistaken."

Claydon stared at me a moment. "Oh, *she* knows," he affirmed with a smile that chilled me.

"You mean to leave the portrait as it is then?" I persisted.

He shrugged his shoulders. "He hasn't sent for me yet!"

A waiter came up with the cigars and Claydon rose and joined another group.

It was just a fortnight later that Grancy's housekeeper telegraphed for me. She met me at the station with the news that he had been "taken bad" and that the doctors were with him. I had to wait for some time in the deserted library before the medical men appeared. They had the baffled manner of empirics who have been superseded by the great Healer; and I lingered only long enough to hear that Grancy was not suffering and that my presence could do him no harm.

I found him seated in his arm-chair in the little study. He held out his hand with a smile.

"You see she was right after all," he said.

"She?" I repeated, perplexed for the moment.

"My wife." He indicated the picture. "Of course I knew she had no hope from the first. I saw that"—he lowered his voice—"after Claydon had been here. But I wouldn't believe it at first!"

I caught his hands in mine. "For God's sake don't believe it now!" I adjured him.

He shook his head gently. "It's too late," he said. "I might have known that she knew."

"But, Grancy, listen to me," I began; and then I stopped. What could I say that would convince him? There was no common ground of argument on which we could meet; and after all it would be easier for him to die feeling that she *had* known. Strangely enough, I saw that Claydon had missed his mark.

V

GRANCY'S will named me as one of his executors; and my associate, having other duties on his hands, begged me to assume the task of carrying out our friend's wishes. This placed me under the necessity of informing Claydon that the portrait of Mrs. Grancy had been bequeathed to him; and he replied by the next post that he would send for the picture at once. I was staying in the deserted house when the portrait was taken away; and as the door closed on it I felt that Grancy's presence had vanished too. Was it his turn to follow her now, and could one ghost haunt another?

After that, for a year or two, I heard nothing more of the picture, and though I met Claydon from time to time we had little to say to each other. I had no definable grievance against the man and I tried to remember that he had done a fine thing in sacrificing his best picture to a friend; but my resentment had all the tenacity of unreason.

One day, however, a lady whose portrait he had just finished begged me to go with her to see it. To refuse was impossible, and I went with the less reluctance that I knew I was not the only friend she had invited. The others were all grouped around the easel when I entered, and after contributing my share to the chorus of approval I turned away and began to stroll about the studio. Claydon was something of a collector and his things were generally worth looking at. The studio was a long tapestried room with a curtained archway at one end. The curtains were looped back, showing a smaller apartment, with books and flowers and a few fine bits of bronze and porcelain. The tea-table standing in this inner room proclaimed that it was open to inspection, and I wandered in. A *bleu poudré* vase first attracted me; then I turned to examine a slender bronze Ganymede, and in so doing found myself face to face with Mrs. Grancy's portrait. I stared up at her blankly and she smiled back at me in all the recovered radiance of youth. The artist had effaced every trace of his later touches and the original picture had reappeared. It throned alone on the paneled wall, asserting a brilliant supremacy over its carefully-chosen surroundings. I felt in an instant that the whole room was tributary to it: that Claydon had heaped his treasures at the feet of the woman he loved. Yes—it was the woman he had loved and not the picture; and my instinctive resentment was explained.

Suddenly I felt a hand on my shoulder.

"Ah, how could you?" I cried, turning on him.

"How could I?" he retorted. "How could I not? Doesn't she belong to me now?"

I moved away impatiently.

"Wait a moment," he said with a detaining gesture. "The others have gone and I want to say a word to you.—Oh, I know what you've thought of me—I can guess! You think I killed Grancy, I suppose?"

I was startled by his sudden vehemence. "I think you tried to do a cruel thing," I said.

"Ah—what a little way you others see into life!" he murmured. "Sit down a moment—here, where we can look at her—and I'll tell you."

He threw himself on the ottoman beside me and sat gazing up at the picture, with his hands clasped about his knee.

"Pygmalion," he began slowly, "turned his statue into a real woman; *I* turned my real woman into a picture. Small compensation, you think—but you don't know how much of a woman belongs to you after you've painted her!—Well, I made the best of it, at any rate—I gave her the best I had in me; and she gave me in return what such a woman gives by merely being. And after all she rewarded me enough by making me paint as I shall never paint again! There was one side of her, though, that was mine alone, and that was her beauty; for no one else understood it. To Grancy even it was the mere expression of herself—what language is to thought. Even when he saw the picture he didn't guess my secret—he was so sure she was all his! As though a man should think he owned the moon because it was reflected in the pool at his door.

"Well—when he came home and sent for me to change the picture it was like asking me to commit murder. He wanted me to make an old woman of her—of her who had been so divinely, unchangeably young! As if any man who really loved a woman would ask her to sacrifice her youth and beauty for his sake! At first I told him I couldn't do it—but afterward, when he left me alone with the picture, something queer happened. I suppose it was because I was always so confoundedly fond of Grancy that it went against me to refuse what he asked. Anyhow, as I sat looking up at her, she seemed to say, 'I'm not yours but his, and I want you to make me what he wishes.' And so I did it. I could have cut my hand off when the work was done—I daresay he told you I never would go back and look at it. He thought I was too busy—he never understood.

"Well—and then last year he sent for me again—you remember. It was after his illness, and he told me he'd grown twenty years older and that he wanted her to grow older too—he didn't want her to be left behind. The doctors all thought he was going to get well at that time, and he thought so too; and so did I when I first looked at him. But when I turned to the picture—ah, now I don't ask you to believe me; but I swear it was *her* face that told me he was dying, and that she wanted him to know it! She had a message for him and she made me deliver it."

He rose abruptly and walked toward the portrait; then he sat down beside me again.

"Cruel? Yes, it seemed so to me at first; and this time, if I resisted, it was for *his* sake and not for mine. But all the while I felt her eyes drawing me, and gradually she made me understand. If she'd been there in the flesh (she seemed to say) wouldn't she have seen before any of us that he was dying? Wouldn't he have read the news first in her face? And wouldn't it be horrible if now he should discover it instead in strange eyes?—Well—that was what she wanted of me and I did it—I kept them together to the last!" He looked up at the picture again. "But now she belongs to me," he repeated. . . .

# THE CONFESSIONAL

WHEN I WAS a young man I thought a great deal of local color. At that time it was still a pigment of recent discovery, and supposed to have a peculiarly stimulating effect on the mental eye. As an aid to the imagination its value was perhaps overrated; but as an object of pursuit to that vagrant faculty, it had all the merits claimed for it. I certainly never hunted any game better worth my powder; and to a young man with rare holidays and long working hours, its value was enhanced by the fact that one might bring it down at any turn, if only one kept one's eye alert and one's hand on the trigger.

Even the large manufacturing city where, for some years, my young enthusiasms were chained to an accountant's desk, was not without its romantic opportunities. Many of the mill-hands at Dunstable were Italians, and a foreign settlement had formed itself in that unsavory and unsanitary portion of the town known as the Point. The Point, like more aristocratic communities, had its residential and commercial districts, its church, its theatre and its restaurant. When the craving for local color was on me it was my habit to resort to the restaurant, a low-browed wooden building with the appetizing announcement:

*"Aristiù di montone"*

pasted in one of its fly-blown window-panes. Here the consumption of tough macaroni or of an ambiguous *frittura* sufficed to transport me to the Cappello d'Oro in Venice, while my cup of coffee and a wasp-waisted cigar with a straw in it turned my greasy table-cloth into the marble top of one of the little round tables under the arcade of the Caffè Pedrotti at Padua. This feat of the imagination was materially aided by Agostino, the hollow-eyed and low-collared waiter, whose slimy napkin never lost its Latin flourish and whose zeal for my comfort was not infrequently displayed by his testing the warmth of my soup with his finger. Through Agostino I became acquainted with the inner history of the colony, heard the details of its feuds and vendettas, and learned to know by sight the leading characters in these domestic dramas.

The restaurant was frequented by the chief personages of the community: the overseer of the Italian hands at the Meriton Mills, the doctor, his wife the *levatrice* (a plump Neapolitan with greasy ringlets, a plush picture-hat, and a charm against the evil-eye hanging in a crease of her neck) and lastly by Don Egidio, the *parocco* of the little church across the street. The doctor and his wife came only on feast days, but the overseer and Don Egidio were regular patrons. The former was a quiet saturnine-looking man, of accomplished manners but reluctant speech, and I depended for my diversion chiefly on Don Egidio, whose large loosely-hung lips were always ajar for conversation. The remarks issuing from them were richly tinged by the gutturals of the Bergamasque dialect, and it needed but a slight acquaintance with Italian types to detect the Lombard peasant under the priest's rusty cassock. This inference was confirmed by Don Egidio's telling me that he came from a village of Val Camonica, the radiant valley which extends northward from the lake of Iseo to the Adamello glaciers. His step-father had been a laborer on one of the fruit-farms of a Milanese count who owned large estates in the Val Camonica; and that gentleman, taking a fancy to the lad, whom he had seen at work in his orchards, had removed him to his villa on the lake of Iseo and had subsequently educated him for the Church.

It was doubtless to this picturesque accident that Don Egidio owed the mingling of ease and simplicity that gave an inimitable charm to his stout shabby presence. It was as though some wild mountain-fruit had been transplanted to the Count's orchards and had mellowed under cultivation without losing its sylvan flavor. I have never seen the social art carried farther without suggestion of artifice. The fact that Don Egidio's amenities were mainly exercised on the mill-hands composing his parish proved the genuineness of his gift. It is easier to simulate gentility among gentlemen than among navvies; and the plain man is a touchstone who draws out all the alloy in the gold.

Among his parishioners Don Egidio ruled with the cheerful despotism of the good priest. On cardinal points he was inflexible, but in minor matters he had that elasticity of judgment which enables the Catholic discipline to fit itself to every inequality of the human conscience. There was no appeal from his verdict; but his judgment-seat was a revolving chair from which he could view the same act at various angles. His influence was acknowledged not only by his flock, but by the policeman at the corner, the "bar-keep'" in the dive, the ward politician in the corner grocery. The general verdict of Dunstable was that the Point would have been hell without the priest. It was perhaps not precisely heaven with him; but such light of the upper sky as pierced its murky atmosphere was reflected from Don Egidio's countenance. It is hardly possible for any one to exercise such influence without taking pleasure in it; and on the whole the priest was probably a contented man; though it does not follow that he was a happy one. On this point the first stages of our acquaintance yielded much food for conjecture. At first sight Don Egidio was the image of cheerfulness. He had all the physical indications of a mind at ease: the leisurely rolling gait, the ready laugh, the hospitable eye of the man whose sympathies are always on the latch. It took me some time to discover under his surface garrulity the impenetrable reticence of his profession, and under his enjoyment of trifles a leveling melancholy which made all enjoyment trifling. Don Egidio's aspect and conversation were so unsuggestive of psychological complexities that I set down this trait to poverty or home-sickness. There are few classes of men more frugal in tastes and habit than the village priest in Italy; but Don Egidio, by his own account, had been introduced, at an impressionable age, to a way of living that must have surpassed his wildest dreams of self-indulgence. To whatever privations his parochial work had since accustomed him, the influences of that earlier life were too perceptible in his talk not to have made a profound impression on his tastes; and he remained, for all his apostolic simplicity, the image of the family priest who has his seat at the rich man's table.

It chanced that I had used one of my short European holidays to explore afoot the romantic passes connecting the Valtelline with the lake of Iseo; and my remembrance of that enchanting region made it seem impossible that Don Egidio should ever look without a reminiscent pang on the grimy perspective of his parochial streets. The transition was too complete, too ironical, from those rich glades and Titianesque acclivities to the brick hovels and fissured sidewalks of the Point.

This impression was confirmed when Don Egidio, in response to my urgent invitation, paid his first visit to my modest lodgings. He called one winter evening, when a wood-fire in its happiest humor was giving a factitious luster to my book-shelves and bringing out the values of the one or two old prints and Chinese porcelains that accounted for the perennial shabbiness of my wardrobe.

"Ah," said he with a murmur of satisfaction, as he laid aside his shiny hat and bulging umbrella, "it is a long time since I have been in a *casa signorile*."

My remembrance of his own room (he lodged with the doctor and the *levatrice*) saved this epithet from the suggestion of irony and kept me silent while he sank into my arm-chair with the deliberation of a tired traveller lowering himself gently into a warm bath.

"Good! good!" he repeated, looking about him. "Books, porcelains, objects of *virtù*—I am glad to see that there are still such things in the world!" And he turned a genial eye on the glass of Marsala that I had poured out for him.

Don Egidio was the most temperate of men and never exceeded his one glass; but he liked to sit by the hour puffing at my Cabanas, which I suspected him of preferring to the black weed of his native country. Under the influence of my tobacco he became even more blandly garrulous, and I sometimes fancied that of all the obligations of his calling none could have placed such a strain on him as that of preserving the secrets of the confessional. He often talked of his early life at the Count's villa, where he had been educated with his patron's two sons till he was of age to be sent to the seminary; and I could see that the years spent in simple and familiar intercourse with his benefactors had been the most vivid chapter in his experience. The Italian peasant's inarticulate tenderness for the beauty of his birthplace had been specialized in him by contact with cultivated tastes, and he could tell me not only that the Count had a "stupendous" collection of pictures, but that the chapel of the villa contained a sepulchral monument by Bambaja, and that the art-critics were divided as to the authenticity of the Leonardo in the family palace at Milan.

On all these subjects he was inexhaustibly voluble; but there was one point which he always avoided, and that was his reason for coming to America. I remember the round turn with which he brought me up when I questioned him.

"A priest," said he, "is a soldier and must obey orders like a soldier." He set down his glass of Marsala and strolled across the room. "I had not observed," he went on, "that you have here a photograph of the Sposalizio of the Brera. What a picture! *È stupendo!*" and he turned back to his seat and smilingly lit a fresh cigar.

I saw at once that I had hit on a point where his native garrulity was protected by the chain-mail of religious discipline that every Catholic priest wears beneath his cassock. I had too much respect for my friend to wish to penetrate his armor, and now and then I almost fancied he was grateful to me for not putting his reticence to the test.

Don Egidio must have been past sixty when I made his acquaintance; but it was not till the close of an exceptionally harsh winter, some five or six years after our first meeting, that I began to think of him as an old man. It was as though the long-continued cold had cracked and shriveled him. He had grown bent and hollow-chested and his lower lip shook like an unhinged door. The summer heat did little to revive him, and in September, when I came home from my vacation, I found him just recovering from an attack of pneumonia. That autumn he did not care to venture often into the night air, and now and then I used to go and sit with him in his little room, to which I had contributed the unheard-of luxuries of an easy-chair and a gas stove.

My engagements, however, made these visits infrequent, and several weeks had elapsed without my seeing the *parocco* when, one snowy November morning, I ran across him in the railway-station. I was on my way to New York for the day and had just time to wave a greeting to him as I jumped into the railway-carriage; but a moment later, to my surprise, I saw him stiffly clambering into the same train. I found him seated in the common car, with his umbrella between his knees and a bundle done up in a red cotton handkerchief on the seat at his side. The caution with which, at my approach, he transferred this bundle to his arms caused me to glance at it in surprise; and he answered my look by saying with a smile:

"They are flowers for the dead—the most exquisite flowers—from the greenhouses of Mr. Meriton—*si figuri!*" And he waved a descriptive hand. "One of my lads, Gianpietro, is employed by the gardener there, and every year on this day he brings me a beautiful bunch of flowers—for such a purpose it is no sin," he added, with the charming Italian pliancy of judgment.

"And why are you travelling in this snowy weather, *signor parocco?*" I asked, as he ended with a cough.

He fixed me gravely with his simple shallow eye. "Because it is the day of the dead, my son," he said, "and I go to place these on the grave of the noblest man that ever lived."

"You are going to New York?"

"To Brooklyn—"

I hesitated a moment, wishing to question him, yet uncertain whether his replies were curtailed by the persistency of his cough or by the desire to avoid interrogation.

"This is no weather to be travelling with such a cough," I said at length.

He made a deprecating gesture.

"I have never missed the day—not once in eighteen years. But for me he would have no one!" He folded his hands on his umbrella and looked away from me to hide the trembling of his lip.

I resolved on a last attempt to storm his confidence. "Your friend is buried in Calvary cemetery?"

He signed an assent.

"That is a long way for you to go alone, *signor parocco.* The streets are sure to be slippery and there is an icy wind blowing. Give me your flowers and let me send them to the cemetery by a messenger. I give you my word they shall reach their destination safely."

He turned a quiet look on me. "My son, you are young," he said, "and you don't know how the dead need us." He drew his breviary from his pocket and opened it with a smile. "*Mi scusi?*" he murmured.

The business which had called me to town obliged me to part from him as soon as the train entered the station, and in my dash for the street I left his unwieldy figure laboring far behind me through the crowd on the platform. Before we separated, however, I had learned that he was returning to Dunstable by the four o'clock train, and had resolved to dispatch my business in time to travel home with him. When I reached Wall Street I was received with the news that the man I had appointed to meet was ill and detained in the country. My business was "off" and I found myself with the rest of the day at my disposal. I had no difficulty in deciding how to employ my time. I was at an age when, in such contingencies, there is always a feminine alternative; and even now I don't know how it was that, on my way to a certain hospitable luncheon-table, I suddenly found myself in a cab which was carrying me at full-speed to the Twenty-third Street ferry. It was not till I had bought my ticket and seated myself in the varnished tunnel of the ferry-boat that I was aware of having been diverted from my purpose by an overmastering anxiety for Don Egidio. I rapidly calculated that he had not more than an hour's advance on me, and that, allowing for my greater agility and for the fact that I had a cab at my call, I was likely to reach the cemetery in time to see him under shelter before the gusts of sleet that were already sweeping across the river had thickened to a snow-storm.

At the gates of the cemetery I began to take a less sanguine view of my attempt. The commemorative anniversary had filled the silent avenues with visitors, and I felt the futility of my quest as I tried to fix the gatekeeper's attention on my delineation of a stout Italian priest with a bad cough and a bunch of flowers tied up in a red cotton handkerchief. The gate-keeper showed that delusive desire to oblige that is certain to send its victims in the wrong direction; but I had the presence of mind to go exactly contrary to his indication, and thanks to this precaution I came, after half an hour's search, on the figure of my poor parocco, kneeling on the wet ground in one of the humblest by-ways of the great necropolis. The mound before which he knelt was strewn with the spoils of Mr. Meriton's conservatories, and on the weather-worn tablet at its head I read the inscription:

IL CONTE SIVIANO
DA MILANO.
*Super flumina Babylonis, illic sedimus et flevimus.*

So engrossed was Don Egidio that for some moments I stood behind him unobserved; and when he rose and faced me, grief had left so little room for any minor emotion that he looked at me almost without surprise.

"Don Egidio," I said, "I have a carriage waiting for you at the gate. You must come home with me."

He nodded quietly and I drew his hand through my arm.

He turned back to the grave. "One moment, my son," he said. "It may be for the last time." He stood motionless, his eyes on the heaped-up flowers which were already bruised and blackened by the cold. "To leave him alone—after sixty years! But God is everywhere—" he murmured as I led him away.

On the journey home he did not care to talk, and my chief concern was to keep him wrapped in my greatcoat and to see that his bed was made ready as soon as I had restored him to his lodgings. The *levatrice* brought a quilted coverlet from her own room and hovered over him as gently as though he had been of the sex to require her services; while Agostino, at my summons, appeared with a bowl of hot soup that was heralded down the street by a reviving waft of garlic. To these ministrations I left the *parocco*, intending to call for news of him the next evening; but an unexpected pressure of work kept me late at my desk, and the following day some fresh obstacle delayed me.

On the third afternoon, as I was leaving the office, an agate-eyed infant from the Point hailed me with a message from the doctor. The *parocco* was worse and had asked for me. I jumped into the nearest car and ten minutes later was running up the doctor's greasy stairs.

To my dismay I found Don Egidio's room cold and untenanted; but I was reassured a moment later by the appearance of the *levatrice*, who announced that she had transferred the blessed man to her own apartment, where he could have the sunlight and a good bed to lie in. There in fact he lay, weak but smiling, in a setting which contrasted oddly enough with his own monastic surroundings: a cheerful grimy room, hung with anecdotic chromos, photographs of lady-patients proudly presenting their offspring to the camera, and innumerable Neapolitan *santolini* decked out with shriveled palm-leaves.

The *levatrice* whispered that the good man had the pleurisy, and that, as she phrased it, he was nearing his last mile-stone. I saw that he was in fact in a bad way, but his condition did not indicate any pressing danger, and I had the presentiment that he would still, as the saying is, put up a good fight. It was clear, however, that he knew what turn the conflict must take, and the solemnity with which he welcomed me showed that my summons was a part of that spiritual strategy with which the Catholic opposes the surprise of death.

"My son," he said, when the *levatrice* had left us, "I have a favor to ask you. You found me yesterday bidding good-bye to my best friend." His cough interrupted him. "I have never told you," he went on, "the name of the family in which I was brought up. It was Siviano, and that was the grave of the Count's eldest son, with whom I grew up as a brother. For eighteen years he has lain in that strange ground—*in terra aliena*—and when I die, there will be no one to care for his grave."

I saw what he waited for. "I will care for it, *signor parocco*."

"I knew I should have your promise, my child; and what you promise you keep. But my friend is a stranger to you—you are young and at your age life is a mistress who kisses away sad memories. Why should you remember the grave of a stranger? I cannot lay such a claim on you. But I will tell you his story—and then I think that neither joy nor grief will let you forget him; for when you rejoice you will remember how he sorrowed; and when you sorrow the thought of him will be like a friend's hand in yours."

## II

YOU tell me (Don Egidio began) that you know our little lake; and if you have seen it you will understand why it always used to remind me of the "garden enclosed" of the Canticles.

*Hortus inclusus; columba mea in foraminibus petrae:*

The words used to come back to me whenever I returned from a day's journey across the mountains, and looking down saw the blue lake far below, hidden in its hills like a happy secret in a stern heart. We were never envious of the glory of the great lakes. They are like the show pictures that some nobleman hangs in his public gallery; but our Iseo is the treasure that he hides in his inner chamber.

You tell me you saw it in summer, when it looks up like a saint's eye, reflecting the whole of heaven. It was then too that I first saw it. My future friend, the old Count, had found me at work on one of his fruit-farms up the valley, and hearing that I was ill-treated by my step-father—a drunken peddler from the Val Mastellone, whom my poor mother a year or two earlier had come across at the fair of Lovere—he had taken me home with him to Iseo. I used to serve mass in our hill-village of Cerveno, and the village children called me "the little priest" because when my work was done I often crept back to the church to get away from my step-father's blows and curses. "I will make a real priest of him," the Count declared; and that afternoon, perched on the box of his travelling-carriage, I was whirled away from the dark scenes of my childhood into a world, where, as it seemed to me, everyone was as happy as an angel on a *presepio*.

I wonder if you remember the Count's villa? It lies on the shore of the lake, facing the green knoll of Monte Isola, and overlooked by the village of Siviano and by the old parish-church where I said mass for fifteen happy years. The village hangs on a ledge of the mountain; but the villa dips its foot in the lake, smiling at its reflection like a bather lingering on the brink. What Paradise it seemed to me that day! In our church up the valley there hung an old brown picture, with a Saint Sebastian in the foreground; and behind him the most wonderful palace, with terraced gardens adorned with statues and fountains, where fine folk in resplendent dresses walked up and down without heeding the blessed martyr's pangs. The Count's villa, with its terraces, its roses, its marble steps descending to the lake, reminded me of that palace; only instead of being inhabited by wicked people engrossed in their selfish pleasures it was the home of the kindest friends that ever took a poor lad by the hand.

The old Count was a widower when I first knew him. He had been twice married, and his first wife had left him two children, a son and a daughter. The eldest, Donna Marianna, was then a girl of twenty, who kept her father's house and was a mother to the two lads. She was not handsome or learned, and had no taste for the world; but she was like the lavender-plant in a poor man's window—just a little gray flower, but a sweetness that fills the whole house. Her brother, Count Roberto, had been ailing from his birth, and was a studious lad with a melancholy musing face such as you may see in some of Titian's portraits of young men. He looked like an exiled prince dressed in mourning. There was one child by the second marriage, Count Andrea, a boy of my own age, handsome as a Saint George, but not as kind as the others. No doubt, being younger, he was less able to understand why an uncouth peasant lad should have been brought to his father's table; and the others were so fearful of hurting my feelings that, but for his teasing, I might never have mended my clumsy manners or learned how to behave in the presence of my betters. Count Andrea was not sparing in such lessons, and Count Roberto, in spite of his weak arms, chastised his brother roundly when he thought the discipline had been too severe; but for my part it seemed to me natural enough that such a godlike being should lord it over a poor clodhopper like myself.

Well—I will not linger over the beginning of my new life for my story has to do with its close. Only I should like to make you understand what the change meant to me—an ignorant peasant lad, coming from hard words and blows and a smoke-blackened hut in the hills to that great house full of rare and beautiful things, and of beings who seemed to me even more rare and beautiful. Do you wonder I was ready to kiss the ground they trod, and would have given the last drop of my blood to serve them?

In due course I was sent to the seminary at Lodi; and on holidays I used to visit the family in Milan. Count Andrea was growing up to be one of the handsomest young men imaginable, but a trifle wild; and the old Count married him in haste to the daughter of a Venetian noble, who brought as her dower a great estate in Istria. The Countess Gemma, as this lady was called, was as light as thistledown and had an eye like a baby's; but while she was cooing for the moon her pretty white hands were always stealing toward something within reach that she had not been meant to have. The old Count was not alert enough to follow these maneuvers; and the Countess hid her designs under a torrent of guileless chatter, as pick-pockets wear long sleeves to conceal their movements. Her only fault, he used to say, was that one of her aunts had married an Austrian; and this event having taken place before she was born he laughingly acquitted her of any direct share in it. She confirmed his good opinion of her by giving her husband two sons; and Roberto showing no inclination to marry, these boys naturally came to be looked on as the heirs of the house.

Meanwhile I had finished my course of studies, and the old Count, on my twenty-first birthday, had appointed me priest of the parish of Siviano. It was the year of Count Andrea's marriage and there were great festivities at the villa. Three years later the old Count died, to the sorrow of his two eldest children. Donna Marianna and Count Roberto closed their apartments in the palace at Milan and withdrew for a year to Siviano. It was then that I first began to know my friend. Before that I had loved him without understanding him; now I learned of what metal he was made. His bookish tastes inclined him to a secluded way of living; and his younger brother perhaps fancied that he would not care to assume the charge of the estate. But if Andrea thought this he was disappointed. Roberto resolutely took up the tradition of his father's rule, and, as if conscious of lacking the old Count's easy way with the peasants, made up for it by a redoubled zeal for their welfare. I have seen him toil for days to adjust some trifling difficulty that his father would have set right with a ready word; like the sainted bishop who, when a beggar asked him for a penny, cried out: "Alas, my brother, I have not a penny in my purse; but here are two gold pieces, if they can be made to serve you instead!" We had many conferences over the condition of his people, and he often sent me up the valley to look into the needs of the peasantry on the fruit-farms. No grievance was too trifling for him to consider it, no abuse too deep-seated for him to root it out; and many an hour that other men of his rank would have given to books or pleasure was devoted to adjusting a quarrel about boundary-lines or to weighing the merits of a complaint against the tax-collector. I often said that he was as much his people's priest as I; and he smiled and answered that every landowner was a king and that in old days the king was always a priest.

Donna Marianna was urgent with him to marry, but he always declared that he had a family in his tenantry, and that, as for a wife, she had never let him feel the want of one. He had that musing temper which gives a man a name for coldness; though in fact he may all the while be storing fuel for a great conflagration. But to me he whispered another reason for not marrying. A man, he said, does not take wife and rejoice while his mother is on her death-bed; and Italy, his mother, lay dying, with the foreign vultures waiting to tear her apart.

You are too young to know anything of those days, my son; and how can any one understand them who did not live through them? Italy lay dying indeed; but Lombardy was her heart, and the heart still beat, and sent the faint blood creeping to her cold extremities. Her torturers, weary of their work, had allowed her to fall into a painless stupor; but just as she was sinking from sleep to death, heaven sent Radetsky to scourge her back to consciousness; and at the first sting of his lash she sprang maimed and bleeding to her feet.

Ah, those days, those days, my son! Italy—Italy—was the word on our lips; but the thought in our hearts was just Austria. We clamored for liberty, unity, the franchise; but under our breath we prayed only to smite the white-coats. Remove the beam from our eye, we cried, and we shall see our salvation clearly enough! We priests in the north were all liberals and worked with the nobles and the men of letters. Gioberti was our breviary and his Holiness the new Pope was soon to be the Tancred of our crusade. But meanwhile, mind you, all this went on in silence, underground as it were, while on the surface Lombardy still danced, feasted, married, and took office under the Austrian. In the iron-mines up our valley there used to be certain miners who stayed below ground for months at a time; and, like one of these, Roberto remained buried in his purpose, while life went its way overhead. Though I was not in his confidence I knew well enough where his thoughts were, for he went among us with the eye of a lover, the visionary look of one who hears a Voice. We all heard that Voice, to be sure, mingling faintly with the other noises of life; but to Roberto it was already as the roar of mighty waters, drowning every other sound with its thunder.

On the surface, as I have said, things looked smooth enough. An Austrian cardinal throned in Milan and an Austrian-hearted Pope ruled in Rome. In Lombardy, Austria couched like a beast of prey, ready to spring at our throats if we stirred or struggled. The

Moderates, to whose party Count Roberto belonged, talked of prudence, compromise, the education of the masses; but if their words were a velvet sheath their thought was a dagger. For many years, as you know, the Milanese had maintained an outward show of friendliness with their rulers. The nobles had accepted office under the vice-roy, and in the past there had been frequent intermarriage between the two aristocracies. But now, one by one, the great houses had closed their doors against official society. Though some of the younger and more careless, those who must dance and dine at any cost, still went to the palace and sat beside the enemy at the opera, fashion was gradually taking sides against them, and those who had once been laughed at as old fogeys were now applauded as patriots. Among these, of course, was Count Roberto, who for several years had refused to associate with the Austrians, and had silently resented his easy-going brother's disregard of political distinctions. Andrea and Gemma belonged to the moth tribe, who flock to the brightest light; and Gemma's Istrian possessions, and her family's connection with the Austrian nobility, gave them a pretext for fluttering about the vice-regal candle. Roberto let them go their way, but his own course was a tacit protest against their conduct. They were always welcome at the palazzo Siviano; but he and Donna Marianna withdrew from society in order to have an excuse for not showing themselves at the Countess Gemma's entertainments. If Andrea and Gemma were aware of his disapproval they were clever enough to ignore it; for the rich elder brother who paid their debts and never meant to marry was too important a person to be quarreled with on political grounds. They seemed to think that if he married it would be only to spite them; and they were persuaded that their future depended on their giving him no cause to take such reprisals. I shall never be more than a plain peasant at heart and I have little natural skill in discerning hidden motives; but the experience of the confessional gives every priest a certain insight into the secret springs of action, and I often wondered that the worldly wisdom of Andrea and Gemma did not help them to a clearer reading of their brother's character. For my part I knew that, in Roberto's heart, no great passion could spring from a mean motive; and I had always thought that if he ever loved any woman as he loved Italy, it must be from his country's hand that he received his bride. And so it came about.

Have you ever noticed, on one of those still autumn days before a storm, how here and there a yellow leaf will suddenly detach itself from the bough and whirl through the air as though some warning of the gale had reached it? So it was then in Lombardy. All round was the silence of decay; but now and then a word, a look, a trivial incident, fluttered ominously through the stillness. It was in '45. Only a year earlier the glorious death of the Bandiera brothers had sent a long shudder through Italy. In the Romagna, Renzi and his comrades had tried to uphold by action the protest set forth in the "Manifesto of Rimini"; and their failure had sowed the seed which d'Azeglio and Cavour were to harvest. Everywhere the forces were silently gathering; and nowhere was the hush more profound, the least reverberation more audible, than in the streets of Milan.

It was Count Roberto's habit to attend early mass in the Cathedral; and one morning, as he was standing in the aisle, a young girl passed him with her father. Roberto knew the father, a beggarly Milanese of the noble family of Intelvi, who had cut himself off from his class by accepting an appointment in one of the government offices. As the two went by he saw a group of Austrian officers looking after the girl, and heard one of them say: "Such a choice morsel as that is too good for slaves;" and another answer with a laugh: "Yes, it's a dish for the master's table!"

The girl heard too. She was as white as a wind-flower and he saw the words come out on her cheek like the red mark from a blow. She whispered to her father, but he shook his head and drew her away without so much as a glance at the Austrians. Roberto heard mass and then hastened out and placed himself in the porch of the Cathedral. A moment later the officers appeared, and they too stationed themselves near the doorway. Presently the girl came out on her father's arm. Her admirers stepped forward to greet Intelvi; and the cringing wretch stood there exchanging compliments with them, while their insolent stare devoured his daughter's beauty. She, poor thing, shook like a leaf, and her eyes, in avoiding theirs, suddenly encountered Roberto's. Her look was a wounded bird that flew to him for shelter. He carried it away in his breast and its live warmth beat against his heart. He thought that Italy had looked at him through those eyes; for love is the wiliest of masqueraders and has a thousand disguises at his command.

Within a month Faustina Intelvi was his wife. Donna Marianna and I rejoiced; for we knew he had chosen her because he loved her, and she seemed to us almost worthy of such a choice. As for Count Andrea and his wife, I leave you to guess what ingredients were mingled in the kiss with which they welcomed the bride. They were all smiles at Roberto's marriage, and had only words of praise for his wife. Donna Marianna, who had sometimes taxed me with suspecting their motives, rejoiced in this fresh proof of their magnanimity; but for my part I could have wished to see them a little less kind. All such twilight fears, however, vanished in the flush of my friend's happiness. Over some natures love steals gradually, as the morning light widens across a valley; but it had flashed on Roberto like the leap of dawn to a snow-peak. He walked the world with the wondering step of a blind man suddenly restored to sight; and once he said to me with a laugh: "Love makes a Columbus of every one of us!"

And the Countess—? The Countess, my son, was eighteen, and her husband was forty. Count Roberto had the heart of a poet, but he walked with a limp and his skin was sallow. Youth plucks the fruit for its color rather than its flavor; and first love does not serenade its mistress on a church-organ. In Italy girls are married as land is sold; if two estates adjoin two lives are united. As for the portionless girl, she is a knick-knack that goes to the highest bidder. Faustina was handed over to her purchaser as if she had been a picture for his gallery; and the transaction doubtless seemed as natural to her as to her parents. She walked to the altar like an Iphigenia; but pallor becomes a bride, and it looks well for a daughter to weep on leaving her mother. Perhaps it would have been different if she had guessed that the threshold of her new home was carpeted with love and its four corners hung with tender thoughts of her; but her husband was a silent man, who never called attention to his treasures.

The great palace in Milan was a gloomy house for a girl to enter. Roberto and his sister lived in it as if it had been a monastery, going nowhere and receiving only those who labored for the Cause. To Faustina, accustomed to the easy Austrian society, the Sunday evening receptions at the palazzo Siviano must have seemed as dreary as a scientific congress. It pleased Roberto to regard her as a victim of barbarian insolence, an embodiment of his country desecrated by the desire of the enemy; but though, like any handsome penniless girl, Faustina had now and then been exposed to a free look or a familiar word, I doubt if she connected such incidents with the political condition of Italy. She knew, of course, that in marrying Siviano she was entering a house closed against the Austrian. One of Siviano's first cares had been to pension his father-in-law, with the stipulation that Intelvi should resign his appointment and give up all relations with the government; and the old hypocrite, only too glad to purchase idleness on such terms, embraced the liberal cause with a zeal which left his daughter no excuse for half-heartedness. But he found it less easy than he had expected to recover a footing among his own people. In spite of his patriotic bluster the Milanese held aloof from him; and being the kind of man who must always take his glass in company he gradually drifted back to his old associates. It was impossible to forbid Faustina to visit her parents; and in their house she breathed an air that was at least tolerant of Austria.

But I must not let you think that the young Countess appeared ungrateful or unhappy. She was silent and shy, and it needed a more enterprising temper than Roberto's to break down the barrier between them. They seemed to talk to one another through a convent-grating, rather than across a hearth; but if Roberto had asked more of her than she could give, outwardly she was a model wife. She chose me at once as her confessor and I watched over the first steps of her new life. Never was younger sister tenderer to her elder than she to Donna Marianna; never was young wife more mindful of her religious duties, kinder to her dependents, more charitable to the poor; yet to be with her was like living in a room with shuttered windows. She was always the caged bird, the transplanted flower: for all Roberto's care she never bloomed or sang.

Donna Marianna was the first to speak of it. "The child needs more light and air," she said.

"Light? Air?" Roberto repeated. "Does she not go to mass every morning? Does she not drive on the Corso every evening?"

Donna Marianna was not called clever, but her heart was wiser than most women's heads.

"At our age, brother," said she, "the windows of the mind face north and look out on a landscape full of lengthening shadows. Faustina needs another outlook. She is as pale as a hyacinth grown in a cellar."

Roberto himself turned pale and I saw that she had uttered his own thought.

"You want me to let her go to Gemma's!" he exclaimed.

"Let her go wherever there is a little careless laughter."

"Laughter—now!" he cried, with a gesture toward the somber line of portraits above his head.

"Let her laugh while she can, my brother."

That evening after dinner he called Faustina to him.

"My child," he said, "go and put on your jewels. Your sister Gemma gives a ball to-night and the carriage waits to take you there. I am too much of a recluse to be at ease in such scenes, but I have sent word to your father to go with you."

Andrea and Gemma welcomed their young sister-in-law with effusion, and from that time she was often in their company. Gemma forbade any mention of politics in her drawing-room, and it was natural that Faustina should be glad to escape from the solemn conclaves of the palazzo Siviano to a house where life went as gaily as in that villa above Florence where Boccaccio's careless story-tellers took refuge from the plague. But meanwhile the political distemper was rapidly spreading, and in spite of Gemma's Austrian affiliations it was no longer possible for her to receive the enemy openly. It was whispered that her door was still ajar to her old friends; but the rumor may have risen from the fact that one of the Austrian cavalry officers stationed at Milan was her own cousin, the son of the aunt on whose misalliance the old Count had so often bantered her. No one could blame the Countess Gemma for not turning her own flesh and blood out of doors; and the social famine to which the officers of the garrison were reduced made it natural that young Welkenstern should press the claims of consanguinity.

All this must have reached Roberto's ears; but he made no sign and his wife came and went as she pleased. When they returned the following year to the old dusky villa at

Siviano she was like the voice of a brook in a twilight wood: one could not look at her without ransacking the spring for new similes to paint her freshness. With Roberto it was different. I found him older, more preoccupied and silent; but I guessed that his preoccupations were political, for when his eye rested on his wife it cleared like the lake when a cloud shadow lifts from it.

Count Andrea and his wife occupied an adjoining villa; and during the villeggiatura the two households lived almost as one family. Roberto, however, was often absent in Milan, called thither on business of which the nature was not hard to guess. Sometimes he brought back guests to the villa; and on these occasions Faustina and Donna Marianna went to Count Andrea's for the day. I have said that I was not in his confidence; but he knew my sympathies were with the liberals and now and then he let fall a word of the work going on underground. Meanwhile the new Pope had been elected, and from Piedmont to Calabria we hailed in him the Banner that was to lead our hosts to war.

So time passed and we reached the last months of '47. The villa on Iseo had been closed since the end of August. Roberto had no great liking for his gloomy palace in Milan, and it had been his habit to spend nine months of the year at Siviano; but he was now too much engrossed in his work to remain away from Milan, and his wife and sister had joined him there as soon as the midsummer heat was over. During the autumn he had called me once or twice to the city to consult me on business connected with his fruit-farms; and in the course of our talks he had sometimes let fall a hint of graver matters. It was in July of that year that a troop of Croats had marched into Ferrara, with muskets and cannon loaded. The lighted matches of their cannon had fired the sleeping hate of Austria, and the whole country now echoed the Lombard cry: "Out with the barbarian!" All talk of adjustment, compromise, reorganization, shriveled on lips that the live coal of patriotism had touched. Italy for the Italians, and then—monarchy, federation, republic, it mattered not what!

The oppressor's grip had tightened on our throats and the clear-sighted saw well enough that Metternich's policy was to provoke a rebellion and then crush it under the Croat heel. But it was too late to cry prudence in Lombardy. With the first days of the new year the tobacco riots had drawn blood in Milan. Soon afterward the Lions' Club was closed, and edicts were issued forbidding the singing of Pio Nono's hymn, the wearing of white and blue, the collecting of subscriptions for the victims of the riots. To each prohibition Milan returned a fresh defiance. The ladies of the nobility put on mourning for the rioters who had been shot down by the soldiery. Half the members of the Guardia Nobile resigned and Count Borromeo sent back his Golden Fleece to the Emperor. Fresh regiments were continually pouring into Milan and it was no secret that Radetsky was strengthening the fortifications. Late in January several leading liberals were arrested and sent into exile, and two weeks later martial law was proclaimed in Milan. At the first arrests several members of the liberal party had hastily left Milan, and I was not surprised to hear, a few days later, that orders had been given to reopen the villa at Siviano. The Count and Countess arrived there early in February.

It was seven months since I had seen the Countess, and I was struck with the change in her appearance.

She was paler than ever, and her step had lost its lightness. Yet she did not seem to share her husband's political anxieties; one would have said that she was hardly aware of them. She seemed wrapped in a veil of lassitude, like Iseo on a still gray morning, when dawn is blood-red on the mountains but a mist blurs its reflection in the lake. I felt as though her soul were slipping away from me, and longed to win her back to my care; but she made her ill-health a pretext for not coming to confession, and for the present I could only wait and carry the thought of her to the altar. She had not been long at Siviano before I discovered that this drooping mood was only one phase of her humor. Now and then she flung back the cowl of melancholy and laughed life in the eye; but next moment she was in shadow again, and her muffled thoughts had given us the slip. She was like the lake on one of those days when the wind blows twenty ways and every promontory holds a gust in ambush.

Meanwhile there was a continual coming and going of messengers between Siviano and the city. They came mostly at night, when the household slept, and were away again with the last shadows; but the news they brought stayed and widened, shining through every cranny of the old house. The whole of Lombardy was up. From Pavia to Mantua, from Como to Brescia, the streets ran blood like the arteries of one great body. At Pavia and Padua the universities were closed. The frightened viceroy was preparing to withdraw from Milan to Verona, and Radetsky continued to pour his men across the Alps, till a hundred thousand were massed between the Piave and the Ticino. And now every eye was turned to Turin. Ah, how we watched for the blue banner of Piedmont on the mountains! Charles Albert was pledged to our cause; his whole people had armed to rescue us, the streets echoed with *avanti, Savoia!* and yet Savoy was silent and hung back. Each day was a life-time strained to the cracking-point with hopes and disappointments. We reckoned the hours by rumors, the very minutes by hearsay. Then suddenly—ah, it was worth living through!—word came to us that Vienna was in revolt. The points of the compass had shifted and our sun had risen in the north. I shall never forget that day at the villa. Roberto sent for me early, and I found him smiling and resolute, as becomes a soldier on the eve of action. He had made all his preparations to leave for Milan and was awaiting a summons from his party. The whole household felt that great events impended, and Donna Marianna, awed and tearful, had pleaded with her brother that they should all receive the sacrament together the next morning. Roberto and his sister had been to confession the previous day, but the Countess Faustina had again excused herself. I did not see her while I was with the Count, but as I left the house she met me in the laurel-walk. The morning was damp and cold, and she had drawn a black scarf over her hair, and walked with a listless dragging step; but at my approach she lifted her head quickly and signed to me to follow her into one of the recesses of clipped laurel that bordered the path.

"Don Egidio," she said, "you have heard the news?"

I assented.

"The Count goes to Milan tomorrow?"

"It seems probable, your excellency."

"There will be fighting—we are on the eve of war, I mean?"

"We are in God's hands, your excellency."

"In God's hands!" she murmured. Her eyes wandered and for a moment we stood silent; then she drew a purse from her pocket. "I was forgetting," she exclaimed. "This is for that poor girl you spoke to me about the other day—what was her name? The girl who met the Austrian soldier at the fair at Peschiera—"

"Ah, Vannina," I said; "but she is dead, your excellency."

"Dead!" She turned white and the purse dropped from her hand. I picked it up and held it out to her, but she put back my hand. "That is for masses, then," she said; and with that she moved away toward the house.

I walked on to the gate; but before I had reached it I heard her step behind me.

"Don Egidio!" she called; and I turned back.

"You are coming to say mass in the chapel tomorrow morning?"

"That is the Count's wish."

She wavered a moment. "I am not well enough to walk up to the village this afternoon," she said at length. "Will you come back later and hear my confession here?"

"Willingly, your excellency."

"Come at sunset then." She looked at me gravely. "It is a long time since I have been to confession," she added.

"My child, the door of heaven is always unlatched."

She made no answer and I went my way.

I returned to the villa a little before sunset, hoping for a few words with Roberto. I felt with Faustina that we were on the eve of war, and the uncertainty of the outlook made me treasure every moment of my friend's company. I knew he had been busy all day, but hoped to find that his preparations were ended and that he could spare me a half hour. I was not disappointed; for the servant who met me asked me to follow him to the Count's apartment. Roberto was sitting alone, with his back to the door, at a table spread with maps and papers. He stood up and turned an ashen face on me.

"Roberto!" I cried, as if we had been boys together.

He signed to me to be seated.

"Egidio," he said suddenly, "my wife has sent for you to confess her?"

"The Countess met me on my way home this morning and expressed a wish to receive the sacrament tomorrow morning with you and Donna Marianna, and I promised to return this afternoon to hear her confession."

Roberto sat silent, staring before him as though he hardly heard. At length he raised his head and began to speak.

"You have noticed lately that my wife has been ailing?" he asked.

"Everyone must have seen that the Countess is not in her usual health. She has seemed nervous, out of spirits—I have fancied that she might be anxious about your excellency."

He leaned across the table and laid his wasted hand on mine. "Call me Roberto," he said.

There was another pause before he went on. "Since I saw you this morning," he said slowly, "something horrible has happened. After you left I sent for Andrea and Gemma to tell them the news from Vienna and the probability of my being summoned to Milan before night. You know as well as I that we have reached a crisis. There will be fighting within twenty-four hours, if I know my people; and war may follow sooner than we think. I felt it my duty to leave my affairs in Andrea's hands, and to entrust my wife to his care. Don't look startled," he added with a faint smile. "No reasonable man goes on a journey without setting his house in order; and if things take the turn I expect it may be some months before you see me back at Siviano.—But it was not to hear this that I sent for you." He pushed his chair aside and walked up and down the room with his short limping step. "My God!" he broke out wildly, "how can I say it?—When Andrea had heard me, I saw him exchange a glance with his wife, and she said with that infernal sweet voice of hers, 'Yes, Andrea, it is our duty.'

"'Your duty?' I asked. 'What is your duty?'

"Andrea wetted his lips with his tongue and looked at her again; and her look was like a blade in his hand.

"'Your wife has a lover,' he said.

"She caught my arm as I flung myself on him. He is ten times stronger than I, but you remember how I made him howl for mercy in the old days when he used to bully you.

"'Let me go,' I said to his wife. 'He must live to unsay it.'

"Andrea began to whimper. 'Oh, my poor brother, I would give my heart's blood to unsay it!'

"'The secret has been killing us,' she chimed in.

"'The secret? Whose secret? How dare you—?'

"Gemma fell on her knees like a tragedy actress. 'Strike me—kill me—it is I who am the offender! It was at my house that she met him—'

"'Him?'

"'Franz Welkenstern—my cousin,' she wailed.

"I suppose I stood before them like a stunned ox, for they repeated the name again and again, as if they were not sure of my having heard it.—Not hear it!" he cried suddenly, dropping into a chair and hiding his face in his hands. "Shall I ever on earth hear anything else again?"

He sat a long time with his face hidden and I waited. My head was like a great bronze bell with one thought for the clapper.

After a while he went on in a low deliberate voice, as though his words were balancing themselves on the brink of madness. With strange composure he repeated each detail of his brother's charges: the meetings in the Countess Gemma's drawing-room, the innocent friendliness of the two young people, the talk of mysterious visits to a villa outside the Porta Ticinese, the ever-widening circle of scandal that had spread about their names. At first, Andrea said, he and his wife had refused to listen to the reports which reached them. Then, when the talk became too loud, they had sent for Welkenstern, remonstrated with him, implored him to exchange into another regiment; but in vain. The young officer indignantly denied the reports and declared that to leave his post at such a moment would be desertion.

With a laborious accuracy Roberto went on, detailing one by one each incident of the hateful story, till suddenly he cried out, springing from his chair—"And now to leave her with this lie unburied!"

His cry was like the lifting of a grave-stone from my breast. "You must not leave her!" I exclaimed.

He shook his head. "I am pledged."

"This is your first duty."

"It would be any other man's; not an Italian's."

I was silent: in those days the argument seemed unanswerable.

At length I said: "No harm can come to her while you are away. Donna Marianna and I are here to watch over her. And when you come back—"

He looked at me gravely. "*If* I come back—"

"Roberto!"

"We are men, Egidio; we both know what is coming. Milan is up already; and there is a rumor that Charles Albert is moving. This year the spring rains will be red in Italy."

"In your absence not a breath shall touch her!"

"And if I never come back to defend her? They hate her as hell hates, Egidio!—They kept repeating, 'He is of her own age and youth draws youth—.' She is in their way, Egidio!"

"Consider, my son. They do not love her, perhaps; but why should they hate her at such cost? She has given you no child."

"No child!" He paused. "But what if—? She has ailed lately!" he cried, and broke off to grapple with the stabbing thought.

"Roberto! Roberto!" I adjured him.

He jumped up and gripped my arm.

"Egidio! You believe in her?"

"She's as pure as a lily on the altar!"

"Those eyes are wells of truth—and she has been like a daughter to Marianna. Egidio! do I look like an old man?"

"Quiet yourself, Roberto," I entreated.

"Quiet myself? With this sting in my blood? A lover—and an Austrian lover! Oh, Italy, Italy, my bride!"

"I stake my life on her truth," I cried, "and who knows better than I? Has her soul not lain before me like the bed of a clear stream?"

"And if what you saw there was only the reflection of your faith in her?"

"My son, I am a priest, and the priest penetrates to the soul as the angel passed through the walls of Peter's prison. I see the truth in her heart as I see Christ in the host!"

"No, no, she is false!" he cried.

I sprang up terrified. "Roberto, be silent!"

He looked at me with a wild incredulous smile. "Poor simple man of God!" he said.

"I would not exchange my simplicity for yours—the dupe of envy's first malicious whisper!"

"Envy—you think that?"

"Is it questionable?"

"You would stake your life on it?"

"My life!"

"Your faith?"

"My faith!"

"Your vows as a priest?"

"My vows—" I stopped and stared at him. He had risen and laid his hand on my shoulder.

"You see now what I would be at," he said quietly. "I must take your place presently—"

"My place—?"

"When my wife comes down. You understand me."

"Ah, now you are quite mad!" I cried breaking away from him.

"Am I?" he returned, maintaining his strange composure. "Consider a moment. She has not confessed to you before since our return from Milan—"

"Her ill-health—"

He cut me short with a gesture. "Yet to-day she sends for you—"

"In order that she may receive the sacrament with you on the eve of your first separation."

"If that is her only reason her first words will clear her. I must hear those words, Egidio!"

"You are quite mad," I repeated.

"Strange," he said slowly. "You stake your life on my wife's innocence, yet you refuse me the only means of vindicating it!"

"I would give my life for any one of you—but what you ask is not mine to give."

"The priest first—the man afterward?" he sneered.

"Long afterward!"

He measured me with a contemptuous eye. "We laymen are ready to give the last shred of flesh from our bones, but you priests intend to keep your cassocks whole."

"I tell you my cassock is not mine," I repeated.

"And, by God," he cried, "you are right; for it's mine! Who put it on your back but my father? What kept it there but my charity? Peasant! beggar! Hear his holiness pontificate!"

"Yes," I said, "I was a peasant and a beggar when your father found me; and if he had left me one I might have been excused for putting my hand to any ugly job that my betters required of me; but he made me a priest, and so set me above all of you, and laid on me the charge of your souls as well as mine."

He sat down shaken with dreadful tears. "Ah," he broke out, "would you have answered me thus when we were boys together, and I stood between you and Andrea?"

"If God had given me the strength."

"You call it strength to make a woman's soul your stepping-stone to heaven?"

"Her soul is in my care, not yours, my son. She is safe with me."

"She? But I? I go out to meet death, and leave a worse death behind me!" He leaned over and clutched my arm. "It is not for myself I plead but for her—for her, Egidio! Don't you see to what a hell you condemn her if I don't come back? What chance has she against that slow unsleeping hate? Their lies will fasten themselves to her and suck out her life. You and Marianna are powerless against such enemies."

"You leave her in God's hands, my son."

"Easily said—but, ah, priest, if you were a man! What if their poison works in me and I go to battle thinking that every Austrian bullet may be sent by her lover's hand? What if I die not only to free Italy but to free my wife as well?"

I laid my hand on his shoulder. "My son, I answer for her. Leave your faith in her in my hands and I will keep it whole."

He stared at me strangely. "And what if your own fail you?"

"In her? Never. I call every saint to witness!"

"And yet—and yet—ah, this is a blind," he shouted; "you know all and perjure yourself to spare me!"

At that, my son, I felt a knife in my breast. I looked at him in anguish and his gaze was a wall of metal. Mine seemed to slip away from it, like a clawless thing struggling up the sheer side of a precipice.

"You know all," he repeated, "and you dare not let me hear her!"

"I dare not betray my trust."

He waved the answer aside.

"Is this a time to quibble over church discipline? If you believed in her you would save her at any cost!"

I said to myself, "Eternity can hold nothing worse than this for me—" and clutched my resolve again like a cross to my bosom.

Just then there was a hand on the door and we heard Donna Marianna.

"Faustina has sent to know if the *signor parocco* is here."

"He is here. Bid her come down to the chapel." Roberta spoke quietly, and closed the door on her so that she should not see his face. We heard her patter away across the brick floor of the *salone*.

Roberto turned to me. "Egidio!" he said; and all at once I was no more than a straw on the torrent of his will.

The chapel adjoined the room in which we sat. He opened the door, and in the twilight I saw the light glimmering before the Virgin's shrine and the old carved confessional standing like a cowled watcher in its corner. But I saw it all in a dream; for nothing in heaven or earth was real to me but the iron grip on my shoulder.

"Quick!" he said and drove me forward. I heard him shoot back the bolt of the outer door and a moment later I stood alone in the garden. The sun had set and the cold spring dusk was falling. Lights shone here and there in the long front of the villa; the statues glimmered gray among the thickets. Through the window-pane of the chapel I caught the faint red gleam of the Virgin's lamp; but I turned my back on it and walked away.

All night I lay like a heretic on the fire. Before dawn there came a call from the villa. The Count had received a second summons from Milan and was to set out in an hour. I hurried down the cold dewy path to the lake. All was new and hushed and strange as on the day of resurrection; and in the dark twilight of the garden alleys the statues stared at me like the shrouded dead.

In the *salone*, where the old Count's portrait hung, I found the family assembled. Andrea and Gemma sat together, a little pinched, I thought, but decent and self-contained, like mourners who expect to inherit. Donna Marianna drooped near them, with something black over her head and her face dim with weeping. Roberto received me calmly and then turned to his sister.

"Go fetch my wife," he said.

While she was gone there was silence. We could hear the cold drip of the garden-fountain and the patter of rats in the wall. Andrea and his wife stared out of window and Roberto sat in his father's carved seat at the head of the long table. Then the door opened and Faustina entered.

When I saw her I stopped breathing. She seemed no more than the shell of herself, a hollow thing that grief has voided. Her eyes returned our images like polished agate, but conveyed to her no sense of our presence. Marianna led her to a seat, and she crossed her hands and nailed her dull gaze on Roberto. I looked from one to another, and in that spectral light it seemed to me that we were all souls come to judgment and naked to each other as to God. As to my own wrongdoing, it weighed on me no more than dust. The only feeling I had room for was fear—a fear that seemed to fill my throat and lungs and bubble coldly over my drowning head.

Suddenly Roberto began to speak. His voice was clear and steady, and I clutched at his words to drag myself above the surface of my terror. He touched on the charge that had been made against his wife—he did not say by whom—the foul rumor that had made itself heard on the eve of their first parting. Duty, he said, had sent him a double summons; to fight for his country and for his wife. He must clear his wife's name before he was worthy to draw sword for Italy. There was no time to tame the slander before throttling it; he had to take the shortest way to its throat. At this point he looked at me and my soul shook. Then he turned to Andrea and Gemma.

"When you came to me with this rumor," he said quietly, "you agreed to consider the family honor satisfied if I could induce Don Egidio to let me take his place and overhear my wife's confession, and if that confession convinced me of her innocence. Was this the understanding?"

Andrea muttered something and Gemma tapped a sullen foot.

"After you had left," Roberto continued, "I laid the case before Don Egidio and threw myself on his mercy." He looked at me fixedly. "So strong was his faith in my wife's innocence that for her sake he agreed to violate the sanctity of the confessional. I took his place."

Marianna sobbed and crossed herself and a strange look flitted over Faustina's face.

There was a moment's pause; then Roberto, rising, walked across the room to his wife and took her by the hand.

"Your seat is beside me, Countess Siviano," he said, and led her to the empty chair by his own.

Gemma started to her feet, but her husband pulled her down again.

"Jesus! Mary!" We heard Donna Marianna moan.

Roberto raised his wife's hand to his lips. "You forgive me," he said, "the means I took to defend you?" And turning to Andrea he added slowly: "I declare my wife innocent and my honor satisfied. You swear to stand by my decision?"

What Andrea stammered out, what hissing serpents of speech Gemma's clinched teeth bit back, I never knew—for my eyes were on Faustina, and her face was a wonder to behold.

She had let herself be led across the room like a blind woman, and had listened without change of feature to her husband's first words; but as he ceased her frozen gaze broke and her whole body seemed to melt against his breast. He put his arm out, but she slipped to his feet and Marianna hastened forward to raise her up. At that moment we heard the stroke of oars across the quiet water and saw the Count's boat touch the landing-steps. Four strong oarsmen from Monte Isola were to row him down to Iseo, to take horse for Milan, and his servant, knapsack on shoulder, knocked warningly at the terrace window.

"No time to lose, excellency!" he cried.

Roberto turned and gripped my hand. "Pray for me," he said low; and with a brief gesture to the others ran down the terrace to the boat.

Marianna was bathing Faustina with happy tears.

"Look up, dear! Think how soon he will come back! And there is the sunrise—see!"

Andrea and Gemma had slunk away like ghosts at cock-crow, and a red dawn stood over Milan.

If that sun rose red it set scarlet. It was the first of the Five Days in Milan—the Five Glorious Days, as they are called. Roberto reached the city just before the gates closed. So much we knew—little more. We heard of him in the Broletto (whence he must have escaped when the Austrians blew in the door) and in the Casa Vidiserti, with Casati, Cattaneo and the rest; but after the barricading began we could trace him only as having been seen here and there in the thick of the fighting, or tending the wounded under Bertani's orders. His place, one would have said, was in the council-chamber, with the soberer heads; but that was an hour when every man gave his blood where it was most needed, and Cernuschi, Dandolo, Anfossi, della Porta fought shoulder to shoulder with students, artisans and peasants. Certain it is that he was seen on the fifth day; for among the volunteers who swarmed after Manara in his assault on the Porta Tosa was a servant of palazzo Siviano; and this fellow swore he had seen his master charge with Manara in the last assault—had watched him, sword in hand, press close to the gates, and then, as they swung open before the victorious dash of our men, had seen him drop and disappear in the inrushing tide of peasants that almost swept the little company off its feet. After that we heard nothing. There was savage work in Milan in those days, and more than one well-known figure lay lost among the heaps of dead hacked and disfeatured by Croat blades.

At the villa, we waited breathless. News came to us hour by hour: the very wind seemed to carry it, and it was swept to us on the incessant rush of the rain. On the twenty-third Radetsky had fled from Milan, to face Venice rising in his path. On the twenty-fourth the first Piedmontese had crossed the Ticino, and Charles Albert himself was in Pavia on the twenty-ninth. The bells of Milan had carried the word from Turin to Naples, from Genoa to Ancona, and the whole country was pouring like a flood-tide into Lombardy. Heroes sprang up from the bloody soil as thick as wheat after rain, and every day carried some new name to us; but never the one for which we prayed and waited. Weeks passed. We heard of Pastrengo, Goito, Rivoli; of Radetsky hemmed into the Quadrilateral, and our troops closing in on him from Rome, Tuscany and Venetia. Months passed—and we heard of Custozza. We saw Charles Albert's broken forces flung back from the Mincio to the Oglio, from the Oglio to the Adda. We followed the dreadful retreat from Milan, and saw our rescuers dispersed like dust before the wind. But all the while no word came to us of Roberto.

These were dark days in Lombardy; and nowhere darker than in the old villa on Iseo. In September Donna Marianna and the young Countess put on black, and Count Andrea and his wife followed their example. In October the Countess gave birth to a daughter. Count Andrea then took possession of the palazzo Siviano, and the two women remained at the villa. I have no heart to tell you of the days that followed. Donna Marianna wept and prayed incessantly, and it was long before the baby could snatch a smile from her. As for the Countess Faustina, she went among us like one of the statues in the garden. The child had a wet-nurse from the village, and it was small wonder there was no milk for it in that marble breast. I spent much of my time at the villa, comforting Donna Marianna as best I could; but sometimes, in the long winter evenings, when we three sat in the dimly-lit *salone*, with the old Count's portrait overhead, and I looked up and saw the Countess Faustina in the tall carved seat beside her husband's empty chair, my spine grew chill and I felt a cold wind in my hair.

The end of it was that in the spring I went to see my bishop and laid my sin before him. He was a saintly and merciful old man, and gave me a patient hearing.

"You believed the lady innocent?" he asked when I had ended.

"Monsignore, on my soul!"

"You thought to avert a great calamity from the house to which you owed more than your life?"

"It was my only thought."

He laid his hand on my shoulder.

"Go home, my son. You shall learn my decision."

Three months later I was ordered to resign my living and go to America, where a priest was needed for the Italian mission church in New York. I packed my possessions and set sail from Genoa. I knew no more of America than any peasant up in the hills. I fully expected to be speared by naked savages on landing; and for the first few months after my arrival I wished at least once a day that such a blessed fate had befallen me. But it is no part of my story to tell you what I suffered in those early days. The Church had dealt with me mercifully, as is her wont, and her punishment fell far below my deserts.

I had been some four years in New York, and no longer thought of looking back from the plough, when one day word was brought me that an Italian professor lay ill and had asked for a priest. There were many Italian refugees in New York at that time, and the greater number, being well-educated men, earned a living by teaching their language, which was then included among the accomplishments of fashionable New York. The messenger led me to a poor boarding-house and up to a small bare room on the top floor. On the visiting-card nailed to the door I read the name "De Roberti, Professor of Italian." Inside, a gray-haired haggard man tossed on the narrow bed. He turned a glazed eye on me as I entered, and I recognized Roberto Siviano.

I steadied myself against the door-post and stood staring at him without a word.

"What's the matter?" asked the doctor who was bending over the bed. I stammered that the sick man was an old friend.

"He wouldn't know his oldest friend just now," said the doctor. "The fever's on him; but it will go down toward sunset."

I sat down at the head of the bed and took Roberto's hand in mine.

"Is he going to die?" I asked.

"I don't believe so; but he wants nursing."

"I will nurse him."

The doctor nodded and went out. I sat in the little room, with Roberto's burning hand in mine. Gradually his skin cooled, the fingers grew quiet, and the flush faded from his sallow cheek-bones. Toward dusk he looked up at me and smiled.

"Egidio," he said quietly.

I administered the sacrament, which he received with the most fervent devotion; then he fell into a deep sleep.

During the weeks that followed I had no time to ask myself the meaning of it all. My one business was to keep him alive if I could. I fought the fever day and night, and at length it yielded. For the most part he raved or lay unconscious; but now and then he knew me for a moment, and whispered "Egidio" with a look of peace.

I had stolen many hours from my duties to nurse him; and as soon as the danger was past I had to go back to my parish work. Then it was that I began to ask myself what had brought him to America; but I dared not face the answer.

On the fourth day I snatched a moment from my work and climbed to his room. I found him sitting propped against his pillows, weak as a child but clear-eyed and quiet. I ran forward, but his look stopped me.

"*Signor parocco*," he said, "the doctor tells me that I owe my life to your nursing, and I have to thank you for the kindness you have shown to a friendless stranger."

"A stranger?" I gasped.

He looked at me steadily. "I am not aware that we have met before," he said.

For a moment I thought the fever was on him; but a second glance convinced me that he was master of himself.

"Roberto!" I cried, trembling.

"You have the advantage of me," he said civilly. "But my name is Roberti, not Roberto."

The floor swam under me and I had to lean against the wall.

"You are not Count Roberto Siviano of Milan?"

"I am Tommaso de Roberti, professor of Italian, from Modena."

"And you have never seen me before?"

"Never that I know of."

"Were you never at Siviano, on the lake of Iseo?" I faltered.

He said calmly: "I am unacquainted with that part of Italy."

My heart grew cold and I was silent.

"You mistook me for a friend, I suppose?" he added.

"Yes," I cried, "I mistook you for a friend;" and with that I fell on my knees by his bed and cried like a child.

Suddenly I felt a touch on my shoulder. "Egidio," said he in a broken voice, "look up."

I raised my eyes, and there was his old smile above me, and we clung to each other without a word. Presently, however, he drew back, and put me quietly aside.

"Sit over there, Egidio. My bones are like water and I am not good for much talking yet."

"Let us wait, Roberto. Sleep now—we can talk tomorrow."

"No. What I have to say must be said at once." He examined me thoughtfully. "You have a parish here in New York?"

I assented.

"And my work keeps me here. I have pupils. It is too late to make a change."

"A change?"

He continued to look at me calmly. "It would be difficult for me," he explained, "to find employment in a new place."

"But why should you leave here?"

"I shall have to," he returned deliberately, "if you persist in recognizing in me your former friend Count Siviano."

"Roberto!"

He lifted his hand. "Egidio," he said, "I am alone here, and without friends. The companionship, the sympathy of my parish priest would be a consolation in this strange city; but it must not be the companionship of the *parocco* of Siviano. You understand?"

"Roberto," I cried, "it is too dreadful to understand!"

"Be a man, Egidio," said he with a touch of impatience. "The choice lies with you, and you must make it now. If you are willing to ask no questions, to name no names, to make no allusions to the past, let us live as friends together, in God's name! If not, as soon as my legs can carry me I must be off again. The world is wide, luckily—but why should we be parted?"

I was on my knees at his side in an instant. "We must never be parted!" I cried. "Do as you will with me. Give me your orders and I obey—have I not always obeyed you?"

I felt his hand close sharply on mine. "Egidio!" he admonished me.

"No—no—I shall remember. I shall say nothing—"

"Think nothing?"

"Think nothing," I said with a last effort.

"God bless you!" he answered.

My son, for eight years I kept my word to him. We met daily almost, we ate and walked and talked together, we lived like David and Jonathan—but without so much as a glance at the past. How he had escaped from Milan—how he had reached New York—I never knew. We talked often of Italy's liberation—as what Italians would not?—but never touched on his share in the work. Once only a word slipped from him; and that was when one day he asked me how it was that I had been sent to America. The blood rushed to my face, and before I could answer he had raised a silencing hand.

"I see," he said; "it was *your* penance too."

During the first years he had plenty of work to do, but he lived so frugally that I guessed he had some secret use for his earnings. It was easy to conjecture what it was.

All over the world Italian exiles were toiling and saving to further the great cause. He had political friends in New York, and sometimes he went to other cities to attend meetings and make addresses. His zeal never slackened; and but for me he would often have gone hungry that some shivering patriot might dine. I was with him heart and soul, but I had the parish on my shoulders, and perhaps my long experience of men had made me a little less credulous than Christian charity requires; for I could have sworn that some of the heroes who hung on him had never had a whiff of Austrian blood, and would have fed out of the same trough with the white-coats if there had been polenta enough to go round. Happily my friend had no such doubts. He believed in the patriots as devoutly as in the cause; and if some of his hard-earned dollars travelled no farther than the nearest wine-cellar or cigar-shop, he never suspected the course they took.

His health was never the same after the fever; and by and by he began to lose his pupils, and the patriots cooled off as his pockets fell in. Toward the end I took him to live in my shabby attic. He had grown weak and had a troublesome cough, and he spent the greater part of his days indoors. Cruel days they must have been to him, but he made no sign, and always welcomed me with a cheerful word. When his pupils dropped off, and his health made it difficult for him to pick up work outside, he set up a letter-writer's sign, and used to earn a few pennies by serving as amanuensis to my poor parishioners; but it went against him to take their money, and half the time he did the work for nothing. I knew it was hard for him to live on charity, as he called it, and I used to find what jobs I could for him among my friends the *negozianti*, who would send him letters to copy, accounts to make up and what not; but we were all poor together, and the master had licked the platter before the dog got it.

So lived that just man, my son; and so, after eight years of exile, he died one day in my arms. God had let him live long enough to see Solferino and Villa-franca; and was perhaps never more merciful than in sparing him Monte Rotondo and Mentana. But these are things of which it does not become me to speak. The new Italy does not wear the face of our visions; but it is written that God shall know His own, and it cannot be that He shall misread the hearts of those who dreamed of fashioning her in His image.

As for my friend, he is at peace, I doubt not; and his just life and holy death intercede for me, who sinned for his sake alone.

## THE DESCENT OF MAN (1904)

### THE DESCENT OF MAN

WHEN PROFESSOR LINYARD came back from his holiday in the Maine woods the air of rejuvenation he brought with him was due less to the influences of the climate than to the companionship he had enjoyed on his travels. To Mrs. Linyard's observant eye he had appeared to set out alone; but an invisible traveller had in fact accompanied him, and if his heart beat high it was simply at the pitch of his adventure: for the Professor had eloped with an idea.

No one who has not tried the experiment can divine its exhilaration. Professor Linyard would not have changed places with any hero of romance pledged to a flesh-and-blood abduction. The most fascinating female is apt to be encumbered with luggage and scruples: to take up a good deal of room in the present and overlap inconveniently into the future; whereas an idea can accommodate itself to a single molecule of the brain or expand to the circumference of the horizon. The Professor's companion had to the utmost this quality of adaptability. As the express train whirled him away from the somewhat inelastic circle of Mrs. Linyard's affections, his idea seemed to be sitting opposite him, and their eyes met every moment or two in a glance of joyous complicity; yet when a friend of the family presently joined him and began to talk about college matters, the idea slipped out of sight in a flash, and the Professor would have had no difficulty in proving that he was alone.

But if, from the outset, he found his idea the most agreeable of fellow-travellers, it was only in the aromatic solitude of the woods that he tasted the full savor of his adventure. There, during the long cool August days, lying full length on the pine-needles and gazing up into the sky, he would meet the eyes of his companion bending over him like a nearer heaven. And what eyes they were!—clear yet unfathomable, bubbling with inexhaustible laughter, yet drawing their freshness and sparkle from the central depths of thought! To a man who for twenty years had faced an eye reflecting the obvious with perfect accuracy, these escapes into the inscrutable had always been peculiarly inviting; but hitherto the Professor's mental infidelities had been restricted by an unbroken and relentless domesticity. Now, for the first time since his marriage, chance had given him six weeks to himself, and he was coming home with his lungs full of liberty.

It must not be inferred that the Professor's domestic relations were defective: they were in fact so complete that it was almost impossible to get away from them. It is the happy husbands who are really in bondage; the little rift within the lute is often a passage to freedom. Marriage had given the Professor exactly what he had sought in it; a comfortable lining to life. The impossibility of rising to sentimental crises had made him scrupulously careful not to shirk the practical obligations of the bond. He took as it were a sociological view of his case, and modestly regarded himself as a brick in that foundation on which the state is supposed to rest. Perhaps if Mrs. Linyard had cared about entomology, or had taken sides in the war over the transmission of acquired characteristics, he might have had a less impersonal notion of marriage; but he was unconscious of any deficiency in their relation, and if consulted would probably have declared that he didn't want any woman bothering with his beetles. His real life had always lain in the universe of thought, in that enchanted region which, to those who have lingered there, comes to have so much more color and substance than the painted curtain hanging before it. The Professor's particular veil of Maia was a narrow strip of homespun woven in a monotonous pattern; but he had only to lift it to step into an empire.

This unseen universe was thronged with the most seductive shapes: the Professor moved Sultan-like through a seraglio of ideas. But of all the lovely apparitions that wove their spells about him, none had ever worn quite so persuasive an aspect as this latest favorite. For the others were mostly rather grave companions, serious-minded and elevating enough to have passed muster in a Ladies' Debating Club; but this new fancy of the Professor's was simply one embodied laugh. It was, in other words, the smile of relaxation at the end of a long day's toil: the flash of irony that the laborious mind projects, irresistibly, over labor conscientiously performed. The Professor had always been a hard worker. If he was an indulgent friend to his ideas, he was also a stern task-master to them. For, in addition to their other duties, they had to support his family: to pay the butcher and baker, and provide for Jack's schooling and Millicent's dresses. The Professor's household was a modest one, yet it tasked his ideas to keep it up to his wife's standard. Mrs. Linyard was not an exacting wife, and she took enough pride in her husband's attainments to pay for her honors by turning Millicent's dresses and darning Jack's socks, and going to the College receptions year after year in the same black silk with shiny seams. It consoled her to see an occasional mention of Professor Linyard's remarkable monograph on the Ethical Reactions of the Infusoria, or an allusion to his investigations into the Unconscious Cerebration of the Amoeba.

Still there were moments when the healthy indifference of Jack and Millicent reacted on the maternal sympathies; when Mrs. Linyard would have made her husband a railway-director, if by this transformation she might have increased her boy's allowance and given her daughter a new hat, or a set of furs such as the other girls were wearing. Of such moments of rebellion the Professor himself was not wholly unconscious. He could not indeed understand why anyone should want a new hat; and as to an allowance, he had had much less money at college than Jack, and had yet managed to buy a microscope and collect a few "specimens"; while Jack was free from such expensive tastes! But the Professor did not let his want of sympathy interfere with the discharge of his paternal obligations. He worked hard to keep the wants of his family gratified, and it was precisely in the endeavor to attain this end that he at length broke down and had to cease from work altogether.

To cease from work was not to cease from thought of it; and in the unwonted pause from effort the Professor found himself taking a general survey of the field he had travelled. At last it was possible to lift his nose from the loom, to step a moment in front of the tapestry he had been weaving. From this first inspection of the pattern so long wrought over from behind, it was natural to glance a little farther and seek its reflection in the public eye. It was not indeed of his special task that he thought in this connection. He was but one of the great army of weavers at work among the threads of that cosmic woof; and what he sought was the general impression their labor had produced.

When Professor Linyard first plied his microscope, the audience of the man of science had been composed of a few fellow-students, sympathetic or hostile as their habits of mind predetermined, but versed in the jargon of the profession and familiar with the point of departure. In the intervening quarter of a century, however, this little group had been swallowed up in a larger public. Every one now read scientific books and expressed an opinion on them. The ladies and the clergy had taken them up first; now they had passed to the school-room and the kindergarten. Daily life was regulated on scientific principles; the daily papers had their "Scientific Jottings"; nurses passed examinations in hygienic science, and babies were fed and dandled according to the new psychology.

The very fact that scientific investigation still had, to some minds, a flavor of heterodoxy, gave it a perennial interest. The mob had broken down the walls of tradition to batten in the orchard of forbidden knowledge. The inaccessible goddess whom the Professor had served in his youth now offered her charms in the market-place. And yet it was not the same goddess after all, but a pseudo-science masquerading in the garb of the real divinity. This false goddess had her ritual and her literature. She had her sacred books, written by false priests and sold by millions to the faithful. In the most successful of these works, ancient dogma and modern discovery were depicted in a close embrace under the lime-lights of a hazy transcendentalism; and the tableau never failed of its effect. Some of the books designed on this popular model had lately fallen into the Professor's hands, and they filled him with mingled rage and hilarity. The rage soon died: he came to regard this mass of pseudo-literature as protecting the truth from desecration. But the hilarity remained, and flowed into the form of his idea. And the idea—the divine, incomparable idea—was simply that he should avenge his goddess by satirizing her false interpreters. He would write a skit on the "popular" scientific book; he would so heap platitude on platitude, fallacy on fallacy, false analogy on false analogy, so use his superior knowledge to abound in the sense of the ignorant, that even the gross crowd would join in the laugh against its augurs. And the laugh should be something more than the distension of mental muscles; it should be the trumpet-blast bringing down the walls of ignorance, or at least the little stone striking the giant between the eyes.

II

THE Professor, on presenting his card, had imagined that it would command prompt access to the publisher's sanctuary; but the young man who read his name was not moved to immediate action. It was clear that Professor Linyard of Hillbridge University was not a specific figure to the purveyors of popular literature. But the publisher was an old friend; and when the card had finally drifted to his office on the languid tide of routine he came forth at once to greet his visitor.

The warmth of his welcome convinced the Professor that he had been right in bringing his manuscript to Ned Harviss. He and Harviss had been at Hillbridge together, and the future publisher had been one of the wildest spirits in that band of college outlaws which yearly turns out so many inoffensive citizens and kind husbands and fathers. The Professor knew the taming qualities of life. He was aware that many of his most reckless comrades had been transformed into prudent capitalists or cowed wage-earners; but he was almost sure that he could count on Harviss. So rare a sense of irony, so keen a perception of relative values, could hardly have been blunted even by twenty years' intercourse with the obvious.

The publisher's appearance was a little disconcerting. He looked as if he had been fattened on popular fiction; and his fat was full of optimistic creases. The Professor seemed to see him bowing into his office a long train of spotless heroines laden with the maiden tribute of the hundredth thousand volume.

Nevertheless, his welcome was reassuring. He did not disown his early enormities, and capped his visitor's tentative allusions by such flagrant references to the past that the Professor produced his manuscript without a scruple.

"What—you don't mean to say you've been doing something in our line?"

The Professor smiled. "You publish scientific books sometimes, don't you?"

The publisher's optimistic creases relaxed a little. "H'm—it all depends—I'm afraid you're a little *too* scientific for us. We have a big sale for scientific breakfast foods, but not for the concentrated essences. In your case, of course, I should be delighted to stretch a point; but in your own interest I ought to tell you that perhaps one of the educational houses would do you better."

The Professor leaned back, still smiling luxuriously.

"Well, look it over—I rather think you'll take it."

"Oh, we'll *take* it, as I say; but the terms might not—"

"No matter about the terms—"

The publisher threw his head back with a laugh. "I had no idea that science was so profitable; we find our popular novelists are the hardest hands at a bargain."

"Science is disinterested," the Professor corrected him. "And I have a fancy to have you publish this thing."

"That's immensely good of you, my dear fellow. Of course your name goes with a certain public—and I rather like the originality of our bringing out a work so out of our line. I daresay it may boom us both." His creases deepened at the thought, and he shone encouragingly on the Professor's leave-taking.

Within a fortnight, a line from Harviss recalled the Professor to town. He had been looking forward with immense zest to this second meeting; Harviss' college roar was in his tympanum, and he pictured himself following up the protracted chuckle which would follow his friend's progress through the manuscript. He was proud of the adroitness with which he had kept his secret from Harviss, had maintained to the last the pretense of a serious work, in order to give the keener edge to his reader's enjoyment. Not since undergraduate days had the Professor tasted such a draught of pure fun as his anticipations now poured for him.

This time his card brought instant admission. He was bowed into the office like a successful novelist, and Harviss grasped him with both hands.

"Well—do you mean to take it?" he asked, with a lingering coquetry.

"Take it? Take it, my dear fellow? It's in press already—you'll excuse my not waiting to consult you? There will be no difficulty about terms, I assure you, and we had barely time to catch the autumn market. My dear Linyard, why didn't you tell me?" His voice sank to a reproachful solemnity, and he pushed forward his own arm-chair.

The Professor dropped into it with a chuckle. "And miss the joy of letting you find out?"

"Well—it *was* a joy." Harviss held out a box of his best cigars. "I don't know when I've had a bigger sensation. It was so deucedly unexpected—and, my dear fellow, you've brought it so exactly to the right shop."

"I'm glad to hear you say so," said the Professor modestly.

Harviss laughed in rich appreciation. "I don't suppose you had a doubt of it; but of course I was quite unprepared. And it's so extraordinarily out of your line—"

The Professor took off his glasses and rubbed them with a slow smile.

"Would you have thought it so—at college?"

Harviss stared. "At college?—Why, you were the most iconoclastic devil—"

There was a perceptible pause. The Professor restored his glasses and looked at his friend. "Well—?" he said simply.

"Well—?" echoed the other, still staring. "Ah—I see; you mean that that's what explains it. The swing of the pendulum, and so forth. Well, I admit it's not an uncommon phenomenon. I've conformed myself, for example; most of our crowd have, I believe; but somehow I hadn't expected it of you."

The close observer might have detected a faint sadness under the official congratulation of his tone; but the Professor was too amazed to have an ear for such fine shades.

"Expected it of me? Expected what of me?" he gasped. "What in heaven do you think this thing is?" And he struck his fist on the manuscript which lay between them.

Harviss had recovered his optimistic creases. He rested a benevolent eye on the document.

"Why, your apologia—your confession of faith, I should call it. You surely must have seen which way you were going? You can't have written it in your sleep?"

"Oh, no, I was wide awake enough," said the Professor faintly.

"Well, then, why are you staring at me as if I were not?" Harviss leaned forward to lay a reassuring hand on his visitor's worn coat-sleeve. "Don't mistake me, my dear Linyard. Don't fancy there was the least unkindness in my allusion to your change of front. What is growth but the shifting of the stand-point? Why should a man be expected to look at life with the same eyes at twenty and at—our age? It never occurred to me that you could feel the least delicacy in admitting that you have come round a little—have fallen into line, so to speak."

But the Professor had sprung up as if to give his lungs more room to expand; and from them there issued a laugh which shook the editorial rafters.

"Oh, Lord, oh Lord—is it really as good as that?" he gasped.

Harviss had glanced instinctively toward the electric bell on his desk; it was evident that he was prepared for an emergency.

"My dear fellow—" he began in a soothing tone.

"Oh, let me have my laugh out, do," implored the Professor. "I'll—I'll quiet down in a minute; you needn't ring for the young man." He dropped into his chair again, and grasped its arms to steady his shaking. "This is the best laugh I've had since college," he brought out between his paroxysms. And then, suddenly, he sat up with a groan. "But if it's as good as that it's a failure!" he exclaimed.

Harviss, stiffening a little, examined the tip of his cigar. "My dear Linyard," he said at length, "I don't understand a word you're saying."

The Professor succumbed to a fresh access, from the vortex of which he managed to fling out—"But that's the very core of the joke!"

Harviss looked at him resignedly. "What is?"

"Why, your not seeing—your not understanding—"

"Not understanding what?"

"Why, what the book is meant to be." His laughter subsided again and he sat gazing thoughtfully at the publisher. "Unless it means," he wound up, "that I've over-shot the mark."

"If I am the mark, you certainly have," said Harviss, with a glance at the clock.

The Professor caught the glance and interpreted it. "The book is a skit," he said, rising.

The other stared. "A skit? It's not serious, you mean?"

"Not to me—but it seems you've taken it so."

"You never told me—" began the publisher in a ruffled tone.

"No, I never told you," said the Professor.

Harviss sat staring at the manuscript between them. "I don't pretend to be up in such recondite forms of humor," he said, still stiffly. "Of course you address yourself to a very small class of readers."

"Oh, infinitely small," admitted the Professor, extending his hand toward the manuscript.

Harviss appeared to be pursuing his own train of thought. "That is," he continued, "if you insist on an ironical interpretation."

"If I insist on it—what do you mean?"

The publisher smiled faintly. "Well—isn't the book susceptible of another? If I read it without seeing—"

"Well?" murmured the other, fascinated.

"—Why shouldn't the rest of the world?" declared Harviss boldly. "I represent the Average Reader—that's my business, that's what I've been training myself to do for the last twenty years. It's a mission like another—the thing is to do it thoroughly; not to cheat and compromise. I know fellows who are publishers in business hours and dilettantes the rest of the time. Well, they never succeed: convictions are just as necessary in business as in religion. But that's not the point—I was going to say that if you'll let me handle this book as a genuine thing I'll guarantee to make it go."

The Professor stood motionless, his hand still on the manuscript.

"A genuine thing?" he echoed.

"A serious piece of work—the expression of your convictions. I tell you there's nothing the public likes as much as convictions—they'll always follow a man who believes in his own ideas. And this book is just on the line of popular interest. You've got hold of a big thing. It's full of hope and enthusiasm: it's written in the religious key. There are passages in it that would do splendidly in a Birthday Book—things that popular preachers would quote in their sermons. If you'd wanted to catch a big public you couldn't have gone about it in a better way. The thing's perfect for my purpose—I wouldn't let you alter a word of it. It'll sell like a popular novel if you'll let me handle it in the right way."

## III

WHEN the Professor left Harviss' office, the manuscript remained behind. He thought he had been taken by the huge irony of the situation—by the enlarged circumference of the joke. In its original form, as Harviss had said, the book would have addressed itself to a very limited circle: now it would include the world. The elect would understand; the crowd would not; and his work would thus serve a double purpose. And, after all, nothing was changed in the situation; not a word of the book was to be altered. The change was merely in the publisher's point of view, and in the "tip" he was to give the reviewers. The Professor had only to hold his tongue and look serious.

These arguments found a strong reinforcement in the large premium which expressed Harviss' sense of his opportunity. As a satire, the book would have brought its author nothing; in fact, its cost would have come out of his own pocket, since, as Harviss assured him, no publisher would have risked taking it. But as a profession of faith, as the recantation of an eminent biologist, whose leanings had hitherto been supposed to be toward a cold determinism, it would bring in a steady income to author and publisher. The offer found the Professor in a moment of financial perplexity. His illness, his unwonted holiday, the necessity of postponing a course of well-paid lectures, had combined to diminish his resources; and when Harviss offered him an advance of a thousand dollars the esoteric savor of the joke became irresistible. It was still as a joke that he persisted in regarding the transaction; and though he had pledged himself not to betray the real intent of the book, he held *in petto* the notion of some day being able to take the public into his confidence. As for the initiated, they would know at once: and however long a face he pulled, his colleagues would see the tongue in his cheek. Meanwhile it fortunately happened that, even if the book should achieve the kind of triumph prophesied by Harviss, it would not appreciably injure its author's professional standing. Professor Linyard was known chiefly as a microscopist. On the structure and habits of a certain class of coleoptera he was the most distinguished living authority; but none save his intimate friends knew what generalizations on the destiny of man he had drawn from these special studies. He might have published a treatise on the Filioque without disturbing the confidence of those on whose approval his reputation rested; and moreover he was sustained by the thought that one glance at his book would let them into its secret. In fact, so sure was he of this that he wondered the astute Harviss had cared to risk such speedy exposure. But Harviss had probably reflected that even in this reverberating age the opinions of the laboratory do not easily reach the street; and the Professor, at any rate, was not bound to offer advice on this point.

The determining cause of his consent was the fact that the book was already in press. The Professor knew little about the workings of the press, but the phrase gave him a sense of finality, of having been caught himself in the toils of that mysterious engine. If he had had time to think the matter over, his scruples might have dragged him back; but his conscience was eased by the futility of resistance.

## IV

MRS. LINYARD did not often read the papers; and there was therefore a special significance in her approaching her husband one evening after dinner with a copy of the *New York Investigator* in her hand. Her expression lent solemnity to the act: Mrs. Linyard had a limited but distinctive set of expressions, and she now looked as she did when the President of the University came to dine.

"You didn't tell me of this, Samuel," she said in a slightly tremulous voice.

"Tell you of what?" returned the Professor, reddening to the margin of his baldness.

"That you had published a book—I might never have heard of it if Mrs. Pease hadn't brought me the paper."

Her husband rubbed his eye-glasses with a groan. "Oh, you would have heard of it," he said gloomily.

Mrs. Linyard stared. "Did you wish to keep it from me, Samuel?" And as he made no answer, she added with irresistible pride: "Perhaps you don't know what beautiful things have been said about it."

He took the paper with a reluctant hand. "Has Pease been saying beautiful things about it?"

"The Professor? Mrs. Pease didn't say he had mentioned it."

The author heaved a sigh of relief. His book, as Harviss had prophesied, had caught the autumn market: had caught and captured it. The publisher had conducted the campaign like an experienced strategist. He had completely surrounded the enemy. Every newspaper, every periodical, held in ambush an advertisement of *The Vital Thing*. Weeks in advance the great commander had begun to form his lines of attack. Allusions to the remarkable significance of the coming work had appeared first in the scientific and literary reviews, spreading thence to the supplements of the daily journals. Not a moment passed without a quickening touch to the public consciousness: seventy millions of people were forced to remember at least once a day that Professor Linyard's book was on the verge of appearing. Slips emblazoned with the question: *Have you read "The Vital Thing"?* fell from the pages of popular novels and whitened the floors of crowded street-cars. The query, in large lettering, assaulted the traveller at the railway bookstall, confronted him on the walls of "elevated" stations, and seemed, in its ascending scale, about to supplant the interrogations as to soap and stove-polish which animate our rural scenery.

On the day of publication, the Professor had withdrawn to his laboratory. The shriek of the advertisements was in his ears, and his one desire was to avoid all knowledge of the event they heralded. A reaction of self-consciousness had set in, and if Harviss' check had sufficed to buy up the first edition of *The Vital Thing* the Professor would gladly have devoted it to that purpose. But the sense of inevitableness gradually subdued him, and he received his wife's copy of the *Investigator* with a kind of impersonal curiosity. The review was a long one, full of extracts: he saw, as he glanced over them, how well they would look in a volume of "Selections." The reviewer began by thanking his author "for sounding with no uncertain voice that note of ringing optimism, of faith in man's destiny and the supremacy of good, which has too long been silenced by the whining chorus of a decadent nihilism. . . . It is well," the writer continued, "when such reminders come to us not from the moralist but from the man of science—when from the desiccating atmosphere of the laboratory there rises this glorious cry of faith and reconstruction."

The review was minute and exhaustive. Thanks no doubt to Harviss' diplomacy, it had been given to the *Investigator's* "best man," and the Professor was startled by the bold eye with which his emancipated fallacies confronted him. Under the reviewer's handling they made up admirably as truths, and their author began to understand Harviss' regret that they should be used for any less profitable purpose.

The *Investigator*, as Harviss phrased it, "set the pace," and the other journals followed, finding it easier to let their critical man-of-all-work play a variation on the first reviewer's theme than to secure an expert to "do" the book afresh. But it was evident that the Professor had captured his public, for all the resources of the profession could not, as Harviss gleefully pointed out, have carried the book so straight to the heart of the nation. There was something noble in the way in which Harviss belittled his own share in the achievement, and insisted on the inutility of shoving a book which had started with such headway on.

"All I ask you is to admit that I saw what would happen," he said with a touch of professional pride. "I knew you'd struck the right note—I knew they'd be quoting you from Maine to San Francisco. Good as fiction? It's better—it'll keep going longer."

"Will it?" said the Professor with a slight shudder. He was resigned to an ephemeral triumph, but the thought of the book's persistency frightened him.

"I should say so! Why, you fit in everywhere—science, theology, natural history— and then the all-for-the-best element which is so popular just now. Why, you come right in with the How-to-Relax series, and they sell way up in the millions. And then the book's so full of tenderness—there are such lovely things in it about flowers and children. I didn't know an old Dryasdust like you could have such a lot of sentiment in him. Why, I actually caught myself sniveling over that passage about the snowdrops piercing the frozen earth; and my wife was saying the other day that, since she's read *The Vital Thing*, she begins to think you must write the 'What-Cheer Column,' in the *Inglenook*." He threw back his head with a laugh which ended in the inspired cry: "And, by George, sir, when the thing begins to slow off we'll start somebody writing against it, and that will run us straight into another hundred thousand."

And as earnest of this belief he drew the Professor a supplementary check.

V

MRS. LINYARD'S knock cut short the importunities of the lady who had been trying to persuade the Professor to be taken by flashlight at his study table for the Christmas number of the *Inglenook*. On this point the Professor had fancied himself impregnable; but the unwonted smile with which he welcomed his wife's intrusion showed that his defences were weakening.

The lady from the *Inglenook* took the hint with professional promptness, but said brightly, as she snapped the elastic around her note-book: "I shan't let you forget me, Professor."

The groan with which he followed her retreat was interrupted by his wife's question:

"Do they pay you for these interviews, Samuel?"

The Professor looked at her with sudden attention. "Not directly," he said, wondering at her expression.

She sank down with a sigh. "Indirectly, then?"

"What is the matter, my dear? I gave you Harviss' second check the other day—"

Her tears arrested him. "Don't be hard on the boy, Samuel! I really believe your success has turned his head."

"The boy—what boy? My success—? Explain yourself, Susan!"

"It's only that Jack has—has borrowed some money—which he can't repay. But you mustn't think him altogether to blame, Samuel. Since the success of your book he has been asked about so much—it's given the children quite a different position. Millicent says that wherever they go the first question asked is, 'Are you any relation of the author of *The Vital Thing?*' Of course we're all very proud of the book; but it entails obligations which you may not have thought of in writing it."

The Professor sat gazing at the letters and newspaper clippings on the study-table which he had just successfully defended from the camera of the *Inglenook*. He took up an envelope bearing the name of a popular weekly paper.

"I don't know that the Inglenook would help much," he said, "but I suppose this might."

Mrs. Linyard's eyes glowed with maternal avidity.

"What is it, Samuel?"

"A series of 'Scientific Sermons' for the Round-the-Gas-Log column of *The Woman's World*. I believe that journal has a larger circulation than any other weekly, and they pay in proportion."

He had not even asked the extent of Jack's indebtedness. It had been so easy to relieve recent domestic difficulties by the timely production of Harviss' two checks, that it now seemed natural to get Mrs. Linyard out of the room by promising further reinforcements. The Professor had indignantly rejected Harviss' suggestion that he should follow up his success by a second volume on the same lines. He had sworn not to lend more than a passive support to the fraud of *The Vital Thing;* but the temptation to free himself from Mrs. Linyard prevailed over his last scruples, and within an hour he was at work on the "Scientific Sermons."

The Professor was not an unkind man. He really enjoyed making his family happy; and it was his own business if his reward for so doing was that it kept them out of his way. But the success of "The Vital Thing" gave him more than this negative satisfaction. It enlarged his own existence and opened new doors into other lives. The Professor, during fifty virtuous years, had been cognizant of only two types of women: the fond and foolish, whom one married, and the earnest and intellectual, whom one did not. Of the two, he infinitely preferred the former, even for conversational purposes. But as a social instrument woman was unknown to him; and it was not till he was drawn into the world on the tide of his literary success that he discovered the deficiencies in his classification of the sex. Then he learned with astonishment of the existence of a third type: the woman who is fond without foolishness and intellectual without earnestness. Not that the Professor inspired, or sought to inspire, sentimental emotions; but he expanded in the warm atmosphere of personal interest which some of his new acquaintances contrived to create about him. It was delightful to talk of serious things in a setting of frivolity, and to be personal without being domestic.

Even in this new world, where all subjects were touched on lightly, and emphasis was the only indelicacy, the Professor found himself constrained to endure an occasional reference to his book. It was unpleasant at first; but gradually he slipped into the habit of hearing it talked of, and grew accustomed to telling pretty women just how "it had first come to him."

Meanwhile the success of the "Scientific Sermons" was facilitating his family relations. His photograph in the *Inglenook*, to which the lady of the note-book had succeeded in appending a vivid interview, carried his fame to circles inaccessible even to *The Vital Thing;* and the Professor found himself the man of the hour. He soon grew used to the functions of the office, and gave out hundred-dollar interviews on every subject, from labor strikes to Babism, with a frequency which reacted agreeably on the domestic exchequer. Presently his head began to figure in the advertising pages of the magazines. Admiring readers learned the name of the only breakfast-food in use at his table, of the ink with which "The Vital Thing" had been written, the soap with which the author's hands were washed, and the tissue-builder which fortified him for further effort. These confidences endeared the Professor to millions of readers, and his head passed in due course from the magazine and the newspaper to the biscuit-tin and the chocolate box.

## VI

THE Professor, all the while, was leading a double life. While the author of *The Vital Thing* reaped the fruits of popular approval, the distinguished microscopist continued his laboratory work unheeded save by the few who were engaged in the same line of investigations. His divided allegiance had not hitherto affected the quality of his work: it seemed to him that he returned to the laboratory with greater zest after an afternoon in a drawing-room where readings from "The Vital Thing" had alternated with plantation melodies and tea. He had long ceased to concern himself with what his colleagues thought of his literary career. Of the few whom he frequented, none had referred to *The Vital Thing;* and he knew enough of their lives to guess that their silence might as fairly be attributed to indifference as to disapproval. They were intensely interested in the Professor's views on beetles, but they really cared very little what he thought of the Almighty.

The Professor entirely shared their feelings, and one of his chief reasons for cultivating the success which accident had bestowed on him, was that it enabled him to command a greater range of appliances for his real work. He had known what it was to lack books and instruments; and *The Vital Thing* was the magic wand which summoned them to his aid. For some time he had been feeling his way along the edge of a discovery: balancing himself with professional skill on a plank of hypothesis flung across an abyss of uncertainty. The conjecture was the result of years of patient gathering of facts: its corroboration would take months more of comparison and classification. But at the end of the vista victory loomed. The Professor felt within himself that assurance of ultimate justification which, to the man of science, makes a life-time seem the mere comma between premise and deduction. But he had reached the point where his conjectures required formulation. It was only by giving them expression, by exposing them to the comment and criticism of his associates, that he could test their final value; and this inner assurance was confirmed by the only friend whose confidence he invited.

Professor Pease, the husband of the lady who had opened Mrs. Linyard's eyes to the triumph of *The Vital Thing*, was the repository of her husband's scientific experiences. What he thought of "The Vital Thing" had never been divulged; and he was capable of such vast exclusions that it was quite possible that pervasive work had not yet reached him. In any case, it was not likely to affect his judgment of the author's professional capacity.

"You want to put that all in a book, Linyard," was Professor Pease's summing-up. "I'm sure you've got hold of something big; but to see it clearly yourself you ought to outline it for others. Take my advice—chuck everything else and get to work tomorrow. It's time you wrote a book, anyhow."

*It's time you wrote a book, anyhow!* The words smote the Professor with mingled pain and ecstasy: he could have wept over their significance. But his friend's other phrase reminded him with a start of Harviss. "You have got hold of a big thing—" it had been the publisher's first comment on "The Vital Thing." But what a world of meaning lay between the two phrases! It was the world in which the powers who fought for the Professor were destined to wage their final battle; and for the moment he had no doubt of the outcome.

"By George, I'll do it, Pease!" he said, stretching his hand to his friend.

The next day he went to town to see Harviss. He wanted to ask for an advance on the new popular edition of *The Vital Thing.* He had determined to drop a course of supplementary lectures at the University, and to give himself up for a year to his book. To do this, additional funds were necessary; but thanks to *The Vital Thing* they would be forthcoming.

The publisher received him as cordially as usual; but the response to his demand was not as prompt as his previous experience had entitled him to expect.

"Of course we'll be glad to do what we can for you, Linyard; but the fact is, we've decided to give up the idea of the new edition for the present."

"You've given up the new edition?"

"Why, yes—we've done pretty well by *The Vital Thing,* and we're inclined to think it's *your* turn to do something for it now."

The Professor looked at him blankly. "What can I do for it?" he asked—"what *more*" his accent added.

"Why, put a little new life in it by writing something else. The secret of perpetual motion hasn't yet been discovered, you know, and it's one of the laws of literature that books which start with a rush are apt to slow down sooner than the crawlers. We've kept *The Vital Thing* going for eighteen months—but, hang it, it ain't so vital any more. We simply couldn't see our way to a new edition. Oh, I don't say it's dead yet—but it's moribund, and you're the only man who can resuscitate it."

The Professor continued to stare. "I—what can I do about it?" he stammered.

"Do? Why write another like it—go it one better: you know the trick. The public isn't tired of you by any means; but you want to make yourself heard again before anybody else cuts in. Write another book—write two, and we'll sell them in sets in a box: The Vital Thing Series. That will take tremendously in the holidays. Try and let us have a new volume by October—I'll be glad to give you a big advance if you'll sign a contract on that."

The Professor sat silent: there was too cruel an irony in the coincidence.

Harviss looked up at him in surprise.

"Well, what's the matter with taking my advice—you're not going out of literature, are you?"

The Professor rose from his chair. "No—I'm going into it," he said simply.

"Going into it?"

"I'm going to write a real book—a serious one."

"Good Lord! Most people think *The Vital Thing* is serious."

"Yes—but I mean something different."

"In your old line—beetles and so forth?"

"Yes," said the Professor solemnly.

Harviss looked at him with equal gravity. "Well, I'm sorry for that," he said, "because it takes you out of our bailiwick. But I suppose you've made enough money out of *The Vital Thing* to permit yourself a little harmless amusement. When you want more cash come back to us—only don't put it off too long, or some other fellow will have stepped into your shoes. Popularity don't keep, you know; and the hotter the success the quicker the commodity perishes."

He leaned back, cheerful and sententious, delivering his axioms with conscious kindliness.

The Professor, who had risen and moved to the door, turned back with a wavering step.

"When did you say another volume would have to be ready?" he faltered.

"I said October—but call it a month later. You don't need any pushing nowadays."

"And—you'd have no objection to letting me have a little advance now? I need some new instruments for my real work."

Harviss extended a cordial hand. "My dear fellow, that's talking—I'll write the check while you wait; and I daresay we can start up the cheap edition of *The Vital Thing* at the same time, if you'll pledge yourself to give us the book by November.—How much?" he asked, poised above his checkbook.

In the street, the Professor stood staring about him, uncertain and a little dazed.

"After all, it's only putting it off for six months," he said to himself; "and I can do better work when I get my new instruments."

He smiled and raised his hat to the passing victoria of a lady in whose copy of *The Vital Thing* he had recently written:

*Labor est etiam ipsa voluptas.*

## THE MISSION OF JANE

LETHBURY, SURVEYING his wife across the dinner table, found his transient conjugal glance arrested by an indefinable change in her appearance.

"How smart you look! Is that a new gown?" he asked.

Her answering look seemed to deprecate his charging her with the extravagance of wasting a new gown on him, and he now perceived that the change lay deeper than any accident of dress. At the same time, he noticed that she betrayed her consciousness of it by a delicate, almost frightened blush. It was one of the compensations of Mrs. Lethbury's protracted childishness that she still blushed as prettily as at eighteen. Her body had been privileged not to outstrip her mind, and the two, as it seemed to Lethbury, were destined to travel together through an eternity of girlishness.

"I don't know what you mean," she said.

Since she never did, he always wondered at her bringing this out as a fresh grievance against him; but his wonder was unresentful, and he said good-humoredly: "You sparkle so that I thought you had on your diamonds."

She sighed and blushed again.

"It must be," he continued, "that you've been to a dressmaker's opening. You're absolutely brimming with illicit enjoyment."

She stared again, this time at the adjective. His adjectives always embarrassed her: their unintelligibleness savored of impropriety.

"In short," he summed up, "you've been doing something that you're thoroughly ashamed of."

To his surprise she retorted: "I don't see why I should be ashamed of it!"

Lethbury leaned back with a smile of enjoyment. When there was nothing better going he always liked to listen to her explanations.

"Well—?" he said.

She was becoming breathless and ejaculatory. "Of course you'll laugh—you laugh at everything!"

"That rather blunts the point of my derision, doesn't it?" he interjected; but she rushed on without noticing:

"It's so easy to laugh at things."

"Ah," murmured Lethbury with relish, "that's Aunt Sophronia's, isn't it?"

Most of his wife's opinions were heirlooms, and he took a quaint pleasure in tracing their descent. She was proud of their age, and saw no reason for discarding them while they were still serviceable. Some, of course, were so fine that she kept them for state occasions, like her great-grandmother's Crown Derby; but from the lady known as Aunt Sophronia she had inherited a stout set of every-day prejudices that were practically as good as new; whereas her husband's, as she noticed, were always having to be replaced. In the early days she had fancied there might be a certain satisfaction in taxing him with the fact; but she had long since been silenced by the reply: "My dear, I'm not a rich man, but I never use an opinion twice if I can help it."

She was reduced, therefore, to dwelling on his moral deficiencies; and one of the most obvious of these was his refusal to take things seriously. On this occasion, however, some ulterior purpose kept her from taking up his taunt.

"I'm not in the least ashamed!" she repeated, with the air of shaking a banner to the wind; but the domestic atmosphere being calm, the banner drooped unheroically.

"That," said Lethbury judicially, "encourages me to infer that you ought to be, and that, consequently, you've been giving yourself the unusual pleasure of doing something I shouldn't approve of."

She met this with an almost solemn directness. "No," she said. "You won't approve of it. I've allowed for that."

"Ah," he exclaimed, setting down his liqueur-glass. "You've worked out the whole problem, eh?"

"I believe so."

"That's uncommonly interesting. And what is it?"

She looked at him quietly. "A baby."

If it was seldom given her to surprise him, she had attained the distinction for once.

"A baby?"

"Yes."

"A—human baby?"

"Of course!" she cried, with the virtuous resentment of the woman who has never allowed dogs in the house.

Lethbury's puzzled stare broke into a fresh smile. "A baby I shan't approve of? Well, in the abstract I don't think much of them, I admit. Is this an abstract baby?"

Again she frowned at the adjective; but she had reached a pitch of exaltation at which such obstacles could not deter her.

"It's the loveliest baby—" she murmured.

"Ah, then it's concrete. It exists. In this harsh world it draws its breath in pain—"

"It's the healthiest child I ever saw!" she indignantly corrected.

"You've seen it, then?"

Again the accusing blush suffused her. "Yes—I've seen it."

"And to whom does the paragon belong?"

And here indeed she confounded him. "To me—I hope," she declared.

He pushed his chair back with an inarticulate murmur. "To you—?"

"To *us*," she corrected.

"Good Lord!" he said. If there had been the least hint of hallucination in her transparent gaze—but no: it was as clear, as shallow, as easily fathomable as when he had first suffered the sharp surprise of striking bottom in it.

It occurred to him that perhaps she was trying to be funny: he knew that there is nothing more cryptic than the humor of the unhumorous.

"Is it a joke?" he faltered.

"Oh, I hope not. I want it so much to be a reality—"

He paused to smile at the limitations of a world in which jokes were not realities, and continued gently: "But since it is one already—"

"To us, I mean: to you and me. I want—" her voice wavered, and her eyes with it. "I have always wanted so dreadfully . . . it has been such a disappointment . . . not to . . . "

"I see," said Lethbury slowly.

But he had not seen before. It seemed curious, now, that he had never thought of her taking it in that way, had never surmised any hidden depths beneath her outspread obviousness. He felt as though he had touched a secret spring in her mind.

There was a moment's silence, moist and tremulous on her part, awkward and slightly irritated on his.

"You've been lonely, I suppose?" he began. It was odd, having suddenly to reckon with the stranger who gazed at him out of her trivial eyes.

"At times," she said.

"I'm sorry."

"It was not your fault. A man has so many occupations; and women who are clever—or very handsome—I suppose that's an occupation too. Sometimes I've felt that when dinner was ordered I had nothing to do till the next day."

"Oh," he groaned.

"It wasn't your fault," she insisted. "I never told you—but when I chose that rose-bud paper for the front room upstairs, I always thought—"

"Well—?"

"It would be such a pretty paper—for a baby—to wake up in. That was years ago, of course; but it was rather an expensive paper . . . and it hasn't faded in the least . . . " she broke off incoherently.

"It hasn't faded?"

"No—and so I thought . . . as we don't use the room for anything . . . now that Aunt Sophronia is dead . . . I thought I might . . . you might . . . oh, Julian, if you could only have seen it just waking up in its crib!"

"Seen what—where? You haven't got a baby upstairs?"

"Oh, no—not *yet*," she said, with her rare laugh—the girlish bubbling of merriment that had seemed one of her chief graces in the early days. It occurred to him that he had not given her enough things to laugh about lately. But then she needed such very elementary things: it was as difficult to amuse her as a savage. He concluded that he was not sufficiently simple.

"Alice," he said, almost solemnly, "what *do* you mean?"

She hesitated a moment: he saw her gather her courage for a supreme effort. Then she said slowly, gravely, as though she were pronouncing a sacramental phrase:

"I'm so lonely without a little child—and I thought perhaps you'd let me adopt one. . . . It's at the hospital . . . its mother is dead . . . and I could . . . pet it, and dress it, and do things for it . . . and it's such a good baby . . . you can ask any of the nurses . . . it would never, *never* bother you by crying . . . "

## II

LETHBURY accompanied his wife to the hospital in a mood of chastened wonder. It did not occur to him to oppose her wish. He knew, of course, that he would have to bear the brunt of the situation: the jokes at the club, the inquiries, the explanations. He saw himself in the comic role of the adopted father, and welcomed it as an expiation. For in his rapid reconstruction of the past he found himself cutting a shabbier figure than he cared to admit. He had always been intolerant of stupid people, and it was his punishment to be convicted of stupidity. As his mind traversed the years between his marriage and this unexpected assumption of paternity, he saw, in the light of an overheated imagination, many signs of unwonted crassness. It was not that he had ceased to think his wife stupid: she *was* stupid, limited, inflexible; but there was a pathos in the struggles of her swaddled mind, in its blind reachings toward the primal emotions. He had always thought she would have been happier with a child; but he had thought it mechanically, because it had so often been thought before, because it was in the nature of things to think it of every woman, because his wife was so eminently one of a species that she fitted into all the generalizations on the sex. But he had regarded this generalization as merely typical of the triumph of tradition over experience. Maternity was no doubt the supreme function of primitive woman, the one end to which her whole organism tended; but the law of increasing complexity had operated in both sexes, and he had not seriously supposed that, outside the world of Christmas fiction and anecdotic art, such truisms had any special hold on the feminine imagination. Now he saw that the arts in question were kept alive by the vitality of the sentiments they appealed to.

Lethbury was in fact going through a rapid process of readjustment. His marriage had been a failure, but he had preserved toward his wife the exact fidelity of act that is sometimes supposed to excuse any divagation of feeling; so that, for years, the tie between them had consisted mainly in his abstaining from making love to other women. The abstention had not always been easy, for the world is surprisingly well-stocked with the kind of woman one ought to have married but did not; and Lethbury had not escaped the solicitation of such alternatives. His immunity had been purchased at the cost of taking refuge in the somewhat rarified atmosphere of his perceptions; and his world being thus limited, he had given unusual care to its details, compensating himself for the narrowness of his horizon by the minute finish of his foreground. It was a world of fine shadings and the nicest proportions, where impulse seldom set a blundering foot, and the feast of reason was undisturbed by an intemperate flow of soul. To such a banquet his wife naturally remained uninvited. The diet would have disagreed with her, and she would probably have objected to the other guests. But Lethbury, miscalculating her needs, had hitherto supposed that he had made ample provision for them, and was consequently at liberty to enjoy his own fare without any reproach of mendicancy at his gates. Now he beheld her pressing a starved face against the windows of his life, and in his imaginative reaction he invested her with a pathos borrowed from the sense of his own shortcomings.

In the hospital, the imaginative process continued with increasing force. He looked at his wife with new eyes. Formerly she had been to him a mere bundle of negations, a labyrinth of dead walls and bolted doors. There was nothing behind the walls, and the doors led no-whither: he had sounded and listened often enough to be sure of that. Now he felt like a traveller who, exploring some ancient ruin, comes on an inner cell, intact amid the general dilapidation, and painted with images which reveal the forgotten uses of the building.

His wife stood by a white crib in one of the wards. In the crib lay a child, a year old, the nurse affirmed, but to Lethbury's eye a mere dateless fragment of humanity projected against a background of conjecture. Over this anonymous particle of life Mrs. Lethbury leaned, such ecstasy reflected in her face as strikes up, in Correggio's Night-piece, from the child's body to the mother's countenance. It was a light that irradiated and dazzled her. She looked up at an inquiry of Lethbury's, but as their glances met he perceived that she no longer saw him, that he had become as invisible to her as she had long been to him. He had to transfer his question to the nurse.

"What is the child's name?" he asked.

"We call her Jane," said the nurse.

### III

LETHBURY, at first, had resisted the idea of a legal adoption; but when he found that his wife's curiously limited imagination prevented her regarding the child as hers till it had been made so by process of law, he promptly withdrew his objection. On one point only he remained inflexible; and that was the changing of the waif's name. Mrs. Lethbury, almost at once, had expressed a wish to rechristen it: she fluctuated between Muriel and Gladys, deferring the moment of decision like a lady wavering between two bonnets. But Lethbury was unyielding. In the general surrender of his prejudices this one alone held out.

"But Jane is so dreadful," Mrs. Lethbury protested.

"Well, we don't know that *she* won't be dreadful. She may grow up a Jane."

His wife exclaimed reproachfully. "The nurse says she's the loveliest—"

"Don't they always say that?" asked Lethbury patiently. He was prepared to be inexhaustibly patient now that he had reached a firm foothold of opposition.

"It's cruel· to call her Jane," Mrs. Lethbury pleaded.

"It's ridiculous to call her Muriel."

"The nurse is *sure* she must be a lady's child."

Lethbury winced: he had tried, all along, to keep his mind off the question of antecedents.

"Well, let her prove it," he said, with a rising sense of exasperation. He wondered how he could ever have allowed himself to be drawn into such a ridiculous business; for the first time he felt the full irony of it. He had visions of coming home in the afternoon to a house smelling of linseed and paregoric, and of being greeted by a chronic howl as he went upstairs to dress for dinner. He had never been a club-man, but he saw himself becoming one now.

The worst of his anticipations were unfulfilled. The baby was surprisingly well and surprisingly quiet. Such infantile remedies as she absorbed were not potent enough to be perceived beyond the nursery; and when Lethbury could be induced to enter that sanctuary, there was nothing to jar his nerves in the mild pink presence of his adopted daughter. Jars there were, indeed: they were probably inevitable in the disturbed routine of the household; but they occurred between Mrs. Lethbury and the nurses, and Jane contributed to them only a placid stare which might have served as a rebuke to the combatants.

In the reaction from his first impulse of atonement, Lethbury noted with sharpened perceptions the effect of the change on his wife's character. He saw already the error of supposing that it could work any transformation in her. It simply magnified her existing qualities. She was like a dried sponge put in water: she expanded, but she did not change her shape. From the stand-point of scientific observation it was curious to see how her stored instincts responded to the pseudo-maternal call. She overflowed with the petty maxims of the occasion. One felt in her the epitome, the consummation, of centuries of animal maternity, so that this little woman, who screamed at a mouse and was nervous about burglars, came to typify the cave-mother rending her prey for her young.

It was less easy to regard philosophically the practical effects of her borrowed motherhood. Lethbury found with surprise that she was becoming assertive and definite. She no longer represented the negative side of his life; she showed, indeed, a tendency to inconvenient affirmations. She had gradually expanded her assumption of motherhood till it included his own share in the relation, and he suddenly found himself regarded as the father of Jane. This was a contingency he had not foreseen, and it took all his philosophy to accept it; but there were moments of compensation. For Mrs. Lethbury was undoubtedly happy for the first time in years; and the thought that he had tardily contributed to this end reconciled him to the irony of the means.

At first he was inclined to reproach himself for still viewing the situation from the outside, for remaining a spectator instead of a participant. He had been allured, for a moment, by the vision of severed hands meeting over a cradle, as the whole body of domestic fiction bears witness to their doing; and the fact that no such conjunction took place he could explain only on the ground that it was a borrowed cradle. He did not dislike the little girl. She still remained to him a hypothetical presence, a query rather than a fact; but her nearness was not unpleasant, and there were moments when her tentative utterances, her groping steps, seemed to loosen the dry accretions enveloping his inner self. But even at such moments—moments which he invited and caressed—she did not bring him nearer to his wife. He now perceived that he had made a certain place in his life for Mrs. Lethbury, and that she no longer fitted into it. It was too late to enlarge the space, and so she overflowed and encroached. Lethbury struggled against the sense of submergence. He let down barrier after barrier, yielded privacy after privacy; but his wife's personality continued to dilate. She was no longer herself alone: she was herself and Jane. Gradually, in a monstrous fusion of identity, she became herself, himself and Jane; and instead of trying to adapt her to a spare crevice of his character, he found himself carelessly squeezed into the smallest compartment of the domestic economy.

IV

HE continued to tell himself that he was satisfied if his wife was happy; and it was not till the child's tenth year that he felt a doubt of her happiness.

Jane had been a preternaturally good child. During the eight years of her adoption she had caused her foster-parents no anxiety beyond those connected with the usual succession of youthful diseases. But her unknown progenitors had given her a robust constitution, and she passed unperturbed through measles, chicken-pox and whooping-cough. If there was any suffering it was endured vicariously by Mrs. Lethbury, whose temperature rose and fell with the patient's, and who could not hear Jane sneeze without visions of a marble angel weeping over a broken column. But though Jane's prompt recoveries continued to belie such premonitions, though her existence continued to move forward on an even keel of good health and good conduct, Mrs. Lethbury's satisfaction showed no corresponding advance. Lethbury, at first, was disposed to add her disappointment to the long list of feminine inconsistencies with which the sententious observer of life builds up his favorite induction; but circumstances presently led him to take a kindlier view of the case.

Hitherto his wife had regarded him as a negligible factor in Jane's evolution. Beyond providing for his adopted daughter, and effacing himself before her, he was not expected to contribute to her well-being. But as time passed he appeared to his wife in a new light. It was he who was to educate Jane. In matters of the intellect, Mrs. Lethbury was the first to declare her deficiencies—to proclaim them, even, with a certain virtuous superiority. She said she did not pretend to be clever, and there was no denying the truth of the assertion. Now, however, she seemed less ready, not to own her limitations, but to glory in them. Confronted with the problem of Jane's instruction, she stood in awe of the child.

"I have always been stupid, you know," she said to Lethbury with a new humility, "and I'm afraid I shan't know what is best for Jane. I'm sure she has a wonderfully good mind, and I should reproach myself if I didn't give her every opportunity." She looked at him helplessly. "You must tell me what ought to be done."

Lethbury was not unwilling to oblige her. Somewhere in his mental lumber-room there rusted a theory of education such as usually lingers among the impedimenta of the childless. He brought this out, refurbished it, and applied it to Jane. At first he thought his wife had not overrated the quality of the child's mind. Jane seemed extraordinarily intelligent. Her precocious definiteness of mind was encouraging to her inexperienced preceptor. She had no difficulty in fixing her attention, and he felt that every fact he imparted was being etched in metal. He helped his wife to engage the best teachers, and for a while continued to take an ex-official interest in his adopted daughter's studies. But gradually his interest waned. Jane's ideas did not increase with her acquisitions. Her young mind remained a mere receptacle for facts: a kind of cold-storage from which anything that had been put there could be taken out at a moment's notice, intact but congealed. She developed, moreover, an inordinate pride in the capacity of her mental storehouse, and a tendency to pelt her public with its contents. She was overheard to jeer at her nurse for not knowing when the Saxon Heptarchy had fallen, and she alternately dazzled and depressed Mrs. Lethbury by the wealth of her chronological allusions. She showed no interest in the significance of the facts she amassed: she simply collected dates as another child might have collected stamps or marbles. To her foster-mother she seemed a prodigy of wisdom; but Lethbury saw, with a secret movement of sympathy, how the aptitudes in which Mrs. Lethbury gloried were slowly estranging her from their possessor.

"She is getting too clever for me," his wife said to him, after one of Jane's historical flights, "but I am so glad that she will be a companion to you."

Lethbury groaned in spirit. He did not look forward to Jane's companionship. She was still a good little girl: but there was something automatic and formal in her goodness, as though it were a kind of moral calisthenics that she went through for the sake of showing her agility. An early consciousness of virtue had moreover constituted her the natural guardian and adviser of her elders. Before she was fifteen she had set about reforming the household. She took Mrs. Lethbury in hand first; then she extended her efforts to the servants, with consequences more disastrous to the domestic harmony; and lastly she applied herself to Lethbury. She proved to him by statistics that he smoked too much, and that it was injurious to the optic nerve to read in bed. She took him to task for not going to church more regularly, and pointed out to him the evils of desultory reading. She suggested that a regular course of study encourages mental concentration, and hinted that inconsecutiveness of thought is a sign of approaching age.

To her adopted mother her suggestions were equally pertinent. She instructed Mrs. Lethbury in an improved way of making beef stock, and called her attention to the unhygienic qualities of carpets. She poured out distracting facts about bacilli and vegetable mold, and demonstrated that curtains and picture-frames are a hot-bed of animal organisms. She learned by heart the nutritive ingredients of the principal articles of diet, and revolutionized the cuisine by an attempt to establish a scientific average between starch and phosphates. Four cooks left during this experiment, and Lethbury fell into the habit of dining at his club.

Once or twice, at the outset, he had tried to check Jane's ardor; but his efforts resulted only in hurting his wife's feelings. Jane remained impervious, and Mrs. Lethbury resented any attempt to protect her from her daughter. Lethbury saw that she was consoled for the sense of her own inferiority by the thought of what Jane's intellectual companionship must be to him; and he tried to keep up the illusion by enduring with what grace he might the blighting edification of Jane's discourse.

V

AS Jane grew up, he sometimes avenged himself by wondering if his wife was still sorry that they had not called her Muriel. Jane was not ugly; she developed, indeed, a kind of categorical prettiness that might have been a projection of her mind. She had a creditable collection of features, but one had to take an inventory of them to find out that she was good-looking. The fusing grace had been omitted.

Mrs. Lethbury took a touching pride in her daughter's first steps in the world. She expected Jane to take by her complexion those whom she did not capture by her learning. But Jane's rosy freshness did not work any perceptible ravages. Whether the young men guessed the axioms on her lips and detected the encyclopedia in her eye, or whether they simply found no intrinsic interest in these features, certain it is, that, in spite of her mother's heroic efforts, and of incessant calls on Lethbury's purse, Jane, at the end of her first season, had dropped hopelessly out of the running. A few duller girls found her interesting, and one or two young men came to the house with the object of meeting other young women; but she was rapidly becoming one of the social supernumeraries who are asked out only because they are on people's lists.

The blow was bitter to Mrs. Lethbury; but she consoled herself with the idea that Jane had failed because she was too clever. Jane probably shared this conviction; at all events she betrayed no consciousness of failure. She had developed a pronounced taste for society, and went out, unweariedly and obstinately, winter after winter, while Mrs. Lethbury toiled in her wake, showering attentions on oblivious hostesses. To Lethbury there was something at once tragic and exasperating in the sight of their two figures, the one conciliatory, the other dogged, both pursuing with unabated zeal the elusive prize of popularity. He even began to feel a personal stake in the pursuit, not as it concerned Jane, but as it affected his wife. He saw that the latter was the victim of Jane's disappointment: that Jane was not above the crude satisfaction of "taking it out" of her mother. Experience checked the impulse to come to his wife's defence; and when his resentment was at its height, Jane disarmed him by giving up the struggle.

Nothing was said to mark her capitulation; but Lethbury noticed that the visiting ceased, and that the dressmaker's bills diminished. At the same time, Mrs. Lethbury made it known that Jane had taken up charities; and before long Jane's conversation confirmed this announcement. At first Lethbury congratulated himself on the change; but Jane's domesticity soon began to weigh on him. During the day she was sometimes absent on errands of mercy; but in the evening she was always there. At first she and Mrs. Lethbury sat in the drawing-room together, and Lethbury smoked in the library; but presently Jane formed the habit of joining him there, and he began to suspect that he was included among the objects of her philanthropy.

Mrs. Lethbury confirmed the suspicion. "Jane has grown very serious-minded lately," she said. "She imagines that she used to neglect you, and she is trying to make up for it. Don't discourage her," she added innocently.

Such a plea delivered Lethbury helpless to his daughter's ministrations: and he found himself measuring the hours he spent with her by the amount of relief they must be affording her mother. There were even moments when he read a furtive gratitude in Mrs. Lethbury's eye.

But Lethbury was no hero, and he had nearly reached the limit of vicarious endurance when something wonderful happened. They never quite knew afterward how it had come about, or who first perceived it; but Mrs. Lethbury one day gave tremulous voice to their inferences.

"Of course," she said, "he comes here because of Elise." The young lady in question, a friend of Jane's, was possessed of attractions which had already been found to explain the presence of masculine visitors.

Lethbury risked a denial. "I don't think he does," he declared.

"But Elise is thought very pretty," Mrs. Lethbury insisted.

"I can't help that," said Lethbury doggedly.

He saw a faint light in his wife's eyes; but she remarked carelessly: "Mr. Budd would be a very good match for Elise."

Lethbury could hardly repress a chuckle: he was so exquisitely aware that she was trying to propitiate the gods.

For a few weeks neither said a word; then Mrs. Lethbury once more reverted to the subject.

"It is a month since Elise went abroad," she said.

"Is it?"

"And Mr. Budd seems to come here just as often—"

"Ah," said Lethbury with heroic indifference; and his wife hastily changed the subject.

Mr. Winstanley Budd was a young man who suffered from an excess of manner. Politeness gushed from him in the driest seasons. He was always performing feats of drawing-room chivalry, and the approach of the most unobtrusive female threw him into attitudes which endangered the furniture. His features, being of the cherubic order, did not lend themselves to this role; but there were moments when he appeared to dominate them, to force them into compliance with an aquiline ideal. The range of Mr. Budd's social benevolence made its object hard to distinguish. He spread his cloak so indiscriminately that one could not always interpret the gesture, and Jane's impassive manner had the effect of increasing his demonstrations: she threw him into paroxysms of politeness.

At first he filled the house with his amenities; but gradually it became apparent that his most dazzling effects were directed exclusively to Jane. Lethbury and his wife held their breath and looked away from each other. They pretended not to notice the frequency of Mr. Budd's visits, they struggled against an imprudent inclination to leave the young people too much alone. Their conclusions were the result of indirect observation, for neither of them dared to be caught watching Mr. Budd: they behaved like naturalists on the trail of a rare butterfly.

In his efforts not to notice Mr. Budd, Lethbury centered his attentions on Jane; and Jane, at this crucial moment, wrung from him a reluctant admiration. While her parents went about dissembling their emotions, she seemed to have none to conceal. She betrayed neither eagerness nor surprise; so complete was her unconcern that there were moments when Lethbury feared it was obtuseness, when he could hardly help whispering to her that now was the moment to lower the net.

Meanwhile the velocity of Mr. Budd's gyrations increased with the ardor of courtship: his politeness became incandescent, and Jane found herself the center of a pyrotechnical display culminating in the "set piece" of an offer of marriage.

Mrs. Lethbury imparted the news to her husband one evening after their daughter had gone to bed. The announcement was made and received with an air of detachment, as though both feared to be betrayed into unseemly exultation; but Lethbury, as his wife ended, could not repress the inquiry, "Have they decided on a day?"

Mrs. Lethbury's superior command of her features enabled her to look shocked. "What can you be thinking of? He only offered himself at five!"

"Of course—of course—" stammered Lethbury—"but nowadays people marry after such short engagements—"

"Engagement!" said his wife solemnly. "There is no engagement."

Lethbury dropped his cigar. "What on earth do you mean?"

"Jane is thinking it over."

"*Thinking it over?*"

"She has asked for a month before deciding."

Lethbury sank back with a gasp. Was it genius or was it madness? He felt incompetent to decide; and Mrs. Lethbury's next words showed that she shared his difficulty.

"Of course I don't want to hurry Jane—"

"Of course not," he acquiesced.

"But I pointed out to her that a young man of Mr. Budd's impulsive temperament might—might be easily discouraged—"

"Yes; and what did she say?"

"She said that if she was worth winning she was worth waiting for."

## VI

THE period of Mr. Budd's probation could scarcely have cost him as much mental anguish as it caused his would-be parents-in-law.

Mrs. Lethbury, by various ruses, tried to shorten the ordeal, but Jane remained inexorable; and each morning Lethbury came down to breakfast with the certainty of finding a letter of withdrawal from her discouraged suitor.

When at length the decisive day came, and Mrs. Lethbury, at its close, stole into the library with an air of chastened joy, they stood for a moment without speaking; then Mrs. Lethbury paid a fitting tribute to the proprieties by faltering out: "It will be dreadful to have to give her up—"

Lethbury could not repress a warning gesture; but even as it escaped him, he realized that his wife's grief was genuine.

"Of course, of course," he said, vainly sounding his own emotional shallows for an answering regret. And yet it was his wife who had suffered most from Jane!

He had fancied that these sufferings would be effaced by the milder atmosphere of their last weeks together; but felicity did not soften Jane. Not for a moment did she relax her dominion: she simply widened it to include a new subject. Mr. Budd found himself under orders with the others; and a new fear assailed Lethbury as he saw Jane assume prenuptial control of her betrothed. Lethbury had never felt any strong personal interest in Mr. Budd; but, as Jane's prospective husband, the young man excited his sympathy. To his surprise, he found that Mrs. Lethbury shared the feeling.

"I'm afraid he may find Jane a little exacting," she said, after an evening dedicated to a stormy discussion of the wedding arrangements. "She really ought to make some concessions. If he wants to be married in a black frock-coat instead of a dark gray one—" She paused and looked doubtfully at Lethbury.

"What can I do about it?" he said.

"You might explain to him—tell him that Jane isn't always—"

Lethbury made an impatient gesture. "What are you afraid of? His finding her out or his not finding her out?"

Mrs. Lethbury flushed. "You put it so dreadfully!"

Her husband mused for a moment; then he said with an air of cheerful hypocrisy: "After all, Budd is old enough to take care of himself."

But the next day Mrs. Lethbury surprised him. Late in the afternoon she entered the library, so breathless and inarticulate that he scented a catastrophe.

"I've done it!" she cried.

"Done what?"

"Told him." She nodded toward the door. "He's just gone. Jane is out, and I had a chance to talk to him alone."

Lethbury pushed a chair forward and she sank into it.

"What did you tell him? That she is *not* always—"

Mrs. Lethbury lifted a tragic eye. "No; I told him that she always *is*—"

"Always *is*—?"

"Yes."

There was a pause. Lethbury made a call on his hoarded philosophy. He saw Jane suddenly reinstated in her evening seat by the library fire; but an answering chord in him thrilled at his wife's heroism.

"Well—what did he say?"

Mrs. Lethbury's agitation deepened. It was clear that the blow had fallen.

"He . . . he said . . . that we . . . had never understood Jane . . . or appreciated her . . . " The final syllables were lost in her handkerchief, and she left him marveling at the mechanism of a woman.

After that, Lethbury faced the future with an undaunted eye. They had done their duty—at least his wife had done hers—and they were reaping the usual harvest of ingratitude with a zest seldom accorded to such reaping. There was a marked change in Mr. Budd's manner, and his increasing coldness sent a genial glow through Lethbury's system. It was easy to bear with Jane in the light of Mr. Budd's disapproval.

There was a good deal to be borne in the last days, and the brunt of it fell on Mrs. Lethbury. Jane marked her transition to the married state by an appropriate but incongruous display of nerves. She became sentimental, hysterical and reluctant. She quarreled with her betrothed and threatened to return the ring. Mrs. Lethbury had to intervene, and Lethbury felt the hovering sword of destiny. But the blow was suspended. Mr. Budd's chivalry was proof against all his bride's caprices, and his devotion throve on her cruelty. Lethbury feared that he was too faithful, too enduring, and longed to urge him to vary his tactics. Jane presently reappeared with the ring on her finger, and consented to try on the wedding-dress; but her uncertainties, her reactions, were prolonged till the final day.

When it dawned, Lethbury was still in an ecstasy of apprehension. Feeling reasonably sure of the principal actors, he had centered his fears on incidental possibilities. The clergyman might have a stroke, or the church might burn down, or there might be something wrong with the license. He did all that was humanly possible to avert such contingencies, but there remained that incalculable factor known as the hand of God. Lethbury seemed to feel it groping for him.

At the altar it almost had him by the nape. Mr. Budd was late; and for five immeasurable minutes Lethbury and Jane faced a churchful of conjecture. Then the bridegroom appeared, flushed but chivalrous, and explaining to his father-in-law under cover of the ritual that he had torn his glove and had to go back for another.

"You'll be losing the ring next," muttered Lethbury; but Mr. Budd produced this article punctually, and a moment or two later was bearing its wearer captive down the aisle.

At the wedding breakfast Lethbury caught his wife's eye fixed on him in mild disapproval, and understood that his hilarity was exceeding the bounds of fitness. He pulled himself together, and tried to subdue his tone; but his jubilation bubbled over like a champagne-glass perpetually refilled. The deeper his draughts, the higher it rose.

It was at the brim when, in the wake of the dispersing guests, Jane came down in her travelling-dress and fell on her mother's neck.

"I can't leave you!" she wailed, and Lethbury felt as suddenly sobered as a man under a douche. But if the bride was reluctant her captor was relentless. Never had Mr. Budd been more dominant, more aquiline. Lethbury's last fears were dissipated as the young man snatched Jane from her mother's bosom and bore her off to the brougham.

The brougham rolled away, the last milliner's girl forsook her post by the awning, the red carpet was folded up, and the house door closed. Lethbury stood alone in the hall with his wife. As he turned toward her, he noticed the look of tired heroism in her eyes, the deepened lines of her face. They reflected his own symptoms too accurately not to appeal to him. The nervous tension had been horrible. He went up to her, and an answering impulse made her lay a hand on his arm. He held it there a moment.

"Let us go off and have a jolly little dinner at a restaurant," he proposed.

There had been a time when such a suggestion would have surprised her to the verge of disapproval; but now she agreed to it at once.

"Oh, that would be so nice," she murmured with a great sigh of relief and assuagement.

Jane had fulfilled her mission after all: she had drawn them together at last.

## THE OTHER TWO

WAYTHORN, on the drawing-room hearth, waited for his wife to come down to dinner.

It was their first night under his own roof, and he was surprised at his thrill of boyish agitation. He was not so old, to be sure—his glass gave him little more than the five-and-thirty years to which his wife confessed—but he had fancied himself already in the temperate zone; yet here he was listening for her step with a tender sense of all it symbolized, with some old trail of verse about the garlanded nuptial door-posts floating through his enjoyment of the pleasant room and the good dinner just beyond it.

They had been hastily recalled from their honeymoon by the illness of Lily Haskett, the child of Mrs. Waythorn's first marriage. The little girl, at Waythorn's desire, had been transferred to his house on the day of her mother's wedding, and the doctor, on their arrival, broke the news that she was ill with typhoid, but declared that all the symptoms were favorable. Lily could show twelve years of unblemished health, and the case promised to be a light one. The nurse spoke as reassuringly, and after a moment of alarm Mrs. Waythorn had adjusted herself to the situation. She was very fond of Lily—her affection for the child had perhaps been her decisive charm in Waythorn's eyes—but she had the perfectly balanced nerves which her little girl had inherited, and no woman ever wasted less tissue in unproductive worry. Waythorn was therefore quite prepared to see her come in presently, a little late because of a last look at Lily, but as serene and well-appointed as if her good-night kiss had been laid on the brow of health. Her composure was restful to him; it acted as ballast to his somewhat unstable sensibilities. As he pictured her bending over the child's bed he thought how soothing her presence must be in illness: her very step would prognosticate recovery.

His own life had been a gray one, from temperament rather than circumstance, and he had been drawn to her by the unperturbed gayety which kept her fresh and elastic at an age when most women's activities are growing either slack or febrile. He knew what was said about her; for, popular as she was, there had always been a faint undercurrent of detraction. When she had appeared in New York, nine or ten years earlier, as the pretty Mrs. Haskett whom Gus Varick had unearthed somewhere—was it in Pittsburgh or Utica?—society, while promptly accepting her, had reserved the right to cast a doubt on its own discrimination. Inquiry, however, established her undoubted connection with a socially reigning family, and explained her recent divorce as the natural result of a runaway match at seventeen; and as nothing was known of Mr. Haskett it was easy to believe the worst of him.

Alice Haskett's remarriage with Gus Varick was a passport to the set whose recognition she coveted, and for a few years the Varicks were the most popular couple in town. Unfortunately the alliance was brief and stormy, and this time the husband had his champions. Still, even Varick's stanchest supporters admitted that he was not meant for matrimony, and Mrs. Varick's grievances were of a nature to bear the inspection of the New York courts. A New York divorce is in itself a diploma of virtue, and in the semi-widowhood of this second separation Mrs. Varick took on an air of sanctity, and was allowed to confide her wrongs to some of the most scrupulous ears in town. But when it was known that she was to marry Waythorn there was a momentary reaction. Her best friends would have preferred to see her remain in the role of the injured wife, which was as becoming to her as crape to a rosy complexion. True, a decent time had elapsed, and it was not even suggested that Waythorn had supplanted his predecessor. Still, people shook their heads over him, and one grudging friend, to whom he affirmed that he took the step with his eyes open, replied oracularly: "Yes—and with your ears shut."

Waythorn could afford to smile at these innuendoes. In the Wall Street phrase, he had "discounted" them. He knew that society has not yet adapted itself to the consequences of divorce, and that till the adaptation takes place every woman who uses the freedom the law accords her must be her own social justification. Waythorn had an amused confidence in his wife's ability to justify herself. His expectations were fulfilled, and before the wedding took place Alice Varick's group had rallied openly to her support. She took it all imperturbably: she had a way of surmounting obstacles without seeming to be aware of them, and Waythorn looked back with wonder at the trivialities over which he had worn his nerves thin. He had the sense of having found refuge in a richer, warmer nature than his own, and his satisfaction, at the moment, was humorously summed up in the thought that his wife, when she had done all she could for Lily, would not be ashamed to come down and enjoy a good dinner.

The anticipation of such enjoyment was not, however, the sentiment expressed by Mrs. Waythorn's charming face when she presently joined him. Though she had put on her most engaging tea gown she had neglected to assume the smile that went with it, and Waythorn thought he had never seen her look so nearly worried.

"What is it?" he asked. "Is anything wrong with Lily?"

"No; I've just been in and she's still sleeping." Mrs. Waythorn hesitated. "But something tiresome has happened."

He had taken her two hands, and now perceived that he was crushing a paper between them.

"This letter?"

"Yes—Mr. Haskett has written—I mean his lawyer has written."

Waythorn felt himself flush uncomfortably. He dropped his wife's hands.

"What about?"

"About seeing Lily. You know the courts—"

"Yes, yes," he interrupted nervously.

Nothing was known about Haskett in New York. He was vaguely supposed to have remained in the outer darkness from which his wife had been rescued, and Waythorn was one of the few who were aware that he had given up his business in Utica and followed her to New York in order to be near his little girl. In the days of his wooing, Waythorn had often met Lily on the doorstep, rosy and smiling, on her way "to see papa."

"I am so sorry," Mrs. Waythorn murmured.

He roused himself. "What does he want?"

"He wants to see her. You know she goes to him once a week."

"Well—he doesn't expect her to go to him now, does he?"

"No—he has heard of her illness; but he expects to come here."

"*Here?*"

Mrs. Waythorn reddened under his gaze. They looked away from each other. "I'm afraid he has the right....You'll see...." She made a proffer of the letter. Waythorn moved away with a gesture of refusal. He stood staring about the softly lighted room, which a moment before had seemed so full of bridal intimacy.

"I'm so sorry," she repeated. "If Lily could have been moved—"

"That's out of the question," he returned impatiently.

"I suppose so."

Her lip was beginning to tremble, and he felt himself a brute.

"He must come, of course," he said. "When is—his day?"

"I'm afraid—tomorrow."

"Very well. Send a note in the morning."

The butler entered to announce dinner.

Waythorn turned to his wife. "Come—you must be tired. It's beastly, but try to forget about it," he said, drawing her hand through his arm.

"You're so good, dear. I'll try," she whispered back.

Her face cleared at once, and as she looked at him across the flowers, between the rosy candle-shades, he saw her lips waver back into a smile.

"How pretty everything is!" she sighed luxuriously.

He turned to the butler. "The champagne at once, please. Mrs. Waythorn is tired."

In a moment or two their eyes met above the sparkling glasses. Her own were quite clear and untroubled: he saw that she had obeyed his injunction and forgotten.

## II

WAYTHORN, the next morning, went down town earlier than usual. Haskett was not likely to come till the afternoon, but the instinct of flight drove him forth. He meant to stay away all day—he had thoughts of dining at his club. As his door closed behind him he reflected that before he opened it again it would have admitted another man who had as much right to enter it as himself, and the thought filled him with a physical repugnance.

He caught the elevated at the employees' hour, and found himself crushed between two layers of pendulous humanity. At Eighth Street the man facing him wriggled out and another took his place. Waythorn glanced up and saw that it was Gus Varick. The men were so close together that it was impossible to ignore the smile of recognition on Varick's handsome overblown face. And after all—why not? They had always been on good terms, and Varick had been divorced before Waythorn's attentions to his wife began. The two exchanged a word on the perennial grievance of the congested trains, and when a seat at their side was miraculously left empty the instinct of self-preservation made Waythorn slip into it after Varick.

The latter drew the stout man's breath of relief. "Lord—I was beginning to feel like a pressed flower." He leaned back, looking unconcernedly at Waythorn. "Sorry to hear that Sellers is knocked out again."

"Sellers?" echoed Waythorn, starting at his partner's name.

Varick looked surprised. "You didn't know he was laid up with the gout?"

"No. I've been away—I only got back last night." Waythorn felt himself reddening in anticipation of the other's smile.

"Ah—yes; to be sure. And Sellers's attack came on two days ago. I'm afraid he's pretty bad. Very awkward for me, as it happens, because he was just putting through a rather important thing for me."

"Ah?" Waythorn wondered vaguely since when Varick had been dealing in "important things." Hitherto he had dabbled only in the shallow pools of speculation, with which Waythorn's office did not usually concern itself.

It occurred to him that Varick might be talking at random, to relieve the strain of their propinquity. That strain was becoming momentarily more apparent to Waythorn, and when, at Cortlandt Street, he caught sight of an acquaintance, and had a sudden vision of the picture he and Varick must present to an initiated eye, he jumped up with a muttered excuse.

"I hope you'll find Sellers better," said Varick civilly, and he stammered back: "If I can be of any use to you—" and let the departing crowd sweep him to the platform.

At his office he heard that Sellers was in fact ill with the gout, and would probably not be able to leave the house for some weeks.

"I'm sorry it should have happened so, Mr. Waythorn," the senior clerk said with affable significance. "Mr. Sellers was very much upset at the idea of giving you such a lot of extra work just now."

"Oh, that's no matter," said Waythorn hastily. He secretly welcomed the pressure of additional business, and was glad to think that, when the day's work was over, he would have to call at his partner's on the way home.

He was late for luncheon, and turned in at the nearest restaurant instead of going to his club. The place was full, and the waiter hurried him to the back of the room to capture the only vacant table. In the cloud of cigar-smoke Waythorn did not at once distinguish his neighbors; but presently, looking about him, he saw Varick seated a few feet off. This time, luckily, they were too far apart for conversation, and Varick, who faced another way, had probably not even seen him; but there was an irony in their renewed nearness.

Varick was said to be fond of good living, and as Waythorn sat dispatching his hurried luncheon he looked across half enviously at the other's leisurely degustation of his meal. When Waythorn first saw him he had been helping himself with critical deliberation to a bit of Camembert at the ideal point of liquefaction, and now, the cheese removed, he was just pouring his *café double* from its little two-storied earthen pot. He poured slowly, his ruddy profile bent above the task, and one beringed white hand steadying the lid of the coffee-pot; then he stretched his other hand to the decanter of cognac at his elbow, filled a liqueur-glass, took a tentative sip, and poured the brandy into his coffee-cup.

Waythorn watched him in a kind of fascination. What was he thinking of—only of the flavor of the coffee and the liqueur? Had the morning's meeting left no more trace in his thoughts than on his face? Had his wife so completely passed out of his life that even this odd encounter with her present husband, within a week after her remarriage, was no more than an incident in his day? And as Waythorn mused, another idea struck him: had Haskett ever met Varick as Varick and he had just met? The recollection of Haskett perturbed him, and he rose and left the restaurant, taking a circuitous way out to escape the placid irony of Varick's nod.

It was after seven when Waythorn reached home. He thought the footman who opened the door looked at him oddly.

"How is Miss Lily?" he asked in haste.

"Doing very well, sir. A gentleman—"

"Tell Barlow to put off dinner for half an hour," Waythorn cut him off, hurrying upstairs.

He went straight to his room and dressed without seeing his wife. When he reached the drawing-room she was there, fresh and radiant. Lily's day had been good; the doctor was not coming back that evening.

At dinner Waythorn told her of Sellers's illness and of the resulting complications. She listened sympathetically, adjuring him not to let himself be overworked, and asking vague feminine questions about the routine of the office. Then she gave him the chronicle of Lily's day; quoted the nurse and doctor, and told him who had called to inquire. He had never seen her more serene and unruffled. It struck him, with a curious pang, that she was very happy in being with him, so happy that she found a childish pleasure in rehearsing the trivial incidents of her day.

After dinner they went to the library, and the servant put the coffee and liqueurs on a low table before her and left the room. She looked singularly soft and girlish in her rosy pale dress, against the dark leather of one of his bachelor armchairs. A day earlier the contrast would have charmed him.

He turned away now, choosing a cigar with affected deliberation.

"Did Haskett come?" he asked, with his back to her.

"Oh, yes—he came."

"You didn't see him, of course?"

She hesitated a moment. "I let the nurse see him."

That was all. There was nothing more to ask. He swung round toward her, applying a match to his cigar. Well, the thing was over for a week, at any rate. He would try not to think of it. She looked up at him, a trifle rosier than usual, with a smile in her eyes.

"Ready for your coffee, dear?"

He leaned against the mantelpiece, watching her as she lifted the coffee-pot. The lamplight struck a gleam from her bracelets and tipped her soft hair with brightness. How light and slender she was, and how each gesture flowed into the next! She seemed a creature all compact of harmonies. As the thought of Haskett receded, Waythorn felt himself yielding again to the joy of possessorship. They were his, those white hands with their flitting motions, his the light haze of hair, the lips and eyes. . . .

She set down the coffee-pot, and reaching for the decanter of cognac, measured off a liqueur-glass and poured it into his cup.

Waythorn uttered a sudden exclamation.

"What is the matter?" she said, startled.

"Nothing; only—I don't take cognac in my coffee."

"Oh, how stupid of me," she cried.

Their eyes met, and she blushed a sudden agonized red.

### III

TEN days later, Mr. Sellers, still house-bound, asked Waythorn to call on his way down town.

The senior partner, with his swaddled foot propped up by the fire, greeted his associate with an air of embarrassment.

"I'm sorry, my dear fellow; I've got to ask you to do an awkward thing for me."

Waythorn waited, and the other went on, after a pause apparently given to the arrangement of his phrases: "The fact is, when I was knocked out I had just gone into a rather complicated piece of business for—Gus Varick."

"Well?" said Waythorn, with an attempt to put him at his ease.

"Well—it's this way: Varick came to me the day before my attack. He had evidently had an inside tip from somebody, and had made about a hundred thousand. He came to me for advice, and I suggested his going in with Vanderlyn."

"Oh, the deuce!" Waythorn exclaimed. He saw in a flash what had happened. The investment was an alluring one, but required negotiation. He listened intently while Sellers put the case before him, and, the statement ended, he said: "You think I ought to see Varick?"

"I'm afraid I can't as yet. The doctor is obdurate. And this thing can't wait. I hate to ask you, but no one else in the office knows the ins and outs of it."

Waythorn stood silent. He did not care a farthing for the success of Varick's venture, but the honor of the office was to be considered, and he could hardly refuse to oblige his partner.

"Very well," he said, "I'll do it."

That afternoon, apprised by telephone, Varick called at the office. Waythorn, waiting in his private room, wondered what the others thought of it. The newspapers, at the time of Mrs. Waythorn's marriage, had acquainted their readers with every detail of her previous matrimonial ventures, and Waythorn could fancy the clerks smiling behind Varick's back as he was ushered in.

Varick bore himself admirably. He was easy without being undignified, and Waythorn was conscious of cutting a much less impressive figure. Varick had no head for business, and the talk prolonged itself for nearly an hour while Waythorn set forth with scrupulous precision the details of the proposed transaction.

"I'm awfully obliged to you," Varick said as he rose. "The fact is I'm not used to having much money to look after, and I don't want to make an ass of myself—" He smiled, and Waythorn could not help noticing that there was something pleasant about his smile. "It feels uncommonly queer to have enough cash to pay one's bills. I'd have sold my soul for it a few years ago!"

Waythorn winced at the allusion. He had heard it rumored that a lack of funds had been one of the determining causes of the Varick separation, but it did not occur to him that Varick's words were intentional. It seemed more likely that the desire to keep clear of embarrassing topics had fatally drawn him into one. Waythorn did not wish to be outdone in civility.

"We'll do the best we can for you," he said. "I think this is a good thing you're in."

"Oh, I'm sure it's immense. It's awfully good of you—" Varick broke off, embarrassed. "I suppose the thing's settled now—but if—"

"If anything happens before Sellers is about, I'll see you again," said Waythorn quietly. He was glad, in the end, to appear the more self-possessed of the two.

The course of Lily's illness ran smooth, and as the days passed Waythorn grew used to the idea of Haskett's weekly visit. The first time the day came round, he stayed out late, and questioned his wife as to the visit on his return. She replied at once that Haskett had merely seen the nurse downstairs, as the doctor did not wish any one in the child's sick-room till after the crisis.

The following week Waythorn was again conscious of the recurrence of the day, but had forgotten it by the time he came home to dinner. The crisis of the disease came a few days later, with a rapid decline of fever, and the little girl was pronounced out of danger. In the rejoicing which ensued the thought of Haskett passed out of Waythorn's mind and one afternoon, letting himself into the house with a latchkey, he went straight to his library without noticing a shabby hat and umbrella in the hall.

In the library he found a small effaced-looking man with a thinnish gray beard sitting on the edge of a chair. The stranger might have been a piano-tuner, or one of those mysteriously efficient persons who are summoned in emergencies to adjust some detail of the domestic machinery. He blinked at Waythorn through a pair of gold-rimmed spectacles and said mildly: "Mr. Waythorn, I presume? I am Lily's father."

Waythorn flushed. "Oh—" he stammered uncomfortably. He broke off, disliking to appear rude. Inwardly he was trying to adjust the actual Haskett to the image of him projected by his wife's reminiscences. Waythorn had been allowed to infer that Alice's first husband was a brute.

"I am sorry to intrude," said Haskett, with his over-the-counter politeness.

"Don't mention it," returned Waythorn, collecting himself. "I suppose the nurse has been told?"

"I presume so. I can wait," said Haskett. He had a resigned way of speaking, as though life had worn down his natural powers of resistance.

Waythorn stood on the threshold, nervously pulling off his gloves.

"I'm sorry you've been detained. I will send for the nurse," he said; and as he opened the door he added with an effort: "I'm glad we can give you a good report of Lily." He winced as the we slipped out, but Haskett seemed not to notice it.

"Thank you, Mr. Waythorn. It's been an anxious time for me."

"Ah, well, that's past. Soon she'll be able to go to you." Waythorn nodded and passed out.

In his own room, he flung himself down with a groan. He hated the womanish sensibility which made him suffer so acutely from the grotesque chances of life. He had known when he married that his wife's former husbands were both living, and that amid the multiplied contacts of modern existence there were a thousand chances to one that he would run against one or the other, yet he found himself as much disturbed by his brief encounter with Haskett as though the law had not obligingly removed all difficulties in the way of their meeting.

Waythorn sprang up and began to pace the room nervously. He had not suffered half so much from his two meetings with Varick. It was Haskett's presence in his own house that made the situation so intolerable. He stood still, hearing steps in the passage.

"This way, please," he heard the nurse say. Haskett was being taken upstairs, then: not a corner of the house but was open to him. Waythorn dropped into another chair, staring vaguely ahead of him. On his dressing-table stood a photograph of Alice, taken when he had first known her. She was Alice Varick then—how fine and exquisite he had thought her! Those were Varick's pearls about her neck. At Waythorn's instance they had been returned before her marriage. Had Haskett ever given her any trinkets—and what had become of them, Waythorn wondered? He realized suddenly that he knew very little of Haskett's past or present situation; but from the man's appearance and manner of speech he could reconstruct with curious precision the surroundings of Alice's first marriage. And it startled him to think that she had, in the background of her life, a phase of existence so different from anything with which he had connected her. Varick, whatever his faults, was a gentleman, in the conventional, traditional sense of the term: the sense which at that moment seemed, oddly enough, to have most meaning to Waythorn. He and Varick had the same social habits, spoke the same language, understood the same allusions. But this other man...it was grotesquely uppermost in Waythorn's mind that Haskett had worn a made-up tie attached with an elastic. Why should that ridiculous detail symbolize the whole man? Waythorn was exasperated by his own paltriness, but the fact of the tie expanded, forced itself on him, became as it were the key to Alice's past. He could see her, as Mrs. Haskett, sitting in a "front parlor" furnished in plush, with a pianola, and a copy of *Ben Hur* on the center table. He could see her going to the theatre with Haskett—or perhaps even to a "Church Sociable"—she in a "picture hat" and Haskett in a black frock-coat, a little creased, with the made-up tie on an elastic. On the way home they would stop and look at the illuminated shop-windows, lingering over the photographs of New York actresses. On Sunday afternoons Haskett would take her for a walk, pushing Lily ahead of them in a white enameled perambulator, and Waythorn had a vision of the people they would stop and talk to. He could fancy how pretty Alice must have looked, in a dress adroitly constructed from the hints of a New York fashion-paper; how she must have looked down on the other women, chafing at her life, and secretly feeling that she belonged in a bigger place.

For the moment his foremost thought was one of wonder at the way in which she had shed the phase of existence which her marriage with Haskett implied. It was as if her whole aspect, every gesture, every inflection, every allusion, were a studied negation of that period of her life. If she had denied being married to Haskett she could hardly have stood more convicted of duplicity than in this obliteration of the self which had been his wife.

Waythorn started up, checking himself in the analysis of her motives. What right had he to create a fantastic effigy of her and then pass judgment on it? She had spoken vaguely of her first marriage as unhappy, had hinted, with becoming reticence, that Haskett had wrought havoc among her young illusions....It was a pity for Waythorn's peace of mind that Haskett's very inoffensiveness shed a new light on the nature of those illusions. A man would rather think that his wife has been brutalized by her first husband than that the process has been reversed.

IV

"MR. WAYTHORN, I don't like that French governess of Lily's."

Haskett, subdued and apologetic, stood before Waythorn in the library, revolving his shabby hat in his hand.

Waythorn, surprised in his armchair over the evening paper, stared back perplexedly at his visitor.

"You'll excuse my asking to see you," Haskett continued. "But this is my last visit, and I thought if I could have a word with you it would be a better way than writing to Mrs. Waythorn's lawyer."

Waythorn rose uneasily. He did not like the French governess either; but that was irrelevant.

"I am not so sure of that," he returned stiffly; "but since you wish it I will give your message to—my wife." He always hesitated over the possessive pronoun in addressing Haskett.

The latter sighed. "I don't know as that will help much. She didn't like it when I spoke to her."

Waythorn turned red. "When did you see her?" he asked.

"Not since the first day I came to see Lily—right after she was taken sick. I remarked to her then that I didn't like the governess."

Waythorn made no answer. He remembered distinctly that, after that first visit, he had asked his wife if she had seen Haskett. She had lied to him then, but she had respected his wishes since; and the incident cast a curious light on her character. He was sure she would not have seen Haskett that first day if she had divined that Waythorn would object, and the fact that she did not divine it was almost as disagreeable to the latter as the discovery that she had lied to him.

"I don't like the woman," Haskett was repeating with mild persistency. "She ain't straight, Mr. Waythorn—she'll teach the child to be underhand. I've noticed a change in Lily—she's too anxious to please—and she don't always tell the truth. She used to be the straightest child, Mr. Waythorn—" He broke off, his voice a little thick. "Not but what I want her to have a stylish education," he ended.

Waythorn was touched. "I'm sorry, Mr. Haskett; but frankly, I don't quite see what I can do."

Haskett hesitated. Then he laid his hat on the table, and advanced to the hearth-rug, on which Waythorn was standing. There was nothing aggressive in his manner; but he had the solemnity of a timid man resolved on a decisive measure.

"There's just one thing you can do, Mr. Waythorn," he said. "You can remind Mrs. Waythorn that, by the decree of the courts, I am entitled to have a voice in Lily's bringing up." He paused, and went on more deprecatingly: "I'm not the kind to talk about enforcing my rights, Mr. Waythorn. I don't know as I think a man is entitled to rights he hasn't known how to hold on to; but this business of the child is different. I've never let go there—and I never mean to."

The scene left Waythorn deeply shaken. Shamefacedly, in indirect ways, he had been finding out about Haskett; and all that he had learned was favorable. The little man, in order to be near his daughter, had sold out his share in a profitable business in Utica, and accepted a modest clerkship in a New York manufacturing house. He boarded in a shabby street and had few acquaintances. His passion for Lily filled his life. Waythorn felt that this exploration of Haskett was like groping about with a dark-lantern in his wife's past; but he saw now that there were recesses his lantern had not explored. He had never inquired into the exact circumstances of his wife's first matrimonial rupture. On the surface all had been fair. It was she who had obtained the divorce, and the court had given her the child. But Waythorn knew how many ambiguities such a verdict might cover. The mere fact that Haskett retained a right over his daughter implied an unsuspected compromise. Waythorn was an idealist. He always refused to recognize unpleasant contingencies till he found himself confronted with them, and then he saw them followed by a special train of consequences. His next days were thus haunted, and he determined to try to lay the ghosts by conjuring them up in his wife's presence.

When he repeated Haskett's request a flame of anger passed over her face; but she subdued it instantly and spoke with a slight quiver of outraged motherhood.

"It is very ungentlemanly of him," she said.

The word grated on Waythorn. "That is neither here nor there. It's a bare question of rights."

She murmured: "It's not as if he could ever be a help to Lily—"

Waythorn flushed. This was even less to his taste. "The question is," he repeated, "what authority has he over her?"

She looked downward, twisting herself a little in her seat. "I am willing to see him—I thought you objected," she faltered.

In a flash he understood that she knew the extent of Haskett's claims. Perhaps it was not the first time she had resisted them.

"My objecting has nothing to do with it," he said coldly; "if Haskett has a right to be consulted you must consult him."

She burst into tears, and he saw that she expected him to regard her as a victim.

Haskett did not abuse his rights. Waythorn had felt miserably sure that he would not. But the governess was dismissed, and from time to time the little man demanded an interview with Alice. After the first outburst she accepted the situation with her usual adaptability. Haskett had once reminded Waythorn of the piano-tuner, and Mrs. Waythorn, after a month or two, appeared to class him with that domestic familiar. Waythorn could not but respect the father's tenacity. At first he had tried to cultivate the suspicion that Haskett might be "up to" something, that he had an object in securing a foothold in the house. But in his heart Waythorn was sure of Haskett's single-mindedness; he even guessed in the latter a mild contempt for such advantages as his relation with the Waythorns might offer. Haskett's sincerity of purpose made him invulnerable, and his successor had to accept him as a lien on the property.

Mr. Sellers was sent to Europe to recover from his gout, and Varick's affairs hung on Waythorn's hands. The negotiations were prolonged and complicated; they necessitated frequent conferences between the two men, and the interests of the firm forbade Waythorn's suggesting that his client should transfer his business to another office.

Varick appeared well in the transaction. In moments of relaxation his coarse streak appeared, and Waythorn dreaded his geniality; but in the office he was concise and clear-headed, with a flattering deference to Waythorn's judgment. Their business relations being so affably established, it would have been absurd for the two men to ignore each other in society. The first time they met in a drawing-room, Varick took up their intercourse in the same easy key, and his hostess's grateful glance obliged Waythorn to respond to it. After that they ran across each other frequently, and one evening at a ball Waythorn, wandering through the remoter rooms, came upon Varick seated beside his wife. She colored a little, and faltered in what she was saying; but Varick nodded to Waythorn without rising, and the latter strolled on.

In the carriage, on the way home, he broke out nervously: "I didn't know you spoke to Varick."

Her voice trembled a little. "It's the first time—he happened to be standing near me; I didn't know what to do. It's so awkward, meeting everywhere—and he said you had been very kind about some business."

"That's different," said Waythorn.

She paused a moment. "I'll do just as you wish," she returned pliantly. "I thought it would be less awkward to speak to him when we meet."

Her pliancy was beginning to sicken him. Had she really no will of her own—no theory about her relation to these men? She had accepted Haskett—did she mean to accept Varick? It was "less awkward," as she had said, and her instinct was to evade difficulties or to circumvent them. With sudden vividness Waythorn saw how the instinct had developed. She was "as easy as an old shoe"—a shoe that too many feet had worn. Her elasticity was the result of tension in too many different directions. Alice Haskett— Alice Varick—Alice Waythorn—she had been each in turn, and had left hanging to each name a little of her privacy, a little of her personality, a little of the inmost self where the unknown god abides.

"Yes—it's better to speak to Varick," said Waythorn wearily.

V

THE winter wore on, and society took advantage of the Waythorns' acceptance of Varick. Harassed hostesses were grateful to them for bridging over a social difficulty, and Mrs. Waythorn was held up as a miracle of good taste. Some experimental spirits could not resist the diversion of throwing Varick and his former wife together, and there were those who thought he found a zest in the propinquity. But Mrs. Waythorn's conduct remained irreproachable. She neither avoided Varick nor sought him out. Even Waythorn could not but admit that she had discovered the solution of the newest social problem.

He had married her without giving much thought to that problem. He had fancied that a woman can shed her past like a man. But now he saw that Alice was bound to hers both by the circumstances which forced her into continued relation with it, and by the traces it had left on her nature. With grim irony Waythorn compared himself to a member of a syndicate. He held so many shares in his wife's personality and his predecessors were his partners in the business. If there had been any element of passion in the transaction he would have felt less deteriorated by it. The fact that Alice took her change of husbands like a change of weather reduced the situation to mediocrity. He could have forgiven her for blunders, for excesses; for resisting Hackett, for yielding to Varick; for anything but her acquiescence and her tact. She reminded him of a juggler tossing knives; but the knives were blunt and she knew they would never cut her.

And then, gradually, habit formed a protecting surface for his sensibilities. If he paid for each day's comfort with the small change of his illusions, he grew daily to value the comfort more and set less store upon the coin. He had drifted into a dulling propinquity with Haskett and Varick and he took refuge in the cheap revenge of satirizing the situation. He even began to reckon up the advantages which accrued from it, to ask himself if it were not better to own a third of a wife who knew how to make a man happy than a whole one who had lacked opportunity to acquire the art. For it *was* an art, and made up, like all others, of concessions, eliminations and embellishments; of lights judiciously thrown and shadows skillfully softened. His wife knew exactly how to manage the lights, and he knew exactly to what training she owed her skill. He even tried to trace the source of his obligations, to discriminate between the influences which had combined to produce his domestic happiness: he perceived that Haskett's commonness had made Alice worship good breeding, while Varick's liberal construction of the marriage bond had taught her to value the conjugal virtues; so that he was directly indebted to his predecessors for the devotion which made his life easy if not inspiring.

From this phase he passed into that of complete acceptance. He ceased to satirize himself because time dulled the irony of the situation and the joke lost its humor with its sting. Even the sight of Haskett's hat on the hall table had ceased to touch the springs of epigram. The hat was often seen there now, for it had been decided that it was better for Lily's father to visit her than for the little girl to go to his boarding-house. Waythorn, having acquiesced in this arrangement, had been surprised to find how little difference it made. Haskett was never obtrusive, and the few visitors who met him on the stairs were unaware of his identity. Waythorn did not know how often he saw Alice, but with himself Haskett was seldom in contact.

One afternoon, however, he learned on entering that Lily's father was waiting to see him. In the library he found Haskett occupying a chair in his usual provisional way. Waythorn always felt grateful to him for not leaning back.

"I hope you'll excuse me, Mr. Waythorn," he said rising. "I wanted to see Mrs. Waythorn about Lily, and your man asked me to wait here till she came in."

"Of course," said Waythorn, remembering that a sudden leak had that morning given over the drawing room to the plumbers.

He opened his cigar case and held it out to his visitor, and Haskett's acceptance seemed to mark a fresh stage in their intercourse. The spring evening was chilly, and Waythorn invited his guest to draw up his chair to the fire. He meant to find an excuse to leave Haskett in a moment; but he was tired and cold, and after all the little man no longer jarred on him.

The two were enclosed in the intimacy of their blended cigar-smoke when the door opened and Varick walked into the room. Waythorn rose abruptly. It was the first time that Varick had come to the house, and the surprise of seeing him, combined with the singular inopportuneness of his arrival, gave a new edge to Waythorn's blunted sensibilities. He stared at his visitor without speaking.

Varick seemed too preoccupied to notice his host's embarrassment.

"My dear fellow," he exclaimed in his most expansive tone, "I must apologize for tumbling in on you in this way, but I was too late to catch you down town, and so I thought—"

He stopped short, catching sight of Haskett, and his sanguine color deepened to a flush which spread vividly under his scant blond hair. But in a moment he recovered himself and nodded slightly. Haskett returned the bow in silence, and Waythorn was still groping for speech when the footman came in carrying a tea table.

The intrusion offered a welcome vent to Waythorn's nerves. "What the deuce are you bringing this here for?" he said sharply.

"I beg your pardon, sir, but the plumbers are still in the drawing-room, and Mrs. Waythorn said she would have tea in the library." The footman's perfectly respectful tone implied a reflection on Waythorn's reasonableness.

"Oh, very well," said the latter resignedly, and the footman proceeded to open the folding tea-table and set out its complicated appointments. While this interminable process continued the three men stood motionless, watching it with a fascinated stare, till Waythorn, to break the silence, said to Varick: "Won't you have a cigar?"

He held out the case he had just tendered to Haskett, and Varick helped himself with a smile. Waythorn looked about for a match, and finding none, proffered a light from his own cigar. Haskett, in the background, held his ground mildly, examining his cigar-tip now and then, and stepping forward at the right moment to knock its ashes into the fire.

The footman at last withdrew, and Varick immediately began: "If I could just say half a word to you about this business—"

"Certainly," stammered Waythorn; "in the dining-room—"

But as he placed his hand on the door it opened from without, and his wife appeared on the threshold.

She came in fresh and smiling, in her street dress and hat, shedding a fragrance from the boa which she loosened in advancing.

"Shall we have tea in here, dear?" she began; and then she caught sight of Varick. Her smile deepened, veiling a slight tremor of surprise. "Why, how do you do?" she said with a distinct note of pleasure.

As she shook hands with Varick she saw Haskett standing behind him. Her smile faded for a moment, but she recalled it quickly, with a scarcely perceptible side-glance at Waythorn.

"How do you do, Mr. Haskett?" she said, and shook hands with him a shade less cordially.

The three men stood awkwardly before her, till Varick, always the most self-possessed, dashed into an explanatory phrase.

"We—I had to see Waythorn a moment on business," he stammered, brick-red from chin to nape.

Haskett stepped forward with his air of mild obstinacy. "I am sorry to intrude; but you appointed five o'clock—" he directed his resigned glance to the time-piece on the mantel.

She swept aside their embarrassment with a charming gesture of hospitality.

"I'm so sorry—I'm always late; but the afternoon was so lovely." She stood drawing her gloves off, propitiatory and graceful, diffusing about her a sense of ease and familiarity in which the situation lost its grotesqueness. "But before talking business," she added brightly, "I'm sure every one wants a cup of tea."

She dropped into her low chair by the tea-table, and the two visitors, as if drawn by her smile, advanced to receive the cups she held out.

She glanced about for Waythorn, and he took the third cup with a laugh.

## THE QUICKSAND

AS MRS. QUENTIN'S victoria, driving homeward, turned from the Park into Fifth Avenue, she divined her son's tall figure walking ahead of her in the twilight. His long stride covered the ground more rapidly than usual, and she had a premonition that, if he were going home at that hour, it was because he wanted to see her.

Mrs. Quentin, though not a fanciful woman, was sometimes aware of a sixth sense enabling her to detect the faintest vibrations of her son's impulses. She was too shrewd to fancy herself the one mother in possession of this faculty, but she permitted herself to think that few could exercise it more discreetly. If she could not help overhearing Alan's thoughts, she had the courage to keep her discoveries to herself, the tact to take for granted nothing that lay below the surface of their spoken intercourse: she knew that most people would rather have their letters read than their thoughts. For this superfeminine discretion Alan repaid her by—being Alan. There could have been no completer reward. He was the key to the meaning of life, the justification of what must have seemed as incomprehensible as it was odious, had it not all-sufficingly ended in himself. He was a perfect son, and Mrs. Quentin had always hungered for perfection.

Her house, in a minor way, bore witness to the craving. One felt it to be the result of a series of eliminations: there was nothing fortuitous in its blending of line and color. The almost morbid finish of every material detail of her life suggested the possibility that a diversity of energies had, by some pressure of circumstance, been forced into the channel of a narrow dilettantism. Mrs. Quentin's fastidiousness had, indeed, the flaw of being too one-sided. Her friends were not always worthy of the chairs they sat in, and she overlooked in her associates defects she would not have tolerated in her bric-a-brac. Her house was, in fact, never so distinguished as when it was empty; and it was at its best in the warm fire-lit silence that now received her.

Her son, who had overtaken her on the door-step, followed her into the drawing-room, and threw himself into an armchair near the fire, while she laid off her furs and busied herself about the tea table. For a while neither spoke; but glancing at him across the kettle, his mother noticed that he sat staring at the embers with a look she had never seen on his face, though its arrogant young outline was as familiar to her as her own thoughts. The look extended itself to his negligent attitude, to the droop of his long fine hands, the dejected tilt of his head against the cushions. It was like the moral equivalent of physical fatigue: he looked, as he himself would have phrased it, dead-beat, played out. Such an air was so foreign to his usual bright indomitableness that Mrs. Quentin had the sense of an unfamiliar presence, in which she must observe herself, must raise hurried barriers against an alien approach. It was one of the drawbacks of their excessive intimacy that any break in it seemed a chasm.

She was accustomed to let his thoughts circle about her before they settled into speech, and she now sat in motionless expectancy, as though a sound might frighten them away.

At length, without turning his eyes from the fire, he said: "I'm so glad you're a nice old-fashioned intuitive woman. It's painful to see them think."

Her apprehension had already preceded him. "Hope Fenno—?" she faltered.

He nodded. "She's been thinking—hard. It was very painful—to me, at least; and I don't believe she enjoyed it: she said she didn't." He stretched his feet to the fire. "The result of her cogitations is that she won't have me. She arrived at this by pure ratiocination—it's not a question of feeling, you understand. I'm the only man she's ever loved—but she won't have me. What novels did you read when you were young, dear? I'm convinced it all turns on that. If she'd been brought up on Trollope and Whyte-Melville, instead of Tolstoi and Mrs. Ward, we should have now been vulgarly sitting on a sofa, trying on the engagement-ring."

Mrs. Quentin at first was kept silent by the mother's instinctive anger that the girl she has not wanted for her son should have dared to refuse him. Then she said, "Tell me, dear."

"My good woman, she has scruples."

"Scruples?"

"Against the paper. She objects to me in my official capacity as owner of the *Radiator*."

His mother did not echo his laugh.

"She had found a solution, of course—she overflows with expedients. I was to chuck the paper, and we were to live happily ever afterward on canned food and virtue. She even had an alternative ready—women are so full of resources! I was to turn the Radiator into an independent organ, and run it at a loss to show the public what a model newspaper ought to be. On the whole, I think she fancied this plan more than the other—it commended itself to her as being more uncomfortable and aggressive. It's not the fashion nowadays to be good by stealth."

Mrs. Quentin said to herself, "I didn't know how much he cared!" Aloud she murmured, "You must give her time."

"Time?"

"To move out the old prejudices and make room for new ones."

"My dear mother, those she has are brand-new; that's the trouble with them. She's tremendously up-to-date. She takes in all the moral fashion-papers, and wears the newest thing in ethics."

Her resentment lost its way in the intricacies of his metaphor. "Is she so very religious?"

"You dear archaic woman! She's hopelessly irreligious; that's the difficulty. You can make a religious woman believe almost anything: there's the habit of credulity to work on. But when a girl's faith in the Deluge has been shaken, it's very hard to inspire her with confidence. She makes you feel that, before believing in you, it's her duty as a conscientious agnostic to find out whether you're not obsolete, or whether the text isn't corrupt, or somebody hasn't proved conclusively that you never existed, anyhow."

Mrs. Quentin was again silent. The two moved in that atmosphere of implications and assumptions where the lightest word may shake down the dust of countless stored impressions; and speech was sometimes more difficult between them than had their union been less close.

Presently she ventured, "It's impossible?"

"Impossible?"

She seemed to use her words cautiously, like weapons that might slip and inflict a cut. "What she suggests."

Her son, raising himself, turned to look at her for the first time. Their glance met in a shock of comprehension. He was with her against the girl, then! Her satisfaction overflowed in a murmur of tenderness.

"Of course not, dear. One can't change—change one's life...."

"One's self," he emended. "That's what I tell her. What's the use of my giving up the paper if I keep my point of view?"

The psychological distinction attracted her. "Which is it she minds most?"

"Oh, the paper—for the present. She undertakes to modify the point of view afterward. All she asks is that I shall renounce my heresy: the gift of grace will come later."

Mrs. Quentin sat gazing into her untouched cup. Her son's first words had produced in her the hallucinated sense of struggling in the thick of a crowd that he could not see. It was horrible to feel herself hemmed in by influences imperceptible to him; yet if anything could have increased her misery it would have been the discovery that her ghosts had become visible.

As though to divert his attention, she precipitately asked, "Are you—?"

His answer carried the shock of an evocation. "I merely asked her what she thought of *you*."

"Of me?"

"She admires you immensely, you know."

For a moment Mrs. Quentin's cheek showed the lingering light of girlhood: praise transmitted by her son acquired something of the transmitter's merit. "Well—?" she smiled.

"Well—you didn't make my father give up the *Radiator*, did you?"

His mother, stiffening, made a circuitous return: "She never comes here. How can she know me?"

"She's so poor! She goes out so little." He rose and leaned against the mantel-piece, dislodging with impatient fingers a slender bronze wrestler poised on a porphyry base, between two warm-toned Spanish ivories. "And then her mother—" he added, as if involuntarily.

"Her mother has never visited me," Mrs. Quentin finished for him.

He shrugged his shoulders. "Mrs. Fenno has the scope of a wax doll. Her rule of conduct is taken from her grandmother's sampler."

"But the daughter is so modern—and yet—"

"The result is the same? Not exactly. *She* admires you—oh, immensely!" He replaced the bronze and turned to his mother with a smile. "Aren't you on some hospital committee together? What especially strikes her is your way of doing good. She says philanthropy is not a line of conduct, but a state of mind—and it appears that you are one of the elect."

As, in the vague diffusion of physical pain, relief seems to come with the acuter pang of a single nerve, Mrs. Quentin felt herself suddenly eased by a rush of anger against the girl. "If she loved you—" she began.

His gesture checked her. "I'm not asking you to get her to do that."

The two were again silent, facing each other in the disarray of a common catastrophe—as though their thoughts, at the summons of danger, had rushed naked into action. Mrs. Quentin, at this revealing moment, saw for the first time how many elements of her son's character had seemed comprehensible simply because they were familiar: as, in reading a foreign language, we take the meaning of certain words for granted till the context corrects us. Often as in a given case, her maternal musings had figured his conduct, she now found herself at a loss to forecast it; and with this failure of intuition came a sense of the subserviency which had hitherto made her counsels but the anticipation of his wish. Her despair escaped in the moan, "What *is* it you ask me?"

"To talk to her."

"Talk to her?"

"Show her—tell her—make her understand that the paper has always been a thing outside your life—that hasn't touched you—that needn't touch *her*. Only, let her hear you—watch you—be with you—she'll see...she can't help seeing..."

His mother faltered. "But if she's given you her reasons—?"

"Let her give them to you! If she can—when she sees you...." His impatient hand again displaced the wrestler. "I care abominably," he confessed.

## II

ON the Fenno threshold a sudden sense of the futility of the attempt had almost driven Mrs. Quentin back to her carriage; but the door was already opening, and a parlor-maid who believed that Miss Fenno was in led the way to the depressing drawing-room. It was the kind of room in which no member of the family is likely to be found except after dinner or after death. The chairs and tables looked like poor relations who had repaid their keep by a long career of grudging usefulness: they seemed banded together against intruders in a sullen conspiracy of discomfort. Mrs. Quentin, keenly susceptible to such influences, read failure in every angle of the upholstery. She was incapable of the vulgar error of thinking that Hope Fenno might be induced to marry Alan for his money; but between this assumption and the inference that the girl's imagination might be touched by the finer possibilities of wealth, good taste admitted a distinction. The Fenno furniture, however, presented to such reasoning the obtuseness of its black-walnut chamferings; and something in its attitude suggested that its owners would be as uncompromising. The room showed none of the modern attempts at palliation, no apologetic draping of facts; and Mrs. Quentin, provisionally perched on a green-reps Gothic sofa with which it was clearly impossible to establish any closer relations, concluded that, had Mrs. Fenno needed another seat of the same size, she would have set out placidly to match the one on which her visitor now languished.

To Mrs. Quentin's fancy, Hope Fenno's opinions, presently imparted in a clear young voice from the opposite angle of the Gothic sofa, partook of the character of their surroundings. The girl's mind was like a large light empty place, scantily furnished with a few massive prejudices, not designed to add to any one's comfort but too ponderous to be easily moved. Mrs. Quentin's own intelligence, in which its owner, in an artistically shaded half-light, had so long moved amid a delicate complexity of sensations, seemed in comparison suddenly close and crowded; and in taking refuge there from the glare of the young girl's candor, the older woman found herself stumbling in an unwonted obscurity. Her uneasiness resolved itself into a sense of irritation against her listener. Mrs. Quentin knew that the momentary value of any argument lies in the capacity of the mind to which it is addressed, and as her shafts of persuasion spent themselves against Miss Fenno's obduracy, she said to herself that, since conduct is governed by emotions rather than ideas, the really strong people are those who mistake their sensations for opinions. Viewed in this light, Miss Fenno was certainly very strong: there was an unmistakable ring of finality in the tone with which she declared:

"It's impossible."

Mrs. Quentin's answer veiled the least shade of feminine resentment. "I told Alan that, where he had failed, there was no chance of my making an impression."

Hope Fenno laid on her visitor's an almost reverential hand. "Dear Mrs. Quentin, it's the impression you make that confirms the impossibility."

Mrs. Quentin waited a moment: she was perfectly aware that, where her feelings were concerned, her sense of humor was not to be relied on. "Do I make such an odious impression?" she asked at length, with a smile that seemed to give the girl her choice of two meanings.

"You make such a beautiful one! It's too beautiful—it obscures my judgment."

Mrs. Quentin looked at her thoughtfully. "Would it be permissible, I wonder, for an older woman to suggest that, at your age, it isn't always a misfortune to have what one calls one's judgment temporarily obscured?"

Miss Fenno flushed. "I try not to judge others—"

"You judge Alan."

"Ah, *he* is not others," she murmured, with an accent that touched the older woman.

"You judge his mother."

"I don't; I don't!"

Mrs. Quentin pressed her point. "You judge yourself, then, as you would be in my position—and your verdict condemns me."

"How can you think it? It's because I appreciate the difference in our point of view that I find it so difficult to defend myself—"

"Against what?"

"The temptation to imagine that I might be as *you* are—feeling as I do."

Mrs. Quentin rose with a sigh. "My child, in my day love was less subtle." She added, after a moment, "Alan is a perfect son."

"Ah, that again—that makes it worse!"

"Worse?"

"Just as your goodness does, your sweetness, your immense indulgence in letting me discuss things with you in a way that must seem almost an impertinence."

Mrs. Quentin's smile was not without irony. "You must remember that I do it for Alan."

"That's what I love you for!" the girl instantly returned; and again her tone touched her listener.

"And yet you're sacrificing him—and to an idea!"

"Isn't it to ideas that all the sacrifices that were worth-while have been made?"

"One may sacrifice one's self."

Miss Fenno's color rose. "That's what I'm doing," she said gently.

Mrs. Quentin took her hand. "I believe you are," she answered. "And it isn't true that I speak only for Alan. Perhaps I did when I began; but now I want to plead for you too—against yourself." She paused, and then went on with a deeper note: "I have let you, as you say, speak your mind to me in terms that some women might have resented, because I wanted to show you how little, as the years go on, theories, ideas, abstract conceptions of life, weigh against the actual, against the particular way in which life presents itself to us—to women especially. To decide beforehand exactly how one ought to behave in given circumstances is like deciding that one will follow a certain direction in crossing an unexplored country. Afterward we find that we must turn out for the obstacles—cross the rivers where they're shallowest—take the tracks that others have beaten—make all sorts of unexpected concessions. Life is made up of compromises: that is what youth refuses to understand. I've lived long enough to doubt whether any real good ever came of sacrificing beautiful facts to even more beautiful theories. Do I seem casuistical? I don't know—there may be losses either way...but the love of the man one loves...of the child one loves... that makes up for everything...."

She had spoken with a thrill which seemed to communicate itself to the hand her listener had left in hers. Her eyes filled suddenly, but through their dimness she saw the girl's lips shape a last desperate denial:

"Don't you see it's because I feel all this that I mustn't—that I can't?"

III

MRS. QUENTIN, in the late spring afternoon, had turned in at the doors of the Metropolitan Museum. She had been walking in the Park, in a solitude oppressed by the ever-present sense of her son's trouble, and had suddenly remembered that some one had added a Beltraffio to the collection. It was an old habit of Mrs. Quentin's to seek in the enjoyment of the beautiful the distraction that most of her acquaintances appeared to find in each other's company. She had few friends, and their society was welcome to her only in her more superficial moods; but she could drug anxiety with a picture as some women can soothe it with a bonnet.

During the six months that had elapsed since her visit to Miss Fenno she had been conscious of a pain of which she had supposed herself no longer capable: as a man will continue to feel the ache of an amputated arm. She had fancied that all her centers of feeling had been transferred to Alan; but she now found herself subject to a kind of dual suffering, in which her individual pang was the keener in that it divided her from her son's. Alan had surprised her: she had not foreseen that he would take a sentimental rebuff so hard. His disappointment took the uncommunicative form of a sterner application to work. He threw himself into the concerns of the *Radiator* with an aggressiveness that almost betrayed itself in the paper. Mrs. Quentin never read the *Radiator*, but from the glimpses of it reflected in the other journals she gathered that it was at least not being subjected to the moral reconstruction which had been one of Miss Fenno's alternatives.

Mrs. Quentin never spoke to her son of what had happened. She was superior to the cheap satisfaction of avenging his injury by depreciating its cause. She knew that in sentimental sorrows such consolations are as salt in the wound. The avoidance of a subject so vividly present to both could not but affect the closeness of their relation. An invisible presence hampered their liberty of speech and thought. The girl was always between them; and to hide the sense of her intrusion they began to be less frequently together. It was then that Mrs. Quentin measured the extent of her isolation. Had she ever dared to forecast such a situation, she would have proceeded on the conventional theory that her son's suffering must draw her nearer to him; and this was precisely the relief that was denied her. Alan's uncommunicativeness extended below the level of speech, and his mother, reduced to the helplessness of dead-reckoning, had not even the solace of adapting her sympathy to his needs. She did not know what he felt: his course was incalculable to her. She sometimes wondered if she had become as incomprehensible to him; and it was to find a moment's refuge from the dogging misery of such conjectures that she had now turned in at the Museum.

The long line of mellow canvases seemed to receive her into the rich calm of an autumn twilight. She might have been walking in an enchanted wood where the footfall of care never sounded. So deep was the sense of seclusion that, as she turned from her prolonged communion with the new Beltraffio, it was a surprise to find she was not alone.

A young lady who had risen from the central ottoman stood in suspended flight as Mrs. Quentin faced her. The older woman was the first to regain her self-possession.

"Miss Fenno!" she said.

The girl advanced with a blush. As it faded, Mrs. Quentin noticed a change in her. There had always been something bright and banner-like in her aspect, but now her look drooped, and she hung at half-mast, as it were. Mrs. Quentin, in the embarrassment of surprising a secret that its possessor was doubtless unconscious of betraying, reverted hurriedly to the Beltraffio.

"I came to see this," she said. "It's very beautiful."

Miss Fenno's eye travelled incuriously over the mystic blue reaches of the landscape. "I suppose so," she assented; adding, after another tentative pause, "You come here often, don't you?"

"Very often," Mrs. Quentin answered. "I find pictures a great help."

"A help?"

"A rest, I mean...if one is tired or out of sorts."

"Ah," Miss Fenno murmured, looking down.

"This Beltraffio is new, you know," Mrs. Quentin continued. "What a wonderful background, isn't it? Is he a painter who interests you?"

The girl glanced again at the dusky canvas, as though in a final endeavor to extract from it a clue to the consolations of art. "I don't know," she said at length; "I'm afraid I don't understand pictures." She moved nearer to Mrs. Quentin and held out her hand.

"You're going?"

"Yes."

Mrs. Quentin looked at her. "Let me drive you home," she said, impulsively. She was feeling, with a shock of surprise, that it gave her, after all, no pleasure to see how much the girl had suffered.

Miss Fenno stiffened perceptibly. "Thank you; I shall like the walk."

Mrs. Quentin dropped her hand with a corresponding movement of withdrawal, and a momentary wave of antagonism seemed to sweep the two women apart. Then, as Mrs. Quentin, bowing slightly, again addressed herself to the picture, she felt a sudden touch on her arm.

"Mrs. Quentin," the girl faltered, "I really came here because I saw your carriage."

Her eyes sank, and then fluttered back to her hearer's face. "I've been horribly unhappy!" she exclaimed.

Mrs. Quentin was silent. If Hope Fenno had expected an immediate response to her appeal, she was disappointed. The older woman's face was like a veil dropped before her thoughts.

"I've thought so often," the girl went on precipitately, "of what you said that day you came to see me last autumn. I think I understand now what you meant—what you tried to make me see.... Oh, Mrs. Quentin," she broke out, "I didn't mean to tell you this—I never dreamed of it till this moment—but you *do* remember what you said, don't you? You must remember it! And now that I've met you in this way, I can't help telling you that I believe—I begin to believe—that you were right, after all."

Mrs. Quentin had listened without moving; but now she raised her eyes with a slight smile. "Do you wish me to say this to Alan?" she asked.

The girl flushed, but her glance braved the smile. "Would he still care to hear it?" she said fearlessly.

Mrs. Quentin took momentary refuge in a renewed inspection of the Beltraffio; then, turning, she said, with a kind of reluctance: "He would still care."

"Ah!" broke from the girl.

During this exchange of words the two speakers had drifted unconsciously toward one of the benches. Mrs. Quentin glanced about her: a custodian who had been hovering in the doorway sauntered into the adjoining gallery, and they remained alone among the silvery Vandykes and flushed bituminous Halses. Mrs. Quentin sank down on the bench and reached a hand to the girl.

"Sit by me," she said.

Miss Fenno dropped beside her. In both women the stress of emotion was too strong for speech. The girl was still trembling, and Mrs. Quentin was the first to regain her composure.

"You say you've suffered," she began at last. "Do you suppose I haven't?"

"I knew you had. That made it so much worse for me—that I should have been the cause of your suffering for Alan!"

Mrs. Quentin drew a deep breath. "Not for Alan only," she said. Miss Fenno turned on her a wondering glance. "Not for Alan only. That pain every woman expects—and knows how to bear. We all know our children must have such disappointments, and to suffer with them is not the deepest pain. It's the suffering apart—in ways they don't understand." She breathed deeply. "I want you to know what I mean. You were right—that day—and I was wrong."

"Oh," the girl faltered.

Mrs. Quentin went on in a voice of passionate lucidity. "I knew it then—I knew it even while I was trying to argue with you—I've always known it! I didn't want my son to marry you till I heard your reasons for refusing him; and then—then I longed to see you his wife!"

"Oh, Mrs. Quentin!"

"I longed for it; but I knew it mustn't be."

"Mustn't be?"

Mrs. Quentin shook her head sadly, and the girl, gaining courage from this mute negation, cried with an uncontrollable escape of feeling:

"It's because you thought me hard, obstinate narrow-minded? Oh, I understand that so well! My self-righteousness must have seemed so petty! A girl who could sacrifice a man's future to her own moral vanity—for it *was* a form of vanity; you showed me that plainly enough—how you must have despised me! But I am not that girl now—indeed I'm not. I'm not impulsive—I think things out. I've thought this out. I know Alan loves me—I know *how* he loves me—and I believe I can help him—oh, not in the ways I had fancied before—but just merely by loving him." She paused, but Mrs. Quentin made no sign. "I see it all so differently now. I see what an influence love itself may be—how my believing in him, loving him, accepting him just as he is, might help him more than any theories, any arguments. I might have seen this long ago in looking at *you*—as he often told me—in seeing how you'd kept yourself apart from—from—Mr. Quentin's work and his—been always the beautiful side of life to them—kept their faith alive in spite of themselves—not by interfering, preaching, reforming, but by—just loving them and being there—" She looked at Mrs. Quentin with a simple nobleness. "It isn't as if I cared for the money, you know; if I cared for that, I should be afraid—"

"You will care for it in time," Mrs. Quentin said suddenly.

Miss Fenno drew back, releasing her hand. "In time?"

"Yes; when there's nothing else left." She stared a moment at the pictures. "My poor child," she broke out, "I've heard all you say so often before!"

"You've heard it?"

"Yes—from myself. I felt as you do, I argued as you do, I acted as I mean to prevent your doing, when I married Alan's father."

The long empty gallery seemed to reverberate with the girl's startled exclamation—"Oh, Mrs. Quentin—"

"Hush; let me speak. Do you suppose I'd do this if you were the kind of pink-and-white idiot he ought to have married? It's because I see you're alive, as I was, tingling with beliefs, ambitions, energies, as I was—that I can't see you walled up alive, as I was, without stretching out a hand to save you!" She sat gazing rigidly forward, her eyes on the pictures, speaking in the low precipitate tone of one who tries to press the meaning of a lifetime into a few breathless sentences.

"When I met Alan's father," she went on, "I knew nothing of his—his work. We met abroad, where I had been living with my mother. That was twenty-six years ago, when the *Radiator* was less—less notorious than it is now. I knew my husband owned a newspaper—a great newspaper—and nothing more. I had never seen a copy of the *Radiator*; I had no notion what it stood for, in politics—or in other ways. We were married in Europe, and a few months afterward we came to live here. People were already beginning to talk about the *Radiator*. My husband, on leaving college, had bought it with some money an old uncle had left him, and the public at first was merely curious to see what an ambitious, stirring young man without any experience of journalism was going to make out of his experiment. They found first of all that he was going to make a great deal of money out of it. I found that out too. I was so happy in other ways that it didn't make much difference at first; though it was pleasant to be able to help my mother, to be generous and charitable, to live in a nice house, and wear the handsome gowns he liked to see me in. But still it didn't really count—it counted so little that when, one day, I learned what the *Radiator* was, I would have gone out into the streets barefooted rather than live another hour on the money it brought in. . . ." Her voice sank, and she paused to steady it. The girl at her side did not speak or move. "I shall never forget that day," she began again. "The paper had stripped bare some family scandal—some miserable bleeding secret that a dozen unhappy people had been struggling to keep out of print— that *would* have been kept out if my husband had not—Oh, you must guess the rest! I can't go on!"

She felt a hand on hers. "You mustn't go on, Mrs. Quentin," the girl whispered.

"Yes, I must—I must! You must be made to understand." She drew a deep breath. "My husband was not like Alan. When he found out how I felt about it he was surprised at first—but gradually he began to see—or at least I fancied he saw—the hatefulness of it. At any rate he saw how I suffered, and he offered to give up the whole thing—to sell the paper. It couldn't be done all of a sudden, of course—he made me see that—for he had put all his money in it, and he had no special aptitude for any other kind of work. He was a born journalist—like Alan. It was a great sacrifice for him to give up the paper, but he promised to do it—in time—when a good opportunity offered. Meanwhile, of course, he wanted to build it up, to increase the circulation—and to do that he had to keep on in the same way—he made that clear to me. I saw that we were in a vicious circle. The paper, to sell well, had to be made more and more detestable and disgraceful. At first I rebelled—but somehow—I can't tell you how it was—after that first concession the ground seemed to give under me: with every struggle I sank deeper. And then—then Alan was born. He was such a delicate baby that there was very little hope of saving him. But money did it—the money from the paper. I took him abroad to see the best physicians—I took him to a warm climate every winter. In hot weather the doctors recommended sea air, and we had a yacht and cruised every summer. I owed his life to the *Radiator*. And when he began to grow stronger the habit was formed—the habit of luxury. He could not get on without the things he had always been used to. He pined in bad air; he drooped under monotony and discomfort; he throve on variety, amusement, travel, every kind of novelty and excitement. And all I wanted for him his inexhaustible foster-mother was there to give!

"My husband said nothing, but he must have seen how things were going. There was no more talk of giving up the *Radiator*. He never reproached me with my inconsistency, but I thought he must despise me, and the thought made me reckless. I determined to ignore the paper altogether—to take what it gave as though I didn't know where it came from. And to excuse this I invented the theory that one may, so to speak, purify money by putting it to good uses. I gave away a great deal in charity—I indulged myself very little at first. All the money that was not spent on Alan I tried to do good with. But gradually, as my boy grew up, the problem became more complicated. How was I to protect Alan from the contamination I had let him live in? I couldn't preach by example—couldn't hold up his father as a warning, or denounce the money we were living on. All I could do was to disguise the inner ugliness of life by making it beautiful outside—to build a wall of beauty between him and the facts of life, turn his tastes and interests another way, hide the *Radiator* from him as a smiling woman at a ball may hide a cancer in her breast! Just as Alan was entering college his father died. Then I saw my way clear. I had loved my husband—and yet I drew my first free breath in years. For the *Radiator* had been left to Alan outright—there was nothing on earth to prevent his selling it when he came of age. And there was no excuse for his not selling it. I had brought him up to depend on money, but the paper had given us enough money to gratify all his tastes. At last we could turn on the monster that had nourished us. I felt a savage joy in the thought—I could hardly bear to wait till Alan came of age. But I had never spoken to him of the paper, and I didn't dare speak of it now. Some false shame kept me back, some vague belief in his ignorance. I would wait till he was twenty-one, and then we should be free.

"I waited—the day came, and I spoke. You can guess his answer, I suppose. He had no idea of selling the *Radiator*. It wasn't the money he cared for—it was the career that tempted him. He was a born journalist, and his ambition, ever since he could remember, had been to carry on his father's work, to develop, to surpass it. There was nothing in the world as interesting as modern journalism. He couldn't imagine any other kind of life that wouldn't bore him to death. A newspaper like the *Radiator* might be made one of the biggest powers on earth, and he loved power, and meant to have all he could get. I listened to him in a kind of trance. I couldn't find a word to say. His father had had scruples—he had none. I seemed to realize at once that argument would be useless. I don't know that I even tried to plead with him—he was so bright and hard and inaccessible! Then I saw that he was, after all, what I had made him—the creature of my concessions, my connivances, my evasions. That was the price I had paid for him—I had kept him at that cost!

"Well—I *had* kept him, at any rate. That was the feeling that survived. He was my boy, my son, my very own—till some other woman took him. Meanwhile the old life must go on as it could. I gave up the struggle. If at that point he was inaccessible, at others he was close to me. He has always been a perfect son. Our tastes grew together— we enjoyed the same books, the same pictures, the same people. All I had to do was to look at him in profile to see the side of him that was really mine. At first I kept thinking of the dreadful other side—but gradually the impression faded, and I kept my mind turned from it, as one does from a deformity in a face one loves. I thought I had made my last compromise with life—had hit on a *modus vivendi* that would last my time.

"And then he met you. I had always been prepared for his marrying, but not a girl like you. I thought he would choose a sweet thing who would never pry into his closets— he hated women with ideas! But as soon as I saw you I knew the struggle would have to begin again. He is so much stronger than his father—he is full of the most monstrous convictions. And he has the courage of them, too—you saw last year that his love for you never made him waver. He believes in his work; he adores it—it is a kind of hideous idol to which he would make human sacrifices! He loves you still—I've been honest with you—but his love wouldn't change him. It is you who would have to change—to die gradually, as I have died, till there is only one live point left in me. Ah, if one died completely—that's simple enough! But something persists—remember that—a single point, an aching nerve of truth. Now and then you may drug it—but a touch wakes it again, as your face has waked it in me. There's always enough of one's old self left to suffer with...."

She stood up and faced the girl abruptly. "What shall I tell Alan?" she said.

Miss Fenno sat motionless, her eyes on the ground. Twilight was falling on the gallery—a twilight which seemed to emanate not so much from the glass dome overhead as from the crepuscular depths into which the faces of the pictures were receding. The custodian's step sounded warningly down the corridor. When the girl looked up she was alone.

## THE DILETTANTE

IT WAS on an impulse hardly needing the arguments he found himself advancing in its favor, that Thursdale, on his way to the club, turned as usual into Mrs. Vervain's street.

The "as usual" was his own qualification of the act; a convenient way of bridging the interval—in days and other sequences—that lay between this visit and the last. It was characteristic of him that he instinctively excluded his call two days earlier, with Ruth Gaynor, from the list of his visits to Mrs. Vervain: the special conditions attending it had made it no more like a visit to Mrs. Vervain than an engraved dinner invitation is like a personal letter. Yet it was to talk over his call with Miss Gaynor that he was now returning to the scene of that episode; and it was because Mrs. Vervain could be trusted to handle the talking over as skillfully as the interview itself that, at her corner, he had felt the dilettante's irresistible craving to take a last look at a work of art that was passing out of his possession.

On the whole, he knew no one better fitted to deal with the unexpected than Mrs. Vervain. She excelled in the rare art of taking things for granted, and Thursdale felt a pardonable pride in the thought that she owed her excellence to his training. Early in his career Thursdale had made the mistake, at the outset of his acquaintance with a lady, of telling her that he loved her and exacting the same avowal in return. The latter part of that episode had been like the long walk back from a picnic, when one has to carry all the crockery one has finished using: it was the last time Thursdale ever allowed himself to be encumbered with the debris of a feast. He thus incidentally learned that the privilege of loving her is one of the least favors that a charming woman can accord; and in seeking to avoid the pitfalls of sentiment he had developed a science of evasion in which the woman of the moment became a mere implement of the game. He owed a great deal of delicate enjoyment to the cultivation of this art. The perils from which it had been his refuge became naively harmless: was it possible that he who now took his easy way along the levels had once preferred to gasp on the raw heights of emotion? Youth is a high-colored season; but he had the satisfaction of feeling that he had entered earlier than most into that chiaroscuro of sensation where every half-tone has its value.

As a promoter of this pleasure no one he had known was comparable to Mrs. Vervain. He had taught a good many women not to betray their feelings, but he had never before had such fine material to work in. She had been surprisingly crude when he first knew her; capable of making the most awkward inferences, of plunging through thin ice, of recklessly undressing her emotions; but she had acquired, under the discipline of his reticences and evasions, a skill almost equal to his own, and perhaps more remarkable in that it involved keeping time with any tune he played and reading at sight some uncommonly difficult passages.

It had taken Thursdale seven years to form this fine talent; but the result justified the effort. At the crucial moment she had been perfect: her way of greeting Miss Gaynor had made him regret that he had announced his engagement by letter. It was an evasion that confessed a difficulty; a deviation implying an obstacle, where, by common consent, it was agreed to see none; it betrayed, in short, a lack of confidence in the completeness of his method. It had been his pride never to put himself in a position which had to be quitted, as it were, by the back door; but here, as he perceived, the main portals would have opened for him of their own accord. All this, and much more, he read in the finished naturalness with which Mrs. Vervain had met Miss Gaynor. He had never seen a better piece of work: there was no over-eagerness, no suspicious warmth, above all (and this gave her art the grace of a natural quality) there were none of those damnable implications whereby a woman, in welcoming her friend's betrothed, may keep him on pins and needles while she laps the lady in complacency. So masterly a performance, indeed, hardly needed the offset of Miss Gaynor's door-step words—"To be so kind to me, how she must have liked you!"—though he caught himself wishing it lay within the bounds of fitness to transmit them, as a final tribute, to the one woman he knew who was unfailingly certain to enjoy a good thing. It was perhaps the one drawback to his new situation that it might develop good things which it would be impossible to hand on to

Margaret Vervain.

The fact that he had made the mistake of underrating his friend's powers, the consciousness that his writing must have betrayed his distrust of her efficiency, seemed an added reason for turning down her street instead of going on to the club. He would show her that he knew how to value her; he would ask her to achieve with him a feat infinitely rarer and more delicate than the one he had appeared to avoid. Incidentally, he would also dispose of the interval of time before dinner: ever since he had seen Miss Gaynor off, an hour earlier, on her return journey to Buffalo, he had been wondering how he should put in the rest of the afternoon. It was absurd, how he missed the girl....Yes, that was it; the desire to talk about her was, after all, at the bottom of his impulse to call on Mrs. Vervain! It was absurd, if you like—but it was delightfully rejuvenating. He could recall the time when he had been afraid of being obvious: now he felt that this return to the primitive emotions might be as restorative as a holiday in the Canadian woods. And it was precisely by the girl's candor, her directness, her lack of complications, that he was taken. The sense that she might say something rash at any moment was positively exhilarating: if she had thrown her arms about him at the station he would not have given a thought to his crumpled dignity. It surprised Thursdale to find what freshness of heart he brought to the adventure; and though his sense of irony prevented his ascribing his intactness to any conscious purpose, he could but rejoice in the fact that his sentimental economies had left him such a large surplus to draw upon.

Mrs. Vervain was at home—as usual. When one visits the cemetery one expects to find the angel on the tombstone, and it struck Thursdale as another proof of his friend's good taste that she had been in no undue haste to change her habits. The whole house appeared to count on his coming; the footman took his hat and overcoat as naturally as though there had been no lapse in his visits; and the drawing-room at once enveloped him in that atmosphere of tacit intelligence which Mrs. Vervain imparted to her very furniture.

It was a surprise that, in this general harmony of circumstances, Mrs. Vervain should herself sound the first false note.

"You?" she exclaimed; and the book she held slipped from her hand.

It was crude, certainly; unless it were a touch of the finest art. The difficulty of classifying it disturbed Thursdale's balance.

"Why not?" he said, restoring the book. "Isn't it my hour?" And as she made no answer, he added gently, "Unless it's some one else's?"

She laid the book aside and sank back into her chair. "Mine, merely," she said.

"I hope that doesn't mean that you're unwilling to share it?"

"With you? By no means. You're welcome to my last crust."

He looked at her reproachfully. "Do you call this the last?"

She smiled as he dropped into the seat across the hearth. "It's a way of giving it more flavor!"

He returned the smile. "A visit to you doesn't need such condiments."

She took this with just the right measure of retrospective amusement.

"Ah, but I want to put into this one a very special taste," she confessed.

Her smile was so confident, so reassuring, that it lulled him into the imprudence of saying, "Why should you want it to be different from what was always so perfectly right?"

She hesitated. "Doesn't the fact that it's the last constitute a difference?"

"The last—my last visit to you?"

"Oh, metaphorically, I mean—there's a break in the continuity."

Decidedly, she was pressing too hard: unlearning his arts already!

"I don't recognize it," he said. "Unless you make me—" he added, with a note that slightly stirred her attitude of languid attention.

She turned to him with grave eyes. "You recognize no difference whatever?"

"None—except an added link in the chain."

"An added link?"

"In having one more thing to like you for—your letting Miss Gaynor see why I had already so many." He flattered himself that this turn had taken the least hint of fatuity from the phrase.

Mrs. Vervain sank into her former easy pose. "Was it that you came for?" she asked, almost gaily.

"If it is necessary to have a reason—that was one."

"To talk to me about Miss Gaynor?"

"To tell you how she talks about you."

"That will be very interesting—especially if you have seen her since her second visit to me."

"Her second visit?" Thursdale pushed his chair back with a start and moved to another. "She came to see you again?"

"This morning, yes—by appointment."

He continued to look at her blankly. "You sent for her?"

"I didn't have to—she wrote and asked me last night. But no doubt you have seen her since."

Thursdale sat silent. He was trying to separate his words from his thoughts, but they still clung together inextricably. "I saw her off just now at the station."

"And she didn't tell you that she had been here again?"

"There was hardly time, I suppose—there were people about—" he floundered.

"Ah, she'll write, then."

He regained his composure. "Of course she'll write: very often, I hope. You know I'm absurdly in love," he cried audaciously.

She tilted her head back, looking up at him as he leaned against the chimney-piece. He had leaned there so often that the attitude touched a pulse which set up a throbbing in her throat. "Oh, my poor Thursdale!" she murmured.

"I suppose it's rather ridiculous," he owned; and as she remained silent, he added, with a sudden break—"Or have you another reason for pitying me?"

Her answer was another question. "Have you been back to your rooms since you left her?"

"Since I left her at the station? I came straight here."

"Ah, yes—you *could*: there was no reason—" Her words passed into a silent musing.

Thursdale moved nervously nearer. "You said you had something to tell me?"

"Perhaps I had better let her do so. There may be a letter at your rooms."

"A letter? What do you mean? A letter from *her*? What has happened?"

His paleness shook her, and she raised a hand of reassurance. "Nothing has happened—perhaps that is just the worst of it. You always *hated*, you know," she added incoherently, "to have things happen: you never would let them."

"And now—?"

"Well, that was what she came here for: I supposed you had guessed. To know if anything had happened."

"Had happened?" He gazed at her slowly. "Between you and me?" he said with a rush of light.

The words were so much cruder than any that had ever passed between them that the color rose to her face; but she held his startled gaze.

"You know girls are not quite as unsophisticated as they used to be. Are you surprised that such an idea should occur to her?"

His own color answered hers: it was the only reply that came to him.

Mrs. Vervain went on, smoothly: "I supposed it might have struck you that there were times when we presented that appearance."

He made an impatient gesture. "A man's past is his own!"

"Perhaps—it certainly never belongs to the woman who has shared it. But one learns such truths only by experience; and Miss Gaynor is naturally inexperienced."

"Of course—but—supposing her act a natural one—" he floundered lamentably among his innuendoes—"I still don't see—how there was anything—"

"Anything to take hold of? There wasn't—"

"Well, then—?" escaped him, in crude satisfaction; but as she did not complete the sentence he went on with a faltering laugh: "She can hardly object to the existence of a mere friendship between us!"

"But she does," said Mrs. Vervain.

Thursdale stood perplexed. He had seen, on the previous day, no trace of jealousy or resentment in his betrothed: he could still hear the candid ring of the girl's praise of Mrs. Vervain. If she were such an abyss of insincerity as to dissemble distrust under such frankness, she must at least be more subtle than to bring her doubts to her rival for solution. The situation seemed one through which one could no longer move in a penumbra, and he let in a burst of light with the direct query: "Won't you explain what you mean?"

Mrs. Vervain sat silent, not provokingly, as though to prolong his distress, but as if, in the attenuated phraseology he had taught her, it was difficult to find words robust enough to meet his challenge. It was the first time he had ever asked her to explain anything; and she had lived so long in dread of offering elucidations which were not wanted, that she seemed unable to produce one on the spot.

At last she said slowly: "She came to find out if you were really free."

Thursdale colored again. "Free?" he stammered, with a sense of physical disgust at contact with such crassness.

"Yes—if I had quite done with you." She smiled in recovered security. "It seems she likes clear outlines; she has a passion for definitions."

"Yes—well?" he said, wincing at the echo of his own subtlety.

"Well—and when I told her that you had never belonged to me, she wanted me to define *my* status—to know exactly where I had stood all along."

Thursdale sat gazing at her intently; his hand was not yet on the clue. "And even when you had told her that—"

"Even when I had told her that I had had no status—that I had never stood anywhere, in any sense she meant," said Mrs. Vervain, slowly—"even then she wasn't satisfied, it seems."

He uttered an uneasy exclamation. "She didn't believe you, you mean?"

"I mean that she *did* believe me: too thoroughly."

"Well, then—in God's name, what did she want?"

"Something more—those were the words she used."

"Something more? Between—between you and me? Is it a conundrum?" He laughed awkwardly.

"Girls are not what they were in my day; they are no longer forbidden to contemplate the relation of the sexes."

"So it seems!" he commented. "But since, in this case, there wasn't any—" he broke off, catching the dawn of a revelation in her gaze.

"That's just it. The unpardonable offence has been—in our not offending."

He flung himself down despairingly. "I give it up!—What did you tell her?" he burst out with sudden crudeness.

"The exact truth. If I had only known," she broke off with a beseeching tenderness, "won't you believe that I would still have lied for you?"

"Lied for me? Why on earth should you have lied for either of us?"

"To save you—to hide you from her to the last! As I've hidden you from myself all these years!" She stood up with a sudden tragic import in her movement. "You believe me capable of that, don't you? If I had only guessed—but I have never known a girl like her; she had the truth out of me with a spring."

"The truth that you and I had never—"

"Had never—never in all these years! Oh, she knew why—she measured us both in a flash. She didn't suspect me of having haggled with you—her words pelted me like hail. 'He just took what he wanted—sifted and sorted you to suit his taste. Burnt out the gold and left a heap of cinders. And you let him—you let yourself be cut in bits'—she mixed her metaphors a little—'be cut in bits, and used or discarded, while all the while every drop of blood in you belonged to him! But he's Shylock—and you have bled to death of the pound of flesh he has cut out of you.' But she despises me the most, you know—far the most—" Mrs. Vervain ended.

The words fell strangely on the scented stillness of the room: they seemed out of harmony with its setting of afternoon intimacy, the kind of intimacy on which at any moment, a visitor might intrude without perceptibly lowering the atmosphere. It was as though a grand opera-singer had strained the acoustics of a private music-room.

Thursdale stood up, facing his hostess. Half the room was between them, but they seemed to stare close at each other now that the veils of reticence and ambiguity had fallen.

His first words were characteristic. "She *does* despise me, then?" he exclaimed.

"She thinks the pound of flesh you took was a little too near the heart."

He was excessively pale. "Please tell me exactly what she said of me."

"She did not speak much of you: she is proud. But I gather that while she understands love or indifference, her eyes have never been opened to the many intermediate shades of feeling. At any rate, she expressed an unwillingness to be taken with reservations—she thinks you would have loved her better if you had loved some one else first. The point of view is original—she insists on a man with a past!"

"Oh, a past—if she's serious—I could rake up a past!" he said with a laugh.

"So I suggested: but she has her eyes on his particular portion of it. She insists on making it a test case. She wanted to know what you had done to me; and before I could guess her drift I blundered into telling her."

Thursdale drew a difficult breath. "I never supposed—your revenge is complete," he said slowly.

He heard a little gasp in her throat. "My revenge? When I sent for you to warn you—to save you from being surprised as *I* was surprised?"

"You're very good—but it's rather late to talk of saving me." He held out his hand in the mechanical gesture of leave-taking.

"How you must care!—for I never saw you so dull," was her answer. "Don't you see that it's not too late for me to help you?" And as he continued to stare, she brought out sublimely: "Take the rest—in imagination! Let it at least be of that much use to you. Tell her I lied to her—she's too ready to believe it! And so, after all, in a sense, I sha'n't have been wasted."

His stare hung on her, widening to a kind of wonder. She gave the look back brightly, unblushingly, as though the expedient were too simple to need oblique approaches. It was extraordinary how a few words had swept them from an atmosphere of the most complex dissimulations to this contact of naked souls.

It was not in Thursdale to expand with the pressure of fate; but something in him cracked with it, and the rift let in new light. He went up to his friend and took her hand.

"You would do it—you would do it!"

She looked at him, smiling, but her hand shook.

"Good-bye," he said, kissing it.

"Good-bye? You are going—?"

"To get my letter."

"Your letter? The letter won't matter, if you will only do what I ask."

He returned her gaze. "I might, I suppose, without being out of character. Only, don't you see that if your plan helped me it could only harm her?"

"Harm *her*?"

"To sacrifice you wouldn't make me different. I shall go on being what I have always been—sifting and sorting, as she calls it. Do you want my punishment to fall on *her*?"

She looked at him long and deeply. "Ah, if I had to choose between you—!"

"You would let her take her chance? But I can't, you see. I must take my punishment alone."

She drew her hand away, sighing. "Oh, there will be no punishment for either of you."

"For either of us? There will be the reading of her letter for me."

She shook her head with a slight laugh. "There will be no letter."

Thursdale faced about from the threshold with fresh life in his look. "No letter? You don't mean—"

"I mean that she's been with you since I saw her—she's seen you and heard your voice. If there is a letter, she has recalled it—from the first station, by telegraph."

He turned back to the door, forcing an answer to her smile. "But in the mean while I shall have read it," he said.

The door closed on him, and she hid her eyes from the dreadful emptiness of the room.

## THE RECKONING

THE MARRIAGE LAW of the new dispensation will be: *Thou shalt not be unfaithful— to thyself.*

A discreet murmur of approval filled the studio, and through the haze of cigarette smoke Mrs. Clement Westall, as her husband descended from his improvised platform, saw him merged in a congratulatory group of ladies. Westall's informal talks on "The New Ethics" had drawn about him an eager following of the mentally unemployed—

those who, as he had once phrased it, liked to have their brain-food cut up for them. The talks had begun by accident. Westall's ideas were known to be "advanced," but hitherto their advance had not been in the direction of publicity. He had been, in his wife's opinion, almost pusillanimously careful not to let his personal views endanger his professional standing. Of late, however, he had shown a puzzling tendency to dogmatize, to throw down the gauntlet, to flaunt his private code in the face of society; and the relation of the sexes being a topic always sure of an audience, a few admiring friends had persuaded him to give his after-dinner opinions a larger circulation by summing them up in a series of talks at the Van Sideren studio.

The Herbert Van Siderens were a couple who subsisted, socially, on the fact that they had a studio. Van Sideren's pictures were chiefly valuable as accessories to the *mise en scène* which differentiated his wife's "afternoons" from the blighting functions held in long New York drawing-rooms, and permitted her to offer their friends whiskey-and-soda instead of tea. Mrs. Van Sideren, for her part, was skilled in making the most of the kind of atmosphere which a lay-figure and an easel create; and if at times she found the illusion hard to maintain, and lost courage to the extent of almost wishing that Herbert could paint, she promptly overcame such moments of weakness by calling in some fresh talent, some extraneous re-enforcement of the "artistic" impression. It was in quest of such aid that she had seized on Westall, coaxing him, somewhat to his wife's surprise, into a flattered participation in her fraud. It was vaguely felt, in the Van Sideren circle, that all the audacities were artistic, and that a teacher who pronounced marriage immoral was somehow as distinguished as a painter who depicted purple grass and a green sky. The Van Sideren set were tired of the conventional color-scheme in art and conduct.

Julia Westall had long had her own views on the immorality of marriage; she might indeed have claimed her husband as a disciple. In the early days of their union she had secretly resented his disinclination to proclaim himself a follower of the new creed; had been inclined to tax him with moral cowardice, with a failure to live up to the convictions for which their marriage was supposed to stand. That was in the first burst of propagandism, when, womanlike, she wanted to turn her disobedience into a law. Now she felt differently. She could hardly account for the change, yet being a woman who never allowed her impulses to remain unaccounted for, she tried to do so by saying that she did not care to have the articles of her faith misinterpreted by the vulgar. In this connection, she was beginning to think that almost everyone was vulgar; certainly there were few to whom she would have cared to intrust the defence of so esoteric a doctrine. And it was precisely at this point that Westall, discarding his unspoken principles, had chosen to descend from the heights of privacy, and stand hawking his convictions at the street-corner!

It was Una Van Sideren who, on this occasion, unconsciously focused upon herself Mrs. Westall's wandering resentment. In the first place, the girl had no business to be there. It was "horrid"—Mrs. Westall found herself slipping back into the old feminine vocabulary—simply "horrid" to think of a young girl's being allowed to listen to such talk. The fact that Una smoked cigarettes and sipped an occasional cocktail did not in the least tarnish a certain radiant innocency which made her appear the victim, rather than the accomplice, of her parents' vulgarities. Julia Westall felt in a hot helpless way that something ought to be done—that someone ought to speak to the girl's mother. And just then Una glided up.

"Oh, Mrs. Westall, how beautiful it was!" Una fixed her with large limpid eyes. "You believe it all, I suppose?" she asked with seraphic gravity.

"All—what, my dear child?"

The girl shone on her. "About the higher life—the freer expansion of the individual—the law of fidelity to one's self," she glibly recited.

Mrs. Westall, to her own wonder, blushed a deep and burning blush.

"My dear Una," she said, "you don't in the least understand what it's all about!"

Miss Van Sideren stared, with a slowly answering blush. "Don't you, then?" she murmured.

Mrs. Westall laughed. "Not always—or altogether! But I should like some tea, please."

Una led her to the corner where innocent beverages were dispensed. As Julia received her cup she scrutinized the girl more carefully. It was not such a girlish face, after all—definite lines were forming under the rosy haze of youth. She reflected that Una must be six-and-twenty, and wondered why she had not married. A nice stock of ideas she would have as her dower! If *they* were to be a part of the modern girl's trousseau—

Mrs. Westall caught herself up with a start. It was as though some one else had been speaking—a stranger who had borrowed her own voice: she felt herself the dupe of some fantastic mental ventriloquism. Concluding suddenly that the room was stifling and Una's tea too sweet, she set down her cup, and looked about for Westall: to meet his eyes had long been her refuge from every uncertainty. She met them now, but only, as she felt, in transit; they included her parenthetically in a larger flight. She followed the flight, and it carried her to a corner to which Una had withdrawn—one of the palmy nooks to which Mrs. Van Sideren attributed the success of her Saturdays. Westall, a moment later, had overtaken his look, and found a place at the girl's side. She bent forward, speaking eagerly; he leaned back, listening, with the depreciatory smile which acted as a filter to flattery, enabling him to swallow the strongest doses without apparent grossness of appetite. Julia winced at her own definition of the smile.

On the way home, in the deserted winter dusk, Westall surprised his wife by a sudden boyish pressure of her arm. "Did I open their eyes a bit? Did I tell them what you wanted me to?" he asked gaily.

Almost unconsciously, she let her arm slip from his. "What I wanted—?"

"Why, haven't you—all this time?" She caught the honest wonder of his tone. "I somehow fancied you'd rather blamed me for not talking more openly—before—You've made me feel, at times, that I was sacrificing principles to expediency."

She paused a moment over her reply; then she asked quietly: "What made you decide not to—any longer?"

She felt again the vibration of a faint surprise. "Why—the wish to please you!" he answered, almost too simply.

"I wish you would not go on, then," she said abruptly.

He stopped in his quick walk, and she felt his stare through the darkness.

"Not go on—?"

"Call a hansom, please. I'm tired," broke from her with a sudden rush of physical weariness.

Instantly his solicitude enveloped her. The room had been infernally hot—and then that confounded cigarette smoke—he had noticed once or twice that she looked pale—she mustn't come to another Saturday. She felt herself yielding, as she always did, to the warm influence of his concern for her, the feminine in her leaning on the man in him with a conscious intensity of abandonment. He put her in the hansom, and her hand stole into his in the darkness. A tear or two rose, and she let them fall. It was so delicious to cry over imaginary troubles!

That evening, after dinner, he surprised her by reverting to the subject of his talk. He combined a man's dislike of uncomfortable questions with an almost feminine skill in eluding them; and she knew that if he returned to the subject he must have some special reason for doing so.

"You seem not to have cared for what I said this afternoon. Did I put the case badly?"

"No—you put it very well."

"Then what did you mean by saying that you would rather not have me go on with it?"

She glanced at him nervously, her ignorance of his intention deepening her sense of helplessness.

"I don't think I care to hear such things discussed in public."

"I don't understand you," he exclaimed. Again the feeling that his surprise was genuine gave an air of obliquity to her own attitude. She was not sure that she understood herself.

"Won't you explain?" he said with a tinge of impatience.

Her eyes wandered about the familiar drawing-room which had been the scene of so many of their evening confidences. The shaded lamps, the quiet-colored walls hung with mezzotints, the pale spring flowers scattered here and there in Venice glasses and bowls of old Sevres, recalled, she hardly knew why, the apartment in which the evenings of her first marriage had been passed—a wilderness of rosewood and upholstery, with a picture of a Roman peasant above the mantel-piece, and a Greek slave in "statuary marble" between the folding-doors of the back drawing-room. It was a room with which she had never been able to establish any closer relation than that between a traveller and a railway station; and now, as she looked about at the surroundings which stood for her deepest affinities—the room for which she had left that other room—she was startled by the same sense of strangeness and unfamiliarity. The prints, the flowers, the subdued tones of the old porcelains, seemed to typify a superficial refinement that had no relation to the deeper significances of life.

Suddenly she heard her husband repeating his question.

"I don't know that I can explain," she faltered.

He drew his arm-chair forward so that he faced her across the hearth. The light of a reading-lamp fell on his finely drawn face, which had a kind of surface-sensitiveness akin to the surface-refinement of its setting.

"Is it that you no longer believe in our ideas?" he asked.

"In our ideas—?"

"The ideas I am trying to teach. The ideas you and I are supposed to stand for." He paused a moment. "The ideas on which our marriage was founded."

The blood rushed to her face. He had his reasons, then—she was sure now that he had his reasons! In the ten years of their marriage, how often had either of them stopped to consider the ideas on which it was founded? How often does a man dig about the basement of his house to examine its foundation? The foundation is there, of course—the house rests on it—but one lives abovestairs and not in the cellar. It was she, indeed, who in the beginning had insisted on reviewing the situation now and then, on recapitulating the reasons which justified her course, on proclaiming, from time to time, her adherence to the religion of personal independence; but she had long ceased to feel the need of any such ideal standards, and had accepted her marriage as frankly and naturally as though it had been based on the primitive needs of the heart, and needed no special sanction to explain or justify it.

"Of course I still believe in our ideas!" she exclaimed.

"Then I repeat that I don't understand. It was a part of your theory that the greatest possible publicity should be given to our view of marriage. Have you changed your mind in that respect?"

She hesitated. "It depends on circumstances—on the public one is addressing. The set of people that the Van Siderens get about them don't care for the truth or falseness of a doctrine. They are attracted simply by its novelty."

"And yet it was in just such a set of people that you and I met, and learned the truth from each other."

"That was different."

"In what way?"

"I thought you considered it one of the deepest social wrongs that such things never *are* discussed before young girls; but that is beside the point, for I don't remember seeing any young girl in my audience to-day—"

"Except Una Van Sideren!"

He turned slightly and pushed back the lamp at his elbow.

"Oh, Miss Van Sideren—naturally—"

"Why naturally?"

"The daughter of the house—would you have had her sent out with her governess?"

"If I had a daughter I should not allow such things to go on in my house!"

Westall, stroking his mustache, leaned back with a faint smile. "I fancy Miss Van Sideren is quite capable of taking care of herself."

"No girl knows how to take care of herself—till it's too late."

"And yet you would deliberately deny her the surest means of self-defence?"

"What do you call the surest means of self-defence?"

"Some preliminary knowledge of human nature in its relation to the marriage tie."

She made an impatient gesture. "How should you like to marry that kind of a girl?"

"Immensely—if she were my kind of girl in other respects."

She took up the argument at another point.

"You are quite mistaken if you think such talk does not affect young girls. Una was in a state of the most absurd exaltation—" She broke off, wondering why she had spoken.

Westall reopened a magazine which he had laid aside at the beginning of their discussion. "What you tell me is immensely flattering to my oratorical talent—but I fear you overrate its effect. I can assure you that Miss Van Sideren doesn't have to have her thinking done for her. She's quite capable of doing it herself."

"You seem very familiar with her mental processes!" flashed unguardedly from his wife.

He looked up quietly from the pages he was cutting.

"I should like to be," he answered. "She interests me."

## II

IF there be a distinction in being misunderstood, it was one denied to Julia Westall when she left her first husband. Everyone was ready to excuse and even to defend her. The world she adorned agreed that John Arment was "impossible," and hostesses gave a sigh of relief at the thought that it would no longer be necessary to ask him to dine.

There had been no scandal connected with the divorce: neither side had accused the other of the offence euphemistically described as "statutory." The Arments had indeed been obliged to transfer their allegiance to a State which recognized desertion as a cause for divorce, and construed the term so liberally that the seeds of desertion were shown to exist in every union. Even Mrs. Arment's second marriage did not make traditional morality stir in its sleep. It was known that she had not met her second husband till after she had parted from the first, and she had, moreover, replaced a rich man by a poor one. Though Clement Westall was acknowledged to be a rising lawyer, it was generally felt that his fortunes would not rise as rapidly as his reputation. The Westalls would probably always have to live quietly and go out to dinner in cabs. Could there be better evidence of Mrs. Arment's complete disinterestedness?

If the reasoning by which her friends justified her course was somewhat cruder and less complex than her own elucidation of the matter, both explanations led to the same conclusion: John Arment was impossible. The only difference was that, to his wife, his impossibility was something deeper than a social disqualification. She had once said, in ironical defence of her marriage, that it had at least preserved her from the necessity of sitting next to him at dinner; but she had not then realized at what cost the immunity was purchased. John Arment was impossible; but the sting of his impossibility lay in the fact that he made it impossible for those about him to be other than himself. By an unconscious process of elimination he had excluded from the world everything of which he did not feel a personal need: had become, as it were, a climate in which only his own requirements survived. This might seem to imply a deliberate selfishness; but there was nothing deliberate about Arment. He was as instinctive as an animal or a child. It was this childish element in his nature which sometimes for a moment unsettled his wife's estimate of him. Was it possible that he was simply undeveloped, that he had delayed, somewhat longer than is usual, the laborious process of growing up? He had the kind of sporadic shrewdness which causes it to be said of a dull man that he is "no fool"; and it was this quality that his wife found most trying. Even to the naturalist it is annoying to have his deductions disturbed by some unforeseen aberrancy of form or function; and how much more so to the wife whose estimate of herself is inevitably bound up with her judgment of her husband!

Arment's shrewdness did not, indeed, imply any latent intellectual power; it suggested, rather, potentialities of feeling, of suffering, perhaps, in a blind rudimentary way, on which Julia's sensibilities naturally declined to linger. She so fully understood her own reasons for leaving him that she disliked to think they were not as comprehensible to her husband. She was haunted, in her analytic moments, by the look of perplexity, too inarticulate for words, with which he had acquiesced to her explanations.

These moments were rare with her, however. Her marriage had been too concrete a misery to be surveyed philosophically. If she had been unhappy for complex reasons, the unhappiness was as real as though it had been uncomplicated. Soul is more bruisable than flesh, and Julia was wounded in every fiber of her spirit. Her husband's personality seemed to be closing gradually in on her, obscuring the sky and cutting off the air, till she felt herself shut up among the decaying bodies of her starved hopes. A sense of having been decoyed by some world-old conspiracy into this bondage of body and soul filled her with despair. If marriage was the slow life-long acquittal of a debt contracted in ignorance, then marriage was a crime against human nature. She, for one, would have no share in maintaining the pretense of which she had been a victim: the pretense that a man and a woman, forced into the narrowest of personal relations, must remain there till the end, though they may have outgrown the span of each other's natures as the mature tree outgrows the iron brace about the sapling.

It was in the first heat of her moral indignation that she had met Clement Westall. She had seen at once that he was "interested," and had fought off the discovery, dreading any influence that should draw her back into the bondage of conventional relations. To ward off the peril she had, with an almost crude precipitancy, revealed her opinions to him. To her surprise, she found that he shared them. She was attracted by the frankness of a suitor who, while pressing his suit, admitted that he did not believe in marriage. Her worst audacities did not seem to surprise him: he had thought out all that she had felt, and they had reached the same conclusion. People grew at varying rates, and the yoke that was an easy fit for the one might soon become galling to the other. That was what divorce was for: the readjustment of personal relations. As soon as their necessarily transitive nature was recognized they would gain in dignity as well as in harmony. There would be no farther need of the ignoble concessions and connivances, the perpetual sacrifice of personal delicacy and moral pride, by means of which imperfect marriages were now held together. Each partner to the contract would be on his mettle, forced to live up to the highest standard of self-development, on pain of losing the other's respect and affection. The low nature could no longer drag the higher down, but must struggle to rise, or remain alone on its inferior level. The only necessary condition to a harmonious marriage was a frank recognition of this truth, and a solemn agreement between the contracting parties to keep faith with themselves, and not to live together for a moment after complete accord had ceased to exist between them. The new adultery was unfaithfulness to self.

It was, as Westall had just reminded her, on this understanding that they had married. The ceremony was an unimportant concession to social prejudice: now that the door of divorce stood open, no marriage need be an imprisonment, and the contract therefore no longer involved any diminution of self-respect. The nature of their attachment placed them so far beyond the reach of such contingencies that it was easy to discuss them with an open mind; and Julia's sense of security made her dwell with a tender insistence on Westall's promise to claim his release when he should cease to love her. The exchange of these vows seemed to make them, in a sense, champions of the new law, pioneers in the forbidden realm of individual freedom: they felt that they had somehow achieved beatitude without martyrdom.

This, as Julia now reviewed the past, she perceived to have been her theoretical attitude toward marriage. It was unconsciously, insidiously, that her ten years of happiness with Westall had developed another conception of the tie; a reversion, rather, to the old instinct of passionate dependency and possessorship that now made her blood revolt at the mere hint of change. Change? Renewal? Was that what they had called it, in their foolish jargon? Destruction, extermination rather—this rending of a myriad fibers interwoven with another's being! Another? But he was not other! He and she were one, one in the mystic sense which alone gave marriage its significance. The new law was not for them, but for the disunited creatures forced into a mockery of union. The gospel she had felt called on to proclaim had no bearing on her own case. . . . She sent for the doctor and told him she was sure she needed a nerve tonic.

She took the nerve tonic diligently, but it failed to act as a sedative to her fears. She did not know what she feared; but that made her anxiety the more pervasive. Her husband had not reverted to the subject of his Saturday talks. He was unusually kind and considerate, with a softening of his quick manner, a touch of shyness in his consideration, that sickened her with new fears. She told herself that it was because she looked badly— because he knew about the doctor and the nerve tonic—that he showed this deference to her wishes, this eagerness to screen her from moral draughts; but the explanation simply cleared the way for fresh inferences.

The week passed slowly, vacantly, like a prolonged Sunday. On Saturday the morning post brought a note from Mrs. Van Sideren. Would dear Julia ask Mr. Westall to come half an hour earlier than usual, as there was to be some music after his "talk"? Westall was just leaving for his office when his wife read the note. She opened the drawing-room door and called him back to deliver the message.

He glanced at the note and tossed it aside. "What a bore! I shall have to cut my game of racquets. Well, I suppose it can't be helped. Will you write and say it's all right?"

Julia hesitated a moment, her hand stiffening on the chair-back against which she leaned.

"You mean to go on with these talks?" she asked.

"I—why not?" he returned; and this time it struck her that his surprise was not quite unfeigned. The discovery helped her to find words.

"You said you had started them with the idea of pleasing me—"

"Well?"

"I told you last week that they didn't please me."

"Last week? Oh—" He seemed to make an effort of memory. "I thought you were nervous then; you sent for the doctor the next day."

"It was not the doctor I needed; it was your assurance—"

"My assurance?"

Suddenly she felt the floor fail under her. She sank into the chair with a choking throat, her words, her reasons slipping away from her like straws down a whirling flood.

"Clement," she cried, "isn't it enough for you to know that I hate it?"

He turned to close the door behind them; then he walked toward her and sat down. "What is it that you hate?" he asked gently.

She had made a desperate effort to rally her routed argument.

"I can't bear to have you speak as if—as if—our marriage—were like the other kind—the wrong kind. When I heard you there, the other afternoon, before all those inquisitive gossiping people, proclaiming that husbands and wives had a right to leave each other whenever they were tired—or had seen someone else—"

Westall sat motionless, his eyes fixed on a pattern of the carpet.

"You *have* ceased to take this view, then?" he said as she broke off. "You no longer believe that husbands and wives are justified in separating—under such conditions?"

"Under such conditions?" she stammered. "Yes—I still believe that—but how can we judge for others? What can we know of the circumstances—?"

He interrupted her. "I thought it was a fundamental article of our creed that the special circumstances produced by marriage were not to interfere with the full assertion of individual liberty." He paused a moment. "I thought that was your reason for leaving Arment."

She flushed to the forehead. It was not like him to give a personal turn to the argument.

"It was my reason," she said simply.

"Well, then—why do you refuse to recognize its validity now?"

"I don't—I don't—I only say that one can't judge for others."

He made an impatient movement. "This is mere hair-splitting. What you mean is that, the doctrine having served your purpose when you needed it, you now repudiate it."

"Well," she exclaimed, flushing again, "what if I do? What does it matter to us?"

Westall rose from his chair. He was excessively pale, and stood before his wife with something of the formality of a stranger.

"It matters to me," he said in a low voice, "because I do *not* repudiate it."

"Well—?"

"And because I had intended to invoke it as"—

He paused and drew his breath deeply. She sat silent, almost deafened by her heart-beats.—"as a complete justification of the course I am about to take."

Julia remained motionless. "What course is that?" she asked.

He cleared his throat. "I mean to claim the fulfilment of your promise."

For an instant the room wavered and darkened; then she recovered a torturing acuteness of vision. Every detail of her surroundings pressed upon her: the tick of the clock, the slant of sunlight on the wall, the hardness of the chair-arms that she grasped, were a separate wound to each sense.

"My promise—" she faltered.

"Your part of our mutual agreement to set each other free if one or the other should wish to be released."

She was silent again. He waited a moment, shifting his position nervously; then he said, with a touch of irritability: "You acknowledge the agreement?"

The question went through her like a shock. She lifted her head to it proudly. "I acknowledge the agreement," she said.

"And—you don't mean to repudiate it?"

A log on the hearth fell forward, and mechanically he advanced and pushed it back.

"No," she answered slowly, "I don't mean to repudiate it."

There was a pause. He remained near the hearth, his elbow resting on the mantel-shelf. Close to his hand stood a little cup of jade that he had given her on one of their wedding anniversaries. She wondered vaguely if he noticed it.

"You intend to leave me, then?" she said at length.

His gesture seemed to deprecate the crudeness of the allusion.

"To marry someone else?"

Again his eye and hand protested. She rose and stood before him.

"Why should you be afraid to tell me? Is it Una Van Sideren?"

He was silent.

"I wish you good luck," she said.

### III

SHE looked up, finding herself alone. She did not remember when or how he had left the room, or how long afterward she had sat there. The fire still smoldered on the hearth, but the slant of sunlight had left the wall.

Her first conscious thought was that she had not broken her word, that she had fulfilled the very letter of their bargain. There had been no crying out, no vain appeal to the past, no attempt at temporizing or evasion. She had marched straight up to the guns.

Now that it was over, she sickened to find herself alive. She looked about her, trying to recover her hold on reality. Her identity seemed to be slipping from her, as it disappears in a physical swoon. "This is my room—this is my house," she heard herself saying. Her room? Her house? She could almost hear the walls laugh back at her.

She stood up, weariness in every bone. The silence of the room frightened her. She remembered, now, having heard the front door close a long time ago: the sound suddenly re-echoed through her brain. Her husband must have left the house, then—her *husband*? She no longer knew in what terms to think: the simplest phrases had a poisoned edge. She sank back into her chair, overcome by a strange weakness. The clock struck ten—it was only ten o'clock! Suddenly she remembered that she had not ordered dinner . . . or were they dining out that evening? Dinner—*dining out*—the old meaningless phraseology pursued her! She must try to think of herself as she would think of someone else, a someone dissociated from all the familiar routine of the past, whose wants and habits must gradually be learned, as one might spy out the ways of a strange animal. . . .

The clock struck another hour—eleven. She stood up again and walked to the door: she thought she would go upstairs to her room. *Her* room? Again the word derided her. She opened the door, crossed the narrow hall, and walked up the stairs. As she passed, she noticed Westall's sticks and umbrellas: a pair of his gloves lay on the hall table. The same stair-carpet mounted between the same walls; the same old French print, in its narrow black frame, faced her on the landing. This visual continuity was intolerable. Within, a gaping chasm; without, the same untroubled and familiar surface. She must get away from it before she could attempt to think. But, once in her room, she sat down on the lounge, a stupor creeping over her. . . .

Gradually her vision cleared. A great deal had happened in the interval—a wild marching and countermarching of emotions, arguments, ideas—a fury of insurgent impulses that fell back spent upon themselves. She had tried, at first, to rally, to organize these chaotic forces. There must be help somewhere, if only she could master the inner tumult. Life could not be broken off short like this, for a whim, a fancy; the law itself would side with her, would defend her. The law? What claim had she upon it? She was the prisoner of her own choice: she had been her own legislator, and she was the predestined victim of the code she had devised. But this was grotesque, intolerable—a mad mistake, for which she could not be held accountable! The law she had despised was still there, might still be invoked . . . invoked, but to what end? Could she ask it to chain Westall to her side? *She* had been allowed to go free when she claimed her freedom— should she show less magnanimity than she had exacted? Magnanimity? The word lashed her with its irony—one does not strike an attitude when one is fighting for life! She would threaten, grovel, cajole . . . she would yield anything to keep her hold on happiness. Ah, but the difficulty lay deeper! The law could not help her—her own apostasy could not help her. She was the victim of the theories she renounced. It was as though some giant machine of her own making had caught her up in its wheels and was grinding her to atoms. . . .

It was afternoon when she found herself out-of-doors. She walked with an aimless haste, fearing to meet familiar faces. The day was radiant, metallic: one of those searching American days so calculated to reveal the shortcomings of our street-cleaning and the excesses of our architecture. The streets looked bare and hideous; everything stared and glittered. She called a passing hansom, and gave Mrs. Van Sideren's address.

She did not know what had led up to the act; but she found herself suddenly resolved to speak, to cry out a warning. It was too late to save herself—but the girl might still be told. The hansom rattled up Fifth Avenue; she sat with her eyes fixed, avoiding recognition. At the Van Siderens' door she sprang out and rang the bell. Action had cleared her brain, and she felt calm and self-possessed. She knew now exactly what she meant to say.

The ladies were both out . . . the parlor-maid stood waiting for a card. Julia, with a vague murmur, turned away from the door and lingered a moment on the sidewalk. Then she remembered that she had not paid the cab-driver. She drew a dollar from her purse and handed it to him. He touched his hat and drove off, leaving her alone in the long empty street. She wandered away westward, toward strange thoroughfares, where she was not likely to meet acquaintances. The feeling of aimlessness had returned. Once she found herself in the afternoon torrent of Broadway, swept past tawdry shops and flaming theatrical posters, with a succession of meaningless faces gliding by in the opposite direction. . . .

A feeling of faintness reminded her that she had not eaten since morning. She turned into a side street of shabby houses, with rows of ash-barrels behind bent area railings. In a basement window she saw the sign Ladies' Restaurant: a pie and a dish of doughnuts lay against the dusty pane like petrified food in an ethnological museum. She entered, and a young woman with a weak mouth and a brazen eye cleared a table for her near the window. The table was covered with a red and white cotton cloth and adorned with a bunch of celery in a thick tumbler and a salt-cellar full of grayish lumpy salt. Julia ordered tea, and sat a long time waiting for it. She was glad to be away from the noise and confusion of the streets. The low-ceilinged room was empty, and two or three waitresses with thin pert faces lounged in the background staring at her and whispering together. At last the tea was brought in a discolored metal teapot. Julia poured a cup and drank it hastily. It was black and bitter, but it flowed through her veins like an elixir. She was almost dizzy with exhilaration. Oh, how tired, how unutterably tired she had been!

She drank a second cup, blacker and bitterer, and now her mind was once more working clearly. She felt as vigorous, as decisive, as when she had stood on the Van Siderens' door-step—but the wish to return there had subsided. She saw now the futility of such an attempt—the humiliation to which it might have exposed her . . . The pity of it was that she did not know what to do next. The short winter day was fading, and she realized that she could not remain much longer in the restaurant without attracting notice. She paid for her tea and went out into the street. The lamps were alight, and here and there a basement shop cast an oblong of gas-light across the fissured pavement. In the dusk there was something sinister about the aspect of the street, and she hastened back toward Fifth Avenue. She was not used to being out alone at that hour.

At the corner of Fifth Avenue she paused and stood watching the stream of carriages. At last a policeman caught sight of her and signed to her that he would take her across. She had not meant to cross the street, but she obeyed automatically, and presently found herself on the farther corner. There she paused again for a moment; but she fancied the policeman was watching her, and this sent her hastening down the nearest side street... After that she walked a long time, vaguely . . . Night had fallen, and now and then, through the windows of a passing carriage, she caught the expanse of an evening waistcoat or the shimmer of an opera cloak. . . .

Suddenly she found herself in a familiar street. She stood still a moment, breathing quickly. She had turned the corner without noticing whither it led; but now, a few yards ahead of her, she saw the house in which she had once lived—her first husband's house.

The blinds were drawn, and only a faint translucence marked the windows and the transom above the door. As she stood there she heard a step behind her, and a man walked by in the direction of the house. He walked slowly, with a heavy middle-aged gait, his head sunk a little between the shoulders, the red crease of his neck visible above the fur collar of his overcoat. He crossed the street, went up the steps of the house, drew forth a latch-key, and let himself in. . . .

There was no one else in sight. Julia leaned for a long time against the area-rail at the corner, her eyes fixed on the front of the house. The feeling of physical weariness had returned, but the strong tea still throbbed in her veins and lit her brain with an unnatural clearness. Presently she heard another step draw near, and moving quickly away, she too crossed the street and mounted the steps of the house. The impulse which had carried her there prolonged itself in a quick pressure of the electric bell—then she felt suddenly weak and tremulous, and grasped the balustrade for support. The door opened and a young footman with a fresh inexperienced face stood on the threshold. Julia knew in an instant that he would admit her.

"I saw Mr. Arment going in just now," she said. "Will you ask him to see me for a moment?"

The footman hesitated. "I think Mr. Arment has gone up to dress for dinner, madam."

Julia advanced into the hall. "I am sure he will see me—I will not detain him long," she said. She spoke quietly, authoritatively, in the tone which a good servant does not mistake. The footman had his hand on the drawing-room door.

"I will tell him, madam. What name, please?"

Julia trembled: she had not thought of that. "Merely say a lady," she returned carelessly.

The footman wavered and she fancied herself lost; but at that instant the door opened from within and John Arment stepped into the hall. He drew back sharply as he saw her, his florid face turning sallow with the shock; then the blood poured back to it, swelling the veins on his temples and reddening the lobes of his thick ears.

It was long since Julia had seen him, and she was startled at the change in his appearance. He had thickened, coarsened, settled down into the enclosing flesh. But she noted this insensibly: her one conscious thought was that, now she was face to face with him, she must not let him escape till he had heard her. Every pulse in her body throbbed with the urgency of her message.

She went up to him as he drew back. "I must speak to you," she said.

Arment hesitated, red and stammering. Julia glanced at the footman, and her look acted as a warning. The instinctive shrinking from a "scene" predominated over every other impulse, and Arment said slowly: "Will you come this way?"

He followed her into the drawing-room and closed the door. Julia, as she advanced, was vaguely aware that the room at least was unchanged: time had not mitigated its horrors. The contadina still lurched from the chimney-breast, and the Greek slave obstructed the threshold of the inner room. The place was alive with memories: they started out from every fold of the yellow satin curtains and glided between the angles of the rosewood furniture. But while some subordinate agency was carrying these impressions to her brain, her whole conscious effort was centered in the act of dominating Arment's will. The fear that he would refuse to hear her mounted like fever to her brain. She felt her purpose melt before it, words and arguments running into each other in the heat of her longing. For a moment her voice failed her, and she imagined herself thrust out before she could speak; but as she was struggling for a word, Arment pushed a chair forward, and said quietly: "You are not well."

The sound of his voice steadied her. It was neither kind nor unkind—a voice that suspended judgment, rather, awaiting unforeseen developments. She supported herself against the back of the chair and drew a deep breath.

"Shall I send for something?" he continued, with a cold embarrassed politeness.

Julia raised an entreating hand. "No—no—thank you. I am quite well."

He paused midway toward the bell and turned on her. "Then may I ask—?"

"Yes," she interrupted him. "I came here because I wanted to see you. There is something I must tell you."

Arment continued to scrutinize her. "I am surprised at that," he said. "I should have supposed that any communication you may wish to make could have been made through our lawyers."

"Our lawyers!" She burst into a little laugh. "I don't think they could help me—this time."

Arment's face took on a barricaded look. "If there is any question of help—of course—"

It struck her, whimsically, that she had seen that look when some shabby devil called with a subscription-book. Perhaps he thought she wanted him to put his name down for so much in sympathy—or even in money . . . The thought made her laugh again. She saw his look change slowly to perplexity. All his facial changes were slow, and she remembered, suddenly, how it had once diverted her to shift that lumbering scenery with a word. For the first time it struck her that she had been cruel. "There *is* a question of help," she said in a softer key: "you can help me; but only by listening . . . I want to tell you something . . . "

Arment's resistance was not yielding. "Would it not be easier to—write?" he suggested.

She shook her head. "There is no time to write . . . and it won't take long." She raised her head and their eyes met. "My husband has left me," she said.

"Westall—?" he stammered, reddening again.

"Yes. This morning. Just as I left you. Because he was tired of me."

The words, uttered scarcely above a whisper, seemed to dilate to the limit of the room. Arment looked toward the door; then his embarrassed glance returned to Julia.

"I am very sorry," he said awkwardly.

"Thank you," she murmured.

"But I don't see—"

"No—but you will—in a moment. Won't you listen to me? Please!" Instinctively she had shifted her position putting herself between him and the door. "It happened this morning," she went on in short breathless phrases. "I never suspected anything—I thought we were—perfectly happy . . . Suddenly he told me he was tired of me . . . there is a girl he likes better... He has gone to her . . . " As she spoke, the lurking anguish rose upon her, possessing her once more to the exclusion of every other emotion. Her eyes ached, her throat swelled with it, and two painful tears burnt a way down her face.

Arment's constraint was increasing visibly. "This—this is very unfortunate," he began. "But I should say the law—"

"The law?" she echoed ironically. "When he asks for his freedom?"

"You are not obliged to give it."

"You were not obliged to give me mine—but you did."

He made a protesting gesture.

"You saw that the law couldn't help you—didn't you?" she went on. "That is what I see now. The law represents material rights—it can't go beyond. If we don't recognize an inner law . . . the obligation that love creates . . . being loved as well as loving . . . there is nothing to prevent our spreading ruin unhindered . . . is there?" She raised her head plaintively, with the look of a bewildered child. "That is what I see now...what I wanted to tell you. He leaves me because he's tired . . . but I was not tired; and I don't understand why he is. That's the dreadful part of it—the not understanding: I hadn't realized what it meant. But I've been thinking of it all day, and things have come back to me—things I hadn't noticed...when you and I . . . " She moved closer to him, and fixed her eyes on his with the gaze that tries to reach beyond words. "I see now that *you* didn't understand—did you?"

Their eyes met in a sudden shock of comprehension: a veil seemed to be lifted between them. Arment's lip trembled.

"No," he said, "I didn't understand."

She gave a little cry, almost of triumph. "I knew it! I knew it! You wondered—you tried to tell me—but no words came . . . You saw your life falling in ruins . . . the world slipping from you . . . and you couldn't speak or move!"

She sank down on the chair against which she had been leaning. "Now I know—now I know," she repeated.

"I am very sorry for you," she heard Arment stammer.

She looked up quickly. "That's not what I came for. I don't want you to be sorry. I came to ask you to forgive me . . . for not understanding that *you* didn't understand . . . That's all I wanted to say." She rose with a vague sense that the end had come, and put out a groping hand toward the door.

Arment stood motionless. She turned to him with a faint smile.

"You forgive me?"

"There is nothing to forgive—"

"Then will you shake hands for good-by?" She felt his hand in hers: it was nerveless, reluctant.

"Good-by," she repeated. "I understand now."

She opened the door and passed out into the hall. As she did so, Arment took an impulsive step forward; but just then the footman, who was evidently alive to his obligations, advanced from the background to let her out. She heard Arment fall back. The footman threw open the door, and she found herself outside in the darkness.

## EXPIATION

"I CAN NEVER," said Mrs. Fetherel, "hear the bell ring without a shudder."

Her unruffled aspect—she was the kind of woman whose emotions never communicate themselves to her clothes—and the conventional background of the New York drawing-room, with its pervading implication of an imminent tea-tray and of an atmosphere in which the social functions have become purely reflex, lent to her declaration a relief not lost on her cousin Mrs. Clinch, who, from the other side of the fireplace, agreed with a glance at the clock, that it *was* the hour for bores.

"Bores!" cried Mrs. Fetherel impatiently. "If I shuddered at them, I should have a chronic ague!"

She leaned forward and laid a sparkling finger on her cousin's shabby black knee. "I mean the newspaper clippings," she whispered.

Mrs. Clinch returned a glance of intelligence. "They've begun already?"

"Not yet; but they're sure to now, at any minute, my publisher tells me."

Mrs. Fetherel's look of apprehension sat oddly on her small features, which had an air of neat symmetry somehow suggestive of being set in order every morning by the housemaid. Someone (there were rumors that it was her cousin) had once said that Paula Fetherel would have been very pretty if she hadn't looked so like a moral axiom in a copybook hand.

Mrs. Clinch received her confidence with a smile. "Well," she said, "I suppose you were prepared for the consequences of authorship?"

Mrs. Fetherel blushed brightly. "It isn't their coming," she owned—"it's their coming *now*."

"Now?"

"The Bishop's in town."

Mrs. Clinch leaned back and shaped her lips to a whistle which deflected in a laugh. "Well!" she said.

"You see!" Mrs. Fetherel triumphed.

"Well—weren't you prepared for the Bishop?"

"Not now—at least, I hadn't thought of his seeing the clippings."

"And why should he see them?"

"Bella—*won't* you understand? It's John."

"John?"

"Who has taken the most unexpected tone—one might almost say out of perversity."

"Oh, perversity—" Mrs. Clinch murmured, observing her cousin between lids wrinkled by amusement. "What tone has John taken?"

Mrs. Fetherel threw out her answer with the desperate gesture of a woman who lays bare the traces of a marital fist. "The tone of being proud of my book."

The measure of Mrs. Clinch's enjoyment overflowed in laughter.

"Oh, you may laugh," Mrs. Fetherel insisted, "but it's no joke to me. In the first place, John's liking the book is so—so—such a false note—it puts me in such a ridiculous position; and then it has set him watching for the reviews—who would ever have suspected John of knowing that books were *reviewed*? Why, he's actually found out about the Clipping Bureau, and whenever the postman rings I hear John rush out of the library to see if there are any yellow envelopes. Of course, when they do come he'll bring them into the drawing-room and read them aloud to everybody who happens to be here—and the Bishop is sure to happen to be here!"

Mrs. Clinch repressed her amusement. "The picture you draw is a lurid one," she conceded, "but your modesty strikes me as abnormal, especially in an author. The chances are that some of the clippings will be rather pleasant reading. The critics are not all union men."

Mrs. Fetherel stared. "Union men?"

"Well, I mean they don't all belong to the well-known Society-for-the-Persecution-of-Rising-Authors. Some of them have even been known to defy its regulations and say a good word for a new writer."

"Oh, I dare say," said Mrs. Fetherel, with the laugh her cousin's epigram exacted. "But you don't quite see my point. I'm not at all nervous about the success of my book— my publisher tells me I have no need to be—but I am afraid of its being a *succès de scandale*."

"Mercy!" said Mrs. Clinch, sitting up.

The butler and footman at this moment appeared with the tea-tray, and when they had withdrawn, Mrs. Fetherel, bending her brightly rippled head above the kettle, continued in a murmur of avowal, "The title, even, is a kind of challenge."

"*Fast and Loose*," Mrs. Clinch mused. "Yes, it ought to take."

"I didn't choose it for that reason!" the author protested. "I should have preferred something quieter—less pronounced; but I was determined not to shirk the responsibility of what I had written. I want people to know beforehand exactly what kind of book they are buying."

"Well," said Mrs. Clinch, "that's a degree of conscientiousness that I've never met with before. So few books fulfill the promise of their titles that experienced readers never expect the fare to come up to the menu."

"*Fast and Loose* will be no disappointment on that score," her cousin significantly returned. "I've handled the subject without gloves. I've called a spade a spade."

"You simply make my mouth water! And to think I haven't been able to read it yet because every spare minute of my time has been given to correcting the proofs of 'How the Birds Keep Christmas'! There's an instance of the hardships of an author's life!"

Mrs. Fetherel's eye clouded. "Don't joke, Bella, please. I suppose to experienced authors there's always something absurd in the nervousness of a new writer, but in my case so much is at stake; I've put so much of myself into this book and I'm so afraid of being misunderstood . . . of being, as it were, in advance of my time . . . like poor Flaubert....I *know* you'll think me ridiculous . . . and if only my own reputation were at stake, I should never give it a thought . . . but the idea of dragging John's name through the mire . . . "

Mrs. Clinch, who had risen and gathered her cloak about her, stood surveying from her genial height her cousin's agitated countenance.

"Why did you use John's name, then?"

"That's another of my difficulties! I *had* to. There would have been no merit in publishing such a book under an assumed name; it would have been an act of moral cowardice. *Fast and Loose* is not an ordinary novel. A writer who dares to show up the hollowness of social conventions must have the courage of her convictions and be willing to accept the consequences of defying society. Can you imagine Ibsen or Tolstoy writing under a false name?" Mrs. Fetherel lifted a tragic eye to her cousin. "You don't know, Bella, how often I've envied you since I began to write. I used to wonder sometimes—you won't mind my saying so?—why, with all your cleverness, you hadn't taken up some more exciting subject than natural history; but I see now how wise you were. Whatever happens, you will never be denounced by the press!"

"Is that what you're afraid of?" asked Mrs. Clinch, as she grasped the bulging umbrella which rested against her chair. "My dear, if I had ever had the good luck to be denounced by the press, my brougham would be waiting at the door for me at this very moment, and I shouldn't have to ruin this umbrella by using it in the rain. Why, you innocent, if I'd ever felt the slightest aptitude for showing up social conventions, do you suppose I should waste my time writing 'Nests Ajar' and 'How to Smell the Flowers'? There's a fairly steady demand for pseudo-science and colloquial ornithology, but it's nothing, simply nothing, to the ravenous call for attacks on social institutions—especially by those inside the institutions!"

There was often, to her cousin, a lack of taste in Mrs. Clinch's pleasantries, and on this occasion they seemed more than usually irrelevant.

"'Fast and Loose' was not written with the idea of a large sale."

Mrs. Clinch was unperturbed. "Perhaps that's just as well," she returned, with a philosophic shrug. "The surprise will be all the pleasanter, I mean. For of course it's going to sell tremendously; especially if you can get the press to denounce it."

"Bella, how *can* you? I sometimes think you say such things expressly to tease me; and yet I should think you of all women would understand my purpose in writing such a book. It has always seemed to me that the message I had to deliver was not for myself alone, but for all the other women in the world who have felt the hollowness of our social shams, the ignominy of bowing down to the idols of the market, but have lacked either the courage or the power to proclaim their independence; and I have fancied, Bella dear, that, however severely society might punish me for revealing its weaknesses, I could count on the sympathy of those who, like you"—Mrs. Fetherel's voice sank—"have passed through the deep waters."

Mrs. Clinch gave herself a kind of canine shake, as though to free her ample shoulders from any drop of the element she was supposed to have traversed.

"Oh, call them muddy rather than deep," she returned; "and you'll find, my dear, that women who've had any wading to do are rather shy of stirring up mud. It sticks—especially on white clothes."

Mrs. Fetherel lifted an undaunted brow. "I'm not afraid," she proclaimed; and at the same instant she dropped her tea-spoon with a clatter and shrank back into her seat. "There's the bell," she exclaimed, "and I know it's the Bishop!"

It was in fact the Bishop of Ossining, who, impressively announced by Mrs. Fetherel's butler, now made an entry that may best be described as not inadequate to the expectations the announcement raised. The Bishop always entered a room well; but, when unannounced, or preceded by a Low Church butler who gave him his surname, his appearance lacked the impressiveness conferred on it by the due specification of his diocesan dignity. The Bishop was very fond of his niece Mrs. Fetherel, and one of the traits he most valued in her was the possession of a butler who knew how to announce a bishop.

Mrs. Clinch was also his niece; but, aside from the fact that she possessed no butler at all, she had laid herself open to her uncle's criticism by writing insignificant little books which had a way of going into five or ten editions, while the fruits of his own episcopal leisure—"The Wail of Jonah" (twenty cantos in blank verse), and "Through a Glass Brightly; or, How to Raise Funds for a Memorial Window"—inexplicably languished on the back shelves of a publisher noted for his dexterity in pushing "devotional goods." Even this indiscretion the Bishop might, however, have condoned, had his niece thought fit to turn to him for support and advice at the painful juncture of her history when, in her own words, it became necessary for her to invite Mr. Clinch to look out for another situation. Mr. Clinch's misconduct was of the kind especially designed by Providence to test the fortitude of a Christian wife and mother, and the Bishop was absolutely distended with seasonable advice and edification; so that when Bella met his tentative exhortations with the curt remark that she preferred to do her own housecleaning unassisted, her uncle's grief at her ingratitude was not untempered with sympathy for Mr. Clinch.

It is not surprising, therefore, that the Bishop's warmest greetings were always reserved for Mrs. Fetherel; and on this occasion Mrs. Clinch thought she detected, in the salutation which fell to her share, a pronounced suggestion that her own presence was superfluous—a hint which she took with her usual imperturbable good humor.

## II

LEFT alone with the Bishop, Mrs. Fetherel sought the nearest refuge from conversation by offering him a cup of tea. The Bishop accepted with the preoccupied air of a man to whom, for the moment, tea is but a subordinate incident. Mrs. Fetherel's nervousness increased; and knowing that the surest way of distracting attention from one's own affairs is to affect an interest in those of one's companion, she hastily asked if her uncle had come to town on business.

"On business—yes—" said the Bishop in an impressive tone. "I had to see my publisher, who has been behaving rather unsatisfactorily in regard to my last book."

"Ah—your last book?" faltered Mrs. Fetherel, with a sickening sense of her inability to recall the name or nature of the work in question, and a mental vow never again to be caught in such ignorance of a colleague's productions.

"'Through a Glass Brightly,'" the Bishop explained, with an emphasis which revealed his detection of her predicament. "You may remember that I sent you a copy last Christmas?"

"Of course I do!" Mrs. Fetherel brightened. "It was that delightful story of the poor consumptive girl who had no money, and two little brothers to support—"

"Sisters—idiot sisters—" the Bishop gloomily corrected.

"I mean sisters; and who managed to collect money enough to put up a beautiful memorial window to her—her grandfather, whom she had never seen—"

"But whose sermons had been her chief consolation and support during her long struggle with poverty and disease." The Bishop gave the satisfied sigh of the workman who reviews his completed task. "A touching subject, surely; and I believe I did it justice; at least, so my friends assured me."

"Why, yes—I remember there was a splendid review of it in the *Reredos!*" cried Mrs. Fetherel, moved by the incipient instinct of reciprocity.

"Yes—by my dear friend Mrs. Gollinger, whose husband, the late Dean Gollinger, was under very particular obligations to me. Mrs. Gollinger is a woman of rare literary acumen, and her praise of my book was unqualified; but the public wants more highly seasoned fare, and the approval of a thoughtful churchwoman carries less weight than the sensational comments of an illiterate journalist." The Bishop lent a meditative eye on his spotless gaiters. "At the risk of horrifying you, my dear," he added, with a slight laugh, "I will confide to you that my best chance of a popular success would be to have my book denounced by the press."

"Denounced?" gasped Mrs. Fetherel. "On what ground?"

"On the ground of immorality." The Bishop evaded her startled gaze. "Such a thing is inconceivable to you, of course; but I am only repeating what my publisher tells me. If, for instance, a critic could be induced—I mean, if a critic were to be found, who called in question the morality of my heroine in sacrificing her own health and that of her idiot sisters in order to put up a memorial window to her grandfather, it would probably raise a general controversy in the newspapers, and I might count on a sale of ten or fifteen thousand within the next year. If he described her as morbid or decadent, it might even run to twenty thousand; but that is more than I permit myself to hope. In fact, I should be satisfied with any general charge of immorality." The Bishop sighed again. "I need hardly tell you that I am actuated by no mere literary ambition. Those whose opinion I most value have assured me that the book is not without merit; but, though it does not become me to dispute their verdict, I can truly say that my vanity as an author is not at stake. I have, however, a special reason for wishing to increase the circulation of 'Through a Glass Brightly'; it was written for a purpose—a purpose I have greatly at heart—"

"I know," cried his niece sympathetically. "The chantry window—?"

"Is still empty, alas! and I had great hopes that, under Providence, my little book might be the means of filling it. All our wealthy parishioners have given lavishly to the cathedral, and it was for this reason that, in writing 'Through a Glass,' I addressed my appeal more especially to the less well-endowed, hoping by the example of my heroine to stimulate the collection of small sums throughout the entire diocese, and perhaps beyond it. I am sure," the Bishop feelingly concluded, "the book would have a wide-spread influence if people could only be induced to read it!"

His conclusion touched a fresh thread of association in Mrs. Fetherel's vibrating nerve-centers. "I never thought of that!" she cried.

The Bishop looked at her inquiringly.

"That one's books may not be read at all! How dreadful!" she exclaimed.

He smiled faintly. "I had not forgotten that I was addressing an authoress," he said. "Indeed, I should not have dared to inflict my troubles on any one not of the craft."

Mrs. Fetherel was quivering with the consciousness of her involuntary self-betrayal. "Oh, Uncle!" she murmured.

"In fact," the Bishop continued, with a gesture which seemed to brush away her scruples, "I came here partly to speak to you about your novel. 'Fast and Loose,' I think you call it?"

Mrs. Fetherel blushed assentingly.

"And is it out yet?" the Bishop continued.

"It came out about a week ago. But you haven't touched your tea, and it must be quite cold. Let me give you another cup..."

"My reason for asking," the Bishop went on, with the bland inexorableness with which, in his younger days, he had been known to continue a sermon after the senior warden had looked four times at his watch—"my reason for asking is, that I hoped I might not be too late to induce you to change the title."

Mrs. Fetherel set down the cup she had filled. "The title?" she faltered.

The Bishop raised a reassuring hand. "Don't misunderstand me, dear child; don't for a moment imagine that I take it to be in anyway indicative of the contents of the book. I know you too well for that. My first idea was that it had probably been forced on you by an unscrupulous publisher—I know too well to what ignoble compromises one may be driven in such cases! . . . " He paused, as though to give her the opportunity of confirming this conjecture, but she preserved an apprehensive silence, and he went on, as though taking up the second point in his sermon—"Or, again, the name may have taken your fancy without your realizing all that it implies to minds more alive than yours to offensive innuendoes. It is—ahem—excessively suggestive, and I hope I am not too late to warn you of the false impression it is likely to produce on the very readers whose approbation you would most value. My friend Mrs. Gollinger, for instance—"

Mrs. Fetherel, as the publication of her novel testified, was in theory a woman of independent views; and if in practice she sometimes failed to live up to her standard, it was rather from an irresistible tendency to adapt herself to her environment than from any conscious lack of moral courage. The Bishop's exordium had excited in her that sense of opposition which such admonitions are apt to provoke; but as he went on she felt herself gradually enclosed in an atmosphere in which her theories vainly gasped for breath. The

Bishop had the immense dialectical advantage of invalidating any conclusions at variance with his own by always assuming that his premises were among the necessary laws of thought. This method, combined with the habit of ignoring any classifications but his own, created an element in which the first condition of existence was the immediate adoption of his standpoint; so that his niece, as she listened, seemed to feel Mrs. Gollinger's Mechlin cap spreading its conventual shadow over her rebellious brow and the *Revue de Paris* at her elbow turning into a copy of the *Reredos*. She had meant to assure her uncle that she was quite aware of the significance of the title she had chosen, that it had been deliberately selected as indicating the subject of her novel, and that the book itself had been written indirect defiance of the class of readers for whose susceptibilities she was alarmed. The words were almost on her lips when the irresistible suggestion conveyed by the Bishop's tone and language deflected them into the apologetic murmur, "Oh, uncle, you mustn't think—I never meant—" How much farther this current of reaction might have carried her, the historian is unable to computer, for at this point the door opened and her husband entered the room.

"The first review of your book!" he cried, flourishing a yellow envelope. "My dear Bishop, how lucky you're here!"

Though the trials of married life have been classified and catalogued with exhaustive accuracy, there is one form of conjugal misery which has perhaps received inadequate attention; and that is the suffering of the versatile woman whose husband is not equally adapted to all her moods. Every woman feels for the sister who is compelled to wear a bonnet which does not "go" with her gown; but how much sympathy is given to her whose husband refuses to harmonize with the pose of the moment? Scant justice has, for instance, been done to the misunderstood wife whose husband persists in understanding her; to the submissive helpmate whose taskmaster shuns every opportunity of browbeating her; and to the generous and impulsive being whose bills are paid with philosophic calm. Mrs. Fetherel, as wives go, had been fairly exempt from trials of this nature, for her husband, if undistinguished by pronounced brutality or indifference, had at least the negative merit of being her intellectual inferior. Landscape gardeners, who are aware of the usefulness of a valley in emphasizing the height of a hill, can form an idea of the account to which an accomplished woman may turn such deficiencies; and it need scarcely be said that Mrs. Fetherel had made the most of her opportunities. It was agreeably obvious to everyone, Fetherel included, that he was not the man to appreciate such a woman; but there are no limits to man's perversity, and he did his best to invalidate this advantage by admiring her without pretending to understand her. What she most suffered from was this fatuous approval: the maddening sense that, however she conducted herself, he would always admire her. Had he belonged to the class whose conversational supplies are drawn from the domestic circle, his wife's name would never have been off his lips; and to Mrs. Fetherel's sensitive perceptions his frequent silences were indicative of the fact that she was his one topic.

It was, in part, the attempt to escape this persistent approbation that had driven Mrs. Fetherel to authorship. She had fancied that even the most infatuated husband might be counted onto resent, at least negatively, an attack on the sanctity of the hearth; and her anticipations were heightened by a sense of the unpardonableness of her act. Mrs. Fetherel's relations with her husband were in fact complicated by an irrepressible tendency to be fond of him; and there was a certain pleasure in the prospect of a situation that justified the most explicit expiation.

These hopes Fetherel's attitude had already defeated. He read the book with enthusiasm, he pressed it on his friends, he sent a copy to his mother; and his very soul now hung on the verdict of the reviewers. It was perhaps this proof of his general ineptitude that made his wife doubly alive to his special defects; so that his inopportune entrance was aggravated by the very sound of his voice and the hopeless aberration of his smile. Nothing, to the observant, is more indicative of a man's character and circumstances than his way of entering a room. The Bishop of Ossining, for instance, brought with him not only an atmosphere of episcopal authority, but an implied opinion on the verbal inspiration of the Scriptures, and on the attitude of the church toward divorce; while the appearance of Mrs. Fetherel's husband produced an immediate impression of domestic felicity. His mere aspect implied that there was a well-filled nursery upstairs; that this wife, if she did not sew on his buttons, at least superintended the performance of that task; that they both went to church regularly, and that they dined with his mother every Sunday evening punctually at seven o'clock.

All this and more was expressed in the affectionate gesture with which he now raised the yellow envelope above Mrs. Fetherel's clutch; and knowing the uselessness of begging him not to be silly, she said, with a dry despair, "You're boring the Bishop horribly."

Fetherel turned a radiant eye on that dignitary. "She bores us all horribly, doesn't she, sir?" he exulted.

"Have you read it?" said his wife, uncontrollably.

"Read it? Of course not—it's just this minute come. I say, Bishop, you're not going—?"

"Not till I've heard this," said the Bishop, settling himself in his chair with an indulgent smile.

His niece glanced at him despairingly. "Don't let John's nonsense detain you," she entreated.

"Detain him? That's good," guffawed Fetherel. "It isn't as long as one of his sermons—won't take me five minutes to read. Here, listen to this, ladies and gentlemen: 'In this age of festering pessimism and decadent depravity, it is no surprise to the nauseated reviewer to open one more volume saturated with the fetid emanations of the sewer—'"

Fetherel, who was not in the habit of reading aloud, paused with a gasp, and the Bishop glanced sharply at his niece, who kept her gaze fixed on the tea-cup she had not yet succeeded in transferring to his hand.

"'Of the sewer,'" her husband resumed; "'but his wonder is proportionately great when he lights on a novel as sweetly inoffensive as Paula Fetherel's *Fast and Loose*. Mrs. Fetherel is, we believe, a new hand at fiction, and her work reveals frequent traces of inexperience; but these are more than atoned for by her pure, fresh view of life and her altogether unfashionable regard for the reader's moral susceptibilities. Let no one be induced by its distinctly misleading title to forego the enjoyment of this pleasant picture of domestic life, which, in spite of a total lack of force in character-drawing and of consecutiveness in incident, may be described as a distinctly pretty story.'"

## III

IT was several weeks later that Mrs. Clinch once more brought the plebeian aroma of heated tram-cars and muddy street-crossings into the violet-scented atmosphere of her cousin's drawing room.

"Well," she said, tossing a damp bundle of proof into the corner of a silk-cushioned bergère, "I've read it at last and I'm not so awfully shocked!"

Mrs. Fetherel, who sat near the fire with her head propped on a languid hand, looked up without speaking.

"Mercy, Paula," said her visitor, "you're ill."

Mrs. Fetherel shook her head. "I was never better," she said, mournfully.

"Then may I help myself to tea? Thanks."

Mrs. Clinch carefully removed her mended glove before taking a buttered tea-cake; then she glanced again at her cousin.

"It's not what I said just now—?" she ventured.

"Just now?"

"About *Fast and Loose*? I came to talk it over."

Mrs. Fetherel sprang to her feet. "I never," she cried dramatically, "want to hear it mentioned again!"

"Paula!" exclaimed Mrs. Clinch, setting down her cup.

Mrs. Fetherel slowly turned on her an eye brimming with the incommunicable; then, dropping into her seat again, she added, with a tragic laugh, "There's nothing left to say."

"Nothing—?" faltered Mrs. Clinch, longing for another tea-cake, but feeling the inappropriateness of the impulse in an atmosphere so charged with the portentous. "Do you mean that everything *has* been said?" She looked tentatively at her cousin. "Haven't they been nice?"

"They've been odious—odious—" Mrs. Fetherel burst out, with an ineffectual clutch at her handkerchief. "It's been perfectly intolerable!"

Mrs. Clinch, philosophically resigning herself to the propriety of taking no more tea, crossed over to her cousin and laid a sympathizing hand on that lady's agitated shoulder.

"It *is* a bore at first," she conceded; "but you'll be surprised to see how soon one gets used to it."

"I shall—never—get—used to it—" Mrs. Fetherel brokenly declared.

"Have they been so very nasty—all of them?"

"Every one of them!" the novelist sobbed.

"I'm so sorry, dear; it *does* hurt, I know—but hadn't you rather expected it?"

"Expected it?" cried Mrs. Fetherel, sitting up.

Mrs. Clinch felt her way warily. "I only mean, dear, that I fancied from what you said before the book came out—that you rather expected—that you'd rather discounted—"

"Their recommending it to everybody as a perfectly harmless story?"

"Good gracious! Is *that* what they've done?"

Mrs. Fetherel speechlessly nodded.

"Every one of them?"

"Every one."

"Phew!" said Mrs. Clinch, with an incipient whistle.

"Why, you've just said it yourself!" her cousin suddenly reproached her.

"Said what?"

"That you weren't so *awfully* shocked—"

"I? Oh, well—you see, you'd keyed me up to such a pitch that it wasn't quite as bad as I expected—"

Mrs. Fetherel lifted a smile steeled for the worst. "Why not say at once," she suggested, "that it's a distinctly pretty story?"

"They haven't said *that*?"

"They've all said it."

"My poor Paula!"

"Even the Bishop—"

"The Bishop called it a pretty story?"

"He wrote me—I've his letter somewhere. The title rather scared him—he wanted me to change it; but when he'd read the book he wrote that it was all right and that he'd sent several copies to his friends."

"The old hypocrite!" cried Mrs. Clinch. "That was nothing but professional jealousy."

"Do you think so?" cried her cousin, brightening.

"Sure of it, my dear. His own books don't sell, and he knew the quickest way to kill yours was to distribute it through the diocese with his blessing."

"Then you don't really think it's a pretty story?"

"Dear me, no! Not nearly as bad as that—"

"You're so good, Bella—but the reviewers?"

"Oh, the reviewers," Mrs. Clinch jeered. She gazed meditatively at the cold remains of her tea-cake. "Let me see," she said, suddenly; "do you happen to remember if the first review came out in an important paper?"

"Yes—the *Radiator*."

"That's it! I thought so. Then the others simply followed suit: they often do if a big paper sets the pace. Saves a lot of trouble. Now if you could only have got the *Radiator* to denounce you—"

"That's what the Bishop said!" cried Mrs. Fetherel.

"He did?"

"He said his only chance of selling 'Through a Glass Brightly' was to have it denounced on the ground of immorality."

"H'm," said Mrs. Clinch. "I thought he knew a trick or two." She turned an illuminated eye on her cousin. "You ought to get *him* to denounce *Fast and Loose*!" she cried.

Mrs. Fetherel looked at her suspiciously. "I suppose every book must stand or fall on its own merits," she said in an unconvinced tone.

"Bosh! That view is as extinct as the post-chaise and the packet-ship—it belongs to the time when people read books. Nobody does that now; the reviewer was the first to set the example, and the public were only too thankful to follow it. At first they read the reviews; now they read only the publishers' extracts from them. Even these are rapidly being replaced by paragraphs borrowed from the vocabulary of commerce. I often have to look twice before I am sure if I am reading a department-store advertisement or the announcement of a new batch of literature. The publishers will soon be having their 'fall and spring openings' and their 'special importations for Horse-Show Week.' But the Bishop is right, of course—nothing helps a book like a rousing attack on its morals; and as the publishers can't exactly proclaim the impropriety of their own wares, the task has to be left to the press or the pulpit."

"The pulpit—?" Mrs. Fetherel mused.

"Why, yes—look at those two novels in England last year—"

Mrs. Fetherel shook her head hopelessly. "There is so much more interest in literature in England than here."

"Well, we've got to make the supply create the demand. The Bishop could run your novel up into the hundred thousands in no time."

"But if he can't make his own sell—?"

"My dear, a man can't very well preach against his own writings!"

Mrs. Clinch rose and picked up her proofs.

"I'm awfully sorry for you, Paula dear," she concluded, "but I can't help being thankful that there's no demand for pessimism in the field of natural history. Fancy having to write 'The Fall of a Sparrow,' or 'How the Plants Misbehave!'"

## IV

MRS. FETHEREL, driving up to the Grand Central Station one morning about five months later, caught sight of the distinguished novelist, Archer Hynes, hurrying into the waiting-room ahead of her. Hynes, on his side, recognizing her brougham, turned back to greet her as the footman opened the carriage door.

"My dear colleague! Is it possible that we are traveling together?"

Mrs. Fetherel blushed with pleasure. Hynes had given her two columns of praise in the *Sunday Meteor*, and she had not yet learned to disguise her gratitude.

"I am going to Ossining," she said, smilingly.

"So am I. Why, this is almost as good as an elopement."

"And it will end where elopements ought to—in church."

"In church? You're not going to Ossining to go to church?"

"Why not? There's a special ceremony in the cathedral—the chantry window is to be unveiled."

"The chantry window? How picturesque! What is a chantry? And why do you want to see it unveiled? Are you after copy—doing something in the Huysmans manner? 'La Cathédrale,' eh?"

"Oh, no." Mrs. Fetherel hesitated. "I'm going simply to please my uncle," she said, at last.

"Your uncle?"

"The Bishop, you know." She smiled.

"The Bishop—the Bishop of Ossining? Why, wasn't he the chap who made that ridiculous attack on your book? Is that prehistoric ass your uncle? Upon my soul, I think you're mighty forgiving to travel all the way to Ossining for one of his stained-glass sociables!"

Mrs. Fetherel's smile flowed into a gentle laugh. "Oh, I've never allowed that to interfere with our friendship. My uncle felt dreadfully about having to speak publicly against my book—it was a great deal harder for him than for me—but he thought it his duty to do so. He has the very highest sense of duty."

"Well," said Hynes, with a shrug, "I don't know that he didn't do you a good turn. Look at that!"

They were standing near the book-stall, and he pointed to a placard surmounting the counter and emblazoned with the conspicuous announcement: "*Fast and Loose.* New

Edition with Author's Portrait. Hundred and Fiftieth Thousand."

Mrs. Fetherel frowned impatiently. "How absurd! They've no right to use my picture as a poster!"

"There's our train," said Hynes; and they began to push their way through the crowd surging toward one of the inner doors.

As they stood wedged between circumferent shoulders, Mrs. Fetherel became conscious of the fixed stare of a pretty girl who whispered eagerly to her companion: "Look Myrtle! That's Paula Fetherel right behind us—I knew her in a minute!"

"Gracious—where?" cried the other girl, giving her head a twist which swept her Gainsborough plumes across Mrs. Fetherel's face.

The first speaker's words had carried beyond her companion's ear, and a lemon-colored woman in spectacles, who clutched a copy of the "Journal of Psychology" on one drab-cotton-gloved hand, stretched her disengaged hand across the intervening barrier of humanity.

"Have I the privilege of addressing the distinguished author of *Fast and Loose*? If so, let me thank you in the name of the Woman's Psychological League of Peoria for your magnificent courage in raising the standard of revolt against—"

"You can tell us the rest in the car," said a fat man, pressing his good-humored bulk against the speaker's arm.

Mrs. Fetherel, blushing, embarrassed and happy, slipped into the space produced by this displacement, and a few moments later had taken her seat in the train.

She was a little late, and the other chairs were already filled by a company of elderly ladies and clergymen who seemed to belong to the same party, and were still busy exchanging greetings and settling themselves in their places.

One of the ladies, at Mrs. Fetherel's approach, uttered an exclamation of pleasure and advanced with outstretched hand. "My dear Mrs. Fetherel! I am so delighted to see you here. May I hope you are going to the unveiling of the chantry window? The dear Bishop so hoped that you would do so! But perhaps I ought to introduce myself. I am Mrs. Gollinger"—she lowered her voice expressively—"one of your uncle's oldest friends, one who has stood close to him through all this sad business, and who knows what he suffered when he felt obliged to sacrifice family affection to the call of duty."

Mrs. Fetherel, who had smiled and colored slightly at the beginning of this speech, received its close with a deprecating gesture.

"Oh, pray don't mention it," she murmured. "I quite understood how my uncle was placed—I bore him no ill will for feeling obliged to preach against my book."

"He understood that, and was so touched by it! He has often told me that it was the hardest task he was ever called upon to perform—and, do you know, he quite feels that this unexpected gift of the chantry window is in some way a return for his courage in preaching that sermon."

Mrs. Fetherel smiled faintly. "Does he feel that?"

"Yes; he really does. When the funds for the window were so mysteriously placed at his disposal, just as he had begun to despair of raising them, he assured me that he could not help connecting the fact with his denunciation of your book."

"Dear Uncle!" sighed Mrs. Fetherel. "Did he say that?"

"And now," continued Mrs. Gollinger, with cumulative rapture—"now that you are about to show, by appearing at the ceremony to-day, that there has been no break in your friendly relations, the dear Bishop's happiness will be complete. He was so longing to have you come to the unveiling!"

"He might have counted on me," said Mrs. Fetherel, still smiling.

"Ah, that is so beautifully forgiving of you!" cried Mrs. Gollinger, enthusiastically. "But then, the Bishop has always assured me that your real nature was very different from that which—if you will pardon my saying so—seems to be revealed by your brilliant but—er—rather subversive book. 'If you only knew my niece, dear Mrs. Gollinger,' he always said, 'you would see that her novel was written in all innocence of heart;' and to tell you the truth, when I first read the book I didn't think it so very, *very* shocking. It wasn't till the dear Bishop had explained to me—but, dear me, I mustn't take up your time in this way when so many others are anxious to have a word with you."

Mrs. Fetherel glanced at her in surprise, and Mrs. Gollinger continued, with a playful smile: "You forget that your face is familiar to thousands whom you have never seen. We all recognized you the moment you entered the train, and my friends here are so eager to make your acquaintance—even those"—her smile deepened—"who thought the dear Bishop not *quite unjustified* in his attack on your remarkable novel."

V

A RELIGIOUS light filled the chantry of Ossining Cathedral, filtering through the linen curtain which veiled the central window, and mingling with the blaze of tapers on the richly adorned altar.

In this devout atmosphere, agreeably laden with the incense-like aroma of Easter lilies and forced lilacs, Mrs. Fetherel knelt with a sense of luxurious satisfaction. Beside her sat Archer Hynes, who had remembered that there was to be a church scene in his next novel, and that his impressions of the devotional environment needed refreshing. Mrs. Fetherel was very happy. She was conscious that her entrance had sent a thrill through the female devotees who packed the chantry, and she had humor enough to enjoy the thought that, but for the good Bishop's denunciation of her book, the heads of his flock would not have been turned so eagerly in her direction. Moreover, as she had entered she had caught sight of a society reporter, and she knew that her presence, and the fact that she was accompanied by Hynes, would be conspicuously proclaimed in the morning papers. All these evidences of the success of her handiwork might have turned a calmer head than Mrs. Fetherel's; and though she had now learned to dissemble her gratification, it still filled her inwardly with a delightful glow.

The Bishop was somewhat late in appearing, and she employed the interval in meditating on the plot of her next novel, which was already partly sketched out, but for which she had been unable to find a satisfactory denouement. By a not uncommon process of ratiocination, Mrs. Fetherel's success had convinced her of her vocation. She was sure now that it was her duty to lay bare the secret plague-spots of society, and she was resolved that there should be no doubt as to the purpose of her new book. Experience had shown her that where she had fancied she was calling a spade a spade she had in fact been alluding in guarded terms to the drawing-room shovel. She was determined not to repeat the same mistake, and she flattered herself that her coming novel would not need an episcopal denunciation to insure its sale, however likely it was to receive this crowning evidence of success.

She had reached this point in her meditations when the choir burst into song and the ceremony of the unveiling began. The Bishop, almost always felicitous in his addresses to the fair sex, was never more so than when he was celebrating the triumph of one of his cherished purposes. There was a peculiar mixture of Christian humility and episcopal exultation in the manner with which he called attention to the Creator's promptness in responding to his demand for funds, and he had never been more happily inspired than in eulogizing the mysterious gift of the chantry window.

Though no hint of the donor's identity had been allowed to escape him, it was generally understood that the Bishop knew who had given the window, and the congregation awaited in a flutter of suspense the possible announcement of a name. None came, however, though the Bishop deliciously titillated the curiosity of his flock by circling ever closer about the interesting secret. He would not disguise from them, he said, that the heart which had divined his inmost wish had been a woman's—is it not to woman's intuitions that more than half the happiness of earth is owing? What man is obliged to learn by the laborious process of experience, woman's wondrous instinct tells her at a glance; and so it had been with this cherished scheme, this unhoped-for completion of their beautiful chantry. So much, at least, he was allowed to reveal; and indeed, had he not done so, the window itself would have spoken for him, since the first glance at its touching subject and exquisite design would show it to have originated in a woman's heart. This tribute to the sex was received with an audible sigh of contentment, and the Bishop, always stimulated by such evidence of his sway over his hearers, took up his theme with gathering eloquence.

Yes—a woman's heart had planned the gift, a woman's hand had executed it, and, might he add, without too far withdrawing the veil in which Christian beneficence ever loved to drape its acts—might he add that, under Providence, a book, a simple book, a mere tale, in fact, had had its share in the good work for which they were assembled to give thanks?

At this unexpected announcement, a ripple of excitement ran through the assemblage, and more than one head was abruptly turned in the direction of Mrs. Fetherel, who sat listening in an agony of wonder and confusion. It did not escape the observant novelist at her side that she drew down her veil to conceal an uncontrollable blush, and this evidence of dismay caused him to fix an attentive gaze on her, while from her seat across the aisle, Mrs. Gollinger sent a smile of unctuous approval.

"A book—a simple book—" the Bishop's voice went on above this flutter of mingled emotions. "What is a book? Only a few pages and a little ink—and yet one of the mightiest instruments which Providence has devised for shaping the destinies of man . .. one of the most powerful influences for good or evil which the Creator has placed in the hands of his creatures . . . "

The air seemed intolerably close to Mrs. Fetherel, and she drew out her scent-bottle, and then thrust it hurriedly away, conscious that she was still the center of an unenviable attention. And all the while the Bishop's voice droned on...

"And of all forms of literature, fiction is doubtless that which has exercised the greatest sway, for good or ill, over the passions and imagination of the masses. Yes, my friends, I am the first to acknowledge it—no sermon, however eloquent, no theological treatise, however learned and convincing, has ever inflamed the heart and imagination like a novel—a simple novel. Incalculable is the power exercised over humanity by the great magicians of the pen—a power ever enlarging its boundaries and increasing its responsibilities as popular education multiplies the number of readers....Yes, it is the novelist's hand which can pour balm on countless human sufferings, or inoculate mankind with the festering poison of a corrupt imagination. . . . "

Mrs. Fetherel had turned white, and her eyes were fixed with a blind stare of anger on the large-sleeved figure in the center of the chancel.

"And too often, alas, it is the poison and not the balm which the unscrupulous hand of genius proffers to its unsuspecting readers. But, my friends, why should I continue? None know better than an assemblage of Christian women, such as I am now addressing, the beneficent or baleful influences of modern fiction; and so, when I say that this beautiful chantry window of ours owes its existence in part to the romancer's pen"—the Bishop paused, and bending forward, seemed to seek a certain face among the countenances eagerly addressed to his—"when I say that this pen, which for personal reasons it does not become me to celebrate unduly—"

Mrs. Fetherel at this point half rose, pushing back her chair, which scraped loudly over the marble floor; but Hynes involuntarily laid a warning hand on her arm, and she sank down with a confused murmur about the heat.

"—When I confess that this pen, which for once at least has proved itself so much mightier than the sword, is that which was inspired to trace the simple narrative of 'Through a Glass Brightly'"—Mrs. Fetherel looked up with a gasp of mingled relief and anger—"when I tell you, my dear friends, that it was your Bishop's own work which first roused the mind of one of his flock to the crying need of a chantry window, I think you will admit that I am justified in celebrating the triumphs of the pen, even though it be the modest instrument which your own Bishop wields."

The Bishop paused impressively, and a faint gasp of surprise and disappointment was audible throughout the chantry. Something very different from this conclusion had been expected, and even Mrs. Gollinger's lips curled with a slightly ironic smile. But Archer Hynes's attention was chiefly reserved for Mrs. Fetherel, whose face had changed with astonishing rapidity from surprise to annoyance, from annoyance to relief, and then back again to something very like indignation.

The address concluded, the actual ceremony of the unveiling was about to take place, and the attention of the congregation soon reverted to the chancel, where the choir had grouped themselves beneath the veiled window, prepared to burst into a chant of praise as the Bishop drew back the hanging. The moment was an impressive one, and every eye was fixed on the curtain. Even Hynes's gaze strayed to it for a moment, but soon returned to his neighbor's face; and then he perceived that Mrs. Fetherel, alone of all the persons present, was not looking at the window. Her eyes were fixed in an indignant stare on the Bishop; a flush of anger burned becomingly under her veil, and her hands nervously crumpled the beautifully printed program of the ceremony.

Hynes broke into a smile of comprehension. He glanced at the Bishop, and back at the Bishop's niece; then, as the episcopal hand was solemnly raised to draw back the curtain, he bent and whispered in Mrs. Fetherel's ear:

"Why, you gave it yourself! You wonderful woman, of course you gave it yourself!"

Mrs. Fetherel raised her eyes to his with a start. Her blush deepened and her lips shaped a hasty "No"; but the denial was deflected into the indignant murmur—"It wasn't *his* silly book that did it anyhow!"

## THE LADY'S MAID'S BELL

IT WAS the autumn after I had the typhoid. I'd been three months in hospital, and when I came out I looked so weak and tottery that the two or three ladies I applied to were afraid to engage me. Most of my money was gone, and after I'd boarded for two months, hanging about the employment-agencies, and answering any advertisement that looked any way respectable, I pretty nearly lost heart, for fretting hadn't made me fatter, and I didn't see why my luck should ever turn. It did though—or I thought so at the time. A Mrs. Railton, a friend of the lady that first brought me out to the States, met me one day and stopped to speak to me: she was one that had always a friendly way with her. She asked me what ailed me to look so white, and when I told her, "Why, Hartley," says she, "I believe I've got the very place for you. Come in tomorrow and we'll talk about it."

The next day, when I called, she told me the lady she'd in mind was a niece of hers, a Mrs. Brympton, a youngish lady, but something of an invalid, who lived all the year round at her country-place on the Hudson, owing to not being able to stand the fatigue of town life.

"Now, Hartley," Mrs. Railton said, in that cheery way that always made me feel things must be going to take a turn for the better—"now understand me; it's not a cheerful place I'm sending you to. The house is big and gloomy; my niece is nervous, vaporish; her husband—well, he's generally away; and the two children are dead. A year ago, I would as soon have thought of shutting a rosy active girl like you into a vault; but you're not particularly brisk yourself just now, are you? and a quiet place, with country air and wholesome food and early hours, ought to be the very thing for you. Don't mistake me," she added, for I suppose I looked a trifle downcast; "you may find it dull, but you won't be unhappy. My niece is an angel. Her former maid, who died last spring, had been with her twenty years and worshipped the ground she walked on. She's a kind mistress to all, and where the mistress is kind, as you know, the servants are generally good-humored, so you'll probably get on well enough with the rest of the household. And you're the very woman I want for my niece: quiet, well-mannered, and educated above your station. You read aloud well, I think? That's a good thing; my niece likes to be read to. She wants a maid that can be something of a companion: her last was, and I can't say how she misses her. It's a lonely life . . . Well, have you decided?"

"Why, ma'am," I said, "I'm not afraid of solitude."

"Well, then, go; my niece will take you on my recommendation. I'll telegraph her at once and you can take the afternoon train. She has no one to wait on her at present, and I don't want you to lose any time."

I was ready enough to start, yet something in me hung back; and to gain time I asked, "And the gentleman, ma'am?"

"The gentleman's almost always away, I tell you," said Mrs. Ralston, quick-like—"and when he's there," says she suddenly, "you've only to keep out of his way."

I took the afternoon train and got out at D—— station at about four o'clock. A groom in a dog-cart was waiting, and we drove off at a smart pace. It was a dull October day, with rain hanging close overhead, and by the time we turned into the Brympton Place woods the daylight was almost gone. The drive wound through the woods for a mile or two, and came out on a gravel court shut in with thickets of tall black-looking shrubs. There were no lights in the windows, and the house *did* look a bit gloomy.

I had asked no questions of the groom, for I never was one to get my notion of new masters from their other servants: I prefer to wait and see for myself. But I could tell by the look of everything that I had got into the right kind of house, and that things were done handsomely. A pleasant-faced cook met me at the back door and called the house-maid to show me up to my room. "You'll see madam later," she said. "Mrs. Brympton has a visitor."

I hadn't fancied Mrs. Brympton was a lady to have many visitors, and somehow the words cheered me. I followed the house-maid upstairs, and saw, through a door on the upper landing, that the main part of the house seemed well-furnished, with dark paneling and a number of old portraits. Another flight of stairs led us up to the servants' wing. It was almost dark now, and the house-maid excused herself for not having brought a light. "But there's matches in your room," she said, "and if you go careful you'll be all right. Mind the step at the end of the passage. Your room is just beyond."

I looked ahead as she spoke, and half-way down the passage, I saw a woman standing. She drew back into a doorway as we passed, and the house-maid didn't appear to notice her. She was a thin woman with a white face, and a darkish stuff gown and apron. I took her for the housekeeper and thought it odd that she didn't speak, but just gave me a long look as she went by. My room opened into a square hall at the end of the passage. Facing my door was another which stood open: the house-maid exclaimed when she saw it.

"There—Mrs. Blinder's left that door open again!" said she, closing it.

"Is Mrs. Blinder the housekeeper?"

"There's no housekeeper: Mrs. Blinder's the cook."

"And is that her room?"

"Laws, no," said the house-maid, cross-like. "That's nobody's room. It's empty, I mean, and the door hadn't ought to be open. Mrs. Brympton wants it kept locked."

She opened my door and led me into a neat room, nicely furnished, with a picture or two on the walls; and having lit a candle she took leave, telling me that the servants'-hall tea was at six, and that Mrs. Brympton would see me afterward.

I found them a pleasant-spoken set in the servants' hall, and by what they let fall I gathered that, as Mrs. Railton had said, Mrs. Brympton was the kindest of ladies; but I didn't take much notice of their talk, for I was watching to see the pale woman in the dark gown come in. She didn't show herself, however, and I wondered if she ate apart; but if she wasn't the housekeeper, why should she? Suddenly it struck me that she might be a trained nurse, and in that case her meals would of course be served in her room. If Mrs. Brympton was an invalid it was likely enough she had a nurse. The idea annoyed me, I own, for they're not always the easiest to get on with, and if I'd known, I shouldn't have taken the place. But there I was, and there was no use pulling a long face over it; and not being one to ask questions, I waited to see what would turn up.

When tea was over, the house-maid said to the footman: "Has Mr. Ranford gone?" and when he said yes, she told me to come up with her to Mrs. Brympton.

Mrs. Brympton was lying down in her bedroom. Her lounge stood near the fire and beside it was a shaded lamp. She was a delicate-looking lady, but when she smiled I felt there was nothing I wouldn't do for her. She spoke very pleasantly, in a low voice, asking me my name and age and so on, and if I had everything I wanted, and if I wasn't afraid of feeling lonely in the country.

"Not with you I wouldn't be, madam," I said, and the words surprised me when I'd spoken them, for I'm not an impulsive person; but it was just as if I'd thought aloud.

She seemed pleased at that, and said she hoped I'd continue in the same mind; then she gave me a few directions about her toilet, and said Agnes the house-maid would show me next morning where things were kept.

"I am tired tonight, and shall dine upstairs," she said. "Agnes will bring me my tray, that you may have time to unpack and settle yourself; and later you may come and undress me."

"Very well, ma'am," I said. "You'll ring, I suppose?"

I thought she looked odd.

"No—Agnes will fetch you," says she quickly, and took up her book again.

Well—that was certainly strange: a lady's maid having to be fetched by the house-maid whenever her lady wanted her! I wondered if there were no bells in the house; but the next day I satisfied myself that there was one in every room, and a special one ringing from my mistress's room to mine; and after that it did strike me as queer that, whenever Mrs. Brympton wanted anything, she rang for Agnes, who had to walk the whole length of the servants' wing to call me.

But that wasn't the only queer thing in the house. The very next day I found out that Mrs. Brympton had no nurse; and then I asked Agnes about the woman I had seen in the passage the afternoon before. Agnes said she had seen no one, and I saw that she thought I was dreaming. To be sure, it was dusk when we went down the passage, and she had excused herself for not bringing a light; but I had seen the woman plain enough to know her again if we should meet. I decided that she must have been a friend of the cook's, or of one of the other women-servants: perhaps she had come down from town for a night's visit, and the servants wanted it kept secret. Some ladies are very stiff about having their servants' friends in the house overnight. At any rate, I made up my mind to ask no more questions.

In a day or two, another odd thing happened. I was chatting one afternoon with Mrs. Blinder, who was a friendly disposed woman, and had been longer in the house than the other servants, and she asked me if I was quite comfortable and had everything I needed. I said I had no fault to find with my place or with my mistress, but I thought it odd that in so large a house there was no sewing-room for the lady's maid.

"Why," says she, "there *is* one; the room you're in is the old sewing-room."

"Oh," said I; "and where did the other lady's maid sleep?"

At that she grew confused, and said hurriedly that the servants' rooms had all been changed about last year, and she didn't rightly remember.

That struck me as peculiar, but I went on as if I hadn't noticed: "Well, there's a vacant room opposite mine, and I mean to ask Mrs. Brympton if I mayn't use that as a sewing-room."

To my astonishment, Mrs. Blinder went white, and gave my hand a kind of squeeze. "Don't do that, my dear," said she, trembling-like. "To tell you the truth, that was Emma Saxon's room, and my mistress has kept it closed ever since her death."

"And who was Emma Saxon?"

"Mrs. Brympton's former maid."

"The one that was with her so many years?" said I, remembering what Mrs. Railton had told me.

Mrs. Blinder nodded.

"What sort of woman was she?"

"No better walked the earth," said Mrs. Blinder. "My mistress loved her like a sister."

"But I mean—what did she look like?"

Mrs. Blinder got up and gave me a kind of angry stare. "I'm no great hand at describing," she said; "and I believe my pastry's rising." And she walked off into the kitchen and shut the door after her.

## II

I HAD been near a week at Brympton before I saw my master. Word came that he was arriving one afternoon, and a change passed over the whole household. It was plain that nobody loved him below stairs. Mrs. Blinder took uncommon care with the dinner that night, but she snapped at the kitchen-maid in a way quite unusual with her; and Mr. Wace, the butler, a serious, slow-spoken man, went about his duties as if he'd been getting ready for a funeral. He was a great Bible-reader, Mr. Wace was, and had a beautiful assortment of texts at his command; but that day he used such dreadful language that I was about to leave the table, when he assured me it was all out of Isaiah; and I noticed that whenever the master came Mr. Wace took to the prophets.

About seven, Agnes called me to my mistress's room; and there I found Mr. Brympton. He was standing on the hearth; a big fair bull-necked man, with a red face and little bad-tempered blue eyes: the kind of man a young simpleton might have thought handsome, and would have been like to pay dear for thinking it.

He swung about when I came in, and looked me over in a trice. I knew what the look meant, from having experienced it once or twice in my former places. Then he turned his back on me, and went on talking to his wife; and I knew what *that* meant, too. I was not the kind of morsel he was after. The typhoid had served me well enough in one way: it kept that kind of gentleman at arm's length.

"This is my new maid, Hartley," says Mrs. Brympton in her kind voice; and he nodded and went on with what he was saying.

In a minute or two he went off, and left my mistress to dress for dinner, and I noticed as I waited on her that she was white, and chill to the touch.

Mr. Brympton took himself off the next morning, and the whole house drew a long breath when he drove away. As for my mistress, she put on her hat and furs (for it was a fine winter morning) and went out for a walk in the gardens, coming back quite fresh and rosy, so that for a minute, before her color faded, I could guess what a pretty young lady she must have been, and not so long ago, either.

She had met Mr. Ranford in the grounds, and the two came back together, I remember, smiling and talking as they walked along the terrace under my window. That was the first time I saw Mr. Ranford, though I had often heard his name mentioned in the hall. He was a neighbor, it appeared, living a mile or two beyond Brympton, at the end of the village; and as he was in the habit of spending his winters in the country he was almost the only company my mistress had at that season. He was a slight tall gentleman of about thirty, and I thought him rather melancholy-looking till I saw his smile, which had a kind of surprise in it, like the first warm day in spring. He was a great reader, I heard, like my mistress, and the two were forever borrowing books of one another, and sometimes (Mr. Wace told me) he would read aloud to Mrs. Brympton by the hour, in the big dark library where she sat in the winter afternoons. The servants all liked him, and perhaps that's more of a compliment than the masters suspect. He had a friendly word for every one of us, and we were all glad to think that Mrs. Brympton had a pleasant companionable gentleman like that to keep her company when the master was away. Mr. Ranford seemed on excellent terms with Mr. Brympton too; though I couldn't but wonder that two gentlemen so unlike each other should be so friendly. But then I knew how the real quality can keep their feelings to themselves.

As for Mr. Brympton, he came and went, never staying more than a day or two, cursing the dullness and the solitude, grumbling at everything, and (as I soon found out) drinking a deal more than was good for him. After Mrs. Brympton left the table he would sit half the night over the old Brympton port and madeira, and once, as I was leaving my mistress's room rather later than usual, I met him coming up the stairs in such a state that I turned sick to think of what some ladies have to endure and hold their tongues about.

The servants said very little about their master; but from what they let drop I could see it had been an unhappy match from the beginning. Mr. Brympton was coarse, loud and pleasure-loving; my mistress quiet, retiring, and perhaps a trifle cold. Not that she was not always pleasant-spoken to him: I thought her wonderfully forbearing; but to a gentleman as free as Mr. Brympton I daresay she seemed a little offish.

Well, things went on quietly for several weeks. My mistress was kind, my duties were light, and I got on well with the other servants. In short, I had nothing to complain of; yet there was always a weight on me. I can't say why it was so, but I know it was not the loneliness that I felt. I soon got used to that; and being still languid from the fever, I was thankful for the quiet and the good country air. Nevertheless, I was never quite easy in my mind. My mistress, knowing I had been ill, insisted that I should take my walk regular, and often invented errands for me:—a yard of ribbon to be fetched from the village, a letter posted, or a book returned to Mr. Ranford. As soon as I was out of doors my spirits rose, and I looked forward to my walks through the bare moist-smelling woods; but the moment I caught sight of the house again my heart dropped down like a stone in a well. It was not a gloomy house exactly, yet I never entered it but a feeling of gloom came over me.

Mrs. Brympton seldom went out in winter; only on the finest days did she walk an hour at noon on the south terrace. Excepting Mr. Ranford, we had no visitors but the doctor, who drove over from D—— about once a week. He sent for me once or twice to give me some trifling direction about my mistress, and though he never told me what her illness was, I thought, from a waxy look she had now and then of a morning, that it might be the heart that ailed her. The season was soft and unwholesome, and in January we had a long spell of rain. That was a sore trial to me, I own, for I couldn't go out, and sitting over my sewing all day, listening to the drip, drip of the eaves, I grew so nervous that the least sound made me jump. Somehow, the thought of that locked room across the passage began to weigh on me. Once or twice, in the long rainy nights, I fancied I heard noises there; but that was nonsense, of course, and the daylight drove such notions out of my head. Well, one morning Mrs. Brympton gave me quite a start of pleasure by telling me she wished me to go to town for some shopping. I hadn't known till then how low my spirits had fallen. I set off in high glee, and my first sight of the crowded streets and the cheerful-looking shops quite took me out of myself. Toward afternoon, however, the noise and confusion began to tire me, and I was actually looking forward to the quiet of Brympton, and thinking how I should enjoy the drive home through the dark woods, when I ran across an old acquaintance, a maid I had once been in service with. We had lost sight of each other for a number of years, and I had to stop and tell her what had happened to me in the interval. When I mentioned where I was living she rolled up her eyes and pulled a long face.

"What! The Mrs. Brympton that lives all the year at her place on the Hudson? My dear, you won't stay there three months."

"Oh, but I don't mind the country," says I, offended somehow at her tone. "Since the fever I'm glad to be quiet."

She shook her head. "It's not the country I'm thinking of. All I know is she's had four maids in the last six months, and the last one, who was a friend of mine, told me nobody could stay in the house."

"Did she say why?" I asked.

"No—she wouldn't give me her reason. But she says to me, 'Mrs. Ansey,' she says, 'if ever a young woman as you know of thinks of going there, you tell her it's not worth while to unpack her boxes.'"

"Is she young and handsome?" said I, thinking of Mr. Brympton.

"Not her! She's the kind that mothers engage when they've gay young gentlemen at college."

Well, though I knew the woman was an idle gossip, the words stuck in my head, and my heart sank lower than ever as I drove up to Brympton in the dusk. There *was* something about the house—I was sure of it now...

When I went in to tea I heard that Mr. Brympton had arrived, and I saw at a glance that there had been a disturbance of some kind. Mrs. Blinder's hand shook so that she could hardly pour the tea, and Mr. Wace quoted the most dreadful texts full of brimstone. Nobody said a word to me then, but when I went up to my room Mrs. Blinder followed me.

"Oh, my dear," says she, taking my hand, "I'm so glad and thankful you've come back to us!"

That struck me, as you may imagine. "Why," said I, "did you think I was leaving for good?"

"No, no, to be sure," said she, a little confused, "but I can't a-bear to have madam left alone for a day even." She pressed my hand hard, and, "Oh, Miss Hartley," says she, "be good to your mistress, as you're a Christian woman." And with that she hurried away, and left me staring.

A moment later Agnes called me to Mrs. Brympton. Hearing Mr. Brympton's voice in her room, I went round by the dressing-room, thinking I would lay out her dinner-gown before going in. The dressing-room is a large room with a window over the portico that looks toward the gardens. Mr. Brympton's apartments are beyond. When I went in, the door into the bedroom was ajar, and I heard Mr. Brympton saying angrily:—"One would suppose he was the only person fit for you to talk to."

"I don't have many visitors in winter," Mrs. Brympton answered quietly.

"You have *me!*" he flung at her, sneering.

"You are here so seldom," said she.

"Well—whose fault is that? You make the place about as lively as a family vault—"

With that I rattled the toilet-things, to give my mistress warning and she rose and called me in.

The two dined alone, as usual, and I knew by Mr. Wace's manner at supper that things must be going badly. He quoted the prophets something terrible, and worked on the kitchen-maid so that she declared she wouldn't go down alone to put the cold meat in the ice-box. I felt nervous myself, and after I had put my mistress to bed I was half-tempted to go down again and persuade Mrs. Blinder to sit up awhile over a game of cards. But I heard her door closing for the night, and so I went on to my own room. The rain had begun again, and the drip, drip, drip seemed to be dropping into my brain. I lay awake listening to it, and turning over what my friend in town had said. What puzzled me was that it was always the maids who left . . . .

After a while I slept; but suddenly a loud noise wakened me. My bell had rung. I sat up, terrified by the unusual sound, which seemed to go on jangling through the darkness.

My hands shook so that I couldn't find the matches. At length I struck a light and jumped out of bed. I began to think I must have been dreaming; but I looked at the bell against the wall, and there was the little hammer still quivering.

I was just beginning to huddle on my clothes when I heard another sound. This time it was the door of the locked room opposite mine softly opening and closing. I heard the sound distinctly, and it frightened me so that I stood stock still. Then I heard a footstep hurrying down the passage toward the main house. The floor being carpeted, the sound was very faint, but I was quite sure it was a woman's step. I turned cold with the thought of it, and for a minute or two I dursn't breathe or move. Then I came to my senses.

"Alice Hartley," says I to myself, "someone left that room just now and ran down the passage ahead of you. The idea isn't pleasant, but you may as well face it. Your mistress has rung for you, and to answer her bell you've got to go the way that other woman has gone."

Well—I did it. I never walked faster in my life, yet I thought I should never get to the end of the passage or reach Mrs. Brympton's room. On the way I heard nothing and saw nothing: all was dark and quiet as the grave. When I reached my mistress's door the silence was so deep that I began to think I must be dreaming, and was half-minded to turn back. Then a panic seized me, and I knocked.

There was no answer, and I knocked again, loudly. To my astonishment the door was opened by Mr. Brympton. He started back when he saw me, and in the light of my candle his face looked red and savage.

"*You?*" he said, in a queer voice. "*How many of you are there, in God's name?*"

At that I felt the ground give under me; but I said to myself that he had been drinking, and answered as steadily as I could: "May I go in, sir? Mrs. Brympton has rung for me."

"You may all go in, for what I care," says he, and, pushing by me, walked down the hall to his own bedroom. I looked after him as he went, and to my surprise I saw that he walked as straight as a sober man.

I found my mistress lying very weak and still, but she forced a smile when she saw me, and signed to me to pour out some drops for her. After that she lay without speaking, her breath coming quick, and her eyes closed. Suddenly she groped out with her hand, and "*Emma,*" says she, faintly.

"It's Hartley, madam," I said. "Do you want anything?"

She opened her eyes wide and gave me a startled look.

"I was dreaming," she said. "You may go, now, Hartley, and thank you kindly. I'm quite well again, you see." And she turned her face away from me.

### III

THERE was no more sleep for me that night, and I was thankful when daylight came.

Soon afterward, Agnes called me to Mrs. Brympton. I was afraid she was ill again, for she seldom sent for me before nine, but I found her sitting up in bed, pale and drawn-looking, but quite herself.

"Hartley," says she quickly, "will you put on your things at once and go down to the village for me? I want this prescription made up—" here she hesitated a minute and blushed—"and I should like you to be back again before Mr. Brympton is up."

"Certainly, madam," I said.

"And—stay a moment—" she called me back as if an idea had just struck her—

"while you're waiting for the mixture, you'll have time to go on to Mr. Ranford's with this note."

It was a two-mile walk to the village, and on my way I had time to turn things over in my mind. It struck me as peculiar that my mistress should wish the prescription made up without Mr. Brympton's knowledge; and, putting this together with the scene of the night before, and with much else that I had noticed and suspected, I began to wonder if the poor lady was weary of her life, and had come to the mad resolve of ending it. The idea took such hold on me that I reached the village on a run, and dropped breathless into a chair before the chemist's counter. The good man, who was just taking down his shutters, stared at me so hard that it brought me to myself.

"Mr. Limmel," I says, trying to speak indifferent, "will you run your eye over this, and tell me if it's quite right?"

He put on his spectacles and studied the prescription.

"Why, it's one of Dr. Walton's," says he. "What should be wrong with it?"

"Well—is it dangerous to take?"

"Dangerous—how do you mean?"

I could have shaken the man for his stupidity.

"I mean—if a person was to take too much of it—by mistake of course—" says I, my heart in my throat.

"Lord bless you, no. It's only lime-water. You might feed it to a baby by the bottleful."

I gave a great sigh of relief, and hurried on to Mr. Ranford's. But on the way another thought struck me. If there was nothing to conceal about my visit to the chemist's, was it my other errand that Mrs. Brympton wished me to keep private? Somehow, that thought frightened me worse than the other. Yet the two gentlemen seemed fast friends, and I would have staked my head on my mistress's goodness. I felt ashamed of my suspicions, and concluded that I was still disturbed by the strange events of the night. I left the note at Mr. Ranford's—and, hurrying back to Brympton, slipped in by a side door without being seen, as I thought.

An hour later, however, as I was carrying in my mistress's breakfast, I was stopped in the hall by Mr. Brympton.

"What were you doing out so early?" he says, looking hard at me.

"Early—me, sir?" I said, in a tremble.

"Come, come," he says, an angry red spot coming out on his forehead, "didn't I see you scuttling home through the shrubbery an hour or more ago?"

I'm a truthful woman by nature, but at that a lie popped out ready-made. "No, sir, you didn't," said I, and looked straight back at him.

He shrugged his shoulders and gave a sullen laugh. "I suppose you think I was drunk last night?" he asked suddenly.

"No, sir, I don't," I answered, this time truthfully enough.

He turned away with another shrug. "A pretty notion my servants have of me!" I heard him mutter as he walked off.

Not till I had settled down to my afternoon's sewing did I realize how the events of the night had shaken me. I couldn't pass that locked door without a shiver. I knew I had heard someone come out of it, and walk down the passage ahead of me. I thought of speaking to Mrs. Blinder or to Mr. Wace, the only two in the house who appeared to have an inkling of what was going on, but I had a feeling that if I questioned them they would deny everything, and that I might learn more by holding my tongue and keeping my eyes open. The idea of spending another night opposite the locked room sickened me, and once I was seized with the notion of packing my trunk and taking the first train to town; but it wasn't in me to throw over a kind mistress in that manner, and I tried to go on with my sewing as if nothing had happened.

I hadn't worked ten minutes before the sewing-machine broke down. It was one I had found in the house, a good machine, but a trifle out of order: Mrs. Blinder said it had never been used since Emma Saxon's death. I stopped to see what was wrong, and as I was working at the machine a drawer which I had never been able to open slid forward and a photograph fell out. I picked it up and sat looking at it in a maze. It was a woman's likeness, and I knew I had seen the face somewhere—the eyes had an asking look that I had felt on me before. And suddenly I remembered the pale woman in the passage.

I stood up, cold all over, and ran out of the room. My heart seemed to be thumping in the top of my head, and I felt as if I should never get away from the look in those eyes. I went straight to Mrs. Blinder. She was taking her afternoon nap, and sat up with a jump when I came in.

"Mrs. Blinder," said I, "who is that?" And I held out the photograph.

She rubbed her eyes and stared.

"Why, Emma Saxon," says she. "Where did you find it?"

I looked hard at her for a minute. "Mrs. Blinder," I said, "I've seen that face before."

Mrs. Blinder got up and walked over to the looking-glass. "Dear me! I must have been asleep," she says. "My front is all over one ear. And now do run along, Miss Hartley, dear, for I hear the clock striking four, and I must go down this very minute and put on the Virginia ham for Mr. Brympton's dinner."

IV

TO all appearances, things went on as usual for a week or two. The only difference was that Mr. Brympton stayed on, instead of going off as he usually did, and that Mr. Ranford never showed himself. I heard Mr. Brympton remark on this one afternoon when he was sitting in my mistress's room before dinner:

"Where's Ranford?" says he. "He hasn't been near the house for a week. Does he keep away because I'm here?"

Mrs. Brympton spoke so low that I couldn't catch her answer.

"Well," he went on, "two's company and three's trumpery; I'm sorry to be in Ranford's way, and I suppose I shall have to take myself off again in a day or two and give him a show." And he laughed at his own joke.

The very next day, as it happened, Mr. Ranford called. The footman said the three were very merry over their tea in the library, and Mr. Brympton strolled down to the gate with Mr. Ranford when he left.

I have said that things went on as usual; and so they did with the rest of the household; but as for myself, I had never been the same since the night my bell had rung. Night after night I used to lie awake, listening for it to ring again, and for the door of the locked room to open stealthily. But the bell never rang, and I heard no sound across the passage. At last the silence began to be more dreadful to me than the most mysterious sounds. I felt that *someone* were cowering there, behind the locked door, watching and listening as I watched and listened, and I could almost have cried out, "Whoever you are, come out and let me see you face to face, but don't lurk there and spy on me in the darkness!"

Feeling as I did, you may wonder I didn't give warning. Once I very nearly did so; but at the last moment something held me back. Whether it was compassion for my mistress, who had grown more and more dependent on me, or unwillingness to try a new place, or some other feeling that I couldn't put a name to, I lingered on as if spell-bound, though every night was dreadful to me, and the days but little better.

For one thing, I didn't like Mrs. Brympton's looks. She had never been the same since that night, no more than I had. I thought she would brighten up after Mr. Brympton left, but though she seemed easier in her mind, her spirits didn't revive, nor her strength either. She had grown attached to me, and seemed to like to have me about; and Agnes told me one day that, since Emma Saxon's death, I was the only maid her mistress had taken to. This gave me a warm feeling for the poor lady, though after all there was little I could do to help her.

After Mr. Brympton's departure, Mr. Ranford took to coming again, though less often than formerly. I met him once or twice in the grounds, or in the village, and I couldn't but think there was a change in him too; but I set it down to my disordered fancy.

The weeks passed, and Mr. Brympton had now been a month absent. We heard he was cruising with a friend in the West Indies, and Mr. Wace said that was a long way off, but though you had the wings of a dove and went to the uttermost parts of the earth, you couldn't get away from the Almighty. Agnes said that as long as he stayed away from Brympton, the Almighty might have him and welcome; and this raised a laugh, though Mrs. Blinder tried to look shocked, and Mr. Wace said the bears would eat us.

We were all glad to hear that the West Indies were a long way off, and I remember that, in spite of Mr. Wace's solemn looks, we had a very merry dinner that day in the hall. I don't know if it was because of my being in better spirits, but I fancied Mrs. Brympton looked better too, and seemed more cheerful in her manner. She had been for a walk in the morning, and after luncheon she lay down in her room, and I read aloud to her. When she dismissed me I went to my own room feeling quite bright and happy, and for the first time in weeks walked past the locked door without thinking of it. As I sat down to my work I looked out and saw a few snow-flakes falling. The sight was pleasanter than the eternal rain, and I pictured to myself how pretty the bare gardens would look in their white mantle. It seemed to me as if the snow would cover up all the dreariness, indoors as well as out.

The fancy had hardly crossed my mind when I heard a step at my side. I looked up, thinking it was Agnes.

"Well, Agnes—" said I, and the words froze on my tongue; for there, in the door, stood *Emma Saxon*.

I don't know how long she stood there. I only know I couldn't stir or take my eyes from her. Afterward I was terribly frightened, but at the time it wasn't fear I felt, but something deeper and quieter. She looked at me long and long, and her face was just one dumb prayer to me—but how in the world was I to help her? Suddenly she turned, and I heard her walk down the passage. This time I wasn't afraid to follow—I felt that I must know what she wanted. I sprang up and ran out. She was at the other end of the passage, and I expected her to take the turn toward my mistress's room; but instead of that she pushed open the door that led to the backstairs. I followed her down the stairs, and across the passageway to the back door. The kitchen and hall were empty at that hour, the servants being off duty, except for the footman, who was in the pantry. At the door she stood still a moment, with another look at me; then she turned the handle, and stepped out. For a minute I hesitated. Where was she leading me to? The door had closed softly after her, and I opened it and looked out, half-expecting to find that she had disappeared. But I saw her a few yards off, hurrying across the court-yard to the path through the woods. Her figure looked black and lonely in the snow, and for a second my heart failed me and I thought of turning back. But all the while she was drawing me after her; and catching up an old shawl of Mrs. Blinder's I ran out into the open.

Emma Saxon was in the wood-path now. She walked on steadily, and I followed at the same pace, till we passed out of the gates and reached the high-road. Then she struck across the open fields to the village. By this time the ground was white, and as she climbed the slope of a bare hill ahead of me I noticed that she left no foot-prints behind her. At sight of that, my heart shriveled up within me, and my knees were water. Somehow, it was worse here than indoors. She made the whole countryside seem lonely as the grave, with none but us two in it, and no help in the wide world.

Once I tried to go back; but she turned and looked at me, and it was as if she had dragged me with ropes. After that I followed her like a dog. We came to the village, and she led me through it, past the church and the blacksmith's shop, and down the lane to Mr. Ranford's. Mr. Ranford's house stands close to the road: a plain old-fashioned building, with a flagged path leading to the door between box-borders. The lane was deserted, and as I turned into it, I saw Emma Saxon pause under the old elm by the gate. And now another fear came over me. I saw that we had reached the end of our journey, and that it was my turn to act. All the way from Brympton I had been asking myself what she wanted of me, but I had followed in a trance, as it were, and not till I saw her stop at Mr. Ranford's gate did my brain begin to clear itself. It stood a little way off in the snow, my heart beating fit to strangle me, and my feet frozen to the ground; and she stood under the elm and watched me.

I knew well enough that she hadn't led me there for nothing. I felt there was something I ought to say or do—but how was I to guess what it was? I had never thought harm of my mistress and Mr. Ranford, but I was sure now that, from one cause or another, some dreadful thing hung over them. *She* knew what it was; she would tell me if she could; perhaps she would answer if I questioned her.

It turned me faint to think of speaking to her; but I plucked up heart and dragged myself across the few yards between us. As I did so, I heard the house-door open, and saw Mr. Ranford approaching. He looked handsome and cheerful, as my mistress had looked that morning, and at sight of him the blood began to flow again in my veins.

"Why, Hartley," said he, "what's the matter? I saw you coming down the lane just now, and came out to see if you had taken root in the snow." He stopped and stared at me. "What are you looking at?" he says.

I turned toward the elm as he spoke, and his eyes followed me; but there was no one there. The lane was empty as far as the eye could reach.

A sense of helplessness came over me. She was gone, and I had not been able to guess what she wanted. Her last look had pierced me to the marrow; and yet it had not told me! All at once, I felt more desolate than when she had stood there watching me. It seemed as if she had left me all alone to carry the weight of the secret I couldn't guess. The snow went round me in great circles, and the ground fell away from me....

A drop of brandy and the warmth of Mr. Ranford's fire soon brought me to, and I insisted on being driven back at once to Brympton. It was nearly dark, and I was afraid my mistress might be wanting me. I explained to Mr. Ranford that I had been out for a walk and had been taken with a fit of giddiness as I passed his gate. This was true enough; yet I never felt more like a liar than when I said it.

When I dressed Mrs. Brympton for dinner she remarked on my pale looks and asked what ailed me. I told her I had a headache, and she said she would not require me again that evening, and advised me to go to bed.

It was a fact that I could scarcely keep on my feet; yet I had no fancy to spend a solitary evening in my room. I sat downstairs in the hall as long as I could hold my head up; but by nine I crept upstairs, too weary to care what happened if I could but get my head on a pillow. The rest of the household went to bed soon afterward; they kept early hours when the master was away, and before ten I heard Mrs. Blinder's door close, and Mr. Wace's soon after.

It was a very still night, earth and air all muffled in snow. Once in bed I felt easier, and lay quiet, listening to the strange noises that come out in a house after dark. Once I thought I heard a door open and close again below: it might have been the glass door that led to the gardens. I got up and peered out of the window; but it was in the dark of the moon, and nothing visible outside but the streaking of snow against the panes.

I went back to bed and must have dozed, for I jumped awake to the furious ringing of my bell. Before my head was clear I had sprung out of bed, and was dragging on my clothes. *It is going to happen now*, I heard myself saying; but what I meant I had no notion. My hands seemed to be covered with glue—I thought I should never get into my clothes. At last I opened my door and peered down the passage. As far as my candle-flame carried, I could see nothing unusual ahead of me. I hurried on, breathless; but as I pushed open the baize door leading to the main hall my heart stood still, for there at the head of the stairs was Emma Saxon, peering dreadfully down into the darkness.

For a second I couldn't stir; but my hand slipped from the door, and as it swung shut the figure vanished. At the same instant there came another sound from below stairs—a stealthy mysterious sound, as of a latch-key turning in the house-door. I ran to Mrs. Brympton's room and knocked.

There was no answer, and I knocked again. This time I heard someone moving in the room; the bolt slipped back and my mistress stood before me. To my surprise I saw that she had not undressed for the night. She gave me a startled look.

"What is this, Hartley?" she says in a whisper. "Are you ill? What are you doing here at this hour?"

"I am not ill, madam; but my bell rang."

At that she turned pale, and seemed about to fall.

"You are mistaken," she said harshly; "I didn't ring. You must have been dreaming." I had never heard her speak in such a tone. "Go back to bed," she said, closing the door on me.

But as she spoke I heard sounds again in the hall below: a man's step this time; and the truth leaped out on me.

"Madam," I said, pushing past her, "there is someone in the house—"

"Someone—?"

"Mr. Brympton, I think—I hear his step below—"

A dreadful look came over her, and without a word, she dropped flat at my feet. I fell on my knees and tried to lift her: by the way she breathed I saw it was no common faint. But as I raised her head there came quick steps on the stairs and across the hall: the door was flung open, and there stood Mr. Brympton, in his travelling-clothes, the snow dripping from him. He drew back with a start as he saw me kneeling by my mistress.

"What the devil is this?" he shouted. He was less high-colored than usual, and the red spot came out on his forehead.

"Mrs. Brympton has fainted, sir," said I.

He laughed unsteadily and pushed by me. "It's a pity she didn't choose a more convenient moment. I'm sorry to disturb her, but—"

I raised myself up, aghast at the man's action.

"Sir," said I, "are you mad? What are you doing?"

"Going to meet a friend," said he, and seemed to make for the dressing room.

At that my heart turned over. I don't know what I thought or feared; but I sprang up and caught him by the sleeve.

"Sir, sir," said I, "for pity's sake look at your wife!"

He shook me off furiously.

"It seems that's done for me," says he, and caught hold of the dressing room door.

At that moment I heard a slight noise inside. Slight as it was, he heard it too, and tore the door open; but as he did so he dropped back. On the threshold stood Emma Saxon. All was dark behind her, but I saw her plainly, and so did he. He threw up his hands as if to hide his face from her; and when I looked again she was gone.

He stood motionless, as if the strength had run out of him; and in the stillness my mistress suddenly raised herself, and opening her eyes fixed a look on him. Then she fell back, and I saw the death-flutter pass over her face. . . .

We buried her on the third day, in a driving snow-storm. There were few people in the church, for it was bad weather to come from town, and I've a notion my mistress was one that hadn't many near friends. Mr. Ranford was among the last to come, just before they carried her up the aisle. He was in black, of course, being such a friend of the family, and I never saw a gentleman so pale. As he passed me, I noticed that he leaned a trifle on a stick he carried; and I fancy Mr. Brympton noticed it too, for the red spot came out sharp on his forehead, and all through the service he kept staring across the church at Mr. Ranford, instead of following the prayers as a mourner should.

When it was over and we went out to the graveyard, Mr. Ranford had disappeared, and as soon as my poor mistress's body was underground, Mr. Brympton jumped into the carriage nearest the gate and drove off without a word to any of us. I heard him call out, "To the station," and we servants went back alone to the house.

## A VENETIAN NIGHT'S ENTERTAINMENT

THIS IS the story that, in the dining-room of the old Beacon Street house (now the Aldebaran Club), Judge Anthony Bracknell, of the famous East India firm of Bracknell & Saulsbee, when the ladies had withdrawn to the oval parlor (and Maria's harp was throwing its gauzy web of sound across the Common), used to relate to his grandsons, about the year that Bonaparte marched upon Moscow.

### I

"HIM VENICE!" said the Lascar with the big earrings; and Tony Bracknell, leaning on the high gunwale of his father's East Indiaman, the Hepzibah B., saw far off, across the morning sea, a faint vision of towers and domes dissolved in golden air.

It was a rare February day of the year 1760, and a young Tony, newly of age, and bound on the grand tour aboard the crack merchantman of old Bracknell's fleet, felt his heart leap up as the distant city trembled into shape. *Venice!* The name, since childhood, had been a magician's wand to him. In the hall of the old Bracknell house at Salem there hung a series of yellowing prints which Uncle Richard Saulsbee had brought home from one of his long voyages: views of heathen mosques and palaces, of the Grand Turk's Seraglio, of St. Peter's Church in Rome; and, in a corner—the corner nearest the rack where the old flintlocks hung—a busy merry populous scene, entitled: St. Mark's Square in Venice. This picture, from the first, had singularly taken little Tony's fancy. His unformulated criticism on the others was that they lacked action. True, in the view of St. Peter's an experienced-looking gentleman in a full-bottomed wig was pointing out the fairly obvious monument to a bashful companion, who had presumably not ventured to raise his eyes to it; while, at the doors of the Seraglio, a group of turbaned infidels observed with less hesitancy the approach of a veiled lady on a camel. But in Venice so many things were happening at once—more, Tony was sure, than had ever happened in Boston in a twelve-month or in Salem in a long lifetime. For here, by their garb, were people of every nation on earth, Chinamen, Turks, Spaniards, and many more, mixed with a parti-colored throng of gentry, lackeys, chapmen, hucksters, and tall personages in parsons' gowns who stalked through the crowd with an air of mastery, a string of parasites at their heels. And all these people seemed to be diverting themselves hugely, chaffering with the hucksters, watching the antics of trained dogs and monkeys, distributing doles to maimed beggars or having their pockets picked by slippery-looking fellows in black—the whole with such an air of ease and good-humor that one felt the cut-purses to be as much a part of the show as the tumbling acrobats and animals.

As Tony advanced in years and experience this childish mumming lost its magic; but not so the early imaginings it had excited. For the old picture had been but the spring-board of fancy, the first step of a cloud-ladder leading to a land of dreams. With these dreams the name of Venice remained associated; and all that observation or report subsequently brought him concerning the place seemed, on a sober warranty of fact, to confirm its claim to stand midway between reality and illusion. There was, for instance, a slender Venice glass, gold-powdered as with lily-pollen or the dust of sunbeams, that, standing in the corner cabinet betwixt two Lowestoft caddies, seemed, among its lifeless neighbors, to palpitate like an impaled butterfly. There was, farther, a gold chain of his mother's, spun of that same sun-pollen, so thread-like, impalpable, that it slipped through the fingers like light, yet so strong that it carried a heavy pendant which seemed held in air as if by magic. Magic! That was the word which the thought of Venice evoked. It was the kind of place, Tony felt, in which things elsewhere impossible might naturally happen, in which two and two might make five, a paradox elope with a syllogism, and a conclusion give the lie to its own premise. Was there ever a young heart that did not, once and again, long to get away into such a world as that? Tony, at least, had felt the longing from the first hour when the axioms in his horn-book had brought home to him his heavy responsibilities as a Christian and a sinner. And now here was his wish taking shape before him, as the distant haze of gold shaped itself into towers and domes across the morning sea!

The Reverend Ozias Mounce, Tony's governor and bear-leader, was just putting a hand to the third clause of the fourth part of a sermon on Free-Will and Predestination as the Hepzibah B.'s anchor rattled overboard. Tony, in his haste to be ashore, would have made one plunge with the anchor; but the Reverend Ozias, on being roused from his lucubrations, earnestly protested against leaving his argument in suspense. What was the trifle of an arrival at some papistical foreign city, where the very churches wore turbans like so many Moslem idolaters, to the important fact of Mr. Mounce's summing up his conclusions before the Muse of Theology took flight? He should be happy, he said, if the tide served, to visit Venice with Mr. Bracknell the next morning.

The next morning, ha! Tony murmured a submissive "Yes, sir," winked at the subjugated captain, buckled on his sword, pressed his hat down with a flourish, and before the Reverend Ozias had arrived at his next deduction, was skimming merrily shoreward in the Hepzibah's gig.

A moment more and he was in the thick of it! Here was the very world of the old print, only suffused with sunlight and color, and bubbling with merry noises. What a scene it was! A square enclosed in fantastic painted buildings, and peopled with a throng as fantastic: a bawling, laughing, jostling, sweating mob, parti-colored, parti-speeched, crackling and sputtering under the hot sun like a dish of fritters over a kitchen fire. Tony, agape, shouldered his way through the press, aware at once that, spite of the tumult, the shrillness, the gesticulation, there was no undercurrent of clownishness, no tendency to horse-play, as in such crowds on market-day at home, but a kind of facetious suavity which seemed to include everybody in the circumference of one huge joke. In such an air the sense of strangeness soon wore off, and Tony was beginning to feel himself vastly at home, when a lift of the tide bore him against a droll-looking bell-ringing fellow who carried above his head a tall metal tree hung with sherbet-glasses. The encounter set the glasses spinning and three or four spun off and clattered to the stones. The sherbet-seller called on all the saints, and Tony, clapping a lordly hand to his pocket, tossed him a ducat by mistake for a sequin. The fellow's eyes shot out of their orbits, and just then a personable-looking young man who had observed the transaction stepped up to Tony and said pleasantly, in English:

"I perceive, sir, that you are not familiar with our currency."

"Does he want more?" says Tony, very lordly; whereat the other laughed and replied: "You have given him enough to retire from his business and open a gaming-house over the arcade."

Tony joined in the laugh, and this incident bridging the preliminaries, the two young men were presently hobnobbing over a glass of Canary in front of one of the coffee-houses about the square. Tony counted himself lucky to have run across an English-speaking companion who was good-natured enough to give him a clue to the labyrinth; and when he had paid for the Canary (in the coin his friend selected) they set out again to view the town. The Italian gentleman, who called himself Count Rialto, appeared to have a very numerous acquaintance, and was able to point out to Tony all the chief dignitaries of the state, the men of ton and ladies of fashion, as well as a number of other characters of a kind not openly mentioned in taking a census of Salem.

Tony, who was not averse from reading when nothing better offered, had perused the *Merchant of Venice* and Mr. Otway's fine tragedy; but though these pieces had given him a notion that the social usages of Venice differed from those at home, he was unprepared for the surprising appearance and manners of the great people his friend named to him. The gravest Senators of the Republic went in prodigious striped trousers, short cloaks and feathered hats. One nobleman wore a ruff and doctor's gown, another a black velvet tunic slashed with rose color; while the President of the dreaded Council of Ten was a terrible strutting fellow with a rapier-like nose, a buff leather jerkin and a trailing scarlet cloak that the crowd was careful not to step on.

It was all vastly diverting, and Tony would gladly have gone on forever; but he had given his word to the captain to be at the landing-place at sunset, and here was dusk already creeping over the skies! Tony was a man of honor; and having pressed on the Count a handsome damascened dagger selected from one of the goldsmiths' shops in a narrow street lined with such wares, he insisted on turning his face toward the Hepzibah's gig. The Count yielded reluctantly; but as they came out again on the square they were caught in a great throng pouring toward the doors of the cathedral.

"They go to Benediction," said the Count. "A beautiful sight, with many lights and flowers. It is a pity you cannot take a peep at it."

Tony thought so too, and in another minute a legless beggar had pulled back the leathern flap of the cathedral door, and they stood in a haze of gold and perfume that seemed to rise and fall on the mighty undulations of the organ. Here the press was as thick as without; and as Tony flattened himself against a pillar, he heard a pretty voice at his elbow:—"Oh, sir, oh, sir, your sword!"

He turned at sound of the broken English, and saw a girl who matched the voice trying to disengage her dress from the tip of his scabbard. She wore one of the voluminous black hoods which the Venetian ladies affected, and under its projecting eaves her face spied out at him as sweet as a nesting bird.

In the dusk their hands met over the scabbard, and as she freed herself a shred of her lace flounce clung to Tony's enchanted fingers. Looking after her, he saw she was on the arm of a pompous-looking graybeard in a long black gown and scarlet stockings, who, on perceiving the exchange of glances between the young people, drew the lady away with a threatening look.

The Count met Tony's eye with a smile. "One of our Venetian beauties," said he; "the lovely Polixena Cador. She is thought to have the finest eyes in Venice."

"She spoke English," stammered Tony.

"Oh—ah—precisely: she learned the language at the Court of Saint James's, where her father, the Senator, was formerly accredited as Ambassador. She played as an infant with the royal princes of England."

"And that was her father?"

"Assuredly: young ladies of Donna Polixena's rank do not go abroad save with their parents or a duenna."

Just then a soft hand slid into Tony's. His heart gave a foolish bound, and he turned about half-expecting to meet again the merry eyes under the hood; but saw instead a slender brown boy, in some kind of fanciful page's dress, who thrust a folded paper between his fingers and vanished in the throng. Tony, in a tingle, glanced surreptitiously at the Count, who appeared absorbed in his prayers. The crowd, at the ringing of a bell, had in fact been overswept by a sudden wave of devotion; and Tony seized the moment to step beneath a lighted shrine with his letter.

"I am in dreadful trouble and implore your help. Polixena"—he read; but hardly had he seized the sense of the words when a hand fell on his shoulder, and a stern-looking man in a cocked hat, and bearing a kind of rod or mace, pronounced a few words in Venetian.

Tony, with a start, thrust the letter in his breast, and tried to jerk himself free; but the harder he jerked the tighter grew the other's grip, and the Count, presently perceiving what had happened, pushed his way through the crowd, and whispered hastily to his companion: "For God's sake, make no struggle. This is serious. Keep quiet and do as I tell you."

Tony was no chickenheart. He had something of a name for pugnacity among the lads of his own age at home, and was not the man to stand in Venice what he would have resented in Salem; but the devil of it was that this black fellow seemed to be pointing to the letter in his breast; and this suspicion was confirmed by the Count's agitated whisper:

"This is one of the agents of the Ten. For God's sake, no outcry." He exchanged a word or two with the mace-bearer and again turned to Tony. "You have been seen concealing a letter about your person—"

"And what of that?" says Tony furiously.

"Gently, gently, my master. A letter handed to you by the page of Donna Polixena Cador.—A black business! Oh, a very black business! This Cador is one of the most powerful nobles in Venice—I beseech you, not a word, sir! Let me think—deliberate—"

His hand on Tony's shoulder, he carried on a rapid dialogue with the potentate in the cocked hat.

"I am sorry, sir—but our young ladies of rank are as jealously guarded as the Grand Turk's wives, and you must be answerable for this scandal. The best I can do is to have you taken privately to the Palazzo Cador, instead of being brought before the Council. I have pleaded your youth and inexperience"—Tony winced at this—"and I think the business may still be arranged."

Meanwhile the agent of the Ten had yielded his place to a sharp-featured shabby-looking fellow in black, dressed somewhat like a lawyer's clerk, who laid a grimy hand on Tony's arm, and with many apologetic gestures steered him through the crowd to the doors of the church. The Count held him by the other arm, and in this fashion they emerged on the square, which now lay in darkness save for the many lights twinkling under the arcade and in the windows of the gaming rooms above it.

Tony by this time had regained voice enough to declare that he would go where they pleased, but that he must first say a word to the mate of the Hepzibah, who had now been awaiting him some two hours or more at the landing place.

The Count repeated this to Tony's custodian, but the latter shook his head and rattled off a sharp denial.

"Impossible, sir," said the Count. "I entreat you not to insist. Any resistance will tell against you in the end."

Tony fell silent. With a rapid eye he was measuring his chances of escape. In wind and limb he was more than a mate for his captors, and boyhood's ruses were not so far behind him but he felt himself equal to outwitting a dozen grown men; but he had the sense to see that at a cry the crowd would close in on him. Space was what he wanted: a clear ten yards, and he would have laughed at Doge and Council. But the throng was thick as glue, and he walked on submissively, keeping his eye alert for an opening. Suddenly the mob swerved aside after some new show. Tony's fist shot out at the black fellow's chest, and before the latter could right himself the young New Englander was showing a clean pair of heels to his escort. On he sped, cleaving the crowd like a flood-tide in Gloucester bay, diving under the first arch that caught his eye, dashing down a lane to an unlit water-way, and plunging across a narrow hump-back bridge which landed him in a black pocket between walls. But now his pursuers were at his back, reinforced by the yelping mob. The walls were too high to scale, and for all his courage Tony's breath came short as he paced the masonry cage in which ill-luck had landed him. Suddenly a gate opened in one of the walls, and a slip of a servant wench looked out and beckoned him. There was no time to weigh chances. Tony dashed through the gate, his rescuer slammed and bolted it, and the two stood in a narrow paved well between high houses.

## II

THE servant picked up a lantern and signed to Tony to follow her. They climbed a squalid stairway of stone, felt their way along a corridor, and entered a tall vaulted room feebly lit by an oil-lamp hung from the painted ceiling. Tony discerned traces of former splendor in his surroundings, but he had no time to examine them, for a figure started up at his approach and in the dim light he recognized the girl who was the cause of all his troubles.

She sprang toward him with outstretched hands, but as he advanced her face changed and she shrank back abashed.

"This is a misunderstanding—a dreadful misunderstanding," she cried out in her pretty broken English. "Oh, how does it happen that you are here?"

"Through no choice of my own, madam, I assure you!" retorted Tony, not over-pleased by his reception.

"But why—how—how did you make this unfortunate mistake?"

"Why, madam, if you'll excuse my candor, I think the mistake was yours—"

"Mine?"

"—in sending me a letter—"

"*You*—a letter?"

"—by a simpleton of a lad, who must needs hand it to me under your father's very nose—"

The girl broke in on him with a cry. "What! It was *you* who received my letter?" She swept round on the little maid-servant and submerged her under a flood of Venetian. The latter volleyed back in the same jargon, and as she did so, Tony's astonished eye detected in her the doubleted page who had handed him the letter in Saint Mark's.

"What!" he cried, "the lad was this girl in disguise?"

Polixena broke off with an irrepressible smile; but her face clouded instantly and she returned to the charge.

"This wicked, careless girl—she has ruined me, she will be my undoing! Oh, sir, how can I make you understand? The letter was not intended for you—it was meant for the English Ambassador, an old friend of my mother's, from whom I hoped to obtain assistance—oh, how can I ever excuse myself to you?"

"No excuses are needed, madam," said Tony, bowing; "though I am surprised, I own, that any one should mistake me for an ambassador."

Here a wave of mirth again overran Polixena's face. "Oh, sir, you must pardon my poor girl's mistake. She heard you speaking English, and—and—I had told her to hand the letter to the handsomest foreigner in the church." Tony bowed again, more profoundly. "The English Ambassador," Polixena added simply, "is a very handsome man."

"I wish, madam, I were a better proxy!"

She echoed his laugh, and then clapped her hands together with a look of anguish. "Fool that I am! How can I jest at such a moment? I am in dreadful trouble, and now perhaps I have brought trouble on you also—Oh, my father! I hear my father coming!" She turned pale and leaned tremblingly upon the little servant.

Footsteps and loud voices were in fact heard outside, and a moment later the red-stockinged Senator stalked into the room attended by half-a-dozen of the magnificoes whom Tony had seen abroad in the square. At sight of him, all clapped hands to their swords and burst into furious outcries; and though their jargon was unintelligible to the young man, their tones and gestures made their meaning unpleasantly plain. The Senator, with a start of anger, first flung himself on the intruder; then, snatched back by his companions, turned wrathfully on his daughter, who, at his feet, with outstretched arms and streaming face, pleaded her cause with all the eloquence of young distress. Meanwhile the other nobles gesticulated vehemently among themselves, and one, a truculent-looking personage in ruff and Spanish cape, stalked apart, keeping a jealous eye on Tony. The latter was at his wit's end how to comport himself, for the lovely Polixena's tears had quite drowned her few words of English, and beyond guessing that the magnificoes meant him a mischief he had no notion what they would be at.

At this point, luckily, his friend Count Rialto suddenly broke in on the scene, and was at once assailed by all the tongues in the room. He pulled a long face at sight of Tony, but signed to the young man to be silent, and addressed himself earnestly to the Senator. The latter, at first, would not draw breath to hear him; but presently, sobering, he walked apart with the Count, and the two conversed together out of earshot.

"My dear sir," said the Count, at length turning to Tony with a perturbed countenance, "it is as I feared, and you are fallen into a great misfortune."

"A great misfortune! A great trap, I call it!" shouted Tony, whose blood, by this time, was boiling; but as he uttered the word the beautiful Polixena cast such a stricken look on him that he blushed up to the forehead.

"Be careful," said the Count, in a low tone. "Though his Illustriousness does not speak your language, he understands a few words of it, and—"

"So much the better!" broke in Tony; "I hope he will understand me if I ask him in plain English what is his grievance against me."

The Senator, at this, would have burst forth again; but the Count, stepping between, answered quickly: "His grievance against you is that you have been detected in secret correspondence with his daughter, the most noble Polixena Cador, the betrothed bride of this gentleman, the most illustrious Marquess Zanipolo—" and he waved a deferential hand at the frowning hidalgo of the cape and ruff.

"Sir," said Tony, "if that is the extent of my offence, it lies with the young lady to set me free, since by her own avowal—" but here he stopped short, for, to his surprise, Polixena shot a terrified glance at him.

"Sir," interposed the Count, "we are not accustomed in Venice to take shelter behind a lady's reputation."

"No more are we in Salem," retorted Tony in a white heat. "I was merely about to remark that, by the young lady's avowal, she has never seen me before."

Polixena's eyes signaled her gratitude, and he felt he would have died to defend her.

The Count translated his statement, and presently pursued: "His Illustriousness observes that, in that case, his daughter's misconduct has been all the more reprehensible."

"Her misconduct? Of what does he accuse her?"

"Of sending you, just now, in the church of Saint Mark's, a letter which you were seen to read openly and thrust in your bosom. The incident was witnessed by his Illustriousness the Marquess Zanipolo, who, in consequence, has already repudiated his unhappy bride."

Tony stared contemptuously at the black Marquess. "If his Illustriousness is so lacking in gallantry as to repudiate a lady on so trivial a pretext, it is he and not I who should be the object of her father's resentment."

"That, my dear young gentleman, is hardly for you to decide. Your only excuse being your ignorance of our customs, it is scarcely for you to advise us how to behave in matters of punctilio."

It seemed to Tony as though the Count were going over to his enemies, and the thought sharpened his retort.

"I had supposed," said he, "that men of sense had much the same behavior in all countries, and that, here as elsewhere, a gentleman would be taken at his word. I solemnly affirm that the letter I was seen to read reflects in no way on the honor of this young lady, and has in fact nothing to do with what you suppose."

As he had himself no notion what the letter was about, this was as far as he dared commit himself.

There was another brief consultation in the opposing camp, and the Count then said:—"We all know, sir, that a gentleman is obliged to meet certain enquiries by a denial; but you have at your command the means of immediately clearing the lady. Will you show the letter to her father?"

There was a perceptible pause, during which Tony, while appearing to look straight before him, managed to deflect an interrogatory glance toward Polixena. Her reply was a faint negative motion, accompanied by unmistakable signs of apprehension.

"Poor girl!" he thought, "she is in a worse case than I imagined, and whatever happens I must keep her secret."

He turned to the Senator with a deep bow. "I am not," said he, "in the habit of showing my private correspondence to strangers."

The Count interpreted these words, and Donna Polixena's father, dashing his hand on his hilt, broke into furious invective, while the Marquess continued to nurse his outraged feelings aloof.

The Count shook his head funereally. "Alas, sir, it is as I feared. This is not the first time that youth and propinquity have led to fatal imprudence. But I need hardly, I suppose, point out the obligation incumbent upon you as a man of honor."

Tony stared at him haughtily, with a look which was meant for the Marquess. "And what obligation is that?"

"To repair the wrong you have done—in other words, to marry the lady."

Polixena at this burst into tears, and Tony said to himself: "Why in heaven does she not bid me show the letter?" Then he remembered that it had no superscription, and that the words it contained, supposing them to have been addressed to himself, were hardly of a nature to disarm suspicion. The sense of the girl's grave plight effaced all thought of his own risk, but the Count's last words struck him as so preposterous that he could not repress a smile.

"I cannot flatter myself," said he, "that the lady would welcome this solution."

The Count's manner became increasingly ceremonious. "Such modesty," he said, "becomes your youth and inexperience; but even if it were justified it would scarcely alter the case, as it is always assumed in this country that a young lady wishes to marry the man whom her father has selected."

"But I understood just now," Tony interposed, "that the gentleman yonder was in that enviable position."

"So he was, till circumstances obliged him to waive the privilege in your favor."

"He does me too much honor; but if a deep sense of my unworthiness obliges me to decline—"

"You are still," interrupted the Count, "laboring under a misapprehension. Your choice in the matter is no more to be consulted than the lady's. Not to put too fine a point on it, it is necessary that you should marry her within the hour."

Tony, at this, for all his spirit, felt the blood run thin in his veins. He looked in silence at the threatening visages between himself and the door, stole a side-glance at the high barred windows of the apartment, and then turned to Polixena, who had fallen sobbing at her father's feet.

"And if I refuse?" said he.

The Count made a significant gesture. "I am not so foolish as to threaten a man of your mettle. But perhaps you are unaware what the consequences would be to the lady."

Polixena, at this, struggling to her feet, addressed a few impassioned words to the Count and her father; but the latter put her aside with an obdurate gesture.

The Count turned to Tony. "The lady herself pleads for you—at what cost you do not guess—but as you see it is vain. In an hour his Illustriousness's chaplain will be here. Meanwhile his Illustriousness consents to leave you in the custody of your betrothed."

He stepped back, and the other gentlemen, bowing with deep ceremony to Tony, stalked out one by one from the room. Tony heard the key turn in the lock, and found himself alone with Polixena.

III

THE girl had sunk into a chair, her face hidden, a picture of shame and agony. So moving was the sight that Tony once again forgot his own extremity in the view of her distress. He went and kneeled beside her, drawing her hands from her face.

"Oh, don't make me look at you!" she sobbed; but it was on his bosom that she hid from his gaze. He held her there a breathing-space, as he might have clasped a weeping child; then she drew back and put him gently from her.

"What humiliation!" she lamented.

"Do you think I blame you for what has happened?"

"Alas, was it not my foolish letter that brought you to this plight? And how nobly you defended me! How generous it was of you not to show the letter! If my father knew I had written to the Ambassador to save me from this dreadful marriage his anger against me would be even greater."

"Ah—it was that you wrote for?" cried Tony with unaccountable relief.

"Of course—what else did you think?"

"But is it too late for the Ambassador to save you?"

"From *you?*" A smile flashed through her tears. "Alas, yes." She drew back and hid her face again, as though overcome by a fresh wave of shame.

Tony glanced about him. "If I could wrench a bar out of that window—" he muttered.

"Impossible! The court is guarded. You are a prisoner, alas.—Oh, I must speak!" She sprang up and paced the room. "But indeed you can scarce think worse of me than you do already—"

"I think ill of you?"

"Alas, you must! To be unwilling to marry the man my father has chosen for me—"

"Such a beetle-browed lout! It would be a burning shame if you married him."

"Ah, you come from a free country. Here a girl is allowed no choice."

"It is infamous, I say—infamous!"

"No, no—I ought to have resigned myself, like so many others."

"Resigned yourself to that brute! Impossible!"

"He has a dreadful name for violence—his gondolier has told my little maid such tales of him! But why do I talk of myself, when it is of you I should be thinking?"

"Of me, poor child?" cried Tony, losing his head.

"Yes, and how to save you—for I *can* save you! But every moment counts—and yet what I have to say is so dreadful."

"Nothing from your lips could seem dreadful."

"Ah, if he had had your way of speaking!"

"Well, now at least you are free of him," said Tony, a little wildly; but at this she stood up and bent a grave look on him.

"No, I am not free," she said; "but you are, if you will do as I tell you."

Tony, at this, felt a sudden dizziness; as though, from a mad flight through clouds and darkness, he had dropped to safety again, and the fall had stunned him.

"What am I to do?" he said.

"Look away from me, or I can never tell you."

He thought at first that this was a jest, but her eyes commanded him, and reluctantly he walked away and leaned in the embrasure of the window. She stood in the middle of the room, and as soon as his back was turned she began to speak in a quick monotonous voice, as though she were reciting a lesson.

"You must know that the Marquess Zanipolo, though a great noble, is not a rich man. True, he has large estates, but he is a desperate spendthrift and gambler, and would sell his soul for a round sum of ready money.—If you turn round I shall not go on!—He wrangled horribly with my father over my dowry—he wanted me to have more than either of my sisters, though one married a Procurator and the other a grandee of Spain. But my father is a gambler too—oh, such fortunes as are squandered over the arcade yonder! And so—and so—don't turn, I implore you—oh, do you begin to see my meaning?"

She broke off sobbing, and it took all his strength to keep his eyes from her.

"Go on," he said.

"Will you not understand? Oh, I would say anything to save you! You don't know us Venetians—we're all to be bought for a price. It is not only the brides who are marketable—sometimes the husbands sell themselves too. And they think you rich—my father does, and the others—I don't know why, unless you have shown your money too freely—and the English are all rich, are they not? And—oh, oh—do you understand? Oh, I can't bear your eyes!"

She dropped into a chair, her head on her arms, and Tony in a flash was at her side.

"My poor child, my poor Polixena!" he cried, and wept and clasped her.

"You *are* rich, are you not? You would promise them a ransom?" she persisted.

"To enable you to marry the Marquess?"

"To enable you to escape from this place. Oh, I hope I may never see your face again." She fell to weeping once more, and he drew away and paced the floor in a fever.

Presently she sprang up with a fresh air of resolution, and pointed to a clock against the wall. "The hour is nearly over. It is quite true that my father is gone to fetch his chaplain. Oh, I implore you, be warned by me! There is no other way of escape."

"And if I do as you say—?"

"You are safe! You are free! I stake my life on it."

"And you—you are married to that villain?"

"But I shall have saved you. Tell me your name, that I may say it to myself when I am alone."

"My name is Anthony. But you must not marry that fellow."

"You forgive me, Anthony? You don't think too badly of me?"

"I say you must not marry that fellow."

She laid a trembling hand on his arm. "Time presses," she adjured him, "and I warn you there is no other way."

For a moment he had a vision of his mother, sitting very upright, on a Sunday evening, reading Dr. Tillotson's sermons in the best parlor at Salem; then he swung round on the girl and caught both her hands in his. "Yes, there is," he cried, "if you are willing. Polixena, let the priest come!"

She shrank back from him, white and radiant. "Oh, hush, be silent!" she said.

"I am no noble Marquess, and have no great estates," he cried. "My father is a plain India merchant in the colony of Massachusetts—but if you—"

"Oh, hush, I say! I don't know what your long words mean. But I bless you, bless you, bless you on my knees!" And she knelt before him, and fell to kissing his hands.

He drew her up to his breast and held her there.

"You are willing, Polixena?" he said.

"No, no!" She broke from him with outstretched hands. "I am not willing. You mistake me. I must marry the Marquess, I tell you!"

"On my money?" he taunted her; and her burning blush rebuked him.

"Yes, on your money," she said sadly.

"Why? Because, much as you hate him, you hate me still more?"

She was silent.

"If you hate me, why do you sacrifice yourself for me?" he persisted.

"You torture me! And I tell you the hour is past."

"Let it pass. I'll not accept your sacrifice. I will not lift a finger to help another man to marry you."

"Oh, madman, madman!" she murmured.

Tony, with crossed arms, faced her squarely, and she leaned against the wall a few feet off from him. Her breast throbbed under its lace and falbalas, and her eyes swam with terror and entreaty.

"Polixena, I love you!" he cried.

A blush swept over her throat and bosom, bathing her in light to the verge of her troubled brows.

"I love you! I love you!" he repeated.

And now she was on his breast again, and all their youth was in their lips. But her embrace was as fleeting as a bird's poise and before he knew it he clasped empty air, and half the room was between them.

She was holding up a little coral charm and laughing. "I took it from your fob," she said. "It is of no value, is it? And I shall not get any of the money, you know."

She continued to laugh strangely, and the rouge burned like fire in her ashen face.

"What are you talking of?" he said.

"They never give me anything but the clothes I wear. And I shall never see you again, Anthony!" She gave him a dreadful look. "Oh, my poor boy, my poor love—*'I love you, I love you, Polixena!'*"

He thought she had turned light-headed, and advanced to her with soothing words; but she held him quietly at arm's length, and as he gazed he read the truth in her face.

He fell back from her, and a sob broke from him as he bowed his head on his hands.

"Only, for God's sake, have the money ready, or there may be foul play here," she said.

As she spoke there was a great tramping of steps outside and a burst of voices on the threshold.

"It is all a lie," she gasped out, "about my marriage, and the Marquess, and the Ambassador, and the Senator—but not, oh, not about your danger in this place—or about my love," she breathed to him. And as the key rattled in the door she laid her lips on his brow.

The key rattled, and the door swung open—but the black-cassocked gentleman who stepped in, though a priest indeed, was no votary of idolatrous rites, but that sound orthodox divine, the Reverend Ozias Mounce, looking very much perturbed at his surroundings, and very much on the alert for the Scarlet Woman. He was supported, to his evident relief, by the captain of the Hepzibah B., and the procession was closed by an escort of stern-looking fellows in cocked hats and small-swords, who led between them Tony's late friends the magnificoes, now as sorry a looking company as the law ever landed in her net.

The captain strode briskly into the room, uttering a grunt of satisfaction as he clapped eyes on Tony.

"So, Mr. Bracknell," said he, "you have been seeing the Carnival with this pack of mummers, have you? And this is where your pleasuring has landed you? H'm—a pretty establishment, and a pretty lady at the head of it." He glanced about the apartment and doffed his hat with mock ceremony to Polixena, who faced him like a princess.

"Why, my girl," said he, amicably, "I think I saw you this morning in the square, on the arm of the Pantaloon yonder; and as for that Captain Spavent—" and he pointed a derisive finger at the Marquess—"I've watched him drive his bully's trade under the arcade ever since I first dropped anchor in these waters. Well, well," he continued, his indignation subsiding, "all's fair in Carnival, I suppose, but this gentleman here is under sailing orders, and I fear we must break up your little party."

At this Tony saw Count Rialto step forward, looking very small and explanatory, and uncovering obsequiously to the captain.

"I can assure you, sir," said the Count in his best English, "that this incident is the result of an unfortunate misunderstanding, and if you will oblige us by dismissing these myrmidons, any of my friends here will be happy to offer satisfaction to Mr. Bracknell and his companions."

Mr. Mounce shrank visibly at this, and the captain burst into a loud guffaw.

"Satisfaction?" says he. "Why, my cock, that's very handsome of you, considering the rope's at your throats. But we'll not take advantage of your generosity, for I fear Mr. Bracknell has already trespassed on it too long. You pack of galley-slaves, you!" he spluttered suddenly, "decoying young innocents with that devil's bait of yours—" His eye fell on Polixena, and his voice softened unaccountably. "Ah, well, we must all see the Carnival once, I suppose," he said. "All's well that ends well, as the fellow says in the play; and now, if you please, Mr. Bracknell, if you'll take the reverend gentleman's arm there, we'll bid adieu to our hospitable entertainers, and right about face for the Hepzibah."

UNCOLLECTED STORIES (1904-1908)

THE LETTER

As first published in *Harper's Monthly Magazine*, April, 1904

COLONEL ALINGDON died in Florence in 1890.

For many years he had lived withdrawn from the world in which he had once played so active and even turbulent a part. The study of Tuscan art was his only pursuit, and it was to help him in the classification of his notes and documents that I was first called to his villa. Colonel Alingdon had then the look of a very old man, though his age can hardly have exceeded seventy. He was small and bent, with a finely wrinkled face which still wore the tan of youthful exposure. But for this dusky redness it would have been hard to reconstruct from the shrunken recluse, with his low fastidious voice and carefully tended hands, an image of that young knight of adventure whose sword had been at the service of every uprising which stirred the uneasy soil of Italy in the first half of the nineteenth century.

Though I was more of a proficient in Colonel Alingdon's later than his earlier pursuits, the thought of his soldiering days was always coming between me and the pacific work of his old age. As we sat collating papers and comparing photographs, I had the feeling that this dry and quiet old man had seen even stranger things than people said: that he knew more of the inner history of Europe than half the diplomatists of his day.

I was not alone in this conviction; and the friend who had engaged me for Colonel Alingdon had appended to his instructions the injunction to "get him to talk." But this was what no one could do. Colonel Alingdon was ready to discuss by the hour the date of a Giottesque triptych, or the attribution of a disputed master; but on the history of his early life he was habitually silent.

It was perhaps because I recognized this silence and respected it that it afterward came to be broken for me. Or it was perhaps merely because, as the failure of Colonel Alingdon's sight cut him off from his work, he felt the natural inclination of age to revert from the empty present to the crowded past. For one cause or another he *did* talk to me in the last year of his life; and I felt myself mingled, to an extent inconceivable to the mere reader of history, with the passionate scenes of the Italian struggle for liberty. Colonel Alingdon had been mixed with it in all its phases: he had known the last Carbonari and the Young Italy of Mazzini; he had been in Perugia when the mercenaries of a liberal Pope slaughtered women and children in the streets; he had been in Sicily with the Thousand, and in Milan during the Cinque Giornate.

"They say the Italians didn't know how to fight," he said one day, musingly—"that the French had to come down and do their work for them. People forget how long it was since they had had any fighting to do. But they hadn't forgotten how to suffer and hold their tongues; how to die and take their secrets with them. The Italian war of independence was really carried on underground: it was one of those awful silent struggles which are so much more terrible than the roar of a battle. It's a deuced sight easier to charge with your regiment than to lie rotting in an Austrian prison and know that if you give up the name of a friend or two you can go back scot-free to your wife and children. And thousands and thousands of Italians had the choice given them—and hardly one went back."

He sat silent, his meditative fingertips laid together, his eyes fixed on the past which was the now only thing clearly visible to them.

"And the women?" I said. "Were they as brave as the men?"

I had not spoken quite at random. I had always heard that there had been as much of love as of war in Colonel Alingdon's early career, and I hoped that my question might give a personal turn to his reminiscences.

"The women?" he repeated. "They were braver—for they had more to bear and less to do. Italy could never have been saved without them."

His eye had kindled and I detected in it the reflection of some vivid memory. It was then that I asked him what was the bravest thing he had ever known of a woman's doing.

The question was such a vague one that I hardly knew why I had put it, but to my surprise he answered almost at once, as though I had touched on a subject of frequent meditation.

"The bravest thing I ever saw done by a woman," he said, "was brought about by an act of my own—and one of which I am not particularly proud. For that reason I have never spoken of it before—there was a time when I didn't even care to think of it—but all that is past now. She died years ago, and so did the Jack Alingdon she knew, and in telling you the story I am no more than the mouthpiece of an old tradition which some ancestor might have handed down to me."

He leaned back, his clear blind gaze fixed smilingly on me, and I had the feeling that, in groping through the labyrinth of his young adventures, I had come unawares upon their central point.

## II

WHEN I was in Milan in '47 an unlucky thing happened to me.

I had been sent there to look over the ground by some of my Italian friends in England. As an English officer I had no difficulty in getting into Milanese society, for England had for years been the refuge of the Italian fugitives, and I was known to be working in their interests. It was just the kind of job I liked, and I never enjoyed life more than I did in those days. There was a great deal going on—good music, balls and theatres. Milan kept up her gayety to the last. The English were shocked by the *insouciance* of a race who could dance under the very nose of the usurper; but those who understood the situation knew that Milan was playing Brutus, and playing it uncommonly well.

I was in the thick of it all—it was just the atmosphere to suit a young fellow of nine-and-twenty, with a healthy passion for waltzing and fighting. But, as I said, an unlucky thing happened to me. I was fool enough to fall in love with Donna Candida Falco. You have heard of her, of course: you know the share she had in the great work. In a different way she was what the terrible Princess Belgioioso had been to an earlier generation. But Donna Candida was not terrible. She was quiet, discreet and charming. When I knew her she was a widow of thirty, her husband, Andrea Falco, having died ten years previously, soon after their marriage. The marriage had been notoriously unhappy, and his death was a release to Donna Candida. Her family were of Modena, but they had come to live in Milan soon after the execution of Ciro Menotti and his companions. You remember the details of that business? The Duke of Modena, one of the most adroit villains in Europe, had been bitten with the hope of uniting the Italian states under his rule. It was a vision of Italian liberation—of a sort. A few madmen were dazzled by it, and Ciro Menotti was one of them. You know the end. The Duke of Modena, who had counted on Louis

Philippe's backing, found that that astute sovereign had betrayed him to Austria. Instantly, he saw that his first business was to get rid of the conspirators he had created. There was nothing easier than for a Hapsburg Este to turn on a friend. Ciro Menotti had staked his life for the Duke—and the Duke took it. You may remember that, on the night when seven hundred men and a cannon attacked Menotti's house, the Duke was seen looking on at the slaughter from an arcade across the square.

Well, among the lesser fry taken that night was a lad of eighteen, Emilio Verna, who was the only brother of Donna Candida. The Verna family was one of the most respected in Modena. It consisted, at that time, of the mother, Countess Verna, of young Emilio and his sister. Count Verna had been in Spielberg in the twenties. He had never recovered from his sufferings there, and died in exile, without seeing his wife and children again. Countess Verna had been an ardent patriot in her youth, but the failure of the first attempts against Austria had discouraged her. She thought that in losing her husband she had sacrificed enough for her country, and her one idea was to keep Emilio on good terms with the government. But the Verna blood was not tractable, and his father's death was not likely to make Emilio a good subject of the Estes. Not that he had as yet taken any active share in the work of the conspirators: he simply hadn't had time. At his trial there was nothing to show that he had been in Menotti's confidence; but he had been seen once or twice coming out of what the ducal police called "suspicious" houses, and in his desk were found some verses to Italy. That was enough to hang a man in Modena, and Emilio Verna was hanged.

The Countess never recovered from the blow. The circumstances of her son's death were too abominable, to unendurable. If he had risked his life in the conspiracy, she might have been reconciled to his losing it. But he was a mere child, who had sat at home, chafing but powerless, while his seniors plotted and fought. He had been sacrificed to the Duke's insane fear, to his savage greed for victims, and the Countess Verna was not to be consoled.

As soon as possible, the mother and daughter left Modena for Milan. There they lived in seclusion till Candida's marriage. During her girlhood she had had to accept her mother's view of life: to shut herself up in the tomb in which the poor woman brooded over her martyrs. But that was not the girl's way of honoring the dead. At the moment when the first shot was fired on Menotti's house she had been reading Petrarch's *Ode to the Lords of Italy*, and the lines

> *l'antico valor*
> *Ne l'italici cor non è ancor morto*

had lodged like a bullet in her brain. From the day of her marriage she began to take a share in the silent work which was going on throughout Italy. Milan was at that time the center of the movement, and Candida Falco threw herself into it with all the passion which her unhappy marriage left unsatisfied. At first she had to act with great reserve, for her husband was a prudent man, who did not care to have his habits disturbed by political complications; but after his death there was nothing to restrain her, except the exquisite tact which enabled her to work night and day in the Italian cause without giving the Austrian authorities a pretext for interference.

When I first knew Donna Candida, her mother was still living: a tragic woman, prematurely bowed, like an image of death in the background of the daughter's brilliant life. The Countess, since her son's death, had become a patriot again, though in a narrower sense than Candida. The mother's first thought was that her dead must be avenged, the daughter's that Italy must be saved; but from different motives they worked for the same end. Candida felt for the Countess that protecting tenderness with which Italian children so often regard their parents, a feeling heightened by the reverence which the mother's sufferings inspired. Countess Verna, as the wife and mother of martyrs, had done what Candida longed to do: she had given her utmost to Italy. There must have been moments when the self-absorption of her grief chilled her daughter's ardent spirit; but Candida revered in her mother the image of their afflicted country.

"It was too terrible," she said, speaking of what the Countess had suffered after Emilio's death. "All the circumstances were too unmerciful. It seemed as if God had turned His face from my mother; as if she had been singled out to suffer more than any of the others. All the other families received some message or token of farewell from the prisoners. One of them bribed the jailer to carry a letter—another sent a lock of hair by the chaplain. But Emilio made no sign, sent no word. My mother felt as though he had turned his back on us. She used to sit for hours, saying again and again, 'Why was he the only one to forget his mother?' I tried to comfort her, but it was useless: she had suffered too much. Now I never reason with her; I listen, and let her ease her poor heart. Do you know, she still asks me sometimes if I think he may have left a letter—if there is no way of finding out if he left one? She forgets that I have tried again and again: that I have sent bribes and messages to the jailer, the chaplain, to every one who came near him. The answer is always the same—no one has ever heard of a letter. I suppose the poor boy was stunned, and did not think of writing. Who knows what was passing through his poor bewildered brain? But it would have been a great help to my mother to have a word from him. If I had known how to imitate his writing I should have forged a letter."

I knew enough of the Italians to understand how her boy's silence must have aggravated the Countess's grief. Precious as a message from a dying son would be to any mother, such signs of tenderness have to the Italians a peculiar significance. The Latin race is rhetorical: it possesses the gift of death-bed eloquence, the knack of saying the effective thing on momentous occasions. The letters which the Italian patriots sent home from their prisons or from the scaffold are not the halting farewells that anguish would have wrung from a less expressive race: they are veritable "compositions," saved from affectation only by the fact that fluency and sonority are a part of the Latin inheritance. Such letters, passed from hand to hand among the bereaved families, were not only a comfort to the survivors but an incentive to fresh sacrifices. They were the "seed of the martyrs" with which Italy was being sown; and I knew what it meant to the Countess Verna to have no such treasure in her bosom, to sit silent while other mothers quoted their sons' last words.

I said just now that it was an unlucky day for me when I fell in love with Donna Candida; and no doubt you have guessed the reason. She was in love with some one else. It was the old situation of Heine's song. That other loved another—loved Italy, and with an undivided passion. His name was Fernando Briga, and at that time he was one of the foremost liberals in Italy. He came of a middle-class Modenese family. His father was a doctor, a prudent man, engrossed in his profession and unwilling to compromise it by meddling in politics. His irreproachable attitude won the confidence of the government, and the Duke conferred on him the sinister office of physician to the prisons of Modena. It was this Briga who attended Emilio Falco, and several of the other prisoners who were executed at the same time.

Under shelter of his father's loyalty young Fernando conspired in safety. He was studying medicine, and every one supposed him to be absorbed in his work; but as a matter of fact he was fast ripening into one of Mazzini's ablest lieutenants. His career belongs to history, so I need not enlarge on it here. In 1847 he was in Milan, and had become one of the leading figures in the liberal group which was working for a coalition with Piedmont. Like all the ablest men of his day, he had cast off Mazziniism and pinned his faith to the house of Savoy. The Austrian government had an eye on him, but he had inherited his father's prudence, though he used it for nobler ends, and his discretion enabled him to do far more for the cause than a dozen enthusiasts could have accomplished. No one understood this better than Donna Candida. She had a share of his caution, and he trusted her with secrets which he would not have confided to many men. Her drawing-room was the center of the Piedmontese party, yet so clever was she in averting suspicion that more than one hunted conspirator hid in her house, and was helped across the Alps by her agents.

Briga relied on her as he did on no one else; but he did not love her, and she knew it. Still, she was young, she was handsome, and he loved no one else: how could she give up hoping? From her intimate friends she made no secret of her feelings: Italian women are not reticent in such matters, and Donna Candida was proud of loving a hero. You will see at once that I had no chance; but if she could not give up hope, neither could I. Perhaps in her desire to secure my services for the cause she may have shown herself overkind; or perhaps I was still young enough to set down to my own charms a success due to quite different causes. At any rate, I persuaded myself that if I could manage to do something conspicuous for Italy I might yet make her care for me. With such an incentive you will not wonder that I worked hard; but though Donna Candida was full of gratitude she continued to adore my rival.

One day we had a hot scene. I began, I believe, by reproaching her with having led me on; and when she defended herself, I retaliated by taunting her with Briga's indifference. She grew pale at that, and said it was enough to love a hero, even without hope of return; and as she said it she herself looked so heroic, so radiant, so unattainably the woman I wanted, that a sneer may have escaped me:—was she so sure then that Briga was a hero? I remember her proud silence and our wretched parting. I went away feeling that at last I had really lost her; and the thought made me savage and vindictive.

Soon after, as it happened, came the Five Days, and Milan was free. I caught a distant glimpse of Donna Candida in the hospital to which I was carried after the fight; but my wound was a slight one and in twenty-four hours I was about again on crutches. I hoped she might send for me, but she did not, and I was too sulky to make the first advance. A day or two later I heard there had been a commotion in Modena, and not being in fighting trim I got leave to go over there with one or two men whom the Modenese liberals had called in to help them. When we arrived the precious Duke had been swept out and a provisional government set up. One of my companions, who was a Modenese, was made a member, and knowing that I wanted something to do, he commissioned me to look up some papers in the ducal archives. It was fascinating work, for in the pursuit of my documents I uncovered the hidden springs of his late Highness's paternal administration. The principal papers relative to the civil and criminal administration of Modena have since been published, and the world knows how that estimable sovereign cared for the material and spiritual welfare of his subjects.

Well—in the course of my search, I came across a file of old papers marked: "Taken from political prisoners. A.D. 1831." It was the year of Menotti's conspiracy, and everything connected with that date was thrilling. I loosened the band and ran over the letters. Suddenly I came across one which was docketed: "Given by Doctor Briga's son to the warder of His Highness's prisons." *Doctor Briga's son?* That could be no other than Fernando: I knew he was an only child. But how came such a paper into his hands, and how had it passed from them into those of the Duke's warder? My own hands shook as I opened the letter—I felt the man suddenly in my power.

Then I began to read. "My adored mother, even in this lowest circle of hell all hearts are not closed to pity, and I have been given the hope that these last words of farewell may reach you. . . . " My eyes ran on over pages of plaintive rhetoric. "Embrace for me my adored Candida...let her never forget the cause for which her father and brother perished...let her keep alive in her breast the thought of Spielberg and Reggio. Do not grieve that I die so young . . . though not with those heroes in deed I was with them in spirit, and am worthy to be enrolled in the sacred phalanx . . . " and so on. Before I reached the signature I knew the letter was from Emilio Verna.

I put it in my pocket, finished my work and started immediately for Milan. I didn't quite know what I meant to do—my head was in a whirl. I saw at once what must have happened. Fernando Briga, then a lad of fifteen or sixteen, had attended his father in prison during Emilio Verna's last hours, and the latter, perhaps aware of the lad's liberal sympathies, had found an opportunity of giving him the letter. But why had Briga given it up to the warder? That was the puzzling question. The docket said: "*Given by* Doctor Briga's son"—but it might mean "taken from." Fernando might have been seen to receive the letter and might have been searched on leaving the prison. But that would not account for his silence afterward. How was it that, if he knew of the letter, he had never told Emilio's family of it? There was only one explanation. If the letter had been taken from him by force he would have had no reason for concealing its existence; and his silence was clear proof that he had given it up voluntarily, no doubt in the hope of standing well with the authorities. But then he was a traitor and a coward; the patriot of 'forty-eight had begun life as an informer! But does innate character ever change so radically that the lad who has committed a base act at fifteen may grow up into an honorable man? A good man may be corrupted by life, but can the years turn a born sneak into a hero?

You may fancy how I answered my own questions. . . . If Briga had been false and cowardly then, was he not sure to be false and cowardly still? In those days there were traitors under every coat, and more than one brave fellow had been sold to the police by his best friend. . . . You will say that Briga's record was unblemished, that he had exposed himself to danger too frequently, had stood by his friends too steadfastly, to permit of a rational doubt of his good faith. So reason might have told me in a calmer moment, but she was not allowed to make herself heard just then. I was young, I was angry, I chose to think I had been unfairly treated, and perhaps at my rival's instigation. It was not unlikely that Briga knew of my love for Donna Candida, and had encouraged her to use it in the good cause. Was she not always at his bidding? My blood boiled at the thought, and reaching Milan in a rage I went straight to Donna Candida.

I had measured the exact force of the blow I was going to deal. The triumph of the liberals in Modena had revived public interest in the unsuccessful struggle of their predecessors, the men who, sixteen years earlier, had paid for the same attempt with their lives. The victors of '48 wished to honor the vanquished of '32. All the families exiled by the ducal government were hastening back to recover possession of their confiscated property and of the graves of their dead. Already it had been decided to raise a monument to Menotti and his companions. There were to be speeches, garlands, a public holiday: the thrill of the commemoration would run through Europe. You see what it would have meant to the poor Countess to appear on the scene with her boy's letter in her hand; and you see also what the memorandum on the back of the letter would have meant to Donna Candida. Poor Emilio's farewell would be published in all the journals of Europe: the finding of the letter would be on every one's lips. And how conceal those fatal words on the back? At the moment, it seemed to me that fortune could not have given me a handsomer chance of destroying my rival than in letting me find the letter which he stood convicted of having suppressed.

My sentiment was perhaps not a strictly honorable one; yet what could I do but give the letter to Donna Candida? To keep it back was out of the question; and with the best will in the world I could not have erased Briga's name from the back. The mistake I made was in thinking it lucky that the paper had fallen into my hands.

Donna Candida was alone when I entered. We had parted in anger, but she held out her hand with a smile of pardon, and asked what news I brought from Modena. The smile exasperated me: I felt as though she were trying to get me into her power again.

"I bring you a letter from your brother," I said, and handed it to her. I had purposely turned the superscription downward, so that she should not see it.

She uttered an incredulous cry and tore the letter open. A light struck up from it into her face as she read—a radiance that smote me to the soul. For a moment I longed to snatch the paper from her and efface the name on the back. It hurt me to think how short-lived her happiness must be.

Then she did a fatal thing. She came up to me, caught my two hands and kissed them. "Oh, thank you—bless you a thousand times! He died thinking of us—he died loving Italy!"

I put her from me gently: it was not the kiss I wanted, and the touch of her lips hardened me.

She shone on me through her happy tears. "What happiness—what consolation you have brought my poor mother! This will take the bitterness from her grief. And that it should come to her now! Do you know, she had a presentiment of it? When we heard of the Duke's flight her first word was: 'Now we may find Emilio's letter.' At heart she was always sure that he had written—I suppose some blessed instinct told her so." She dropped her face on her hands, and I saw her tears fall on the wretched letter.

In a moment she looked up again, with eyes that blessed and trusted me. "Tell me where you found it," she said.

I told her.

"Oh, the savages! They took it from him—"

My opportunity had come. "No," I said, "it appears they did *not* take it from him."

"Then how—"

I waited a moment. "The letter," I said, looking full at her, "was given up to the warder of the prison by the son of Doctor Briga."

She stared, repeating the words slowly. "The son of Doctor Briga? But that is—Fernando," she said.

"I have always understood," I replied, "that your friend was an only son."

I had expected an outcry of horror; if she had uttered it I could have forgiven her anything. But I heard, instead, an incredulous exclamation: my statement was really too preposterous! I saw that her mind had flashed back to our last talk, and that she charged me with something too nearly true to be endurable.

"My brother's letter? Given to the prison warder by Fernando Briga? My dear Captain Alingdon—on what authority do you expect me to believe such a tale?"

Her incredulity had in it an evident implication of bad faith, and I was stung to a quick reply.

"If you will turn over the letter you will see."

She continued to gaze at me a moment: then she obeyed. I don't think I ever admired her more than I did then. As she read the name a tremor crossed her face; and that was all. Her mind must have reached out instantly to the farthest consequences of the discovery, but the long habit of self-command enabled her to steady her muscles at once. If I had not been on the alert I should have seen no hint of emotion.

For a while she looked fixedly at the back of the letter; then she raised her eyes to mine.

"Can you tell me who wrote this?" she asked.

Her composure irritated me. She had rallied all her forces to Briga's defence, and I felt as though my triumph were slipping from me.

"Probably one of the clerks of the archives," I answered. "It is written in the same hand as all the other memoranda relating to the political prisoners of that year."

"But it is a lie!" she exclaimed. "He was never admitted to the prisons."

"Are you sure?"

"How should he have been?"

"He might have gone as his father's assistant."

"But if he had seen my poor brother he would have told me long ago."

"Not if he had really given up this letter," I retorted.

I supposed her quick intelligence had seized this from the first; but I saw now that it came to her as a shock. She stood motionless, clenching the letter in her hands, and I could guess the rapid travel of her thoughts.

Suddenly she came up to me. "Colonel Alingdon," she said, "you have been a good friend of mine, though I think you have not liked me lately. But whether you like me or not, I know you will not deceive me. On your honor, do you think this memorandum may have been written later than the letter?"

I hesitated. If she had cried out once against Briga I should have wished myself out of the business; but she was too sure of him.

"On my honor," I said, "I think it hardly possible. The ink has faded to the same degree."

She made a rapid comparison and folded the letter with a gesture of assent.

"It may have been written by an enemy," I went on, wishing to clear myself of any appearance of malice.

She shook her head. "He was barely fifteen—and his father was on the side of the government. Besides, this would have served him with the government, and the liberals would never have known of it."

This was unanswerable—and still not a word of revolt against the man whose condemnation she was pronouncing!

"Then—" I said with a vague gesture.

She caught me up. "Then—?"

"You have answered my objections," I returned.

"Your objections?"

"To thinking that Signor Briga could have begun his career as a patriot by betraying a friend."

I had brought her to the test at last, but my eyes shrank from her face as I spoke. There was a dead silence, which I broke by adding lamely: "But no doubt Signor Briga could explain."

She lifted her head, and I saw that my triumph was to be short. She stood erect, a few paces from me, resting her hand on a table, but not for support.

"Of course he can explain," she said; "do you suppose I ever doubted it? But—" she paused a moment, fronting me nobly—"he need not, for I understand it all now."

"Ah," I murmured with a last flicker of irony.

"I understand," she repeated. It was she, now, who sought my eyes and held them. "It is quite simple—he could not have done otherwise."

This was a little too oracular to be received with equanimity. I suppose I smiled.

"He could not have done otherwise," she repeated with tranquil emphasis. "He merely did what is every Italian's duty—he put Italy before himself and his friends." She waited a moment, and then went on with growing passion: "Surely you must see what I mean? He was evidently in the prison with his father at the time of my poor brother's death. Emilio perhaps guessed that he was a friend—or perhaps appealed to him because he was young and looked kind. But don't you see how dangerous it would have been for Briga to bring this letter to us, or even to hide it in his father's house? It is true that he was not yet suspected of liberalism, but he was already connected with Young Italy, and it is just because he managed to keep himself so free of suspicion that he was able to do such good work for the cause." She paused, and then went on with a firmer voice. "You don't know the danger we all lived in. The government spies were everywhere. The laws were set aside as the Duke pleased—was not Emilio hanged for having an ode to Italy in his desk? After Menotti's conspiracy the Duke grew mad with fear—he was haunted by the dread of assassination. The police, to prove their zeal, had to trump up false charges and arrest innocent persons—you remember the case of poor Ricci? Incriminating papers were smuggled into people's houses—they were condemned to death on the paid evidence of brigands and galley-slaves. The families of the revolutionists were under the closest observation and were shunned by all who wished to stand well with the government. If Briga had been seen going into our house he would at once have been suspected. If he had hidden Emilio's letter at home, its discovery might have ruined his family as well as himself. It was his duty to consider all these things. In those days no man could serve two masters, and he had to choose between endangering the cause and failing to serve a friend. He chose the latter—and he was right."

I stood listening, fascinated by the rapidity and skill with which she had built up the hypothesis of Briga's defence. But before she ended a strange thing happened—her argument had convinced me. It seemed to me quite likely that Briga had in fact been actuated by the motives she suggested.

I suppose she read the admission in my face, for hers lit up victoriously.

"You see?" she exclaimed. "Ah, it takes one brave man to understand another."

Perhaps I winced a little at being thus coupled with her hero; at any rate, some last impulse of resistance made me say: "I should be quite convinced, if Briga had only spoken of the letter afterward. If brave people understand each other, I cannot see why he should have been afraid of telling you the truth."

She colored deeply, and perhaps not quite resentfully.

"You are right," she said; "he need not have been afraid. But he does not know me as I know him. I was useful to Italy, and he may have feared to risk my friendship."

"You are the most generous woman I ever knew!" I exclaimed.

She looked at me intently. "You also are generous," she said.

I stiffened instantly, suspecting a purpose behind her praise. "I have given you small proof of it!" I said.

She seemed surprised. "In bringing me this letter? What else could you do?" She sighed deeply. "You can give me proof enough now."

She had dropped into a chair, and I saw that we had reached the most difficult point in our interview.

"Captain Alingdon," she said, "does anyone else know of this letter?"

"No. I was alone in the archives when I found it."

"And you spoke of it to no one?"

"To no one."

"Then no one must know."

I bowed. "It is for you to decide."

She paused. "Not even my mother," she continued, with a painful blush.

I looked at her in amazement. "Not even—?"

She shook her head sadly. "You think me a cruel daughter? Well—*he* was a cruel friend. What he did was done for Italy: shall I allow myself to be surpassed?"

I felt a pang of commiseration for the mother. "But you will at least tell the Countess—"

Her eyes filled with tears. "My poor mother—don't make it more difficult for me!"

"But I don't understand—"

"Don't you see that she might find it impossible to forgive him? She has suffered so much! And I can't risk that—for in her anger she might speak. And even if she forgave him, she might be tempted to show the letter. Don't you see that, even now, a word of this might ruin him? I will trust his fate to no one. If Italy needed him then she needs him far more today."

She stood before me magnificently, in the splendor of her great refusal; then she turned to the writing-table at which she had been seated when I came in. Her sealing-taper was still alight, and she held her brother's letter to the flame.

I watched her in silence while it burned; but one more question rose to my lips.

"You will tell *him*, then, what you have done for him?" I cried.

And at that the heroine turned woman, melted and pressed unhappy hands in mine.

"Don't you see that I can never tell him what I do for him? That is my gift to Italy," she said.

## THE HOUSE OF THE DEAD HAND

### As first published in The Atlantic Monthly, August, 1904

"ABOVE ALL," the letter ended, "don't leave Siena without seeing Doctor Lombard's Leonardo. Lombard is a queer old Englishman, a mystic or a madman (if the two are not synonymous), and a devout student of the Italian Renaissance. He has lived for years in Italy, exploring its remotest corners, and has lately picked up an undoubted Leonardo, which came to light in a farmhouse near Bergamo. It is believed to be one of the missing pictures mentioned by Vasari, and is at any rate, according to the most competent authorities, a genuine and almost untouched example of the best period.

"Lombard is a queer stick, and jealous of showing his treasures; but we struck up a friendship when I was working on the Sodomas in Siena three years ago, and if you will give him the enclosed line you may get a peep at the Leonardo. Probably not more than a peep, though, for I hear he refuses to have it reproduced. I want badly to use it in my monograph on the Windsor drawings, so please see what you can do for me, and if you can't persuade him to let you take a photograph or make a sketch, at least jot down a detailed description of the picture and get from him all the facts you can. I hear that the French and Italian governments have offered him a large advance on his purchase, but that he refuses to sell at any price, though he certainly can't afford such luxuries; in fact, I don't see where he got enough money to buy the picture. He lives in the Via Papa Giulio."

Wyant sat at the table d'hote of his hotel, re-reading his friend's letter over a late luncheon. He had been five days in Siena without having found time to call on Doctor Lombard; not from any indifference to the opportunity presented, but because it was his first visit to the strange red city and he was still under the spell of its more conspicuous wonders—the brick palaces flinging out their wrought-iron torch-holders with a gesture of arrogant suzerainty; the great council-chamber emblazoned with civic allegories; the pageant of Pope Julius on the Library walls; the Sodomas smiling balefully through the dusk of moldering chapels—and it was only when his first hunger was appeased that he remembered that one course in the banquet was still untasted.

He put the letter in his pocket and turned to leave the room, with a nod to its only other occupant, an olive-skinned young man with lustrous eyes and a low collar, who sat on the other side of the table, perusing the *Fanfulla di Domenica*. This gentleman, his daily vis-à-vis, returned the nod with a Latin eloquence of gesture, and Wyant passed on to the ante-chamber, where he paused to light a cigarette. He was just restoring the case to his pocket when he heard a hurried step behind him, and the lustrous-eyed young man advanced through the glass doors of the dining room.

"Pardon me, sir," he said in measured English, and with an intonation of exquisite politeness; "you have let this letter fall."

Wyant, recognizing his friend's note of introduction to Doctor Lombard, took it with a word of thanks, and was about to turn away when he perceived that the eyes of his fellow diner remained fixed on him with a gaze of melancholy interrogation.

"Again pardon me," the young man at length ventured, "but are you by chance the friend of the illustrious Doctor Lombard?"

"No," returned Wyant, with the instinctive Anglo-Saxon distrust of foreign advances. Then, fearing to appear rude, he said with a guarded politeness: "Perhaps, by the way, you can tell me the number of his house. I see it is not given here."

The young man brightened perceptibly. "The number of the house is thirteen; but any one can indicate it to you—it is well known in Siena. It is called," he continued after a moment, "the House of the Dead Hand."

Wyant stared. "What a queer name!" he said.

"The name comes from an antique hand of marble which for many hundred years has been above the door."

Wyant was turning away with a gesture of thanks, when the other added: "If you would have the kindness to ring twice."

"To ring twice?"

"At the doctor's." The young man smiled. "It is the custom."

It was a dazzling March afternoon, with a shower of sun from the mid-blue, and a marshalling of slaty clouds behind the umber-colored hills. For nearly an hour Wyant loitered on the Lizza, watching the shadows race across the naked landscape and the thunder blacken in the west; then he decided to set out for the House of the Dead Hand. The map in his guidebook showed him that the Via Papa Giulio was one of the streets which radiate from the Piazza, and thither he bent his course, pausing at every other step to fill his eye with some fresh image of weather-beaten beauty. The clouds had rolled upward, obscuring the sunshine and hanging like a funereal baldachin above the projecting cornices of Doctor Lombard's street, and Wyant walked for some distance in the shade of the beetling palace fronts before his eye fell on a doorway surmounted by a sallow marble hand. He stood for a moment staring up at the strange emblem. The hand was a woman's—a dead drooping hand, which hung there convulsed and helpless, as though it had been thrust forth in denunciation of some evil mystery within the house, and had sunk struggling into death.

A girl who was drawing water from the well in the court said that the English doctor lived on the first floor, and Wyant, passing through a glazed door, mounted the damp degrees of a vaulted stairway with a plaster Aesculapius moldering in a niche on the landing. Facing the Aesculapius was another door, and as Wyant put his hand on the bell-rope he remembered his unknown friend's injunction, and rang twice.

His ring was answered by a peasant woman with a low forehead and small close-set eyes, who, after a prolonged scrutiny of himself, his card, and his letter of introduction, left him standing in a high, cold ante-chamber floored with brick. He heard her wooden pattens click down an interminable corridor, and after some delay she returned and told him to follow her.

They passed through a long saloon, bare as the ante-chamber, but loftily vaulted, and frescoed with a seventeenth-century Triumph of Scipio or Alexander—martial figures following Wyant with the filmed melancholy gaze of shades in limbo. At the end of this apartment he was admitted to a smaller room, with the same atmosphere of mortal cold, but showing more obvious signs of occupancy. The walls were covered with tapestry which had faded to the gray-brown tints of decaying vegetation, so that the young man felt as though he were entering a sunless autumn wood. Against these hangings stood a few tall cabinets on heavy gilt feet, and at a table in the window three persons were seated: an elderly lady who was warming her hands over a brazier, a girl bent above a strip of needle-work, and an old man.

As the latter advanced toward Wyant, the young man was conscious of staring with unseemly intentness at his small round-backed figure, dressed with shabby disorder and surmounted by a wonderful head, lean, vulpine, eagle-beaked as that of some art-loving despot of the Renaissance: a head combining the venerable hair and large prominent eyes of the humanist with the greedy profile of the adventurer. Wyant, in musing on the Italian portrait-medals of the fifteenth century, had often fancied that only in that period of fierce individualism could types so paradoxical have been produced; yet the subtle craftsmen who committed them to the bronze had never drawn a face more strangely stamped with contradictory passions than that of Doctor Lombard.

"I am glad to see you," he said to Wyant, extending a hand which seemed a mere framework held together by knotted veins. "We lead a quiet life here and receive few visitors, but any friend of Professor Clyde's is welcome." Then, with a gesture which included the two women, he added dryly: "My wife and daughter often talk of Professor Clyde."

"Oh yes—he used to make me such nice toast; they don't understand toast in Italy," said Mrs. Lombard in a high plaintive voice.

It would have been difficult, from Doctor Lombard's manner and appearance to guess his nationality; but his wife was so inconsciently and ineradicably English that even the silhouette of her cap seemed a protest against Continental laxities. She was a stout fair woman, with pale cheeks netted with red lines. A brooch with a miniature portrait sustained a bogwood watch-chain upon her bosom, and at her elbow lay a heap of knitting and an old copy of *The Queen*.

The young girl, who had remained standing, was a slim replica of her mother, with an apple-cheeked face and opaque blue eyes. Her small head was prodigally laden with braids of dull fair hair, and she might have had a kind of transient prettiness but for the sullen droop of her round mouth. It was hard to say whether her expression implied ill-temper or apathy; but Wyant was struck by the contrast between the fierce vitality of the doctor's age and the inanimateness of his daughter's youth.

Seating himself in the chair which his host advanced, the young man tried to open the conversation by addressing to Mrs. Lombard some random remark on the beauties of Siena. The lady murmured a resigned assent, and Doctor Lombard interposed with a smile: "My dear sir, my wife considers Siena a most salubrious spot, and is favorably impressed by the cheapness of the marketing; but she deplores the total absence of muffins and cannel coal, and cannot resign herself to the Italian method of dusting furniture."

"But they don't, you know—they don't dust it!" Mrs. Lombard protested, without showing any resentment of her husband's manner.

"Precisely—they don't dust it. Since we have lived in Siena we have not once seen the cobwebs removed from the battlements of the Mangia. Can you conceive of such housekeeping? My wife has never yet dared to write it home to her aunts at Bonchurch."

Mrs. Lombard accepted in silence this remarkable statement of her views, and her husband, with a malicious smile at Wyant's embarrassment, planted himself suddenly before the young man.

"And now," said he, "do you want to see my Leonardo?"

"*Do* I?" cried Wyant, on his feet in a flash.

The doctor chuckled. "Ah," he said, with a kind of crooning deliberation, "that's the way they all behave—that's what they all come for." He turned to his daughter with another variation of mockery in his smile. "Don't fancy it's for your *beaux yeux*, my dear; or for the mature charms of Mrs. Lombard," he added, glaring suddenly at his wife, who had taken up her knitting and was softly murmuring over the number of her stitches.

Neither lady appeared to notice his pleasantries, and he continued, addressing himself to Wyant: "They all come—they all come; but many are called and few are chosen." His voice sank to solemnity. "While I live," he said, "no unworthy eye shall desecrate that picture. But I will not do my friend Clyde the injustice to suppose that he would send an unworthy representative. He tells me he wishes a description of the picture for his book; and you shall describe it to him—if you can."

Wyant hesitated, not knowing whether it was a propitious moment to put in his appeal for a photograph.

"Well, sir," he said, "you know Clyde wants me to take away all I can of it."

Doctor Lombard eyed him sardonically. "You're welcome to take away all you can carry," he replied; adding, as he turned to his daughter: "That is, if he has your permission, Sybilla."

The girl rose without a word, and laying aside her work, took a key from a secret drawer in one of the cabinets, while the doctor continued in the same note of grim jocularity: "For you must know that the picture is not mine—it is my daughter's."

He followed with evident amusement the surprised glance which Wyant turned on the young girl's impassive figure.

"Sybilla," he pursued, "is a votary of the arts; she has inherited her fond father's passion for the unattainable. Luckily, however, she also recently inherited a tidy legacy from her grandmother; and having seen the Leonardo, on which its discoverer had placed a price far beyond my reach, she took a step which deserves to go down to history: she invested her whole inheritance in the purchase of the picture, thus enabling me to spend my closing years in communion with one of the world's masterpieces. My dear sir, could Antigone do more?"

The object of this strange eulogy had meanwhile drawn aside one of the tapestry hangings, and fitted her key into a concealed door.

"Come," said Doctor Lombard, "let us go before the light fails us."

Wyant glanced at Mrs. Lombard, who continued to knit impassively.

"No, no," said his host, "my wife will not come with us. You might not suspect it from her conversation, but my wife has no feeling for art—Italian art, that is; for no one is fonder of our early Victorian school."

"Frith's Railway Station, you know," said Mrs. Lombard, smiling. "I like an animated picture."

Miss Lombard, who had unlocked the door, held back the tapestry to let her father and Wyant pass out; then she followed them down a narrow stone passage with another door at its end. This door was iron-barred, and Wyant noticed that it had a complicated patent lock. The girl fitted another key into the lock, and Doctor Lombard led the way into a small room. The dark paneling of this apartment was irradiated by streams of yellow light slanting through the disbanded thunder clouds, and in the central brightness hung a picture concealed by a curtain of faded velvet.

"A little too bright, Sybilla," said Doctor Lombard. His face had grown solemn, and his mouth twitched nervously as his daughter drew a linen drapery across the upper part of the window.

"That will do—that will do." He turned impressively to Wyant. "Do you see the pomegranate bud in this rug? Place yourself there—keep your left foot on it, please. And now, Sybilla, draw the cord."

Miss Lombard advanced and placed her hand on a cord hidden behind the velvet curtain.

"Ah," said the doctor, "one moment:

I should like you, while looking at the picture, to have in mind a few lines of verse. Sybilla—"

Without the slightest change of countenance, and with a promptness which proved her to be prepared for the request, Miss Lombard began to recite, in a full round voice like her mother's, St. Bernard's invocation to the Virgin, in the thirty-third canto of the *Paradise*.

"Thank you, my dear," said her father, drawing a deep breath as she ended. "That unapproachable combination of vowel sounds prepares one better than anything I know for the contemplation of the picture."

As he spoke the folds of velvet slowly parted, and the Leonardo appeared in its frame of tarnished gold:

From the nature of Miss Lombard's recitation Wyant had expected a sacred subject, and his surprise was therefore great as the composition was gradually revealed by the widening division of the curtain.

In the background a steel-colored river wound through a pale calcareous landscape; while to the left, on a lonely peak, a crucified Christ hung livid against indigo clouds. The central figure of the foreground, however, was that of a woman seated in an antique chair of marble with bas-reliefs of dancing maenads. Her feet rested on a meadow sprinkled with minute wild-flowers, and her attitude of smiling majesty recalled that of Dosso Dossi's "Circe." She wore a red robe, flowing in closely fluted lines from under a fancifully embroidered cloak. Above her high forehead the crinkled golden hair flowed sideways beneath a veil; one hand drooped on the arm of her chair; the other held up an inverted human skull, into which a young Dionysus, smooth, brown and sidelong as the "St. John" of the Louvre, poured a stream of wine from a high-poised flagon. At the lady's feet lay the symbols of art and luxury: a flute and a roll of music, a platter heaped with grapes and roses, the torso of a Greek statuette, and a bowl overflowing with coins and jewels; behind her, on the chalky hilltop, hung the crucified Christ. A scroll in a corner of the foreground bore the legend: *Lux Mundi*.

Wyant, emerging from the first plunge of wonder, turned inquiringly toward his companions. Neither had moved. Miss Lombard stood with her hand on the cord, her lids lowered, her mouth drooping; the doctor, his strange Thoth-like profile turned toward his guest, was still lost in rapt contemplation of his treasure.

Wyant addressed the young girl.

"You are fortunate," he said, "to be the possessor of anything so perfect."

"It is considered very beautiful," she said coldly.

"Beautiful—*beautiful!*" the doctor burst out. "Ah, the poor, worn out, over-worked word! There are no adjectives in the language fresh enough to describe such pristine brilliancy; all their brightness has been worn off by misuse. Think of the things that have been called beautiful, and then look at *that!*"

"It is worthy of a new vocabulary," Wyant agreed.

"Yes," Doctor Lombard continued, "my daughter is indeed fortunate. She has chosen what Catholics call the higher life—the counsel of perfection. What other private person enjoys the same opportunity of understanding the master? Who else lives under the same roof with an untouched masterpiece of Leonardo's? Think of the happiness of being always under the influence of such a creation; of living into it; of partaking of it in daily and hourly communion! This room is a chapel; the sight of that picture is a sacrament. What an atmosphere for a young life to unfold itself in! My daughter is singularly blessed. Sybilla, point out some of the details to Mr. Wyant; I see that he will appreciate them."

The girl turned her dense blue eyes toward Wyant; then, glancing away from him, she pointed to the canvas.

"Notice the modeling of the left hand," she began in a monotonous voice; "it recalls the hand of the Mona Lisa.

The head of the naked genius will remind you of that of the St. John of the Louvre, but it is more purely pagan and is turned a little less to the right. The embroidery on the cloak is symbolic: you will see that the roots of this plant have burst through the vase. This recalls the famous definition of Hamlet's character in *Wilhelm Meister*. Here are the mystic rose, the flame, and the serpent, emblem of eternity. Some of the other symbols we have not yet been able to decipher."

Wyant watched her curiously; she seemed to be reciting a lesson.

"And the picture itself?" he said. "How do you explain that? *Lux Mundi*—what a curious device to connect with such a subject! What can it mean?"

Miss Lombard dropped her eyes: the answer was evidently not included in her lesson.

"What, indeed?" the doctor interposed. "What does life mean? As one may define it in a hundred different ways, so one may find a hundred different meanings in this picture. Its symbolism is as many-faceted as a well-cut diamond. Who, for instance, is that divine lady? Is it she who is the true *Lux Mundi*—the light reflected from jewels and young eyes, from polished marble and clear waters and statues of bronze? Or is that the Light of the World, extinguished on yonder stormy hill, and is this lady the Pride of Life, feasting blindly on the wine of iniquity, with her back turned to the light which has shone for her in vain? Something of both these meanings may be traced in the picture; but to me it symbolizes rather the central truth of existence: that all that is raised in incorruption is sown in corruption; art, beauty, love, religion; that all our wine is drunk out of skulls, and poured for us by the mysterious genius of a remote and cruel past."

The doctor's face blazed: his bent figure seemed to straighten itself and become taller.

"Ah," he cried, growing more dithyrambic, "how lightly you ask what it means! How confidently you expect an answer! Yet here am I who have given my life to the study of the Renaissance; who have violated its tomb, laid open its dead body, and traced the course of every muscle, bone, and artery; who have sucked its very soul from the pages of poets and humanists; who have wept and believed with Joachim of Flora, smiled and doubted with Aeneas Sylvius Piccolomini; who have patiently followed to its source the least inspiration of the masters, and groped in neolithic caverns and Babylonian ruins for the first unfolding tendrils of the arabesques of Mantegna and Crivelli; and I tell you that I stand abashed and ignorant before the mystery of this picture. It means nothing—it means all things. It may represent the period which saw its creation; it may represent all ages past and to come. There are volumes of meaning in the tiniest emblem on the lady's cloak; the blossoms of its border are rooted in the deepest soil of myth and tradition. Don't ask what it means, young man, but bow your head in thankfulness' for having seen it!"

Miss Lombard laid her hand on his arm.

"Don't excite yourself, father," she said in the detached tone of a professional nurse.

He answered with a despairing gesture. "Ah, it's easy for you to talk. You have years and years to spend with it; I am an old man, and every moment counts!"

"It's bad for you," she repeated with gentle obstinacy.

The doctor's sacred fury had in fact burnt itself out. He dropped into a seat with dull eyes and slackening lips, and his daughter drew the curtain across the picture.

Wyant turned away reluctantly. He felt that his opportunity was slipping from him, yet he dared not refer to Clyde's wish for a photograph. He now understood the meaning of the laugh with which Doctor Lombard had given him leave to carry away all the details he could remember. The picture was so dazzling, so unexpected, so crossed with elusive and contradictory suggestions, that the most alert observer, when placed suddenly before it, must lose his coordinating faculty in a sense of confused wonder. Yet how valuable to Clyde the record of such a work would be! In some ways it seemed to be the summing up of the master's thought, the key to his enigmatic philosophy.

The doctor had risen and was walking slowly toward the door. His daughter unlocked it, and Wyant followed them back in silence to the room in which they had left Mrs. Lombard. That lady was no longer there, and he could think of no excuse for lingering.

He thanked the doctor, and turned to Miss Lombard, who stood in the middle of the room as though awaiting farther orders.

"It is very good of you," he said, "to allow one even a glimpse of such a treasure."

She looked at him with her odd directness. "You will come again?" she said quickly; and turning to her father she added: "You know what Professor Clyde asked. This gentleman cannot give him any account of the picture without seeing it again."

Doctor Lombard glanced at her vaguely; he was still like a person in a trance.

"Eh?" he said, rousing himself with an effort.

"I said, father, that Mr. Wyant must see the picture again if he is to tell Professor Clyde about it," Miss Lombard repeated with extraordinary precision of tone.

Wyant was silent. He had the puzzled sense that his wishes were being divined and gratified for reasons with which he was in no way connected.

"Well, well," the doctor muttered, "I don't say no—I don't say no. I know what Clyde wants—I don't refuse to help him." He turned to Wyant. "You may come again—you may make notes," he added with a sudden effort. "Jot down what occurs to you. I'm willing to concede that."

Wyant again caught the girl's eye, but its emphatic message perplexed him.

"You're very good," he said tentatively, "but the fact is the picture is so mysterious—so full of complicated detail—that I'm afraid no notes I could make would serve Clyde's purpose as well as—as a photograph, say. If you would allow me—"

Miss Lombard's brow darkened, and her father raised his furiously.

"A photograph? A photograph, did you say? Good God, man, not ten people have been allowed to set foot in that room! A *photograph?*"

Wyant saw his mistake, but saw also that he had gone too far to retreat.

"I know, sir, from what Clyde has told me, that you object to having any reproduction of the picture published; but he hoped you might let me take a photograph for his personal use—not to be reproduced in his book, but simply to give him something to work by. I should take the photograph myself, and the negative would of course be yours. If you wished it, only one impression would be struck off, and that one Clyde could return to you when he had done with it."

Doctor Lombard interrupted him with a snarl. "When he had done with it? Just so: I thank thee for that word! When it had been re-photographed, drawn, traced, autotyped, passed about from hand to hand, defiled by every ignorant eye in England, vulgarized by the blundering praise of every art-scribbler in Europe! Bah! I'd as soon give you the picture itself: why don't you ask for that?"

"Well, sir," said Wyant calmly, "if you will trust me with it, I'll engage to take it safely to England and back, and to let no eye but Clyde's see it while it is out of your keeping."

The doctor received this remarkable proposal in silence; then he burst into a laugh.

"Upon my soul!" he said with sardonic good humor.

It was Miss Lombard's turn to look perplexedly at Wyant. His last words and her father's unexpected reply had evidently carried her beyond her depth.

"Well, sir, am I to take the picture?" Wyant smilingly pursued.

"No, young man; nor a photograph of it. Nor a sketch, either; mind that,—nothing that can be reproduced. Sybilla," he cried with sudden passion, "swear to me that the picture shall never be reproduced! No photograph, no sketch—now or afterward. Do you hear me?"

"Yes, father," said the girl quietly.

"The vandals," he muttered, "the desecrators of beauty; if I thought it would ever get into their hands I'd burn it first, by God!" He turned to Wyant, speaking more quietly. "I said you might come back—I never retract what I say. But you must give me your word that no one but Clyde shall see the notes you make."

Wyant was growing warm.

"If you won't trust me with a photograph I wonder you trust me not to show my notes!" he exclaimed.

The doctor looked at him with a malicious smile.

"Humph!" he said; "would they be of much use to anybody?"

Wyant saw that he was losing ground and controlled his impatience.

"To Clyde, I hope, at any rate," he answered, holding out his hand. The doctor shook it without a trace of resentment, and Wyant added: "When shall I come, sir?"

"Tomorrow—tomorrow morning," cried Miss Lombard, speaking suddenly.

She looked fixedly at her father, and he shrugged his shoulders.

"The picture is hers," he said to Wyant.

In the ante-chamber the young man was met by the woman who had admitted him. She handed him his hat and stick, and turned to unbar the door. As the bolt slipped back he felt a touch on his arm.

"You have a letter?" she said in a low tone.

"A letter?" He stared. "What letter?"

She shrugged her shoulders, and drew back to let him pass.

II

AS Wyant emerged from the house he paused once more to glance up at its scarred brick façade. The marble hand drooped tragically above the entrance: in the waning light it seemed to have relaxed into the passiveness of despair, and Wyant stood musing on its hidden meaning. But the Dead Hand was not the only mysterious thing about Doctor Lombard's house. What were the relations between Miss Lombard and her father? Above all, between Miss Lombard and her picture? She did not look like a person capable of a disinterested passion for the arts; and there had been moments when it struck Wyant that she hated the picture.

The sky at the end of the street was flooded with turbulent yellow light, and the young man turned his steps toward the church of San Domenico, in the hope of catching the lingering brightness on Sodoma's St. Catherine.

The great bare aisles were almost dark when he entered, and he had to grope his way to the chapel steps. Under the momentary evocation of the sunset, the saint's figure emerged pale and swooning from the dusk, and the warm light gave a sensual tinge to her ecstasy. The flesh seemed to glow and heave, the eyelids to tremble; Wyant stood fascinated by the accidental collaboration of light and color.

Suddenly he noticed that something white had fluttered to the ground at his feet. He stooped and picked up a small thin sheet of note-paper, folded and sealed like an old-fashioned letter, and bearing the superscription: *To the Count Ottaviano Celsi.*

Wyant stared at this mysterious document. Where had it come from? He was distinctly conscious of having seen it fall through the air, close to his feet. He glanced up at the dark ceiling of the chapel; then he turned and looked about the church. There was only one figure in it, that of a man who knelt near the high altar.

Suddenly Wyant recalled the question of Doctor Lombard's maid-servant. Was this the letter she had asked for? Had he been unconsciously carrying it about with him all the afternoon? Who was Count Ottaviano Celsi, and how came Wyant to have been chosen to act as that nobleman's ambulant letter box?

Wyant laid his hat and stick on the chapel steps and began to explore his pockets, in the irrational hope of finding there some clue to the mystery; but they held nothing which he had not himself put there, and he was reduced to wondering how the letter, supposing some unknown hand to have bestowed it on him, had happened to fall out while he stood motionless before the picture.

At this point he was disturbed by a step on the floor of the aisle, and turning, he saw his lustrous-eyed neighbor of the table d'hote.

The young man bowed and waved an apologetic hand.

"I do not intrude?" he inquired suavely.

Without waiting for a reply, he mounted the steps of the chapel, glancing about him with the affable air of an afternoon caller.

"I see," he remarked with a smile, "that you know the hour at which our saint should be visited."

Wyant agreed that the hour was indeed felicitous.

The stranger stood beamingly before the picture.

"What grace! What poetry!" he murmured, apostrophizing the St. Catherine, but letting his glance slip rapidly about the chapel as he spoke.

Wyant, detecting the maneuver, murmured a brief assent.

"But it is cold here—mortally cold; you do not find it so?" The intruder put on his hat. "It is permitted at this hour—when the church is empty. And you, my dear sir—do you not feel the dampness? You are an artist, are you not? And to artists it is permitted to cover the head when they are engaged in the study of the paintings."

He darted suddenly toward the steps and bent over Wyant's hat.

"Permit me—cover yourself!" he said a moment later, holding out the hat with an ingratiating gesture.

A light flashed on Wyant.

"Perhaps," he said, looking straight at the young man, "you will tell me your name. My own is Wyant."

The stranger, surprised, but not disconcerted, drew forth a coroneted card, which he offered with a low bow. On the card was engraved: *Il Conte Ottaviano Celsi.*

"I am much obliged to you," said Wyant; "and I may as well tell you that the letter which you apparently expected to find in the lining of my hat is not there, but in my pocket."

He drew it out and handed it to its owner, who had grown very pale.

"And now," Wyant continued, "you will perhaps be good enough to tell me what all this means."

There was no mistaking the effect produced on Count Ottaviano by this request. His lips moved, but he achieved only an ineffectual smile.

"I suppose you know," Wyant went on, his anger rising at the sight of the other's discomfiture, "that you have taken an unwarrantable liberty. I don't yet understand what part I have been made to play, but it's evident that you have made use of me to serve some purpose of your own, and I propose to know the reason why."

Count Ottaviano advanced with an imploring gesture.

"Sir," he pleaded, "you permit me to speak?"

"I expect you to," cried Wyant. "But not here," he added, hearing the clank of the verger's keys. "It is growing dark, and we shall be turned out in a few minutes."

He walked across the church, and Count Ottaviano followed him out into the deserted square.

"Now," said Wyant, pausing on the steps.

The count, who had regained some measure of self-possession, began to speak in a high key, with an accompaniment of conciliatory gesture.

"My dear sir—my dear Mr. Wyant—you find me in an abominable position—that, as a man of honor, I immediately confess. I have taken advantage of you—yes! I have counted on your amiability, your chivalry—too far, perhaps? I confess it! But what could I do? It was to oblige a lady"—he laid a hand on his heart—"a lady whom I would die to serve!" He went on with increasing volubility, his deliberate English swept away by a torrent of Italian, through which Wyant, with some difficulty, struggled to a comprehension of the case.

Count Ottaviano, according to his own statement, had come to Siena some months previously, on business connected with his mother's property; the paternal estate being near Orvieto, of which ancient city his father was syndic. Soon after his arrival in Siena the young Count had met the incomparable daughter of Doctor Lombard, and falling deeply in love with her, had prevailed on his parents to ask her hand in marriage. Doctor Lombard had not opposed his suit, but when the question of settlements arose it became known that Miss Lombard, who was possessed of a small property in her own right, had a short time before invested the whole amount in the purchase of the Bergamo Leonardo. Thereupon Count Ottaviano's parents had politely suggested that she should sell the picture and thus recover her independence; and this proposal being met by a curt refusal from Doctor Lombard, they had withdrawn their consent to their son's marriage. The young lady's attitude had hitherto been one of passive submission; she was horribly afraid of her father, and would never venture openly to oppose him; but she had made known to Ottaviano her intention of not giving him up, of waiting patiently till events should take a more favorable turn. She seemed hardly aware, the Count said with a sigh, that the means of escape lay in her own hands; that she was of age, and had a right to sell the picture, and to marry without asking her father's consent. Meanwhile her suitor spared no pains to keep himself before her, to remind her that he, too, was waiting and would never give her up.

Doctor Lombard, who suspected the young man of trying to persuade Sybilla to sell the picture, had forbidden the lovers to meet or to correspond; they were thus driven to clandestine communication, and had several times, the Count ingenuously avowed, made use of the doctor's visitors as a means of exchanging letters.

"And you told the visitors to ring twice?" Wyant interposed.

The young man extended his hands in a deprecating gesture. Could Mr. Wyant blame him? He was young, he was ardent, he was enamored! The young lady had done him the supreme honor of avowing her attachment, of pledging her unalterable fidelity; should he suffer his devotion to be outdone? But his purpose in writing to her, he admitted, was not merely to reiterate his fidelity; he was trying by every means in his power to induce her to sell the picture. He had organized a plan of action; every detail was complete; if she would but have the courage to carry out his instructions he would answer for the result. His idea was that she should secretly retire to a convent of which his aunt was the Mother Superior, and from that stronghold should transact the sale of the Leonardo. He had a purchaser ready, who was willing to pay a large sum; a sum, Count Ottaviano whispered, considerably in excess of the young lady's original inheritance; once the picture sold, it could, if necessary, be removed by force from Doctor Lombard's house, and his daughter, being safely in the convent, would be spared the painful scenes incidental to the removal. Finally, if Doctor Lombard were vindictive enough to refuse his consent to her marriage, she had only to make a *Sommation respectueuse*, and at the end of the prescribed delay no power on earth could prevent her becoming the wife of Count Ottaviano.

Wyant's anger had fallen at the recital of this simple romance. It was absurd to be angry with a young man who confided his secrets to the first stranger he met in the streets, and placed his hand on his heart whenever he mentioned the name of his betrothed. The easiest way out of the business was to take it as a joke. Wyant had played the wall to this new Pyramus and Thisbe, and was philosophic enough to laugh at the part he had unwittingly performed.

He held out his hand with a smile to Count Ottaviano.

"I won't deprive you any longer," he said, "of the pleasure of reading your letter."

"Oh, sir, a thousand thanks! And when you return to the casa Lombard, you will take a message from me—the letter she expected this afternoon?"

"The letter she expected?" Wyant paused. "No, thank you. I thought you understood that where I come from we don't do that kind of thing—knowingly."

"But, sir, to serve a young lady!"

"I'm sorry for the young lady, if what you tell me is true"—the Count's expressive hands resented the doubt—"but remember that if I am under obligations to any one in this matter, it is to her father, who has admitted me to his house and has allowed me to see his picture."

"*His* picture? Hers!"

"Well, the house is his, at all events."

"Unhappily—since to her it is a dungeon!"

"Why doesn't she leave it, then?" exclaimed Wyant impatiently.

The Count clasped his hands. "Ah, how you say that—with what force, with what virility! If you would but say it to *her* in that tone—you, her countryman! She has no one to advise her; the mother is an idiot; the father is terrible; she is in his power; it is my belief that he would kill her if she resisted him. Mr. Wyant, I tremble for her life while she remains in that house!"

"Oh, come," said Wyant lightly, "they seem to understand each other well enough. But in any case, you must see that I can't interfere—at least you would if you were an Englishman," he added with an escape of contempt.

### III

WYANT'S affiliations in Siena being restricted to an acquaintance with his land-lady, he was forced to apply to her for the verification of Count Ottaviano's story.

The young nobleman had, it appeared, given a perfectly correct account of his situation. His father, Count Celsi-Mongirone, was a man of distinguished family and some wealth. He was syndic of Orvieto, and lived either in that town or on his neighboring estate of Mongirone. His wife owned a large property near Siena, and Count Ottaviano, who was the second son, came there from time to time to look into its management. The eldest son was in the army, the youngest in the Church; and an aunt of Count Ottaviano's was Mother Superior of the Visitandine convent in Siena. At one time it had been said that Count Ottaviano, who was a most amiable and accomplished young man, was to marry the daughter of the strange Englishman, Doctor Lombard, but difficulties having arisen as to the adjustment of the young lady's dower, Count Celsi-Mongirone had very properly broken off the match. It was sad for the young man, however, who was said to be deeply in love, and to find frequent excuses for coming to

Siena to inspect his mother's estate.

Viewed in the light of Count Ottaviano's personality the story had a tinge of opera bouffe; but the next morning, as Wyant mounted the stairs of the House of the Dead Hand, the situation insensibly assumed another aspect. It was impossible to take Doctor Lombard lightly; and there was a suggestion of fatality in the appearance of his gaunt dwelling. Who could tell amid what tragic records of domestic tyranny and fluttering broken purposes the little drama of Miss Lombard's fate was being played out? Might not the accumulated influences of such a house modify the lives within it in a manner unguessed by the inmates of a suburban villa with sanitary plumbing and a telephone?

One person, at least, remained unperturbed by such fanciful problems; and that was Mrs. Lombard, who, at Wyant's entrance, raised a placidly wrinkled brow from her knitting. The morning was mild, and her chair had been wheeled into a bar of sunshine near the window, so that she made a cheerful spot of prose in the poetic gloom of her surroundings.

"What a nice morning!" she said; "it must be delightful weather at Bonchurch."

Her dull blue glance wandered across the narrow street with its threatening house fronts, and fluttered back baffled, like a bird with clipped wings. It was evident, poor lady, that she had never seen beyond the opposite houses.

Wyant was not sorry to find her alone. Seeing that she was surprised at his reappearance he said at once: "I have come back to study Miss Lombard's picture."

"Oh, the picture—" Mrs. Lombard's face expressed a gentle disappointment, which might have been boredom in a person of acuter sensibilities. "It's an original Leonardo, you know," she said mechanically.

"And Miss Lombard is very proud of it, I suppose? She seems to have inherited her father's love for art."

Mrs. Lombard counted her stitches, and he went on: "It's unusual in so young a girl. Such tastes generally develop later."

Mrs. Lombard looked up eagerly. "That's what I say! I was quite different at her age, you know. I liked dancing, and doing a pretty bit of fancy-work. Not that I couldn't sketch, too; I had a master down from London. My aunts have some of my crayons hung up in their drawing-room now—I did a view of Kenilworth which was thought pleasing. But I liked a picnic, too, or a pretty walk through the woods with young people of my own age. I say it's more natural, Mr. Wyant; one may have a feeling for art, and do crayons that are worth framing, and yet not give up everything else. I was taught that there were other things."

Wyant, half ashamed of provoking these innocent confidences, could not resist another question. "And Miss Lombard cares for nothing else?"

Her mother looked troubled.

"Sybilla is so clever—she says I don't understand. You know how self-confident young people are! My husband never said that of me, now—he knows I had an excellent education. My aunts were very particular; I was brought up to have opinions, and my husband has always respected them. He says himself that he wouldn't for the world miss hearing my opinion on any subject; you may have noticed that he often refers to my tastes. He has always respected my preference for living in England; he likes to hear me give my reasons for it. He is so much interested in my ideas that he often says he knows just what I am going to say before I speak. But Sybilla does not care for what I think—"

At this point Doctor Lombard entered. He glanced sharply at Wyant. "The servant is a fool; she didn't tell me you were here." His eye turned to his wife. "Well, my dear, what have you been telling Mr. Wyant? About the aunts at Bonchurch, I'll be bound!"

Mrs. Lombard looked triumphantly at Wyant, and her husband rubbed his hooked fingers, with a smile.

"Mrs. Lombard's aunts are very superior women. They subscribe to the circulating library, and borrow *Good Words* and the *Monthly Packet* from the curate's wife across the way. They have the rector to tea twice a year, and keep a page-boy, and are visited by two baronets' wives. They devoted themselves to the education of their orphan niece, and I think I may say without boasting that Mrs. Lombard's conversation shows marked traces of the advantages she enjoyed."

Mrs. Lombard colored with pleasure.

"I was telling Mr. Wyant that my aunts were very particular."

"Quite so, my dear; and did you mention that they never sleep in anything but linen, and that Miss Sophia puts away the furs and blankets every spring with her own hands? Both those facts are interesting to the student of human nature." Doctor Lombard glanced at his watch. "But we are missing an incomparable moment; the light is perfect at this hour."

Wyant rose, and the doctor led him through the tapestried door and down the passageway.

The light was, in fact, perfect, and the picture shone with an inner radiancy, as though a lamp burned behind the soft screen of the lady's flesh. Every detail of the foreground detached itself with jewel-like precision. Wyant noticed a dozen accessories which had escaped him on the previous day.

He drew out his notebook, and the doctor, who had dropped his sardonic grin for a look of devout contemplation, pushed a chair forward, and seated himself on a carved settle against the wall.

"Now, then," he said, "tell Clyde what you can; but the letter killeth."

He sank down, his hands hanging on the arm of the settle like the claws of a dead bird, his eyes fixed on Wyant's notebook with the obvious intention of detecting any attempt at a surreptitious sketch.

Wyant, nettled at this surveillance, and disturbed by the speculations which Doctor Lombard's strange household excited, sat motionless for a few minutes, staring first at the picture and then at the blank pages of the note-book. The thought that Doctor Lombard was enjoying his discomfiture at length roused him, and he began to write.

He was interrupted by a knock on the iron door. Doctor Lombard rose to unlock it, and his daughter entered.

She bowed hurriedly to Wyant, without looking at him.

"Father, had you forgotten that the man from Monte Amiato was to come back this morning with an answer about the bas-relief? He is here now; he says he can't wait."

"The devil!" cried her father impatiently. "Didn't you tell him—"

"Yes; but he says he can't come back. If you want to see him you must come now."

"Then you think there's a chance?—"

She nodded.

He turned and looked at Wyant, who was writing assiduously.

"You will stay here, Sybilla; I shall be back in a moment."

He hurried out, locking the door behind him.

Wyant had looked up, wondering if Miss Lombard would show any surprise at being locked in with him; but it was his turn to be surprised, for hardly had they heard the key withdrawn when she moved close to him, her small face pale and tumultuous.

"I arranged it—I must speak to you," she gasped. "He'll be back in five minutes."

Her courage seemed to fail, and she looked at him helplessly.

Wyant had a sense of stepping among explosives. He glanced about him at the dusky vaulted room, at the haunting smile of the strange picture overhead, and at the pink-and-white girl whispering of conspiracies in a voice meant to exchange platitudes with a curate.

"How can I help you?" he said with a rush of compassion.

"Oh, if you would! I never have a chance to speak to any one; it's so difficult—he watches me—he'll be back immediately."

"Try to tell me what I can do."

"I don't dare; I feel as if he were behind me." She turned away, fixing her eyes on the picture. A sound startled her. "There he comes, and I haven't spoken! It was my only chance; but it bewilders me so to be hurried."

"I don't hear any one," said Wyant, listening. "Try to tell me."

"How can I make you understand? It would take so long to explain." She drew a deep breath, and then with a plunge—"Will you come here again this afternoon—at about five?" she whispered.

"Come here again?"

"Yes—you can ask to see the picture,—make some excuse. He will come with you, of course; I will open the door for you—and—and lock you both in"—she gasped.

"Lock us in?"

"You see? You understand? It's the only way for me to leave the house—if I am ever to do it"—She drew another difficult breath. "The key will be returned—by a safe person—in half an hour,—perhaps sooner—"

She trembled so much that she was obliged to lean against the settle for support.

"Wyant looked at her steadily; he was very sorry for her.

"I can't, Miss Lombard," he said at length.

"You can't?"

"I'm sorry; I must seem cruel; but consider—"

He was stopped by the futility of the word: as well ask a hunted rabbit to pause in its dash for a hole!

Wyant took her hand; it was cold and nerveless.

"I will serve you in any way I can; but you must see that this way is impossible. Can't I talk to you again? Perhaps—"

"Oh," she cried, starting up, "there he comes!"

Doctor Lombard's step sounded in the passage.

Wyant held her fast. "Tell me one thing: he won't let you sell the picture?"

"No—hush!"

"Make no pledges for the future, then; promise me that."

"The future?"

"In case he should die: your father is an old man. You haven't promised?"

She shook her head.

"Don't, then; remember that."

She made no answer, and the key turned in the lock.

As he passed out of the house, its scowling cornice and facade of ravaged brick looked down on him with the startlingness of a strange face, seen momentarily in a crowd, and impressing itself on the brain as part of an inevitable future. Above the doorway, the marble hand reached out like the cry of an imprisoned anguish.

Wyant turned away impatiently.

"Rubbish!" he said to himself. " She isn't walled in; she can get out if she wants to."

IV

WYANT had any number of plans for coming to Miss Lombard's aid: he was elaborating the twentieth when, on the same afternoon, he stepped into the express train for Florence. By the time the train reached Certaldo he was convinced that, in thus hastening his departure, he had followed the only reasonable course; at Empoli, he began to reflect that the priest and the Levite had probably justified themselves in much the same manner.

A month later, after his return to England, he was unexpectedly relieved from these alternatives of extenuation and approval. A paragraph in the morning paper announced the sudden death of Doctor Lombard, the distinguished English dilettante who had long resided in Siena. Wyant's justification was complete. Our blindest impulses become evidence of perspicacity when they fall in with the course of events.

Wyant could now comfortably speculate on the particular complications from which his foresight had probably saved him. The climax was unexpectedly dramatic. Miss Lombard, on the brink of a step which, whatever its issue, would have burdened her with retrospective compunction, had been set free before her suitor's ardor could have had time to cool, and was now doubtless planning a life of domestic felicity on the proceeds of the Leonardo. One thing, however, struck Wyant as odd—he saw no mention of the sale of the picture. He had scanned the papers for an immediate announcement of its transfer to one of the great museums; but presently concluding that Miss Lombard, out of filial piety, had wished to avoid an appearance of unseemly haste in the disposal of her treasure, he dismissed the matter from his mind. Other affairs happened to engage him; the months slipped by, and gradually the lady and the picture dwelt less vividly in his mind.

It was not till five or six years later, when chance took him again to Siena, that the recollection started from some inner fold of memory. He found himself, as it happened, at the head of Doctor Lombard's street, and glancing down that grim thoroughfare, caught an oblique glimpse of the doctor's house front, with the Dead Hand projecting above its threshold.

The sight revived his interest, and that evening, over an admirable *frittata*, he questioned his landlady about Miss Lombard's marriage.

"The daughter of the English doctor? But she has never married, signore."

"Never married? What, then, became of Count Ottaviano?"

"For a long time he waited; but last year he married a noble lady of the Maremma."

"But what happened—why was the marriage broken?"

The landlady enacted a pantomime of baffled interrogation.

"And Miss Lombard still lives in her father's house?"

"Yes, signore; she is still there."

"And the Leonardo—"

"The Leonardo, also, is still there."

The next day, as Wyant entered the House of the Dead Hand, he remembered Count Ottaviano's injunction to ring twice, and smiled mournfully to think that so much subtlety had been vain. But what could have prevented the marriage? If Doctor Lombard's death had been long delayed, time might have acted as a dissolvent, or the young lady's resolve have failed; but it seemed impossible that the white heat of ardor in which Wyant had left the lovers should have cooled in a few short weeks.

As he ascended the vaulted stairway the atmosphere of the place seemed a reply to his conjectures. The same numbing air fell on him, like an emanation from some persistent will-power, a something fierce and imminent which might reduce to impotence every impulse within its range. Wyant could almost fancy a hand on his shoulder, guiding him upward with the ironical intent of confronting him with the evidence of its work.

A strange servant opened the door, and he was presently introduced to the tapestried room, where, from their usual seats in the window, Mrs. Lombard and her daughter advanced to welcome him with faint ejaculations of surprise.

Both had grown oddly old, but in a dry, smooth way, as fruits might shrivel on a shelf instead of ripening on the tree. Mrs. Lombard was still knitting, and pausing now and then to warm her swollen hands above the brazier; and Miss Lombard, in rising, had laid aside a strip of needle-work which might have been the same on which Wyant had first seen her engaged.

Their visitor inquired discreetly how they had fared in the interval, and learned that they had thought of returning to England, but had somehow never done so.

"I am sorry not to see my aunts again," Mrs. Lombard said resignedly; "but Sybilla thinks it best that we should not go this year."

"Next year, perhaps," murmured Miss Lombard, in a voice which seemed to suggest that they had a great waste of time to fill.

She had returned to her seat, and sat bending over her work. Her hair enveloped her head in the same thick braids, but the rose color of her cheeks had turned to blotches of dull red, like some pigment which has darkened in drying.

"And Professor Clyde—is he well?" Mrs. Lombard asked affably; continuing, as her daughter raised a startled eye: "Surely, Sybilla, Mr. Wyant was the gentleman who was sent by Professor Clyde to see the Leonardo?"

Miss Lombard was silent, but Wyant hastened to assure the elder lady of his friend's well-being.

"Ah—perhaps, then, he will come back some day to Siena," she said, sighing. Wyant declared that it was more than likely; and there ensued a pause, which he presently broke by saying to Miss Lombard: "And you still have the picture?"

She raised her eyes and looked at him. "Should you like to see it?" she asked.

On his assenting, she rose, and extracting the same key from the same secret drawer, unlocked the door beneath the tapestry. They walked down the passage in silence, and she stood aside with a grave gesture, making Wyant pass before her into the room. Then she crossed over and drew the curtain back from the picture.

The light of the early afternoon poured full on it: its surface appeared to ripple and heave with a fluid splendor. The colors had lost none of their warmth, the outlines none of their pure precision; it seemed to Wyant like some magical flower which had burst suddenly from the mold of darkness and oblivion.

He turned to Miss Lombard with a movement of comprehension.

"Ah, I understand—you couldn't part with it, after all!" he cried.

"No—I couldn't part with it," she answered.

"It's too beautiful,—too beautiful,"—he assented.

"Too beautiful?" She turned on him with a curious stare. "I have never thought it beautiful, you know."

He gave back the stare. "You have never—"

She shook her head. "It's not that. I hate it; I've always hated it. But he wouldn't let me—he will never let me now."

Wyant was startled by her use of the present tense. Her look surprised him, too: there was a strange fixity of resentment in her innocuous eye. Was it possible that she was laboring under some delusion? Or did the pronoun not refer to her father?

"You mean that Doctor Lombard did not wish you to part with the picture?"

"No—he prevented me; he will always prevent me."

There was another pause. "You promised him, then, before his death—"

"No; I promised nothing. He died too suddenly to make me." Her voice sank to a whisper. "I was free—perfectly free—or I thought I was till I tried."

"Till you tried?"

"To disobey him—to sell the picture. Then I found it was impossible. I tried again and again; but he was always in the room with me."

She glanced over her shoulder as though she had heard a step; and to Wyant, too, for a moment, the room seemed full of a third presence.

"And you can't"—he faltered, unconsciously dropping his voice to the pitch of hers.

She shook her head, gazing at him mystically. "I can't lock him out; I can never lock him out now. I told you I should never have another chance."

Wyant felt the chill of her words like a cold breath in his hair.

"Oh"—he groaned; but she cut him off with a grave gesture.

"It is too late," she said; "but you ought to have helped me that day."

## THE INTRODUCERS

As first published in *Ainslee's*, December, 1905 and January, 1906

AT NINE O'CLOCK on an August morning Mr. Frederick Tilney descended the terrace steps of Sea Lodge and strolled across the lawn to the cliffs.

The upper windows of the long white facade above the terrace were all close-shuttered, for at nine o'clock Newport still sleeps, and he who is stirring enough to venture forth at that unwonted hour may enjoy what no wealth could buy a little later—the privilege of being alone.

Though Mr. Tilney's habits of life, combined with the elegance of his appearance, declared him to be socially disposed, he was not insensible to the rarer pleasures of self-communion, and on this occasion he found peculiar gratification in the thought of having to himself the whole opulent extent of turf and flower border between Ochre Point and Bailey's Beach. The morning was brilliant, with a blue horizon line pure of fog, and such a sparkle on every leaf and grass blade, and on every restless facet of the ever-moving sea, as would have tempted a less sophisticated fancy to visions of wet bows and a leaping stern, or of woodland climbs up the course of a mountain stream.

But it was so long since Mr. Tilney had found a savor in such innocent diversions, that the unblemished fairness of the morning suggested to him only a lazy well-being associated with escape from social duties, and the chance to finish the French novel over which he had fallen asleep at three o'clock that morning.

It was odd how he was growing to value his rare opportunities of being alone. He who in his earlier years had depended on the stimulus of companionship as the fagged diner-out depends on the fillip of his first glass of champagne, was now beginning to watch for and cherish every momentary escape from the crowd. It had grown to such a passion with him, this craving to have the world to himself, that he had overcome the habit of late rising, and learned to curtail the complications of his toilet, in order to secure a half hour of solitude before he was caught back into the whizzing social machinery.

"And talk of the solitude of the desert, it's nothing to the Newport cliffs at this hour," he mused, as he threw himself down on a shaded seat invitingly placed near the path which follows the shore. "Sometimes I feel as if the sea, and the cliffs, and the skyline out there, were all a part of the stupid show—the expensive stage setting of a rottenly cheap play—to be folded up and packed away with the rest of the rubbish when the performance is over; and it's good to come out and find it here at this hour, all by itself, and not giving a hang for the ridiculous goings-on of which it happens to be made the temporary background. Well—there's one comfort: none of the other fools really see it— it's here only for those who seek it out at such an hour—and as I'm the only human being who does, it's here only for me, and belongs only to me, and not to the impenetrable asses who think they own it because they've paid for it at so many thousand dollars a foot!"

And Mr. Tilney, throwing out his chest with the irrepressible pride of possessorship, cast an eye of approval along the windings of the deserted path which skirted the lawn of Sea Lodge and lost itself in the trim shrubberies of the adjoining estate.

"Yes—it's mine—all mine—and this is the only real possessorship, after all! No fear of intruders at this hour—no need of warning signposts, and polite requests to keep to the path. I don't suppose anybody ever walked along this path at my hour, and I don't care who walks here for the rest of the day!" But at this point his meditations were interrupted by the sight of a white gleam through the adjacent foliage; and a moment later all his theories as to the habits of his neighbors had been rudely shattered by the appearance of a lady who, under the sheltering arch of a wide lace sunshade, was advancing indolently toward his seat.

"Why, you've got my bench!" she exclaimed, passing before him, with merriment and indignation mingling in her eyes as sun and wind contended on the ripples behind her.

"*Your* bench?" echoed Tilney, rising at her approach, and dissembling his annoyance under a fair pretense of hospitality. "If ever I thought anything on earth was mine, it's this bench."

The lady, who was young, tall and critical-looking, drew her straight brows together and smilingly pondered his assertion.

"I suppose you thought that because it happens to stand in the grounds of Sea Lodge instead of Cliffwood—*we* haven't any benches, by the way; but my theory is a little different, as it happens. I think things belong only to the people who know how to appreciate them."

"Why, so do I—if the bench isn't mine, at least the theory is!" Tilney protested.

"Well, it's mine too, and it makes the bench mine, you see," the young lady argued with earnestness, "because hitherto I've been the only person who appreciated sitting on it at this hour."

"Ah, hitherto, perhaps—but not since I arrived here last week. I haven't missed a morning," Tilney declared.

She smiled. "That explains the misunderstanding. I've been away for a week, and before that no one ever ever sat on my bench at this hour."

"And since then no one has ever ever sat on *my* bench at this hour; but, my dear Miss Grantham," Tilney gallantly concluded, "I shall be only too honored if you will make the first exception to this rule by sitting on it in my company this morning."

Miss Grantham was evidently a young lady of judicial temper, for she weighed this assertion as carefully as the other, before answering, with a slight tinge of condescension: "I don't know that you have any more right to ask me to sit on my bench, than I have to ask you to sit on *yours*, but for my part I am magnanimous enough to assume just for once that it's ours."

Tilney bowed his thanks and seated himself at her side. "I realize how magnanimous it is of you," he returned, "for, just as you came round the corner, I was saying to myself that this bench was really the only thing in the world I could call my own—"

"And now I've taken half of it away from you! But then," she rejoined, "you've taken the other half from *me;* and as I was under the same delusion as yourself, we are both in the same situation, and had better accommodate ourselves as best we can to the diminished glory of joint ownership."

"It would be ungrateful of me to reject so reasonable a proposal; but in return for my consent, would you mind telling me how you happen to attach such excessive importance to the ownership of this bench?"

"It isn't the bench alone—it's the bench and the hour. They are the only things I have to myself."

Tilney met her lovely eyes with a look of intelligence. "Ah, that's surprising—very surprising."

"Why so?" she exclaimed, a little resentfully.

"Because it's so exactly my own feeling."

Miss Grantham smiled and caressed the folds of her lace gown. "And is it so surprising that we should happen to have the same feelings?"

"Not in all respects, I trust; but I never suspected you of an inclination for solitude."

She returned his scrutiny with a glance as penetrating. "Well, you don't look like a recluse yourself; yet I think I should have guessed that you sometimes have a longing to be alone."

"A longing? Good heavens, it's a passion, it's becoming a mania!"

"Ah, how well I understand that. It's the only thing that can tear me from my bed!"

"I confess one doesn't associate you with the sunrise," he said, letting his glance rest with amusement on the intricate simplicity of her apparel.

"And you!" she smiled back at him. "If our friends were to be told that Fred Tilney and Belle Grantham were to be found sitting on the cliffs at nine o'clock in the morning, the day after the Summerton ball—"

"And that they had come there, not to meet each other, but to escape from every one else—"

"Oh, there's the point: that's what makes it interesting. If we're in the same box why shouldn't we be on the same bench?"

"It requires no argument to convince me that we should. But *are* we in the same box? You see I've just come, and when I saw you last night I supposed you were stopping with the Summertons."

She shook her head. "No, I'm next door, at Cliffwood, for the summer."

"At Cliffwood? With the Bixbys?" He glanced at the fantastic chimneys and profusely carved gables which made the neighboring villa rise from its shrubberies like a *pièce montée* from a flower-decked dish.

"Well, why not, if *you're* at Sea Lodge with Mr. Magraw?"

"Oh, I'm only a poor itinerant devil—"

"And what am I but a circulating beauty? Didn't you know I'd gone into the business too? I hope you won't let professional jealousy interfere with our friendship."

"I'm not sure that I can help it, if you've really gone into the business. But when I last saw you—where was it?—oh, in Athens—"

"Things were different, were they not?" she interposed. "I was sketching and you were archaeologizing—do you remember that divine day at Delphi? Not that you took much notice of me, by the way—"

"Wasn't one warned off the premises by the report that you were engaged to Lord Pytchley?"

She colored, and negligently dropped her sunshade between her eyes and his. "Well, I wasn't, you see—and my sketches were not good enough to sell. So I've taken to this kind of thing instead. But I thought you meant to stick to your digging."

He hesitated. "I was very keen about it for a time; but I had a touch of the sun out in Greece that summer; and a rich fellow picked me up on his steam yacht and carried me off to the Black Sea and then to a salmon river in Norway. I meant to go back, but I dawdled, and the first thing I knew they put another chap in my place. And now I'm Hutchins Magraw's secretary."

He sat staring absently at the distant skyline, and perceiving that he was no longer conscious of her presence she quietly shifted her sunshade and let her eyes rest for a moment on his moody profile.

"Yes—that's what I call it, too. I'm Mrs. Bixby's secretary—or Sadie's, I forget which. But how much writing do you do?"

"Well, not much. The butler attends to the invitations."

"I merely keep an eye on Sadie's spelling, and see that she doesn't sign herself 'lovingly' to young men. Mrs. Bixby has no correspondents, and the dinner invitations are engraved."

"And what are your other duties?"

"Oh, the usual things—reminding Mrs. Bixby not to speak of her husband as *Mr. Bixby,* not to send in her cards when people are at home, not to let the butler say 'fine claret' in a sticky whisper in people's ears, not to speak of town as 'the city,' and not to let Mr. Bixby tell what things cost. Mrs. Bixby takes the bit in her teeth at times, but Sadie is such a dear adaptable creature that, when I've broken her of trying to relieve her callers of their hats, I shall really have nothing left to do. That habit is hard to eradicate, because she is such a good girl, and it was so carefully inculcated at her finishing school."

Tilney reflected. "Magraw is a good fellow too. There's really nothing to do except to tone him down a little—as you say, one feels as if one didn't earn one's keep."

She flashed round upon him instantly. "Ah, but I didn't say that. I said the ostensible duties were easy—but how about the others?"

He looked at her a little consciously. "What do you mean by the others?"

"I don't know how far you live up to your duties, but I'm horribly conscientious about mine. And of course what we're both paid for is to be introducers," she said.

"Introducers?" He colored slightly and, flinging his arm over the back of the bench, turned to command a fuller view of her face. "Yes, that is what we're paid for, I suppose."

"And that's what I hate about it, don't you?"

"Uncommonly," he assented with emphasis.

It isn't that the Bixbys are not nice people—they are, deep down, you know—or at least they would be, if they were leading a real life among their real friends. But the very fact that one is abetting them to lead a false life, and renounce and deny their past, and impose themselves on people who wouldn't look at them if it were not for their money, and who rather resent their intrusion as it is—well, if one oughtn't to be paid well for doing such a job as that, I don't know what it is to work for my living!"

Tilney continued to observe with appreciation the dramatic play of feature by means of which she expressed her rising disgust at her task; but when she ended he merely said in a detached tone: "It's charming how you've preserved your illusions."

"My illusions? Why, I haven't enough left for decency!"

"Oh, yes, you have. About the Bixbys, and what they would be if one hadn't egged them on. Why not say to yourself that, if they were not vulgar at heart, they would never have let themselves be taken in by this kind of humbug?"

"Is that what you say about Mr. Magraw?"

"I've told you that Magraw is a good fellow. But when I ran across him he was simply aching to see the show, and all I've done is to get him a seat in the front row."

"Yes—but are you not expected to do something more for him?"

"Something more—in what line?"

"Well, I think the Bixbys expect me to make a match for Sadie."

"The deuce they do! Well, we'll marry her to my man."

Miss Grantham uttered a cry of dismay. "Don't suggest it even in joke! Don't you see what a catastrophe it would be?"

"Why should it be a catastrophe?"

"Don't you really see? In the first place we should both be out of a job, and in the second, I should earn the everlasting enmity of the Bixbys. What they want for Sadie is not money but position. Mrs. Bixby tells me that every day."

Tilney received this in meditative silence: then he said with a slight laugh: "Well, if position is all they want, why don't you choose *me* as your candidate?"

Miss Grantham did not echo his laugh; she simply concentrated her gaze on his with a slowly deepening interest before answering: "It's a funny idea—but I believe they might do worse."

Tilney's hilarity increased.

"At any rate," she continued, without noticing it, "there's one thing that you and no one else can do for them, and I really believe that Mrs. Bixby, in her present mood, would be capable of rewarding you with her daughter's hand."

"Good heavens! Then I should have to take a look at Miss Bixby before doing it."

"Oh, Sadie's charming. Didn't you notice her last night at the ball? I managed to smuggle her in, though I couldn't get the others invited. What Mrs. Bixby wants," Miss Grantham earnestly continued, "what she's absolutely sickening for at this moment, is to have Sadie invited to Aline Leicester's little Louis XV dance tomorrow night. And you are the only person in Newport who can do it. I didn't even have a chance to try—for the very day my invitation came I happened to meet Aline, and she said at once: 'Belle, I see the Bixbys in your eye; but I don't see them in my ballroom.' After that, I tried a little wire-pulling, but it simply made her more obstinate—you know her latest pose is to snub the new millionaires; and you are the only person who can persuade her to make an exception for the Bixbys. Aline's family feeling is tremendously strong, and every one knows you are her favorite cousin."

Tilney listened attentively to this plea; but when it had ended he said, with a discouraging gesture: "I was just going to try to get an invitation for Magraw!"

"Lump them together, then—it will be just as easy; and if you *should* want Mr. Bixby to do anything for you—such as putting you on to a good tip—"

"Thanks, but I've been put on to too many good tips. If it weren't for the good tips I've had, I should be living like a gentleman on my income."

"Well, you'll make Mrs. Bixby think you the most eligible young man in Newport. And if you could persuade Aline to ask Sadie to the dinner before the dance—"

"*Comme vous y allez!* What would be my return for that?"

She rose with a charming gesture. "Who knows, after all? Perhaps only the pleasure of doing me a very great favor."

"That settles it. I'll do what I can. But how about getting your costumes at such short notice?"

"Oh, we cabled out to Worth on the chance." She held out her hand for good-by. "If only there were something I could do for *you!*"

"Well, there is, as it happens," he rejoined with a smile. "If I succeed in my attempt, let Magraw dance the cotillon with you at Aline's."

She hesitated, visibly embarrassed. "I should be delighted, of course. I'm engaged already, but that's nothing. Only—I'm going to be horribly frank—the Bixbys are rather a heavy load, and I'm not sure I can carry your friend too!"

"Oh, yes, you can. That's my reason for asking you. You see, I really can't help Magraw much. It takes a woman to give a man a start. Aline will say, 'Oh, bring him, if you choose'—but when he comes she won't take any notice of him, or introduce him to any of the nice women. He was too shy to go to the Summertons' last night—he's really very shy under his loudness—so Aline's dance will be his first appearance in Newport; and if he's seen dancing the cotillon with you, at a little *sauterie* like that, with only a handful of people in the room, why, he's made, and my hard work is over for the season."

She smiled. "If you take a fancy to Sadie, perhaps it's over for life."

"And if *you*—by George! No, I don't think I want you to dance the cotillon with Magraw."

"Why not? Do you grudge me a comfortable home for my old age?"

He stood gazing at her as though for the first time his eyes took in the full measure of her grace.

"No—but I grudge *him* even a cotillon with you."

"Ah, you and I were not made to dance cotillons with one another; or do anything together, except conspire at sunrise for each other's material advancement. And that reminds me—I shan't see you again to-day, for we are going to Narragansett on Mr. Bixby's yacht, and to-night we have a dinner at home. But if you succeed with Aline, will you send me a line in the evening?"

He shook his head as they clasped hands once more. "No; but I'll tell you about it here tomorrow morning."

"Very well—I'll be punctual!" she called out to him, as she sped away through the shrubbery.

II

IT was, in fact, Miss Grantham who was first on the scene the next morning; and so eager was she to learn the result of the mission with which she had charged her friend, that, instead of profiting by her few moments of solitude, she sat watching the path and chafing at Mr. Tilney's delay.

When he arrived, politeness restrained the question on her lips; but his first word was to assure her of his success. "You are to bring Miss Bixby to the dinner," he announced.

"Oh, thank you, thank you—you're wonderful!" she exclaimed; "and if there's anything in the world I can do—" She paused suddenly, remembering her side of the compact, and added with nobility: "If it is of any possible advantage to Mr. Magraw to make my acquaintance, I shall be very glad—"

She had already observed in Tilney a marked depression of manner, which even this handsome reaffirmation of her purpose did not dispel.

"Oh," he merely said, "I did not mean to hold you so closely to your bargain—" and with that he seated himself at her side, and lapsed into a state of dumb preoccupation.

Miss Grantham suffered this as long as it was possible for a young lady of spirit to endure; then she determined to make Mr. Tilney aware of her presence by withdrawing it.

"I am afraid," she said, rising with a smile, "that, though you welcomed me so handsomely yesterday, my being here seriously interferes with your enjoyment of the hour, and I am going to propose a compromise. Since it is agreed that we are joint proprietors of this bench, and entitled to an equal share of its advantages, and since our sitting on it together practically negatives those advantages, I suggest that we occupy it on alternate mornings—and to show my gratitude for the favor you have done me, I will set the example by withdrawing today."

Tilney met her smile with a look of unrelieved melancholy. "I don't wonder," he said, "that you find solitude less oppressive than my company; but since our purpose in seeking this bench is to snatch an hour's quiet enjoyment, and since enjoyment of any sort is impossible to me to-day, it is obviously you who are entitled to remain here, and I who ought to take myself away." And he held out his hand in farewell.

Miss Grantham detained it in hers. "To have you surrender your rights because you are too miserable to enjoy them, leaves me with no heart to profit by my own; and if you wish me to remain you must stay also, and tell me what it is that troubles you."

She reseated herself as she spoke, and Tilney, with a deprecating gesture, resumed his place at her side.

"My dear Miss Grantham, the subject is too trifling to mention; I was only trying to calculate how long one could live in Venice on a hundred dollars."

"Why in Venice—and why a hundred dollars?"

"Because, when my passage is paid, it will be all the ready money I possess, and I have always heard that one could live very moderately in Venice."

Miss Grantham flushed and threw a quick glance at him. "You're not thinking of deserting?" she cried, reproachfully.

The young man returned her look. "Deserting—whom?" he inquired.

"Well, me, if you choose! You can't think the comfort it's been to me, since yesterday, to know that there were two of us. I understand now how humane it is to chain convicts together!"

Tilney considered this with a faint smile. "How long have you been at it?" he asked.

"At the Bixbys? I joined them last April in Paris."

"Ah, well—I've been six months with Magraw. It wasn't so bad when we were yachting and knocking about the world—but since we've taken to society it has become unendurable."

"Yes. I didn't mind ordering the Bixbys' dresses as much as I mind providing opportunities for their wearing them."

"I don't so much mind trotting Magraw about—though you know it's nonsense about your having to dance with him this evening—"

"No matter about that. What is it that bothers you?"

"The whole preposterous situation. Magraw's the best fellow in the world—but there are moments when he takes me for the butler."

"Oh, I know," she sympathized. "Mrs. Bixby—"

"That isn't the worst, though: it's the reaction. He took me for the butler yesterday afternoon—and in the evening I found a ruby scarf pin on my dressing table."

But her sympathy was ready for any demand on it. "I know, I know—" she reiterated; and then, breaking off, she added with a mounting color: "You know I couldn't go to the dance to-night if Mrs. Bixby didn't pay for my dress."

"Oh, the cases are not the same; and it's different for a woman."

"Why are the cases not the same? And why should I not be humiliated by what humiliates you?"

He shrugged his shoulders ironically. "I'm not humiliated by anything that poor Magraw does to me; I'm humiliated by what I do to *him!*"

"What you do?"

"Yes. What right have I to behave like a gentleman, and return his scarf pins?"

"At least you do return them? And I can't return the dresses. Oh, it's detestable either way!" she exclaimed.

"Yes, especially when one succumbs to the weakness of hating them instead of one's self. I hate Magraw this morning," he confessed.

She rose with an impatient glance at her watch. "Dear me, I must go. I promised Sadie to see the dressmaker at half-past nine: she's coming to alter our fancy dresses. You see I felt sure you would get Sadie's invitation. I want you to know her," she continued. "She's really a very nice girl. I should like her immensely if I didn't have to accept so many favors from her."

"Ah, you've just expressed my feeling about Magraw. I really should like your opinion of him," he added.

"Well, you shall have it—tomorrow morning."

"Here?" he rejoined with sudden interest.

"Why not? You know I mean to dance with him this evening."


The morning after the dance it was Miss Grantham's turn to arrive late at the tryst; and when she did so, it was with the air of having a duty to discharge rather than a pleasure to enjoy.

"Mr. Tilney," she said, advancing resolutely to the bench on which he sat awaiting her, "my only object in coming this morning is—"

He rose with extended hand. "To let me thank you, I hope, for the generous way in which you fulfilled your share of the compact? It was awfully good of you to be so nice to Magraw."

She colored vividly, but held his gaze. "As it happens, I *liked* Mr. Magraw. But if I had known the means you had used to obtain his invitation—"

Tilney colored in turn, but they continued to face each other boldly.

"Did Aline betray me? How like a woman!" he exclaimed.

"I can quite understand," Miss Grantham witheringly continued, "the importance you attached to having Mr. Magraw invited to your cousin's dance. *You had to make some return for the scarf pin.* But to use my name as a pretext—to tell Aline Leicester that I was trying to marry Mr. Magraw!"

"Oh, I didn't say *trying*—I said you meant to," Tilney corrected.

"As if that made it any better! To let that man think—"

"He'll never hear of it; and you don't seem to realize that it's not easy to extract an invitation from Aline."

"I don't know that it was absolutely necessary that Mr. Magraw should receive one!"

Tilney, at this, raised his head with a challenging air. "You appeared to think it absolutely necessary that Miss Bixby should."

"Well—I don't see—"

"You don't see how I got *hers?* I dare say you'll think the same method is even more objectionable when the situation is reversed—"

She stared at him with growing disapproval. "You don't mean to say that you let Aline think you wanted to marry Sadie Bixby?"

"I told you there was nothing I wouldn't stoop to. I suppose you think that horribly low."

Her stare resolved itself into a faint sound of laughter. "Good heavens, how enchanted Mrs. Bixby will be!"

"The deuce she will—but of course the joke can easily be explained."

"To whom? To Mrs. Bixby? I'm glad you think so. I should have said it would be difficult."

"Oh, Mrs. Bixby will never hear of it. I told Aline in the strictest confidence—"

"Everyone at the dance was congratulating me on my conquest of Mr. Magraw. I don't see why Aline should keep one secret and not the other."

Tilney's brow darkened ominously. "Well, at any rate, I'll soon undeceive Magraw!"

"A thousand thanks. And I suppose you leave it to me to undeceive Sadie? She talked of you all the way home. Of course, you're almost the only decent man she's met."

"Ah, then the remedy is simple enough. You've only to introduce a few others."

"Yes, I've thought of that." Miss Grantham examined him with a cold smile. "But are you quite sure you want me to?"

Tilney met her question with another. "What on earth do you mean?"

"I'm not stupid in such cases, and I could see that Sadie was interested. Did you find her so perfectly impossible?"

"Impossible? I thought her very pretty."

"That's going to the other extreme—but she certainly looked her best last night. Still, before deciding, I should want you to see her by daylight—and without the paint—"

"Oh, she had on very little paint. One could see her own color through it."

"Yes—she has an unfortunate way of getting red—"

"At that age I should call it blushing."

Miss Grantham's face grew suddenly stern. "Of course," she said, "I should never forgive myself if you were only trifling with Sadie—"

Tilney paused. "But if I were in earnest—?" he suggested.

She gazed at him intently for a moment. "After all, I might be saving her from something worse!"

III

FOR TWO mornings after that Tilney, to his secret regret, had the bench on the cliffs to himself. On the third morning he was detained indoors somewhat later than usual on pressing business of his employer's; and when he emerged from the house he was surprised, and considerably dismayed, to find his seat tenanted by the incongruous figure of Mr. Hutchins Magraw.

Given his patron's unmatutinal habits, and rooted indifference to the beauties of nature, it was impossible to conceive what whim had drawn him to so unlikely a spot at so improbable an hour; and Tilney's first impulse was to approach the seat, and allay his curiosity by direct inquiry. Hardly, however, had he begun to advance when the flutter of a white skirt through the Cliffwood shrubberies caused him to retreat abruptly into the covert of lilac bushes edging the lawn. It was by a mere accident, of course, that an unknown female, wearing a white gown, happened to be walking along the path from that particular direction. The path was open to the public, and there was no reason to assume any coincidence between—

Tilney drew a sharp breath. Mr. Magraw had risen and was advancing in the direction of the approaching petticoat; and as it was impossible for him to recognize its wearer from where he sat, it was obvious that he expected some one, and that the invisible female was no casual stroller drawn forth by the beauty of the morning. The next moment this conjecture was unpleasantly confirmed; for Miss Grantham emerged from the shrubbery, and placed her hand in Mr. Magraw's without perceptible surprise. He, then, had also been expected; and she had actually had the effrontery to select, as the scene of their tryst, the seat which, by every right of friendship, should have been kept sacred to her conversations with Fred Tilney!

"The idea of telling him about my bench!" Resentment of her perfidy was for the moment uppermost in Tilney's breast, or was, at any rate, the only sentiment to which he chose to give explicit expression. But other considerations surged indignantly beneath it—wonder at woman's unaccountableness, disgust at her facility, disappointment, above all, that this one little episode, saved from the wreckage of many shattered illusions, should have had so premature and unpoetic an ending.

"Magraw—if only it hadn't been Magraw!"

He had meant to turn away and reenter the house; but a feeling of mingled curiosity and wretchedness kept him rooted in his hiding place, while he followed with his eyes the broad swaggering back of Mr. Hutchins Magraw, as it attended Miss Grantham's slender silhouette across the lawn.

"I hadn't realized how disgustingly fat the man has grown. One would think a fellow with that outline would know better than to rig himself out in a check a foot square, and impale his double chin on the points of that preposterous collar! It's odd how little the most fastidious women notice such details. If they did, fewer men would make themselves ridiculous. Why are they standing there, looking up at the house? Perhaps, after all, it was an accident, their meeting. No—they're making straight for the bench—by George, I believe they were looking at the house to make sure I wasn't coming! Don't be alarmed, my dear Miss Grantham, I've no desire to interfere with your amusements. I see now, though, why Magraw was in such a hurry to have me balance his bank book this morning. Just a dodge to keep me indoors, of course. It's beastly bad taste, anyhow, to make a poor devil like me go over a bank book with such an indecently big balance. That's the kind of thing that makes a man turn socialist. Why the devil should Magraw have all those millions while I—well, to be sure, poor devil, he needs them all to make up for his other deficiencies. I'd like to see how long Belle Grantham would share that bench with him if it weren't for his bank account! It must be hard work to talk to Magraw at nine o'clock in the morning. I wonder what the deuce she's saying to him?"

The two objects of Tilney's contemplation had by this time settled themselves on the seat which their observer still chose to call his own, and something in their attitudes seemed to announce that theirs was no transient alighting, but the deliberate installation which precedes an earnest talk.

"Well, she could talk to anybody, at any hour of the day or night! That's her trade, poor girl, as much as it is mine. Only I can't see why she should give Magraw *my* particular hour. Now that I've given him such a good start they've plenty of other chances of meeting. But perhaps she's afraid of competition, and wants to clinch the business by this morning interview. Poor girl! How she must hate it at heart! I'll do her the justice to say that if she had enough to keep body and soul together she'd never look at a Magraw. But if this hand-to-mouth life is hard on a man it's ten times worse for a woman—and her day is over sooner, too. Poor girl! No wonder she shrinks at the idea of growing old in such a trade. To see people cooling off, and the newcomers crowding her out—how can I blame her for being afraid to face such a future? Why, I ought to do what I can to help her—but to help her to Magraw! Bah—there's something rotten in our social system; but it isn't her fault, and only a primitive ass of a man would be fool enough to blame her, instead of pitying her as a fellow victim."

At this point Miss Grantham started up with an apprehensive gesture with which Tilney was painfully familiar. "She's had to look at her watch to realize how time was flying! She doesn't seem to find it goes so slowly with Magraw. Perhaps my pity's wasted, after all. That's the way she always lingers on after she has said she couldn't possibly stay another minute. Poor Magraw! She's playing him for all she's worth, and I don't suppose he even knows he's on the hook. Oh, I don't blame her—not in the least!— only I think she might have chosen another place for their meetings. Hardened wretch as I am, I was beginning to have a sentiment for that bench—it would never have occurred to me to sit there with Miss Bixby, for instance. It's queer how a woman's taste deteriorates when she associates with common men—but I mean to let Miss Grantham know that, though she's welcome to Magraw, she can't have my bench into the bargain!"

By this time the couple under observation had completed their lingering adieux, the gentleman returning across the lawn to his house, while the lady retraced her way toward Cliffwood. Tilney remained in concealment while Mr. Magraw strode by within a few feet, the fatuous smile of self-complacency upon his lips; then the young man, emerging behind his patron's back, struck across the lawn and overtook Miss Grantham as she turned into the adjoining grounds.

She paused as she became aware of Tilney's approach, and cast a rapid glance in the direction from which he had come; but he had taken care not to show himself till Magraw had vanished in the shrubberies, and he was quick to note the look of reassurance in Miss Grantham's eyes. She held out her hand, blushing slightly, but self-possessed.

*"J'ai failli attendre!"* she quoted with an indulgent smile; and the smile had well-nigh stung her companion to immediate retaliation. But he meditated a subtler revenge, and dissembling his resentment, asked innocently: "Have you been here long?"

"It has certainly seemed so," she replied in the same tone.

"Well, at any rate, my involuntary delay has enabled you to enjoy what you originally came out to seek;" and, in reply to her puzzled glance, he added pointedly: "The pleasures of solitude."

Unmoved by the thrust, she turned a smiling look on him. "But what if you have made them lose their flavor?"

"Then it was almost worth my while to have stayed away!"

She held out her hand. "The experiment was so successful that you need not try it again," she said sweetly. "But time flies, and I must hasten back into captivity."

He detained her hand to ask sentimentally: "I hope you are not losing your taste for freedom?" and she replied, as she hastened away: "Come and see—come and see tomorrow!"

He stood in the path where she had left him, and slowly drew from his pocket Mr. Magraw's latest gift—a jeweled cigarette case. He took out the cigarettes, transferred them to his pocket, and then, with a free swing of the arm, flung their receptacle into the sea.

"Do *you* come and see tomorrow!" he muttered, addressing himself to Miss Grantham's retreating figure; then he lit a cigarette, and walked rapidly back to Sea Lodge.

"I shouldn't have thought it of her!" he said as he entered the house.

## IV

TWO mornings later Tilney, with a beating heart, descended the terrace of Sea Lodge, and once more directed himself toward the bench on the cliff.

He was not only on time, but a few minutes before the hour; yet it was something of a surprise to him to find the bench still untenanted. He seated himself, lit a cigarette with deliberation, and drew from his pocket a note stamped Cliffwood and bearing the date of the previous evening.

"Dear Mr. Tilney," it ran, "Much as I dislike to intrude upon the solitude which I know you value so highly, I must ask you to spare me a few moments tomorrow morning; and I send this line in advance in order that my coming may not interfere with *any other arrangements*.

Yours sincerely,
Belle Grantham."

Tilney reread this note with an air of considerable complacency; then he laid it carefully back in his notecase, and rose to meet Miss Grantham as she made her appearance around the curve of the path.

The morning was chilly, and veiled in a slight haze, too translucent to be called a fog, but perceptible enough to cast a faint grayness over sea and sky. Seen in this tempered light, Miss Grantham's face seemed to lose its usual vivacity and be subdued to the influence of the atmosphere; and her manner of greeting Tilney had the same tinge of soberness.

"I must excuse myself," she began, "for again intruding on your privacy—"

"*My* privacy?" Tilney gallantly interposed. "Was it not long since understood between us that the privacy of this spot belongs as much to you as to me?"

"Long since—yes," she replied; "but so much has happened in the interval." She paused, and added in a significant tone: "Since I came here yesterday morning, and found you sitting on this bench with Sadie Bixby."

Tilney feigned a successful show of embarrassment. "You came here yesterday morning—?"

"By appointment, as you evidently do *not* remember," she continued coldly. "It is a mistake one does not make twice, and my only object in asking to see you this morning—"

"One moment," Tilney interposed. "Before you go on, I must say in my own defense that I assumed our compact about the use of this seat had been abrogated when I came out the day before yesterday, and found *you* sharing it with Magraw."

There was no mistaking the effect of this thrust. Her color rose painfully, and she forced a laugh as she replied: "The day before yesterday? Ah, yes—that was the morning you were so late. Mr. Magraw saw me from the house, and took pity on my deserted state."

Tilney colored also at this fresh evidence of her duplicity.

"I beg your pardon—but does not your memory deceive you? It seemed to me that Magraw was waiting on the bench, and that it was *you* who took pity—if I am not mistaken."

She drew herself up and flashed an outraged glance at him. "You were watching us, then?" she exclaimed.

"Oh—*watching!* I was merely repairing to our seat at my usual hour."

"At your usual hour? But Mr. Magraw told me you were not coming—that you would be busy all the morning with some writing—" She broke off, seeing herself more deeply involved with each word.

"Some writing he had given me to do? Precisely," Tilney answered with scorn. "Only, he had underrated either my impatience to see you, or my head for figures—or both."

She received this in an embarrassed silence, and softened by her embarrassment he added: "It is not for me to discuss your arrangements; but I confess I wondered a little that you chose our bench as a meeting place."

She hesitated a moment, and then said in a deprecating tone: "It is the only place where I can see anyone alone!"

"And you wished to see Magraw alone?"

Their eyes met defiantly, but hers fell first as she answered: "Yes—I did wish to."

Tilney bowed ceremoniously. "In that case, of course, nothing remains to be said."

They had both remained standing during this short colloquy, but she now seated herself and signed to him to do the same.

"Yes—something remains for me to say; and it was for the purpose of saying it that I asked you to meet me this morning."

Tilney, without replying, placed himself at the opposite end of the bench.

"What I wish to ask," she continued in a decisive tone, "is your object in meeting Miss Bixby here yesterday."

The temerity of the question was so surprising to her companion that for a moment he gazed at her without speaking; then he replied with a faint smile: "If there is any right of priority in such inquiries, perhaps I am entitled to ask first what was your object in meeting Magraw here the day before that."

She repressed her impatience, and returned gently: "The cases are surely not quite alike; but I thought I had already given you my answer."

"That you wished to see him alone? Well, I had the same object in asking Miss Bixby to meet me."

"But you must see that in the case of a young girl—especially a girl as inexperienced as Sadie—"

Tilney raised his hand with a deprecating gesture. "Are you not falling into the conventional mistake of assuming that a man cannot seek to be alone with a young girl except for the purpose of making love to her?"

"Well, what other purpose—?"

He looked at her calmly. "Then it was to promote that purpose that you asked Magraw to meet you here the day before I met Miss Bixby?"

It was Miss Grantham's turn to color, and she fulfilled the obligation handsomely. "I see no object in such cross-questioning—"

"Ah, pardon me, but it was you who began it."

"It was my duty to question you about Sadie. You can't imagine I do it for my pleasure—but her parents are too inexperienced to protect her."

"To protect her? Then you consider me hopelessly detrimental—?"

Miss Grantham drew a quick breath. "Why not have told me at once that you wished to marry her? Every one is saying so, of course; but I could not help remembering that your intentions have not always been so—"

"Specific?" he suggested ironically.

"Well, you are still unmarried," she observed.

"Yes," he said musingly. "It takes a pretty varied experience of life to find out that there are worse states than marriage."

Miss Grantham rose with a smile. "Since you have found it out," she said generously, "I can congratulate you with perfect sincerity. Sadie is a dear little creature—"

"But too good for me? Is that what you meant to add?"

"No, for when you find out how good she is you'll want to be worthy of her."

He received this in silence, but when she held out her hand for good-by he said: "I wonder if it's not my duty to protect Magraw? He hasn't even an inexperienced parent."

She met his smile steadily, but he felt the sudden resistance of her hand. "Mr. Magraw," she returned, withdrawing it, "would be quite safe if Sadie were."

"If Sadie—?"

She broke into a laugh. "If you're planning to take the bread out of my mouth, I must do something in the way of self-preservation." And as he remained silent, feeling a rather tragic import under her pleasantry, she added wearily: "I can't begin this kind of thing over again—I simply can't!"

Tilney's discouraged gesture showed his comprehension of her words. "To whom do you say it?" he exclaimed.

"Well, then, let us drop phrases, and admit frankly that we're trying to marry each other's wards—or whatever you choose to call them!"

He did not answer, and she continued, with a kind of nervous animation: "And that we'll do all we can—that we *honorably* can—to help each other's plans, and see each other through."

The young man still remained silent, his eyes absently fixed on the line of sea from which the veil of mist was gradually receding; and before he had found a reply a footman, hastening across the lawn from the house, broke in upon his meditations.

"Beg pardon, sir, but Mr. Magraw wishes you to come in immediately, sir, to answer the telephone for him."

Tilney turned abruptly toward his companion. "By heaven, yes, we'll see each other through!" he exclaimed.

Though Tilney and Miss Grantham had parted without any reference to future meetings at the same spot, each was now drawn to the bench on the cliffs by a new motive—the not unpardonable desire to see if the other had again extended its hospitality to a third party.

Their mutual reconnoitering did not, for several mornings, carry them farther than the most distant point from which the bench was visible; when, perceiving it to be untenanted, they respectively retreated, without having discovered each other's maneuver.

The fifth day, however, was so foggy that distant espionage was impossible; and Tilney's suspicions having been aroused by the unusual amount of correspondence with which his patron had burdened him overnight, he determined to ascertain by direct inspection if the sanctity of the bench had again been violated. It would have been hard to say why, in his own thoughts, he still applied such terms to the possibility of Miss Grantham's resorting to the spot in company with her suitor. Tilney fully acquiesced in the inevitableness of the course they had agreed upon; but if his reason accepted the consequences, his sensibilities made the process unpleasant to contemplate. He would have been prepared to append his signature to a matrimonial contract drawn up between Miss Grantham and his employer; but it irritated him that an arrangement so purely utilitarian should be disguised under the charming futilities of courtship.

"The real grossness is not in viewing marriage as a business partnership, but in pretending that one doesn't," he summed up, as he crossed the damp lawn with the waves of gray fog coiling around him like a phantom sea.

Through their pale surges he could just discern, as he approached the bench, an indeterminate outline hovering near it; and the outline proclaiming itself, on nearer inspection, as of his own sex, Tilney was about to turn aside when another figure appeared from the direction of Cliffwood.

"It's odd," he mused, trying to philosophize upon his own discomfiture—"it's odd how the fog distorts a silhouette. I could have sworn I should have known hers anywhere, and yet this deceptive vapor—or my nerves, or the two together—make her look so much shorter—and I'll swear I never saw her swing her arm as she walked. I suppose it comes from associating with a bounder like—"

He drew back with a suppressed exclamation as the small feminine outline showed more clearly through a partial break in the fog.

"Why, it looks—no, it can't be! Hanged if I know, she's so bundled up. Well, it's not *she*, at any rate; and if Magraw, at this stage of the proceedings, has the indecency to be meeting other women here, it's almost my duty to the poor girl to let her know before it's too late to break with him."

He was surprised at the immediate sense of lightness which this conclusion produced in him. He was sorry for Miss Grantham, of course, when she'd so nearly landed her man; but, hang it, there were as good fish in the sea—and meanwhile she must, at all costs, be saved from the humiliation of committing herself farther. His first impulse had been the somewhat cruel one of putting the unvarnished facts before her; but farther reflection made him shrink from this course, and cast about for some more humane expedient.

"If she could only be made to think that she can do better than Magraw—and she ought to, with half a chance, poor child! I can't be wholly sorry that she should not be sacrificed to this particular monster—not that Magraw's not a good fellow in himself; I daresay the Minotaur was liked in his own set—but he should have stayed there, that's all."

While engaged in these considerations, Tilney had prudently withdrawn into the Cliffwood shrubberies; and he was just deciding to effect his escape through the Bixbys' grounds, rather than run the chance of being discovered by the tenants of the bench, when, on issuing from his retreat, he beheld the indistinct gleam of a white dress half way down the Cliffwood lawn. This time, even though the fog had thickened, there was no mistaking the form and movement of the shrouded figure; or was it some subtler sense than that of sight that so positively assured him of Miss Grantham's nearness? At any rate, he advanced to meet her without a moment's hesitation, determined to protect her, by whatever expedient, from the embarrassment of interrupting the colloquy on the bench. He had but a moment in which to consider how this should be effected; but it was not the first time he had trusted to his gift of improvisation in delicate situations, and he was now sustained by the unwonted sense of his complete disinterestedness. The progress of his own affairs had in fact made it impossible for him to interfere from personal motives; and he thus had the support of knowing that his intervention was quite unaffected by selfish considerations.

"I'm almost glad," he reflected, "that I am committed, if one of the first consequences is to enable me to act as her friend, without any afterthought, or any possibility of her suspecting me of not playing fair. One of my reasons for wanting to settle my own future has always been the desire to help her; and little Sadie is far too good a girl not to understand—"

At this point he found himself face to face with Miss Grantham, who, suddenly discerning him through the fog, drew back with a slight start of surprise.

"I had a feeling that I might meet you this morning," he said in a tone of undisguised pleasure; and even as he spoke, his half-formed plan for her rescue began to dissolve in the glow of happiness which her nearness always produced. He was annoyed to find that his self-control was so completely at the mercy of her presence; but he could no more resist the sudden reaction of his pulses from reason to feeling than he could dispel the softly enveloping fog which seemed to act as the accomplice of his wishes.

"If I can only make her think she can do better than Magraw," he kept mechanically repeating to himself; but the only expedient that occurred to him was one which both prudence and honor rejected.

Miss Grantham's first words threw his ideas into still deeper confusion.

"Mr. Tilney," she said, without heeding his greeting, "are you, or are you not, engaged to Sadie Bixby?"

The abruptness of the inquiry, and the sternness of her tone, had a not wholly unpleasing effect on the young man; but their only perceptible result was to reduce him to an embarrassed silence.

Miss Grantham gave a faint laugh. "I suppose I may consider myself answered? And in that case, I have only to apologize for asking so indiscreet a question—"

Tilney cleared his throat nervously. "I am not aware that I have either answered your question or shown that I regarded it as indiscreet—"

"Your silence did both," she returned with some impatience. He made no reply, and after a moment's pause she added, with a sudden assumption of playfulness: "Well, if this is really to be our last meeting, as I suppose it is—shall we not celebrate it by sitting together for a few moments on our dear old bench?"

As she spoke she began to move in the direction of the seat, apparently assuming that her companion would offer no opposition to her proposal. But Tilney, with a vague exclamation, laid his hand on her arm. "Don't you think it's rather too damp to sit out of doors?"

He reddened under the laugh with which she met this incongruous objection.

"My poor friend—would she really mind so much? I was foolish enough to think you might give me this last morning—"

"The whole day is at your service," he interposed nervously, "but—"

"Ah, yes; there will always be a *but* between us now. No wonder men get on so much better than women; they are so much more prudent! Now, even if I were engaged to Mr. Magraw—" She broke off, and he fancied he could see her flush through the fog.

He turned on her abruptly. "*Are* you? There's the point!" he exclaimed.

She drew back, slightly disconcerted, but recovering herself at once, added in the same playful tone: "I was about to say that, even if I *were*, I should not feel there was any disloyalty to my future in giving this last hour to *our* past."

Her light emphasis on the pronoun threw him into a glow of pleasure, through which discretion and foresight loomed as remote as objects in the fog; but when she added, with a half-sad laugh: "I should not hesitate to go back to our bench for the last time—" he broke out, with a fresh leap of apprehension: "Ah, but you couldn't, if it meant to you what it does to me!"

He had spoken the words haphazardly, snatching at them as the readiest means of diverting her purpose; but once uttered they seemed to fill the whole air, and to create a silence which neither speaker had, for a moment, the courage to fill.

Womanlike, Miss Grantham was the first to recover her self-possession. "I am sure," she said sweetly, "that we shall both look back often on our quiet morning talks, and I can't think that the persons with whom our futures may be associated will be defrauded by our treasuring such memories."

She spoke with a sadness so poignant to Tilney that for a moment he stood without replying, and during the pause she again advanced a few steps nearer to the bench.

The young man broke into a scornful laugh. "*Defrauded?* Good heavens—one can't defraud people of treasures they are utterly incapable of valuing!"

She caught this up with a vehemence that surprised him. "Oh, do you feel that too? It's just what I mean," she exclaimed.

"Feel it—?" He stopped before her, blocking her way. "Do you suppose I've felt anything else, night or day, since the accursed day when we agreed—?"

He interrupted himself with a last effort at self-control, and she replied in a low tone of exquisite pleading: "Well, then, if you *do* feel it, why not go back for a moment to our bench?"

Tilney groaned. "Can't we talk as well here? Let us walk a little way—we shall be alone anywhere in this fog." ("Anywhere but on that confounded bench," he mentally added.)

Miss Grantham uttered an ironical exclamation. "Ah, you've promised her, I see. Was it one of the conditions? In that case, of course—"

"There were no conditions—and if there had been—"

"Oh, be careful! I want to talk of our past, and not of our future."

Tilney groaned again. "If only it *could* be our future—Belle, what a beastly bad turn we've done each other, after all!"

"Don't let us talk of the present, either, please." She laid a restraining touch on his arm. "Why should we give each other this pain when it's too late?"

"Too late?" He paused, remembering that, for him at least, it was too late; but an irresistible impulse prompted him to add: "If it hadn't been, tell me at least—*would you have dared to*, Belle?"

They stood looking at each other, mysteriously isolated in the magic circle of the fog.

"Dared? I am daring more now—more than I have courage for!" she murmured, half to herself.

The admission had well-nigh broken down the last barriers of Tilney's self-restraint; but at the moment of surrender he suddenly recalled his own state of bondage. He had but to lead Miss Grantham to the bench, and she would find herself free; but when she turned to reward him as liberators expect to be rewarded, with what a sorry countenance must he refuse her gift!

He dropped the hand he had caught in his, and said in a low voice: "You were right just now, and I was wrong. We must not even talk of our past, lest we should be tempted to think of our present or our future. I happen to know that I am not doing anyone a serious wrong in speaking to you as I have; but my own case is different."

"Your own case is different?" Miss Grantham interposed, with a sudden change of voice and expression. "If you think you can make love to me without doing Mr. Magraw a serious wrong, I should like to know why I may not listen to you without—"

Tilney received her attack with a disarming humility. "I said the cases were different, because, in a moment of incredible folly, I have tried to attract the interest of a trustful, affectionate girl—"

Miss Grantham interrupted him with a laugh. "Do you mean that," she asked ironically, "for a description of Sadie Bixby?"

Her tone aroused an incongruous flash of resentment in Tilney. "I see no difficulty," he returned, "in identifying the young lady from my words."

"If you really believe them to apply to her, I cannot see how you can excuse yourself for being here with me at this moment!" She laughed again, and then, to Tilney's surprise, drew nearer, and once more laid her hand on his arm.

"My poor friend, it is I who am the real offender, and not you. Believe me, I would not have let you speak to me as you have to-day, if I had not known—if I had not almost felt it my duty to be kind to you—to do what I could to atone—"

"To be kind to me? To atone? What on earth are you talking about?" exclaimed Tilney, startled by this unexpected echo of his inmost thoughts.

"Alas, it was a foolish impulse, and one which only our old friendship could justify. I forgot for a moment that I was not free, in my desire to prepare you—to console you in advance—for a blow—"

"A blow? You're not *married?*" burst from Tilney.

She paused, and gazed at him wonderingly but not unkindly.

"I was speaking of yourself—yourself and Sadie. I feel myself so deeply to blame—"

Tilney interrupted her with an air of inexpressible relief. "We're both to blame for abetting each other in such suicidal folly. As if either of us was made to give up life and liberty for a bank-balance! But I don't reproach you, Belle—it was more my fault than yours; and I deserve that I should be the one to pay the penalty!"

"The penalty? The penalty of marrying Sadie?" she breathlessly interposed.

"Of marrying any one but you!" he returned recklessly; and at the retort, a veil of sadness fell suddenly upon her eager face.

"It's too late to think of that now; but if you really feel as you say—"

Tilney again cut her short. "It's too late for me, I know; but if *you* really feel as you say, thank Heaven, Belle, it's not too late for you!"

She drew back a step, and both paused, as though dazed by the shock of their flying words. But as Tilney again approached her, she raised her hand and said gravely: "I don't know what you mean, but I can explain what *I* mean if you'll only—"

"One moment, please. I can explain, too, if you'll only—"

He caught her hand, and began to lead her hurriedly across the lawn to the bench.

"Only what?" she panted, trying to keep pace with his flying strides; and he called back across his shoulder: "Only come to the bench—and be quick!"

"To the bench? Why, haven't I been trying all this time to take you there?" she cried after him, between tears and laughter.

"Yes; but I didn't know; at least *you* didn't know—"

"Didn't know what?"

"Whom you'd find there!"

She pulled back at this, detaining him forcibly. "Good heavens," she gasped, "do you mean to say that *you've* known all this time?"

"Do you think I should have dared to say what I have if I hadn't—?"

"Hadn't known about Sadie—?"

"*Sadie?* I suppose you mean Magraw?"

"Mr. Magraw?" She stopped short, and snatched her hand away with an indignant gesture.

"Mr. Tilney, who do you think is sitting on that bench?"

He faced around on her with equal indignation. "I don't *think*, I know. Magraw is sitting there with a woman."

"You're utterly mistaken! I happen to know that it's Sadie Bixby who is sitting there with a man."

There was a long pause between them, charged with a gradual rush of inner enlightenment; then Tilney suddenly burst into a huge, world-defying laugh.

"Well, then, don't you see—?"

"I don't see anything more than if the fog were inside me!" she wailed.

"Don't you see that Magraw and Miss Bixby must be sitting there together, and that, in that case, nothing remains for you and me but to find a new seat for ourselves?"

## LES METTEURS EN SCÈNE

As first published in the *Revue des Deux Mondes*, October 1908

IT WAS tea time at the Hotel Nouveau-Luxe.

For several moments now Jean Le Fanois had been standing in the doorway of one of the small Louis XV drawing rooms that opened onto the spacious lounge. Of medium height, lean and well-built in his impeccably tailored frock coat, he had the knowing and slightly impertinent air of the aristocratic Parisian too long caught up in the exotic, noisy world of first-class hotels and fashionable cabarets. From time to time, however, his pale, finely chiseled face was clouded by an anxious expression, which the carefree smile he bestowed on passing acquaintances did little to hide.

Several times he glanced impatiently at his watch; then his expression cleared, and he advanced rapidly to meet a young woman who had just appeared on the threshold of the lounge. Exquisite and slender in a street dress of understated elegance, she balanced on a long, slim neck the head of an ephebe. Her exceedingly pale pink lips and large limpid eyes complemented an intelligent forehead crowned with a soft haze of indecisively blond hair. Glancing about for the young man, she made her way across the room alone, with the confident air, the serenely audacious carriage, of the young American used to making her own way in life. A closer scrutiny, however, revealed that the slightly naive air of independence characteristic of her compatriots was tempered in her by a nuance of Parisian refinement—as if a florid complexion had been softened by a film of tulle. Contact with another civilization had affected her in a totally different way than it had Le Fanois; she had gained, in this cosmopolitan exchange, as much as he seemed to have lost.

The young man approached her with a brotherly gesture of familiarity. "You're alone! Did your friends leave you in the lurch?" he asked her, shaking her hand.

Miss Lambart smiled reassuringly as she scanned the room. "No, I don't think so. I was supposed to find Mrs. Smithers and her daughter in one of the drawing rooms over there." She pointed with her tortoise-shell lorgnette toward the series of rooms just off the lounge. "If we look for them . . . ," she continued, but Le Fanois held her back.

"No, wait a moment," he said, lowering his voice and propelling the young woman to one of the large glassed-in bays overlooking the hotel garden. "Tell me what you told them about me and just what role I'm supposed to play." He hesitated; then, with a vaguely ironic smile, "In brief, what stage of social ambition have your friends reached?"

Miss Lambart smiled too. "They still seem quite naive to me," she said; "but one always has to be on one's guard. The most naïve are sometimes the most distrustful." She threw him a teasing glance. "Do you remember that pretty widow in Trouville—you know, from last year? If you'd been willing to present her to the Duchess of Sestre, what a marvelous trick you would have played!"

The young man shrugged slightly. "She was simply asking too much," he returned. "And then—and then was she really a widow as we understand it here, or had she simply mislaid her last husband? Your country is so vast that such accidents must be common. Decidedly, her past was much too nebulous!"

The girl broke into a chuckle that revealed her even pearl-white teeth beneath pale pink lips that were a bit too thin. "Well, as far as 'nebulous pasts' go, I can't answer for Mrs. Smithers' because I've never raised the veil that surrounds it. But I *will* vouch for the fact that her daughter is charming and that you're terribly finicky if you don't agree."

The young man shot her an indefinable glance which seemed to color his customary mockery with a nuance of affection.

"As charming as you are?" he asked banteringly.

Miss Lambart frowned and her eyes suddenly turned a cold metallic gray. "Now then, my dear fellow, you're not speaking in character. Besides," she went on, self-possessed and smiling once again, "it's my job to point such things out to you. As I was saying, I believe that for the moment Mrs. Smithers' ambitions are rather amorphous. Like many Americans who find themselves rich overnight, she wasn't able to establish the proper social connections in New York. So half out of spite and half out of sheer desire to spend her money, she jumped aboard the first available steamer with her daughter, no doubt hoping to acquire immediate social standing in a world where people are received in society without embarrassing inquiries into their past, provided they are wealthy and come from far enough away! As you know, it's only recently that I met Mrs. Smithers—on the liner that brought me back here—and she admitted to me with positively *noble* frankness that she wanted to establish ties with the French aristocracy, since her own aristocratic tastes made life in a plebeian society unbearable. Look, there she is," she added with a subtly malicious smile.

Le Fanois turned around and saw a large woman with pale, puffy features and a complicated coiffure, on which was poised a hat laden with the remains of an entire aviary of exotic birds. She advanced toward them, her shoulders weighed down by a magnificent silver fox coat, her movements impeded by the folds of a lavishly embroidered dress, trailing in her wake a tall, rosy girl. Dressed with the same exaggerated elegance as her mother, the girl held in her hands a sable muff, a gold purse set with precious stones and a diamond-studded lorgnette, and her incredibly blond hair was crowned with a floral abundance as varied as the ornithological trimmings of the maternal bonnet. "Here are Mrs. Smithers and her daughter Catherine," Blanche Lambart repeated, and Le Fanois, following her toward the new arrivals, could not suppress a sigh;

"Oh, those poor people . . . those poor people!"

## II

FOR almost ten years, Jean Le Fanois had led the tiresome and ambiguous life of a promoter of "nouveaux riches" in Parisian society. He had let himself be drawn into it little by little, as a result of accidental dealings with an extremely wealthy American at a time when he himself was down on his luck. How could this luxury-craving boy, accustomed from early youth to the easy-going and costly life of the Parisian clubman, have resisted the unhoped-for windfall such a relationship represented? His new friend, goodhearted and simple-minded, asked only to enjoy his millions in the company of a few choice friends. A dabbler in art collecting, like many of his compatriots, he was able to appreciate the artistic tastes of Le Fanois and commissioned him to furnish and decorate the elegant town house he had just bought from a bankrupt adventurer. Jean was delighted with the opportunity to distinguish himself in the role of enlightened amateur and, in acquiring handsome works of art for his friend, he experienced a little of the pleasure he would have had in buying them for himself. Then he learned that the stakes in this game included more durable rewards than mere altruistic pleasure. He received large sums of money from secondhand dealers highly pleased with the client he brought them; and although this arrangement embarrassed him slightly the first time it was proposed, he quickly grew accustomed to it, especially in view of the fact that sizeable gambling losses had seriously depreciated his modest fortune.

He enjoyed in more disinterested fashion the idle, luxurious life in which he found himself involved. The compatriots surrounding his friend led a completely empty existence, devoid of fixed occupations and stable relationships—but how artfully they hid its yawning emptiness under the appearances of frantic activity! Cruises on yachts, automobile trips sumptuous dinners in fashionable restaurants, afternoons of elegant strolling at Bagatelle or Saint-James, trips to the race track and to art exhibits, evenings at those small theaters designed for tourists in the know: all of these expensive and monotonous diversions followed in succession time and time again without exhausting a need to be busy inherited from enterprising and tenacious ancestors, who had directed the same furious activity toward amassing fortunes that their descendants devoted to squandering them. Needless to say, Le Fanois was often bored in this childish and shifting milieu. Yet he found such sweet compensations in it! Not only did his transactions with antique dealers enable him to purchase at a fraction of their worth some of the exquisite objects with which he liked to surround himself, but his parasitic existence saved him a considerable sum of money, which finally allowed him to organize a life of his own.

One fine day his Maecenas died, leaving his entire fortune to American relatives—to the great disappointment of Le Fanois. Happily, a successor soon appeared on the scene, and little by little the young man became accustomed to the role of "metteur en scène"— his own definition—serving as advisor extraordinary to foreign pilgrims quickened by the pious desire to spend their millions for the benefit of idle Parisians.

His family ties and charming personality had enabled him to remain in contact with the exclusive social circles that keep their distance from the madding crowd; Le Fanois acted as intermediary between the renegades from this milieu, each of them tormented by a craving for luxury and movement, and the explorers from the New World who longed to penetrate their closed society.

His task had not assumed significant proportions, however—he had not really turned professional—until he met Miss Blanche Lambart at a gathering of the foreign colony. Her fine intelligence and open-minded-ness had struck him immediately; he had frequented her compatriots too long not to realize promptly that she came from more refined stock than most Americans who try to storm Parisian society. Everything about her betrayed a careful education, an abundance of social graces, the habit of moving in elegant circles. He had soon guessed, however, that like himself, she lived at the expense of people she despised.

At the time of their meeting, Miss Lambart was the traveling companion of a wealthy widow from Chicago who had visions of an advantageous marriage. In no time at all, Le Fanois and Miss Lambart had joined forces to present her to society and look for a husband who met her specifications. But it seems that the widow was as ungrateful as Le Fanois' patron; for the moment she was married she dismissed Miss Lambart who was forced to search for another benefactress. Having found one without delay, she once again asked Le Fanois' assistance in introducing her protégée to society.

Their unspoken agreement was three or four years old now. Le Fanois still did not know what pressing circumstances had prompted her to choose such a life. Was it the taste for luxury or the need for perpetual motion that so often motivated her fellow-countrymen? Did she come from one of those small towns whose sad, monotonous atmosphere he had heard described, where the women die of boredom in idle solitude while their husbands pile up a fortune that neither of them can enjoy? Le Fanois thought he detected in her, rather, a casualty of New York society, too poor to resist the luxury that surrounded her, yet too proud and particular to tie herself down to a second-rate marriage. But whatever her past, Le Fanois found her attractive in a unique and undefinable way. He had never spoken to her of love. In spite of her free manner and ultramodern vocabulary, he sensed in her an almost aggressive uprightness, that shielded her from his advances even more effectively than her deliberately ironic way of speaking.

So they simply remained the best of friends, enjoying their meetings and at the same time protecting themselves from the humiliation of their secret complicity by openly and cynically making fun of it.

Blanche Lambart had guessed right; Mrs. Smithers and her daughter were naïve souls.

Catherine in particular asked no more than to enjoy herself, aspired to no more stable happiness. She wanted to go to the races and the theater, to display her lovely outfits at the American colony's dances and to meet the greatest possible number of waltzers. Mrs. Smithers, however, already envisioned for her daughter the inevitable "marriage to a French count." But she realized only too well that she could not set her plan in motion by herself. Won over immediately by Miss Lambart's charm, she entrusted to her the creation of an existence consonant with her social aspirations. The young woman secured the services of Le Fanois, and before long the two of them had installed Mrs. Smithers in the town house formerly owned by Le Fanois' first patron and decorated by Le Fanois himself. Next they arranged a splendid succession of dinners and balls, to which Le Fanois' friends flocked with a pleasure they sometimes forgot to express to the hostess. But they did take notice of Catherine. In spite of her awkwardness, her twangy voice, her ear-splitting laugh, she projected such freshness and youthful radiance that her lack of savoir-faire was soon forgotten. She was a "nice girl" and her naïveté and joviality were much appreciated.

"After all the designing women you've sent us over here, that child is a real relief,"

Le Fanois remarked jestingly to Blanche. "I think her very faults will help us to marry her off."

They were sitting at the tea table in Miss Lambart's tiny sitting room. Two years ago she had been able to move into an unpretentious fifth-floor apartment, where she received callers with the independence of a married woman.

("What else could I do?" she would say. "I have no source of income, no husband and no companion, so I have to be all three to myself.")

She smiled at the young man's mild impertinence.

"I admit that the Americans we send you are not always models of democratic pride," she said. "But are they any worse than the husbands you unearth for them so effortlessly?"

He did not reply and she went on: "I don't know if we'll find it quite as easy to settle Catherine. I share your opinion of her and I wouldn't want to see her unhappily married for anything in the world."

Le Fanois mused for a moment. Then he said:

"What would you say to Jean de Sestre?"

She started. "You mean the young prince? He's the eldest son, isn't he? That means he'll be the Duke of Sestre!"

"Exactly."

"And you think . . ."

"I think he's sincerely smitten with our charming Catherine and I don't foresee any difficulty in obtaining his parents' consent."

She blinked at him as dumbfounded as ever.

"Now that's what's called a splendid match!" she said. "And he's a fine person, isn't he?"

"He's no genius, but I think he'll be an exemplary husband. You'll be able to entrust your protégée to him without fear."

Miss Lambart seemed lost in thought. Then she got up with a sigh and took several steps across the tiny room.

"What's the matter?" the young man inquired, tilting his head against the back of his chair to follow her graceful movements more easily.

She came toward him and leaned against the mantelpiece.

"Well, I . . . it's just that I keep thinking about the awful power of money. Quite an original thought, isn't it? But I can't help it when I look at that sweet young thing, who is certainly goodhearted enough, but who, when you come right down to it, is neither beautiful, witty, imaginative nor charming. And yet all she has to do is reach out her hand—oh! that pudgy red paw—and pluck herself a name from the social register, security for life and the heart of a respectable young man!"

Le Fanois was still gazing at her, with that indefinable gleam that sometimes came to his eyes when she was present.

"While you, poor dear, who have all that . . ."

"Oh, be quiet!" she interrupted.

A brick-red flush crept to her temples, and she returned abruptly to her place at the tea table.

Le Fanois shrugged.

"I thought we could be frank with one another."

Her smile was full of bitterness.

"Very well, then. I'm worn out, I've had enough. But I've lived too long among the rich and the happy—the need for luxury is in my blood. And when I think that I'll have to start over again—put up another good fight . . . ! Once Catherine is married, Mrs. Smithers will probably go back to America to conquer New York. If not, Catherine's position will make my services quite expendable." An ironic laugh burst from her throat. "Believe me, I've had enough!"

Le Fanois looked at her for a moment with a faintly sad expression; then he reassumed his bantering tone:

"Well, perhaps this time they'll give you a dowry, and I'll make a fine match for you."

Their eyes met again; then she said smilingly:

"Oh! the dowry . . . the dowry I've dreamed of! How much do you think I would need to find a suitable husband?"

He seemed to reflect on it.

"A suitable husband? Why, for an income of sixty thousand francs, I solemnly promise to find you a man who adores you."

She blushed a little, laughing incredulously.

"A man who adores me? Does such a person exist?"

"Trust me," he said as he rose from his chair. "And in the meantime, we're agreed, aren't we, that you'll feel out Mrs. Smithers while I take care of the de Sestres. I think our little affair is all but settled.

## IV

TEN days later, the two friends found themselves together again, this time in one of the gilded drawing rooms of the Smithers town house. Mrs. Smithers and her daughter had decided to go for a long drive, and Blanche had telephoned the young man to let him know she would wait for him alone at their house.

"My dear colleague," he said, shaking her hand, "it seems that your half of our venture has dragged on a bit! I had no difficulty at all with mine—I've just been waiting for a sign from you."

Miss Lambart motioned him to an armchair opposite her own.

"And I couldn't give you a sign till this morning. It's been a fight to the finish."

"A fight? What do you mean? They don't want my suitor?"

"Mrs. Smithers wants nothing more, as you might suspect." She smiled wanly. "But Catherine has other ideas."

"What! That brainless girl?" Le Fanois frowned. "What happened?"

Blanche hesitated, playing distractedly with the silk tassels that fringed the lapels of her dress. Finally she said, "Well, in spite of myself, I sided with Catherine—I protected her from her mother."

Le Fanois looked at her aghast.

"But what in the world does the child want? I'm completely lost."

"On the contrary. You've *arrived*, my friend, because it's *you* she wants."

The words, borne on her mocking laugh, struck him like a challenger's glove. He bolted from his chair, his face suddenly ashen, and began stroking his moustache nervously as if to hide his contorted lips.

"What? What do you mean by that?" he stammered.

"Just what I said. Catherine intends to marry the man she loves, and that man is you."

He stood before her, bearing down with both hands on the bronze-laden table that separated them.

"Me? She loves *me?"* he repeated.

Blanche's laugh was tinged with a distinct note of mockery.

"Oh, come now! You can't be *that* surprised."

"Surprised? I'm flabbergasted!" He glanced at her suddenly. "Wait a minute. You don't think . . . "

"Oh, of course not! I'm well aware that you laid your cards on the table. Only, it's not the first time, is it, that someone has fallen in love with you without your assistance?"

He shrugged disdainfully; then he turned on his heel, paced the room once or twice, and came back to where Blanche was sitting.

"But the mother—the mother would never give her consent, would she?" he asked abruptly.

A sudden rush of color inflamed Blanche Lambart's cheeks. She stood up.

"Then it's all right with you?" she said, looking straight into his eyes.

He reddened too, and began to twist his gloves between his agitated fingers. "All right with me? I have no idea. I was only asking . . . "

"In that case, the matter is settled. I have obtained Mrs. Smithers permission."

He looked at her, dumbfounded.

"You've obtained her permission? But how? It's unbelievable!"

"Not at all. She's a good woman at heart, and she adores Catherine. She wouldn't make her unhappy for anything in the world. The two of us broke down her resistance in no time. Catherine will marry for love—and Mrs. Smithers herself will make the brilliant match."

Le Fanois gasped at this final surprise.

"Good Lord, you mean that *she* wants to marry Sestre?"

"Oh no! I don't think she intends to replace her daughter. But we should certainly be able to find someone her own age. You'll take care of it won't you? She's really not too bad since she lost weight and began to wear dark colors."

Blanche suddenly broke off. "I hear the doorbell. They've come back."

And, as Le Fanois looked around, searching for a way to escape without being seen, Blanche smiled and went on:

"No, don't go. You know we don't stand on ceremony in this household. Besides, I promised Catherine I would keep you here."

She added softly as she left him. "She's desperately in love with you. You'll be good to her, won't you?"

V

SIX weeks later, Jean Le Fanois was again pacing Mrs. Smithers' gilded salon.

This time, he was alone; but, when he had crisscrossed the room several times and paced back and forth before the handsome bronze clock on the mantelpiece, he heard the soft rustle of a skirt behind him and turned to greet Miss Lambart.

It was the first time they had seen each other since the engagement.

The very day after her last conversation with him, she had left for London to visit some friends. In spite of Mrs. Smithers' supplications, she prolonged her stay far beyond the date set for her return. She wrote that she had caught a bad case of influenza, then alleged a slow convalescence which made her fear the strain of the trip home.

Her decision was finally triggered by a telegram stating that Catherine Smithers had become critically ill, and she had only been back for a few hours when Le Fanois arrived.

The moment she appeared, he was struck by the extreme pallor of her thin features, as drawn from anxiety over Catherine as from the traces of her own indisposition.

"It's really serious, then?" the young man asked after shaking hands with her.

"I'm afraid so. The poor child has double pneumonia, and her fever is raging."

They continued to speak in hushed tones of Catherine's illness. Pneumonia had set in only the day before, complicating what had been a neglected cold. Mrs. Smithers, half out of her mind, never left her daughter's bedside. Four doctors and three nurses gave her the finest of care and the mother, in despair, spoke of calling in a specialist from New York. For the time being, the symptoms were quite serious. However, the doctors would not be able to make their prognosis for twenty-four hours.

"The poor girl often asks for you, but they're afraid your visit might upset her. So Mrs. Smithers asked me to take her a message for you."

Le Fanois had tears in his eyes.

"The poor child! Tell her, tell her that I . . . " He hesitated and suddenly seemed uncomfortable under Miss Lambart's serene gaze.

The hint of a sardonic smile crossed her pale lips.

"I'll know what to tell her," she replied with a slightly bitter intonation.

Le Fanois looked at her; then he took her hand and kissed it.

"Would you?" he said. And she left him.

Two days later Catherine died. Her mother, having imagined till the very last minute that she could save her by sheer force of money, was profoundly shaken by the disaster, which seemed to show her for the time the impotence of her millions. She questioned Blanche and Le Fanois over and over again: "What more could I have spent?" and blamed herself for not having sent for the specialist from New York, forgetting that Catherine had died before he could have arrived. Nevertheless, she was consoled a bit when she learned that Parisian high society, touched by the girl's tragic death, was bent on attending the funeral and she sent for a hundred copies of the *Paris Herald* to send to her friends in America.

Le Fanois and Miss Lambart did not see each other after the funeral. Greatly saddened by Catherine's death, Blanche had been forced to stay in bed by a recurrence of influenza; and the very next day Mrs. Smithers had asked Le Fanois to accompany her to Cannes, where she spoke of hiding her sorrow, in spite of the fact that the social season was at its height. The young man could hardly refuse the woman who was to have been his mother-in-law, so Miss Lambart remained alone in the luxurious hotel where she had stayed since her return from London.

Weeks slipped by. Mrs. Smithers did not write a word, so that Blanche, knowing that her patroness found spelling an insurmountable obstacle, finally wrote to Le Fanois to ask how she was. His answer was a week in arriving. Then he wrote from Barcelona, where he and Mrs. Smithers had gone by car in the hope that she would be diverted by a brief excursion in Spain.

Several days later, Blanche received from San Sebastian a card hastily scribbled by Mrs. Smithers, telling her that she would be home shortly and instructing her to order a selection of "suitable" outfits from the couturiers of the rue de la Paix. In a postscript, she asked her to pick up at the jewelers her long strand of black pearls, "the only ornament she would dream of wearing." Miss Lambart carried out her orders and moved back into the town house on the eve of Mrs. Smithers' return.

The next day at tea time Blanche was expecting a visit from Le Fanois, whom she had asked to stop by. When he appeared, paler and thinner than usual in his mourning clothes, she went to meet him with, a sad smile somehow touched with tenderness. Le Fanois was struck by the soft luminosity of her wide gray eyes. For the first time in her life, she seemed unafraid to take off the mask of irony that usually blurred her lovely features.

She put her hand in his and looked at him lingeringly.

"I've been so anxious to talk with you! I have so many things to tell you," she said in a soft, affectionate tone of voice, motioning him to the armchair next to hers.

He sat down without saying a word and for a moment both were silent. Then, in a voice quavering with emotion, she began to speak of Catherine.

Le Fanois' face clouded and he made an almost irritated gesture.

"What's the matter?" asked Blanche, astonished.

He stumbled over his words. "It's . . . that that innocent child's love weighs me down. I . . . I'm ashamed I couldn't love her in return—the way I wanted to . . . the way she deserved. Please, let's not talk about it anymore."

Miss Lambart replied, smiling:

"She never suspected a thing. She thought you were sincerely in love."

He reddened.

"Can't you see I'm ashamed of that too?"

She continued to gaze at him with a tender smile.

"Let's talk about Mrs. Smithers, then. I only saw her for a minute this morning. She was so busy with her dressmakers that I beat a hasty retreat."

Le Fanois lowered his eyes.

"She seems better now. She's looking for activities to occupy her time," he said casually.

"Yes, and I think she'll succeed. She spoke of an intimate luncheon she hopes to give next week for a grand duke passing through Paris. . . . Don't you think I'm right?" she went on, as Le Fanois remained silent. 'Don't you think Mrs. Smithers will find a good catch?"

"Really, this is hardly the moment to think about such things."

"You don't think so? Well, I disagree. It seems to me that the poor woman needs to be diverted. She sincerely loved her daughter, but she doesn't know how to live with her sorrow. Besides, mourning suits her quite well. Her black dresses make her appear thinner, and she looks ten years younger since she stopped dyeing her hair. Was that your bright idea?"

Le Fanois frowned and uttered a short irritated burst of laughter.

"My dear girl, do you think I have nothing better to do than to supervise Mrs. Smithers' hairdresser?"

Miss Lambart smiled.

"If it bothers you to talk about Mrs. Smithers, why don't we talk about me for a while?"

Immediately he seemed more at ease.

"About you? That's a subject I never tire of."

She was seated before him, slender and delicate in a dark dress which brought out the transparent pallor of her skin, making her lips seem even redder than they were. Golden highlights shimmered on her blond hair. Le Fanois decided she had never looked prettier, more captivating. When he felt her eyes softly meet his, however, he glanced away.

"Yes," she continued, "I want to talk to you about myself. I have some news—big news—to tell you."

His head jerked up.

"You're getting married?"

"Perhaps. It's possible. I really don't know!"

She still enveloped him in her calm, sweet gaze, which seemed infused with an inner light.

"You asked me just a moment ago not to bring up the love of the poor child we're grieving over. However, I have to tell you that she was so ecstatic over your love for her that she wanted a little of her happiness to spill over onto others. The poor dear . . . She knew I was the one who had pleaded your cause with her mother—that I had fought for it loyally —and the very day she got sick she called me to her room to let me know how grateful she was."

Le Fanois had pushed back his chair. He rose halfway, almost involuntarily, then changed his mind and sat down again.

"Go on," he said in a low voice.

"She was so choked with emotion that she could hardly speak; but I knew instinctively what she wanted to tell me, and I hugged her and told her to be still for a moment and calm down. Then she answered that she couldn't enjoy her own happiness without doing her best to ensure my own. She knew I had almost no means of support and couldn't bear the idea of my continuing to live at others' expense. She had learned that a girl can't get married without a dowry in France, and she begged me to accept a gift that her feverish hand slipped into mine. I was already worried by the way she looked, so I accepted her present and kissed her without even glancing at the paper. The next day pneumonia set in, and three days later she was dead. I had put the paper away in my writing case, and I only looked at it the day after the burial."

She stopped for a moment; then she slipped her hand under the lace of her bodice and withdrew a folded piece of paper that she gave to Le Fanois.

"Look," she said, her voice trembling.

He unfolded the piece of paper automatically, and was astounded by what he saw.

"A million dollars, a million dollars . . . ." he stammered.

"Yes indeed! It's hard to believe how wealthy these people are. They give you a gift of a million dollars as if they were paying their butcher's bill."

She said nothing, and their eyes met.

"It's like a fairy tale, isn't it?" she said with a short, high-pitched laugh.

Le Fanois had risen and given back the paper with a faintly trembling hand.

Again they fell silent. He had gone to lean against the mantelpiece, while Blanche, still seated, kept her hands crossed on her lap and her head slightly bowed. Le Fanois spoke first.

"I'm so happy for you! You don't doubt it, do you?" he said with obvious emotion, but without moving toward Blanche.

She raised her head slowly and looked at him, blushing.

"Have you forgotten your promise?" she asked with a smile.

"My promise?"

Le Fanois' cheeks flushed crimson.

She continued to gaze at him with her tender, fathomless eyes, as if to decipher what was going on inside him. But, as he still said nothing and stood propped against the fireplace with no apparent intention of coming toward her, she turned pale all of a sudden and stood up.

"I see that you *have* forgotten it—just my luck!" she said, struggling to maintain a lively tone of voice as her eyes filled with tears.

At the sound of her voice, Le Fanois wheeled around and came toward her, seizing her wrists with a violent movement.

"No, no! I haven't forgotten it, I haven't forgotten," he cried, pulling her toward him.

She uttered a cry of joy and fright; then, just as she was about to yield to his embrace, she looked at him again and jerked backward, pushing him away with all the force of her stiffened arms.

"What is it? What's the matter?" she cried in a terror-stricken voice.

Le Fanois still clutched her wrists in a vise-like grip, and they stood stock-still for an instant, their eyes riveted on each other.

"Jean, what's the matter? Say something, I implore you!" she gasped.

Suddenly he let go of her hands and turned away from her with a hopeless gesture.

"The matter is . . . that I have engaged to marry the mother," he said, with a bitter laugh.

## THE HERMIT AND THE WILD WOMAN (1908)

### THE HERMIT AND THE WILD WOMAN

THE Hermit lived in a cave in the hollow of a hill. Below him was a glen, with a stream in a coppice of oaks and alders, and on the farther side of the valley, half a day's journey distant, another hill, steep and bristling, which raised aloft a little walled town with Ghibelline swallow-tails notched against the sky.

When the Hermit was a lad, and lived in the town, the crenellations of the walls had been square-topped, and a Guelf lord had flown his standard from the keep. Then one day a steel-colored line of men-at-arms rode across the valley, wound up the hill and battered in the gates. Stones and Greek fire rained from the ramparts, shields clashed in the streets, blade sprang at blade in passages and stairways, pikes and lances dripped above huddled flesh, and all the still familiar place was a stew of dying bodies. The boy fled from it in horror. He had seen his father go forth and not come back, his mother drop dead from an arquebuse shot as she leaned from the platform of the tower, his little sister fall with a slit throat across the altar steps of the chapel—and he ran, ran for his life, through the slippery streets, over warm twitching bodies, between legs of soldiers carousing, out of the gates, past burning farmsteads, trampled wheat-fields, orchards stripped and broken, till the still woods received him and he fell face down on the unmutilated earth.

He had no wish to go back. His longing was to live hidden from life. Up the hillside he found a hollow in the rock, and built before it a porch of boughs bound together with withies. He fed on nuts and roots, and on trout which he caught with his hands under the stones in the stream. He had always been a quiet boy, liking to sit at his mother's feet and watch the flowers grow on her embroidery frame, while the chaplain read aloud the histories of the Desert Fathers from a great silver-clasped volume. He would rather have been bred a clerk and scholar than a knight's son, and his happiest moments were when he served mass for the chaplain in the early morning, and felt his heart flutter up and up like a lark, up and up till it was lost in infinite space and brightness. Almost as happy were the hours when he sat beside the foreign painter who came over the mountains to paint the chapel, and under whose brush celestial faces grew out of the rough wall as if he had sown some magic seed which flowered while you watched it. With the appearing of every gold-rimmed face the boy felt he had won another friend, a friend who would come and bend above him at night, keeping off the ugly visions which haunted his pillow— visions of the gnawing monsters about the church-porch, evil-faced bats and dragons, giant worms and winged bristling hogs, a devil's flock who crept down from the stone-work at night and hunted the souls of sinful children through the town. With the growth of the picture the bright mailed angels thronged so close about the boy's bed that between their interwoven wings not a snout or a claw could force itself; and he would turn over sighing on his pillow, which felt as soft and warm as if it had been lined with down from those sheltering pinions.

All these thoughts came back to him now in his cave on the cliff-side. The stillness seemed to enclose him with wings, to fold him away from life and evil. He was never restless or discontented. He loved the long silent empty days, each one as like the other as pearls in a well-matched string. Above all he liked to have time to save his soul. He had been greatly troubled about his soul since a band of Flagellants had passed through the town, exhibiting their gaunt scourged bodies and exhorting the people to turn from soft raiment and delicate fare, from marriage and money-getting and dancing and games, and think only how they might escape the devil's talons and the great red blaze of hell. For days that red blaze hung on the edge of the boy's thoughts like the light of a burning city across a plain. There seemed to be so many pitfalls to avoid—so many things were wicked which one might have supposed to be harmless. How could a child of his age tell? He dared not for a moment think of anything else. And the scene of sack and slaughter from which he had fled gave shape and distinctness to that blood-red vision. Hell was like that, only a million million times worse. Now he knew how flesh looked when devils' pincers tore it, how the shrieks of the damned sounded, and how roasting bodies smelled. How could a Christian spare one moment of his days and nights from the long, long struggle to keep safe from the wrath to come?

Gradually the horror faded, leaving only a tranquil pleasure in the minute performance of his religious duties. His mind was not naturally given to the contemplation of evil, and in the blessed solitude of his new life his thoughts dwelt more and more on the beauty of holiness. His desire was to be perfectly good, and to live in love and charity with his fellow-men; and how could one do this without fleeing from them?

At first his life was difficult, for in the winter season he was put to great straits to feed himself; and there were nights when the sky was like an iron vault, and a hoarse wind rattled the oak wood in the valley, and a great fear came on him that was worse than any cold. But in time it became known to his townsfolk and to the peasants in the neighboring valleys that he had withdrawn to the wilderness to lead a godly life; and after that his worst hardships were over, for pious persons brought him gifts of oil and dried fruit, one good woman gave him seeds from her garden, another spun for him a hodden gown, and others would have brought him all manner of food and clothing, had he not refused to accept anything but for his bare needs. The good woman who had given him the seeds showed him also how to build a little garden on the southern ledge of his cliff, and all one summer the Hermit carried up soil from the streamside, and the next he carried up water to keep his garden green. After that the fear of solitude quite passed from him, for he was so busy all day long that at night he had much ado to fight off the demon of sleep, which Saint Aresenius the Abbot has denounced as the chief foe of the solitary. His memory kept good store of prayers and litanies, besides long passages from the Mass and other offices, and he marked the hours of his day by different acts of devotion. On Sundays and feast days, when the wind was set his way, he could hear the church bells from his native town, and these helped him to follow the worship of the faithful, and to bear in mind the seasons of the liturgical year; and what with carrying up water from the river, digging in the garden, gathering fagots for his fire, observing his religious duties, and keeping his thoughts continually upon the salvation of his soul, the Hermit knew not a moment's idleness.

At first, during his night vigils, he had felt a great fear of the stars, which seemed to set a cruel watch upon him, as though they spied out the frailty of his heart and took the measure of his littleness. But one day a wandering clerk, to whom he chanced to give a night's shelter, explained to him that, in the opinion of the most learned doctors of theology, the stars were inhabited by the spirits of the blessed, and this thought brought great consolation to the Hermit. Even on winter nights, when the eagle's wings clanged among the peaks, and he heard the long howl of wolves about the sheep-cotes in the valley, he no longer felt any fear, but thought of those sounds as representing the evil voices of the world, and hugged himself in the solitude of his cave. Sometimes, to keep himself awake, he composed lauds in honor of Christ and the saints, and they seemed to him so pleasant that he feared to forget them, so after much debate with himself he decided to ask a friendly priest from the valley, who sometimes visited him, to write down the lauds; and the priest wrote them down on comely sheepskin, which the Hermit dried and prepared with his own hands. When the Hermit saw them written down they appeared to him so beautiful that he feared to commit the sin of vanity if he looked at them too often, so he hid them between two smooth stones in his cave, and vowed that he would take them out only once in the year, at Easter, when our Lord has risen and it is meet that Christians should rejoice. And this vow he faithfully kept; but, alas, when Easter drew near, he found he was looking forward to the blessed festival less because of our Lord's rising than because he should then be able to read his pleasant lauds written on fair sheepskin; and thereupon he took a vow that he would not look upon the lauds till he lay dying.

So the Hermit, for many years, lived to the glory of God and in great peace of mind.

II

ONE day he resolved to set forth on a visit to the Saint of the Rock, who lived on the other side of the mountains. Travellers had brought the Hermit report of this solitary, how he lived in great holiness and austerity in a desert place among the hills, where snow lay all winter, and in summer the sun beat down cruelly. The Saint, it appeared, had vowed that he would withdraw from the world to a spot where there was neither shade nor water, lest he should be tempted to take his ease and think less continually upon his Maker; but wherever he went he found a spreading tree or a gushing spring, till at last he climbed up to the bare heights where nothing grows, and where the only water comes from the melting of the snow in spring. Here he found a tall rock rising from the ground, and in it he scooped a hollow with his own hands, laboring for five years and wearing his fingers to the bone. Then he seated himself in the hollow, which faced the west, so that in winter he should have small warmth of the sun and in summer be consumed by it; and there he had sat without moving for years beyond number.

The Hermit was greatly drawn by the tale of such austerities, which in his humility he did not dream of emulating, but desired, for his soul's good, to contemplate and praise;

so one day he bound sandals to his feet, cut an alder staff from the stream, and set out to visit the Saint of the Rock.

It was the pleasant spring season, when seeds are shooting and the bud is on the tree. The Hermit was troubled at the thought of leaving his plants without water, but he could not travel in winter by reason of the snows, and in summer he feared the garden would suffer even more from his absence. So he set out, praying that rain might fall while he was away, and hoping to return again in five days. The peasants laboring in the fields left their work to ask his blessing; and they would even have followed him in great numbers had he not told them that he was bound on a pilgrimage to the Saint of the Rock, and that it behooved him to go alone, as one solitary seeking another. So they respected his wish, and he went on and entered the forest. In the forest he walked for two days and slept for two nights. He heard the wolves crying, and foxes rustling in the covert, and once, at twilight, a shaggy brown man peered at him through the leaves and galloped away with a soft padding of hoofs; but the Hermit feared neither wild beasts nor evil-doers, nor even the fauns and satyrs who linger in unhallowed forest depths where the Cross has not been raised; for he said: "If I die, I die to the glory of God, and if I live it must be to the same end." Only he felt a secret pang at the thought that he might die without seeing his lauds again. But the third day, without misadventure, he came out on another valley.

Then he began to climb the mountain, first through brown woods of beech and oak, then through pine and broom, and then across red stony ledges where only a pinched growth of lentiscus and briar spread in patches over the rock. By this time he thought to have reached his goal, but for two more days he fared on through the same scene, with the sky close over him and the green valleys of earth receding far below. Sometimes for hours he saw only the red glistering slopes tufted with thin bushes, and the hard blue heaven so close that it seemed his hand could touch it; then at a turn of the path the rocks rolled apart, the eye plunged down a long pine-clad defile, and beyond it the forest flowed in mighty undulations to a plain shining with cities and another mountain-range many days' journey away. To some eyes this would have been a terrible spectacle, reminding the wayfarer of his remoteness from his kind, and of the perils which lurk in waste places and the weakness of man against them; but the Hermit was so mated to solitude, and felt such love for all things created, that to him the bare rocks sang of their Maker and the vast distance bore witness to His greatness. So His servant journeyed on unafraid.

But one morning, after a long climb over steep and difficult slopes, the wayfarer halted suddenly at a bend of the way; for beyond the defile at his feet there was no plain shining with cities, but a bare expanse of shaken silver that reached away to the rim of the world; and the Hermit knew it was the sea. Fear seized him then, for it was terrible to see that great plain move like a heaving bosom, and, as he looked on it, the earth seemed also to heave beneath him. But presently he remembered how Christ had walked the waves, and how even Saint Mary of Egypt, who was a great sinner, had crossed the waters of Jordan dry-shod to receive the Sacrament from the Abbot Zosimus; and then the Hermit's heart grew still, and he sang as he went down the mountain: "The sea shall praise Thee, O Lord."

All day he kept seeing it and then losing it; but toward night he came to a cleft of the hills, and lay down in a pine-wood to sleep. He had now been six days gone, and once and again he thought anxiously of his herbs; but he said to himself: "What though my garden perish, if I see a holy man face to face and praise God in his company?" So he was never long cast down.

Before daylight he was afoot under the stars; and leaving the wood where he had slept, began climbing the face of a tall cliff, where he had to clutch the jutting ledges with his hands, and with every step he gained, a rock seemed thrust forth to hurl him back. So, footsore and bleeding, he reached a little stony plain as the sun dropped to the sea; and in the red light he saw a hollow rock, and the Saint sitting in the hollow.

The Hermit fell on his knees, praising God; then he rose and ran across the plain to the rock. As he drew near he saw that the Saint was a very old man, clad in goatskin, with a long white beard. He sat motionless, his hands on his knees, and two red eye-sockets turned to the sunset. Near him was a young boy in skins who brushed the flies from his face; but they always came back, and settled on the rheum which ran from his eyes.

He did not appear to hear or see the approach of the Hermit, but sat quite still till the boy said: "Father, here is a pilgrim."

Then he lifted up his voice and asked angrily who was there and what the stranger sought.

The Hermit answered: "Father, the report of your holy practices came to me a long way off, and being myself a solitary, though not worthy to be named with you for godliness, it seemed fitting that I should cross the mountains to visit you, that we might sit together and speak in praise of solitude."

The Saint replied: "You fool, how can two sit together and praise solitude, since by so doing they put an end to the thing they praise?"

The Hermit, at that, was sorely abashed, for he had thought his speech out on the way, reciting it many times over; and now it appeared to him vainer than the crackling of thorns under a pot.

Nevertheless he took heart and said: "True, Father; but may not two sinners sit together and praise Christ, who has taught them the blessings of solitude?"

But the other only answered: "If you had really learned the blessings of solitude you would not squander them in idle wandering." And, the Hermit not knowing how to reply, he said again: "If two sinners meet they can best praise Christ by going each his own way in silence."

After that he shut his lips and continued motionless while the boy brushed the flies from his eye-sockets; but the Hermit's heart sank, and for the first time he felt all the weariness of the way he had fared, and the great distance dividing him from home.

He had meant to take counsel with the Saint concerning his lauds, and whether he ought to destroy them; but now he had no heart to say another word, and turning away he began to descend the mountain. Presently he heard steps running behind him, and the boy came up and pressed a honeycomb in his hand.

"You have come a long way and must be hungry," he said; but before the Hermit could thank him he had hastened back to his task. So the Hermit crept down the mountain till he reached the wood where he had slept before; and there he made his bed again, but he had no mind to eat before sleeping, for his heart hungered more than his body; and his salt tears made the honeycomb bitter.

### III

ON the fourteenth day he came to the valley below his cliff, and saw the walls of his native town against the sky. He was footsore and heavy of heart, for his long pilgrimage had brought him only weariness and humiliation, and as no drop of rain had fallen he knew that his garden must have perished. So he climbed the cliff heavily and reached his cave at the angelus.

But there a great wonder awaited him. For though the scant earth of the hillside was parched and crumbling, his garden-soil reeked with moisture, and his plants had shot up, fresh and glistening, to a height they had never before attained. More wonderful still, the tendrils of the gourd had been trained about his door, and kneeling down he saw that the earth had been loosened between the rows of sprouting vegetables, and that every leaf sparkled with drops as though the rain had but newly ceased. Then it appeared to the Hermit that he beheld a miracle, but doubting his own deserts he refused to believe himself worthy of such grace, and went within doors to ponder on what had befallen him. And on his bed of rushes he saw a young woman sleeping, clad in an outlandish garment, with strange amulets about her neck.

The sight was very terrifying to the Hermit, for he recalled how often the demon, in tempting the Desert Fathers, had taken the form of a woman for their undoing; but he reflected that, since there was nothing pleasing to him in the sight of this female, who was brown as a nut and lean with wayfaring, he ran no great danger in looking at her. At first he took her for a wandering Egyptian, but as he looked he perceived, among the heathen charms, an Agnus Dei in her bosom; and this so surprised him that he bent over and called on her to wake.

She sprang up with a start, but seeing the Hermit's gown and staff, and his face above her, lay quiet and said to him: "I have watered your garden daily in return for the beans and oil that I took from your store."

"Who are you, and how do you come here?" asked the Hermit.

She said: "I am a wild woman and live in the woods."

And when he pressed her again to tell him why she had sought shelter in his cave, she said that the land to the south, whence she came, was full of armed companies and bands of marauders, and that great license and bloodshed prevailed there; and this the Hermit knew to be true, for he had heard of it on his homeward journey. The Wild Woman went on to tell him that she had been hunted through the woods like an animal by a band of drunken men-at-arms, Landsknechts from the north by their barbarous dress and speech, and at length, starving and spent, had come on his cave and hidden herself from her pursuers. "For," she said, "I fear neither wild beasts nor the woodland people, charcoal burners, Egyptians, wandering minstrels or chapmen; even the highway robbers do not touch me, because I am poor and brown; but these armed men flown with blood and wine are more terrible than wolves and tigers."

And the Hermit's heart melted, for he thought of his little sister lying with her throat slit across the altar steps, and of the scenes of blood and rapine from which he had fled away into the wilderness. So he said to the stranger that it was not meet he should house her in his cave, but that he would send a messenger to the town across the valley, and beg a pious woman there to give her lodging and work in her household. "For," said he, "I perceive by the blessed image about your neck that you are not a heathen wilding, but a child of Christ, though so far astray from Him in the desert."

"Yes," she said, "I am a Christian, and know as many prayers as you; but I will never set foot in city walls again, lest I be caught and put back into the convent."

"What," cried the Hermit with a start, "you are a runagate nun?" And he crossed himself, and again thought of the demon.

She smiled and said: "It is true I was once a cloistered woman, but I will never willingly be one again. Now drive me forth if you like; but I cannot go far, for I have a wounded foot, which I got in climbing the cliff with water for your garden." And she pointed to a deep cut in her foot.

At that, for all his fear, the Hermit was moved to pity, and washed the cut and bound it up; and as he did so he bethought him that perhaps his strange visitor had been sent to him not for his soul's undoing but for her own salvation. And from that hour he earnestly yearned to save her.

But it was not fitting that she should remain in his cave; so, having given her water to drink and a handful of lentils, he raised her up and putting his staff in her hand guided her to a hollow not far off in the face of the cliff. And while he was doing this he heard the sunset bells ring across the valley, and set about reciting the *Angelus Domini nuntiavit Mariae;* and she joined in very piously, with her hands folded, not missing a word.

Nevertheless the thought of her wickedness weighed on him, and the next day when he went to carry her food he asked her to tell him how it came about that she had fallen into such abominable sin. And this is the story she told.

IV

I WAS born (said she) in the north country, where the winters are long and cold, where snow sometimes falls in the valleys, and the high mountains for months are white with it. My father's castle is in a tall green wood, where the winds always rustle, and a cold river runs down from the ice-gorges. South of us was the wide plain, glowing with heat, but above us were stony passes where the eagle nests and the storms howl; in winter great fires roared in our chimneys, and even in summer there was always a cool air off the gorges. But when I was a child my mother went southward in the great Empress's train and I went with her. We travelled many days, across plains and mountains, and saw Rome, where the Pope lives in a golden palace, and many other cities, till we came to the great Emperor's court. There for two years or more we lived in pomp and merriment, for it was a wonderful court, full of mimes, magicians, philosophers and poets; and the Empress's ladies spent their days in mirth and music, dressed in light silken garments, walking in gardens of roses, and bathing in a great cool marble tank, while the Emperor's eunuchs guarded the approach to the gardens. Oh, those baths in the marble tank, my Father! I used to lie awake through the whole hot southern night, and think of that plunge at sunrise under the last stars. For we were in a burning country, and I pined for the tall green woods and the cold stream of my father's valley; and when I had cooled my limbs in the tank I lay all day in the scant cypress shade and dreamed of my next bath.

My mother pined for the coolness till she died; then the Empress put me in a convent and I was forgotten. The convent was on the side of a bare yellow hill, where bees made a hot buzzing in the thyme. Below was the sea, blazing with a million shafts of light; and overhead a blinding sky, which reflected the sun's glitter like a huge baldric of steel. Now the convent was built on the site of an old pleasure-house which a holy Princess had given to our Order; and a part of the house was left standing with its court and garden. The nuns had built all about the garden; but they left the cypresses in the middle, and the long marble tank where the Princess and her ladies had bathed. The tank, however, as you may conceive, was no longer used as a bath; for the washing of the body is an indulgence forbidden to cloistered virgins; and our Abbess, who was famed for her austerities, boasted that, like holy Sylvia the nun, she never touched water save to bathe her finger-tips before receiving the Sacrament. With such an example before them, the nuns were obliged to conform to the same pious rule, and many, having been bred in the convent from infancy, regarded all ablutions with horror, and felt no temptation to cleanse the filth from their flesh; but I, who had bathed daily, had the freshness of clear water in my veins, and perished slowly for want of it, like your garden herbs in a drought.

My cell did not look on the garden, but on the steep mule-path leading up the cliff, where all day long the sun beat as if with flails of fire, and I saw the sweating peasants toil up and down behind their thirsty asses, and the beggars whining and scraping their sores in the heat. Oh, how I hated to look out through the bars on that burning world! I used to turn away from it, sick with disgust, and lying on my hard bed, stare up by the hour at the ceiling of my cell. But flies crawled in hundreds on the ceiling, and the hot noise they made was worse than the glare. Sometimes, at an hour when I knew myself unobserved, I tore off my stifling gown, and hung it over the grated window, that I might no longer see the shaft of hot sunlight lying across my cell, and the dust dancing in it like fat in the fire. But the darkness choked me, and I struggled for breath as though I lay at the bottom of a pit; so that at last I would spring up, and dragging down the dress, fling myself on my knees before the Cross, and entreat our Lord to give me the gift of holiness, that I might escape the everlasting fires of hell, of which this heat was like an awful foretaste. For if I could not endure the scorching of a summer's day, with what constancy could I meet the thought of the flame that dieth not?

This longing to escape the heat of hell made me apply myself to a devouter way of living, and I reflected that if my bodily distress were somewhat eased I should be able to throw myself with greater zeal into the practice of vigils and austerities. And at length, having set forth to the Abbess that the sultry air of my cell induced in me a grievous heaviness of sleep, I prevailed on her to lodge me in that part of the building which overlooked the garden.

For a few days I was quite happy, for instead of the dusty mountainside, and the sight of the sweating peasants and their asses, I looked out on dark cypresses and rows of budding vegetables. But presently I found I had not bettered myself. For with the approach of midsummer the garden, being all enclosed with buildings, grew as stifling as my cell. All the green things in it withered and dried off, leaving trenches of bare red earth, across which the cypresses cast strips of shade too narrow to cool the aching heads of the nuns who sought shelter there; and I began to think sorrowfully of my former cell, where now and then there came a sea-breeze, hot and languid, yet alive, and where at least I could look out upon the sea. But this was not the worst; for when the dog-days came I found that the sun, at a certain hour, cast on the ceiling of my cell the reflection of the ripples on the garden-tank; and to say how I suffered from this sight is not within the power of speech. It was indeed agony to watch the clear water rippling and washing above my head, yet feel no solace of it on my limbs: as though I had been a senseless brazen image lying at the bottom of a well. But the image, if it felt no refreshment, would have suffered no torture; whereas every inch of my skin throbbed with thirst, and every vein was a mouth of Dives praying for a drop of water. Oh, Father, how shall I tell you the grievous pains that I endured? Sometimes I so feared the sight of the mocking ripples overhead that I hid my eyes from their approach, lying face down on my burning bed till I knew that they were gone; yet on cloudy days, when they did not come, the heat was even worse to bear.

By day I hardly dared trust myself in the garden, for the nuns walked there, and one fiery noon they found me hanging so close above the tank that they snatched me away, crying out that I had tried to destroy myself. The scandal of this reaching the Abbess, she sent for me to know what demon had beset me; and when I wept and said, the longing to bathe my burning body, she broke into great anger and cried out: "Do you not know that this is a sin well-nigh as great as the other, and condemned by all the greatest saints? For a nun may be tempted to take her life through excess of self-scrutiny and despair of her own worthiness; but this desire to indulge the despicable body is one of the lusts of the flesh, to be classed with concupiscence and adultery." And she ordered me to sleep every night for a month in my heavy gown, with a veil upon my face.

Now, Father, I believe it was this penance that drove me to sin. For we were in the dog-days, and it was more than flesh could bear. And on the third night, after the portress had passed, and the lights were out, I rose and flung off my veil and gown, and knelt in my window fainting. There was no moon, but the sky was full of stars. At first the garden was all blackness; but as I looked I saw a faint twinkle between the cypress-trunks, and I knew it was the starlight on the tank. The water! The water! It was there close to me—only a few bolts and bars were between us.

The portress was a heavy sleeper, and I knew where her keys hung, on a nail just within the door of her cell. I stole thither, unlatched the door, seized the keys and crept barefoot down the corridor. The bolts of the cloister-door were stiff and heavy, and I dragged at them till the veins in my wrists were bursting. Then I turned the key and it cried out in the ward. I stood still, my whole body beating with fear lest the hinges too should have a voice—but no one stirred, and I pushed open the door and slipped out. The garden was as airless as a pit, but at least I could stretch my arms in it; and, oh, my Father, the sweetness of the stars! The stones in the path cut my feet as I ran, but I thought of the joy of bathing them in the tank, and that made the wounds sweet to me.... My Father, I have heard of the temptations which in times past assailed the holy Solitaries of the desert, flattering the reluctant flesh beyond resistance; but none, I think, could have surpassed in ecstasy that first touch of the water on my limbs. To prolong the joy I let myself slip in slowly, resting my hands on the edge of the tank, and smiling to see my body, as I lowered it, break up the shining black surface and shatter the starbeams into splinters. And the water, my Father, seemed to crave me as I craved it. Its ripples rose about me, first in furtive touches, then in a long embrace that clung and drew me down; till at length they lay like kisses on my lips. It was no frank comrade like the mountain pools of my childhood, but a secret playmate compassionating my pains and soothing them with noiseless hands. From the first I thought of it as an accomplice—its whisper seemed to promise me secrecy if I would promise it love. And I went back and back to it, my Father; all day I lived in the thought of it; each night I stole to it with fresh thirst. . . .

But at length the old portress died, and a young lay-sister took her place. She was a light sleeper, and keen-eared; and I knew the danger of venturing to her cell. I knew the danger, but when darkness came I felt the water drawing me. The first night I fought on my bed and held out; but the second I crept to her door. She made no motion when I entered, but rose up secretly and stole after me; and the second night she warned the Abbess, and the two came on me as I stood by the tank.

I was punished with terrible penances: fasting, scourging, imprisonment, and the privation of drinking water; for the Abbess stood amazed at the obduracy of my sin, and was resolved to make me an example to my fellows. For a month I endured the pains of hell; then one night the Saracen pirates fell on our convent. On a sudden the darkness was full of flames and blood; but while the other nuns ran hither and thither, clinging to the Abbess's feet or shrieking on the steps of the altar, I slipped through an unwatched postern and made my way to the hills. The next day the Emperor's soldiery descended on the carousing heathen, slew them and burned their vessels on the beach; the Abbess and nuns were rescued, the convent walls rebuilt, and peace restored to the holy precincts. All this I heard from a shepherdess of the hills, who found me in my hiding, and brought me honeycomb and water. In her simplicity she offered to lead me home to the convent; but while she slept I laid off my wimple and scapular, and stealing her cloak fled away lest she should betray me. And since then I have wandered alone over the face of the world, living in woods and desert places, often hungry, often cold and sometimes fearful; yet resigned to any hardship, and with a front for any peril, if only I may sleep under the free heaven and wash the dust from my body in cool water.

V

THE Hermit, as may be supposed, was much perturbed by this story, and dismayed that such sinfullness should cross his path. His first motion was to drive the woman forth, for he knew the heinousness of the craving for water, and how Saint Jerome, Saint Augustine and other holy doctors have taught that they who would purify the soul must not be distraught by the vain cares of bodily cleanliness; yet, remembering the lust that drew him to his lauds, he dared not judge his sister's fault too harshly.

Moreover he was moved by the Wild Woman's story of the hardships she had suffered, and the godless company she had been driven to keep—Egyptians, jugglers, outlaws and even sorcerers, who are masters of the pagan lore of the East, and still practice their dark rites among the simple folk of the hills. Yet she would not have him think wholly ill of this vagrant people, from whom she had often received food and comfort; and her worst danger, as he learned with shame, had come from the *girovaghi* or wandering monks, who are the scourge and shame of Christendom; carrying their ribald idleness from one monastery to another, and leaving on their way a trail of thieving, revelry and worse. Once or twice the Wild Woman had nearly fallen into their hands; but had been saved by her own quick wit and skill in woodcraft. Once, so she assured the Hermit, she had found refuge with a faun and his female, who fed and sheltered her in their cave, where she slept on a bed of leaves with their shaggy nurslings; and in this cave she had seen a stock or idol of wood, extremely seamed and ancient, before which the wood-creatures, when they thought she slept, laid garlands and the wild bees' honeycomb.

She told him also of a hill village of weavers, where she lived many weeks, and learned to ply their trade in return for her lodging; and where wayfaring men in the guise of cobblers, charcoal-burners or goatherds came and taught strange doctrines at midnight in the poor hovels. What they taught she could not clearly tell, save that they believed each soul could commune directly with its Maker, without need of priest or intercessor; also she had heard from some of their disciples that there are two Gods, one of good and one of evil, and that the God of evil has his throne in the Pope's palace in Rome. But in spite of these dark teachings they were a mild and merciful folk, full of loving-kindness toward poor persons and wayfarers; so that her heart grieved for them when one day a Dominican monk appeared in the village with a company of soldiers, and some of the weavers were seized and dragged to prison, while others, with their wives and babes, fled to the winter woods. She fled with them, fearing to be charged with their heresy, and for months they lay hid in desert places, the older and weaker, who fell sick from want and exposure, being devoutly ministered to by their brethren, and dying in the sure faith of heaven.

All this she related modestly and simply, not as one who joys in a godless life, but as having been drawn into it through misadventure; and she told the Hermit that when she heard the sound of church bells she never failed to say an *Ave* or a *Pater;* and that often, as she lay in the midnight darkness of the forest, she had hushed her fears by reciting the versicles from the Evening Hour:

*Keep us, O Lord, as the apple of the eye,*
*Protect us under the shadow of Thy wings.*

The wound in her foot healed slowly; and the Hermit, while it was mending, repaired daily to her cave, reasoning with her in love and charity, and exhorting her to return to the cloister. But this she persistently refused to do; and fearing lest she attempt to fly before her foot was healed, and so expose herself to hunger and ill-usage, he promised not to betray her presence, or to take any measures toward restoring her to her Order.

He began indeed to doubt whether she had any calling to the life enclosed; yet her gentleness and innocency of mind made him feel that she might be won back to holy living, if only her freedom were assured. So after many inward struggles (since his promise forbade his taking counsel with any concerning her) he resolved to let her remain in the cave till some light should come to him. And one day, visiting her about the hour of *Nones* (for it became his pious habit to say the evening office with her), he found her engaged with a little goatherd, who in a sudden seizure had fallen from a rock above her cave, and lay senseless and full of blood at her feet. And the Hermit saw with wonder how skillfully she bound up his cuts and restored his senses, giving him to drink of a liquor she had distilled from the wild simples of the mountain; whereat the boy opened his eyes and praised God, as one restored by heaven. Now it was known that this lad was subject to possessions, and had more than once dropped lifeless while he heeded his flock; and the Hermit, knowing that only great saints or unclean necromancers can loosen devils, feared that the Wild Woman had exorcised the spirits by means of unholy spells. But she told him that the goatherd's sickness was caused only by the heat of the sun, and that, such seizures being common in the hot countries whence she came, she had learned from a wise woman how to stay them by a decoction of the *carduus benedictus*, made in the third night of the waxing moon, but without the aid of magic.

"But," she continued, "you need not fear my bringing scandal on your holy retreat, for by the arts of the same wise woman my own wound is well-nigh healed, and tonight at sunset I set forth on my travels."

The Hermit's heart grew heavy as she spoke, and it seemed to him that her own look was sorrowful. And suddenly his perplexities were lifted from him, and he saw what was God's purpose with the Wild Woman.

"Why," said he, "do you fly from this place, where you are safe from molestation, and can look to the saving of your soul? Is it that your feet weary for the road, and your spirits are heavy for lack of worldly discourse?"

She replied that she had no wish to travel, and felt no repugnance to solitude. "But," said she, "I must go forth to beg my bread, since in this wilderness there is none but yourself to feed me; and moreover, when it is known that I have healed the goatherd, curious folk and scandal-mongers may seek me out, and, learning whence I come, drag me back to the cloister."

Then the Hermit answered her and said: "In the early days, when the faith of Christ was first preached, there were holy women who fled to the desert and lived there in solitude, to the glory of God and the edification of their sex. If you are minded to embrace so austere a life, contenting you with such sustenance as the wilderness yields, and wearing out your days in prayer and vigil, it may be that you shall make amends for the great sin you have committed, and live and die in the peace of the Lord Jesus."

He spoke thus, knowing that if she left him and returned to her roaming, hunger and fear might drive her to fresh sin; whereas in a life of penance and reclusion her eyes might be opened to her iniquity, and her soul snatched back from ruin.

He saw that his words moved her, and she seemed about to consent, and embrace a life of holiness; but suddenly she fell silent, and looked down on the valley at their feet.

"A stream flows in the glen below us," she said. "Do you forbid me to bathe in it in the heat of summer?"

"It is not I that forbid you, my daughter, but the laws of God," said the Hermit; "yet see how miraculously heaven protects you—for in the hot season, when your lust is upon you, our stream runs dry, and temptation will be removed from you. Moreover on these heights there is no excess of heat to madden the body, but always, before dawn and at the angelus, a cool breeze which refreshes it like water."

And after thinking long on this, and again receiving his promise not to betray her, the Wild Woman agreed to embrace a life of reclusion; and the Hermit fell on his knees, worshipping God and rejoicing to think that, if he saved his sister from sin, his own term of probation would be shortened.

## VI

THEREAFTER for two years the Hermit and the Wild Woman lived side by side, meeting together to pray on the great feast-days of the year, but on all other days dwelling apart, engaged in pious practices.

At first the Hermit, knowing the weakness of woman, and her little aptitude for the life apart, had feared that he might be disturbed by the nearness of his penitent; but she faithfully held to his commands, abstaining from all sight of him save on the Days of Obligation; and when they met, so modest and devout was her demeanor that she raised his soul to fresh fervency. And gradually it grew sweet to him to think that, near by though unseen, was one who performed the same tasks at the same hours; so that, whether he tended his garden, or recited his chaplet, or rose under the stars to repeat the midnight office, he had a companion in all his labors and devotions.

Meanwhile the report had spread abroad that a holy woman who cast out devils had made her dwelling in the Hermit's cliff; and many sick persons from the valley sought her out, and went away restored by her. These poor pilgrims brought her oil and flour, and with her own hands she made a garden like the Hermit's, and planted it with corn and lentils; but she would never take a trout from the brook, or receive the gift of a snared wild-fowl, for she said that in her vagrant life the wild creatures of the wood had befriended her, and as she had slept in peace among them, so now she would never suffer them to be molested.

In the third year came a plague, and death walked the cities, and many poor peasants fled to the hills to escape it. These the Hermit and his penitent faithfully tended, and so skillful were the Wild Woman's ministrations that the report of them reached the town across the valley, and a deputation of burgesses came with rich offerings, and besought her to descend and comfort their sick. The Hermit, seeing her depart on so dangerous a mission, would have accompanied her, but she bade him remain and tend those who fled to the hills; and for many days his heart was consumed in prayer for her, and he feared lest every fugitive should bring him word of her death.

But at length she returned, wearied-out but whole, and covered with the blessings of the townsfolk; and thereafter her name for holiness spread as wide as the Hermit's.

Seeing how constant she remained in her chosen life, and what advance she had made in the way of perfection, the Hermit now felt that it behooved him to exhort her again to return to the convent; and more than once he resolved to speak with her, but his heart hung back. At length he bethought him that by failing in this duty he imperiled his own soul, and thereupon, on the next feast-day, when they met, he reminded her that in spite of her good works she still lived in sin and excommunicate, and that, now she had once more tasted the sweets of godliness, it was her duty to confess her fault and give herself up to her superiors.

She heard him meekly, but when he had spoken she was silent and her tears ran over; and looking at her he wept also, and said no more. And they prayed together, and returned each to his cave.

It was not till late winter that the plague abated; and the spring and early summer following were heavy with rains and great heat. When the Hermit visited his penitent at the feast of Pentecost, she appeared to him so weak and wasted that, when they had recited the *Veni, sancte spiritus*, and the proper psalms, he taxed her with too great rigor of penitential practices; but she replied that her weakness was not due to an excess of discipline, but that she had brought back from her labors among the sick a heaviness of body which the intemperance of the season no doubt increased. The evil rains continued, falling chiefly at night, while by day the land reeked with heat and vapors; so that lassitude fell on the Hermit also, and he could hardly drag himself down to the spring whence he drew his drinking-water. Thus he fell into the habit of going down to the glen before cockcrow, after he had recited Matins; for at that hour the rain commonly ceased, and a faint air was stirring. Now because of the wet season the stream had not gone dry, and instead of replenishing his flagon slowly at the trickling spring, the Hermit went down to the waterside to fill it; and once, as he descended the steep slope of the glen, he heard the covert rustle, and saw the leaves stir as though something moved behind them. As he looked silence fell, and the leaves grew still; but his heart was shaken, for it seemed to him that what he had seen in the dusk had a human semblance, such as the wood-people wear. And he was loth to think that such unhallowed beings haunted the glen.

A few days passed, and again, descending to the stream, he saw a figure flit by him through the covert; and this time a deeper fear entered into him; but he put away the thought, and prayed fervently for all souls in temptation. And when he spoke with the Wild Woman again, on the feast of the Seven Maccabees, which falls on the first day of August, he was smitten with fear to see her wasted looks, and besought her to cease from laboring and let him minister to her in her weakness. But she denied him gently, and replied that all she asked of him was to keep her steadfastly in his prayers.

Before the feast of the Assumption the rains ceased, and the plague, which had begun to show itself, was stayed; but the ardency of the sun grew greater, and the Hermit's cliff was a fiery furnace. Never had such heat been known in those regions; but the people did not murmur, for with the cessation of the rain their crops were saved and the pestilence banished; and these mercies they ascribed in great part to the prayers and macerations of the two holy anchorets. Therefore on the eve of the Assumption they sent a messenger to the Hermit, saying that at daylight on the morrow the townspeople and all the dwellers in the valley would come forth, led by their Bishop, who bore the Pope's blessing to the two solitaries, and who was mindful to celebrate the Mass of the Assumption in the Hermit's cave in the cliffside. At the blessed word the Hermit was well-nigh distraught with joy, for he felt this to be a sign from heaven that his prayers were heard, and that he had won the Wild Woman's grace as well as his own. And all night he prayed that on the morrow she might confess her fault and receive the Sacrament with him.

Before dawn he recited the psalms of the proper nocturn; then he girded on his gown and sandals, and went forth to meet the Bishop in the valley.

As he went downward daylight stood on the mountains, and he thought he had never seen so fair a dawn. It filled the farthest heaven with brightness, and penetrated even to the woody crevices of the glen, as the grace of God had entered into the obscurest folds of his heart. The morning airs were hushed, and he heard only the sound of his own footfall, and the murmur of the stream which, though diminished, still poured a swift current between the rocks; but as he reached the bottom of the glen a sound of chanting came to him, and he knew that the pilgrims were at hand. His heart leapt up and his feet hastened forward; but at the streamside they were suddenly stayed, for in a pool where the water was still deep he saw the shining of a woman's body—and on a stone hard by lay the Wild Woman's gown and sandals.

Fear and rage possessed the Hermit's heart, and he stood as one smitten speechless, covering his eyes from the shame. But the song of the approaching pilgrims swelled ever louder and nearer, and finding voice he cried to the Wild Woman to come forth and hide herself from the people.

She made no answer, but in the dusk he saw her limbs sway with the swaying of the water, and her eyes were turned to him as if in mockery. At the sight blind fury filled him, and clambering over the rocks to the pool's edge he bent down and caught her by the shoulder. At that moment he could have strangled her with his hands, so abhorrent to him was the touch of her flesh; but as he cried out on her, heaping her with cruel names, he saw that her eyes returned his look without wavering; and suddenly it came to him that she was dead. Then through all his anger and fear a great pang smote him; for here was his work undone, and one he had loved in Christ laid low in her sin, in spite of all his labors.

One moment pity possessed him; the next he bethought him how the people would find him bending above the body of a naked woman, whom he had held up to them as holy, but whom they might now well take for the secret instrument of his undoing; and beholding how at her touch all the slow edifice of his holiness was demolished, and his soul in mortal jeopardy, he felt the earth reel round him and his sight grew red.

Already the head of the procession had entered the glen, and the stillness shook with the great sound of the *Salve Regina*. When the Hermit opened his eyes once more the air was quivering with thronged candle-flames, which glittered on the gold thread of priestly vestments, and on the blazing monstrance beneath its canopy; and close above him was bent the Bishop's face.

The Hermit struggled to his knees.

"My Father in God," he cried, "behold, for my sins I have been visited by a demon—" But as he spoke he perceived that those about him no longer heeded him, and that the Bishop and all his clergy had fallen on their knees about the pool. Then the Hermit, following their gaze, saw that the brown waters of the pool covered the Wild Woman's limbs as with a garment, and that about her floating head a great light floated; and to the utmost edges of the throng a cry of praise went up, for many were there whom the Wild

Woman had healed and comforted, and who read God's mercy in this wonder. But fresh fear fell on the Hermit, for he had cursed a dying saint, and denounced her aloud to all the people; and this new anguish, coming so close upon the other, smote down his weakened frame, so that his limbs failed him and he sank once more to the ground.

The earth reeled about him, and the bending faces grew remote; but as he forced his weak voice once more to proclaim his sins he felt the blessed touch of absolution, and the holy oils of the last voyage laid on his lips and eyes. Peace returned to him then, and with it a great longing to look once more upon his lauds, as he had dreamed of doing at his last hour; but he was too far gone to make this longing known, and so tried to banish it from his mind. Yet in his weakness the wish held him, and the tears ran down his face.

Then, as he lay there, feeling the earth slip from under him, and the Everlasting Arms replace it, he heard a great peal of voices that seemed to come down from the sky and mingle with the singing of the throng; and the words of the chant were the words of his own lauds, so long hidden in the secret of his breast, and now rejoicing above him through the spheres. And his soul rose on the chant, and soared with it to the seat of mercy.

## THE LAST ASSET

"THE DEVIL!" Paul Garnett exclaimed as he re-read his note; and the dry old gentleman who was at the moment his only neighbor in the quiet restaurant they both frequented, remarked with a smile: "You don't seem particularly annoyed at meeting him."

Garnett returned the smile. "I don't know why I apostrophized him, for he's not in the least present—except inasmuch as he may prove to be at the bottom of anything unexpected."

The old gentleman who, like Garnett, was an American, and spoke in the thin rarefied voice which seems best fitted to emit sententious truths, twisted his lean neck toward the younger man and cackled out shrewdly: "Ah, it's generally a woman who is at the bottom of the unexpected. Not," he added, leaning forward with deliberation to select a tooth-pick, "that that precludes the devil's being there too."

Garnett uttered the requisite laugh, and his neighbor, pushing back his plate, called out with a perfectly unbending American intonation: "Gassong! L'addition, silver play."

His repast, as usual, had been a simple one, and he left only thirty centimes in the plate on which his account was presented; but the waiter, to whom he was evidently a familiar presence, received the tribute with Latin affability, and hovered helpfully about the table while the old gentleman cut and lighted his cigar.

"Yes," the latter proceeded, revolving the cigar meditatively between his thin lips, "they're generally both in the same hole, like the owl and the prairie-dog in the natural history books of my youth. I believe it was all a mistake about the owl and the prairie-dog, but it isn't about the unexpected. The fact is, the unexpected is the devil—the sooner you find that out, the happier you'll be." He leaned back, tilting his smooth bald head against the blotched mirror behind him, and rambling on with gentle garrulity while Garnett attacked his omelet.

"Get your life down to routine—eliminate surprises. Arrange things so that, when you get up in the morning, you'll know exactly what is going to happen to you during the day—and the next day and the next. I don't say it's funny—it ain't. But it's better than being hit on the head by a brick-bat. That's why I always take my meals at this restaurant. I know just how much onion they put in things—if I went to the next place I shouldn't.

And I always take the same streets to come here—I've been doing it for ten years now. I know at which crossings to look out—I know what I'm going to see in the shop-windows. It saves a lot of wear and tear to know what's coming. For a good many years I never *did* know, from one minute to another, and now I like to think that everything's cut-and-dried, and nothing unexpected can jump out at me like a tramp from a ditch."

He paused calmly to knock the ashes from his cigar, and Garnett said with a smile: "Doesn't such a plan of life cut off nearly all the possibilities?"

The old gentleman made a contemptuous motion. "Possibilities of what? Of being multifariously miserable? There are lots of ways of being miserable, but there's only one way of being comfortable, and that is to stop running round after happiness. If you make up your mind not to be happy there's no reason why you shouldn't have a fairly good time."

"That was Schopenhauer's idea, I believe," the young man said, pouring his wine with the smile of youthful incredulity.

"I guess he hadn't the monopoly," responded his friend. "Lots of people have found out the secret—the trouble is that so few live up to it."

He rose from his seat, pushing the table forward, and standing passive while the waiter advanced with his shabby overcoat and umbrella. Then he nodded to Garnett, lifted his hat politely to the broad-bosomed lady behind the desk, and passed out into the street.

Garnett looked after him with a musing smile. The two had exchanged views on life for two years without so much as knowing each other's names. Garnett was a newspaper correspondent whose work kept him mainly in London, but on his periodic visits to Paris he lodged in a dingy hotel of the Latin Quarter, the chief merit of which was its nearness to the cheap and excellent restaurant where the two Americans had made acquaintance. But Garnett's assiduity in frequenting the place arose, in the end, less from the excellence of the food than from the enjoyment of his old friend's conversation. Amid the flashy sophistications of the Parisian life to which Garnett's trade introduced him, the American sage's conversation had the crisp and homely flavor of a native dish—one of the domestic compounds for which the exiled palate is supposed to yearn. It was a mark of the old man's impersonality that, in spite of the interest he inspired, Garnett had never got beyond idly wondering who he might be, where he lived, and what his occupations were. He was presumably a bachelor—a man of family ties, however relaxed, though he might have been as often absent from home would not have been as regularly present in the same place—and there was about him a boundless desultoriness which renewed Garnett's conviction that there is no one on earth as idle as an American who is not busy. From certain allusions it was plain that he had lived many years in Paris, yet he had not taken the trouble to adapt his tongue to the local inflections, but spoke French with the accent of one who has formed his conception of the language from a phrase book.

The city itself seemed to have made as little impression on him as its speech. He appeared to have no artistic or intellectual curiosities, to remain untouched by the complex appeal of Paris, while preserving, perhaps the more strikingly from his very detachment, that odd American astuteness which seems the fruit of innocence rather than of experience. His nationality revealed itself again in a mild interest in the political problems of his adopted country, though they appeared to preoccupy him only as illustrating the boundless perversity of mankind. The exhibition of human folly never ceased to divert him, and though his examples of it seemed mainly drawn from the columns of one exiguous daily paper, he found there matter for endless variations on his favorite theme. If this monotony of topic did not weary the younger man, it was because he fancied he could detect under it the tragic implication of the fixed idea—of some great moral upheaval which had flung his friend stripped and starving on the desert island of the little cafe where they met. He hardly knew wherein he read this revelation—whether in the resigned shabbiness of the sage's dress, the impartial courtesy of his manner, or the shade of apprehension which lurked, indescribably, in his guileless yet suspicious eye. There were moments when Garnett could only define him by saying that he looked like a man who had seen a ghost.

## II

AN apparition almost as startling had come to Garnett himself in the shape of the mauve note received from his *concierge* as he was leaving the hotel for luncheon.

Not that, on the face of it, a missive announcing Mrs. Sam Newell's arrival at Ritz's, and her need of his presence there that afternoon at five, carried any special mark of the portentous. It was not her being at Ritz's that surprised him. The fact that she was chronically hard up, and had once or twice lately been so brutally confronted with the consequences as to accept—indeed solicit—a loan of five pounds from him: this circumstance, as Garnett knew, would never be allowed to affect the general tenor of her existence. If one came to Paris, where could one go but to Ritz's? Did he see her in some grubby hole across the river? Or in a family *pension* near the Place de l'Etoile? There was no affectation in her tendency to gravitate toward what was costliest and most conspicuous. In doing so she obeyed one of the profoundest instincts of her nature, and it was another instinct which taught her to gratify the first at any cost, even to that of dipping into the pocket of an impecunious newspaper correspondent. It was a part of her strength—and of her charm too—that she did such things naturally, openly, without any of the ugly grimaces of dissimulation or compunction.

Her recourse to Garnett had of course marked a specially low ebb in her fortunes. Save in moments of exceptional dearth she had richer sources of supply; and he was nearly sure that, by running over the "society column" of the Paris Herald, he should find an explanation, not perhaps of her presence at Ritz's, but of her means of subsistence there. What really perplexed him was not the financial but the social aspect of the case. When Mrs. Newell had left London in July she had told him that, between Cowes and Scotland, she and Hermy were provided for till the middle of October: after that, as she put it, they would have to look about. Why, then, when she had in her hand the opportunity of living for three months at the expense of the British aristocracy, did she rush off to Paris at heaven knew whose expense in the beginning of September? She was not a woman to act incoherently; if she made mistakes they were not of that kind. Garnett felt sure she would never willingly relax her hold on her distinguished friends—was it possible that it was they who had somewhat violently let go of her?

As Garnett reviewed the situation he began to see that this possibility had for some time been latent in it. He had felt that something might happen at any moment—and was not this the something he had obscurely foreseen? Mrs. Newell really moved too fast: her position was as perilous as that of an invading army without a base of supplies. She used up everything too quickly—friends, credit, influence, forbearance. It was so easy for her to acquire all these—what a pity she had never learned to keep them! He himself, for instance—the most insignificant of her acquisitions—was beginning to feel like a squeezed sponge at the mere thought of her; and it was this sense of exhaustion, of the inability to provide more, either materially or morally, which had provoked his exclamation on opening her note. From the first days of their acquaintance her prodigality had amazed him, but he had believed it to be surpassed by the infinity of her resources. If she exhausted old supplies she always found new ones to replace them. When one set of people began to find her impossible, another was always beginning to find her indispensable. Yes—but there were limits—there were only so many sets of people, at least in her social classification, and when she came to an end of them, what then? Was this flight to Paris a sign that she had come to an end—was she going to try Paris because London had failed her? The time of year precluded such a conjecture. Mrs. Newell's Paris was non-existent in September. The town was a desert of gaping trippers—he could as soon think of her seeking social restoration at Margate.

For a moment it occurred to him that she might have to come over to replenish her wardrobe; but he knew her dates too well to dwell long on this hope. It was in April and December that she visited the dress-makers: before December, he had heard her explain, one got nothing but "the American fashions." Mrs. Newell's scorn of all things American was somewhat illogically coupled with the determination to use her own Americanism to the utmost as a means of social advance. She had found out long ago that, on certain lines, it paid in London to be American, and she had manufactured for herself a personality independent of geographical or social demarcations, and presenting that remarkable blend of plantation dialect, Bowery slang and hyperbolic statement, which is the British nobility's favorite idea of an unadulterated Americanism. Mrs. Newell, for all her talents, was not naturally either humorous or hyperbolic, and there were times when it would doubtless have been a relief to her to be as monumentally stolid as some of the persons whose dullness it was her fate to enliven. It was perhaps the need of relaxing which had drawn her into her odd intimacy with Garnett, with whom she did not have to be either scrupulously English or artificially American, since the impression she made on him was of no more consequence than that which she produced on her footman. Garnett was perfectly aware that he owed his success to his insignificance, but the fact affected him only as adding one more element to his knowledge of Mrs. Newell's character. He was as ready to sacrifice his personal vanity in such a cause as he had been, at the outset of their acquaintance, to sacrifice his professional pride to the opportunity of knowing her.

When he had accepted the position of "London correspondent" (with an occasional side-glance at Paris) to the New York *Searchlight*, he had not understood that his work was to include the obligation of "interviewing"; indeed, had the possibility presented itself in advance, he would have met it by unpacking his valise and returning to the drudgery of his assistant-editorship in New York. But when, after three months in Europe, he received a letter from his chief, suggesting that he should enliven the Sunday *Searchlight* by a series of "Talks with Smart Americans in London" (beginning, say, with Mrs. Sam Newell), the change of focus already enabled him to view the proposal without passion. For his life on the edge of the great world-caldron of art, politics and pleasure— of that high-spiced brew which is nowhere else so subtly and variously compounded— had bred in him an eager appetite to taste of the heady mixture. He knew he should never have the full spoon at his lips, but he recalled the peasant-girl in one of Browning's plays, who has once eaten polenta cut with a knife which has carved an ortolan. Might not Mrs. Newell, who had so successfully cut a way into the dense and succulent mass of English society, serve as the knife to season his polenta?

He had expected, as the result of the interview, to which she promptly, almost eagerly, assented, no more than the glimpse of brightly lit vistas which a waiting messenger may catch through open doors; but instead he had found himself drawn at once into the inner sanctuary, not of London society, but of Mrs. Newell's relation to it. She had been candidly charmed by the idea of the interview: it struck him that she was conscious of the need of being freshened up. Her appearance was brilliantly fresh, with the inveterate freshness of the toilet-table; her paint was as impenetrable as armor. But her personality was a little tarnished: she was in want of social renovation. She had been doing and saying the same things for too long a time. London, Cowes, Homburg, Scotland, Monte Carlo—that had been the round since Hermy was a baby. Hermy was her daughter, Miss Hermione Newell, who was called in presently to be shown off to the interviewer and add a paragraph to the celebration of her mother's charms.

Miss Newell's appearance was so full of an unassisted freshness that for a moment Garnett made the mistake of fancying that she could fill a paragraph of her own. But he soon found that her vague personality was merely tributary to her parent's; that her youth and grace were, in some mysterious way, her mother's rather than her own. She smiled obediently on Garnett, but could contribute little beyond her smile and the general sweetness of her presence, to the picture of Mrs. Newell's existence which it was the young man's business to draw. And presently he found that she had left the room without his noticing it.

He learned in time that this unnoticeableness was the most conspicuous thing about her. Burning at best with a mild light, she became invisible in the glare of her mother's personality. It was in fact only as a product of her environment that poor Hermione struck the imagination. With the smartest woman in London as her guide and example she had never developed a taste for dress, and with opportunities for enlightenment from which Garnett's fancy recoiled she remained simple, unsuspicious and tender, with an inclination to good works and afternoon church, a taste for the society of dull girls, and a clinging fidelity to old governesses and retired nurse-maids. Mrs. Newell, whose boast it was that she looked facts in the face, frankly owned that she had not been able to make anything of Hermione. "If she has a role I haven't discovered it," she confessed to Garnett. "I've tried everything, but she doesn't fit in anywhere."

Mrs. Newell spoke as if her daughter were a piece of furniture acquired without due reflection, and for which no suitable place could be found. She got, of course, what she could out of Hermione, who wrote her notes, ran her errands, saw tiresome people for her, and occupied an intermediate office between that of lady's maid and secretary; but such small returns on her investment were not what Mrs. Newell had counted on. What was the use of producing and educating a handsome daughter if she did not, in some more positive way, contribute to her parent's advancement?

### III

"IT'S about Hermy," Mrs. Newell said, rising from the heap of embroidered cushions which formed the background of her afternoon repose.

Her sitting room at Ritz's was full of penetrating warmth and fragrance. Long-stemmed roses filled the vases on the chimney-piece, in which a fire sparkled with that effect of luxury which fires produce when the weather is not cold enough to justify them. On the writing-table, among notes and cards, and signed photographs of celebrities, Mrs. Newell's gold inkstand, her jeweled penholder, her heavily-monogrammed despatch-box, gave back from their expensive surfaces the glint of the flame, which sought out and magnified the orient of the pearls among the lady's laces and found a mirror in the pinky polish of her finger-tips. It was just such a scene as a little September fire, lit for show and not for warmth, would delight to dwell on and pick out in all its opulent details; and even Garnett, inured to Mrs. Newell's capacity for extracting manna from the desert, reflected that she must have found new fields to glean.

"It's about Hermy," she repeated, making room for him among the cushions. "I had to see you at once. We came over yesterday from London."

Garnett, seating himself, continued his leisurely survey of the room. In the glitter of Mrs. Newell's magnificence Hermione, as usual, faded out of sight, and he hardly noticed her mother's allusion.

"I have never seen you more resplendent," he remarked.

She received the tribute with complacency. "The rooms are not bad, are they? We came over with the Woolsey Hubbards (you've heard of them, of course?—they're from Detroit), and really they do things very decently. Their motor-car met us at Boulogne, and the courier always wires ahead to have the rooms filled with flowers. This salon, is really a part of their suite. I simply couldn't have afforded it myself."

She delivered these facts in a high decisive voice, which had a note akin to the clink of her many bracelets and the rattle of her ringed hands against the enameled cigarette-case which she extended to Garnett after helping herself from its contents.

"You are always meeting such charming people," said Garnett with mild irony; and, reverting to her first remark, he bethought himself to add: "I hope Miss Hermione is not ill?"

"Ill? She was never ill in her life," exclaimed Mrs. Newell, as though her daughter had been accused of an indelicacy.

"It was only that you said you had come over on her account."

"So I have. Hermione is to be married."

Mrs. Newell brought out the words impressively, drawing back to observe their effect on her visitor. It was such that he received them with a long silent stare, which finally passed into a cry of wonder. "Married? For heaven's sake, to whom?"

Mrs. Newell continued to regard him with a smile so serene and victorious that he saw she took his somewhat unseemly astonishment as a merited tribute to her genius. Presently she extended a glittering hand and took a sheet of note paper from the blotter.

"You can have that put in tomorrow's *Herald*," she said.

Garnett, receiving the paper, read in Hermione's own finished hand: "A marriage has been arranged, and will shortly take place, between the Comte Louis du Trayas, son of the Marquis du Trayas de la Baume, and Miss Hermione Newell, daughter of Samuel C. Newell Esq. of Elmira, N. Y. Comte Louis du Trayas belongs to one of the oldest and most distinguished families in France, and is equally well connected in England, being the nephew of Lord Saint Priscoe and a cousin of the Countess of Morningfield, whom he frequently visits at Adham and Portlow."

The perusal of this document filled Garnett with such deepening wonder that he could not, for the moment, even do justice to the strangeness of its being written out for publication in the bride's own hand. Hermione a bride! Hermione a future countess! Hermione on the brink of a marriage which would give her not only a great "situation" in the Parisian world but a footing in some of the best houses in England! Regardless of its unflattering implications, Garnett prolonged his stare of mute amazement till Mrs. Newell somewhat sharply exclaimed—"Well, didn't I always tell you that she would marry a Frenchman?"

Garnett, in spite of himself, smiled at this revised version of his hostess's frequent assertion that Hermione was too goody-goody to take in England, but that with her little dowdy air she might very well "go off" in the Faubourg if only a *dot* could be raked up for her—and the recollection flashed a new light on the versatility of Mrs. Newell's genius.

"But how did you do it—?" was on the tip of his tongue; and he had barely time to give the query the more conventional turn of: "How did it happen?"

"Oh, we were up at Glaish with the Edmund Fitzarthurs. Lady Edmund is a sort of cousin of the Morningfields', who have a shooting-lodge near Glaish—a place called Portlow—and young Trayas was there with them. Lady Edmund, who is a dear, drove Hermy over to Portlow, and the thing was done in no time. He simply fell over head and ears in love with her. You know Hermy is really very handsome in her peculiar way. I don't think you have ever appreciated her," Mrs. Newell summed up with a note of exquisite reproach.

"I've appreciated her, I assure you; but one somehow didn't think of her marrying—so soon."

"Soon? She's three and twenty; but you've no imagination," said Mrs. Newell; and Garnett inwardly admitted that he had not enough to soar to the heights of her invention. For the marriage, of course, was an invention of her own, a superlative stroke of business, in which he was sure the principal parties had all been passive agents, in which everyone, from the bankrupt and disreputable Fitzarthurs to the rich and immaculate Morningfields, had by some mysterious sleight of hand been made to fit into Mrs. Newell's designs. But it was not enough for Garnett to marvel at her work—he wanted to understand it, to take it apart, to find out how the trick had been done. It was true that Mrs. Newell had always said Hermy might go off in the Faubourg if she had a *dot*—but even Mrs. Newell's juggling could hardly conjure up a *dot:* such feats as she was able to perform in this line were usually made to serve her own urgent necessities. And besides, who was likely to take sufficient interest in Hermione to supply her with the means of marrying a French nobleman? The flowers ordered in advance by the Woolsey Hubbards' courier made Garnett wonder if that accomplished functionary had also wired over to have Miss Newell's settlements drawn up. But of all the comments hovering on his lips the only one he could decently formulate was the remark that he supposed Mrs. Newell and her daughter had come over to see the young man's family and make the final arrangements.

"Oh, they're made—everything is settled," said Mrs. Newell, looking him squarely in the eye. "You're wondering, of course, about the *dot*—Frenchmen never go off their heads to the extent of forgetting *that;* or at least their parents don't allow them to."

Garnett murmured a vague assent, and she went on without the least appearance of resenting his curiosity: "It all came about so fortunately. Only fancy, just the week they met I got a little legacy from an aunt in Elmira—a good soul I hadn't seen or heard of for years. I suppose I ought to have put on mourning for her, by the way, but it would have eaten up a good bit of the legacy, and I really needed it all for poor Hermy. Oh, it's not a fortune, you understand—but the young man is madly in love, and has always had his own way, so after a lot of correspondence it's been arranged. They saw Hermy this morning, and they're enchanted."

"And the marriage takes place very soon?"

"Yes, in a few weeks, here. His mother is an invalid and couldn't have gone to England. Besides, the French don't travel. And as Hermy has become a Catholic—"

"Already?"

Mrs. Newell stared. "It doesn't take long. And it suits Hermy exactly—she can go to church so much oftener. So I thought," Mrs. Newell concluded with dignity, "that a wedding at Saint Philippe du Roule would be the most suitable thing at this season."

"Dear me," said Garnett, "I am left breathless—I can't catch up with you. I suppose even the day is fixed, though Miss Hermione doesn't mention it," and he indicated the official announcement in his hand.

Mrs. Newell laughed. "Hermy had to write that herself, poor dear, because my scrawl's too hideous—but I dictated it. No, the day isn't fixed—that's why I sent for you." There was a splendid directness about Mrs. Newell. It would never have occurred to her to pretend to Garnett that she had summoned him for the pleasure of his company.

"You've sent for me—to fix the day?" he enquired humorously.

"To remove the last obstacle to its being fixed."

"I? What kind of an obstacle could I have the least effect on?"

Mrs. Newell met his banter with a look which quelled it. "I want you to find her father."

"Her father? Miss Hermione's—?"

"My husband, of course. I suppose you know he's living."

Garnett blushed at his own clumsiness. "I—yes—that is, I really knew nothing—" he stammered, feeling that each word added to it. If Hermione was unnoticeable, Mr. Newell had always been invisible. The young man had never so much as given him a thought, and it was awkward to come on him so suddenly at a turn of the talk.

"Well, he is—living here in Paris," said Mrs. Newell, with a note of asperity which seemed to imply that her friend might have taken the trouble to post himself on this point.

"In Paris? But in that case isn't it quite simple—?"

"To find him? I daresay it won't be difficult, though he is rather mysterious. But the point is that I can't go to him—and that if I write to him he won't answer."

"Ah," said Garnett thoughtfully.

"And so you've got to find him for me, and tell him."

"Tell him what?"

"That he must come to the wedding—that we must show ourselves together at church and at the breakfast."

She delivered the behest in her sharp imperative key, the tone of the born commander. But for once Garnett ventured to question her orders.

"And supposing he won't come?"

"He must if he cares for his daughter's happiness. She can't be married without him." "Can't be married?"

"The French are like that—especially the old families. I was given to understand at once that my husband must appear—if only to establish the fact that we're not divorced."

"Ah—you're *not*, then?" escaped from Garnett.

"Mercy, no! Divorce is stupid. They don't like it in Europe. And in this case it would have been the end of Hermy's marriage. They wouldn't think of letting their son marry the child of divorced parents."

"How fortunate, then—"

"Yes; but I always think of such things beforehand. And of course I've told them that my husband will be present."

"You think he will consent?"

"No; not at first; but you must make him. You must tell him how sweet Hermione is—and you must see Louis, and be able to describe their happiness. You must dine here to-night—he is coming. We're all dining with the Hubbards, and they expect you. They have given Hermy some very good diamonds—though I should have preferred a check, as she'll be horribly poor. But I think Kate Hubbard means to do something about the trousseau—Hermy is at Paquin's with her now. You've no idea how delightful all our friends have been.—Ah, here is one of them now," she broke off smiling, as the door opened to admit, without preliminary announcement, a gentleman so glossy and ancient, with such a fixed unnatural freshness of smile and eye, that he gave Garnett the effect of having been embalmed and then enameled. It needed not the exotic-looking ribbon in the visitor's button-hole, nor Mrs. Newell's introduction of him as her friend Baron Schenkelderff, to assure Garnett of his connection with a race as ancient as his appearance.

Baron Schenkelderff greeted his hostess with paternal playfulness, and the young man with an ease which might have been acquired on the Stock Exchange and in the dressing-rooms of "leading ladies." He spoke a faultless, colorless English, from which one felt he might pass with equal mastery to half a dozen other languages. He enquired patronizingly for the excellent Hubbards, asked his hostess if she did not mean to give him a drop of tea and a cigarette, remarked that he need not ask if Hermione was still closeted with the dress-maker, and, on the waiter's coming in answer to his ring, ordered the tea himself, and added a request for *fine champagne*. It was not the first time that Garnett had seen such minor liberties taken in Mrs. Newell's drawing-room, but they had hitherto been taken by persons who had at least the superiority of knowing what they were permitting themselves, whereas the young man felt almost sure that Baron Schenkelderff's manner was the most distinguished he could achieve; and this deepened the disgust with which, as the minutes passed, he yielded to the conviction that the Baron was Mrs. Newell's "aunt."

IV

GARNETT had always foreseen that Mrs. Newell might someday ask him to do something he should greatly dislike. He had never gone so far as to conjecture what it might be, but had simply felt that if he allowed his acquaintance with her to pass from spectatorship to participation he must be prepared to find himself, at any moment, in a queer situation.

The moment had come; and he was relieved to find that he could meet it by refusing her request. He had not always been sure that she would leave him this alternative. She had a way of involving people in her complications without their being aware of it, and Garnett had pictured himself in holes so tight that there might not be room for a wriggle. Happily in this case he could still move freely. Nothing compelled him to act as an intermediary between Mrs. Newell and her husband, and it was preposterous to suppose that, even in a life of such perpetual upheaval as hers, there were no roots which struck deeper than her casual intimacy with himself. She had simply laid hands on him because he happened to be within reach, and he would put himself out of reach by leaving for London on the morrow.

Having thus inwardly asserted his independence, he felt free to let his fancy dwell on the strangeness of the situation. He had always supposed that Mrs. Newell, in her flight through life, must have thrown a good many victims to the wolves, and had assumed that Mr. Newell had been among the number. That he had been dropped overboard at an early stage in the lady's career seemed probable from the fact that neither his wife nor his daughter ever mentioned him. Mrs. Newell was incapable of reticence, and if her husband had still been an active element in her life he would certainly have figured in her conversation. Garnett, if he thought of the matter at all, had concluded that divorce must long since have eliminated Mr. Newell; but he now saw how he had underrated his friend's faculty for using up the waste material of life. She had always struck him as the most extravagant of women, yet it turned out that by a miracle of thrift she had for years kept a superfluous husband on the chance that he might some day be useful to her. The day had come, and Mr. Newell was to be called from his obscurity. Garnett wondered what had become of him in the interval, and in what shape he would respond to the evocation. The fact that his wife feared he might not respond to it at all, seemed to show that his exile was voluntary, or had at least come to appear preferable to other alternatives; but if that were the case it was curious that he should not have taken legal means to free himself. He could hardly have had his wife's motives for wishing to maintain the vague tie between them; but conjecture lost itself in trying to picture what his point of view was likely to be, and Garnett, on his way to the Hubbards' dinner that evening, could not help regretting that circumstances denied him the opportunity of meeting so enigmatic a person. The young man's knowledge of Mrs. Newell's methods made him feel that her husband might be an interesting study. This, however, did not affect his resolve to keep clear of the business. He entered the Hubbards' dining-room with the firm intention of refusing to execute Mrs. Newell's commission, and if he changed his mind in the course of the evening it was not owing to that lady's persuasions.

Garnett's curiosity as to the Hubbards' share in Hermione's marriage was appeased before he had been seated five minutes at their table.

Mrs. Woolsey Hubbard was an expansive blonde, whose ample but disciplined outline seemed the result of a well-matched struggle between her cook and her corset-maker. She talked a great deal of what was appropriate in dress and conduct, and seemed to regard Mrs. Newell as a final arbiter on both points. To do or to wear anything inappropriate would have been extremely mortifying to Mrs. Hubbard, and she was evidently resolved, at the price of eternal vigilance, to prove her familiarity with what she frequently referred to as "the right thing." Mr. Hubbard appeared to have no such preoccupations. Garnett, if called upon to describe him, would have done so by saying that he was the American who always pays. The young man, in the course of his foreign wanderings, had come across many fellow-citizens of Mr. Hubbard's type, in the most diverse company and surroundings; and wherever they were to be found, they always had their hands in their pockets. Mr. Hubbard's standard of gentility was the extent of a man's capacity to "foot the bill"; and as no one but an occasional compatriot cared to dispute the privilege with him, he seldom had reason to doubt his social superiority.

Garnett, nevertheless, did not believe that this lavish pair were, as Mrs. Newell would have phrased it, "putting up" Hermione's *dot*. They would go very far in diamonds, but they would hang back from securities. Their readiness to pay was indefinably mingled with a dread of being expected to, and their prodigalities would take flight at the first hint of coercion. Mrs. Newell, who had had a good deal of experience in managing this type of millionaire, could be trusted not to arouse their susceptibilities, and Garnett was therefore certain that the chimerical legacy had been extracted from other pockets. There were none in view but those of Baron Schenkelderff, who, seated at Mrs. Hubbard's right, with a new order in his button-hole, and a fresh glaze upon his features, enchanted that lady by his careless references to crowned heads and his condescending approval of the champagne. Garnett was more than ever certain that it was the Baron who was paying; and it was this conviction which made him suddenly feel that, at any cost, Hermione's marriage must take place. He had felt no special interest in the marriage except as one more proof of Mrs. Newell's extraordinary capacity; but now it appealed to him from the girl's own stand-point. For he saw, with a touch of compunction, that in the mephitic air of her surroundings a love-story of surprising freshness had miraculously flowered. He had only to intercept the glances which the young couple exchanged to find himself transported to the candid region of romance. It was evident that Hermione adored and was adored; that the lovers believed in each other and in every one about them, and that even the legacy of the defunct aunt had not been too great a strain on their faith in human nature.

His first glance at the Comte Louis du Trayas showed Garnett that, by some marvel of fitness, Hermione had happened upon a kindred nature. If the young man's long mild features and short-sighted glance revealed no special force of character, they showed a benevolence and simplicity as incorruptible as her own, and declared that their possessor, whatever his failings, would never imperil the illusions she had so miraculously preserved. The fact that the girl took her good fortune naturally, and did not regard herself as suddenly snatched from the jaws of death, added poignancy to the situation; for if she missed this way of escape, and was thrown back on her former life, the day of discovery could not be long deferred. It made Garnett shiver to think of her growing old between her mother and Schenkelderff, or such successors of the Baron's as might probably attend on Mrs. Newell's waning fortunes; for it was clear to him that the Baron marked the first stage in his friend's decline. When Garnett took leave that evening he had promised Mrs. Newell that he would try to find her husband.

V

IF Mr. Newell read in the papers the announcement of his daughter's marriage it did not cause him to lift the veil of seclusion in which his wife represented him as shrouded.

A round of the American banks in Paris failed to give Garnett his address, and it was only in chance talk with one of the young secretaries of the Embassy that he was put on Mr. Newell's track. The secretary's father, it appeared, had known the Newells some twenty years earlier. He had had business relations with Mr. Newell, who was then a man of property, with factories or something of the kind, the narrator thought, somewhere in Western New York. There had been at this period, for Mrs. Newell, a phase of large hospitality and showy carriages in Washington and at Narragansett. Then her husband had had reverses, had lost heavily in Wall Street, and had finally drifted abroad and been lost to sight. The young man did not know at what point in his financial decline Mr. Newell had parted company with his wife and daughter; "though you may bet your hat," he philosophically concluded, "that the old girl hung on as long as there were any pickings." He did not himself know Mr. Newell's address, but opined that it might be extracted from a certain official at the Consulate, if Garnett could give a sufficiently good reason for the request; and here in fact Mrs. Newell's emissary learned that her husband was to be found in an obscure street of the Luxembourg quarter.

In order to be near the scene of action, Garnett went to breakfast at his usual haunt, determined to dispatch his business as early in the day as politeness allowed. The head waiter welcomed him to a table near that of the transatlantic sage, who sat in his customary corner, his head tilted back against the blistered mirror at an angle suggesting that in a freer civilization his feet would have sought the same level. He greeted Garnett affably and the two exchanged their usual generalizations on life till the sage rose to go; whereupon it occurred to Garnett to accompany him. His friend took the offer in good part, merely remarking that he was going to the Luxembourg gardens, where it was his invariable habit, on good days, to feed the sparrows with the remains of his breakfast roll; and Garnett replied that, as it happened, his own business lay in the same direction.

"Perhaps, by the way," he added, "you can tell me how to find the rue Panonceaux where I must go presently. I thought I knew this quarter fairly well, but I have never heard of it."

His companion came to a sudden halt on the narrow sidewalk, to the confusion of the dense and desultory traffic which marks the old streets of the Latin quarter. He fixed his mild eye on Garnett and gave a twist to the cigar which lingered in the corner of his mouth.

"The rue Panonceaux? It is an out-of-the-way hole, but I can tell you how to find it," he answered.

He made no motion to do so, however, but continued to bend on the young man the full force of his interrogative gaze; then he added abruptly: "Would you mind telling me your object in going there?"

Garnett looked at him with surprise: a question so unblushingly personal was strangely out of keeping with his friend's usual attitude of detachment. Before he could reply, however, the other had quietly continued: "Do you happen to be in search of Samuel C. Newell?"

"Why, yes, I am," said Garnett with a start of conjecture.

His companion uttered a sigh. "I supposed so," he said resignedly; "and in that case," he added, "we may as well have the matter out in the Luxembourg."

Garnett had halted before him with deepening astonishment. "But you don't mean to tell me—?" he stammered.

The little man made a motion of assent. "I am Samuel C. Newell," he said drily; "and if you have no objection, I prefer not to break through my habit of feeding the sparrows. We are five minutes late as it is."

He quickened his pace without awaiting any reply from Garnett, who walked beside him in unsubdued wonder till they reached the Luxembourg gardens, where Mr. Newell, making for one of the less frequented alleys, seated himself on a bench and drew the fragment of a roll from his pocket. His coming was evidently expected, for a shower of little dusky bodies at once descended on him, and the gravel fluttered with battling wings and beaks as he distributed his dole.

It was not till the ground was white with crumbs, and the first frenzy of his pensioners appeased, that he turned to Garnett and said: "I presume, sir, that you come from my wife."

Garnett colored with embarrassment: the more simply the old man took his mission the more complicated it appeared to himself.

"From your wife—and from Miss Newell," he said at length. "You have perhaps heard that she is to be married."

"Oh, yes—I read the *Herald* pretty faithfully," said Miss Newell's parent, shaking out another handful of crumbs.

Garnett cleared his throat. "Then you have no doubt thought it natural that, under the circumstances, they should wish to communicate with you."

The sage continued to fix his attention on the sparrows. "My wife," he remarked, "might have written to me."

"Mrs. Newell was afraid she might not hear from you in reply."

"In reply? Why should she? I suppose she merely wishes to announce the marriage. She knows I have no money left to buy wedding-presents," said Mr. Newell astonishingly.

Garnett felt his color deepen: he had a vague sense of standing as the representative of something guilty and enormous, with which he had rashly identified himself.

"I don't think you understand," he said. "Mrs. Newell and your daughter have asked me to see you because they are anxious that you should consent to appear at the wedding."

Mr. Newell, at this, ceased to give his attention to the birds, and turned a compassionate gaze upon Garnett.

"My dear sir—I don't know your name—" he remarked, "would you mind telling me how long you have been acquainted with Mrs. Newell?" And without waiting for an answer he added judicially: "If you wait long enough she will ask you to do some very disagreeable things for her."

This echo of his own thoughts gave Garnett a sharp twinge of discomfort, but he made shift to answer good-humoredly: "If you refer to my present errand, I must tell you that I don't find it disagreeable to do anything which may be of service to Miss Hermione."

Mr. Newell fumbled in his pocket, as though searching unavailingly for another morsel of bread; then he said: "From her point of view I shall not be the most important person at the ceremony."

Garnett smiled. "That is hardly a reason—" he began; but he was checked by the brevity of tone with which his companion replied: "I am not aware that I am called upon to give you my reasons."

"You are certainly not," the young man rejoined, "except in so far as you are willing to consider me as the messenger of your wife and daughter."

"Oh, I accept your credentials," said the other with his dry smile; "what I don't recognize is their right to send a message."

This reduced Garnett to silence, and after a moment's pause Mr. Newell drew his watch from his pocket.

"I am sorry to cut the conversation short, but my days are mapped out with a certain regularity, and this is the hour for my nap." He rose as he spoke and held out his hand with a glint of melancholy humor in his small clear eyes.

"You dismiss me, then? I am to take back a refusal?" the young man exclaimed.

"My dear sir, those ladies have got on very well without me for a number of years: I imagine they can put through this wedding without my help."

"You are mistaken, then; if it were not for that I shouldn't have undertaken this errand."

Mr. Newell paused as he was turning away. "Not for what?" he enquired.

"The fact that, as it happens, the wedding can't be put through without your help."

Mr. Newell's thin lips formed a noiseless whistle. "They've got to have my consent, have they? Well, is he a good young man?"

"The bridegroom?" Garnett echoed in surprise. "I hear the best accounts of him—and Miss Newell is very much in love."

Her parent met this with an odd smile. "Well, then, I give my consent—it's all I've got left to give," he added philosophically.

Garnett hesitated. "But if you consent—if you approve—why do you refuse your daughter's request?"

Mr. Newell looked at him a moment. "Ask Mrs. Newell!" he said. And as Garnett was again silent, he turned away with a slight gesture of leave-taking.

But in an instant the young man was at his side. "I will not ask your reasons, sir," he said, "but I will give you mine for being here. Miss Newell cannot be married unless you are present at the ceremony. The young man's parents know that she has a father living, and they give their consent only on condition that he appears at her marriage. I believe it is customary in old French families—."

"Old French families be damned!" said Mr. Newell with sudden vigour. "She had better marry an American." And he made a more decided motion to free himself from Garnett's importunities.

But his resistance only strengthened the young man's. The more unpleasant the latter's task became, the more unwilling he grew to see his efforts end in failure. During the three days which had been consumed in his quest it had become clear to him that the bridegroom's parents, having been surprised into a reluctant consent, were but too ready to withdraw it on the plea of Mr. Newell's non-appearance. Mrs. Newell, on the last edge of tension, had confided to Garnett that the Morningfields were "being nasty"; and he could picture the whole powerful clan, on both sides of the Channel, arrayed in a common resolve to exclude poor Hermione from their ranks. The very inequality of the contest stirred his blood, and made him vow that in this case at least the sins of the parents should not be visited on the children. In his talk with the young secretary he had obtained some glimpses of Baron Schenkelderff's past which fortified this resolve. The Baron, at one time a familiar figure in a much-observed London set, had been mixed up in an ugly money-lending business ending in suicide, which had excluded him from the society most accessible to his race. His alliance with Mrs. Newell was doubtless a desperate attempt at rehabilitation, a forlorn hope on both sides, but likely to be an enduring tie because it represented, to both partners, their last chance of escape from social extinction. That Hermione's marriage was a mere stake in their game did not in the least affect Garnett's view of its urgency. If on their part it was a sordid speculation, to her it had the freshness of the first wooing. If it made of her a mere pawn in their hands, it would put her, so Garnett hoped, beyond farther risk of such base uses; and to achieve this had become a necessity to him.

The sense that, if he lost sight of Mr. Newell, the latter might not easily be found again, nerved Garnett to hold his ground in spite of the resistance he encountered; and he tried to put the full force of his plea into the tone with which he cried: "Ah, you don't know your daughter!"

## VI

MRS. NEWELL, that afternoon, met him on the threshold of her sitting-room with a "Well?" of pent-up anxiety.

In the room itself, Baron Schenkelderff sat with crossed legs and head thrown back, in an attitude which he did not see fit to alter at the young man's approach.

Garnett hesitated; but it was not the summariness of the Baron's greeting which he resented.

"You've found him?" Mrs. Newell exclaimed.

"Yes; but—"

She followed his glance and answered it with a slight shrug. "I can't take you into my room, because there's a dress-maker there, and she won't go because she is waiting to be paid. Schenkelderff," she exclaimed, "you're not wanted; please go and look out of the window."

The Baron rose and, lighting a cigarette, laughingly retired to the embrasure. Mrs. Newell flung herself down and signed to Garnett to take a seat at her side.

"Well—you've found him? You've talked with him?"

"Yes; I have talked with him—for an hour."

She made an impatient movement. "That's too long! Does he refuse?"

"He doesn't consent."

"Then you mean—?"

"He wants time to think it over."

"Time? There *is* no time—did you tell him so?"

"I told him so; but you must remember that he has plenty. He has taken twenty-four hours."

Mrs. Newell groaned. "Oh, that's too much. When he thinks things over he always refuses."

"Well, he would have refused at once if I had not agreed to the delay."

She rose nervously from her seat and pressed her hands to her forehead. "It's too hard, after all I've done! The trousseau is ordered—think how disgraceful! You must have managed him badly; I'll go and see him myself."

The Baron, at this, turned abruptly from his study of the Place Vendome.

"My dear creature, for heaven's sake don't spoil everything!" he exclaimed.

Mrs. Newell colored furiously. "What's the meaning of that brilliant speech?"

"I was merely putting myself in the place of a man on whom you have ceased to smile."

He picked up his hat and stick, nodded knowingly to Garnett, and walked toward the door with an air of creaking jauntiness.

But on the threshold Mrs. Newell waylaid him.

"Don't go—I must speak to you," she said, following him into the antechamber; and Garnett remembered the dress-maker who was not to be dislodged from her bedroom.

In a moment Mrs. Newell returned, with a small flat packet which she vainly sought to dissemble in an inaccessible pocket.

"He makes everything too odious!" she exclaimed; but whether she referred to her husband or the Baron it was left to Garnett to decide.

She sat silent, nervously twisting her cigarette-case between her fingers, while her visitor rehearsed the details of his conversation with Mr. Newell. He did not indeed tell her the arguments he had used to shake her husband's resolve, since in his eloquent sketch of Hermione's situation there had perforce entered hints unflattering to her mother; but he gave the impression that his hearer had in the end been moved, and for that reason had consented to defer his refusal.

"Ah, it's not that—it's to prolong our misery!" Mrs. Newell exclaimed; and after a moment she added drearily: "He has been waiting for such an opportunity for years."

It seemed needless for Garnett to protract his visit, and he took leave with the promise to report at once the result of his final talk with Mr. Newell. But as he was passing through the ante-chamber a side-door opened and Hermione stood before him. Her face was flushed and shaken out of its usual repose of line, and he saw at once that she had been waiting for him.

"Mr. Garnett!" she said in a whisper.

He paused, considering her with surprise: he had never supposed her capable of such emotion as her voice and eyes revealed.

"I want to speak to you; we are quite safe here. Mamma is with the dress-maker," she explained, closing the door behind her, while Garnett laid aside his hat and stick.

"I am at your service," he said.

"You have seen my father? Mamma told me that you were to see him to-day," the girl went on, standing close to him in order that she might not have to raise her voice.

"Yes; I have seen him," Garnett replied with increasing wonder. Hermione had never before mentioned her father to him, and it was by a slight stretch of veracity that he had included her name in her mother's plea to Mr. Newell. He had supposed her to be either unconscious of the transaction, or else too much engrossed in her own happiness to give it a thought; and he had forgiven her the last alternative in consideration of the abnormal character of her filial relations. But now he saw that he must readjust his view of her.

"You went to ask him to come to my wedding; I know about it," Hermione continued. "Of course it is the custom—people will think it odd if he does not come." She paused, and then asked: "Does he consent?"

"No; he has not yet consented."

"Ah, I thought so when I saw Mamma just now!"

"But he hasn't quite refused—he has promised to think it over."

"But he hated it—he hated the idea?"

Garnett hesitated. "It seemed to arouse painful associations."

"Ah, it would—it would!" she exclaimed.

He was astonished at the passion of her accent; astonished still more at the tone with which she went on, laying her hand on his arm: "Mr. Garnett, he must not be asked—he has been asked too often to do things that he hated!"

Garnett looked at the girl with a shock of awe. What abysses of knowledge did her purity hide?

"But, my dear Miss Hermione—" he began.

"I know what you are going to say," she interrupted him. "It is necessary that he should be present at the marriage or the du Trayas will break it off. They don't want it very much, at any rate," she added with a strange candor, "and they will not be sorry, perhaps—for of course Louis would have to obey them."

"So I explained to your father," Garnett assured her.

"Yes—yes; I knew you would put it to him. But that makes no difference, Mr. Garnett. He must not be forced to come unwillingly."

"But if he sees the point—after all, no one can force him!"

"No; but if it is painful to him—if it reminds him too much . . . Oh, Mr. Garnett, I was not a child when he left us. . . . I was old enough to see . . . to see how it must hurt him even now to be reminded. Peace was all he asked for, and I want him to be left in peace!"

Garnett paused in deep embarrassment. "My dear child, there is no need to remind you that your own future—"

She had a gesture that recalled her mother. "My future must take care of itself; he must not be made to see us!" she said imperatively. And as Garnett remained silent she went on: "I have always hoped he did not hate me, but he would hate me now if he were forced to see me."

"Not if he could see you at this moment!" he exclaimed.

She lifted her face with swimming eyes.

"Well, go to him, then; tell him what I have said to you!"

Garnett continued to stand before her, deeply struck. "It might be the best thing," he reflected inwardly; but he did not give utterance to the thought. He merely put out his hand, holding Hermione's in a long pressure.

"I will do whatever you wish," he replied.

"You understand that I am in earnest?" she urged tenaciously.

"I am quite sure of it."

"Then I want you to repeat to him what I have said—I want him to be left undisturbed. I don't want him ever to hear of us again!"

The next day, at the appointed hour, Garnett resorted to the Luxembourg gardens, which Mr. Newell had named as a meeting-place in preference to his own lodgings. It was clear that he did not wish to admit the young man any further into his privacy than the occasion required, and the extreme shabbiness of his dress hinted that pride might be the cause of his reluctance.

Garnett found him feeding the sparrows, but he desisted at the young man's approach, and said at once: "You will not thank me for bringing you all this distance."

"If that means that you are going to send me away with a refusal, I have come to spare you the necessity," Garnett answered.

Mr. Newell turned on him a glance of undisguised wonder, in which an undertone of disappointment might almost have been detected.

"Ah—they've got no use for me, after all?" he said ironically.

Garnett, in reply, related without comment his conversation with Hermione, and the message with which she had charged him. He remembered her words exactly and repeated them without modification, heedless of what they implied or revealed.

Mr. Newell listened with an immovable face, occasionally casting a crumb to his flock. When Garnett ended he asked: "Does her mother know of this?"

"Assuredly not!" cried Garnett with a movement of disgust.

"You must pardon me; but Mrs. Newell is a very ingenious woman." Mr. Newell shook out his remaining crumbs and turned thoughtfully toward Garnett.

"You believe it's quite clear to Hermione that these people will use my refusal as a pretext for backing out of the marriage?"

"Perfectly clear—she told me so herself."

"Doesn't she consider the young man rather chickenhearted?"

"No; he has already put up a big fight for her, and you know the French look at these things differently. He's only twenty-three and his marrying against his parents' approval is in itself an act of heroism."

"Yes; I believe they look at it that way," Mr. Newell assented. He rose and picked up the half-smoked cigar which he had laid on the bench beside him.

"What do they wear at these French weddings, anyhow? A dress-suit, isn't it?" he asked.

The question was such a surprise to Garnett that for the moment he could only stammer out—"You consent then? I may go and tell her?"

"You may tell my girl—yes." He gave a vague laugh and added: "One way or another, my wife always gets what she wants."

## VII

MR. NEWELL'S consent brought with it no accompanying concessions. In the first flush of his success Garnett had pictured himself as bringing together the father and daughter, and hovering in an attitude of benediction over a family group in which Mrs. Newell did not very distinctly figure.

But Mr. Newell's conditions were inflexible. He would "see the thing through" for his daughter's sake; but he stipulated that in the meantime there should be no meetings or farther communications of any kind. He agreed to be ready when Garnett called for him, at the appointed hour on the wedding-day; but until then he begged to be left alone. To this decision he adhered immovably, and when Garnett conveyed it to Hermione she accepted it with a deep look of understanding. As for Mrs. Newell she was too much engrossed in the nuptial preparations to give her husband another thought. She had gained her point, she had disarmed her foes, and in the first flush of success she had no time to remember by what means her victory had been won. Even Garnett's services received little recognition, unless he found them sufficiently compensated by the new look in Hermione's eyes.

The principal figures in Mrs. Newell's foreground were the Woolsey Hubbards and Baron Schenkelderff. With these she was in hourly consultation, and Mrs. Hubbard went about aureoled with the importance of her close connection with an "aristocratic marriage," and dazzled by the Baron's familiarity with the intricacies of the Almanach de Gotha. In his society and Mrs. Newell's, Mrs. Hubbard evidently felt that she had penetrated to the sacred precincts where "the right thing" flourished in its native soil. As for Hermione, her look of happiness had returned, but with an undertint of melancholy, visible perhaps only to Garnett, but to him always hauntingly present. Outwardly she sank back into her passive self, resigned to serve as the brilliant lay-figure on which Mrs. Newell hung the trophies of conquest. Preparations for the wedding were zealously pressed. Mrs. Newell knew the danger of giving people time to think things over, and her fears about her husband being allayed, she began to dread a new attempt at evasion on the part of the bridegroom's family.

"The sooner it's over the sounder I shall sleep!" she declared to Garnett; and all the mitigations of art could not conceal the fact that she was desperately in need of that restorative. There were moments, indeed, when he was sorrier for her than for her husband or her daughter; so black and unfathomable appeared the abyss into which she must slip back if she lost her hold on this last spar of safety.

But she did not lose her hold; his own experience, as well as her husband's declaration, might have told him that she always got what she wanted. How much she had wanted this particular thing was shown by the way in which, on the last day, when all peril was over, she bloomed out in renovated splendor. It gave Garnett a shivering sense of the ugliness of the alternative which had confronted her.

The day came; the showy coupé provided by Mrs. Newell presented itself punctually at Garnett's door, and the young man entered it and drove to the rue Panonceaux. It was a little melancholy back street, with lean old houses sweating rust and damp, and glimpses of pit-life gardens, black and sunless, between walls bristling with iron spikes. On the narrow pavement a blind man pottered along led by a red-eyed poodle: a little farther on a disheveled woman sat grinding coffee on the threshold of a *buvette*. The bridal carriage stopped before one of the doorways, with a clatter of hoofs and harness which drew the neighborhood to its windows, and Garnett started to mount the ill-smelling stairs to the fourth floor, on which he learned from the *concierge* that Mr. Newell lodged. But half-way up he met the latter descending, and they turned and went down together.

Hermione's parent wore his usual imperturbable look, and his eye seemed as full as ever of generalizations on human folly; but there was something oddly shrunken and submerged in his appearance, as though he had grown smaller or his clothes larger. And on the last hypothesis Garnett paused—for it became evident to him that Mr. Newell had hired his dress-suit.

Seated at the young man's side on the satin cushions, he remained silent while the carriage rolled smoothly and rapidly through the net-work of streets leading to the Boulevard Saint-Germain; only once he remarked, glancing at the elaborate fittings of the coupe: "Is this Mrs. Newell's carriage?"

"I believe so—yes," Garnett assented, with the guilty sense that in defining that lady's possessions it was impossible not to trespass on those of her friends.

Mr. Newell made no farther comment, but presently requested his companion to rehearse to him once more the exact duties which were to devolve on him during the coming ceremony. Having mastered these he remained silent, fixing a dry speculative eye on the panorama of the brilliant streets, till the carriage drew up at the entrance of Saint Philippe du Roule.

With the same air of composure he followed his guide through the mob of spectators, and up the crimson velvet steps, at the head of which, but for a word from Garnett, a formidable Suisse, glittering with cocked hat and mace, would have checked the advance of the small crumpled figure so oddly out of keeping with the magnificence of the bridal party. The French fashion prescribing that the family *cortège* shall follow the bride to the altar, the vestibule of the church was thronged with the participators in the coming procession; but if Mr. Newell felt any nervousness at his sudden projection into this unfamiliar group, nothing in his look or manner betrayed it. He stood beside Garnett till a white-favored carriage, dashing up to the church with a superlative glitter of highly groomed horseflesh and silver-plated harness, deposited the snowy apparition of the bride, supported by her mother; then, as Hermione entered the vestibule, he went forward quietly to meet her.

The girl, wrapped in the haze of her bridal veil, and a little confused, perhaps, by the anticipation of the meeting, paused a moment, as if in doubt, before the small oddly-clad figure which blocked her path—a horrible moment to Garnett, who felt a pang of misery at this satire on the infallibility of the filial instinct. He longed to make some sign, to break in some way the pause of uncertainty; but before he could move he saw Mrs. Newell give her daughter a sharp push, he saw a blush of compunction flood Hermione's face, and the girl, throwing back her veil, bent her tall head and flung her arms about her father.

Mr. Newell emerged unshaken from the embrace: it seemed to have no effect beyond giving an odder twist to his tie. He stood beside his daughter till the church doors were thrown open; then, at a sign from the verger, he gave her his arm, and the strange couple, with the long train of fashion and finery behind them, started on their march to the altar.

Garnett had already slipped into the church and secured a post of vantage which gave him a side-view over the assemblage. The building was thronged—Mrs. Newell had attained her ambition and given Hermione a smart wedding. Garnett's eye travelled curiously from one group to another—from the numerous representatives of the bridegroom's family, all stamped with the same air of somewhat dowdy distinction, the air of having had their thinking done for them for so long that they could no longer perform the act individually, and the heterogeneous company of Mrs. Newell's friends, who presented, on the opposite side of the nave, every variety of individual conviction in dress and conduct. Of the two groups the latter was decidedly the more interesting to Garnett, who observed that it comprised not only such recent acquisitions as the Woolsey Hubbards and the Baron, but also sundry more important figures which of late had faded to the verse of Mrs. Newell's horizon. Hermione's marriage had drawn them back, bad once more made her mother a social entity, had in short already accomplished the object for which it had been planned and executed.

And as he looked about him Garnett saw that all the other actors in the show faded into insignificance beside the dominant figure of Mrs. Newell, became mere marionettes pulled hither and thither by the hidden wires of her intention. One and all they were there to serve her ends and accomplish her purpose: Schenkelderff and the Hubbards to pay for the show, the bride and bridegroom to seal and symbolize her social rehabilitation, Garnett himself as the humble instrument adjusting the different parts of the complicated machinery, and her husband, finally, as the last stake in her game, the last asset on which she could draw to rebuild her fallen fortunes. At the thought Garnett was filled with a deep disgust for what the scene signified, and for his own share in it. He had been her tool and dupe like the others; if he imagined that he was serving Hermione, it was for her mother's ends that he had worked. What right had he to sentimentalize a marriage founded on such base connivances, and how could he have imagined that in so doing he was acting a disinterested part?

While these thoughts were passing through his mind the ceremony had already begun, and the principal personages in the drama were ranged before him in the row of crimson velvet chairs which fills the foreground of a Catholic marriage. Through the glow of lights and the perfumed haze about the altar, Garnett's eyes rested on the central figures of the group, and gradually the others disappeared from his view and his mind. After all, neither Mrs. Newell's schemes nor his own share in them could ever unsanctify Hermione's marriage. It was one more testimony to life's indefatigable renewals, to nature's secret of drawing fragrance from corruption; and as his eyes turned from the girl's illuminated presence to the resigned and stoical figure sunk in the adjoining chair, it occurred to him that he had perhaps worked better than he knew in placing them, if only for a moment, side by side.

## IN TRUST

IN THE GOOD DAYS, just after we all left college, Ned Halidon and I used to listen, laughing and smoking, while Paul Ambrose set forth his plans.

They were immense, these plans, involving, as it sometimes seemed, the ultimate aesthetic redemption of the whole human race; and provisionally restoring the sense of beauty to those unhappy millions of our fellow country-men who, as Ambrose movingly pointed out, now live and die in surroundings of unperceived and unmitigated ugliness.

"I want to bring the poor starved wretches back to their lost inheritance, to the divine past they've thrown away—I want to make 'em hate ugliness so that they'll smash nearly everything in sight," he would passionately exclaim, stretching his arms across the shabby black-walnut writing-table and shaking his thin consumptive fist in the fact of all the accumulated ugliness in the world.

"You might set the example by smashing that table," I once suggested with youthful brutality; and Paul, pulling himself up, cast a surprised glance at me, and then looked slowly about the parental library.

His parents were dead, and he had inherited the house in Seventeenth Street, where his grandfather Ambrose had lived in a setting of black walnut and pier glasses, giving Madeira dinners, and saying to his guests, as they rejoined the ladies across a florid waste of Aubusson: "This, sir, is Dabney's first study for the Niagara—the Grecian Slave in the bay window was executed for me in Rome twenty years ago by my old friend Ezra Stimpson—" by token of which he passed for a Maecenas in the New York of the 'forties,' and a poem had once been published in the Keepsake or the Book of Beauty "On a picture in the possession of Jonathan Ambrose, Esqre."

Since then the house had remained unchanged. Paul's father, a frugal liver and hard-headed manipulator of investments, did not inherit old Jonathan's artistic sensibilities, and was content to live and die in the unmodified black walnut and red rep of his predecessor. It was only in Paul that the grandfather's aesthetic faculty revived, and Mrs. Ambrose used often to say to her husband, as they watched the little pale-browed boy poring over an old number of the *Art Journal:* "Paul will know how to appreciate your father's treasures."

In recognition of these transmitted gifts Paul, on leaving Harvard, was sent to Paris with a tutor, and established in a studio in which nothing was ever done. He could not paint, and recognized the fact early enough to save himself much wasted labor and his friends many painful efforts in dissimulation. But he brought back a touching enthusiasm for the forms of beauty which an old civilization had revealed to him and an apostolic ardor in the cause of their dissemination.

He had paused in his harangue to take in my ill-timed parenthesis, and the color mounted slowly to his thin cheekbones.

"It *is* an ugly room," he owned, as though he had noticed the library for the first time.

The desk was carved at the angles with the heads of helmeted knights with long black-walnut moustaches. The red cloth top was worn threadbare, and patterned like a map with islands and peninsulas of ink; and in its center throned a massive bronze inkstand representing a Syrian maiden slumbering by a well beneath a palm tree.

"The fact is," I said, walking home that evening with Ned Halidon, "old Paul will never do anything, for the simple reason that he's too stingy."

Ned, who was an idealist, shook his handsome head. "It's not that, my dear fellow. He simply doesn't see things when they're too close to him. I'm glad you woke him up to that desk."

The next time I dined with Paul he said, when we entered the library, and I had gently rejected one of his cheap cigars in favor of a superior article of my own: "Look here, I've been looking round for a decent writing-table. I don't care, as a rule, to turn out old things, especially when they've done good service, but I see now that this is too monstrous—"

"For an apostle of beauty to write his evangel on," I agreed, "it is a little inappropriate, except as an awful warning."

Paul colored. "Well, but, my dear fellow, I'd no idea how much a table of this kind costs. I find I can't get anything decent—the plainest mahogany—under a hundred and fifty." He hung his head, and pretended not to notice that I was taking out my own cigar.

"Well, what's a hundred and fifty to you?" I rejoined. "You talk as if you had to live on a book-keeper's salary, with a large family to support."

He smiled nervously and twirled the ring on his thin finger. "I know—I know—that's all very well. But for twenty tables that I *don't* buy I can send some fellow abroad and unseal his eyes."

"Oh, hang it, do both!" I exclaimed impatiently; but the writing-table was never bought. The library remained as it was, and so did the contention between Halidon and myself, as to whether this inconsistent acceptance of his surroundings was due, on our friend's part, to a congenital inability to put his hand in his pocket, or to a real unconsciousness of the ugliness that happened to fall inside his point of vision.

"But he owned that the table was ugly," I agreed.

"Yes, but not till you'd called his attention to the fact; and I'll wager he became unconscious of it again as soon as your back was turned."

"Not before he'd had time to look at a lot of others, and make up his mind that he couldn't afford to buy one."

"That was just his excuse. He'd rather be thought mean than insensible to ugliness. But the truth is that he doesn't mind the table and is used to it. He knows his way about the drawers."

"But he could get another with the same number of drawers."

"Too much trouble," argued Halidon.

"Too much money," I persisted.

"Oh, hang it, now, if he were mean would he have founded three travelling scholarships and be planning this big Academy of Arts?"

"Well, he's mean to himself, at any rate."

"Yes; and magnificently, royally generous to all the world besides!" Halidon exclaimed with one of his great flushes of enthusiasm.

But if, on the whole, the last word remained with Halidon, and Ambrose's personal chariness seemed a trifling foible compared to his altruistic breadth of intention, yet neither of us could help observing, as time went on, that the habit of thrift was beginning to impede the execution of his schemes of art-philanthropy. The three travelling scholarships had been founded in the first blaze of his ardor, and before the personal management of his property had awakened in him the sleeping instincts of parsimony. But as his capital accumulated, and problems of investment and considerations of interest began to encroach upon his visionary hours, we saw a gradual arrest in the practical development of his plan.

"For every thousand dollars he talks of spending on his work, I believe he knocks off a cigar, or buys one less newspaper," Halidon grumbled affectionately; "but after all," he went on, with one of the quick revivals of optimism that gave a perpetual freshness to his spirit, "after all, it makes one admire him all the more when one sees such a nature condemned to be at war with the petty inherited instinct of greed."

Still, I could see it was a disappointment to Halidon that the great project of the Academy of Arts should languish on paper long after all its details had been discussed and settled to the satisfaction of the projector, and of the expert advisers he had called in council.

"He's quite right to do nothing in a hurry—to take advice and compare ideas and points of view—to collect and classify his material in advance," Halidon argued, in answer to a taunt of mine about Paul's perpetually reiterated plea that he was still waiting for So-and-so's report; "but now that the plan's mature—and such a plan! You'll grant it's magnificent?—I should think he'd burn to see it carried out, instead of pottering over it till his enthusiasm cools and the whole business turns stale on his hands."

That summer Ambrose went to Europe, and spent his holiday in a frugal walking-tour through Brittany. When he came back he seemed refreshed by his respite from business cares and from the interminable revision of his cherished scheme; while contact with the concrete manifestations of beauty had, as usual, renewed his flagging ardor.

"By Jove," he cried, "whenever I indulged my unworthy eyes in a long gaze at one of those big things—picture or church or statue—I kept saying to myself: 'You lucky devil, you, to be able to provide such a sight as that for eyes that can make some good use of it! Isn't it better to give fifty fellows a chance to paint or carve or build, than to be able to daub canvas or punch clay in a corner all by yourself?'"

"Well," I said, when he had worked off his first ebullition, "when is the foundation stone to be laid?"

His excitement dropped. "The foundation stone—?"

"When are you going to touch the electric button that sets the thing going?"

Paul, with his hands in his sagging pockets, began to pace the library hearth-rug—I can see him now, setting his shabby red slippers between its ramified cabbages.

"My dear fellow, there are one or two points to be considered still—one or two new suggestions I picked up over there—"

I sat silent, and he paused before me, flushing to the roots of his thin hair. "You think I've had time enough—that I ought to have put the thing through before this? I suppose you're right; I can see that even Ned Halidon thinks so; and he has always understood my difficulties better than you have."

This exasperated me. "Ned would have put it through years ago!" I broke out.

Paul pulled at his straggling moustache. "You mean he has more executive capacity? More—no, it's not that; he's not afraid to spend money, and I am!" he suddenly exclaimed.

He had never before alluded to this weakness to either of us, and I sat abashed, suffering from his evident distress. But he remained planted before me, his little legs wide apart, his eyes fixed on mine in an agony of voluntary self-exposure.

"That's my trouble, and I know it. Big sums frighten me—I can't look them in the face. By George, I wish Ned had the carrying out of this scheme—I wish he could spend my money for me!" His face was lit by the reflection of a passing thought. "Do you know, I shouldn't wonder if I dropped out of the running before either of you chaps, and in case I do I've half a mind to leave everything in trust to Halidon, and let him put the job through for me."

"Much better have your own fun with it," I retorted; but he shook his head, saying with a sigh as he turned away: "It's *not* fun to me—that's the worst of it."

Halidon, to whom I could not help repeating our talk, was amused and touched by his friend's thought.

"Heaven knows what will become of the scheme, if Paul doesn't live to carry it out. There are a lot of hungry Ambrose cousins who will make one gulp of his money, and never give a dollar to the work. Jove, it *would* be a fine thing to have the carrying out of such a plan—but he'll do it yet, you'll see he'll do it yet!" cried Ned, his old faith in his friend flaming up again through the wet blanket of fact.

## II

PAUL AMBROSE did not die and leave his fortune to Halidon, but the following summer he did something far more unexpected. He went abroad again, and came back married. Now our busy fancy had never seen Paul married. Even Ned recognized the vague unlikelihood of such a metamorphosis.

"He'd stick at the parson's fee—not to mention the best man's scarf-pin. And I should hate," Ned added sentimentally, "to see 'the touch of a woman's hand' desecrate the sublime ugliness of the ancestral home. Think of such a house made 'cozy'!"

But when the news came he would own neither to surprise nor to disappointment.

"Goodbye, poor Academy!" I exclaimed, tossing over the bridegroom's eight-page rhapsody to Halidon, who had received its duplicate by the same post.

"Now, why the deuce do you say that?" he growled. "I never saw such a beast as you are for imputing mean motives."

To defend myself from this accusation I put out my hand and recovered Paul's letter.

"Here: listen to this. 'Studying art in Paris when I met her—"the vision and the faculty divine, but lacking the accomplishment," etc. . . . A little ethereal profile, like one of Piero della Francesca's angels . . . not rich, thank heaven, *but not afraid of money*, and already enamored of my project for fertilizing my sterile millions . . . '"

"Well, why the deuce—?" Ned began again, as though I had convicted myself out of my friend's mouth; and I could only grumble obscurely: "It's all too pat."

He brushed aside my misgivings. "Thank heaven, she can't paint, any how. And now that I think of it, Paul's just the kind of chap who ought to have a dozen children."

"Ah, then indeed: goodbye, poor Academy!" I croaked.

The lady was lovely, of that there could be no doubt; and if Paul now for a time forgot the Academy, his doing so was but a vindication of his sex. Halidon had only a glimpse of the returning couple before he was himself snatched up in one of the chariots of adventure that seemed perpetually waiting at his door. This time he was going to the far East in the train of a "special mission," and his head was humming with new hopes and ardors; but he had time for a last word with me about Ambrose.

"You'll see—you'll see!" he summed up hopefully as we parted; and what I was to see was, of course, the crowning pinnacle of the Academy lifting itself against the horizon of the immediate future.

It was in the nature of things that I should, meanwhile, see less than formerly of the projector of that unrealized structure. Paul had a personal dread of society, but he wished to show his wife to the world, and I was not often a spectator on these occasions. Paul indeed, good fellow, tried to maintain the pretense of an unbroken intercourse, and to this end I was asked to dine now and then; but when I went I found guests of a new type, who, after dinner, talked of sport and stocks, while their host blinked at them silently through the smoke of his cheap cigars.

The first innovation that struck me was a sudden improvement in the quality of the cigars. Was this Daisy's doing? (Mrs. Ambrose was Daisy.) It was hard to tell—she produced her results so noiselessly. With her fair bent head and vague smile, she seemed to watch life flow by without, as yet, trusting anything of her own to its current. But she was watching, at any rate, and anything might come of that. Such modifications as she produced were as yet almost imperceptible to any but the trained observer. I saw that Paul wished her to be well dressed, but also that he suffered her to drive in a hired brougham, and to have her door opened by the raw-boned Celt who had bumped down the dishes on his bachelor table. The drawing-room curtains were renewed, but this change served only to accentuate the enormities of the carpet, and perhaps discouraged Mrs. Ambrose from farther experiments. At any rate, the desecrating touch that Halidon had affected to dread made no other inroads on the serried ugliness of the Ambrose interior.

In the early summer, when Ned returned, the Ambroses had flown to Europe again— and the Academy was still on paper.

"Well, what do you make of her?" the traveller asked, as we sat over our first dinner together.

"Too many things—and they don't hang together. Perhaps she's still in the chrysalis stage."

"Has Paul chucked the scheme altogether?"

"No. He sent for me and we had a talk about it just before he sailed."

"And what impression did you get?"

"That he had waited to send for me till just before he sailed."

"Oh, there you go again!" I offered no denial, and after a pause he asked: "Did *she* ever talk to you about it?"

"Yes. Once or twice—in snatches."

"Well—?"

"She thinks it all *too* beautiful. She would like to see beauty put within the reach of everyone."

"And the practical side—?"

"She says she doesn't understand business."

Halidon rose with a shrug. "Very likely you frightened her with your ugly sardonic grin."

"It's not my fault if my smile doesn't add to the sum-total of beauty."

"Well," he said, ignoring me, "next winter we shall see."

But the next winter did not bring Ambrose back. A brief line, written in November from the Italian lakes, told me that he had "a rotten cough," and that the doctors were packing him off to Egypt. Would I see the architects for him, and explain to the trustees? (The Academy already had trustees, and all the rest of its official hierarchy.) And would they all excuse his not writing more than a word? He was really too groggy—but a little warm weather would set him up again, and he would certainly come home in the spring.

He came home in the spring—in the hold of the ship, with his widow several decks above. The funeral services were attended by all the officers of the Academy, and by two of the young fellows who had won the travelling scholarships, and who shed tears of genuine grief when their benefactor was committed to the grave.

After that there was a pause of suspense—and then the newspapers announced that the late Paul Ambrose had left his entire estate to his widow. The board of the Academy dissolved like a summer cloud, and the secretary lighted his pipe for a year with the official paper of the still-born institution.

After a decent lapse of time I called at the house in Seventeenth Street, and found a man attaching a real-estate agent's sign to the window and a van-load of luggage backing away from the door. The care-taker told me that Mrs. Ambrose was sailing the next morning. Not long afterward I saw the library table with the helmeted knights standing before an auctioneer's door in University Place; and I looked with a pang at the familiar ink-stains, in which I had so often traced the geography of Paul's visionary world.

Halidon, who had picked up another job in the Orient, wrote me an elegiac letter on Paul's death, ending with—"And what about the Academy?" and for all answer I sent him a newspaper clipping recording the terms of the will, and another announcing the sale of the house and Mrs. Ambrose's departure for Europe.

Though Ned and I corresponded with tolerable regularity I received no direct answer to this communication till about eighteen months later, when he surprised me by a letter dated from Florence. It began: "Though she tells me you have never understood her—" and when I had reached that point I laid it down and stared out of my office window at the chimney-pots and the dirty snow on the roof.

"Ned Halidon and Paul's wife!" I murmured; and, incongruously enough, my next thought was: "I wish I'd bought the library table that day."

The letter went on with waxing eloquence: "I could not stand the money if it were not that, to her as well as to me, it represents the sacred opportunity of at last giving speech to his inarticulateness ..."

"Oh, damn it, they're too glib!" I muttered, dashing the letter down; then, controlling my unreasoning resentment, I read on. "You remember, old man, those words of his that you repeated to me three or four years ago: 'I've half a mind to leave my money in trust to Ned'? Well, it has come to me in trust—as if in mysterious fulfillment of his thought; and, oh, dear chap—" I dashed the letter down again, and plunged into my work.

### III

WON'T you own yourself a beast, dear boy?" Halidon asked me gently, one afternoon of the following spring.

I had escaped for a six weeks' holiday, and was lying outstretched beside him in a willow chair on the terrace of their villa above Florence.

My eyes turned from the happy vale at our feet to the illuminated face beside me. A little way off, at the other end of the terrace, Mrs. Halidon was bending over a pot of carnations on the balustrade.

"Oh, cheerfully," I assented.

"You see," he continued, glowing, "living here costs us next to nothing, and it was quite *her* idea, our founding that fourth scholarship in memory of Paul."

I had already heard of the fourth scholarship, but I may have betrayed my surprise at the plural pronoun, for the blood rose under Ned's sensitive skin, and he said with an embarrassed laugh: "Ah, she so completely makes me forget that it's not mine too."

"Well, the great thing is that you both think of it chiefly as his."

"Oh, chiefly—altogether. I should be no more than a wretched parasite if I didn't live first of all for that!"

Mrs. Halidon had turned and was advancing toward us with the slow step of leisurely enjoyment. The bud of her beauty had at last unfolded: her vague enigmatical gaze had given way to the clear look of the woman whose hand is on the clue of life.

"*She's* not living for anything but her own happiness," I mused, "and why in heaven's name should she? But Ned—"

"My wife," Halidon continued, his eyes following mine, "my wife feels it too, even more strongly. You know a woman's sensitiveness. She's—there's nothing she wouldn't do for his memory—because—in other ways. . . . You understand," he added, lowering his tone as she drew nearer, "that as soon as the child is born we mean to go home for good, and take up his work—Paul's work."

Mrs. Halidon recovered slowly after the birth of her child: the return to America was deferred for six months, and then again for a whole year. I heard of the Halidons as established first at Biarritz, then in Rome. The second summer Ned wrote me a line from St. Moritz. He said the place agreed so well with his wife—who was still delicate—that they were "thinking of building a house there: a mere cleft in the rocks, to hide our happiness in when it becomes too exuberant"—and the rest of the letter, very properly, was filled with a rhapsody upon his little daughter. He spoke of her as Paula.

The following year the Halidons reappeared in New York, and I heard with surprise that they had taken the Brereton house for the winter.

"Well, why not?" I argued with myself. "After all, the money is hers: as far as I know the will didn't even hint at a restriction. Why should I expect a pretty woman with two children" (for now there was an heir) "to spend her fortune on a visionary scheme that its originator hadn't the heart to carry out?"

"Yes," cried the devil's advocate—"but Ned?"

My first impression of Halidon was that he had thickened—thickened all through. He was heavier, physically, with the ruddiness of good living rather than of hard training; he spoke more deliberately, and had less frequent bursts of subversive enthusiasm. Well, he was a father, a householder—yes, and a capitalist now. It was fitting that his manner should show a sense of these responsibilities. As for Mrs. Halidon, it was evident that the only responsibilities she was conscious of were those of the handsome woman and the accomplished hostess. She was handsomer than ever, with her two babies at her knee—perfect mother as she was perfect wife. Poor Paul! I wonder if he ever dreamed what a flower was hidden in the bud?

Not long after their arrival, I dined alone with the Halidons, and lingered on to smoke with Ned while his wife went alone to the opera. He seemed dull and out of sorts, and complained of a twinge of gout.

"Fact is, I don't get enough exercise—I must look about for a horse."

He had gone afoot for a good many years, and kept his clear skin and quick eye on that homely regimen—but I had to remind myself that, after all, we were both older; and also that the Halidons had champagne every evening.

"How do you like these cigars? They're some I've just got out from London, but I'm not quite satisfied with them myself," he grumbled, pushing toward me the silver box and its attendant taper.

I leaned to the flame, and our eyes met as I lit my cigar. Ned flushed and laughed uneasily. "Poor Paul! Were you thinking of those execrable weeds of his?—I wonder how I knew you were? Probably because I have been wanting to talk to you of our plan—I sent Daisy off alone so that we might have a quiet evening. Not that she isn't interested, only the technical details bore her."

I hesitated. "Are there many technical details left to settle?"

Halidon pushed his armchair back from the fire-light, and twirled his cigar between his fingers. "I didn't suppose there were till I began to look into things a little more closely. You know I never had much of a head for business, and it was chiefly with you that Paul used to go over the figures."

"The figures—?"

"There it is, you see." He paused. "Have you any idea how much this thing is going to cost?"

"Approximately, yes."

"And have you any idea how much we—how much Daisy's fortune amounts to?"

"None whatever," I hastened to assert.

He looked relieved. "Well, we simply can't do it—and live."

"Live?"

"Paul didn't *live*," he said impatiently. "I can't ask a woman with two children to think of—hang it, she's under no actual obligation—" He rose and began to walk the floor. Presently he paused and halted in front of me, defensively, as Paul had once done years before. "It's not that I've lost the sense of my obligation—it grows keener with the growth of my happiness; but my position's a delicate one—"

"Ah, my dear fellow—"

"You *do* see it? I knew you would." (Yes, he was duller!) "That's the point. I can't strip my wife and children to carry out a plan—a plan so nebulous that even its inventor.... The long and short of it is that the whole scheme must be re-studied, reorganized. Paul lived in a world of dreams."

I rose and tossed my cigar into the fire. "There were some things he never dreamed of," I said.

Halidon rose too, facing me uneasily. "You mean—?"

"That *you* would taunt him with not having spent that money."

He pulled himself up with darkening brows; then the muscles of his forehead relaxed, a flush suffused it, and he held out his hand in boyish penitence.

"I stand a good deal from you," he said.

He kept up his idea of going over the Academy question—threshing it out once for all, as he expressed it; but my suggestion that we should provisionally resuscitate the extinct board did not meet with his approval.

"Not till the whole business is settled. I shouldn't have the face—Wait till I can go to them and say: 'We're laying the foundation stone on such a day.'"

We had one or two conferences, and Ned speedily lost himself in a maze of figures. His nimble fancy was recalcitrant to mental discipline, and he excused his inattention with the plea that he had no head for business.

"All I know is that it's a colossal undertaking, and that short of living on bread and water—" and then we turned anew to the hard problem of retrenchment.

At the close of the second conference we fixed a date for a third, when Ned's business adviser was to be called in; but before the day came, I learned casually that the Halidons had gone south. Some weeks later Ned wrote me from Florida, apologizing for his remissness. They had rushed off suddenly—his wife had a cough, he explained.

When they returned in the spring, I heard that they had bought the Brereton house, for what seemed to my inexperienced ears a very large sum. But Ned, whom I met one day at the club, explained to me convincingly that it was really the most economical thing they could do. "You don't understand about such things, dear boy, living in your Diogenes tub; but wait till there's a Mrs. Diogenes. I can assure you it's a lot cheaper than building, which is what Daisy would have preferred, and of course," he added, his color rising as our eyes met, "of course, once the Academy's going, I shall have to make my head-quarters here; and I suppose even you won't grudge me a roof over my head."

The Brereton roof was a vast one, with a marble balustrade about it; and I could quite understand, without Ned's halting explanation, that "under the circumstances" it would be necessary to defer what he called "our work—" "Of course, after we've rallied from this amputation, we shall grow fresh supplies—I mean my wife's investments will," he laughingly corrected, "and then we'll have no big outlays ahead and shall know exactly where we stand. After all, my dear fellow, charity begins at home!"

## IV

THE Halidons floated off to Europe for the summer. In due course their return was announced in the social chronicle, and walking up Fifth Avenue one afternoon I saw the back of the Brereton house sheathed in scaffolding, and realized that they were adding a wing.

I did not look up Halidon, nor did I hear from him till the middle of the winter. Once or twice, meanwhile, I had seen him in the back of his wife's opera box; but Mrs. Halidon had grown so resplendent that she reduced her handsome husband to a supernumerary. In January the papers began to talk of the Halidon ball; and in due course I received a card for it. I was not a frequenter of balls, and had no intention of going to this one; but when the day came some obscure impulse moved me to set aside my rule, and toward midnight I presented myself at Ned's illuminated portals.

I shall never forget his look when I accosted him on the threshold of the big new ballroom. With celibate egoism I had rather fancied he would be gratified by my departure from custom; but one glance showed me my mistake. He smiled warmly, indeed, and threw into his hand-clasp an artificial energy of welcome—"You of all people—my dear fellow! Have you seen Daisy?"—but the look behind the smile made me feel cold in the crowded room.

Nor was Mrs. Halidon's greeting calculated to restore my circulation. "Have you come to spy on us?" her frosty smile seemed to say; and I crept home early, wondering if she had not found me out.

It was the following week that Halidon turned up one day in my office. He looked pale and thinner, and for the first time I noticed a dash of gray in his hair. I was startled at the change in him, but I reflected that it was nearly a year since we had looked at each other by daylight, and that my shaving-glass had doubtless a similar tale to tell.

He fidgeted about the office, told me a funny story about his little boy, and then dropped into a chair.

"Look here," he said, "I want to go into business."

"Business?" I stared.

"Well, why not? I suppose men have gone to work, even at my age, and not made a complete failure of it. The fact is, I want to make some money." He paused, and added: "I've heard of an opportunity to pick up for next to nothing a site for the Academy, and if I could lay my hands on a little cash—"

"Do you want to speculate?" I interposed.

"Heaven forbid! But don't you see that, if I had a fixed job—so much a quarter—I could borrow the money and pay it off gradually?"

I meditated upon this astounding proposition. "Do you really think it's wise to buy a site before—"

"Before what?"

"Well—seeing ahead a little?"

His face fell for a moment, but he rejoined cheerfully: "It's an exceptional chance, and after all, I *shall* see ahead if I can get regular work. I can put by a little every month, and by and bye, when our living expenses diminish, my wife means to come forward—her idea would be to give the building—"

He broke off and drummed on the table, waiting nervously for me to speak. He did not say on what grounds he still counted on a diminution of his household expenses, and I had not the cruelty to press this point; but I murmured, after a moment: "I think you're right—I should try to buy the land."

We discussed his potentialities for work, which were obviously still an unknown quantity, and the conference ended in my sending him to a firm of real-estate brokers who were looking out for a partner with a little money to invest. Halidon had a few thousands of his own, which he decided to embark in the venture; and thereafter, for the remaining months of the winter, he appeared punctually at a desk in the brokers' office, and sketched plans of the Academy on the back of their business paper. The site for the future building had meanwhile been bought, and I rather deplored the publicity which Ned gave to the fact; but, after all, since this publicity served to commit him more deeply, to pledge him conspicuously to the completion of his task, it was perhaps a wise instinct of self-coercion that had prompted him.

It was a dull winter in realty, and toward spring, when the market began to revive, one of the Halidon children showed symptoms of a delicate throat, and the fashionable doctor who humored the family ailments counseled—nay, commanded—a prompt flight to the Mediterranean.

"He says a New York spring would be simply criminal—and as for those ghastly southern places, my wife won't hear of them; so we're off. But I shall be back in July, and I mean to stick to the office all summer."

He was true to his word, and reappeared just as all his friends were deserting town. For two torrid months he sat at his desk, drawing fresh plans of the Academy, and waiting for the wind-fall of a "big deal"; but in September he broke down from the effect of the unwonted confinement, and his indignant wife swept him off to the mountains.

"Why Ned should work when we have the money—I wish he would sell that wretched piece of land!" And sell it he did one day: I chanced on a record of the transaction in the realty column of the morning paper. He afterward explained the sale to me at length. Owing to some spasmodic effort at municipal improvement, there had been an unforeseen rise in the adjoining property, and it would have been foolish—yes, I agreed that it would have been foolish. He had made $10,000 on the sale, and that would go toward paying off what he had borrowed for the original purchase. Meanwhile he could be looking about for another site.

Later in the winter he told me it was a bad time to look. His position in the real-estate business enabled him to follow the trend of the market, and that trend was obstinately upward. But of course there would be a reaction—and he was keeping his eyes open.

As the resuscitated Academy scheme once more fell into abeyance, I saw Halidon less and less frequently; and we had not met for several months, when one day of June, my morning paper startled me with the announcement that the President had appointed Edward Halidon of New York to be Civil Commissioner of our newly acquired Eastern possession, the Mañana Islands. "The unhealthy climate of the islands, and the defective sanitation of the towns, make it necessary that vigorous measures should be taken to protect the health of the American citizens established there, and it is believed that Mr. Halidon's large experience of Eastern life and well-known energy of character—" I read the paragraph twice; then I dropped the paper, and projected myself through the subway to Halidon's office. But he was not there; he had not been there for a month. One of the clerks believed he was in Washington.

"It's true, then!" I said to myself. "But Mrs. Halidon in the Mañanas—?"

A day or two later Ned appeared in my office. He looked better than when we had last met, and there was a determined line about his lips.

"My wife? Heaven forbid! You don't suppose I should think of taking her? But the job is a tremendously interesting one, and it's the kind of work I believe I can do—the only kind," he added, smiling rather ruefully.

"But my dear Ned—"

He faced me with a look of quiet resolution. "I think I've been through all the *buts*. It's an infernal climate, of course, but then I am used to the East—I know what precautions to take. And it would be a big thing to clean up that Augean stable."

"But consider your wife and children—"

He met this with deliberation. "I *have* considered my children—that's the point. I don't want them to be able to say, when they look back: 'He was content to go on living on that money—'"

"My dear Ned—"

"That's the one thing they *shan't* say of me," he pressed on vehemently. "I've tried other ways—but I'm no good at business. I see now that I shall never make money enough to carry out the scheme myself; but at least I can clear out, and not go on being *his* pensioner—seeing his dreams turned into horses and carpets and clothes—"

He broke off, and leaning on my desk hid his face in his hands. When he looked up again his flush of wrath had subsided.

"Just understand me—it's not *her* fault. Don't fancy I'm trying for an instant to shift the blame. A woman with children simply obeys the instinct of her sex; she puts them first—and I wouldn't have it otherwise. As far as she's concerned there were no conditions attached—there's no reason why she should make any sacrifice." He paused, and added painfully: "The trouble is, I can't make her see that I am differently situated."

"But, Ned, the climate—what are you going to gain by chucking yourself away?"

He lifted his brows. "That's a queer argument from *you*. And, besides, I'm up to the tricks of all those ague-holes. And I've *got* to live, you see: I've got something to put through." He saw my look of enquiry, and added with a shy, poignant laugh—how I hear it still!—: "I don't mean only the job in hand, though that's enough in itself; but Paul's work—you understand.—It won't come in *my* day, of course—I've got to accept that— but my boy's a splendid chap" (the boy was three), "and I tell you what it is, old man, I believe when he grows up *he'll put it through*."

Halidon went to the Mañanas, and for two years the journals brought me incidental reports of the work he was accomplishing. He certainly had found a job to his hand: official words of commendation rang through the country, and there were lengthy newspaper leaders on the efficiency with which our representative was prosecuting his task in that lost corner of our colonies. Then one day a brief paragraph announced his death—"one of the last victims of the pestilence he had so successfully combated."

That evening, at my club, I heard men talking of him. One said: "What's the use of a fellow wasting himself on a lot of savages?" and another wiseacre opined: "Oh, he went off because there was friction at home. A fellow like that, who knew the East, would have got through all right if he'd taken the proper precautions. I saw him before he left, and I never saw a man look less as if he wanted to live."

I turned on the last speaker, and my voice made him drop his lighted cigar on his complacent knuckles.

"I never knew a man," I exclaimed, "who had better reasons for wanting to live!"

A handsome youth mused: "Yes, his wife is very beautiful—but it doesn't follow—"
And then someone nudged him, for they knew I was Halidon's friend.

## THE PRETEXT

MRS. RANSOM, when the front door had closed on her visitor, passed with a spring from the drawing-room to the narrow hall, and thence up the narrow stairs to her bedroom.

Though slender, and still light of foot, she did not always move so quickly: hitherto, in her life, there had not been much to hurry for, save the recurring domestic tasks that compel haste without fostering elasticity; but some impetus of youth revived, communicated to her by her talk with Guy Dawnish, now found expression in her girlish flight upstairs, her girlish impatience to bolt herself into her room with her throbs and her blushes.

Her blushes? Was she really blushing?

She approached the cramped eagle-topped mirror above her plain prim dressing-table: just such a meager concession to the weakness of the flesh as every old-fashioned house in Wentworth counted among its relics. The face reflected in this unflattering surface—for even the mirrors of Wentworth erred on the side of depreciation—did not seem, at first sight, a suitable theatre for the display of the tenderer emotions, and its owner blushed more deeply as the fact was forced upon her.

Her fair hair had grown too thin—it no longer quite hid the blue veins in her candid forehead—a forehead that one seemed to see turned toward professorial desks, in large bare halls where a snowy winter light fell uncompromisingly on rows of "thoughtful women." Her mouth was thin, too, and a little strained; her lips were too pale; and there were lines in the corners of her eyes. It was a face which had grown middle-aged while it waited for the joys of youth.

Well—but if she could still blush? Instinctively she drew back a little, so that her scrutiny became less microscopic, and the pretty lingering pink threw a veil over her pallor, the hollows in her temples, the faint wrinkles of inexperience about her lips and eyes. How a little color helped! It made her eyes so deep and shining. She saw now why bad women rouged. . . . Her redness deepened at the thought.

But suddenly she noticed for the first time that the collar of her dress was cut too low. It showed the shrunken lines of the throat. She rummaged feverishly in a tidy scentless drawer, and snatching out a bit of black velvet, bound it about her neck. Yes—that was better. It gave her the relief she needed. Relief—contrast—that was it! She had never had any, either in her appearance or in her setting. She was as flat as the pattern of the wall-paper—and so was her life. And all the people about her had the same look. Wentworth was the kind of place where husbands and wives gradually grew to resemble each other—one or two of her friends, she remembered, had told her lately that she and Ransom were beginning to look alike. . . .

But why had she always, so tamely, allowed her aspect to conform to her situation? Perhaps a gayer exterior would have provoked a brighter fate. Even now—she turned back to the glass, loosened the tight strands of hair above her brow, ran the fine end of the comb under them with a rapid frizzing motion, and then disposed them, more lightly and amply, above her eager face. Yes—it was really better; it made a difference. She smiled at herself with a timid coquetry, and her lips seemed rosier as she smiled. Then she laid down the comb and the smile faded. It made a difference, certainly—but was it right to try to make one's hair look thicker and wavier than it really was? Between that and rouging the ethical line seemed almost impalpable, and the specter of her rigid New England ancestry rose reprovingly before her. She was sure that none of her grandmothers had ever simulated a curl or encouraged a blush. A blush, indeed! What had any of them ever had to blush for in all their frozen lives? And what, in Heaven's name, had she? She sat down in the stiff mahogany rocking-chair beside her work-table and tried to collect herself. From childhood she had been taught to "collect herself"—but never before had her small sensations and aspirations been so widely scattered, diffused over so vague and uncharted an expanse. Hitherto they had lain in neatly sorted and easily accessible bundles on the high shelves of a perfectly ordered moral consciousness. And now—now that for the first time they *needed* collecting—now that the little winged and scattered bits of self were dancing madly down the vagrant winds of fancy, she knew no spell to call them to the fold again. The best way, no doubt—if only her bewilderment permitted—was to go back to the beginning—the beginning, at least, of to-day's visit—to recapitulate, word for word and look for look. . . .

She clasped her hands on the arms of the chair, checked its swaying with a firm thrust of her foot, and fixed her eyes upon the inward vision. . . .

To begin with, what had made to-day's visit so different from the others? It became suddenly vivid to her that there had been many, almost daily, others, since Guy Dawnish's coming to Wentworth. Even the previous winter—the winter of his arrival from England—his visits had been numerous enough to make Wentworth aware that—very naturally—Mrs. Ransom was "looking after" the stray young Englishman committed to her husband's care by an eminent Q. C. whom the Ransoms had known on one of their brief London visits, and with whom Ransom had since maintained professional relations. All this was in the natural order of things, as sanctioned by the social code of Wentworth. Every one was kind to Guy Dawnish—some rather importunately so, as Margaret Ransom had smiled to observe—but it was recognized as fitting that she should be kindest, since he was in a sense her property, since his people in England, by profusely acknowledging her kindness, had given it the domestic sanction without which, to Wentworth, any social relation between the sexes remained unhallowed and to be viewed askance. Yes! And even this second winter, when the visits had become so much more frequent, so admitted a part of the day's routine, there had not been, from any one, a hint of surprise or of conjecture.

Mrs. Ransom smiled with a faint bitterness. She was protected by her age, no doubt—her age and her past, and the image her mirror gave back to her....

Her door handle turned suddenly, and the bolt's resistance was met by an impatient knock.

"Margaret!"

She started up, her brightness fading, and unbolted the door to admit her husband.

"Why are you locked in? Why, you're not dressed yet!" he exclaimed.

It was possible for Ransom to reach his dressing-room by a slight circuit through the passage; but it was characteristic of the relentless domesticity of their relation that he chose, as a matter of course, the directer way through his wife's bedroom. She had never before been disturbed by this practice, which she accepted as inevitable, but had merely adapted her own habits to it, delaying her hasty toilet till he was safely in his room, or completing it before she heard his step on the stair; since a scrupulous traditional prudery had miraculously survived this massacre of all the privacies.

"Oh, I shan't dress this evening—I shall just have some tea in the library after you've gone," she answered absently. "Your things are laid out," she added, rousing herself.

He looked surprised. "The dinner's at seven. I suppose the speeches will begin at nine. I thought you were coming to hear them."

She wavered. "I don't know. I think not. Mrs. Sperry's ill, and I've no one else to go with."

He glanced at his watch. "Why not get hold of Dawnish? Wasn't he here just now? Why didn't you ask him?"

She turned toward her dressing table, and straightened the comb and brush with a nervous hand. Her husband had given her, that morning, two tickets for the ladies' gallery in Hamblin Hall, where the great public dinner of the evening was to take place—a banquet offered by the faculty of Wentworth to visitors of academic eminence—and she had meant to ask Dawnish to go with her: it had seemed the most natural thing to do, till the end of his visit came, and then, after all, she had not spoken. . . .

"It's too late now," she murmured, bending over her pin cushion.

"Too late? Not if you telephone him."

Her husband came toward her, and she turned quickly to face him, lest he should suspect her of trying to avoid his eye. To what duplicity was she already committed!

Ransom laid a friendly hand on her arm: "Come along, Margaret. You know I speak for the bar." She was aware, in his voice, of a little note of surprise at his having to remind her of this.

"Oh, yes. I meant to go, of course—"

"Well, then—" He opened his dressing-room door, and caught a glimpse of the retreating house-maid's skirt. "Here's Maria now. Maria! Call up Mr. Dawnish—at Mrs. Creswell's, you know. Tell him Mrs. Ransom wants him to go with her to hear the speeches this evening—the *speeches*, you understand?—and he's to call for her at a quarter before nine."

Margaret heard the Irish "Yessir" on the stairs, and stood motionless, while her husband added loudly: "And bring me some towels when you come up." Then he turned back into his wife's room.

"Why, it would be a thousand pities for Guy to miss this. He's so interested in the way we do things over here—and I don't know that he's ever heard me speak in public." Again the slight note of fatuity! Was it possible that Ransom was fatuous?

He paused in front of her, his short-sighted unobservant glance concentrating itself unexpectedly on her face.

"You're not going like that, are you?" he asked, with glaring eye-glasses.

"Like what?" she faltered, lifting a conscious hand to the velvet at her throat.

"With your hair in such a fearful mess. Have you been shampooing it? You look like the Brant girl at the end of a tennis match."

The Brant girl was their horror—the horror of all right-thinking Wentworth; a laced, whale-boned, frizzle-headed, high-heeled daughter of iniquity, who came—from New York, of course—on long, disturbing, tumultuous visits to a Wentworth aunt, working havoc among the freshmen, and leaving, when she departed, an angry wake of criticism that ruffled the social waters for weeks. *She*, too, had tried her hand at Guy—with ludicrous unsuccess. And now, to be compared to her—to be accused of looking "New Yorky!" Ah, there are times when husbands are obtuse; and Ransom, as he stood there, thick and yet juiceless, in his dry legal middle age, with his wiry dust-colored beard, and his perpetual *pince-nez*, seemed to his wife a sudden embodiment of this traditional attribute. Not that she had ever fancied herself, poor soul, a "*femme incomprise*." She had, on the contrary, prided herself on being understood by her husband, almost as much as on her own complete comprehension of him. Wentworth laid a good deal of stress on "motives"; and Margaret Ransom and her husband had dwelt in a complete community of motive. It had been the proudest day of her life when, without consulting her, he had refused an offer of partnership in an eminent New York firm because he preferred the distinction of practicing in Wentworth, of being known as the legal representative of the University. Wentworth, in fact, had always been the bond between the two; they were united in their veneration for that estimable seat of learning, and in their modest yet vivid consciousness of possessing its tone. The Wentworth "tone" is unmistakable: it permeates every part of the social economy, from the coiffure of the ladies to the preparation of the food. It has its sumptuary laws as well as its curriculum of learning. It sits in judgment not only on its own townsmen but on the rest of the world—enlightening, criticizing, ostracizing a heedless universe—and non-conformity to Wentworth standards involves obliteration from Wentworth's consciousness.

In a world without traditions, without reverence, without stability, such little expiring centers of prejudice and precedent make an irresistible appeal to those instincts for which a democracy has neglected to provide. Wentworth, with its "tone," its backward references, its inflexible aversions and condemnations, its hard moral outline preserved intact against a whirling background of experiment, had been all the poetry and history of Margaret Ransom's life. Yes, what she had really esteemed in her husband was the fact of his being so intense an embodiment of Wentworth; so long and closely identified, for instance, with its legal affairs, that he was almost a part of its university existence, that of course, at a college banquet, he would inevitably speak for the bar!

It was wonderful of how much consequence all this had seemed till now. . . .

## II

WHEN, punctually at ten minutes to seven, her husband had emerged from the house, Margaret Ransom remained seated in her bedroom, addressing herself anew to the difficult process of self-collection. As an aid to this endeavor, she bent forward and looked out of the window, following Ransom's figure as it receded down the elm-shaded street. He moved almost alone between the prim flowerless grass-plots, the white porches, the protrusion of irrelevant shingled gables, which stamped the empty street as part of an American college town. She had always been proud of living in Hill Street, where the university people congregated, proud to associate her husband's retreating back, as he walked daily to his office, with backs literary and pedagogic, backs of which it was whispered, for the edification of duly impressed visitors: "Wait till that old boy turns—that's so-and-so."

This had been her world, a world destitute of personal experience, but filled with a rich sense of privilege and distinction, of being not as those millions were who, denied the inestimable advantage of living at Wentworth, pursued elsewhere careers foredoomed to futility.

And now—!

She rose and turned to her work table where she had dropped, on entering, the handful of photographs that Guy Dawnish had left with her. While he sat so close, pointing out and explaining, she had hardly taken in the details; but now, on the full tones of his low young voice, they came back with redoubled distinctness. This was Guise Abbey, his uncle's place in Wiltshire, where, under his grandfather's rule, Guy's own boyhood had been spent: a long gabled Jacobean facade, many-chimneyed, ivy-draped, overhung (she felt sure) by the boughs of a venerable rookery. And in this other picture— the walled garden at Guise—that was his uncle, Lord Askern, a hale gouty-looking figure, planted robustly on the terrace, a gun on his shoulder and a couple of setters at his feet. And here was the river below the park, with Guy "punting" a girl in a flapping hat— how Margaret hated the flap that hid the girl's face! And here was the tennis-court, with Guy among a jolly cross-legged group of youths in flannels, and pretty girls about the tea-table under the big lime: in the center the curate handing bread and butter, and in the middle distance a footman approaching with more cups.

Margaret raised this picture closer to her eyes, puzzling, in the diminished light, over the face of the girl nearest to Guy Dawnish—bent above him in profile, while he laughingly lifted his head. No hat hid this profile, which stood out clearly against the foliage behind it.

"And who is that handsome girl?" Margaret had said, detaining the photograph as he pushed it aside, and struck by the fact that, of the whole group, he had left only this member unnamed.

"Oh, only Gwendolen Matcher—I've always known her—. Look at this: the almshouses at Guise. Aren't they jolly?"

And then—without her having had the courage to ask if the girl in the punt were also Gwendolen Matcher—they passed on to photographs of his rooms at Oxford, of a cousin's studio in London—one of Lord Askern's grandsons was "artistic"—of the rose-hung cottage in Wales to which, on the old Earl's death, his daughter-in-law, Guy's mother, had retired.

Every one of the photographs opened a window on the life Margaret had been trying to picture since she had known him—a life so rich, so romantic, so packed—in the mere casual vocabulary of daily life—with historic reference and poetic allusion, that she felt almost oppressed by this distant whiff of its air. The very words he used fascinated and bewildered her. He seemed to have been born into all sorts of connections, political, historical, official, that made the Ransom situation at Wentworth as featureless as the top shelf of a dark closet. Someone in the family had "asked for the Chiltern Hundreds"—one uncle was an Elder Brother of the Trinity House—someone else was the Master of a College—someone was in command at Devonport—the Army, the Navy, the House of Commons, the House of Lords, the most venerable seats of learning, were all woven into the dense background of this young man's light unconscious talk. For the unconsciousness was unmistakable. Margaret was not without experience of the transatlantic visitor who sounds loud names and evokes reverberating connections. The poetry of Guy Dawnish's situation lay in the fact that it was so completely a part of early associations and accepted facts. Life was like that in England—in Wentworth of course (where he had been sent, through his uncle's influence, for two years' training in the neighboring electrical works at Smedden)—in Wentworth, though "immensely jolly," it was different. The fact that he was qualifying to be an electrical engineer—with the hope of a secretaryship at the London end of the great Smedden Company—that, at best, he was returning home to a life of industrial "grind," this fact, though avowedly a bore, did not disconnect him from that brilliant pinnacled past, that many-faceted life in which the brightest episodes of the whole body of English fiction seemed collectively reflected. Of course he would have to work—younger sons' sons almost always had to—but his uncle Askern (like Wentworth) was "immensely jolly," and Guise always open to him, and his other uncle, the Master, a capital old boy too—and in town he could always put up with his clever aunt, Lady Caroline Duckett, who had made a "beastly marriage" and was horribly poor, but who knew everybody jolly and amusing, and had always been particularly kind to him.

It was not—and Margaret had not, even in her own thoughts, to defend herself from the imputation—it was not what Wentworth would have called the "material side" of her friend's situation that captivated her. She was austerely proof against such appeals: her enthusiasms were all of the imaginative order. What subjugated her was the unexampled prodigality with which he poured for her the same draught of tradition of which Wentworth held out its little teacupful. He besieged her with a million Wentworths in one—saying, as it were: "All these are mine for the asking—and I choose you instead!"

For this, she told herself somewhat dizzily, was what it came to—the summing-up toward which her conscientious efforts at self-collection had been gradually pushing her: with all this in reach, Guy Dawnish was leaving Wentworth reluctantly.

"I *was* a bit lonely here at first—but *now!"* And again: "It will be jolly, of course, to see them all again—but there are some things one doesn't easily give up...."

If he had known only Wentworth, it would have been wonderful enough that he should have chosen her out of all Wentworth—but to have known that other life, and to set her in the balance against it—poor Margaret Ransom, in whom, at the moment, nothing seemed of weight but her years! Ah, it might well produce, in nerves and brain, and poor unpracticed pulses, a flushed tumult of sensation, the rush of a great wave of life, under which memory struggled in vain to reassert itself, to particularize again just what his last words—the very last—had been. . . .

When consciousness emerged, quivering, from this retrospective assault, it pushed Margaret Ransom—feeling herself a mere leaf in the blast—toward the writing-table from which her innocent and voluminous correspondence habitually flowed. She had a letter to write now—much shorter but more difficult than any she had ever been called on to indite.

"Dear Mr. Dawnish," she began, "since telephoning you just now I have decided not—"

Maria's voice, at the door, announced that tea was in the library: "And I s'pose it's the brown silk you'll wear to the speaking?"

In the usual order of the Ransom existence, its mistress's toilet was performed unassisted; and the mere enquiry—at once friendly and deferential—projected, for Margaret, a strong light on the importance of the occasion. That she should answer: "But I am not going," when the going was so manifestly part of a household solemnity about which the thoughts below stairs fluttered in proud participation; that in face of such participation she should utter a word implying indifference or hesitation—nay, revealing herself the transposed, uprooted thing she had been on the verge of becoming; to do this was—well! infinitely harder than to perform the alternative act of tearing up the sheet of note-paper under her reluctant pen.

Yes, she said, she would wear the brown silk. . . .

## III

ALL the heat and glare from the long illuminated table, about which the fumes of many courses still hung in a savory fog, seemed to surge up to the ladies' gallery, and concentrate themselves in the burning cheeks of a slender figure withdrawn behind the projection of a pillar.

It never occurred to Margaret Ransom that she was sitting in the shade. She supposed that the full light of the chandeliers was beating on her face—and there were moments when it seemed as though all the heads about the great horse-shoe below, bald, shaggy, sleek, close-thatched, or thinly latticed, were equipped with an additional pair of eyes, set at an angle which enabled them to rake her face as relentlessly as the electric burners.

In the lull after a speech, the gallery was fluttering with the rustle of programs consulted, and Mrs. Sheff (the Brant girl's aunt) leaned forward to say enthusiastically: "And now we're to hear Mr. Ransom!"

A louder buzz rose from the table, and the heads (without relaxing their upward vigilance) seemed to merge, and flow together, like an attentive flood, toward the upper end of the horse-shoe, where all the threads of Margaret Ransom's consciousness were suddenly drawn into what seemed a small speck, no more—a black speck that rose, hung in air, dissolved into gyrating gestures, became distended, enormous, preponderant—became her husband "speaking."

"It's the heat—" Margaret gasped, pressing her handkerchief to her whitening lips, and finding just strength enough left to push back farther into the shadow.

She felt a touch on her arm. "It is horrible—shall we go?" a voice suggested; and, "Yes, yes, let us go," she whispered, feeling, with a great throb of relief, *that* to be the only possible, the only conceivable, solution. To sit and listen to her husband *now*—how could she ever have thought she could survive it? Luckily, under the lingering hubbub from below, his opening words were inaudible, and she had only to run the gauntlet of sympathetic feminine glances, shot after her between waving fans and programs, as, guided by Guy Dawnish, she managed to reach the door. It was really so hot that even Mrs. Sheff was not much surprised—till long afterward. . . .

The winding staircase was empty, half dark and blessedly silent. In a committee room below Dawnish found the inevitable water jug, and filled a glass for her, while she leaned back, confronted only by a frowning college President in an emblazoned frame. The academic frown descended on her like an anathema when she rose and followed her companion out of the building.

Hamblin Hall stands at the end of the long green "Campus" with its sextuple line of elms—the boast and the singularity of Wentworth. A pale spring moon, rising above the dome of the University library at the opposite end of the elm-walk, diffused a pearly mildness in the sky, melted to thin haze the shadows of the trees, and turned to golden yellow the lights of the college windows. Against this soft suffusion of light the Library cupola assumed a Bramantesque grace, the white steeple of the congregational church became a campanile topped by a winged spirit, and the scant porticoes of the older halls the colonnades of classic temples.

"This is better—" Dawnish said, as they passed down the steps and under the shadow of the elms.

They moved on a little way in silence before he began again: "You're too tired to walk. Let us sit down a few minutes."

Her feet, in truth, were leaden, and not far off a group of park benches, encircling the pedestal of a patriot in bronze, invited them to rest. But Dawnish was guiding her toward a lateral path which bent, through shrubberies, toward a strip of turf between two of the buildings.

"It will be cooler by the river," he said, moving on without waiting for a possible protest. None came: it seemed easier, for the moment, to let herself be led without any conventional feint of resistance. And besides, there was nothing wrong about *this*—the wrong would have been in sitting up there in the glare, pretending to listen to her husband, a dutiful wife among her kind. . . .

The path descended, as both knew, to the chosen, the inimitable spot of Wentworth: that fugitive curve of the river, where, before hurrying on to glut the brutal industries of South Wentworth and Smedden, it simulated for a few hundred yards the leisurely pace of an ancient university stream, with willows on its banks and a stretch of turf extending from the grounds of Hamblin Hall to the boat houses at the farther bend. Here too were benches, beneath the willows, and so close to the river that the voice of its gliding softened and filled out the reverberating silence between Margaret and her companion, and made her feel that she knew why he had brought her there.

"Do you feel better?" he asked gently as he sat down beside her.

"Oh, yes. I only needed a little air."

"I'm so glad you did. Of course the speeches were tremendously interesting—but I prefer this. What a good night!"

"Yes."

There was a pause, which now, after all, the soothing accompaniment of the river seemed hardly sufficient to fill.

"I wonder what time it is. I ought to be going home," Margaret began at length.

"Oh, it's not late. They'll be at it for hours in there—yet."

She made a faint inarticulate sound. She wanted to say: "No—Robert's speech was to be the last—" but she could not bring herself to pronounce Ransom's name, and at the moment no other way of refuting her companion's statement occurred to her.

The young man leaned back luxuriously, reassured by her silence.

"You see it's my last chance—and I want to make the most of it."

"Your last chance?" How stupid of her to repeat his words on that cooing note of interrogation! It was just such a lead as the Brant girl might have given him.

"To be with you—like this. I haven't had so many. And there's less than a week left."

She attempted to laugh. "Perhaps it will sound longer if you call it five days."

The flatness of that, again! And she knew there were people who called her intelligent. Fortunately he did not seem to notice it; but her laugh continued to sound in her own ears—the coquettish chirp of middle age! She decided that if he spoke again—if he *said anything*—she would make no farther effort at evasion: she would take it directly, seriously, frankly—she would not be doubly disloyal.

"Besides," he continued, throwing his arm along the back of the bench, and turning toward her so that his face was like a dusky bas-relief with a silver rim—"besides, there's something I've been wanting to tell you."

The sound of the river seemed to cease altogether: the whole world became silent.

Margaret had trusted her inspiration farther than it appeared likely to carry her. Again she could think of nothing happier than to repeat, on the same witless note of interrogation: "To tell me?"

"You only."

The constraint, the difficulty, seemed to be on his side now: she divined it by the renewed shifting of his attitude—he was capable, usually, of such fine intervals of immobility—and by a confusion in his utterance that set her own voice throbbing in her throat.

"You've been so perfect to me," he began again. "It's not my fault if you've made me feel that you would understand everything—make allowances for everything—see just how a man may have held out, and fought against a thing as long as he had the strength.... This may be my only chance; and I can't go away without telling you."

He had turned from her now, and was staring at the river, so that his profile was projected against the moonlight in all its beautiful young dejection.

There was a slight pause, as though he waited for her to speak; then she leaned forward and laid her hand on his.

"If I have really been—if I have done for you even the least part of what you say ... what you imagine . . . will you do for me, now, just one thing in return?"

He sat motionless, as if fearing to frighten away the shy touch on his hand, and she left it there, conscious of her gesture only as part of the high ritual of their farewell.

"What do you want me to do?" he asked in a low tone.

"*Not* to tell me!" she breathed on a deep note of entreaty.

"*Not* to tell you—?"

"Anything—*anything*—just to leave our . . . our friendship ... as it has been—as—as a painter, if a friend asked him, might leave a picture—not quite finished, perhaps . . . but all the more exquisite. . . . "

She felt the hand under hers slip away, recover itself, and seek her own, which had flashed out of reach in the same instant—felt the start that swept him round on her as if he had been caught and turned about by the shoulders.

"You—*you*—?" he stammered, in a strange voice full of fear and tenderness; but she held fast, so centered in her inexorable resolve that she was hardly conscious of the effect her words might be producing.

"Don't you see," she hurried on, "don't you *feel* how much safer it is—yes, I'm willing to put it so!—how much safer to leave everything undisturbed . . . just as . . . as it has grown of itself . . . without trying to say: 'It's this or that'. . . ? It's what we each choose to call it to ourselves, after all, isn't it? Don't let us try to find a name that . . . that we should both agree upon . . . we probably shouldn't succeed." She laughed abruptly. "And ghosts vanish when one names them!" she ended with a break in her voice.

When she ceased her heart was beating so violently that there was a rush in her ears like the noise of the river after rain, and she did not immediately make out what he was answering. But as she recovered her lucidity she said to herself that, whatever he was saying, she must not hear it; and she began to speak again, half playfully, half appealingly, with an eloquence of entreaty, an ingenuity in argument, of which she had never dreamed herself capable. And then, suddenly, strangling hands seemed to reach up from her heart to her throat, and she had to stop.

Her companion remained motionless. He had not tried to regain her hand, and his eyes were away from her, on the river. But his nearness had become something formidable and exquisite—something she had never before imagined. A flush of guilt swept over her—vague reminiscences of French novels and of opera plots. This was what such women felt, then . . . this was "shame.". . . Phrases of the newspaper and the pulpit danced before her. . . . She dared not speak, and his silence began to frighten her. Had ever a heart beat so wildly before in Wentworth?

He turned at last, and taking her two hands, quite simply, kissed them one after the other.

"I shall never forget—" he said in a confused voice, unlike his own.

A return of strength enabled her to rise, and even to let her eyes meet his for a moment.

"Thank you," she said, simply also.

She turned away from the bench, regaining the path that led back to the college buildings, and he walked beside her in silence. When they reached the elm walk it was dotted with dispersing groups. The "speaking" was over, and Hamblin Hall had poured its audience out into the moonlight. Margaret felt a rush of relief, followed by a receding wave of regret. She had the distinct sensation that her hour—her one hour—was over.

One of the groups just ahead broke up as they approached, and projected Ransom's solid bulk against the moonlight.

"My husband," she said, hastening forward; and she never afterward forgot the look of his back—heavy, round-shouldered, yet a little pompous—in a badly fitting overcoat that stood out at the neck and hid his collar. She had never before noticed how he dressed.

IV

THEY met again, inevitably, before Dawnish left; but the thing she feared did not happen—he did not try to see her alone.

It even became clear to her, in looking back, that he had deliberately avoided doing so; and this seemed merely an added proof of his "understanding," of that deep undefinable communion that set them alone in an empty world, as if on a peak above the clouds.

The five days passed in a flash; and when the last one came, it brought to Margaret Ransom an hour of weakness, of profound disorganization, when old barriers fell, old convictions faded—when to be alone with him for a moment became, after all, the one craving of her heart. She knew he was coming that afternoon to say "good-by"—and she knew also that Ransom was to be away at South Wentworth. She waited alone in her pale little drawing-room, with its scant kakemonos, its one or two chilly reproductions from the antique, its slippery Chippendale chairs. At length the bell rang, and her world became a rosy blur—through which she presently discerned the austere form of Mrs. Sperry, wife of the Professor of Paleontology, who had come to talk over with her the next winter's program for the Higher Thought Club. They debated the question for an hour, and when Mrs. Sperry departed Margaret had a confused impression that the course was to deal with the influence of the First Crusade on the development of European architecture—but the sentient part of her knew only that Dawnish had not come.

He "bobbed in," as he would have put it, after dinner—having, it appeared, run across Ransom early in the day, and learned that the latter would be absent till evening. Margaret was in the study with her husband when the door opened and Dawnish stood there. Ransom—who had not had time to dress—was seated at his desk, a pile of shabby law books at his elbow, the light from a hanging lamp falling on his grayish stubble of hair, his sallow forehead and spectacled eyes. Dawnish, towering higher than usual against the shadows of the room, and refined by his unusual pallor, hung a moment on the threshold, then came in, explaining himself profusely—laughing, accepting a cigar, letting Ransom push an arm-chair forward—a Dawnish she had never seen, ill at ease, ejaculatory, yet somehow more mature, more obscurely in command of himself.

Margaret drew back, seating herself in the shade, in such a way that she saw her husband's head first, and beyond it their visitor's, relieved against the dusk of the book shelves. Her heart was still—she felt no throbbing in her throat or temples: all her life seemed concentrated in the hand that lay on her knee, the hand he would touch when they said good-by.

Afterward her heart rang all the changes, and there was a mood in which she reproached herself for cowardice—for having deliberately missed her one moment with him, the moment in which she might have sounded the depths of life, for joy or anguish. But that mood was fleeting and infrequent. In quieter hours she blushed for it—she even trembled to think that he might have guessed such a regret in her. It seemed to convict her of a lack of fineness that he should have had, in his youth and his power, a tenderer, surer sense of the peril of a rash touch—should have handled the case so much more delicately.

At first her days were fire and the nights long solemn vigils. Her thoughts were no longer vulgarized and defaced by any notion of "guilt," of mental disloyalty. She was ashamed now of her shame. What had happened was as much outside the sphere of her marriage as some transaction in a star. It had simply given her a secret life of incommunicable joys, as if all the wasted springs of her youth had been stored in some hidden pool, and she could return there now to bathe in them.

After that there came a phase of loneliness, through which the life about her loomed phantasmal and remote. She thought the dead must feel thus, repeating the vain gestures of the living beside some Stygian shore. She wondered if any other woman had lived to whom *nothing had ever happened?* And then his first letter came. . . .

It was a charming letter—a perfect letter. The little touch of awkwardness and constraint under its boyish spontaneity told her more than whole pages of eloquence. He spoke of their friendship—of their good days together. . . . Ransom, chancing to come in while she read, noticed the foreign stamps; and she was able to hand him the letter, saying gaily: "There's a message for you," and knowing all the while that *her* message was safe in her heart.

On the days when the letters came the outlines of things grew indistinct, and she could never afterward remember what she had done or how the business of life had been carried on. It was always a surprise when she found dinner on the table as usual, and Ransom seated opposite to her, running over the evening paper.

But though Dawnish continued to write, with all the English loyalty to the outward observances of friendship, his communications came only at intervals of several weeks, and between them she had time to repossess herself, to regain some sort of normal contact with life. And the customary, the recurring, gradually reclaimed her, the net of habit tightened again—her daily life became real, and her one momentary escape from it an exquisite illusion. Not that she ceased to believe in the miracle that had befallen her: she still treasured the reality of her one moment beside the river. What reason was there for doubting it? She could hear the ring of truth in young Dawnish's voice: "It's not my fault if you've made me feel that you would understand everything. . . . " No! she believed in her miracle, and the belief sweetened and illumined her life; but she came to see that what was for her the transformation of her whole being might well have been, for her companion, a mere passing explosion of gratitude, of boyish good-fellowship touched with the pang of leave-taking. She even reached the point of telling herself that it was "better so": this view of the episode so defended it from the alternating extremes of self-reproach and derision, so enshrined it in a pale immortality to which she could make her secret pilgrimages without reproach.

For a long time she had not been able to pass by the bench under the willows—she even avoided the elm walk till autumn had stripped its branches. But every day, now, she noted a step toward recovery; and at last a day came when, walking along the river, she said to herself, as she approached the bench: "I used not to be able to pass here without thinking of him; *and now I am not thinking of him at all!*"

This seemed such convincing proof of her recovery that she began, as spring returned, to permit herself, now and then, a quiet session on the bench—a dedicated hour from which she went back fortified to her task.

She had not heard from her friend for six weeks or more—the intervals between his letters were growing longer. But that was "best" too, and she was not anxious, for she knew he had obtained the post he had been preparing for, and that his active life in London had begun. The thought reminded her, one mild March day, that in leaving the house she had thrust in her reticule a letter from a Wentworth friend who was abroad on a holiday. The envelope bore the London post mark, a fact showing that the lady's face was turned toward home. Margaret seated herself on her bench, and began to read the letter.

The London described was that of shops and museums—as remote as possible from the setting of Guy Dawnish's existence. But suddenly Margaret's eye fell on his name, and the page began to tremble in her hands.

"I heard such a funny thing yesterday about your friend Mr. Dawnish. We went to a tea at Professor Bunce's (I do wish you knew the Bunces—their atmosphere is so *uplifting*), and there I met that Miss Bruce-Pringle who came out last year to take a course in histology at the Annex. Of course she asked about you and Mr. Ransom, and then she told me she had just seen Mr. Dawnish's aunt—the clever one he was always talking about, Lady Caroline something—and that they were all in a dreadful state about him. I wonder if you knew he was engaged when he went to America? He never mentioned it to us. She said it was not a positive engagement, but an understanding with a girl he has always been devoted to, who lives near their place in Wiltshire; and both families expected the marriage to take place as soon as he got back. It seems the girl is an heiress (you know *how low* the English ideals are compared with ours), and Miss Bruce-Pringle said his relations were perfectly delighted at his 'being provided for,' as she called it. Well, when he got back he asked the girl to release him; and she and her family were furious, and so were his people; but he holds out, and won't marry her, and won't give a reason, except that he has 'formed an unfortunate attachment.' Did you ever hear anything so peculiar? His aunt, who is quite wild about it, says it must have happened at Wentworth, because he didn't go anywhere else in America. Do you suppose it *could* have been the Brant girl? But why 'unfortunate' when everybody knows she would have jumped at him?"

Margaret folded the letter and looked out across the river. It was not the same river, but a mystic current shot with moonlight. The bare willows wove a leafy veil above her head, and beside her she felt the nearness of youth and tempestuous tenderness. It had all happened just here, on this very seat by the river—it had come to her, and passed her by, and she had not held out a hand to detain it. . . .

Well! Was it not, by that very abstention, made more deeply and ineffaceably hers? She could argue thus while she had thought the episode, on his side, a mere transient effect of propinquity; but now that she knew it had altered the whole course of his life, now that it took on substance and reality, asserted a separate existence outside of her own troubled consciousness—now it seemed almost cowardly to have missed her share in it.

She walked home in a dream. Now and then, when she passed an acquaintance, she wondered if the pain and glory were written on her face. But Mrs. Sperry, who stopped her at the corner of Maverick Street to say a word about the next meeting of the Higher Thought Club, seemed to remark no change in her.

When she reached home Ransom had not yet returned from the office, and she went straight to the library to tidy his writing-table. It was part of her daily duty to bring order out of the chaos of his papers, and of late she had fastened on such small recurring tasks as some one falling over a precipice might snatch at the weak bushes in its clefts.

When she had sorted the letters she took up some pamphlets and newspapers, glancing over them to see if they were to be kept. Among the papers was a page torn from a London *Times* of the previous month. Her eye ran down its columns and suddenly a paragraph flamed out.

"We are requested to state that the marriage arranged between Mr. Guy Dawnish, son of the late Colonel the Hon. Roderick Dawnish, of Malby, Wilts, and Gwendolen, daughter of Samuel Matcher, Esq. of Armingham Towers, Wilts, will not take place."

Margaret dropped the paper and sat down, hiding her face against the stained baize of the desk. She remembered the photograph of the tennis-court at Guise—she remembered the handsome girl at whom Guy Dawnish looked up, laughing. A gust of tears shook her, loosening the dry surface of conventional feeling, welling up from unsuspected depths. She was sorry—very sorry, yet so glad—so ineffably, impenitently glad.

## V

THERE came a reaction in which she decided to write to him. She even sketched out a letter of sisterly, almost motherly, remonstrance, in which she reminded him that he "still had all his life before him." But she reflected that so, after all, had she; and that seemed to weaken the argument.

In the end she decided not to send the letter. He had never spoken to her of his engagement to Gwendolen Matcher, and his letters had contained no allusion to any sentimental disturbance in his life. She had only his few broken words, that night by the river, on which to build her theory of the case. But illuminated by the phrase "an unfortunate attachment" the theory towered up, distinct and immovable, like some high landmark by which travellers shape their course. She had been loved—extraordinarily loved. But he had chosen that she should know of it by his silence rather than by his speech. He had understood that only on those terms could their transcendant communion continue—that he must lose her to keep her. To break that silence would be like spilling a cup of water in a waste of sand. There would be nothing left for her thirst.

Her life, thenceforward, was bathed in a tranquil beauty. The days flowed by like a river beneath the moon—each ripple caught the brightness and passed it on. She began to take a renewed interest in her familiar round of duties. The tasks which had once seemed colorless and irksome had now a kind of sacrificial sweetness, a symbolic meaning into which she alone was initiated. She had been restless—had longed to travel; now she felt that she should never again care to leave Wentworth. But if her desire to wander had ceased, she travelled in spirit, performing invisible pilgrimages in the footsteps of her friend. She regretted that her one short visit to England had taken her so little out of London—that her acquaintance with the landscape had been formed chiefly through the windows of a railway carriage. She threw herself into the architectural studies of the Higher Thought Club, and distinguished herself, at the spring meetings, by her fluency, her competence, her inexhaustible curiosity on the subject of the growth of English Gothic. She ransacked the shelves of the college library, she borrowed photographs of the cathedrals, she pored over the folio pages of "The Seats of Noblemen and Gentlemen." She was like some banished princess who learns that she has inherited a domain in her own country, who knows that she will never see it, yet feels, wherever she walks, its soil beneath her feet.

May was half over, and the Higher Thought Club was to hold its last meeting, previous to the college festivities which, in early June, agreeably disorganized the social routine of Wentworth. The meeting was to take place in Margaret Ransom's drawing-room, and on the day before she sat upstairs preparing for her dual duties as hostess and orator—for she had been invited to read the final paper of the course.

In order to sum up with precision her conclusions on the subject of English Gothic she had been rereading an analysis of the structural features of the principal English cathedrals; and she was murmuring over to herself the phrase: "The longitudinal arches of Lincoln have an approximately elliptical form," when there came a knock on the door, and Maria's voice announced: "There's a lady down in the parlor."

Margaret's soul dropped from the heights of the shadowy vaulting to the dead level of an afternoon call at Wentworth.

"A lady? Did she give no name?"

Maria became confused. "She only said she was a lady—" and in reply to her mistress's look of mild surprise: "Well, ma'am, she told me so three or four times over."

Margaret laid her book down, leaving it open at the description of Lincoln, and slowly descended the stairs. As she did so, she repeated to herself: "The longitudinal arches are elliptical."

On the threshold below, she had the odd impression that her bare and inanimate drawing-room was brimming with life and noise—an impression produced, as she presently perceived, by the resolute forward dash—it was almost a pounce—of the one small figure restlessly measuring its length.

The dash checked itself within a yard of Margaret, and the lady—a stranger—held back long enough to stamp on her hostess a sharp impression of sallowness, leanness, keenness, before she said, in a voice that might have been addressing an unruly committee meeting: "I am Lady Caroline Duckett—a fact I found it impossible to make clear to the young woman who let me in."

A warm wave rushed up from Margaret's heart to her throat and forehead. She held out both hands impulsively. "Oh, I'm so glad—I'd no idea—"

Her voice sank under her visitor's impartial scrutiny.

"I don't wonder," said the latter drily. "I suppose she didn't mention, either, that my object in calling here was to see Mrs. Ransom?"

"Oh, yes—won't you sit down?" Margaret pushed a chair forward. She seated herself at a little distance, brain and heart humming with a confused interchange of signals. This dark sharp woman was his aunt—the "clever aunt" who had had such a hard life, but had always managed to keep her head above water. Margaret remembered that Guy had spoken of her kindness—perhaps she would seem kinder when they had talked together a little. Meanwhile the first impression she produced was of an amplitude out of all proportion to her somewhat scant exterior. With her small flat figure, her shabby heterogeneous dress, she was as dowdy as any Professor's wife at Wentworth; but her dowdiness (Margaret borrowed a literary analogy to define it), her dowdiness was somehow "of the center." Like the insignificant emissary of a great power, she was to be judged rather by her passports than her person.

While Margaret was receiving these impressions, Lady Caroline, with quick bird-like twists of her head, was gathering others from the pale void spaces of the drawing-room. Her eyes, divided by a sharp nose like a bill, seemed to be set far enough apart to see at separate angles; but suddenly she bent both of them on Margaret.

"This *is* Mrs. Ransom's house?" she asked, with an emphasis on the verb that gave a distinct hint of unfulfilled expectations.

Margaret assented.

"Because your American houses, especially in the provincial towns, all look so remarkably alike, that I thought I might have been mistaken; and as my time is extremely limited—in fact I'm sailing on Wednesday—"

She paused long enough to let Margaret say: "I had no idea you were in America."

Lady Caroline made no attempt to take this up. "And so much of it," she carried on her sentence, "has been wasted in talking to people I really hadn't the slightest desire to see, that you must excuse me if I go straight to the point."

Margaret felt a sudden tension of the heart. "Of course," she said while a voice within her cried: "He is dead—he has left me a message."

There was another pause; then Lady Caroline went on, with increasing asperity: "So that—in short—if I *could* see Mrs. Ransom at once—"

Margaret looked up in surprise. "I am Mrs. Ransom," she said.

The other stared a moment, with much the same look of cautious incredulity that had marked her inspection of the drawing-room. Then light came to her.

"Oh, I beg your pardon. I should have said that I wished to see Mrs. *Robert* Ransom, not Mrs. Ransom. But I understood that in the States you don't make those distinctions." She paused a moment, and then went on, before Margaret could answer: "Perhaps, after all, it's as well that I should see you instead, since you're evidently one of the household—your son and his wife live with you, I suppose? Yes, on the whole, then, it's better—I shall be able to talk so much more frankly." She spoke as if, as a rule, circumstances prevented her giving rein to this propensity. "And frankness, of course, is the only way out of this—this extremely tiresome complication. You know, I suppose, that my nephew thinks he's in love with your daughter-in-law?"

Margaret made a slight movement, but her visitor pressed on without heeding it. "Oh, don't fancy, please, that I'm pretending to take a high moral ground—though his mother does, poor dear! I can perfectly imagine that in a place like this—I've just been driving about it for two hours—a young man of Guy's age would *have* to provide himself with some sort of distraction, and he's not the kind to go in for anything objectionable. Oh, we quite allow for that—we should allow for the whole affair, if it hadn't so preposterously ended in his throwing over the girl he was engaged to, and upsetting an arrangement that affected a number of people besides himself. I understand that in the States it's different—the young people have only themselves to consider. In England—in our class, I mean—a great deal may depend on a young man's making a good match; and in Guy's case I may say that his mother and sisters (I won't include myself, though I might) have been simply stranded—thrown overboard—by his freak. You can understand how serious it is when I tell you that it's that and nothing else that has brought me all the way to America. And my first idea was to go straight to your daughter-in-law, since her influence is the only thing we can count on now, and put it to her fairly, as I'm putting it to you. But, on the whole, I dare say it's better to see you first—you might give me an idea of the line to take with her. I'm prepared to throw myself on her mercy!"

Margaret rose from her chair, outwardly rigid in proportion to her inward tremor.

"You don't understand—" she began.

Lady Caroline brushed the interruption aside. "Oh, but I do—completely! I cast no reflection on your daughter-in-law. Guy has made it quite clear to us that his attachment is—has, in short, not been rewarded. But don't you see that that's the worst part of it? There'd be much more hope of his recovering if Mrs. Robert Ransom had—had—"

Margaret's voice broke from her in a cry. "I am Mrs. Robert Ransom," she said.

If Lady Caroline Duckett had hitherto given her hostess the impression of a person not easily silenced, this fact added sensibly to the effect produced by the intense stillness which now fell on her.

She sat quite motionless, her large bangled hands clasped about the meager fur boa she had unwound from her neck on entering, her rusty black veil pushed up to the edge of a "fringe" of doubtful authenticity, her thin lips parted on a gasp that seemed to sharpen itself on the edges of her teeth. So overwhelming and helpless was her silence that Margaret began to feel a motion of pity beneath her indignation—a desire at least to facilitate the excuses which must terminate their disastrous colloquy. But when Lady Caroline found voice she did not use it to excuse herself.

"You *can't* be," she said, quite simply.

"Can't be?" Margaret stammered, with a flushing cheek.

"I mean, it's some mistake. Are there *two* Mrs. Robert Ransoms in the same town? Your family arrangements are so extremely puzzling." She had a farther rush of enlightenment. "Oh, I see! I ought of course to have asked for Mrs. Robert Ransom *Junior!*"

The idea sent her to her feet with a haste which showed her impatience to make up for lost time.

"There is no other Mrs. Robert Ransom at Wentworth," said Margaret.

"No other—no 'Junior'? Are you *sure?*" Lady Caroline fell back into her seat again. "Then I simply don't see," she murmured helplessly.

Margaret's blush had fixed itself on her throbbing forehead. She remained standing, while her strange visitor continued to gaze at her with a perturbation in which the consciousness of indiscretion had evidently as yet no part.

"I simply don't see," she repeated.

Suddenly she sprang up, and advancing to Margaret laid an inspired hand on her arm. "But, my dear woman, you can help us out all the same; you can help us to find out *who it is*—and you will, won't you? Because, as it's not you, you can't in the least mind what I've been saying—"

Margaret, freeing her arm from her visitor's hold, drew back a step; but Lady Caroline instantly rejoined her.

"Of course, I can see that if it *had* been, you might have been annoyed: I dare say I put the case stupidly—but I'm so bewildered by this new development—by his using you all this time as a pretext—that I really don't know where to turn for light on the mystery—"

She had Margaret in her imperious grasp again, but the latter broke from her with a more resolute gesture.

"I'm afraid I have no light to give you," she began; but once more Lady Caroline caught her up.

"Oh, but do please understand me! I condemn Guy most strongly for using your name—when we all know you'd been so amazingly kind to him! I haven't a word to say in his defence—but of course the important thing now is: *who is the woman, since you're not?*"

The question rang out loudly, as if all the pale puritan corners of the room flung it back with a shudder at the speaker. In the silence that ensued Margaret felt the blood ebbing back to her heart; then she said, in a distinct and level voice: "I know nothing of the history of Mr. Dawnish."

Lady Caroline gave a stare and a gasp. Her distracted hand groped for her boa and she began to wind it mechanically about her long neck.

"It would really be an enormous help to us—and to poor Gwendolen Matcher," she persisted pleadingly. "And you'd be doing Guy himself a good turn."

Margaret remained silent and motionless while her visitor drew on one of the worn gloves she had pulled off to adjust her veil. Lady Caroline gave the veil a final twitch.

"I've come a tremendously long way," she said, "and, since it isn't you, I can't think why you won't help me. . . ."

When the door had closed on her visitor Margaret Ransom went slowly up the stairs to her room. As she dragged her feet from one step to another, she remembered how she had sprung up the same steep flight after that visit of Guy Dawnish's when she had looked in the glass and seen on her face the blush of youth.

When she reached her room she bolted the door as she had done that day, and again looked at herself in the narrow mirror above her dressing-table. It was just a year since then—the elms were budding again, the willows hanging their green veil above the bench by the river. But there was no trace of youth left in her face—she saw it now as others had doubtless always seen it. If it seemed as it did to Lady Caroline Duckett, what look must it have worn to the fresh gaze of young Guy Dawnish?

A pretext—she had been a pretext. He had used her name to screen some one else— or perhaps merely to escape from a situation of which he was weary. She did not care to conjecture what his motive had been—everything connected with him had grown so remote and alien. She felt no anger—only an unspeakable sadness, a sadness which she knew would never be appeased.

She looked at herself long and steadily; she wished to clear her eyes of all illusions. Then she turned away and took her usual seat beside her work-table. From where she sat she could look down the empty elm-shaded street, up which, at this hour every day, she was sure to see her husband's figure advancing. She would see it presently—she would see it for many years to come. She had a sudden aching sense of the length of the years that stretched before her. Strange that one who was not young should still, in all likelihood, have so long to live!

Nothing was changed in the setting of her life, perhaps nothing would ever change in it. She would certainly live and die in Wentworth. And meanwhile the days would go on as usual, bringing the usual obligations. As the word flitted through her brain she remembered that she had still to put the finishing touches to the paper she was to read the next afternoon at the meeting of the Higher Thought Club.

The book she had been reading lay face downward beside her, where she had left it an hour ago. She took it up, and slowly and painfully, like a child laboriously spelling out the syllables, she went on with the rest of the sentence:

—"And they spring from a level not much above that of the springing of the transverse and diagonal ribs, which are so arranged as to give a convex curve to the surface of the vaulting conoid."

## THE VERDICT

I HAD ALWAYS THOUGHT Jack Gisburn rather a cheap genius—though a good fellow enough—so it was no great surprise to me to hear that, in the height of his glory, he had dropped his painting, married a rich widow, and established himself in a villa on the Riviera. (Though I rather thought it would have been Rome or Florence.)

"The height of his glory"—that was what the women called it. I can hear Mrs. Gideon Thwing—his last Chicago sitter—deploring his unaccountable abdication. "Of course it's going to send the value of my picture 'way up; but I don't think of that, Mr. Rickham—the loss to Arrt is all I think of." The word, on Mrs. Thwing's lips, multiplied its *rs* as though they were reflected in an endless vista of mirrors. And it was not only the Mrs. Thwings who mourned. Had not the exquisite Hermia Croft, at the last Grafton Gallery show, stopped me before Gisburn's "Moon-dancers" to say, with tears in her eyes: "We shall not look upon its like again"?

Well!—even through the prism of Hermia's tears I felt able to face the fact with equanimity. Poor Jack Gisburn! The women had made him—it was fitting that they should mourn him. Among his own sex fewer regrets were heard, and in his own trade hardly a murmur. Professional jealousy? Perhaps. If it were, the honor of the craft was vindicated by little Claude Nutley, who, in all good faith, brought out in the Burlington a very handsome "obituary" on Jack—one of those showy articles stocked with random technicalities that I have heard (I won't say by whom) compared to Gisburn's painting. And so—his resolve being apparently irrevocable—the discussion gradually died out, and, as Mrs. Thwing had predicted, the price of "Gisburns" went up.

It was not till three years later that, in the course of a few weeks' idling on the Riviera, it suddenly occurred to me to wonder why Gisburn had given up his painting. On reflection, it really was a tempting problem. To accuse his wife would have been too easy—his fair sitters had been denied the solace of saying that Mrs. Gisburn had "dragged him down." For Mrs. Gisburn—as such—had not existed till nearly a year after Jack's resolve had been taken. It might be that he had married her—since he liked his ease—because he didn't want to go on painting; but it would have been hard to prove that he had given up his painting because he had married her.

Of course, if she had not dragged him down, she had equally, as Miss Croft contended, failed to "lift him up"—she had not led him back to the easel. To put the brush into his hand again—what a vocation for a wife! But Mrs. Gisburn appeared to have disdained it—and I felt it might be interesting to find out why.

The desultory life of the Riviera lends itself to such purely academic speculations; and having, on my way to Monte Carlo, caught a glimpse of Jack's balustraded terraces between the pines, I had myself borne thither the next day.

I found the couple at tea beneath their palm-trees; and Mrs. Gisburn's welcome was so genial that, in the ensuing weeks, I claimed it frequently. It was not that my hostess was "interesting": on that point I could have given Miss Croft the fullest reassurance. It was just because she was *not* interesting—if I may be pardoned the bull—that I found her so. For Jack, all his life, had been surrounded by interesting women: they had fostered his art, it had been reared in the hot-house of their adulation. And it was therefore instructive to note what effect the "deadening atmosphere of mediocrity" (I quote Miss Croft) was having on him.

I have mentioned that Mrs. Gisburn was rich; and it was immediately perceptible that her husband was extracting from this circumstance a delicate but substantial satisfaction. It is, as a rule, the people who scorn money who get most out of it; and Jack's elegant disdain of his wife's big balance enabled him, with an appearance of perfect good-breeding, to transmute it into objects of art and luxury. To the latter, I must add, he remained relatively indifferent; but he was buying Renaissance bronzes and eighteenth-century pictures with a discrimination that bespoke the amplest resources.

"Money's only excuse is to put beauty into circulation," was one of the axioms he laid down across the Sevres and silver of an exquisitely appointed luncheon-table, when, on a later day, I had again run over from Monte Carlo; and Mrs. Gisburn, beaming on him, added for my enlightenment: "Jack is so morbidly sensitive to every form of beauty."

Poor Jack! It had always been his fate to have women say such things of him: the fact should be set down in extenuation. What struck me now was that, for the first time, he resented the tone. I had seen him, so often, basking under similar tributes—was it the conjugal note that robbed them of their savor? No—for, oddly enough, it became apparent that he was fond of Mrs. Gisburn—fond enough not to see her absurdity. It was his own absurdity he seemed to be wincing under—his own attitude as an object for garlands and incense.

"My dear, since I've chucked painting people don't say that stuff about me—they say it about Victor Grindle," was his only protest, as he rose from the table and strolled out onto the sunlit terrace.

I glanced after him, struck by his last word. Victor Grindle was, in fact, becoming the man of the moment—as Jack himself, one might put it, had been the man of the hour. The younger artist was said to have formed himself at my friend's feet, and I wondered if a tinge of jealousy underlay the latter's mysterious abdication. But no – for it was not till after that event that the fashionable drawing rooms had begun to display their "Grindles."

I turned to Mrs. Gisburn, who had lingered to give a lump of sugar to her spaniel in the dining-room.

"Why *has* he chucked painting?" I asked abruptly.

She raised her eyebrows with a hint of good-humored surprise.

"Oh, he doesn't *have* to now, you know; and I want him to enjoy himself," she said quite simply.

I looked about the spacious white-paneled room, with its *famille-verte* vases repeating the tones of the pale damask curtains, and its eighteenth-century pastels in delicate faded frames.

"Has he chucked his pictures too? I haven't seen a single one in the house."

A slight shade of constraint crossed Mrs. Gisburn's open countenance. "It's his ridiculous modesty, you know. He says they're not fit to have about; he's sent them all away except one—my portrait—and that I have to keep upstairs."

His ridiculous modesty—Jack's modesty about his pictures? My curiosity was growing like the bean-stalk. I said persuasively to my hostess: "I must really see your portrait, you know."

She glanced out almost timorously at the terrace where her husband, lounging in a hooded chair, had lit a cigar and drawn the Russian deerhound's head between his knees.

"Well, come while he's not looking," she said, with a laugh that tried to hide her nervousness; and I followed her between the marble Emperors of the hall, and up the wide stairs with terra-cotta nymphs poised among flowers at each landing.

In the dimmest corner of her boudoir, amid a profusion of delicate and distinguished objects, hung one of the familiar oval canvases, in the inevitable garlanded frame. The mere outline of the frame called up all Gisburn's past!

Mrs. Gisburn drew back the window-curtains, moved aside a *jardinière* full of pink azaleas, pushed an arm-chair away, and said: "If you stand here you can just manage to see it. I had it over the mantel-piece, but he wouldn't let it stay."

Yes—I could just manage to see it—the first portrait of Jack's I had ever had to strain my eyes over! Usually they had the place of honor—say the central panel in a pale yellow or *rose Dubarry* drawing-room, or a monumental easel placed so that it took the light through curtains of old Venetian point. The more modest place became the picture better; yet, as my eyes grew accustomed to the half-light, all the characteristic qualities came out—all the hesitations disguised as audacities, the tricks of prestidigitation by which, with such consummate skill, he managed to divert attention from the real business of the picture to some pretty irrelevance of detail. Mrs. Gisburn, presenting a neutral surface to work on—forming, as it were, so inevitably the background of her own picture—had lent herself in an unusual degree to the display of this false virtuosity. The picture was one of Jack's "strongest," as his admirers would have put it—it represented, on his part, a swelling of muscles, a congesting of veins, a balancing, straddling and straining, that reminded one of the circus-clown's ironic efforts to lift a feather. It met, in short, at every point the demand of lovely woman to be painted "strongly" because she was tired of being painted "sweetly"—and yet not to lose an atom of the sweetness.

"It's the last he painted, you know," Mrs. Gisburn said with pardonable pride. "The last but one," she corrected herself—"but the other doesn't count, because he destroyed it."

"Destroyed it?" I was about to follow up this clue when I heard a footstep and saw Jack himself on the threshold.

As he stood there, his hands in the pockets of his velveteen coat, the thin brown waves of hair pushed back from his white forehead, his lean sunburnt cheeks furrowed by a smile that lifted the tips of a self-confident moustache, I felt to what a degree he had the same quality as his pictures—the quality of looking cleverer than he was.

His wife glanced at him deprecatingly, but his eyes travelled past her to the portrait.

"Mr. Rickham wanted to see it," she began, as if excusing herself. He shrugged his shoulders, still smiling.

"Oh, Rickham found me out long ago," he said lightly; then, passing his arm through mine: "Come and see the rest of the house."

He showed it to me with a kind of naive suburban pride: the bath-rooms, the speaking-tubes, the dress-closets, the trouser-presses—all the complex simplifications of the millionaire's domestic economy. And whenever my wonder paid the expected tribute he said, throwing out his chest a little: "Yes, I really don't see how people manage to live without that."

Well—it was just the end one might have foreseen for him. Only he was, through it all and in spite of it all—as he had been through, and in spite of, his pictures—so handsome, so charming, so disarming, that one longed to cry out: "Be dissatisfied with your leisure!" as once one had longed to say: "Be dissatisfied with your work!"

But, with the cry on my lips, my diagnosis suffered an unexpected check.

"This is my own lair," he said, leading me into a dark plain room at the end of the florid vista. It was square and brown and leathery: no "effects"; no bric-a-brac, none of the air of posing for reproduction in a picture weekly—above all, no least sign of ever having been used as a studio.

The fact brought home to me the absolute finality of Jack's break with his old life.

"Don't you ever dabble with paint any more?" I asked, still looking about for a trace of such activity.

"Never," he said briefly.

"Or water-color—or etching?"

His confident eyes grew dim, and his cheeks paled a little under their handsome sunburn.

"Never think of it, my dear fellow—any more than if I'd never touched a brush."

And his tone told me in a flash that he never thought of anything else.

I moved away, instinctively embarrassed by my unexpected discovery; and as I turned, my eye fell on a small picture above the mantel-piece—the only object breaking the plain oak paneling of the room.

"Oh, by Jove!" I said.

It was a sketch of a donkey—an old tired donkey, standing in the rain under a wall.

"By Jove—a Stroud!" I cried.

He was silent; but I felt him close behind me, breathing a little quickly.

"What a wonder! Made with a dozen lines—but on everlasting foundations. You lucky chap, where did you get it?"

He answered slowly: "Mrs. Stroud gave it to me."

"Ah—I didn't know you even knew the Strouds. He was such an inflexible hermit."

"I didn't—till after.... She sent for me to paint him when he was dead."

"When he was dead? You?"

I must have let a little too much amazement escape through my surprise, for he answered with a deprecating laugh: "Yes—she's an awful simpleton, you know, Mrs. Stroud. Her only idea was to have him done by a fashionable painter—ah, poor Stroud! She thought it the surest way of proclaiming his greatness—of forcing it on a purblind public. And at the moment I was *the* fashionable painter."

"Ah, poor Stroud—as you say. Was *that* his history?"

"That was his history. She believed in him, gloried in him—or thought she did. But she couldn't bear not to have all the drawing-rooms with her. She couldn't bear the fact that, on varnishing days, one could always get near enough to see his pictures. Poor woman! She's just a fragment groping for other fragments. Stroud is the only whole I ever knew."

"You ever knew? But you just said—"

Gisburn had a curious smile in his eyes.

"Oh, I knew him, and he knew me—only it happened after he was dead."

I dropped my voice instinctively. "When she sent for you?"

"Yes—quite insensible to the irony. She wanted him vindicated—and by me!"

He laughed again, and threw back his head to look up at the sketch of the donkey. "There were days when I couldn't look at that thing—couldn't face it. But I forced myself to put it here; and now it's cured me—cured me. That's the reason why I don't dabble any more, my dear Rickham; or rather Stroud himself is the reason."

For the first time my idle curiosity about my companion turned into a serious desire to understand him better.

"I wish you'd tell me how it happened," I said.

He stood looking up at the sketch, and twirling between his fingers a cigarette he had forgotten to light. Suddenly he turned toward me.

"I'd rather like to tell you—because I've always suspected you of loathing my work."

I made a deprecating gesture, which he negatived with a good-humored shrug.

"Oh, I didn't care a straw when I believed in myself—and now it's an added tie between us!"

He laughed slightly, without bitterness, and pushed one of the deep arm-chairs forward. "There: make yourself comfortable—and here are the cigars you like."

He placed them at my elbow and continued to wander up and down the room, stopping now and then beneath the picture.

"How it happened? I can tell you in five minutes—and it didn't take much longer to happen.... I can remember now how surprised and pleased I was when I got Mrs. Stroud's note. Of course, deep down, I had always *felt* there was no one like him—only I had gone with the stream, echoed the usual platitudes about him, till I half got to think he was a failure, one of the kind that are left behind. By Jove, and he was left behind—because he had come to stay! The rest of us had to let ourselves be swept along or go under, but he was high above the current—on everlasting foundations, as you say.

"Well, I went off to the house in my most egregious mood—rather moved, Lord forgive me, at the pathos of poor Stroud's career of failure being crowned by the glory of my painting him! Of course I meant to do the picture for nothing—I told Mrs. Stroud so when she began to stammer something about her poverty. I remember getting off a prodigious phrase about the honor being *mine*—oh, I was princely, my dear Rickham! I was posing to myself like one of my own sitters.

"Then I was taken up and left alone with him. I had sent all my traps in advance, and I had only to set up the easel and get to work. He had been dead only twenty-four hours, and he died suddenly, of heart disease, so that there had been no preliminary work of destruction—his face was clear and untouched. I had met him once or twice, years before, and thought him insignificant and dingy. Now I saw that he was superb.

"I was glad at first, with a merely aesthetic satisfaction: glad to have my hand on such a 'subject.' Then his strange life-likeness began to affect me queerly—as I blocked the head in I felt as if he *were* watching me do it. The sensation was followed by the thought: if he were watching me, what would he say to my way of working? My strokes began to go a little wild—I felt nervous and uncertain.

"Once, when I looked up, I seemed to see a smile behind his close grayish beard—as if he had the secret, and were amusing himself by holding it back from me. That exasperated me still more. The secret? Why, I had a secret worth twenty of his! I dashed at the canvas furiously, and tried some of my bravura tricks. But they failed me, they crumbled. I saw that he wasn't watching the showy bits—I couldn't distract his attention; he just kept his eyes on the hard passages between. Those were the ones I had always shirked, or covered up with some lying paint. And how he saw through my lies!

"I looked up again, and caught sight of that sketch of the donkey hanging on the wall near his bed. His wife told me afterward it was the last thing he had done—just a note taken with a shaking hand, when he was down in Devonshire recovering from a previous heart attack. Just a note! But it tells his whole history. There are years of patient scornful persistence in every line. A man who had swum with the current could never have learned that mighty up-stream stroke. . . .

"I turned back to my work, and went on groping and muddling; then I looked at the donkey again. I saw that, when Stroud laid in the first stroke, he knew just what the end would be. He had possessed his subject, absorbed it, recreated it. When had I done that with any of my things? They hadn't been born of me—I had just adopted them. . . .

"Hang it, Rickham, with that face watching me I couldn't do another stroke. The plain truth was, I didn't know where to put it—*I had never known*. Only, with my sitters and my public, a showy splash of color covered up the fact—I just threw paint into their faces.... Well, paint was the one medium those dead eyes could see through—see straight to the tottering foundations underneath. Don't you know how, in talking a foreign language, even fluently, one says half the time not what one wants to but what one can? Well—that was the way I painted; and as he lay there and watched me, the thing they called my 'technique' collapsed like a house of cards. He didn't sneer, you understand, poor Stroud—he just lay there quietly watching, and on his lips, through the gray beard, I seemed to hear the question: 'Are you sure you know where you're coming out?'

"If I could have painted that face, with that question on it, I should have done a great thing. The next greatest thing was to see that I couldn't—and that grace was given me. But, oh, at that minute, Rickham, was there anything on earth I wouldn't have given to have Stroud alive before me, and to hear him say: 'It's not too late—I'll show you how'?

"It *was* too late—it would have been, even if he'd been alive. I packed up my traps, and went down and told Mrs. Stroud. Of course I didn't tell her *that*—it would have been Greek to her. I simply said I couldn't paint him, that I was too moved. She rather liked the idea—she's so romantic! It was that that made her give me the donkey. But she was terribly upset at not getting the portrait—she did so want him 'done' by someone showy! At first I was afraid she wouldn't let me off—and at my wits' end I suggested Grindle. Yes, it was I who started Grindle: I told Mrs. Stroud he was the 'coming' man, and she told somebody else, and so it got to be true. . . . And he painted Stroud without wincing; and she hung the picture among her husband's things. . . ."

He flung himself down in the arm-chair near mine, laid back his head, and clasping his arms beneath it, looked up at the picture above the chimney-piece.

"I like to fancy that Stroud himself would have given it to me, if he'd been able to say what he thought that day."

And, in answer to a question I put half-mechanically—"Begin again?" he flashed out. "When the one thing that brings me anywhere near him is that I knew enough to leave off?"

He stood up and laid his hand on my shoulder with a laugh. "Only the irony of it is that I *am* still painting—since Grindle's doing it for me! The Strouds stand alone, and happen once—but there's no exterminating our kind of art."

## THE POT-BOILER

THE STUDIO faced north, looking out over a dismal reach of roofs and chimneys, and rusty fire-escapes hung with heterogeneous garments. A crust of dirty snow covered the level surfaces, and a December sky with more snow in it lowered above them.

The room was bare and gaunt, with blotched walls and a stained uneven floor. On a divan lay a pile of "properties"—limp draperies, an Algerian scarf, a moth-eaten fan of peacock feathers. The janitor had forgotten to fill the coal-scuttle over-night, and the cast-iron stove projected its cold flanks into the room like a black iceberg. Ned Stanwell, who had just added his hat and great-coat to the miscellaneous heap on the divan, turned from the empty stove with a shiver.

"By Jove, this is a little too much like the last act of *Bohème*," he said, slipping into his coat again after a vain glance at the coal-scuttle. Much solitude, and a lively habit of mind, had bred in him the habit of audible soliloquy, and having flung a shout for the janitor down the seven flights dividing the studio from the basement, he turned back, picking up the thread of his monologue. "Exactly like *Bohème*, really—that crack in the wall is much more like a stage-crack than a real one—just the sort of crack Mungold would paint if he were doing a Humble Interior."

Mungold, the fashionable portrait-painter of the hour, was the favorite object of the younger men's irony.

"It only needs Kate Arran to be borne in dying," Stanwell continued with a laugh. "Much more likely to be poor little Caspar, though," he concluded.

His neighbor across the landing—the little sculptor, Caspar Arran, humorously called "Gasper" on account of his bronchial asthma—had lately been joined by a sister, Kate Arran, a strapping girl, fresh from the country, who had installed herself in the little room off her brother's studio, keeping house for him with a chafing-dish and a coffee-machine, to the mirth and envy of the other young men in the building.

Poor little Gasper had been very bad all the autumn, and it was surmised that his sister's presence, which he spoke of growlingly, as a troublesome necessity devolved on him by the inopportune death of an aunt, was really an indication of his failing ability to take care of himself. Kate Arran took his complaints with unfailing good-humor, darned his socks, brushed his clothes, fed him with steaming broths and foaming milk-punches, and listened with reverential assent to his interminable disquisitions on art. Everyone in the house was sorry for little Gasper, and the other fellows liked him all the more because it was so impossible to like his sculpture; but his talk was a bore, and when his colleagues ran in to see him they were apt to keep a hand on the door-knob and to plead a pressing engagement. At least they had been till Kate came; but now they began to show a disposition to enter and sit down. Caspar, who was no fool, perceived the change, and perhaps detected its cause; at any rate, he showed no special gratification at the increased cordiality of his friends, and Kate, who followed him in everything, took this as a sign that guests were to be discouraged.

There was one exception, however: Ned Stanwell, who was deplorably good-natured, had always lent a patient ear to Caspar, and he now reaped his reward by being taken into Kate's favor. Before she had been a month in the building they were on confidential terms as to Caspar's health, and lately Stanwell had penetrated farther, even to the inmost recesses of her anxiety about her brother's career. Caspar had recently had a bad blow in the refusal of his *magnum opus*—a vast allegorical group—by the Commissioners of the Minneapolis Exhibition. He took the rejection with Promethean irony, proclaimed it as the clinching proof of his ability, and abounded in reasons why, even in an age of such crass artistic ignorance, a refusal so egregious must react to the advantage of its object. But his sister's indignation, if as glowing, was a shade less hopeful. Of course Caspar was going to succeed—she knew it was only a question of time—but she paled at the word and turned imploring eyes on Stanwell. *Was there time enough?* It was the one element in the combination that she could not count on; and Stanwell, reddening under her look of interrogation, and cursing his own glaring robustness, would affirm that of course, of course, of course, by everything that was holy there was time enough—with the mental reservation that there wouldn't be, even if poor Caspar lived to be a hundred.

"Vos dat you yelling for the shanitor, Mr. Sdanwell?" inquired an affable voice through the doorway; and Stanwell, turning with a laugh, confronted the squat figure of a middle-aged man in an expensive fur coat, who looked as if his face secreted the oil which he used on his hair.

"Hullo, Shepson—I should say I *was* yelling. Did you ever feel such an atmosphere? That fool has forgotten to light the stove. Come in, but for heaven's sake don't take off your coat."

Mr. Shepson glanced about the studio with a look which seemed to say that, where so much else was lacking, the absence of a fire hardly added to the general sense of destitution.

"Vell, you ain't as vell fixed as Mr. Mungold—ever been to his studio, Mr. Sdanwell? De most *exquisite* blush hangings, and a gas fire, shoost as natural—"

"Oh, hang it, Shepson, do you call *that* a studio? It's like a manicure's parlor—or a beauty-doctor's. By George," broke off Stanwell, "and that's just what he is!"

"A beauty doctor?"

"Yes—oh, well, you wouldn't see," murmured Stanwell, mentally storing his epigram for more appreciative ears. "But you didn't come just to make me envious of Mungold's studio, did you?" And he pushed forward a chair for his visitor.

The latter, however, declined it with an affable motion. "Of gourse not, of gourse not—but Mr. Mungold is a sensible man. He makes a lot of money, you know."

"Is that what you came to tell me?" said Stanwell, still humorously.

"My gootness, no—I was downstairs looking at Holbrook's sdained class, and I shoost thought I'd sdep up a minute and take a beep at your vork."

"Much obliged, I'm sure—especially as I assume that you don't want any of it." Try as he would, Stanwell could not keep a note of eagerness from his voice. Mr. Shepson caught the note, and eyed him shrewdly through gold-rimmed glasses.

"Vell, vell, vell—I'm not prepared to commit myself. Shoost let me take a look round, vill you?"

"With the greatest pleasure—and I'll give another shout for the coal."

Stanwell went out on the landing, and Mr. Shepson, left to himself, began a meditative progress about the room. On an easel facing the improvised dais stood a canvas on which a young woman's head had been blocked in. It was just in that happy state of semi-evocation when a picture seems to detach itself from the grossness of its medium and live a wondrous moment in the actual; and the quality of the head in question—a vigorous dusky youthfulness, a kind of virgin majesty—lent itself to this illusion of vitality. Stanwell, who had re-entered the studio, could not help drawing a sharp breath as he saw the picture-dealer pausing with tilted head before this portrait: it seemed, at one moment, so impossible that he should not be struck with it, at the next so incredible that he should be.

Shepson cocked his parrot eye at the canvas with a desultory "Vat's dat?" which sent a twinge through the young man.

"That? Oh—a sketch of a young lady," stammered Stanwell, flushing at the imbecility of his reply. "It's Miss Arran, you know," he added, "the sister of my neighbor here, the sculptor."

"Sgulpture? There's no market for modern sgulpture except tombstones," said Shepson disparagingly, passing on as if he included the sister's portrait in his condemnation of her brother's trade.

Stanwell smiled, but more at himself than Shepson. How could he ever have supposed that the gross fool would see anything in his sketch of Kate Arran? He stood aside, straining after detachment, while the dealer continued his round of exploration, waddling up to the canvases on the walls, prodding with his stick at those stacked in corners, prying and peering sideways like a great bird rummaging for seed. He seemed to find little nutriment in the course of his search, for the sounds he emitted expressed a weary distaste for misdirected effort, and he completed his round without having thought it worth-while to draw a single canvas from its obscurity.

As his visits always had the same result, Stanwell was reduced to wondering why he had come again; but Shepson was not the man to indulge in vague roamings through the field of art, and it was safe to conclude that his purpose would in due course reveal itself. His tour brought him at length face to face with the painter, where he paused, clasping his plump gloved hands behind his back, and shaking an admonitory head.

"Gleffer—very gleffer, of course—I suppose you'll let me know when you want to sell anything?"

"Let you know?" gasped Stanwell, to whom the room grew so glowingly hot that he thought for a moment the janitor must have made up the fire.

Shepson gave a dry laugh. "Vell, it doesn't sdrike me that you want to now—doing this kind of thing, you know!" And he swept a comprehensive hand about the studio.

"Ah," said Stanwell, who could not keep a note of flatness out of his laugh.

"See here, Mr. Sdanwell, vot do you do it for? If you do it for yourself and the other fellows, vell and good—only don't ask me round. I sell pictures, I don't theorize about them. Ven you vant to sell, gome to me with what my gustomers vant. You can do it—you're smart enough. You can do most anything. Vere's dat bortrait of Gladys Glyde dat you showed at the Fake Club last autumn? Dat little thing in de Romney style? Dat vas a little shem, now," exclaimed Mr. Shepson, whose pronunciation became increasingly Semitic in moments of excitement.

Stanwell stared. Called upon a few months previously to contribute to an exhibition of skits on well-known artists, he had used the photograph of a favorite music-hall "star" as the basis of a picture in the pseudo-historical style affected by the popular portrait-painters of the day.

"That thing?" he said contemptuously. "How on earth did you happen to see it?"

"I see everything," returned the dealer with an oracular smile. "If you've got it here let me look at it, please."

It cost Stanwell a few minutes' search to unearth his skit—a clever blending of dash and sentimentality, in just the right proportion to create the impression of a powerful brush subdued to mildness by the charms of the sitter. Stanwell had thrown it off in a burst of imitative frenzy, beginning for the mere joy of the satire, but gradually fascinated by the problem of producing the requisite mingling of attributes. He was surprised now to see how well he had caught the note, and Shepson's face reflected his approval.

"By George! Dat's something like," the dealer ejaculated.

"Like what? Like Mungold?" Stanwell laughed.

"Like business! Like a big order for a bortrait, Mr. Sdanwell—dat's what it's like!" cried Shepson, swinging round on him.

Stanwell's stare widened. "An order for me?"

"Vy not? Accidents *vill* happen," said Shepson jocosely. "De fact is, Mrs. Archer Millington wants to be bainted—you know her sdyle? Well, she prides herself on her likeness to little Gladys. And so ven she saw dat bicture of yours at de Fake Show she made a note of your name, and de udder day she sent for me and she says: 'Mr. Shepson, I'm tired of Mungold—all my friends are done by Mungold. I vant to break away and be orishinal—I vant to be done by the bainter that did Gladys Glyde."

Shepson waited to observe the result of this overwhelming announcement, and Stanwell, after a momentary halt of surprise, brought out laughingly: "But this *is* a Mungold. Is this what she calls being original?"

"Shoost exactly," said Shepson, with unexpected acuteness. "That's vat dey all want—something different from what all deir friends have got, but shoost like it all de same. Dat's de public all over! Mrs. Millington don't want a Mungold, because everybody's got a Mungold, but she wants a picture that's in the same sdyle, because dat's de sdyle, and she's afraid of any oder!"

Stanwell was listening with real enjoyment. "Ah, you know your public," he murmured.

"Vell, you do, too, or you couldn't have painted dat," the dealer retorted. "And I don't say dey're wrong—mind dat. I like a bretty picture myself. And I understand the way dey feel. Dey're villing to let Sargent take liberties vid them, because it's like being punched in de ribs by a King; but if anybody else baints them, they vant to look as sweet as an obituary." He turned earnestly to Stanwell. "The thing is to attract their notice. Vonce you got it they von't gif you dime to sleep. And dat's why I'm here to-day—you've attracted Mrs. Millington's notice, and vonce you're hung in dat new ball-room—dat's vere she vants you, in a big gold panel—vonce you're dere, vy, you'll be like the Pianola—no home gompleat without you. And I ain't going to charge you any commission on the first job!"

He stood before the painter, exuding a mixture of deference and patronage in which either element might predominate as events developed; but Stanwell could see in the incident only the stuff for a good story.

"My dear Shepson," he said, "what are you talking about? This is no picture of mine. Why don't you ask me to do you a Corot at once? I hear there's a great demand for them still in the West. Or an Arthur Schracker—I can do Schracker as well as Mungold," he added, turning around a small canvas at which a paint-pot seemed to have been hurled with violence from a considerable distance.

Shepson ignored the allusion to Corot, but screwed his eyes at the picture. "Ah, Schracker—vell, the Schracker sdyle would take first rate if you were a foreigner—but, for goodness sake, don't try it on Mrs. Millington!"

Stanwell pushed the two skits aside. "Oh, you can trust me," he cried humorously. "The pearls and the eyes very large—the extremities very small. Isn't that about the size of it?"

"Dat's it—dat's it. And the check as big as you vant to make it! Mrs. Millington vants the picture finished in time for her first barty in the new ball-room, and if you rush the job she won't sdickle at an extra thousand. Vill you come along with me now and arrange for your first sitting?"

He stood before the young man, urgent, paternal, and so imbued with the importance of his mission that his face stretched to a ludicrous length of dismay when Stanwell, administering a good-humored push to his shoulder, cried gaily: "My dear fellow, it will make my price rise still higher when the lady hears I'm too busy to take any orders at present—and that I'm actually obliged to turn you out now because I'm expecting a sitter!"

It was part of Shepson's business to have a quick ear for the note of finality, and he offered no resistance to Stanwell's friendly impulse; but on the threshold he paused to murmur, with a regretful glance at the denuded studio: "You could haf done it, Mr. Sdanwell—you could haf done it!"

## II

KATE ARRAN was Stanwell's sitter; but the janitor had hardly filled the stove when she came in to say that she could not sit. Caspar had had a bad night: he was depressed and feverish, and in spite of his protests she had resolved to fetch the doctor. Care sat on her usually tranquil features, and Stanwell, as he offered to go for the doctor, wished he could have caught in his picture the wide gloom of her brow. There was always a kind of Biblical breadth in the expression of her emotions, and today she suggested a text from Isaiah.

"But you're not busy?" she hesitated; in the full voice which seemed tuned to a solemn rhetoric.

"I meant to be—with you. But since that's off I'm quite unemployed."

She smiled interrogatively. "I thought perhaps you had an order. I met Mr. Shepson rubbing his hands on the landing."

"Was he rubbing his hands? Well, it was not over me. He says that from the style of my pictures he doesn't suppose I want to sell."

She looked at him superbly. "Well, do you?"

He embraced his bleak walls in a circular gesture. "Judge for yourself!"

"Ah, but it's splendidly furnished!"

"With rejected pictures, you mean?"

"With ideals!" she exclaimed in a tone caught from her brother, and which would have been irritating to Stanwell if it had not been moving.

He gave a slight shrug and took up his hat; but she interposed to say that if it didn't make any difference she would prefer to have him go and sit with poor Caspar, while she ran for the doctor and did some household errands by the way. Stanwell divined in her request the need for a brief respite from Caspar, and though he shivered at the thought of her facing the cold in the scant jacket which had been her only wear since he had known her, he let her go without a protest, and betook himself to Arran's studio.

He found the little sculptor dressed and roaming fretfully about the melancholy room in which he and his plastic off-spring lodged together. In one corner, where Kate's chair and work-table stood, a scrupulous order prevailed; but the rest of the apartment had the dreary untidiness, the damp grey look, which the worker in clay usually creates about him. In the center of this desert stood the shrouded image of Caspar's disappointment: the colossal rejected group as to which his friends could seldom remember whether it represented Jove hurling a Titan from Olympus or Science Subjugating Religion. Caspar was the sworn foe of religion, which he appeared to regard as indirectly connected with his inability to sell his statues.

The sculptor was too ill to work, and Stanwell's appearance loosed the pent-up springs of his talk.

"Hullo! What are you doing here? I thought Kate had gone over to sit to you. She wanted a little fresh air? I should say enough of it came in through these windows. How like a woman, when she's agreed to do a certain thing, to make up her mind at once that she's got to do another! They don't call it caprice—it's always duty: that's the humor of it. I'll be bound Kate alleged a pressing engagement. Sorry she should waste your time so, my dear fellow. Here am I with plenty of it to burn—look at my hand shake; I can't do a thing! Well, luckily nobody wants me to—posterity may suffer, but the present generation isn't worrying. The present generation wants to be carved in sugar-candy, or painted in maple syrup. It doesn't want to be told the truth about itself or about anything in the universe. The prophets have always lived in a garret, my dear fellow—only the ravens don't always find out their address! Speaking of ravens, though, Kate told me she saw old Shepson coming out of your place—I say, old man, you're not meditating an apostasy? You're not doing the kind of thing that Shepson would look at?"

Stanwell laughed. "Oh, he looked at them—but only to confirm his reasons for rejecting them."

"Ha! ha! That's right—he wanted to refresh his memory with their badness. But how on earth did he happen to have any doubts on the subject? I should as soon have thought of his coming in here!"

Stanwell winced at the analogy, but replied in Caspar's key: "Oh, he's not as sure of any of us as he is of you!"

The sculptor received this tribute with a joyous expletive. "By God, no, he's sure of me, as you say! He and his tribe know that I'll starve in my tracks sooner than make a concession—a single concession. A fellow came after me once to do an angel on a tombstone—an angel leaning against a broken column, and looking as if it was waiting for the elevator and wondering why in hell it didn't come. He said he wanted me to show that the deceased was pining to get to heaven. As she was his wife I didn't dispute the proposition, but when I asked him what he understood by *heaven* he grabbed his hat and walked out of the studio. *He* didn't wait for the elevator."

Stanwell listened with a practiced smile. The story of the man who had come to order the angel was so familiar to Arran's friends that its only interest consisted in waiting to see what variation he would give to the retort which had put the mourner to flight. It was generally supposed that this visit represented the sculptor's nearest approach to an order, and one of his fellow-craftsmen had been heard to remark that if Caspar *had* made the tombstone, the lady under it would have tried harder than ever to get to heaven. To Stanwell's present mood, however, there was something more than usually irritating in the gratuitous assumption that Arran had only to derogate from his altitude to have a press of purchasers at his door.

"Well—what did you gain by kicking your widower out?" he objected. "Why can't a man do two kinds of work—one to please himself and the other to boil the pot?"

Caspar stopped in his jerky walk—the stride of a tall man attempted with short legs (it sometimes appeared to Stanwell to symbolize his artistic endeavour).

"Why can't a man—why can't he? You ask me that, Stanwell?" he blazed out.

"Yes; and what's more, I'll answer you: it isn't everybody who can adapt his art as he wants to!"

Caspar stood before him, gasping with incredulous scorn. "Adapt his art? As he wants to? Unhappy wretch, what lingo are you talking? If you mean that it isn't every honest man who can be a renegade—"

"That's just what I do mean: he can't unless he's clever enough to see the other side."

The deep groan with which Caspar met this casuistry was cut short by a knock at the studio door, which thereupon opened to admit a small dapperly-dressed man with a silky moustache and mildly-bulging eyes.

"Ah, Mungold," exclaimed Stanwell, to cover the gloomy silence with which Arran received the new-comer; whereat the latter, with the air of a man who does not easily believe himself unwelcome, bestowed a sympathetic pressure on the sculptor's hand.

"My dear chap, I've just met Miss Arran, and she told me you were laid up with a bad cold, so I thought I'd pop in and cheer you up a little."

He looked about him with a smile evidently intended as the first act in his beneficent program.

Mr. Mungold, freshly soaped and scented, with a neat glaze of gentility extending from his varnished boot-tips to his glossy hat, looked like the "flattered" portrait of a common man—just such an idealized presentment as his own brush might have produced. As a rule, however, he devoted himself to the portrayal of the other sex, painting ladies in syrup, as Arran said, with marsh-mallow children leaning against their knees. He was as quick as a dressmaker at catching new ideas, and the style of his pictures changed as rapidly as that of the fashion-plates. One year all his sitters were done on oval canvases, with gauzy draperies and a background of clouds; the next they were seated under an immemorial elm, caressing enormous dogs obviously constructed out of door-mats. Whatever their occupation they always looked straight out of the canvas, giving the impression that their eyes were fixed on an invisible camera. This gave rise to the rumor that Mungold "did" his portraits from photographs; it was even said that he had invented a way of transferring an enlarged photograph to the canvas, so that all that remained was to fill in the colors. If he heard of this charge he took it calmly, but probably it had not reached the high spheres in which he moved, and in which he was esteemed for painting pearls better, and making unsuggestive children look lovelier, than any of his fellow-craftsmen. Mr. Mungold, in fact, deemed it a part of his professional duty to study his sitters in their home-life; and as this life was chiefly led in the homes of others, he was too busy dining out and going to the opera to mingle much with his colleagues. But as no one is wholly consistent, Mr. Mungold had lately belied his ambitions by falling in love with Kate Arran; and with that gentle persistency which made him so wonderful in managing obstreperous infantile sitters, he had contrived to establish a precarious footing in her brother's studio.

Part of his success was due to the fact that he could not easily think himself the object of a rebuff. If it seemed to hit him he regarded it as deflected from its aim, and brushed it aside with a discreet gesture. A touch of comedy was lent to the situation by the fact that, till Kate Arran's coming, Mungold had always served as her brother's Awful Example. It was a mark of Arran's lack of humor that he persisted in regarding the little man as a conscious apostate, instead of perceiving that he painted as he could, in a world which really looked to him like a vast confectioner's window. Stanwell had never quite divined how Mungold had won over the sister, to whom her brother's prejudices were a religion; but he suspected the painter of having united a deep belief in Caspar's gifts with the occasional offer of opportune delicacies—the port-wine or game which Kate had no other means of procuring for her patient.

Stanwell, persuaded that Mungold would stick to his post till Miss Arran's return, felt himself freed from his promise to the latter and left the incongruous pair to themselves. There had been a time when it amused him to see Caspar submerge the painter in a torrent of turbid eloquence, and to watch poor Mungold sputtering under the rush of denunciation, yet emitting little bland phrases of assent, like a gentleman drowning correctly, in gloves and eye-glasses. But Stanwell was beginning to find less food for gaiety than for envy in the contemplation of his colleague. After all, Mungold held his ground, he did not go under. Spite of his manifest absurdity he had succeeded in propitiating the sister, in making himself tolerated by the brother; and the fact that his success was due to the ability to purchase port-wine and game was not in this case a mitigating circumstance. Stanwell knew that the Arrans really preferred him to Mungold, but the knowledge only sharpened his envy of the latter, whose friendship could command visible tokens of expression, while poor Stanwell's remained gloomily inarticulate. As he returned to his over-populated studio and surveyed anew the pictures of which Shepson had not offered to relieve him, he found himself wishing, not for Mungold's lack of scruples, for he believed him to be the most scrupulous of men, but for that happy mean of talent which so completely satisfied the artistic requirements of the inartistic. Mungold was not to be despised as an apostate—he was to be congratulated as a man whose aptitudes were exactly in line with the taste of the persons he liked to dine with.

At this point in his meditations, Stanwell's eye fell on the portrait of Miss Gladys Glyde. It was really, as Shepson said, as good as a Mungold; yet it could never be made to serve the same purpose, because it was the work of a man who knew it was bad art. That at least would have been Caspar Arran's contention—poor Caspar, who produced as bad art in the service of the loftiest convictions! The distinction began to look like mere casuistry to Stanwell. He had never been very proud of his own adaptability. It had seemed to him to indicate the lack of an individual stand-point, and he had tried to counteract it by the cultivation of an aggressively personal style. But the cursed knack was in his fingers—he was always at the mercy of some other man's sensations, and there were moments when he blushed to remember that his grandfather had spent a laborious life-time in Rome, copying the Old Masters for a generation which lacked the facile resource of the camera. Now, however, it struck him that the ancestral versatility might be a useful inheritance. In art, after all, the greatest of them did what they could; and if a man could do several things instead of one, why should he not profit by the multiplicity of his gifts? If one had two talents why not serve two masters?

## III

STANWELL, while seeing Caspar through the attack which had been the cause of his sister's arrival, had struck up a friendship with the young doctor who climbed the patient's seven flights with unremitting fidelity. The two, since then, had continued to exchange confidences regarding the sculptor's health, and Stanwell, anxious to waylay the doctor after his visit, left the studio door ajar, and went out when he heard a sound of leave-taking across the landing. But it appeared that the doctor had just come, and that it was Mungold who was making his adieux.

The latter at once assumed that Stanwell had been on the alert for him, and met the supposed advance by affably inviting himself into the studio.

"May I come and take a look around, my dear fellow? I have been meaning to drop in for an age—" Mungold always spoke with a girlish emphasis and effusiveness—"but I have been so busy getting up Mrs. Van Orley's tableaux—English eighteenth century portraits, you know—that really, what with that and my sittings, I've hardly had time to think. And then you know you owe me about a dozen visits! But you're a savage—you don't pay visits. You stay here and *piocher*—which is wiser, as the results prove. Ah, you're very strong—immensely strong!" He paused in the middle of the studio, glancing about a little apprehensively, as though he thought the stored energy of the pictures might result in an explosion. "Very original—very striking—ah, Miss Arran! A powerful head; but—excuse the suggestion—isn't there just the least little lack of sweetness? You don't think she has the sweet type? Perhaps not—but could she be so lovely if she were not intensely feminine? Just at present, though, she is not looking her best—she is horribly tired. I am afraid there is very little money left—and poor dear Caspar is so impossible:

he won't hear of a loan. Otherwise I should be most happy—. But I came just now to propose a piece of work—in fact to give him an order. Mrs. Archer Millington has built a new ball-room, as I daresay you may have seen in the papers, and she has been kind enough to ask me for some hints—oh, merely as a friend: I don't presume to do more than advise. But her decorator wants to do something with Cupids—something light and playful, you understand. And so I ventured to say that I knew a very clever sculptor— well, I *do* believe Caspar has talent—latent talent, you know—and at any rate a job of that sort would be a big lift for him. At least I thought he would regard it so; but you should have heard him when I showed him the decorator's sketch. He asked me what the Cupids were to be done in—lard? And if I thought he had had his training at a confectioner's? And I don't know what more besides—but he worked himself up to such a degree that he brought on a frightful fit of coughing, and Miss Arran, I'm afraid, was rather annoyed with me when she came in, though I'm sure an order from Mrs. Archer Millington is not a thing that would annoy most people!"

Mr. Mungold paused, breathless with the rehearsal of his wrongs, and Stanwell said with a smile: "You know poor Caspar is terribly stiff on the purity of the artist's aim."

"The artist's aim?" Mr. Mungold stared. "What is the artist's aim but to please—isn't that the purpose of all true art? But his theories are so extravagant. I really don't know what I shall say to Mrs. Millington—she is not used to being refused. I suppose I had better put it on the ground of ill-health." The artist glanced at his handsome repeater. "Dear me, I promised to be at Mrs. Van Orley's before twelve o'clock. We are to settle about the curtain before luncheon. My dear fellow, it has been a privilege to see your work. By the way, *you* have never done any modeling, I suppose? You're so extraordinarily versatile—I didn't know whether you might care to undertake the Cupids yourself."

Stanwell had to wait a long time for the doctor; and when the latter came out he looked grave. Worse? No, he couldn't say that Caspar was worse—but then he wasn't any better. There was nothing mortal the matter, but the question was how long he could hold out. It was the kind of case where there is no use in drugs—he had just scribbled a prescription to quiet Miss Arran.

"It's the cold, I suppose," Stanwell groaned. "He ought to be shipped off to Florida."

The doctor made a negative gesture. "Florida be hanged! What he wants is to sell his group. That would set him up quicker than sitting on the equator."

"Sell his group?" Stanwell echoed. "But he's so indifferent to recognition—he believes in himself so thoroughly. I thought at first he would be hard hit when the Exhibition Committee refused it, but he seems to regard that as another proof of its superiority."

His visitor turned on him the penetrating eye of the confessor. "Indifferent to recognition? He's eating his heart out for it. Can't you see that all that talk is just so much whistling to keep his courage up? The name of his disease is failure—and I can't write the prescription that will cure that complaint. But if somebody would come along and take a fancy to those two naked parties who are breaking each other's heads, we'd have Mr. Caspar putting on a pound a day."

The truth of this diagnosis became suddenly vivid to Stanwell. How dull of him not to have seen before that it was not cold or privation which was killing Caspar—not anxiety for his sister's future, nor the ache of watching her daily struggle—but simply the cankering thought that he might die before he had made himself known! It was his vanity that was starving to death, and all Mungold's hampers could not appease that hunger. Stanwell was not shocked by the discovery—he was only the more sorry for the little man, who was, after all, denied that solace of self-sufficiency which his talk so noisily proclaimed. His lot seemed hard enough when Stanwell had pictured him as buoyed up by the scorn of public opinion—it became tragic if he was denied that support. The artist wondered if Kate had guessed her brother's secret, or if she were still the dupe of his stoicism. Stanwell was sure that the sculptor would take no one into his confidence, and least of all his sister, whose faith in his artistic independence was the chief prop of that tottering pose. Kate's penetration was not great, and Stanwell recalled the incredulous smile with which she had heard him defend poor Mungold's "sincerity" against Caspar's assaults; but she had the insight of the heart, and where her brother's happiness was concerned she might have seen deeper than any of them. It was this last consideration which took the strongest hold on Stanwell—he felt Caspar's sufferings chiefly through the thought of his sister's possible disillusionment.

IV

WITHIN three months two events had set the studio building talking. Stanwell had painted a full-length portrait of Mrs. Archer Millington, and Caspar Arran had received an order to execute his group in marble.

The name of the sculptor's patron had not been divulged. The order came through Shepson, who explained that an American customer living abroad, having seen a photograph of the group in one of the papers, had at once cabled home to secure it. He intended to bestow it on a public building in America, and not wishing to advertise his munificence, had preferred that even the sculptor should remain ignorant of his name. The group bought by an enlightened compatriot for the adornment of a civic building in his native land! There could hardly be a more complete vindication of unappreciated genius, and Caspar made the most of the argument. He was not exultant, he was sublimely magnanimous. He had always said that he could afford to await the Verdict of Posterity, and his unknown patron's act clearly shadowed forth that impressive decision. Happily it also found expression in a check which it would have taken more philosophy to await. The group was paid for in advance, and Kate's joy in her brother's recognition was deliciously mingled with the thrill of ordering him some new clothes, and coaxing him out to dine succulently at a neighboring restaurant. Caspar flourished insufferably on this regime: he began to strike the attitude of the recognized Great Master, who gives advice and encouragement to the struggling neophyte. He held himself up as an example of the reward of disinterestedness, of the triumph of the artist who clings obstinately to his ideals.

"A man must believe in his star—look at Napoleon! It's the dogged trust in one's convictions that tells—it always ends by forcing the public into line. Only be sure you make no concessions—don't give in to any of their humbug! An artist who listens to the critics is ruined—they never have any use for the poor devils who do what they tell them to. Run after fame and she'll keep you running, but stay in your own corner and do your own work, and by George, sir, she'll come crawling up to you and ask to have her likeness done!"

These exhortations were chiefly directed to Stanwell, partly because the inmates of the other studios were apt to elude them, partly also because the rumors concerning Stanwell's portrait of Mrs. Millington had begun to disquiet the sculptor. At first he had taken a condescending interest in the fact of his friend's receiving an order, and had admonished him not to lose the chance of "showing up" his sitter and her environment. It was a splendid opportunity for a fellow with a "message" to be introduced into the tents of the Philistine, and Stanwell was charged to drive a long sharp nail into the enemy's skull. But presently Arran began to suspect that the portrait was not as comminatory as he could have wished. Mungold, the most kindly of rivals, let drop a word of injudicious praise: the picture, he said, promised to be delightfully "in keeping" with the decorations of the ball-room, and the lady's gown harmonized exquisitely with the window-curtains. Stanwell, called to account by his monitor, reminded the latter that he himself had been selected by Mungold to do the Cupids for Mrs. Millington's ball-room, and that the friendly artist's praise could, therefore, not be taken as positive evidence of incapacity.

"Ah, but I didn't do them—I kicked him out!" Caspar rejoined; and Stanwell could only plead that, even in the cause of art, one could hardly kick a lady.

"Ah, that's the worst of it. If the women get at you you're lost. You're young, you're impressionable, you won't mind my saying that you're not built for a stoic, and hang it, they'll coddle you, they'll enervate you, they'll sentimentalize you, they'll make a Mungold of you!"

"Poor Mungold," Stanwell laughed. "If he lived the life of an anchorite he couldn't help painting pictures that would please Mrs. Millington."

"Whereas you could," Kate interjected, raising her head from the ironing-board where, Sphinx-like, magnificent, she swung a splendid arm above her brother's shirts.

"Oh, well, perhaps I shan't please her; perhaps I shall elevate her taste."

Caspar directed a groan to his sister. "That's what they all think at first—Childe Roland to the Dark Tower came. But inside the Dark Tower there's the Venusberg. Oh, I don't mean that you'll be taken with truffles and plush footmen, like Mungold. But praise, my poor Ned—praise is a deadly drug! It's the absinthe of the artist—and they'll stupefy you with it. You'll wallow in the mire of success."

Stanwell raised a protesting hand. "Really, for one order, you're a little lurid!"

"One? Haven't you already had a dozen others?"

"Only one other, so far—and I'm not sure I shall do that."

"Not sure—wavering already! That's the way the mischief begins. If the women get a fad for you they'll work you like a galley-slave. You'll have to do your round of 'copy' every morning. What becomes of inspiration then? How are you going to loaf and invite the soul? Don't barter your birthright for a mess of pottage! Oh, I understand the temptation—I know the taste of money and success. But look at me, Stanwell. You know how long I had to wait for recognition. Well, now it's come to me I don't mean to let it knock me off my feet. I don't mean to let myself be overworked; I have already made it known that I will not be bullied into taking more orders than I can do full justice to. And my sister is with me, God bless her; Kate would rather go on ironing my shirts in a garret than see me prostitute my art!"

Kate's glance radiantly confirmed this declaration of independence, and Stanwell, with his evasive laugh, asked her if, meanwhile, she should object to his investing a part of his ill-gotten gains in theatre tickets for the party that evening.

It appeared that Stanwell had also been paid in advance, and well paid; for he began to permit himself various mild distractions, in which he generally contrived to have the Arrans share. It seemed perfectly natural to Kate that Caspar's friends should spend their money for his recreation, and by one of the most touching sophistries of her sex she thus reconciled herself to the anomaly of taking a little pleasure on her own account. Mungold was less often in the way, for she had never been able to forgive him for proposing that Caspar should do Mrs. Millington's Cupids; and for a few radiant weeks Stanwell had the undisputed enjoyment of her pride in her brother's achievement.

Stanwell had "rushed through" Mrs. Millington's portrait in time for the opening of her new ball-room; and it was perhaps in return for this favor that she consented to let the picture be exhibited at a big Portrait Show which was held in April for the benefit of a fashionable charity.

In Mrs. Millington's ball-room the picture had been seen and approved only by the distinguished few who had access to that social sanctuary; but on the walls of the exhibition it became a center of comment and discussion. One of the immediate results of this publicity was a visit from Shepson, with two or three orders in his pocket, as he put it. He surveyed the studio with fresh disgust, asked Stanwell why he did not move, and was impressed rather than downcast on learning that the painter had not decided whether he would take any more orders that spring.

"You might haf a studio at Newport," he suggested. "It would be rather new to do your sitters out of doors, with the sea behind them—showing they had a blace on the gliffs!"

The picture produced a different and less flattering effect on the critics. They gave it, indeed, more space than they had ever before accorded to the artist's efforts, but their estimate seemed to confirm Caspar Arran's forebodings, and Stanwell had perhaps never despised them so little as when he read their comments on his work. On the whole, however, neither praise nor blame disquieted him greatly. He was engrossed in the contemplation of Kate Arran's happiness, and basking in the refracted warmth it shed about her. The doctor's prognostications had come true. Caspar was putting on a pound a week, and had plunged into a fresh "creation" more symbolic and encumbering than the monument of which he had been so opportunely relieved. If there was any cloud on Stanwell's enjoyment of life, it was caused by the discovery that success had quadrupled Caspar's artistic energies. Meanwhile it was delightful to see Kate's joy in her brother's recovered capacity for work, and to listen to the axioms which, for Stanwell's guidance, she deduced from the example of Caspar's heroic pursuit of the ideal. There was nothing repellent in Kate's borrowed didacticism, and if it sometimes bored Stanwell to hear her quote her brother, he was sure it would never bore him to be quoted by her himself; and there were moments when he felt he had nearly achieved that distinction.

Caspar was not addicted to the visiting of art exhibitions. He took little interest in any productions save his own, and was moreover disposed to believe that good pictures, like clever criminals, are apt to go unhung. Stanwell therefore thought it unlikely that his portrait of Mrs. Millington would be seen by Kate, who was not given to independent explorations in the field of art; but one day, on entering the exhibition—which he had hitherto rather nervously shunned—he saw the Arrans at the end of the gallery in which the portrait hung. They were not looking at it, they were moving away from it, and to Stanwell's quickened perceptions their attitude seemed almost that of flight. For a moment he thought of flying too; then a desperate resolve nerved him to meet them, and stemming the crowd, he made a circuit which brought him face to face with their retreat.

The room in which they met was momentarily empty, and there was nothing to intervene between the shock of their inter-changed glances. Caspar was flushed and bristling: his little body quivered like a machine from which the steam has just been turned off. Kate lifted a stricken glance. Stanwell read in it the reflection of her brother's tirade, but she held out her hand in silence.

For a moment Caspar was silent too; then, with a terrible smile: "My dear fellow, I congratulate you; Mungold will have to look to his laurels," he said.

The shot delivered, he stalked away with his seven-league stride, and Kate moved tragically through the room in his wake.

V

SHEPSON took up his hat with a despairing gesture. "Vell, I gif you up—I gif you up!" he said.

"Don't—yet," protested Stanwell from the divan.

It was winter again, and though the janitor had not forgotten the fire, the studio gave no other evidence of its master's increasing prosperity. If Stanwell spent his money it was not upon himself.

He leaned back against the wall, his hands in his pockets, a cigarette between his lips, while Shepson paced the dirty floor or halted impatiently before an untouched canvas on the easel.

"I tell you vat it is, Mr. Sdanwell, I can't make you out!" he lamented. "Last vinter you got a sdart that vould have kept most men going for years. After making dat hit vith Mrs. Millington's picture you could have bainted half the town. And here you are sitting on your divan and saying you can't make up your mind to take another order. Vell, I can only say that if you take much longer to make it up, you'll find some other chap has cut in and got your job. Mrs. Van Orley has been waiting since last August, and she dells me you haven't even answered her letter."

"How could I? I didn't know if I wanted to paint her."

"My goodness! Don't you know if you vant three thousand tollars?"

Stanwell surveyed his cigarette. "No, I'm not sure I do," he said.

Shepson flung out his hands. "Ask more den—but do it quick!" he exclaimed.

Left to himself, Stanwell stood in silent contemplation of the canvas on which the dealer had riveted his reproachful gaze. It had been destined to reflect the opulent image of Mrs. Alpheus Van Orley, but some secret reluctance of Stanwell's had stayed the execution of the task. He had painted two of Mrs. Millington's friends in the spring, had been much praised and liberally paid for his work, and then, declining several recent orders to be executed at Newport, had surprised his friends by remaining quietly in town. It was not till August that he hired a little cottage on the New Jersey coast and invited the Arrans to visit him. They accepted the invitation, and the three had spent together six weeks of seashore idleness, during which Stanwell's modest rafters shook with Caspar's denunciations of his host's venality, and the brightness of Kate's gratitude was tempered by a tinge of reproach. But her grief over Stanwell's apostasy could not efface the fact that he had offered her brother the means of escape from town, and Stanwell himself was consoled by the reflection that but for Mrs. Millington's portrait he could not have performed even this trifling service for his friends.

When the Arrans left him in September he went to pay a few visits in the country, and on his return, a month later, to the studio building he found that things had not gone well with Caspar. The little sculptor had caught cold, and the labor and expense of converting his gigantic offspring into marble seemed to hang heavily upon him. He and Kate were living in a damp company of amorphous clay monsters, unfinished witnesses to the creative frenzy which had seized him after the sale of his group; and the doctor had urged that his patient should be removed to warmer and drier lodgings. But to uproot

Caspar was impossible, and his sister could only feed the stove, and swaddle him in mufflers and felt slippers.

Stanwell found that during his absence Mungold had reappeared, fresh and rosy from a summer in Europe, and as prodigal as ever of the only form of attention which Kate could be counted on not to resent. The game and champagne reappeared with him, and he seemed as ready as Stanwell to lend a patient ear to Caspar's homilies. But Stanwell could see that, even now, Kate had not forgiven him for the Cupids. Stanwell himself had spent the early winter months in idleness. The sight of his tools filled him with a strange repugnance, and he absented himself as much as possible from the studio. But Shepson's visit roused him to the fact that he must decide on some definite course of action. If he wished to follow up his success of the previous spring he must refuse no more orders: he must not let Mrs. Van Orley slip away from him. He knew there were competitors enough ready to profit by his hesitations, and since his success was the result of a whim, a whim might undo it. With a sudden gesture of decision he caught up his hat and left the studio.

On the landing he met Kate Arran. She too was going out, drawn forth by the sudden radiance of the January afternoon. She met him with a smile which seemed the answer to his uncertainties, and he asked abruptly if she had time to take a walk with him.

Yes; for once she had time, for Mr. Mungold was sitting with Caspar, and had promised to remain till she came in. It mattered little to Stanwell that Mungold was with Caspar as long as he himself was with Kate; and he instantly soared to the suggestion that they should prolong the painter's vigil by taking the "elevated" to the Park. In this too his companion acquiesced after a moment of surprise: she seemed in a consenting mood, and Stanwell augured well from the fact.

The Park was clothed in the double glitter of snow and sunshine. They roamed the hard white alleys to a continuous tinkle of sleigh-bells, and Kate brightened with the exhilaration of the scene. It was not often that she permitted herself such an escape from routine, and in this new environment, which seemed to detach her from her daily setting, Stanwell had his first complete vision of her. To the girl also their unwonted isolation seemed to create a sense of fuller communion, for she began presently, as they reached the leafless solitude of the Ramble, to speak with sudden freedom of her brother. It appeared that the orders against which Caspar had so heroically steeled himself were slow in coming: he had received no commission since the sale of his group, and he was beginning to suffer from a reaction of discouragement. Oh, it was not the craving for popularity—Stanwell knew how far above that he stood. But it had been exquisite, yes, exquisite to him to find himself believed in, understood. He had fancied that the purchase of the group was the dawn of a tardy recognition—and now the darkness of indifference had set in again, no one spoke of him, no one wrote of him, no one cared.

"If he were in good health it would not matter—he would throw off such weakness, he would live only for the joy of his work; but he is losing ground, his strength is failing, and he is so afraid there will not be time enough left—time enough for full recognition," she explained.

The quiver in her voice silenced Stanwell: he was afraid of echoing it with his own. At length he said: "Oh, more orders will come. Success is a gradual growth."

"Yes, *real* success," she said, with a solemn note in which he caught—and forgave— a reflection on his own facile triumphs.

"But when the orders do come," she continued, "will he have strength to carry them out? Last winter the doctor thought he only needed work to set him up; now he talks of rest instead! He says we ought to go to a warm climate—but how can Caspar leave the group?"

"Oh, hang the group—let him chuck the order!" cried Stanwell.

She looked at him tragically. "The money is spent," she said.

Stanwell colored to the roots of his hair. "But ill-health—ill-health excuses everything. If he goes away now he will come back good for twice the amount of work in the spring. A sculptor is not expected to deliver a statue on a given day, like a package of groceries! You must do as the doctor says—you must make him chuck everything and go."

They had reached a windless nook above the lake, and, pausing in the stress of their talk, she let herself sink on a bench beside the path. The movement encouraged him, and he seated himself at her side.

"You must take him away at once," he repeated urgently. "He must be made comfortable—you must both be free from worry. And I want you to let me manage it for you—"

He broke off, silenced by her rising blush, her protesting murmur.

"Oh, stop, please; let me explain. I'm not talking of lending you money; I'm talking of giving you—myself. The offer may be just as unacceptable, but it's of a kind to which it's customary to accord it a hearing. I should have made it a year ago—the first day I saw you, I believe!—but that, then, it wasn't in my power to make things easier for you. But now, you know, I've had a little luck. Since I painted Mrs. Millington things have changed. I believe I can get as many orders as I choose—there are two or three people waiting now. What's the use of it all, if it doesn't bring me a little happiness? And the only happiness I know is the kind that you can give me."

He paused, suddenly losing the courage to look at her, so that her pained murmur was framed for him in a glittering vision of the frozen lake. He turned with a start and met the refusal in her eyes.

"No—really no?" he repeated.

She shook her head silently.

"I could have helped you—I could have helped you!" he sighed.

She flushed distressfully, but kept her eyes on his.

"It's just that—don't you see?" she reproached him.

"Just that—the fact that I could be of use to you?"

"The fact that, as you say, things have changed since you painted Mrs. Millington. I haven't seen the later portraits, but they tell me—"

"Oh, they're just as bad!" Stanwell jeered.

"You've sold your talent, and you know it: that's the dreadful part. You did it deliberately," she cried with passion.

"Oh, deliberately," he interjected.

"And you're not ashamed—you talk of going on."

"I'm not ashamed; I talk of going on."

She received this with a long shuddering sigh, and turned her eyes away from him.

"Oh, why—why—why?" she lamented.

It was on the tip of Stanwell's tongue to answer, "That I might say to you what I am just saying now—" but he replied instead: "A man may paint bad pictures and be a decent fellow. Look at Mungold, after all!"

The adjuration had an unexpected effect. Kate's color faded suddenly, and she sat motionless, with a stricken face.

"There's a difference—" she began at length abruptly; "the difference you've always insisted on. Mr. Mungold paints as well as he can. He has no idea that his pictures are— less good than they might be."

"Well—?"

"So he can't be accused of doing what he does for money—of sacrificing anything better." She turned on him with troubled eyes. "It was you who made me understand that, when Caspar used to make fun of him."

Stanwell smiled. "I'm glad you still think me a better painter than Mungold. But isn't it hard that for that very reason I should starve in a hole? If I painted badly enough you'd see no objection to my living at the Waldorf!"

"Ah, don't joke about it," she murmured. "Don't triumph in it."

"I see no reason to at present," said Stanwell drily. "But I won't pretend to be ashamed when I'm not. I think there are occasions when a man is justified in doing what I've done."

She looked at him solemnly. "What occasions?"

"Why, when he wants money, hang it!"

She drew a deep breath. "Money—money? Has Caspar's example been nothing to you, then?"

"It hasn't proved to me that I must starve while Mungold lives on truffles!"

Again her face changed and she stirred uneasily, and then rose to her feet.

"There is no occasion which can justify an artist's sacrificing his convictions!" she exclaimed.

Stanwell rose too, facing her with a mounting urgency which sent a flush to his cheek.

"Can't you conceive such an occasion in my case? The wish, I mean, to make things easier for Caspar—to help you in any way you might let me?"

Her face reflected his blush, and she stood gazing at him with a wounded wonder.

"Caspar and I—you imagine we could live on money earned in that way?"

Stanwell made an impatient gesture. "You've got to live on something—or he has, even if you don't include yourself!"

Her blush deepened miserably, but she held her head high.

"That's just it—that's what I came here to say to you." She stood a moment gazing away from him at the lake.

He looked at her in surprise. "You came here to say something to me?"

"Yes. That we've got to live on something, Caspar and I, as you say; and since an artist cannot sacrifice his convictions, the sacrifice must—I mean—I wanted you to know that I have promised to marry Mr. Mungold."

"Mungold!" Stanwell cried with a sharp note of irony; but her white look checked it on his lips.

"I know all you are going to say," she murmured, with a kind of nobleness which moved him even through his sense of its grotesqueness. "But you must see the distinction, because you first made it clear to me. I can take money earned in good faith—I can let Caspar live on it. I can marry Mr. Mungold; because, though his pictures are bad, he does not prostitute his art."

She began to move away from him slowly, and he followed her in silence along the frozen path.

When Stanwell re-entered his studio the dusk had fallen. He lit his lamp and rummaged out some writing-materials. Having found them, he wrote to Shepson to say that he could not paint Mrs. Van Orley, and did not care to accept any more orders for the present. He sealed and stamped the letter and flung it over the banisters for the janitor to post; then he dragged out his unfinished head of Kate Arran, replaced it on the easel, and sat down before it with a grim smile.

## THE BEST MAN

DUSK HAD FALLEN, and the circle of light shed by the lamp of Governor Mornway's writing-table just rescued from the surrounding dimness his own imposing bulk, thrown back in a deep chair in the lounging attitude habitual to him at that hour.

When the Governor of Midsylvania rested he rested completely. Five minutes earlier he had been bowed over his office desk, an Atlas with the State on his shoulders; now, his working hours over, he had the air of a man who has spent his day in desultory pleasure, and means to end it in the enjoyment of a good dinner. This freedom from care threw into relief the hovering fidgetiness of his sister, Mrs. Nimick, who, just outside the circle of lamplight, haunted the warm gloom of the hearth, from which the wood fire now and then sent up an exploring flash into her face.

Mrs. Nimick's presence did not usually minister to repose; but the Governor's serenity was too deep to be easily disturbed, and he felt the calmness of a man who knows there is a mosquito in the room, but has drawn the netting close about his head. This calmness reflected itself in the accent with which he said, throwing himself back to smile up at his sister: "You know I am not going to make any appointments for a week."

It was the day after the great reform victory which had put John Mornway for the second time at the head of his State, a triumph compared with which even the mighty battle of his first election sank into insignificance, and he leaned back with the sense of unassailable placidity which follows upon successful effort.

Mrs. Nimick murmured an apology. "I didn't understand—I saw in this morning's papers that the Attorney-General was reappointed."

"Oh, Fleetwood—his reappointment was involved in the campaign. He's one of the principles I represent!"

Mrs. Nimick smiled a little tartly. "It seems odd to some people to think of Mr. Fleetwood in connection with principles."

The Governor's smile had no answering acerbity; the mention of his Attorney-General's name had set his blood humming with the thrill of the fight, and he wondered how it was that Fleetwood had not already been in to clasp hands with him over their triumph.

"No," he said, good-humoredly, "two years ago Fleetwood's name didn't stand for principles of any sort; but I believed in him, and look what he's done for me! I thought he was too big a man not to see in time that statesmanship is a finer thing than practical politics, and now that I've given him a chance to make the discovery, he's on the way to becoming just such a statesman as the country needs."

"Oh, it's a great deal easier and pleasanter to believe in people," replied Mrs. Nimick, in a tone full of occult allusion, "and, of course, we all knew that Mr. Fleetwood would have a hearing before anyone else."

The Governor took this imperturbably. "Well, at any rate, he isn't going to fill all the offices in the State; there will probably be one or two to spare after he has helped himself, and when the time comes I'll think over your man. I'll consider him."

Mrs. Nimick brightened. "It would make *such* a difference to Jack—it might mean anything to the poor boy to have Mr. Ashford appointed!"

The Governor held up a warning hand.

"Oh, I know, one mustn't say that, or at least you mustn't listen. You're so dreadfully afraid of nepotism. But I'm not asking for anything for Jack—I have never asked for a crust for any of us, thank Heaven! No one can point to *me*—" Mrs. Nimick checked herself suddenly and continued in a more impersonal tone: "But there's no harm, surely, in my saying a word for Mr. Ashford, when I know that he's actually under consideration, and I don't see why the fact that Jack is in his office should prevent my speaking."

"On the contrary," said the Governor, "it implies, on your part, a personal knowledge of Mr. Ashford's qualifications which may be of great help to me in reaching a decision."

Mrs. Nimick never quite knew how to meet him when he took that tone, and the flickering fire made her face for a moment the picture of uncertainty; then at all hazards she launched out: "Well, I have Ella's promise, at any rate."

The Governor sat upright. "Ella's promise?"

"To back me up. She thoroughly approves of him!"

The Governor smiled. "You talk as if Ella had a political salon and distributed *lettres de cachet!* I'm glad she approves of Ashford; but if you think my wife makes my appointments for me—" He broke off with a laugh at the superfluity of such a protest.

Mrs. Nimick reddened. "One never knows how you will take the simplest thing. What harm is there in my saying that Ella approves of Mr. Ashford? I thought you liked her to take an interest in your work."

"I like it immensely. But I shouldn't care to have it take that form."

"What form?"

"That of promising to use her influence to get people appointed. But you always talk of politics in the vocabulary of European courts. Thank Heaven, Ella has less imagination. She has her sympathies, of course, but she doesn't think they can affect the distribution of offices."

Mrs. Nimick gathered up her furs with an air at once crestfallen and resentful. "I'm sorry—I always seem to say the wrong thing. I'm sure I came with the best intentions—it's natural that your sister should want to be with you at such a happy moment."

"Of course it is, my dear," exclaimed the Governor genially, as he rose to grasp the hands with which she was nervously adjusting her wraps.

Mrs. Nimick, who lived a little way out of town, and whose visits to her brother were apparently achieved at the cost of immense effort and mysterious complications, had come to congratulate him on his victory, and to sound him regarding the nomination to a coveted post of the lawyer in whose firm her eldest son was a clerk. In the urgency of the latter errand she had rather lost sight of the former, but her face softened as the Governor, keeping both her hands in his, said in the voice which always seemed to put the most generous interpretation on her motives: "I was sure you would be one of the first to give me your blessing."

"Oh, your success—no one feels it more than I do!" sighed Mrs. Nimick, always at home in the emotional key. "I keep in the background. I make no noise, I claim no credit, but whatever happens, no one shall ever prevent my rejoicing in my brother's success!"

Mrs. Nimick's felicitations were always couched in the conditional, with a side-glance at dark contingencies, and the Governor, smiling at the familiar construction, returned cheerfully: "I don't see why anyone should want to deprive you of that privilege."

"They couldn't—they couldn't—" Mrs. Nimick heroically affirmed.

"Well, I'm in the saddle for another two years at any rate, so you had better put in all the rejoicing you can."

"Whatever happens—whatever happens!" cried Mrs. Nimick, melting on his bosom.

"The only thing likely to happen at present is that you will miss your train if I let you go on saying nice things to me much longer."

Mrs. Nimick at this dried her eyes, renewed her clutch on her draperies, and stood glancing sentimentally about the room while her brother rang for the carriage.

"I take away a lovely picture of you," she murmured. "It's wonderful what you've made of this hideous house."

"Ah, not I, but Ella—there she *does* reign undisputed," he acknowledged, following her glance about the library, which wore an air of permanent habitation, of slowly formed intimacy with its inmates, in marked contrast to the gaudy impersonality of the usual executive apartment.

"Oh, she's wonderful, quite wonderful. I see she has got those imported damask curtains she was looking at the other day at Fielding's. When I am asked how she does it all, I always say it's beyond me!"

"It's an art like another," smiled the Governor. "Ella has been used to living in tents and she has the knack of giving them a wonderful look of permanence."

"She certainly makes the most extraordinary bargains—all the knack in the world won't take the place of such curtains and carpets."

"Are they good? I'm glad to hear it. But all the good curtains and carpets won't make a house comfortable to live in. There's where the knack comes in, you see."

He recalled with a shudder the lean Congressional years—the years before his marriage—when Mrs. Nimick had lived with him in Washington, and the daily struggle in the House had been combined with domestic conflicts almost equally recurrent. The offer of a foreign mission, though disconnecting him from active politics, had the advantage of freeing him from his sister's tutelage, and in Europe, where he remained for two years, he had met the lady who was to become his wife. Mrs. Renfield was the widow of one of the diplomatists who languish in perpetual first secretary-ship at our various embassies. Her life had given her ease without triviality, and a sense of the importance of politics seldom found in ladies of her nationality. She regarded a public life as the noblest and most engrossing of careers, and combined with great social versatility an equal gift for reading blue-books and studying debates. So sincere was the latter taste that she passed without regret from the amenities of a European life well stocked with picturesque intimacies to the rawness of the Midsylvanian capital. She helped Mornway in his fight for the Governorship as a man likes to be helped by a woman—by her tact, her good looks, her memory for faces, her knack of saying the right thing to the right person, and her capacity for obscure hard work in the background of his public activity. But, above all, she helped him by making his private life smooth and harmonious. For a man careless of personal ease, Mornway was singularly alive to the domestic amenities. Attentive service, well-ordered dinners, brightly burning fires, and a scent of flowers in the house—these material details, which had come to seem the extension of his wife's personality, the inevitable result of her nearness, were as agreeable to him after five years of marriage as in the first surprise of his introduction to them. Mrs. Nimick had kept house jerkily and vociferously; Ella performed the same task silently and imperceptibly, and the results were all in favor of the latter method. Though neither the Governor nor his wife had large means, the household, under Mrs. Mornway's guidance, took on an air of sober luxury as agreeable to her husband as it was exasperating to her sister-in-law. The domestic machinery ran without a jar. There were no upheavals, no debts, no squalid cookless hiatuses between intervals of showy hospitality; the household moved along on lines of quiet elegance and comfort, behind which only the eye of the housekeeping sex could have detected a gradually increasing scale of expense.

Such an eye was now projected on the Governor's surroundings, and its explorations were summed up in the tone in which Mrs. Nimick repeated from the threshold: "I always say I don't see how she does it!"

The tone did not escape the Governor, but it disturbed him no more than the buzz of a baffled insect. Poor Grace! It was not his fault if her husband was given to chimerical investments, if her sons were "unsatisfactory," and her cooks would not stay with her; but it was natural that these facts should throw into irritating contrast the ease and harmony of his own domestic life. It made him all the sorrier for his sister to know that her envy did not penetrate to the essence of his happiness, but lingered on those external signs of well-being which counted for so little in the sum total of his advantages. Poor Mrs. Nimick's life seemed doubly thin and mean when one remembered that, beneath its shabby surface, there were no compensating riches of the spirit.

## II

IT was the custodian of his own hidden treasure who at this moment broke in upon his musings. Mrs. Mornway, fresh from her afternoon walk, entered the room with that air of ease and lightness which seemed to diffuse a social warmth about her; fine, slender, pliant, so polished and modeled by an intelligent experience of life that youth seemed clumsy in her presence. She looked down at her husband and shook her head.

"You promised to keep the afternoon to yourself, and I hear Grace has been here."

"Poor Grace—she didn't stay long, and I should have been a brute not to see her."

He leaned back, filling his gaze to the brim with her charming image, which obliterated at a stroke the fretful ghost of Mrs. Nimick.

"She came to congratulate you, I suppose?"

"Yes, and to ask me to do something for Ashford."

"Ah—on account of Jack. What does she want for him?"

The Governor laughed. "She said you were in her confidence—that you were backing her up. She seemed to think your support would ensure her success."

Mrs. Mornway smiled; her smile, always full of delicate implications, seemed to caress her husband while it gently mocked his sister.

"Poor Grace! I suppose you undeceived her."

"As to your influence? I told her it was paramount where it ought to be."

"And where is that?"

"In the choice of carpets and curtains. It seems ours are almost too good."

"Thanks for the compliment! Too good for what?"

"Our station in life, I suppose. At least they seemed to bother Grace."

"Poor Grace! I've always bothered her." She paused, removing her gloves reflectively and laying her long fine hands on his shoulders as she stood behind him. "Then you don't believe in Ashford?" Feeling his slight start, she drew away her hands and raised them to detach her veil.

"What makes you think I don't believe in Ashford?" he asked.

"I asked out of curiosity. I wondered whether you had decided anything."

"No, and I don't mean to for a week. I'm dead beat, and I want to bring a fresh mind to the question. There is hardly one appointment I'm sure of except, of course, Fleetwood's."

She turned away from him, smoothing her hair in the mirror above the mantelpiece. "You're sure of that?" she asked after a moment.

"Of George Fleetwood? And poor Grace thinks you are deep in my counsels! I am as sure of re-appointing Fleetwood as I am that I have just been re-elected myself. I've never made any secret of the fact that if they wanted me back they must have him, too."

"You are tremendously generous!" she murmured.

"Generous? What a strange word to use! Fleetwood is my trump card—the one man I can count on to carry out my ideas through thick and thin."

She mused on this, smiling a little. "That's why I call you generous—when I remember how you disliked him two years ago!"

"What of that? I was prejudiced against him, I own; or rather, I had a just distrust of a man with such a past. But how splendidly he's wiped it out! What a record he has written on the new leaf he promised to turn over if I gave him the chance! Do you know," the Governor interrupted himself with a pleasantly reminiscent laugh, "I was rather annoyed with Grace when she hinted that you had promised to back up Ashford—I told her you didn't aspire to distribute patronage. But she might have reminded me—if she'd known—that it *was* you who persuaded me to give Fleetwood that chance."

Mrs. Mornway turned with a slight heightening of color. "Grace—how could she possibly have known?"

"She couldn't, of course, unless she'd read my weakness in my face. But why do you look so startled at my little joke?"

"It's only that I so dislike Grace's ineradicable idea that I am a wire-puller. Why should she imagine I would help her about Ashford?"

"Oh, Grace has always been a mild and ineffectual conspirator, and she thinks every other woman is built on the same plan. But you *did* get Fleetwood's job for him, you know," he repeated with laughing insistence.

"I had more faith than you in human nature, that's all." She paused a moment, and then added: "Personally, you know, I have always rather disliked him."

"Oh, I never doubted your disinterestedness. But you are not going to turn against your candidate, are you?"

She hesitated. "I am not sure; circumstances alter cases. When you made Fleetwood Attorney-General two years ago he was the inevitable man for the place."

"Well—is there a better one now?"

"I don't say there is—it's not my business to look for him, at any rate. What I mean is that at that time Fleetwood was worth risking anything for—now I don't know that he is."

"But, even if he were not, what do I risk for him now? I don't see your point. Since he didn't cost me my re-election, what can he possibly cost me now I'm in?"

"He's immensely unpopular. He will cost you a great deal of popularity, and you have never pretended to despise that."

"No, nor ever sacrificed anything essential to it. Are you really asking me to offer up Fleetwood to it now?"

"I don't ask you to do anything—except to consider if he is essential. You said you were over-tired and wanted to bring a fresh mind to bear on the other appointments. Why not delay this one too?"

Mornway turned in his chair and looked at her searchingly. "This means something,

Ella. What have you heard?"

"Just what you have, probably, but with more attentive ears. The very record you are so proud of has made George Fleetwood innumerable enemies in the last two years. The Lead Trust people are determined to ruin him, and if his reappointment is attacked you will not be spared."

"Attacked? In the papers, you mean?"

She paused. "You know the *Spy* has always threatened a campaign. And he has a past, as you say."

"Which was public property long before I first appointed him. Nothing could be gained by raking up his old political history. Everybody knows he didn't come to me with clean hands, but to hurt him now the 'Spy' would have to fasten a new scandal on him, and that would not be easy."

"It would be easy to invent one!"

"Unproved accusations don't count much against a man of such proved capacity. The best answer is his record of the last two years. That is what the public looks at."

"The public looks wherever the press points. And besides, you have your own future to consider. It would be a pity to sacrifice such a career as yours for the sake of backing up even as useful a man as George Fleetwood." She paused, as if checked by his gathering frown, but went on with fresh decision: "Oh, I'm not speaking of personal ambition; I'm thinking of the good you can do. Will Fleetwood's reappointment secure the greatest good of the greatest number, if his unpopularity reacts on you to the extent of hindering your career?"

The Governor's brow cleared and he rose with a smile. "My dear, your reasoning is admirable, but we must leave my career to take care of itself. Whatever I may be tomorrow, I am Governor of Midsylvania to-day, and my business as Governor is to appoint as Attorney-General the best man I can find for the place—and that man is George Fleetwood, unless you have a better one to propose."

She met this with perfect good-humor. "No, I have told you already that that is not my business. But I *have* a candidate of my own for another office, so Grace was not quite wrong, after all."

"Well, who is your candidate, and for what office? I only hope you don't want to change cooks!"

"Oh, I do that without your authority, and you never even know it has been done." She hesitated, and then said with a bright directness: "I want you to do something for poor Gregg."

"Gregg? Rufus Gregg?" He stared. "What an extraordinary request! What can I do for a man I've had to kick out for dishonesty?"

"Not much, perhaps; I know it's difficult. But, after all, it was your kicking him out that ruined him."

"It was his dishonesty that ruined him. He was getting a good salary as my stenographer, and if he hadn't sold those letters to the 'Spy' he would have been getting it still."

She wavered. "After all, nothing was proved—he always denied it."

"Good heavens, Ella! Have you ever doubted his guilt?"

"No—no; I don't mean that. But, of course, his wife and children believe in him, and think you were cruel, and he has been out of work so long that they are starving."

"Send them some money, then; I wonder you thought it necessary to ask."

"I shouldn't have thought it so, but money is not what I want. Mrs. Gregg is proud, and it is hard to help her in that way. Couldn't you give him work of some kind—just a little post in a corner?"

"My dear child, the little posts in the corner are just the ones where honesty is essential. A footpad doesn't wait under a street-lamp! Besides, how can I recommend a man whom I have dismissed for theft? I won't say a word to hinder his getting a place, but on my conscience I can't give him one."

She paused and turned toward the door silently, though without any show of resentment; but on the threshold she lingered long enough to say: "Yet you gave Fleetwood his chance!"

"Fleetwood? You class Fleetwood with Gregg? The best man in the State with a little beggarly thieving nonentity? It's evident enough you're new at wire-pulling, or you would show more skill at it!"

She met this with a laugh. "I'm not likely to have much practice if my first attempt is such a failure. Well, I will see if Mrs. Gregg will let me help her a little—I suppose there is nothing else to be done."

"Nothing that we can do. If Gregg wants a place he had better get one on the staff of the *Spy*. He served them better than he did me."

## III

THE Governor stared at the card with a frown. Half an hour had elapsed since his wife had gone upstairs to dress for the big dinner from which official duties excused him, and he was still lingering over the fire before preparing for his own solitary meal. He expected no one that evening but his old friend Hadley Shackwell, with whom it was his long-established habit to talk over his defeats and victories in the first lull after the conflict; and Shackwell was not likely to turn up till nine o'clock. The unwonted stillness of the room, and the knowledge that he had a quiet evening before him, filled the Governor with a luxurious sense of repose. The world seemed to him a good place to be in, and his complacency was shadowed only by the fear that he had perhaps been a trifle over-harsh in refusing his wife's plea for the stenographer. There seemed, therefore, a certain fitness in the appearance of the man's card, and the Governor with a sigh gave orders that Gregg should be admitted.

Gregg was still the soft-stepping scoundrel who invited the toe of honesty, and Mornway, as he entered, was conscious of a sharp revulsion of feeling. But it was impossible to evade the interview, and he sat silent while the man stated his case.

Mrs. Mornway had represented the stenographer as being in desperate straits, and ready to accept any job that could be found, but though his appearance might have seemed to corroborate her account, he evidently took a less hopeless view of his case, and the Governor found with surprise that he had fixed his eye on a clerkship in one of the Government offices, a post which had been half promised him before the incident of the letters. His plea was that the Governor's charge, though unproved, had so injured his reputation that he could only hope to clear himself by getting some sort of small job under the Administration. After that, it would be easy for him to obtain any employment he wanted.

He met Mornway's refusal with civility, but remarked after a moment: "I hadn't expected this, Governor. Mrs. Mornway led me to think that something might be arranged."

The Governor's tone was brief. "Mrs. Mornway is sorry for your wife and children, and for their sake would be glad to find work for you, but she could not have led you to think that there was any chance of your getting a clerkship."

"Well, that's just it; she said she thought she could manage it."

"You have misinterpreted my wife's interest in your family. Mrs. Mornway has nothing to do with the distribution of Government offices." The Governor broke off, annoyed to find himself asseverating for the second time so obvious a fact.

There was a moment's silence; then Gregg said, still in a perfectly equable tone: "You've always been hard on me, Governor, but I don't bear malice. You accused me of selling those letters to the *Spy*—"

The Governor made an impatient gesture.

"You couldn't prove your case," Gregg went on imperturbably, "but you were right in one respect. I *was* on confidential terms with the 'Spy.'" He paused and glanced at Mornway, whose face remained immovable. "I'm on the same terms with them still, and I'm ready to let you have the benefit of it if you'll give *me* the chance to retrieve my good name."

In spite of his irritation the Governor could not repress a smile.

"In other words, you will do a dirty trick for me if I undertake to convince people that you are the soul of honor."

Gregg smiled also.

"There are always two ways of putting a thing. Why not call it a plain case of give and take? I want something and can pay for it."

"Not in any coin I have a use for," said Mornway, pushing back his chair.

Gregg hesitated; then he said: "Perhaps you don't mean to reappoint Fleetwood." The Governor was silent, and he continued: "If you do, don't kick me out a second time. I'm not threatening you—I'm speaking as a friend. Mrs. Mornway has been kind to my wife, and I'd like to help her."

The Governor rose, gripping his chair-back sternly. "You will be kind enough to leave my wife's name out of the discussion. I supposed you knew me well enough to know that I don't buy newspaper secrets at any price, least of all at that of the public money!"

Gregg, who had risen also, stood a few feet off, looking at him inscrutably.

"Is that final, Governor?"

"Quite final."

"Well, good evening, then."

IV

SHACKWELL and the Governor sat over the evening embers. It was after ten o'clock, and the servant had carried away the coffee and liqueurs, leaving the two men to their cigars. Mornway had once more lapsed into his arm-chair, and sat with out-stretched feet, gazing comfortably at his friend.

Shackwell was a small dry man of fifty, with a face as sallow and freckled as a winter pear, a limp mustache, and shrewd melancholy eyes.

"I am glad you have given yourself a day's rest," he said, looking at the Governor.

"Well, I don't know that I needed it. There's such exhilaration in victory that I never felt fresher."

"Ah, but the fight's just beginning."

"I know—but I'm ready for it. You mean the campaign against Fleetwood. I understand there is to be a big row. Well, he and I are used to rows."

Shackwell paused, surveying his cigar. "You knew the *Spy* meant to lead the attack?"

"Yes. I was offered a glimpse of the documents this afternoon."

Shackwell started up. "You didn't refuse?"

Mornway related the incident of Gregg's visit. "I could hardly buy my information at that price," he said, "and, besides, it is really Fleetwood's business this time. I suppose he has heard the report, but it doesn't seem to bother him. I rather thought he would have looked in to-day to talk things over, but I haven't seen him."

Shackwell continued to twist his cigar through his sallow fingers without remembering to light it. "You're determined to reappoint Fleetwood?" he asked.

The Governor caught him up. "You're the fourth person who has asked me that to-day! You haven't lost faith in him, have you, Hadley?"

"Not an atom!" said the other with emphasis.

"Well, then, what are you all thinking of, to suppose I can be frightened by a little newspaper talk? Besides, if Fleetwood is not afraid, why should I be?"

"Because you'll be involved in it with him."

The Governor laughed. "What have they got against me now?"

Shackwell, standing up, confronted his friend solemnly. "This—that Fleetwood bought his appointment two years ago."

"Ah—bought it of me? Why didn't it come out at the time?"

"Because it wasn't known. It has only been found out lately."

"Known—found out? This is magnificent! What was my price, and what did I do with the money?"

Shackwell glanced about the room, and his eyes returned to Mornway's face.

"Look here, John, Fleetwood is not the only man in the world."

"The only man?"

"The only Attorney-General. The *Spy* has the Lead Trust behind it and means to put up a savage fight. Mud sticks, and—"

"Hadley, is this a conspiracy? You're saying to me just what Ella said this afternoon."

At the mention of Mrs. Mornway's name a silence fell between the two men and the Governor moved uneasily in his chair.

"You are not advising me to chuck Fleetwood because the *Spy* is going to accuse me of having sold him his first appointment?" he said at length.

Shackwell drew a deep breath. "You say yourself that Mrs. Mornway gave you the same advice this afternoon."

"Well, what of that? Do you imagine that my wife distrib—" The Governor broke off with an exasperated laugh.

Shackwell, leaning against the mantelpiece, looked down into the embers. "I didn't say the *Spy* meant to accuse *you* of having sold the office."

Mornway stood up slowly, his eyes on his friend's averted face. The ashes dropped from his cigar, scattering a white trail across the carpet which had excited Mrs. Nimick's envy.

"The office is in my gift. If I didn't sell it, who did?" he demanded.

Shackwell laid a hand on his arm. "For heaven's sake, John—"

"Who did, who did?" the Governor violently repeated.

The two men faced each other in the closely curtained silence of the dim luxurious room. Shackwell's eyes again wandered, as if summoning the walls to reply. Then he said, "I have positive information that the *Spy* will say nothing if you don't appoint Fleetwood."

"And what will it say if I do appoint him?"

"That he bought his first appointment from your wife."

The Governor stood silent, immovable, while the blood crept slowly from his strong neck to his lowering brows. Once he laughed, then he set his lips and continued to gaze into the fire. After a while he looked at his cigar and shook the freshly formed cone of ashes carefully upon the hearth. He had just turned again to Shackwell when the door opened and the butler announced: "Mr. Fleetwood."

The room swam about Shackwell, and when he recovered himself, Mornway, with outstretched hand, was advancing quietly to meet his guest.

Fleetwood was a smaller man than the Governor. He was erect and compact, with a face full of dry energy, which seemed to press forward with the spring of his prominent features, as though it were the weapon with which he cleared his way through the world. He was in evening dress, scrupulously appointed, but pale and nervous. Of the two men, it was Mornway who was the more composed.

"I thought I should have seen you before this," he said.

Fleetwood returned his grasp and shook hands with Shackwell.

"I knew you needed to be let alone. I didn't mean to come tonight, but I wanted to say a word to you."

At this, Shackwell, who had fallen into the background, made a motion of leave-taking, but the Governor arrested it.

"We haven't any secrets from Hadley, have we, Fleetwood?"

"Certainly not. I am glad to have him stay. I have simply come to say that I have been thinking over my future arrangements, and that I find it will not be possible for me to continue in office."

There was a long pause, during which Shackwell kept his eyes on Mornway. The Governor had turned pale, but when he spoke his voice was full and firm.

"This is sudden," he said.

Fleetwood stood leaning against a high chair-back, fretting its carved ornaments with restless fingers. "It is sudden—yes. I—there are a variety of reasons."

"Is one of them the fact that you are afraid of what the *Spy* is going to say?"

The Attorney General flushed deeply and moved away a few steps. "I'm sick of mud-throwing," he muttered.

"George Fleetwood!" Mornway exclaimed. He had advanced toward his friend, and the two stood confronting each other, already oblivious of Shackwell's presence.

"It's not only that, of course. I've been frightfully hard-worked. My health has given way—"

"Since yesterday?"

Fleetwood forced a smile. "My dear fellow, what a slave-driver you are! Hasn't a man the right to take a rest?"

"Not a soldier on the eve of battle. You have never failed me before."

"I don't want to fail you now. But it isn't the eve of battle—you're in, and that's the main thing."

"The main thing at present is that you promised to stay in with me, and that I must have your real reason for breaking your word."

Fleetwood made a deprecatory movement. "My dear Governor, if you only knew it, I'm doing you a service in backing out."

"A service—why?"

"Because I'm hated—because the Lead Trust wants my blood, and will have yours too if you appoint me."

"Ah, that's the real reason, then—you're afraid of the *Spy?*"

"Afraid—?"

The Governor continued to speak with dry deliberation. "Evidently, then, you know what they mean to say."

Fleetwood laughed. "One needn't do that to be sure it will be abominable!"

"Who cares how abominable it is if it's untrue?"

Fleetwood shrugged his shoulders and was silent. Shackwell, from a distant seat, uttered a faint protesting sound, but no one heeded him. The Governor stood squarely before Fleetwood, his hands in his pockets. "It *is* true, then?" he demanded.

"What is true?"

"What the *Spy* means to say—that you bought my wife's influence to get your first appointment."

In the silence Shackwell started suddenly to his feet. A sound of carriage-wheels had disturbed the quiet street. They paused and then rolled up the semicircle to the door of the Executive Mansion.

"John!" Shackwell warned him.

The Governor turned impatiently; there was the sound of a servant's steps in the hall, followed by the opening and closing of the outer door.

"Your wife—Mrs. Mornway!" Shackwell cried.

Another step, accompanied by a soft rustle of skirts, was advancing toward the library.

"My wife? Let her come!" said the Governor.

V

SHE stood before them in her bright evening dress, with an arrested brilliancy of aspect like the sparkle of a fountain suddenly caught in ice. Her look moved rapidly from one to the other; then she came forward, while Shackwell slipped behind her to close the door.

"What has happened?" she said.

Shackwell began to speak, but the Governor interposed calmly:

"Fleetwood has come to tell me that he does not wish to remain in office."

"Ah!" she murmured.

There was another silence. Fleetwood broke it by saying: "It is getting late. If you want to see me tomorrow—"

The Governor looked from his face to Ella's. "Yes; good night," he said.

Shackwell moved in Fleetwood's wake to the door. Mrs. Mornway stood with her head high, smiling slightly. She shook hands with each of the men in turn; then she moved toward the sofa and laid aside her shining cloak. All her gestures were calm and noble, but as she raised her hand to unclasp the cloak her husband uttered a sudden exclamation.

"Where did you get that bracelet? I don't remember it."

"This?" She looked at him with astonishment. "It belonged to my mother. I don't often wear it."

"Ah—I shall suspect everything now," he groaned.

He turned away and flung himself with bowed head in the chair behind his writing-table. He wanted to collect himself, to question her, to get to the bottom of the hideous abyss over which his imagination hung. But what was the use? What did the facts matter? He had only to put his memories together—they led him straight to the truth. Every incident of the day seemed to point a leering finger in the same direction, from Mrs. Nimick's allusion to the imported damask curtains to Gregg's confident appeal for rehabilitation.

"If you imagine that my wife distributes patronage—" he heard himself repeating inanely, and the walls seemed to reverberate with the laughter which his sister and Gregg had suppressed. He heard Ella rise from the sofa and lifted his head sharply.

"Sit still!" he commanded. She sank back without speaking, and he hid his face again. The past months, the past years, were dancing a witches' dance about him. He remembered a hundred significant things. . . . *Oh, God*, he cried to himself, *if only she does not lie about it!* Suddenly he recalled having pitied Mrs. Nimick because she could not penetrate to the essence of his happiness. Those were the very words he had used! He heard himself laugh aloud. The clock struck—it went on striking interminably. At length he heard his wife rise again and say with sudden authority: "John, you must speak."

Authority—she spoke to him with authority! He laughed again, and through his laugh he heard the senseless rattle of the words, "If you imagine that my wife distributes patronage . . . "

He looked up and saw her standing before him. If only she would not lie about it! He said: "You see what has happened."

"I suppose someone has told you about the *Spy*."

"Who told you? Gregg?" he interposed.

"Yes," she said quietly.

"That was why you wanted—?"

"Why I wanted you to help him? Yes."

"Oh, God! . . . He wouldn't take money?"

"No, he wouldn't take money."

He sat silent, looking at her, noting with a morbid minuteness the exquisite finish of her dress, that finish which seemed so much a part of herself that it had never before struck him as a merely purchasable accessory. He knew so little what a woman's dresses cost! For a moment he lost himself in vague calculations; finally, he said: "What did you do it for?"

"Do what?"

"Take money from Fleetwood."

She paused a moment and then said: "If you will let me explain—"

And then he saw that, all along, he had thought she would be able to disprove it! A smothering blackness closed in on him, and he had a physical struggle for breath. Then he forced himself to his feet and said: "He was your lover?"

"Oh, no, no, *no!*" she cried with conviction. He hardly knew whether the shadow lifted or deepened; the fact that he instantly believed her seemed only to increase his bewilderment. Presently he found that she was still speaking, and he began to listen to her, catching a phrase now and then through the deafening clamor of his thoughts.

It amounted to this—that just after her husband's first election, when Fleetwood's claims for the Attorney-Generalship were being vainly pressed by a group of his political backers, Mrs. Mornway had chanced to sit next to him once or twice at dinner. One day, on the strength of these meetings, he had called and asked her frankly if she would not help him with her husband. He had made a clean breast of his past, but had said that, under a man like Mornway, he felt he could wipe out his political sins and purify himself while he served the party. She knew the party needed his brains, and she believed in him—she was sure he would keep his word. She would have spoken in his favor in any case—she would have used all her influence to overcome her husband's prejudice—and it was by a mere accident that, in the course of one of their talks, he happened to give her a "tip" (his past connections were still useful for such purposes), a "tip" which, in the first invading pressure of debt after Mornway's election, she had not had the courage to refuse. Fleetwood had made some money for her—yes, about thirty thousand dollars. She had repaid what he had lent her, and there had been no further transactions of the kind between them. But it appeared that Gregg, before his dismissal, had got hold of an old check-book which gave a hint of the story, and had pieced the rest together with the help of a clerk in Fleetwood's office. The *Spy* was in possession of the facts, but did not mean to use them if Fleetwood was not reappointed, the Lead Trust having no personal grudge against Mornway.

Her story ended there, and she sat silent while he continued to look at her. So much had perished in the wreck of his faith that he did not attach much value to what remained. It scarcely mattered that he believed her when the truth was so sordid. There had been, after all, nothing to envy him for but what Mrs. Nimick had seen; the core of his life was as mean and miserable as his sister's. . . .

His wife rose at length, pale but still calm. She had a kind of external dignity which she wore like one of her rich dresses. It seemed as little a part of her now as the finery of which his gaze contemptuously reckoned the cost.

"John—" she said, laying her hand on his shoulder.

He looked up wearily. "You had better go to bed," he interjected.

"Don't look at me in that way. I am prepared for your being angry with me—I made a dreadful mistake and must bear my punishment: any punishment you choose to inflict. But you must think of yourself first—you must spare yourself. Why should you be so horribly unhappy? Don't you see that since Mr. Fleetwood has behaved so well we are quite safe? And I swear to you I have paid back every penny of the money."

## VI

THREE days later Shackwell was summoned by telephone to the Governor's office in the Capitol. There had been, in the interval, no communication between the two men, and the papers had been silent or noncommittal.

In the lobby Shackwell met Fleetwood leaving the building. For a moment the Attorney-General seemed about to speak; then he nodded and passed on, leaving to Shackwell the impression of a face more than ever thrust forward like a weapon.

The Governor sat behind his desk in the clear autumn sunlight. In contrast to Fleetwood he seemed relaxed and unwieldy, and the face he turned to his friend had a gray look of convalescence. Shackwell wondered, with a start of apprehension, if he and Fleetwood had been together.

He relieved himself of his overcoat without speaking, and when he turned again toward Mornway he was surprised to find the latter watching him with a smile.

"It's good to see you, Hadley," the Governor said.

"I waited to be sent for; I knew you'd let me know when you wanted me," Shackwell replied.

"I didn't send for you on purpose. If I had, I might have asked your advice, and I didn't want to ask anybody's advice but my own." The Governor spoke steadily, but in a voice a trifle too well disciplined to be natural. "I've had a three days' conference with myself," he continued, "and now that everything is settled I want you to do me a favor."

"Yes?" Shackwell assented. The private issues of the affair were still wrapped in mystery to him, but he had never had a moment's doubt as to its public solution, and he had no difficulty in conjecturing the nature of the service he was to render. His heart ached for Mornway, but he was glad the inevitable step was to be taken without further delay.

"Everything is settled," the Governor repeated, "and I want you to notify the press that I have decided to reappoint Fleetwood."

Shackwell bounded from his seat. "Good heavens!" he ejaculated.

"To reappoint Fleetwood," the Governor repeated, "because at the present juncture of affairs he is the only man for the place. The work we began together is not finished, and I can't finish it without him. Remember the vistas opened by the Lead Trust investigation—he knows where they lead and no one else does. We must put that inquiry through, no matter what it costs us, and that is why I have sent for you to take this letter to the *Spy*."

Shackwell's hand drew back from the proffered envelope.

"You say you don't want my advice, but you can't expect me to go on such an errand with my eyes shut. What on earth are you driving at? Of course Fleetwood will persist in refusing."

Mornway smiled. "He did persist—for three hours. But when he left here just now he had given me his word to accept."

Shackwell groaned. "Then I am dealing with two madmen instead of one."

The Governor laughed. "My poor Hadley, you're worse than I expected. I thought you would understand me."

"Understand you? How can I, in heaven's name, when I don't understand the situation?

"The situation—the situation?" Mornway repeated slowly. "Whose? His or mine? I don't either—I haven't had time to think of them."

"What on earth have you been thinking of then?"

The Governor rose, with a gesture toward the window, through which, below the slope of the Capitol grounds, the roofs and steeples of the city spread their smoky mass to the mild air.

"Of all that is left," he said. "Of everything except Fleetwood and myself."

"Ah—" Shackwell murmured.

Mornway turned back and sank into his seat. "Don't you see that was all I had to turn to? The State—the country—it's big enough, in all conscience, to fill a good deal of a void! My own walls had grown too cramped for me, so I just stepped outside. You have no idea how it simplified matters at once. All I had to do was to say to myself: 'Go ahead, and do the best you can for the country.' The personal issue simply didn't exist."

"Yes—and then?"

"Then I turned over for three days this question of the Attorney-Generalship. I couldn't see that it was changed—how should my feelings have affected it? Fleetwood hasn't betrayed the State. There isn't a scar on his public record—he is still the best man for the place. My business is to appoint the best man I can find, and I can't find any one as good as Fleetwood."

"But—but—your wife?" Shackwell stammered.

The Governor looked up with surprise. Shackwell could almost have sworn that he had indeed forgotten the private issue.

"My wife is ready to face the consequences," he said.

Shackwell returned to his former attitude of incredulity.

"But Fleetwood? Fleetwood has no right to sacrifice—"

"To sacrifice my wife to the State? Oh, let us beware of big words. Fleetwood was inclined to use them at first, but I managed to restore his sense of proportion. I showed him that our private lives are only a few feet square anyhow, and that really, to breathe freely, one must get out of them into the open." He paused and broke out with sudden violence, "My God, Hadley, didn't you see that Fleetwood had to obey me?"

"Yes—I see that," said Shackwell, with reviving obstinacy. "But if you've reached such a height and pulled him up to your side it seems to me that from that standpoint you ought to get an even clearer view of the madness of your position. You say you have decided to sacrifice your own feelings and your wife's—though I'm not so sure of your right to dispose of *her* voice in the matter; but what if you sacrifice the party and the State as well, in this transcendental attempt to distinguish between private and public honor? You'll have to answer that before you can get me to carry this letter."

The Governor did not blanch under the attack.

"I think the letter will answer you," he said calmly.

"The letter?"

"Yes. It's something more than a notification of Fleetwood's reappointment." Mornway paused and looked steadily at his friend. "You're afraid of an investigation—an impeachment? Well, the letter anticipates that."

"How, in heaven's name?"

"By a plain statement of the facts. My wife has told me that she did borrow of Fleetwood. He speculated for her and made a considerable sum, out of which she repaid his loan. The *Spy's* accusation is true. If it can be proved that my wife induced me to appoint Fleetwood, it may be argued that she sold him the appointment. But it can't be proved, and the *Spy* won't waste its breath in trying to, because my statement will take the sting out of its innuendoes. I propose to anticipate its attack by setting forth the facts in its columns, and asking the public to decide between us. On one side is the private fact that my wife, without my knowledge, borrowed money from Fleetwood just before I appointed him to an important post; on the other side is his public record and mine. I want people to see both sides and judge between them, not in the red glare of a newspaper denunciation, but in the plain daylight of common-sense. Charges against the private morality of a public man are usually made in such a blare of headlines and cloud of mud-throwing that the voice he lifts up in his defence can not make itself heard. In this case I want the public to hear what I have to say before the yelping begins. My letter will take the wind out of the *Spy's* sails, and if the verdict goes against me, the case will have been decided on its own merits, and not at the dictation of the writers of scare heads. Even if I don't gain my end, it will be a good thing, for once, for the public to consider dispassionately how far a private calamity should be allowed to affect a career of public usefulness, and the next man who goes through what I am undergoing may have cause to thank me if no one else does."

Shackwell sat silent for a moment, with the ring of the last words in his ears.

Suddenly he rose and held out his hand. "Give me the letter," he said.

The Governor caught him up with a kindling eye. "It's all right, then? You see, and you'll take it?"

Shackwell met his glance with one of melancholy interrogation. "I think I see a magnificent suicide, but it's the kind of way I shouldn't mind dying myself."

He pulled himself silently into his coat and put the letter into one of its pockets, but as he was turning to the door the Governor called after him cheerfully: "By the way, Hadley, aren't you and Mrs. Shackwell giving a big dinner tomorrow?"

Shackwell paused with a look of surprise. "I believe we are—why?"

"Because, if there is room for two more, my wife and I would like to be invited."

Shackwell nodded his assent and turned away without answering. As he came out of the lobby into the clear sunset radiance he saw a victoria drive up the long sweep to the Capitol and pause before the central portion. He descended the steps, and Mrs. Mornway leaned from her furs to greet him.

"I have called for my husband," she said, smiling. "He promised to get away in time for a little turn in the Park before dinner."

## TALES OF MEN AND GHOSTS (1910)

### THE BOLTED DOOR

HUBERT GRANICE, pacing the length of his pleasant lamp-lit library, paused to compare his watch with the clock on the chimney-piece.

Three minutes to eight.

In exactly three minutes Mr. Peter Ascham, of the eminent legal firm of Ascham and Pettilow, would have his punctual hand on the door-bell of the flat. It was a comfort to reflect that Ascham was so punctual—the suspense was beginning to make his host nervous. And the sound of the door-bell would be the beginning of the end—after that there'd be no going back, by God—no going back!

Granice resumed his pacing. Each time he reached the end of the room opposite the door he caught his reflection in the Florentine mirror above the fine old walnut *crédence* he had picked up at Dijon—saw himself spare, quick-moving, carefully brushed and dressed, but furrowed, gray about the temples, with a stoop which he corrected by a spasmodic straightening of the shoulders whenever a glass confronted him: a tired middle-aged man, baffled, beaten, worn out.

As he summed himself up thus for the third or fourth time the door opened and he turned with a thrill of relief to greet his guest. But it was only the man-servant who entered, advancing silently over the mossy surface of the old Turkey rug.

"Mr. Ascham telephones, sir, to say he's unexpectedly detained and can't be here till eight-thirty."

Granice made a curt gesture of annoyance. It was becoming harder and harder for him to control these reflexes. He turned on his heel, tossing to the servant over his shoulder: "Very good. Put off dinner."

Down his spine he felt the man's injured stare. Mr. Granice had always been so mild-spoken to his people—no doubt the odd change in his manner had already been noticed and discussed below stairs. And very likely they suspected the cause. He stood drumming on the writing-table till he heard the servant go out; then he threw himself into a chair, propping his elbows on the table and resting his chin on his locked hands.

Another half hour alone with it!

He wondered irritably what could have detained his guest. Some professional matter, no doubt—the punctilious lawyer would have allowed nothing less to interfere with a dinner engagement, more especially since Granice, in his note, had said: "I shall want a little business chat afterward."

But what professional matter could have come up at that unprofessional hour? Perhaps some other soul in misery had called on the lawyer; and, after all, Granice's note had given no hint of his own need! No doubt Ascham thought he merely wanted to make another change in his will. Since he had come into his little property, ten years earlier, Granice had been perpetually tinkering with his will.

Suddenly another thought pulled him up, sending a flush to his sallow temples. He remembered a word he had tossed to the lawyer some six weeks earlier, at the Century Club. "Yes—my play's as good as taken. I shall be calling on you soon to go over the contract. Those theatrical chaps are so slippery—I won't trust anybody but you to tie the knot for me!" That, of course, was what Ascham would think he was wanted for. Granice, at the idea, broke into an audible laugh—a queer stage-laugh, like the cackle of a baffled villain in a melodrama. The absurdity, the unnaturalness of the sound abashed him, and he compressed his lips angrily. Would he take to soliloquy next?

He lowered his arms and pulled open the upper drawer of the writing-table. In the right-hand corner lay a thick manuscript, bound in paper folders, and tied with a string beneath which a letter had been slipped. Next to the manuscript was a small revolver. Granice stared a moment at these oddly associated objects; then he took the letter from under the string and slowly began to open it. He had known he should do so from the moment his hand touched the drawer. Whenever his eye fell on that letter some relentless force compelled him to reread it.

It was dated about four weeks back, under the letter-head of "The Diversity Theatre."

My Dear Mr. Granice:

I have given the matter my best consideration for the last month, and it's no use—the play won't do. I have talked it over with Miss Melrose—and you know there isn't a gamer artist on our stage—and I regret to tell you she feels just as I do about it. It isn't the poetry that scares her—or me either. We both want to do all we can to help along the poetic drama—we believe the public's ready for it, and we're willing to take a big financial risk in order to be the first to give them what they want. *But we don't believe they could be made to want this.* The fact is, there isn't enough drama in your play to the allowance of poetry—the thing drags all through. You've got a big idea, but it's not out of swaddling clothes.

"If this was your first play I'd say: *Try again.* But it has been just the same with all the others you've shown me. And you remember the result of *The Lee Shore*, where you carried all the expenses of production yourself, and we couldn't fill the theatre for a week. Yet 'The Lee Shore' was a modern problem play—much easier to swing than blank verse. It isn't as if you hadn't tried all kinds—"

Granice folded the letter and put it carefully back into the envelope. Why on earth was he re-reading it, when he knew every phrase in it by heart, when for a month past he had seen it, night after night, stand out in letters of flame against the darkness of his sleepless lids?

*"It has been just the same with all the others you've shown me."*

That was the way they dismissed ten years of passionate unremitting work!

*"You remember the result of 'The Lee Shore.'"*

Good God—as if he were likely to forget it! He re-lived it all now in a drowning flash: the persistent rejection of the play, his sudden resolve to put it on at his own cost, to spend ten thousand dollars of his inheritance on testing his chance of success—the fever of preparation, the dry-mouthed agony of the "first night," the flat fall, the stupid press, his secret rush to Europe to escape the condolence of his friends!

*"It isn't as if you hadn't tried all kinds."*

No—he had tried all kinds: comedy, tragedy, prose and verse, the light curtain-raiser, the short sharp drama, the bourgeois-realistic and the lyrical-romantic—finally deciding that he would no longer "prostitute his talent" to win popularity, but would impose on the public his own theory of art in the form of five acts of blank verse. Yes, he had offered them everything—and always with the same result.

Ten years of it—ten years of dogged work and unrelieved failure. The ten years from forty to fifty—the best ten years of his life! And if one counted the years before, the silent years of dreams, assimilation, preparation—then call it half a man's life-time: half a man's life-time thrown away!

And what was he to do with the remaining half? Well, he had settled that, thank God! He turned and glanced anxiously at the clock. Ten minutes past eight—only ten minutes had been consumed in that stormy rush through his whole past! And he must wait another twenty minutes for Ascham. It was one of the worst symptoms of his case that, in proportion as he had grown to shrink from human company, he dreaded more and more to be alone. . . . But why the devil was he waiting for Ascham? Why didn't he cut the knot himself? Since he was so unutterably sick of the whole business, why did he have to call in an outsider to rid him of this nightmare of living?

He opened the drawer again and laid his hand on the revolver. It was a small slim ivory toy—just the instrument for a tired sufferer to give himself a "hypodermic" with. Granice raised it slowly in one hand, while with the other he felt under the thin hair at the back of his head, between the ear and the nape. He knew just where to place the muzzle: he had once got a young surgeon to show him. And as he found the spot, and lifted the revolver to it, the inevitable phenomenon occurred. The hand that held the weapon began to shake, the tremor communicated itself to his arm, his heart gave a wild leap which sent up a wave of deadly nausea to his throat, he smelt the powder, he sickened at the crash of the bullet through his skull, and a sweat of fear broke out over his forehead and ran down his quivering face. . . .

He laid away the revolver with an oath and, pulling out a cologne-scented handkerchief, passed it tremulously over his brow and temples. It was no use—he knew he could never do it in that way. His attempts at self-destruction were as futile as his snatches at fame! He couldn't make himself a real life, and he couldn't get rid of the life he had. And that was why he had sent for Ascham to help him. . . .

The lawyer, over the Camembert and Burgundy, began to excuse himself for his delay.

"I didn't like to say anything while your man was about—but the fact is, I was sent for on a rather unusual matter—"

"Oh, it's all right," said Granice cheerfully. He was beginning to feel the usual reaction that food and company produced. It was not any recovered pleasure in life that he felt, but only a deeper withdrawal into himself. It was easier to go on automatically with the social gestures than to uncover to any human eye the abyss within him.

"My dear fellow, it's sacrilege to keep a dinner waiting—especially the production of an artist like yours." Mr. Ascham sipped his Burgundy luxuriously. "But the fact is, Mrs.

Ashgrove sent for me."

Granice raised his head with a quick movement of surprise. For a moment he was shaken out of his self-absorption.

*"Mrs. Ashgrove?"*

Ascham smiled. "I thought you'd be interested; I know your passion for *causes célèbres*. And this promises to be one. Of course it's out of our line entirely—we never touch criminal cases. But she wanted to consult me as a friend. Ashgrove was a distant connection of my wife's. And, by Jove, it is a queer case!" The servant re-entered, and Ascham snapped his lips shut.

Would the gentlemen have their coffee in the dining-room?

"No—serve it in the library," said Granice, rising. He led the way back to the curtained confidential room. He was really curious to hear what Ascham had to tell him.

While the coffee and cigars were being served he fidgeted about the library, glancing at his letters—the usual meaningless notes and bills—and picking up the evening paper. As he unfolded it a headline caught his eye.

ROSE MELROSE WANTS TO PLAY POETRY.
THINKS SHE HAS FOUND HER POET."

He read on with a thumping heart—found the name of a young author he had barely heard of, saw the title of a play, a "poetic drama," dance before his eyes, and dropped the paper, sick, disgusted. It was true, then—she *was* "game"—it was not the manner but the matter she mistrusted!

Granice turned to the servant, who seemed to be purposely lingering. "I shan't need you this evening, Flint. I'll lock up myself."

He fancied the man's acquiescence implied surprise. What was going on, Flint seemed to wonder, that Mr. Granice should want him out of the way? Probably he would find a pretext for coming back to see. Granice suddenly felt himself enveloped in a network of espionage.

As the door closed he threw himself into an armchair and leaned forward to take a light from Ascham's cigar.

"Tell me about Mrs. Ashgrove," he said, seeming to himself to speak stiffly, as if his lips were cracked.

"Mrs. Ashgrove? Well, there's not much to *tell*."

"And you couldn't if there were?" Granice smiled.

"Probably not. As a matter of fact, she wanted my advice about her choice of counsel. There was nothing especially confidential in our talk."

"And what's your impression, now you've seen her?"

"My impression is, very distinctly, *that nothing will ever be known.*"

"Ah—?" Granice murmured, puffing at his cigar.

"I'm more and more convinced that whoever poisoned Ashgrove knew his business, and will consequently never be found out. That's a capital cigar you've given me."

"You like it? I get them over from Cuba." Granice examined his own reflectively. "Then you believe in the theory that the clever criminals never *are* caught?"

"Of course I do. Look about you—look back for the last dozen years—none of the big murder problems are ever solved." The lawyer ruminated behind his blue cloud. "Why, take the instance in your own family: I'd forgotten I had an illustration at hand! Take old Joseph Lenman's murder—do you suppose that will ever be explained?"

As the words dropped from Ascham's lips his host looked slowly about the library, and every object in it stared back at him with a stale unescapable familiarity. How sick he was of looking at that room! It was as dull as the face of a wife one has wearied of. He cleared his throat slowly; then he turned his head to the lawyer and said: "I could explain the Lenman murder myself."

Ascham's eye kindled: he shared Granice's interest in criminal cases.

"By Jove! You've had a theory all this time? It's odd you never mentioned it. Go ahead and tell me. There are certain features in the Lenman case not unlike this Ashgrove affair, and your idea may be a help."

Granice paused and his eye reverted instinctively to the table drawer in which the revolver and the manuscript lay side by side. What if he were to try another appeal to Rose Melrose? Then he looked at the notes and bills on the table, and the horror of taking up again the lifeless routine of life—of performing the same automatic gestures another day—displaced his fleeting vision.

"I haven't a theory. I *know* who murdered Joseph Lenman."

Ascham settled himself comfortably in his chair, prepared for enjoyment.

"You *know?* Well, who did?" he laughed.

"I did," said Granice, rising.

He stood before Ascham, and the lawyer lay back staring up at him.

Then he broke into another laugh.

"Why, this is glorious! You murdered him, did you? To inherit his money, I suppose? Better and better! Go on, my boy! Unbosom yourself! Tell me all about it! Confession is good for the soul."

Granice waited till the lawyer had shaken the last peal of laughter from his throat; then he repeated doggedly: "I murdered him."

The two men looked at each other for a long moment, and this time Ascham did not laugh.

"Granice!"

"I murdered him—to get his money, as you say."

There was another pause, and Granice, with a vague underlying sense of amusement, saw his guest's look change from pleasantry to apprehension.

"What's the joke, my dear fellow? I fail to see."

"It's not a joke. It's the truth. I murdered him." He had spoken painfully at first, as if there were a knot in his throat; but each time he repeated the words he found they were easier to say.

Ascham laid down his extinct cigar.

"What's the matter? Aren't you well? What on earth are you driving at?"

"I'm perfectly well. But I murdered my cousin, Joseph Lenman, and I want it known that I murdered him."

*"You want it known?"*

"Yes. That's why I sent for you. I'm sick of living, and when I try to kill myself I funk it." He spoke quite naturally now, as if the knot in his throat had been untied.

"Good Lord—good Lord," the lawyer gasped.

"But I suppose," Granice continued, "there's no doubt this would be murder in the first degree? I'm sure of the chair if I own up?"

Ascham drew a long breath; then he said slowly: "Sit down, Granice. Let's talk."

## II

GRANICE told his story simply, connectedly.

He began by a quick survey of his early years—the years of drudgery and privation. His father, a charming man who could never say "no," had so signally failed to say it on certain essential occasions that when he died he left an illegitimate family and a mortgaged estate. His lawful kin found themselves hanging over a gulf of debt, and young Granice, to support his mother and sister, had to leave Harvard and bury himself at eighteen in a broker's office. He loathed his work, and he was always poor, always worried and in ill-health. A few years later his mother died, but his sister, an ineffectual neurasthenic, remained on his hands. His own health gave out, and he had to go away for six months, and work harder than ever when he came back. He had no knack for business, no head for figures, no dimmest insight into the mysteries of commerce. He wanted to travel and write—those were his inmost longings. And as the years dragged on, and he neared middle-age without making any more money, or acquiring any firmer health, a sick despair possessed him. He tried writing, but he always came home from the office so tired that his brain could not work. For half the year he did not reach his dim up-town flat till after dark, and could only "brush up" for dinner, and afterward lie on the lounge with his pipe, while his sister droned through the evening paper. Sometimes he spent an evening at the theatre; or he dined out, or, more rarely, strayed off with an acquaintance or two in quest of what is known as "pleasure." And in summer, when he and Kate went to the sea-side for a month, he dozed through the days in utter weariness. Once he fell in love with a charming girl—but what had he to offer her, in God's name? She seemed to like him, and in common decency he had to drop out of the running. Apparently no one replaced him, for she never married, but grew stoutish, grayish, philanthropic—yet how sweet she had been when he had first kissed her! One more wasted life, he reflected. . . .

But the stage had always been his master-passion. He would have sold his soul for the time and freedom to write plays! It was in him—he could not remember when it had not been his deepest-seated instinct. As the years passed it became a morbid, a relentless obsession—yet with every year the material conditions were more and more against it. He felt himself growing middle-aged, and he watched the reflection of the process in his sister's wasted face. At eighteen she had been pretty, and as full of enthusiasm as he. Now she was sour, trivial, insignificant—she had missed her chance of life. And she had no resources, poor creature, was fashioned simply for the primitive functions she had been denied the chance to fulfill! It exasperated him to think of it—and to reflect that even now a little travel, a little health, a little money, might transform her, make her young and desirable . . . The chief fruit of his experience was that there is no such fixed state as age or youth—there is only health as against sickness, wealth as against poverty; and age or youth as the outcome of the lot one draws.

At this point in his narrative Granice stood up, and went to lean against the mantel-piece, looking down at Ascham, who had not moved from his seat, or changed his attitude of rigid fascinated attention.

"Then came the summer when we went to Wrenfield to be near old Lenman—my mother's cousin, as you know. Some of the family always mounted guard over him—generally a niece or so. But that year they were all scattered, and one of the nieces offered to lend us her cottage if we'd relieve her of duty for two months. It was a nuisance for me, of course, for Wrenfield is two hours from town; but my mother, who was a slave to family observances, had always been good to the old man, so it was natural we should be called on—and there was the saving of rent and the good air for Kate. So we went.

"You never knew Joseph Lenman? Well, picture to yourself an amoeba or some primitive organism of that sort, under a Titan's microscope. He was large, undifferentiated, inert—since I could remember him he had done nothing but take his temperature and read the Churchman. Oh, and cultivate melons—that was his hobby. Not vulgar, out-of-door melons—his were grown under glass. He had miles of it at Wrenfield—his big kitchen-garden was surrounded by blinking battalions of green-houses. And in nearly all of them melons were grown—early melons and late, French, English, domestic—dwarf melons and monsters: every shape, color and variety. They were petted and nursed like children—a staff of trained attendants waited on them. I'm not sure they didn't have a doctor to take their temperature—at any rate the place was full of thermometers. And they didn't sprawl on the ground like ordinary melons; they were trained against the glass like nectarines, and each melon hung in a net which sustained its weight and left it free on all sides to the sun and air.

"It used to strike me sometimes that old Lenman was just like one of his own melons—the pale-fleshed English kind. His life, apathetic and motionless, hung in a net of gold, in an equable warm ventilated atmosphere, high above sordid earthly worries. The cardinal rule of his existence was not to let himself be 'worried.' . . . I remember his advising me to try it myself, one day when I spoke to him about Kate's bad health, and her need of a change. 'I never let myself worry,' he said complacently. 'It's the worst thing for the liver—and you look to me as if you had a liver. Take my advice and be cheerful. You'll make yourself happier and others too.' And all he had to do was to write a check, and send the poor girl off for a holiday!

"The hardest part of it was that the money half-belonged to us already. The old skin-flint only had it for life, in trust for us and the others. But his life was a good deal sounder than mine or Kate's—and one could picture him taking extra care of it for the joke of keeping us waiting. I always felt that the sight of our hungry eyes was a tonic to him.

"Well, I tried to see if I couldn't reach him through his vanity. I flattered him, feigned a passionate interest in his melons. And he was taken in, and used to discourse on them by the hour. On fine days he was driven to the green-houses in his pony-chair, and waddled through them, prodding and leering at the fruit, like a fat Turk in his seraglio. When he bragged to me of the expense of growing them I was reminded of a hideous old Lothario bragging of what his pleasures cost. And the resemblance was completed by the fact that he couldn't eat as much as a mouthful of his melons—had lived for years on buttermilk and toast. 'But, after all, it's my only hobby—why shouldn't I indulge it?' he said sentimentally. As if I'd ever been able to indulge any of mine! On the keep of those melons Kate and I could have lived like gods. . .

"One day toward the end of the summer, when Kate was too unwell to drag herself up to the big house, she asked me to go and spend the afternoon with cousin Joseph. It was a lovely soft September afternoon—a day to lie under a Roman stone-pine, with one's eyes on the sky, and let the cosmic harmonies rush through one. Perhaps the vision was suggested by the fact that, as I entered cousin Joseph's hideous black walnut library, I passed one of the under-gardeners, a handsome full-throated Italian, who dashed out in such a hurry that he nearly knocked me down. I remember thinking it queer that the fellow, whom I had often seen about the melon-houses, did not bow to me, or even seem to see me.

"Cousin Joseph sat in his usual seat, behind the darkened windows, his fat hands folded on his protuberant waistcoat, the last number of the *Churchman* at his elbow, and near it, on a huge dish, a fat melon—the fattest melon I'd ever seen. As I looked at it I pictured the ecstasy of contemplation from which I must have roused him, and congratulated myself on finding him in such a mood, since I had made up my mind to ask him a favor. Then I noticed that his face, instead of looking as calm as an egg-shell, was distorted and whimpering—and without stopping to greet me he pointed passionately to the melon.

"'Look at it, look at it—did you ever see such a beauty? Such firmness—roundness—such delicious smoothness to the touch?' It was as if he had said 'she' instead of 'it,' and when he put out his senile hand and touched the melon I positively had to look the other way.

"Then he told me what had happened. The Italian under-gardener, who had been specially recommended for the melon-houses—though it was against my cousin's principles to employ a Papist—had been assigned to the care of the monster: for it had revealed itself, early in its existence, as destined to become a monster, to surpass its plumpest, pulpiest sisters, carry off prizes at agricultural shows, and be photographed and celebrated in every gardening paper in the land. The Italian had done well—seemed to have a sense of responsibility. And that very morning he had been ordered to pick the melon, which was to be shown next day at the county fair, and to bring it in for Mr. Lenman to gaze on its blonde virginity. But in picking it, what had the damned scoundrelly Jesuit done but drop it—drop it crash on the sharp spout of a watering-pot, so that it received a deep gash in its firm pale rotundity, and was henceforth but a bruised, ruined, fallen melon?

"The old man's rage was fearful in its impotence—he shook, spluttered and strangled with it. He had just had the Italian up and had sacked him on the spot, without wages or character—had threatened to have him arrested if he was ever caught prowling about Wrenfield. 'By God, and I'll do it—I'll write to Washington—I'll have the pauper scoundrel deported! I'll show him what money can do!' As likely as not there was some murderous Black-hand business under it—it would be found that the fellow was a member of a 'gang.' Those Italians would murder you for a quarter. He meant to have the police look into it . . . And then he grew frightened at his own excitement. 'But I must calm myself,' he said. He took his temperature, rang for his drops, and turned to the *Churchman*. He had been reading an article on Nestorianism when the melon was brought in. He asked me to go on with it, and I read to him for an hour, in the dim close room, with a fat fly buzzing stealthily about the fallen melon.

"All the while one phrase of the old man's buzzed in my brain like the fly about the melon. *'I'll show him what money can do!'* Good heaven! If *I* could but show the old man! If I could make him see his power of giving happiness as a new outlet for his monstrous egotism! I tried to tell him something about my situation and Kate's—spoke of my ill-health, my unsuccessful drudgery, my longing to write, to make myself a name—I stammered out an entreaty for a loan. 'I can guarantee to repay you, sir—I've a half-written play as security. . . .'

"I shall never forget his glassy stare. His face had grown as smooth as an egg-shell again—his eyes peered over his fat cheeks like sentinels over a slippery rampart.

"'A half-written play—a play of *yours* as security?' He looked at me almost fearfully, as if detecting the first symptoms of insanity. 'Do you understand anything of business?' he enquired mildly. I laughed and answered: 'No, not much.'

"He leaned back with closed lids. 'All this excitement has been too much for me,' he said. 'If you'll excuse me, I'll prepare for my nap.' And I stumbled out of the room, blindly, like the Italian."

Granice moved away from the mantelpiece, and walked across to the tray set out with decanters and soda-water. He poured himself a tall glass of soda-water, emptied it, and glanced at Ascham's dead cigar.

"Better light another," he suggested.

The lawyer shook his head, and Granice went on with his tale. He told of his mounting obsession—how the murderous impulse had waked in him on the instant of his cousin's refusal, and he had muttered to himself: "By God, if you won't, I'll make you." He spoke more tranquilly as the narrative proceeded, as though his rage had died down once the resolve to act on it was taken. He applied his whole mind to the question of how the old man was to be "disposed of." Suddenly he remembered the outcry: "Those Italians will murder you for a quarter!" But no definite project presented itself: he simply waited for an inspiration.

Granice and his sister moved to town a day or two after the incident of the melon. But the cousins, who had returned, kept them informed of the old man's condition. One day, about three weeks later, Granice, on getting home, found Kate excited over a report from Wrenfield. The Italian had been there again—had somehow slipped into the house, made his way up to the library, and "used threatening language." The house-keeper found cousin Joseph gasping, the whites of his eyes showing "something awful." The doctor was sent for, and the attack warded off; and the police had ordered the Italian from the neighborhood.

But cousin Joseph, thereafter, languished, had "nerves," and lost his taste for toast and butter-milk. The doctor called in a colleague, and the consultation amused and excited the old man—he became once more an important figure. The medical men reassured the family—too completely!—and to the patient they recommended a more varied diet: advised him to take whatever "tempted him." And so one day, tremulously, prayerfully, he decided on a tiny bit of melon. It was brought up with ceremony, and consumed in the presence of the house-keeper and a hovering cousin; and twenty minutes later he was dead. . . .

"But you remember the circumstances," Granice went on; "how suspicion turned at once on the Italian? In spite of the hint the police had given him he had been seen hanging about the house since 'the scene.' It was said that he had tender relations with the kitchen-maid, and the rest seemed easy to explain. But when they looked round to ask him for the explanation he was gone—gone clean out of sight. He had been 'warned' to leave Wrenfield, and he had taken the warning so to heart that no one ever laid eyes on him again."

Granice paused. He had dropped into a chair opposite the lawyer's, and he sat for a moment, his head thrown back, looking about the familiar room. Everything in it had grown grimacing and alien, and each strange insistent object seemed craning forward from its place to hear him.

"It was I who put the stuff in the melon," he said. "And I don't want you to think I'm sorry for it. This isn't 'remorse,' understand. I'm glad the old skin-flint is dead—I'm glad the others have their money. But mine's no use to me any more. My sister married miserably, and died. And I've never had what I wanted."

Ascham continued to stare; then he said: "What on earth was your object, then?"

"Why, to *get* what I wanted—what I fancied was in reach! I wanted change, rest, *life,* for both of us—wanted, above all, for myself, the chance to write! I travelled, got back my health, and came home to tie myself up to my work. And I've slaved at it steadily for ten years without reward—without the most distant hope of success! Nobody will look at my stuff. And now I'm fifty, and I'm beaten, and I know it." His chin dropped forward on his breast. "I want to chuck the whole business," he ended.

III

IT was after midnight when Ascham left.

His hand on Granice's shoulder, as he turned to go—"District Attorney be hanged; see a doctor, see a doctor!" he had cried; and so, with an exaggerated laugh, had pulled on his coat and departed.

Granice turned back into the library. It had never occurred to him that Ascham would not believe his story. For three hours he had explained, elucidated, patiently and painfully gone over every detail—but without once breaking down the iron incredulity of the lawyer's eye.

At first Ascham had feigned to be convinced—but that, as Granice now perceived, was simply to get him to expose himself, to entrap him into contradictions. And when the attempt failed, when Granice triumphantly met and refuted each disconcerting question, the lawyer dropped the mask suddenly, and said with a good-humored laugh: "By Jove, Granice you'll write a successful play yet. The way you've worked this all out is a marvel."

Granice swung about furiously—that last sneer about the play inflamed him. Was all the world in a conspiracy to deride his failure?

"I did it, I did it," he muttered sullenly, his rage spending itself against the impenetrable surface of the other's mockery; and Ascham answered with a smile: "Ever read any of those books on hallucination? I've got a fairly good medico-legal library. I could send you one or two if you like. . . ."

Left alone, Granice cowered down in the chair before his writing-table. He understood that Ascham thought him off his head.

"Good God—what if they all think me crazy?"

The horror of it broke out over him in a cold sweat—he sat there and shook, his eyes hidden in his icy hands. But gradually, as he began to rehearse his story for the thousandth time, he saw again how incontrovertible it was, and felt sure that any criminal lawyer would believe him.

"That's the trouble—Ascham's not a criminal lawyer. And then he's a friend. What a fool I was to talk to a friend! Even if he did believe me, he'd never let me see it—his instinct would be to cover the whole thing up. . .But in that case—if he *did* believe me—he might think it a kindness to get me shut up in an asylum. . . " Granice began to tremble again. "Good heaven! If he should bring in an expert—one of those damned alienists! Ascham and Pettilow can do anything—their word always goes. If Ascham drops a hint that I'd better be shut up, I'll be in a strait-jacket by tomorrow! And he'd do it from the kindest motives—be quite right to do it if he thinks I'm a murderer!"

The vision froze him to his chair. He pressed his fists to his bursting temples and tried to think. For the first time he hoped that Ascham had not believed his story.

"But he did—he did! I can see it now—I noticed what a queer eye he cocked at me. Good God, what shall I do—what shall I do?"

He started up and looked at the clock. Half-past one. What if Ascham should think the case urgent, rout out an alienist, and come back with him? Granice jumped to his feet, and his sudden gesture brushed the morning paper from the table. Mechanically he stooped to pick it up, and the movement started a new train of association.

He sat down again, and reached for the telephone book in the rack by his chair.

"Give me three-o-ten . . . yes."

The new idea in his mind had revived his flagging energy. He would act—act at once. It was only by thus planning ahead, committing himself to some unavoidable line of conduct, that he could pull himself through the meaningless days. Each time he reached a fresh decision it was like coming out of a foggy weltering sea into a calm harbour with lights. One of the queerest phases of his long agony was the intense relief produced by these momentary lulls.

"That the office of the *Investigator?* Yes? Give me Mr. Denver, please . . . Hallo, Denver . . . Yes, Hubert Granice. . . . Just caught you? Going straight home? Can I come and see you . . . yes, now . . . have a talk? It's rather urgent . . . yes, might give you some first-rate 'copy.'. . . All right!" He hung up the receiver with a laugh. It had been a happy thought to call up the editor of the *Investigator*—Robert Denver was the very man he needed . . .

Granice put out the lights in the library—it was odd how the automatic gestures persisted!—went into the hall, put on his hat and overcoat, and let himself out of the flat. In the hall, a sleepy elevator boy blinked at him and then dropped his head on his folded arms. Granice passed out into the street. At the corner of Fifth Avenue he hailed a crawling cab, and called out an up-town address. The long thoroughfare stretched before him, dim and deserted, like an ancient avenue of tombs. But from Denver's house a friendly beam fell on the pavement; and as Granice sprang from his cab the editor's electric turned the corner.

The two men grasped hands, and Denver, feeling for his latch-key, ushered Granice into the brightly-lit hall.

"Disturb me? Not a bit. You might have, at ten tomorrow morning . . . but this is my liveliest hour . . . you know my habits of old."

Granice had known Robert Denver for fifteen years—watched his rise through all the stages of journalism to the Olympian pinnacle of the *Investigator's* editorial office. In the thick-set man with grizzling hair there were few traces left of the hungry-eyed young reporter who, on his way home in the small hours, used to "bob in" on Granice, while the latter sat grinding at his plays. Denver had to pass Granice's flat on the way to his own, and it became a habit, if he saw a light in the window, and Granice's shadow against the blind, to go in, smoke a pipe, and discuss the universe.

"Well—this is like old times—a good old habit reversed." The editor smote his visitor genially on the shoulder. "Reminds me of the nights when I used to rout you out... How's the play, by the way? There is a play, I suppose? It's as safe to ask you that as to say to some men: 'How's the baby?'"

Denver laughed good-naturedly, and Granice thought how thick and heavy he had grown. It was evident, even to Granice's tortured nerves, that the words had not been uttered in malice—and the fact gave him a new measure of his insignificance. Denver did not even know that he had been a failure! The fact hurt more than Ascham's irony.

"Come in—come in." The editor led the way into a small cheerful room, where there were cigars and decanters. He pushed an arm-chair toward his visitor, and dropped into another with a comfortable groan.

"Now, then—help yourself. And let's hear all about it."

He beamed at Granice over his pipe-bowl, and the latter, lighting his cigar, said to himself: "Success makes men comfortable, but it makes them stupid."

Then he turned, and began: "Denver, I want to tell you—"

The clock ticked rhythmically on the mantel-piece. The room was gradually filled with drifting blue layers of smoke, and through them the editor's face came and went like the moon through a moving sky. Once the hour struck—then the rhythmical ticking began again. The atmosphere grew denser and heavier, and beads of perspiration began to roll from Granice's forehead.

"Do you mind if I open the window?"

"No. It *is* stuffy in here. Wait—I'll do it myself." Denver pushed down the upper sash, and returned to his chair. "Well—go on," he said, filling another pipe. His composure exasperated Granice.

"There's no use in my going on if you don't believe me."

The editor remained unmoved. "Who says I don't believe you? And how can I tell till you've finished?"

Granice went on, ashamed of his outburst. "It was simple enough, as you'll see. From the day the old man said to me, 'Those Italians would murder you for a quarter,' I dropped everything and just worked at my scheme. It struck me at once that I must find a way of getting to Wrenfield and back in a night—and that led to the idea of a motor. A motor—that never occurred to you? You wonder where I got the money, I suppose. Well, I had a thousand or so put by, and I nosed around till I found what I wanted—a second-hand racer. I knew how to drive a car, and I tried the thing and found it was all right. Times were bad, and I bought it for my price, and stored it away. Where? Why, in one of those no-questions-asked garages where they keep motors that are not for family use. I had a lively cousin who had put me up to that dodge, and I looked about till I found a queer hole where they took in my car like a baby in a foundling asylum . . . Then I practiced running to Wrenfield and back in a night. I knew the way pretty well, for I'd done it often with the same lively cousin—and in the small hours, too. The distance is over ninety miles, and on the third trial I did it under two hours. But my arms were so lame that I could hardly get dressed the next morning.

"Well, then came the report about the Italian's threats, and I saw I must act at once... I meant to break into the old man's room, shoot him, and get away again. It was a big risk, but I thought I could manage it. Then we heard that he was ill—that there'd been a consultation. Perhaps the fates were going to do it for me! Good Lord, if that could only be!..."

Granice stopped and wiped his forehead: the open window did not seem to have cooled the room.

"Then came word that he was better; and the day after, when I came up from my office, I found Kate laughing over the news that he was to try a bit of melon. The house-keeper had just telephoned her—all Wrenfield was in a flutter. The doctor himself had picked out the melon, one of the little French ones that are hardly bigger than a large tomato—and the patient was to eat it at his breakfast the next morning.

"In a flash I saw my chance. It was a bare chance, no more. But I knew the ways of the house—I was sure the melon would be brought in over night and put in the pantry ice-box. If there were only one melon in the ice-box I could be fairly sure it was the one I wanted. Melons didn't lie around loose in that house—every one was known, numbered, catalogued. The old man was beset by the dread that the servants would eat them, and he took a hundred mean precautions to prevent it. Yes, I felt pretty sure of my melon ... and poisoning was much safer than shooting. It would have been the devil and all to get into the old man's bedroom without his rousing the house; but I ought to be able to break into the pantry without much trouble.

"It was a cloudy night, too—everything served me. I dined quietly, and sat down at my desk. Kate had one of her usual headaches, and went to bed early. As soon as she was gone I slipped out. I had got together a sort of disguise—red beard and queer-looking ulster. I shoved them into a bag, and went round to the garage. There was no one there but a half-drunken machinist whom I'd never seen before. That served me, too. They were always changing machinists, and this new fellow didn't even bother to ask if the car belonged to me. It was a very easy-going place ...

"Well, I jumped in, ran up Broadway, and let the car go as soon as I was out of Harlem. Dark as it was, I could trust myself to strike a sharp pace. In the shadow of a wood I stopped a second and got into the beard and ulster. Then away again—it was just eleven-thirty when I got to Wrenfield.

"I left the car in a dark lane behind the Lenman place, and slipped through the kitchen-garden. The melon-houses winked at me through the dark—I remember thinking that they knew what I wanted to know. . . . By the stable a dog came out growling—but he nosed me out, jumped on me, and went back . . . The house was as dark as the grave. I knew everybody went to bed by ten. But there might be a prowling servant—the kitchen-maid might have come down to let in her Italian. I had to risk that, of course. I crept around by the back door and hid in the shrubbery. Then I listened. It was all as silent as death. I crossed over to the house, pried open the pantry window and climbed in. I had a little electric lamp in my pocket, and shielding it with my cap I groped my way to the ice-box, opened it—and there was the little French melon . . . only one.

"I stopped to listen—I was quite cool. Then I pulled out my bottle of stuff and my syringe, and gave each section of the melon a hypodermic. It was all done inside of three minutes—at ten minutes to twelve I was back in the car. I got out of the lane as quietly as I could, struck a back road that skirted the village, and let the car out as soon as I was beyond the last houses. I only stopped once on the way in, to drop the beard and ulster into a pond. I had a big stone ready to weight them with and they went down plump, like a dead body—and at two o'clock I was back at my desk."

Granice stopped speaking and looked across the smoke-fumes at his listener; but Denver's face remained inscrutable.

At length he said: "Why did you want to tell me this?"

The question startled Granice. He was about to explain, as he had explained to Ascham; but suddenly it occurred to him that if his motive had not seemed convincing to the lawyer it would carry much less weight with Denver. Both were successful men, and success does not understand the subtle agony of failure. Granice cast about for another reason.

"Why, I—the thing haunts me . . . remorse, I suppose you'd call it. . ."

Denver struck the ashes from his empty pipe.

"Remorse? Bosh!" he said energetically.

Granice's heart sank. "You don't believe in—*remorse?*"

"Not an atom: in the man of action. The mere fact of your talking of remorse proves to me that you're not the man to have planned and put through such a job."

Granice groaned. "Well—I lied to you about remorse. I've never felt any."

Denver's lips tightened sceptically about his freshly-filled pipe.

"What *was* your motive, then? You must have had one."

"I'll tell you—" And Granice began again to rehearse the story of his failure, of his loathing for life. "Don't say you don't believe me this time . . . that this isn't a real reason!" he stammered out piteously as he ended.

Denver meditated. "No, I won't say that. I've seen too many queer things. There's always a reason for wanting to get out of life—the wonder is that we find so many for staying in!"

Granice's heart grew light. "Then you *do* believe me?" he faltered.

"Believe that you're sick of the job? Yes. And that you haven't the nerve to pull the trigger? Oh, yes—that's easy enough, too. But all that doesn't make you a murderer— though I don't say it proves you could never have been one."

"I *have* been one, Denver—I swear to you."

"Perhaps." He meditated. "Just tell me one or two things."

"Oh, go ahead. You won't stump me!" Granice heard himself say with a laugh.

"Well—how did you make all those trial trips without exciting your sister's curiosity? I knew your night habits pretty well at that time, remember. You were very seldom out late. Didn't the change in your ways surprise her?"

"No; because she was away at the time. She went to pay several visits in the country soon after we came back from Wrenfield, and was only in town for a night or two before—before I did the job."

"And that night she went to bed early with a headache?"

"Yes—blinding. She didn't know anything when she had that kind. And her room was at the back of the flat."

There was another pause in Denver's interrogatory. "And when you got back—she didn't hear you? You got in without her knowing it?"

"Yes. I went straight to my work—took it up at the word where I'd left off—*why, Denver, don't you remember?*" Granice suddenly, passionately interjected.

"Remember—?"

"Yes; how you found me—when you looked in that morning, between two and three . . . your usual hour . . . ?"

"Yes," the editor nodded.

Granice gave a short laugh. "In my old coat—with my pipe: looked as if I'd been working all night, didn't I? Well, I hadn't been in my chair ten minutes!"

Denver uncrossed his legs and then crossed them again. "I didn't know whether *you* remembered that."

"What?"

"My coming in that particular night—or morning."

Granice swung round in his chair. "Why, man alive! That's why I'm here now. Because it was you who spoke for me at the inquest, when they looked round to see what all the old man's heirs had been doing that night—you who testified to having dropped in and found me at my desk as usual. . . . I thought *that* would appeal to your journalistic sense if nothing else would!"

Denver smiled. "Oh, my journalistic sense is still susceptible enough—and the idea's picturesque, I grant you: asking the man who proved your alibi to establish your guilt."

"That's it—that's it!" Granice's laugh had a ring of triumph.

"Well, but how about the other chap's testimony—I mean that young doctor: what was his name? Ned Ranney. Don't you remember my testifying that I'd met him at the elevated station, and told him I was on my way to smoke a pipe with you, and his saying: 'All right; you'll find him in. I passed the house two hours ago, and saw his shadow against the blind, as usual.' And the lady with the toothache in the flat across the way: she corroborated his statement, you remember."

"Yes; I remember."

Well, then?"

"Simple enough. Before starting I rigged up a kind of mannequin with old coats and a cushion—something to cast a shadow on the blind. All you fellows were used to seeing my shadow there in the small hours—I counted on that, and knew you'd take any vague outline as mine."

"Simple enough, as you say. But the woman with the toothache saw the shadow move—you remember she said she saw you sink forward, as if you'd fallen asleep."

"Yes; and she was right. It *did* move. I suppose some extra-heavy dray must have jolted by the flimsy building—at any rate, something gave my mannequin a jar, and when I came back he had sunk forward, half over the table."

There was a long silence between the two men. Granice, with a throbbing heart, watched Denver refill his pipe. The editor, at any rate, did not sneer and flout him. After all, journalism gave a deeper insight than the law into the fantastic possibilities of life, prepared one better to allow for the incalculableness of human impulses.

"Well?" Granice faltered out.

Denver stood up with a shrug. "Look here, man—what's wrong with you? Make a clean breast of it! Nerves gone to smash? I'd like to take you to see a chap I know—an ex-prize-fighter—who's a wonder at pulling fellows in your state out of their hole—"

"Oh, oh—" Granice broke in. He stood up also, and the two men eyed each other. "You don't believe me, then?"

"This yarn—how can I? There wasn't a flaw in your alibi."

"But haven't I filled it full of them now?"

Denver shook his head. "I might think so if I hadn't happened to know that you *wanted* to. There's the hitch, don't you see?"

Granice groaned. "No, I didn't. You mean my wanting to be found guilty—?"

"Of course! If somebody else had accused you, the story might have been worth looking into. As it is, a child could have invented it. It doesn't do much credit to your ingenuity."

Granice turned sullenly toward the door. What was the use of arguing? But on the threshold a sudden impulse drew him back. "Look here, Denver—I daresay you're right. But will you do just one thing to prove it? Put my statement in the *Investigator*, just as I've made it. Ridicule it as much as you like. Only give the other fellows a chance at it—men who don't know anything about me. Set them talking and looking about. I don't care a damn whether *you* believe me—what I want is to convince the Grand Jury! I oughtn't to have come to a man who knows me—your cursed incredulity is infectious. I don't put my case well, because I know in advance it's discredited, and I almost end by not believing it myself. That's why I can't convince *you*. It's a vicious circle." He laid a hand on Denver's arm. "Send a stenographer, and put my statement in the paper."

But Denver did not warm to the idea. "My dear fellow, you seem to forget that all the evidence was pretty thoroughly sifted at the time, every possible clue followed up. The public would have been ready enough then to believe that you murdered old Lenman—you or anybody else. All they wanted was a murderer—the most improbable would have served. But your alibi was too confoundedly complete. And nothing you've told me has shaken it." Denver laid his cool hand over the other's burning fingers. "Look here, old fellow, go home and work up a better case—then come in and submit it to the *Investigator*."

IV

THE perspiration was rolling off Granice's forehead. Every few minutes he had to draw out his handkerchief and wipe the moisture from his haggard face.

For an hour and a half he had been talking steadily, putting his case to the District Attorney. Luckily he had a speaking acquaintance with Allonby, and had obtained, without much difficulty, a private audience on the very day after his talk with Robert Denver. In the interval between he had hurried home, got out of his evening clothes, and gone forth again at once into the dreary dawn. His fear of Ascham and the alienist made it impossible for him to remain in his rooms. And it seemed to him that the only way of averting that hideous peril was by establishing, in some sane impartial mind, the proof of his guilt. Even if he had not been so incurably sick of life, the electric chair seemed now the only alternative to the strait jacket.

As he paused to wipe his forehead he saw the District Attorney glance at his watch. The gesture was significant, and Granice lifted an appealing hand. "I don't expect you to believe me now—but can't you put me under arrest, and have the thing looked into?"

Allonby smiled faintly under his heavy grayish moustache. He had a ruddy face, full and jovial, in which his keen professional eyes seemed to keep watch over impulses not strictly professional.

"Well, I don't know that we need lock you up just yet. But of course I'm bound to look into your statement—"

Granice rose with an exquisite sense of relief. Surely Allonby wouldn't have said that if he hadn't believed him!

"That's all right. Then I needn't detain you. I can be found at any time at my apartment." He gave the address.

The District Attorney smiled again, more openly. "What do you say to leaving it for an hour or two this evening? I'm giving a little supper at Rector's—quiet, little affair, you understand: just Miss Melrose—I think you know her—and a friend or two; and if you'll join us…"

Granice stumbled out of the office without knowing what reply he had made.

He waited for four days—four days of concentrated horror. During the first twenty-four hours the fear of Ascham's alienist dogged him; and as that subsided, it was replaced by the exasperating sense that his avowal had made no impression on the District Attorney. Evidently, if he had been going to look into the case, Allonby would have been heard from before now. . . . And that mocking invitation to supper showed clearly enough how little the story had impressed him!

Granice was overcome by the futility of any farther attempt to inculpate himself. He was chained to life—a "prisoner of consciousness." Where was it he had read the phrase? Well, he was learning what it meant. In the glaring night-hours, when his brain seemed ablaze, he was visited by a sense of his fixed identity, of his irreducible, inexpugnable *selfness*, keener, more insidious, more unescapable, than any sensation he had ever known. He had not guessed that the mind was capable of such intricacies of self-realization, of penetrating so deep into its own dark windings. Often he woke from his brief snatches of sleep with the feeling that something material was clinging to him, was on his hands and face, and in his throat—and as his brain cleared he understood that it was the sense of his own loathed personality that stuck to him like some thick viscous substance.

Then, in the first morning hours, he would rise and look out of his window at the awakening activities of the street—at the street-cleaners, the ash-cart drivers, and the other dingy workers flitting hurriedly by through the sallow winter light. Oh, to be one of them—any of them—to take his chance in any of their skins! They were the toilers—the men whose lot was pitied—the victims wept over and ranted about by altruists and economists; and how gladly he would have taken up the load of any one of them, if only he might have shaken off his own! But, no—the iron circle of consciousness held them too: each one was hand-cuffed to his own hideous ego. Why wish to be any one man rather than another? The only absolute good was not to be . . . And Flint, coming in to draw his bath, would ask if he preferred his eggs scrambled or poached that morning?

On the fifth day he wrote a long urgent letter to Allonby; and for the succeeding two days he had the occupation of waiting for an answer. He hardly stirred from his rooms, in his fear of missing the letter by a moment; but would the District Attorney write, or send a representative: a policeman, a "secret agent," or some other mysterious emissary of the law?

On the third morning Flint, stepping softly—as if, confound it! his master were ill—entered the library where Granice sat behind an unread newspaper, and proffered a card on a tray.

Granice read the name—J. B. Hewson—and underneath, in pencil, "From the District Attorney's office." He started up with a thumping heart, and signed an assent to the servant.

Mr. Hewson was a slight sallow nondescript man of about fifty—the kind of man of whom one is sure to see a specimen in any crowd. "Just the type of the successful detective," Granice reflected as he shook hands with his visitor.

And it was in that character that Mr. Hewson briefly introduced himself. He had been sent by the District Attorney to have "a quiet talk" with Mr. Granice—to ask him to repeat the statement he had made about the Lenman murder.

His manner was so quiet, so reasonable and receptive, that Granice's self-confidence returned. Here was a sensible man—a man who knew his business—it would be easy enough to make *him* see through that ridiculous alibi! Granice offered Mr. Hewson a cigar, and lighting one himself—to prove his coolness—began again to tell his story.

He was conscious, as he proceeded, of telling it better than ever before. Practice helped, no doubt; and his listener's detached, impartial attitude helped still more. He could see that Hewson, at least, had not decided in advance to disbelieve him, and the sense of being trusted made him more lucid and more consecutive. Yes, this time his words would certainly carry conviction . . .

V

DESPAIRINGLY, Granice gazed up and down the shabby street. Beside him stood a young man with bright prominent eyes, a smooth but not too smoothly-shaven face, and an Irish smile. The young man's nimble glance followed Granice's.

"Sure of the number, are you?" he asked briskly.

"Oh, yes—it was 104."

"Well, then, the new building has swallowed it up—that's certain."

He tilted his head back and surveyed the half-finished front of a brick and limestone flat-house that reared its flimsy elegance above a row of tottering tenements and stables.

"Dead sure?" he repeated.

"Yes," said Granice, discouraged. "And even if I hadn't been, I know the garage was just opposite Leffler's over there." He pointed across the street to a tumble-down stable with a blotched sign on which the words "Livery and Boarding" were still faintly discernible.

The young man dashed across to the opposite pavement. "Well, that's something— may get a clue there. Leffler's—same name there, anyhow. You remember that name?"

"Yes—distinctly."

Granice had felt a return of confidence since he had enlisted the interest of the *Explorer's* "smartest" reporter. If there were moments when he hardly believed his own story, there were others when it seemed impossible that everyone should not believe it; and young Peter McCarren, peering, listening, questioning, jotting down notes, inspired him with an exquisite sense of security. McCarren had fastened on the case at once, "like a leech," as he phrased it—jumped at it, thrilled to it, and settled down to "draw the last drop of fact from it, and had not let go till he had." No one else had treated Granice in that way—even Allonby's detective had not taken a single note. And though a week had elapsed since the visit of that authorized official, nothing had been heard from the District Attorney's office: Allonby had apparently dropped the matter again. But McCarren wasn't going to drop it—not he! He positively hung on Granice's footsteps. They had spent the greater part of the previous day together, and now they were off again, running down fresh clues.

But at Leffler's they got none, after all. Leffler's was no longer a stable. It was condemned to demolition, and in the respite between sentence and execution it had become a vague place of storage, a hospital for broken-down carriages and carts, presided over by a blear-eyed old woman who knew nothing of Flood's garage across the way— did not even remember what had stood there before the new flat-house began to rise.

"Well—we may run Leffler down somewhere; I've seen harder jobs done," said McCarren, cheerfully noting down the name.

As they walked back toward Sixth Avenue he added, in a less sanguine tone: "I'd undertake now to put the thing through if you could only put me on the track of that cyanide."

Granice's heart sank. Yes—there was the weak spot; he had felt it from the first! But he still hoped to convince McCarren that his case was strong enough without it; and he urged the reporter to come back to his rooms and sum up the facts with him again.

"Sorry, Mr. Granice, but I'm due at the office now. Besides, it'd be no use till I get some fresh stuff to work on. Suppose I call you up tomorrow or next day?"

He plunged into a trolley and left Granice gazing desolately after him.

Two days later he reappeared at the apartment, a shade less jaunty in demeanor.

"Well, Mr. Granice, the stars in their courses are against you, as the bard says. Can't get a trace of Flood, or of Leffler either. And you say you bought the motor through Flood, and sold it through him, too?"

"Yes," said Granice wearily.

"Who bought it, do you know?"

Granice wrinkled his brows. "Why, Flood—yes, Flood himself. I sold it back to him three months later."

"Flood? The devil! And I've ransacked the town for Flood. That kind of business disappears as if the earth had swallowed it."

Granice, discouraged, kept silence.

"That brings us back to the poison," McCarren continued, his note-book out. "Just go over that again, will you?"

And Granice went over it again. It had all been so simple at the time—and he had been so clever in covering up his traces! As soon as he decided on poison he looked about for an acquaintance who manufactured chemicals; and there was Jim Dawes, a Harvard classmate, in the dyeing business—just the man. But at the last moment it occurred to him that suspicion might turn toward so obvious an opportunity, and he decided on a more tortuous course. Another friend, Carrick Venn, a student of medicine whom irremediable ill-health had kept from the practice of his profession, amused his leisure with experiments in physics, for the exercise of which he had set up a simple laboratory. Granice had the habit of dropping in to smoke a cigar with him on Sunday afternoons, and the friends generally sat in Venn's work-shop, at the back of the old family house in Stuyvesant Square. Off this work-shop was the cupboard of supplies, with its row of deadly bottles. Carrick Venn was an original, a man of restless curious tastes, and his place, on a Sunday, was often full of visitors: a cheerful crowd of journalists, scribblers, painters, experimenters in divers forms of expression. Coming and going among so many, it was easy enough to pass unperceived; and one afternoon Granice, arriving before Venn had returned home, found himself alone in the work-shop, and quickly slipping into the cupboard, transferred the drug to his pocket.

But that had happened ten years ago; and Venn, poor fellow, was long since dead of his dragging ailment. His old father was dead, too, the house in Stuyvesant Square had been turned into a boarding-house, and the shifting life of New York had passed its rapid sponge over every trace of their obscure little history. Even the optimistic McCarren seemed to acknowledge the hopelessness of seeking for proof in that direction.

"And there's the third door slammed in our faces." He shut his note-book, and throwing back his head, rested his bright inquisitive eyes on Granice's furrowed face.

"Look here, Mr. Granice—you see the weak spot, don't you?"

The other made a despairing motion. "I see so many!"

"Yes: but the one that weakens all the others. Why the deuce do you want this thing known? Why do you want to put your head into the noose?"

Granice looked at him hopelessly, trying to take the measure of his quick light irreverent mind. No one so full of a cheerful animal life would believe in the craving for death as a sufficient motive; and Granice racked his brain for one more convincing. But suddenly he saw the reporter's face soften, and melt to an artless sentimentalism.

"Mr. Granice—has the memory of it always haunted you?"

Granice stared a moment, and then leapt at the opening. "That's it—the memory of it ... always ... "

McCarren nodded vehemently. "Dogged your steps, eh? Wouldn't let you sleep? The time came when you had to make a clean breast of it?"

"I had to. Can't you understand?"

The reporter struck his fist on the table. "God, sir! I don't suppose there's a human being with a drop of warm blood in him that can't picture the deadly horrors of remorse—"

The Celtic imagination was aflame, and Granice mutely thanked him for the word. What neither Ascham nor Denver would accept as a conceivable motive the Irish reporter seized on as the most adequate; and, as he said, once one could find a convincing motive, the difficulties of the case became so many incentives to effort.

"Remorse—*remorse*," he repeated, rolling the word under his tongue with an accent that was a clue to the psychology of the popular drama; and Granice, perversely, said to himself: "If I could only have struck that note I should have been running in six theatres at once."

He saw that from that moment McCarren's professional zeal would be fanned by emotional curiosity; and he profited by the fact to propose that they should dine together, and go on afterward to some music-hall or theatre. It was becoming necessary to Granice to feel himself an object of pre-occupation, to find himself in another mind. He took a kind of gray penumbral pleasure in riveting McCarren's attention on his case; and to feign the grimaces of moral anguish became a passionately engrossing game. He had not entered a theatre for months; but he sat out the meaningless performance in rigid tolerance, sustained by the sense of the reporter's observation.

Between the acts, McCarren amused him with anecdotes about the audience: he knew everyone by sight, and could lift the curtain from every physiognomy. Granice listened indulgently. He had lost all interest in his kind, but he knew that he was himself the real center of McCarren's attention, and that every word the latter spoke had an indirect bearing on his own problem.

"See that fellow over there—the little dried-up man in the third row, pulling his moustache? His memoirs would be worth publishing," McCarren said suddenly in the last *entr'acte*.

Granice, following his glance, recognized the detective from Allonby's office. For a moment he had the thrilling sense that he was being shadowed.

"Caesar, if *he* could talk—!" McCarren continued. "Know who he is, of course? Dr. John B. Stell, the biggest alienist in the country—"

Granice, with a start, bent again between the heads in front of him. "*That* man—the fourth from the aisle? You're mistaken. That's not Dr. Stell."

McCarren laughed. "Well, I guess I've been in court enough to know Stell when I see him. He testifies in nearly all the big cases where they plead insanity."

A cold shiver ran down Granice's spine, but he repeated obstinately:

"That's not Dr. Stell."

"Not Stell? Why, man, I *know* him. Look—here he comes. If it isn't Stell, he won't speak to me."

The little dried-up man was moving slowly up the aisle. As he neared McCarren he made a slight gesture of recognition.

"How'do, Doctor Stell? Pretty slim show, ain't it?" the reporter cheerfully flung out at him. And Mr. J. B. Hewson, with a nod of amicable assent, passed on.

Granice sat benumbed. He knew he had not been mistaken—the man who had just passed was the same man whom Allonby had sent to see him: a physician disguised as a detective. Allonby, then, had thought him insane, like the others—had regarded his confession as the maundering of a maniac. The discovery froze Granice with horror—he seemed to see the madhouse gaping for him.

"Isn't there a man a good deal like him—a detective named J. B. Hewson?"

But he knew in advance what McCarren's answer would be. "Hewson? J. B. Hewson? Never heard of him. But that was J. B. Stell fast enough—I guess he can be trusted to know himself, and you saw he answered to his name."

## VI

SOME days passed before Granice could obtain a word with the District Attorney: he began to think that Allonby avoided him.

But when they were face to face Allonby's jovial countenance showed no sign of embarrassment. He waved his visitor to a chair, and leaned across his desk with the encouraging smile of a consulting physician.

Granice broke out at once: "That detective you sent me the other day—"

Allonby raised a deprecating hand.

"—I know: it was Stell the alienist. Why did you do that, Allonby?"

The other's face did not lose its composure. "Because I looked up your story first—and there's nothing in it."

"Nothing in it?" Granice furiously interposed.

"Absolutely nothing. If there is, why the deuce don't you bring me proofs? I know you've been talking to Peter Ascham, and to Denver, and to that little ferret McCarren of the *Explorer*. Have any of them been able to make out a case for you? No. Well, what am I to do?"

Granice's lips began to tremble. "Why did you play me that trick?"

"About Stell? I had to, my dear fellow: it's part of my business. Stell is a detective, if you come to that—every doctor is."

The trembling of Granice's lips increased, communicating itself in a long quiver to his facial muscles. He forced a laugh through his dry throat. "Well—and what did he detect?"

"In you? Oh, he thinks it's overwork—overwork and too much smoking. If you look in on him some day at his office he'll show you the record of hundreds of cases like yours, and advise you what treatment to follow. It's one of the commonest forms of hallucination. Have a cigar, all the same."

"But, Allonby, I killed that man!"

The District Attorney's large hand, outstretched on his desk, had an almost imperceptible gesture, and a moment later, as if an answer to the call of an electric bell, a clerk looked in from the outer office.

"Sorry, my dear fellow—lot of people waiting. Drop in on Stell some morning," Allonby said, shaking hands.

McCarren had to own himself beaten: there was absolutely no flaw in the alibi. And since his duty to his journal obviously forbade his wasting time on insoluble mysteries, he ceased to frequent Granice, who dropped back into a deeper isolation. For a day or two after his visit to Allonby he continued to live in dread of Dr. Stell. Why might not Allonby have deceived him as to the alienist's diagnosis? What if he were really being shadowed, not by a police agent but by a mad-doctor? To have the truth out, he suddenly determined to call on Dr. Stell.

The physician received him kindly, and reverted without embarrassment to the conditions of their previous meeting. "We have to do that occasionally, Mr. Granice; it's one of our methods. And you had given Allonby a fright."

Granice was silent. He would have liked to reaffirm his guilt, to produce the fresh arguments which had occurred to him since his last talk with the physician; but he feared his eagerness might be taken for a symptom of derangement, and he affected to smile away Dr. Stell's allusion.

"You think, then, it's a case of brain-fag—nothing more?"

"Nothing more. And I should advise you to knock off tobacco. You smoke a good deal, don't you?"

He developed his treatment, recommending massage, gymnastics, travel, or any form of diversion that did not—that in short—

Granice interrupted him impatiently. "Oh, I loathe all that—and I'm sick of travelling."

"H'm. Then some larger interest—politics, reform, philanthropy? Something to take you out of yourself."

"Yes. I understand," said Granice wearily.

"Above all, don't lose heart. I see hundreds of cases like yours," the doctor added cheerfully from the threshold.

On the doorstep Granice stood still and laughed. Hundreds of cases like his—the case of a man who had committed a murder, who confessed his guilt, and whom no one would believe! Why, there had never been a case like it in the world. What a good figure Stell would have made in a play: the great alienist who couldn't read a man's mind any better than that!

Granice saw huge comic opportunities in the type.

But as he walked away, his fears dispelled, the sense of listlessness returned on him. For the first time since his avowal to Peter Ascham he found himself without an occupation, and understood that he had been carried through the past weeks only by the necessity of constant action. Now his life had once more become a stagnant backwater, and as he stood on the street corner watching the tides of traffic sweep by, he asked himself despairingly how much longer he could endure to float about in the sluggish circle of his consciousness.

The thought of self-destruction recurred to him; but again his flesh recoiled. He yearned for death from other hands, but he could never take it from his own. And, aside from his insuperable physical reluctance, another motive restrained him. He was possessed by the dogged desire to establish the truth of his story. He refused to be swept aside as an irresponsible dreamer—even if he had to kill himself in the end, he would not do so before proving to society that he had deserved death from it.

He began to write long letters to the papers; but after the first had been published and commented on, public curiosity was quelled by a brief statement from the District Attorney's office, and the rest of his communications remained unprinted. Ascham came to see him, and begged him to travel. Robert Denver dropped in, and tried to joke him out of his delusion; till Granice, mistrustful of their motives, began to dread the reappearance of Dr. Stell, and set a guard on his lips. But the words he kept back engendered others and still others in his brain. His inner self became a humming factory of arguments, and he spent long hours reciting and writing down elaborate statements of his crime, which he constantly retouched and developed. Then gradually his activity languished under the lack of an audience, the sense of being buried beneath deepening drifts of indifference. In a passion of resentment he swore that he would prove himself a murderer, even if he had to commit another crime to do it; and for a sleepless night or two the thought flamed red on his darkness. But daylight dispelled it. The determining impulse was lacking and he hated too promiscuously to choose his victim . . . So he was thrown back on the unavailing struggle to impose the truth of his story. As fast as one channel closed on him he tried to pierce another through the sliding sands of incredulity. But every issue seemed blocked, and the whole human race leagued together to cheat one man of the right to die.

Thus viewed, the situation became so monstrous that he lost his last shred of self-restraint in contemplating it. What if he were really the victim of some mocking experiment, the center of a ring of holiday-makers jeering at a poor creature in its blind dashes against the solid walls of consciousness? But, no—men were not so uniformly cruel: there were flaws in the close surface of their indifference, cracks of weakness and pity here and there . . .

Granice began to think that his mistake lay in having appealed to persons more or less familiar with his past, and to whom the visible conformities of his life seemed a final disproof of its one fierce secret deviation. The general tendency was to take for the whole of life the slit seen between the blinders of habit: and in his walk down that narrow vista Granice cut a correct enough figure. To a vision free to follow his whole orbit his story would be more intelligible: it would be easier to convince a chance idler in the street than the trained intelligence hampered by a sense of his antecedents. This idea shot up in him with the tropic luxuriance of each new seed of thought, and he began to walk the streets, and to frequent out-of-the-way chop-houses and bars in his search for the impartial stranger to whom he should disclose himself.

At first every face looked encouragement; but at the crucial moment he always held back. So much was at stake, and it was so essential that his first choice should be decisive. He dreaded stupidity, timidity, intolerance. The imaginative eye, the furrowed brow, were what he sought. He must reveal himself only to a heart versed in the tortuous motions of the human will; and he began to hate the dull benevolence of the average face. Once or twice, obscurely, allusively, he made a beginning—once sitting down at a man's side in a basement chop-house, another day approaching a lounger on an east-side wharf. But in both cases the premonition of failure checked him on the brink of avowal. His dread of being taken for a man in the clutch of a fixed idea gave him an unnatural keenness in reading the expression of his interlocutors, and he had provided himself in advance with a series of verbal alternatives, trap-doors of evasion from the first dart of ridicule or suspicion.

He passed the greater part of the day in the streets, coming home at irregular hours, dreading the silence and orderliness of his apartment, and the critical scrutiny of Flint. His real life was spent in a world so remote from this familiar setting that he sometimes had the mysterious sense of a living metempsychosis, a furtive passage from one identity to another—yet the other as unescapably himself!

One humiliation he was spared: the desire to live never revived in him. Not for a moment was he tempted to a shabby pact with existing conditions. He wanted to die, wanted it with the fixed unwavering desire which alone attains its end. And still the end eluded him! It would not always, of course—he had full faith in the dark star of his destiny. And he could prove it best by repeating his story, persistently and indefatigably, pouring it into indifferent ears, hammering it into dull brains, till at last it kindled a spark, and some one of the careless millions paused, listened, believed...

It was a mild March day, and he had been loitering on the west-side docks, looking at faces. He was becoming an expert in physiognomies: his eagerness no longer made rash darts and awkward recoils. He knew now the face he needed, as clearly as if it had come to him in a vision; and not till he found it would he speak. As he walked eastward through the shabby reeking streets he had a premonition that he should find it that morning. Perhaps it was the promise of spring in the air—certainly he felt calmer than for many days . . .

He turned into Washington Square, struck across it obliquely, and walked up University Place. Its heterogeneous passers always allured him—they were less hurried than in Broadway, less enclosed and classified than in Fifth Avenue. He walked slowly, watching for his face.

At Union Square he felt a sudden relapse into discouragement, like a votary who has watched too long for a sign from the altar. Perhaps, after all, he should never find his face . . . The air was languid, and he felt tired. He walked between the bald grass-plots and the twisted trees, making for an empty seat. Presently he passed a bench on which a girl sat alone, and something as definite as the twitch of a cord made him stop before her. He had never dreamed of telling his story to a girl, had hardly looked at the women's faces as they passed. His case was man's work: how could a woman help him? But this girl's face was extraordinary—quiet and wide as a clear evening sky. It suggested a hundred images of space, distance, mystery, like ships he had seen, as a boy, quietly berthed by a familiar wharf, but with the breath of far seas and strange harbors in their shrouds . . . Certainly this girl would understand. He went up to her quietly, lifting his hat, observing the forms—wishing her to see at once that he was "a gentleman."

"I am a stranger to you," he began, sitting down beside her, "but your face is so extremely intelligent that I feel . . . I feel it is the face I've waited for . . . looked for everywhere; and I want to tell you—"

The girl's eyes widened: she rose to her feet. She was escaping him!

In his dismay he ran a few steps after her, and caught her roughly by the arm.

"Here—wait—listen! Oh, don't scream, you fool!" he shouted out.

He felt a hand on his own arm; turned and confronted a policeman. Instantly he understood that he was being arrested, and something hard within him was loosened and ran to tears.

"Ah, you know—you *know* I'm guilty!"

He was conscious that a crowd was forming, and that the girl's frightened face had disappeared. But what did he care about her face? It was the policeman who had really understood him. He turned and followed, the crowd at his heels . . .

## VII

IN the charming place in which he found himself there were so many sympathetic faces that he felt more than ever convinced of the certainty of making himself heard.

It was a bad blow, at first, to find that he had not been arrested for murder; but Ascham, who had come to him at once, explained that he needed rest, and the time to "review" his statements; it appeared that reiteration had made them a little confused and contradictory. To this end he had willingly acquiesced in his removal to a large quiet establishment, with an open space and trees about it, where he had found a number of intelligent companions, some, like himself, engaged in preparing or reviewing statements of their cases, and others ready to lend an interested ear to his own recital.

For a time he was content to let himself go on the tranquil current of this existence; but although his auditors gave him for the most part an encouraging attention, which, in some, went the length of really brilliant and helpful suggestion, he gradually felt a recurrence of his old doubts. Either his hearers were not sincere, or else they had less power to aid him than they boasted. His interminable conferences resulted in nothing, and as the benefit of the long rest made itself felt, it produced an increased mental lucidity which rendered inaction more and more unbearable. At length he discovered that on certain days visitors from the outer world were admitted to his retreat; and he wrote out long and logically constructed relations of his crime, and furtively slipped them into the hands of these messengers of hope.

This gave him a fresh lease of patience, and he now lived only to watch for the visitors' days, and scan the faces that swept by him like stars seen and lost in the rifts of a hurrying sky.

Mostly, these faces were strange and less intelligent than those of his companions. But they represented his last means of access to the world, a kind of subterranean channel on which he could set his "statements" afloat, like paper boats which the mysterious current might sweep out into the open seas of life.

One day, however, his attention was arrested by a familiar contour, a pair of bright prominent eyes, and a chin insufficiently shaved. He sprang up and stood in the path of Peter McCarren.

The journalist looked at him doubtfully, then held out his hand with a startled deprecating, *"Why—?"*

"You didn't know me? I'm so changed?" Granice faltered, feeling the rebound of the other's wonder.

"Why, no; but you're looking quieter—smoothed out," McCarren smiled.

"Yes: that's what I'm here for—to rest. And I've taken the opportunity to write out a clearer statement—"

Granice's hand shook so that he could hardly draw the folded paper from his pocket. As he did so he noticed that the reporter was accompanied by a tall man with grave compassionate eyes. It came to Granice in a wild thrill of conviction that this was the face he had waited for . . .

"Perhaps your friend—he *is* your friend?—would glance over it—or I could put the case in a few words if you have time?" Granice's voice shook like his hand. If this chance escaped him he felt that his last hope was gone. McCarren and the stranger looked at each other, and the former glanced at his watch.

"I'm sorry we can't stay and talk it over now, Mr. Granice; but my friend has an engagement, and we're rather pressed—"

Granice continued to proffer the paper. "I'm sorry—I think I could have explained. But you'll take this, at any rate?"

The stranger looked at him gently. "Certainly—I'll take it." He had his hand out. "Good-bye."

"Good-bye," Granice echoed.

He stood watching the two men move away from him through the long light hall; and as he watched them a tear ran down his face. But as soon as they were out of sight he turned and walked hastily toward his room, beginning to hope again, already planning a new statement. . . .

Outside the building the two men stood still, and the journalist's companion looked up curiously at the long monotonous rows of barred windows.

"So that was Granice?"

"Yes—that was Granice, poor devil," said McCarren.

"Strange case! I suppose there's never been one just like it? He's still absolutely convinced that he committed that murder?"

"Absolutely. Yes."

The stranger reflected. "And there was no conceivable ground for the idea? No one could make out how it started? A quiet conventional sort of fellow like that—where do you suppose he got such a delusion? Did you ever get the least clue to it?"

McCarren stood still, his hands in his pockets, his head cocked up in contemplation of the barred windows. Then he turned his bright hard gaze on his companion.

"That was the queer part of it. I've never spoken of it—but I *did* get a clue."

"By Jove! That's interesting. What was it?"

McCarren formed his red lips into a whistle. "Why—that it wasn't a delusion."

He produced his effect—the other turned on him with a pallid stare.

"He murdered the man all right. I tumbled on the truth by the merest accident, when I'd pretty nearly chucked the whole job."

"He murdered him—murdered his cousin?"

"Sure as you live. Only don't split on me. It's about the queerest business I ever ran into... *Do about it?* Why, what was I to do? I couldn't hang the poor devil, could I? Lord, but I was glad when they collared him, and had him stowed away safe in there!"

The tall man listened with a grave face, grasping Granice's statement in his hand.

"Here—take this; it makes me sick," he said abruptly, thrusting the paper at the reporter; and the two men turned and walked in silence to the gates.

## HIS FATHER'S SON

AFTER HIS WIFE'S DEATH Mason Grew took the momentous step of selling out his business and moving from Wingfield, Connecticut, to Brooklyn.

For years he had secretly nursed the hope of such a change, but had never dared to suggest it to Mrs. Grew, a woman of immutable habits. Mr. Grew himself was attached to Wingfield, where he had grown up, prospered, and become what the local press described as "prominent." He was attached to his ugly brick house with sandstone trimmings and a cast-iron area-railing neatly sanded to match; to the similar row of houses across the street, the "trolley" wires forming a kind of aerial pathway between, and the sprawling vista closed by the steeple of the church which he and his wife had always attended, and where their only child had been baptized.

It was hard to snap all these threads of association, visual and sentimental; yet still harder, now that he was alone, to live so far from his boy. Ronald Grew was practicing law in New York, and there was no more chance of returning to live at Wingfield than of a river's flowing inland from the sea. Therefore to be near him his father must move; and it was characteristic of Mr. Grew, and of the situation generally, that the translation, when it took place, was to Brooklyn, and not to New York.

"Why you bury yourself in that hole I can't think," had been Ronald's comment; and Mr. Grew simply replied that rents were lower in Brooklyn, and that he had heard of a house that would suit him. In reality he had said to himself—being the only recipient of his own confidences—that if he went to New York he might be on the boy's mind; whereas, if he lived in Brooklyn, Ronald would always have a good excuse for not popping over to see him every other day. The sociological isolation of Brooklyn, combined with its geographical nearness, presented in fact the precise conditions that Mr. Grew sought. He wanted to be near enough to New York to go there often, to feel under his feet the same pavement that Ronald trod, to sit now and then in the same theatres, and find on his breakfast table the journals which, with increasing frequency, inserted Ronald's name in the sacred bounds of the society column. It had always been a trial to Mr. Grew to have to wait twenty-four hours to read that "among those present was Mr.

Ronald Grew." Now he had it with his coffee, and left it on the breakfast table to the perusal of a hired girl cosmopolitan enough to do it justice. In such ways Brooklyn attested the advantages of it nearness to New York, while remaining, as regards Ronald's duty to his father, as remote and inaccessible as Wingfield.

It was not that Ronald shirked his filial obligations, but rather because of his heavy sense of them, that Mr. Grew so persistently sought to minimize and lighten them. It was he who insisted, to Ronald, on the immense difficulty of getting from New York to Brooklyn.

"Any way you look at it, it makes a big hole in the day; and there's not much use in the ragged rim left. You say you're dining out next Sunday? Then I forbid you to come over here for lunch. Do you understand me, sir? You disobey at the risk of your father's malediction! Where did you say you were dining? With the Waltham Bankshires again? Why, that's the second time in three weeks, ain't it? Big blow-out, I suppose? Gold plate and orchids—opera singers in afterward? Well, you'd be in a nice box if there was a fog on the river, and you got hung up half-way over. That'd be a handsome return for the attention Mrs. Bankshire has shown you—singling out a whipper-snapper like you twice in three weeks! (What's the daughter's name—Daisy?) No, *sir*—don't you come fooling round here next Sunday, or I'll set the dogs on you. And you wouldn't find me in anyhow, come to think of it. I'm lunching out myself, as it happens—yes, sir, *lunching out*. Is there anything especially comic in my lunching out? I don't often do it, you say? Well, that's no reason why I never should. Who with? Why, with—with old Dr. Bleaker: Dr. Eliphalet Bleaker. No, you wouldn't know about him—he's only an old friend of your mother's and mine."

Gradually Ronald's insistence became less difficult to overcome. With his customary sweetness and tact (as Mr. Grew put it) he began to "take the hint," to give in to "the old gentleman's" growing desire for solitude.

"I'm set in my ways, Ronny, that's about the size of it; I like to go tick-ticking along like a clock. I always did. And when you come bouncing in I never feel sure there's enough for dinner—or that I haven't sent Maria out for the evening. And I don't want the neighbors to see me opening my own door to my son. That's the kind of cringing snob I am. Don't give me away, will you? I want 'em to think I keep four or five powdered flunkeys in the hall day and night—same as the lobby of one of those Fifth Avenue hotels. And if you pop over when you're not expected, how am I going to keep up the bluff?"

Ronald yielded after the proper amount of resistance—his intuitive sense, in every social transaction, of the proper amount of force to be expended, was one of the qualities his father most admired in him. Mr. Grew's perceptions in this line were probably more acute than his son suspected. The souls of short thick-set men, with chubby features, mutton-chop whiskers, and pale eyes peering between folds of fat like almond kernels in half-split shells—souls thus encased do not reveal themselves to the casual scrutiny as delicate emotional instruments. But in spite of the dense disguise in which he walked Mr. Grew vibrated exquisitely in response to every imaginative appeal; and his son Ronald was perpetually stimulating and feeding his imagination.

Ronald in fact constituted his father's one escape from the impenetrable element of mediocrity which had always hemmed him in. To a man so enamored of beauty, and so little qualified to add to its sum total, it was a wonderful privilege to have bestowed on the world such a being. Ronald's resemblance to Mr. Grew's early conception of what he himself would have liked to look might have put new life into the discredited theory of pre-natal influences. At any rate, if the young man owed his beauty, his distinction and his winning manner to the dreams of one of his parents, it was certainly to those of Mr. Grew, who, while outwardly devoting his life to the manufacture and dissemination of Grew's Secure Suspender Buckle, moved in an enchanted inward world peopled with all the figures of romance. In this high company Mr. Grew cut as brilliant a figure as any of its noble phantoms; and to see his vision of himself suddenly projected on the outer world in the shape of a brilliant popular conquering son, seemed, in retrospect, to give to that image a belated objective reality. There were even moments when, forgetting his physiognomy, Mr. Grew said to himself that if he'd had "half a chance" he might have done as well as Ronald; but this only fortified his resolve that Ronald should do infinitely better.

Ronald's ability to do well almost equaled his gift of looking well. Mr. Grew constantly affirmed to himself that the boy was "not a genius"; but, barring this slight deficiency, he was almost everything that a parent could wish. Even at Harvard he had managed to be several desirable things at once—writing poetry in the college magazine, playing delightfully "by ear," acquitting himself honorably in his studies, and yet holding his own in the fashionable sporting set that formed, as it were, the gateway of the temple of Society. Mr. Grew's idealism did not preclude the frank desire that his son should pass through that gateway; but the wish was not prompted by material considerations. It was Mr. Grew's notion that, in the rough and hurrying current of a new civilization, the little pools of leisure and enjoyment must nurture delicate growths, material graces as well as moral refinements, likely to be uprooted and swept away by the rush of the main torrent. He based his theory on the fact that he had liked the few "society" people he had met—had found their manners simpler, their voices more agreeable, their views more consonant with his own, than those of the leading citizens of Wingfield. But then he had met very few.

Ronald's sympathies needed no urging in the same direction. He took naturally, dauntlessly, to all the high and exceptional things about which his father's imagination had so long sheepishly and ineffectually hovered—from the start he *was* what Mr. Grew had dreamed of being. And so precise, so detailed, was Mr. Grew's vision of his own imaginary career, that as Ronald grew up, and began to travel in a widening orbit, his father had an almost uncanny sense of the extent to which that career was enacting itself before him. At Harvard, Ronald had done exactly what the hypothetical Mason Grew would have done, had not his actual self, at the same age, been working his way up in old Slagden's button factory—the institution which was later to acquire fame, and even notoriety, as the birthplace of Grew's Secure Suspender Buckle. Afterward, at a period when the actual Grew had passed from the factory to the bookkeeper's desk, his invisible double had been reading law at Columbia—precisely again what Ronald did! But it was when the young man left the paths laid out for him by the parental hand, and cast himself boldly on the world, that his adventures began to bear the most astonishing resemblance to those of the unrealized Mason Grew. It was in New York that the scene of this hypothetical being's first exploits had always been laid; and it was in New York that Ronald was to achieve his first triumph. There was nothing small or timid about Mr. Grew's imagination; it had never stopped at anything between Wingfield and the metropolis. And the real Ronald had the same cosmic vision as his parent. He brushed aside with a contemptuous laugh his mother's tearful entreaty that he should stay at Wingfield and continue the dynasty of the Grew Suspender Buckle. Mr. Grew knew that in reality Ronald winced at the Buckle, loathed it, blushed for his connection with it. Yet it was the Buckle that had seen him through Groton, Harvard and the Law School, and had permitted him to enter the office of a distinguished corporation lawyer, instead of being enslaved to some sordid business with quick returns. The Buckle had been Ronald's fairy godmother—yet his father did not blame him for abhorring and disowning it. Mr. Grew himself often bitterly regretted having bestowed his own name on the instrument of his material success, though, at the time, his doing so had been the natural expression of his romanticism. When he invented the Buckle, and took out his patent, he and his wife both felt that to bestow their name on it was like naming a battle-ship or a peak of the Andes.

Mrs. Grew had never learned to know better; but Mr. Grew had discovered his error before Ronald was out of school. He read it first in a black eye of his boy's. Ronald's symmetry had been marred by the insolent fist of a fourth former whom he had chastised for alluding to his father as "Old Buckles;" and when Mr. Grew heard the epithet he understood in a flash that the Buckle was a thing to blush for. It was too late then to dissociate his name from it, or to efface from the hoardings of the entire continent the picture of two gentlemen, one contorting himself in the abject effort to repair a broken brace, while the careless ease of the other's attitude proclaimed his trust in the Secure Suspender Buckle. These records were indelible, but Ronald could at least be spared all direct connection with them; and from that day Mr. Grew resolved that the boy should not return to Wingfield.

"You'll see," he had said to Mrs. Grew, "he'll take right hold in New York. Ronald's got my knack for taking hold," he added, throwing out his chest.

"But the way you took hold was in business," objected Mrs. Grew, who was large and literal.

Mr. Grew's chest collapsed, and he became suddenly conscious of his comic face in its rim of sandy whiskers. "That's not the only way," he said, with a touch of wistfulness which escaped his wife's analysis.

"Well, of course you could have written beautifully," she rejoined with admiring eyes.

"*Written?* Me!" Mr. Grew became sardonic.

"Why, those letters—weren't *they* beautiful, I'd like to know?"

The couple exchanged a glance, innocently allusive and amused on the wife's part, and charged with a sudden tragic significance on the husband's.

"Well, I've got to be going along to the office now," he merely said, dragging himself out of his rocking-chair.

This had happened while Ronald was still at school; and now Mrs. Grew slept in the Wingfield cemetery, under a life-size theological virtue of her own choosing, and Mr. Grew's prognostications as to Ronald's ability to "take right hold" in New York were being more and more brilliantly fulfilled.

II

RONALD obeyed his father's injunction not to come to luncheon on the day of the Bankshires' dinner; but in the middle of the following week Mr. Grew was surprised by a telegram from his son.

"Want to see you important matter. Expect me tomorrow afternoon."

Mr. Grew received the telegram after breakfast. To peruse it he had lifted his eye from a paragraph of the morning paper describing a fancy-dress dinner which had taken place the night before at the Hamilton Gliddens' for the house-warming of their new Fifth Avenue palace.

"Among the couples who afterward danced in the Poets' Quadrille were Miss Daisy Bankshire, looking more than usually lovely as Laura, and Mr. Ronald Grew as the young Petrarch."

Petrarch and Laura! Well—if *anything* meant anything, Mr. Grew supposed he knew what that meant. For weeks past he had noticed how constantly the names of the young people appeared together in the society notes he so insatiably devoured. Even the soulless reporter was getting into the habit of coupling them in his lists. And this Laura and Petrarch business was almost an announcement . . .

Mr. Grew dropped the telegram, wiped his eye-glasses, and re-read the paragraph. "Miss Daisy Bankshire . . . more than usually lovely . . . " Yes; she was lovely. He had often seen her photograph in the papers—seen her represented in every conceivable attitude of the mundane game: fondling her prize bull-dog, taking a fence on her thoroughbred, dancing a *gavotte*, all patches and plumes, or fingering a guitar, all tulle and lilies; and once he had caught a glimpse of her at the theatre. Hearing that Ronald was going to a fashionable first-night with the Bankshires, Mr. Grew had for once overcome his repugnance to following his son's movements, and had secured for himself, under the shadow of the balcony, a stall whence he could observe the Bankshire box without fear of detection. Ronald had never known of his father's presence at the play; and for three blessed hours Mr. Grew had watched his boy's handsome dark head bent above the dense fair hair and white averted shoulder that were all he could catch of Miss Bankshire's beauties.

He recalled the vision now; and with it came, as usual, its ghostly double: the vision of his young self bending above such a white shoulder and such shining hair. Needless to say that the real Mason Grew had never found himself in so enviable a situation. The late Mrs. Grew had no more resembled Miss Daisy Bankshire than he had looked like the happy victorious Ronald. And the mystery was that from their dull faces, their dull endearments, the miracle of Ronald should have sprung. It was almost—fantastically—as if the boy had been a changeling, child of a Latmian night, whom the divine companion of Mr. Grew's early reveries had secretly laid in the cradle of the Wingfield bedroom while Mr. And Mrs. Grew slept the deep sleep of conjugal indifference.

The young Mason Grew had not at first accepted this astral episode as the complete cancelling of his claims on romance. He too had grasped at the high-hung glory; and, with his fatal tendency to reach too far when he reached at all, had singled out the prettiest girl in Wingfield. When he recalled his stammered confession of love his face still tingled under her cool bright stare. The wonder of his audacity had struck her dumb; and when she recovered her voice it was to fling a taunt at him.

"Don't be too discouraged, you know—have you ever thought of trying Addie Wicks?"

All Wingfield would have understood the gibe: Addie Wicks was the dullest girl in town. And a year later he had married Addie Wicks…

He looked up from the perusal of Ronald's telegram with this memory in his mind. Now at last his dream was coming true! His boy would taste of the joys that had mocked his thwarted youth and his dull gray middle-age. And it was fitting that they should be realized in Ronald's destiny. Ronald was made to take happiness boldly by the hand and lead it home like a bridegroom. He had the carriage, the confidence, the high faith in his fortune, that compel the wilful stars. And, thanks to the Buckle, he would have the exceptional setting, the background of material elegance, that became his conquering person. Since Mr. Grew had retired from business his investments had prospered, and he had been saving up his income for just such a contingency. His own wants were few: he had transferred the Wingfield furniture to Brooklyn, and his sitting-room was a replica of that in which the long years of his married life had been spent. Even the florid carpet on which Ronald's tottering footsteps had been taken was carefully matched when it became too threadbare. And on the marble center table, with its chenille-fringed cover and bunch of dyed pampas grass, lay the illustrated Longfellow and the copy of Ingersoll's lectures which represented literature to Mr. Grew when he had led home his bride. In the light of Ronald's romance, Mr. Grew found himself re-living, with a strange tremor of mingled pain and tenderness, all the poor prosaic incidents of his own personal history. Curiously enough, with this new splendor on them they began to emit a small faint ray of their own. His wife's armchair, in its usual place by the fire, recalled her placid unperceiving presence, seated opposite to him during the long drowsy years; and he felt her kindness, her equanimity, where formerly he had only ached at her obtuseness. And from the chair he glanced up at the large discolored photograph on the wall above, with a brittle brown wreath suspended on a corner of the frame. The photograph represented a young man with a poetic necktie and untrammelled hair, leaning negligently against a Gothic chair-back, a roll of music in his hand; and beneath was scrawled a bar of Chopin, with the words: *"Adieu, Adèle."*

The portrait was that of the great pianist, Fortuné Dolbrowski; and its presence on the wall of Mr. Grew's sitting-room commemorated the only exquisite hour of his life save that of Ronald's birth. It was some time before the latter memorable event, a few months only after Mr. Grew's marriage, that he had taken his wife to New York to hear the great Dolbrowski. Their evening had been magically beautiful, and even Addie, roused from her habitual inexpressiveness, had quivered into a momentary semblance of life. "I never—I never—" she gasped out helplessly when they had regained their hotel bedroom, and sat staring back entranced at the evening's evocations. Her large immovable face was pink and tremulous, and she sat with her hands on her knees, forgetting to roll up her bonnet-strings and prepare her curl-papers.

"I'd like to *write* him just how I felt—I wish I knew how!" she burst out suddenly in a final effervescence of emotion.

Her husband lifted his head and looked at her.

"Would you? I feel that way too," he said with a sheepish laugh. And they continued to stare at each other shyly through a transfiguring mist of sound.

The scene rose before Mr. Grew as he gazed up at the pianist's photograph. "Well, I owe her that anyhow—poor Addie!" he said, with a smile at the inconsequences of fate. With Ronald's telegram in his hand he was in a mood to count his mercies.

III

"A CLEAR twenty-five thousand a year: that's what you can tell 'em with my compliments," said Mr. Grew, glancing complacently across the center-table at his boy.

It struck him that Ronald's gift for looking his part in life had never so romantically expressed itself. Other young men, at such a moment, would have been red, damp, tight about the collar; but Ronald's cheek was only a shade paler, and the contrast made his dark eyes more expressive.

"A clear twenty-five thousand; yes, sir—that's what I always meant you to have."

Mr. Grew leaned carelessly back, his hands thrust carelessly in his pockets, as though to divert attention from the agitation of his features. He had often pictured himself rolling out that phrase to Ronald, and now that it was actually on his lips he could not control their tremor.

Ronald listened in silence, lifting a nervous hand to his slight dark moustache, as though he, too, wished to hide some involuntary betrayal of emotion. At first Mr. Grew took his silence for an expression of gratified surprise; but as it prolonged itself it became less easy to interpret.

"I—see here, my boy; did you expect more? Isn't it enough?" Mr. Grew cleared his throat. "Do *they* expect more?" he asked nervously. He was hardly able to face the pain of inflicting a disappointment on Ronald at the very moment when he had counted on putting the final touch to his bliss.

Ronald moved uneasily in his chair and his eyes wandered upward to the laurel-wreathed photograph of the pianist above his father's head.

*"Is* it that, Ronald? Speak out, my boy. We'll see, we'll look round—I'll manage somehow."

"No, no," the young man interrupted, abruptly raising his hand as though to silence his father.

Mr. Grew recovered his cheerfulness. "Well, what's the matter than, if *she's* willing?"

Ronald shifted his position again, and finally rose from his seat.

"Father—I—there's something I've got to tell you. I can't take your money."

Mr. Grew sat speechless a moment, staring blankly at his son; then he emitted a puzzled laugh. "My money? What are you talking about? What's this about my money? Why, it ain't *mine*, Ronny; it's all yours—every cent of it!" he cried.

The young man met his tender look with a gaze of tragic rejection.

"No, no, it's not mine—not even in the sense you mean. Not in any sense. Can't you understand my feeling so?"

"Feeling so? I don't know how you're feeling. I don't know what you're talking about. Are you too proud to touch any money you haven't earned? Is that what you're trying to tell me?"

"No. It's not that. You must know—"

Mr. Grew flushed to the rim of his bristling whiskers. "Know? Know *what?* Can't you speak?"

Ronald hesitated, and the two men faced each other for a long strained moment, during which Mr. Grew's congested countenance grew gradually pale again.

"What's the meaning of this? Is it because you've done something . . . something you're ashamed of . . . ashamed to tell me?" he suddenly gasped out; and walking around the table he laid his hand on his son's shoulder. "There's nothing you can't tell me, my boy."

"It's not that. Why do you make it so hard for me?" Ronald broke out with passion. "You must have known this was sure to happen sooner or later."

"Happen? What was sure to hap—?" Mr. Grew's question wavered on his lip and passed into a tremulous laugh. "Is it something I've done that you don't approve of? Is it—is it *the Buckle* you're ashamed of, Ronald Grew?"

Ronald laughed too, impatiently. "The Buckle? No, I'm not ashamed of the Buckle; not any more than you are," he returned with a sudden bright flush. "But I'm ashamed of all I owe to it—all I owe to you—when—when—" He broke off and took a few distracted steps across the room. "You might make this easier for me," he protested, turning back to his father.

"Make what easier? I know less and less what you're driving at," Mr. Grew groaned.

Ronald's walk had once more brought him beneath the photograph on the wall. He lifted his head for a moment and looked at it; then he looked again at Mr. Grew.

"Do you suppose I haven't always known?"

"Known—?"

"Even before you gave me those letters—after my mother's death—even before that, I suspected. I don't know how it began . . . perhaps from little things you let drop . . . you and she . . . and resemblances that I couldn't help seeing . . . in myself . . . How on earth could you suppose I *shouldn't guess?* I always thought you gave me the letters as a way of telling me—"

Mr. Grew rose slowly from his chair. "The letters? Dolbrowski's letters?"

Ronald nodded with white lips. "You must remember giving them to me the day after the funeral."

Mr. Grew nodded back. "Of course. I wanted you to have everything your mother valued."

"Well—how could I help knowing after that?"

"Knowing *what?*" Mr. Grew stood staring helplessly at his son.

Suddenly his look caught at a clue that seemed to confront it with a deeper bewilderment. "You thought—you thought those letters . . . Dolbrowski's letters . . . you thought they meant . . . "

"Oh, it wasn't only the letters. There were so many other signs. My love of music—my—all my feelings about life . . . and art . . . And when you gave me the letters I thought you must mean me to know."

Mr. Grew had grown quiet. His lips were firm, and his small eyes looked out steadily from their creased lids.

"To know that you were Fortuné Dolbrowski's son?"

Ronald made a mute sign of assent.

"I see. And what did you mean to do?"

"I meant to wait till I could earn my living, and then repay you . . . as far as I can ever repay you . . . But now that there's a chance of my marrying . . . and your generosity overwhelms me . . . I'm obliged to speak."

"I see," said Mr. Grew again. He let himself down into his chair, looking steadily and not unkindly at the young man. "Sit down, Ronald. Let's talk."

Ronald made a protesting movement. "Is anything to be gained by it? You can't change me—change what I feel. The reading of those letters transformed my whole life—I was a boy till then: they made a man of me. From that moment I understood myself." He paused, and then looked up at Mr. Grew's face. "Don't imagine I don't appreciate your kindness—your extraordinary generosity. But I can't go through life in disguise. And I want you to know that I have not won Daisy under false pretenses—"

Mr. Grew started up with the first expletive Ronald had ever heard on his lips.

"You damned young fool, you, you haven't *told* her—?"

Ronald raised his head quickly. "Oh, you don't know her, sir! She thinks no worse of me for knowing my secret. She is above and beyond all such conventional prejudices. She's *proud* of my parentage—" he straightened his slim young shoulders—"as I'm proud of it . . . yes, sir, proud of it . . . "

Mr. Grew sank back into his seat with a dry laugh. "Well, you ought to be. You come of good stock. And you're father's son, every inch of you!" He laughed again, as though the humor of the situation grew on him with its closer contemplation.

"Yes, I've always felt that," Ronald murmured, flushing.

"Your father's son, and no mistake." Mr. Grew leaned forward.

"You're the son of as big a fool as yourself. And here he sits, Ronald Grew!"

The young man's flush deepened to crimson; but Mr. Grew checked his reply with a decisive gesture. "Here he sits, with all your young nonsense still alive in him. Don't you see the likeness? If you don't, I'll tell you the story of those letters."

Ronald stared. "What do you mean? Don't they tell their own story?"

"I supposed they did when I gave them to you; but you've given it a twist that needs straightening out." Mr. Grew squared his elbows on the table, and looked at the young man across the gift-books and the dyed pampas grass. "I wrote all the letters that Dolbrowski answered."

Ronald gave back his look in frowning perplexity. *"You* wrote them? I don't understand. His letters are all addressed to my mother."

"Yes. And he thought he was corresponding with her."

"But my mother—what did she think?"

Mr. Grew hesitated, puckering his thick lids. "Well, I guess she kinder thought it was a joke. Your mother didn't think about things much."

Ronald continued to bend a puzzled frown on the question. "I don't understand," he reiterated.

Mr. Grew cleared his throat with a nervous laugh. "Well, I don't know as you ever will—*quite.* But this is the way it came about. I had a toughish time of it when I was young. Oh, I don't mean so much the fight I had to put up to make my way—there was always plenty of fight in me. But inside of myself it was kinder lonesome. And the outside didn't attract callers." He laughed again, with an apologetic gesture toward his broad blinking face. "When I went round with the other young fellows I was always the forlorn hope—the one that had to eat the drumsticks and dance with the left-overs. As sure as there was a blighter at a picnic I had to swing her, and feed her, and drive her home. And all the time I was mad after all the things you've got—poetry and music and all the joy-forever business. So there were the pair of us—my face and my imagination—chained together, and fighting, and hating each other like poison.

"Then your mother came along and took pity on me. It sets up a gawky fellow to find a girl who ain't ashamed to be seen walking with him Sundays. And I was grateful to your mother, and we got along first-rate. Only I couldn't say things to her—and she couldn't answer. Well—one day, a few months after we were married, Dolbrowski came to New York, and the whole place went wild about him. I'd never heard any good music, but I'd always had an inkling of what it must be like, though I couldn't tell you to this day how I knew. Well, your mother read about him in the papers too, and she thought it'd be the swagger thing to go to New York and hear him play—so we went . . . I'll never forget that evening. Your mother wasn't easily stirred up—she never seemed to need to let off steam. But that night she seemed to understand the way I felt. And when we got back to the hotel she said suddenly: 'I'd like to tell him how I feel. I'd like to sit right down and write to him.'

"'Would you?' I said. 'So would I.'

"There was paper and pens there before us, and I pulled a sheet toward me, and began to write. 'Is this what you'd like to say to him?' I asked her when the letter was done. And she got pink and said: 'I don't understand it, but it's lovely.' And she copied it out and signed her name to it, and sent it."

Mr. Grew paused, and Ronald sat silent, with lowered eyes.

"That's how it began; and that's where I thought it would end. But it didn't, because Dolbrowski answered. His first letter was dated January 10, 1872. I guess you'll find I'm correct. Well, I went back to hear him again, and I wrote him after the performance, and he answered again. And after that we kept it up for six months. Your mother always copied the letters and signed them. She seemed to think it was a kinder joke, and she was proud of his answering my letters. But she never went back to New York to hear him, though I saved up enough to give her the treat again. She was too lazy, and she let me go without her. I heard him three times in New York; and in the spring he came to Wingfield and played once at the Academy. Your mother was sick and couldn't go; so I went alone. After the performance I meant to get one of the directors to take me in to see him; but when the time came, I just went back home and wrote to him instead. And the month after, before he went back to Europe, he sent your mother a last little note, and that picture hanging up there…"

Mr. Grew paused again, and both men lifted their eyes to the photograph.

"Is that all?" Ronald slowly asked.

"That's all—every bit of it," said Mr. Grew.

"And my mother—my mother never even spoke to Dolbrowski?"

"Never. She never even saw him but that once in New York at his concert."

The blood crept again to Ronald's face. "Are you sure of that, sir?" he asked in a trembling voice.

"Sure as I am that I'm sitting here. Why, she was too lazy to look at his letters after the first novelty wore off. She copied the answers just to humor me—but she always said she couldn't understand what we wrote."

"But how could you go on with such a correspondence? It's incredible!"

Mr. Grew looked at his son thoughtfully. "I suppose it is, to you. You've only had to put out your hand and get the things I was starving for—music, and good talk, and ideas. Those letters gave me all that. You've read them, and you know that Dolbrowski was not only a great musician but a great man. There was nothing beautiful he didn't see, nothing fine he didn't feel. For six months I breathed his air, and I've lived on it ever since. Do you begin to understand a little now?"

"Yes—a little. But why write in my mother's name? Why make it a sentimental correspondence?"

Mr. Grew reddened to his bald temples. "Why, I tell you it began that way, as a kinder joke. And when I saw that the first letter pleased and interested him, I was afraid to tell him—*I couldn't* tell him. Do you suppose he'd gone on writing if he'd ever seen me, Ronny?"

Ronald suddenly looked at him with new eyes. "But he must have thought your letters very beautiful—to go on as he did," he broke out.

"Well—I did my best," said Mr. Grew modestly.

Ronald pursued his idea. "Where are all your letters, I wonder?

Weren't they returned to you at his death?"

Mr. Grew laughed. "Lord, no. I guess he had trunks and trunks full of better ones. I guess Queens and Empresses wrote to him."

"I should have liked to see your letters," the young man insisted.

"Well, they weren't bad," said Mr. Grew drily. "But I'll tell you one thing, Ronny," he added suddenly. Ronald raised his head with a quick glance, and Mr. Grew continued: "I'll tell you where the best of those letters is—it's in *you*. If it hadn't been for that one look at life I couldn't have made you what you are. Oh, I know you've done a good deal of your own making—but I've been there behind you all the time. And you'll never know the work I've spared you and the time I've saved you. Fortune Dolbrowski helped me do that. I never saw things in little again after I'd looked at 'em with him. And I tried to give you the big view from the stars . . . So that's what became of my letters."

Mr. Grew paused, and for a long time Ronald sat motionless, his elbows on the table, his face dropped on his hands.

Suddenly Mr. Grew's touch fell on his shoulder.

"Look at here, Ronald Grew—do you want me to tell you how you're feeling at this minute? Just a mite let down, after all, at the idea that you ain't the romantic figure you'd got to think yourself . . . Well, that's natural enough, too; but I'll tell you what it proves. It proves you're my son right enough, if any more proof was needed. For it's just the kind of fool nonsense I used to feel at your age—and if there's anybody here to laugh at it's myself, and not you. And you can laugh at me just as much as you like . . . "

## THE DAUNT DIANA

"WHAT'S BECOME OF the Daunt Diana? You mean to say you never heard the sequel?"

Ringham Finney threw himself back into his chair with the smile of the collector who has a good thing to show. He knew he had a good listener, at any rate. I don't think much of Ringham's snuff-boxes, but his anecdotes are usually worth-while. He's a psychologist astray among *bibelots*, and the best bits he brings back from his raids on Christie's and the Hotel Drouot are the fragments of human nature he picks up on those historic battle-fields. If his *flair* in enamel had been half as good we should have heard of the Finney collection by this time.

He really has—queer fatuous investigator!—an unusually sensitive touch for the human texture, and the specimens he gathers into his museum of heterogeneous memories have almost always some mark of the rare and chosen. I felt, therefore, that I was really to be congratulated on the fact that I didn't know what had become of the Daunt Diana, and on having before me a long evening in which to learn. I had just led my friend back, after an excellent dinner at Foyot's, to the shabby pleasant sitting-room of my *Rive Gauche* hotel; and I knew that, once I had settled him in a good arm-chair, and put a box of cigars at his elbow, I could trust him not to budge till I had the story.

II

YOU remember old Neave, of course? Little Humphrey Neave, I mean. We used to see him pottering about Rome years ago. He lived in two tiny rooms over a wine shop, on polenta and lentils, and prowled among the refuse of the Ripetta whenever he had a few coppers to spend. But you've been out of the collector's world for so long that you may not know what happened to him afterward . . .

He was always a queer chap, Neave; years older than you and me, of course—and even when I first knew him, in my raw Roman days, he gave me an extraordinary sense of age and experience. I don't think I've ever known any one who was at once so intelligent and so simple. It's the precise combination that results in romance; and poor little Neave was romantic.

He told me once how he'd come to Rome. He was *originaire* of Mystic, Connecticut—and he wanted to get as far away from it as possible. Rome seemed as far as anything on the same planet could be; and after he'd worried his way through Harvard—with shifts and shavings that you and I can't imagine—he contrived to get sent to Switzerland as tutor to a chap who'd failed in his examinations. With only the Alps between, he wasn't likely to turn back; and he got another fellow to take his pupil home, and struck out on foot for the seven hills.

I'm telling you these early details merely to give you a notion of the man's idealism. There was a cool persistency and a headlong courage in his dash for Rome that one wouldn't have guessed in the little pottering chap we used to know. Once on the spot, he got more tutoring, managed to make himself a name for coaxing balky youths to take their fences, and was finally able to take up the more congenial task of expounding "the antiquities" to cultured travellers. I call it more congenial—but how it must have seared his soul! Fancy unveiling the sacred scars of Time to ladies who murmur: "Was this *actually* the spot—?" while they absently feel for their hatpins! He used to say that nothing kept him at it but the exquisite thought of accumulating the *lire* for his collection. For the Neave collection, my dear fellow, began early, began almost with his Roman life, began in a series of little nameless odds and ends, broken trinkets, torn embroideries, the amputated extremities of maimed marbles: things that even the rag-picker had pitched away when he sifted his haul. But they weren't nameless or meaningless to Neave; his strength lay in his instinct for identifying, putting together, seeing significant relations. He was a regular Cuvier of bric-a-brac. And during those early years, when he had time to brood over trifles and note imperceptible differences, he gradually sharpened his instinct, and made it into the delicate and redoubtable instrument it is. Before he had a thousand francs' worth of *anticaglie* to his name he began to be known as an expert, and the big dealers were glad to consult him. But we're getting no nearer the Daunt Diana . . .

Well, some fifteen years ago, in London, I ran across Neave at Christie's. He was the same little man we'd known, effaced, bleached, indistinct, like a poor "impression"—as unnoticeable as one of his own early finds, yet, like them, with *a quality*, if one had an eye for it. He told me he still lived in Rome, and had contrived, by fierce self-denial, to get a few decent bits together—"piecemeal, little by little, with fasting and prayer; and I mean the fasting literally!" he said.

He had run over to London for his annual "look-round"—I fancy one or another of the big collectors usually paid his journey—and when we met he was on his way to see the Daunt collection. You know old Daunt was a surly brute, and the things weren't easily seen; but he had heard Neave was in London, and had sent—yes, actually sent!—for him to come and give his opinion on a few bits, including the Diana. The little man bore himself discreetly, but you can imagine his pride. In his exultation he asked me to come with him—"Oh, I've the *grandes et petites entrées*, my dear fellow: I've made my conditions—" and so it happened that I saw the first meeting between Humphrey Neave and his fate.

For that collection was his fate: or, one may say, it was embodied in the Diana who was queen and goddess of the realm. Yes—I shall always be glad I was with Neave when he had his first look at the Diana. I see him now, blinking at her through his white lashes, and stroking his seedy wisp of a moustache to hide a twitch of the muscles. It was all very quiet, but it was the *coup de foudre*. I could see that by the way his hands trembled when he turned away and began to examine the other things. You remember Neave's hands—thin, sallow, dry, with long inquisitive fingers thrown out like antennae? Whatever they hold—bronze or lace, hard enamel or brittle glass—they have an air of conforming themselves to the texture of the thing, and sucking out of it, by every finger-tip, the mysterious essence it has secreted. Well, that day, as he moved about among Daunt's treasures, the Diana followed him everywhere. He didn't look back at her—he gave himself to the business he was there for—but whatever he touched, he felt her. And on the threshold he turned and gave her his first free look—the kind of look that says: *"You're mine."*

It amused me at the time—the idea of little Neave making eyes at any of Daunt's belongings. He might as well have coquetted with the Kohinoor. And the same idea seemed to strike him; for as we turned away from the big house in Belgravia he glanced up at it and said, with a bitterness I'd never heard in him: "Good Lord! To think of that lumpy fool having those things to handle! Did you notice his stupid stumps of fingers? I suppose he blunted them gouging nuggets out of the gold fields. And in exchange for the nuggets he gets all that in a year—only has to hold out his callous palm to have that great ripe sphere of beauty drop into it! That's my idea of heaven—to have a great collection drop into one's hand, as success, or love, or any of the big shining things, drop suddenly on some men. And I've had to worry along for nearly fifty years, saving and paring, and haggling and intriguing, to get here a bit and there a bit—and not one perfection in the lot! It's enough to poison a man's life."

The outbreak was so unlike Neave that I remember every word of it: remember, too, saying in answer: "But, look here, Neave, you wouldn't take Daunt's hands for yours, I imagine?"

He stared a moment and smiled. "Have all that, and grope my way through it like a blind cave fish? What a question! But the sense that it's always the blind fish that live in that kind of aquarium is what makes anarchists, sir!" He looked back from the corner of the square, where we had paused while he delivered himself of this remarkable metaphor. "God, I'd like to throw a bomb at that place, and be in at the looting!"

And with that, on the way home, he unpacked his grievance—pulled the bandage off the wound, and showed me the ugly mark it had made on his little white soul.

It wasn't the struggling, stinting, self-denying that galled him—it was the inadequacy of the result. It was, in short, the old tragedy of the discrepancy between a man's wants and his power to gratify them. Neave's taste was too exquisite for his means—was like some strange, delicate, capricious animal, that he cherished and pampered and couldn't satisfy.

"Don't you know those little glittering lizards that die if they're not fed on some wonderful tropical fly? Well, my taste's like that, with one important difference—if it doesn't get its fly, it simply turns and feeds on me. Oh, it doesn't die, my taste—worse luck! It gets larger and stronger and more fastidious, and takes a bigger bite of me—that's all."

That was all. Year by year, day by day, he had made himself into this delicate register of perceptions and sensations—as far above the ordinary human faculty of appreciation as some scientific registering instrument is beyond the rough human senses—only to find that the beauty which alone could satisfy him was unattainable—that he was never to know the last deep identification which only possession can give. He had trained himself in short, to feel, in the rare great thing—such an utterance of beauty as the Daunt Diana, say—a hundred elements of perfection, a hundred *reasons why*, imperceptible, inexplicable even, to the average "artistic" sense; he had reached this point by a long austere process of discrimination and rejection, the renewed great refusals of the intelligence which perpetually asks more, which will make no pact with its self of yesterday, and is never to be beguiled from its purpose by the wiles of the next-best-thing. Oh, it's a poignant case, but not a common one; for the next-best-thing usually wins...

You see, the worst of Neave's state was the fact of his not being a mere collector, even the collector raised to his highest pitch of efficiency. The whole thing was blended in him with poetry—his imagination had romanticized the acquisitive instinct, as the religious feeling of the Middle Ages turned passion into love. And yet his could never be the abstract enjoyment of the philosopher who says: "This or that object is really mine because I'm capable of appreciating it." Neave *wanted* what he appreciated—wanted it with his touch and his sight as well as with his imagination.

It was hardly a year afterward that, coming back from a long tour in India, I picked up a London paper and read the amazing headline: "Mr. Humphrey Neave buys the Daunt collection" . . . I rubbed my eyes and read again. Yes, it could only be our old friend Humphrey. "An American living in Rome . . . one of our most discerning collectors"; there was no mistaking the description. I clapped on my hat and bolted out to see the first dealer I could find; and there I had the incredible details. Neave had come into a fortune—two or three million dollars, amassed by an uncle who had a corset-factory, and who had attained wealth as the creator of the Mystic Super-straight. (Corset-factory sounds odd, by the way, doesn't it? One had fancied that the corset was a personal, a highly specialized garment, more or less shaped on the form it was to modify; but, after all, the Tanagras were all made from two or three molds—and so, I suppose, are the ladies who wear the Mystic Super-straight.)

The uncle had a son, and Neave had never dreamed of seeing a penny of the money; but the son died suddenly, and the father followed, leaving a codicil that gave everything to our friend. Humphrey had to go out to "realize" on the corset-factory; and his description of *that!* . . . Well, he came back with his money in his pocket, and the day he landed old Daunt went to smash. It all fitted in like a Chinese puzzle. I believe Neave drove straight from Euston to Daunt House: at any rate, within two months the collection was his, and at a price that made the trade sit up. Trust old Daunt for that!

I was in Rome the following spring, and you'd better believe I looked him up. A big porter glared at me from the door of the Palazzo Neave: I had almost to produce my passport to get in. But that wasn't Neave's fault—the poor fellow was so beset by people clamoring to see his collection that he had to barricade himself, literally. When I had mounted the state *Scalone*, and come on him, at the end of half a dozen echoing saloons, in the farthest, smallest *réduit* of the vast suite, I received the same welcome that he used to give us in his little den over the wine shop.

"Well—so you've got her?" I said. For I'd caught sight of the Diana in passing, against the bluish blur of an old *verdure*—just the background for her poised loveliness. Only I rather wondered why she wasn't in the room where he sat.

He smiled. "Yes, I've got her," he returned, more calmly than I had expected.

"And all the rest of the loot?"

"Yes. I had to buy the lump."

"Had to? But you wanted to, didn't you? You used to say it was your idea of heaven—to stretch out your hand and have a great ripe sphere of beauty drop into it. I'm quoting your own words, by the way."

Neave blinked and stroked his seedy moustache. "Oh, yes. I remember the phrase. It's true—it is the last luxury." He paused, as if seeking a pretext for his lack of warmth. "The thing that bothered me was having to move. I couldn't cram all the stuff into my old quarters."

"Well, I should say not! This is rather a better setting."

He got up. "Come and take a look round. I want to show you two or three things—new attributions I've made. I'm doing the catalogue over."

The interest of showing me the things seemed to dispel the vague apathy I had felt in him. He grew keen again in detailing his redistribution of values, and above all in convicting old Daunt and his advisers of their repeated aberrations of judgment. "The miracle is that he should have got such things, knowing as little as he did what he was getting. And the egregious asses who bought for him were no better, were worse in fact, since they had all sorts of humbugging wrong reasons for admiring what old Daunt simply coveted because it belonged to some other rich man."

Never had Neave had so wondrous a field for the exercise of his perfected faculty; and I saw then how in the real, the great collector's appreciations the keenest scientific perception is suffused with imaginative sensibility, and how it's to the latter undefinable quality that in the last resort he trusts himself.

Nevertheless, I still felt the shadow of that hovering apathy, and he knew I felt it, and was always breaking off to give me reasons for it. For one thing, he wasn't used to his new quarters—hated their bigness and formality; then the requests to show his things drove him mad. "The women—oh, the women!" he wailed, and interrupted himself to describe a heavy-footed German Princess who had marched past his treasures as if she were inspecting a cavalry regiment, applying an unmodulated *Mugneeficent* to everything from the engraved gems to the Hercules torso.

"Not that she was half as bad as the other kind," he added, as if with a last effort at optimism. "The kind who discriminate and say: 'I'm not sure if it's Botticelli or Cellini I mean, but *one of that school*, at any rate.' And the worst of all are the ones who know—up to a certain point: have the schools, and the dates and the jargon pat, and yet wouldn't know a Phidias if it stood where they hadn't expected it."

He had all my sympathy, poor Neave; yet these were trials inseparable from the collector's lot, and not always without their secret compensations. Certainly they did not wholly explain my friend's attitude; and for a moment I wondered if it were due to some strange disillusionment as to the quality of his treasures. But no! the Daunt collection was almost above criticism; and as we passed from one object to another I saw there was no mistaking the genuineness of Neave's pride in his possessions. The ripe sphere of beauty was his, and he had found no flaw in it as yet . . .

A year later came the amazing announcement—the Daunt collection was for sale. At first we all supposed it was a case of weeding out (though how old Daunt would have raged at the thought of anybody's weeding *his* collection!) But no—the catalogue corrected that idea. Every stick and stone was to go under the hammer. The news ran like wildfire from Rome to Berlin, from Paris to London and New York. Was Neave ruined, then? Wrong again—the dealers nosed that out in no time. He was simply selling because he chose to sell; and in due time the things came up at Christie's.

But you may be sure the trade had found an answer to the riddle; and the answer was that, on close inspection, Neave had found the collection less impeccable than he had supposed. It was a preposterous answer—but then there was no other. Neave, by this time, was pretty generally recognized as having the subtlest *flair* of any collector in Europe, and if he didn't choose to keep the Daunt collection it could be only because he had reason to think he could do better.

In a flash this report had gone the rounds and the buyers were on their guard. I had run over to London to see the thing through, and it was the queerest sale I ever was at. Some of the things held their own, but a lot—and a few of the best among them—went for half their value. You see, they'd been locked up in old Daunt's house for nearly twenty years, and hardly shown to any one, so that the whole younger generation of dealers and collectors knew of them only by hearsay. Then you know the effect of suggestion in such cases. The undefinable sense we were speaking of is a ticklish instrument, easily thrown out of gear by a sudden fall of temperature; and the sharpest experts grow shy and self-distrustful when the cold current of depreciation touches them. The sale was a slaughter—and when I saw the Daunt Diana fall at the wink of a little third-rate *brocanteur* from Vienna I turned sick at the folly of my kind.

For my part, I had never believed that Neave had sold the collection because he'd "found it out"; and within a year my incredulity was justified. As soon as the things were put in circulation they were known for the marvels they are. There was hardly a poor bit in the lot; and my wonder grew at Neave's madness. All over Europe, dealers began to be fighting for the spoils; and all kinds of stuff were palmed off on the unsuspecting as fragments of the Daunt collection!

Meantime, what was Neave doing? For a long time I didn't hear, and chance kept me from returning to Rome. But one day, in Paris, I ran across a dealer who had captured for a song one of the best Florentine bronzes in the Daunt collection—a marvelous *plaquette* of Donatello's. I asked him what had become of it, and he said with a grin: "I sold it the other day," naming a price that staggered me.

"Ye gods! Who paid you that for it?"

His grin broadened, and he answered: "Neave."

*"Neave?* Humphrey Neave?"

"Didn't you know he was buying back his things?"

"Nonsense!"

"He is, though. Not in his own name—but he's doing it."

And he *was,* do you know—and at prices that would have made a sane man shudder! A few weeks later I ran across his tracks in London, where he was trying to get hold of a Penicaud enamel—another of his scattered treasures. Then I hunted him down at his hotel, and had it out with him.

"Look here, Neave, what are you up to?"

He wouldn't tell me at first: stared and laughed and denied. But I took him off to dine, and after dinner, while we smoked, I happened to mention casually that I had a pull over the man who had the Penicaud—and at that he broke down and confessed.

"Yes, I'm buying them back, Finney—it's true." He laughed nervously, twitching his moustache. And then he let me have the story.

"You know how I'd hungered and thirsted for the *real thing*—you quoted my own phrase to me once, about the 'ripe sphere of beauty.' So when I got my money, and Daunt lost his, almost at the same moment, I saw the hand of Providence in it. I knew that, even if I'd been younger, and had more time, I could never hope, nowadays, to form such a collection as *that*. There was the ripe sphere, within reach; and I took it. But when I got it, and began to live with it, I found out my mistake. It was a *marriage de convenance*—there'd been no wooing, no winning. Each of my little old bits—the rubbish I chucked out to make room for Daunt's glories—had its own personal history, the drama of my relation to it, of the discovery, the struggle, the capture, the first divine moment of possession. There was a romantic secret between us. And then I had absorbed its beauties one by one, they had become a part of my imagination, they held me by a hundred threads of far-reaching association. And suddenly I had expected to create this kind of intense personal tie between myself and a roomful of new cold alien presences—things staring at me vacantly from the depths of unknown pasts! Can you fancy a more preposterous hope? Why, my other things, my *own* things, had wooed me as passionately as I wooed them: there was a certain little bronze, a little Venus, who had drawn me, drawn me, drawn me, imploring me to rescue her from her unspeakable surroundings in a vulgar bric-a-brac shop at Biarritz, where she shrank out of sight among sham Sevres and Dutch silver, as one has seen certain women—rare, shy, exquisite—made almost invisible by the vulgar splendors surrounding them. Well! that little Venus, who was just a specious seventeenth century attempt at the 'antique,' but who had penetrated me with her pleading grace, touched me by the easily guessed story of her obscure, anonymous origin, was more to me imaginatively—yes! more than the cold bought beauty of the Daunt Diana . . . "

"The Daunt Diana!" I broke in. "Hold up, Neave—*the Daunt Diana?*"

He smiled contemptuously. "A professional beauty, my dear fellow—expected every head to be turned when she came into a room."

"Oh, Neave," I groaned.

"Yes, I know. You're thinking of what we felt that day we first saw her in London. Many a poor devil has sold his soul as the result of such a first sight! Well, I sold her instead. Do you want the truth about her? *Elle était bête à pleurer.*"

He laughed, and stood up with a little shrug of disenchantment.

"And so you're impenitent?" I paused. "And yet you're buying some of the things back?"

Neave laughed again, ironically. "I knew you'd find me out and call me to account. Well, yes: I'm buying back." He stood before me half sheepish, half defiant. "I'm buying back because there's nothing else as good in the market. And because I've a queer feeling that, this time, they'll be *mine*. But I'm ruining myself at the game!" he confessed.

It was true: Neave was ruining himself. And he's gone on ruining himself ever since, till now the job's nearly done. Bit by bit, year by year, he has gathered in his scattered treasures, at higher prices than the dealers ever dreamed of getting. There are fabulous details in the story of his quest. Now and then I ran across him, and was able to help him recover a fragment; and it was wonderful to see his delight in the moment of reunion. Finally, about two years ago, we met in Paris, and he told me he had got back all the important pieces except the Diana.

"The Diana? But you told me you didn't care for her."

"Didn't care?" He leaned across the restaurant table that divided us. "Well, no, in a sense I didn't. I wanted her to want me, you see; and she didn't then! Whereas now she's crying to me to come to her. You know where she is?" he broke off.

Yes, I knew: in the center of Mrs. Willy P. Goldmark's yellow and gold drawing-room, under a thousand-candle-power chandelier, with reflectors aimed at her from every point of the compass. I had seen her wincing and shivering there in her outraged nudity at one of the Goldmark "crushes."

"But you can't get her, Neave," I objected.

"No, I can't get her," he said.

Well, last month I was in Rome, for the first time in six or seven years, and of course I looked about for Neave. The Palazzo Neave was let to some rich Russians, and the splendid new porter didn't know where the proprietor lived. But I got on his trail easily enough, and it led me to a strange old place in the Trastevere, an ancient crevassed black palace turned tenement house, and fluttering with pauper clothes-lines. I found Neave under the leads, in two or three cold rooms that smelt of the *cuisine* of all his neighbors: a poor shrunken little figure, seedier and shabbier than ever, yet more alive than when we had made the tour of his collection in the Palazzo Neave.

The collection was around him again, not displayed in tall cabinets and on marble tables, but huddled on shelves, perched on chairs, crammed in corners, putting the gleam of bronze, the opalescence of old glass, the pale luster of marble, into all the angles of his low dim rooms. There they were, the proud presences that had stared at him down the vistas of Daunt House, and shone in cold transplanted beauty under his own painted cornices: there they were, gathered in humble promiscuity about his bent shabby figure, like superb wild creatures tamed to become the familiars of some harmless old wizard.

As we went from bit to bit, as he lifted one piece after another, and held it to the light of his low windows, I saw in his hands the same tremor of sensation that I had noticed when he first examined the same objects at Daunt House. All his life was in his finger-tips, and it seemed to communicate life to the exquisite things he touched. But you'll think me infected by his mysticism if I tell you they gained new beauty while he held them . . .

We went the rounds slowly and reverently; and then, when I supposed our inspection was over, and was turning to take my leave, he opened a door I had not noticed, and showed me into a slit of a room beyond. It was a mere monastic cell, scarcely large enough for his narrow iron bed and the chest which probably held his few clothes; but there, in a niche of the bare wall, facing the foot of the bed—there stood the Daunt Diana.

I gasped at the sight and turned to him; and he looked back at me without speaking.

"In the name of magic, Neave, how did you do it?"

He smiled as if from the depths of some secret rapture. "Call it magic, if you like; but I ruined myself doing it," he said.

I stared at him in silence, breathless with the madness and the wonder of it; and suddenly, red to the ears, he flung out his boyish confession. "I lied to you that day in London—the day I said I didn't care for her. I always cared—always worshipped—always wanted her. But she wasn't mine then, and I knew it, and she knew it . . . and now at last we understand each other." He looked at me shyly, and then glanced about the bare cold cell. "The setting isn't worthy of her, I know; she was meant for glories I can't give her; but beautiful things, my dear Finney, like beautiful spirits, live in houses not made with hands . . . "

His face shone with extraordinary sweetness as he spoke; and I saw he'd got hold of the secret we're all after. No, the setting isn't worthy of her, if you like. The rooms are as shabby and mean as those we used to see him in years ago over the wine shop. I'm not sure they're not shabbier and meaner. But she rules there at last, she shines and hovers there above him, and there at night, I doubt not, steals down from her cloud to give him the Latmian kiss.

THE DEBT

YOU REMEMBER—it's not so long ago—the talk there was about Dredge's *Arrival of the Fittest?* The talk has subsided, but the book of course remains: stands up, in fact, as the tallest thing of its kind since—well, I'd almost said since *The Origin of Species.*

I'm not wrong, at any rate, in calling it the most important contribution yet made to the development of the Darwinian theory, or rather to the solution of the awkward problem about which that theory has had to make such a circuit. Dredge's hypothesis will be contested, may one day be disproved; but at least it has swept out of the way all previous conjectures, including of course Lanfear's magnificent attempt; and for our generation of scientific investigators it will serve as the first safe bridge across a murderous black whirlpool.

It's all very interesting—there are few things more stirring to the imagination than that sudden projection of the new hypothesis, light as a cobweb and strong as steel, across the intellectual abyss; but, for an idle observer of human motives, the other, the personal, side of Dredge's case is even more interesting and arresting.

Personal side? You didn't know there was one? Pictured him simply as a thinking machine, a highly specialized instrument of precision, the result of a long series of "adaptations," as his own jargon would put it? Well, I don't wonder—if you've met him. He does give the impression of being something out of his own laboratory: a delicate scientific instrument that reveals wonders to the initiated, and is absolutely useless in an ordinary hand.

In his youth it was just the other way. I knew him twenty years ago, as an awkward lout whom young Archie Lanfear had picked up at college, and brought home for a visit. I happened to be staying at the Lanfears' when the boys arrived, and I shall never forget Dredge's first appearance on the scene. You know the Lanfears always lived very simply. That summer they had gone to Buzzard's Bay, in order that Professor Lanfear might be near the Biological Station at Wood's Hole, and they were picnicking in a kind of sketchy bungalow without any attempt at elegance. But Galen Dredge couldn't have been more awe-struck if he'd been suddenly plunged into a Fifth Avenue ball-room. He nearly knocked his shock head against the low doorway, and in dodging this peril trod heavily on Mabel Lanfear's foot, and became hopelessly entangled in her mother's draperies—though how he managed it I never knew, for Mrs. Lanfear's dowdy muslins ran to no excess of train.

When the Professor himself came in it was ten times worse, and I saw then that Dredge's emotion was a tribute to the great man's proximity. That made the boy interesting, and I began to watch. Archie, always enthusiastic but vague, had said: "Oh, he's a tremendous chap—you'll see—" but I hadn't expected to see quite so clearly. Lanfear's vision, of course, was sharper than mine; and the next morning he had carried Dredge off to the Biological Station. And that was the way it began.

Dredge is the son of a Baptist minister. He comes from East Lethe, New York State, and was working his way through college—waiting at White Mountain hotels in summer—when Archie Lanfear ran across him. There were eight children in the family, and the mother was an invalid. Dredge never had a penny from his father after he was fourteen; but his mother wanted him to be a scholar, and "kept at him," as he put it, in the hope of his going back to "teach school" at East Lethe. He developed slowly, as the scientific mind generally does, and was still adrift about himself and his tendencies when

Archie took him down to Buzzard's Bay. But he had read Lanfear's *Utility and Variation*, and had always been a patient and curious observer of nature. And his first meeting with Lanfear explained him to himself. It didn't, however, enable him to explain himself to others, and for a long time he remained, to all but Lanfear, an object of incredulity and conjecture.

*"Why* my husband wants him about—" poor Mrs. Lanfear, the kindest of women, privately lamented to her friends; for Dredge, at that time—they kept him all summer at the bungalow—had one of the most encumbering personalities you can imagine. He was as inexpressive as he is to-day, and yet oddly obtrusive: one of those uncomfortable presences whose silence is an interruption.

The poor Lanfears almost died of him that summer, and the pity of it was that he never suspected it, but continued to lavish on them a floundering devotion as uncomfortable as the endearments of a dripping dog—all out of gratitude for the Professor's kindness! He was full, in those days, of raw enthusiasms, which he forced on anyone who would listen when his first shyness had worn off. You can't picture him spouting sentimental poetry, can you? Yet I've seen him petrify a whole group of Mrs. Lanfear's callers by suddenly discharging on them, in the strident drawl of Western New York, "Barbara Freitchie" or "The Queen of the May." His taste in literature was uniformly bad, but very definite, and far more assertive than his views on biological questions. In his scientific judgments he showed, even then, a remarkable temperance, a precocious openness to the opposite view; but in literature he was a furious propagandist, aggressive, disputatious, and extremely sensitive to adverse opinion.

Lanfear, of course, had been struck from the first by his gift of accurate observation, and by the fact that his eagerness to learn was offset by his reluctance to conclude. I remember Lanfear's telling me that he had never known a lad of Dredge's age who gave such promise of uniting an aptitude for general ideas with the plodding patience of the accumulator of facts. Of course when Lanfear talked like that of a young biologist his fate was sealed. There could be no question of Dredge's going back to "teach school" at East Lethe. He must take a course in biology at Columbia, spend his vacations at the Wood's Hole laboratory, and then, if possible, go to Germany for a year or two.

All this meant his virtual adoption by the Lanfears. Most of Lanfear's fortune went in helping young students to a start, and he devoted his heaviest subsidies to Dredge.

"Dredge will be my biggest dividend—you'll see!" he used to say, in the chrysalis days when poor Galen was known to the world of science only as a perpetual slouching presence in Mrs. Lanfear's drawing-room. And Dredge, it must be said, took his obligations simply, with that kind of personal dignity, and quiet sense of his own worth, which in such cases saves the beneficiary from abjectness. He seemed to trust himself as fully as Lanfear trusted him.

The comic part of it was that his only idea of making what is known as "a return" was to devote himself to the Professor's family. When I hear pretty women lamenting that they can't coax Professor Dredge out of his laboratory I remember Mabel Lanfear's cry to me: "If Galen would only keep away!" When Mabel fell on the ice and broke her leg, Galen walked seven miles in a blizzard to get a surgeon; but if he did her this service one day in the year, he bored her by being in the way for the other three hundred and sixty-four. One would have imagined at that time that he thought his perpetual presence the greatest gift he could bestow; for, except on the occasion of his fetching the surgeon, I don't remember his taking any other way of expressing his gratitude.

In love with Mabel? Not a bit! But the queer thing was that he did have a passion in those days—a blind, hopeless passion for Mrs. Lanfear! Yes: I know what I'm saying. I mean Mrs. Lanfear, the Professor's wife, poor Mrs. Lanfear, with her tight hair and her loose figure, her blameless brow and earnest eye-glasses, and her perpetual attitude of mild misapprehension. I can see Dredge cowering, long and many-jointed, in a diminutive drawing-room chair, one square-toed shoe coiled round an exposed ankle, his knees clasped in a knot of red knuckles, and his spectacles perpetually seeking Mrs. Lanfear's eye-glasses. I never knew if the poor lady was aware of the sentiment she inspired, but her children observed it, and it provoked them to irreverent mirth. Galen was the predestined butt of Mabel and Archie; and secure in their mother's virtuous obtuseness, and in her worshipper's timidity, they allowed themselves a latitude of banter that sometimes turned their audience cold. Dredge meanwhile was going on obstinately with his work. Now and then he had queer fits of idleness, when he lapsed into a state of sulky inertia from which even Lanfear's admonitions could not rouse him. Once, just before an examination, he suddenly went off to the Maine woods for two weeks, came back, and failed to pass. I don't know if his benefactor ever lost hope; but at times his confidence must have been sorely strained. The queer part of it was that when Dredge emerged from these eclipses he seemed keener and more active than ever. His slowly growing intelligence probably needed its periodical pauses of assimilation; and Lanfear was wonderfully patient.

At last Dredge finished his course and went to Germany; and when he came back he was a new man—was, in fact, the Dredge we all know. He seemed to have shed his blundering, encumbering personality, and come to life as a disembodied intelligence. His fidelity to the Lanfears was unchanged; but he showed it negatively, by his discretions and abstentions. I have an idea that Mabel was less disposed to deride him, might even have been induced to softer sentiments; but I doubt if Dredge even noticed the change. As for his ex-goddess, he seemed to regard her as a motherly household divinity, the guardian genius of the darning needle; but on Professor Lanfear he looked with a deepening reverence. If the rest of the family had diminished in his eyes, its head had grown even greater.

II

FROM that day Dredge's progress continued steadily. If not always perceptible to the untrained eye, in Lanfear's sight it never deviated, and the great man began to associate Dredge with his work, and to lean on him more and more. Lanfear's health was already failing, and in my confidential talks with him I saw how he counted on Galen Dredge to continue and amplify his doctrine. If he did not describe the young man as his predestined Huxley, it was because any such comparison between himself and his great predecessors would have been repugnant to his taste; but he evidently felt that it would be Dredge's role to reveal him to posterity. And the young man seemed at that time to take the same view of his calling. When he was not busy about Lanfear's work he was recording their conversations with the diligence of a biographer and the accuracy of a naturalist. Any attempt to question or minimize Lanfear's theories roused in his disciple the only flashes of wrath I have ever seen a scientific discussion provoke in him. In defending his master he became almost as intemperate as in the early period of his literary passions.

Such filial dedication must have been all the more precious to Lanfear because, about that time, it became evident that Archie would never carry on his father's work. He had begun brilliantly, you may remember, by a little paper on *Limulus Polyphemus* that attracted a good deal of notice when it appeared in the Central Blatt; but gradually his zoological ardor yielded to an absorbing passion for the violin, which was followed by a sudden plunge into physics. At present, after a side-glance at the drama, I understand he's devoting what is left of his father's money to archaeological explorations in Asia Minor.

"Archie's got a delightful little mind," Lanfear used to say to me, rather wistfully, "but it's just a highly polished surface held up to the show as it passes. Dredge's mind takes in only a bit at a time, but the bit stays, and other bits are joined to it, in a hard mosaic of fact, of which imagination weaves the pattern. I saw just how it would be years ago, when my boy used to take my meaning in a flash, and answer me with clever objections, while Galen disappeared into one of his fathomless silences, and then came to the surface like a dripping retriever, a long way beyond Archie's objections, and with an answer to them in his mouth."

It was about this time that the crowning satisfaction of Lanfear's career came to him: I mean, of course, John Weyman's gift to Columbia of the Lanfear Laboratory, and the founding, in connection with it, of a chair of Experimental Evolution. Weyman had always taken an interest in Lanfear's work, but no one had supposed that his interest would express itself so magnificently. The honor came to Lanfear at a time when he was fighting an accumulation of troubles: failing health, the money difficulties resulting from his irrepressible generosity, his disappointment about Archie's career, and perhaps also the persistent attacks of the new school of German zoologists.

"If I hadn't Galen I should feel the game was up," he said to me once, in a fit of half-real, half-mocking despondency. "But he'll do what I haven't time to do myself, and what my boy can't do for me."

That meant that he would answer the critics, and triumphantly affirm Lanfear's theory, which had been rudely shaken, but not dislodged.

"A scientific hypothesis lasts till there's something else to put in its place. People who want to get across a river will use the old bridge till the new one's built. And I don't see anyone who's particularly anxious, in this case, to take a contract for the new one," Lanfear ended; and I remember answering with a laugh: "Not while Horatius Dredge holds the other."

It was generally known that Lanfear had not long to live, and the Laboratory was hardly opened before the question of his successor in the chair of Experimental Evolution began to be a matter of public discussion. It was conceded that whoever followed him ought to be a man of achieved reputation, someone carrying, as the French say, a considerable "baggage." At the same time, even Lanfear's critics felt that he should be succeeded by a man who held his views and would continue his teaching. This was not in itself a difficulty, for German criticism had so far been mainly negative, and there were plenty of good men who, while they questioned the permanent validity of Lanfear's conclusions, were yet ready to accept them for their provisional usefulness. And then there was the added inducement of the Laboratory! The Columbia Professor of Experimental Evolution has at his disposal the most complete instrument of biological research that modern ingenuity has yet produced; and it's not only in theology or politics *que Paris vaut bien une messe!* There was no trouble about finding a candidate; but the whole thing turned on Lanfear's decision, since it was tacitly understood that, by Weyman's wish, he was to select his successor. And what a cry there was when he selected Galen Dredge!

Not in the scientific world, though. The specialists were beginning to know about Dredge. His remarkable paper on Sexual Dimorphism had been translated into several languages, and a furious polemic had broken out over it. When a young fellow can get the big men fighting over him his future is pretty well assured. But Dredge was only thirty-four, and some people seemed to feel that there was a kind of deflected nepotism in Lanfear's choice.

"If he could choose Dredge he might as well have chosen his own son," I've heard it said; and the irony was that Archie—will you believe it?—actually thought so himself! But Lanfear had Weyman behind him, and when the end came the Faculty at once appointed Galen Dredge to the chair of Experimental Evolution.

For the first two years things went quietly, along accustomed lines. Dredge simply continued the course which Lanfear's death had interrupted. He lectured well even then, with a persuasive simplicity surprising in the slow, inarticulate creature one knew him for. But haven't you noticed that certain personalities reveal themselves only in the more impersonal relations of life? It's as if they woke only to collective contacts, and the single consciousness were an unmeaning fragment to them.

If there was anything to criticize in that first part of the course, it was the avoidance of general ideas, of those brilliant rockets of conjecture that Lanfear's students were used to seeing him fling across the darkness. I remember once saying this to Archie, who, having recovered from his absurd disappointment, had returned to his old allegiance to Dredge.

"Oh, that's Galen all over. He doesn't want to jump into the ring till he has a big swishing knock-down argument in his fist. He'll wait twenty years if he has to. That's his strength: he's never afraid to wait."

I thought this shrewd of Archie, as well as generous; and I saw the wisdom of Dredge's course. As Lanfear himself had said, his theory was safe enough till somebody found a more attractive one; and before that day Dredge would probably have accumulated sufficient proof to crystallize the fluid hypothesis.

III

THE third winter I was off collecting in Central America, and didn't get back till Dredge's course had been going for a couple of months. The very day I turned up in town Archie Lanfear descended on me with a summons from his mother. I was wanted at once at a family council.

I found the Lanfear ladies in a state of incoherent distress, which Archie's own indignation hardly made more intelligible. But gradually I put together their fragmentary charges, and learned that Dredge's lectures were turning into an organized assault on his master's doctrine.

"It amounts to just this," Archie said, controlling his women with the masterful gesture of the weak man. "Galen has simply turned round and betrayed my father."

"Just for a handful of silver he left us," Mabel sobbed in parenthesis, while Mrs. Lanfear tearfully cited Hamlet.

Archie silenced them again. "The ugly part of it is that he must have had this up his sleeve for years. He must have known when he was asked to succeed my father what use he meant to make of his opportunity. What he's doing isn't the result of a hasty conclusion: it means years of work and preparation."

Archie broke off to explain himself. He had returned from Europe the week before, and had learned on arriving that Dredge's lectures were stirring the world of science as nothing had stirred it since Lanfear's *Utility and Variation*. And the incredible outrage was that they owed their sensational effect to the fact of being an attempted refutation of Lanfear's great work.

I own that I was staggered: the case looked ugly, as Archie said. And there was a veil of reticence, of secrecy, about Dredge, that always kept his conduct in a half-light of uncertainty. Of some men one would have said off-hand: "It's impossible!" But one couldn't affirm it of him.

Archie hadn't seen him as yet; and Mrs. Lanfear had sent for me because she wished me to be present at the interview between the two men. The Lanfear ladies had a touching belief in Archie's violence: they thought him as terrible as a natural force. My own idea was that if there were any broken bones they wouldn't be Dredge's; but I was too curious as to the outcome not to be glad to offer my services as moderator.

First, however, I wanted to hear one of the lectures; and I went the next afternoon. The hall was jammed, and I saw, as soon as Dredge appeared, what increased security and ease the interest of his public had given him. He had been clear the year before, now he was also eloquent. The lecture was a remarkable effort: you'll find the gist of it in Chapter VII of *The Arrival of the Fittest*. Archie sat at my side in a white rage; he was too clever not to measure the extent of the disaster. And I was almost as indignant as he when we went to see Dredge the next day.

I saw at a glance that the latter suspected nothing; and it was characteristic of him that he began by questioning me about my finds, and only afterward turned to reproach Archie for having been back a week without notifying him.

"You know I'm up to my neck in this job. Why in the world didn't you hunt me up before this?"

The question was exasperating, and I could understand Archie's stammer of wrath.

"Hunt you up? Hunt you up? What the deuce are you made of, to ask me such a question instead of wondering why I'm here now?"

Dredge bent his slow calm scrutiny on his friend's quivering face; then he turned to me.

"What's the matter?" he said simply.

"The matter?" shrieked Archie, his clenched fist hovering excitedly above the desk by which he stood; but Dredge, with unwonted quickness, caught the fist as it descended.

"Careful—I've got a *Kallima* in that jar there." He pushed a chair forward, and added quietly: "Sit down."

Archie, ignoring the gesture, towered pale and avenging in his place; and Dredge, after a moment, took the chair himself.

"The matter?" Archie reiterated with rising passion. "Are you so lost to all sense of decency and honor that you can put that question in good faith? Don't you really *know* what's the matter?"

Dredge smiled slowly. "There are so few things one really *knows.*"

"Oh, damn your scientific hair-splitting! Don't you know you're insulting my father's memory?"

Dredge stared again, turning his spectacles thoughtfully from one of us to the other.

"Oh, that's it, is it? Then you'd better sit down. If you don't see at once it'll take some time to make you."

Archie burst into an ironic laugh.

"I rather think it will!" he conceded.

"Sit down, Archie," I said, setting the example; and he obeyed, with a gesture that made his consent a protest.

Dredge seemed to notice nothing beyond the fact that his visitors were seated. He reached for his pipe, and filled it with the care which the habit of delicate manipulations gave to all the motions of his long, knotty hands.

"It's about the lectures?" he said.

Archie's answer was a deep scornful breath.

"You've only been back a week, so you've only heard one, I suppose?"

"It was not necessary to hear even that one. You must know the talk they're making. If notoriety is what you're after—"

"Well, I'm not sorry to make a noise," said Dredge, putting a match to his pipe.

Archie bounded in his chair. "There's no easier way of doing it than to attack a man who can't answer you!"

Dredge raised a sobering hand. "Hold on. Perhaps you and I don't mean the same thing. Tell me first what's in your mind."

The request steadied Archie, who turned on Dredge a countenance really eloquent with filial indignation.

"It's an odd question for you to ask; it makes me wonder what's in *yours*. Not much thought of my father, at any rate, or you couldn't stand in his place and use the chance he's given you to push yourself at his expense."

Dredge received this in silence, puffing slowly at his pipe.

"Is that the way it strikes you?" he asked at length.

"God! It's the way it would strike most men."

He turned to me. "You too?"

"I can see how Archie feels," I said.

"That I'm attacking his father's memory to glorify myself?"

"Well, not precisely: I think what he really feels is that, if your convictions didn't permit you to continue his father's teaching, you might perhaps have done better to sever your connection with the Lanfear lectureship."

"Then you and he regard the Lanfear lectureship as having been founded to perpetuate a dogma, not to try and get at the truth?"

"Certainly not," Archie broke in. "But there's a question of taste, of delicacy, involved in the case that can't be decided on abstract principles. We know as well as you that my father meant the laboratory and the lectureship to serve the ends of science, at whatever cost to his own special convictions; what we feel—and you don't seem to—is that you're the last man to put them to that use; and I don't want to remind you why."

A slight redness rose through Dredge's sallow skin. "You needn't," he said. "It's because he pulled me out of my hole, woke me up, made me, shoved me off from the shore. Because he saved me ten or twenty years of muddled effort, and put me where I am at an age when my best working years are still ahead of me. Everyone knows that's what your father did for me, but I'm the only person who knows the time and trouble that it took."

It was well said, and I glanced quickly at Archie, who was never closed to generous emotions.

"Well, then—?" he said, flushing also.

"Well, then," Dredge continued, his voice deepening and losing its nasal edge, "I had to pay him back, didn't I?"

The sudden drop flung Archie back on his prepared attitude of irony. "It would be the natural inference—with most men."

"Just so. And I'm not so very different. I knew your father wanted a successor—some one who'd try and tie up the loose ends. And I took the lectureship with that object."

"And you're using it to tear the whole fabric to pieces!"

Dredge paused to re-light his pipe. "Looks that way," he conceded. "This year anyhow."

*"This year—?"* Archie gasped at him.

"Yes. When I took up the job I saw it just as your father left it. Or rather, I didn't see any other way of going on with it. The change came gradually, as I worked."

"Gradually? So that you had time to look round you, to know where you were, to see you were fatally committed to undoing the work he had done?"

"Oh, yes—I had time," Dredge conceded.

"And yet you kept the chair and went on with the course?"

Dredge refilled his pipe, and then turned in his seat so that he looked squarely at Archie.

"What would your father have done in my place?" he asked.

"In your place—?"

"Yes: supposing he'd found out the things I've found out in the last year or two. You'll see what they are, and how much they count, if you'll run over the report of the lectures. If your father'd been alive he might have come across the same facts just as easily."

There was a silence which Archie at last broke by saying: "But he didn't, and you did. There's the difference."

"The difference? What difference? Would your father have suppressed the facts if he'd found them? It's you who insult his memory by implying it! And if I'd brought them to him, would he have used his hold over me to get me to suppress them?"

"Certainly not. But can't you see it's his death that makes the difference? He's not here to defend his case."

Dredge laughed, but not unkindly. "My dear Archie, your father wasn't one of the kind who bother to defend their case. Men like him are the masters, not the servants, of their theories. They respect an idea only as long as it's of use to them; when it's usefulness ends they chuck it out. And that's what your father would have done."

Archie reddened. "Don't you assume a good deal in taking it for granted that he would have had to in this particular case?"

Dredge reflected. Yes: I was going too far. Each of us can only answer for himself. But to my mind your father's theory is refuted."

"And you don't hesitate to be the man to do it?"

"Should I have been of any use if I had? And did your father ever ask anything of me but to be of as much use as I could?"

It was Archie's turn to reflect. "No. That was what he always wanted, of course."

"That's the way I've always felt. The first day he took me away from East Lethe I knew the debt I was piling up against him, and I never had any doubt as to how I'd pay it, or how he'd want it paid. He didn't pick me out and train me for any object but to carry on the light. Do you suppose he'd have wanted me to snuff it out because it happened to light up a fact *he* didn't fancy? I'm using *his* oil to feed my torch with: yes, but it isn't really his torch or mine, or his oil or mine: they belong to each of us till we drop and hand them on."

Archie turned a sobered glance on him. "I see your point. But if the job had to be done I don't see that you need have done it from his chair."

"There's where we differ. If I did it at all I had to do it in the best way, and with all the authority his backing gave me. If I owe your father anything, I owe him that. It would have made him sick to see the job badly done. And don't you see that the way to honor him, and show what he's done for science, was to spare no advantage in my attack on him—that I'm proving the strength of his position by the desperateness of my assault?" Dredge paused and squared his lounging shoulders. "After all," he added, "he's not down yet, and if I leave him standing I guess it'll be some time before anybody else cares to tackle him."

There was a silence between the two men; then Dredge continued in a lighter tone: "There's one thing, though, that we're both in danger of forgetting: and that is how little, in the long run, it all counts either way." He smiled a little at Archie's outraged gesture. "The most we can any of us do—even by such a magnificent effort as your father's—is to turn the great marching army a hair's breadth nearer what seems to us the right direction; if one of us drops out, here and there, the loss of headway's hardly perceptible. And that's what I'm coming to now."

He rose from his seat, and walked across to the hearth; then, cautiously resting his shoulder-blades against the mantel-shelf jammed with miscellaneous specimens, he bent his musing spectacles on Archie.

"Your father would have understood why I've done, what I'm doing; but that's no reason why the rest of you should. And I rather think it's the rest of you who've suffered most from me. He always knew what I was *there for*, and that must have been some comfort even when I was most in the way; but I was just an ordinary nuisance to you and your mother and Mabel. You were all too kind to let me see it at the time, but I've seen it since, and it makes me feel that, after all, the settling of this matter lies with you. If it hurts you to have me go on with my examination of your father's theory, I'm ready to drop the lectures tomorrow, and trust to the Lanfear Laboratory to breed up a young chap who'll knock us both out in time. You've only got to say the word."

There was a pause while Dredge turned and laid his extinguished pipe carefully between a jar of embryo sea-urchins and a colony of regenerating planarians.

Then Archie rose and held out his hand.

"No," he said simply; "go on."

## FULL CIRCLE

GEOFFREY BETTON woke rather late—so late that the winter sunlight sliding across his warm red carpet struck his eyes as he turned on the pillow.

Strett, the valet, had been in, drawn the bath in the adjoining dressing-room, placed the crystal and silver cigarette-box at his side, put a match to the fire, and thrown open the windows to the bright morning air. It brought in, on the glitter of sun, all the shrill crisp morning noises—those piercing notes of the American thoroughfare that seem to take a sharper vibration from the clearness of the medium through which they pass.

Betton raised himself languidly. That was the voice of Fifth Avenue below his windows. He remembered that when he moved into his rooms eighteen months before, the sound had been like music to him: the complex orchestration to which the tune of his new life was set. Now it filled him with horror and weariness, since it had become the symbol of the hurry and noise of that new life. He had been far less hurried in the old days when he had to be up by seven, and down at the office sharp at nine. Now that he got up when he chose, and his life had no fixed framework of duties, the hours hunted him like a pack of bloodhounds.

He dropped back on his pillows with a groan. Yes—not a year ago there had been a positively sensuous joy in getting out of bed, feeling under his bare feet the softness of the sunlit carpet, and entering the shining tiled sanctuary where his great porcelain bath proffered its renovating flood. But then a year ago he could still call up the horror of the communal plunge at his earlier lodgings: the listening for other bathers, the dodging of shrouded ladies in "crimping"-pins, the cold wait on the landing, the reluctant descent into a blotchy tin bath, and the effort to identify one's soap and nail-brush among the promiscuous implements of ablution. That memory had faded now, and Betton saw only the dark hours to which his blue and white temple of refreshment formed a kind of glittering antechamber. For after his bath came his breakfast, and on the breakfast-tray his letters. His letters!

He remembered—and *that* memory had not faded!—the thrill with which he had opened the first missive in a strange feminine hand: the letter beginning: "I wonder if you'll mind an unknown reader's telling you all that your book has been to her?"

*Mind?* Ye gods, he minded now! For more than a year after the publication of *Diadems and Faggots* the letters, the inane indiscriminate letters of condemnation, of criticism, of interrogation, had poured in on him by every post. Hundreds of unknown readers had told him with unsparing detail all that his book had been to them. And the wonder of it was, when all was said and done, that it had really been so little—that when their thick broth of praise was strained through the author's anxious vanity there remained to him so small a sediment of definite specific understanding! No—it was always the same thing, over and over and over again—the same vague gush of adjectives, the same incorrigible tendency to estimate his effort according to each writer's personal preferences, instead of regarding it as a work of art, a thing to be measured by objective standards!

He smiled to think how little, at first, he had felt the vanity of it all. He had found a savor even in the grosser evidences of popularity: the advertisements of his book, the daily shower of "clippings," the sense that, when he entered a restaurant or a theatre, people nudged each other and said "That's Betton." Yes, the publicity had been sweet to him—at first. He had been touched by the sympathy of his fellow-men: had thought indulgently of the world, as a better place than the failures and the dyspeptics would acknowledge. And then his success began to submerge him: he gasped under the thickening shower of letters. His admirers were really unappeasable. And they wanted him to do such preposterous things—to give lectures, to head movements, to be tendered receptions, to speak at banquets, to address mothers, to plead for orphans, to go up in balloons, to lead the struggle for sterilized milk. They wanted his photograph for literary supplements, his autograph for charity bazaars, his name on committees, literary, educational, and social; above all, they wanted his opinion on everything: on Christianity, Buddhism, tight lacing, the drug-habit, democratic government, female suffrage and love. Perhaps the chief benefit of this demand was his incidentally learning from it how few opinions he really had: the only one that remained with him was a rooted horror of all forms of correspondence. He had been unutterably thankful when the letters began to fall off.

*Diadems and Faggots* was now two years old, and the moment was at hand when its author might have counted on regaining the blessed shelter of oblivion—if only he had not written another book! For it was the worst part of his plight that his first success had goaded him to the perpetration of this particular folly—that one of the incentives (hideous thought!) to his new work had been the desire to extend and perpetuate his popularity. And this very week the book was to come out, and the letters, the cursed letters, would begin again!

Wistfully, almost plaintively, he contemplated the breakfast-tray with which Strett presently appeared. It bore only two notes and the morning journals, but he knew that within the week it would groan under its epistolary burden. The very newspapers flung the fact at him as he opened them.

READY ON MONDAY.
GEOFFREY BETTON'S NEW NOVEL
ABUNDANCE.
BY THE AUTHOR OF "DIADEMS AND FAGGOTS."
FIRST EDITION OF ONE HUNDRED AND FIFTY THOUSAND
ALREADY SOLD OUT.
ORDER NOW.

A hundred and fifty thousand volumes! And an average of three readers to each! Half a million of people would be reading him within a week, and every one of them would write to him, and their friends and relations would write too. He laid down the paper with a shudder.

The two notes looked harmless enough, and the calligraphy of one was vaguely familiar. He opened the envelope and looked at the signature: *Duncan Vyse*. He had not seen the name in years—what on earth could Duncan Vyse have to say? He ran over the page and dropped it with a wondering exclamation, which the watchful Strett, re-entering, met by a tentative "Yes, sir?"

"Nothing. Yes—that is—" Betton picked up the note. "There's a gentleman, a Mr. Vyse, coming to see me at ten."

Strett glanced at the clock. "Yes, sir. You'll remember that ten was the hour you appointed for the secretaries to call, sir."

Betton nodded. "I'll see Mr. Vyse first. My clothes, please."

As he got into them, in the state of irritable hurry that had become almost chronic with him, he continued to think about Duncan Vyse. They had seen a lot of each other for the few years after both had left Harvard: the hard happy years when Betton had been grinding at his business and Vyse—poor devil!—trying to write. The novelist recalled his friend's attempts with a smile; then the memory of one small volume came back to him. It was a novel: "The Lifted Lamp." There was stuff in that, certainly. He remembered Vyse's tossing it down on his table with a gesture of despair when it came back from the last publisher. Betton, taking it up indifferently, had sat riveted till daylight. When he ended, the impression was so strong that he said to himself: "I'll tell Apthorn about it—I'll go and see him tomorrow." His own secret literary yearnings gave him a passionate desire to champion Vyse, to see him triumph over the ignorance and timidity of the publishers. Apthorn was the youngest of the guild, still capable of opinions and the courage of them, a personal friend of Betton's, and, as it happened, the man afterward to become known as the privileged publisher of *Diadems and Faggots*. Unluckily the next day something unexpected turned up, and Betton forgot about Vyse and his manuscript. He continued to forget for a month, and then came a note from Vyse, who was ill, and wrote to ask what his friend had done. Betton did not like to say "I've done nothing," so he left the note unanswered, and vowed again: "I'll see Apthorn."

The following day he was called to the West on business, and was gone a month. When he came back, there was another note from Vyse, who was still ill, and desperately hard up. "I'll take anything for the book, if they'll advance me two hundred dollars." Betton, full of compunction, would gladly have advanced the sum himself; but he was hard up too, and could only swear inwardly: "I'll write to Apthorn." Then he glanced again at the manuscript, and reflected: "No—there are things in it that need explaining. I'd better see him."

Once he went so far as to telephone Apthorn, but the publisher was out. Then he finally and completely forgot.

One Sunday he went out of town, and on his return, rummaging among the papers on his desk, he missed "The Lifted Lamp," which had been gathering dust there for half a year. What the deuce could have become of it? Betton spent a feverish hour in vainly increasing the disorder of his documents, and then bethought himself of calling the maid-servant, who first indignantly denied having touched anything ("I can see that's true from the dust," Betton scathingly interjected), and then mentioned with hauteur that a young lady had called in his absence and asked to be allowed to get a book.

"A lady? Did you let her come up?"

"She said somebody'd sent her."

Vyse, of course—Vyse had sent her for his manuscript! He was always mixed up with some woman, and it was just like him to send the girl of the moment to Betton's lodgings, with instructions to force the door in his absence. Vyse had never been remarkable for delicacy. Betton, furious, glanced over his table to see if any of his own effects were missing—one couldn't tell, with the company Vyse kept!—and then dismissed the matter from his mind, with a vague sense of magnanimity in doing so. He felt himself exonerated by Vyse's conduct.

The sense of magnanimity was still uppermost when the valet opened the door to announce "Mr. Vyse," and Betton, a moment later, crossed the threshold of his pleasant library.

His first thought was that the man facing him from the hearth-rug was the very Duncan Vyse of old: small, starved, bleached-looking, with the same sidelong movements, the same queer air of anemic truculence. Only he had grown shabbier, and bald.

Betton held out a hospitable hand.

"This is a good surprise! Glad you looked me up, my dear fellow."

Vyse's palm was damp and bony: he had always had a disagreeable hand.

"You got my note? You know what I've come for?" he said.

"About the secretaryship? (Sit down.) Is that really serious?"

Betton lowered himself luxuriously into one of his vast Maple arm-chairs. He had grown stouter in the last year, and the cushion behind him fitted comfortably into the crease of his nape. As he leaned back he caught sight of his image in the mirror between the windows, and reflected uneasily that Vyse would not find *him* unchanged.

"Serious?" Vyse rejoined. "Why not? Aren't *you?*"

"Oh, perfectly." Betton laughed apologetically. "Only—well, the fact is, you may not understand what rubbish a secretary of mine would have to deal with. In advertising for one I never imagined—I didn't aspire to any one above the ordinary hack."

"I'm the ordinary hack," said Vyse drily.

Betton's affable gesture protested. "My dear fellow—. You see it's not business—what I'm in now," he continued with a laugh.

Vyse's thin lips seemed to form a noiseless *"Isn't* it?" which they instantly transposed into the audibly reply: "I inferred from your advertisement that you want some one to relieve you in your literary work. Dictation, short-hand—that kind of thing?"

"Well, no: not that either. I type my own things. What I'm looking for is somebody who won't be above tackling my correspondence."

Vyse looked slightly surprised. "I should be glad of the job," he then said.

Betton began to feel a vague embarrassment. He had supposed that such a proposal would be instantly rejected. "It would be only for an hour or two a day—if you're doing any writing of your own?" he threw out interrogatively.

"No. I've given all that up. I'm in an office now—business. But it doesn't take all my time, or pay enough to keep me alive."

"In that case, my dear fellow—if you could come every morning; but it's mostly awful bosh, you know," Betton again broke off, with growing awkwardness.

Vyse glanced at him humorously. "What you want me to write?"

"Well, that depends—" Betton sketched the obligatory smile. "But I was thinking of the letters you'll have to answer. Letters about my books, you know—I've another one appearing next week. And I want to be beforehand now—dam the flood before it swamps me. Have you any idea of the deluge of stuff that people write to a successful novelist?"

As Betton spoke, he saw a tinge of red on Vyse's thin cheek, and his own reflected it in a richer glow of shame. "I mean—I mean—" he stammered helplessly.

"No, I haven't," said Vyse; "but it will be awfully jolly finding out."

There was a pause, groping and desperate on Betton's part, sardonically calm on his visitor's.

"You—you've given up writing altogether?" Betton continued.

"Yes; we've changed places, as it were." Vyse paused. "But about these letters—you dictate the answers?"

"Lord, no! That's the reason why I said I wanted somebody—er—well used to writing. I don't want to have anything to do with them—not a thing! You'll have to answer them as if they were written to *you*—" Betton pulled himself up again, and rising in confusion jerked open one of the drawers of his writing-table.

"Here—this kind of rubbish," he said, tossing a packet of letters onto Vyse's knee.

"Oh—you keep them, do you?" said Vyse simply.

"I—well—some of them; a few of the funniest only."

Vyse slipped off the band and began to open the letters. While he was glancing over them Betton again caught his own reflection in the glass, and asked himself what impression he had made on his visitor. It occurred to him for the first time that his high-colored well-fed person presented the image of commercial rather than of intellectual achievement. He did not look like his own idea of the author of *Diadems and Faggots*—and he wondered why.

Vyse laid the letters aside. "I think I can do it—if you'll give me a notion of the tone I'm to take."

"The tone?"

"Yes—that is, if I'm to sign your name."

"Oh, of course: I expect you to sign for me. As for the tone, say just what you'd—well, say all you can without encouraging them to answer."

Vyse rose from his seat. "I could submit a few specimens," he suggested.

"Oh, as to that—you always wrote better than I do," said Betton handsomely.

"I've never had this kind of thing to write. When do you wish me to begin?" Vyse enquired, ignoring the tribute.

"The book's out on Monday. The deluge will begin about three days after. Will you turn up on Thursday at this hour?" Betton held his hand out with real heartiness. "It was great luck for me, your striking that advertisement. Don't be too harsh with my correspondents—I owe them something for having brought us together."

## II

THE deluge began punctually on the Thursday, and Vyse, arriving as punctually, had an impressive pile of letters to attack. Betton, on his way to the Park for a ride, came into the library, smoking the cigarette of indolence, to look over his secretary's shoulder.

"How many of 'em? Twenty? Good Lord! It's going to be worse than *Diadems*. I've just had my first quiet breakfast in two years—time to read the papers and loaf. How I used to dread the sight of my letter-box! Now I shan't know I have one."

He leaned over Vyse's chair, and the secretary handed him a letter.

"Here's rather an exceptional one—lady, evidently. I thought you might want to answer it yourself—"

"Exceptional?" Betton ran over the mauve pages and tossed them down. "Why, my dear man, I get hundreds like that. You'll have to be pretty short with her, or she'll send her photograph."

He clapped Vyse on the shoulder and turned away, humming a tune. "Stay to luncheon," he called back gaily from the threshold.

After luncheon Vyse insisted on showing a few of his answers to the first batch of letters. "If I've struck the note I won't bother you again," he urged; and Betton groaningly consented.

"My dear fellow, they're beautiful—too beautiful. I'll be let in for a correspondence with every one of these people."

Vyse, at this, meditated for a while above a blank sheet. "All right—how's this?" he said, after another interval of rapid writing.

Betton glanced over the page. "By George—by George! Won't she *see* it?" he exulted, between fear and rapture.

"It's wonderful how little people see," said Vyse reassuringly.

The letters continued to pour in for several weeks after the appearance of *Abundance*. For five or six blissful days Betton did not even have his mail brought to him, trusting to Vyse to single out his personal correspondence, and to deal with the rest according to their agreement. During those days he luxuriated in a sense of wild and lawless freedom; then, gradually, he began to feel the need of fresh restraints to break, and learned that the zest of liberty lies in the escape from specific obligations. At first he was conscious only of a vague hunger, but in time the craving resolved into a shame-faced desire to see his letters.

"After all, I hated them only because I had to answer them"; and he told Vyse carelessly that he wished all his letters submitted to him before the secretary answered them.

At first he pushed aside those beginning: "I have just laid down *Abundance* after a third reading," or: "Every day for the last month I have been telephoning my bookseller to know when your novel would be out." But little by little the freshness of his interest revived, and even this stereotyped homage began to arrest his eye. At last a day came when he read all the letters, from the first word to the last, as he had done when *Diadems and Faggots* appeared. It was really a pleasure to read them, now that he was relieved of the burden of replying: his new relation to his correspondents had the glow of a love-affair unchilled by the contingency of marriage.

One day it struck him that the letters were coming in more slowly and in smaller numbers. Certainly there had been more of a rush when *Diadems and Faggots* came out. Betton began to wonder if Vyse were exercising an unauthorized discrimination, and keeping back the communications he deemed least important. This sudden conjecture carried the novelist straight to his library, where he found Vyse bending over the writing-table with his usual inscrutable pale smile. But once there, Betton hardly knew how to frame his question, and blundered into an enquiry for a missing invitation.

"There's a note—a personal note—I ought to have had this morning. Sure you haven't kept it back by mistake among the others?"

Vyse laid down his pen. "The others? But I never keep back any."

Betton had foreseen the answer. "Not even the worst twaddle about my book?" he suggested lightly, pushing the papers about.

"Nothing. I understood you wanted to go over them all first."

"Well, perhaps it's safer," Betton conceded, as if the idea were new to him. With an embarrassed hand he continued to turn over the letters at Vyse's elbow.

"Those are yesterday's," said the secretary; "here are to-day's," he added, pointing to a meager trio.

"H'm—only these?" Betton took them and looked them over lingeringly. "I don't see what the deuce that chap means about the first part of *Abundance* 'certainly justifying the title'—do you?"

Vyse was silent, and the novelist continued irritably: "Damned cheek, his writing, if he doesn't like the book. Who cares what he thinks about it, anyhow?"

And his morning ride was embittered by the discovery that it was unexpectedly disagreeable to have Vyse read any letters which did not express unqualified praise of his books. He began to fancy there was a latent rancor, a kind of baffled sneer, under Vyse's manner; and he decided to return to the practice of having his mail brought straight to his room. In that way he could edit the letters before his secretary saw them.

Vyse made no comment on the change, and Betton was reduced to wondering whether his imperturbable composure were the mask of complete indifference or of a watchful jealousy. The latter view being more agreeable to his employer's self-esteem, the next step was to conclude that Vyse had not forgotten the episode of "The Lifted Lamp," and would naturally take a vindictive joy in any unfavorable judgments passed on his rival's work. This did not simplify the situation, for there was no denying that unfavorable criticisms preponderated in Betton's correspondence. *Abundance* was neither meeting with the unrestricted welcome of *Diadems and Faggots*, nor enjoying the alternative of an animated controversy: it was simply found dull, and its readers said so in language not too tactfully tempered by regretful comparisons with its predecessor. To withhold unfavorable comments from Vyse was, therefore, to make it appear that correspondence about the book had died out; and its author, mindful of his unguarded predictions, found this even more embarrassing. The simplest solution would be to get rid of Vyse; and to this end Betton began to address his energies.

One evening, finding himself unexpectedly disengaged, he asked Vyse to dine; it had occurred to him that, in the course of an after-dinner chat, he might delicately hint his feeling that the work he had offered his friend was unworthy so accomplished a hand.

Vyse surprised him by a momentary hesitation. "I may not have time to dress."

Betton stared. "What's the odds? We'll dine here—and as late as you like."

Vyse thanked him, and appeared, punctually at eight, in all the shabbiness of his daily wear. He looked paler and more shyly truculent than usual, and Betton, from the height of his florid stature, said to himself, with the sudden professional instinct for "type": "He might be an agent of something—a chap who carries deadly secrets."

Vyse, it was to appear, did carry a deadly secret; but one less perilous to society than to himself. He was simply poor—inexcusably, irremediably poor. Everything failed him, had always failed him: whatever he put his hand to went to bits.

This was the confession that, reluctantly, yet with a kind of white-lipped bravado, he flung at Betton in answer to the latter's tentative suggestion that, really, the letter-answering job wasn't worth bothering him with—a thing that any typewriter could do.

"If you mean you're paying me more than it's worth, I'll take less," Vyse rushed out after a pause.

"Oh, my dear fellow—" Betton protested, flushing.

"What *do* you mean, then? Don't I answer the letters as you want them answered?"

Betton anxiously stroked his silken ankle. "You do it beautifully, too beautifully. I mean what I say: the work's not worthy of you. I'm ashamed to ask you—"

"Oh, hang shame," Vyse interrupted. "Do you know why I said I shouldn't have time to dress to-night? Because I haven't any evening clothes. As a matter of fact, I haven't much but the clothes I stand in. One thing after another's gone against me; all the infernal ingenuities of chance. It's been a slow Chinese torture, the kind where they keep you alive to have more fun killing you." He straightened himself with a sudden blush. "Oh, I'm all right now—getting on capitally. But I'm still walking rather a narrow plank; and if I do your work well enough—if I take your idea—"

Betton stared into the fire without answering. He knew next to nothing of Vyse's history, of the mischance or mismanagement that had brought him, with his brains and his training, to so unlikely a pass. But a pang of compunction shot through him as he remembered the manuscript of "The Lifted Lamp" gathering dust on his table for half a year.

"Not that it would have made any earthly difference—since he's evidently never been able to get the thing published." But this reflection did not wholly console Betton, and he found it impossible, at the moment, to tell Vyse that his services were not needed.

### III

DURING the ensuing weeks the letters grew fewer and fewer, and Betton foresaw the approach of the fatal day when his secretary, in common decency, would have to say: "I can't draw my pay for doing nothing."

What a triumph for Vyse!

The thought was intolerable, and Betton cursed his weakness in not having dismissed the fellow before such a possibility arose.

"If I tell him I've no use for him now, he'll see straight through it, of course;—and then, hang it, he looks so poor!"

This consideration came after the other, but Betton, in rearranging them, put it first, because he thought it looked better there, and also because he immediately perceived its value in justifying a plan of action that was beginning to take shape in his mind.

"Poor devil, I'm damned if I don't do it for him!" said Betton, sitting down at his desk.

Three or four days later he sent word to Vyse that he didn't care to go over the letters any longer, and that they would once more be carried directly to the library.

The next time he lounged in, on his way to his morning ride, he found his secretary's pen in active motion.

"A lot today," Vyse told him cheerfully.

His tone irritated Betton: it had the inane optimism of the physician reassuring a discouraged patient.

"Oh, Lord—I thought it was almost over," groaned the novelist.

"No: they've just got their second wind. Here's one from a Chicago publisher—never heard the name—offering you thirty per cent. on your next novel, with an advance royalty of twenty thousand. And here's a chap who wants to syndicate it for a bunch of Sunday papers: big offer, too. That's from Ann Arbor. And this—oh, *this* one's funny!"

He held up a small scented sheet to Betton, who made no movement to receive it.

"Funny? Why's it funny?" he growled.

"Well, it's from a girl—a lady—and she thinks she's the only person who understands *Abundance*—has the clue to it. Says she's never seen a book so misrepresented by the critics—"

"Ha, ha! That *is* good!" Betton agreed with too loud a laugh.

"This one's from a lady, too—married woman. Says she's misunderstood, and would like to correspond."

"Oh, Lord," said Betton.—"What are you looking at?" he added sharply, as Vyse continued to bend his blinking gaze on the letters.

"I was only thinking I'd never seen such short letters from women.

Neither one fills the first page."

"Well, what of that?" queried Betton.

Vyse reflected. "I'd like to meet a woman like that," he said wearily; and Betton laughed again.

The letters continued to pour in, and there could be no farther question of dispensing with Vyse's services. But one morning, about three weeks later, the latter asked for a word with his employer, and Betton, on entering the library, found his secretary with half a dozen documents spread out before him.

"What's up?" queried Betton, with a touch of impatience.

Vyse was attentively scanning the outspread letters.

"I don't know: can't make out." His voice had a faint note of embarrassment. "Do you remember a note signed Hester Macklin that came three or four weeks ago? Married— misunderstood—Western army post—wanted to correspond?"

Betton seemed to grope among his memories; then he assented vaguely.

"A short note," Vyse went on: "the whole story in half a page. The shortness struck me so much—and the directness—that I wrote her: wrote in my own name, I mean."

"In your own name?" Betton stood amazed; then he broke into a groan.

"Good Lord, Vyse—you're incorrigible!"

The secretary pulled his thin moustache with a nervous laugh. "If you mean I'm an ass, you're right. Look here." He held out an envelope stamped with the words: "Dead Letter Office." "My effusion has come back to me marked 'unknown.' There's no such person at the address she gave you."

Betton seemed for an instant to share his secretary's embarrassment; then he burst into an uproarious laugh.

"Hoax, was it? That's rough on you, old fellow!"

Vyse shrugged his shoulders. "Yes; but the interesting question is—why on earth didn't *your* answer come back, too?"

"My answer?"

"The official one—the one I wrote in your name. If she's unknown, what's become of *that?*"

Betton stared at him with eyes wrinkled by amusement. "Perhaps she hadn't disappeared then."

Vyse disregarded the conjecture. "Look here—I believe *all* these letters are a hoax," he broke out.

Betton stared at him with a face that turned slowly red and angry.

"What are you talking about? All what letters?"

"These I've spread out here: I've been comparing them. And I believe they're all written by one man."

Burton's redness turned to a purple that made his ruddy moustache seem pale. "What the devil are you driving at?" he asked.

"Well, just look at it," Vyse persisted, still bent above the letters. "I've been studying them carefully—those that have come within the last two or three weeks—and there's a queer likeness in the writing of some of them. The g's are all like corkscrews. And the same phrases keep recurring—the Ann Arbor news-agent uses the same expressions as the President of the Girls' College at Euphorbia, Maine."

Betton laughed. "Aren't the critics always groaning over the shrinkage of the national vocabulary? Of course we all use the same expressions."

"Yes," said Vyse obstinately. "But how about using the same g's?"

Betton laughed again, but Vyse continued without heeding him: "Look here, Betton—could Strett have written them?"

"Strett?" Betton roared. *"Strett?"* He threw himself into his arm-chair to shake out his mirth at greater ease.

"I'll tell you why. Strett always posts all my answers. He comes in for them every day before I leave. He posted the letter to the misunderstood party—the letter from *you* that the Dead Letter Office didn't return. *I* posted my own letter to her; and that came back."

A measurable silence followed the emission of this ingenious conjecture; then Betton observed with gentle irony: "Extremely neat. And of course it's no business of yours to supply any valid motive for this remarkable attention on my valet's part."

Vyse cast on him a slanting glance.

"If you've found that human conduct's generally based on valid motives—!"

"Well, outside of mad-houses it's supposed to be not quite incalculable."

Vyse had an odd smile under his thin moustache. "Every house is a mad-house at some time or another."

Betton rose with a careless shake of the shoulders. "This one will be if I talk to you much longer," he said, moving away with a laugh.

## IV

BETTON did not for a moment believe that Vyse suspected the valet of having written the letters.

"Why the devil don't he say out what he thinks? He was always a tortuous chap," he grumbled inwardly.

The sense of being held under the lens of Vyse's mute scrutiny became more and more exasperating. Betton, by this time, had squared his shoulders to the fact that *Abundance* was a failure with the public: a confessed and glaring failure. The press told him so openly, and his friends emphasized the fact by their circumlocutions and evasions. Betton minded it a good deal more than he had expected, but not nearly as much as he minded Vyse's knowing it. That remained the central twinge in his diffused discomfort. And the problem of getting rid of his secretary once more engaged him.

He had set aside all sentimental pretexts for retaining Vyse; but a practical argument replaced them. "If I ship him now he'll think it's because I'm ashamed to have him see that I'm not getting any more letters."

For the letters had ceased again, almost abruptly, since Vyse had hazarded the conjecture that they were the product of Strett's devoted pen. Betton had reverted only once to the subject—to ask ironically, a day or two later: "Is Strett writing to me as much as ever?"—and, on Vyse's replying with a neutral head-shake, had added with a laugh: "If you suspect *him* you might as well think I write the letters myself!"

"There are very few today," said Vyse, with his irritating evasiveness; and Betton rejoined squarely: "Oh, they'll stop soon. The book's a failure."

A few mornings later he felt a rush of shame at his own tergiversations, and stalked into the library with Vyse's sentence on his tongue.

Vyse started back with one of his anemic blushes. "I was hoping you'd be in. I wanted to speak to you. There've been no letters the last day or two," he explained.

Betton drew a quick breath of relief. The man had some sense of decency, then! He meant to dismiss himself.

"I told you so, my dear fellow; the book's a flat failure," he said, almost gaily.

Vyse made a deprecating gesture. "I don't know that I should regard the absence of letters as the ultimate test. But I wanted to ask you if there isn't something else I can do on the days when there's no writing." He turned his glance toward the book-lined walls. "Don't you want your library catalogued?" he asked insidiously.

"Had it done last year, thanks." Betton glanced away from Vyse's face. It was piteous, how he needed the job!

"I see. ... Of course this is just a temporary lull in the letters. They'll begin again—as they did before. The people who read carefully read slowly—you haven't heard yet what *they* think."

Betton felt a rush of puerile joy at the suggestion. Actually, he hadn't thought of that! "There *was* a big second crop after *Diadems and Faggots*," he mused aloud.

"Of course. Wait and see," said Vyse confidently.

The letters in fact began again—more gradually and in smaller numbers. But their quality was different, as Vyse had predicted. And in two cases Betton's correspondents, not content to compress into one rapid communication the thoughts inspired by his work, developed their views in a succession of really remarkable letters. One of the writers was a professor in a Western college; the other was a girl in Florida. In their language, their point of view, their reasons for appreciating *Abundance*, they differed almost diametrically; but this only made the unanimity of their approval the more striking. The rush of correspondence evoked by Betton's earlier novel had produced nothing so personal, so exceptional as these communications. He had gulped the praise of *Diadems and Faggots* as undiscriminatingly as it was offered; now he knew for the first time the subtler pleasures of the palate. He tried to feign indifference, even to himself; and to Vyse he made no sign. But gradually he felt a desire to know what his secretary thought of the letters, and, above all, what he was saying in reply to them. And he resented acutely the possibility of Vyse's starting one of his clandestine correspondences with the girl in Florida. Vyse's notorious lack of delicacy had never been more vividly present to Betton's imagination; and he made up his mind to answer the letters himself.

He would keep Vyse on, of course: there were other communications that the secretary could attend to. And, if necessary, Betton would invent an occupation: he cursed his stupidity in having betrayed the fact that his books were already catalogued.

Vyse showed no surprise when Betton announced his intention of dealing personally with the two correspondents who showed so flattering a reluctance to take their leave. But Betton immediately read a criticism in his lack of comment, and put forth, on a note of challenge: "After all, one must be decent!"

Vyse looked at him with an evanescent smile. "You'll have to explain that you didn't write the first answers."

Betton halted. "Well—I—I more or less dictated them, didn't I?"

"Oh, virtually, they're yours, of course."

"You think I can put it that way?"

"Why not?" The secretary absently drew an arabesque on the blotting-pad. "Of course they'll keep it up longer if you write yourself," he suggested.

Betton blushed, but faced the issue. "Hang it all, I shan't be sorry. They interest me. They're remarkable letters." And Vyse, without observation, returned to his writings.

The spring, that year, was delicious to Betton. His college professor continued to address him tersely but cogently at fixed intervals, and twice a week eight serried pages came from Florida. There were other letters, too; he had the solace of feeling that at last *Abundance* was making its way, was reaching the people who, as Vyse said, read slowly because they read intelligently. But welcome as were all these proofs of his restored authority they were but the background of his happiness. His life revolved for the moment about the personality of his two chief correspondents. The professor's letters satisfied his craving for intellectual recognition, and the satisfaction he felt in them proved how completely he had lost faith in himself. He blushed to think that his opinion of his work had been swayed by the shallow judgments of a public whose taste he despised. Was it possible that he had allowed himself to think less well of *Abundance* because it was not to the taste of the average novel-reader? Such false humility was less excusable than the crudest appetite for praise: it was ridiculous to try to do conscientious work if one's self-esteem were at the mercy of popular judgments. All this the professor's letters delicately and indirectly conveyed to Betton, with the result that the author of *Abundance* began to recognize in it the ripest flower of his genius.

But if the professor understood his book, the girl in Florida understood *him;* and Betton was fully alive to the superior qualities of discernment which this process implied. For his lovely correspondent his novel was but the starting-point, the pretext of her discourse: he himself was her real object, and he had the delicious sense, as their exchange of thoughts proceeded, that she was interested in *Abundance* because of its author, rather than in the author because of his book. Of course she laid stress on the fact that his ideas were the object of her contemplation; but Betton's agreeable person had permitted him some insight into the incorrigible subjectiveness of female judgments, and he was pleasantly aware, from the lady's tone, that she guessed him to be neither old nor ridiculous. And suddenly he wrote to ask if he might see her. . . .

The answer was long in coming. Betton fumed at the delay, watched, wondered, fretted; then he received the one word "Impossible."

He wrote back more urgently, and awaited the reply with increasing eagerness. A certain shyness had kept him from once more modifying the instructions regarding his mail, and Strett still carried the letters directly to Vyse. The hour when he knew they were passing under the latter's eyes was now becoming intolerable to Betton, and it was a profound relief when the secretary, suddenly advised of his father's illness, asked permission to absent himself for a fortnight.

Vyse departed just after Betton had dispatched to Florida his second missive of entreaty, and for ten days he tasted the furtive joy of a first perusal of his letters. The answer from Florida was not among them; but Betton said to himself "She's thinking it over," and delay, in that light, seemed favorable. So charming, in fact, was this phase of sentimental suspense that he felt a start of resentment when a telegram apprised him one morning that Vyse would return to his post that day.

Betton had slept later than usual, and, springing out of bed with the telegram in his hand, he learned from the clock that his secretary was due in half an hour. He reflected that the morning's mail must long since be in; and, too impatient to wait for its appearance with his breakfast-tray, he threw on a dressing-gown and went to the library. There lay the letters, half a dozen of them: but his eye flew to one envelope, and as he tore it open a warm wave rocked his heart.

The letter was dated a few days after its writer must have received his own: it had all the qualities of grace and insight to which his unknown friend had accustomed him, but it contained no allusion, however indirect, to the special purport of his appeal. Even a vanity less ingenious than Betton's might have read in the lady's silence one of the most familiar motions of consent; but the smile provoked by this inference faded as he turned to his other letters. For the uppermost bore the superscription "Dead Letter Office," and the document that fell from it was his own last letter from Florida.

Betton studied the ironic "Unknown" for an appreciable space of time; then he broke into a laugh. He had suddenly recalled Vyse's similar experience with "Hester Macklin," and the light he was able to throw on that obscure episode was searching enough to penetrate all the dark corners of his own adventure. He felt a rush of heat to the ears; catching sight of himself in the glass, he saw a red ridiculous congested countenance, and dropped into a chair to hide it between flushed fists. He was roused by the opening of the door, and Vyse appeared on the threshold.

"Oh, I beg pardon—you're ill?" said the secretary.

Betton's only answer was an inarticulate murmur of derision; then he pushed forward the letter with the imprint of the Dead Letter Office.

"Look at that," he jeered.

Vyse peered at the envelope, and turned it over slowly in his hands. Betton's eyes, fixed on him, saw his face decompose like a substance touched by some powerful acid. He clung to the envelope as if to gain time.

"It's from the young lady you've been writing to at Swazee Springs?" he asked at length.

"It's from the young lady I've been writing to at Swazee Springs."

"Well—I suppose she's gone away," continued Vyse, rebuilding his countenance rapidly.

"Yes; and in a community numbering perhaps a hundred and seventy-five souls, including the dogs and chickens, the local post-office is so ignorant of her movements that my letter has to be sent to the Dead Letter Office."

Vyse meditated on this; then he laughed in turn. "After all, the same thing happened to me—with 'Hester Macklin,' I mean," he recalled sheepishly.

"Just so," said Betton, bringing down his clenched fist on the table. *"Just so,"* he repeated, in italics.

He caught his secretary's glance, and held it with his own for a moment. Then he dropped it as, in pity, one releases something scared and squirming.

"The very day my letter was returned from Swazee Springs she wrote me this from there," he said, holding up the last Florida missive.

"Ha! That's funny," said Vyse, with a damp forehead.

"Yes, it's funny; it's funny," said Betton. He leaned back, his hands in his pockets, staring up at the ceiling, and noticing a crack in the cornice. Vyse, at the corner of the writing table, waited.

"Shall I get to work?" he began, after a silence measurable by minutes. Betton's gaze descended from the cornice.

"I've got your seat, haven't I?" he said, rising and moving away from the table.

Vyse, with a quick gleam of relief, slipped into the vacant chair, and began to stir about vaguely among the papers.

"How's your father?" Betton asked from the hearth.

"Oh, better—better, thank you. He'll pull out of it."

"But you had a sharp scare for a day or two?"

"Yes—it was touch and go when I got there."

Another pause, while Vyse began to classify the letters.

"And I suppose," Betton continued in a steady tone, "your anxiety made you forget your usual precautions—whatever they were—about this Florida correspondence, and before you'd had time to prevent it the Swazee post-office blundered?"

Vyse lifted his head with a quick movement. "What do you mean?" he asked, pushing back his chair.

"I mean that you saw I couldn't live without flattery, and that you've been ladling it out to me to earn your keep."

Vyse sat motionless and shrunken, digging the blotting-pad with his pen. "What on earth are you driving at?" he repeated.

"Though why the deuce," Betton continued in the same steady tone, "you should need to do this kind of work when you've got such faculties at your service—those letters were magnificent, my dear fellow! Why in the world don't you write novels, instead of writing to other people about them?"

Vyse straightened himself with an effort. "What are you talking about, Betton? Why the devil do you think *I* wrote those letters?"

Betton held back his answer, with a brooding face. "Because I wrote 'Hester Macklin's'—to myself!"

Vyse sat stock-still, without the least outcry of wonder. "Well—?" he finally said, in a low tone.

"And because you found me out (you see, you can't even feign surprise!)—because you saw through it at a glance, knew at once that the letters were faked. And when you'd foolishly put me on my guard by pointing out to me that they were a clumsy forgery, and had then suddenly guessed that *I* was the forger, you drew the natural inference that I had to have popular approval, or at least had to make *you* think I had it. You saw that, to me, the worst thing about the failure of the book was having *you* know it was a failure. And so you applied your superior—your immeasurably superior—abilities to carrying on the humbug, and deceiving me as I'd tried to deceive you. And you did it so successfully that I don't see why the devil you haven't made your fortune writing novels!"

Vyse remained silent, his head slightly bent under the mounting tide of Betton's denunciation.

"The way you differentiated your people—characterized them—avoided my stupid mistake of making the women's letters too short and logical, of letting my different correspondents use the same expressions: the amount of ingenuity and art you wasted on it! I swear, Vyse, I'm sorry that damned post-office went back on you," Betton went on, piling up the waves of his irony.

But at this height they suddenly paused, drew back on themselves, and began to recede before the spectacle of Vyse's pale distress. Something warm and emotional in Betton's nature—a lurking kindliness, perhaps, for any one who tried to soothe and smooth his writhing ego—softened his eye as it rested on the drooping figure of his secretary.

"Look here, Vyse—I'm not sorry—not altogether sorry this has happened!" He moved slowly across the room, and laid a friendly palm on Vyse's shoulder. "In a queer illogical way it evens up things, as it were. I did you a shabby turn once, years ago—oh, out of sheer carelessness, of course—about that novel of yours I promised to give to Apthorn. If I had given it, it might not have made any difference—I'm not sure it wasn't too good for success—but anyhow, I dare say you thought my personal influence might have helped you, might at least have got you a quicker hearing. Perhaps you thought it was because the thing was so good that I kept it back, that I felt some nasty jealousy of your superiority. I swear to you it wasn't that—I clean forgot it. And one day when I came home it was gone: you'd sent and taken it. And I've always thought since you might have owed me a grudge—and not unjustly; so this . . . this business of the letters . . . the sympathy you've shown . . . for I suppose it is sympathy . . . ?"

Vyse startled and checked him by a queer crackling laugh.

"It's *not* sympathy?" broke in Betton, the moisture drying out of his voice. He withdrew his hand from Vyse's shoulder. "What is it, then? The joy of uncovering my nakedness? An eye for an eye? Is it *that?*"

Vyse rose from his seat, and with a mechanical gesture swept into a heap all the letters he had sorted.

"I'm stone-broke, and wanted to keep my job—that's what it is," he said wearily . . .

## THE LEGEND

ARTHUR BERNALD could never afterward recall just when the first conjecture flashed on him: oddly enough, there was no record of it in the agitated jottings of his diary. But, as it seemed to him in retrospect, he had always felt that the queer man at the Wades' must be John Pellerin, if only for the negative reason that he couldn't imaginably be anyone else. It was impossible, in the confused pattern of the century's intellectual life, to fit the stranger in anywhere, save in the big gap which, some five and twenty years earlier, had been left by Pellerin's unaccountable disappearance; and conversely, such a man as the Wades' visitor couldn't have lived for sixty years without filling, somewhere in space, a nearly equivalent void.

At all events, it was certainly not to Doctor Wade or to his mother that Bernald owed the hint: the good unconscious Wades, one of whose chief charms in the young man's eyes was that they remained so robustly untainted by Pellerinism, in spite of the fact that Doctor Wade's younger brother, Howland, was among its most impudently flourishing high-priests.

The incident had begun by Bernald's running across Doctor Robert Wade one hot summer night at the University Club, and by Wade's saying, in the tone of unprofessional laxity which the shadowy stillness of the place invited: "I got hold of a queer fish at St. Martin's the other day—case of heat-prostration picked up in Central Park. When we'd patched him up I found he had nowhere to go, and not a dollar in his pocket, and I sent him down to our place at Portchester to rebuild."

The opening roused his hearer's attention. Bob Wade had an odd unformulated sense of values that Bernald had learned to trust.

"What sort of chap? Young or old?"

"Oh, every age—full of years, and yet with a lot left. He called himself sixty on the books."

"Sixty's a good age for some kinds of living. And age is of course purely subjective. How has he used his sixty years?"

"Well—part of them in educating himself, apparently. He's a scholar—humanities, languages, and so forth."

"Oh—decayed gentleman," Bernald murmured, disappointed.

"Decayed? Not much!" cried the doctor with his accustomed literalness. "I only mentioned that side of Winterman—his name's Winterman—because it was the side my mother noticed first. I suppose women generally do. But it's only a part—a small part. The man's the big thing."

"Really big?"

"Well—there again. … When I took him down to the country, looking rather like a tramp from a 'Shelter,' with an untrimmed beard, and a suit of reach-me-downs he'd slept round the Park in for a week, I felt sure my mother'd carry the silver up to her room, and send for the gardener's dog to sleep in the hall the first night. But she didn't."

"I see. 'Women and children love him.' Oh, Wade!" Bernald groaned.

"Not a bit of it! You're out again. We don't love him, either of us. But we *feel* him—the air's charged with him. You'll see."

And Bernald agreed that he *would* see, the following Sunday. Wade's inarticulate attempts to characterize the stranger had struck his friend. The human revelation had for Bernald a poignant and ever-renewed interest, which his trade, as the dramatic critic of a daily paper, had hitherto failed to discourage. And he knew that Bob Wade, simple and undefiled by literature—Bernald's specific affliction—had a free and personal way of judging men, and the diviner's knack of reaching their hidden springs. During the days that followed, the young doctor gave Bernald farther details about John Winterman: details not of fact—for in that respect his visitor's reticence was baffling—but of impression. It appeared that Winterman, while lying insensible in the Park, had been robbed of the few dollars he possessed; and on leaving the hospital, still weak and half-blind, he had quite simply and unprotestingly accepted the Wades' offer to give him shelter till such time as he should be strong enough to go to work.

"But what's his work?" Bernald interjected. "Hasn't he at least told you that?"

"Well, writing. Some kind of writing." Doctor Bob always became vague and clumsy when he approached the confines of literature. "He means to take it up again as soon as his eyes get right."

Bernald groaned. "Oh, Lord—that finishes him; and *me!* He's looking for a publisher, of course—he wants a 'favorable notice.' I won't come!"

"He hasn't written a line for twenty years."

"A line of *what?* What kind of literature can one keep corked up for twenty years?"

Wade surprised him. "The real kind, I should say. But I don't know Winterman's line," the doctor added. "He speaks of the things he used to write merely as 'stuff that wouldn't sell.' He has a wonderfully confidential way of *not* telling one things. But he says he'll have to do something for his living as soon as his eyes are patched up, and that writing is the only trade he knows. The queer thing is that he seems pretty sure of selling *now*. He even talked of buying the bungalow of us, with an acre or two about it."

"The bungalow? What's that?"

"The studio down by the shore that we built for Howland when he thought he meant to paint." (Howland Wade, as Bernald knew, had experienced various "calls.") "Since he's taken to writing nobody's been near it. I offered it to Winterman, and he camps there—cooks his meals, does his own house-keeping, and never comes up to the house except in the evenings, when he joins us on the verandah, in the dark, and smokes while my mother knits."

"A discreet visitor, eh?"

"More than he need be. My mother actually wanted him to stay on in the house—in her pink chintz room. Think of it! But he says houses smother him. I take it he's lived for years in the open."

"In the open where?"

"I can't make out, except that it was somewhere in the East. 'East of everything—beyond the day-spring. In places not on the map.' That's the way he put it; and when I said: 'You've been an explorer, then?' he smiled in his beard, and answered: 'Yes; that's it—an explorer.' Yet he doesn't strike me as a man of action: hasn't the hands or the eyes."

"What sort of hands and eyes has he?"

Wade reflected. His range of observation was not large, but within its limits it was exact and could give an account of itself.

"He's worked a lot with his hands, but that's not what they were made for. I should say they were extraordinarily delicate conductors of sensation. And his eye—his eye too. He hasn't used it to dominate people: he didn't care to. He simply looks through 'em all like windows. Makes me feel like the fellows who think they're made of glass. The mitigating circumstance is that he seems to see such a glorious landscape through me."

Wade grinned at the thought of serving such a purpose.

"I see. I'll come on Sunday and be looked through!" Bernald cried.

II

BERNALD came on two successive Sundays; and the second time he lingered till the Tuesday.

"Here he comes!" Wade had said, the first evening, as the two young men, with Wade's mother sat in the sultry dusk, with the Virginian creeper drawing, between the verandah arches, its black arabesques against a moon-lined sky.

Bernald heard a step on the gravel, and saw the red flit of a cigar through the shrubs. Then a loosely-moving figure obscured the patch of sky between the creepers, and the red spark became the center of a dim bearded face, in which Bernald discerned only a broad white gleam of forehead.

It was the young man's subsequent impression that Winterman had not spoken much that first evening; at any rate, Bernald himself remembered chiefly what the Wades had said. And this was the more curious because he had come for the purpose of studying their visitor, and because there was nothing to divert him from that purpose in Wade's halting communications or his mother's artless comments. He reflected afterward that there must have been a mysteriously fertilizing quality in the stranger's silence: it had brooded over their talk like a large moist cloud above a dry country.

Mrs. Wade, apparently apprehensive lest her son should have given Bernald an exaggerated notion of their visitor's importance, had hastened to qualify it before the latter appeared.

"He's not what you or Howland would call intellectual—"(Bernald writhed at the coupling of the names)—"not in the least *literary;* though he told Bob he used to write. I don't think, though, it could have been what Howland would call writing." Mrs. Wade always mentioned her younger son with a reverential drop of the voice. She viewed literature much as she did Providence, as an inscrutably mystery; and she spoke of Howland as a dedicated being, set apart to perform secret rites within the veil of the sanctuary.

"I shouldn't say he had a quick mind," she continued, reverting apologetically to Winterman. "Sometimes he hardly seems to follow what we're saying. But he's got such sound ideas—when he does speak he's never silly. And clever people sometimes *are,* don't you think so?" Bernald groaned an unqualified assent. "And he's so capable. The other day something went wrong with the kitchen range, just as I was expecting some friends of Bob's for dinner; and do you know, when Mr. Winterman heard we were in trouble, he came and took a look, and knew at once what to do? I told him it was a dreadful pity he wasn't married!"

Close on midnight, when the session on the verandah ended, and the two young men were strolling down to the bungalow at Winterman's side, Bernald's mind reverted to the image of the fertilizing cloud. There was something brooding, pregnant, in the silent presence beside him: he had, in place of any circumscribing impression of the individual, a large hovering sense of manifold latent meanings. And he felt a distinct thrill of relief when, half-way down the lawn, Doctor Bob was checked by a voice that called him back to the telephone.

"Now I'll be with him alone!" thought Bernald, with a throb like a lover's.

Under the low rafters of the bungalow Winterman had to grope for the lamp on his desk, and as its light struck up into his face Bernald's sense of the rareness of his opportunity increased. He couldn't have said why, for the face, with its ridged brows, its shabby greyish beard and blunt Socratic nose, made no direct appeal to the eye. It seemed rather like a stage on which remarkable things might be enacted, like some shaggy moorland landscape dependent for form and expression on the clouds rolling over it, and the bursts of light between; and one of these flashed out in the smile with which Winterman, as if in answer to his companion's thought, said simply, as he turned to fill his pipe: "Now we'll talk."

So he'd known all along that they hadn't yet—and had guessed that, with Bernald, one might!

The young man's glow of pleasure was so intense that it left him for a moment unable to meet the challenge; and in that moment he felt the brush of something winged and summoning. His spirit rose to it with a rush; but just as he felt himself poised between the ascending pinions, the door opened and Bob Wade plunged in.

"Too bad! I'm sorry! It was from Howland, to say he can't come tomorrow after all." The doctor panted out his news with honest grief.

"I tried my best to pull it off for you; and my brother wants to come—he's keen to talk to you and see what he can do. But you see he's so tremendously in demand. He'll try for another Sunday later on."

Winterman gave an untroubled nod. "Oh, he'll find me here. I shall work my time out slowly." He pointed to the scattered sheets on the kitchen table which formed his writing desk.

"Not slowly enough to suit us," Wade answered hospitably. "Only, if Howland could have come he might have given you a tip or two—put you on the right track—shown you how to get in touch with the public."

Winterman, his hands in his sagging pockets, lounged against the bare pine walls, twisting his pipe under his beard. "Does your brother enjoy the privilege of that contact?" he questioned gravely.

Wade stared a little. "Oh, of course Howland's not what you'd call a *popular* writer; he despises that kind of thing. But whatever he says goes with—well, with the chaps that count; and everyone tells me he's written the book on Pellerin. You must read it when you get back your eyes." He paused, as if to let the name sink in, but Winterman drew at his pipe with a blank face. "You must have heard of Pellerin, I suppose?" the doctor continued. "I've never read a word of him myself: he's too big a proposition for *me*. But one can't escape the talk about him. I have him crammed down my throat even in hospital. The internes read him at the clinics. He tumbles out of the nurses' pockets. The patients keep him under their pillows. Oh, with most of them, of course, it's just a craze, like the last new game or puzzle: they don't understand him in the least. Howland says that even now, twenty-five years after his death, and with his books in everybody's hands, there are not twenty people who really understand Pellerin; and Howland ought to know, if anybody does. He's—what's their great word?—*interpreted* him. You must get Howland to put you through a course of Pellerin."

And as the young men, having taken leave of Winterman, retraced their way across the lawn, Wade continued to develop the theme of his brother's accomplishments.

"I wish I *could* get Howland to take an interest in Winterman: this is the third Sunday he's chucked us. Of course he does get bored with people consulting him about their writings—but I believe if he could only talk to Winterman he'd see something in him, as we do. And it would be such a god-send to the poor man to have some one to advise him about his work. I'm going to make a desperate effort to get Howland here next Sunday."

It was then that Bernald vowed to himself that he would return the next Sunday at all costs. He hardly knew whether he was prompted by the impulse to shield Winterman from Howland Wade's ineptitude, or by the desire to see the latter abandon himself to the full shamelessness of its display; but of one fact he was blissfully assured—and that was of the existence in Winterman of some quality which would provoke Howland to the amplest exercise of his fatuity. "How he'll draw him—how he'll draw him!" Bernald chuckled, with a security the more unaccountable that his one glimpse of Winterman had shown the latter only as a passive subject for experimentation; and he felt himself avenged in advance for the injury of Howland Wade's existence.

### III

THAT this hope was to be frustrated Bernald learned from Howland Wade's own lips, the day before the two young men were to meet at Portchester.

"I can't really, my dear fellow," the Interpreter lisped, passing a polished hand over the faded smoothness of his face. "Oh, an authentic engagement, I assure you: otherwise, to oblige old Bob I'd submit cheerfully to looking over his foundling's literature. But I'm pledged this week to the Pellerin Society of Kenosha: I had a hand in founding it, and for two years now they've been patiently waiting for a word from me—the *Fiat Lux*, so to speak. You see it's a ministry, Bernald—I assure you, I look upon my calling quite religiously."

As Bernald listened, his disappointment gradually changed to relief. Howland, on trial, always turned out to be too insufferable, and the pleasure of watching his antics was invariably lost in the impulse to put a sanguinary end to them.

"If he'd only keep his beastly pink hands off Pellerin," Bernald groaned, thinking of the thick manuscript condemned to perpetual incarceration in his own desk by the publication of Howland's "definitive" work on the great man. One couldn't, *after* Howland Wade, expose one's self to the derision of writing about Pellerin: the eagerness with which Wade's book had been devoured proved, not that the public had enough appetite for another, but simply that, for a stomach so undiscriminating, anything better than Wade had given it would be too good. And Bernald, in the confidence that his own work was open to this objection, had stoically locked it up. Yet if he had resigned his exasperated intelligence to the fact that Wade's book existed, and was already passing into the immortality of perpetual republication, he could not, after repeated trials, adjust himself to the author's talk about Pellerin. When Wade wrote of the great dead he was egregious, but in conversation he was familiar and fond. It might have been supposed that one of the beauties of Pellerin's hidden life and mysterious taking off would have been to guard him from the fingering of anecdote; but biographers like Howland Wade were born to rise above such obstacles. He might be vague or inaccurate in dealing with the few recorded events of his subject's life; but when he left fact for conjecture no one had a firmer footing. Whole chapters in his volume were constructed in the conditional mood and packed with hypothetical detail; and in talk, by the very law of the process, hypothesis became affirmation, and he was ready to tell you confidentially the exact circumstances of Pellerin's death, and of the "distressing incident" leading up to it. Bernald himself not only questioned the form under which this incident was shaping itself before posterity, but the mere radical fact of its occurrence: he had never been able to discover any break in the dense cloud enveloping Pellerin's later life and its mysterious termination. He had gone away—that was all that any of them knew: he who had so little, at any time, been with them or of them; and his going had so slightly stirred the public consciousness that even the subsequent news of his death, laconically imparted from afar, had dropped unheeded into the universal scrap-basket, to be long afterward fished out, with all its details missing, when some enquiring spirit first became aware, by chance encounter with a two-penny volume in a London book-stall, not only that such a man as John Pellerin had died, but that he had ever lived, or written.

It need hardly be noted that Howland Wade had not been the pioneer in question: his had been the wiser part of swelling the chorus when it rose, and gradually drowning the other voices by his own insistent note. He had pitched the note so screamingly, and held it so long, that he was now the accepted authority on Pellerin, not only in the land which had given birth to his genius but in the Europe which had first acclaimed it; and it was the central point of pain in Bernald's sense of the situation that a man who had so yearned for silence as Pellerin should have his grave piped over by such a voice as Wade's.

Bernald's talk with the Interpreter had revived this ache to the momentary exclusion of other sensations; and he was still sore with it when, the next afternoon, he arrived at Portchester for his second Sunday with the Wades.

At the station he had the surprise of seeing Winterman's face on the platform, and of hearing from him that Doctor Bob had been called away to assist at an operation in a distant town.

"Mrs. Wade wanted to put you off, but I believe the message came too late; so she sent me down to break the news to you," said Winterman, holding out his hand.

Perhaps because they were the first conventional words that Bernald had heard him speak, the young man was struck by the relief his intonation gave them.

"She wanted to send a carriage," Winterman added, "but I told her we'd walk back through the woods." He looked at Bernald with a sudden kindness that flushed the young man with pleasure.

"Are you strong enough? It's not too far?"

"Oh, no. I'm pulling myself together. Getting back to work is the slowest part of the business: not on account of my eyes—I can use them now, though not for reading; but some of the links between things are missing. It's a kind of broken spectrum … here, that boy will look after your bag."

The walk through the woods remained in Bernald's memory as an enchanted hour. He used the word literally, as descriptive of the way in which Winterman's contact changed the face of things, or perhaps restored them to their primitive meanings. And the scene they traversed—one of those little untended woods that still, in America, fringe the tawdry skirts of civilization—acquired, as a background to Winterman, the hush of a spot aware of transcendent visitings. Did he talk, or did he make Bernald talk? The young man never knew. He recalled only a sense of lightness and liberation, as if the hard walls of individuality had melted, and he were merged in the poet's deeper interfusion, yet without losing the least sharp edge of self. This general impression resolved itself afterward into the sense of Winterman's wide elemental range. His thought encircled things like the horizon at sea. He didn't, as it happened, touch on lofty themes—Bernald was gleefully aware that, to Howland Wade, their talk would hardly have been Talk at all—but Winterman's mind, applied to lowly topics, was like a powerful lens that brought out microscopic delicacies and differences.

The lack of Sunday trains kept Doctor Bob for two days on the scene of his surgical duties, and during those two days Bernald seized every moment of communion with his friend's guest. Winterman, as Wade had said, was reticent as to his personal affairs, or rather as to the practical and material conditions to which the term is generally applied. But it was evident that, in Winterman's case, the usual classification must be reversed, and that the discussion of ideas carried one much farther into his intimacy than any specific acquaintance with the incidents of his life.

"That's exactly what Howland Wade and his tribe have never understood about Pellerin: that it's much less important to know how, or even why, he disapp—"

Bernald pulled himself up with a jerk, and turned to look full at his companion. It was late on the Monday evening, and the two men, after an hour's chat on the verandah to the tune of Mrs. Wade's knitting-needles, had bidden their hostess good-night and strolled back to the bungalow together.

"Come and have a pipe before you turn in," Winterman had said; and they had sat on together till midnight, with the door of the bungalow open on a heaving moonlit bay, and summer insects bumping against the chimney of the lamp. Winterman had just bent down to re-fill his pipe from the jar on the table, and Bernald, jerking about to catch him in the yellow circle of lamplight, sat speechless, staring at a fact that seemed suddenly to have substituted itself for Winterman's face, or rather to have taken on its features.

"No, they never saw that Pellerin's ideas *were* Pellerin. ..." He continued to stare at Winterman. "Just as this man's ideas are—why, are Pellerin!"

The thought uttered itself in a kind of inner shout, and Bernald started upright with the violent impact of his conclusion. Again and again in the last forty-eight hours he had exclaimed to himself: "This is as good as Pellerin." Why hadn't he said till now: "This is Pellerin"? . . . Surprising as the answer was, he had no choice but to take it. He hadn't said so simply because Winterman was *better than Pellerin*—that there was so much more of him, so to speak. Yes; but—it came to Bernald in a flash—wouldn't there by this time have been any amount more of Pellerin? . . . The young man felt actually dizzy with the thought. That was it—there was the solution of the haunting problem! This man was Pellerin, and more than Pellerin! It was so fantastic and yet so unanswerable that he burst into a sudden startled laugh.

Winterman, at the same moment, brought his palm down with a sudden crash on the pile of manuscript covering the desk.

"What's the matter?" Bernald gasped.

"My match wasn't out. In another minute the destruction of the library of Alexandria would have been a trifle compared to what you'd have seen." Winterman, with his large deep laugh, shook out the smoldering sheets. "And I should have been a pensioner on Doctor Bob the Lord knows how much longer!"

Bernald pulled himself together. "You've really got going again? The thing's actually getting into shape?"

"This particular thing *is* in shape. I drove at it hard all last week, thinking our friend's brother would be down on Sunday, and might look it over."

Bernald had to repress the tendency to another wild laugh.

"Howland—you meant to show *Howland* what you've done?"

Winterman, looming against the moonlight, slowly turned a dusky shaggy head toward him.

"Isn't it a good thing to do?"

Bernald wavered, torn between loyalty to his friends and the grotesqueness of answering in the affirmative. After all, it was none of his business to furnish Winterman with an estimate of Howland Wade.

"Well, you see, you've never told me what your line *is*," he answered, temporizing.

"No, because nobody's ever told *me*. It's exactly what I want to find out," said the other genially.

"And you expect Wade—?"

"Why, I gathered from our good Doctor that it's his trade. Doesn't he explain—interpret?"

"In his own domain—which is Pellerinism."

Winterman gazed out musingly upon the moon-touched dusk of waters.

"And what *is* Pellerinism?" he asked.

Bernald sprang to his feet with a cry. "Ah, I don't know—but you're Pellerin!"

They stood for a minute facing each other, among the uncertain swaying shadows of the room, with the sea breathing through it as something immense and inarticulate breathed through young Bernald's thoughts; then Winterman threw up his arms with a humorous gesture.

"Don't shoot!" he said.

## IV

DAWN found them there, and the risen sun laid its beams on the rough floor of the bungalow, before either of the men was conscious of the passage of time. Bernald, vaguely trying to define his own state in retrospect, could only phrase it: "I floated ... floated. ..."

The gist of fact at the core of the extraordinary experience was simply that John Pellerin, twenty-five years earlier, had voluntarily disappeared, causing the rumour of his death to be reported to an inattentive world; and that now he had come back to see what that world had made of him.

"You'll hardly believe it of me; I hardly believe it of myself; but I went away in a rage of disappointment, of wounded pride—no, vanity! I don't know which cut deepest—the sneers or the silence—but between them, there wasn't an inch of me that wasn't raw. I had just the one thing in me: the message, the cry, the revelation. But nobody saw and nobody listened. Nobody wanted what I had to give. I was like a poor devil of a tramp looking for shelter on a bitter night, in a town with every door bolted and all the windows dark. And suddenly I felt that the easiest thing would be to lie down and go to sleep in the snow. Perhaps I'd a vague notion that if they found me there at daylight, frozen stiff, the pathetic spectacle might produce a reaction, a feeling of remorse. . . . So I took care to be found! Well, a good many thousand people die every day on the face of the globe; and I soon discovered that I was simply one of the thousands; and when I made that discovery I really died—and stayed dead a year or two. . . . When I came to life again I was off on the under side of the world, in regions unaware of what we know as 'the public.' Have you any notion how it shifts the point of view to wake under new constellations? I advise any who's been in love with a woman under Cassiopeia to go and think about her under the Southern Cross. . . . It's the only way to tell the pivotal truths from the others. . . . I didn't believe in my theory any less—there was my triumph and my vindication! It held out, resisted, measured itself with the stars. But I didn't care a snap of my finger whether anybody else believed in it, or even knew it had been formulated. It escaped out of my books—my poor still-born books—like Psyche from the chrysalis and soared away into the blue, and lived there. I knew then how it frees an idea to be ignored; how apprehension circumscribes and deforms it. . . . Once I'd learned that, it was easy enough to turn to and shift for myself. I was sure now that my idea would live: the good ones are self-supporting. I had to learn to be so; and I tried my hand at a number of things . . . adventurous, menial, commercial. . . . It's not a bad thing for a man to have to live his life—and we nearly all manage to dodge it. Our first round with the Sphinx may strike something out of us—a book or a picture or a symphony; and we're amazed at our feat, and go on letting that first work breed others, as some animal forms reproduce each other without renewed fertilization. So there we are, committed to our first guess at the riddle; and our works look as like as successive impressions of the same plate, each with the lines a little fainter; whereas they ought to be—if we touch earth between times—as different from each other as those other creatures—jellyfish, aren't they, of a kind?—where successive generations produce new forms, and it takes a zoologist to see the hidden likeness. . . .

"Well, I proved my first guess, off there in the wilds, and it lived, and grew, and took care of itself. And I said 'Some day it will make itself heard; but by that time my atoms will have waltzed into a new pattern.' Then, in Cashmere one day, I met a fellow in a caravan, with a dog-eared book in his pocket. He said he never stirred without it—wanted to know where I'd been, never to have heard of it. It was *my guess*—in its twentieth edition! . . . The globe spun round at that, and all of a sudden I was under the old stars. That's the way it happens when the ballast of vanity shifts! I'd lived a third of a life out there, unconscious of human opinion—because I supposed it was unconscious of *me*. But now—now! Oh, it was different. I wanted to know what they said. . . . Not exactly that, either: I wanted to know *what I'd made them say*. There's a difference. . . . And here I am," said John Pellerin, with a pull at his pipe.

So much Bernald retained of his companion's actual narrative; the rest was swept away under the tide of wonder that rose and submerged him as Pellerin—at some indefinitely later stage of their talk—picked up his manuscript and began to read. Bernald sat opposite, his elbows propped on the table, his eyes fixed on the swaying waters outside, from which the moon gradually faded, leaving them to make a denser blackness in the night. As Pellerin read, this density of blackness—which never for a moment seemed inert or unalive—was attenuated by imperceptible degrees, till a greyish pallor replaced it; then the pallor breathed and brightened, and suddenly dawn was on the sea.

Something of the same nature went on in the young man's mind while he watched and listened. He was conscious of a gradually withdrawing light, of an interval of obscurity full of the stir of invisible forces, and then of the victorious flush of day. And as the light rose, he saw how far he had travelled and what wonders the night had prepared. Pellerin had been right in saying that his first idea had survived, had borne the test of time; but he had given his hearer no hint of the extent to which it had been enlarged and modified, of the fresh implications it now unfolded. In a brief flash of retrospection Bernald saw the earlier books dwindle and fall into their place as mere precursors of this fuller revelation; then, with a leap of helpless rage, he pictured Howland Wade's pink hands on the new treasure, and his prophetic feet upon the lecture platform.

"IT won't do—oh, he let him down as gently as possible; but it appears it simply won't do."

Doctor Bob imparted the ineluctable fact to Bernald while the two men, accidentally meeting at their club a few nights later, sat together over the dinner they had immediately agreed to share.

Bernald had left Portchester the morning after his strange discovery, and he and Bob Wade had not seen each other since. And now Bernald, moved by an irresistible instinct of postponement, had waited for his companion to bring up Winterman's name, and had even executed several conversational diversions in the hope of delaying its mention. For how could one talk of Winterman with the thought of Pellerin swelling one's breast?

"Yes; the very day Howland got back from Kenosha I brought the manuscript to town, and got him to read it. And yesterday evening I nailed him, and dragged an answer out of him."

"Then Howland hasn't seen Winterman yet?"

"No. He said: 'Before you let him loose on me I'll go over the stuff, and see if it's at all worth while.'"

Bernald drew a freer breath. "And he found it wasn't?"

"Between ourselves, he found it was of no account at all. Queer, isn't it, when the *man* . . . but of course literature's another proposition. Howland says it's one of the cases where an idea might seem original and striking if one didn't happen to be able to trace its descent. And this is straight out of bosh—by Pellerin. . . . Yes: Pellerin. It seems that everything in the article that isn't pure nonsense is just Pellerinism. Howland thinks poor Winterman must have been tremendously struck by Pellerin's writings, and have lived too much out of the world to know that they've become the text-books of modern thought. Otherwise, of course, he'd have taken more trouble to disguise his plagiarisms."

"I see," Bernald mused. "Yet you say there is an original element?"

"Yes; but unluckily it's no good."

"It's not—conceivably—in any sense a development of Pellerin's idea: a logical step farther?"

*"Logical?* Howland says it's twaddle at white heat."

Bernald sat silent, divided between the fierce satisfaction of seeing the Interpreter rush upon his fate, and the despair of knowing that the state of mind he represented was indestructible. Then both emotions were swept away on a wave of pure joy, as he reflected that now, at last, Howland Wade had given him back John Pellerin.

The possession was one he did not mean to part with lightly; and the dread of its being torn from him constrained him to extraordinary precautions.

"You've told Winterman, I suppose? How did he take it?"

"Why, unexpectedly, as he does most things. You can never tell which way he'll jump. I thought he'd take a high tone, or else laugh it off; but he did neither. He seemed awfully cast down. I wished myself well out of the job when I saw how cut up he was."

Bernald thrilled at the words. Pellerin had shared his pang, then—the "old woe of the world" at the perpetuity of human dullness!

"But what did he say to the charge of plagiarism—if you made it?"

"Oh, I told him straight out what Howland said. I thought it fairer. And his answer to that was the rummest part of all."

"What was it?" Bernald questioned, with a tremor.

"He said: 'That's queer, for I've never read Pellerin.'"

Bernald drew a deep breath of ecstasy. "Well—and I suppose you believed him?"

"I believed him, because I know him. But the public won't—the critics won't. And if it's a pure coincidence it's just as bad for him as if it were a straight steal—isn't it?"

Bernald sighed his acquiescence.

"It bothers me awfully," Wade continued, knitting his kindly brows, "because I could see what a blow it was to him. He's got to earn his living, and I don't suppose he knows how to do anything else. At his age it's hard to start fresh. I put that to Howland—asked him if there wasn't a chance he might do better if he only had a little encouragement. I can't help feeling he's got the essential thing in him. But of course I'm no judge when it comes to books. And Howland says it would be cruel to give him any hope." Wade paused, turned his wineglass about under a meditative stare, and then leaned across the table toward Bernald. "Look here—do you know what I've proposed to Winterman? That he should come to town with me tomorrow and go in the evening to hear Howland lecture to the Uplift Club. They're to meet at Mrs. Beecher Bain's, and Howland is to repeat the lecture that he gave the other day before the Pellerin Society at Kenosha. It will give Winterman a chance to get some notion of what Pellerin was: he'll get it much straighter from Howland than if he tried to plough through Pellerin's books. And then afterward—as if accidentally—I thought I might bring him and Howland together. If Howland could only see him and hear him talk, there's no knowing what might come of it. He couldn't help feeling the man's force, as we do; and he might give him a pointer—tell him what line to take. Anyhow, it would please Winterman, and take the edge off his disappointment. I saw that as soon as I proposed it."


"Someone who's never heard of Pellerin?"

Mrs. Beecher Bain, large, smiling, diffuse, reached out parenthetically from the incoming throng on her threshold to waylay Bernald with the question as he was about to move past her in the wake of his companion.

"Oh, keep straight on, Mr. Winterman!" she interrupted herself to call after the latter. "Into the back drawing-room, please! And remember, you're to sit next to me—in the corner on the left, close under the platform."

She renewed her interrogative clutch on Bernald's sleeve. "Most curious! Doctor Wade has been telling me all about him—how remarkable you all think him. And it's actually true that he's never heard of Pellerin? Of course as soon as Doctor Wade told me *that*, I said 'Bring him!' It will be so extraordinarily interesting to watch the first impression.—Yes, do follow him, dear Mr. Bernald, and be sure that you and he secure the seats next to me. Of course Alice Fosdick insists on being with us. She was wild with excitement when I told her she was to meet some one who'd never heard of Pellerin!"

On the indulgent lips of Mrs. Beecher Bain conjecture speedily passed into affirmation; and as Bernald's companion, broad and shaggy in his visibly new evening clothes, moved down the length of the crowded rooms, he was already, to the ladies drawing aside their skirts to let him pass, the interesting Huron of the fable.

How far he was aware of the character ascribed to him it was impossible for Bernald to discover. He was as unconscious as a tree or a cloud, and his observer had never known anyone so alive to human contacts and yet so secure from them. But the scene was playing such a lively tune on Bernald's own sensibilities that for the moment he could not adjust himself to the probable effect it produced on his companion. The young man, of late, had made but rare appearances in the group of which Mrs. Beecher Bain was one of the most indefatigable hostesses, and the Uplift Club the chief medium of expression. To a critic, obliged by his trade to cultivate convictions, it was the essence of luxury to leave them at home in his hours of ease; and Bernald gave his preference to circles in which less finality of judgment prevailed, and it was consequently less embarrassing to be caught without an opinion.

But in his fresher days he had known the spell of the Uplift Club and the thrill of moving among the Emancipated; and he felt an odd sense of rejuvenation as he looked at the rows of faces packed about the embowered platform from which Howland Wade was presently to hand down the eternal verities. Many of these countenances belonged to the old days, when the gospel of Pellerin was unknown, and it required considerable intellectual courage to avow one's acceptance of the very doctrines he had since demolished. The latter moral revolution seemed to have been accepted as submissively as a change in hair-dressing; and it even struck Bernald that, in the case of many of the assembled ladies, their convictions were rather newer than their clothes.

One of the most interesting examples of this facility of adaptation was actually, in the person of Miss Alice Fosdick, brushing his elbow with exotic amulets, and enveloping him in Arabian odors, as she leaned forward to murmur her sympathetic sense of the situation. Miss Fosdick, who was one of the most advanced exponents of Pellerinism, had large eyes and a plaintive mouth, and Bernald had always fancied that she might have been pretty if she had not been perpetually explaining things.

"Yes, I know—Isabella Bain told me all about him. (He can't hear us, can he?) And I wonder if you realize how remarkably interesting it is that we should have such an opportunity *now*—I mean the opportunity to see the impression of Pellerinism on a perfectly fresh mind. (You must introduce him as soon as the lecture's over.) I explained that to Isabella as soon as she showed me Doctor Wade's note. Of course you see why, don't you?" Bernald made a faint motion of acquiescence, which she instantly swept aside. "At least I think I can *make you see why*. (If you're sure he can't hear?) Why, it's just this—Pellerinism is in danger of becoming a truism. Oh, it's an awful thing to say! But then I'm not afraid of saying awful things! I rather believe it's my mission. What I mean is, that we're getting into the way of taking Pellerin for granted—as we do the air we breathe. We don't sufficiently lead our *conscious life* in him—we're gradually letting him become subliminal." She swayed closer to the young man, and he saw that she was making a graceful attempt to throw her explanatory net over his companion, who, evading Mrs. Bain's hospitable signal, had cautiously wedged himself into a seat between Bernald and the wall.

"*Did* you hear what I was saying, Mr. Winterman? (Yes, I know who you are, of course!) Oh, well, I don't really mind if you did. I was talking about you—about you and Pellerin. I was explaining to Mr. Bernald that what we need at this very minute is a Pellerin revival; and we need someone like you—to whom his message comes as a wonderful new interpretation of life—to lead the revival, and rouse us out of our apathy. . . .

"You see," she went on winningly, "it's not only the big public that needs it (of course *their* Pellerin isn't ours!) It's we, his disciples, his interpreters, who discovered him and gave him to the world—we, the Chosen People, the Custodians of the Sacred Books, as Howland Wade calls us—it's *we*, who are in perpetual danger of sinking back into the old stagnant ideals, and practicing the Seven Deadly Virtues; it's we who need to count our mercies, and realize anew what he's done for us, and what we ought to do for him!

And it's for that reason that I urged Mr. Wade to speak here, in the very inner sanctuary of Pellerinism, exactly as he would speak to the uninitiated—to repeat, simply, his Kenosha lecture, 'What Pellerinism means'; and we ought all, I think, to listen to him with the hearts of little children—just as *you* will, Mr. Winterman—as if he were telling us new things, and we—"

"Alice, *dear—*" Mrs. Bain murmured with a deprecating gesture; and Howland Wade, emerging between the palms, took the center of the platform.

A pang of commiseration shot through Bernald as he saw him there, so innocent and so exposed. His plump pulpy body, which made his evening dress fall into intimate and wrapper-like folds, was like a wide surface spread to the shafts of irony; and the mild ripples of his voice seemed to enlarge the vulnerable area as he leaned forward, poised on confidential finger-tips, to say persuasively: "Let me try to tell you what Pellerinism means."

Bernald moved restlessly in his seat. He had the obscure sense of being a party to something not wholly honorable. He ought not to have come; he ought not to have let his companion come. Yet how could he have done otherwise? John Pellerin's secret was his own. As long as he chose to remain John Winterman it was no one's business to gainsay him; and Bernald's scruples were really justifiable only in respect of his own presence on the scene. But even in this connection he ceased to feel them as soon as Howland Wade began to speak.

## VI

IT had been arranged that Pellerin, after the meeting of the Uplift Club, should join Bernald at his rooms and spend the night there, instead of returning to Portchester. The plan had been eagerly elaborated by the young man, but he had been unprepared for the alacrity with which his wonderful friend accepted it. He was beginning to see that it was a part of Pellerin's wonderfulness to fall in, quite simply and naturally, with any arrangements made for his convenience, or tending to promote the convenience of others. Bernald felt that his extreme docility in such matters was proportioned to the force of resistance which, for nearly half a life-time, had kept him, with his back to the wall, fighting alone against the powers of darkness. In such a scale of values how little the small daily alternatives must weigh!

At the close of Howland Wade's discourse, Bernald, charged with his prodigious secret, had felt the need to escape for an instant from the liberated rush of talk. The interest of watching Pellerin was so perilously great that the watcher felt it might, at any moment, betray him. He lingered in the crowded drawing-room long enough to see his friend enclosed in a mounting tide, above which Mrs. Beecher Bain and Miss Fosdick actively waved their conversational tridents; then he took refuge, at the back of the house, in a small dim library where, in his younger days, he had discussed personal immortality and the problem of consciousness with beautiful girls whose names he could not remember.

In this retreat he surprised Mr. Beecher Bain, a quiet man with a mild brow, who was smoking a surreptitious cigar over the last number of the *Strand*. Mr. Bain, at Bernald's approach, dissembled the Strand under a copy of the *Hibbert Journal*, but tendered his cigar-case with the remark that stocks were heavy again; and Bernald blissfully abandoned himself to this unexpected contact with reality.

On his return to the drawing-room he found that the tide had set toward the supper-table, and when it finally carried him thither it was to land him in the welcoming arms of Bob Wade.

"Hullo, old man! Where have you been all this time?—Winterman? Oh, *he's* talking to Howland: yes, I managed it finally. I believe Mrs. Bain has steered them into the library, so that they shan't be disturbed. I gave her an idea of the situation, and she was awfully kind. We'd better leave them alone, don't you think? I'm trying to get a croquette for Miss Fosdick."

Bernald's secret leapt in his bosom, and he devoted himself to the task of distributing sandwiches and champagne while his pulses danced to the tune of the cosmic laughter. The vision of Pellerin and his Interpreter, face to face at last, had a Cyclopean grandeur that dwarfed all other comedy. "And I shall hear of it presently; in an hour or two he'll be telling me about it. And that hour will be all mine—mine and his!" The dizziness of the thought made it difficult for Bernald to preserve the balance of the supper-plates he was distributing. Life had for him at that moment the completeness which seems to defy disintegration.

The throng in the dining-room was thickening, and Bernald's efforts as purveyor were interrupted by frequent appeals, from ladies who had reached repleteness, that he should sit down a moment and tell them all about his interesting friend. Winterman's fame, trumpeted abroad by Miss Fosdick, had reached the four corners of the Uplift Club, and Bernald found himself fabricating *de toutes pièces* a Winterman legend which should in some degree respond to the Club's demand for the human document. When at length he had acquitted himself of this obligation, and was free to work his way back through the lessening groups into the drawing-room, he was at last rewarded by a glimpse of his friend, who, still densely encompassed, towered in the center of the room in all his sovereign ugliness.

Their eyes met across the crowd; but Bernald gathered only perplexity from the encounter. What were Pellerin's eyes saying to him? What orders, what confidences, what indefinable apprehension did their long look impart? The young man was still trying to decipher their complex message when he felt a tap on the arm, and turned to encounter the rueful gaze of Bob Wade, whose meaning lay clearly enough on the surface of his good blue stare.

"Well, it won't work—it won't work," the doctor groaned.

"What won't?"

"I mean with Howland. Winterman won't. Howland doesn't take to him. Says he's crude—frightfully crude. And you know how Howland hates crudeness."

"Oh, I know," Bernald exulted. It was the word he had waited for—he saw it now! Once more he was lost in wonder at Howland's miraculous faculty for always, as the naturalists said, being true to type.

"So I'm afraid it's all up with his chance of writing. At least *I* can do no more," said Wade, discouraged.

Bernald pressed him for farther details. "Does Winterman seem to mind much? Did you hear his version?"

"His version?"

"I mean what he said to Howland."

"Why no. What the deuce was there for him to say?"

"What indeed? I think I'll take him home," said Bernald gaily.

He turned away to join the circle from which, a few minutes before, Pellerin's eyes had vainly and enigmatically signaled to him; but the circle had dispersed, and Pellerin himself was not in sight.

Bernald, looking about him, saw that during his brief aside with Wade the party had passed into the final phase of dissolution. People still delayed, in diminishing groups, but the current had set toward the doors, and every moment or two it bore away a few more lingerers. Bernald, from his post, commanded the clearing perspective of the two drawing-rooms, and a rapid survey of their length sufficed to assure him that Pellerin was not in either. Taking leave of Wade, the young man made his way back to the drawing-room, where only a few hardened feasters remained, and then passed on to the library which had been the scene of the late momentous colloquy. But the library too was empty, and drifting back uncertainly to the inner drawing-room Bernald found Mrs. Beecher Bain domestically putting out the wax candles on the mantelpiece.

"Dear Mr. Bernald! Do sit down and have a little chat. What a wonderful privilege it has been! I don't know when I've had such an intense impression."

She made way for him, hospitably, in a corner of the sofa to which she had sunk; and he echoed her vaguely: "You *were* impressed, then?"

"I can't express to you how it affected me! As Alice said, it was a resurrection—it was as if John Pellerin were actually here in the room with us!"

Bernald turned on her with a half-audible gasp. "You felt that, dear Mrs. Bain?"

"We all felt it—every one of us! I don't wonder the Greeks—it was the Greeks?—regarded eloquence as a supernatural power. As Alice says, when one looked at Howland Wade one understood what they meant by the Afflatus."

Bernald rose and held out his hand. "Oh, I see—it was Howland who made you feel as if Pellerin were in the room? And he made Miss Fosdick feel so too?"

"Why, of course. But why are you rushing off?"

"Because I must hunt up my friend, who's not used to such late hours."

"Your friend?" Mrs. Bain had to collect her thoughts. "Oh, Mr. Winterman, you mean? But he's gone already."

"Gone?" Bernald exclaimed, with an odd twinge of foreboding. Remembering Pellerin's signal across the crowd, he reproached himself for not having answered it more promptly. Yet it was certainly strange that his friend should have left the house without him.

"Are you quite sure?" he asked, with a startled glance at the clock.

"Oh, perfectly. He went half an hour ago. But you needn't hurry home on his account, for Alice Fosdick carried him off with her. I saw them leave together."

"Carried him off? She took him home with her, you mean?"

"Yes. You know what strange hours she keeps. She told me she was going to give him a Welsh rabbit, and explain Pellerinism to him."

"Oh, if she's going to explain—" Bernald murmured. But his amazement at the news struggled with a confused impatience to reach his rooms in time to be there for his friend's arrival. There could be no stranger spectacle beneath the stars than that of John Pellerin carried off by Miss Fosdick, and listening, in the small hours, to her elucidation of his doctrines; but Bernald knew enough of his sex to be aware that such an experiment may present a less humorous side to its subject than to an impartial observer. Even the Uplift Club and its connotations might benefit by the attraction of the unknown; and it was conceivable that to a traveller from Mesopotamia Miss Fosdick might present elements of interest which she had lost for the frequenters of Fifth Avenue. There was, at any rate, no denying that the affair had become unexpectedly complex, and that its farther development promised to be rich in comedy.

In the charmed contemplation of these possibilities Bernald sat over his fire, listening for Pellerin's ring. He had arranged his modest quarters with the reverent care of a celebrant awaiting the descent of his deity. He guessed Pellerin to be unconscious of visual detail, but sensitive to the happy blending of sensuous impressions: to the intimate spell of lamplight on books, and of a deep chair placed where one could watch the fire. The chair was there, and Bernald, facing it across the hearth, already saw it filled by Pellerin's lounging figure. The autumn dawn came late, and even now they had before them the promise of some untroubled hours. Bernald, sitting there alone in the warm stillness of his room, and in the profounder hush of his expectancy, was conscious of gathering up all his sensibilities and perceptions into one exquisitely-adjusted instrument of notation. Until now he had tasted Pellerin's society only in unpremeditated snatches, and had always left him with a sense, on his own part, of waste and shortcoming. Now, in the lull of this dedicated hour, he felt that he should miss nothing, and forget nothing, of the initiation that awaited him. And catching sight of Pellerin's pipe, he rose and laid it carefully on a table by the armchair...

"No. I've never had any news of him," Bernald heard himself repeating. He spoke in a low tone, and with the automatic utterance that alone made it possible to say the words.

They were addressed to Miss Fosdick, into whose neighborhood chance had thrown him at a dinner, a year or so later than their encounter at the Uplift Club. Hitherto he had successfully, and intentionally, avoided Miss Fosdick, not from any animosity toward that unconscious instrument of fate, but from an intense reluctance to pronounce the words which he knew he should have to speak if they met.

Now, as it turned out, his chief surprise was that she should wait so long to make him speak them. All through the dinner she had swept him along on a rapid current of talk which showed no tendency to linger or turn back upon the past. At first he ascribed her reserve to a sense of delicacy with which he reproached himself for not having previously credited her; then he saw that she had been carried so far beyond the point at which they had last faced each other, that it was by the merest hazard of associated ideas that she was now finally borne back to it. For it appeared that the very next evening, at Mrs. Beecher Bain's, a Hindu Mahatma was to lecture to the Uplift Club on the Limits of the Subliminal; and it was owing to no less a person than Howland Wade that this exceptional privilege had been obtained.

"Of course Howland's known all over the world as the interpreter of Pellerinism, and the Aga Gautch, who had absolutely declined to speak anywhere in public, wrote to Isabella that he could not refuse anything that Mr. Wade asked. Did you know that Howland's lecture, 'What Pellerinism Means,' has been translated into twenty-two languages, and gone into a fifth edition in Icelandic? Why, that reminds me," Miss Fosdick broke off—"I've never heard what became of your queer friend—what was his name?—whom you and Bob Wade accused me of spiriting away after that very lecture. And I've never seen *you* since you rushed into the house the next morning, and dragged me out of bed to know what I'd done with him!"

With a sharp effort Bernald gathered himself together to have it out. "Well, what *did* you do with him?" he retorted.

She laughed her appreciation of his humor. "Just what I told you, of course. I said good-bye to him on Isabella's door-step."

Bernald looked at her. "It's really true, then, that he didn't go home with you?"

She bantered back: "Have you suspected me, all this time, of hiding his remains in the cellar?" And with a droop of her fine lids she added: "I wish he *had* come home with me, for he was rather interesting, and there were things I think I could have explained to him."

Bernald helped himself to a nectarine, and Miss Fosdick continued on a note of amused curiosity: "So you've really never had any news of him since that night?"

"No—I've never had any news of him."

"Not the least little message?"

"Not the least little message."

"Or a rumor or report of any kind?"

"Or a rumor or report of any kind."

Miss Fosdick's interest seemed to be revived by the strangeness of the case. "It's rather creepy, isn't it? What could have happened? You don't suppose he could have been waylaid and murdered?" she asked with brightening eyes.

Bernald shook his head serenely. "No. I'm sure he's safe—quite safe."

"But if you're sure, you must know something."

"No. I know nothing," he repeated.

She scanned him incredulously. "But what's your theory—for you must have a theory? What in the world can have become of him?"

Bernald returned her look and hesitated. "Do you happen to remember the last thing he said to you—the very last, on the door-step, when he left you?"

"The last thing?" She poised her fork above the peach on her plate. "I don't think he said anything. Oh, yes—when I reminded him that he'd solemnly promised to come back with me and have a little talk he said he couldn't because he was going home."

"Well, then, I suppose," said Bernald, "he went home."

She glanced at him as if suspecting a trap. "Dear me, how flat! I always inclined to a mysterious murder. But of course you know more of him than you say."

She began to cut her peach, but paused above a lifted bit to ask, with a renewal of animation in her expressive eyes: "By the way, had you heard that Howland Wade has been gradually getting farther and farther away from Pellerinism? It seems he's begun to feel that there's a Positivist element in it which is narrowing to anyone who has gone at all deeply into the Wisdom of the East. He was intensely interesting about it the other day, and of course I *do* see what he feels. ... Oh, it's too long to tell you now; but if you could manage to come in to tea some afternoon soon—any day but Wednesday—I should so like to explain—"

## THE EYES

WE HAD BEEN PUT in the mood for ghosts, that evening, after an excellent dinner at our old friend Culwin's, by a tale of Fred Murchard's—the narrative of a strange personal visitation.

Seen through the haze of our cigars, and by the drowsy gleam of a coal fire, Culwin's library, with its oak walls and dark old bindings, made a good setting for such evocations; and ghostly experiences at first hand being, after Murchard's brilliant opening, the only kind acceptable to us, we proceeded to take stock of our group and tax each member for a contribution. There were eight of us, and seven contrived, in a manner more or less adequate, to fulfill the condition imposed. It surprised us all to find that we could muster such a show of supernatural impressions, for none of us, excepting Murchard himself and young Phil Frenham—whose story was the slightest of the lot—had the habit of sending our souls into the invisible. So that, on the whole, we had every reason to be proud of our seven "exhibits," and none of us would have dreamed of expecting an eighth from our host.

Our old friend, Mr. Andrew Culwin, who had sat back in his arm-chair, listening and blinking through the smoke circles with the cheerful tolerance of a wise old idol, was not the kind of man likely to be favored with such contacts, though he had imagination enough to enjoy, without envying, the superior privileges of his guests. By age and by education he belonged to the stout Positivist tradition, and his habit of thought had been formed in the days of the epic struggle between physics and metaphysics. But he had been, then and always, essentially a spectator, a humorous detached observer of the immense muddled variety show of life, slipping out of his seat now and then for a brief dip into the convivialities at the back of the house, but never, as far as one knew, showing the least desire to jump on the stage and do a "turn."

Among his contemporaries there lingered a vague tradition of his having, at a remote period, and in a romantic clime, been wounded in a duel; but this legend no more tallied with what we younger men knew of his character than my mother's assertion that he had once been "a charming little man with nice eyes" corresponded to any possible reconstitution of his dry thwarted physiognomy.

"He never can have looked like anything but a bundle of sticks," Murchard had once said of him. "Or a phosphorescent log, rather," some one else amended; and we recognized the happiness of this description of his small squat trunk, with the red blink of the eyes in a face like mottled bark. He had always been possessed of a leisure which he had nursed and protected, instead of squandering it in vain activities. His carefully guarded hours had been devoted to the cultivation of a fine intelligence and a few judiciously chosen habits; and none of the disturbances common to human experience seemed to have crossed his sky. Nevertheless, his dispassionate survey of the universe had not raised his opinion of that costly experiment, and his study of the human race seemed to have resulted in the conclusion that all men were superfluous, and women necessary only because some one had to do the cooking. On the importance of this point his convictions were absolute, and gastronomy was the only science which he revered as dogma. It must be owned that his little dinners were a strong argument in favor of this view, besides being a reason—though not the main one—for the fidelity of his friends.

Mentally he exercised a hospitality less seductive but no less stimulating. His mind was like a forum, or some open meeting-place for the exchange of ideas: somewhat cold and draughty, but light, spacious and orderly—a kind of academic grove from which all the leaves had fallen. In this privileged area a dozen of us were wont to stretch our muscles and expand our lungs; and, as if to prolong as much as possible the tradition of what we felt to be a vanishing institution, one or two neophytes were now and then added to our band.

Young Phil Frenham was the last, and the most interesting, of these recruits, and a good example of Murchard's somewhat morbid assertion that our old friend "liked 'em juicy." It was indeed a fact that Culwin, for all his mental dryness, specially tasted the lyric qualities in youth. As he was far too good an Epicurean to nip the flowers of soul which he gathered for his garden, his friendship was not a disintegrating influence: on the contrary, it forced the young idea to robuster bloom. And in Phil Frenham he had a fine subject for experimentation. The boy was really intelligent, and the soundness of his nature was like the pure paste under a delicate glaze. Culwin had fished him out of a thick fog of family dullness, and pulled him up to a peak in Darien; and the adventure hadn't hurt him a bit. Indeed, the skill with which Culwin had contrived to stimulate his curiosities without robbing them of their young bloom of awe seemed to me a sufficient answer to Murchard's ogreish metaphor. There was nothing hectic in Frenham's efflorescence, and his old friend had not laid even a finger-tip on the sacred stupidities. One wanted no better proof of that than the fact that Frenham still reverenced them in Culwin.

"There's a side of him you fellows don't see. I believe that story about the duel!" he declared; and it was of the very essence of this belief that it should impel him—just as our little party was dispersing—to turn back to our host with the absurd demand: "And now you've got to tell us about *your* ghost!"

The outer door had closed on Murchard and the others; only Frenham and I remained; and the vigilant servant who presided over Culwin's destinies, having brought a fresh supply of soda-water, had been laconically ordered to bed.

Culwin's sociability was a night-blooming flower, and we knew that he expected the nucleus of his group to tighten around him after midnight. But Frenham's appeal seemed to disconcert him comically, and he rose from the chair in which he had just reseated himself after his farewells in the hall.

*"My* ghost? Do you suppose I'm fool enough to go to the expense of keeping one of my own, when there are so many charming ones in my friends' closets?—Take another cigar," he said, revolving toward me with a laugh.

Frenham laughed too, pulling up his slender height before the chimney-piece as he turned to face his short bristling friend.

"Oh," he said, "you'd never be content to share if you met one you really liked."

Culwin had dropped back into his armchair, his shock head embedded in its habitual hollow, his little eyes glimmering over a fresh cigar.

"Liked—*liked?* Good Lord!" he growled.

"Ah, you *have*, then!" Frenham pounced on him in the same instant, with a sidewise glance of victory at me; but Culwin cowered gnomelike among his cushions, dissembling himself in a protective cloud of smoke.

"What's the use of denying it? You've seen everything, so of course you've seen a ghost!" his young friend persisted, talking intrepidly into the cloud. "Or, if you haven't seen one, it's only because you've seen two!"

The form of the challenge seemed to strike our host. He shot his head out of the mist with a queer tortoise-like motion he sometimes had, and blinked approvingly at Frenham.

"That's it," he suddenly flung at us on a shrill jerk of laughter; "it's only because I've seen two!"

The words were so unexpected that they dropped down and down into a fathomless silence, while we continued to stare at each other over Culwin's head, and Culwin stared at his ghosts. At length Frenham, without speaking, threw himself into the chair on the other side of the hearth, and leaned forward with his listening smile ...

## II

"OH, of course they're not show ghosts—a collector wouldn't think anything of them ... Don't let me raise your hopes ... their one merit is their numerical strength: the exceptional fact of their being two. But, as against this, I'm bound to admit that at any moment I could probably have exorcised them both by asking my doctor for a prescription, or my oculist for a pair of spectacles. Only, as I never could make up my mind whether to go to the doctor or the oculist—whether I was afflicted by an optical or a digestive delusion—I left them to pursue their interesting double life, though at times they made mine exceedingly uncomfortable …

"Yes—uncomfortable; and you know how I hate to be uncomfortable! But it was part of my stupid pride, when the thing began, not to admit that I could be disturbed by the trifling matter of seeing two—

"And then I'd no reason, really, to suppose I was ill. As far as I knew I was simply bored—horribly bored. But it was part of my boredom—I remember—that I was feeling so uncommonly well, and didn't know how on earth to work off my surplus energy. I had come back from a long journey—down in South America and Mexico—and had settled down for the winter near New York, with an old aunt who had known Washington Irving and corresponded with N. P. Willis. She lived, not far from Irvington, in a damp Gothic villa, overhung by Norway spruces, and looking exactly like a memorial emblem done in hair. Her personal appearance was in keeping with this image, and her own hair—of which there was little left—might have been sacrificed to the manufacture of the emblem.

"I had just reached the end of an agitated year, with considerable arrears to make up in money and emotion; and theoretically it seemed as though my aunt's mild hospitality would be as beneficial to my nerves as to my purse. But the deuce of it was that as soon as I felt myself safe and sheltered my energy began to revive; and how was I to work it off inside of a memorial emblem? I had, at that time, the agreeable illusion that sustained intellectual effort could engage a man's whole activity; and I decided to write a great book—I forget about what. My aunt, impressed by my plan, gave up to me her Gothic library, filled with classics in black cloth and daguerreotypes of faded celebrities; and I sat down at my desk to make myself a place among their number. And to facilitate my task she lent me a cousin to copy my manuscript.

"The cousin was a nice girl, and I had an idea that a nice girl was just what I needed to restore my faith in human nature, and principally in myself. She was neither beautiful nor intelligent—poor Alice Nowell!—but it interested me to see any woman content to be so uninteresting, and I wanted to find out the secret of her content. In doing this I handled it rather rashly, and put it out of joint—oh, just for a moment! There's no fatuity in telling you this, for the poor girl had never seen anyone but cousins …

"Well, I was sorry for what I'd done, of course, and confoundedly bothered as to how I should put it straight. She was staying in the house, and one evening, after my aunt had gone to bed, she came down to the library to fetch a book she'd mislaid, like any artless heroine on the shelves behind us. She was pink-nosed and flustered, and it suddenly occurred to me that her hair, though it was fairly thick and pretty, would look exactly like my aunt's when she grew older. I was glad I had noticed this, for it made it easier for me to do what was right; and when I had found the book she hadn't lost I told her I was leaving for Europe that week.

"Europe was terribly far off in those days, and Alice knew at once what I meant. She didn't take it in the least as I'd expected—it would have been easier if she had. She held her book very tight, and turned away a moment to wind up the lamp on my desk—it had a ground glass shade with vine leaves, and glass drops around the edge, I remember. Then she came back, held out her hand, and said: 'Good-bye.' And as she said it she looked straight at me and kissed me. I had never felt anything as fresh and shy and brave as her kiss. It was worse than any reproach, and it made me ashamed to deserve a reproach from her. I said to myself: 'I'll marry her, and when my aunt dies she'll leave us this house, and I'll sit here at the desk and go on with my book; and Alice will sit over there with her embroidery and look at me as she's looking now. And life will go on like that for any number of years.' The prospect frightened me a little, but at the time it didn't frighten me as much as doing anything to hurt her; and ten minutes later she had my seal ring on my finger, and my promise that when I went abroad she should go with me.

"You'll wonder why I'm enlarging on this familiar incident. It's because the evening on which it took place was the very evening on which I first saw the queer sight I've spoken of. Being at that time an ardent believer in a necessary sequence between cause and effect I naturally tried to trace some kind of link between what had just happened to me in my aunt's library, and what was to happen a few hours later on the same night; and so the coincidence between the two events always remained in my mind.

"I went up to bed with rather a heavy heart, for I was bowed under the weight of the first good action I had ever consciously committed; and young as I was, I saw the gravity of my situation. Don't imagine from this that I had hitherto been an instrument of destruction. I had been merely a harmless young man, who had followed his bent and declined all collaboration with Providence. Now I had suddenly undertaken to promote the moral order of the world, and I felt a good deal like the trustful spectator who has given his gold watch to the conjurer, and doesn't know in what shape he'll get it back when the trick is over … Still, a glow of self-righteousness tempered my fears, and I said to myself as I undressed that when I'd got used to being good it probably wouldn't make me as nervous as it did at the start. And by the time I was in bed, and had blown out my candle, I felt that I really was getting used to it, and that, as far as I'd got, it was not unlike sinking down into one of my aunt's very softest wool mattresses.

"I closed my eyes on this image, and when I opened them it must have been a good deal later, for my room had grown cold, and the night was intensely still. I was waked suddenly by the feeling we all know—the feeling that there was something near me that hadn't been there when I fell asleep. I sat up and strained my eyes into the darkness. The room was pitch black, and at first I saw nothing; but gradually a vague glimmer at the foot of the bed turned into two eyes staring back at me. I couldn't see the face attached to them—on account of the darkness, I imagined—but as I looked the eyes grew more and more distinct: they gave out a light of their own.

"The sensation of being thus gazed at was far from pleasant, and you might suppose that my first impulse would have been to jump out of bed and hurl myself on the invisible figure attached to the eyes. But it wasn't—my impulse was simply to lie still … I can't say whether this was due to an immediate sense of the uncanny nature of the apparition—to the certainty that if I did jump out of bed I should hurl myself on nothing—or merely to the benumbing effect of the eyes themselves. They were the very worst eyes I've ever seen: a man's eyes—but what a man! My first thought was that he must be frightfully old. The orbits were sunk, and the thick red-lined lids hung over the eyeballs like blinds of which the cords are broken. One lid drooped a little lower than the other, with the effect of a crooked leer; and between these pulpy folds of flesh, with their scant bristle of lashes, the eyes themselves, small glassy disks with an agate-like rim about the pupils, looked like sea-pebbles in the grip of a starfish.

"But the age of the eyes was not the most unpleasant thing about them. What turned me sick was their expression of vicious security. I don't know how else to describe the fact that they seemed to belong to a man who had done a lot of harm in his life, but had always kept just inside the danger lines. They were not the eyes of a coward, but of some one much too clever to take risks; and my gorge rose at their look of base astuteness. Yet even that wasn't the worst; for as we continued to scan each other I saw in them a tinge of faint derision, and felt myself to be its object.

"At that I was seized by an impulse of rage that jerked me out of bed and pitched me straight on the unseen figure at its foot. But of course there wasn't any figure there, and my fists struck at emptiness. Ashamed and cold, I groped about for a match and lit the candles. The room looked just as usual—as I had known it would; and I crawled back to bed, and blew out the lights.

"As soon as the room was dark again the eyes reappeared; and I now applied myself to explaining them on scientific principles. At first I thought the illusion might have been caused by the glow of the last embers in the chimney; but the fire-place was on the other side of my bed, and so placed that the fire could not possibly be reflected in my toilet glass, which was the only mirror in the room. Then it occurred to me that I might have been tricked by the reflection of the embers in some polished bit of wood or metal; and though I couldn't discover any object of the sort in my line of vision, I got up again, groped my way to the hearth, and covered what was left of the fire. But as soon as I was back in bed the eyes were back at its foot.

"They were an hallucination, then: that was plain. But the fact that they were not due to any external dupery didn't make them a bit pleasanter to see. For if they were a projection of my inner consciousness, what the deuce was the matter with that organ? I had gone deeply enough into the mystery of morbid pathological states to picture the conditions under which an exploring mind might lay itself open to such a midnight admonition; but I couldn't fit it to my present case. I had never felt more normal, mentally and physically; and the only unusual fact in my situation—that of having assured the happiness of an amiable girl—did not seem of a kind to summon unclean spirits about my pillow. But there were the eyes still looking at me.

"I shut mine, and tried to evoke a vision of Alice Nowell's. They were not remarkable eyes, but they were as wholesome as fresh water, and if she had had more imagination—or longer lashes—their expression might have been interesting. As it was, they did not prove very efficacious, and in a few moments I perceived that they had mysteriously changed into the eyes at the foot of the bed. It exasperated me more to feel these glaring at me through my shut lids than to see them, and I opened my eyes again and looked straight into their hateful stare …

"And so it went on all night. I can't tell you what that night was, nor how long it lasted. Have you ever lain in bed, hopelessly wide awake, and tried to keep your eyes shut, knowing that if you opened 'em you'd see something you dreaded and loathed? It sounds easy, but it's devilish hard. Those eyes hung there and drew me. I had the *vertige de l'abîme*, and their red lids were the edge of my abyss. … I had known nervous hours before: hours when I'd felt the wind of danger in my neck; but never this kind of strain. It wasn't that the eyes were so awful; they hadn't the majesty of the powers of darkness. But they had—how shall I say?—a physical effect that was the equivalent of a bad smell: their look left a smear like a snail's. And I didn't see what business they had with me, anyhow—and I stared and stared, trying to find out.

"I don't know what effect they were trying to produce; but the effect they *did* produce was that of making me pack my portmanteau and bolt to town early the next morning. I left a note for my aunt, explaining that I was ill and had gone to see my doctor; and as a matter of fact I did feel uncommonly ill—the night seemed to have pumped all the blood out of me. But when I reached town I didn't go to the doctor's. I went to a friend's rooms, and threw myself on a bed, and slept for ten heavenly hours. When I woke it was the middle of the night, and I turned cold at the thought of what might be waiting for me. I sat up, shaking, and stared into the darkness; but there wasn't a break in its blessed surface, and when I saw that the eyes were not there I dropped back into another long sleep.

"I had left no word for Alice when I fled, because I meant to go back the next morning. But the next morning I was too exhausted to stir. As the day went on the exhaustion increased, instead of wearing off like the lassitude left by an ordinary night of insomnia: the effect of the eyes seemed to be cumulative, and the thought of seeing them again grew intolerable. For two days I struggled with my dread; but on the third evening I pulled myself together and decided to go back the next morning. I felt a good deal happier as soon as I'd decided, for I knew that my abrupt disappearance, and the strangeness of my not writing, must have been very painful for poor Alice. That night I went to bed with an easy mind, and fell asleep at once; but in the middle of the night I woke, and there were the eyes...

"Well, I simply couldn't face them; and instead of going back to my aunt's I bundled a few things into a trunk and jumped onto the first steamer for England. I was so dead tired when I got on board that I crawled straight into my berth, and slept most of the way over; and I can't tell you the bliss it was to wake from those long stretches of dreamless sleep and look fearlessly into the darkness, *knowing* that I shouldn't see the eyes ...

"I stayed abroad for a year, and then I stayed for another; and during that time I never had a glimpse of them. That was enough reason for prolonging my stay if I'd been on a desert island. Another was, of course, that I had perfectly come to see, on the voyage over, the folly, complete impossibility, of my marrying Alice Nowell. The fact that I had been so slow in making this discovery annoyed me, and made me want to avoid explanations. The bliss of escaping at one stroke from the eyes, and from this other embarrassment, gave my freedom an extraordinary zest; and the longer I savored it the better I liked its taste.

"The eyes had burned such a hole in my consciousness that for a long time I went on puzzling over the nature of the apparition, and wondering nervously if it would ever come back. But as time passed I lost this dread, and retained only the precision of the image. Then that faded in its turn.

"The second year found me settled in Rome, where I was planning, I believe, to write another great book—a definitive work on Etruscan influences in Italian art. At any rate, I'd found some pretext of the kind for taking a sunny apartment in the Piazza di Spagna and dabbling about indefinitely in the Forum; and there, one morning, a charming youth came to me. As he stood there in the warm light, slender and smooth and hyacinthine, he might have stepped from a ruined altar—one to Antinous, say—but he'd come instead from New York, with a letter (of all people) from Alice Nowell. The letter—the first I'd had from her since our break—was simply a line introducing her young cousin, Gilbert Noyes, and appealing to me to befriend him. It appeared, poor lad, that he 'had talent,' and 'wanted to write'; and, an obdurate family having insisted that his calligraphy should take the form of double entry, Alice had intervened to win him six months' respite, during which he was to travel on a meager pittance, and somehow prove his ultimate ability to increase it by his pen. The quaint conditions of the test struck me first: it seemed about as conclusive as a mediaeval 'ordeal.' Then I was touched by her having sent him to me. I had always wanted to do her some service, to justify myself in my own eyes rather than hers; and here was a beautiful embodiment of my chance.

"I imagine it's safe to lay down the general principle that predestined geniuses don't, as a rule, appear before one in the spring sunshine of the Forum looking like one of its banished gods. At any rate, poor Noyes wasn't a predestined genius. But he *was* beautiful to see, and charming as a comrade too. It was only when he began to talk literature that my heart failed me. I knew all the symptoms so well—the things he had 'in him,' and the things outside him that impinged! There's the real test, after all. It was always—punctually, inevitably, with the inexorableness of a mechanical law—it was *always* the wrong thing that struck him. I grew to find a certain grim fascination in deciding in advance exactly which wrong thing he'd select; and I acquired an astonishing skill at the game …

"The worst of it was that his *bêtise* wasn't of the too obvious sort. Ladies who met him at picnics thought him intellectual; and even at dinners he passed for clever. I, who had him under the microscope, fancied now and then that he might develop some kind of a slim talent, something that he could make 'do' and be happy on; and wasn't that, after all, what I was concerned with? He was so charming—he continued to be so charming—that he called forth all my charity in support of this argument; and for the first few months I really believed there was a chance for him …

"Those months were delightful. Noyes was constantly with me, and the more I saw of him the better I liked him. His stupidity was a natural grace—it was as beautiful, really, as his eye-lashes. And he was so gay, so affectionate, and so happy with me, that telling him the truth would have been about as pleasant as slitting the throat of some artless animal. At first I used to wonder what had put into that radiant head the detestable delusion that it held a brain. Then I began to see that it was simply protective mimicry—an instinctive ruse to get away from family life and an office desk. Not that Gilbert didn't—dear lad!—believe in himself. There wasn't a trace of hypocrisy in his composition. He was sure that his 'call' was irresistible, while to me it was the saving grace of his situation that it wasn't, and that a little money, a little leisure, a little pleasure would have turned him into an inoffensive idler. Unluckily, however, there was no hope of money, and with the grim alternative of the office desk before him he couldn't postpone his attempt at literature. The stuff he turned out was deplorable, and I see now that I knew it from the first. Still, the absurdity of deciding a man's whole future on a first trial seemed to justify me in withholding my verdict, and perhaps even in encouraging him a little, on the ground that the human plant generally needs warmth to flower.

"At any rate, I proceeded on that principle, and carried it to the point of getting his term of probation extended. When I left Rome he went with me, and we idled away a delicious summer between Capri and Venice. I said to myself: 'If he has anything in him, it will come out now; and it *did*. He was never more enchanting and enchanted. There were moments of our pilgrimage when beauty born of murmuring sound seemed actually to pass into his face—but only to issue forth in a shallow flood of the palest ink …

"Well the time came to turn off the tap; and I knew there was no hand but mine to do it. We were back in Rome, and I had taken him to stay with me, not wanting him to be alone in his *pension* when he had to face the necessity of renouncing his ambition. I hadn't, of course, relied solely on my own judgment in deciding to advise him to drop literature. I had sent his stuff to various people—editors and critics—and they had always sent it back with the same chilling lack of comment. Really there was nothing to say.

"I confess I never felt more shabbily than I did on the day when I decided to have it out with Gilbert. It was well enough to tell myself that it was my duty to knock the poor boy's hopes into splinters—but I'd like to know what act of gratuitous cruelty hasn't been justified on that plea? I've always shrunk from usurping the functions of Providence, and when I have to exercise them I decidedly prefer that it shouldn't be on an errand of destruction. Besides, in the last issue, who was I to decide, even after a year's trial, if poor Gilbert had it in him or not?

"The more I looked at the part I'd resolved to play, the less I liked it; and I liked it still less when Gilbert sat opposite me, with his head thrown back in the lamplight, just as Phil's is now ... I'd been going over his last manuscript, and he knew it, and he knew that his future hung on my verdict—we'd tacitly agreed to that. The manuscript lay between us, on my table—a novel, his first novel, if you please!—and he reached over and laid his hand on it, and looked up at me with all his life in the look.

"I stood up and cleared my throat, trying to keep my eyes away from his face and on the manuscript.

"'The fact is, my dear Gilbert,' I began—

"I saw him turn pale, but he was up and facing me in an instant.

"'Oh, look here, don't take on so, my dear fellow! I'm not so awfully cut up as all that!' His hands were on my shoulders, and he was laughing down on me from his full height, with a kind of mortally-stricken gaiety that drove the knife into my side.

"He was too beautifully brave for me to keep up any humbug about my duty. And it came over me suddenly how I should hurt others in hurting him: myself first, since sending him home meant losing him; but more particularly poor Alice Nowell, to whom I had so uneasily longed to prove my good faith and my immense desire to serve her. It really seemed like failing her twice to fail Gilbert.

"But my intuition was like one of those lightning flashes that encircle the whole horizon, and in the same instant I saw what I might be letting myself in for if I didn't tell the truth. I said to myself: 'I shall have him for life'—and I'd never yet seen any one, man or woman, whom I was quite sure of wanting on those terms. Well, this impulse of egotism decided me. I was ashamed of it, and to get away from it I took a leap that landed me straight in Gilbert's arms.

"'The thing's all right, and you're all wrong!' I shouted up at him; and as he hugged me, and I laughed and shook in his incredulous clutch, I had for a minute the sense of self-complacency that is supposed to attend the footsteps of the just. Hang it all, making people happy *has* its charms.

"Gilbert, of course, was for celebrating his emancipation in some spectacular manner; but I sent him away alone to explode his emotions, and went to bed to sleep off mine. As I undressed I began to wonder what their after-taste would be—so many of the finest don't keep! Still, I wasn't sorry, and I meant to empty the bottle, even if it *did* turn a trifle flat.

"After I got into bed I lay for a long time smiling at the memory of his eyes—his blissful eyes... Then I fell asleep, and when I woke the room was deathly cold, and I sat up with a jerk—and there were *the other eyes*...

"It was three years since I'd seen them, but I'd thought of them so often that I fancied they could never take me unawares again. Now, with their red sneer on me, I knew that I had never really believed they would come back, and that I was as defenceless as ever against them ... As before, it was the insane irrelevance of their coming that made it so horrible. What the deuce were they after, to leap out at me at such a time? I had lived more or less carelessly in the years since I'd seen them, though my worst indiscretions were not dark enough to invite the searchings of their infernal glare; but at this particular moment I was really in what might have been called a state of grace; and I can't tell you how the fact added to their horror ...

"But it's not enough to say they were as bad as before: they were worse. Worse by just so much as I'd learned of life in the interval; by all the damnable implications my wider experience read into them. I saw now what I hadn't seen before: that they were eyes which had grown hideous gradually, which had built up their baseness coral-wise, bit by bit, out of a series of small turpitudes slowly accumulated through the industrious years. Yes—it came to me that what made them so bad was that they'd grown bad so slowly …

"There they hung in the darkness, their swollen lids dropped across the little watery bulbs rolling loose in the orbits, and the puff of fat flesh making a muddy shadow underneath—and as their filmy stare moved with my movements, there came over me a sense of their tacit complicity, of a deep hidden understanding between us that was worse than the first shock of their strangeness. Not that I understood them; but that they made it so clear that someday I should … Yes, that was the worst part of it, decidedly; and it was the feeling that became stronger each time they came back to me …

"For they got into the damnable habit of coming back. They reminded me of vampires with a taste for young flesh, they seemed so to gloat over the taste of a good conscience. Every night for a month they came to claim their morsel of mine: since I'd made Gilbert happy they simply wouldn't loosen their fangs. The coincidence almost made me hate him, poor lad, fortuitous as I felt it to be. I puzzled over it a good deal, but couldn't find any hint of an explanation except in the chance of his association with Alice Nowell. But then the eyes had let up on me the moment I had abandoned her, so they could hardly be the emissaries of a woman scorned, even if one could have pictured poor Alice charging such spirits to avenge her. That set me thinking, and I began to wonder if they would let up on me if I abandoned Gilbert. The temptation was insidious, and I had to stiffen myself against it; but really, dear boy! he was too charming to be sacrificed to such demons. And so, after all, I never found out what they wanted…"

### III

THE fire crumbled, sending up a flash which threw into relief the narrator's gnarled red face under its grey-black stubble. Pressed into the hollow of the dark leather armchair, it stood out an instant like an intaglio of yellowish red-veined stone, with spots of enamel for the eyes; then the fire sank and in the shaded lamp-light it became once more a dim Rembrandtish blur.

Phil Frenham, sitting in a low chair on the opposite side of the hearth, one long arm propped on the table behind him, one hand supporting his thrown-back head, and his eyes steadily fixed on his old friend's face, had not moved since the tale began. He continued to maintain his silent immobility after Culwin had ceased to speak, and it was I who, with a vague sense of disappointment at the sudden drop of the story, finally asked: "But how long did you keep on seeing them?"

Culwin, so sunk into his chair that he seemed like a heap of his own empty clothes, stirred a little, as if in surprise at my question. He appeared to have half-forgotten what he had been telling us.

"How long? Oh, off and on all that winter. It was infernal. I never got used to them. I grew really ill."

Frenham shifted his attitude silently, and as he did so his elbow struck against a small mirror in a bronze frame standing on the table behind him. He turned and changed its angle slightly; then he resumed his former attitude, his dark head thrown back on his lifted palm, his eyes intent on Culwin's face. Something in his stare embarrassed me, and as if to divert attention from it I pressed on with another question:

"And you never tried sacrificing Noyes?"

"Oh, no. The fact is I didn't have to. He did it for me, poor infatuated boy!"

"Did it for you? How do you mean?"

"He wore me out—wore everybody out. He kept on pouring out his lamentable twaddle, and hawking it up and down the place till he became a thing of terror. I tried to wean him from writing—oh, ever so gently, you understand, by throwing him with agreeable people, giving him a chance to make himself felt, to come to a sense of what he *really* had to give. I'd foreseen this solution from the beginning—felt sure that, once the first ardor of authorship was quenched, he'd drop into his place as a charming parasitic thing, the kind of chronic Cherubino for whom, in old societies, there's always a seat at table, and a shelter behind the ladies' skirts. I saw him take his place as 'the poet': the poet who doesn't write. One knows the type in every drawing-room. Living in that way doesn't cost much—I'd worked it all out in my mind, and felt sure that, with a little help, he could manage it for the next few years; and meanwhile he'd be sure to marry. I saw him married to a widow, rather older, with a good cook and a well-run house. And I actually had my eye on the widow … Meanwhile I did everything to facilitate the transition—lent him money to ease his conscience, introduced him to pretty women to make him forget his vows. But nothing would do him: he had but one idea in his beautiful obstinate head. He wanted the laurel and not the rose, and he kept on repeating Gautier's axiom, and battering and filing at his limp prose till he'd spread it out over Lord knows how many thousand sloppy pages. Now and then he would send a barrelful to a publisher, and of course it would always come back.

"At first it didn't matter—he thought he was 'misunderstood.' He took the attitudes of genius, and whenever an opus came home he wrote another to keep it company. Then he had a reaction of despair, and accused me of deceiving him, and Lord knows what. I got angry at that, and told him it was he who had deceived himself. He'd come to me determined to write, and I'd done my best to help him. That was the extent of my offence, and I'd done it for his cousin's sake, not his.

"That seemed to strike home, and he didn't answer for a minute. Then he said: 'My time's up and my money's up. What do you think I'd better do?'

"'I think you'd better not be an ass,' I said.

"'What do you mean by being an ass?'

"I took a letter from my desk and held it out to him.

"'I mean refusing this offer of Mrs. Ellinger's: to be her secretary at a salary of five thousand dollars. There may be a lot more in it than that.'

"He flung out his hand with a violence that struck the letter from mine. 'Oh, I know well enough what's in it!' he said, scarlet to the roots of his hair.

"'And what's your answer, if you know?' I asked.

"He made none at the minute, but turned away slowly to the door. There, with his hand on the threshold, he stopped to ask, almost under his breath: 'Then you really think my stuff's no good?'

"I was tired and exasperated, and I laughed. I don't defend my laugh—it was in wretched taste. But I must plead in extenuation that the boy was a fool, and that I'd done my best for him—I really had.

"He went out of the room, shutting the door quietly after him. That afternoon I left for Frascati, where I'd promised to spend the Sunday with some friends. I was glad to escape from Gilbert, and by the same token, as I learned that night, I had also escaped from the eyes. I dropped into the same lethargic sleep that had come to me before when their visitations ceased; and when I woke the next morning, in my peaceful painted room above the ilexes, I felt the utter weariness and deep relief that always followed on that repairing slumber. I put in two blessed nights at Frascati, and when I got back to my rooms in Rome I found that Gilbert had gone … Oh, nothing tragic had happened—the episode never rose to that. He'd simply packed his manuscripts and left for America—for his family and the Wall Street desk. He left a decent little note to tell me of his decision, and behaved altogether, in the circumstances, as little like a fool as it's possible for a fool to behave …"

## IV

CULWIN paused again, and again Frenham sat motionless, the dusky contour of his young head reflected in the mirror at his back.

"And what became of Noyes afterward?" I finally asked, still disquieted by a sense of incompleteness, by the need of some connecting thread between the parallel lines of the tale.

Culwin twitched his shoulders. "Oh, nothing became of him—because he became nothing. There could be no question of 'becoming' about it. He vegetated in an office, I believe, and finally got a clerkship in a consulate, and married drearily in China. I saw him once in Hong Kong, years afterward. He was fat and hadn't shaved. I was told he drank. He didn't recognize me."

"And the eyes?" I asked, after another pause which Frenham's continued silence made oppressive.

Culwin, stroking his chin, blinked at me meditatively through the shadows. "I never saw them after my last talk with Gilbert. Put two and two together if you can. For my part, I haven't found the link."

He rose, his hands in his pockets, and walked over to the table on which reviving drinks had been set out.

"You must be parched after this dry tale. Here, help yourself, my dear fellow. Here, Phil—" He turned back to the hearth.

Frenham still sat in his low chair, making no response to his host's hospitable summons. But as Culwin advanced toward him, their eyes met in a long look; after which, to my intense surprise, the young man, turning suddenly in his seat, flung his arms across the table, and dropped his face upon them.

Culwin, at the unexpected gesture, stopped short, a flush on his face.

"Phil—what the deuce? Why, have the eyes scared *you?* My dear boy—my dear fellow—I never had such a tribute to my literary ability, never!"

He broke into a chuckle at the thought, and halted on the hearth-rug, his hands still in his pockets, gazing down in honest perplexity at the youth's bowed head. Then, as Frenham still made no answer, he moved a step or two nearer.

"Cheer up, my dear Phil! It's years since I've seen them—apparently I've done nothing lately bad enough to call them out of chaos. Unless my present evocation of them has made *you* see them; which would be their worst stroke yet!"

His bantering appeal quivered off into an uneasy laugh, and he moved still nearer, bending over Frenham, and laying his gouty hands on the lad's shoulders.

"Phil, my dear boy, really—what's the matter? Why don't you answer? *Have* you seen the eyes?"

Frenham's face was still pressed against his arms, and from where I stood behind

Culwin I saw the latter, as if under the rebuff of this unaccountable attitude, draw back slowly from his friend. As he did so, the light of the lamp on the table fell full on his perplexed congested face, and I caught its sudden reflection in the mirror behind Frenham's head.

Culwin saw the reflection also. He paused, his face level with the mirror, as if scarcely recognizing the countenance in it as his own. But as he looked his expression gradually changed, and for an appreciable space of time he and the image in the glass confronted each other with a glare of slowly gathering hate. Then Culwin let go of Frenham's shoulders, and drew back a step...

Frenham, his face still hidden, did not stir.

## THE BLOND BEAST

IT HAD BEEN almost too easy—that was young Millner's first feeling, as he stood again on the Spence door-step, the great moment of his interview behind him, and Fifth Avenue rolling its grimy Pactolus at his feet.

Halting there in the winter light, with the clang of the ponderous vestibule doors in his ears, and his eyes carried down the perspective of the packed interminable thoroughfare, he even dared to remember Rastignac's apostrophe to Paris, and to hazard recklessly under his small fair moustache: "Who knows?"

He, Hugh Millner, at any rate, knew a good deal already: a good deal more than he had imagined it possible to learn in half an hour's talk with a man like Orlando G. Spence; and the loud-rumoring city spread out there before him seemed to grin like an accomplice who knew the rest.

A gust of wind, whirling down from the dizzy height of the building on the next corner, drove sharply through his overcoat and compelled him to clutch at his hat. It was a bitter January day, a day of fierce light and air, when the sunshine cut like icicles and the wind sucked one into black gulfs at the street corners. But Millner's complacency was like a warm lining to his shabby coat, and heaving steadied his hat he continued to stand on the Spence threshold, lost in the vision revealed to him from the Pisgah of its marble steps. Yes, it was wonderful what the vision showed him. ... In his absorption he might have frozen fast to the door-step if the Rhadamanthine portals behind him had not suddenly opened to let out a slim fur-coated figure, the figure, as he perceived, of the youth whom he had caught in the act of withdrawal as he entered Mr. Spence's study, and whom the latter, with a wave of his affable hand, had detained to introduce as "my son Draper."

It was characteristic of the odd friendliness of the whole scene that the great man should have thought it worth-while to call back and name his heir to a mere humble applicant like Millner; and that the heir should shed on him, from a pale high-browed face, a smile of such deprecating kindness. It was characteristic, equally, of Millner, that he should at once mark the narrowness of the shoulders sustaining this ingenuous head; a narrowness, as he now observed, imperfectly concealed by the wide fur collar of young Spence's expensive and badly cut coat. But the face took on, as the youth smiled his surprise at their second meeting, a look of almost plaintive good-will: the kind of look that Millner scorned and yet could never quite resist.

"Mr. Millner? Are you—er—waiting?" the lad asked, with an intention of serviceableness that was like a finer echo of his father's resounding cordiality.

"For my motor? No," Millner jested in his frank free voice. "The fact is, I was just standing here lost in the contemplation of my luck"—and as his companion's pale blue eyes seemed to shape a question, "my extraordinary luck," he explained, "in having been engaged as your father's secretary."

"Oh," the other rejoined, with a faint color in his sallow cheek. "I'm so glad," he murmured: "but I was sure—" He stopped, and the two looked kindly at each other.

Millner averted his gaze first, almost fearful of its betraying the added sense of his own strength and dexterity which he drew from the contrast of the other's frailness.

"Sure? How could anyone be sure? I don't believe in it yet!" he laughed out in the irony of his triumph.

The boy's words did not sound like a mere civility—Millner felt in them an homage to his power.

"Oh, yes: I was sure," young Draper repeated. "Sure as soon as I saw you, I mean."

Millner tingled again with this tribute to his physical straightness and bloom. Yes, he looked his part, hang it—he looked it!

But his companion still lingered, a shy sociability in his eye.

"If you're walking, then, can I go along a little way?" And he nodded southward down the shabby gaudy avenue.

That, again, was part of the high comedy of the hour—that Millner should descend the Spence steps at young Spence's side, and stroll down Fifth Avenue with him at the proudest moment of the afternoon; O. G. Spence's secretary walking abroad with O. G. Spence's heir! He had the scientific detachment to pull out his watch and furtively note the hour. Yes—it was exactly forty minutes since he had rung the Spence door-bell and handed his card to a gelid footman, who, openly sceptical of his claim to be received, had left him unceremoniously planted on the cold tessellations of the vestibule.

("Someday," Miller grinned to himself, "I think I'll take that footman as furnace-man—or to do the boots." And he pictured his marble palace rising from the earth to form the mausoleum of a footman's pride.)

Only forty minutes ago! And now he had his opportunity fast! And he never meant to let it go! It was incredible, what had happened in the interval. He had gone up the Spence steps an unknown young man, out of a job, and with no substantial hope of getting into one: a needy young man with a mother and two limp sisters to be helped, and a lengthening figure of debt that stood by his bed through the anxious nights. And he went down the steps with his present assured, and his future lit by the hues of the rainbow above the pot of gold. Certainly a fellow who made his way at that rate had it "in him," and could afford to trust his star.

Descending from this joyous flight he stooped his ear to the discourse of young Spence.

"My father'll work you rather hard, you know: but you look as if you wouldn't mind that."

Millner pulled up his inches with the self-consciousness of the man who had none to waste. "Oh, no, I shan't mind that: I don't mind any amount of work if it leads to something."

"Just so," Draper Spence assented eagerly. "That's what I feel. And you'll find that whatever my father undertakes leads to such awfully fine things."

Millner tightened his lips on a grin. He was thinking only of where the work would lead him, not in the least of where it might land the eminent Orlando G. Spence. But he looked at his companion sympathetically.

"You're a philanthropist like your father, I see?"

"Oh, I don't know." They had paused at a crossing, and young Draper, with a dubious air, stood striking his agate-headed stick against the curb-stone. "I believe in a purpose, don't you?" he asked, lifting his blue eyes suddenly to Millner's face.

"A purpose? I should rather say so! I believe in nothing else," cried Millner, feeling as if his were something he could grip in his hand and swing like a club.

Young Spence seemed relieved. "Yes—I tie up to that. There *is* a Purpose. And so, after all, even if I don't agree with my father on minor points ..." He colored quickly, and looked again at Millner. "I should like to talk to you about this someday."

Millner smothered another smile. "We'll have lots of talks, I hope."

"Oh, if you can spare the time—!" said Draper, almost humbly.

"Why, I shall be there on tap!"

"For father, not me." Draper hesitated, with another self-confessing smile. "Father thinks I talk too much—that I keep going in and out of things. He doesn't believe in analyzing: he thinks it's destructive. But it hasn't destroyed my ideals." He looked wistfully up and down the clanging street. "And that's the main thing, isn't it? I mean, that one should have an Ideal." He turned back almost gaily to Millner. "I suspect you're a revolutionist too!"

"Revolutionist? Rather! I belong to the Red Syndicate and the Black Hand!" Millner joyfully assented.

Young Draper chuckled at the enormity of the joke. "First rate! We'll have incendiary meetings!" He pulled an elaborately armorial watch from his enfolding furs. "I'm so sorry, but I must say good-bye—this is my street," he explained. Millner, with a faint twinge of envy, glanced across at the colonnaded marble edifice in the farther corner. "Going to the club?" he said carelessly.

His companion looked surprised. "Oh, no: I never go *there*. It's too boring." And he brought out, after one of the pauses in which he seemed rather breathlessly to measure the chances of his listener's indulgence: "I'm just going over to a little Bible Class I have in Tenth Avenue."

Millner, for a moment or two, stood watching the slim figure wind its way through the mass of vehicles to the opposite corner; then he pursued his own course down Fifth Avenue, measuring his steps to the rhythmic refrain: "It's too easy—it's too easy—it's too easy!"

His own destination being the small shabby flat off University Place where three tender females awaited the result of his mission, he had time, on the way home, after abandoning himself to a general sense of triumph, to dwell specifically on the various aspects of his achievement. Viewed materially and practically, it was a thing to be proud of; yet it was chiefly on aesthetic grounds—because he had done so exactly what he had set out to do—that he glowed with pride at the afternoon's work. For, after all, any young man with the proper "pull" might have applied to Orlando G. Spence for the post of secretary, and even have penetrated as far as the great man's study; but that he, Hugh Millner, should not only have forced his way to this fastness, but have established, within a short half hour, his right to remain there permanently: well, this, if it proved anything, proved that the first rule of success was to know how to live up to one's principles.

"One must have a plan—one must have a plan," the young man murmured, looking with pity at the vague faces which the crowd bore past him, and feeling almost impelled to detain them and expound his doctrine. But the planlessness of average human nature was of course the measure of his opportunity; and he smiled to think that every purposeless face he met was a guarantee of his own advancement, a rung in the ladder he meant to climb.

Yes, the whole secret of success was to know what one wanted to do, and not to be afraid to do it. His own history was proving that already. He had not been afraid to give up his small but safe position in a real-estate office for the precarious adventure of a private secretaryship; and his first glimpse of his new employer had convinced him that he had not mistaken his calling. When one has a "way" with one—as, in all modesty, Millner knew he had—not to utilize it is a stupid waste of force. And when he had learned that Orlando G. Spence was in search of a private secretary who should be able to give him intelligent assistance in the execution of his philanthropic schemes, the young man felt that his hour had come. It was no part of his plan to associate himself with one of the masters of finance: he had a notion that minnows who go to a whale to learn how to grow bigger are likely to be swallowed in the process. The opportunity of a clever young man with a cool head and no prejudices (this again was drawn from life) lay rather in making himself indispensable to one of the beneficent rich, and in using the timidities and conformities of his patron as the means of his scruples about formulating these principles to himself. It was not for nothing that, in his college days, he had hunted the hypothetical "moral sense" to its lair, and dragged from their concealment the various self-advancing sentiments dissembled under its edifying guise. His strength lay in his precocious insight into the springs of action, and in his refusal to classify them according to the accepted moral and social sanctions. He had to the full the courage of his lack of convictions.

To a young man so untrammelled by prejudice it was self-evident that helpless philanthropists like Orlando G. Spence were just as much the natural diet of the strong as the lamb is of the wolf. It was pleasanter to eat than to be eaten, in a world where, as yet, there seemed to be no third alternative; and any scruples one might feel as to the temporary discomfort of one's victim were speedily dispelled by that larger scientific view which took into account the social destructiveness of the benevolent. Millner was persuaded that every individual woe mitigated by the philanthropy of Orlando G. Spence added just so much to the sum-total of human inefficiency, and it was one of his favorite subjects of speculation to picture the innumerable social evils that may follow upon the rescue of one infant from Mount Taygetus.

"We're all born to prey on each other, and pity for suffering is one of the most elementary stages of egotism. Until one has passed beyond, and acquired a taste for the more complex forms of the instinct—"

He stopped suddenly, checked in his advance by a sallow wisp of a dog which had plunged through the press of vehicles to hurl itself between his legs. Millner did not dislike animals, though he preferred that they should be healthy and handsome. The dog under his feet was neither. Its cringing contour showed an injudicious mingling of races, and its meager coat betrayed the deplorable habit of sleeping in coal-holes and subsisting on an innutritious diet. In addition to these physical disadvantages, its shrinking and inconsequent movements revealed a congenital weakness of character which, even under more favorable conditions, would hardly have qualified it to become a useful member of society; and Millner was not sorry to notice that it moved with a limp of the hind leg that probably doomed it to speedy extinction.

The absurdity of such an animal's attempting to cross Fifth Avenue at the most crowded hour of the afternoon struck him as only less great than the irony of its having been permitted to achieve the feat; and he stood a moment looking at it, and wondering what had moved it to the attempt. It was really a perfect type of the human derelict which Orlando G. Spence and his kind were devoting their millions to perpetuate, and he reflected how much better Nature knew her business in dealing with the superfluous quadruped.

A lady advancing in the opposite direction evidently took a less dispassionate view of the case, for she paused to remark emotionally: "Oh, you poor thing!" while she stooped to caress the object of her sympathy. The dog, with characteristic lack of discrimination, viewed her gesture with suspicion, and met it with a snarl. The lady turned pale and shrank away, a chivalrous male repelled the animal with his umbrella, and two idle boys backed his action by a vigorous "Hi!" The object of these hostile demonstrations, apparently attributing them not to its own unsocial conduct, but merely to the chronic animosity of the universe, dashed wildly around the corner into a side street, and as it did so Millner noticed that the lame leg left a little trail of blood. Irresistibly, he turned the corner to see what would happen next. It was deplorably clear that the animal itself had no plan; but after several inconsequent and contradictory movements it plunged down an area, where it backed up against the iron gate, forlornly and foolishly at bay.

Millner, still following, looked down at it, and wondered. Then he whistled, just to see if it would come; but this only caused it to start up on its quivering legs, with desperate turns of the head that measured the chances of escape.

"Oh, hang it, you poor devil, stay there if you like!" the young man murmured, walking away.

A few yards off he looked back, and saw that the dog had made a rush out of the area and was limping furtively down the street. The idle boys were in the offing, and he disliked the thought of leaving them in control of the situation. Softly, with infinite precautions, he began to follow the dog. He did not know why he was doing it, but the impulse was overmastering. For a moment he seemed to be gaining upon his quarry, but with a cunning sense of his approach it suddenly turned and hobbled across the frozen grass-plot adjoining a shuttered house. Against the wall at the back of the plot it cowered down in a dirty snow-drift, as if disheartened by the struggle. Millner stood outside the railings and looked at it. He reflected that under the shelter of the winter dusk it might have the luck to remain there unmolested, and that in the morning it would probably be dead of cold. This was so obviously the best solution that he began to move away again; but as he did so the idle boys confronted him.

"Ketch yer dog for yer, boss?" they grinned.

Millner consigned them to the devil, and stood sternly watching them till the first stage of the journey had carried them around the nearest corner; then, after pausing to look once more up and down the empty street, laid his hand on the railing, and vaulted over it into the grass-plot. As he did so, he reflected that, since pity for suffering was one of the most elementary forms of egotism, he ought to have remembered that it was necessarily one of the most tenacious.

## II

"MY chief aim in life?" Orlando G. Spence repeated. He threw himself back in his chair, straightened the tortoise-shell pince-nez, on his short blunt nose, and beamed down the luncheon table at the two young men who shared his repast.

His glance rested on his son Draper, seated opposite him behind a barrier of

Georgian silver and orchids; but his words were addressed to his secretary who, stylograph in hand, had turned from the seductions of a mushroom soufflé in order to jot down, for the Sunday *Investigator*, an outline of his employer's views and intentions respecting the newly endowed Orlando G. Spence College for Missionaries. It was Mr. Spence's practice to receive in person the journalists privileged to impart his opinions to a waiting world; but during the last few months—and especially since the vast project of the Missionary College had been in process of development—the pressure of business and beneficence had necessitated Millner's frequent intervention, and compelled the secretary to snatch the sense of his patron's elucubrations between the courses of their hasty meals.

Young Millner had a healthy appetite, and it was not one of his least sacrifices to be so often obliged to curb it in the interest of his advancement; but whenever he waved aside one of the triumphs of Mr. Spence's chef he was conscious of rising a step in his employer's favor. Mr. Spence did not despise the pleasures of the table, though he appeared to regard them as the reward of success rather than as the alleviation of effort; and it increased his sense of his secretary's merit to note how keenly the young man enjoyed the fare which he was so frequently obliged to deny himself. Draper, having subsisted since infancy on a diet of truffles and terrapin, consumed such delicacies with the insensibility of a traveller swallowing a railway sandwich; but Millner never made the mistake of concealing from Mr. Spence his sense of what he was losing when duty constrained him to exchange the fork for the pen.

"My chief aim in life!" Mr. Spence repeated, removing his eye-glass and swinging it thoughtfully on his finger. ("I'm sorry you should miss this soufflé, Millner: it's worth while.) Why, I suppose I might say that my chief aim in life is to leave the world better than I found it. Yes: I don't know that I could put it better than that. To leave the world better than I found it. It wouldn't be a bad idea to use that as a headline. *'Wants to leave the world better than he found it.'* It's exactly the point I should like to make in this talk for the *Investigator* about the College."

Mr. Spence paused, and his glance once more reverted to his son, who, having pushed aside his plate, sat watching Millner with a dreamy intensity.

"And it's the point I want to make with you, too, Draper," his father continued genially, while he turned over with a critical fork the plump and perfectly matched asparagus which a footman was presenting to his notice. "I want to make you feel that nothing else counts in comparison with that—no amount of literary success or intellectual celebrity."

"Oh, I *do* feel that," Draper murmured, with one of his quick blushes, and a glance that wavered between his father and Millner. The secretary kept his eyes on his notes, and young Spence continued, after a pause: "Only the thing is—isn't it?—to try and find out just what *does* make the world better?"

"To *try* to find out?" his father echoed compassionately. "It's not necessary to try very hard. Goodness is what makes the world better."

"Yes, yes, of course," his son nervously interposed; "but the question is, what is good—"

Mr. Spence, with a darkening brow, brought his fist down emphatically on the damask. "I'll thank you not to blaspheme, my son!"

Draper's head reared itself a trifle higher on his thin neck. "I was not going to blaspheme; only there may be different ways—"

"There's where you're mistaken, Draper. There's only one way: there's my way," said

Mr. Spence in a tone of unshaken conviction.

"I know, father; I see what you mean. But don't you see that even your way wouldn't be the right way for you if you ceased to believe that it was?"

His father looked at him with mingled bewilderment and reprobation. "Do you mean to say that the fact of goodness depends on my conception of it, and not on God Almighty's?"

"I do ... yes ... in a specific sense ..." young Draper falteringly maintained; and Mr. Spence turned with a discouraged gesture toward his secretary's suspended pen.

"I don't understand your scientific jargon, Draper; and I don't want to.—What's the next point, Millner? (No; no *Savarin*. Bring the fruit—and the coffee with it.)"

Millner, keenly aware that an aromatic *Savarin au rhum* was describing an arc behind his head previous to being rushed back to the pantry under young Draper's indifferent eye, stiffened himself against this last assault of the enemy, and read out firmly: *"What relation do you consider that a man's business conduct should bear to his religious and domestic life?"*

Mr. Spence mused a moment. "Why, that's a stupid question. It goes over the same ground as the other one. A man ought to do good with his money—that's all. Go on."

At this point the butler's murmur in his ear caused him to push back his chair, and to arrest Millner's interrogatory by a rapid gesture. "Yes; I'm coming. Hold the wire." Mr. Spence rose and plunged into the adjoining "office," where a telephone and a Remington divided the attention of a young lady in spectacles who was preparing for Zenana work in the East.

As the door closed, the butler, having placed the coffee and liqueurs on the table, withdrew in the rear of his battalion, and the two young men were left alone beneath the Rembrandts and Hobbemas on the dining-room walls.

There was a moment's silence between them; then young Spence, leaning across the table, said in the lowered tone of intimacy: "Why do you suppose he dodged that last question?"

Millner, who had rapidly taken an opulent purple fig from the fruit-dish nearest him, paused in surprise in the act of hurrying it to his lips.

"I mean," Draper hastened on, "the question as to the relation between business and private morality. It's such an interesting one, and he's just the person who ought to tackle it."

Millner, dispatching the fig, glanced down at his notes. "I don't think your father meant to dodge the question."

Young Draper continued to look at him.

"You think he imagined that his answer really covers the ground?"

"As much as it needs to be covered."

The son of the house glanced away with a sigh.

"You know things about him that I don't," he said wistfully, but without a tinge of resentment.

"Oh, as to that—(may I give myself some coffee?)" Millner, in his walk around the table to fill his cup, paused a moment to lay an affectionate hand on Draper's shoulder. "Perhaps I know him better, in a sense: outsiders often get a more accurate focus."

Draper seemed to consider this. "And your idea is that he acts on principles he has never thought of testing or defining?"

Millner looked up quickly, and for an instant their glances crossed.

"How do you mean?"

"I mean: that he's an inconscient instrument of goodness, as it were? A—a sort of blindly beneficent force?"

The other smiled. "That's not a bad definition. I know one thing about him, at any rate: he's awfully upset at your having chucked your Bible Class."

A shadow fell on young Spence's candid brow. "I know. But what can I do about it? That's what I was thinking of when I tried to show him that goodness, in a certain sense, is purely subjective: that one can't do good against one's principles." Again his glance appealed to Millner. *"You* understand me, don't you?"

Millner stirred his coffee in a silence not unclouded by perplexity. "Theoretically, perhaps. It's a pretty question, certainly. But I also understand your father's feeling that it hasn't much to do with real life: especially now that he's got to make a speech in connection with the founding of this Missionary College. He may think that any hint of internecine strife will weaken his prestige. Mightn't you have waited a little longer?"

"How could I, when I might have been expected to take a part in this performance? To talk, and say things I didn't mean? That was exactly what made me decide not to wait."

The door opened and Mr. Spence re-entered the room. As he did so his son rose abruptly as if to leave it.

"Where are you off to, Draper?" the banker asked.

"I'm in rather a hurry, sir—"

Mr. Spence looked at his watch. "You can't be in more of a hurry than I am; and I've got seven minutes and a half." He seated himself behind the coffee—tray, lit a cigar, laid his watch on the table, and signed to Draper to resume his place. "No, Millner, don't you go; I want you both." He turned to the secretary. "You know that Draper's given up his Bible Class? I understand it's not from the pressure of engagements—" Mr. Spence's narrow lips took an ironic curve under the straight-clipped stubble of his moustache— "it's on principle, he tells me. He's *principled* against doing good!"

Draper lifted a protesting hand. "It's not exactly that, father—"

"I know: you'll tell me it's some scientific quibble that I don't understand. I've never had time to go in for intellectual hair-splitting. I've found too many people down in the mire who needed a hand to pull them out. A busy man has to take his choice between helping his fellow-men and theorizing about them. I've preferred to help. (You might take that down for the *Investigator*, Millner.) And I thank God I've never stopped to ask what made me want to do good. I've just yielded to the impulse—that's all." Mr. Spence turned back to his son. "Better men than either of us have been satisfied with that creed, my son."

Draper was silent, and Mr. Spence once more addressed himself to his secretary. "Millner, you're a reader: I've caught you at it. And I know this boy talks to you. What have you got to say? Do you suppose a Bible Class ever *hurt* anybody?"

Millner paused a moment, feeling all through his nervous system the fateful tremor of the balance. "That's what I was just trying to tell him, sir—"

"Ah; you were? That's good. Then I'll only say one thing more. Your doing what you've done at this particular moment hurts me more, Draper, than your teaching the gospel of Jesus could possibly have hurt those young men over in Tenth Avenue." Mr. Spence arose and restored his watch to his pocket. "I shall want you in twenty minutes, Millner."

The door closed on him, and for a while the two young men sat silent behind their cigar fumes. Then Draper Spence broke out, with a catch in his throat: "That's what I can't bear, Millner, what I simply can't *bear:* to hurt him, to hurt his faith in *me!* It's an awful responsibility, isn't it, to tamper with anybody's faith in anything?"

III

THE twenty minutes prolonged themselves to forty, the forty to fifty, and the fifty to an hour; and still Millner waited for Mr. Spence's summons.

During the two years of his secretaryship the young man had learned the significance of such postponements. Mr. Spence's days were organized like a railway time-table, and a delay of an hour implied a casualty as far-reaching as the breaking down of an express. Of the cause of the present derangement Hugh Millner was ignorant; and the experience of the last months allowed him to fluctuate between conflicting conjectures. All were based on the indisputable fact that Mr. Spence was "bothered"—had for some time past been "bothered." And it was one of Millner's discoveries that an extremely parsimonious use of the emotions underlay Mr. Spence's expansive manner and fraternal phraseology, and that he did not throw away his feelings any more than (for all his philanthropy) he threw away his money. If he was bothered, then, it could be only because a careful survey of his situation had forced on him some unpleasant fact with which he was not immediately prepared to deal; and any unpreparedness on Mr. Spence's part was also a significant symptom.

Obviously, Millner's original conception of his employer's character had suffered extensive modification; but no final outline had replaced the first conjectural image. The two years spent in Mr. Spence's service had produced too many contradictory impressions to be fitted into any definite pattern; and the chief lesson Millner had learned from them was that life was less of an exact science, and character a more incalculable element, than he had been taught in the schools. In the light of this revised impression, his own footing seemed less secure than he had imagined, and the rungs of the ladder he was climbing more slippery than they had looked from below. He was not without the reassuring sense of having made himself, in certain small ways, necessary to Mr. Spence; and this conviction was confirmed by Draper's reiterated assurance of his father's appreciation. But Millner had begun to suspect that one might be necessary to Mr. Spence one day, and a superfluity, if not an obstacle, the next; and that it would take superhuman astuteness to foresee how and when the change would occur. Every fluctuation of the great man's mood was therefore anxiously noted by the young meteorologist in his service; and this observer's vigilance was now strained to the utmost by the little cloud, no bigger than a man's hand, adumbrated by the banker's unpunctuality.

When Mr. Spence finally appeared, his aspect did not tend to dissipate the cloud. He wore what Millner had learned to call his "back-door face": a blank barred countenance, in which only an occasional twitch of the lids behind his glasses suggested that some one was on the watch. In this mood Mr. Spence usually seemed unconscious of his secretary's presence, or aware of it only as an arm terminating in a pen. Millner, accustomed on such occasions to exist merely as a function, sat waiting for the click of the spring that should set him in action; but the pressure not being applied, he finally hazarded: "Are we to go on with the *Investigator,* sir?"

Mr. Spence, who had been pacing up and down between the desk and the fireplace, threw himself into his usual seat at Millner's elbow.

"I don't understand this new notion of Draper's," he said abruptly. "Where's he got it from? No one ever learned irreligion in my household."

He turned his eyes on Millner, who had the sense of being scrutinized through a ground-glass window which left him visible while it concealed his observer. The young man let his pen describe two or three vague patterns on the blank sheet before him.

"Draper has ideas—" he risked at last.

Mr. Spence looked hard at him. "That's all right," he said. "I want my son to have everything. But what's the point of mixing up ideas and principles? I've seen fellows who did that, and they were generally trying to borrow five dollars to get away from the sheriff. What's all this talk about goodness? Goodness isn't an idea. It's a fact. It's as solid as a business proposition. And it's Draper's duty, as the son of a wealthy man, and the prospective steward of a great fortune, to elevate the standards of other young men—of young men who haven't had his opportunities. The rich ought to preach contentment, and to set the example themselves. We have our cares, but we ought to conceal them. We ought to be cheerful, and accept things as they are—not go about sowing dissent and restlessness. What has Draper got to give these boys in his Bible Class, that's so much better than what he wants to take from them? That's the question I'd like to have answered."

Mr. Spence, carried away by his own eloquence, had removed his *pince-nez* and was twirling it about his extended fore-finger with the gesture habitual to him when he spoke in public. After a pause, he went on, with a drop to the level of private intercourse: "I tell you this because I know you have a good deal of influence with Draper. He has a high opinion of your brains. But you're a practical fellow, and you must see what I mean. Try to make Draper see it. Make him understand how it looks to have him drop his Bible Class just at this particular time. It was his own choice to take up religious teaching among young men. He began with our office-boys, and then the work spread and was blessed. I was almost alarmed, at one time, at the way it took hold of him: when the papers began to talk about him as a formative influence I was afraid he'd lose his head and go into the church. Luckily he tried University Settlement first; but just as I thought he was settling down to that, he took to worrying about the Higher Criticism, and saying he couldn't go on teaching fairy-tales as history. I can't see that any good ever came of criticizing what our parents believed, and it's a queer time for Draper to criticize my belief just as I'm backing it to the extent of five millions."

Millner remained silent; and, as though his silence were an argument, Mr. Spence continued combatively: "Draper's always talking about some distinction between religion and morality. I don't understand what he means. I got my morals out of the Bible, and I guess there's enough left in it for Draper. If religion won't make a man moral, I don't see why irreligion should. And he talks about using his mind—well, can't he use that in Wall Street? A man can get a good deal farther in life watching the market than picking holes in Genesis; and he can do more good too. There's a time for everything; and Draper seems to me to have mixed up week-days with Sunday."

Mr. Spence replaced his eye-glasses, and stretching his hand to the silver box at his elbow, extracted from it one of the long cigars sheathed in gold-leaf which were reserved for his private consumption. The secretary hastened to tender him a match, and for a moment he puffed in silence. When he spoke again it was in a different note.

"I've got about all the bother I can handle just now, without this nonsense of Draper's. That was one of the Trustees of the College with me. It seems the *Flashlight* has been trying to stir up a fuss—" Mr. Spence paused, and turned his *pince-nez* on his secretary. "You haven't heard from them?" he asked.

"From the *Flashlight?* No." Millner's surprise was genuine.

He detected a gleam of relief behind Mr. Spence's glasses. "It may be just malicious talk. That's the worst of good works; they bring out all the meanness in human nature. And then there are always women mixed up in them, and there never was a woman yet who understood the difference between philanthropy and business." He drew again at his cigar, and then, with an unwonted movement, leaned forward and mechanically pushed the box toward Millner. "Help yourself," he said.

Millner, as mechanically, took one of the virginally cinctured cigars, and began to undo its wrappings. It was the first time he had ever been privileged to detach that golden girdle, and nothing could have given him a better measure of the importance of the situation, and of the degree to which he was apparently involved in it. "You remember that San Pablo rubber business? That's what they've been raking up," said Mr. Spence abruptly.

Millner paused in the act of striking a match. Then, with an appreciable effort of the will, he completed the gesture, applied the flame to his cigar, and took a long inhalation. The cigar was certainly delicious.

Mr. Spence, drawing a little closer, leaned forward and touched him on the arm. The touch caused Millner to turn his head, and for an instant the glance of the two men crossed at short range. Millner was conscious, first, of a nearer view than he had ever had of his employer's face, and of its vaguely suggesting a seamed sandstone head, the kind of thing that lies in a corner in the court of a museum, and in which only the round enameled eyes have resisted the wear of time. His next feeling was that he had now reached the moment to which the offer of the cigar had been a prelude. He had always known that, sooner or later, such a moment would come; all his life, in a sense, had been a preparation for it. But in entering Mr. Spence's service he had not foreseen that it would present itself in this form. He had seen himself consciously guiding that gentleman up to the moment, rather than being thrust into it by a stronger hand. And his first act of reflection was the resolve that, in the end, his hand should prove the stronger of the two. This was followed, almost immediately, by the idea that to be stronger than Mr. Spence's it would have to be very strong indeed. It was odd that he should feel this, since—as far as verbal communication went—it was Mr. Spence who was asking for his support. In a theoretical statement of the case the banker would have figured as being at Millner's mercy; but one of the queerest things about experience was the way it made light of theory. Millner felt now as though he were being crushed by some inexorable engine of which he had been playing with the lever. ...

He had always been intensely interested in observing his own reactions, and had regarded this faculty of self-detachment as of immense advantage in such a career as he had planned. He felt this still, even in the act of noting his own bewilderment—felt it the more in contrast to the odd unconsciousness of Mr. Spence's attitude, of the incredible candor of his self-abasement and self-abandonment. It was clear that Mr. Spence was not troubled by the repercussion of his actions in the consciousness of others; and this looked like a weakness—unless it were, instead, a great strength. ...

Through the hum of these swarming thoughts Mr. Spence's voice was going on. "That's the only rag of proof they've got; and they got it by one of those nasty accidents that nobody can guard against. I don't care how conscientiously a man attends to business, he can't always protect himself against meddlesome people. I don't pretend to know how the letter came into their hands; but they've got it; and they mean to use it— and they mean to say that you wrote it for me, and that you knew what it was about when you wrote it. ... They'll probably be after you tomorrow—"

Mr. Spence, restoring his cigar to his lips, puffed at it slowly. In the pause that followed there was an instant during which the universe seemed to Hugh Millner like a sounding-board bent above his single consciousness. If he spoke, what thunders would be sent back to him from that intently listening vastness?

"You see?" said Mr. Spence.

The universal ear bent closer, as if to catch the least articulation of Millner's narrowed lips; but when he opened them it was merely to re-insert his cigar, and for a short space nothing passed between the two men but an exchange of smoke rings.

"What do you mean to do? There's the point," Mr. Spence at length sent through the rings.

Oh, yes, the point was there, as distinctly before Millner as the tip of his expensive cigar: he had seen it coming quite as soon as Mr. Spence. He knew that fate was handing him an ultimatum; but the sense of the formidable echo which his least answer would rouse kept him doggedly, and almost helplessly, silent. To let Mr. Spence talk on as long as possible was no doubt the best way of gaining time; but Millner knew that his silence was really due to his dread of the echo. Suddenly, however, in a reaction of impatience at his own indecision, he began to speak.

The sound of his voice cleared his mind and strengthened his resolve. It was odd how the word seemed to shape the act, though one knew how ancillary it really was. As he talked, it was as if the globe had swung around, and he himself were upright on its axis, with Mr. Spence underneath, on his head. Through the ensuing interchange of concise and rapid speech there sounded in Millner's ears the refrain to which he had walked down Fifth Avenue after his first talk with Mr. Spence: "It's too easy—it's too easy—it's too easy." Yes, it was even easier than he had expected. His sensation was that of the skillful carver who feels his good blade sink into a tender joint.

As he went on talking, this surprised sense of mastery was like wine in his veins. Mr. Spence was at his mercy, after all—that was what it came to; but this new view of the case did not lessen Millner's sense of Mr. Spence's strength, it merely revealed to him his own superiority. Mr. Spence was even stronger than he had suspected. There could be no better proof of that than his faith in Millner's power to grasp the situation, and his tacit recognition of the young man's right to make the most of it. Millner felt that Mr. Spence would have despised him even more for not using his advantage than for not seeing it; and this homage to his capacity nerved him to greater alertness, and made the concluding moments of their talk as physically exhilarating as some hotly contested game.

When the conclusion was reached, and Millner stood at the goal, the golden trophy in his grasp, his first conscious thought was one of regret that the struggle was over. He would have liked to prolong their talk for the purely aesthetic pleasure of making Mr. Spence lose time, and, better still, of making him forget that he was losing it. The sense of advantage that the situation conferred was so great that when Mr. Spence rose it was as if Millner were dismissing him, and when he reached his hand toward the cigar-box it seemed to be one of Millner's cigars that he was taking.

## IV

THERE had been only one condition attached to the transaction: Millner was to speak to Draper about the Bible Class.

The condition was easy to fulfill. Millner was confident of his power to deflect his young friend's purpose; and he knew the opportunity would be given him before the day was over. His professional duties dispatched, he had only to go up to his room to wait. Draper nearly always looked in on him for a moment before dinner: it was the hour most propitious to their elliptic interchange of words and silences.

Meanwhile, the waiting was an occupation in itself. Millner looked about his room with new eyes. Since the first thrill of initiation into its complicated comforts—the shower-bath, the telephone, the many-jointed reading-lamp and the vast mirrored presses through which he was always hunting his scant outfit—Millner's room had interested him no more than a railway-carriage in which he might have been travelling. But now it had acquired a sort of historic significance as the witness of the astounding change in his fate. It was Corsica, it was Brienne—it was the kind of spot that posterity might yet mark with a tablet. Then he reflected that he should soon be leaving it, and the lustre of its monumental mahogany was veiled in pathos. Why indeed should he linger on in bondage? He perceived with a certain surprise that the only thing he should regret would be leaving Draper. ...

It was odd, it was inconsequent, it was almost exasperating, that such a regret should obscure his triumph. Why in the world should he suddenly take to regretting Draper? If there were any logic in human likings, it should be to Mr. Spence that he inclined. Draper, dear lad, had the illusion of an "intellectual sympathy" between them; but that, Millner knew, was an affair of reading and not of character. Draper's temerities would always be of that kind; whereas his own—well, his own, put to the proof, had now definitely classed him with Mr. Spence rather than with Mr. Spence's son. It was a consequence of this new condition—of his having thus distinctly and irrevocably classed himself—that, when Draper at length brought upon the scene his shy shamble and his wistful smile, Millner, for the first time, had to steel himself against them instead of yielding to their charm.

In the new order upon which he had entered, one principle of the old survived: the point of honor between allies. And Millner had promised Mr. Spence to speak to Draper about his Bible Class. ...

Draper, thrown back in his chair, and swinging a loose leg across a meager knee, listened with his habitual gravity. His downcast eyes seemed to pursue the vision which Millner's words evoked; and the words, to their speaker, took on a new sound as that candid consciousness refracted them.

"You know, dear boy, I perfectly see your father's point. It's naturally distressing to him, at this particular time, to have any hint of civil war leak out—"

Draper sat upright, laying his lank legs knee to knee.

"That's it, then? I thought that was it!"

Millner raised a surprised glance. *"What's* it?"

"That it should be at this particular time—"

"Why, naturally, as I say! Just as he's making, as it were, his public profession of faith. You know, to men like your father convictions are irreducible elements—they can't be split up, and differently combined. And your exegetical scruples seem to him to strike at the very root of his convictions."

Draper pulled himself to his feet and shuffled across the room. Then he turned about, and stood before his friend.

"Is it that—or is it this?" he said; and with the word he drew a letter from his pocket and proffered it silently to Millner.

The latter, as he unfolded it, was first aware of an intense surprise at the young man's abruptness of tone and gesture. Usually Draper fluttered long about his point before making it; and his sudden movement seemed as mechanical as the impulsion conveyed by some strong spring. The spring, of course, was in the letter; and to it Millner turned his startled glance, feeling the while that, by some curious cleavage of perception, he was continuing to watch Draper while he read.

"Oh, the beasts!" he cried.

He and Draper were face to face across the sheet which had dropped between them. The youth's features were tightened by a smile that was like the ligature of a wound. He looked white and withered.

"Ah—you knew, then?"

Millner sat still, and after a moment Draper turned from him, walked to the hearth, and leaned against the chimney, propping his chin on his hands. Millner, his head thrown back, stared up at the ceiling, which had suddenly become to him the image of the universal sounding-board hanging over his consciousness.

"You knew, then?" Draper repeated.

Millner remained silent. He had perceived, with the surprise of a mathematician working out a new problem, that the lie which Mr. Spence had just bought of him was exactly the one gift he could give of his own free will to Mr. Spence's son. This discovery gave the world a strange new topsy-turvyness, and set Millner's theories spinning about his brain like the cabin furniture of a tossing ship.

"You *knew*," said Draper, in a tone of quiet affirmation.

Millner righted himself, and grasped the arms of his chair as if that too were reeling. "About this blackguardly charge?"

Draper was studying him intently. "What does it matter if it's blackguardly?"

"Matter—?" Millner stammered.

"It's that, of course, in any case. But the point is whether it's true or not." Draper bent down, and picking up the crumpled letter, smoothed it out between his fingers. "The point, is, whether my father, when he was publicly denouncing the peonage abuses on the San Pablo plantations over a year ago, had actually sold out his stock, as he announced at the time; or whether, as they say here—how do they put it?—he had simply transferred it to a dummy till the scandal should blow over, and has meanwhile gone on drawing his forty per cent interest on five thousand shares? There's the point."

Millner had never before heard his young friend put a case with such unadorned precision. His language was like that of Mr. Spence making a statement to a committee meeting; and the resemblance to his father flashed out with ironic incongruity.

"You see why I've brought this letter to you—I couldn't go to him with it!" Draper's voice faltered, and the resemblance vanished as suddenly as it had appeared.

"No; you couldn't go to him with it," said Millner slowly.

"And since they say here that *you* know: that they've got your letter proving it—" The muscles of Draper's face quivered as if a blinding light had been swept over it. "For God's sake, Millner—it's all right?"

"It's all right," said Millner, rising to his feet.

Draper caught him by the wrist. "You're sure—you're absolutely sure?"

"Sure. They know they've got nothing to go on."

Draper fell back a step and looked almost sternly at his friend. "That's not what I mean. I don't care a straw what they think they've got to go on. I want to know if my father's all right. If he is, they can say what they please."

Millner, again, felt himself under the concentrated scrutiny of the ceiling. "Of course, of course. I understand."

"You understand? Then why don't you answer?"

Millner looked compassionately at the boy's struggling face. Decidedly, the battle was to the strong, and he was not sorry to be on the side of the legions. But Draper's pain was as awkward as a material obstacle, as something that one stumbled over in a race.

"You know what I'm driving at, Millner." Again Mr. Spence's committee-meeting tone sounded oddly through his son's strained voice. "If my father's so awfully upset about my giving up my Bible Class, and letting it be known that I do so on conscientious grounds, is it because he's afraid it may be considered a criticism on something *he* has done which—which won't bear the test of the doctrines he believes in?"

Draper, with the last question, squared himself in front of Millner, as if suspecting that the latter meant to evade it by flight. But Millner had never felt more disposed to stand his ground than at that moment.

"No—by Jove, no! It's not *that*." His relief almost escaped him in a cry, as he lifted his head to give back Draper's look.

"On your honor?" the other passionately pressed him.

"Oh, on anybody's you like—on *yours!*" Millner could hardly restrain a laugh of relief. It was vertiginous to find himself spared, after all, the need of an altruistic lie: he perceived that they were the kind he least liked.

Draper took a deep breath. "You don't—Millner, a lot depends on this—you don't really think my father has any ulterior motive?"

"I think he has none but his horror of seeing you go straight to perdition!"

They looked at each other again, and Draper's tension was suddenly relieved by a free boyish laugh. "It's his convictions—it's just his funny old convictions?"

"It's that, and nothing else on earth!"

Draper turned back to the arm-chair he had left, and let his narrow figure sink down into it as into a bath. Then he looked over at Millner with a smile. "I can see that I've been worrying him horribly. So he really thinks I'm on the road to perdition? Of course you can fancy what a sick minute I had when I thought it might be this other reason—the damnable insinuation in this letter." Draper crumpled the paper in his hand, and leaned forward to toss it into the coals of the grate. "I ought to have known better, of course. I ought to have remembered that, as you say, my father can't conceive how conduct may be independent of creed. That's where I was stupid—and rather base. But that letter made me dizzy—I couldn't think. Even now I can't very clearly. I'm not sure what my convictions require of me: they seem to me so much less to be considered than his! When I've done half the good to people that he has, it will be time enough to begin attacking their beliefs. Meanwhile—meanwhile I can't touch his. ..." Draper leaned forward, stretching his lank arms along his knees. His face was as clear as a spring sky. "I won't touch them, Millner—Go and tell him so. ..."

## V

IN the study a half hour later Mr. Spence, watch in hand, was doling out his minutes again. The peril conjured, he had recovered his dominion over time. He turned his commanding eye-glasses on Millner.

"It's all settled, then? Tell Draper I'm sorry not to see him again to-night—but I'm to speak at the dinner of the Legal Relief Association, and I'm due there in five minutes. You and he dine alone here, I suppose? Tell him I appreciate what he's done. Some day he'll see that to leave the world better than we find it is the best we can hope to do.

(You've finished the notes for the *Investigator?* Be sure you don't forget that phrase.) Well, good evening: that's all, I think."

Smooth and compact in his glossy evening clothes, Mr. Spence advanced toward the study door; but as he reached it, his secretary stood there before him.

"It's not quite all, Mr. Spence."

Mr. Spence turned on him a look in which impatience was faintly tinged with apprehension. "What else is there? It's two and a half minutes to eight."

Millner stood his ground. "It won't take longer than that. I want to tell you that, if you can conveniently replace me, I'd like—there are reasons why I shall have to leave you."

Millner was conscious of reddening as he spoke. His redness deepened under Mr. Spence's dispassionate scrutiny. He saw at once that the banker was not surprised at his announcement.

"Well, I suppose that's natural enough. You'll want to make a start for yourself now. Only, of course, for the sake of appearances—"

"Oh, certainly," Millner hastily agreed.

"Well, then: is that all?" Mr. Spence repeated.

"Nearly." Millner paused, as if in search of an appropriate formula. But after a moment he gave up the search, and pulled from his pocket an envelope which he held out to his employer. "I merely want to give this back."

The hand which Mr. Spence had extended dropped to his side, and his sand-colored face grew chalky. "Give it back?" His voice was as thick as Millner's. "What's happened? Is the bargain off?"

"Oh, no. I've given you my word."

"Your word?" Mr. Spence lowered at him. "I'd like to know what that's worth!"

Millner continued to hold out the envelope. "You do know, now. It's worth *that*. It's worth my place."

Mr. Spence, standing motionless before him, hesitated for an appreciable space of time. His lips parted once or twice under their square-clipped stubble, and at last emitted: "You'd better say at once how much more you want."

Millner broke into a laugh. "Oh, I've got all I want—all and more!"

"What—from the others? Are you crazy?"

"No, you are," said Millner with a sudden recovery of composure. "But you're safe—you're as safe as you'll ever be. Only I don't care to take this for making you so."

Mr. Spence slowly moistened his lips with his tongue, and removing his *pince-nez*, took a long hard look at Millner.

"I don't understand. What other guarantee have I got?"

"That I mean what I say?" Millner glanced past the banker's figure at his rich densely colored background of Spanish leather and mahogany. He remembered that it was from this very threshold that he had first seen Mr. Spence's son.

"What guaranty? You've got Draper!" he said.

## AFTERWARD

"Oh, THERE *is* one, of course, but you'll never know it."

The assertion, laughingly flung out six months earlier in a bright June garden, came back to Mary Boyne with a sharp perception of its latent significance as she stood, in the December dusk, waiting for the lamps to be brought into the library.

The words had been spoken by their friend Alida Stair, as they sat at tea on her lawn at Pangbourne, in reference to the very house of which the library in question was the central, the pivotal "feature." Mary Boyne and her husband, in quest of a country place in one of the southern or southwestern counties, had, on their arrival in England, carried their problem straight to Alida Stair, who had successfully solved it in her own case; but it was not until they had rejected, almost capriciously, several practical and judicious suggestions that she threw it out: "Well, there's Lyng, in Dorsetshire. It belongs to Hugo's cousins, and you can get it for a song."

The reason she gave for its being obtainable on these terms—its remoteness from a station, its lack of electric light, hot-water pipes, and other vulgar necessities—were exactly those pleading in its favor with two romantic Americans perversely in search of the economic drawbacks which were associated, in their tradition, with unusual architectural felicities.

"I should never believe I was living in an old house unless I was thoroughly uncomfortable," Ned Boyne, the more extravagant of the two, had jocosely insisted; "the least hint of 'convenience' would make me think it had been bought out of an exhibition, with the pieces numbered, and set up again." And they had proceeded to enumerate, with humorous precision, their various suspicions and exactions, refusing to believe that the house their cousin recommended was *really* Tudor till they learned it had no heating system, or that the village church was literally in the grounds till she assured them of the deplorable uncertainty of the water supply.

"It's too uncomfortable to be true!" Edward Boyne had continued to exult as the avowal of each disadvantage was successively wrung from her; but he had cut short his rhapsody to ask, with a sudden relapse to distrust: "And the ghost? You've been concealing from us the fact that there is no ghost!"

Mary, at the moment, had laughed with him, yet almost with her laugh, being possessed of several sets of independent perceptions, had noted a sudden flatness of tone in Alida's answering hilarity.

"Oh, Dorsetshire's full of ghosts, you know."

"Yes, yes; but that won't do. I don't want to have to drive ten miles to see somebody else's ghost. I want one of my own on the premises. Is there a ghost at Lyng?"

His rejoinder had made Alida laugh again, and it was then that she had flung back tantalizingly: "Oh, there *is* one, of course, but you'll never know it."

"Never know it?" Boyne pulled her up. "But what in the world constitutes a ghost except the fact of its being known for one?"

"I can't say. But that's the story."

"That there's a ghost, but that nobody knows it's a ghost?"

"Well—not till afterward, at any rate."

"Till afterward?"

"Not till long, long afterward."

"But if it's once been identified as an unearthly visitant, why hasn't its *signalement* been handed down in the family? How has it managed to preserve its incognito?"

Alida could only shake her head. "Don't ask me. But it has."

"And then suddenly—" Mary spoke up as if from some cavernous depth of divination—"suddenly, long afterward, one says to one's self, *'That was it?'*"

She was oddly startled at the sepulchral sound with which her question fell on the banter of the other two, and she saw the shadow of the same surprise flit across Alida's clear pupils. "I suppose so. One just has to wait."

"Oh, hang waiting!" Ned broke in. "Life's too short for a ghost who can only be enjoyed in retrospect. Can't we do better than that, Mary?"

But it turned out that in the event they were not destined to, for within three months of their conversation with Mrs. Stair they were established at Lyng, and the life they had yearned for to the point of planning it out in all its daily details had actually begun for them.

It was to sit, in the thick December dusk, by just such a wide-hooded fireplace, under just such black oak rafters, with the sense that beyond the mullioned panes the downs were darkening to a deeper solitude: it was for the ultimate indulgence in such sensations that Mary Boyne had endured for nearly fourteen years the soul-deadening ugliness of the Middle West, and that Boyne had ground on doggedly at his engineering till, with a suddenness that still made her blink, the prodigious windfall of the Blue Star Mine had put them at a stroke in possession of life and the leisure to taste it. They had never for a moment meant their new state to be one of idleness; but they meant to give themselves only to harmonious activities. She had her vision of painting and gardening (against a background of gray walls), he dreamed of the production of his long-planned book on the "Economic Basis of Culture"; and with such absorbing work ahead no existence could be too sequestered; they could not get far enough from the world, or plunge deep enough into the past.

Dorsetshire had attracted them from the first by a semblance of remoteness out of all proportion to its geographical position. But to the Boynes it was one of the ever-recurring wonders of the whole incredibly compressed island—a nest of counties, as they put it— that for the production of its effects so little of a given quality went so far: that so few miles made a distance, and so short a distance a difference.

"It's that," Ned had once enthusiastically explained, "that gives such depth to their effects, such relief to their least contrasts. They've been able to lay the butter so thick on every exquisite mouthful."

The butter had certainly been laid on thick at Lyng: the old gray house, hidden under a shoulder of the downs, had almost all the finer marks of commerce with a protracted past. The mere fact that it was neither large nor exceptional made it, to the Boynes, abound the more richly in its special sense—the sense of having been for centuries a deep, dim reservoir of life. The life had probably not been of the most vivid order: for long periods, no doubt, it had fallen as noiselessly into the past as the quiet drizzle of autumn fell, hour after hour, into the green fish-pond between the yews; but these back-waters of existence sometimes breed, in their sluggish depths, strange acuities of emotion, and Mary Boyne had felt from the first the occasional brush of an intenser memories.

The feeling had never been stronger than on the December afternoon when, waiting in the library for the belated lamps, she rose from her seat and stood among the shadows of the hearth. Her husband had gone off, after luncheon, for one of his long tramps on the downs. She had noticed of late that he preferred to be unaccompanied on these occasions;

and, in the tried security of their personal relations, had been driven to conclude that his book was bothering him, and that he needed the afternoons to turn over in solitude the problems left from the morning's work. Certainly the book was not going as smoothly as she had imagined it would, and the lines of perplexity between his eyes had never been there in his engineering days. Then he had often looked fagged to the verge of illness, but the native demon of "worry" had never branded his brow. Yet the few pages he had so far read to her—the introduction, and a synopsis of the opening chapter—gave evidences of a firm possession of his subject, and a deepening confidence in his powers.

The fact threw her into deeper perplexity, since, now that he had done with "business" and its disturbing contingencies, the one other possible element of anxiety was eliminated. Unless it were his health, then? But physically he had gained since they had come to Dorsetshire, grown robuster, ruddier, and fresher-eyed. It was only within a week that she had felt in him the undefinable change that made her restless in his absence, and as tongue-tied in his presence as though it were *she* who had a secret to keep from him!

The thought that there was a secret somewhere between them struck her with a sudden smart rap of wonder, and she looked about her down the dim, long room.

"Can it be the house?" she mused.

The room itself might have been full of secrets. They seemed to be piling themselves up, as evening fell, like the layers and layers of velvet shadow dropping from the low ceiling, the dusky walls of books, the smoke-blurred sculpture of the hooded hearth.

"Why, of course—the house is haunted!" she reflected.

The ghost—Alida's imperceptible ghost—after figuring largely in the banter of their first month or two at Lyng, had been gradually discarded as too ineffectual for imaginative use. Mary had, indeed, as became the tenant of a haunted house, made the customary inquiries among her few rural neighbors, but, beyond a vague, "They dü say so, Ma'am," the villagers had nothing to impart. The elusive specter had apparently never had sufficient identity for a legend to crystallize about it, and after a time the Boynes had laughingly set the matter down to their profit-and-loss account, agreeing that Lyng was one of the few houses good enough in itself to dispense with supernatural enhancements.

"And I suppose, poor, ineffectual demon, that's why it beats its beautiful wings in vain in the void," Mary had laughingly concluded.

"Or, rather," Ned answered, in the same strain, "why, amid so much that's ghostly, it can never affirm its separate existence as *the* ghost." And thereupon their invisible housemate had finally dropped out of their references, which were numerous enough to make them promptly unaware of the loss.

Now, as she stood on the hearth, the subject of their earlier curiosity revived in her with a new sense of its meaning—a sense gradually acquired through close daily contact with the scene of the lurking mystery. It was the house itself, of course, that possessed the ghost-seeing faculty, that communed visually but secretly with its own past; and if one could only get into close enough communion with the house, one might surprise its secret, and acquire the ghost-sight on one's own account. Perhaps, in his long solitary hours in this very room, where she never trespassed till the afternoon, her husband *had* acquired it already, and was silently carrying the dread weight of whatever it had revealed to him. Mary was too well-versed in the code of the spectral world not to know that one could not talk about the ghosts one saw: to do so was almost as great a breach of good-breeding as to name a lady in a club. But this explanation did not really satisfy her. "What, after all, except for the fun of the frisson," she reflected, "would he really care for any of their old ghosts?" And thence she was thrown back once more on the fundamental dilemma: the fact that one's greater or less susceptibility to spectral influences had no particular bearing on the case, since, when one *did* see a ghost at Lyng, one did not know it.

"Not till long afterward," Alida Stair had said. Well, supposing Ned *had* seen one when they first came, and had known only within the last week what had happened to him? More and more under the spell of the hour, she threw back her searching thoughts to the early days of their tenancy, but at first only to recall a gay confusion of unpacking, settling, arranging of books, and calling to each other from remote corners of the house as treasure after treasure of their habitation revealed itself to them. It was in this particular connection that she presently recalled a certain soft afternoon of the previous October, when, passing from the first rapturous flurry of exploration to a detailed inspection of the old house, she had pressed (like a novel heroine) a panel that opened at her touch, on a narrow flight of stairs leading to an unsuspected flat ledge of the roof—the roof which, from below, seemed to slope away on all sides too abruptly for any but practised feet to scale.

The view from this hidden coign was enchanting, and she had flown down to snatch Ned from his papers and give him the freedom of her discovery. She remembered still how, standing on the narrow ledge, he had passed his arm about her while their gaze flew to the long, tossed horizon-line of the downs, and then dropped contentedly back to trace the arabesque of yew hedges about the fish-pond, and the shadow of the cedar on the lawn.

"And now the other way," he had said, gently turning her about within his arm; and closely pressed to him, she had absorbed, like some long, satisfying draft, the picture of the gray-walled court, the squat lions on the gates, and the lime-avenue reaching up to the highroad under the downs.

It was just then, while they gazed and held each other, that she had felt his arm relax, and heard a sharp "Hullo!" that made her turn to glance at him.

Distinctly, yes, she now recalled she had seen, as she glanced, a shadow of anxiety, of perplexity, rather, fall across his face; and, following his eyes, had beheld the figure of a man—a man in loose, grayish clothes, as it appeared to her—who was sauntering down the lime-avenue to the court with the tentative gait of a stranger seeking his way. Her short-sighted eyes had given her but a blurred impression of slightness and grayness, with something foreign, or at least unlocal, in the cut of the figure or its garb; but her husband had apparently seen more—seen enough to make him push past her with a sharp "Wait!" and dash down the twisting stairs without pausing to give her a hand.

A slight tendency to dizziness obliged her, after a provisional clutch at the chimney against which they had been leaning, to follow him down more cautiously; and when she had reached the attic landing she paused again for a less definite reason, leaning over the oak banister to strain her eyes through the silence of the brown, sun-flecked depths below. She lingered there till, somewhere in those depths, she heard the closing of a door; then, mechanically impelled, she went down the shallow flights of steps till she reached the lower hall.

The front door stood open on the mild sunlight of the court, and hall and court were empty. The library door was open, too, and after listening in vain for any sound of voices within, she quickly crossed the threshold, and found her husband alone, vaguely fingering the papers on his desk.

He looked up, as if surprised at her precipitate entrance, but the shadow of anxiety had passed from his face, leaving it even, as she fancied, a little brighter and clearer than usual.

"What was it? Who was it?" she asked.

"Who?" he repeated, with the surprise still all on his side.

"The man we saw coming toward the house."

He seemed to reflect. "The man? Why, I thought I saw Peters; I dashed after him to say word about the stable drains, but he had disappeared before I could get down."

Boyne shrugged his shoulders. "So I thought; but he must have got up steam in the interval. What do you say to our trying a scramble up Meldon Steep before sunset?"

That was all. At the time the occurrence had been less than nothing, had, indeed, been immediately obliterated by the magic of their first vision from Meldon Steep, a height which they had dreamed of climbing ever since they had first seen its bare spine heaving itself above the low roof of Lyng. Doubtless it was the mere fact of the other incident's having occurred on the very day of their ascent to Meldon that had kept it stored away in the unconscious fold of association from which it now emerged; for in itself it had no mark of the portentous. At the moment there could have been nothing more natural than that Ned should dash himself from the roof in the pursuit of dilatory tradesmen. It was the period when they were always on the watch for one or the other of the specialists employed about the place; always lying in wait for them, and dashing out at them with questions, reproaches, or reminders. And certainly in the distance the gray figure had looked like Peters.

Yet now, as she reviewed the rapid scene, she felt her husband's explanation of it to have been invalidated by the look of anxiety on his face. Why had the familiar appearance of Peters made him anxious? Why, above all, if it was of such prime necessity to confer with that authority on the subject of the stable-drains, had the failure to find him produced such a look of relief? Mary could not say that any one of these considerations had occurred to her at the time, yet, from the promptness with which they now marshaled themselves at her summons, she had a sudden sense that they must all along have been there, waiting their hour.

II

WEARY with her thoughts, she moved toward the window. The library was now completely dark, and she was surprised to see how much faint light the outer world still held.

As she peered out into it across the court, a figure shaped itself in the tapering perspective of bare lines: it looked a mere blot of deeper gray in the grayness, and for an instant, as it moved toward her, her heart thumped to the thought, "It's the ghost!"

She had time, in that long instant, to feel suddenly that the man of whom, two months earlier, she had a brief distant vision from the roof was now, at his predestined hour, about to reveal himself as *not* having been Peters; and her spirit sank under the impending fear of the disclosure. But almost with the next tick of the clock the ambiguous figure, gaining substance and character, showed itself even to her weak sight as her husband's; and she turned away to meet him, as he entered, with the confession of her folly.

"It's really too absurd," she laughed out from the threshold, "but I never *can* remember!"

"Remember what?" Boyne questioned as they drew together.

"That when one sees the Lyng ghost one never knows it."

Her hand was on his sleeve, and he kept it there, but with no response in his gesture or in the lines of his fagged, preoccupied face.

"Did you think you'd seen it?" he asked, after an appreciable interval.

"Why, I actually took *you* for it, my dear, in my mad determination to spot it!"

"Me—just now?" His arm dropped away, and he turned from her with a faint echo of her laugh. "Really, dearest, you'd better give it up, if that's the best you can do."

"Yes, I give it up—I give it up. Have *you?*" she asked, turning round on him abruptly.

The parlor-maid had entered with letters and a lamp, and the light struck up into Boyne's face as he bent above the tray she presented.

"Have you?" Mary perversely insisted, when the servant had disappeared on her errand of illumination.

"Have I what?" he rejoined absently, the light bringing out the sharp stamp of worry between his brows as he turned over the letters.

"I never tried," he said, tearing open the wrapper of a newspaper.

"Well, of course," Mary persisted, "the exasperating thing is that there's no use trying, since one can't be sure till so long afterward."

He was unfolding the paper as if he had hardly heard her; but after a pause, during which the sheets rustled spasmodically between his hands, he lifted his head to say abruptly, "Have you any idea *how long?*"

Mary had sunk into a low chair beside the fireplace. From her seat she looked up, startled, at her husband's profile, which was darkly projected against the circle of lamplight.

"No; none. *Have you?*" she retorted, repeating her former phrase with an added keenness of intention.

Boyne crumpled the paper into a bunch, and then inconsequently turned back with it toward the lamp.

"Lord, no! I only meant," he explained, with a faint tinge of impatience, "is there any legend, any tradition, as to that?"

"Not that I know of," she answered; but the impulse to add, "What makes you ask?" was checked by the reappearance of the parlor-maid with tea and a second lamp.

With the dispersal of shadows, and the repetition of the daily domestic office, Mary Boyne felt herself less oppressed by that sense of something mutely imminent which had darkened her solitary afternoon. For a few moments she gave herself silently to the details of her task, and when she looked up from it she was struck to the point of bewilderment by the change in her husband's face. He had seated himself near the farther lamp, and was absorbed in the perusal of his letters; but was it something he had found in them, or merely the shifting of her own point of view, that had restored his features to their normal aspect? The longer she looked, the more definitely the change affirmed itself. The lines of painful tension had vanished, and such traces of fatigue as lingered were of the kind easily attributable to steady mental effort. He glanced up, as if drawn by her gaze, and met her eyes with a smile.

"I'm dying for my tea, you know; and here's a letter for you," he said.

She took the letter he held out in exchange for the cup she proffered him, and, returning to her seat, broke the seal with the languid gesture of the reader whose interests are all enclosed in the circle of one cherished presence.

Her next conscious motion was that of starting to her feet, the letter falling to them as she rose, while she held out to her husband a long newspaper clipping.

"Ned! What's this? What does it mean?"

He had risen at the same instant, almost as if hearing her cry before she uttered it; and for a perceptible space of time he and she studied each other, like adversaries watching for an advantage, across the space between her chair and his desk.

"What's what? You fairly made me jump!" Boyne said at length, moving toward her with a sudden, half-exasperated laugh. The shadow of apprehension was on his face again, not now a look of fixed foreboding, but a shifting vigilance of lips and eyes that gave her the sense of his feeling himself invisibly surrounded.

Her hand shook so that she could hardly give him the clipping.

"This article—from the *Waukesha Sentinel*—that a man named Elwell has brought suit against you—that there was something wrong about the Blue Star Mine. I can't understand more than half."

They continued to face each other as she spoke, and to her astonishment, she saw that her words had the almost immediate effect of dissipating the strained watchfullness of his look.

"Oh, *that!*" He glanced down the printed slip, and then folded it with the gesture of one who handles something harmless and familiar. "What's the matter with you this afternoon, Mary? I thought you'd got bad news."

She stood before him with her undefinable terror subsiding slowly under the reassuring touch of his composure.

"You knew about this, then—it's all right?"

"Certainly I knew about it; and it's all right."

"But what *is* it? I don't understand. What does this man accuse you of?"

"Oh, pretty nearly every crime in the calendar." Boyne had tossed the clipping down, and thrown himself comfortably into an arm-chair near the fire. "Do you want to hear the story? It's not particularly interesting—just a squabble over interests in the Blue Star."

"But who is this Elwell? I don't know the name."

"Oh, he's a fellow I put into it—gave him a hand up. I told you all about him at the time."

"I daresay. I must have forgotten." Vainly she strained back among her memories. "But if you helped him, why does he make this return?"

"Probably some shyster lawyer got hold of him and talked him over. It's all rather technical and complicated. I thought that kind of thing bored you."

His wife felt a sting of compunction. Theoretically, she deprecated the American wife's detachment from her husband's professional interests, but in practice she had always found it difficult to fix her attention on Boyne's report of the transactions in which his varied interests involved him. Besides, she had felt from the first that, in a community where the amenities of living could be obtained only at the cost of efforts as arduous as her husband's professional labors, such brief leisure as they could command should be used as an escape from immediate preoccupations, a flight to the life they always dreamed of living. Once or twice, now that this new life had actually drawn its magic circle about them, she had asked herself if she had done right; but hitherto such conjectures had been no more than the retrospective excursions of an active fancy. Now, for the first time, it startled her a little to find how little she knew of the material foundation on which her happiness was built.

She glanced again at her husband, and was reassured by the composure of his face; yet she felt the need of more definite grounds for her reassurance.

"But doesn't this suit worry you? Why have you never spoken to me about it?"

He answered both questions at once: "I didn't speak of it at first because it *did* worry me—annoyed me, rather. But it's all ancient history now. Your correspondent must have got hold of a back number of the *Sentinel*."

She felt a quick thrill of relief. "You mean it's over? He's lost his case?"

There was a just perceptible delay in Boyne's reply. "The suit's been withdrawn—that's all."

But she persisted, as if to exonerate herself from the inward charge of being too easily put off. "Withdrawn because he saw he had no chance?"

"Oh, he had no chance," Boyne answered.

She was still struggling with a dimly felt perplexity at the back of her thoughts.

"How long ago was it withdrawn?"

He paused, as if with a slight return of his former uncertainty. "I've just had the news now; but I've been expecting it."

"Just now—in one of your letters?"

"Yes; in one of my letters."

She made no answer, and was aware only, after a short interval of waiting, that he had risen, and strolling across the room, had placed himself on the sofa at her side. She felt him, as he did so, pass an arm about her, she felt his hand seek hers and clasp it, and turning slowly, drawn by the warmth of his cheek, she met the smiling clearness of his eyes.

"It's all right—it's all right?" she questioned, through the flood of her dissolving doubts; and "I give you my word it never was righter!" he laughed back at her, holding her close.

III

ONE of the strangest things she was afterward to recall out of all the next day's incredible strangeness was the sudden and complete recovery of her sense of security.

It was in the air when she woke in her low-ceilinged, dusky room; it accompanied her downstairs to the breakfast-table, flashed out at her from the fire, and re-duplicated itself brightly from the flanks of the urn and the sturdy flutings of the Georgian teapot. It was as if, in some roundabout way, all her diffused apprehensions of the previous day, with their moment of sharp concentration about the newspaper article,—as if this dim questioning of the future, and startled return upon the past,—had between them liquidated the arrears of some haunting moral obligation. If she had indeed been careless of her husband's affairs, it was, her new state seemed to prove, because her faith in him instinctively justified such carelessness; and his right to her faith had overwhelmingly affirmed itself in the very face of menace and suspicion. She had never seen him more untroubled, more naturally and unconsciously in possession of himself, than after the cross-examination to which she had subjected him: it was almost as if he had been aware of her lurking doubts, and had wanted the air cleared as much as she did.

It was as clear, thank Heaven! as the bright outer light that surprised her almost with a touch of summer when she issued from the house for her daily round of the gardens. She had left Boyne at his desk, indulging herself, as she passed the library door, by a last peep at his quiet face, where he bent, pipe in his mouth, above his papers, and now she had her own morning's task to perform. The task involved on such charmed winter days almost as much delighted loitering about the different quarters of her demesne as if spring were already at work on shrubs and borders. There were such inexhaustible possibilities still before her, such opportunities to bring out the latent graces of the old place, without a single irreverent touch of alteration, that the winter months were all too short to plan what spring and autumn executed. And her recovered sense of safety gave, on this particular morning, a peculiar zest to her progress through the sweet, still place. She went first to the kitchen-garden, where the espaliered pear-trees drew complicated patterns on the walls, and pigeons were fluttering and preening about the silvery-slated roof of their cot. There was something wrong about the piping of the hothouse, and she was expecting an authority from Dorchester, who was to drive out between trains and make a diagnosis of the boiler. But when she dipped into the damp heat of the greenhouses, among the spiced scents and waxy pinks and reds of old-fashioned exotics,—even the flora of Lyng was in the note!—she learned that the great man had not arrived, and the day being too rare to waste in an artificial atmosphere, she came out again and paced slowly along the springy turf of the bowling-green to the gardens behind the house. At their farther end rose a grass terrace, commanding, over the fish-pond and the yew hedges, a view of the long house-front, with its twisted chimney-stacks and the blue shadows of its roof angles, all drenched in the pale gold moisture of the air.

Seen thus, across the level tracery of the yews, under the suffused, mild light, it sent her, from its open windows and hospitably smoking chimneys, the look of some warm human presence, of a mind slowly ripened on a sunny wall of experience. She had never before had so deep a sense of her intimacy with it, such a conviction that its secrets were all beneficent, kept, as they said to children, "for one's good," so complete a trust in its power to gather up her life and Ned's into the harmonious pattern of the long, long story it sat there weaving in the sun.

She heard steps behind her, and turned, expecting to see the gardener, accompanied by the engineer from Dorchester. But only one figure was in sight, that of a youngish, slightly built man, who, for reasons she could not on the spot have specified, did not remotely resemble her preconceived notion of an authority on hot-house boilers. The new-comer, on seeing her, lifted his hat, and paused with the air of a gentleman—perhaps a traveler—desirous of having it immediately known that his intrusion is involuntary. The local fame of Lyng occasionally attracted the more intelligent sight-seer, and Mary half-expected to see the stranger dissemble a camera, or justify his presence by producing it. But he made no gesture of any sort, and after a moment she asked, in a tone responding to the courteous deprecation of his attitude: "Is there any one you wish to see?"

"I came to see Mr. Boyne," he replied. His intonation, rather than his accent, was faintly American, and Mary, at the familiar note, looked at him more closely. The brim of his soft felt hat cast a shade on his face, which, thus obscured, wore to her short-sighted gaze a look of seriousness, as of a person arriving "on business," and civilly but firmly aware of his rights.

Past experience had made Mary equally sensible to such claims; but she was jealous of her husband's morning hours, and doubtful of his having given any one the right to intrude on them.

"Have you an appointment with my husband?" she asked.

The visitor hesitated, as if unprepared for the question.

"I think he expects me," he replied.

It was Mary's turn to hesitate. "You see this is his time for work: he never sees anyone in the morning."

He looked at her a moment without answering; then, as if accepting her decision, he began o move away. As he turned, Mary saw him pause and glance up at the peaceful house front. Something in his air suggested weariness and disappointment, the dejection of the traveler who has come from far off and whose hours are limited by the timetable. It occurred to her that if this were the case her refusal might have made his errand vain, and a sense of compunction caused her to hasten after him.

"May I ask if you have come a long way?"

He gave her the same grave look. "Yes—I have come a long way."

"Then, if you'll go to the house, no doubt my husband will see you now. You'll find him in the library."

She did not know why she had added the last phrase, except from a vague impulse to atone for her previous inhospitality. The visitor seemed about to express his thanks, but her attention was distracted by the approach of the gardener with a companion who bore all the marks of being the expert from Dorchester.

"This way," she said, waving the stranger to the house; and an instant later she had forgotten him in the absorption of her meeting with the boiler maker.

The encounter with this authority led to such far-reaching issues that they resulted in his finding it expedient to ignore his train, and beguiled Mary into spending the remainder of the morning in absorbed confabulation among the greenhouses. She was startled to find, when the colloquy ended, that it was nearly luncheon-time, and she half expected, as she hurried back to the house, to see her husband coming out to meet her. But she found no one in the court but an under-gardener raking the gravel, and the hall, when she entered it, was so silent that she guessed Boyne to be still at work.

Not wishing to disturb him, she turned into the drawing-room, and there, at her writing-table, lost herself in renewed calculations of the outlay to which the morning's conference had committed her. The knowledge that she could permit herself such follies had not yet lost its novelty; and somehow, in contrast to the vague apprehensions of the previous days, it now seemed an element of her recovered security, of the sense that, as Ned had said, things in general had never been "righter."

She was still luxuriating in a lavish play of figures when the parlor-maid, from the threshold, roused her with a dubiously worded inquiry as to the expediency of serving luncheon. It was one of their jokes that Trimmle announced luncheon as if she were divulging a state secret, and Mary, intent upon her papers, merely murmured an absent-minded assent.

She felt Trimmle wavering expressively on the threshold as if in rebuke of such offhand acquiescence; then her retreating steps sounded down the passage, and Mary, pushing away her papers, crossed the hall, and went to the library door. It was still closed, and she wavered in her turn, disliking to disturb her husband, yet anxious that he should not exceed his normal measure of work. As she stood there, balancing her impulses, the esoteric Trimmle returned with the announcement of luncheon, and Mary, thus impelled, opened the door and went into the library.

Boyne was not at his desk, and she peered about her, expecting to discover him at the book-shelves, somewhere down the length of the room; but her call brought no response, and gradually it became clear to her that he was not there.

She turned back to the parlormaid.

"Mr. Boyne must be upstairs. Please tell him that luncheon is ready."

Trimmle appeared to hesitate between the obvious duty of obeying orders and an equally obvious conviction of the foolishness of the injunction laid upon her. The struggle resulted in her saying doubtfully, "If you please, Madam, Mr. Boyne's not upstairs."

"Not in his room? Are you sure?"

"I'm sure, Madam."

Mary consulted the clock. "Where is he, then?"

"He's gone out," Trimmle announced, with the superior air of one who has respectfully waited for the question that a well-ordered mind would have put first.

Mary's conjecture had been right, then. Boyne must have gone to the gardens to meet her, and since she had missed him, it was clear that he had taken the shorter way by the south door, instead of going round to the court. She crossed the hall to the glass portal opening directly on the yew garden, but the parlor-maid, after another moment of inner conflict, decided to bring out recklessly, "Please, Madam, Mr. Boyne didn't go that way."

Mary turned back. "Where *did* he go? And when?"

"He went out of the front door, up the drive, Madam." It was a matter of principle with Trimmle never to answer more than one question at a time.

"Up the drive? At this hour?" Mary went to the door herself, and glanced across the court through the long tunnel of bare limes. But its perspective was as empty as when she had scanned it on entering the house.

"Did Mr. Boyne leave no message?" she asked.

Trimmle seemed to surrender herself to a last struggle with the forces of chaos.

"No, Madam. He just went out with the gentleman."

"The gentleman? What gentleman?" Mary wheeled about, as if to front this new factor.

"The gentleman who called, Madam," said Trimmle, resignedly.

"When did a gentleman call? Do explain yourself, Trimmle!"

Only the fact that Mary was very hungry, and that she wanted to consult her husband about the greenhouses, would have caused her to lay so unusual an injunction on her attendant; and even now she was detached enough to note in Trimmle's eye the dawning defiance of the respectful subordinate who has been pressed too hard.

"I couldn't exactly say the hour, Madam, because I didn't let the gentleman in," she replied, with the air of magnanimously ignoring the irregularity of her mistress's course.

"You didn't let him in?"

"No, Madam. When the bell rang I was dressing, and Agnes—"

"Go and ask Agnes, then," said Mary.

Trimmle still wore her look of patient magnanimity. "Agnes would not know, Madam, for she had unfortunately burnt her hand in trying the wick of the new lamp from town—" Trimmle, as Mary was aware, had always been opposed to the new lamp—"and so Mrs. Dockett sent the kitchen-maid instead."

Mary looked again at the clock. "It's after two! Go and ask the kitchen-maid if Mr. Boyne left any word."

She went into luncheon without waiting, and Trimmle presently brought her there the kitchen-maid's statement that the gentleman had called about one o'clock, that Mr. Boyne had gone out with him without leaving any message. The kitchen-maid did not even know the caller's name, for he had written it on a slip of paper, which he had folded and handed to her, with the injunction to deliver it at once to Mr. Boyne.

Mary finished her luncheon, still wondering, and when it was over, and Trimmle had brought the coffee to the drawing-room, her wonder had deepened to a first faint tinge of disquietude. It was unlike Boyne to absent himself without explanation at so unwonted an hour, and the difficulty of identifying the visitor whose summons he had apparently obeyed made his disappearance the more unaccountable. Mary Boyne's experience as the wife of a busy engineer, subject to sudden calls and compelled to keep irregular hours, had trained her to the philosophic acceptance of surprises; but since Boyne's withdrawal from business he had adopted a Benedictine regularity of life. As if to make up for the dispersed and agitated years, with their "stand-up" lunches and dinners rattled down to the joltings of the dining-car, he cultivated the last refinements of punctuality and monotony, discouraging his wife's fancy for the unexpected; and declaring that to a delicate taste there were infinite gradations of pleasure in the fixed recurrences of habit.

Still, since no life can completely defend itself from the unforeseen, it was evident that all Boyne's precautions would sooner or later prove unavailable, and Mary concluded that he had cut short a tiresome visit by walking with his caller to the station, or at least accompanying him for part of the way.

This conclusion relieved her from farther preoccupation, and she went out herself to take up her conference with the gardener. Thence she walked to the village post-office, a mile or so away; and when she turned toward home, the early twilight was setting in.

She had taken a footpath across the downs, and as Boyne, meanwhile, had probably returned from the station by the highroad, there was little likelihood of their meeting on the way. She felt sure, however, of his having reached the house before her; so sure that, when she entered it herself, without even pausing to inquire of Trimmle, she made directly for the library. But the library was still empty, and with an unwonted precision of visual memory she immediately observed that the papers on her husband's desk lay precisely as they had lain when she had gone in to call him to luncheon.

Then of a sudden she was seized by a vague dread of the unknown. She had closed the door behind her on entering, and as she stood alone in the long, silent, shadowy room, her dread seemed to take shape and sound, to be there audibly breathing and lurking among the shadows. Her short-sighted eyes strained through them, half-discerning an actual presence, something aloof, that watched and knew; and in the recoil from that intangible propinquity she threw herself suddenly on the bell-rope and gave it a desperate pull.

The sharp summons brought Trimmle in precipitately with a lamp, and Mary breathed again at this sobering reappearance of the usual.

"You may bring tea if Mr. Boyne is in," she said, to justify her ring.

"Very well, Madam. But Mr. Boyne is not in," said Trimmle, putting down the lamp.

"Not in? You mean he's come back and gone out again?"

"No, Madam. He's never been back."

The dread stirred again, and Mary knew that now it had her fast.

"Not since he went out with—the gentleman?"

"Not since he went out with the gentleman."

"But who *was* the gentleman?" Mary gasped out, with the sharp note of some one trying to be heard through a confusion of meaningless noises.

"That I couldn't say, Madam." Trimmle, standing there by the lamp, seemed suddenly to grow less round and rosy, as though eclipsed by the same creeping shade of apprehension.

"But the kitchenmaid knows—wasn't it the kitchen-maid who let him in?"

"She doesn't know either, Madam, for he wrote his name on a folded paper."

Mary, through her agitation, was aware that they were both designating the unknown visitor by a vague pronoun, instead of the conventional formula which, till then, had kept their allusions within the bounds of custom. And at the same moment her mind caught at the suggestion of the folded paper.

"But he must have a name! Where is the paper?"

She moved to the desk, and began to turn over the scattered documents that littered it. The first that caught her eye was an unfinished letter in her husband's hand, with his pen lying across it, as though dropped there at a sudden summons.

"My dear Parvis,"—who was Parvis?—"I have just received your letter announcing Elwell's death, and while I suppose there is now no farther risk of trouble, it might be safer—"

She tossed the sheet aside, and continued her search; but no folded paper was discoverable among the letters and pages of manuscript which had been swept together in a promiscuous heap, as if by a hurried or a startled gesture.

"But the kitchenmaid *saw* him. Send her here," she commanded, wondering at her dullness in not thinking sooner of so simple a solution.

Trimmle vanished in a flash, as if thankful to be out of the room, and when she reappeared, conducting the agitated underling, Mary had regained her self-possession, and had her questions ready.

The gentleman was a stranger, yes—that she understood. But what had he said? And, above all, what had he looked like? The first question was easily enough answered, for the disconcerting reason that he had said so little—had merely asked for Mr. Boyne, and, scribbling something on a bit of paper, had requested that it should at once be carried in to him.

"Then you don't know what he wrote? You're not sure it *was* his name?"

The kitchenmaid was not sure, but supposed it was, since he had written it in answer to her inquiry as to whom she should announce.

"And when you carried the paper in to Mr. Boyne, what did he say?"

The kitchen-maid did not think that Mr. Boyne had said anything, but she could not be sure, for just as she had handed him the paper and he was opening it, she had become aware that the visitor had followed her into the library, and she had slipped out, leaving the two gentlemen together.

"But then, if you left them in the library, how do you know that they went out of the house?"

This question plunged the witness into momentary inarticulateness, from which she was rescued by Trimmle, who, by means of ingenious circumlocutions, elicited the statement that before she could cross the hall to the back passage she had heard the gentlemen behind her, and had seen them go out of the front door together.

"Then, if you saw the gentleman twice, you must be able to tell me what he looked like."

But with this final challenge to her powers of expression it became clear that the limit of the kitchen-maid's endurance had been reached. The obligation of going to the front door to "show in" a visitor was in itself so subversive of the fundamental order of things that it had thrown her faculties into hopeless disarray, and she could only stammer out, after various panting efforts at evocation, "His hat, mum, was different-like, as you might say—"

"Different? How different?" Mary flashed out at her, her own mind, in the same instant, leaping back to an image left on it that morning, but temporarily lost under layers of subsequent impressions.

"His hat had a wide brim, you mean? and his face was pale—a youngish face?" Mary pressed her, with a white-lipped intensity of interrogation. But if the kitchen-maid found any adequate answer to this challenge, it was swept away for her listener down the rushing current of her own convictions. The stranger—the stranger in the garden! Why had Mary not thought of him before? She needed no one now to tell her that it was he who had called for her husband and gone away with him. But who was he, and why had Boyne obeyed him?

## IV

IT leaped out at her suddenly, like a grin out of the dark, that they had often called England so little—"such a confoundedly hard place to get lost in."

*A confoundedly hard place to get lost in!* That had been her husband's phrase. And now, with the whole machinery of official investigation sweeping its flash-lights from shore to shore, and across the dividing straits; now, with Boyne's name blazing from the walls of every town and village, his portrait (how that wrung her!) hawked up and down the country like the image of a hunted criminal; now the little compact, populous island, so policed, surveyed, and administered, revealed itself as a Sphinx-like guardian of abysmal mysteries, staring back into his wife's anguished eyes as if with the malicious joy of knowing something they would never know!

In the fortnight since Boyne's disappearance there had been no word of him, no trace of his movements. Even the usual misleading reports that raise expectancy in tortured bosoms had been few and fleeting. No one but the bewildered kitchen-maid had seen him leave the house, and no one else had seen "the gentleman" who accompanied him. All inquiries in the neighborhood failed to elicit the memory of a stranger's presence that day in the neighborhood of Lyng. And no one had met Edward Boyne, either alone or in company, in any of the neighboring villages, or on the road across the downs, or at either of the local railway-stations. The sunny English noon had swallowed him as completely as if he had gone out into Cimmerian night.

Mary, while every external means of investigation was working at its highest pressure, had ransacked her husband's papers for any trace of antecedent complications, of entanglements or obligations unknown to her, that might throw a faint ray into the darkness. But if any such had existed in the background of Boyne's life, they had disappeared as completely as the slip of paper on which the visitor had written his name. There remained no possible thread of guidance except—if it were indeed an exception— the letter which Boyne had apparently been in the act of writing when he received his mysterious summons. That letter, read and reread by his wife, and submitted by her to the police, yielded little enough to feed conjecture.

"I have just heard of Elwell's death, and while I suppose there is now no farther risk of trouble, it might be safer—" That was all. The "risk of trouble" was easily explained by the newspaper clipping which had apprised Mary of the suit brought against her husband by one of his associates in the Blue Star enterprise. The only new information conveyed in the letter was the fact of its showing Boyne, when he wrote it, to be still apprehensive of the results of the suit, though he had assured his wife that it had been withdrawn, and though the letter itself declared that the plaintiff was dead. It took several weeks of exhaustive cabling to fix the identity of the "Parvis" to whom the fragmentary communication was addressed, but even after these inquiries had shown him to be a Waukesha lawyer, no new facts concerning the Elwell suit were elicited. He appeared to have had no direct concern in it, but to have been conversant with the facts merely as an acquaintance, and possible intermediary; and he declared himself unable to divine with what object Boyne intended to seek his assistance.

This negative information, sole fruit of the first fortnight's feverish search, was not increased by a jot during the slow weeks that followed. Mary knew that the investigations were still being carried on, but she had a vague sense of their gradually slackening, as the actual march of time seemed to slacken. It was as though the days, flying horror-struck from the shrouded image of the one inscrutable day, gained assurance as the distance lengthened, till at last they fell back into their normal gait. And so with the human imaginations at work on the dark event. No doubt it occupied them still, but week by week and hour by hour it grew less absorbing, took up less space, was slowly but inevitably crowded out of the foreground of consciousness by the new problems perpetually bubbling up from the vaporous caldron of human experience.

Even Mary Boyne's consciousness gradually felt the same lowering of velocity. It still swayed with the incessant oscillations of conjecture; but they were slower, more rhythmical in their beat. There were moments of overwhelming lassitude when, like the victim of some poison which leaves the brain clear, but holds the body motionless, she saw herself domesticated with the Horror, accepting its perpetual presence as one of the fixed conditions of life.

These moments lengthened into hours and days, till she passed into a phase of stolid acquiescence. She watched the familiar routine of life with the incurious eye of a savage on whom the meaningless processes of civilization make but the faintest impression. She had come to regard herself as part of the routine, a spoke of the wheel, revolving with its motion; she felt almost like the furniture of the room in which she sat, an insensate object to be dusted and pushed about with the chairs and tables. And this deepening apathy held her fast at Lyng, in spite of the urgent entreaties of friends and the usual medical recommendation of "change." Her friends supposed that her refusal to move was inspired by the belief that her husband would one day return to the spot from which he had vanished, and a beautiful legend grew up about this imaginary state of waiting. But in reality she had no such belief: the depths of anguish inclosing her were no longer lighted by flashes of hope. She was sure that Boyne would never come back, that he had gone out of her sight as completely as if Death itself had waited that day on the threshold. She had even renounced, one by one, the various theories as to his disappearance which had been advanced by the press, the police, and her own agonized imagination. In sheer lassitude her mind turned from these alternatives of horror, and sank back into the blank fact that he was gone.

No, she would never know what had become of him—no one would ever know. But the house *knew;* the library in which she spent her long, lonely evenings knew. For it was here that the last scene had been enacted, here that the stranger had come, and spoken the word which had caused Boyne to rise and follow him. The floor she trod had felt his tread; the books on the shelves had seen his face; and there were moments when the intense consciousness of the old, dusky walls seemed about to break out into some audible revelation of their secret. But the revelation never came, and she knew it would never come. Lyng was not one of the garrulous old houses that betray the secrets entrusted to them. Its very legend proved that it had always been the mute accomplice, the incorruptible custodian of the mysteries it had surprised. And Mary Boyne, sitting face to face with its portentous silence, felt the futility of seeking to break it by any human means.

## V

"I DON'T say it *wasn't* straight, yet don't say it *was* straight. It was business."

Mary, at the words, lifted her head with a start, and looked intently at the speaker.

When, half an hour before, a card with "Mr. Parvis" on it had been brought up to her, she had been immediately aware that the name had been a part of her consciousness ever since she had read it at the head of Boyne's unfinished letter. In the library she had found awaiting her a small neutral-tinted man with a bald head and gold eye-glasses, and it sent a strange tremor through her to know that this was the person to whom her husband's last known thought had been directed.

Parvis, civilly, but without vain preamble,—in the manner of a man who has his watch in his hand,—had set forth the object of his visit. He had "run over" to England on business, and finding himself in the neighborhood of Dorchester, had not wished to leave it without paying his respects to Mrs. Boyne; without asking her, if the occasion offered, what she meant to do about Bob Elwell's family.

The words touched the spring of some obscure dread in Mary's bosom. Did her visitor, after all, know what Boyne had meant by his unfinished phrase? She asked for an elucidation of his question, and noticed at once that he seemed surprised at her continued ignorance of the subject. Was it possible that she really knew as little as she said?

"I know nothing—you must tell me," she faltered out; and her visitor thereupon proceeded to unfold his story. It threw, even to her confused perceptions, and imperfectly initiated vision, a lurid glare on the whole hazy episode of the Blue Star Mine. Her husband had made his money in that brilliant speculation at the cost of "getting ahead" of some one less alert to seize the chance; the victim of his ingenuity was young Robert Elwell, who had "put him on" to the Blue Star scheme.

Parvis, at Mary's first startled cry, had thrown her a sobering glance through his impartial glasses.

"Bob Elwell wasn't smart enough, that's all; if he had been, he might have turned round and served Boyne the same way. It's the kind of thing that happens every day in business. I guess it's what the scientists call the survival of the fittest," said Mr. Parvis, evidently pleased with the aptness of his analogy.

Mary felt a physical shrinking from the next question she tried to frame; it was as though the words on her lips had a taste that nauseated her.

"But then—you accuse my husband of doing something dishonorable?"

Mr. Parvis surveyed the question dispassionately. "Oh, no, I don't. I don't even say it wasn't straight." He glanced up and down the long lines of books, as if one of them might have supplied him with the definition he sought. "I don't say it *wasn't* straight, and yet I don't say it *was* straight. It was business." After all, no definition in his category could be more comprehensive than that.

Mary sat staring at him with a look of terror. He seemed to her like the indifferent, implacable emissary of some evil power.

"But Mr. Elwell's lawyers apparently did not take your view, since I suppose the suit was withdrawn by their advice."

"Oh, yes, they knew he hadn't a leg to stand on, technically. It was when they advised him to withdraw the suit that he got desperate. You see, he'd borrowed most of the money he lost in the Blue Star, and he was up a tree. That's why he shot himself when they told him he had no show."

The horror was sweeping over Mary in great, deafening waves.

"He shot himself? He killed himself because of that?"

"Well, he didn't kill himself, exactly. He dragged on two months before he died." Parvis emitted the statement as unemotionally as a gramophone grinding out its record.

"You mean that he tried to kill himself, and failed? And tried again?"

"Oh, he didn't have to *try* again," said Parvis, grimly.

They sat opposite each other in silence, he swinging his eye-glass thoughtfully about his finger, she, motionless, her arms stretched along her knees in an attitude of rigid tension.

"But if you knew all this," she began at length, hardly able to force her voice above a whisper, "how is it that when I wrote you at the time of my husband's disappearance you said you didn't understand his letter?"

Parvis received this without perceptible discomfiture. "Why, I didn't understand it—strictly speaking. And it wasn't the time to talk about it, if I had. The Elwell business was settled when the suit was withdrawn. Nothing I could have told you would have helped you to find your husband."

Mary continued to scrutinize him. "Then why are you telling me now?"

Still Parvis did not hesitate. "Well, to begin with, I supposed you knew more than you appear to—I mean about the circumstances of Elwell's death. And then people are talking of it now; the whole matter's been raked up again. And I thought, if you didn't know, you ought to."

She remained silent, and he continued: "You see, it's only come out lately what a bad state Elwell's affairs were in. His wife's a proud woman, and she fought on as long as she could, going out to work, and taking sewing at home, when she got too sick—something with the heart, I believe. But she had his bedridden mother to look after, and the children, and she broke down under it, and finally had to ask for help. That attracted attention to the case, and the papers took it up, and a subscription was started. Everybody out there liked Bob Elwell, and most of the prominent names in the place are down on the list, and people began to wonder why—"

Parvis broke off to fumble in an inner pocket. "Here," he continued, "here's an account of the whole thing from the *Sentinel*—a little sensational, of course. But I guess you'd better look it over."

He held out a newspaper to Mary, who unfolded it slowly, remembering, as she did so, the evening when, in that same room, the perusal of a clipping from the *Sentinel* had first shaken the depths of her security.

As she opened the paper, her eyes, shrinking from the glaring head-lines, "Widow of Boyne's Victim Forced to Appeal for Aid," ran down the column of text to two portraits inserted in it. The first was her husband's, taken from a photograph made the year they had come to England. It was the picture of him that she liked best, the one that stood on the writing-table up-stairs in her bedroom. As the eyes in the photograph met hers, she felt it would be impossible to read what was said of him, and closed her lids with the sharpness of the pain.

"I thought if you felt disposed to put your name down—" she heard Parvis continue.

She opened her eyes with an effort, and they fell on the other portrait. It was that of a youngish man, slightly built, in rough clothes, with features somewhat blurred by the shadow of a projecting hat-brim. Where had she seen that outline before? She stared at it confusedly, her heart hammering in her throat and ears. Then she gave a cry.

"This is the man—the man who came for my husband!"

She heard Parvis start to his feet, and was dimly aware that she had slipped backward into the corner of the sofa, and that he was bending above her in alarm. With an intense effort she straightened herself, and reached out for the paper, which she had dropped.

"It's the man! I should know him anywhere!" she cried in a voice that sounded in her own ears like a scream.

Parvis's answer seemed to come to her from far off, down endless, fog-muffled windings.

"Mrs. Boyne, you're not very well. Shall I call somebody? Shall I get a glass of water?"

"No, no, no!" She threw herself toward him, her hand frantically clenching the newspaper. "I tell you, it's the man! I know him! He spoke to me in the garden!"

Parvis took the journal from her, directing his glasses to the portrait. "It can't be, Mrs. Boyne. It's Robert Elwell."

"Robert Elwell?" Her white stare seemed to travel into space. "Then it was Robert Elwell who came for him."

"Came for Boyne? The day he went away?" Parvis's voice dropped as hers rose. He bent over, laying a fraternal hand on her, as if to coax her gently back into her seat. "Why, Elwell was dead! Don't you remember?"

Mary sat with her eyes fixed on the picture, unconscious of what he was saying.

"Don't you remember Boyne's unfinished letter to me—the one you found on his desk that day? It was written just after he'd heard of Elwell's death." She noticed an odd shake in Parvis's unemotional voice. "Surely you remember that!" he urged her.

Yes, she remembered: that was the profoundest horror of it. Elwell had died the day before her husband's disappearance; and this was Elwell's portrait; and it was the portrait of the man who had spoken to her in the garden. She lifted her head and looked slowly about the library. The library could have borne witness that it was also the portrait of the man who had come in that day to call Boyne from his unfinished letter. Through the misty surgings of her brain she heard the faint boom of half-forgotten words—words spoken by Alida Stair on the lawn at Pangbourne before Boyne and his wife had ever seen the house at Lyng, or had imagined that they might one day live there.

"This was the man who spoke to me," she repeated.

She looked again at Parvis. He was trying to conceal his disturbance under what he imagined to be an expression of indulgent commiseration; but the edges of his lips were blue. "He thinks me mad; but I'm not mad," she reflected; and suddenly there flashed upon her a way of justifying her strange affirmation.

She sat quiet, controlling the quiver of her lips, and waiting till she could trust her voice to keep its habitual level; then she said, looking straight at Parvis: "Will you answer me one question, please? When was it that Robert Elwell tried to kill himself?"

"When—when?" Parvis stammered.

"Yes; the date. Please try to remember."

She saw that he was growing still more afraid of her. "I have a reason," she insisted gently.

"Yes, yes. Only I can't remember. About two months before, I should say."

"I want the date," she repeated.

Parvis picked up the newspaper. "We might see here," he said, still humoring her. He ran his eyes down the page. "Here it is. Last October—the—"

She caught the words from him. "The 20th, wasn't it?" With a sharp look at her, he verified. "Yes, the 20th. Then you *did* know?"

"I know now." Her white stare continued to travel past him. "Sunday, the 20th—that was the day he came first."

Parvis's voice was almost inaudible. "Came *here* first?"

"Yes."

"You saw him twice, then?"

"Yes, twice." She breathed it at him with dilated eyes. "He came first on the 20th of October. I remember the date because it was the day we went up Meldon Steep for the first time." She felt a faint gasp of inward laughter at the thought that but for that she might have forgotten.

Parvis continued to scrutinize her, as if trying to intercept her gaze.

"We saw him from the roof," she went on. "He came down the lime-avenue toward the house. He was dressed just as he is in that picture. My husband saw him first. He was frightened, and ran down ahead of me; but there was no one there. He had vanished."

"Elwell had vanished?" Parvis faltered.

"Yes." Their two whispers seemed to grope for each other. "I couldn't think what had happened. I see now. He *tried* to come then; but he wasn't dead enough—he couldn't reach us. He had to wait for two months; and then he came back again—and Ned went with him."

She nodded at Parvis with the look of triumph of a child who has successfully worked out a difficult puzzle. But suddenly she lifted her hands with a desperate gesture, pressing them to her bursting temples.

"Oh, my God! I sent him to Ned—I told him where to go! I sent him to this room!" she screamed out.

She felt the walls of the room rush toward her, like inward falling ruins; and she heard Parvis, a long way off, as if through the ruins, crying to her, and struggling to get at her. But she was numb to his touch, she did not know what he was saying. Through the tumult she heard but one clear note, the voice of Alida Stair, speaking on the lawn at Pangbourne.

"You won't know till afterward," it said. "You won't know till long, long afterward."

## THE LETTERS

UP THE HILL from the station at St. Cloud, Lizzie West climbed in the cold spring sunshine. As she breasted the incline, she noticed the first waves of wisteria over courtyard railings and the high lights of new foliage against the walls of ivy-matted gardens; and she thought again, as she had thought a hundred times before, that she had never seen so beautiful a spring.

She was on her way to the Deerings' house, in a street near the hilltop; and every step was dear and familiar to her. She went there five times a week to teach little Juliet Deering, the daughter of Mr. Vincent Deering, the distinguished American artist. Juliet had been her pupil for two years, and day after day, during that time, Lizzie West had mounted the hill in all weathers; sometimes with her umbrella bent against a driving rain, sometimes with her frail cotton parasol unfurled beneath a fiery sun, sometimes with the snow soaking through her patched boots or a bitter wind piercing her thin jacket, sometimes with the dust whirling about her and bleaching the flowers of the poor little hat that *had* to "carry her through" till next summer.

At first the ascent had seemed tedious enough, as dull as the trudge to her other lessons. Lizzie was not a heaven-sent teacher; she had no born zeal for her calling, and though she dealt kindly and dutifully with her pupils, she did not fly to them on winged feet. But one day something had happened to change the face of life, and since then the climb to the Deering house had seemed like a dream-flight up a heavenly stairway.

Her heart beat faster as she remembered it—no longer in a tumult of fright and self-reproach, but softly, peacefully, as if brooding over a possession that none could take from her.

It was on a day of the previous October that she had stopped, after Juliet's lesson, to ask if she might speak to Juliet's papa. One had always to apply to Mr. Deering if there was anything to be said about the lessons. Mrs. Deering lay on her lounge up-stairs, reading greasy relays of dog-eared novels, the choice of which she left to the cook and the nurse, who were always fetching them for her from the *cabinet de lecture*; and it was understood in the house that she was not to be "bothered" about Juliet. Mr. Deering's interest in his daughter was fitful rather than consecutive; but at least he was approachable, and listened sympathetically, if a little absently, stroking his long, fair mustache, while Lizzie stated her difficulty or put in her plea for maps or copybooks.

"Yes, yes—of course—whatever you think right," he would always assent, sometimes drawing a five-franc piece from his pocket, and laying it carelessly on the table, or oftener saying, with his charming smile: "Get what you please, and just put it on your account, you know."

But this time Lizzie had not come to ask for maps or copy-books, or even to hint, in crimson misery,—as once, poor soul! she had had to do,—that Mr. Deering had overlooked her last little account had probably not noticed that she had left it, some two months earlier, on a corner of his littered writing-table. That hour had been bad enough, though he had done his best to make it easy to carry it off gallantly and gaily; but this was infinitely worse. For she had come to complain of her pupil; to say that, much as she loved little Juliet, it was useless, unless Mr. Deering could "do something," to go on with the lessons.

"It wouldn't be honest—I should be robbing you; I'm not sure that I haven't already," she half laughed, through mounting tears, as she put her case. Little Juliet would not work, would not obey. Her poor, little, drifting existence floated aimlessly between the kitchen and the *lingerie*, and all the groping tendrils of her curiosity were fastened about the doings of the backstairs.

It was the same kind of curiosity that Mrs. Deering, overhead in her drug-scented room, lavished on her dog-eared novels and on the "society notes" of the morning paper; but since Juliet's horizon was not yet wide enough to embrace these loftier objects, her interest was centered in the anecdotes that Celeste and Suzanne brought back from the market and the library. That these were not always of an edifying nature the child's artless prattle too often betrayed; but unhappily they occupied her fancy to the complete exclusion of such nourishing items as dates and dynasties, and the sources of the principal European rivers.

At length the crisis became so acute that poor Lizzie felt herself bound to resign her charge or ask Mr. Deering's intervention; and for Juliet's sake she chose the harder alternative. It was hard to speak to him not only because one hated still more to ascribe it to such vulgar causes, but because one blushed to bring them to the notice of a spirit engaged with higher things. Mr. Deering was very busy at that moment: he had a new picture "on." And Lizzie entered the studio with the flutter of one profanely intruding on some sacred rite; she almost heard the rustle of retreating wings as she approached.

And then—and then—how differently it had all turned out! Perhaps it wouldn't have, if she hadn't been such a goose—she who so seldom cried, so prided herself on a stoic control of her little twittering cageful of "feelings." But if she had cried, it was because he had looked at her so kindly, so softly, and because she had nevertheless felt him so pained and shamed by what she said. The pain, of course, lay for both in the implication behind her words—in the one word they left unspoken. If little Juliet was as she was, it was because of the mother up-stairs—the mother who had given her child her futile impulses, and grudged her the care that might have guided them. The wretched case so obviously revolved in its own vicious circle that when Mr. Deering had murmured, "Of course if my wife were not an invalid," they both turned with a simultaneous spring to the flagrant "bad example" of Celeste and Suzanne, fastening on that with a mutual insistence that ended in his crying out, "All the more, then, how can you leave her to them?"

"But if I do her no good?" Lizzie wailed; and it was then that,—when he took her hand and assured her gently, "But you do, you do!"—it was then that, in the traditional phrase, she "broke down," and her conventional protest quivered off into tears.

"You do *me* good, at any rate—you make the house seem less like a desert," she heard him say; and the next moment she felt herself drawn to him, and they kissed each other through her weeping.

They kissed each other—there was the new fact. One does not, if one is a poor little teacher living in Mme. Clopin's Pension Suisse at Passy, and if one has pretty brown hair and eyes that reach out trustfully to other eyes—one does not, under these common but defenseless conditions, arrive at the age of twenty-five without being now and then kissed,—waylaid once by a noisy student between two doors, surprised once by one's gray-bearded professor as one bent over the "theme" he was correcting,—but these episodes, if they tarnish the surface, do not reach the heart: it is not the kiss endured, but the kiss returned, that lives. And Lizzie West's first kiss was for Vincent Deering.

As she drew back from it, something new awoke in her—something deeper than the fright and the shame, and the penitent thought of Mrs. Deering. A sleeping germ of life thrilled and unfolded, and started out blindly to seek the sun.

She might have felt differently, perhaps,—the shame and penitence might have prevailed,—had she not known him so kind and tender, and guessed him so baffled, poor, and disappointed. She knew the failure of his married life, and she divined a corresponding failure in his artistic career. Lizzie, who had made her own faltering snatch at the same laurels, brought her thwarted proficiency to bear on the question of his pictures, which she judged to be extremely brilliant, but suspected of having somehow failed to affirm their merit publicly. She understood that he had tasted an earlier moment of success: a *mention*, a medal, something official and tangible; then the tide of publicity had somehow set the other way, and left him stranded in a noble isolation. It was extraordinary and unbelievable that any one so naturally eminent and exceptional should have been subject to the same vulgar necessities that governed her own life, should have known poverty and obscurity and indifference. But she gathered that this had been the case, and felt that it formed the miraculous link between them. For through what medium less revealing than that of shared misfortune would he ever have perceived so inconspicuous an object as herself? And she recalled now how gently his eyes had rested on her from the first—the gray eyes that might have seemed mocking if they had not been so gentle.

She remembered how kindly he had met her the first day, when Mrs. Deering's inevitable headache had prevented her from receiving the new teacher, and how his few questions had at once revealed his interest in the little stranded, compatriot, doomed to earn a precarious living so far from her native shore. Sweet as the moment of unburdening had been, she wondered afterward what had determined it: how she, so shy and sequestered, had found herself letting slip her whole poverty-stricken story, even to the avowal of the ineffectual "artistic" tendencies that had drawn her to Paris, and had then left her there to the dry task of tuition. She wondered at first, but she understood now; she understood everything after he had kissed her. It was simply because he was as kind as he was great.

She thought of this now as she mounted the hill in the spring sunshine, and she thought of all that had happened since. The intervening months, as she looked back at them, were merged in a vast golden haze, through which here and there rose the outline of a shining island. The haze was the general enveloping sense of his love, and the shining islands were the days they had spent together. They had never kissed again under his own roof. Lizzie's professional honor had a keen edge, but she had been spared the vulgar necessity of making him feel it. It was of the essence of her fatality that he always "understood" when his failing to do so might have imperiled his hold on her.

But her Thursdays and Sundays were free, and it soon became a habit to give them to him. She knew, for her peace of mind, only too much about pictures, and galleries and churches had been the one bright outlet from the grayness of her personal atmosphere. For poetry, too, and the other imaginative forms of literature, she had always felt more than she had hitherto had occasion to betray; and now all these folded sympathies shot out their tendrils to the light. Mr. Deering knew how to express with unmatched clearness and competence the thoughts that trembled in her mind: to talk with him was to soar up into the azure on the outspread wings of his intelligence, and look down dizzily yet distinctly, on all the wonders and glories of the world. She was a little ashamed, sometimes, to find how few definite impressions she brought back from these flights; but that was doubtless because her heart beat so fast when he was near, and his smile made his words like a long quiver of light. Afterward, in quieter hours, fragments of their talk emerged in her memory with wondrous precision, every syllable as minutely chiseled as some of the delicate objects in crystal or ivory that he pointed out in the museums they frequented. It was always a puzzle to Lizzie that some of their hours should be so blurred and others so vivid.

She was reliving all these memories with unusual distinctness, for it was a fortnight since she had seen her friend. Mrs. Deering, some six weeks previously, had gone to visit a relation at St.-Raphael; and, after she had been a month absent, her husband and the little girl had joined her. Lizzie's adieux to Deering had been made on a rainy afternoon in the damp corridors of the Aquarium at the Trocadéro. She could not receive him at her own *pension*. That a teacher should be visited by the father of a pupil, especially when that father was still, as Madame Clopin said, *si bien*, was against that lady's austere Helvetian code. From Deering's first tentative hint of another solution Lizzie had recoiled in a wild unreasoned flurry of all her scruples, he took her "No, no, *no!"* as he took all her twists and turns of conscience, with eyes half-tender and half-mocking, and an instant acquiescence which was the finest homage to the "lady" she felt he divined and honored in her.

So they continued to meet in museums and galleries, or to extend, on fine days, their explorations to the suburbs, where now and then, in the solitude of grove or garden, the kiss renewed itself, fleeting, isolated, or prolonged in a shy, silent pressure of the hand. But on the day of his leave-taking the rain kept them under cover; and as they threaded the subterranean windings of the Aquarium, and Lizzie looked unseeingly at the monstrous faces glaring at her through walls of glass, she felt like a poor drowned wretch at the bottom of the sea, with all her glancing, sunlit memories rolling over her like the waves of its surface.

"You'll never see him again—never see him again," the waves boomed in her ears through his last words; and when she had said good-by to him at the corner, and had scrambled, wet and shivering, into the Passy omnibus, its great, grinding wheels took up the derisive burden—"Never see him, never see him again."

All that was only two weeks ago, and here she was, as happy as a lark, mounting the hill to his door in the spring sunshine. So weak a heart did not deserve such a radiant fate; and Lizzie said to herself that she would never again distrust her star.

## II

THE cracked bell tinkled sweetly through her heart as she stood listening for the scamper of Juliet's feet. Juliet, anticipating the laggard Suzanne, almost always opened the door for her governess, not from any unnatural zeal to hasten the hour of her studies, but from the irrepressible desire to see what was going on in the street. But on this occasion Lizzie listened vainly for a step, and at length gave the bell another twitch. Doubtless some unusually absorbing incident had detained the child below-stairs; thus only could her absence be explained. A third ring produced no response, and Lizzie, full of dawning fears, drew back to look up at the shabby, blistered house. She saw that the studio shutters stood wide, and then noticed, without surprise, that Mrs. Deering's were still unopened. No doubt Mrs. Deering was resting after the fatigue of the journey. Instinctively Lizzie's eyes turned again to the studio; and as she looked, she saw Deering at the window. He caught sight of her, and an instant later came to the door. He looked paler than usual, and she noticed that he wore a black coat.

"I rang and rang—where is Juliet?"

He looked at her gravely, almost solemnly; then, without answering, he led her down the passage to the studio, and closed the door when she had entered.

"My wife is dead—she died suddenly ten days ago. Didn't you see it in the papers?"

Lizzie, with a little cry, sank down on the rickety divan. She seldom saw a newspaper, since she could not afford one for her own perusal, and those supplied to the Pension Clopin were usually in the hands of its more privileged lodgers till long after the hour when she set out on her morning round.

"No; I didn't see it," she stammered.

Deering was silent. He stood a little way off, twisting an unlit cigarette in his hand, and looking down at her with a gaze that was both constrained and hesitating.

She, too, felt the constraint of the situation, the impossibility of finding words that, after what had passed between them, should seem neither false nor heartless; and at last she exclaimed, standing up: "Poor little Juliet! Can't I go to her?"

"Juliet is not here. I left her at St.-Raphael with the relations with whom my wife was staying."

"Oh," Lizzie murmured, feeling vaguely that this added to the difficulty of the moment. How differently she had pictured their meeting!

"I'm so—so sorry for her!" she faltered out.

Deering made no reply, but, turning on his heel, walked the length of the studio, and then halted vaguely before the picture on the easel. It was the landscape he had begun the previous autumn, with the intention of sending it to the Salon that spring. But it was still unfinished—seemed, indeed, hardly more advanced than on the fateful October day when Lizzie, standing before it for the first time, had confessed her inability to deal with Juliet. Perhaps the same thought struck its creator, for he broke into a dry laugh, and turned from the easel with a shrug.

Under his protracted silence Lizzie roused herself to the fact that, since her pupil was absent, there was no reason for her remaining any longer; and as Deering again moved toward her she said with an effort: "I'll go, then. You'll send for me when she comes back?"

Deering still hesitated, tormenting the cigarette between his fingers.

"She's not coming back—not at present."

Lizzie heard him with a drop of the heart. Was everything to be changed in their lives? But of course; how could she have dreamed it would be otherwise? She could only stupidly repeat: "Not coming back? Not this spring?"

"Probably not, since are friends are so good as to keep her. The fact is, I've got to go to America. My wife left a little property, a few pennies, that I must go and see to—for the child."

Lizzie stood before him, a cold knife in her breast. "I see—I see," she reiterated, feeling all the while that she strained her eyes into impenetrable blackness.

"It's a nuisance, having to pull up stakes," he went on, with a fretful glance about the studio.

She lifted her eyes slowly to his face. "Shall you be gone long?" she took courage to ask.

"There again—I can't tell. It's all so frightfully mixed up." He met her look for an incredibly long, strange moment. "I hate to go!" he murmured abruptly.

Lizzie felt a rush of moisture to her lashes, and the old, familiar wave of weakness at her heart. She raised her hand to her face with an instinctive gesture, and as she did so he held out his arms.

"Come here, Lizzie!" he said.

And she went—went with a sweet, wild throb of liberation, with the sense that at last the house was his, that she was his, if he wanted her; that never again would that silent, rebuking presence in the room above constrain and shame her rapture.

He pushed back her veil and covered her face with kisses. "Don't cry, you little goose!" he said.

### III

THAT they must see each other again before his departure, in someplace less exposed than their usual haunts, was as clear to Lizzie as it appeared to be to Deering. His expressing the wish seemed, indeed, the sweetest testimony to the quality of his feeling, since, in the first weeks of the most perfunctory widower hood, a man of his stamp is presumed to abstain from light adventures. If, then, at such a moment, he wished so much to be quietly and gravely with her, it could be only for reasons she did not call by name, but of which she felt the sacred tremor in her heart; and it would have seemed incredibly vain and vulgar to put forward, at such a crisis, the conventional objections by means of which such little exposed existences defend the treasure of their freshness.

In such a mood as this one may descend from the Passy omnibus at the corner of the Pont de la Concorde (she had not let him fetch her in a cab) with a sense of dedication almost solemn, and may advance to meet one's fate, in the shape of a gentleman of melancholy elegance, with an auto-taxi at his call, as one has advanced to the altar-steps in some girlish bridal vision.

Even the experienced waiter ushering them into an upper room of the quiet restaurant on the Seine could hardly have supposed their quest for seclusion to be based on sentimental motives, so soberly did Deering give his orders, while his companion sat small and grave at his side. She did not, indeed, mean to let her private pang obscure their hour together: she was already learning that Deering shrank from sadness. He should see that she had courage and gaiety to face their coming separation, and yet give herself meanwhile to this completer nearness; but she waited, as always, for him to strike the opening note.

Looking back at it later, she wondered at the mild suavity of the hour. Her heart was unversed in happiness, but he had found the tone to lull her apprehensions, and make her trust her fate for any golden wonder. Deepest of all, he gave her the sense of something tacit and confirmed between them, as if his tenderness were a habit of the heart hardly needing the support of outward proof.

Such proof as he offered came, therefore, as a kind of crowning luxury, the flower of a profoundly rooted sentiment; and here again the instinctive reserves and defenses would have seemed to vulgarize what his trust ennobled. But if all the tender casuistries of her heart were at his service, he took no grave advantage of them. Even when they sat alone after dinner, with the lights of the river trembling through their one low window, and the vast rumor of Paris inclosing them in a heart of silence, he seemed, as much as herself, under the spell of hallowing influences. She felt it most of all as she yielded to the arm he presently put about her, to the long caress he laid on her lips and eyes: not a word or gesture missed the note of quiet union, or cast a doubt, in retrospect, on the pact they sealed with their last look.

That pact, as she reviewed it through a sleepless night, seemed to have consisted mainly, on his part, in pleadings for full and frequent news of her, on hers in the assurance that it should be given as often as he asked it. She had felt an intense desire not to betray any undue eagerness, any crude desire to affirm and define her hold on him. Her life had given her a certain acquaintance with the arts of defense: girls in her situation were commonly supposed to know them all, and to use them as occasion called. But Lizzie's very need of them had intensified her disdain. Just because she was so poor, and had always, materially, so to count her change and calculate her margin, she would at least know the joy of emotional prodigality, would give her heart as recklessly as the rich their millions. She was sure now that Deering loved her, and if he had seized the occasion of their farewell to give her some definitely worded sign of his feeling—if, more plainly he had asked her to marry him,—his doing so would have seemed less like a proof of his sincerity than of his suspecting in her the need of a verbal warrant. That he had abstained seemed to show that he trusted her as she trusted him, and that they were one most of all in this deep security of understanding.

She had tried to make him divine all this in the chariness of her promise to write. She would write; of course she would. But he would be busy, preoccupied, on the move: it was for him to let her know when he wished a word, to spare her the embarrassment of ill-timed intrusions.

"Intrusions?" He had smiled the word away. "You can't well intrude, my darling, on a heart where you're already established, to the complete exclusion of other lodgers." And then, taking her hands, and looking up from them into her happy, dizzy eyes: "You don' know much about being in love, do you, Lizzie?" he laughingly ended.

It seemed easy enough to reject this imputation in a kiss; but she wondered afterward if she had not deserved it. Was she really cold and conventional, and did other women give more richly and recklessly? She found that it was possible to turn about every one of her reserves and delicacies so that they looked like selfish scruples and petty pruderies, and at this game she came in time to exhaust all the resources of an over-abundant casuistry.

Meanwhile the first days after Deering's departure wore a soft, refracted light like the radiance lingering after sunset. *He*, at any rate, was taxable with no reserves, no calculations, and his letters of farewell, from train and steamer, filled her with long murmurs and echoes of his presence. How he loved her, how he loved her—and how he knew how to tell her so!

She was not sure of possessing the same aptitude. Unused to the expression of personal emotion, she fluctuated between the impulse to pour out all she felt and the fear lest her extravagance should amuse or even bore him. She never lost the sense that what was to her the central crisis of experience must be a mere episode in a life so predestined as his to romantic accidents. All that she felt and said would be subjected to the test of comparison with what others had already given him: from all quarters of the globe she saw passionate missives winging their way toward Deering, for whom her poor little swallow-flight of devotion could certainly not make a summer. But such moments were succeeded by others in which she raised her head and dared inwardly to affirm her conviction that no woman had ever loved him just as she had, and that none, therefore, had probably found just such things to say to him. And this conviction strengthened the other less solidly based belief that he also, for the same reason, had found new accents to express his tenderness, and that the three letters she wore all day in her shabby blouse, and hid all night beneath her pillow, surpassed not only in beauty, but in quality, all he had ever penned for other eyes.

They gave her, at any rate, during the weeks that she wore them on her heart, sensations even more complex and delicate than Deering's actual presence had ever occasioned. To be with him was always like breasting a bright, rough sea, that blinded while it buoyed her: but his letters formed a still pool of contemplation, above which she could bend, and see the reflection of the sky, and the myriad movements of life that flitted and gleamed below the surface. The wealth of his hidden life—that was what most surprised her! It was incredible to her now that she had had no inkling of it, but had kept on blindly along the narrow track of habit, like a traveler climbing a road in a fog, who suddenly finds himself on a sunlit crag between blue leagues of sky and dizzy depths of valley. And the odd thing was that all the people about her—the whole world of the Passy pension—were still plodding along the same dull path, preoccupied with the pebbles underfoot, and unconscious of the glory beyond the fog!

There were wild hours when she longed to cry out to them what one saw from the summit—and hours of tremulous abasement when she asked herself why *her* feet had been guided there, while others, no doubt as worthy, stumbled and blundered in obscurity. She felt, in particular, a sudden urgent pity for the two or three other girls at Mme. Clopin's—girls older, duller, less alive than she, and by that very token more appealingly flung upon her sympathy. Would they ever know? Had they ever known?— those were the questions that haunted her as she crossed her companions on the stairs, faced them at the dinner-table, and listened to their poor, pining talk in the dim-lit slippery-seated *salon*. One of the girls was Swiss, the other English; the third, Andora

Macy, was a young lady from the Southern States who was studying French with the ultimate object of imparting it to the inmates of a girls' school at Macon, Georgia.

Andora Macy was pale, faded, immature. She had a drooping Southern accent, and a manner which fluctuated between arch audacity and fits of panicky hauteur. She yearned to be admired, and feared to be insulted; and yet seemed tragically conscious that she was destined to miss both these extremes of sensation, or to enjoy them only at second hand in the experiences of her more privileged friends.

It was perhaps for this reason that she took a wistful interest in Lizzie, who had shrunk from her at first, as the depressing image of her own probable future, but to whom she had now suddenly become an object of sentimental pity.

IV

MISS MACY's room was next to Miss West's, and the Southerner's knock often appealed to Lizzie's hospitality when Mme. Clopin's early curfew had driven her boarders from the *salon*. It sounded thus one evening just as Lizzie, tired from an unusually long day of tuition, was in the act of removing her dress. She was in too indulgent a mood to withhold her "Come in," and as Miss Macy crossed the threshold, Lizzie felt that Vincent Deering's first letter—the letter from the train—had slipped from her loosened bodice to the floor.

Miss Macy, as promptly noting the fact, darted forward to recover the letter. Lizzie stooped also, fiercely jealous of her touch; but the other reached the precious paper first, and as she seized it, Lizzie knew that she had seen whence it fell, and was weaving round the incident a rapid web of romance.

Lizzie blushed with annoyance. "It's too stupid, having no pockets! If one gets a letter as she is going out in the morning, she has to carry it in her blouse all day."

Miss Macy looked at her with swimming eyes. "It's warm from your heart!" she breathed, reluctantly yielding up the missive.

Lizzie laughed, for she knew better: she knew it was the letter that had warmed her heart. Poor Andora Macy! *She* would never know. Her bleak bosom would never take fire from such a contact. Lizzie looked at her with kind eyes, secretly chafing at the injustice of fate.

The next evening, on her return home, she found Andora hovering in the entrance hall.

"I thought you'd like me to put this in your own hand," Miss Macy whispered significantly, pressing a letter upon Lizzie. "I couldn't *bear* to see it lying on the table with the others."

It was Deering's letter from the steamer. Lizzie blushed to the forehead, but without resenting Andora's divination. She could not have breathed a word of her bliss, but she was not altogether sorry to have it guessed, and pity for Andora's destitution yielded to the pleasure of using it as a mirror for her own abundance.

Deering wrote again on reaching New York, a long, fond, dissatisfied letter, vague in its indication of his own projects, specific in the expression of his love. Lizzie brooded over every syllable of it till they formed the undercurrent of all her waking thoughts, and murmured through her midnight dreams; but she would have been happier if they had shed some definite light on the future.

That would come, no doubt, when he had had time to look about and get his bearings. She counted up the days that must elapse before she received his next letter, and stole down early to peep at the papers, and learn when the next American mail was due. At length the happy date arrived, and she hurried distractedly through the day's work, trying to conceal her impatience by the endearments she bestowed upon her pupils. It was easier, in her present mood, to kiss them than to keep them at their grammars.

That evening, on Mme. Clopin's threshold, her heart beat so wildly that she had to lean a moment against the door-post before entering. But on the hall table, where the letters lay, there was none for her.

She went over them with a feverish hand, her heart dropping down and down, as she had sometimes fallen down an endless stairway in a dream—the very same stairway up which she had seemed to fly when she climbed the long hill to Deering's door. Then it suddenly struck her that Andora might have found and secreted her letter, and with a spring she was on the actual stairs and rattling Miss Macy's door handle.

"You've a letter for me, haven't you?" she panted.

Miss Macy enclosed her in attenuated arms. "Oh, darling, did you expect one to-day?"

"Do give it to me!" Lizzie pleaded with burning eyes.

"But I haven't any! There hasn't been a sign of a letter for you."

"I know there is. There *must* be," Lizzie persisted, stamping her foot.

"But, dearest, I've *watched* for you, and there's been nothing, absolutely nothing."

Day after day, for the ensuing weeks, the same scene reenacted itself with endless variations. Lizzie, after the first sharp spasm of disappointment, made no effort to conceal her anxiety from Miss Macy, and the fond Andora was charged to keep a vigilant eye upon the postman's coming, and to spy on the *bonne* for possible negligence or perfidy. But these elaborate precautions remained fruitless, and no letter from Deering came.

During the first fortnight of silence Lizzie exhausted all the ingenuities of explanation. She marveled afterward at the reasons she had found for Deering's silence: there were moments when she almost argued herself into thinking it more natural than his continuing to write. There was only one reason which her intelligence consistently rejected, and that was the possibility that he had forgotten her, that the whole episode had faded from his mind like a breath from a mirror. From that she resolutely turned her thoughts, aware that if she suffered herself to contemplate it, the motive power of life would fail, and she would no longer understand why she rose up in the morning and lay down at night.

If she had had leisure to indulge her anguish she might have been unable to keep such speculations at bay. But she had to be up and working: the *blanchisseuse* had to be paid, and Mme. Clopin's weekly bill, and all the little "extras" that even her frugal habits had to reckon with. And in the depths of her thought dwelt the dogging fear of illness and incapacity, goading her to work while she could. She hardly remembered the time when she had been without that fear; it was second nature now, and it kept her on her feet when other incentives might have failed. In the blankness of her misery she felt no dread of death; but the horror of being ill and "dependent" was in her blood.

In the first weeks of silence she wrote again and again to Deering, entreating him for a word, for a mere sign of life. From the first she had shrunk from seeming to assert any claim on his future, yet in her aching bewilderment she now charged herself with having been too possessive, too exacting in her tone. She told herself that his fastidiousness shrank from any but a "light touch," and that hers had not been light enough. She should have kept to the character of the "little friend," the artless consciousness in which tormented genius may find an escape from its complexities; and instead, she had dramatized their relation, exaggerated her own part in it, presumed, forsooth, to share the front of the stage with him, instead of being content to serve as scenery or chorus.

But though, to herself, she admitted, and even insisted on, the episodical nature of the experience, on the fact that for Deering it could be no more than an incident, she was still convinced that his sentiment for her, however fugitive, had been genuine.

His had not been the attitude of the unscrupulous male seeking a vulgar "advantage." For a moment he had really needed her, and if he was silent now, it was perhaps because he feared that she had mistaken the nature of the need and built vain hopes on its possible duration.

It was of the very essence of Lizzie's devotion that it sought instinctively the larger freedom of its object; she could not conceive of love under any form of exaction or compulsion. To make this clear to Deering became an overwhelming need, and in a last short letter she explicitly freed him from whatever sentimental obligation its predecessors might have seemed to impose. In this studied communication she playfully accused herself of having unwittingly sentimentalized their relation, affirming, in self-defense, a retrospective astuteness, a sense of the impermanence of the tenderer sentiments, that almost put Deering in the fatuous position of having mistaken coquetry for surrender. And she ended gracefully with a plea for the continuance of the friendly regard which she had "always understood" to be the basis of their sympathy. The document, when completed, seemed to her worthy of what she conceived to be Deering's conception of a woman of the world, and she found a spectral satisfaction in the thought of making her final appearance before him in that distinguished character. But she was never destined to learn what effect the appearance produced; for the letter, like those it sought to excuse, remained unanswered.

V

THE fresh spring sunshine which had so often attended Lizzie Weston her dusty climb up the hill of St.-Cloud beamed on her, some two years later, in a scene and a situation of altered import.

Its rays, filtered through the horse chestnuts of the Champs Elysées, shone on the graveled circle about Laurent's restaurant; and Miss West, seated at a table within that privileged space, presented to the light a hat much better able to sustain its scrutiny than those which had shaded the brow of Juliet Deering's instructress.

Her dress was in keeping with the hat, and both belonged to a situation rich in such possibilities as the act of a leisurely luncheon at Laurent's in the opening week of the Salon. Her companions, of both sexes, confirmed and emphasized this impression by an elaborateness of garb and an ease of attitude implying the largest range of selection between the forms of Parisian idleness; and even Andora Macy, seated opposite, as in the place of co-hostess or companion, reflected, in coy grays and mauves, the festal note of the occasion.

This note reverberated persistently in the ears of a solitary gentleman straining for glimpses of the group from a table wedged in the remotest corner of the garden; but to Miss West herself the occurrence did not rise above the usual. For nearly a year she had been acquiring the habit of such situations, and the act of offering a luncheon at Laurent's to her cousins, the Harvey Mearses of Providence, and their friend Mr. Jackson Benn, produced in her no emotion beyond the languid glow which Mr. Benn's presence was beginning to impart to such scenes.

"It's frightful, the way you've got used to it," Andora Macy had wailed in the first days of her friend's transfigured fortune, when Lizzie West had waked one morning to find herself among the heirs of an old and miserly cousin whose testamentary dispositions had formed, since her earliest childhood, the subject of pleasantry and conjecture in her own improvident family. Old Hezron Mears had never given any sign of life to the luckless Wests; had perhaps hardly been conscious of including them in the carefully drawn will which, following the old American convention, scrupulously divided his hoarded millions among his kin. It was by a mere genealogical accident that Lizzie, falling just within the golden circle, found herself possessed of a pittance sufficient to release her from the prospect of a long gray future in Mme. Clopin's *pension*.

The release had seemed wonderful at first; yet she presently found that it had destroyed her former world without giving her anew one. On the ruins of the old *pension* life bloomed the only flower that had ever sweetened her path; and beyond the sense of present ease, and the removal of anxiety for the future, her reconstructed existence blossomed with no compensating joys. She had hoped great things from the opportunity to rest, to travel, to look about her, above all, in various artful feminine ways, to be "nice" to the companions of her less privileged state; but such widenings of scope left her, as it were, but the more conscious of the empty margin of personal life beyond them. It was not till she woke to the leisure of her new days that she had the full sense of what was gone from them.

Their very emptiness made her strain to pack them with transient sensations: she was like the possessor of an unfurnished house, with random furniture and bric-a-brac perpetually pouring in "on approval." It was in this experimental character that Mr. Jackson Benn had fixed her attention, and the languid effort of her imagination to adjust him to her requirements was seconded by the fond complicity of Andora and the smiling approval of her cousins. Lizzie did not discourage these demonstrations: she suffered serenely Andora's allusions to Mr. Benn's infatuation, and Mrs. Mears's casual boast of his business standing. All the better if they could drape his narrow square-shouldered frame and round unwinking countenance in the trailing mists of sentiment: Lizzie looked and listened, not unhopeful of the miracle.

"I never saw anything like the way these Frenchmen stare! Doesn't it make you nervous, Lizzie?" Mrs. Mears broke out suddenly, ruffling her feather boa about an outraged bosom. Mrs. Mears was still in that stage of development when her countrywomen taste to the full the peril of being exposed to the gaze of the licentious Gaul.

Lizzie roused herself from the contemplation of Mr. Benn's round baby cheeks and the square blue jaw resting on his perpendicular collar. "Is someone staring at me?" she asked with a smile.

"Don't turn round, whatever you do! There—just over there, between the rhododendrons—the tall fair man alone at that table. Really, Harvey, I think you ought to speak to the head-waiter, or something; though I suppose in one of these places they'd only laugh at you," Mrs. Mears shudderingly concluded.

Her husband, as if inclining to this probability, continued the undisturbed dissection of his chicken wing; but Mr. Benn, perhaps aware that his situation demanded a more punctilious attitude, sternly revolved upon the parapet of his high collar in the direction of Mrs. Mears's glance.

"What, that fellow all alone over there? Why, *he's* not French; he's an American," he then proclaimed with a perceptible relaxing of the facial muscles.

"Oh!" murmured Mrs. Mears, as perceptibly disappointed, and Mr. Benn continued carelessly: "He came over on the steamer with me. He's some kind of an artist—a fellow named Deering. He was staring at me, I guess: wondering whether I was going to remember him. Why, how d' 'e do? How are you? Why, yes, of course; with pleasure— my friends, Mrs. Harvey Mears—Mr. Mears; my friends Miss Macy and Miss West."

"I have the pleasure of knowing Miss West," said Vincent Deering with a smile.

## VI

EVEN through his smile Lizzie had seen, in the first moment, how changed he was; and the impression of the change deepened to the point of pain when, a few days later, in reply to his brief note, she accorded him a private hour.

That the first sight of his writing—the first answer to his letters—should have come, after three long years, in the shape of this impersonal line, too curt to be called humble, yet confessing to a consciousness of the past by the studied avoidance of its language! As she read, her mind flashed back over what she had dreamed his letters would be, over the exquisite answers she had composed above his name. There was nothing exquisite in the conventional lines before her; but dormant nerves began to throb again at the mere touch of the paper he had touched, and she threw the little note into the fire before she dared to reply to it.

Now that he was actually before her again, he became, as usual, the one live spot in her consciousness. Once more her tormented throbbing self sank back passive and numb, but now with all its power of suffering mysteriously transferred to the presence, so known, yet so unknown, at the opposite corner of her hearth. She was still Lizzie West, and he was still Vincent Deering; but the Styx rolled between them, and she saw his face through its fog. It was his face, really, rather than his words, that told her, as she furtively studied it, the tale of failure and slow discouragement which had so blurred its handsome lines. She kept afterward no precise memory of the actual details of his narrative: the pain it evidently cost him to impart it was so much the sharpest fact in her new vision of him. Confusedly, however, she gathered that on reaching America he had found his wife's small property gravely impaired; and that, while lingering on to secure what remained of it, he had contrived to sell a picture or two, and had even known a brief moment of success, during which he received orders and set up a studio. But inexplicably the tide had ebbed, his work remained on his hands, and a tedious illness, with its miserable sequel of debt, soon wiped out his small advantage. There followed a period of eclipse, still more vaguely pictured, during which she was allowed to infer that he had tried his hand at divers means of livelihood, accepting employment from a fashionable house-decorator, designing wall-papers, illustrating magazine articles, and acting for a time, she dimly understood, as the social tout of a new hotel desirous of advertising its restaurant. These disjointed facts were strung on a slender thread of personal allusions—references to friends who had been kind (jealously, she guessed them to be women), and to enemies who had darkly schemed against him. But, true to his tradition of "correctness," he carefully avoided the mention of names, and left her trembling conjectures to grope dimly through an alien crowded world in which there seemed little room for her small shy presence.

As she listened, her private pang was merged in the intolerable sense of his unhappiness. Nothing he had said explained or excused his conduct to her; but he had suffered, he had been lonely, had been humiliated, and she suddenly felt, with a fierce maternal rage, that there was no conceivable justification for any scheme of things in which such facts were possible. She could not have said why: she simply knew that it hurt too much to see him hurt.

Gradually it came to her that her unconsciousness of any personal grievance was due to her having so definitely determined her own future. She was glad she had decided, as she now felt she had, to marry Jackson Benn, if only for the sense of detachment it gave her in dealing with the case of Vincent Deering. Her personal safety insured her the requisite impartiality, and justified her in dwelling as long as she chose on the last lines of a chapter to which her own act had deliberately fixed the close. Any lingering hesitations as to the finality of her decision were dispelled by the imminent need of making it known to Deering; and when her visitor paused in his reminiscences to say, with a sigh, "But many things have happened to you too," his words did not so much evoke the sense of her altered fortunes as the image of the protector to whom she was about to in trust them.

"Yes, many things; it's three years," she answered.

Deering sat leaning forward, in his sad exiled elegance, his eyes gently bent on hers; and at his side she saw the solid form of Mr. Jackson Benn, with shoulders preternaturally squared by the cut of his tight black coat, and a tall shiny collar sustaining his baby cheeks and hard blue chin. Then the vision faded as Deering began to speak.

"Three years," he repeated, musingly taking up her words. "I've so often wondered what they'd brought you."

She lifted her head with a quick blush, and the terrified wish that he should not, at the cost of all his notions of correctness, lapse into the blunder of becoming "personal."

"You've wondered?" She smiled back bravely.

"Do you suppose I haven't?" His look dwelt on her. "Yes, I daresay that *was* what you thought of me."

She had her answer pat—"Why, frankly, you know, I *didn't* think of you." But the mounting tide of her poor dishonored memories swept it indignantly away. If it was his correctness to ignore, it could never be hers to disavow.

"*Was* that what you thought of me?" she heard him repeat in a tone of sad insistence; and at that, with a quick lift of her head, she resolutely answered: "How could I know what to think? I had no word from you."

If she had expected, and perhaps almost hoped, that this answer would create a difficulty for him, the gaze of quiet fortitude with which he met it proved that she had underestimated his resources.

"No, you had no word. I kept my vow," he said.

"Your vow?"

"That you *shouldn't* have a word—not a syllable. Oh, I kept it through everything!"

Lizzie's heart was sounding in her ears the old confused rumor of the sea of life, but through it she desperately tried to distinguish the still small voice of reason.

"What was your vow? Why shouldn't I have had a syllable from you?"

He sat motionless, still holding her with a look so gentle that it almost seemed forgiving.

Then abruptly he rose, and crossing the space between them, sat down in a chair at her side. The deliberation of his movement might have implied a forgetfullness of changed conditions, and Lizzie, as if thus viewing it, drew slightly back; but he appeared not to notice her recoil, and his eyes, at last leaving her face, slowly and approvingly made the round of the small bright drawing-room. "This is charming. Yes, things *have* changed for you," he said.

A moment before she had prayed that he might be spared the error of a vain return upon the past. It was as if all her retrospective tenderness, dreading to see him at such a disadvantage, rose up to protect him from it. But his evasiveness exasperated her, and suddenly she felt the inconsistent desire to hold him fast, face to face with his own words.

Before she could reiterate her question, however, he had met her with another.

"You *did* think of me, then? Why are you afraid to tell me that you did?"

The unexpectedness of the challenge wrung an indignant cry from her. "Didn't my letters tell you so enough?"

"Ah—your letters—" Keeping her gaze on his in a passion of unrelenting fixity, she could detect in him no confusion, not the least quiver of a sensitive nerve. He only gazed back at her more sadly.

"They went everywhere with me—your letters," he said.

"Yet you never answered them." At last the accusation trembled to her lips.

"Yet I never answered them."

"Did you ever so much as read them, I wonder?"

All the demons of self-torture were up in her now, and she loosed them on him, as if to escape from their rage.

Deering hardly seemed to hear her question. He merely shifted his attitude, leaning a little nearer to her, but without attempting, by the least gesture, to remind her of the privileges which such nearness had once implied.

"There were beautiful, wonderful things in them," he said, smiling.

She felt herself stiffen under his smile. "You've waited three years to tell me so!"

He looked at her with grave surprise. "And do you resent my telling you even now?"

His parries were incredible. They left her with a breathless sense of thrusting at emptiness, and a desperate, almost vindictive desire to drive him against the wall and pin him there.

"No. Only I wonder you should take the trouble to tell me, when at the time—"

And now, with a sudden turn, he gave her the final surprise of meeting her squarely on her own ground.

"When at the time I didn't? But how *could* I—at the time?"

"Why couldn't you? You've not yet told me?"

He gave her again his look of disarming patience. "Do I need to? Hasn't my whole wretched story told you?"

"Told me why you never answered my letters?"

"Yes, since I could only answer them in one way—by protesting my love and my longing."

There was a long pause of resigned expectancy on his part, on hers, of a wild confused reconstruction of her shattered past. "You mean, then, that you didn't write because—"

"Because I found, when I reached America, that I was a pauper; that my wife's money was gone, and that what I could earn—I've so little gift that way!—was barely enough to keep Juliet clothed and educated. It was as if an iron door had been suddenly locked and barred between us."

Lizzie felt herself driven back, panting upon the last defenses of her incredulity. "You might at least have told me—have explained. Do you think I shouldn't have understood?"

He did not hesitate. "You would have understood. It wasn't that."

"What was it then?" she quavered.

"It's wonderful you shouldn't see! Simply that I couldn't write you that. Anything else—not that!"

"And so you preferred to let me suffer?"

There was a shade of reproach in his eyes. "I suffered too," he said.

It was his first direct appeal to her compassion, and for a moment it nearly unsettled the delicate poise of her sympathies, and sent them trembling in the direction of scorn and irony. But even as the impulse rose, it was stayed by another sensation. Once again, as so often in the past, she became aware of a fact which, in his absence, she always failed to reckon with—the fact of the deep irreducible difference between his image in her mind and his actual self, the mysterious alteration in her judgment produced by the inflections of his voice, the look of his eyes, the whole complex pressure of his personality. She had phrased it once self-reproachfully by saying to herself that she "never could remember him," so completely did the sight of him supersede the counterfeit about which her fancy wove its perpetual wonders. Bright and breathing as that counterfeit was, it became a gray figment of the mind at the touch of his presence; and on this occasion the immediate result was to cause her to feel his possible unhappiness with an intensity beside which her private injury paled.

"I suffered horribly," he repeated, "and all the more that I couldn't make a sign, couldn't cry out my misery. There was only one escape from it all—to hold my tongue, and pray that you might hate me."

The blood rushed to Lizzie's forehead. "Hate you—you prayed that I might hate you?"

He rose from his seat, and moving closer, lifted her hand gently in his. "Yes; because your letters showed me that, if you didn't, you'd be unhappier still."

Her hand lay motionless, with the warmth of his flowing through it, and her thoughts, too—her poor fluttering stormy thoughts—felt themselves suddenly penetrated by the same soft current of communion.

"And I meant to keep my resolve," he went on, slowly releasing his clasp. "I meant to keep it even after the random stream of things swept me back here in your way; but when I saw you the other day, I felt that what had been possible at a distance was impossible now that we were near each other. How was it possible to see you and want you to hate me?"

He had moved away, but not to resume his seat. He merely paused at a little distance, his hand resting on a chair-back, in the transient attitude that precedes departure.

Lizzie's heart contracted. He was going, then, and this was his farewell. He was going, and she could find no word to detain him but the senseless stammer "I never hated you."

He considered her with his faint grave smile. "It's not necessary, at any rate, that you should do so now. Time and circumstances have made me so harmless—that's exactly why I've dared to venture back. And I wanted to tell you how I rejoice in your good fortune. It's the only obstacle between us that I can't bring myself to wish away."

Lizzie sat silent, spellbound, as she listened, by the sudden evocation of Mr. Jackson Benn. He stood there again, between herself and Deering, perpendicular and reproachful, but less solid and sharply outlined than before, with a look in his small hard eyes that desperately wailed for reembodiment.

Deering was continuing his farewell speech. "You're rich now, you're free. You will marry." She vaguely saw him holding out his hand.

"It's not true that I'm engaged!" she broke out. They were the last words she had meant to utter; they were hardly related to her conscious thoughts; but she felt her whole will suddenly gathered up in the irrepressible impulse to repudiate and fling away from her forever the spectral claim of Mr. Jackson Benn.

## VII

IT was the firm conviction of Andora Macy that every object in the Vincent Deerings' charming little house at Neuilly had been expressly designed for the Deerings' son to play with.

The house was full of pretty things, some not obviously applicable to the purpose; but Miss Macy's casuistry was equal to the baby's appetite, and the baby's mother was no match for them in the art of defending her possessions. There were moments, in fact, when Lizzie almost fell in with Andora's summary division of her works of art into articles safe or unsafe for the baby to lick, or resisted it only to the extent of occasionally substituting some less precious or less perishable object for the particular fragility on which her son's desire was fixed. And it was with this intention that, on a certain fair spring morning—which wore the added luster of being the baby's second birthday—she had murmured, with her mouth in his curls, and one hand holding a bit of Chelsea above his dangerous clutch: "Wouldn't he rather have that beautiful shiny thing over there in Aunt Andorra's hand?"

The two friends were together in Lizzie's little morning-room—the room she had chosen, on acquiring the house, because, when she sat there, she could hear Deering's step as he paced up and down before his easel in the studio she had built for him. His step had been less regularly audible than she had hoped, for, after three years of wedded bliss, he had somehow failed to settle down to the great work which was to result from that privileged state; but even when she did not hear him she knew that he was there, above her head, stretched out on the old divan from Passy, and smoking endless cigarettes while he skimmed the morning papers; and the sense of his nearness had not yet lost its first keen edge of wonder.

Lizzie herself, on the day in question, was engaged in a more arduous task than the study of the morning's news. She had never unlearned the habit of orderly activity, and the trait she least understood in her husband's character was his way of letting the loose ends of life hang as they would. She had been disposed at first to ascribe this to the chronic incoherence of his first *ménage;* but now she knew that, though he basked under her beneficent rule, he would never feel any active impulse to further its work. He liked to see things fall into place about him at a wave of her wand; but his enjoyment of her household magic in no way diminished his smiling irresponsibility, and it was with one of its least amiable consequences that his wife and her friend were now dealing.

Before them stood two travel-worn trunks and a distended portmanteau, which had shed their contents in heterogeneous heaps over Lizzie's rosy carpet. They represented the hostages left by her husband on his somewhat precipitate departure from a New York boarding-house, and indignantly redeemed by her on her learning, in a curt letter from his landlady, that the latter was not disposed to regard them as an equivalent for the arrears of Deering's board.

Lizzie had not been shocked by the discovery that her husband had left America in debt. She had too sad an acquaintance with the economic strain to see any humiliation in such accidents; but it offended her sense of order that he should not have liquidated his obligation in the three years since their marriage. He took her remonstrance with his usual disarming grace, and left her to forward the liberating draft, though her delicacy had provided him with a bank-account which assured his personal independence. Lizzie had discharged the duty without repugnance, since she knew that his delegating it to her was the result of his good-humored indolence and not of any design on her exchequer. Deering was not dazzled by money; his altered fortunes had tempted him to no excesses: he was simply too lazy to draw the check, as he had been too lazy to remember the debt it canceled.

"No, dear! No!" Lizzie lifted the Chelsea figure higher. "Can't you find something for him, Andora, among that rubbish over there? Where's the beaded bag you had in your hand just now? I don't think it could hurt him to lick that."

Miss Macy, bag in hand, rose from her knees, and stumbled through the slough of frayed garments and old studio properties. Before the group of mother and son she fell into a raptured attitude.

"Do look at him reach for it, the tyrant! Isn't he just like the young Napoleon?"

Lizzie laughed and swung her son in air. "Dangle it before him, Andora. If you let him have it too quickly, he won't care for it. He's just like any man, I think."

Andora slowly lowered the shining bag till the heir of the Deerings closed his masterful fist upon it. "There—my Chelsea's safe!" Lizzie smiled, setting her boy on the floor, and watching him stagger away with his booty.

Andora stood beside her, watching too. "Have you any idea where that bag came from, Lizzie?"

Mrs. Deering, bent above a pile of dis-collared shirts, shook an inattentive head. "I never saw such wicked washing! There isn't one that's fit to mend. The bag? No; I've not the least idea."

Andora surveyed her dramatically. "Doesn't it make you utterly miserable to think that some woman may have made it for him?"

Lizzie, bowed in anxious scrutiny above the shirts, broke into an unruffled laugh. "Really, Andora, really—six, seven, nine; no, there isn't even a dozen. There isn't a whole dozen of *anything*. I don't see how men live alone!"

Andora broodingly pursued her theme. "Do you mean to tell me it doesn't make you jealous to handle these things of his that other women may have given him?"

Lizzie shook her head again, and, straightening herself with a smile, tossed a bundle in her friend's direction. "No, it doesn't make me the least bit jealous. Here, count these socks for me, like a darling."

Andora moaned, "Don't you feel *anything at all?*" as the socks landed in her hollow bosom; but Lizzie, intent upon her task, tranquilly continued to unfold and sort. She felt a great deal as she did so, but her feelings were too deep and delicate for the simplifying process of speech. She only knew that each article she drew from the trunks sent through her the long tremor of Deering's touch. It was part of her wonderful new life that everything belonging to him contained an infinitesimal fraction of himself—a fraction becoming visible in the warmth of her love as certain secret elements become visible in rare intensities of temperature. And in the case of the objects before her, poor shabby witnesses of his days of failure, what they gave out acquired a special poignancy from its contrast to his present cherished state. His shirts were all in round dozens now, and washed as carefully as old lace. As for his socks, she knew the pattern of every pair, and would have liked to see the washerwoman who dared to mislay one, or bring it home with the colors "run"! And in these homely tokens of his well-being she saw the symbol of what her tenderness had brought him. He was safe in it, encompassed by it, morally and materially, and she defied the embattled powers of malice to reach him through the armor of her love. Such feelings, however, were not communicable, even had one desired to express them: they were no more to be distinguished from the sense of life itself than bees from the lime-blossoms in which they murmur.

"Oh, do *look* at him, Lizzie! He's found out how to open the bag!"

Lizzie lifted her head to smile a moment at her son, who sat throned on a heap of studio rubbish, with Andora before him on adoring knees. She thought vaguely, "Poor Andora!" and then resumed the discouraged inspection of a button less white waistcoat. The next sound she was aware of was a fluttered exclamation from her friend.

"Why, Lizzie, do you know what he used the bag for? To keep your letters in!"

Lizzie looked up more quickly. She was aware that Andora's pronoun had changed its object, and was now applied to Deering. And it struck her as odd, and slightly disagreeable, that a letter of hers should be found among the rubbish abandoned in her husband's New York lodgings.

"How funny! Give it to me, please."

"Give the bag to Aunt Andora, darling! Here—look inside, and see what else a big big, boy can find there! Yes, here's another! Why, why—"

Lizzie rose with a shade of impatience and crossed the floor to the romping group beside the other trunk.

"What is it? Give me the letters, please." As she spoke, she suddenly recalled the day when, in Mme. Clopin's *pension*, she had addressed a similar behest to Andora Macy.

Andora had lifted a look of startled conjecture. "Why, this one's never been opened! Do you suppose that awful woman could have kept it from him?"

Lizzie laughed. Andora's imaginings were really puerile. "What awful woman? His landlady? Don't be such a goose, Andora. How can it have been kept back from him, when we've found it here among his things?"

"Yes; but then why was it never opened?"

Andora held out the letter, and Lizzie took it. The writing was hers; the envelop bore the Passy postmark; and it was unopened. She stood looking at it with a sudden sharp drop of the heart.

"Why, so are the others—all unopened!" Andora threw out on a rising note; but Lizzie, stooping over, stretched out her hand.

"Give them to me, please."

"Oh, Lizzie, Lizzie—" Andora, still on her knees, continued to hold back the packet, her pale face paler with anger and compassion. "Lizzie, they're the letters I used to post for you—the letters he never answered! *Look!*"

"Give them back to me, please."

The two women faced each other, Andora kneeling, Lizzie motionless before her, the letters in her hand. The blood had rushed to her face, humming in her ears, and forcing itself into the veins of her temples like hot lead. Then it ebbed, and she felt cold and weak.

"It must have been some plot—some conspiracy!" Andora cried, so fired by the ecstasy of invention that for the moment she seemed lost to all but the esthetic aspect of the case.

Lizzie turned away her eyes with an effort, and they rested on the boy, who sat at her feet placidly sucking the tassels of the bag. His mother stooped and extracted them from his rosy mouth, which a cry of wrath immediately filled. She lifted him in her arms, and for the first time no current of life ran from his body into hers. He felt heavy and clumsy, like some other woman's child; and his screams annoyed her.

"Take him away, please, Andora."

"Oh, Lizzie, Lizzie!" Andora wailed.

Lizzie held out the child, and Andora, struggling to her feet, received him.

"I know just how you feel," she gasped out above the baby's head.

Lizzie, in some dark hollow of herself, heard the echo of a laugh. Andora always thought she knew how people felt!

"Tell Marthe to take him with her when she fetches Juliet home from school."

"Yes, yes." Andora gloated over her. "If you'd only give way, my darling!"

The baby, howling, dived over Andora's shoulder for the bag.

"Oh, *take* him!" his mother ordered.

Andora, from the door, cried out: "I'll be back at once. Remember, love, you're not alone!"

But Lizzie insisted, "Go with them—I wish you to go with them," in the tone to which Miss Macy had never learned the answer.

The door closed on her outraged back, and Lizzie stood alone. She looked about the disordered room, which offered a dreary image of the havoc of her life. An hour or two ago everything about her had been so exquisitely ordered, without and within; her thoughts and emotions had lain outspread before her like delicate jewels laid away symmetrically in a collector's cabinet. Now they had been tossed down helter-skelter among the rubbish there on the floor, and had themselves turned to rubbish like the rest. Yes, there lay her life at her feet, among all that tarnished trash.

She knelt and picked up her letters, ten in all, and examined the flaps of the envelops. Not one had been opened—not one. As she looked, every word she had written fluttered to life, and every feeling prompting it sent a tremor through her. With vertiginous speed and microscopic vision she was reliving that whole period of her life, stripping bare again the black ruin over which the drift of three happy years had fallen.

She laughed at Andora's notion of a conspiracy—of the letters having been "kept back." She required no extraneous aid in deciphering the mystery: her three years' experience of Deering shed on it all the light she needed. And yet a moment before she had believed herself to be perfectly happy! Now it was the worst part of her anguish that it did not really surprise her.

She knew so well how it must have happened. The letters had reached him when he was busy, occupied with something else, and had been put aside to be read at some future time—a time which never came. Perhaps on his way to America, on the steamer, even, he had met "someone else"—the "someone" who lurks, veiled and ominous, in the background of every woman's thoughts about her lover. Or perhaps he had been merely forgetful. She had learned from experience that the sensations which he seemed to feel with the most exquisite intensity left no reverberations in his mind—that he did not relive either his pleasures or his pains. She needed no better proof of that than the lightness of his conduct toward his daughter. He seemed to have taken it for granted that Juliet would remain indefinitely with the friends who had received her after her mother's death, and it was at Lizzie's suggestion that the little girl was brought home and that they had established themselves at Neuilly to be near her school. But Juliet once with them, he became the model of a tender father, and Lizzie wondered that he had not felt the child's absence, since he seemed so affectionately aware of her presence.

Lizzie had noted all this in Juliet's case, but had taken for granted that her own was different; that she formed, for Deering, the exception which every woman secretly supposes herself to form in the experience of the man she loves. Certainly, she had learned by this time that she could not modify his habits, but she imagined that she had deepened his sensibilities, had furnished him with an "ideal"—angelic function! And she now saw that the fact of her letters—her unanswered letters—having, on his own assurance, "meant so much" to him, had been the basis on which this beautiful fabric was reared.

There they lay now, the letters, precisely as when they had left her hands. He had not had time to read them; and there had been a moment in her past when that discovery would have been the sharpest pang imaginable to her heart. She had traveled far beyond that point. She could have forgiven him now for having forgotten her; but she could never forgive him for having deceived her.

She sat down, and looked again vaguely about the room. Suddenly she heard his step overhead, and her heart contracted. She was afraid he was coming down to her. She sprang up and bolted the door; then she dropped into the nearest chair, tremulous and exhausted, as if the pushing of the bolt had required an immense muscular effort. A moment later she heard him on the stairs, and her tremor broke into a cold fit of shaking. "I loathe you—I loathe you!" she cried.

She listened apprehensively for his touch on the handle of the door. He would come in, humming a tune, to ask some idle question and lay a caress on her hair. But no, the door was bolted; she was safe. She continued to listen, and the step passed on. He had not been coming to her, then. He must have gone downstairs to fetch something—another newspaper, perhaps. He seemed to read little else, and she sometimes wondered when he had found time to store the material that used to serve for their famous "literary" talks. The wonder shot through her again, barbed with a sneer. At that moment it seemed to her that everything he had ever done and been was a lie.

She heard the house door close, and started up. Was he going out? It was not his habit to leave the house in the morning.

She crossed the room to the window, and saw him walking, with a quick decided step, between the budding lilacs to the gate. What could have called him forth at that unwonted hour? It was odd that he should not have told her. The fact that she thought it odd suddenly showed her how closely their lives were interwoven. She had become a habit to him, and he was fond of his habits. But to her it was as if a stranger had opened the gate and gone out. She wondered what he would feel if he knew that she felt *that*.

"In an hour he will know," she said to herself, with a kind of fierce exultation; and immediately she began to dramatize the scene. As soon as he came in she meant to call him up to her room and hand him the letters without a word. For a moment she gloated on the picture; then her imagination recoiled from it. She was humiliated by the thought of humiliating him. She wanted to keep his image intact; she would not see him.

He had lied to her about her letters—had lied to her when he found it to his interest to regain her favor. Yes, there was the point to hold fast. He had sought her out when he learned that she was rich. Perhaps he had come back from America on purpose to marry her; no doubt he had come back on purpose. It was incredible that she had not seen this at the time. She turned sick at the thought of her fatuity and of the grossness of his arts. Well, the event proved that they were all he needed. But why had he gone out at such an hour? She was irritated to find herself still preoccupied by his comings and goings.

Turning from the window, she sat down again. She wondered what she meant to do next…No, she would not show him the letters; she would simply leave them on his table and go away. She would leave the house with her boy and Andora. It was a relief to feel a definite plan forming itself in her mind—something that her uprooted thoughts could fasten on. She would go away, of course; and meanwhile, in order not to see him, she would feign a headache, and remain in her room till after luncheon. Then she and Andora would pack a few things, and fly with the child while he was dawdling about up-stairs in the studio. When one's house fell, one fled from the ruins: nothing could be simpler, more inevitable.

Her thoughts were checked by the impossibility of picturing what would happen next. Try as she would, she could not see herself and the child away from Deering. But that, of course, was because of her nervous weakness. She had youth, money, energy: all the trumps were on her side. It was much more difficult to imagine what would become of Deering. He was so dependent on her, and they had been so happy together! The fact struck her as illogical, and even immoral, and yet she knew he had been happy with her. It never happened like that in novels: happiness "built on a lie" always crumbled, and buried the presumptuous architect beneath the ruins. According to the laws of every novel she had ever read, Deering, having deceived her once, would inevitably have gone on deceiving her. Yet she knew he had not gone on deceiving her…

She tried again to picture her new life. Her friends, of course, would rally about her. But the prospect left her cold; she did not want them to rally. She wanted only one thing—the life she had been living before she had given her baby the embroidered bag to play with. Oh, why had she given him the bag? She had been so happy, they had all been so happy! Every nerve in her clamored for her lost happiness, angrily, unreasonably, as the boy had clamored for his bag! It was horrible to know too much; there was always blood in the foundations. Parents "kept things" from children—protected them from all the dark secrets of pain and evil. And was any life livable unless it were thus protected? Could anyone look in the Medusa's face and live?

But why should she leave the house, since it was hers? Here, with her boy and Andora, she could still make for herself the semblance of a life. It was Deering who would have to go; he would understand that as soon as he saw the letters.

She pictured him in the act of going—leaving the house as he had left it just now. She saw the gate closing on him for the last time. Now her vision was acute enough: she saw him as distinctly as if he were in the room. Ah, he would not like returning to the old life of privations and expedients! And yet she knew he would not plead with her.

Suddenly a new thought rushed through her mind. What if Andora had rushed to him with the tale of the discovery of the letters—with the "Fly, you are discovered!" of romantic fiction? What if he *had* left her for good? It would not be unlike him, after all. Under his wonderful gentleness he was always evasive and inscrutable. He might have said to himself that he would forestall her action, and place himself at once on the defensive. It might be that she *had* seen him go out of the gate for the last time.

She looked about the room again, as if this thought had given it a new aspect. Yes, this alone could explain her husband's going out. It was past twelve o'clock, their usual luncheon hour, and he was scrupulously punctual at meals, and gently reproachful if she kept him waiting. Only some unwonted event could have caused him to leave the house at such an hour and with such marks of haste. Well, perhaps it was better that Andora should have spoken. She mistrusted her own courage; she almost hoped the deed had been done for her. Yet her next sensation was one of confused resentment. She said to herself, "Why has Andora interfered?" She felt baffled and angry, as though her prey had escaped her. If Deering had been in the house, she would have gone to him instantly and overwhelmed him with her scorn. But he had gone out, and she did not know where he had gone, and oddly mingled with her anger against him was the latent instinct of vigilance, the solicitude of the woman accustomed to watch over the man she loves. It would be strange never to feel that solicitude again, never to hear him say, with his hand on her hair: "Why, you foolish child, were you worried? Am I late?"

The sense of his touch was so real that she stiffened herself against it, flinging back her head as if to throw off his hand. The mere thought of his caress was hateful; yet she felt it in all her traitorous veins. Yes, she felt it, but with horror and repugnance. It was something she wanted to escape from, and the fact of struggling against it was what made its hold so strong. It was as though her mind were sounding her body to make sure of its allegiance, spying on it for any secret movement of revolt...

To escape from the sensation, she rose and went again to the window. No one was in sight. But presently the gate began to swing back, and her heart gave a leap—she knew not whether up or down. A moment later the gate opened slowly to admit a perambulator, propelled by the nurse and flanked by Juliet and Andora. Lizzie's eyes rested on the familiar group as if she had never seen it before, and she stood motionless, instead of flying down to meet the children.

Suddenly there was a step on the stairs, and she heard Andora's agitated knock. She unbolted the door, and was strained to her friend's emaciated bosom.

"My darling!" Miss Macy cried. "Remember you have your child—and me!"

Lizzie loosened herself gently. She looked at Andora with a feeling of estrangement which she could not explain.

"Have you spoken to my husband?" she asked, drawing coldly back.

"Spoken to him? No." Andora stared at her in genuine wonder.

"Then you haven't met him since he left me?"

"No, my love. Is he out? I haven't met him."

Lizzie sat down with a confused sense of relief, which welled up to her throat and made speech difficult.

Suddenly light came to Andora. "I understand, dearest. You don't feel able to see him yourself. You want me to go to him for you." She looked about her, scenting the battle. "You're right, darling. As soon as he comes in I'll go to him. The sooner we get it over the better."

She followed Lizzie, who without answering her had turned mechanically back to the window. As they stood there, the gate moved again, and Deering entered the garden.

"There he is now!" Lizzie felt Andora's fervent clutch upon her arm. "Where are the letters? I will go down at once. You allow me to speak for you? You trust my woman's heart? Oh, believe me, darling," Miss Macy panted, "I shall know just what to say to him!"

"What to say to him?" Lizzie absently repeated.

As her husband advanced up the path she had a sudden trembling vision of their three years together. Those years were her whole life; everything before them had been colorless and unconscious, like the blind life of the plant before it reaches the surface of the soil. They had not been exactly what she dreamed; but if they had taken away certain illusions, they had left richer realities in their stead. She understood now that she had gradually adjusted herself to the new image of her husband as he was, as he would always be. He was not the hero of her dream, but he was the man she loved, and who had loved her. For she saw now, in this last wide flash of pity and initiation, that, as a solid marble may be made out of worthless scraps of mortar, glass and pebbles, so out of mean mixed substances may be fashioned a love that will bear the stress of life.

More urgently, she felt the pressure of Miss Macy's hand.

"I shall hand him the letters without a word. You may rely, love, on my sense of dignity. I know everything you're feeling at this moment!"

Deering had reached the door-step. Lizzie continued to watch him in silence till he disappeared under the glazed roof of the porch below the window; then she turned and looked almost compassionately at her friend.

"Oh, poor Andora, you don't know anything—you don't know anything at all!" she said.

## XINGU (1916)

### XINGU

MRS. BALLINGER is one of the ladies who pursue Culture in bands, as though it were dangerous to meet alone. To this end she had founded the Lunch Club, an association composed of herself and several other indomitable huntresses of erudition. The Lunch Club, after three or four winters of lunching and debate, had acquired such local distinction that the entertainment of distinguished strangers became one of its accepted functions; in recognition of which it duly extended to the celebrated "Osric Dane," on the day of her arrival in Hillbridge, an invitation to be present at the next meeting.

The club was to meet at Mrs. Ballinger's. The other members, behind her back, were of one voice in deploring her unwillingness to cede her rights in favor of Mrs. Plinth, whose house made a more impressive setting for the entertainment of celebrities; while, as Mrs. Leveret observed, there was always the picture-gallery to fall back on.

Mrs. Plinth made no secret of sharing this view. She had always regarded it as one of her obligations to entertain the Lunch Club's distinguished guests. Mrs. Plinth was almost as proud of her obligations as she was of her picture-gallery; she was in fact fond of implying that the one possession implied the other, and that only a woman of her wealth could afford to live up to a standard as high as that which she had set herself. An all-round sense of duty, roughly adaptable to various ends, was, in her opinion, all that Providence exacted of the more humbly stationed; but the power which had predestined Mrs. Plinth to keep a footman clearly intended her to maintain an equally specialized staff of responsibilities. It was the more to be regretted that Mrs. Ballinger, whose obligations to society were bounded by the narrow scope of two parlormaids, should have been so tenacious of the right to entertain Osric Dane.

The question of that lady's reception had for a month past profoundly moved the members of the Lunch Club. It was not that they felt themselves unequal to the task, but that their sense of the opportunity plunged them into the agreeable uncertainty of the lady who weighs the alternatives of a well-stocked wardrobe. If such subsidiary members as Mrs. Leveret were fluttered by the thought of exchanging ideas with the author of *The Wings of Death*, no forebodings disturbed the conscious adequacy of Mrs. Plinth, Mrs. Ballinger and Miss Van Vluyck. *The Wings of Death* had, in fact, at Miss Van Vluyck's suggestion, been chosen as the subject of discussion at the last club meeting, and each member had thus been enabled to express her own opinion or to appropriate whatever sounded well in the comments of the others.

Mrs. Roby alone had abstained from profiting by the opportunity; but it was now openly recognized that, as a member of the Lunch Club, Mrs. Roby was a failure. "It all comes," as Miss Van Vluyck put it, "of accepting a woman on a man's estimation." Mrs. Roby, returning to Hillbridge from a prolonged sojourn in exotic lands—the other ladies no longer took the trouble to remember where—had been heralded by the distinguished biologist, Professor Foreland, as the most agreeable woman he had ever met; and the members of the Lunch Club, impressed by an encomium that carried the weight of a diploma, and rashly assuming that the Professor's social sympathies would follow the line of his professional bent, had seized the chance of annexing a biological member. Their disillusionment was complete. At Miss Van Vluyck's first off-hand mention of the pterodactyl Mrs. Roby had confusedly murmured: "I know so little about meters—" and after that painful betrayal of incompetence she had prudently withdrawn from farther participation in the mental gymnastics of the club.

"I suppose she flattered him," Miss Van Vluyck summed up—"or else it's the way she does her hair."

The dimensions of Miss Van Vluyck's dining-room having restricted the membership of the club to six, the nonconductiveness of one member was a serious obstacle to the exchange of ideas, and some wonder had already been expressed that Mrs. Roby should care to live, as it were, on the intellectual bounty of the others. This feeling was increased by the discovery that she had not yet read *The Wings of Death*. She owned to having heard the name of Osric Dane; but that—incredible as it appeared—was the extent of her acquaintance with the celebrated novelist. The ladies could not conceal their surprise; but Mrs. Ballinger, whose pride in the club made her wish to put even Mrs. Roby in the best possible light, gently insinuated that, though she had not had time to acquaint herself with *The Wings of Death*, she must at least be familiar with its equally remarkable predecessor, *The Supreme Instant*.

Mrs. Roby wrinkled her sunny brows in a conscientious effort of memory, as a result of which she recalled that, oh, yes, she *had* seen the book at her brother's, when she was staying with him in Brazil, and had even carried it off to read one day on a boating party; but they had all got to shying things at each other in the boat, and the book had gone overboard, so she had never had the chance—

The picture evoked by this anecdote did not increase Mrs. Roby's credit with the club, and there was a painful pause, which was broken by Mrs. Plinth's remarking:

"I can understand that, with all your other pursuits, you should not find much time for reading; but I should have thought you might at least have *got up The Wings of Death* before Osric Dane's arrival."

Mrs. Roby took this rebuke good-humoredly. She had meant, she owned, to glance through the book; but she had been so absorbed in a novel of Trollope's that—

"No one reads Trollope now," Mrs. Ballinger interrupted.

Mrs. Roby looked pained. "I'm only just beginning," she confessed.

"And does he interest you?" Mrs. Plinth enquired.

"He amuses me."

"Amusement," said Mrs. Plinth, "is hardly what I look for in my choice of books."

"Oh, certainly, *The Wings of Death* is not amusing," ventured Mrs. Leveret, whose manner of putting forth an opinion was like that of an obliging salesman with a variety of other styles to submit if his first selection does not suit.

"Was it *meant* to be?" enquired Mrs. Plinth, who was fond of asking questions that she permitted no one but herself to answer. "Assuredly not."

"Assuredly not—that is what I was going to say," assented Mrs. Leveret, hastily rolling up her opinion and reaching for another. "It was meant to—to elevate."

Miss Van Vluyck adjusted her spectacles as though they were the black cap of condemnation. "I hardly see," she interposed, "how a book steeped in the bitterest pessimism can be said to elevate however much it may instruct."

"I meant, of course, to instruct," said Mrs. Leveret, flurried by the unexpected distinction between two terms which she had supposed to be synonymous. Mrs. Leveret's enjoyment of the Lunch Club was frequently marred by such surprises; and not knowing her own value to the other ladies as a mirror for their mental complacency she was sometimes troubled by a doubt of her worthiness to join in their debates. It was only the fact of having a dull sister who thought her clever that saved her, from a sense of hopeless inferiority.

"Do they get married in the end?" Mrs. Roby interposed.

"They—who?" the Lunch Club collectively exclaimed.

"Why, the girl and man. It's a novel, isn't it? I always think that's the one thing that matters. If they're parted it spoils my dinner."

Mrs. Plinth and Mrs. Ballinger exchanged scandalized glances, and the latter said: "I should hardly advise you to read *The Wings of Death* in that spirit. For my part, when there are so many books one *has* to read; I wonder how any one can find time for those that are merely amusing."

"The beautiful part of it," Laura Glyde murmured, "is surely just this—that no one can tell *how The Wings of Death* ends. Osric Dane, overcome by the awful significance of her own meaning, has mercifully veiled it—perhaps even from herself—as Apelles, in representing the sacrifice of Iphigenia, veiled the face or Agamemnon."

"What's that? Is it poetry?" whispered Mrs. Leveret to Mrs. Plinth, who, disdaining a definite reply, said coldly: "You should look it up. I always make it a point to look things up." Her tone added—"though I might easily have it done for me by the footman."

"I was about to say," Miss Van Vluyck resumed, "that it must always be a question whether a book *can* instruct unless it elevates."

"Oh—" murmured Mrs. Leveret, now feeling herself hopelessly astray.

"I don't know," said Mrs. Ballinger, scenting in Miss Van Vluyck's tone a tendency to depreciate the coveted distinction of entertaining Osric Dane; "I don't know that such a question can seriously be raised as to a book which has attracted more attention among thoughtful people than any novel since *Robert Elsmere*."

"Oh, but don't you see," exclaimed Laura Glyde, "that it's just the dark hopelessness of it all—the wonderful tone-scheme of black on black—that makes it such an artistic achievement? It reminded me when I read it of Prince Rupert's *manière noire*...the book is etched, not painted, yet one feels the color values so intensely...."

"Who is *he?*" Mrs. Leveret whispered to her neighbor. "Someone she's met abroad?"

"The wonderful part of the book," Mrs. Ballinger conceded, "is that it may be looked at from so many points of view. I hear that as a study of determinism Professor Lupton ranks it with *The Data of Ethics*."

"I'm told that Osric Dane spent ten years in preparatory studies before beginning to write it," said Mrs. Plinth. "She looks up everything—verifies everything. It has always been my principle, as you know. Nothing would induce me, now, to put aside a book before I'd finished it, just because I can buy as many more as I want."

"And what do *you* think of *The Wings of Death*?" Mrs. Roby abruptly asked her.

It was the kind of question that might be termed out of order, and the ladies glanced at each other as though disclaiming any share in such a breach of discipline. They all knew there was nothing Mrs. Plinth so much disliked as being asked her opinion of a book. Books were written to read; if one read them what more could be expected? To be questioned in detail regarding the contents of a volume seemed to her as great an outrage as being searched for smuggled laces at the Custom House. The club had always respected this idiosyncrasy of Mrs. Plinth's. Such opinions as she had were imposing and substantial: her mind, like her house, was furnished with monumental "pieces" that were not meant to be disarranged; and it was one of the unwritten rules of the Lunch Club that, within her own province, each member's habits of thought should be respected. The meeting therefore closed with an increased sense, on the part of the other ladies, of Mrs. Roby's hopeless unfitness to be one of them.

## II

MRS. LEVERET, on the eventful day, arrived early at Mrs. Ballinger's, her volume of *Appropriate Allusions* in her pocket.

It always flustered Mrs. Leveret to be late at the Lunch Club: she liked to collect her thoughts and gather a hint, as the others assembled, of the turn the conversation was likely to take. To-day, however, she felt herself completely at a loss; and even the familiar contact of *Appropriate Allusions*, which stuck into her as she sat down, failed to give her any reassurance. It was an admirable little volume, compiled to meet all the social emergencies; so that, whether on the occasion of Anniversaries, joyful or melancholy (as the classification ran), of Banquets, social or municipal, or of Baptisms, Church of England or sectarian, its student need never be at a loss for a pertinent reference. Mrs. Leveret, though she had for years devoutly conned its pages, valued it, however, rather for its moral support than for its practical services; for though in the privacy of her own room she commanded an army of quotations, these invariably deserted her at the critical moment, and the only phrase she retained—*Canst thou draw out leviathan with a hook?*—was one she had never yet found occasion to apply.

Today she felt that even the complete mastery of the volume would hardly have insured her self-possession; for she thought it probable that, even if she *did*, in some miraculous way, remember an Allusion, it would be only to find that Osric Dane used a different volume (Mrs. Leveret was convinced that literary people always carried them), and would consequently not recognize her quotations.

Mrs. Leveret's sense of being adrift was intensified by the appearance of Mrs. Ballinger's drawing-room. To a careless eye its aspect was unchanged; but those acquainted with Mrs. Ballinger's way of arranging her books would instantly have detected the marks of recent perturbation. Mrs. Ballinger's province, as a member of the Lunch Club, was the Book of the Day. On that, whatever it was, from a novel to a treatise on experimental psychology, she was confidently, authoritatively "up." What became of last year's books, or last week's even; what she did with the "subjects" she had previously professed with equal authority; no one had ever yet discovered. 'Her mind was an hotel where facts came and went like transient lodgers, without leaving their address behind, and frequently without paying for their board. It was Mrs. Ballinger's boast that she was "abreast with the Thought of the Day," and her pride that this advanced position should be expressed by the books on her table. These volumes, frequently renewed, and almost always damp from the press, bore names generally unfamiliar to Mrs. Leveret, and giving her, as she furtively scanned them, a disheartening glimpse of new fields of knowledge to be breathlessly traversed in Mrs. Ballinger's wake. But to-day a number of maturer-looking volumes were adroitly mingled with the *primeurs* of the press—Karl Marx jostled Professor Bergson, and the *Confessions of St. Augustine* lay beside the last work on "Mendelism"; so that even to Mrs. Leveret's fluttered perceptions it was clear that Mrs. Ballinger didn't in the least know what Osric Dane was likely to talk about, and had taken measures to be prepared for anything. Mrs. Leveret felt like a passenger on an ocean steamer who is told that there is no immediate danger, but that she had better put on her life-belt.

It was a relief to be roused from these forebodings by Miss Van Vluyck's arrival.

"Well, my dear," the new-comer briskly asked her hostess, "what subjects are we to discuss to-day?"

Mrs. Ballinger was furtively replacing a volume of Wordsworth by a copy of Verlaine. "I hardly know," she said, somewhat nervously. "Perhaps we had better leave that to circumstances."

"Circumstances?" said Miss Van Vluyck drily. "That means, I suppose, that Laura Glyde will take the floor as usual, and we shall be deluged with literature."

Philanthropy and statistics were Miss Van Vluyck's province, and she resented any tendency to divert their guest's attention from these topics.

Mrs. Plinth at this moment appeared.

"Literature?" she protested in a tone of remonstrance. "But this is perfectly unexpected. I understood we were to talk of Osric Dane's novel."

Mrs. Ballinger winced at the discrimination, but let it pass. "We can hardly make that our chief subject—at least not too intentionally," she suggested. "Of course we can let our talk *drift* in that direction; but we ought to have some other topic as an introduction, and that is what I wanted to consult you about. The fact is, we know so little of Osric Dane's tastes and interests that it is difficult to make any special preparation."

"It may be difficult," said Mrs. Plinth with decision, "but it is necessary. I know what that happy-go-lucky principle leads to. As I told one of my nieces the other day, there are certain emergencies for which a lady should always be prepared. It's in shocking taste to wear colors when one pays a visit of condolence, or a last year's dress when there are reports that one's husband is on the wrong side of the market; and so it is with conversation. All I ask is that I should know beforehand what is to be talked about; then I feel sure of being able to say the proper thing."

"I quite agree with you," Mrs. Ballinger assented; "but—"

And at that instant, heralded by the fluttered parlourmaid, Osric Dane appeared upon the threshold.

Mrs. Leveret told her sister afterward that she had known at a glance what was coming. She saw that Osric Dane was not going to meet them half way. That distinguished personage had indeed entered with an air of compulsion not calculated to promote the easy exercise of hospitality. She looked as though she were about to be photographed for a new edition of her books.

The desire to propitiate a divinity is generally in inverse ratio to its responsiveness, and the sense of discouragement produced by Osric Dane's entrance visibly increased the Lunch Club's eagerness to please her. Any lingering idea that she might consider herself under an obligation to her entertainers was at once dispelled by her manner: as Mrs. Leveret said afterward to her sister, she had a way of looking at you that made you feel as if there was something wrong with your hat. This evidence of greatness produced such an immediate impression on the ladies that a shudder of awe ran through them when Mrs. Roby, as their hostess led the great personage into the dining-room, turned back to whisper to the others: "What a brute she is!"

The hour about the table did not tend to revise this verdict. It was passed by Osric Dane in the silent deglutition of Mrs. Bollinger's menu, and by the members of the club in the emission of tentative platitudes which their guest seemed to swallow as perfunctorily as the successive courses of the luncheon.

Mrs. Ballinger's reluctance to fix a topic had thrown the club into a mental disarray which increased with the return to the drawing-room, where the actual business of discussion was to open. Each lady waited for the other to speak; and there was a general shock of disappointment when their hostess opened the conversation by the painfully commonplace enquiry. "Is this your first visit to Hillbridge?"

Even Mrs. Leveret was conscious that this was a bad beginning; and a vague impulse of deprecation made Miss Glyde interject: "It is a very small place indeed."

Mrs. Plinth bristled. "We have a great many representative people," she said, in the tone of one who speaks for her order.

Osric Dane turned to her. "What do they represent?" she asked.

Mrs. Plinth's constitutional dislike to being questioned was intensified by her sense of unpreparedness; and her reproachful glance passed the question on to Mrs. Ballinger.

"Why," said that lady, glancing in turn at the other members, "as a community I hope it is not too much to say that we stand for culture."

"For art—" Miss Glyde interjected.

"For art and literature," Mrs. Ballinger emended.

"And for sociology, I trust," snapped Miss Van Vluyck.

"We have a standard," said Mrs. Plinth, feeling herself suddenly secure on the vast expanse of a generalization; and Mrs. Leveret, thinking there must be room for more than one on so broad a statement, took courage to murmur: "Oh, certainly; we have a standard."

"The object of our little club," Mrs. Ballinger continued, "is to concentrate the highest tendencies of Hillbridge—to centralize and focus its intellectual effort."

This was felt to be so happy that the ladies drew an almost audible breath of relief.

"We aspire," the President went on, "to be in touch with whatever is highest in art, literature and ethics."

Osric Dane again turned to her. "What ethics?" she asked.

A tremor of apprehension encircled the room. None of the ladies required any preparation to pronounce on a question of morals; but when they were called ethics it was different. The club, when fresh from the *Encyclopedia Britannica*, the *Reader's Handbook* or Smith's *Classical Dictionary*, could deal confidently with any subject; but when taken unawares it had been known to define agnosticism as a heresy of the Early Church and Professor Froude as a distinguished histologist; and such minor members as Mrs. Leveret still secretly regarded ethics as something vaguely pagan.

Even to Mrs. Ballinger, Osric Dane's question was unsettling, and there was a general sense of gratitude when Laura Glyde leaned forward to say, with her most sympathetic accent: "You must excuse us, Mrs. Dane, for not being able, just at present, to talk of anything but *The Wings of Death*."

"Yes," said Miss Van Vluyck, with a sudden resolve to carry the war into the enemy's camp. "We are so anxious to know the exact purpose you had in mind in writing your wonderful book."

"You will find," Mrs. Plinth interposed, "that we are not superficial readers."

"We are eager to hear from you," Miss Van Vluyck continued, "if the pessimistic tendency of the book is an expression of your own convictions or—"

"Or merely," Miss Glyde thrust in, "a somber background brushed in to throw your figures into more vivid relief. *Are* you not primarily plastic?"

"*I* have always maintained," Mrs. Ballinger interposed, "that you represent the purely objective method—"

Osric Dane helped herself critically to coffee. "How do you define objective?" she then enquired.

There was a flurried pause before Laura Glyde intensely murmured: "In reading *you* we don't define, we feel."

Osric Dane smiled. "The cerebellum," she remarked, "is not infrequently the seat of the literary emotions." And she took a second lump of sugar.

The sting that this remark was vaguely felt to conceal was almost neutralized by the satisfaction of being addressed in such technical language.

"Ah, the cerebellum," said Miss Van Vluyck complacently. "The club took a course in psychology last winter."

"Which psychology?" asked Osric Dane.

There was an agonizing pause, during which each member of the club secretly deplored the distressing inefficiency of the others. Only Mrs. Roby went on placidly sipping her chartreuse. At last Mrs. Ballinger said, with an attempt at a high tone: "Well, really, you know, it was last year that we took psychology, and this winter we have been so absorbed in—"

She broke off, nervously trying to recall some of the club's discussions; but her faculties seemed to be paralyzed by the petrifying stare of Osric Dane. What *had* the club been absorbed in? Mrs. Ballinger, with a vague purpose of gaining time, repeated slowly: "We've been so intensely absorbed in—"

Mrs. Roby put down her liqueur glass and drew near the group with a smile.

"In Xingu?" she gently prompted.

A thrill ran through the other members. They exchanged confused glances, and then, with one accord, turned a gaze of mingled relief and interrogation on their rescuer. The expression of each denoted a different phase of the same emotion. Mrs. Plinth was the first to compose her features to an air of reassurance: after a moment's hasty adjustment her look almost implied that it was she who had given the word to Mrs. Ballinger.

"Xingu, of course!" exclaimed the latter with her accustomed promptness, while Miss Van Vluyck and Laura Glyde seemed to be plumbing the depths of memory, and Mrs. Leveret, feeling apprehensively for *Appropriate Allusions*, was somehow reassured by the uncomfortable pressure of its bulk against her person.

Osric Dane's change of countenance was no less striking than that of her entertainers. She too put down her coffee-cup, but with a look of distinct annoyance; she too wore, for a brief moment, what Mrs. Roby afterward described as the look of feeling for something in the back of her head; and before she could dissemble these momentary signs of weakness, Mrs. Roby, turning to her with a deferential smile, had said: "And we've been so hoping that to-day you would tell us just what you think of it."

Osric Dane received the homage of the smile as a matter of course; but the accompanying question obviously embarrassed her, and it became clear to her observers that she was not quick at shifting her facial scenery. It was as though her countenance had so long been set in an expression of unchallenged superiority that the muscles had stiffened, and refused to obey her orders.

"Xingu—" she said, as if seeking in her turn to gain time.

Mrs. Roby continued to press her. "Knowing how engrossing the subject is, you will understand how it happens that the club has let everything else go to the wall for the moment. Since we took up Xingu I might almost say—were it not for your books—that nothing else seems to us worth remembering."

Osric Dane's stern features were darkened rather than lit up by an uneasy smile. "I am glad to hear that you make one exception," she gave out between narrowed lips.

"Oh, of course," Mrs. Roby said prettily; "but as you have shown us that—so very naturally!—you don't care to talk of your own things, we really can't let you off from telling us exactly what you think about Xingu; especially," she added, with a still more persuasive smile, "as some people say that one of your last books was saturated with it."

It was an *it*, then—the assurance sped like fire through the parched minds of the other members. In their eagerness to gain the least little clue to Xingu they almost forgot the joy of assisting at the discomfiture of Mrs. Dane.

The latter reddened nervously under her antagonist's challenge. "May I ask," she faltered out, "to which of my books you refer?"

Mrs. Roby did not falter. "That's just what I want you to tell us; because, though I was present, I didn't actually take part."

"Present at what?" Mrs. Dane took her up; and for an instant the trembling members of the Lunch Club thought that the champion Providence had raised up for them had lost a point. But Mrs. Roby explained herself gaily: "At the discussion, of course. And so we're dreadfully anxious to know just how it was that you went into the Xingu."

There was a portentous pause, a silence so big with incalculable dangers that the members with one accord checked the words on their lips, like soldiers dropping their arms to watch a single combat between their leaders. Then Mrs. Dane gave expression to their inmost dread by saying sharply: "Ah—you say *the* Xingu, do you?"

Mrs. Roby smiled undauntedly. "It *is* a shade pedantic, isn't it? Personally, I always drop the article; but I don't know how the other members feel about it."

The other members looked as though they would willingly have dispensed with this appeal to their opinion, and Mrs. Roby, after a bright glance about the group, went on: "They probably think, as I do, that nothing really matters except the thing itself—except Xingu."

No immediate reply seemed to occur to Mrs. Dane, and Mrs. Ballinger gathered courage to say: "Surely everyone must feel that about Xingu."

Mrs. Plinth came to her support with a heavy murmur of assent, and Laura Glyde sighed out emotionally: "I have known cases where it has changed a whole life."

"It has done me worlds of good," Mrs. Leveret interjected, seeming to herself to remember that she had either taken it or read it the winter before.

"Of course," Mrs. Roby admitted, "the difficulty is that one must give up so much time to it. It's very long."

"I can't imagine," said Miss Van Vluyck, "grudging the time given to such a subject."

"And deep in places," Mrs. Roby pursued; (so then it was a book!) "And it isn't easy to skip."

"I never skip," said Mrs. Plinth dogmatically.

"Ah, it's dangerous to, in Xingu. Even at the start there are places where one can't. One must just wade through."

"I should hardly call it *wading,*" said Mrs. Ballinger sarcastically.

Mrs. Roby sent her a look of interest. "Ah—you always found it went swimmingly?"

Mrs. Ballinger hesitated. "Of course there are difficult passages," she conceded.

"Yes; some are not at all clear—even," Mrs. Roby added, "if one is familiar with the original."

"As I suppose you are?" Osric Dane interposed, suddenly fixing her with a look of challenge.

Mrs. Roby met it by a deprecating gesture. "Oh, it's really not difficult up to a certain point; though some of the branches are very little known, and it's almost impossible to get at the source."

"Have you ever tried?" Mrs. Plinth enquired, still distrustful of Mrs. Roby's thoroughness.

Mrs. Roby was silent for a moment; then she replied with lowered lids: "No—but a friend of mine did; a very brilliant man; and he told me it was best for women—not to...."

A shudder ran around the room. Mrs. Leveret coughed so that the parlormaid, who was handing the cigarettes, should not hear; Miss Van Vluyck's face took on a nauseated expression, and Mrs. Plinth looked as if she were passing someone she did not care to bow to. But the most remarkable result of Mrs. Roby's words was the effect they produced on the Lunch Club's distinguished guest. Osric Dane's impassive features suddenly softened to an expression of the warmest human sympathy, and edging her chair toward Mrs. Roby's she asked: "Did he really? And—did you find he was right?"

Mrs. Ballinger, in whom annoyance at Mrs. Roby's unwonted assumption of prominence was beginning to displace gratitude for the aid she had rendered, could not consent to her being allowed, by such dubious means, to monopolize the attention of their guest. If Osric Dane had not enough self-respect to resent Mrs. Roby's flippancy, at least the Lunch Club would do so in the person of its President.

Mrs. Ballinger laid her hand on Mrs. Roby's arm. "We must not forget," she said with a frigid amiability, "that absorbing as Xingu is to us, it may be less interesting to—"

"Oh, no, on the contrary, I assure you," Osric Dane intervened.

"—to others," Mrs. Ballinger finished firmly; "and we must not allow our little meeting to end without persuading Mrs. Dane to say a few words to us on a subject which, to-day, is much more present in all our thoughts. I refer, of course, to *The Wings of Death*."

The other members, animated by various degrees of the same sentiment, and encouraged by the humanised mien of their redoubtable guest, repeated after Mrs. Ballinger: "Oh, yes, you really *must* talk to us a little about your book."

Osric Dane's expression became as bored, though not as haughty, as when her work had been previously mentioned. But before she could respond to Mrs. Ballinger's request, Mrs. Roby had risen from her seat, and was pulling down her veil over her frivolous nose.

"I'm so sorry," she said, advancing toward her hostess with outstretched hand, "but before Mrs. Dane begins I think I'd better run away. Unluckily, as you know, I haven't read her books, so I should be at a terrible disadvantage among you all, and besides, I've an engagement to play bridge."

If Mrs. Roby had simply pleaded her ignorance of Osric Dane's works as a reason for withdrawing, the Lunch Club, in view of her recent prowess, might have approved such evidence of discretion; but to couple this excuse with the brazen announcement that she was foregoing the privilege for the purpose of joining a bridge-party was only one more instance of her deplorable lack of discrimination.

The ladies were disposed, however, to feel that her departure—now that she had performed the sole service she was ever likely to render them—would probably make for greater order and dignity in the impending discussion, besides relieving them of the sense of self-distrust which her presence always mysteriously produced. Mrs. Ballinger therefore restricted herself to a formal murmur of regret, and the other members were just grouping themselves comfortably about Osric Dane when the latter, to their dismay, started up from the sofa on which she had been seated.

"Oh wait—do wait, and I'll go with you!" she called out to Mrs. Roby; and, seizing the hands of the disconcerted members, she administered a series of farewell pressures with the mechanical haste of a railway-conductor punching tickets.

"I'm so sorry—I'd quite forgotten—" she flung back at them from the threshold; and as she joined Mrs. Roby, who had turned in surprise at her appeal, the other ladies had the mortification of hearing her say, in a voice which she did not take the pains to lower: "If you'll let me walk a little way with you, I should so like to ask you a few more questions about Xingu...."

III

THE incident had been so rapid that the door closed on the departing pair before the other members had time to understand what was happening. Then a sense of the indignity put upon them by Osric Dane's unceremonious desertion began to contend with the confused feeling that they had been cheated out of their due without exactly knowing how or why.

There was a silence, during which Mrs. Ballinger, with a perfunctory hand, rearranged the skillfully grouped literature at which her distinguished guest had not so much as glanced; then Miss Van Vluyck tartly pronounced: "Well, I can't say that I consider Osric Dane's departure a great loss."

This confession crystallized the resentment of the other members, and Mrs. Leveret exclaimed: "I do believe she came on purpose to be nasty!"

It was Mrs. Plinth's private opinion that Osric Dane's attitude toward the Lunch Club might have been very different had it welcomed her in the majestic setting of the Plinth drawing-rooms; but not liking to reflect on the inadequacy of Mrs. Ballinger's establishment she sought a roundabout satisfaction in depreciating her lack of foresight.

"I said from the first that we ought to have had a subject ready. It's what always happens when you're unprepared. Now if we'd only got up Xingu—"

The slowness of Mrs. Plinth's mental processes was always allowed for by the club; but this instance of it was too much for Mrs. Ballinger's equanimity.

"Xingu!" she scoffed. "Why, it was the fact of our knowing so much more about it than she did—unprepared though we were—that made Osric Dane so furious. I should have thought that was plain enough to everybody!"

This retort impressed even Mrs. Plinth, and Laura Glyde, moved by an impulse of generosity, said: "Yes, we really ought to be grateful to Mrs. Roby for introducing the topic. It may have made Osric Dane furious, but at least it made her civil."

"I am glad we were able to show her," added Miss Van Vluyck, "that a broad and up-to-date culture is not confined to the great intellectual centers."

This increased the satisfaction of the other members, and they began to forget their wrath against Osric Dane in the pleasure of having contributed to her discomfiture.

Miss Van Vluyck thoughtfully rubbed her spectacles. "What surprised me most," she continued, "was that Fanny Roby should be so up on Xingu."

This remark threw a slight chill on the company, but Mrs. Ballinger said with an air of indulgent irony: "Mrs. Roby always has the knack of making a little go a long way;

still, we certainly owe her a debt for happening to remember that she'd heard of Xingu." And this was felt by the other members to be a graceful way of cancelling once for all the club's obligation to Mrs. Roby.

Even Mrs. Leveret took courage to speed a timid shaft of irony. "I fancy Osric Dane hardly expected to take a lesson in Xingu at Hillbridge!"

Mrs. Ballinger smiled. "When she asked me what we represented—do you remember?—I wish I'd simply said we represented Xingu!"

All the ladies laughed appreciatively at this sally, except Mrs. Plinth, who said, after a moment's deliberation: "I'm not sure it would have been wise to do so."

Mrs. Ballinger, who was already beginning to feel as if she had launched at Osric Dane the retort which had just occurred to her, turned ironically on Mrs. Plinth. "May I ask why?" she enquired.

Mrs. Plinth looked grave. "Surely," she said, "I understood from Mrs. Roby herself that the subject was one it was as well not to go into too deeply?"

Miss Van Vluyck rejoined with precision: "I think that applied only to an investigation of the origin of the—of the—"; and suddenly she found that her usually accurate memory had failed her. "It's a part of the subject I never studied myself/," she concluded.

"Nor I," said Mrs. Ballinger.

Laura Glyde bent toward them with widened eyes. "And yet it seems—doesn't it?—the part that is fullest of an esoteric fascination?"

"I don't know on what you base that," said Miss Van Vluyck argumentatively.

"Well, didn't you notice how intensely interested Osric Dane became as soon as she heard what the brilliant foreigner—he was a foreigner, wasn't he?—had told Mrs. Roby about the origin—the origin of the rite—or whatever you call it?"

Mrs. Plinth looked disapproving, and Mrs. Ballinger visibly wavered. Then she said: "It may not be desirable to touch on the—on that part of the subject in general conversation; but, from the importance it evidently has to a woman of Osric Dane's distinction, I feel as if we ought not to be afraid to discuss it among ourselves—without gloves—though with closed doors, if necessary."

"I'm quite of your opinion," Miss Van Vluyck came briskly to her support; "on condition, that is, that all grossness of language is avoided."

"Oh, I'm sure we shall understand without that," Mrs. Leveret tittered; and Laura Glyde added significantly: "I fancy we can read between the lines," while Mrs. Ballinger rose to assure herself that the doors were really closed.

Mrs. Plinth had not yet given her adhesion. "I hardly see," she began, "what benefit is to be derived from investigating such peculiar customs—"

But Mrs. Ballinger's patience had reached the extreme limit of tension. "This at least," she returned; "that we shall not be placed again in the humiliating position of finding ourselves less up on our own subjects than Fanny Roby!"

Even to Mrs. Plinth this argument was conclusive. She peered furtively about the room and lowered her commanding tones to ask: "Have you got a copy?"

"A—a copy?" stammered Mrs. Ballinger. She was aware that the other members were looking at her expectantly, and that this answer was inadequate, so she supported it by asking another question. "A copy of what?"

Her companions bent their expectant gaze on Mrs. Plinth, who, in turn, appeared less sure of herself than usual. "Why, of—of—the book," she explained.

"What book?" snapped Miss Van Vluyck, almost as sharply as Osric Dane.

Mrs. Ballinger looked at Laura Glyde, whose eyes were interrogatively fixed on Mrs. Leveret. The fact of being deferred to was so new to the latter that it filled her with an insane temerity. "Why, Xingu, of course!" she exclaimed.

A profound silence followed this challenge to the resources of Mrs. Ballinger's library, and the latter, after glancing nervously toward the Books of the Day, returned with dignity: "It's not a thing one cares to leave about."

"I should think *not!*" exclaimed Mrs. Plinth.

"It *is* a book, then?" said Miss Van Vluyck.

This again threw the company into disarray, and Mrs. Ballinger, with an impatient sigh, rejoined: "Why—there *is* a book—naturally...."

"Then why did Miss Glyde call it a religion?"

Laura Glyde started up. "A religion? I never—"

"Yes, you did," Miss Van Vluyck insisted; "you spoke of rites; and Mrs. Plinth said it was a custom."

Miss Glyde was evidently making a desperate effort to recall her statement; but accuracy of detail was not her strongest point. At length she began in a deep murmur: "Surely they used to do something of the kind at the Eleusinian mysteries—"

"Oh—" said Miss Van Vluyck, on the verge of disapproval; and Mrs. Plinth protested: "I understood there was to be no indelicacy!"

Mrs. Ballinger could not control her irritation. "Really, it is too bad that we should not be able to talk the matter over quietly among ourselves. Personally, I think that if one goes into Xingu at all—"

"Oh, so do I!" cried Miss Glyde.

"And I don't see how one can avoid doing so, if one wishes to keep up with the Thought of the Day—"

Mrs. Leveret uttered an exclamation of relief. "There—that's it!" she interposed.

"What's it?" the President took her up.

"Why—it's a—a Thought: I mean a philosophy."

This seemed to bring a certain relief to Mrs. Ballinger and Laura Glyde, but Miss Van Vluyck said: "Excuse me if I tell you that you're all mistaken. Xingu happens to be a language."

"A language!" the Lunch Club cried.

"Certainly. Don't you remember Fanny Roby's saying that there were several branches, and that some were hard to trace? What could that apply to but dialects?"

Mrs. Ballinger could no longer restrain a contemptuous laugh. "Really, if the Lunch Club has reached such a pass that it has to go to Fanny Roby for instruction on a subject like Xingu, it had almost better cease to exist!"

"It's really her fault for not being clearer," Laura Glyde put in.

"Oh, clearness and Fanny Roby!" Mrs. Ballinger shrugged. "I daresay we shall find she was mistaken on almost every point."

"Why not look it up?" said Mrs. Plinth.

As a rule this recurrent suggestion of Mrs. Plinth's was ignored in the heat of discussion, and only resorted to afterward in the privacy of each member's home. But on the present occasion the desire to ascribe their own confusion of thought to the vague and contradictory nature of Mrs. Roby's statements caused the members of the Lunch Club to utter a collective demand for a book of reference.

At this point the production of her treasured volume gave Mrs. Leveret, for a moment, the unusual experience of occupying the center front; but she was not able to hold it long, for *Appropriate Allusions* contained no mention of Xingu.

"Oh, that's not the kind of thing we want!" exclaimed Miss Van Vluyck. She cast a disparaging glance over Mrs. Ballinger's assortment of literature, and added impatiently: "Haven't you any useful books?"

"Of course I have," replied Mrs. Ballinger indignantly; "I keep them in my husband's dressing-room."

From this region, after some difficulty and delay, the parlormaid produced the W-Z volume of an *Encyclopedia* and, in deference to the fact that the demand for it had come from Miss Van Vluyck, laid the ponderous tome before her.

There was a moment of painful suspense while Miss Van Vluyck rubbed her spectacles, adjusted them, and turned to Z; and a murmur of surprise when she said: "It isn't here."

"I suppose," said Mrs. Plinth, "it's not fit to be put in a book of reference."

"Oh, nonsense!" exclaimed Mrs. Ballinger. "Try X."

Miss Van Vluyck turned back through the volume, peering short-sightedly up and down the pages, till she came to a stop and remained motionless, like a dog on a point.

"Well, have you found it?" Mrs. Ballinger enquired after a considerable delay.

"Yes. I've found it," said Miss Van Vluyck in a queer voice.

Mrs. Plinth hastily interposed: "I beg you won't read it aloud if there's anything offensive."

Miss Van Vluyck, without answering, continued her silent scrutiny.

"Well, what *is* it?" exclaimed Laura Glyde excitedly.

*"Do* tell us!" urged Mrs. Leveret, feeling that she would have something awful to tell her sister.

Miss Van Vluyck pushed the volume aside and turned slowly toward the expectant group.

"It's a river."

"A *river?"*

"Yes: in Brazil. Isn't that where she's been living?"

"Who? Fanny Roby? Oh, but you must be mistaken. You've been reading the wrong thing," Mrs. Ballinger exclaimed, leaning over her to seize the volume.

"It's the only Xingu in the *Encyclopedia;* and she *has* been living in Brazil," Miss Van Vluyck persisted.

"Yes: her brother has a consulship there," Mrs. Leveret interposed.

"But it's too ridiculous! I—we—why we *all* remember studying Xingu last year—or the year before last," Mrs. Ballinger stammered.

"I thought I did when *you* said so," Laura Glyde avowed.

*"I* said so?" cried Mrs. Ballinger.

"Yes. You said it had crowded everything else out of your mind."

"Well *you* said it had changed your whole life!"

"For that matter. Miss Van Vluyck said she had never grudged the time she'd given it."

Mrs. Plinth interposed: "I made it clear that I knew nothing whatever of the original."

Mrs. Ballinger broke off the dispute with a groan. "Oh, what does it all matter if she's been making fools of us? I believe Miss Van Vluyck's right—she was talking of the river all the while!"

"How could she? It's too preposterous," Miss Glyde exclaimed.

"Listen." Miss Van Vluyck had repossessed herself of the Encyclopedia, and restored her spectacles to a nose reddened by excitement. "'The Xingu, one of the principal rivers of Brazil, rises on the plateau of Mato Grosso, and flows in a northerly direction for a length of no less than one thousand one hundred and eighteen miles, entering the Amazon near the mouth of the latter river. The upper course of the Xingu is auriferous and fed by numerous branches. Its source was first discovered in 1884 by the German explorer von den Steinen, after a difficult and dangerous expedition through a region inhabited by tribes still in the Stone Age of culture.'"

The ladies received this communication in a state of stupefied silence from which Mrs. Leveret was the first to rally. "She certainly *did* speak of its having branches."

The word seemed to snap the last thread of their incredulity. "And of its great length," gasped Mrs. Ballinger.

"She said it was awfully deep, and you couldn't skip—you just had to wade through," Miss Glyde added.

The idea worked its way more slowly through Mrs. Plinth's compact resistances. "How could there be anything improper about a river?" she inquired.

"Improper?"

"Why, what she said about the source—that it was corrupt?"

"Not corrupt, but hard to get at," Laura Glyde corrected. "Some one who'd been there had told her so. I daresay it was the explorer himself—doesn't it say the expedition was dangerous?"

"'Difficult and dangerous,'" read Miss Van Vluyck.

Mrs. Ballinger pressed her hands to her throbbing temples. "There's nothing she said that wouldn't apply to a river—to this river!" She swung about excitedly to the other members. "Why, do you remember her telling us that she hadn't read *The Supreme Instant* because she'd taken it on a boating party while she was staying with her brother, and someone had 'shied' it overboard—'shied' of course was her own expression."

The ladies breathlessly signified that the expression had not escaped them.

"Well—and then didn't she tell Osric Dane that one of her books was simply saturated with Xingu? Of course it was, if one of Mrs. Roby's rowdy friends had thrown it into the river!"

This surprising reconstruction of the scene in which they had just participated left the members of the Lunch Club inarticulate. At length, Mrs. Plinth, after visibly laboring with the problem, said in a heavy tone: "Osric Dane was taken in too."

Mrs. Leveret took courage at this. "Perhaps that's what Mrs. Roby did it for. She said Osric Dane was a brute, and she may have wanted to give her a lesson."

Miss Van Vluyck frowned. "It was hardly worth-while to do it at our expense."

"At least," said Miss Glyde with a touch of bitterness, "she succeeded in interesting her, which was more than we did."

"What chance had we?" rejoined Mrs. Ballinger.

"Mrs. Roby monopolized her from the first. And *that*, I've no doubt, was her purpose—to give Osric Dane a false impression of her own standing in the club. She would hesitate at nothing to attract attention: we all know how she took in poor Professor Foreland."

"She actually makes him give bridge-teas every Thursday," Mrs. Leveret piped up.

Laura Glyde struck her hands together. "Why, this is Thursday, and it's *there* she's gone, of course; and taken Osric with her!"

"And they're shrieking over us at this moment," said Mrs. Ballinger between her teeth.

This possibility seemed too preposterous to be admitted. "She would hardly dare," said Miss Van Vluyck, "confess the imposture to Osric Dane."

"I'm not so sure: I thought I saw her make a sign as she left. If she hadn't made a sign, why should Osric Dane have rushed out after her?"

"Well, you know, we'd all been telling her how wonderful Xingu was, and she said she wanted to find out more about it," Mrs. Leveret said, with a tardy impulse of justice to the absent.

This reminder, far from mitigating the wrath of the other members, gave it a stronger impetus.

"Yes—and that's exactly what they're both laughing over now," said Laura Glyde ironically.

Mrs. Plinth stood up and gathered her expensive furs about her monumental form. "I have no wish to criticize," she said; "but unless the Lunch Club can protect its members against the recurrence of such—such unbecoming scenes, I for one—"

"Oh, so do I!" agreed Miss Glyde, rising also.

Miss Van Vluyck closed the Encyclopedia and proceeded to button herself into her jacket "My time is really too valuable—" she began.

"I fancy we are all of one mind," said Mrs. Ballinger, looking searchingly at Mrs. Leveret, who looked at the others.

"I always deprecate anything like a scandal—" Mrs. Plinth continued.

"She has been the cause of one today!" exclaimed Miss Glyde.

Mrs. Leveret moaned: "I don't see how she *could!*" and Miss Van Vluyck said, picking up her note-book: "Some women stop at nothing."

"—But if," Mrs. Plinth took up her argument impressively, "anything of the kind had happened in *my* house" (it never would have, her tone implied), "I should have felt that I owed it to myself either to ask for Mrs. Roby's resignation—or to offer mine."

"Oh, Mrs. Plinth—" gasped the Lunch Club.

"Fortunately for me," Mrs. Plinth continued with an awful magnanimity, "the matter was taken out of my hands by our President's decision that the right to entertain distinguished guests was a privilege vested in her office; and I think the other members will agree that, as she was alone in this opinion, she ought to be alone in deciding on the best way of effacing its—its really deplorable consequences."

A deep silence followed this outbreak of Mrs. Plinth's long-stored resentment.

"I don't see why *I* should be expected to ask her to resign—" Mrs. Ballinger at length began; but Laura Glyde turned back to remind her: "You know she made you say that you'd got on swimmingly in Xingu."

An ill-timed giggle escaped from Mrs. Leveret, and Mrs. Ballinger energetically continued "—but you needn't think for a moment that I'm afraid to!"

The door of the drawing-room closed on the retreating backs of the Lunch Club, and the President of that distinguished association, seating herself at her writing-table, and pushing away a copy of *The Wings of Death* to make room for her elbow, drew forth a sheet of the club's note-paper, on which she began to write: "My dear Mrs. Roby—"

## COMING HOME

THE YOUNG MEN of our American Relief Corps are beginning to come back from the front with stories.

There was no time to pick them up during the first months—the whole business was too wild and grim. The horror has not decreased, but nerves and sight are beginning to be disciplined to it. In the earlier days, moreover, such fragments of experience as one got were torn from their setting like bits of flesh scattered by shrapnel. Now things that seemed disjointed are beginning to link themselves together, and the broken bones of history are rising from the battlefields.

I can't say that, in this respect, all the members of the Relief Corps have made the most of their opportunity. Some are unobservant, or perhaps simply inarticulate; others, when going beyond the bald statistics of their job, tend to drop into sentiment and cinema scenes; and none but H. Macy Greer has the gift of making the thing told seem as true as if one had seen it. So it is on H. Macy Greer that I depend, and when his motor dashes him back to Paris for supplies I never fail to hunt him down and coax him to my rooms for dinner and a long cigar.

Greer is a small hard-muscled youth, with pleasant manners, a sallow face, straight hemp-colored hair and grey eyes of unexpected inwardness. He has a voice like thick soup, and speaks with the slovenly drawl of the new generation of Americans, dragging his words along like reluctant dogs on a string, and depriving his narrative of every shade of expression that intelligent intonation gives. But his eyes see so much that they make one see even what his foggy voice obscures.

Some of his tales are dark and dreadful, some are unutterably sad, and some end in a huge laugh of irony. I am not sure how I ought to classify the one I have written down here.

II

ON my first dash to the Northern fighting line—Greer told me the other night—I carried supplies to an ambulance where the surgeon asked me to have a talk with an officer who was badly wounded and fretting for news of his people in the east of France.

He was a young Frenchman, a cavalry lieutenant, trim and slim, with a pleasant smile and obstinate blue eyes that I liked. He looked as if he could hold on tight when it was worth his while. He had had a leg smashed, poor devil, in the first fighting in Flanders, and had been dragging on for weeks in the squalid camp-hospital where I found him. He didn't waste any words on himself, but began at once about his family. They were living, when the war broke out, at their country-place in the Vosges; his father and mother, his sister, just eighteen, and his brother Alain, two years younger. His father, the Comte de Réchamp, had married late in life, and was over seventy: his mother, a good deal younger, was crippled with rheumatism; and there was, besides—to round off the group—a helpless but intensely alive and domineering old grandmother about whom all the others revolved. You know how French families hang together, and throw out branches that make new roots but keep hold of the central trunk, like that tree—what's it called?—that they give pictures of in books about the East.

Jean de Réchamp—that was my lieutenant's name—told me his family was a typical case. "We're very *province*," he said. "My people live at Réchamp all the year. We have a house at Nancy—rather a fine old hotel—but my parents go there only once in two or three years, for a few weeks. That's our 'season.'. . . Imagine the point of view! Or rather don't, because you couldn't. . . ." (He had been about the world a good deal, and known something of other angles of vision.)

Well, of this helpless exposed little knot of people he had had no word—simply nothing—since the first of August. He was at home, staying with them at Réchamp, when war broke out. He was mobilized the first day, and had only time to throw his traps into a cart and dash to the station. His depot was on the other side of France, and communications with the East by mail and telegraph were completely interrupted during the first weeks. His regiment was sent at once to the fighting line, and the first news he got came to him in October, from a communiqué in a Paris paper a month old, saying: "The enemy yesterday retook Réchamp." After that, dead silence: and the poor devil left in the trenches to digest that *"retook"!*

There are thousands and thousands of just such cases; and men bearing them, and cracking jokes, and hitting out as hard as they can. Jean de Réchamp knew this, and tried to crack jokes too—but he got his leg smashed just afterward, and ever since he'd been lying on a straw pallet under a horse-blanket, saying to himself: *"Réchamp retaken."*

"Of course," he explained with a weary smile, "as long as you can tot up your daily bag in the trenches it's a sort of satisfaction—though I don't quite know why; anyhow, you're so dead-beat at night that no dreams come. But lying here staring at the ceiling one goes through the whole business once an hour, at the least: the attack, the slaughter, the ruins...and worse.... Haven't I seen and heard things enough on *this* side to know what's been happening on the other? Don't try to sugar the dose. I *like* it bitter."

I was three days in the neighborhood, and I went back every day to see him. He liked to talk to me because he had a faint hope of my getting news of his family when I returned to Paris. I hadn't much myself, but there was no use telling him so. Besides, things change from day to day, and when we parted I promised to get word to him as soon as I could find out anything. We both knew, of course, that that would not be till Réchamp was taken a third time—by his own troops; and perhaps soon after that, I should be able to get there, or near there, and make enquiries myself. To make sure that I should forget nothing, he drew the family photographs from under his pillow, and handed them over: the little witch-grandmother, with a face like a withered walnut, the father, a fine broken-looking old boy with a Roman nose and a weak chin, the mother, in crape, simple, serious and provincial, the little sister ditto, and Alain, the young brother—just the age the brutes have been carrying off to German prisons—an over-grown thread-paper boy with too much forehead and eyes, and not a muscle in his body. A charming-looking family, distinguished and amiable; but all, except the grandmother, rather usual. The kind of people who come in sets.

As I pocketed the photographs I noticed that another lay face down by his pillow. "Is that for me too?" I asked.

He colored and shook his head, and I felt I had blundered. But after a moment he turned the photograph over and held it out.

"It's the young girl I am engaged to. She was at Réchamp visiting my parents when war was declared; but she was to leave the day after I did. . . ." He hesitated. "There may have been some difficulty about her going. . . . I should like to be sure she got away. . . . Her name is Yvonne Malo."

He did not offer me the photograph, and I did not need it. That girl had a face of her own! Dark and keen and splendid: a type so different from the others that I found myself staring. If he had not said *"ma fiancée"* I should have understood better. After another pause he went on: "I will give you her address in Paris. She has no family: she lives alone—she is a musician. Perhaps you may find her there." His color deepened again as he added: "But I know nothing—I have had no news of her either."

To ease the silence that followed I suggested: "But if she has no family, wouldn't she have been likely to stay with your people, and wouldn't that be the reason of your not hearing from her?"

"Oh, no—I don't think she stayed." He seemed about to add: "If she could help it," but shut his lips and slid the picture out of sight.

As soon as I got back to Paris I made enquiries, but without result. The Germans had been pushed back from that particular spot after a fortnight's intermittent occupation; but their lines were close by, across the valley, and Réchamp was still in a net of trenches. No one could get to it, and apparently no news could come from it. For the moment, at any rate, I found it impossible to get in touch with the place.

My enquiries about Mlle. Malo were equally unfruitful. I went to the address Réchamp had given me, somewhere off in Passy, among gardens, in what they call a "Square," no doubt because it's oblong: a kind of long narrow court with aesthetic-looking studio buildings round it. Mlle. Malo lived in one of them, on the top floor, the concierge said, and I looked up and saw a big studio window, and a roof-terrace with dead gourds dangling from a pergola. But she wasn't there, she hadn't been there, and they had no news of her. I wrote to Réchamp of my double failure, he sent me back a line of thanks; and after that for a long while I heard no more of him.

By the beginning of November the enemy's hold had begun to loosen in the Argonne and along the Vosges, and one day we were sent off to the East with a couple of ambulances. Of course we had to have military chauffeurs, and the one attached to my ambulance happened to be a fellow I knew. The day before we started, in talking over our route with him, I said: "I suppose we can manage to get to Réchamp now?" He looked puzzled—it was such a little place that he'd forgotten the name. "Why do you want to get there?" he wondered. I told him, and he gave an exclamation. "Good God! Of course—but how extraordinary! Jean de Réchamp's here now, in Paris, too lame for the front, and driving a motor." We stared at each other, and he went on: "He must take my place—he must go with you. I don't know how it can be done; but done it shall be."

Done it was, and the next morning at daylight I found Jean de Réchamp at the wheel of my car. He looked another fellow from the wreck I had left in the Flemish hospital; all made over, and burning with activity, but older, and with lines about his eyes. He had had news from his people in the interval, and had learned that they were still at Réchamp, and well. What was more surprising was that Mlle. Malo was with them—had never left. Alain had been got away to England, where he remained; but none of the others had budged. They had fitted up an ambulance in the château, and Mlle. Malo and the little sister were nursing the wounded. There were not many details in the letters, and they had been a long time on the way; but their tone was so reassuring that Jean could give himself up to unclouded anticipation. You may fancy if he was grateful for the chance I was giving him; for of course he couldn't have seen his people in any other way.

Our permits, as you know, don't as a rule let us into the firing-line: we only take supplies to second-line ambulances, and carry back the badly wounded in need of delicate operations. So I wasn't in the least sure we should be allowed to go to Réchamp—though I had made up my mind to get there, anyhow.

We were about a fortnight on the way, coming and going in Champagne and the

Argonne, and that gave us time to get to know each other. It was bitter cold, and after our long runs over the lonely frozen hills we used to crawl into the café of the inn—if there was one—and talk and talk. We put up in fairly rough places, generally in a farm house or a cottage packed with soldiers; for the villages have all remained empty since the autumn, except when troops are quartered in them. Usually, to keep warm, we had to go up after supper to the room we shared, and get under the blankets with our clothes on. Once some jolly Sisters of Charity took us in at their Hospice, and we slept two nights in an ice-cold whitewashed cell—but what tales we heard around their kitchen-fire! The Sisters had stayed alone to face the Germans, had seen the town burn, and had made the Teutons turn the hose on the singed roof of their Hospice and beat the fire back from it. It's a pity those Sisters of Charity can't marry. . . .

Réchamp told me a lot in those days. I don't believe he was talkative before the war, but his long weeks in hospital, starving for news, had unstrung him. And then he was mad with excitement at getting back to his own place. In the interval he'd heard how other people caught in their country-houses had fared—you know the stories we all refused to believe at first, and that we now prefer not to think about.... Well, he'd been thinking about those stories pretty steadily for some months; and he kept repeating: "My people say they're all right—but they give no details."

"You see," he explained, "there never were such helpless beings. Even if there had been time to leave, they couldn't have done it. My mother had been having one of her worst attacks of rheumatism—she was in bed, helpless, when I left. And my grandmother, who is a demon of activity in the house, won't stir out of it. We haven't been able to coax her into the garden for years. She says it's draughty; and you know how we all feel about draughts! As for my father, he hasn't had to decide anything since the Comte de Chambord refused to adopt the tricolor. My father decided that he was right, and since then there has been nothing particular for him to take a stand about. But I know how he behaved just as well as if I'd been there—he kept saying: 'One must act—one must act!' and sitting in his chair and doing nothing. Oh, I'm not disrespectful: they were *like* that in his generation! Besides—it's better to laugh at things, isn't it?" And suddenly his face would darken....

On the whole, however, his spirits were good till we began to traverse the line of ruined towns between Sainte Menehould and Bar-le-Duc. "This is the way the devils came," he kept saying to me; and I saw he was hard at work picturing the work they must have done in his own neighborhood.

"But since your sister writes that your people are safe!"

"They may have made her write that to reassure me. They'd heard I was badly wounded. And, mind you, there's never been a line from my mother."

"But you say your mother's hands are so lame that she can't hold a pen. And wouldn't Mlle. Malo have written you the truth?"

At that his frown would lift. "Oh, yes. She would despise any attempt at concealment."

"Well, then—what the deuce is the matter?"

"It's when I see these devils' traces—" he could only mutter.

One day, when we had passed through a particularly devastated little place, and had got from the curé some more than usually abominable details of things done there, Réchamp broke out to me over the kitchen-fire of our night's lodging. "When I hear things like that I don't believe anybody who tells me my people are all right!"

"But you know well enough," I insisted, "that the Germans are not all alike—that it all depends on the particular officer. . . ."

"Yes, yes, I know," he assented, with a visible effort at impartiality. "Only, you see—as one gets nearer. . . ." He went on to say that, when he had been sent from the ambulance at the front to a hospital at Moulins, he had been for a day or two in a ward next to some wounded German soldiers—bad cases, they were—and had heard them talking. They didn't know he knew German, and he had heard things. . . . There was one name always coming back in their talk, von Scharlach, Oberst von Scharlach. One of them, a young fellow, said: "I wish now I'd cut my hand off rather than do what he told us to that night. . . . Every time the fever comes I see it all again. I wish I'd been struck dead first." They all said "Scharlach" with a kind of terror in their voices, as if he might hear them even there, and come down on them horribly. Réchamp had asked where their regiment came from, and had been told: From the Vosges. That had set his brain working, and whenever he saw a ruined village, or heard a tale of savagery, the Scharlach nerve began to quiver. At such times it was no use reminding him that the Germans had had at least three hundred thousand men in the East in August. He simply didn't listen. . . .

III

THE day before we started for Réchamp his spirits flew up again, and that night he became confidential. "You've been such a friend to me that there are certain things— seeing what's ahead of us—that I should like to explain"; and, noticing my surprise, he went on: "I mean about my people. The state of mind in my *milieu* must be so remote from anything you're used to in your happy country.... But perhaps I can make you understand. . . ."

I saw that what he wanted was to talk to me of the girl he was engaged to. Mlle. Malo, left an orphan at ten, had been the ward of a neighbor of the Réchamps', a chap with an old name and a starred château, who had lost almost everything else at baccarat before he was forty, and had repented, had the gout and studied agriculture for the rest of his life. The girl's father was a rather brilliant painter, who died young, and her mother, who followed him in a year or two, was a Pole: you may fancy that, with such antecedents, the girl was just the mixture to shake down quietly into French country life with a gouty and repentant guardian. The Marquis de Corvenaire—that was his name— brought her down to his place, got an old maid sister to come and stay, and really, as far as one knows, brought his ward up rather decently. Now and then she used to be driven over to play with the young Réchamps, and Jean remembered her as an ugly little girl in a plaid frock, who used to invent wonderful games and get tired of playing them just as the other children were beginning to learn how. But her domineering ways and searching questions did not meet with his mother's approval, and her visits were not encouraged. When she was seventeen her guardian died and left her a little money. The maiden sister had gone dotty, there was nobody to look after Yvonne, and she went to Paris, to an aunt, broke loose from the aunt when she came of age, set up her studio, travelled, painted, played the violin, knew lots of people; and never laid eyes on Jean de Réchamp till about a year before the war, when her guardian's place was sold, and she had to go down there to see about her interest in the property.

The old Réchamps heard she was coming, but didn't ask her to stay. Jean drove over to the shut-up chateau, however, and found Mlle. Malo lunching on a corner of the kitchen table. She exclaimed: "My little Jean!" flew to him with a kiss for each cheek, and made him sit down and share her omelet. . . . The ugly little girl had shed her chrysalis—and you may fancy if he went back once or twice!

Mlle. Malo was staying at the chateau all alone, with the farmer's wife to come in and cook her dinner: not a soul in the house at night but herself and her brindled sheep dog. She had to be there a week, and Jean suggested to his people to ask her to Réchamp. But at Réchamp they hesitated, coughed, looked away, said the spare rooms were all upside down, and the valet-de-chambre laid up with the mumps, and the cook short-handed—till finally the irrepressible grandmother broke out: "A young girl who chooses to live alone—probably prefers to live alone!"

There was a deadly silence, and Jean did not raise the question again; but I can imagine his blue eyes getting obstinate.

Soon after Mlle. Malo's return to Paris he followed her and began to frequent the Passy studio. The life there was unlike anything he had ever seen—or conceived as possible, short of the prairies. He had sampled the usual varieties of French womankind, and explored most of the social layers; but he had missed the newest, that of the artistic-emancipated. I don't know much about that set myself, but from his descriptions I should say they were a good deal like intelligent Americans, except that they don't seem to keep art and life in such water-tight compartments. But his great discovery was the new girl. Apparently he had never before known any but the traditional type, which predominates in the provinces, and still persists, he tells me, in the last fastnesses of the Faubourg St. Germain. The girl who comes and goes as she pleases, reads what she likes, has opinions about what she reads, who talks, looks, behaves with the independence of a married woman—and yet has kept the Diana-freshness—think how she must have shaken up such a man's inherited view of things! Mlle. Malo did far more than make Réchamp fall in love with her: she turned his world topsy-turvy, and prevented his ever again squeezing himself into his little old pigeon-hole of prejudices.

Before long they confessed their love—just like any young couple of Anglo-Saxons—and Jean went down to Réchamp to ask permission to marry her. Neither you nor I can quite enter into the state of mind of a young man of twenty-seven who has knocked about all over the globe, and been in and out of the usual sentimental coils—and who has to ask his parents' leave to get married! Don't let us try: it's no use. We should only end by picturing him as an incorrigible ninny. But there isn't a man in France who wouldn't feel it his duty to take that step, as Jean de Réchamp did. All we can do is to accept the premise and pass on.

Well—Jean went down and asked his father and his mother and his old grandmother if they would permit him to marry Mlle. Malo; and they all with one voice said they wouldn't. There was an uproar, in fact; and the old grandmother contributed the most piercing note to the concert. Marry Mlle. Malo! A young girl who lived alone! Travelled! Spent her time with foreigners—with musicians and painters! *A young girl!* Of course, if she had been a married woman—that is, a widow—much as they would have preferred a young girl for Jean, or even, if widow it had to be, a widow of another type—still, it was conceivable that, out of affection for him, they might have resigned themselves to his choice. But a young girl—bring such a young girl to Réchamp! Ask them to receive her under the same roof with their little Simone, their innocent Alain. . . .

He had a bad hour of it; but he held his own, keeping silent while they screamed, and stiffening as they began to wobble from exhaustion. Finally he took his mother apart, and tried to reason with her. His arguments were not much use, but his resolution impressed her, and he saw it. As for his father, nobody was afraid of Monsieur de Réchamp. When he said: "Never—never while I live, and there is a roof on Réchamp!" they all knew he had collapsed inside. But the grandmother was terrible. She was terrible because she was so old, and so clever at taking advantage of it. She could bring on a valvular heart attack by just sitting still and holding her breath, as Jean and his mother had long since found out; and she always treated them to one when things weren't going as she liked. Madame de Réchamp promised Jean that she would intercede with her mother-in-law; but she hadn't much faith in the result, and when she came out of the old lady's room she whispered: "She's just sitting there holding her breath."

The next day Jean himself advanced to the attack. His grandmother was the most intelligent member of the family, and she knew he knew it, and liked him for having found it out; so when he had her alone she listened to him without resorting to any valvular tricks. "Of course," he explained, "you're much too clever not to understand that the times have changed, and manners with them, and that what a woman was criticized for doing yesterday she is ridiculed for not doing to-day. Nearly all the old social thou-shalt-nots have gone: intelligent people nowadays don't give a fig for them, and that simple fact has abolished them. They only existed as long as there was some one left for them to scare." His grandmother listened with a sparkle of admiration in her ancient eyes. "And of course," Jean pursued, "that can't be the real reason for your opposing my marriage—a marriage with a young girl you've always known, who has been received here—"

"Ah, that's it—we've always known her!" the old lady snapped him up.

"What of that? I don't see—"

"Of course you don't. You're here so little: you don't hear things...."

"What things?"

"Things in the air. . . that blow about. . . . You were doing your military service at the time. . . ."

"At what time?"

She leaned forward and laid a warning hand on his arm. "Why did Corvenaire leave her all that money—*why?*"

"But why not—why shouldn't he?" Jean stammered, indignant. Then she unpacked her bag—a heap of vague insinuations, baseless conjectures, village tattle, all, at the last analysis, based, as he succeeded in proving, and making her own, on a word launched at random by a discharged maid-servant who had retailed her grievance to the cure's housekeeper. "Oh, she does what she likes with Monsieur le Marquis, the young miss! *She* knows how. . . ." On that single phrase the neighborhood had raised a slander built of adamant.

Well, I'll give you an idea of what a determined fellow Réchamp is, when I tell you he pulled it down—or thought he did. He kept his temper, hunted up the servant's record, proved her a liar and dishonest, cast grave doubts on the discretion of the cure's housekeeper, and poured such a flood of ridicule over the whole flimsy fable, and those who had believed in it, that in sheer shamefacedness at having based her objection on such grounds, his grandmother gave way, and brought his parents toppling down with her.

All this happened a few weeks before the war, and soon afterward Mlle. Malo came down to Réchamp. Jean had insisted on her coming: he wanted her presence there, as his betrothed, to be known to the neighbourhood. As for her, she seemed delighted to come. I could see from Réchamp's tone, when he reached this part of his story, that he rather thought I should expect its heroine to have shown a becoming reluctance—to have stood on her dignity. He was distinctly relieved when he found I expected no such thing.

"She's simplicity itself—it's her great quality. Vain complications don't exist for her, because she doesn't see them. . . that's what my people can't be made to understand. . . ."

I gathered from the last phrase that the visit had not been a complete success, and this explained his having let out, when he first told me of his fears for his family, that he was sure Mlle. Malo would not have remained at Réchamp if she could help it. Oh, no, decidedly, the visit was not a success. . . .

"You see," he explained with a half-embarrassed smile, "it was partly her fault. Other girls as clever, but less—how shall I say?—less proud, would have adapted themselves, arranged things, avoided startling allusions. She wouldn't stoop to that; she talked to my family as naturally as she did to me. You can imagine for instance, the effect of her saying: 'One night, after a supper at Montmartre, I was walking home with two or three pals'—. It was her way of affirming her convictions, and I adored her for it—but I wished she wouldn't!"

And he depicted, to my joy, the neighbors rumbling over to call in heraldic barouches (the mothers alone—with embarrassed excuses for not bringing their daughters), and the agony of not knowing, till they were in the room, if Yvonne would receive them with lowered lids and folded hands, sitting by in a *pose de fiancée* while the elders talked; or if she would take the opportunity to air her views on the separation of Church and State, or the necessity of making divorce easier. "It's not," he explained, "that she really takes much interest in such questions: she's much more absorbed in her music and painting. But anything her eye lights on sets her mind dancing—as she said to me once: 'It's your mother's friends' bonnets that make me stand up for divorce!'" He broke off abruptly to add: "Good God, how far off all that nonsense seems!"

## IV

THE next day we started for Réchamp, not sure if we could get through, but bound to, anyhow! It was the coldest day we'd had, the sky steel, the earth iron, and a snow-wind howling down on us from the north. The Vosges are splendid in winter. In summer they are just plump puddingy hills; when the wind strips them they turn to mountains. And we seemed to have the whole country to ourselves—the black firs, the blue shadows, the beech-woods cracking and groaning like rigging, the bursts of snowy sunlight from cold clouds. Not a soul in sight except the sentinels guarding the railways, muffled to the eyes, or peering out of their huts of pine-boughs at the cross-roads. Every now and then we passed a long string of seventy-fives, or a train of supply wagons or army ambulances, and at intervals a cavalryman cantered by, his cloak bellied out by the gale; but of ordinary people about the common jobs of life, not a sign.

The sense of loneliness and remoteness that the absence of the civil population produces everywhere in eastern France is increased by the fact that all the names and distances on the mile-stones have been scratched out and the sign-posts at the cross-roads thrown down. It was done, presumably, to throw the enemy off the track in September: and the signs have never been put back. The result is that one is forever losing one's way, for the soldiers quartered in the district know only the names of their particular villages, and those on the march can tell you nothing about the places they are passing through. We had got badly off our road several times during the trip, but on the last day's run Réchamp was in his own country, and knew every yard of the way—or thought he did. We had turned off the main road, and were running along between rather featureless fields and woods, crossed by a good many wood-roads with nothing to distinguish them; but he continued to push ahead, saying: "We don't turn till we get to a manor-house on a stream, with a big paper-mill across the road." He went on to tell me that the mill-owners lived in the manor, and were old friends of his people: good old local stock, who had lived there for generations and done a lot for the neighbourhood.

"It's queer I don't see their village-steeple from this rise. The village is just beyond the house. How the devil could I have missed the turn?" We ran on a little farther, and suddenly he stopped the motor with a jerk. We were at a cross-road, with a stream running under the bank on our right. The place looked like an abandoned stoneyard. I never saw completer ruin. To the left, a fortified gate gaped on emptiness; to the right, a mill-wheel hung in the stream. Everything else was as flat as your dinner-table.

"Was this what you were trying to see from that rise?" I asked; and I saw a tear or two running down his face.

"They were the kindest people: their only son got himself shot the first month in Champagne—"

He had jumped out of the car and was standing staring at the level waste. "The house was there—there was a splendid lime in the court. I used to sit under it and have a glass of *vin gris de Lorraine* with the old people.... Over there, where that cinder-heap is, all their children are buried." He walked across to the grave-yard under a blackened wall—a bit of the apse of the vanished church—and sat down on a grave-stone. "If the devils have done this *here*—so close to us," he burst out, and covered his face.

An old woman walked toward us down the road. Réchamp jumped up and ran to meet her. "Why, Marie Jeanne, what are you doing in these ruins?" The old woman looked at him with unastonished eyes. She seemed incapable of any surprise. "They left my house standing. I'm glad to see Monsieur," she simply said. We followed her to the one house left in the waste of stones. It was a two-roomed cottage, propped against a cow-stable, but fairly decent, with a curtain in the window and a cat on the sill. Réchamp caught me by the arm and pointed to the door-panel. "Oberst von Scharlach" was scrawled on it. He turned as white as your tablecloth, and hung on to me a minute; then he spoke to the old woman. "The officers were quartered here: that was the reason they spared your house?"

She nodded. "Yes: I was lucky. But the gentlemen must come in and have a mouthful."

Réchamp's finger was on the name. "And this one—this was their commanding officer?"

"I suppose so. Is it somebody's name?" She had evidently never speculated on the meaning of the scrawl that had saved her.

"You remember him—their captain? Was his name Scharlach?" Réchamp persisted.

Under its rich weathering the old woman's face grew as pale as his. "Yes, that was his name—I heard it often enough."

"Describe him, then. What was he like? Tall and fair? They're all that—but what else? What in particular?"

She hesitated, and then said: "This one wasn't fair. He was dark, and had a scar that drew up the left corner of his mouth."

Réchamp turned to me. "It's the same. I heard the men describing him at Moulins."

We followed the old woman into the house, and while she gave us some bread and wine she told us about the wrecking of the village and the factory. It was one of the most damnable stories I've heard yet. Put together the worst of the typical horrors and you'll have a fair idea of it. Murder, outrage, torture: Scharlach's program seemed to be fairly comprehensive. She ended off by saying: "His orderly showed me a silver-mounted flute he always travelled with, and a beautiful paint-box mounted in silver too. Before he left he sat down on my door-step and made a painting of the ruins. . . ."

Soon after leaving this place of death we got to the second lines and our troubles began. We had to do a lot of talking to get through the lines, but what Réchamp had just seen had made him eloquent. Luckily, too, the ambulance doctor, a charming fellow, was short of tetanus-serum, and I had some left; and while I went over with him to the pine-branch hut where he hid his wounded I explained Réchamp's case, and implored him to get us through. Finally it was settled that we should leave the ambulance there—for in the lines the ban against motors is absolute—and drive the remaining twelve miles. A sergeant fished out of a farmhouse a toothless old woman with a furry horse harnessed to a two-wheeled trap, and we started off by round-about wood-tracks. The horse was in no hurry, nor the old lady either; for there were bits of road that were pretty steadily currycombed by shell, and it was to everybody's interest not to cross them before twilight. Jean de Réchamp's excitement seemed to have dropped: he sat beside me dumb as a fish, staring straight ahead of him. I didn't feel talkative either, for a word the doctor had let drop had left me thinking. "That poor old granny mind the shells? Not she!" he had said when our crazy chariot drove up. "She doesn't know them from snow-flakes any more. Nothing matters to her now, except trying to outwit a German. They're all like that where Scharlach's been—you've heard of him? She had only one boy—half-witted: he cocked a broom handle at them, and they burnt him. Oh, she'll take you to Réchamp safe enough."

"Where Scharlach's been"—so he had been as close as this to Réchamp! I was wondering if Jean knew it, and if that had sealed his lips and given him that flinty profile. The old horse's woolly flanks jogged on under the bare branches and the old woman's bent back jogged in time with it She never once spoke or looked around at us. "It isn't the noise we make that'll give us away," I said at last; and just then the old woman turned her head and pointed silently with the osier-twig she used as a whip. Just ahead of us lay a heap of ruins: the wreck, apparently, of a great château and its dependencies. "Lermont!" Réchamp exclaimed, turning white. He made a motion to jump out and then dropped back into the seat. "What's the use?" he muttered. He leaned forward and touched the old woman's shoulder.

"I hadn't heard of this—when did it happen?"

"In September."

*"They* did it?"

"Yes. Our wounded were there. It's like this everywhere in our country."

I saw Jean stiffening himself for the next question. "At Réchamp, too?"

She relapsed into indifference. "I haven't been as far as Réchamp."

"But you must have seen people who'd been there—you must have heard."

"I've heard the masters were still there—so there must be something standing. Maybe though," she reflected, "they're in the cellars. . . ."

We continued to jog on through the dusk.

## V

"THERE'S the steeple!" Réchamp burst out.

Through the dimness I couldn't tell which way to look; but I suppose in the thickest midnight he would have known where he was. He jumped from the trap and took the old horse by the bridle. I made out that he was guiding us into a long village street edged by houses in which every light was extinguished. The snow on the ground sent up a pale reflection, and I began to see the gabled outline of the houses and the steeple at the head of the street. The place seemed as calm and unchanged as if the sound of war had never reached it. In the open space at the end of the village Réchamp checked the horse.

"The elm—there's the old elm in front of the church!" he shouted in a voice like a boy's. He ran back and caught me by both hands. "It was true, then—nothing's touched!" The old woman asked: "Is this Réchamp?" and he went back to the horse's head and turned the trap toward a tall gate between park walls. The gate was barred and padlocked, and not a gleam showed through the shutters of the porter's lodge; but Réchamp, after listening a minute or two, gave a low call twice repeated, and presently the lodge door opened, and an old man peered out. Well—I leave you to brush in the rest. Old family servant, tears and hugs and so on. I know you affect to scorn the cinema, and this was it, tremolo and all. Hang it! This war's going to teach us not to be afraid of the obvious.

We piled into the trap and drove down a long avenue to the house. Black as the grave, of course; but in another minute the door opened, and there, in the hall, was another servant, screening a light—and then more doors opened on another cinema-scene: fine old drawing-room with family portraits, shaded lamp, domestic group about the fire. They evidently thought it was the servant coming to announce dinner, and not a head turned at our approach. I could see them all over Jean's shoulder: a grey-haired lady knitting with stiff fingers, an old gentleman with a high nose and a weak chin sitting in a big carved armchair and looking more like a portrait than the portraits; a pretty girl at his feet, with a dog's head in her lap, and another girl, who had a Red Cross on her sleeve, at the table with a book. She had been reading aloud in a rich veiled voice, and broke off her last phrase to say: "Dinner. . . ." Then she looked up and saw Jean. Her dark face remained perfectly calm, but she lifted her hand in a just perceptible gesture of warning, and instantly understanding he drew back and pushed the servant forward in his place.

"Madame la Comtesse—it is someone outside asking for Mademoiselle."

The dark girl jumped up and ran out into the hall. I remember wondering: "Is it because she wants to have him to herself first—or because she's afraid of their being startled?" I wished myself out of the way, but she took no notice of me, and going straight to Jean flung her arms about him. I was behind him and could see her hands about his neck, and her brown fingers tightly locked. There wasn't much doubt about those two. . . .

The next minute she caught sight of me, and I was being rapidly tested by a pair of the finest eyes I ever saw—I don't apply the term to their setting, though that was fine too, but to the look itself, a look at once warm and resolute, all-promising and all-penetrating. I really can't do with fewer adjectives. . . .

Réchamp explained me, and she was full of thanks and welcome; not excessive, but—well, I don't know—eloquent! She gave every intonation all it could carry, and without the least emphasis: that's the wonder.

She went back to "prepare" the parents, as they say in melodrama; and in a minute or two we followed. What struck me first was that these insignificant and inadequate people had the command of the grand gesture—had *la ligne*. The mother had laid aside her knitting—*not* dropped it—and stood waiting with open arms. But even in clasping her son she seemed to include me in her welcome. I don't know how to describe it; but they never let me feel I was in the way. I suppose that's part of what you call distinction; knowing instinctively how to deal with unusual moments.

All the while, I was looking about me at the fine secure old room, in which nothing seemed altered or disturbed, the portraits smiling from the walls, the servants beaming in the doorway—and wondering how such things could have survived in the trail of death and havoc we had been following.

The same thought had evidently struck Jean, for he dropped his sister's hand and turned to gaze about him too.

"Then nothing's touched—*nothing?* I don't understand," he stammered.

Monsieur de Réchamp raised himself majestically from his chair, crossed the room and lifted Yvonne Malo's hand to his lips. "Nothing is touched—thanks to this hand and this brain."

Madame de Réchamp was shining on her son through tears. "Ah, yes—we owe it all to Yvonne."

"All, all! Grandmamma will tell you!" Simone chimed in; and Yvonne, brushing aside their praise with a half-impatient laugh, said to her betrothed: "But your grandmother! You must go up to her at once."

A wonderful specimen, that grandmother: I was taken to see her after dinner. She sat by the fire in a bare paneled bedroom, bolt upright in an armchair with ears, a knitting-table at her elbow with a shaded candle on it. She was even more withered and ancient than she looked in her photograph, and I judge she'd never been pretty; but she somehow made me feel as if I'd got through with prettiness. I don't know exactly what she reminded me of: a dried bouquet, or something rich and clovy that had turned brittle through long keeping in a sandal-wood box. I suppose her sandal-wood box had been Good Society. Well, I had a rare evening with her. Jean and his parents were called down to see the curé, who had hurried over to the château when he heard of the young man's arrival; and the old lady asked me to stay on and chat with her. She related their experiences with uncanny detachment, seeming chiefly to resent the indignity of having been made to descend into the cellar—"to avoid French shells, if you'll believe it: the Germans had the decency not to bombard us," she observed impartially. I was so struck by the absence of rancor in her tone that finally, out of sheer curiosity, I made an allusion to the horror of having the enemy under one's roof. "Oh, I might almost say I didn't see them," she returned. "I never go downstairs any longer; and they didn't do me the honor of coming beyond my door. A glance sufficed them—an old woman like me!" she added with a phosphorescent gleam of coquetry.

"But they searched the château, surely?"

"Oh, a mere form; they were very decent—very decent," she almost snapped at me. "There was a first moment, of course, when we feared it might be hard to get Monsieur de Réchamp away with my young grandson; but Mlle. Malo managed that very cleverly. They slipped off while the officers were dining." She looked at me with the smile of some arch old lady in a Louis XV pastel. "My grandson Jean's fiancée is a very clever young woman: in my time no young girl would have been so sure of herself, so cool and quick. After all, there is something to be said for the new way of bringing up girls. My poor daughter-in-law, at Yvonne's age, was a bleating baby: she is so still, at times. The convent doesn't develop character. I'm glad Yvonne was not brought up in a convent." And this champion of tradition smiled on me more intensely.

Little by little I got from her the story of the German approach: the distracted fugitives pouring in from the villages north of Réchamp, the sound of distant cannonading, and suddenly, the next afternoon, after a reassuring lull, the sight of a single spiked helmet at the end of the drive. In a few minutes a dozen followed: mostly officers; then all at once the place hummed with them. There were supply wagons and motors in the court, bundles of hay, stacks of rifles, artillery-men unharnessing and rubbing down their horses. The crowd was hot and thirsty, and in a moment the old lady, to her amazement, saw wine and cider being handed about by the Réchamp servants. "Or so at least I was told," she added, correcting herself, "for it's not my habit to look out of the window. I simply sat here and waited." Her seat, as she spoke, might have been a curule chair.

Downstairs, it appeared, Mlle. Malo had instantly taken her measures. *She* didn't sit and wait. Surprised in the garden with Simone, she had made the girl walk quietly back to the house and receive the officers with her on the doorstep. The officer in command—captain, or whatever he was—had arrived in a bad temper, cursing and swearing, and growling out menaces about spies. The day was intensely hot, and possibly he had had too much wine. At any rate Mlle. Malo had known how to "put him in his place"; and when he and the other officers entered they found the dining-table set out with refreshing drinks and cigars, melons, strawberries and iced coffee. "The clever creature! She even remembered that they liked whipped cream with their coffee!"

The effect had been miraculous. The captain—what was his name? Yes, Chariot, Chariot—Captain Chariot had been specially complimentary on the subject of the whipped cream and the cigars. Then he asked to see the other members of the family, and Mlle. Malo told him there were only two—"two old women!" He made a face at that, and said all the same he should like to meet them; and she answered: "'One is your hostess, the Comtesse de Réchamp, who is ill in bed'—for my poor daughter-in-law was lying in bed paralyzed with rheumatism—'and the other her mother-in-law, a very old lady who never leaves her room.'"

"But aren't there any men in the family?" he had then asked; and she had said: "Oh yes—two. The Comte de Réchamp and his son."

"And where are they?"

"In England. Monsieur de Réchamp went a month ago to take his son on a trip."

The officer said: "I was told they were here to-day"; and Mlle. Malo replied: "You had better have the house searched and satisfy yourself."

He laughed and said: "The idea *had* occurred to me." She laughed also, and sitting down at the piano struck a few chords. Captain Chariot, who had his foot on the threshold, turned back—Simone had described the scene to her grandmother afterward. "Some of the brutes, it seems, are musical," the old lady explained; "and this was one of them. While he was listening, some soldiers appeared in the court carrying another who seemed to be wounded. It turned out afterward that he'd been climbing a garden wall after fruit, and cut himself on the broken glass at the top; but the blood was enough—they raised the usual dreadful outcry about an ambush, and a lieutenant clattered into the room where Mlle. Malo sat playing Stravinsky." The old lady paused for her effect, and I was conscious of giving her all she wanted.

"Well—?"

"Will you believe it? It seems she looked at her watch-bracelet and said: 'Do you gentlemen dress for dinner? I do—but we've still time for a little Moussorgsky'—or whatever wild names they call themselves—'if you'll make those people outside hold their tongues.' Our captain looked at her again, laughed, gave an order that sent the lieutenant right about, and sat down beside her at the piano. Imagine my stupor, dear sir: the drawing-room is directly under this room, and in a moment I heard two voices coming up to me. Well, I won't conceal from you that his was the finest. But then I always adored a baritone." She folded her shriveled hands among their laces. "After that, the Germans were *très bien—très bien*. They stayed two days, and there was nothing to complain of. Indeed, when the second detachment came, a week later, they never even entered the gates. Orders had been left that they should be quartered elsewhere. Of course we were lucky in happening on a man of the world like Captain Chariot."

"Yes, very lucky. It's odd, though, his having a French name."

"Very. It probably accounts for his breeding," she answered placidly; and left me marveling at the happy remoteness of old age.

## VI

THE next morning early Jean de Réchamp came to my room. I was struck at once by the change in him: he had lost his first glow, and seemed nervous and hesitating. I knew what he had come for: to ask me to postpone our departure for another twenty-four hours. By rights we should have been off that morning; but there had been a sharp brush a few kilometers away, and a couple of poor devils had been brought to the château whom it would have been death to carry farther that day and criminal not to hurry to a base hospital the next morning. "We've simply *got* to stay till tomorrow: you're in luck," I said laughing.

He laughed back, but with a frown that made me feel I had been a brute to speak in that way of a respite due to such a cause.

"The men will pull through, you know—trust Mlle. Malo for that!" I said.

His frown did not lift. He went to the window and drummed on the pane.

"Do you see that breach in the wall, down there behind the trees? It's the only scratch the place has got. And think of Lermont! It's incredible—simply incredible!"

"But it's like that everywhere, isn't it? Everything depends on the officer in command."

"Yes: that's it, I suppose. I haven't had time to get a consecutive account of what happened: they're all too excited. Mlle. Malo is the only person who can tell me exactly how things went." He swung about on me. "Look here, it sounds absurd, what I'm asking; but try to get me an hour alone with her, will you?"

I stared at the request, and he went on, still half-laughing: "You see, they all hang on me; my father and mother, Simone, the curé, the servants. The whole village is coming up presently: they want to stuff their eyes full of me. It's natural enough, after living here all these long months cut off from everything. But the result is I haven't said two words to her yet."

"Well, you shall," I declared; and with an easier smile he turned to hurry down to a mass of thanksgiving which the curé was to celebrate in the private chapel. "My parents wanted it," he explained; "and after that the whole village will be upon us. But later—"

"Later I'll effect a diversion; I swear I will," I assured him.

By daylight, decidedly, Mlle. Malo was less handsome than in the evening. It was my first thought as she came toward me, that afternoon, under the limes. Jean was still indoors, with his people, receiving the village; I rather wondered she hadn't stayed there with him. Theoretically, her place was at his side; but I knew she was a young woman who didn't live by rule, and she had already struck me as having a distaste for superfluous expenditures of feeling.

Yes, she was less effective by day. She looked older for one thing; her face was pinched, and a little sallow and for the first time I noticed that her cheek-bones were too high. Her eyes, too, had lost their velvet depth: fine eyes still, but not unfathomable. But the smile with which she greeted me was charming: it ran over her tired face like a lamp-lighter kindling flames as he runs.

"I was looking for you," she said. "Shall we have a little talk? The reception is sure to last another hour: every one of the villagers is going to tell just what happened to him or her when the Germans came."

"And you've run away from the ceremony?"

"I'm a trifle tired of hearing the same adventures retold," she said, still smiling.

"But I thought there *were* no adventures—that that was the wonder of it?"

She shrugged. "It makes their stories a little dull, at any rate; we've not a hero or a martyr to show." She had strolled farther from the house as we talked, leading me in the direction of a bare horse-chestnut walk that led toward the park.

"Of course Jean's got to listen to it all, poor boy; but *I* needn't," she explained.

I didn't know exactly what to answer and we walked on a little way in silence; then she said: "If you'd carried him off this morning he would have escaped all this fuss." After a pause she added slowly: "On the whole, it might have been as well."

"To carry him off?"

"Yes." She stopped and looked at me. "I wish you *would.*"

"Would?—Now?"

"Yes, now: as soon as you can. He's really not strong yet—he's drawn and nervous." ("So are you," I thought.) "And the excitement is greater than you can perhaps imagine—"

I gave her back her look. "Why, I think I *can* imagine...."

She colored up through her sallow skin and then laughed away her blush. "Oh, I don't mean the excitement of seeing *me!* But his parents, his grandmother, the curé, all the old associations—"

I considered for a moment; then I said: "As a matter of fact, you're about the only person he *hasn't* seen."

She checked a quick answer on her lips, and for a moment or two we faced each other silently. A sudden sense of intimacy, of complicity almost, came over me. What was it that the girl's silence was crying out to me?

"If I take him away now he won't have seen you at all," I continued.

She stood under the bare trees, keeping her eyes on me. "Then take him away now!" she retorted; and as she spoke I saw her face change, decompose into deadly apprehension and as quickly regain its usual calm. From where she stood she faced the courtyard, and glancing in the same direction I saw the throng of villagers coming out of the château. "Take him away—take him away at once!" she passionately commanded; and the next minute Jean de Réchamp detached himself from the group and began to limp down the walk in our direction.

What was I to do? I can't exaggerate the sense of urgency Mlle. Malo's appeal gave me, or my faith in her sincerity. No one who had seen her meeting with Réchamp the night before could have doubted her feeling for him: if she wanted him away it was not because she did not delight in his presence. Even now, as he approached, I saw her face veiled by a faint mist of emotion: it was like watching a fruit ripen under a midsummer sun. But she turned sharply from the house and began to walk on.

"Can't you give me a hint of your reason?" I suggested as I followed.

"My reason? I've given it!" I suppose I looked incredulous, for she added in a lower voice: "I don't want him to hear—yet—about all the horrors."

"The horrors? I thought there had been none here."

"All around us—" Her voice became a whisper. "Our friends. . . our neighbors. . . every one. . . ."

"He can hardly avoid hearing of that, can he? And besides, since you're all safe and happy. . . . Look here," I broke off, "he's coming after us. Don't we look as if we were running away?"

She turned around, suddenly paler; and in a stride or two Réchamp was at our side. He was pale too; and before I could find a pretext for slipping away he had begun to speak. But I saw at once that he didn't know or care if I was there.

"What was the name of the officer in command who was quartered here?" he asked, looking straight at the girl.

She raised her eye-brows slightly. "Do you mean to say that after listening for three hours to every inhabitant of Réchamp you haven't found that out?"

"They all call him something different. My grandmother says he had a French name: she calls him Chariot."

"Your grandmother was never taught German: his name was the Oberst von Scharlach." She did not remember my presence either: the two were still looking straight in each other's eyes.

Réchamp had grown white to the lips: he was rigid with the effort to control himself.

"Why didn't you tell me it was Scharlach who was here?" he brought out at last in a low voice.

She turned her eyes in my direction. "I was just explaining to Mr. Greer—"

"To Mr. Greer?" He looked at me too, half-angrily.

"I know the stories that are about," she continued quietly; "and I was saying to your friend that, since we had been so happy as to be spared, it seemed useless to dwell on what has happened elsewhere."

"Damn what happened elsewhere! I don't yet know what happened here."

I put a hand on his arm. Mlle. Malo was looking hard at me, but I wouldn't let her see I knew it. "I'm going to leave you to hear the whole story now," I said to Réchamp.

"But there isn't any story for him to hear!" she broke in. She pointed at the serene front of the château, looking out across its gardens to the unscarred fields. "We're safe; the place is untouched. Why brood on other horrors—horrors we were powerless to help?"

Réchamp held his ground doggedly. "But the man's name is a curse and an abomination. Wherever he went he spread ruin."

"So they say. Mayn't there be a mistake? Legends grow up so quickly in these dreadful times. Here—" she looked about her again at the peaceful scene—"here he behaved as you see. For heaven's sake be content with that!"

"Content?" He passed his hand across his forehead. "I'm blind with joy. . . or should be, if only. . . ."

She looked at me entreatingly, almost desperately, and I took hold of Réchamp's arm with a warning pressure.

"My dear fellow, don't you see that Mlle. Malo has been under a great strain? *La joie fait peur*—that's the trouble with both of you!"

He lowered his head. "Yes, I suppose it is." He took her hand And kissed it. "I beg your pardon. Greer's right: we're both on edge."

"Yes: I'll leave you for a little while, if you and Mr Greer will excuse me." She included us both in a quiet look that seemed to me extremely noble, and walked lowly away toward the château. Réchamp stood gazing after her for a moment; then he dropped down on one of benches at the edge of the path. He covered his face with his hands. "Scharlach—Scharlach!" I heard him repeat.

We sat there side by side for ten minutes or more without speaking. Finally I said: "Look here, Réchamp—she's right and you're wrong. I shall be sorry I brought you here if you don't see it before it's too late."

His face was still hidden; but presently he dropped his hands and answered me. "I do see. She's saved everything for me—my people and my house, and the ground we're standing on. And I worship it because she walks on it!"

"And so do your people: the war's done that for you, anyhow," I reminded him.

VII

THE morning after we were off before dawn. Our time allowance was up, and it was thought advisable, on account of our wounded, to slip across the exposed bit of road in the dark.

Mlle. Malo was downstairs when we started, pale in her white dress, but calm and active. We had borrowed a farmer's cart in which our two men could be laid on a mattress, and she had stocked our trap with food and remedies. Nothing seemed to have been forgotten. While I was settling the men I suppose Réchamp turned back into the hall to bid her good-bye; anyhow, when she followed him out a moment later he looked quieter and less strained. He had taken leave of his parents and his sister upstairs, and Yvonne Malo stood alone in the dark driveway, watching us as we drove away.

There was not much talk between us during our slow drive back to the lines. We had to go it a snail's pace, for the roads were rough; and there was time for meditation. I knew well enough what my companion was thinking about and my own thoughts ran on the same lines. Though the story of the German occupation of Réchamp had been retold to us a dozen times the main facts did not vary. There were little discrepancies of detail, and gaps in the narrative here and there; but all the household, from the astute ancestress to the last bewildered pantry-boy, were at one in saying that Mlle. Malo's coolness and courage had saved the chateau and the village. The officer in command had arrived full of threats and insolence: Mlle. Malo had placated and disarmed him, turned his suspicions to ridicule, entertained him and his comrades at dinner, and contrived during that time— or rather while they were making music afterward (which they did for half the night, it seemed)—that Monsieur de Réchamp and Alain should slip out of the cellar in which they had been hidden, gain the end of the gardens through an old hidden passage, and get off in the darkness. Meanwhile Simone had been safe upstairs with her mother and grandmother, and none of the officers lodged in the château had—after a first hasty inspection—set foot in any part of the house but the wing assigned to them. On the third morning they had left, and Scharlach, before going, had put in Mlle. Malo's hands a letter requesting whatever officer should follow him to show every consideration to the family of the Comte de Réchamp, and if possible—owing to the grave illness of the Countess—avoid taking up quarters in the château: a request which had been scrupulously observed.

Such were the amazing but undisputed facts over which Réchamp and I, in our different ways, were now pondering. He hardly spoke, and when he did it was only to make some casual reference to the road or to our wounded soldiers; but all the while I sat at his side I kept hearing the echo of the question he was inwardly asking himself, and hoping to God he wouldn't put it to me. . . .

It was nearly noon when we finally reached the lines, and the men had to have a rest before we could start again; but a couple of hours later we landed them safely at the base hospital. From there we had intended to go back to Paris; but as we were starting there came an unexpected summons to another point of the front, where there had been a successful night-attack, and a lot of Germans taken in a blown-up trench. The place was fifty miles away, and off my beat, but the number of wounded on both sides was exceptionally heavy, and all the available ambulances had already started. An urgent call had come for more, and there was nothing for it but to go; so we went.

We found things in a bad mess at the second line shanty-hospital where they were dumping the wounded as fast as they could bring them in. At first we were told that none were fit to be carried farther that night; and after we had done what we could we went off to hunt up a shake-down in the village. But a few minutes later an orderly overtook us with a message from the surgeon. There was a German with an abdominal wound who was in a bad way, but might be saved by an operation if he could be got back to the base before midnight. Would we take him at once and then come back for others?

There is only one answer to such requests, and a few minutes later we were back at the hospital, and the wounded man was being carried out on a stretcher. In the shaky lantern gleam I caught a glimpse of a livid face and a torn uniform, and saw that he was an officer, and nearly done for. Réchamp had climbed to the box, and seemed not to be noticing what was going on at the back of the motor. I understood that he loathed the job, and wanted not to see the face of the man we were carrying; so when we had got him settled I jumped into the ambulance beside him and called out to Réchamp that we were ready. A second later an *infirmier* ran up with a little packet and pushed it into my hand. "His papers," he explained. I pocketed them and pulled the door shut, and we were off.

The man lay motionless on his back, conscious, but desperately weak. Once I turned my pocket-lamp on him and saw that he was young—about thirty—with damp dark hair and a thin face. He had received a flesh-wound above the eyes, and his forehead was bandaged, but the rest of the face uncovered. As the light fell on him he lifted his eyelids and looked at me: his look was inscrutable.

For half an hour or so I sat there in the dark, the sense of that face pressing close on me. It was a damnable face—meanly handsome, basely proud. In my one glimpse of it I had seen that the man was suffering atrociously, but as we slid along through the night he made no sound. At length the motor stopped with a violent jerk that drew a single moan from him. I turned the light on him, but he lay perfectly still, lips and lids shut, making no sign; and I jumped out and ran round to the front to see what had happened.

The motor had stopped for lack of gasoline and was stock still in the deep mud. Réchamp muttered something about a leak in his tank. As he bent over it, the lantern flame struck up into his face, which was set and businesslike. It struck me vaguely that he showed no particular surprise.

"What's to be done?" I asked.

"I think I can tinker it up; but we've got to have more essence to go on with."

I stared at him in despair: it was a good hour's walk back to the lines, and we weren't so sure of getting any gasoline when we got there! But there was no help for it; and as Réchamp was dead lame, no alternative but for me to go.

I opened the ambulance door, gave another look at the motionless man inside and took out a remedy which I handed over to Réchamp with a word of explanation. "You know how to give a hypo? Keep a close eye on him and pop this in if you see a change—not otherwise."

He nodded. "Do you suppose he'll die?" he asked below his breath.

"No, I don't. If we get him to the hospital before morning I think he'll pull through."

"Oh, all right." He unhooked one of the motor lanterns and handed it over to me. "I'll do my best," he said as I turned away.

Getting back to the lines through that pitch-black forest, and finding somebody to bring the gasoline back for me was about the weariest job I ever tackled. I couldn't imagine why it wasn't daylight when we finally got to the place where I had left the motor. It seemed to me as if I had been gone twelve hours when I finally caught sight of the grey bulk of the car through the thinning darkness.

Réchamp came forward to meet us, and took hold of my arm as I was opening the door of the car. "The man's dead," he said.

I had lifted up my pocket lamp, and its light fell on Réchamp's face, which was perfectly composed, and seemed less gaunt and drawn than at any time since we had started on our trip.

"Dead? Why—how? What happened? Did you give him the hypodermic?" I stammered, taken aback.

"No time to. He died in a minute."

"How do you know he did? Were you with him?"

"Of course I was with him," Réchamp retorted, with a sudden harshness which made me aware that I had grown harsh myself. But I had been almost sure the man wasn't anywhere near death when I left him. I opened the door of the ambulance and climbed in with my lantern. He didn't appear to have moved, but he was dead sure enough—had been for two or three hours, by the feel of him. It must have happened not long after I left. . . . Well, I'm not a doctor, anyhow. . . .

I don't think Réchamp and I exchanged a word during the rest of that run. But it was my fault and not his if we didn't. By the mere rub of his sleeve against mine as we sat side by side on the motor I knew he was conscious of no bar between us: he had somehow got back, in the night's interval, to a state of wholesome stolidity, while I, on the contrary, was tingling all over with exposed nerves.

I was glad enough when we got back to the base at last, and the grim load we carried was lifted out and taken into the hospital. Réchamp waited in the courtyard beside his car, lighting a cigarette in the cold early sunlight; but I followed the bearers and the surgeon into the whitewashed room where the dead man was laid out to be undressed. I had a burning spot at the pit of my stomach while his clothes were ripped off him and the bandages undone: I couldn't take my eyes from the surgeon's face. But the surgeon, with a big batch of wounded on his hands, was probably thinking more of the living than the dead; and besides, we were near the front, and the body before him was an enemy's.

He finished his examination and scribbled something in a note-book. "Death must have taken place nearly five hours ago," he merely remarked: it was the conclusion I had already come to myself.

"And how about the papers?" the surgeon continued. "You have them, I suppose?

This way, please."

We left the half-stripped body on the blood-stained oil-cloth, and he led me into an office where a functionary sat behind a littered desk.

"The papers? Thank you. You haven't examined them? Let us see, then."

I handed over the leather notecase I had thrust into my pocket the evening before, and saw for the first time its silver-edged corners and the coronet in one of them. The official took out the papers and spread them on the desk between us. I watched him absently while he did so.

Suddenly he uttered an exclamation. "Ah—that's a haul!" he said, and pushed a bit of paper toward me. On it was engraved the name: Oberst Graf Benno von Scharlach. . . .

"A good riddance," said the surgeon over my shoulder.

I went back to the courtyard and saw Réchamp still smoking his cigarette in the cold sunlight. I don't suppose I'd been in the hospital ten minutes; but I felt as old as Methuselah.

My friend greeted me with a smile. "Ready for breakfast?" he said, and a little chill ran down my spine.... But I said: "Oh, all right—come along. . . ."

For, after all, I *knew* there wasn't a paper of any sort on that man when he was lifted into my ambulance the night before: the French officials attend to their business too carefully for me not to have been sure of that. And there wasn't the least shred of evidence to prove that he hadn't died of his wounds during the unlucky delay in the forest; or that Réchamp had known his tank was leaking when we started out from the lines.

"I could do with a *café complet*, couldn't you?" Réchamp suggested, looking straight at me with his good blue eyes; and arm in arm we started off to hunt for the inn. . . .

## AUTRES TEMPS...

MRS. LIDCOTE, as the huge menacing mass of New York defined itself far off across the waters, shrank back into her corner of the deck and sat listening with a kind of unreasoning terror to the steady onward drive of the screws.

She had set out on the voyage quietly enough,—in what she called her "reasonable" mood,—but the week at sea had given her too much time to think of things and had left her too long alone with the past.

When she was alone, it was always the past that occupied her. She couldn't get away from it, and she didn't any longer care to. During her long years of exile she had made her terms with it, had learned to accept the fact that it would always be there, huge, obstructing, encumbering, bigger and more dominant than anything the future could ever conjure up. And, at any rate, she was sure of it, she understood it, knew how to reckon with it; she had learned to screen and manage and protect it as one does an afflicted member of one's family.

There had never been any danger of her being allowed to forget the past. It looked out at her from the face of every acquaintance, it appeared suddenly in the eyes of strangers when a word enlightened them: "Yes, *the* Mrs. Lidcote, don't you know?" It had sprung at her the first day out, when, across the dining-room, from the captain's table, she had seen Mrs. Lorin Boulger's revolving eye-glass pause and the eye behind it grow as blank as a dropped blind. The next day, of course, the captain had asked: "You know your ambassadress, Mrs. Boulger?" and she had replied that, No, she seldom left Florence, and hadn't been to Rome for more than a day since the Boulgers had been sent to Italy. She was so used to these phrases that it cost her no effort to repeat them. And the captain had promptly changed the subject.

No, she didn't, as a rule, mind the past, because she was used to it and understood it. It was a great concrete fact in her path that she had to walk around every time she moved in any direction. But now, in the light of the unhappy event that had summoned her from Italy,—the sudden unanticipated news of her daughter's divorce from Horace Pursh and remarriage with Wilbour Barkley—the past, her own poor miserable past, started up at her with eyes of accusation, became, to her disordered fancy, like the afflicted relative suddenly breaking away from nurses and keepers and publicly parading the horror and misery she had, all the long years, so patiently screened and secluded.

Yes, there it had stood before her through the agitated weeks since the news had come—during her interminable journey from India, where Leila's letter had overtaken her, and the feverish halt in her apartment in Florence, where she had had to stop and gather up her possessions for a fresh start—there it had stood grinning at her with a new balefullness which seemed to say: "Oh, but you've got to look at me *now,* because I'm not only your own past but Leila's present."

Certainly it was a master stroke of those arch-ironists of the shears and spindle to duplicate her own story in her daughter's. Mrs. Lidcote had always somewhat grimly fancied that, having so signally failed to be of use to Leila in other ways, she would at least serve her as a warning. She had even abstained from defending herself, from making the best of her case, had stoically refused to plead extenuating circumstances, lest Leila's impulsive sympathy should lead to deductions that might react disastrously on her own life. And now that very thing had happened, and Mrs. Lidcote could hear the whole of New York saying with one voice: "Yes, Leila's done just what her mother did. With such an example what could you expect?"

Yet if she had been an example, poor woman, she had been an awful one; she had been, she would have supposed, of more use as a deterrent than a hundred blameless mothers as incentives. For how could anyone who had seen anything of her life in the last eighteen years have had the courage to repeat so disastrous an experiment?

Well, logic in such cases didn't count, example didn't count, nothing probably counted but having the same impulses in the blood; and that was the dark inheritance she had bestowed upon her daughter. Leila hadn't consciously copied her; she had simply "taken after" her, had been a projection of her own long-past rebellion.

Mrs. Lidcote had deplored, when she started, that the Utopia was a slow steamer, and would take eight full days to bring her to her unhappy daughter; but now, as the moment of reunion approached, she would willingly have turned the boat about and fled back to the high seas. It was not only because she felt still so unprepared to face what New York had in store for her, but because she needed more time to dispose of what the Utopia had already given her. The past was bad enough, but the present and future were worse, because they were less comprehensible, and because, as she grew older, surprises and inconsequences troubled her more than the worst certainties.

There was Mrs. Boulger, for instance. In the light, or rather the darkness, of new developments, it might really be that Mrs. Boulger had not meant to cut her, but had simply failed to recognize her. Mrs. Lidcote had arrived at this hypothesis simply by listening to the conversation of the persons sitting next to her on deck—two lively young women with the latest Paris hats on their heads and the latest New York ideas in them. These ladies, as to whom it would have been impossible for a person with Mrs. Lidcote's old-fashioned categories to determine whether they were married or unmarried, "nice" or "horrid," or any one or other of the definite things which young women, in her youth and her society, were conveniently assumed to be, had revealed a familiarity with the world of New York that, again according to Mrs. Lidcote's traditions, should have implied a recognized place in it. But in the present fluid state of manners what did anything imply except what their hats implied—that no one could tell what was coming next?

They seemed, at any rate, to frequent a group of idle and opulent people who executed the same gestures and revolved on the same pivots as Mrs. Lidcote's daughter and her friends: their Coras, Matties and Mabels seemed at any moment likely to reveal familiar patronymics, and once one of the speakers, summing up a discussion of which Mrs. Lidcote had missed the beginning, had affirmed with headlong confidence: "Leila? Oh, *Leila's* all right."

Could it be *her* Leila, the mother had wondered, with a sharp thrill of apprehension? If only they would mention surnames! But their talk leaped elliptically from allusion to allusion, their unfinished sentences dangled over bottomless pits of conjecture, and they gave their bewildered hearer the impression not so much of talking only of their intimates, as of being intimate with every one alive.

Her old friend Franklin Ide could have told her, perhaps; but here was the last day of the voyage, and she hadn't yet found courage to ask him. Great as had been the joy of discovering his name on the passenger-list and seeing his friendly bearded face in the throng against the taffrail at Cherbourg, she had as yet said nothing to him except, when they had met: "Of course I'm going out to Leila."

She had said nothing to Franklin Ide because she had always instinctively shrunk from taking him into her confidence. She was sure he felt sorry for her, sorrier perhaps than any one had ever felt; but he had always paid her the supreme tribute of not showing it. His attitude allowed her to imagine that compassion was not the basis of his feeling for her, and it was part of her joy in his friendship that it was the one relation seemingly unconditioned by her state, the only one in which she could think and feel and behave like any other woman.

Now, however, as the problem of New York loomed nearer, she began to regret that she had not spoken, had not at least questioned him about the hints she had gathered on the way. He did not know the two ladies next to her, he did not even, as it chanced, know Mrs. Lorin Boulger; but he knew New York, and New York was the sphinx whose riddle she must read or perish.

Almost as the thought passed through her mind his stooping shoulders and grizzled head detached themselves against the blaze of light in the west, and he sauntered down the empty deck and dropped into the chair at her side.

"You're expecting the Barkleys to meet you, I suppose?" he asked.

It was the first time she had heard any one pronounce her daughter's new name, and it occurred to her that her friend, who was shy and inarticulate, had been trying to say it all the way over and had at last shot it out at her only because he felt it must be now or never.

"I don't know. I cabled, of course. But I believe she's at—they're at—*his* place somewhere."

"Oh, Barkley's; yes, near Lenox, isn't it? But she's sure to come to town to meet you."

He said it so easily and naturally that her own constraint was relieved, and suddenly, before she knew what she meant to do, she had burst out: "She may dislike the idea of seeing people."

Ide, whose absent short-sighted gaze had been fixed on the slowly gliding water, turned in his seat to stare at his companion.

"Who? Leila?" he said with an incredulous laugh.

Mrs. Lidcote flushed to her faded hair and grew pale again. "It took *me* a long time— to get used to it," she said.

His look grew gently commiserating. "I think you'll find—" he paused for a word— "that things are different now—altogether easier."

"That's what I've been wondering—ever since we started." She was determined now to speak. She moved nearer, so that their arms touched, and she could drop her voice to a murmur. "You see, it all came on me in a flash. My going off to India and Siam on that long trip kept me away from letters for weeks at a time; and she didn't want to tell me beforehand—oh, I understand *that*, poor child! You know how good she's always been to me; how she's tried to spare me. And she knew, of course, what a state of horror I'd be in. She knew I'd rush off to her at once and try to stop it. So she never gave me a hint of anything, and she even managed to muzzle Susy Suffern—you know Susy is the one of the family who keeps me informed about things at home. I don't yet see how she prevented Susy's telling me; but she did. And her first letter, the one I got up at Bangkok, simply said the thing was over—the divorce, I mean—and that the very next day she'd— well, I suppose there was no use waiting; and *he* seems to have behaved as well as possible, to have wanted to marry her as much as—"

"Who? Barkley?" he helped her out. "I should say so! Why what do you suppose—" He interrupted himself. "He'll be devoted to her, I assure you."

"Oh, of course; I'm sure he will. He's written me—really beautifully. But it's a terrible strain on a man's devotion. I'm not sure that Leila realizes—"

Ide sounded again his little reassuring laugh. "I'm not sure that you realize. *They're* all right."

It was the very phrase that the young lady in the next seat had applied to the unknown "Leila," and its recurrence on Ide's lips flushed Mrs. Lidcote with fresh courage.

"I wish I knew just what you mean. The two young women next to me—the ones with the wonderful hats—have been talking in the same way."

"What? About Leila?"

"About *a* Leila; I fancied it might be mine. And about society in general. All their friends seem to be divorced; some of them seem to announce their engagements before they get their decree. One of them—*her* name was Mabel—as far as I could make out, her husband found out that she meant to divorce him by noticing that she wore a new engagement ring."

"Well, you see Leila did everything 'regularly,' as the French say," Ide rejoined.

"Yes; but are these people in society? The people my neighbors talk about?"

He shrugged his shoulders. "It would take an arbitration commission a good many sittings to define the boundaries of society nowadays. But at any rate they're in New York; and I assure you you're *not*; you're farther and farther from it."

"But I've been back there several times to see Leila." She hesitated and looked away from him. Then she brought out slowly: "And I've never noticed—the least change—in— in my own case—"

"Oh," he sounded deprecatingly, and she trembled with the fear of having gone too far. But the hour was past when such scruples could restrain her. She must know where she was and where Leila was. "Mrs. Boulger still cuts me," she brought out with an embarrassed laugh.

"Are you sure? You've probably cut *her;* if not now, at least in the past. And in a cut if you're not first you're nowhere. That's what keeps up so many quarrels."

The word roused Mrs. Lidcote to a renewed sense of realities. "But the Pursues," she said—"the Pursues are so strong! There are so many of them, and they all back each other up, just as my husband's family did. I know what it means to have a clan against one. They're stronger than any number of separate friends. The Pursues will *never* forgive Leila for leaving Horace. Why, his mother opposed his marrying her because of—of me. She tried to get Leila to promise that she wouldn't see me when they went to Europe on their honeymoon. And now she'll say it was my example."

Her companion, vaguely stroking his beard, mused a moment upon this; then he asked, with seeming irrelevance, "What did Leila say when you wrote that you were coming?"

"She said it wasn't the least necessary, but that I'd better come, because it was the only way to convince me that it wasn't."

"Well, then, that proves she's not afraid of the Purshes."

She breathed a long sigh of remembrance. "Oh, just at first, you know—one never is."

He laid his hand on hers with a gesture of intelligence and pity. "You'll see, you'll see," he said.

A shadow lengthened down the deck before them, and a steward stood there, proffering a Marconigram.

"Oh, now I shall know!" she exclaimed.

She tore the message open, and then let it fall on her knees, dropping her hands on it in silence.

Ide's enquiry roused her: "It's all right?"

"Oh, quite right. Perfectly. She can't come; but she's sending Susy Suffern. She says Susy will explain." After another silence she added, with a sudden gush of bitterness: "As if I needed any explanation!"

She felt Ide's hesitating glance upon her. "She's in the country?"

"Yes. 'Prevented last moment. Longing for you, expecting you. Love from both.' Don't you *see*, the poor darling, that she couldn't face it?"

"No, I don't." He waited. "Do you mean to go to her immediately?"

"It will be too late to catch a train this evening; but I shall take the first tomorrow morning." She considered a moment. "'Perhaps it's better. I need a talk with Susy first. She's to meet me at the dock, and I'll take her straight back to the hotel with me."

As she developed this plan, she had the sense that Ide was still thoughtfully, even gravely, considering her. When she ceased, he remained silent a moment; then he said almost ceremoniously: "If your talk with Miss Suffern doesn't last too late, may I come and see you when it's over? I shall be dining at my club, and I'll call you up at about ten, if I may. I'm off to Chicago on business tomorrow morning, and it would be a satisfaction to know, before I start, that your cousin's been able to reassure you, as I know she will."

He spoke with a shy deliberateness that, even to Mrs. Lidcote's troubled perceptions, sounded a long-silenced note of feeling. Perhaps the breaking down of the barrier of reticence between them had released unsuspected emotions in both. The tone of his appeal moved her curiously and loosened the tight strain of her fears.

"Oh, yes, come—do come," she said, rising. The huge threat of New York was imminent now, dwarfing, under long reaches of embattled masonry, the great deck she stood on and all the little specks of life it carried. One of them, drifting nearer, took the shape of her maid, followed by luggage-laden stewards, and signing to her that it was time to go below. As they descended to the main deck, the throng swept her against Mrs. Lorin Boulger's shoulder, and she heard the ambassadress call out to some one, over the vexed sea of hats: "So sorry! I should have been delighted, but I've promised to spend Sunday with some friends at Lenox."

## II

SUSY SUFFERN'S explanation did not end till after ten o'clock, and she had just gone when Franklin Ide, who, complying with an old New York tradition, had caused himself to be preceded by a long white box of roses, was shown into Mrs. Lidcote's sitting-room.

He came forward with his shy half-humorous smile and, taking her hand, looked at her for a moment without speaking.

"It's all right," he then pronounced.

Mrs. Lidcote returned his smile. "It's extraordinary. Everything's changed. Even Susy has changed; and you know the extent to which Susy used to represent the old New York. There's no old New York left, it seems. She talked in the most amazing way. She snaps her fingers at the Pursues. She told me—me, that every woman had a right to happiness and that self-expression was the highest duty. She accused me of misunderstanding Leila; she said my point of view was conventional! She was bursting with pride at having been in the secret, and wearing a brooch that Wilbour Barkley'd given her!"

Franklin Ide had seated himself in the arm-chair she had pushed forward for him under the electric chandelier. He threw back his head and laughed. "What did I tell you?"

"Yes; but I can't believe that Susy's not mistaken. Poor dear, she has the habit of lost causes; and she may feel that, having stuck to me, she can do no less than stick to Leila."

"But she didn't—did she?—openly defy the world for you? She didn't snap her fingers at the Lidcotes?"

Mrs. Lidcote shook her head, still smiling. "No. It was enough to defy *my* family. It was doubtful at one time if they would tolerate her seeing me, and she almost had to disinfect herself after each visit. I believe that at first my sister-in-law wouldn't let the girls come down when Susy dined with her."

"Well, isn't your cousin's present attitude the best possible proof that times have changed?"

"Yes, yes; I know." She leaned forward from her sofa-corner, fixing her eyes on his thin kindly face, which gleamed on her indistinctly through her tears. "If it's true, it's—it's dazzling. She says Leila's perfectly happy. It's as if an angel had gone about lifting gravestones, and the buried people walked again, and the living didn't shrink from them."

"That's about it," he assented.

She drew a deep breath, and sat looking away from him down the long perspective of lamp-fringed streets over which her windows hung.

"I can understand how happy you must be," he began at length.

She turned to him impetuously. "Yes, yes; I'm happy. But I'm lonely, too—lonelier than ever. I didn't take up much room in the world before; but now—where is there a corner for me? Oh. since I've begun to confess myself, why shouldn't I go on? Telling you this lifts a gravestone from *me!* You see, before this, Leila needed me. She was unhappy, and I knew it, and though we hardly ever talked of it I felt that, in a way, the thought that I'd been through the same thing, and down to the dregs of it, helped her. And her needing me helped *me*. And when the news of her marriage came my first thought was that now she'd need me more than ever, that she'd have no one but me to turn to. Yes, under all my distress there was a fierce joy in that. It was so new and wonderful to feel again that there was one person who wouldn't be able to get on without me! And now what you and Susy tell me seems to have taken my child from me; and just at first that's all I can feel."

"Of course it's all you feel." He looked at her musingly. "Why didn't Leila come to meet you?"

"That was really my fault. You see, I'd cabled that I was not sure of being able to get off on the Utopia, and apparently my second cable was delayed, and when she received it she'd already asked some people over Sunday—one or two of her old friends, Susy says. I'm so glad they should have wanted to go to her at once; but naturally I'd rather have been alone with her."

"You still mean to go, then?"

"Oh, I must. Susy wanted to drag me off to Ridgefield with her over Sunday, and Leila sent me word that of course I might go if I wanted to, and that I was not to think of her; but I know how disappointed she would be. Susy said she was afraid I might be upset at her having people to stay, and that, if I minded, she wouldn't urge me to come. But if *they* don't mind, why should I? And of course, if they're willing to go to Leila it must mean—"

"Of course. I'm glad you recognize that," Franklin Ide exclaimed abruptly. He stood up and went over to her, taking her hand with one of his quick gestures. "There's something I want to say to you," he began—

The next morning, in the train, through all the other contending thoughts in Mrs. Lidcote's mind there ran the warm undercurrent of what Franklin Ide had wanted to say to her.

He had wanted, she knew, to say it once before, when, nearly eight years earlier, the hazard of meeting at the end of a rainy autumn in a deserted Swiss hotel had thrown them for a fortnight into unwonted propinquity. They had walked and talked together, borrowed each other's books and newspapers, spent the long chill evenings over the fire in the dim lamplight of her little pitch-pine sitting-room; and she had been wonderfully comforted by his presence, and hard frozen places in her had melted, and she had known that she would be desperately sorry when he went. And then, just at the end, in his odd indirect way, he had let her see that it rested with her to have him stay. She could still relive the sleepless night she had given to that discovery. It was preposterous, of course, to think of repaying his devotion by accepting such a sacrifice; but how find reasons to convince him? She could not bear to let him think her less touched, less inclined to him than she was: the generosity of his love deserved that she should repay it with the truth. Yet how let him see what she felt, and yet refuse what he offered? How confess to him what had been on her lips when he made the offer: "I've seen what it did to one man; and there must never, never be another"? The tacit ignoring of her past had been the element in which their friendship lived, and she could not suddenly, to him of all men, begin to talk of herself like a guilty woman in a play. Somehow, in the end, she had managed it, had averted a direct explanation, had made him understand that her life was over, that she existed only for her daughter, and that a more definite word from him would have been almost a breach of delicacy. She was so used to be having as if her life were over! And, at any rate, he had taken her hint, and she had been able to spare her sensitiveness and his.

The next year, when he came to Florence to see her, they met again in the old friendly way; and that till now had continued to be the tenor of their intimacy.

And now, suddenly and unexpectedly, he had brought up the question again, directly this time, and in such a form that she could not evade it: putting the renewal of his plea, after so long an interval, on the ground that, on her own showing, her chief argument against it no longer existed.

"You tell me Leila's happy. If she's happy, she doesn't need you—need you, that is, in the same way as before. You wanted, I know, to be always in reach, always free and available if she should suddenly call you to her or take refuge with you. I understood that—I respected it. I didn't urge my case because I saw it was useless. You couldn't, I understood well enough, have felt free to take such happiness as life with me might give you while she was unhappy, and, as you imagined, with no hope of release. Even then I didn't feel as you did about it; I understood better the trend of things here. But ten years ago the change hadn't really come; and I had no way of convincing you that it was coming. Still, I always fancied that Leila might not think her case was closed, and so I chose to think that ours wasn't either. Let me go on thinking so, at any rate, till you've seen her, and confirmed with your own eyes what Susy Suffern tells you."

## III

ALL through what Susy Suffern told and retold her during their four-hours' flight to the hills this plea of Ide's kept coming back to Mrs. Lidcote. She did not yet know what she felt as to its bearing on her own fate, but it was something on which her confused thoughts could stay themselves amid the welter of new impressions, and she was inexpressibly glad that he had said what he had, and said it at that particular moment. It helped her to hold fast to her identity in the rush of strange names and new categories that her cousin's talk poured out on her.

With the progress of the journey Miss Suffern's communications grew more and more amazing. She was like a cicerone preparing the mind of an inexperienced traveller for the marvels about to burst on it.

"You won't know Leila. She's had her pearls reset. Sargent's to paint her. Oh, and I was to tell you that she hopes you won't mind being the least bit squeezed over Sunday. The house was built by Wilbour's father, you know, and it's rather old-fashioned—only ten spare bedrooms. Of course that's small for what they mean to do, and she'll show you the new plans they've had made. Their idea is to keep the present house as a wing. She told me to explain—she's so dreadfully sorry not to be able to give you a sitting-room just at first. They're thinking of Egypt for next winter, unless, of course, Wilbour gets his appointment. Oh, didn't she write you about that? Why, he wants Rome, you know—the second secretaryship. Or, rather, he wanted England; but Leila insisted that if they went abroad she must be near you. And of course what she says is law. Oh, they quite hope they'll get it. You see Horace's uncle is in the Cabinet,—one of the assistant secretaries,—and I believe he has a good deal of pull—"

"Horace's uncle? You mean Wilbour's, I suppose," Mrs. Lidcote interjected, with a gasp of which a fraction was given to Miss Suffern's flippant use of the language.

"Wilbour's? No, I don't. I mean Horace's. There's no bad feeling between them, I assure you. Since Horace's engagement was announced—you didn't know Horace was engaged? Why, he's marrying one of Bishop Thorbury's girls: the red-haired one who wrote the novel that every one's talking about, *This Flesh of Mine*. They're to be married in the cathedral. Of course Horace can, because it was Leila who—but, as I say, there's not the *least* feeling, and Horace wrote himself to his uncle about Wilbour."

Mrs. Lidcote's thoughts fled back to what she had said to Ide the day before on the deck of the Utopia. "I didn't take up much room before, but now where is there a corner for me?" Where indeed in this crowded, topsy-turvy world, with its headlong changes and helter-skelter readjustments, its new tolerances and indifferences and accommodations, was there room for a character fashioned by slower sterner processes and a life broken under their inexorable pressure? And then, in a flash, she viewed the chaos from a new angle, and order seemed to move upon the void. If the old processes were changed, her case was changed with them; she, too, was a part of the general readjustment, a tiny fragment of the new pattern worked out in bolder freer harmonies. Since her daughter had no penalty to pay, was not she herself released by the same stroke? The rich arrears of youth and joy were gone; but was there not time enough left to accumulate new stores of happiness? That, of course, was what Franklin Ide had felt and had meant her to feel. He had seen at once what the change in her daughter's situation would make in her view of her own. It was almost—wondrously enough!—as if Leila's folly had been the means of vindicating hers.

Everything else for the moment faded for Mrs. Lidcote in the glow of her daughter's embrace. It was unnatural, it was almost terrifying, to find herself standing on a strange threshold, under an unknown roof, in a big hall full of pictures, flowers, firelight, and hurrying servants, and in this spacious unfamiliar confusion to discover Leila, bareheaded, laughing, authoritative, with a strange young man jovially echoing her welcome and transmitting her orders; but once Mrs. Lidcote had her child on her breast, and her child's "It's all right, you old darling!" in her ears, every other feeling was lost in the deep sense of well-being that only Leila's hug could give.

The sense was still with her, warming her veins and pleasantly fluttering her heart, as she went up to her room after luncheon. A little constrained by the presence of visitors, and not altogether sorry to defer for a few hours the "long talk" with her daughter for which she somehow felt herself tremulously unready, she had withdrawn, on the plea of fatigue, to the bright luxurious bedroom into which Leila had again and again apologized for having been obliged to squeeze her. The room was bigger and finer than any in her small apartment in Florence; but it was not the standard of affluence implied in her daughter's tone about it that chiefly struck her, nor yet the finish and complexity of its appointments. It was the look it shared with the rest of the house, and with the perspective of the gardens beneath its windows, of being part of an "establishment"—of something solid, avowed, founded on sacraments and precedents and principles. There was nothing about the place, or about Leila and Wilbour, that suggested either passion or peril: their relation seemed as comfortable as their furniture and as respectable as their balance at the bank.

This was, in the whole confusing experience, the thing that confused Mrs. Lidcote most, that gave her at once the deepest feeling of security for Leila and the strongest sense of apprehension for herself. Yes, there was something oppressive in the completeness and compactness of Leila's well-being. Ide had been right: her daughter did not need her. Leila, with her first embrace, had unconsciously attested the fact in the same phrase as Ide himself and as the two young women with the hats. "It's all right, you old darling!" she had said; and her mother sat alone, trying to fit herself into the new scheme of things which such a certainty betokened.

Her first distinct feeling was one of irrational resentment. If such a change was to come, why had it not come sooner? Here was she, a woman not yet old, who had paid with the best years of her life for the theft of the happiness that her daughter's contemporaries were taking as their due. There was no sense, no sequence, in it. She had had what she wanted, but she had had to pay too much for it. She had had to pay the last bitterest price of learning that love has a price: that it is worth so much and no more. She had known the anguish of watching the man she loved discover this first, and of reading the discovery in his eyes. It was a part of her history that she had not trusted herself to think of for a long time past: she always took a big turn about that haunted corner. But now, at the sight of the young man downstairs, so openly and jovially Leila's, she was overwhelmed at the senseless waste of her own adventure, and wrung with the irony of perceiving that the success or failure of the deepest human experiences may hang on a matter of chronology.

Then gradually the thought of Ide returned to her. "I chose to think that our case wasn't closed," he had said. She had been deeply touched by that. To every one else her case had been closed so long! Finis was scrawled all over her. But here was one man who had believed and waited, and what if what he believed in and waited for were coming true? If Leila's "all right" should really foreshadow hers?

As yet, of course, it was impossible to tell. She had fancied, indeed, when she entered the drawing-room before luncheon, that a too-sudden hush had fallen on the assembled group of Leila's friends, on the slender vociferous young women and the lounging golf-stockinged young men. They had all received her politely, with the kind of petrified politeness that may be either a tribute to age or a protest at laxity; but to them, of course, she must be an old woman because she was Leila's mother, and in a society so dominated by youth the mere presence of maturity was a constraint.

One of the young girls, however, had presently emerged from the group, and, attaching herself to Mrs. Lidcote, had listened to her with a blue gaze of admiration which gave the older woman a sudden happy consciousness of her long-forgotten social graces. It was agreeable to find herself attracting this young Charlotte Wynn, whose mother had been among her closest friends, and in whom something of the soberness and softness of the earlier manners had survived. But the little colloquy, broken up by the announcement of luncheon, could of course result in nothing more definite than this reminiscent emotion.

No, she could not yet tell how her own case was to be fitted into the new order of things; but there were more people—"older people" Leila had put it—arriving by the afternoon train, and that evening at dinner she would doubtless be able to judge. She began to wonder nervously who the new-comers might be. Probably she would be spared the embarrassment of finding old acquaintances among them; but it was odd that her daughter had mentioned no names.

Leila had proposed that, later in the afternoon, Wilbour should take her mother for a drive: she said she wanted them to have a "nice, quiet talk." But Mrs. Lidcote wished her talk with Leila to come first, and had, moreover, at luncheon, caught stray allusions to an impending tennis-match in which her son-in-law was engaged. Her fatigue had been a sufficient pretext for declining the drive, and she had begged Leila to think of her as peacefully resting in her room till such time as they could snatch their quiet moment.

"Before tea, then, you duck!" Leila with a last kiss had decided; and presently Mrs. Lidcote, through her open window, had heard the fresh loud voices of her daughter's visitors chiming across the gardens from the tennis court.

IV

LEILA had come and gone, and they had had their talk. It had not lasted as long as Mrs. Lidcote wished, for in the middle of it Leila had been summoned to the telephone to receive an important message from town, and had sent word to her mother that she couldn't come back just then, as one of the young ladies had been called away unexpectedly and arrangements had to be made for her departure. But the mother and daughter had had almost an hour together, and Mrs. Lidcote was happy. She had never seen Leila so tender, so solicitous. The only thing that troubled her was the very excess of this solicitude, the exaggerated expression of her daughter's annoyance that their first moments together should have been marred by the presence of strangers.

"Not strangers to me, darling, since they're friends of yours," her mother had assured her.

"Yes; but I know your feeling, you queer wild mother. I know how you've always hated people." (*Hated people!* Had Leila forgotten why?) "And that's why I told Susy that if you preferred to go with her to Ridgefield on Sunday I should perfectly understand, and patiently wait for our good hug. But you didn't really mind them at luncheon, did you, dearest?"

Mrs. Lidcote, at that, had suddenly thrown a startled look at her daughter. "I don't mind things of that kind any longer," she had simply answered.

"But that doesn't console me for having exposed you to the bother of it, for having let you come here when I ought to have *ordered* you off to Ridgefield with Susy. If Susy hadn't been stupid she'd have made you go there with her. I hate to think of you up here all alone."

Again Mrs. Lidcote tried to read something more than a rather obtuse devotion in her daughter's radiant gaze. "I'm glad to have had a rest this afternoon, dear; and later—"

"Oh, yes, later, when all this fuss is over, we'll more than make up for it, shan't we, you precious darling?" And at this point Leila had been summoned to the telephone, leaving Mrs. Lidcote to her conjectures.

These were still floating before her in cloudy uncertainty when Miss Suffern tapped at the door.

"You've come to take me down to tea? I'd forgotten how late it was," Mrs. Lidcote exclaimed.

Miss Suffern, a plump peering little woman, with prim hair and a conciliatory smile, nervously adjusted the pendent bugles of her elaborate black dress. Miss Suffern was always in mourning, and always commemorating the demise of distant relatives by wearing the discarded wardrobe of their next of kin. "It isn't *exactly* mourning," she would say; "but it's the only stitch of black poor Julia had—and of course George was only my mother's step-cousin."

As she came forward Mrs. Lidcote found herself humorously wondering whether she were mourning Horace Pursh's divorce in one of his mother's old black satins.

"Oh, *did* you mean to go down for tea?" Susy Suffern peered at her, a little fluttered. "Leila sent me up to keep you company. She thought it would be cozier for you to stay here. She was afraid you were feeling rather tired."

"I was; but I've had the whole afternoon to rest in. And this wonderful sofa to help me."

"Leila told me to tell you that she'd rush up for a minute before dinner, after everybody had arrived; but the train is always dreadfully late. She's in despair at not giving you a sitting-room; she wanted to know if I thought you really minded."

"Of course I don't mind. It's not like Leila to think I should." Mrs. Lidcote drew aside to make way for the housemaid, who appeared in the doorway bearing a table spread with a bewildering variety of tea cakes.

"Leila saw to it herself," Miss Suffern murmured as the door closed. "Her one idea is that you should feel happy here."

It struck Mrs. Lidcote as one more mark of the subverted state of things that her daughter's solicitude should find expression in the multiplicity of sandwiches and the piping-hotness of muffins; but then everything that had happened since her arrival seemed to increase her confusion.

The note of a motor horn down the drive gave another turn to her thoughts. "Are those the new arrivals already?" she asked.

"Oh, dear, no; they won't be here till after seven." Miss Suffern craned her head from the window to catch a glimpse of the motor. "It must be Charlotte leaving."

"Was it the little Wynn girl who was called away in a hurry? I hope it's not on account of illness."

"Oh, no; I believe there was some mistake about dates. Her mother telephoned her that she was expected at the Stepleys, at Fishkill, and she had to be rushed over to Albany to catch a train."

Mrs. Lidcote meditated. "I'm sorry. She's a charming young thing. I hoped I should have another talk with her this evening after dinner."

"Yes; it's too bad." Miss Suffern's gaze grew vague. "You *do* look tired, you know," she continued, seating herself at the tea-table and preparing to dispense its delicacies. "You must go straight back to your sofa and let me wait on you. The excitement has told on you more than you think, and you mustn't fight against it any longer. Just stay quietly up here and let yourself go. You'll have Leila to yourself on Monday."

Mrs. Lidcote received the tea-cup which her cousin proffered, but showed no other disposition to obey her injunctions. For a moment she stirred her tea in silence; then she asked: "Is it your idea that I should stay quietly up here till Monday?"

Miss Suffern set down her cup with a gesture so sudden that it endangered an adjacent plate of scones. When she had assured herself of the safety of the scones she looked up with a fluttered laugh. "Perhaps, dear, by tomorrow you'll be feeling differently. The air here, you know—"

"Yes, I know." Mrs. Lidcote bent forward to help herself to a scone. "Who's arriving this evening?" she asked.

Miss Suffern frowned and peered. "You know my wretched head for names. Leila told me—but there are so many—"

"So many? She didn't tell me she expected a big party."

"Oh, not big: but rather outside of her little group. And of course, as it's the first time, she's a little excited at having the older set."

"The older set? Our contemporaries, you mean?"

"Why—yes." Miss Suffern paused as if to gather herself up for a leap. "The Ashton Gileses," she brought out.

"The Ashton Gileses? Really? I shall be glad to see Mary Giles again. It must be eighteen years," said Mrs. Lidcote steadily.

"Yes," Miss Suffern gasped, precipitately refilling her cup.

"The Ashton Gileses; and who else?"

"Well, the Sam Fresbies. But the most important person, of course, is Mrs. Lorin Boulger."

"Mrs. Boulger? Leila didn't tell me she was coming."

"Didn't she? I suppose she forgot everything when she saw you. But the party was got up for Mrs. Boulger. You see, it's very important that she should—well, take a fancy to Leila and Wilbour; his being appointed to Rome virtually depends on it. And you know Leila insists on Rome in order to be near you. So she asked Mary Giles, who's intimate with the Boulgers, if the visit couldn't possibly be arranged; and Mary's cable caught Mrs. Boulger at Cherbourg. She's to be only a fortnight in America; and getting her to come directly here was rather a triumph."

"Yes; I see it was," said Mrs. Lidcote.

"You know, she's rather—rather fussy; and Mary was a little doubtful if—"

"If she would, on account of Leila?" Mrs. Lidcote murmured.

"Well, yes. In her official position. But luckily she's a friend of the Barkleys. And finding the Gileses and Fresbies here will make it all right. The times have changed!" Susy Suffern indulgently summed up.

Mrs. Lidcote smiled. "Yes; a few years ago it would have seemed improbable that I should ever again be dining with Mary Giles and Harriet Fresbie and Mrs. Lorin Boulger."

Miss Suffern did not at the moment seem disposed to enlarge upon this theme; and after an interval of silence Mrs. Lidcote suddenly resumed: "Do they know I'm here, by the way?"

The effect of her question was to produce in Miss Suffern an exaggerated access of peering and frowning. She twitched the tea-things about, fingered her bugles, and, looking at the clock, exclaimed amazedly: "Mercy! Is it seven already?"

"Not that it can make any difference, I suppose," Mrs. Lidcote continued. "But did Leila tell them I was coming?"

Miss Suffern looked at her with pain. "Why, you don't suppose, dearest, that Leila would do anything—"

Mrs. Lidcote went on: "For, of course, it's of the first importance, as you say, that Mrs. Lorin Boulger should be favorably impressed, in order that Wilbour may have the best possible chance of getting Rome."

"I *told* Leila you'd feel that, dear. You see, it's actually on *your* account—so that they may get a post near you—that Leila invited Mrs. Boulger."

"Yes, I see that." Mrs. Lidcote, abruptly rising from her seat, turned her eyes to the clock. "But, as you say, it's getting late. Oughtn't we to dress for dinner?"

Miss Suffern, at the suggestion, stood up also, an agitated hand among her bugles. "I do wish I could persuade you to stay up here this evening. I'm sure Leila'd be happier if you would. Really, you're much too tired to come down."

"What nonsense, Susy!" Mrs. Lidcote spoke with a sudden sharpness, her hand stretched to the bell. "When do we dine? At half-past eight? Then I must really send you packing. At my age it takes time to dress."

Miss Suffern, thus projected toward the threshold, lingered there to repeat: "Leila'll never forgive herself if you make an effort you're not up to." But Mrs. Lidcote smiled on her without answering, and the icy light-wave propelled her through the door.

V

MRS. LIDCOTE, though she had made the gesture of ringing for her maid, had not done so.

When the door closed, she continued to stand motionless in the middle of her soft spacious room. The fire which had been kindled at twilight danced on the brightness of silver and mirrors and sober gilding; and the sofa toward which she had been urged by Miss Suffern heaped up its cushions in inviting proximity to a table laden with new books and papers. She could not recall having ever been more luxuriously housed, or having ever had so strange a sense of being out alone, under the night, in a wind-beaten plain. She sat down by the fire and thought.

A knock on the door made her lift her head, and she saw her daughter on the threshold. The intricate ordering of Leila's fair hair and the flying folds of her dressing gown showed that she had interrupted her dressing to hasten to her mother; but once in the room she paused a moment, smiling uncertainly, as though she had forgotten the object of her haste.

Mrs. Lidcote rose to her feet. "Time to dress, dearest? Don't scold! I shan't be late."

"To dress?" Leila stood before her with a puzzled look. "Why, I thought, dear—I mean, I hoped you'd decided just to stay here quietly and rest."

Her mother smiled. "But I've been resting all the afternoon!"

"Yes, but—you know you *do* look tired. And when Susy told me just now that you meant to make the effort—"

"You came to stop me?"

"I came to tell you that you needn't feel in the least obliged—"

"Of course. I understand that."

There was a pause during which Leila, vaguely averting herself from her mother's scrutiny, drifted toward the dressing-table and began to disturb the symmetry of the brushes and bottles laid out on it. "Do your visitors know that I'm here?" Mrs. Lidcote suddenly went on.

"Do they—Of course—why, naturally," Leila rejoined, absorbed in trying to turn the stopper of a salts-bottle.

"Then won't they think it odd if I don't appear?"

"Oh, not in the least, dearest. I assure you they'll *all* understand." Leila laid down the bottle and turned back to her mother, her face alight with reassurance.

Mrs. Lidcote stood motionless, her head erect, her smiling eyes on her daughter's. "Will they think it odd if I *do?"*

Leila stopped short, her lips half parted to reply. As she paused, the color stole over her bare neck, swept up to her throat, and burst into flame in her cheeks. Thence it sent its devastating crimson up to her very temples, to the lobes of her ears, to the edges of her eyelids, beating all over her in fiery waves, as if fanned by some imperceptible wind.

Mrs. Lidcote silently watched the conflagration; then she turned away her eyes with a slight laugh. "I only meant that I was afraid it might upset the arrangement of your dinner-table if I didn't come down. If you can assure me that it won't, I believe I'll take you at your word and go back to this irresistible sofa." She paused, as if waiting for her daughter to speak; then she held out her arms. "Run off and dress, dearest; and don't have me on your mind." She clasped Leila close, pressing a long kiss on the last afterglow of her subsiding blush. "I do feel the least bit overdone, and if it won't inconvenience you to have me drop out of things, I believe I'll basely take to my bed and stay there till your party scatters. And now run off, or you'll be late; and make my excuses to them all."

VI

THE Barkleys' visitors had dispersed, and Mrs. Lidcote, completely restored by her two days' rest, found herself, on the following Monday alone with her children and Miss Suffern.

There was a note of jubilation in the air, for the party had "gone off" so extraordinarily well, and so completely, as it appeared, to the satisfaction of Mrs. Lorin Boulger, that Wilbour's early appointment to Rome was almost to be counted on. So certain did this seem that the prospect of a prompt reunion mitigated the distress with which Leila learned of her mother's decision to return almost immediately to Italy. No one understood this decision; it seemed to Leila absolutely unintelligible that Mrs. Lidcote should not stay on with them till their own fate was fixed, and Wilbour echoed her astonishment.

"Why shouldn't you, as Leila says, wait here till we can all pack up and go together?"

Mrs. Lidcote smiled her gratitude with her refusal. "After all, it's not yet sure that you'll be packing up."

"Oh, you ought to have seen Wilbour with Mrs. Boulger," Leila triumphed.

"No, you ought to have seen Leila with her," Leila's husband exulted.

Miss Suffern enthusiastically appended: "I *do* think inviting Harriet Fresbie was a stroke of genius!"

"Oh, we'll be with you soon," Leila laughed. "So soon that it's really foolish to separate."

But Mrs. Lidcote held out with the quiet firmness which her daughter knew it was useless to oppose. After her long months in India, it was really imperative, she declared, that she should get back to Florence and see what was happening to her little place there; and she had been so comfortable on the Utopia that she had a fancy to return by the same ship. There was nothing for it, therefore, but to acquiesce in her decision and keep her with them till the afternoon before the day of the Utopia's sailing. This arrangement fitted in with certain projects which, during her two days' seclusion, Mrs. Lidcote had silently matured. It had become to her of the first importance to get away as soon as she could, and the little place in Florence, which held her past in every fold of its curtains and between every page of its books, seemed now to her the one spot where that past would be endurable to look upon.

She was not unhappy during the intervening days. The sight of Leila's well-being, the sense of Leila's tenderness, were, after all, what she had come for; and of these she had had full measure. Leila had never been happier or more tender; and the contemplation of her bliss, and the enjoyment of her affection, were an absorbing occupation for her mother. But they were also a sharp strain on certain overtightened chords, and Mrs. Lidcote, when at last she found herself alone in the New York hotel to which she had returned the night before embarking, had the feeling that she had just escaped with her life from the clutch of a giant hand.

She had refused to let her daughter come to town with her; she had even rejected Susy Suffern's company. She wanted no viaticum but that of her own thoughts; and she let these come to her without shrinking from them as she sat in the same high-hung sitting-room in which, just a week before, she and Franklin Ide had had their memorable talk.

She had promised her friend to let him hear from her, but she had not kept her promise. She knew that he had probably come back from Chicago, and that if he learned of her sudden decision to return to Italy it would be impossible for her not to see him before sailing; and as she wished above all things not to see him she had kept silent, intending to send him a letter from the steamer.

There was no reason why she should wait till then to write it. The actual moment was more favorable, and the task, though not agreeable, would at least bridge over an hour of her lonely evening. She went up to the writing-table, drew out a sheet of paper and began to write his name. And as she did so, the door opened and he came in.

The words she met him with were the last she could have imagined herself saying when they had parted. "How in the world did you know that I was here?"

He caught her meaning in a flash. "You didn't want me to, then?" He stood looking at her. "I suppose I ought to have taken your silence as meaning that. But I happened to meet Mrs. Wynn, who is stopping here, and she asked me to dine with her and Charlotte, and Charlotte's young man. They told me they'd seen you arriving this afternoon, and I couldn't help coming up."

There was a pause between them, which Mrs. Lidcote at last surprisingly broke with the exclamation: "Ah, she *did* recognize me, then!"

"Recognize you?" He stared. "Why—"

"Oh, I saw she did, though she never moved an eyelid. I saw it by Charlotte's blush. The child has the prettiest blush. I saw that her mother wouldn't let her speak to me."

Ide put down his hat with an impatient laugh. "Hasn't Leila cured you of your delusions?"

She looked at him intently. "Then you don't think Margaret Wynn meant to cut me?"

"I think your ideas are absurd."

She paused for a perceptible moment without taking this up; then she said, at a tangent: "I'm sailing tomorrow early. I meant to write to you—there's the letter I'd begun."

Ide followed her gesture, and then turned his eyes back to her face. "You didn't mean to see me, then, or even to let me know that you were going till you'd left?"

"I felt it would be easier to explain to you in a letter—"

"What in God's name is there to explain?" She made no reply, and he pressed on: "It can't be that you're worried about Leila, for Charlotte Wynn told me she'd been there last week, and there was a big party arriving when she left: Fresbies and Gileses, and Mrs. Lorin Boulger—all the board of examiners! If Leila has passed *that*, she's got her degree."

Mrs. Lidcote had dropped down into a corner of the sofa where she had sat during their talk of the week before. "I was stupid," she began abruptly. "I ought to have gone to Ridgefield with Susy. I didn't see till afterward that I was expected to."

"You were expected to?"

"Yes. Oh, it wasn't Leila's fault. She suffered—poor darling; she was distracted. But she'd asked her party before she knew I was arriving."

"Oh, as to that—" Ide drew a deep breath of relief. "I can understand that it must have been a disappointment not to have you to herself just at first. But, after all, you were among old friends or their children: the Gileses and Fresbies—and little Charlotte Wynn." He paused a moment before the last name, and scrutinized her hesitatingly. "Even if they came at the wrong time, you must have been glad to see them all at Leila's."

She gave him back his look with a faint smile. "I didn't see them."

"You didn't see them?"

"No. That is, excepting little Charlotte Wynn. That child is exquisite. We had a talk before luncheon the day I arrived. But when her mother found out that I was staying in the house she telephoned her to leave immediately, and so I didn't see her again."

The color rushed to Ide's sallow face. "I don't know where you get such ideas!"

She pursued, as if she had not heard him: "Oh, and I saw Mary Giles for a minute too. Susy Suffern brought her up to my room the last evening, after dinner, when all the others were at bridge. She meant it kindly—but it wasn't much use."

"But what were you doing in your room in the evening after dinner?"

"Why, you see, when I found out my mistake in coming,—how embarrassing it was for Leila, I mean—I simply told her I was very tired, and preferred to stay upstairs till the party was over."

Ide, with a groan, struck his hand against the arm of his chair. "I wonder how much of all this you simply imagined!"

"I didn't imagine the fact of Harriet Fresbie's not even asking if she might see me when she knew I was in the house. Nor of Mary Giles's getting Susy, at the eleventh hour, to smuggle her up to my room when the others wouldn't know where she'd gone; nor poor Leila's ghastly fear lest Mrs. Lorin Boulger, for whom the party was given, should guess I was in the house, and prevent her husband's giving Wilbour the second secretaryship because she'd been obliged to spend a night under the same roof with his mother-in-law!"

Ide continued to drum on his chair-arm with exasperated fingers. "You don't *know* that any of the acts you describe are due to the causes you suppose."

Mrs. Lidcote paused before replying, as if honestly trying to measure the weight of this argument. Then she said in a low tone: "I know that Leila was in an agony lest I should come down to dinner the first night. And it was for me she was afraid, not for herself. Leila is never afraid for herself."

"But the conclusions you draw are simply preposterous. There are narrow-minded women everywhere, but the women who were at Leila's knew perfectly well that their going there would give her a sort of social sanction, and if they were willing that she should have it, why on earth should they want to withhold it from you?"

"That's what I told myself a week ago, in this very room, after my first talk with Susy Suffern." She lifted a misty smile to his anxious eyes. "That's why I listened to what you said to me the same evening, and why your arguments half convinced me, and made me think that what had been possible for Leila might not be impossible for me. If the new dispensation had come, why not for me as well as for the others? I can't tell you the flight my imagination took!"

Franklin Ide rose from his seat and crossed the room to a chair near her sofa-corner. "All I cared about was that it seemed—for the moment—to be carrying you toward me," he said.

"I cared about that, too. That's why I meant to go away without seeing you." They gave each other grave look for look. "Because, you see, I was mistaken," she went on. "We were both mistaken. You say it's preposterous that the women who didn't object to accepting Leila's hospitality should have objected to meeting me under her roof. And so it is; but I begin to understand why. It's simply that society is much too busy to revise its own judgments. Probably no one in the house with me stopped to consider that my case and Leila's were identical. They only remembered that I'd done something which, at the time I did it, was condemned by society. My case has been passed on and classified: I'm the woman who has been cut for nearly twenty years. The older people have half-forgotten why, and the younger ones have never really known: it's simply become a tradition to cut me. And traditions that have lost their meaning are the hardest of all to destroy."

Ide sat motionless while she spoke. As she ended, he stood up with a short laugh and walked across the room to the window. Outside, the immense black prospect of New York, strung with its myriad lines of light, stretched away into the smoky edges of the night. He showed it to her with a gesture.

"What do you suppose such words as you've been using—'society,' 'tradition,' and the rest—mean to all the life out there?"

She came and stood by him in the window. "Less than nothing, of course. But you and I are not out there. We're shut up in a little tight round of habit and association, just as we're shut up in this room. Remember, I thought I'd got out of it once; but what really happened was that the other people went out, and left me in the same little room. The only difference was that I was there alone. Oh, I've made it habitable now, I'm used to it; but I've lost any illusions I may have had as to an angel's opening the door."

Ide again laughed impatiently. "Well, if the door won't open, why not let another prisoner in? At least it would be less of a solitude—"

She turned from the dark window back into the vividly lighted room.

"It would be more of a prison. You forget that I know all about that. We're all imprisoned, of course—all of us middling people, who don't carry our freedom in our brains. But we've accommodated ourselves to our different cells, and if we're moved suddenly into new ones we're likely to find a stone wall where we thought there was thin air, and to knock ourselves senseless against it. I saw a man do that once."

Ide, leaning with folded arms against the window frame, watched her in silence as she moved restlessly about the room, gathering together some scattered books and tossing a handful of torn letters into the paper basket. When she ceased, he rejoined: "All you say is based on preconceived theories. Why didn't you put them to the test by coming down to meet your old friends? Don't you see the inference they would naturally draw from your hiding yourself when they arrived? It looked as though you were afraid of them—or as though you hadn't forgiven them. Either way, you put them in the wrong instead of waiting to let them put you in the right. If Leila had buried herself in a desert do you suppose society would have gone to fetch her out? You say you were afraid for Leila and that she was afraid for you. Don't you see what all these complications of feeling mean? Simply that you were too nervous at the moment to let things happen naturally, just as you're too nervous now to judge them rationally." He paused and turned his eyes to her face. "Don't try to just yet. Give yourself a little more time. Give *me* a little more time. I've always known it would take time."

He moved nearer, and she let him have her hand.

With the grave kindness of his face so close above her she felt like a child roused out of frightened dreams and finding a light in the room.

"Perhaps you're right—" she heard herself begin; then something within her clutched her back, and her hand fell away from him.

"I know I'm right: trust me," he urged. "We'll talk of this in Florence soon."

She stood before him, feeling with despair his kindness, his patience and his unreality. Everything he said seemed like a painted gauze let down between herself and the real facts of life; and a sudden desire seized her to tear the gauze into shreds.

She drew back and looked at him with a smile of superficial reassurance. "You *are* right—about not talking any longer now. I'm nervous and tired, and it would do no good. I brood over things too much. As you say, I must try not to shrink from people." She turned away and glanced at the clock. "Why, it's only ten! If I send you off I shall begin to brood again; and if you stay we shall go on talking about the same thing. Why shouldn't we go down and see Margaret Wynn for half an hour?"

She spoke lightly and rapidly, her brilliant eyes on his face. As she watched him, she saw it change, as if her smile had thrown a too vivid light upon it.

"Oh, no—not to-night!" he exclaimed.

"Not tonight? Why, what other night have I, when I'm off at dawn? Besides, I want to show you at once that I mean to be more sensible—that I'm not going to be afraid of people any more. And I should really like another glimpse of little Charlotte." He stood before her, his hand in his beard, with the gesture he had in moments of perplexity. "Come!" she ordered him gaily, turning to the door.

He followed her and laid his hand on her arm. "Don't you think—hadn't you better let me go first and see? They told me they'd had a tiring day at the dressmaker's* I daresay they have gone to bed."

"But you said they'd a young man of Charlotte's dining with them. Surely he wouldn't have left by ten? At any rate, I'll go down with you and see. It takes so long if one «ends a servant first" She put him gently aside, and then paused as a new thought struck her. "Or wait; my maid's in the next room. I'll tell her to go and ask if Margaret will receive me. Yes, that's much the best way."

She turned back and went toward the door that led to her bedroom; but before she could open it she felt Ide's quick touch again.

"I believe—I remember now—Charlotte's young man was suggesting that they should all go out—to a music hall or something of the sort. I'm sure—I'm positively sure that you won't find them."

Her hand dropped from the door, his dropped from her arm, and as they drew back and faced each other she saw the blood rise slowly through his sallow skin, redden his neck and ears, encroach upon the edges of his beard, and settle in dull patches under his kind troubled eyes. She had seen the same blush on another face, and the same impulse of compassion she had then felt made her turn her gaze away again.

A knock on the door broke the silence, and a porter put his head' into the room.

"It's only just to know how many pieces there'll be to go down to the steamer in the morning."

With the words she felt that the veil of painted gauze was torn in tatters, and that she was moving again among the grim edges of reality.

"Oh, dear," she exclaimed, "I never *can* remember! Wait a minute; I shall have to ask my maid."

She opened her bedroom door and called out: "Annette!"

## KERFOL

"YOU OUGHT TO buy it," said my host; "it's just the place for a solitary-minded devil like you. And it would be rather worth-while to own the most romantic house in Brittany. The present people are dead broke, and it's going for a song—you ought to buy it."

It was not with the least idea of living up to the character my friend Lanrivain ascribed to me (as a matter of fact, under my unsociable exterior I have always had secret yearnings for domesticity) that I took his hint one autumn afternoon and went to Kerfol. My friend was motoring over to Quimper on business: he dropped me on the way, at a cross-road on a heath, and said: "First turn to the right and second to the left. Then straight ahead till you see an avenue. If you meet any peasants, don't ask your way. They don't understand French, and they would pretend they did and mix you up. I'll be back for you here by sunset—and don't forget the tombs in the chapel."

I followed Lanrivain's directions with the hesitation occasioned by the usual difficulty of remembering whether he had said the first turn to the right and second to the left, or the contrary. If I had met a peasant I should certainly have asked, and probably been sent astray; but I had the desert landscape to myself, and so stumbled on the right turn and walked across the heath till I came to an avenue. It was so unlike any other avenue I have ever seen that I instantly knew it must be *the* avenue. The grey-trunked trees sprang up straight to a great height and then interwove their pale-grey branches in a long tunnel through which the autumn light fell faintly. I know most trees by name, but I haven't to this day been able to decide what those trees were. They had the tall curve of elms, the tenuity of poplars, the ashen color of olives under a rainy sky; and they stretched ahead of me for half a mile or more without a break in their arch. If ever I saw an avenue that unmistakably led to something, it was the avenue at Kerfol. My heart beat a little as I began to walk down it.

Presently the trees ended and I came to a fortified gate in a long wall. Between me and the wall was an open space of grass, with other grey avenues radiating from it. Behind the wall were tall slate roofs mossed with silver, a chapel belfry, the top of a keep. A moat filled with wild shrubs and brambles surrounded the place; the drawbridge had been replaced by a stone arch, and the portcullis by an iron gate. I stood for a long time on the hither side of the moat, gazing about me, and letting the influence of the place sink in. I said to myself: "If I wait long enough, the guardian will turn up and show me the tombs—" and I rather hoped he wouldn't turn up too soon.

I sat down on a stone and lit a cigarette. As soon as I had done it, it struck me as a puerile and portentous thing to do, with that great blind house looking down at me, and all the empty avenues converging on me. It may have been the depth of the silence that made me so conscious of my gesture. The squeak of my match sounded as loud as the scraping of a brake, and I almost fancied I heard it fall when I tossed it onto the grass. But there was more than that: a sense of irrelevance, of littleness, of futile bravado, in sitting there puffing my cigarette-smoke into the face of such a past.

I knew nothing of the history of Kerfol—I was new to Brittany, and Lanrivain had never mentioned the name to me till the day before—but one couldn't as much as glance at that pile without feeling in it a long accumulation of history. What kind of history I was not prepared to guess: perhaps only that sheer weight of many associated lives and deaths which gives a majesty to all old houses. But the aspect of Kerfol suggested something more—a perspective of stern and cruel memories stretching away, like its own grey avenues, into a blur of darkness.

Certainly no house had ever more completely and finally broken with the present. As it stood there, lifting its proud roofs and gables to the sky, it might have been its own funeral monument. "Tombs in the chapel? The whole place is a tomb!" I reflected. I hoped more and more that the guardian would not come. The details of the place, however striking, would seem trivial compared with its collective impressiveness; and I wanted only to sit there and be penetrated by the weight of its silence.

"It's the very place for you!" Lanrivain had said; and I was overcome by the almost blasphemous frivolity of suggesting to any living being that Kerfol was the place for him. "Is it possible that anyone could *not* see—?" I wondered. I did not finish the thought: what I meant was undefinable. I stood up and wandered toward the gate. I was beginning to want to know more; not to *see* more—I was by now so sure it was not a question of seeing—but to feel more: feel all the place had to communicate. "But to get in one will have to rout out the keeper," I thought reluctantly, and hesitated. Finally I crossed the bridge and tried the iron gate. It yielded, and I walked through the tunnel formed by the thickness of the *chemin de ronde*. At the farther end, a wooden barricade had been laid across the entrance, and beyond it was a court enclosed in noble architecture. The main building faced me; and I now saw that one half was a mere ruined front, with gaping windows through which the wild growths of the moat and the trees of the park were visible. The rest of the house was still in its robust beauty. One end abutted on the round tower, the other on the small traceried chapel, and in an angle of the building stood a graceful well-head crowned with mossy urns. A few roses grew against the walls, and on an upper window-sill I remember noticing a pot of fuchsias.

My sense of the pressure of the invisible began to yield to my architectural interest. The building was so fine that I felt a desire to explore it for its own sake. I looked about the court, wondering in which corner the guardian lodged. Then I pushed open the barrier and went in. As I did so, a dog barred my way. He was such a remarkably beautiful little dog that for a moment he made me forget the splendid place he was defending. I was not sure of his breed at the time, but have since learned that it was Chinese, and that he was of a rare variety called the "Sleeve-dog." He was very small and golden brown, with large brown eyes and a ruffled throat: he looked like a large tawny chrysanthemum. I said to myself: "These little beasts always snap and scream, and somebody will be out in a minute."

The little animal stood before me, forbidding, almost menacing: there was anger in his large brown eyes. But he made no sound, he came no nearer. Instead, as I advanced, he gradually fell back, and I noticed that another dog, a vague rough brindled thing, had limped up on a lame leg. "There'll be a hubbub now," I thought; for at the same moment a third dog, a long-haired white mongrel, slipped out of a doorway and joined the others. All three stood looking at me with grave eyes; but not a sound came from them. As I advanced they continued to fall back on muffled paws, still watching me. "At a given point, they'll all charge at my ankles: it's one of the jokes that dogs who live together put up on one," I thought. I was not alarmed, for they were neither large nor formidable. But they let me wander about the court as I pleased, following me at a little distance—always the same distance—and always keeping their eyes on me. Presently I looked across at the ruined facade, and saw that in one of its empty window-frames another dog stood: a white pointer with one brown ear. He was an old grave dog, much more experienced than the others; and he seemed to be observing me with a deeper intentness.

"I'll hear from *him*," I said to myself; but he stood in the window-frame, against the trees of the park, and continued to watch me without moving. I stared back at him for a time, to see if the sense that he was being watched would not rouse him. Half the width of the court lay between us, and we gazed at each other silently across it. But he did not stir, and at last I turned away. Behind me I found the rest of the pack, with a newcomer added: a small black greyhound with pale agate-colored eyes. He was shivering a little, and his expression was more timid than that of the others. I noticed that he kept a little behind them. And still there was not a sound.

I stood there for fully five minutes, the circle about me—waiting, as they seemed to be waiting. At last I went up to the little golden-brown dog and stooped to pat him. As I did so, I heard myself give a nervous laugh. The little dog did not start, or growl, or take his eyes from me—he simply slipped back about a yard, and then paused and continued to look at me. "Oh, hang it!" I exclaimed, and walked across the court toward the well.

As I advanced, the dogs separated and slid away into different corners of the court. I examined the urns on the well, tried a locked door or two, and looked up and down the dumb façade; then I faced about toward the chapel. When I turned I perceived that all the dogs had disappeared except the old pointer, who still watched me from the window. It was rather a relief to be rid of that cloud of witnesses; and I began to look about me for a way to the back of the house. "Perhaps there'll be somebody in the garden," I thought. I found a way across the moat, scrambled over a wall smothered in brambles, and got into the garden. A few lean hydrangeas and geraniums pined in the flower-beds, and the ancient house looked down on them indifferently. Its garden side was plainer and severer than the other: the long granite front, with its few windows and steep roof, looked like a fortress-prison. I walked around the farther wing, went up some disjointed steps, and entered the deep twilight of a narrow and incredibly old box-walk. The walk was just wide enough for one person to slip through, and its branches met overhead. It was like the ghost of a box-walk, its lustrous green all turning to the shadowy greyness of the avenues. I walked on and on, the branches hitting me in the face and springing back with a dry rattle; and at length I came out on the grassy top of the *chemin de ronde*. I walked along it to the gate-tower, looking down into the court, which was just below me. Not a human being was in sight; and neither were the dogs. I found a flight of steps in the thickness of the wall and went down them; and when I emerged again into the court, there stood the circle of dogs, the golden-brown one a little ahead of the others, the black greyhound shivering in the rear.

"Oh, hang it—you uncomfortable beasts, you!" I exclaimed, my voice startling me with a sudden echo. The dogs stood motionless, watching me. I knew by this time that they would not try to prevent my approaching the house, and the knowledge left me free to examine them. I had a feeling that they must be horribly cowed to be so silent and inert. Yet they did not look hungry or ill-treated. Their coats were smooth and they were not thin, except the shivering greyhound. It was more as if they had lived a long time with people who never spoke to them or looked at them: as though the silence of the place had gradually benumbed their busy inquisitive natures. And this strange passivity, this almost human lassitude, seemed to me sadder than the misery of starved and beaten animals. I should have liked to rouse them for a minute, to coax them into a game or a scamper; but the longer I looked into their fixed and weary eyes the more preposterous the idea became. With the windows of that house looking down on us, how could I have imagined such a thing? The dogs knew better: *they* knew what the house would tolerate and what it would not. I even fancied that they knew what was passing through my mind, and pitied me for my frivolity. But even that feeling probably reached them through a thick fog of listlessness. I had an idea that their distance from me was as nothing to my remoteness from them. The impression they produced was that of having in common one memory so deep and dark that nothing that had happened since was worth either a growl or a wag.

"I say," I broke out abruptly, addressing myself to the dumb circle, "do you know what you look like, the whole lot of you? You look as if you'd seen a ghost—that's how you look! I wonder if there *is* a ghost here, and nobody but you left for it to appear to?" The dogs continued to gaze at me without moving. . . .

It was dark when I saw Lanrivain's motor lamps at the cross-roads—and I wasn't exactly sorry to see them. I had the sense of having escaped from the loneliest place in the whole world, and of not liking loneliness—to that degree—as much as I had imagined I should. My friend had brought his solicitor back from Quimper for the night, and seated beside a fat and affable stranger I felt no inclination to talk of Kerfol....

But that evening, when Lanrivain and the solicitor were closeted in the study, Madame de Lanrivain began to question me in the drawing room.

"Well—are you going to buy Kerfol?" she asked, tilting up her gay chin from her embroidery.

"I haven't decided yet. The fact is, I couldn't get into the house," I said, as if I had simply postponed my decision, and meant to go back for another look.

"You couldn't get in? Why, what happened? The family are mad to sell the place, and the old guardian has orders—"

"Very likely. But the old guardian wasn't there."

"What a pity! He must have gone to market. But his daughter—?"

"There was nobody about. At least I saw no one."

"How extraordinary! Literally nobody?"

"Nobody but a lot of dogs—a whole pack of them—who seemed to have the place to themselves."

Madame de Lanrivain let the embroidery slip to her knee and folded her hands on it. For several minutes she looked at me thoughtfully.

"A pack of dogs—you *saw* them?"

"Saw them? I saw nothing else!"

"How many?" She dropped her voice a little. "I've always wondered—"

I looked at her with surprise: I had supposed the place to be familiar to her. "Have you never been to Kerfol?" I asked.

"Oh, yes: often. But never on that day."

"What day?"

"I'd quite forgotten—and so had Hervé, I'm sure. If we'd remembered, we never should have sent you to-day—but then, after all, one doesn't half believe that sort of thing, does one?"

"What sort of thing?" I asked, involuntarily sinking my voice to the level of hers. Inwardly I was thinking: "I *knew* there was something. . . ."

Madame de Lanrivain cleared her throat and produced a reassuring smile. "Didn't Hervé tell you the story of Kerfol? An ancestor of his was mixed up in it. You know every Breton house has its ghost-story; and some of them are rather unpleasant."

"Yes—but those dogs?"

"Well, those dogs are the ghosts of Kerfol. At least, the peasants say there's one day in the year when a lot of dogs appear there; and that day the keeper and his daughter go off to Morlaix and get drunk. The women in Brittany drink dreadfully." She stooped to match a silk; then she lifted her charming inquisitive Parisian face. "Did you *really* see a lot of dogs? There isn't one at Kerfol." she said.

## II

LANRIVAIN, the next day, hunted out a shabby calf volume from the back of an upper shelf of his library.

"Yes—here it is. What does it call itself? *A History of the Assizes of the Duchy of Brittany. Quimper,* 1702. The book was written about a hundred years later than the Kerfol affair; but I believe the account is transcribed pretty literally from the judicial records. Anyhow, it's queer reading. And there's a Hervé de Lanrivain mixed up in it— not exactly my style, as you'll see. But then he's only a collateral. Here, take the book up to bed with you. I don't exactly remember the details; but after you've read it I'll bet anything you'll leave your light burning all night!"

I left my light burning all night, as he had predicted; but it was chiefly because, till near dawn, I was absorbed in my reading. The account of the trial of Anne de Cornault, wife of the lord of Kerfol, was long and closely printed. It was, as my friend had said, probably an almost literal transcription of what took place in the court-room; and the trial lasted nearly a month. Besides, the type of the book was very bad. . . .

At first I thought of translating the old record. But it is full of wearisome repetitions, and the main lines of the story are forever straying off into side issues. So I have tried to disentangle it, and give it here in a simpler form. At times, however, I have reverted to the text because no other words could have conveyed so exactly the sense of what I felt at Kerfol; and nowhere have I added anything of my own.

## III

IT was in the year 16— that Yves de Cornault, lord of the domain of Kerfol, went to the *pardon* of Locronan to perform his religious duties. He was a rich and powerful noble, then in his sixty-second year, but hale and sturdy, a great horseman and hunter and a pious man. So all his neighbors attested. In appearance he was short and broad, with a swarthy face, legs slightly bowed from the saddle, a hanging nose and broad hands with black hairs on them. He had married young and lost his wife and son soon after, and since then had lived alone at Kerfol. Twice a year he went to Morlaix, where he had a handsome house by the river, and spent a week or ten days there; and occasionally he rode to Rennes on business. Witnesses were found to declare that during these absences he led a life different from the one he was known to lead at Kerfol, where he busied himself with his estate, attended mass daily, and found his only amusement in hunting the wild boar and water-fowl. But these rumors are not particularly relevant, and it is certain that among people of his own class in the neighbourhood he passed for a stern and even austere man, observant of his religious obligations, and keeping strictly to himself. There was no talk of any familiarity with the women on his estate, though at that time the nobility were very free with their peasants. Some people said he had never looked at a woman since his wife's death; but such things are hard to prove, and the evidence on this point was not worth much.

Well, in his sixty-second year, Yves de Cornault went to the pardon at Locronan, and saw there a young lady of Douarnenez, who had ridden over pillion behind her father to do her duty to the saint. Her name was Anne de Barrigan, and she came of good old Breton stock, but much less great and powerful than that of Yves de Cornault; and her father had squandered his fortune at cards, and lived almost like a peasant in his little granite manor on the moors.... I have said I would add nothing of my own to this bald statement of a strange case; but I must interrupt myself here to describe the young lady who rode up to the lych-gate of Locronan at the very moment when the Baron de Cornault was also dismounting there. I take my description from a faded drawing in red crayon, sober and truthful enough to be by a late pupil of the Clouets, which hangs in Lanrivain's study, and is said to be a portrait of Anne de Barrigan. It is unsigned and has no mark of identity but the initials A. B., and the date 16—, the year after her marriage. It represents a young woman with a small oval face, almost pointed, yet wide enough for a full mouth with a tender depression at the corners. The nose is small, and the eyebrows are set rather high, far apart, and as lightly penciled as the eyebrows in a Chinese painting. The forehead is high and serious, and the hair, which one feels to be fine and thick and fair, is drawn off it and lies close like a cap. The eyes are neither large nor small, hazel probably, with a look at once shy and steady. A pair of beautiful long hands are crossed below the lady's breast. . . .

The chaplain of Kerfol, and other witnesses, averred that when the Baron came back from Locronan he jumped from his horse, ordered another to be instantly saddled, called to a young page to come with him, and rode away that same evening to the south. His steward followed the next morning with coffers laden on a pair of pack mules. The following week Yves de Cornault rode back to Kerfol, sent for his vassals and tenants, and told them he was to be married at All Saints to Anne de Barrigan of Douarnenez. And on All Saints' Day the marriage took place.

As to the next few years, the evidence on both sides seems to show that they passed happily for the couple. No one was found to say that Yves de Cornault had been unkind to his wife, and it was plain to all that he was content with his bargain. Indeed, it was admitted by the chaplain and other witnesses for the prosecution that the young lady had a softening influence on her husband, and that he became less exacting with his tenants, less harsh to peasants and dependents, and less subject to the fits of gloomy silence which had darkened his widowhood. As to his wife, the only grievance her champions could call up in her behalf was that Kerfol was a lonely place, and that when her husband was away on business at Rennes or Morlaix—whither she was never taken—she was not allowed so much as to walk in the park unaccompanied. But no one asserted that she was unhappy, though one servant-woman said she had surprised her crying, and had heard her say that she was a woman accursed to have no child, and nothing in life to call her own. But that was a natural enough feeling in a wife attached to her husband; and certainly it must have been a great grief to Yves de Cornault that she bore no son. Yet he never made her feel her childlessness as a reproach—she admits this in her evidence—but seemed to try to make her forget it by showering gifts and favors on her. Rich though he was, he had never been openhanded; but nothing was too fine for his wife, in the way of silks or gems or linen, or whatever else she fancied. Every wandering merchant was welcome at Kerfol, and when the master was called away he never came back without bringing his wife a handsome present—something curious and particular—from Morlaix or Rennes or Quimper. One of the waiting-women gave, in cross-examination, an interesting list of one year's gifts, which I copy. From Morlaix, a carved ivory junk, with Chinamen at the oars, that a strange sailor had brought back as a votive offering for Notre Dame de la Clarté, above Ploumanac'h; from Quimper, an embroidered gown, worked by the nuns of the Assumption; from Rennes, a silver rose that opened and showed an amber Virgin with a crown of garnets; from Morlaix, again, a length of Damascus velvet shot with gold, bought of a Jew from Syria; and for Michaelmas that same year, from Rennes, a necklet or bracelet of round stones—emeralds and pearls and rubies—strung like beads on a fine gold chain. This was the present that pleased the lady best, the woman said. Later on, as it happened, it was produced at the trial, and appears to have struck the Judges and the public as a curious and valuable jewel.

The very same winter, the Baron absented himself again, this time as far as Bordeaux, and on his return he brought his wife something even odder and prettier than the bracelet. It was a winter evening when he rode up to Kerfol and, walking into the hall, found her sitting by the hearth, her chin on her hand, looking into the fire. He carried a velvet box in his hand and, setting it down, lifted the lid and let out a little golden-brown dog.

Anne de Cornault exclaimed with pleasure as the little creature bounded toward her. "Oh, it looks like a bird or a butterfly!" she cried as she picked it up; and the dog put its paws on her shoulders and looked at her with eyes "like a Christian's." After that she would never have it out of her sight, and petted and talked to it as if it had been a child—as indeed it was the nearest thing to a child she was to know. Yves de Cornault was much pleased with his purchase. The dog had been brought to him by a sailor from an East India merchantman, and the sailor had bought it of a pilgrim in a bazaar at Jaffa, who had stolen it from a nobleman's wife in China: a perfectly permissible thing to do, since the pilgrim was a Christian and the nobleman a heathen doomed to hell-fire. Yves de Cornault had paid a long price for the dog, for they were beginning to be in demand at the French court, and the sailor knew he had got hold of a good thing; but Anne's pleasure was so great that, to see her laugh and play with the little animal, her husband would doubtless have given twice the sum.

So far, all the evidence is at one, and the narrative plain sailing; but now the steering becomes difficult. I will try to keep as nearly as possible to Anne's own statements; though toward the end, poor thing. . . .

Well, to go back. The very year after the little brown dog was brought to Kerfol, Yves de Cornault, one winter night, was found dead at the head of a narrow flight of stairs leading down from his wife's rooms to a door opening on the court. It was his wife who found him and gave the alarm, so distracted, poor wretch, with fear and horror—for his blood was all over her—that at first the roused household could not make out what she was saying, and thought she had suddenly gone mad. But there, sure enough, at the top of the stairs lay her husband, stone dead, and head foremost, the blood from his wounds dripping down to the steps below him. He had been dreadfully scratched and gashed about the face and throat, as if with curious pointed weapons; and one of his legs had a deep tear in it which had cut an artery, and probably caused his death. But how did he come there, and who had murdered him?

His wife declared that she had been asleep in her bed, and hearing his cry had rushed out to find him lying on the stairs; but this was immediately questioned. In the first place, it was proved that from her room she could not have heard the struggle on the stairs, owing to the thickness of the walls and the length of the intervening passage; then it was evident that she had not been in bed and asleep, since she was dressed when she roused the house, and her bed had not been slept in. Moreover, the door at the bottom of the stairs was ajar, and it was noticed by the chaplain (an observant man) that the dress she wore was stained with blood about the knees, and that there were traces of small blood-stained hands low down on the staircase walls, so that it was conjectured that she had really been at the postern-door when her husband fell and, feeling her way up to him in the darkness on her hands and knees, had been stained by his blood dripping down on her. Of course it was argued on the other side that the blood-marks on her dress might have been caused by her kneeling down by her husband when she rushed out of her room; but there was the open door below, and the fact that the finger-marks in the staircase all pointed upward.

The accused held to her statement for the first two days, in spite of its improbability; but on the third day word was brought to her that Hervé de Lanrivain, a young nobleman of the neighbourhood, had been arrested for complicity in the crime. Two or three witnesses thereupon came forward to say that it was known throughout the country that Lanrivain had formerly been on good terms with the lady of Cornault; but that he had been absent from Brittany for over a year, and people had ceased to associate their names. The witnesses who made this statement were not of a very reputable sort. One was an old herb-gatherer suspected of witchcraft, another a drunken clerk from a neighboring parish, the third a half-witted shepherd who could be made to say anything; and it was clear that the prosecution was not satisfied with its case, and would have liked to find more definite proof of Lanrivain's complicity than the statement of the herb-gatherer, who swore to having seen him climbing the wall of the park on the night of the murder. One way of patching out incomplete proofs in those days was to put some sort of pressure, moral or physical, on the accused person. It is not clear what pressure was put on Anne de Cornault; but on the third day, when she was brought in court, she "appeared weak and wandering," and after being encouraged to collect herself and speak the truth, on her honour and the wounds of her Blessed Redeemer, she confessed that she had in fact gone down the stairs to speak with Hervé de Lanrivain (who denied everything), and had been surprised there by the sound of her husband's fall. That was better; and the prosecution rubbed its hands with satisfaction. The satisfaction increased when various dependents living at Kerfol were induced to say—with apparent sincerity—that during the year or two preceding his death their master had once more grown uncertain and irascible, and subject to the fits of brooding silence which his household had learned to dread before his second marriage. This seemed to show that things had not been going well at Kerfol; though no one could be found to say that there had been any signs of open disagreement between husband and wife.

Anne de Cornault, when questioned as to her reason for going down at night to open the door to Hervé de Lanrivain, made an answer which must have sent a smile around the court. She said it was because she was lonely and wanted to talk with the young man. Was this the only reason? she was asked; and replied: "Yes, by the Cross over your Lordships' heads." "But why at midnight?" the court asked. "Because I could see him in no other way." I can see the exchange of glances across the ermine collars under the Crucifix.

Anne de Cornault, further questioned, said that her married life had been extremely lonely: "desolate" was the word she used. It was true that her husband seldom spoke harshly to her; but there were days when he did not speak at all. It was true that he had never struck or threatened her; but he kept her like a prisoner at Kerfol, and when he rode away to Morlaix or Quimper or Rennes he set so close a watch on her that she could not pick a flower in the garden without having a waiting-woman at her heels. "I am no Queen, to need such honors," she once said to him; and he had answered that a man who has a treasure does not leave the key in the lock when he goes out. "Then take me with you," she urged; but to this he said that towns were pernicious places, and young wives better off at their own firesides.

"But what did you want to say to Hervé de Lanrivain?" the court asked; and she answered: "To ask him to take me away."

"Ah—you confess that you went down to him with adulterous thoughts?"

"No."

"Then why did you want him to take you away?"

"Because I was afraid for my life."

"Of whom were you afraid?"

"Of my husband."

"Why were you afraid of your husband?"

"Because he had strangled my little dog."

Another smile must have passed around the courtroom: in days when any nobleman had a right to hang his peasants—and most of them exercised it—pinching a pet animal's wind-pipe was nothing to make a fuss about.

At this point one of the Judges, who appears to have had a certain sympathy for the accused, suggested that she should be allowed to explain herself in her own way; and she thereupon made the following statement.

The first years of her marriage had been lonely; but her husband had not been unkind to her. If she had had a child she would not have been unhappy; but the days were long, and it rained too much.

It was true that her husband, whenever he went away and left her, brought her a handsome present on his return; but this did not make up for the loneliness. At least nothing had, till he brought her the little brown dog from the East: after that she was much less unhappy. Her husband seemed pleased that she was so fond of the dog; he gave her leave to put her jeweled bracelet around its neck, and to keep it always with her.

One day she had fallen asleep in her room, with the dog at her feet, as his habit was. Her feet were bare and resting on his back. Suddenly she was waked by her husband: he stood beside her, smiling not unkindly.

"You look like my great-grandmother, Juliane de Cornault, lying in the chapel with her feet on a little dog," he said.

The analogy sent a chill through her, but she laughed and answered: "Well, when I am dead you must put me beside her, carved in marble, with my dog at my feet."

"Oho—we'll wait and see," he said, laughing also, but with his black brows close together. "The dog is the emblem of fidelity."

"And do you doubt my right to lie with mine at my feet?"

"When I'm in doubt I find out," he answered. "I am an old man," he added, "and people say I make you lead a lonely life. But I swear you shall have your monument if you earn it."

"And I swear to be faithful," she returned, "if only for the sake of having my little dog at my feet."

Not long afterward he went on business to the Quimper Assizes; and while he was away his aunt, the widow of a great nobleman of the duchy, came to spend a night at Kerfol on her way to the *pardon* of Ste. Barbe. She was a woman of piety and consequence, and much respected by Yves de Cornault, and when she proposed to Anne to go with her to Ste. Barbe no one could object, and even the chaplain declared himself in favor of the pilgrimage. So Anne set out for Ste. Barbe, and there for the first time she talked with Hervé de Lanrivain. He had come once or twice to Kerfol with his father, but she had never before exchanged a dozen words with him. They did not talk for more than five minutes now: it was under the chestnuts, as the procession was coming out of the chapel. He said: "I pity you," and she was surprised, for she had not supposed that anyone thought her an object of pity. He added: "Call for me when you need me," and she smiled a little, but was glad afterward, and thought often of the meeting.

She confessed to having seen him three times afterward: not more. How or where she would not say—one had the impression that she feared to implicate someone. Their meetings had been rare and brief; and at the last he had told her that he was starting the next day for a foreign country, on a mission which was not without peril and might keep him for many months absent. He asked her for a remembrance, and she had none to give him but the collar about the little dog's neck. She was sorry afterward that she had given it, but he was so unhappy at going that she had not had the courage to refuse.

Her husband was away at the time. When he returned a few days later he picked up the animal to pet it, and noticed that its collar was missing. His wife told him that the dog had lost it in the undergrowth of the park, and that she and her maids had hunted a whole day for it. It was true, she explained to the court, that she had made the maids search for the necklet—they all believed the dog had lost it in the park. . . .

Her husband made no comment, and that evening at supper he was in his usual mood, between good and bad: you could never tell which. He talked a good deal, describing what he had seen and done at Rennes; but now and then he stopped and looked hard at her, and when she went to bed she found her little dog strangled on her pillow. The little thing was dead, but still warm; she stooped to lift it, and her distress turned to horror when she discovered that it had been strangled by twisting twice round its throat the necklet she had given to Lanrivain.

The next morning at dawn she buried the dog in the garden, and hid the necklet in her breast. She said nothing to her husband, then or later, and he said nothing to her; but that day he had a peasant hanged for stealing a faggot in the park, and the next day he nearly beat to death a young horse he was breaking.

Winter set in, and the short days passed, and the long nights, one by one; and she heard nothing of Hervé de Lanrivain. It might be that her husband had killed him; or merely that he had been robbed of the necklet. Day after day by the hearth among the spinning maids, night after night alone on her bed, she wondered and trembled. Sometimes at table her husband looked across at her and smiled; and then she felt sure that Lanrivain was dead. She dared not try to get news of him, for she was sure her husband would find out if she did: she had an idea that he could find out anything. Even when a witch woman who was a noted seer, and could show you the whole world in her crystal, came to the castle for a night's shelter, and the maids flocked to her, Anne held back.

The winter was long and black and rainy. One day, in Yves de Cornault's absence, some gypsies came to Kerfol with a troop of performing dogs. Anne bought the smallest and cleverest, a white dog with a feathery coat and one blue and one brown eye. It seemed to have been ill-treated by the gypsies, and clung to her plaintively when she took it from them. That evening her husband came back, and when she went to bed she found the dog strangled on her pillow.

After that she said to herself that she would never have another dog; but one bitter cold evening a poor lean greyhound was found whining at the castle-gate, and she took him in and forbade the maids to speak of him to her husband. She hid him in a room that no one went to, smuggled food to him from her own plate, made him a warm bed to lie on and petted him like a child.

Yves de Cornault came home, and the next day she found the greyhound strangled on her pillow. She wept in secret, but said nothing, and resolved that even if she met a dog dying of hunger she would never bring him into the castle; but one day she found a young sheepdog, a brindled puppy with good blue eyes, lying with a broken leg in the snow of the park. Yves de Cornault was at Rennes, and she brought the dog in, warmed and fed it, tied up its leg and hid it in the castle till her husband's return. The day before, she gave it to a peasant woman who lived a long way off, and paid her handsomely to care for it and say nothing; but that night she heard a whining and scratching at her door, and when she opened it the lame puppy, drenched and shivering, jumped up on her with little sobbing barks. She hid him in her bed, and the next morning was about to have him taken back to the peasant woman when she heard her husband ride into the court. She shut the dog in a chest, and went down to receive him. An hour or two later, when she returned to her room, the puppy lay strangled on her pillow. . . .

After that she dared not make a pet of any other dog; and her loneliness became almost unendurable. Sometimes, when she crossed the court of the castle, and thought no one was looking, she stopped to pat the old pointer at the gate. But one day as she was caressing him her husband came out of the chapel; and the next day the old dog was gone. . . .

This curious narrative was not told in one sitting of the court, or received without impatience and incredulous comment. It was plain that the Judges were surprised by its puerility, and that it did not help the accused in the eyes of the public. It was an odd tale, certainly; but what did it prove? That Yves de Cornault disliked dogs, and that his wife, to gratify her own fancy, persistently ignored this dislike. As for pleading this trivial disagreement as an excuse for her relations—whatever their nature—with her supposed accomplice, the argument was so absurd that her own lawyer manifestly regretted having let her make use of it, and tried several times to cut short her story. But she went on to the end, with a kind of hypnotized insistence, as though the scenes she evoked were so real to her that she had forgotten where she was and imagined herself to be reliving them.

At length the Judge who had previously shown a certain kindness to her said (leaning forward a little, one may suppose, from his row of dozing colleagues): "Then you would have us believe that you murdered your husband because he would not let you keep a pet dog?"

"I did not murder my husband."

"Who did, then? Hervé de Lanrivain?"

"No."

"Who then? Can you tell us?"

"Yes, I can tell you. The dogs—" At that point she was carried out of the court in a swoon.

It was evident that her lawyer tried to get her to abandon this line of defense. Possibly her explanation, whatever it was, had seemed convincing when she poured it out to him in the heat of their first private colloquy; but now that it was exposed to the cold daylight of judicial scrutiny, and the banter of the town, he was thoroughly ashamed of it, and would have sacrificed her without a scruple to save his professional reputation. But the obstinate Judge—who perhaps, after all, was more inquisitive than kindly—evidently wanted to hear the story out, and she was ordered, the next day, to continue her deposition.

She said that after the disappearance of the old watchdog nothing particular happened for a month or two. Her husband was much as usual: she did not remember any special incident. But one evening a pedlar woman came to the castle and was selling trinkets to the maids. She had no heart for trinkets, but she stood looking on while the women made their choice. And then, she did not know how, but the pedlar coaxed her into buying for herself a pear-shaped pomander with a strong scent in it—she had once seen something of the kind on a gypsy woman. She had no desire for the pomander, and did not know why she had bought it. The pedlar said that whoever wore it had the power to read the future; but she did not really believe that, or care much either. However, she bought the thing and took it up to her room, where she sat turning it about in her hand. Then the strange scent attracted her and she began to wonder what kind of spice was in the box. She opened it and found a grey bean rolled in a strip of paper; and on the paper she saw a sign she knew, and a message from Hervé de Lanrivain, saying that he was at home again and would be at the door in the court that night after the moon had set. . . .

She burned the paper and sat down to think. It was nightfall, and her husband was at home. . . . She had no way of warning Lanrivain, and there was nothing to do but to wait. . . .

At this point I fancy the drowsy court-room beginning to wake up. Even to the oldest hand on the bench there must have been a certain relish in picturing the feelings of a woman on receiving such a message at nightfall from a man living twenty miles away, to whom she had no means of sending a warning. . . .

She was not a clever woman, I imagine; and as the first result of her cogitation she appears to have made the mistake of being, that evening, too kind to her husband. She could not ply him with wine, according to the traditional expedient, for though he drank heavily at times he had a strong head; and when he drank beyond its strength it was because he chose to, and not because a woman coaxed him. Not his wife, at any rate— she was an old story by now. As I read the case, I fancy there was no feeling for her left in him but the hatred occasioned by his supposed dishonor.

At any rate, she tried to call up her old graces; but early in the evening he complained of pains and fever, and left the hall to go up to the closet where he sometimes slept. His servant carried him a cup of hot wine, and brought back word that he was sleeping and not to be disturbed; and an hour later, when Anne lifted the tapestry and listened at his door, she heard his loud regular breathing. She thought it might be a feint, and stayed a long time barefooted in the passage, her ear to the crack; but the breathing went on too steadily and naturally to be other than that of a man in a sound sleep. She crept back to her room reassured, and stood in the window watching the moon set through the trees of the park. The sky was misty and starless, and after the moon went down the night was black as pitch. She knew the time had come, and stole along the passage, past her husband's door—where she stopped again to listen to his breathing—to the top of the stairs. There she paused a moment, and assured herself that no one was following her; then she began to go down the stairs in the darkness. They were so steep and winding that she had to go very slowly, for fear of stumbling. Her one thought was to get the door unbolted, tell Lanrivain to make his escape, and hasten back to her room. She had tried the bolt earlier in the evening, and managed to put a little grease on it; but nevertheless, when she drew it, it gave a squeak. . . not loud, but it made her heart stop; and the next minute, overhead, she heard a noise. . . .

"What noise?" the prosecution interposed.

"My husband's voice calling out my name and cursing me."

"What did you hear after that?"

"A terrible scream and a fall."

"Where was Hervé de Lanrivain at this time?"

"He was standing outside in the court. I just made him out in the darkness. I told him for God's sake to go, and then I pushed the door shut."

"What did you do next?"

"I stood at the foot of the stairs and listened."

"What did you hear?"

"I heard dogs snarling and panting." (Visible discouragement of the bench, boredom of the public, and exasperation of the lawyer for the defense. Dogs again—! But the inquisitive Judge insisted.)

"What dogs?"

She bent her head and spoke so low that she had to be told to repeat her answer: "I don't know."

"How do you mean—you don't know?"

"I don't know what dogs. . . ."

The Judge again intervened: "Try to tell us exactly what happened. How long did you remain at the foot of the stairs?"

"Only a few minutes."

"And what was going on meanwhile overhead?"

"The dogs kept on snarling and panting. Once or twice he cried out. I think he moaned once. Then he was quiet."

"Then what happened?"

"Then I heard a sound like the noise of a pack when the wolf is thrown to them— gulping and lapping."

(There was a groan of disgust and repulsion through the court, and another attempted intervention by the distracted lawyer. But the inquisitive Judge was still inquisitive.)

"And all the while you did not go up?"

"Yes—I went up then—to drive them off."

"The dogs?"

"Yes."

"Well—?"

"When I got there it was quite dark. I found my husband's flint and steel and struck a spark. I saw him lying there. He was dead."

"And the dogs?"

"The dogs were gone."

"Gone—where to?"

"I don't know. There was no way out—and there were no dogs at Kerfol."

She straightened herself to her full height, threw her arms above her head, and fell down on the stone floor with a long scream. There was a moment of confusion in the court-room. Someone on the bench was heard to say: "This is clearly a case for the ecclesiastical authorities"—and the prisoner's lawyer doubtless jumped at the suggestion.

After this, the trial loses itself in a maze of cross-questioning and squabbling. Every witness who was called corroborated Anne de Cornault's statement that there were no dogs at Kerfol: had been none for several months. The master of the house had taken a dislike to dogs, there was no denying it But, on the other hand, at the inquest, there had been long and bitter discussions as to the nature of the dead man's wounds. One of the surgeons called in had spoken of marks that looked like bites. The suggestion of witchcraft was revived, and the opposing lawyers hurled tomes of necromancy at each other.

At last Anne de Cornault was brought back into court—at the instance of the same Judge—and asked if she knew where the dogs she spoke of could have come from. On the body of her Redeemer she swore that she did not. Then the Judge put his final question: "If the dogs you think you heard had been known to you, do you think you would have recognized them by their barking?"

"Yes."

"Did you recognize them?"

"Yes."

"What dogs do you take them to have been?"

"My dead dogs," she said in a whisper. . . . She was taken out of court, not to reappear there again. There was some kind of ecclesiastical investigation, and the end of the business was that the Judges disagreed with each other, and with the ecclesiastical committee, and that

Anne de Cornault was finally handed over to the keeping of her husband's family, who shut her up in the keep of Kerfol, where she is said to have died many years later, a harmless madwoman.

So ends her story. As for that of Hervé de Lanrivain, I had only to apply to his collateral descendant for its subsequent details. The evidence against the young man being insufficient, and his family influence in the duchy considerable, he was set free, and left soon afterward for Paris. He was probably in no mood for a worldly life, and he appears to have come almost immediately under the influence of the famous M. Arnauld d'Andilly and the gentlemen of Port Royal. A year or two later he was received into their Order, and without achieving any particular distinction he followed its good and evil fortunes till his death some twenty years later. Lanrivain showed me a portrait of him by a pupil of Philippe de Champaigne: sad eyes, an impulsive mouth and a narrow brow. Poor Hervé de Lanrivain: it was a grey ending. Yet as I looked at his stiff and sallow effigy, in the dark dress of the Jansenists, I almost found myself envying his fate. After all, in the course of his life two great things had happened to him: he had loved romantically, and he must have talked with Pascal. . . .

THE LONG RUN

*The shade of those our days that had no tongue.*

IT WAS LAST WINTER, after a twelve years' absence from New York, that I saw again, at one of the Jim Cumnors' dinners, my old friend Halston Merrick.

The Cumnors' house is one of the few where, even after such a lapse of time, one can be sure of finding familiar faces and picking up old threads; where for a moment one can abandon one's self to the illusion that New York humanity is a shade less unstable than its bricks and mortar. And that evening in particular I remember feeling that there could be no pleasanter way of re-entering the confused and careless world to which I was returning than through the quiet softly-lit dining room in which Mrs. Cumnor, with a characteristic sense of my needing to be broken in gradually, had contrived to assemble so many friendly faces.

I was glad to see them all, including the three or four I did not know, or failed to recognize, but had no difficulty in passing as in the tradition and of the group; but I was most of all glad—as I rather wonderingly found—to set eyes again on Halston Merrick.

He and I had been at Harvard together, for one thing, and had shared there curiosities and ardors a little outside the current tendencies: had, on the whole, been more critical than our comrades, and less amenable to the accepted. Then, for the next following years, Merrick had been a vivid and promising figure in young American life. Handsome, careless, and free, he had wandered and tasted and compared. After leaving Harvard he had spent two years at Oxford; then he had accepted a private secretaryship to our Ambassador in England, and had come back from this adventure with a fresh curiosity about public affairs at home, and the conviction that men of his kind should play a larger part in them. This led, first, to his running for a State Senatorship which he failed to get, and ultimately to a few months of intelligent activity in a municipal office. Soon after being deprived of this post by a change of party he had published a small volume of delicate verse, and, a year later, an odd uneven brilliant book on Municipal Government. After that one hardly knew where to look for his next appearance; but chance rather disappointingly solved the problem by killing off his father and placing Halston at the head of the Merrick Iron Foundry at Yonkers.

His friends had gathered that, whenever this regrettable contingency should occur, he meant to dispose of the business and continue his life of free experiment. As often happens in just such cases, however, it was not the moment for a sale, and Merrick had to take over the management of the foundry. Some two years later he had a chance to free himself; but when it came he did not choose to take it. This tame sequel to an inspiriting start was disappointing to some of us, and I was among those disposed to regret Merrick's drop to the level of the prosperous. Then I went away to a big engineering job in China, and from there to Africa, and spent the next twelve years out of sight and sound of New York doings.

During that long interval I heard of no new phase in Merrick's evolution, but this did not surprise me, as I had never expected from him actions resonant enough to cross the globe. All I knew—and this did surprise me—was that he had not married, and that he was still in the iron business. All through those years, however, I never ceased to wish, in certain situations and at certain turns of thought, that Merrick were in reach, that I could tell this or that to Merrick. I had never, in the interval, found any one with just his quickness of perception and just his sureness of response.

After dinner, therefore, we irresistibly drew together. In Mrs. Cumnor's big easy drawing-room cigars were allowed, and there was no break in the communion of the sexes; and, this being the case, I ought to have sought a seat beside one of the ladies among whom we were allowed to remain. But, as had generally happened of old when Merrick was in sight, I found myself steering straight for him past all minor ports of call.

There had been no time, before dinner, for more than the barest expression of satisfaction at meeting, and our seats had been at opposite ends of the longish table, so that we got our first real look at each other in the secluded corner to which Mrs. Cumnor's vigilance now directed us.

Merrick was still handsome in his stooping tawny way: handsomer perhaps, with thinnish hair and more lines in his face, than in the young excess of his good looks. He was very glad to see me and conveyed his gladness by the same charming smile; but as soon as we began to talk I felt a change. It was not merely the change that years and experience and altered values bring. There was something more fundamental the matter with Merrick, something dreadful, unforeseen, unaccountable: Merrick had grown conventional and dull.

In the glow of his frank pleasure in seeing me I was ashamed to analyze the nature of the change; but presently our talk began to flag—fancy a talk with Merrick flagging!—

and self-deception became impossible as I watched myself handing out platitudes with the gesture of the salesman offering something to a purchaser "equally good." The worst of it was that Merrick—Merrick, who had once felt everything!—didn't seem to feel the lack of spontaneity in my remarks, but hung on' them with a harrowing faith in the resuscitating power of our past. It was as if he hugged the empty vessel of our friendship without perceiving that the last drop of its essence was dry.

But after all, I am exaggerating. Through my surprise and disappointment I felt a certain sense of well-being in the mere physical presence of my old friend. I liked looking at the way his dark hair waved away from the forehead, at the tautness of his dry brown cheek, the thoughtful backward tilt of his head, the way his brown eyes mused upon the scene through lowered lids. All the past was in his way of looking and sitting, and I wanted to stay near him, and felt that he wanted me to stay; but the devil of it was that neither of us knew what to talk about.

It was this difficulty which caused me, after a while, since I could not follow Merrick's talk, to follow his eyes in their roaming circuit of the room.

At the moment when our glances joined, his had paused on a lady seated at some distance from our corner. Immersed, at first, in the satisfaction of finding myself again with Merrick, I had been only half aware of this lady, as of one of the few persons present whom I did not know, or had failed to remember. There was nothing in her appearance to challenge my attention or to excite my curiosity, and I don't suppose I should have looked at her again if I had not noticed that my friend was doing so.

She was a woman of about forty-seven, with fair faded hair and a young figure. Her gray dress was handsome but ineffective, and her pale and rather serious face wore a small unvarying smile which might have been pinned on with her ornaments. She was one of the women in whom increasing years show rather what they have taken than what they have bestowed, and only on looking closely did one see that what they had taken must have been good of its kind.

Phil Cumnor and another man were talking to her, and the very intensity of the attention she bestowed on them betrayed the straining of rebellious thoughts. She never let her eyes stray or her smile drop; and at the proper moment I saw she was ready with the proper sentiment.

The party, like most of those that Mrs. Cumnor gathered about her, was not composed of exceptional beings. The people of the old vanished New York set were not exceptional: they were mostly cut on the same convenient and unobtrusive pattern; but they were often exceedingly "nice." And this obsolete quality marked every look and gesture of the lady I was scrutinizing.

While these reflections were passing through my mind I was aware that Merrick's eyes rested still on her. I took a cross-section of his look and found in it neither surprise nor absorption, but only a certain sober pleasure just about at the emotional level of the rest of the room. If he continued to look at her, his expression seemed to say, it was only because, all things considered, there were fewer reasons for looking at anybody else.

This made me wonder what were the reasons for looking at *her;* and as a first step toward enlightenment I said:—"I'm sure I've seen the lady over there in gray—"

Merrick detached his eyes and turned them on me with a wondering look.

"Seen her? You know her." He waited. *"Don't* you know her? It's Mrs. Reardon."

I wondered that he should wonder, for I could not remember, in the Cumnor group or elsewhere, having known any one of the name he mentioned.

"But perhaps," he continued, "you hadn't heard of her marriage? You knew her as

Mrs. Trant."

I gave him back his stare. "Not Mrs. Philip Trant?"

"Yes; Mrs. Philip Trant."

"Not Paulina?"

"Yes—Paulina," he said, with a just perceptible delay before the name.

In my surprise I continued to stare at him. He averted his eyes from mine after a moment, and I saw that they had strayed back to her. "You find her so changed?" he asked.

Something in his voice acted as a warning signal, and I tried to reduce my astonishment to less unbecoming proportions. "I don't find that she looks much older."

"No. Only different?" he suggested, as if there were nothing new to him in my perplexity.

"Yes—awfully different."

"I suppose we're all awfully different. To you, I mean—coming from so far?"

"I recognized all the rest of you," I said, hesitating. "And she used to be the one who stood out most."

There was a flash, a wave, a stir of something deep down in his eyes. "Yes," he said. *"That's* the difference."

"I see it is. She—she looks worn down. Soft but blurred, like the figures in that tapestry behind her."

He glanced at her again, as if to test the exactness of my analogy.

"Life wears everybody down," he said.

"Yes—except those it makes more distinct. They're the rare ones, of course; but she *was* rare."

He stood up suddenly, looking old and tired. "I believe I'll be off. I wish you'd come down to my place for Sunday. . . . No, don't shake hands—I want to slide away unawares."

He had backed away to the threshold and was turning the noiseless door-knob. Even Mrs. Cumnor's doorknobs had tact and didn't tell.

"Of course I'll come," I promised warmly. In the last ten minutes he had begun to interest me again.

"All right Good-bye." Half through the door he paused to add: *"She* remembers you. You ought to speak to her."

"I'm going to. But tell me a little more." I thought I saw a shade of constraint on his face, and did not add, as I had meant to: "Tell me—because she interests me—what wore her down?" Instead, I asked: "How soon after Trant's death did she remarry?"

He seemed to make an effort of memory. "It was seven years ago, I think."

"And is Reardon here to-night?"

"Yes; over there, talking to Mrs. Cumnor."

I looked across the broken groupings and saw a large glossy man with straw-colored hair and a red face, whose shirt and shoes and complexion seemed all to have received a coat of the same expensive varnish.

As I looked there was a drop in the talk about us, and I heard Mr. Reardon pronounce in a big booming voice: "What I say is: what's the good of disturbing things? Thank the Lord, I'm content with what I've got!"

"Is *that* her husband? What's he like?"

"Oh, the best fellow in the world," said Merrick, going.

## II

MERRICK had a little place at Riverdale, where he went occasionally to be near the Iron Works, and where he hid his week-ends when the world was too much with him.

Here, on the following Saturday afternoon I found him awaiting me in a pleasant setting of books and prints and faded parental furniture.

We dined late, and smoked and talked afterward in his book-walled study till the terrier on the hearth-rug stood up and yawned for bed. When we took the hint and moved toward the staircase I felt, not that I had found the old Merrick again, but that I was on his track, had come across traces of his passage here and there in the thick jungle that had grown up between us. But I had a feeling that when I finally came on the man himself he might be dead. . . .

As we started upstairs he turned back with one of his abrupt shy movements, and walked into the study.

"Wait a bit!" he called to me.

I waited, and he came out in a moment carrying a limp folio.

"It's typewritten. Will you take a look at it? I've been trying to get to work again," he explained, thrusting the manuscript into my hand.

"What? Poetry, I hope?" I exclaimed.

He shook his head with a gleam of derision. "No—just general considerations. The fruit of fifty years of inexperience."

He showed me to my room and said good night.

The following afternoon we took a long walk inland, across the hills, and I said to Merrick what I could of his book. Unluckily there wasn't much to say. The essays were judicious, polished and cultivated; but they lacked the freshness and audacity of his youthful work. I tried to conceal my opinion behind the usual generalizations, but he broke through these feints with a quick thrust to the heart of my meaning.

"It's worn down—blurred? Like the figures in the Cumnors' tapestry?"

I hesitated. "It's a little too damned resigned," I said.

"Ah," he exclaimed, "so am I. Resigned." He switched the bare brambles by the roadside. "A man can't serve two masters."

"You mean business and literature?"

"No; I mean theory and instinct. The gray tree and the green. You've got to choose which fruit you'll try; and you don't know till afterward which of the two has the dead core."

"How can anybody be sure that only one of them has?"

"I'm sure," said Merrick sharply.

We turned back to the subject of his essays, and I was astonished at the detachment with which he criticized and demolished them. Little by little, as we talked, his old perspective, his old standards came back to him; but with the difference that they no longer seemed like functions of his mind but merely like attitudes assumed or dropped at will. He could still, with an effort, put himself at the angle from which he had formerly seen things; but it was with the effort of a man climbing mountains after a sedentary life in the plain.

I tried to cut the talk short, but he kept coming back to it with nervous insistence, forcing me into the last retrenchments of hypocrisy, and anticipating the verdict I held back. I perceived that a great deal—immensely more than I could see a reason for—had hung for him on my opinion of his book.

Then, as suddenly, his insistence dropped and, as if ashamed of having forced, himself so long on my attention, he began to talk rapidly and uninterestingly of other things.

We were alone again that evening, and after dinner, wishing to efface the impression of the afternoon, and above all to show that I wanted him to talk about himself, I reverted to his work. "You must need an outlet of that sort. When a man's once had it in him, as you have—and when other things begin to dwindle—"

He laughed. "Your theory is that a man ought to be able to return to the Muse as he comes back to his wife after he's ceased to interest other women?"

"No; as he comes back to his wife after the day's work is done." A new thought came to me as I looked at him. "You ought to have had one," I added.

He laughed again. "A wife, you mean? So that there'd have been someone waiting for me even if the Muse decamped?" He went on after a pause: "I've a notion that the kind of woman worth coming back to wouldn't be much more patient than the Muse. But as it happens I never tried—because, for fear they'd chuck me, I put them both out of doors together."

He turned his head and looked past me with a queer expression at the low paneled door at my back. "Out of that very door they went—the two of 'em, on a rainy night like this: and one stopped and looked back, to see if I wasn't going to call her—and I didn't—and so they both went."

III

"THE Muse?" (said Merrick, refilling my glass and stooping to pat the terrier as he went back to his chair)—"well, you've met the Muse in the little volume of sonnets you used to like; and you've met the woman too, and you used to like *her;* though you didn't know her when you saw her the other evening. . . .

"No, I won't ask you how she struck you when you talked to her: I know. She struck you like that stuff I gave you to read last night She's conformed—I've conformed—the mills have caught us and ground us: ground us, oh, exceedingly small!

"But you remember what she was; and that's the reason why I'm telling you this now. . . .

"You may recall that after my father's death I tried to sell the Works. I was impatient to free myself from anything that would keep me tied to New York. I don't dislike my trade, and I've made, in the end, a fairly good thing of it; but industrialism was not, at that time, in the line of my tastes, and I know now that it wasn't what I was meant for. Above all, I wanted to get away, to see new places and rub up against different ideas. I had reached a time of life—the top of the first hill, so to speak—where the distance draws one, and everything in the foreground seems tame and stale. I was sick to death of the particular set of conformities I had grown up among; sick of being a pleasant popular young man with a long line of dinners on my list, and the dead certainty of meeting the same people, or their prototypes, at all of them.

"Well—I failed to sell the Works, and that increased my discontent. I went through moods of cold unsociability, alternating with sudden flushes of curiosity, when I gloated over stray scraps of talk overheard in railway stations and omnibuses, when strange faces that I passed in the street tantalized me with fugitive promises. I wanted to be among things that were unexpected and unknown; and it seemed to me that nobody about me understood in the least what I felt, but that somewhere just out of reach there was someone who *did*, and whom I must find or despair. . . .

"It was just then that, one evening, I saw Mrs. Trant for the first time.

"Yes: I know—you wonder what I mean. I'd known her, of course, as a girl; I'd met her several times after her marriage; and I'd lately been thrown with her, quite intimately and continuously, during a succession of country-house visits. But I had never, as it happened, really *seen* her. . . .

"It was at a dinner at the Cumnors'; and there she was, in front of the very tapestry we saw her against the other evening, with people about her, and her face turned from me, and nothing noticeable or different in her dress or manner; and suddenly she stood out for me against the familiar unimportant background, and for the first time I saw a meaning in the stale phrase of a picture's walking out of its frame. For, after all, most people *are* just that to us: pictures, furniture, the inanimate accessories of our little island-area of sensation. And then sometimes one of these graven images moves and throws out live filaments toward us, and the line they make draws us across the world as the moon-track seems to draw a boat across the water. . . .

"There she stood; and as this queer sensation came over me I felt that she was looking steadily at me, that her eyes were voluntarily, consciously resting on me with the weight of the very question I was asking.

"I went over and joined her, and she turned and walked with me into the music-room. Earlier in the evening someone had been singing, and there were low lights there, and a few couples still sitting in those confidential corners of which Mrs. Cumnor has the art; but we were under no illusion as to the nature of these presences. We knew that they were just painted in, and that the whole of life was in us two, flowing back and forward between us. We talked, of course; we had the attitudes, even the words, of the others: I remember her telling me her plans for the spring and asking me politely about mine! As if there were the least sense in plans, now that this thing had happened!

"When we went back into the drawing-room I had said nothing to her that I might not have said to any other woman of the party; but when we shook hands I knew we should meet the next day—and the next. . . .

"That's the way, I take it, that Nature has arranged the beginning of the great enduring loves; and likewise of the little epidermal flurries. And how is a man to know where he is going?

"From the first my feeling for Paulina Trant seemed to me a grave business; but then the Enemy is given to producing that illusion. Many a man—I'm talking of the kind with imagination—has thought he was seeking a soul when all he wanted was a closer view of its tenement. And I tried—honestly tried—to make myself think I was in the latter case. Because, in the first place, I didn't, just then, want a big disturbing influence in my life; and because I didn't want to be a dupe; and because Paulina Trant was not, according to hearsay, the kind of woman for whom it was worth-while to bring up the big batteries. . . .

"But my resistance was only half-hearted. What I really felt—*all* I really felt—was the flood of joy that comes of heightened emotion. She had given me that, and I wanted her to give it to me again. That's as near as I've ever come to analyzing my state in the beginning.

"I knew her story, as no doubt you know it: the current version, I mean. She had been poor and fond of enjoyment, and she had married that pompous stick Philip Trant because she needed a home, and perhaps also because she wanted a little luxury. Queer how we sneer at women for wanting the thing that gives them half their attraction!

"People shook their heads over the marriage, and divided, prematurely, into Philip's partisans and hers: for no one thought it would work. And they were almost disappointed when, after all, it did. She and her wooden consort seemed to get on well enough. There was a ripple, at one time, over her friendship with young Jim Dalham, who was always with her during a summer at Newport and an autumn in Italy; then the talk died out, and she and Trant were seen together, as before, on terms of apparent good fellowship.

"This was the more surprising because, from the first, Paulina had never made the least attempt to change her tone or subdue her colours. In the gray Trant atmosphere she flashed with prismatic fires. She smoked, she talked subversively, she did as she liked and went where she chose, and danced over the Trant prejudices and the Trant principles as if they'd been a ball-room floor; and all without apparent offence to her solemn husband and his cloud of cousins. I believe her frankness and directness struck them dumb. She moved like a kind of primitive Una through the virtuous rout, and never got a finger-mark on her freshness.

"One of the finest things about her was the fact that she never, for an instant, used her situation as a means of enhancing her attraction. With a husband like Trant it would have been so easy! He was a man who always saw the small sides of big things. He thought most of life compressible into a set of by-laws and the rest unmentionable; and with his stiff frock-coated and tall-hatted mind, instinctively distrustful of intelligences in another dress, with his arbitrary classification of whatever he didn't understand into 'the kind of thing I don't approve of,' 'the kind of thing that isn't done,' and—deepest depth of all—'the kind of thing I'd rather not discuss,' he lived in bondage to a shadowy moral etiquette of which the complex rites and awful penalties had cast an abiding gloom upon his manner.

"A woman like his wife couldn't have asked a better foil; yet I'm sure she never consciously used his dullness to relieve her brilliancy. She may have felt that the case spoke for itself. But I believe her reserve was rather due to a lively sense of justice, and to the rare habit (you said she was rare) of looking at facts as they are, without any throwing of sentimental lime-lights. She knew Trant could no more help being Trant than she could help being herself—and there was an end of it. I've never known a woman who 'made up' so little mentally. . . .

"Perhaps her very reserve, the fierceness of her implicit rejection of sympathy, exposed her the more to—well, to what happened when we met. She said afterward that it was like having been shut up for months in the hold of a ship, and coming suddenly on deck on a day that was all flying blue and silver. . . .

"I won't try to tell you what she was. It's easier to tell you what her friendship made of me; and I can do that best by adopting her metaphor of the ship. Haven't you, sometimes, at the moment of starting on a journey, some glorious plunge into the unknown, been tripped up by the thought: 'If only one hadn't to come back'? Well, with her one had the sense that one would never have to come back; that the magic ship, would always carry one farther. And what an air one breathed on it! And, oh, the wind, and the islands, and the sunsets!

"I said just now 'her friendship'; and I used the word advisedly. Love is deeper than friendship, but friendship is a good deal wider. The beauty of our relation was that it included both dimensions. Our thoughts met as naturally as our eyes: it was almost as if we loved each other because we liked each other. The quality of a love may be tested by the amount of friendship it contains, and in our case there was no dividing line between loving and liking, no disproportion between them, no barrier against which desire beat in vain or from which thought fell back unsatisfied. Ours was a robust passion that could give an open-eyed account of itself, and not a beautiful madness shrinking away from the proof. . . .

"For the first months friendship sufficed us, or rather gave us so much by the way that we were in no hurry to reach what we knew it was leading to. But we were moving there nevertheless, and one day we found ourselves on the borders. It came about through a sudden decision of Trant's to start on a long tour with his wife. We had never foreseen that: he seemed rooted in his New York habits and convinced that the whole social and financial machinery of the metropolis would cease to function if he did not keep an eye on it through the columns of his morning paper, and pronounce judgment on it in the afternoon at his club. But something new had happened to him: he caught a cold, which was followed by a touch of pleurisy, and instantly he perceived the intense interest and importance which ill-health may add to life. He took the fullest advantage of it. A discerning doctor recommended travel in a warm climate; and suddenly, the morning paper, the afternoon club, Fifth Avenue, Wall Street, all the complex phenomena of the metropolis, faded into insignificance, and the rest of the terrestrial globe, from being a mere geographical hypothesis, useful in enabling one to determine the latitude of New York, acquired reality and magnitude as a factor in the convalescence of Mr. Philip Trant.

"His wife was absorbed in preparations for the journey. To move him was like mobilizing an army, and weeks before the date set for their departure it was almost as if she were already gone.

"This foretaste of separation showed us what we were to each other. Yet I was letting her go—and there was no help for it, no way of preventing it. Resistance was as useless as the vain struggles in a nightmare. She was Trant's and not mine: part of his luggage when he travelled as she was part of his household furniture when he stayed at home. . . .

"The day she told me that their passages were taken—it was on a November afternoon, in her drawing-room in town—I turned away from her and, going to the window, stood looking out at the torrent of traffic interminably pouring down Fifth Avenue. I watched the senseless machinery of life revolving in the rain and mud, and tried to picture myself performing my small function in it after she had gone from me.

"'It can't be—it can't be!' I exclaimed.

"'What can't be?'

"I came back into the room and sat down by her. 'This—this—' I hadn't any words. 'Two weeks!' I said. 'What's two weeks?"

"She answered, vaguely, something about their thinking of Spain for the spring—

"'Two weeks—two weeks!' I repeated. 'And the months we've lost—the days that belonged to us!'

"'Yes,' she said, 'I'm thankful it's settled.'

"Our words seemed irrelevant, haphazard. It was as if each were answering a secret voice, and not what the other was saying.

"'Don't you *feel* anything at all?' I remember bursting out at her. As I asked it the tears were streaming down her face. I felt angry with her, and was almost glad to note that her lids were red and that she didn't cry becomingly. I can't express my sensation to you except by saying that she seemed part of life's huge league against me. And suddenly I thought of an afternoon we had spent together in the country, on a ferny hill-side, when we had sat under a beech-tree, and her hand had lain palm upward in the moss, close to mine, and I had watched a little black-and-red beetle creeping over it. . . .

"The bell rang, and we heard the voice of a visitor and the click of an umbrella in the umbrella-stand.

"She rose to go into the inner drawing-room, and I caught her suddenly by the wrist. 'You understand,' I said, 'that we can't go on like this?'

"'I understand,' she answered, and moved away to meet her visitor. As I went out I heard her saying in the other room: 'Yes, we're really off on the twelfth.'"

IV

"I WROTE her a long letter that night, and waited two days for a reply.

"On the third day I had a brief line saying that she was going to spend Sunday with some friends who had a place near Riverdale, and that she would arrange to see me while she was there. That was all.

"It was on a Saturday that I received the note and I came out here the same night. The next morning was rainy, and I was in despair, for I had counted on her asking me to take her for a drive or a long walk. It was hopeless to try to say what I had to say to her in the drawing-room of a crowded country-house. And only eleven days were left!

"I stayed indoors all the morning, fearing to go out lest she should telephone me. But no sign came, and I grew more and more restless and anxious. She was too free and frank for coquetry, but her silence and evasiveness made me feel that, for some reason, she did not wish to hear what she knew I meant to say. Could it be that she was, after all, more conventional, less genuine, than I had thought? I went again and again over the whole maddening round of conjecture; but the only conclusion I could rest in was that, if she loved me as I loved her, she would be as determined as I was to let no obstacle come between us during the days that were left.

"The luncheon hour came and passed, and there was no word from her. I had ordered my trap to be ready, so that I might drive over as soon as she summoned me; but the hours dragged on, the early twilight came, and I sat here in this very chair, or measured up and down, up and down, the length of this very rug—and still there was no message and no letter.

"It had grown quite dark, and I had ordered away, impatiently, the servant who came in with the lamps: I couldn't *bear* any definite sign that the day was over! And I was standing there on the rug, staring at the door, and noticing a bad crack in its panel, when I heard the sound of wheels on the gravel. A word at last, no doubt—a line to explain. . . . I didn't seem to care much for her reasons, and I stood where I was and continued to stare at the door. And suddenly it opened and she came in.

"The servant followed her with a light, and then went out and closed the door. Her face looked pale in the lamplight, but her voice was as clear as a bell.

"'Well,' she said, 'you see I've come.'

"I started toward her with hands outstretched. 'You've come—you've come!' I stammered.

"Yes; it was like her to come in that way—without dissimulation or explanation or excuse. It was like her, if she gave at all, to give not furtively or in haste, but openly, deliberately, without stinting the measure or counting the cost. But her quietness and serenity disconcerted me. She did not look like a woman who has yielded impetuously to an uncontrollable impulse. There was something almost solemn in her face.

"The effect of it stole over me as I looked at her, suddenly subduing the huge flush of gratified longing.

"'You're here, here, here!' I kept repeating, like a child singing over a happy word.

"'You said,' she continued, in her grave clear voice, 'that we couldn't go on as we were—'

"'Ah, it's divine of you!' I held out my arms to her.

"She didn't draw back from them, but her faint smile said, 'Wait,' and lifting her hands she took the pins from her hat, and laid the hat on the table.

"As I saw her dear head bare in the lamp-light, with the thick hair waving away from the parting, I forgot everything but the bliss and wonder of her being here—here, in my house, on my hearth—that fourth rose from the corner of the rug is the exact spot where she was standing. . . .

"I drew her to the fire, and made her sit down in the chair you're in, and knelt down by her, and hid my face on her knees. She put her hand on my head, and I was happy to the depths of my soul.

"'Oh, I forgot—' she exclaimed suddenly. I lifted my head and our eyes met. Hers were smiling.

"She reached out her hand, opened the little bag she had tossed down with her hat, and drew a small object from it. 'I left my trunk at the station. Here's the check. Can you send for it?' she asked.

"Her trunk—she wanted me to send for her trunk! Oh, yes—I see your smile, your 'lucky man!' Only, you see, I didn't love her in that way. I knew she couldn't come to my house without running a big risk of discovery, and my tenderness for her, my impulse to shield her, was stronger, even then, than vanity or desire. Judged from the point of view of those emotions I fell terribly short of my part. I hadn't any of the proper feelings. Such an act of romantic folly was so unlike her that it almost irritated me, and I found myself desperately wondering how I could get her to reconsider her plan without—well, without seeming to want her to.

"It's not the way a novel hero feels; it's probably not the way a man in real life ought to have felt. But it's the way I felt—and she saw it.

"She put her hands on my shoulders and looked at me with deep, deep eyes. 'Then you didn't expect me to stay?' she asked.

"I caught her hands and pressed them to me, stammering out that I hadn't dared to dream. . . .

"'You thought I'd come—just for an hour?'

"'How could I dare think more? I adore you, you know, for what you've done! But it would be known if you—if you stayed on. My servants—everybody about here knows you. I've no right to expose you to the risk.' She made no answer, and I went on tenderly: 'Give me, if you will, the next few hours: there's a train that will get you to town by midnight. And then we'll arrange something—in town—where it's safer for you—more easily managed. . . . It's beautiful, it's heavenly of you to have come; but I love you too much—I must take care of you and think for you—'

"I don't suppose it ever took me so long to say so few words, and though they were profoundly sincere they sounded unutterably shallow, irrelevant and grotesque. She made no effort to help me out, but sat silent, listening, with her meditative smile. 'It's my duty, dearest, as a man,' I rambled on. The more I love you the more I'm bound—'

"'Yes; but you don't understand,' she interrupted.

"She rose as she spoke, and I got up also, and we stood and looked at each other.

"'I haven't come for a night; if you want me I've come for always,' she said.

"Here again, if I give you an honest account of my feelings I shall write myself down as the poor-spirited creature I suppose I am. There wasn't, I swear, at the moment, a grain of selfishness, of personal reluctance, in my feeling. I worshipped every hair of her head—when we were together I was happy, when I was away from her something was gone from every good thing; but I had always looked on our love for each other, our possible relation to each other, as such situations are looked on in what is called society. I had supposed her, for all her freedom and originality, to be just as tacitly subservient to that view as I was: ready to take what she wanted on the terms on which society concedes such taking, and to pay for it by the usual restrictions, concealments and hypocrisies. In short, I supposed that she would 'play the game'—look out for her own safety, and expect me to look out for it. It sounds cheap enough, put that way—but it's the rule we live under, all of us. And the amazement of finding her suddenly outside of it, oblivious of it, unconscious of it, left me, for an awful minute, stammering at her like a graceless dolt. . . . Perhaps it wasn't even a minute; but in it she had gone the whole round of my thoughts.

"'It's raining,' she said, very low. 'I suppose you can telephone for a trap?'

"There was no irony or resentment in her voice. She walked slowly across the room and paused before the Brangwyn etching over there. 'That's a good impression. *Will* you telephone, please?' she repeated.

"I found my voice again, and with it the power of movement. I followed her and dropped at her feet. 'You can't go like this!' I cried.

"She looked down on me from heights and heights. 'I can't stay like this,' she answered.

"I stood up and we faced each other like antagonists. 'You don't know,' I accused her passionately, 'in the least what you're asking me to ask of you!'

"'Yes, I do: *everything,'* she breathed.

"'And it's got to be that or nothing?'

"'Oh, on both sides,' she reminded me.

"'*Not* on both sides. It's not fair. That's why—'

"'Why you won't?'

"'Why I cannot—may not!'

"'Why you'll take a night and not a life?'

"The taunt, for a woman usually so sure of her aim, fell so short of the mark that its only effect was to increase my conviction of her helplessness. The very intensity of my longing for her made me tremble where she was fearless. I had to protect her first, and think of my own attitude afterward.

"She was too discerning not to see this too. Her face softened, grew inexpressibly appealing, and she dropped again into that chair you're in, leaned forward, and looked up with her grave smile.

"'You think I'm beside myself—raving? (You're not thinking of yourself, I know.) I'm not: I never was saner. Since I've known you I've often thought this might happen. This thing between us isn't an ordinary thing. If it had been we shouldn't, all these months, have drifted. We should have wanted to skip to the last page—and then throw down the book. We shouldn't have felt we could *trust* the future as we did. We were in no hurry because we knew we shouldn't get tired; and when two people feel that about each other they must live together—or part. I don't see what else they can do. A little trip along the coast won't answer. It's the high seas—or else being tied up to Lethe wharf. And I'm for the high seas, my dear!'

"Think of sitting here—here, in this room, in this chair—and listening to that, and seeing the tight on her hair, and hearing the sound of her voice! I don't suppose there ever was a scene just like it. . . .

"She was astounding—inexhaustible; through all my anguish of resistance I found a kind of fierce joy in following her. It was lucidity at white heat: the last sublimation of passion. She might have been an angel arguing a point in the empyrean if she hadn't been, so completely, a woman pleading for her life. . . .

"Her life: that was the thing at stake! She couldn't do with less of it than she was capable of; and a woman's life is inextricably part of the man's she cares for.

"That was why, she argued, she couldn't accept the usual solution: couldn't enter into the only relation that society tolerates between people situated like ourselves. Yes: she knew all the arguments on *that* side: didn't I suppose she'd been over them and over them? She knew (for hadn't she often said it of others?) what is said of the woman who, by throwing in her lot with her lover's, binds him to a lifelong duty which has the irksomeness without the dignity of marriage. Oh, she could talk on that side with the best of them: only she asked me to consider the other—the side of the man and woman who love each other deeply and completely enough to want their lives enlarged, and not diminished, by their love. What, in such a case—she reasoned—must be the inevitable effect of concealing, denying, disowning, the central fact, the motive power of one's existence? She asked me to picture the course of such a love: first working as a fever in the blood, distorting and deflecting everything, making all other interests insipid, all other duties irksome, and then, as the acknowledged claims of life regained their hold, gradually dying—the poor starved passion!—for want of the wholesome necessary food of common living and doing, yet leaving life impoverished by the loss of all it might have been.

"'I'm not talking, dear—' I see her now, leaning toward me with shining eyes: 'I'm not talking of the people who haven't enough to fill their days, and to whom a little mystery, a little maneuvering, gives an illusion of importance that they can't afford to miss; I'm talking of you and me, with all our tastes and curiosities and activities; and I ask you what our love would become if we had to keep it apart from our lives, like a pretty useless animal that we went to peep at and feed with sweetmeats through its cage?'

"I won't, my dear fellow, go into the other side of our strange duel: the arguments I used were those that most men in my situation would have felt bound to use, and that most women in Paulina's accept instinctively, without even formulating them. The exceptionalness, the significance, of the case lay wholly in the fact that she had formulated them all and then rejected them. . . .

"There was one point I didn't, of course, touch on; and that was the popular conviction (which I confess I shared) that when a man and a woman agree to defy the world together the man really sacrifices much more than the woman. I was not even conscious of thinking of this at the time, though it may have lurked somewhere in the shadow of my scruples for her; but she dragged it out into the daylight and held me face to face with it.

"'Remember, I'm not attempting to lay down any general rule,' she insisted; 'I'm not theorizing about Man and Woman, I'm talking about you and me. How do I know what's best for the woman in the next house? Very likely she'll bolt when it would have been better for her to stay at home. And it's the same with the man: he'll probably do the wrong thing. It's generally the weak heads that commit follies, when it's the strong ones that ought to: and my point is that you and I are both strong enough to behave like fools if we want to. . . .

"'Take your own case first—because, in spite of the sentimentalists, it's the man who stands to lose most. You'll have to give up the Iron Works: which you don't much care about—because it won't be particularly agreeable for us to live in New York: which you don't care much about either. But you won't be sacrificing what is called "a career." You made up your mind long ago that your best chance of self-development, and consequently of general usefullness, lay in thinking rather than doing; and, when we first met, you were already planning to sell out your business, and travel and write. Well! Those ambitions are of a kind that won't be harmed by your dropping out of your social setting. On the contrary, such work as you want to do ought to gain by it, because you'll be brought nearer to life-as-it-is, in contrast to life-as-a-visiting-list. . . .'

"She threw back her head with a sudden laugh. 'And the joy of not having any more visits to make! I wonder if you've ever thought of *that?* Just at first, I mean; for society's getting so deplorably lax that, little by little, it will edge up to us—you'll see! I don't want to idealize the situation, dearest, and I won't conceal from you that in time we shall be called on. But, oh, the fun we shall have had in the interval! And then, for the first time we shall be able to dictate our own terms, one of which will be that no bores need apply. Think of being cured of all one's chronic bores! We shall feel as jolly as people do after a successful operation.'

"I don't know why this nonsense sticks in my mind when some of the graver things we said are less distinct. Perhaps it's because of a certain iridescent quality of feeling that made her gaiety seem like sunshine through a shower. . . .

"'You ask me to think of myself?' she went on. 'But the beauty of our being together will be that, for the first time, I shall dare to! Now I have to think of all the tedious trifles I can pack the days with, because I'm afraid—I'm afraid—to hear the voice of the real me, down below, in the windowless underground hole where I keep her. . . .

"'Remember again, please, it's not Woman, it's Paulina Trant, I'm talking of. The woman in the next house may have all sorts of reasons—honest reasons—for staying there. There may be someone there who needs her badly: for whom the light would go out if she went. Whereas to Philip I've been simply—well, what New York was before he decided to travel: the most important thing in life till he made up his mind to leave it; and now merely the starting-place of several lines of steamers. Oh, I didn't have to love you to know that! I only had to live with *him*. . . . If he lost his eye-glasses he'd think it was the fault of the eye-glasses; he'd really feel that the eyeglasses had been careless. And he'd be convinced that no others would suit him quite as well. But at the optician's he'd probably be told that he needed something a little different, and after that he'd feel that the old eye-glasses had never suited him at all, and that that was their fault too. . . .'

"At one moment—but I don't recall when—I remember she stood up with one of her quick movements, and came toward me, holding out her arms. 'Oh, my dear, I'm pleading for my life; do you suppose I shall ever want for arguments?' she cried. . . .

"After that, for a bit, nothing much remains with me except a sense of darkness and of conflict. The one spot of daylight in my whirling brain was the conviction that I couldn't—whatever happened—profit by the sudden impulse she had acted on, and allow her to take, in a moment of passion, a decision that was to shape her whole life. I couldn't so much as lift my little finger to keep her with me then, unless I were prepared to accept for her as well as for myself the full consequences of the future she had planned for us. . .

"Well—there's the point: I wasn't. I felt in her—poor fatuous idiot that I was!—that lack of objective imagination which had always seemed to me to account, at least in part, for many of the so-called heroic qualities in women. When their feelings are involved they simply can't look ahead. Her unfaltering logic notwithstanding, I felt this about Paulina as I listened. She had a specious air of knowing where she was going, but she didn't. She seemed the genius of logic and understanding, but the demon of illusion spoke through her lips. . . .

"I said just now that I hadn't, at the outset, given my own side of the case a thought. It would have been truer to say that I hadn't given it a *separate* thought. But I couldn't think of her without seeing myself as a factor—the chief factor—in her problem, and without recognizing that whatever the experiment made of me, that it must fatally, in the end, make of her. If I couldn't carry the thing through she must break down with me: we should have to throw our separate selves into the melting-pot of this mad adventure, and be 'one' in a terrible indissoluble completeness of which marriage is only an imperfect counterpart. . . .

"There could be no better proof of her extraordinary power over me, and of the way she had managed to clear the air of sentimental illusion, than the fact that I presently found myself putting this before her with a merciless precision of touch.

"'If we love each other enough to do a thing like this, we must love each other enough to see just what it is we're going to do.'

"So I invited her to the dissecting-table, and I see now the fearless eye with which she approached the cadaver. 'For that's what it is, you know,' she flashed out at me, at the end of my long demonstration. 'It's a dead body, like all the instances and examples and hypothetical cases that ever were! What do you expect to learn from *that?* The first great anatomist was the man who stuck his knife in a heart that was beating; and the only way to find out what doing a thing will be like is to do it!'

"She looked away from me suddenly, as if she were fixing her eyes on some vision on the outer rim of consciousness. 'No: there's one other way,' she exclaimed; 'and that is, *not* to do it! To abstain and refrain; and then see what we become, or what we don't become, in the long run, and to draw our inferences. That's the game that almost everybody about us is playing, I suppose; there's hardly one of the dull people one meets at dinner who hasn't had, just once, the chance of a berth on a ship that was off for the Happy Isles, and hasn't refused it for fear of sticking on a sandbank!

"'I'm doing my best, you know,' she continued, 'to see the sequel as you see it, as you believe it's your duty to me to see it. I know the instances you're thinking of: the listless couples wearing out their lives in shabby watering places, and hanging on the favour of hotel acquaintances; or the proud quarrelling wretches shut up alone in a fine house because they're too good for the only society they can get, and trying to cheat their boredom by squabbling with their tradesmen and spying on their servants. No doubt there are such cases; but I don't recognize either of us in those dismal figures. Why, to do it would be to admit that our life, yours and mine, is in the people about us and not in ourselves; that we're parasites and not self-sustaining creatures; and that the lives we're leading now are so brilliant, full and satisfying that what we should have to give up would surpass even the blessedness of being together!'

"At that stage, I confess, the solid ground of my resistance began to give way under me. It was not that my convictions were shaken, but that she had swept me into a world whose laws were different, where one could reach out in directions that the slave of gravity hasn't pictured. But at the same time my opposition hardened from reason into instinct. I knew it was her voice, and not her logic, that was unsettling me. I knew that if she'd written out her thesis and sent it me by post I should have made short work of it;

and again the part of me which I called by all the finest names: my chivalry, my unselfishness, my superior masculine experience, cried out with one voice: 'You can't let a woman use her graces to her own undoing—you can't, for her own sake, let her eyes convince you when her reasons don't!'

"And then, abruptly, and for the first time, a doubt entered me: a doubt of her perfect moral honesty. I don't know how else to describe my feeling that she wasn't playing fair, that in coming to my house, in throwing herself at my head (I called things by their names), she had perhaps not so much obeyed an irresistible impulse as deeply, deliberately reckoned on the dissolvent effect of her generosity, her rashness and her beauty. . . .

"From the moment that this mean doubt raised its head in me I was once more the creature of all the conventional scruples: I was repeating, before the looking-glass of my self-consciousness, all the stereotyped gestures of the 'man of honor.'. . . Oh, the sorry figure I must have cut! You'll understand my dropping the curtain on it as quickly as I can. . . .

"Yet I remember, as I made my point, being struck by its impressiveness. I was suffering and enjoying my own suffering. I told her that, whatever step we decided to take, I owed it to her to insist on its being taken soberly, deliberately—

"('No: it's "advisedly," isn't it? Oh, I was thinking of the Marriage Service,' she interposed with a faint laugh.)

"—That if I accepted, there, on the spot, her headlong beautiful gift of herself, I should feel I had taken an unfair advantage of her, an advantage which she would be justified in reproaching me with afterward; that I was not afraid to tell her this because she was intelligent enough to know that my scruples were the surest proof of the quality of my love; that I refused to owe my happiness to an unconsidered impulse; that we must see each other again, in her own house, in less agitating circumstances, when she had had time to reflect on my words, to study her heart and look into the future. . . .

"The factitious exhilaration produced by uttering these beautiful sentiments did not last very long, as you may imagine. It fell, little by little, under her quiet gaze, a gaze in which there was neither contempt nor irony nor wounded pride, but only a tender wistfullness of interrogation; and I think the acutest point in my suffering was reached when she said, as I ended: 'Oh; yes, of course I understand.'

"'If only you hadn't come to me here!' I blurted out in the torture of my soul.

"She was on the threshold when I said it, and she turned and laid her hand gently on mine. 'There was no other way,' she said; and at the moment it seemed to me like some hackneyed phrase in a novel that she had used without any sense of its meaning.

"I don't remember what I answered or what more we either of us said. At the end a desperate longing to take her in my arms and keep her with me swept aside everything else, and I went up to her, pleading, stammering, urging I don't know what. . . . But she held me back with a quiet look, and went. I had ordered the carriage, as she asked me to; and my last definite recollection is of watching her drive off in the rain. . . .

"I had her promise that she would see me, two days later, at her house in town, and that we should then have what I called 'a decisive talk'; but I don't think that even at the moment I was the dupe of my phrase. I knew, and she knew, that the end had come. . . ."

## V

"IT was about that time (Merrick went on after a long pause) that I definitely decided not to sell the Works, but to stick to my job and conform my life to it.

"I can't describe to you the rage of conformity that possessed me. Poetry, ideas—all the picture-making processes stopped. A kind of dull self-discipline seemed to me the only exercise worthy of a reflecting mind. I *had* to justify my great refusal, and I tried to do it by plunging myself up to the eyes into the very conditions I had been instinctively struggling to get away from. The only possible consolation would have been to find in a life of business routine and social submission such moral compensations as may reward the citizen if they fail the man; but to attain to these I should have had to accept the old delusion that the social and the individual man are two. Now, on the contrary, I found soon enough that I couldn't get one part of my machinery to work effectively while another wanted feeding: and that in rejecting what had seemed to me a negation of action I had made all my action negative.

"The best solution, of course, would have been to fall in love with another woman; but it was long before I could bring myself to wish that this might happen to me. . . . Then, at length, I suddenly and violently desired it; and as such impulses are seldom without some kind of imperfect issue I contrived, a year or two later, to work myself up into the wished-for state. . . . She was a woman in society, and with all the awe of that institution that Paulina lacked. Our relation was consequently one of those unavowed affairs in which triviality is the only alternative to tragedy. Luckily we had, on both sides, risked only as much as prudent people stake in a drawing-room game; and when the match was over I take it that we came out fairly even.

"My gain, at all events, was of an unexpected kind. The adventure had served only to make me understand Paulina's abhorrence of such experiments, and at every turn of the slight intrigue I had felt how exasperating and belittling such a relation was bound to be between two people who, had they been free, would have mated openly. And so from a brief phase of imperfect forgetting I was driven back to a deeper and more understanding remembrance. . . .

"This second incarnation of Paulina was one of the strangest episodes of the whole strange experience. Things she had said during our extraordinary talk, things I had hardly heard at the time, came back to me with singular vividness and a fuller meaning. I hadn't any longer the cold consolation of believing in my own perspicacity: I saw that her insight had been deeper and keener than mine.

"I remember, in particular, starting up in bed one sleepless night as there flashed into my head the meaning of her last words: 'There was no other way'; the phrase I had half-smiled at at the time, as a parrot-like echo of the novel-heroine's stock farewell. I had never, up to that moment, wholly understood why Paulina had come to my house that night. I had never been able to make that particular act—which could hardly, in the light of her subsequent conduct, be dismissed as a blind surge of passion—square with my conception of her character. She was at once the most spontaneous and the steadiest-minded woman I had ever known, and the last to wish to owe any advantage to surprise, to unpreparedness, to any play on the spring of sex. The better I came, retrospectively, to know her, the more sure I was of this, and the less intelligible her act appeared. And then, suddenly, after a night of hungry restless thinking, the flash of enlightenment came. She had come to my house, had brought her trunk with her, had thrown herself at my head with all possible violence and publicity, in order to give me a pretext, a loophole, an honorable excuse, for doing and saying—why, precisely what I had said and done!

"As the idea came to me it was as if some ironic hand had touched an electric button, and all my fatuous phrases had leapt out on me in fire.

"Of course she had known all along just the kind of thing I should say if I didn't at once open my arms to her; and to save my pride, my dignity, my conception of the figure I was cutting in her eyes, she had recklessly and magnificently provided me with the decentest pretext a man could have for doing a pusillanimous thing. . . .

"With that discovery the whole case took a different aspect. It hurt less to think of Paulina—and yet it hurt more. The tinge of bitterness, of doubt, in my thoughts of her had had a tonic quality. It was harder to go on persuading myself that I had done right as, bit by bit, my theories crumbled under the test of time. Yet, after all, as she herself had said, one could judge of results only in the long run. . . .

"The Trants stayed away for two years; and about a year after they got back, you may remember, Trant was killed in a railway accident. You know Fate's way of untying a knot after everybody has given up tugging at it!

"Well—there I was, completely justified: all my weaknesses turned into merits! I had 'saved' a weak woman from herself, I had kept her to the path of duty, I had spared her the humiliation of scandal and the misery of self-reproach; and now I had only to put out my hand and take my reward.

"I had avoided Paulina since her return, and she had made no effort to see me. But after Trant's death I wrote her a few lines, to which she sent a friendly answer; and when a decent interval had elapsed, and I asked if I might call on her, she answered at once that she would see me.

"I went to her house with the fixed intention of asking her to marry me—and I left it without having done so. Why? I don't know that I can tell you. Perhaps you would have had to sit there opposite her, knowing what I did and feeling as I did, to understand why. She was kind, she was compassionate—I could see she didn't want to make it hard for me. Perhaps she even wanted to make it easy. But there, between us, was the memory of the gesture I hadn't made, forever parodying the one I was attempting! There wasn't a word I could think of that hadn't an echo in it of words of hers I had been deaf to; there wasn't an appeal I could make that didn't mock the appeal I had rejected. I sat there and talked of her husband's death, of her plans, of my sympathy; and I knew she understood; and knowing that, in a way, made it harder. . . . The door-bell rang and the footman came in to ask if she would receive other visitors. She looked at me a moment and said 'Yes,' and I got up and shook hands and went away.

"A few days later she sailed for Europe, and the next time we met she had married Reardon. . . ."

## VI

IT was long past midnight, and the terrier's hints became imperious.

Merrick rose from his chair, pushed back a fallen log and put up the fender. He walked across the room and stared a moment at the Brangwyn etching before which Paulina Trant had paused at a memorable turn of their talk. Then he came back and laid his hand on my shoulder.

"She summed it all up, you know, when she said that one way of finding out whether a risk is worth taking is *not* to take it, and then to see what one becomes in the long run, and draw one's inferences. The long run—well, we've run it, she and I. I know what I've become, but that's nothing to the misery of knowing what she's become. She had to have some kind of life, and she married Reardon. Reardon's a very good fellow in his way; but the worst of it is that it's not her way. . . .

"No: the worst of it is that now she and I meet as friends. We dine at the same houses, we talk about the same people, we play bridge together, and I lend her books. And sometimes Reardon slaps me on the back and says: 'Come in and dine with us, old man! What you want is to be cheered up!' And I go and dine with them, and he tells me how jolly comfortable she makes him, and what an ass I am not to marry; and she presses on me a second helping of *poulet Maryland*, and I smoke one of Reardon's cigars, and at half-past ten I get into my overcoat, and walk back alone to my rooms. . . ."

## THE TRIUMPH OF NIGHT

IT WAS CLEAR that the sleigh from Weymore had not come; and the shivering young traveller from Boston, who had counted on jumping into it when he left the train at Northridge Junction, found himself standing alone on the open platform, exposed to the full assault of night-fall and winter.

The blast that swept him came off New Hampshire snow-fields and ice-hung forests. It seemed to have traversed interminable leagues of frozen silence, filling them with the same cold roar and sharpening its edge against the same bitter black-and-white landscape. Dark, searching and sword-like, it alternately muffled and harried its victim, like a bull-fighter now whirling his cloak and now planting his darts. This analogy brought home to the young man the fact that he himself had no cloak, and that the overcoat in which he had faced the relatively temperate air of Boston seemed no thicker than a sheet of paper on the bleak heights of Northridge. George Faxon said to himself that the place was uncommonly well-named. It clung to an exposed ledge over the valley from which the train had lifted him, and the wind combed it with teeth of steel that he seemed actually to hear scraping against the wooden sides of the station. Other building there was none: the village lay far down the road, and thither—since the Weymore sleigh had not come—Faxon saw himself under the necessity of plodding through several feet of snow.

He understood well enough what had happened: his hostess had forgotten that he was coming. Young as Faxon was, this sad lucidity of soul had been acquired as the result of long experience, and he knew that the visitors who can least afford to hire a carriage are almost always those whom their hosts forget to send for. Yet to say that Mrs. Culme had forgotten him was too crude a way of putting it Similar incidents led him to think that she had probably told her maid to tell the butler to telephone the coachman to tell one of the grooms (if no one else needed him) to drive over to Northridge to fetch the new secretary; but on a night like this, what groom who respected his rights would fail to forget the order?

Faxon's obvious course was to struggle through the drifts to the village, and there rout out a sleigh to convey him to Weymore; but what if, on his arrival at Mrs. Culme's, no one remembered to ask him what this devotion to duty had cost? That, again, was one of the contingencies he had expensively learned to look out for, and the perspicacity so acquired told him it would be cheaper to spend the night at the Northridge inn, and advise Mrs. Culme of his presence there by telephone. He had reached this decision, and was about to entrust his luggage to a vague man with a lantern, when his hopes were raised by the sound of bells.

Two sleighs were just dashing up to the station, and from the foremost there sprang a young man muffled in furs.

"Weymore?—No, these are not the Weymore sleighs."

The voice was that of the youth who had jumped to the platform—a voice so agreeable that, in spite of the words, it fell consolingly on Faxon's ears. At the same moment the wandering station-lantern, casting a transient light on the speaker, showed his features to be in the pleasantest harmony with his voice. He was very fair and very young—hardly in the twenties, Faxon thought—but his face, though full of a morning freshness, was a trifle too thin and fine-drawn, as though a vivid spirit contended in him with a strain of physical weakness. Faxon was perhaps the quicker to notice such delicacies of balance because his own temperament hung on lightly quivering nerves, which yet, as he believed, would never quite swing him beyond a normal sensibility.

"You expected a sleigh from Weymore?" the newcomer continued, standing beside Faxon like a slender column of fur.

Mrs. Culme's secretary explained his difficulty, and the other brushed it aside with a contemptuous "Oh, *Mrs. Culme!*" that carried both speakers a long way toward reciprocal understanding.

"But then you must be—" The youth broke off with a smile of interrogation.

"The new secretary? Yes. But apparently there are no notes to be answered this evening." Faxon's laugh deepened the sense of solidarity which had so promptly established itself between the two.

His friend laughed also. "Mrs. Culme," he explained, "was lunching at my uncle's to-day, and she said you were due this evening. But seven hours is a long time for Mrs. Culme to remember anything."

"Well," said Faxon philosophically, "I suppose that's one of the reasons why she needs a secretary. And I've always the inn at Northridge," he concluded.

"Oh, but you haven't, though! It burned down last week."

"The deuce it did!" said Faxon; but the humor of the situation struck him before its inconvenience. His life, for years past, had been mainly a succession of resigned adaptations, and he had learned, before dealing practically with his embarrassments, to extract from most of them a small tribute of amusement.

"Oh, well, there's sure to be somebody in the place who can put me up."

"No one *you* could put up with. Besides, Northridge is three miles off, and our place—in the opposite direction—is a little nearer." Through the darkness, Faxon saw his friend sketch a gesture of self-introduction. "My name's Frank Rainer, and I'm staying with my uncle at Overdale. I've driven over to meet two friends of his, who are due in a few minutes from New York. If you don't mind waiting till they arrive I'm sure Overdale can do you better than Northridge. We're only down from town for a few days, but the house is always ready for a lot of people."

"But your uncle—?" Faxon could only object, with the odd sense, through his embarrassment, that it would be magically dispelled by his invisible friend's next words.

"Oh, my uncle—you'll see! I answer for *him!* I daresay you've heard of him—John Lavington?"

John Lavington! There was a certain irony in asking if one had heard of John Lavington! Even from a post of observation as obscure as that of Mrs. Culme's secretary the rumor of John Lavington's money, of his pictures, his politics, his charities and his hospitality, was as difficult to escape as the roar of a cataract in a mountain solitude. It might almost have been said that the one place in which one would not have expected to come upon him was in just such a solitude as now surrounded the speakers—at least in this deepest hour of its desertedness. But it was just like Lavington's brilliant ubiquity to put one in the wrong even there.

"Oh, yes, I've heard of your uncle."

"Then you *will* come, won't you? We've only five minutes to wait." young Rainer urged, in the tone that dispels scruples by ignoring them; and Faxon found himself accepting the invitation as simply as it was offered.

A delay in the arrival of the New York train lengthened their five minutes to fifteen; and as they paced the icy platform Faxon began to see why it had seemed the most natural thing in the world to accede to his new acquaintance's suggestion. It was because Frank Rainer was one of the privileged beings who simplify human intercourse by the atmosphere of confidence and good humor they diffuse. He produced this effect, Faxon noted, by the exercise of no gift but his youth, and of no art but his sincerity; and these qualities were revealed in a smile of such sweetness that Faxon felt, as never before, what Nature can achieve when she deigns to match the face with the mind.

He learned that the young man was the ward, and the only nephew, of John Lavington, with whom he had made his home since the death of his mother, the great man's sister. Mr. Lavington, Rainer said, had been "a regular brick" to him—"But then he is to everyone, you know"—and the young fellow's situation seemed in fact to be perfectly in keeping with his person. Apparently the only shade that had ever rested on him was cast by the physical weakness which Faxon had already detected. Young Rainer had been threatened with tuberculosis, and the disease was so far advanced that, according to the highest authorities, banishment to Arizona or New Mexico was inevitable. "But luckily my uncle didn't pack me off, as most people would have done, without getting another opinion. Whose? Oh, an awfully clever chap, a young doctor with a lot of new ideas, who simply laughed at my being sent away, and said I'd do perfectly well in New York if I didn't dine out too much, and if I dashed off occasionally to Northridge for a little fresh air. So it's really my uncle's doing that I'm not in exile—and I feel no end better since the new chap told me I needn't bother." Young Rainer went on to confess that he was extremely fond of dining out, dancing and similar distractions; and Faxon, listening to him, was inclined to think that the physician who had refused to cut him off altogether from these pleasures was probably a better psychologist than his seniors.

"All the same you ought to be careful, you know." The sense of elder-brotherly concern that forced the words from Faxon made him, as he spoke, slip his arm through Frank Rainer 's.

The latter met the movement with a responsive pressure. "Oh, I *am:* awfully, awfully. And then my uncle has such an eye on me!"

"But if your uncle has such an eye on you, what does he say to your swallowing knives out here in this Siberian wild?"

Rainer raised his fur collar with a careless gesture. "It's not that that does it—the cold's good for me."

"And it's not the dinners and dances? What is it, then?" Faxon good-humoredly insisted; to which his companion answered with a laugh: "Well, my uncle says it's being bored; and I rather think he's right!"

His laugh ended in a spasm of coughing and a struggle for breath that made Faxon, still holding his arm, guide him hastily into the shelter of the fireless waiting room.

Young Rainer had dropped down on the bench against the wall and pulled off one of his fur gloves to grope for a handkerchief. He tossed aside his cap and drew the handkerchief across his forehead, which was intensely white, and beaded with moisture, though his face retained a healthy glow. But Faxon's gaze remained fastened to the hand he had uncovered: it was so long, so colorless, so wasted, so much older than the brow he passed it over.

"It's queer—a healthy face but dying hands," the secretary mused: he somehow wished young Rainer had kept on his glove.

The whistle of the express drew the young men to their feet, and the next moment two heavily-furred gentlemen had descended to the platform and were breasting the rigor of the night. Frank Rainer introduced them as Mr. Grisben and Mr. Balch, and Faxon, while their luggage was being lifted into the second sleigh, discerned them, by the roving lantern-gleam, to be an elderly grey-headed pair, of the average prosperous business cut.

They saluted their host's nephew with friendly familiarity, and Mr. Grisben, who seemed the spokesman of the two, ended his greeting with a genial—"and many many more of them, dear boy!" which suggested to Faxon that their arrival coincided with an anniversary. But he could not press the enquiry, for the seat allotted him was at the coachman's side, while Frank Rainer joined his uncle's guests inside the sleigh.

A swift flight (behind such horses as one could be sure of John Lavington's having) brought them to tall gateposts, an illuminated lodge, and an avenue on which the snow had been leveled to the smoothness of marble. At the end of the avenue the long house loomed up, its principal bulk dark, but one wing sending out a ray of welcome; and the next moment Faxon was receiving a violent impression of warmth and light, of hot-house plants, hurrying servants, a vast spectacular oak hall like a stage-setting, and, in its unreal middle distance, a small figure, correctly dressed, conventionally featured, and utterly unlike his rather florid conception of the great John Lavington.

The surprise of the contrast remained with him through his hurried dressing in the large luxurious bedroom to which he had been shown. "I don't see where he comes in," was the only way he could put it, so difficult was it to fit the exuberance of Lavington's public personality into his host's contracted frame and manner. Mr. Laving ton, to whom Faxon's case had been rapidly explained by young Rainer, had welcomed him with a sort of dry and stilted cordiality that exactly matched his narrow face, his stiff hand, and the whiff of scent on his evening handkerchief. "Make yourself at home—at home!" he had repeated, in a tone that suggested, on his own part, a complete inability to perform the feat he urged on his visitor. "Any friend of Frank's. . . delighted. . . make yourself thoroughly at home!"

## II

IN spite of the balmy temperature and complicated conveniences of Faxon's bedroom, the injunction was not easy to obey. It was wonderful luck to have found a night's shelter under the opulent roof of Overdale, and he tasted the physical satisfaction to the full. But the place, for all its ingenuities of comfort, was oddly cold and unwelcoming. He couldn't have said why, and could only suppose that Mr. Lavington's intense personality—intensely negative, but intense all the same—must, in some occult way, have penetrated every corner of his dwelling. Perhaps, though, it was merely that Faxon himself was tired and hungry, more deeply chilled than he had known till he came in from the cold, and unutterably sick of all strange houses, and of the prospect of perpetually treading other people's stairs.

"I hope you're not famished?" Rainer's slim figure was in the doorway. "My uncle has a little business to attend to with Mr. Grisben, and we don't dine for half an hour. Shall I fetch you, or can you find your way down? Come straight to the dining-room—the second door on the left of the long gallery."

He disappeared, leaving a ray of warmth behind him, and Faxon, relieved, lit a cigarette and sat down by the fire.

Looking about with less haste, he was struck by a detail that had escaped him. The room was full of flowers—a mere "bachelor's room," in the wing of a house opened only for a few days, in the dead middle of a New Hampshire winter! Flowers were everywhere, not in senseless profusion, but placed with the same conscious art that he had remarked in the grouping of the blossoming shrubs in the hall. A vase of arums stood on the writing-table, a cluster of strange-hued carnations on the stand at his elbow, and from bowls of glass and porcelain clumps of freesia-bulbs diffused their melting fragrance. The fact implied acres of glass—but that was the least interesting part of it. The flowers themselves, their quality, selection and arrangement, attested on some one's part—and on whose but John Lavington's?—a solicitous and sensitive passion for that particular form of beauty. Well, it simply made the man, as he had appeared to Faxon, all the harder to understand!

The half hour elapsed, and Faxon, rejoicing at the prospect of food, set out to make his way to the dining-room. He had not noticed the direction he had followed in going to his room, and was puzzled, when he left it, to find that two staircases, of apparently equal importance, invited him. He chose the one to his right, and reached, at its foot, a long gallery such as Rainer had described. The gallery was empty, the doors down its length were closed; but Rainer had said: "The second to the left," and Faxon, after pausing for some chance enlightenment which did not come, laid his hand on the second knob to the left.

The room he entered was square, with dusky picture-hung walls. In its center, about a table lit by veiled lamps, he fancied Mr. Lavington and his guests to be already seated at dinner; then he perceived that the table was covered not with viands but with papers, and that he had blundered into what seemed to be his host's study. As he paused Frank Rainer looked up.

"Oh, here's Mr. Faxon. Why not ask him—?"

Mr. Lavington, from the end of the table, reflected his nephew's smile in a glance of impartial benevolence.

"Certainly. Come in, Mr. Faxon. If you won't think it a liberty—"

Mr. Grisben, who sat opposite his host, turned his head toward the door. "Of course Mr. Faxon's an American citizen?"

Frank Rainer laughed. "That's all right! . . . Oh, no, not one of your pin-pointed pens, Uncle Jack! Haven't you got a quill somewhere?"

Mr. Balch, who spoke slowly and as if reluctantly, in a muffled voice of which there seemed to be very little left, raised his hand to say: "One moment: you acknowledge this to be—?"

"My last will and testament?" Rainer's laugh redoubled. "Well, I won't answer for the 'last.' It's the first, anyway."

"It's a mere formula," Mr. Balch explained.

"Well, here goes." Rainer dipped his quill in the inkstand his uncle had pushed in his direction, and dashed a gallant signature across the document.

Faxon, understanding what was expected of him, and conjecturing that the young man was signing his will on the attainment of his majority, had placed himself behind Mr. Grisben, and stood awaiting his turn to affix his name to the instrument. Rainer, having signed, was about to push the paper across the table to Mr. Balch; but the latter, again raising his hand, said in his sad imprisoned voice: "The seal—?"

"Oh, does there have to be a seal?"

Faxon, looking over Mr. Grisben at John Lavington, saw a faint frown between his impassive eyes. "Really, Frank!" He seemed, Faxon thought, slightly irritated by his nephew's frivolity.

"Who's got a seal?" Frank Rainer continued, glancing about the table. "There doesn't seem to be one here."

Mr. Grisben interposed. "A wafer will do. Lavington, you have a wafer?"

Mr. Lavington had recovered his serenity. "There must be some in one of the drawers. But I'm ashamed to say I don't know where my secretary keeps these things. He ought to have seen to it that a wafer was sent with the document."

"Oh, hang it—" Frank Rainer pushed the paper aside: "It's the hand of God—and I'm as hungry as a wolf. Let's dine first, Uncle Jack."

"I think I've a seal upstairs," said Faxon.

Mr. Lavington sent him a barely perceptible smile. "So sorry to give you the trouble—"

"Oh, I say, don't send him after it now. Let's wait till after dinner!"

Mr. Lavington continued to smile on his guest, and the latter, as if under the faint coercion of the smile, turned from the room and ran upstairs. Having taken the seal from his writing-case he came down again, and once more opened the door of the study. No one was speaking when he entered—they were evidently awaiting his return with the mute impatience of hunger, and he put the seal in Rainer's reach, and stood watching while Mr. Grisben struck a match and held it to one of the candles flanking the inkstand. As the wax descended on the paper Faxon remarked again the strange emaciation, the premature physical weariness, of the hand that held it: he wondered if Mr. Lavington had ever noticed his nephew's hand, and if it were not poignantly visible to him now.

With this thought in his mind, Faxon raised his eyes to look at Mr. Lavington. The great man's gaze rested on Frank Rainer with an expression of untroubled benevolence; and at the same instant Faxon's attention was attracted by the presence in the room of another person, who must have joined the group while he was upstairs searching for the seal. The new-comer was a man of about Mr. Lavington's age and figure, who stood just behind his chair, and who, at the moment when Faxon first saw him, was gazing at young Rainer with an equal intensity of attention. The likeness between the two men—perhaps increased by the fact that the hooded lamps on the table left the figure behind the chair in shadow—struck Faxon the more because of the contrast in their expression. John Lavington, during his nephew's clumsy attempt to drop the wax and apply the seal, continued to fasten on him a look of half-amused affection; while the man behind the chair, so oddly reduplicating the lines of his features and figure, turned on the boy a face of pale hostility.

The impression was so startling that Faxon forgot what was going on about him. He was just dimly aware of young Reiner's exclaiming; "Your turn, Mr. Grisben!" of Mr. Grisben's protesting: "No—no; Mr. Faxon first," and of the pen's being thereupon transferred to his own hand. He received it with a deadly sense of being unable to move, or even to understand what was expected of him, till he became conscious of Mr. Grisben's paternally pointing out the precise spot on which he was to leave his autograph.

The effort to fix his attention and steady his hand prolonged the process of signing, and when he stood up—a strange weight of fatigue on all his limbs—the figure behind Mr. Lavington's chair was gone.

Faxon felt an immediate sense of relief. It was puzzling that the man's exit should have been so rapid and noiseless, but the door behind Mr. Lavington was screened by a tapestry hanging, and Faxon concluded that the unknown looker-on had merely had to raise it to pass out. At any rate he was gone, and with his withdrawal the strange weight was lifted. Young Rainer was lighting a cigarette, Mr. Balch inscribing his name at the foot of the document, Mr. Lavington—his eyes no longer on his nephew—examining a strange white-winged orchid in the vase at his elbow. Everything suddenly seemed to have grown natural and simple again, and Faxon found himself responding with a smile to the affable gesture with which his host declared: "And now, Mr. Faxon, we'll dine."

III

"I WONDER how I blundered into the wrong room just now; I thought you told me to take the second door to the left," Faxon said to Frank Rainer as they followed the older men down the gallery.

"So I did; but I probably forgot to tell you which staircase to take. Coming from your bedroom, I ought to have said the fourth door to the right. It's a puzzling house, because my uncle keeps adding to it from year to year. He built this room last summer for his modern pictures."

Young Rainer, pausing to open another door, touched an electric button which sent a circle of light about the walls of a long room hung with canvases of the French Impressionist school.

Faxon advanced, attracted by a shimmering Monet, but Rainer laid a hand on his arm.

"He bought that last week. But come along—I'll show you all this after dinner. Or *he* will, rather—he loves it."

"Does he really love things?"

Rainer stared, clearly perplexed at the question. "Rather! Flowers and pictures especially! Haven't you noticed the flowers? I suppose you think his manner's cold; it seems so at first; but he's really awfully keen about things."

Faxon looked quickly at the speaker. "Has your uncle a brother?"

"Brother? No—never had. He and my mother were the only ones."

"Or any relation who—who looks like him? Who might be mistaken for him?"

"Not that I ever heard of. Does he remind you of some one?"

"Yes."

"That's queer. We'll ask him if he's got a double. Come on!"

But another picture had arrested Faxon, and some minutes elapsed before he and his young host reached the dining-room. It was a large room, with the same conventionally handsome furniture and delicately grouped flowers; and Faxon's first glance showed him that only three men were seated about the dining-table. The man who had stood behind Mr. Lavington's chair was not present, and no seat awaited him.

When the young men entered, Mr. Grisben was speaking, and his host, who faced the door, sat looking down at his untouched soup-plate and turning the spoon about in his small dry hand.

"It's pretty late to call them rumors—they were devilish close to facts when we left town this morning," Mr. Grisben was saying, with an unexpected incisiveness of tone.

Mr. Lavington laid down his spoon and smiled interrogatively. "Oh, facts—what *are* facts? Just the way a thing happens to look at a given minute. . . ."

"You haven't heard anything from town?" Mr. Grisben persisted.

"Not a syllable. So you see. . . . Balch, a little more of that *petite marmite*. Mr. Faxon . . . between Frank and Mr. Grisben, please."

The dinner progressed through a series of complicated courses, ceremoniously dispensed by a prelatical butler attended by three tall footmen, and it was evident that Mr. Lavington took a certain satisfaction in the pageant. That, Faxon reflected, was probably the joint in his armor—that and the flowers. He had changed the subject—not abruptly but firmly—when the young men entered, but Faxon perceived that it still possessed the thoughts of the two elderly visitors, and Mr. Balch presently observed, in a voice that seemed to come from the last survivor down a mine-shaft: "If it *does* come, it will be the biggest crash since '93."

Mr. Lavington looked bored but polite. "Wall Street can stand crashes better than it could then. It's got a robuster constitution."

"Yes; but—"

"Speaking of constitutions," Mr. Grisben intervened: "Frank, are you taking care of yourself?"

A flush rose to young Rainer's cheeks.

"Why, of course! Isn't that what I'm here for?"

"You're here about three days in the month, aren't you? And the rest of the time it's crowded restaurants and hot ballrooms in town. I thought you were to be shipped off to New Mexico?"

"Oh, I've got a new man who says that's rot."

"Well, you don't look as if your new man were right," said Mr. Grisben bluntly.

Faxon saw the lad's color fade, and the rings of shadow deepen under his gay eyes. At the same moment his uncle turned to him with a renewed intensity of attention. There was such solicitude in Mr. Lavington's gaze that it seemed almost to fling a shield between his nephew and Mr. Grisben's tactless scrutiny.

"We think Frank's a good deal better," he began; "this new doctor—"

The butler, coming up, bent to whisper a word in his ear, and the communication caused a sudden change in Mr. Lavington's expression. His face was naturally so colorless that it seemed not so much to pale as to fade, to dwindle and recede into something blurred and blotted-out. He half rose, sat down again and sent a rigid smile about the table.

"Will you excuse me? The telephone. Peters, go on with the dinner." With small precise steps he walked out of the door which one of the footmen had thrown open.

A momentary silence fell on the group; then Mr. Grisben once more addressed himself to Rainer. "You ought to have gone, my boy; you ought to have gone."

The anxious look returned to the youth's eyes. "My uncle doesn't think so, really."

"You're not a baby, to be always governed by your uncle's opinion. You came of age to-day, didn't you? Your uncle spoils you . . . that's what's the matter. . . ."

The thrust evidently went home, for Rainer laughed and looked down with a slight accession of color.

"But the doctor—"

"Use your common sense, Frank! You had to try twenty doctors to find one to tell you what you wanted to be told."

A look of apprehension overshadowed Rainer', gaiety. "Oh, come—I say!... What would *you* do?" he stammered.

"Pack up and jump on the first train." Mr. Grisben leaned forward and laid his hand kindly on the young man's arm. "Look here: my nephew Jim Grisben is out there ranching on a big scale. He'll take you in and be glad to have you. You say your new doctor thinks it won't do you any good; but he doesn't pretend to say it will do you harm, does he? Well, then—give it a trial. It'll take you out of hot theatres and night restaurants, anyhow. . . . And all the rest of it. . . . Eh, Balch?"

"Go!" said Mr. Balch hollowly. "Go *at once,"* he added, as if a closer look at the youth's face had impressed on him the need of backing up his friend.

Young Rainer had turned ashy-pale. He tried to stiffen his mouth into a smile. "Do I look as bad as all that?"

Mr. Grisben was helping himself to terrapin. "You look like the day after an earthquake," he said.

The terrapin had encircled the table, and been deliberately enjoyed by Mr. Lavington's three visitors (Rainer, Faxon noticed, left his plate untouched) before the door was thrown open to readmit their host.

Mr. Lavington advanced with an air of recovered composure. He seated himself, picked up his napkin and consulted the gold-monogrammed menu. "No, don't bring back the filet. . . . Some terrapin; yes. . . ." He looked affably about the table. "Sorry to have deserted you, but the storm has played the deuce with the wires, and I had to wait a long time before I could get a good connection. It must be blowing up for a blizzard."

"Uncle Jack," young Rainer broke out, "Mr. Grisben's been lecturing me."

Mr. Lavington was helping himself to terrapin. "Ah—what about?"

"He thinks I ought to have given New Mexico a show."

"I want him to go straight out to my nephew at Santa Paz and stay there till his next birthday." Mr. Lavington signed to the butler to hand the terrapin to Mr. Grisben, who, as he took a second helping, addressed himself again to Rainer. "Jim's in New York now, and going back the day after tomorrow in Olyphant's private car. I'll ask Olyphant to squeeze you in if you'll go. And when you've been out there a week or two, in the saddle all day and sleeping nine hours a night, I suspect you won't think much of the doctor who prescribed New York."

Faxon spoke up, he knew not why. "I was out there once: it's a splendid life. I saw a fellow—oh, a really *bad* case—who'd been simply made over by it."

"It *does* sound jolly," Rainer laughed, a sudden eagerness in his tone.

His uncle looked at him gently. "Perhaps Grisben's right. It's an opportunity—"

Faxon glanced up with a start: the figure dimly perceived in the study was now more visibly and tangibly planted behind Mr. Lavington's chair.

"That's right, Frank: you see your uncle approves. And the trip out there with Olyphant isn't a thing to be missed. So drop a few dozen dinners and be at the Grand Central the day after tomorrow at five."

Mr. Grisben's pleasant grey eye sought corroboration of his host, and Faxon, in a cold anguish of suspense, continued to watch him as he turned his glance on Mr. Lavington. One could not look at Lavington without seeing the presence at his back, and it was clear that, the next minute, some change in Mr. Grisben's expression must give his watcher a clue.

But Mr. Grisben's expression did not change: the gaze he fixed on his host remained unperturbed, and the clue he gave was the startling one of not seeming to see the other figure.

Faxon's first impulse was to look away, to look anywhere else, to resort again to the champagne glass the watchful butler had already brimmed; but some fatal attraction, at war in him with an overwhelming physical resistance, held his eyes upon the spot they feared.

The figure was still standing, more distinctly, and therefore more resemblingly, at Mr. Lavington's back; and while the latter continued to gaze affectionately at his nephew, his counterpart, as before, fixed young Rainer with eyes of deadly menace.

Faxon, with what felt like an actual wrench of the muscles, dragged his own eyes from the sight to scan the other countenances about the table; but not one revealed the least consciousness of what he saw, and a sense of mortal isolation sank upon him.

"It's worth considering, certainly—" he heard Mr. Lavington continue; and as Rainer's face lit up, the face behind his uncle's chair seemed to gather into its look all the fierce weariness of old unsatisfied hates. That was the thing that, as the minutes laboured by, Faxon was becoming most conscious of. The watcher behind the chair was no longer merely malevolent: he had grown suddenly, unutterably tired. His hatred seemed to well up out of the very depths of balked effort and thwarted hopes, and the fact made him more pitiable, and yet more dire.

Faxon's look reverted to Mr. Lavington, as if to surprise in him a corresponding change. At first none was visible: his pinched smile was screwed to his blank face like a gas-light to a white-washed wall. Then the fixity of the smile became ominous: Faxon saw that its wearer was afraid to let it go. It was evident that Mr. Lavington was unutterably tired too, and the discovery sent a colder current through Faxon's veins. Looking down at his untouched plate, he caught the soliciting twinkle of the champagne glass; but the sight of the wine turned him sick.

"Well, we'll go into the details presently," he heard Mr. Lavington say, still on the question of his nephew's future. "Let's have a cigar first. No—not here, Peters." He turned his smile on Faxon. "When we've had coffee I want to show you my pictures."

"Oh, by the way, Uncle Jack—Mr. Faxon wants to know if you've got a double?"

"A double?" Mr. Lavington, still smiling, continued to address himself to his guest. "Not that I know of. Have you seen one, Mr. Faxon?"

Faxon thought: "My God, if I look up now they'll *both* be looking at me!" To avoid raising his eyes he made as though to lift the glass to his lips; but his hand sank inert, and he looked up. Mr. Lavington's glance was politely bent on him, but with a loosening of the strain about his heart he saw that the figure behind the chair still kept its gaze on Rainer.

"Do you think you've seen my double, Mr. Faxon?"

Would the other face turn if he said yes? Faxon felt a dryness in his throat. "No," he answered.

"Ah? It's possible I've a dozen. I believe I'm extremely usual-looking," Mr. Lavington went on conversationally; and still the other face watched Rainer.

"It was . . . a mistake . . . a confusion of memory. . . ." Faxon heard himself stammer. Mr. Lavington pushed back his chair, and as he did so Mr. Grisben suddenly leaned forward.

"Lavington! What have, we been thinking of? We haven't drunk Frank's health!"

Mr. Lavington reseated himself. "My dear boy! . . . Peters, another bottle. . . ." He turned to his nephew. "After such a sin of omission I don't presume to propose the toast myself . . . but Frank knows. . . . Go ahead, Grisben!"

The boy shone on his uncle. "No, no, Uncle Jack! Mr. Grisben won't mind. Nobody but *you*—today!"

The butler was replenishing the glasses. He filled Mr. Lavington's last, and Mr. Lavington put out his small hand to raise it. . . . As he did so, Faxon looked away.

"Well, then—All the good I've wished you in all the past years. . . . I put it into the prayer that the coming ones may be healthy and happy and many . . . and *many,* dear boy!"

Faxon saw the hands about him reach out for their glasses. Automatically, he reached for his. His eyes were still on the table, and he repeated to himself with a trembling vehemence: "I won't look up! I won't. . . . I won't. . . ."

His finders clasped the glass and raised it to the level of his lips. He saw the other hands making the same motion. He heard Mr. Grisben's genial "Hear! Hear!" and Mr. Batch's hollow echo. He said to himself, as the rim of the glass touched his lips: "I won't look up! I swear I won't!—" and he looked.

The glass was so full that it required an extraordinary effort to hold it there, brimming and suspended, during the awful interval before he could trust his hand to lower it again, untouched, to the table. It was this merciful preoccupation which saved him, kept him from crying out, from losing his hold, from slipping down into the bottomless blackness that gaped for him. As long as the problem of the glass engaged him he felt able to keep his seat, manage his muscles, fit unnoticeably into the group; but as the glass touched the table his last link with safety snapped. He stood up and dashed out of the room.

IV

IN the gallery, the instinct of self-preservation helped him to turn back and sign to young Rainer not to follow. He stammered out something about a touch of dizziness, and joining them presently; and the boy nodded sympathetically and drew back.

At the foot of the stairs Faxon ran against a servant. "I should like to telephone to Weymore," he said with dry lips.

"Sorry, sir; wires all down. We've been trying the last hour to get New York again for Mr. Lavington."

Faxon shot on to his room, burst into it, and bolted the door. The lamplight lay on furniture, flowers, books; in the ashes a log still glimmered. He dropped down on the sofa and hid his face. The room was profoundly silent, the whole house was still: nothing about him gave a hint of what was going on, darkly and dumbly, in the room he had flown from, and with the covering of his eyes oblivion and reassurance seemed to fall on him. But they fell for a moment only; then his lids opened again to the monstrous vision. There it was, stamped on his pupils, a part of him forever, an indelible horror burnt into his body and brain. But why into his—just his? Why had he alone been chosen to see what he had seen? What business was it of *his,* in God's name? Any one of the others, thus enlightened, might have exposed the horror and defeated it; but *he,* the one weaponless and defenceless spectator, the one whom none of the others would believe or understand if he attempted to reveal what he knew—*he* alone had been singled out as the victim of this dreadful initiation!

Suddenly he sat up, listening: he had heard a step on the stairs. Some one, no doubt, was coming to see how he was—to urge him, if he felt better, to go down and join the smokers. Cautiously he opened his door; yes, it was young Rainer's step. Faxon looked down the passage, remembered the other stairway and darted to it. All he wanted was to get out of the house. Not another instant would he breathe its abominable air! What business was it of *his,* in God's name?

He reached the opposite end of the lower gallery, and beyond it saw the hall by which he had entered. It was empty, and on a long table he recognized his coat and cap. He got into his coat, unbolted the door, and plunged into the purifying night.

The darkness was deep, and the cold so intense that for an instant it stopped his breathing. Then he perceived that only a thin snow was falling, and resolutely he set his face for flight. The trees along the avenue marked his way as he hastened with long strides over the beaten snow. Gradually, while he walked, the tumult in his brain subsided. The impulse to fly still drove him forward, but he began feel that he was flying from a terror of his own creating, and that the most urgent reason for escape was the need of hiding his state, of shunning other eyes till he should regain his balance.

He had spent the long hours in the train in fruitless broodings on a discouraging situation, and he remembered how his bitterness had turned to exasperation when he found that the Weymore sleigh was not awaiting him. It was absurd, of course; but, though he had joked with Rainer over Mrs. Culme's forgetfullness, to confess it had cost a pang. That was what his rootless life had brought him to: for lack of a personal stake in things his sensibility was at the mercy of such trifles. . . . Yes; that, and the cold and fatigue, the absence of hope and the haunting sense of starved aptitudes, all these had brought him to the perilous verge over which, once or twice before, his terrified brain had hung.

Why else, in the name of any imaginable logic, human or devilish, should he, a stranger, be singled out for this experience? What could it mean to him, how was he related to it, what bearing had it on his case? . . . Unless, indeed, it was just because he was a stranger—a stranger everywhere—because he had no personal life, no warm screen of private egotisms to shield him from exposure, that he had developed this abnormal sensitiveness to the vicissitudes of others. The thought pulled him up with a shudder. No! Such a fate was too abominable; all that was strong and sound in him rejected it. A thousand times better regard himself as ill, disorganized, deluded, than as the predestined victim of such warnings!

He reached the gates and paused before the darkened lodge. The wind had risen and was sweeping the snow into his race. The cold had him in its grasp again, and he stood uncertain. Should he put his sanity to the test and go back? He turned and looked down the dark drive to the house. A single ray shone through the trees, evoking a picture of the lights, the flowers, the faces grouped about that fatal room. He turned and plunged out into the road. . . .

He remembered that, about a mile from Overdale, the coachman had pointed out the road to Northridge; and he began to walk in that direction. Once in the road he had the gale in his face, and the wet snow on his moustache and eye-lashes instantly hardened to ice. The same ice seemed to be driving a million blades into his throat and lungs, but he pushed on, the vision of the warm room pursuing him.

The snow in the road was deep and uneven. He stumbled across ruts and sank into drifts, and the wind drove against him like a granite cliff. Now and then he stopped, gasping, as if an invisible hand had tightened an iron band about his body; then he started again, stiffening himself against the stealthy penetration of the cold. The snow continued to descend out of a pall of inscrutable darkness, and once or twice he paused, fearing he had missed the road to Northridge; but, seeing no sign of a turn, he ploughed on.

At last, feeling sure that he had walked for more than a mile, he halted and looked back. The act of turning brought immediate relief, first because it put his back to the wind, and then because, far down the road, it showed him the gleam of a lantern. A sleigh was coming—a sleigh that might perhaps give him a lift to the village! Fortified by the hope, he began to walk back toward the light. It came forward very slowly, with unaccountable zigzags and waverings; and even when he was within a few yards of it he could catch no sound of sleigh-bells. Then it paused and became stationary by the roadside, as though carried by a pedestrian who had stopped, exhausted by the cold. The thought made Faxon hasten on, and a moment later he was stooping over a motionless figure huddled against the snow-bank. The lantern had dropped from its bearer's hand, and Faxon, fearfully raising it, threw its light into the face of Frank Rainer.

"Rainer! What on earth are you doing here?"

The boy smiled back through his pallor. "What are *you*, I'd like to know?" he retorted; and, scrambling to his feet with a clutch oh Faxon's arm, he added gaily: "Well, I've run you down!"

Faxon stood confounded, his heart sinking. The lad's face was grey.

"What madness—" he began.

"Yes, it *is*. What on earth did you do it for?"

"I? Do what? . . . Why I. . . . I was just taking a walk. . . . I often walk at night. . . ."

Frank Rainer burst into a laugh. "On such nights? Then you hadn't bolted?"

"Bolted?"

"Because I'd done something to offend you? My uncle thought you had."

Faxon grasped his arm. "Did your uncle send you after me?"

"Well, he gave me an awful rowing for not going up to your room with you when you said you were ill. And when we found you'd gone we were frightened—and he was awfully upset—so I said I'd catch you. . . . You're *not* ill, are you?"

"Ill? No. Never better." Faxon picked up the lantern. "Come; let's go back. It was awfully hot in that dining room."

"Yes; I hoped it was only that."

They trudged on in silence for a few minutes; then Faxon questioned: "You're not too done up?"

"Oh, no. It's a lot easier with the wind behind us."

"All right Don't talk any more."

They pushed ahead, walking, in spite of the light that guided them, more slowly than Faxon had walked alone into the gale. The fact of his companion's stumbling against a drift gave Faxon a pretext for saying: "Take hold of my arm," and Rainer obeying, gasped out: "I'm blown!"

"So am I. Who wouldn't be?"

"What a dance you led me! If it hadn't been for one of the servants happening to see you—"

"Yes; all right. And now, won't you kindly shut up?"

Rainer laughed and hung on him. "Oh, the cold doesn't hurt me. . . ."

For the first few minutes after Rainer had overtaken him, anxiety for the lad had been Faxon's only thought. But as each laboring step carried them nearer to the spot he had been fleeing, the reasons for his flight grew more ominous and more insistent. No, he was not ill, he was not distraught and deluded—he was the instrument singled out to warn and save; and here he was, irresistibly driven, dragging the victim back to his doom!

The intensity of the conviction had almost checked his steps. But what could he do or say? At all costs he must get Rainer out of the cold, into the house and into his bed. After that he would act.

The snowfall was thickening, and as they reached a stretch of the road between open fields the wind took them at an angle, lashing their faces with barbed thongs. Rainer stopped to take breath, and Faxon felt the heavier pressure of his arm.

"When we get to the lodge, can't we telephone to the stable for a sleigh?"

"If they're not all asleep at the lodge."

"Oh, I'll manage. Don't talk!" Faxon ordered; and they plodded on. . . .

At length the lantern ray showed ruts that curved away from the road under tree-darkness.

Faxon's spirits rose. "There's the gate! We'll be there in five minutes."

As he spoke he caught, above the boundary hedge, the gleam of a light at the farther end of the dark avenue. It was the same light that had shone on the scene of which every detail was burnt into his brain; and he felt again its overpowering reality. No—he couldn't let the boy go back!

They were at the lodge at last, and Faxon was hammering on the door. He said to himself: "I'll get him inside first, and make them give him a hot drink. Then I'll see—I'll find an argument. . . ."

There was no answer to his knocking, and after an interval Rainer said: "Look here—we'd better go on."

"No!"

"I can, perfectly—"

"You shan't go to the house, I say!" Faxon redoubled his blows, and at length steps sounded on the stairs. Rainer was leaning against the lintel, and as the door opened the light from the hall flashed on his pale face and fixed eyes. Faxon caught him by the arm and drew him in.

"It *was* cold out there." he sighed; and then, abruptly, as if invisible shears at a single stroke had cut every muscle in his body, he swerved, drooped on Faxon's arm, and seemed to sink into nothing at his feet.

The lodgekeeper and Faxon bent over him, and somehow, between them, lifted him into the kitchen and laid him on a sofa by the stove.

The lodge-keeper, stammering: "I'll ring up the house," dashed out of the room. But Faxon heard the words without heeding them: omens mattered nothing now, beside this woe fulfilled. He knelt down to undo the fur collar about Rainer's throat, and as he did so he felt a warm moisture on his hands. He held them up, and they were red. . . .

## V

THE palms threaded their endless line along the yellow river. The little steamer lay at the wharf, and George Faxon, sitting in the verandah of the wooden hotel, idly watched the coolies carrying the freight across the gangplank.

He had been looking at such scenes for two months. Nearly five had elapsed since he had descended from the train at Northridge and strained his eyes for the sleigh that was to take him to Weymore: Weymore, which he was never to behold! . . . Part of the interval—the first part—was still a great grey blur. Even now he could not be quite sure how he had got back to Boston, reached the house of a cousin, and been thence transferred to a quiet room looking out on snow under bare trees. He looked out a long time at the same scene, and finally one day a man he had known at Harvard came to see him and invited him to go out on a business trip to the Malay Peninsula.

"You've had a bad shake-up, and it'll do you no end of good to get away from things."

When the doctor came the next day it turned out that he knew of the plan and approved it. "You ought to be quiet for a year. Just loaf and look at the landscape," he advised.

Faxon felt the first faint stirrings of curiosity.

"What's been the matter with me, anyway?"

"Well, overwork, I suppose. You must have been bottling up for a bad breakdown before you started for New Hampshire last December. And the shock of that poor boy's death did the rest."

Ah, yes—Rainer had died. He remembered. . . .

He started for the East, and gradually, by imperceptible degrees, life crept back into his weary bones and leaden brain. His friend was patient and considerate, and they travelled slowly and talked little. At first Faxon had felt a great shrinking from whatever touched on familiar things. He seldom looked at a newspaper and he never opened a letter without a contraction of the heart. It was not that he had any special cause for apprehension, but merely that a great trail of darkness lay on everything. He had looked too deep down into the abyss. . . . But little by little health and energy returned to him, and with them the common promptings of curiosity. He was beginning to wonder how the world was going, and when, presently, the hotel-keeper told him there were no letters for him in the steamer's mail-bag, he felt a distinct sense of disappointment. His friend had gone into the jungle on a long excursion, and he was lonely, unoccupied and wholesomely bored. He got up and strolled into the stuffy reading room.

There he found a game of dominoes, a mutilated picture-puzzle, some copies of *Zion's Herald* and a pile of New York and London newspapers.

He began to glance through the papers, and was disappointed to find that they were less recent than he had hoped. Evidently the last numbers had been carried off by luckier travellers. He continued to turn them over, picking out the American ones first. These, as it happened, were the oldest: they dated back to December and January. To Faxon, however, they had all the flavor of novelty, since they covered the precise period during which he had virtually ceased to exist. It had never before occurred to him to wonder what had happened in the world during that interval of obliteration; but now he felt a sudden desire to know.

To prolong the pleasure, he began by sorting the papers chronologically, and as he found and spread out the earliest number, the date at the top of the page entered into his consciousness like a key slipping into a lock. It was the seventeenth of December: the date of the day after his arrival at Northridge. He glanced at the first page and read in blazing characters: "Reported Failure of Opal Cement Company. Lavington's name involved. Gigantic Exposure of Corruption Shakes Wall Street to Its Foundations."

He read on, and when he had finished the first paper he turned to the next. There was a gap of three days, but the Opal Cement "Investigation" still held the center of the stage. From its complex revelations of greed and ruin his eye wandered to the death notices, and he read: "Rainer. Suddenly, at Northridge, New Hampshire, Francis John, only son of the late . . ."

His eyes clouded, and he dropped the newspaper and sat for a long time with his face in his hands. When he looked up again he noticed that his gesture had pushed the other papers from the table and scattered them at his feet. The uppermost lay spread out before him, and heavily his eyes began their search again. "John Lavington comes forward with plan for reconstructing Company. Offers to put in ten millions of his own—The proposal under consideration by the District Attorney."

Ten millions . . . ten millions of his own. But if John Lavington was ruined? . . . Faxon stood up with a cry. That was it, then—that was what the warning meant! And if he had not fled from it, dashed wildly away from it into the night, he might have broken the spell of iniquity, the powers of darkness might not have prevailed! He caught up the pile of newspapers and began to glance through each in turn for the head-line: "Wills Admitted to Probate." In the last of all he found the paragraph he sought, and it stared up at him as if with Rainer's dying eyes.

That—*that* was what he had done! The powers of pity had singled him out to warn and save, and he had closed his ears to their call, and washed his hands of it, and fled. Washed his hands of it! That was the word. It caught him back to the dreadful moment in the lodge when, raising himself up from Rainer's side, he had looked at his hands and seen that they were red. . . .

## THE CHOICE

STILLING, THAT NIGHT after dinner, had surpassed himself. He always did, Wrayford reflected, when the small fry from Highfield came to dine. He, Cobham Stilling, who had to find his bearings and keep to his level in the big heedless ironic world of New York, dilated and grew vast in the congenial medium of Highfield. The Red House was the biggest house of the Highfield summer colony, and Cobham Stilling was its biggest man. No one else within a radius of a hundred miles (on a conservative estimate) had as many horses, as many greenhouses, as many servants, and assuredly no one else had three motors and a motorboat for the lake.

The motorboat was Stilling's latest hobby, and he rode—or steered—it in and out of the conversation all the evening, to the obvious edification of every one present save his wife and his visitor, Austin Wrayford. The interest of the latter two who, from opposite ends of the drawing-room, exchanged a fleeting glance when Stilling again launched his craft on the thin current of the talk—the interest of Mrs. Stilling and Wrayford had already lost its edge by protracted contact with the subject.

But the dinner-guests—the Rector, Mr. Swordsley, his wife Mrs. Swordsley, Lucy and Agnes Granger, their brother Addison, and young Jack Emmerton from Harvard—were all, for divers reasons, stirred to the proper pitch of feeling. Mr. Swordsley, no doubt, was saying to himself: "If my good parishioner here can afford to buy a motorboat, in addition to all the other expenditures which an establishment like this must entail, I certainly need not scruple to appeal to him again for a contribution for our Galahad Club." The Granger girls, meanwhile, were evoking visions of lakeside picnics, not unadorned with the presence of young Mr. Emmerton; while that youth himself speculated as to whether his affable host would let him, when he came back on his next vacation, "learn to run the thing himself"; and Mr. Addison Granger, the elderly bachelor brother of the volatile Lucy and Agnes, mentally formulated the precise phrase in which, in his next letter to his cousin Professor Spildyke of the University of East Latmos, he should allude to "our last delightful trip in my old friend Cobham Stilling's ten-thousand-dollar motor-launch"—for East Latmos was still in that primitive stage of culture on which five figures impinge.

Isabel Stilling, sitting beside Mrs. Swordsley, her bead slightly bent above the needlework with which on these occasions it was her old-fashioned habit to employ herself—Isabel also had doubtless her reflections to make. As Wrayford leaned back in his corner and looked at her across the wide flower-filled drawing-room he noted, first of all—for the how many hundredth time?—the play of her hands above the embroidery-frame, the shadow of the thick dark hair on her forehead, the lids over her somewhat full grey eyes. He noted all this with a conscious deliberateness of enjoyment, taking in unconsciously, at the same time, the particular quality in her attitude, in the fall of her dress and the turn of her head, which had set her for him, from the first day, in a separate world; then he said to himself: "She is certainly thinking: 'Where on earth will Cobham get the money to pay for it?'"

Stilling, cigar in mouth and thumbs in his waistcoat pockets, was impressively perorating from his usual dominant position on the hearth-rug.

"I said: 'If I have the thing at all, I want the best that can be got.' That's my way, you know, Swordsley; I suppose I'm what you'd call fastidious. Always was, about everything, from cigars to wom—" his eye met the apprehensive glance of Mrs. Swordsley, who looked like her husband with his clerical coat cut slightly lower—"so I said: 'If I have the thing at all, I want the best that can be got.' Nothing makeshift for me, no second-best. I never cared for the cheap and showy. I always say frankly to a man: 'If you can't give me a first-rate cigar, for the Lord's sake let me smoke my own.'" He paused to do so. "Well, if you have my standards, you can't buy a thing in a minute. You must look round, compare, select. I found there were lots of motor-boats on the market, just as there's lots of stuff called champagne. But I said to myself: 'Ten to one there's only one fit to buy, just as there's only one champagne fit for a gentleman to drink.' Argued like a lawyer, eh, Austin?" He tossed this to Wrayford. "Take me for one of your own trade, wouldn't you? Well, I'm not such a fool as I look. I suppose you fellows who are tied to the treadmill—excuse me, Swordsley, but work's work, isn't it?—I suppose you think a man like me has nothing to do but take it easy: loll through life like a woman. By George, sir, I'd like either of you to see the time it takes—I won't say the *brains*—but just the time it takes to pick out a good motor-boat. Why, I went—"

Mrs. Stilling set her embroidery-frame noiselessly on the table at her side, and turned her head toward Wrayford. "Would you mind ringing for the tray?"

The interruption helped Mrs. Swordsley to waver to her feet. "I'm afraid we ought really to be going; my husband has an early service tomorrow."

Her host intervened with a genial protest. "Going already? Nothing of the sort! Why, the night's still young, as the poet says. Long way from here to the rectory? Nonsense! In our little twenty-horse car we do it in five minutes—don't we, Belle? Ah, you're walking, to be sure—" Stilling's indulgent gesture seemed to concede that, in such a case, allowances must be made, and that he was the last man not to make them. "Well, then, Swordsley—" He held out a thick red hand that seemed to exude beneficence, and the clergyman, pressing it, ventured to murmur a suggestion.

"What, that Galahad Club again? Why, I thought my wife—Isabel, didn't we—No? Well, it must have been my mother, then. Of course, you know, anything my good mother gives is—well—virtually—You haven't asked her? Sure? I could have sworn; I get so many of these appeals. And in these times, you know, we have to go cautiously. I'm sure you recognize that yourself, Swordsley. With my obligations—here now, to show you don't bear malice, have a brandy and soda before you go. Nonsense, man! This brandy isn't liquor; it's liqueur. I picked it up last year in London—last of a famous lot from Lord St. Oswyn's cellar. Laid down here, it stood me at—Eh?" he broke off as his wife moved toward him. "Ah, yes, of course. Miss Lucy, Miss Agnes—a drop of soda-water? Look here, Addison, you won't refuse my tipple, I know. Well, take a cigar, at any rate, Swordsley. And, by the way, I'm afraid you'll have to go round the long way by the avenue to-night. Sorry, Mrs. Swordsley, but I forgot to tell them to leave the gate into the lane unlocked. Well, it's a jolly night, and I daresay you won't mind the extra turn along the lake. And, by Jove! if the moon's out, you'll have a glimpse of the motorboat. She's moored just out beyond our boat-house; and it's a privilege to look at her, I can tell you!"

The dispersal of his guests carried Stilling out into the hall, where his pleasantries reverberated under the oak rafters while the Granger girls were being muffled for the drive and the carriages summoned from the stables.

By a common impulse Mrs. Stilling and Wrayford had moved together toward the fire-place, which was hidden by a tall screen from the door into the hall. Wrayford leaned his elbow against the mantel-piece, and Mrs. Stilling stood beside him, her clasped hands hanging down before her.

"Have you anything more to talk over with him?" she asked.

"No. We wound it all up before dinner. He doesn't want to talk about it any more than he can help."

"It's so bad?"

"No; but this time he's got to pull up."

She stood silent, with lowered lids. He listened a moment, catching Stilling's farewell shout; then he moved a little nearer, and laid his hand on her arm.

"In an hour?"

She made an imperceptible motion of assent.

"I'll tell you about it then. The key's as usual?"

She signed another "Yes" and walked away with her long drifting step as her husband came in from the hall. He went up to the tray and poured himself out a tall glass of brandy and soda.

"The weather is turning queer—black as pitch. I hope the Swordsleys won't walk into the lake—involuntary immersion, eh? He'd come out a Baptist, I suppose. What'd the Bishop do in such a case? There's a problem for a lawyer, my boy!"

He clapped his hand on Wrayford's thin shoulder and then walked over to his wife, who was gathering up her embroidery silks and dropping them into her work-bag. Stilling took her by the arms and swung her playfully about so that she faced the lamplight.

"What's the matter with you tonight?"

"The matter?" she echoed, coloring a little, and standing very straight in her desire not to appear to shrink from his touch.

"You never opened your lips. Left me the whole job of entertaining those blessed people. Didn't she, Austin?"

Wrayford laughed and lit a cigarette.

"There! You see even Austin noticed it. What's the matter, I say? Aren't they good enough for you? I don't say they're particularly exciting; but, hang it! I like to ask them here—I like to give people pleasure."

"I didn't mean to be dull," said Isabel.

"Well, you must learn to make an effort. Don't treat people as if they weren't in the room just because they don't happen to amuse you. Do you know what they'll think? They'll think it's because you've got a bigger house and more money than they have. Shall

I tell you something? My mother said she'd noticed the same thing in you lately. She said she sometimes felt you looked down on her for living in a small house. Oh, she was half joking, of course; but you see you do give people that impression. I can't understand treating any one in that way. The more I have myself, the more I want to make other people happy."

Isabel gently freed herself and laid the work-bag on her embroidery-frame. "I have a headache; perhaps that made me stupid. I'm going to bed." She turned toward Wrayford and held out her hand. "Good night."

"Good night," he answered, opening the door for her.

When he turned back into the room, his host was pouring himself a third glass of brandy and soda.

"Here, have a nip, Austin? Gad, I need it badly, after the shaking up you gave me this afternoon." Stilling laughed and carried his glass to the hearth, where he took up his usual commanding position. "Why the deuce don't you drink something? You look as glum as Isabel. One would think you were the chap that had been hit by this business."

Wrayford threw himself into the chair from which Mrs. Stilling had lately risen. It was the one she usually sat in, and to his fancy a faint scent of her clung to it. He leaned back and looked up at Stilling.

"Want a cigar?" the latter continued. "Shall we go into the den and smoke?"

Wrayford hesitated. "If there's anything more you want to ask me about—"

"Gad, no! I had full measure and running over this afternoon. The deuce of it is, I don't see where the money's all gone to. Luckily I've got plenty of nerve; I'm not the kind of man to sit down and snivel because I've been touched in Wall Street."

Wrayford got to his feet again. "Then, if you don't want me, I think I'll go up to my room and put some finishing touches to a brief before I turn in. I must get back to town tomorrow afternoon."

"All right, then." Stilling set down his empty glass, and held out his hand with a tinge of alacrity. "Good night, old man."

They shook hands, and Wrayford moved toward the door.

"I say, Austin—stop a minute!" his host called after him. Wrayford turned, and the two men faced each other across the hearth-rug. Stilling's eyes shifted uneasily.

"There's one thing more you can do for me before you leave. Tell Isabel about that loan; explain to her that she's got to sign a note for it."

Wrayford, in his turn, flushed slightly. "You want me to tell her?"

"Hang it! I'm soft-hearted—that's the worst of me."

Stilling moved toward the tray, and lifted the brandy decanter. "And she'll take it better from you; she'll *have* to take it from you. She's proud. You can take her out for a row tomorrow morning—look here, take her out in the motor-launch if you like. I meant to have a spin in it myself; but if you'll tell her—"

Wrayford hesitated. "All right, I'll tell her."

"Thanks a lot, my dear fellow. And you'll make her see it wasn't my fault, eh? Women are awfully vague about money, and she'll think it's all right if you back me up."

Wrayford nodded. "As you please."

"And, Austin—there's just one more thing. You needn't say anything to Isabel about the other business—I mean about my mother's securities."

"Ah?" said Wrayford, pausing.

Stilling shifted from one foot to the other. "I'd rather put that to the old lady myself. I can make it clear to her. She idolizes me, you know—and, hang it! I've got a good record.

Up to now, I mean. My mother's been in clover since I married; I may say she's been my first thought. And I don't want her to hear of this beastly business from Isabel. Isabel's a little harsh at times—and of course this isn't going to make her any easier to live with."

"Very well," said Wrayford.

Stilling, with a look of relief, walked toward the window which opened on the terrace. "Gad! what a queer night! Hot as the kitchen-range. Shouldn't wonder if we had a squall before morning. I wonder if that infernal skipper took in the launch's awnings before he went home."

Wrayford stopped with his hand on the door. "Yes, I saw him do it. She's shipshape for the night."

"Good! That saves me a run down to the shore."

"Good night, then," said Wrayford.

"Good night, old man. You'll tell her?"

"I'll tell her."

"And mum about my mother!" his host called after him.

## II

THE darkness had thinned a little when Wrayford scrambled down the steep path to the shore. Though the air was heavy the threat of a storm seemed to have vanished, and now and then the moon's edge showed above a torn slope of cloud.

But in the thick shrubbery about the boathouse the darkness was still dense, and Wrayford had to strike a match before he could find the lock and insert his key. He left the door unlatched, and groped his way in. How often he had crept into this warm pine-scented obscurity, guiding himself by the edge of the bench along the wall, and hearing the soft lap of water through the gaps in the flooring! He knew just where one had to duck one's head to avoid the two canoes swung from the rafters, and just where to put his hand on the latch of the farther door that led to the broad balcony above the lake.

The boathouse represented one of Stilling's abandoned whims. He had built it some seven years before, and for a time it had been the scene of incessant nautical exploits. Stilling had rowed, sailed, paddled indefatigably, and all Highfield had been impressed to bear him company, and to admire his versatility. Then motors had come in, and he had forsaken aquatic sports for the flying chariot. The canoes of birch-bark and canvas had been hoisted to the roof, the sail-boat had rotted at her moorings, and the movable floor of the boat-house, ingeniously contrived to slide back on noiseless runners, had lain undisturbed through several seasons. Even the key of the boat-house had been mislaid— by Isabel's fault, her husband said—and the locksmith had to be called in to make a new one when the purchase of the motor-boat made the lake once more the center of Stilling's activity.

As Wrayford entered he noticed that a strange oily odor overpowered the usual scent of dry pine-wood; and at the next step his foot struck an object that rolled noisily across the boards. He lighted another match, and found he had overturned a can of grease which the boatman had no doubt been using to oil the runners of the sliding floor.

Wrayford felt his way down the length of the boathouse, and softly opening the balcony door looked out on the lake. A few yards away, he saw the launch lying at anchor in the veiled moonlight; and just below him, on the black water, was the dim outline of the skiff which the boatman kept to paddle out to her. The silence was so intense that Wrayford fancied he heard a faint rustling in the shrubbery on the high bank behind the boat-house, and the crackle of gravel on the path descending to it.

He closed the door again and turned back into the darkness; and as he did so the other door, on the land-side, swung inward, and he saw a figure in the dim opening. Just enough light entered through the round holes above the respective doors to reveal Mrs. Stilling's cloaked outline, and to guide her to him as he advanced. But before they met she stumbled and gave a little cry.

"What is it?" he exclaimed.

"My foot caught; the floor seemed to give way under me. Ah, of course—" she bent down in the darkness—"I saw the men oiling it this morning."

Wrayford caught her by the arm. "Do take care! It might be dangerous if it slid too easily. The water's deep under here."

"Yes; the water's very deep. I sometimes wish—" She leaned against him without finishing her sentence, and he put both arms about her.

"Hush!" he said, his lips on hers.

Suddenly she threw her head back and seemed to listen.

"What's the matter? What do you hear?"

"I don't know." He felt her trembling. "I'm not sure this place is as safe as it used to be—"

Wrayford held her to him reassuringly. "But the boatman sleeps down at the village; and who else should come here at this hour?"

"Cobham might. He thinks of nothing but the launch.'"

"He won't tonight. I told him I'd seen the skipper put her shipshape, and that satisfied him."

"Ah—he did think of coming, then?"

"Only for a minute, when the sky looked so black half an hour ago, and he was afraid of a squall. It's clearing now, and there's no danger."

He drew her down on the bench, and they sat a moment or two in silence, her hands in his. Then she said: "You'd better tell me."

Wrayford gave a faint laugh. "Yes, I suppose I had. In fact, he asked me to."

"He asked you to?"

"Yes."

She uttered an exclamation of contempt. "He's afraid!"

Wrayford made no reply, and she went on: "I'm not. Tell me everything, please."

"Well, he's chucked away a pretty big sum again—"

"How?"

"He says he doesn't know. He's been speculating, I suppose. The madness of making him your trustee!"

She drew her hands away. "You know why I did it. When we married I didn't want to put him in the false position of the man who contributes nothing and accepts everything; I wanted people to think the money was partly his."

"I don't know what you've made people think; but you've been eminently successful in one respect. *He* thinks it's all his—and he loses it as if it were."

"There are worse things. What was it that he wished you to tell me?"

"That you've got to sign another promissory note—for fifty thousand this time."

"Is that all?"

Wrayford hesitated; then he said: "Yes—for the present."

She sat motionless, her head bent, her hand resting passively in his.

He leaned nearer. "What did you mean just now, by worse things?"

She hesitated. "Haven't you noticed that he's been drinking a great deal lately?"

"Yes; I've noticed."

They were both silent; then Wrayford broke out, with sudden vehemence: "And yet you won't—"

"Won't?"

"Put an end to it. Good God! Save what's left of your life."

She made no answer, and in the stillness the throb of the water underneath them sounded like the beat of a tormented heart.

"Isabel—" Wrayford murmured. He bent over to kiss her. "Isabel! I can't stand it! listen—"

"No; no. I've thought of everything. There's the boy—the boy's fond of him. He's not a bad father."

"Except in the trifling matter of ruining his son."

"And there's his poor old mother. He's a good son, at any rate; he'd never hurt her. And I know her. If I left him, she'd never take a penny of my money. What she has of her own is not enough to live on; and how could he provide for her? If I put him out of doors, I should be putting his mother out too."

"You could arrange that—there are always ways."

"Not for her! She's proud. And then she believes in him. Lots of people believe in him, you know. It would kill her if she ever found out."

Wrayford made an impatient movement. "It will kill you if you stay with him to prevent her finding out."

She laid her other hand on his. "Not while I have you."

"Have me? In this way?"

"In any way."

"My poor girl—poor child!"

"Unless you grow tired—unless your patience gives out."

He was silent, and she went on insistently: "Don't you suppose I've thought of that too—foreseen it?"

"Well—and then?" he exclaimed.

"I've accepted that too."

He dropped her hands with a despairing gesture. "Then, indeed, I waste my breath!"

She made no answer, and for a time they sat silent again, a little between them. At length he asked: "You're not crying?"

"No."

"I can't see your face, it's grown so dark."

"Yes. The storm must be coming." She made a motion as if to rise.

He drew close and put his arm about her. "Don't leave me yet. You know I must go tomorrow." He broke off with a laugh. "I'm to break the news to you tomorrow morning, by the way; I'm to take you out in the motor launch and break it to you." He dropped her hands and stood up. "Good God! How can I go and leave you here with him?"

"You've done it often."

"Yes; but each time it's more damnable. And then I've always had a hope—"

She rose also. "Give it up! Give it up!"

"You've none, then, yourself?"

She was silent, drawing the folds of her cloak about her.

"None—none?" he insisted.

He had to bend his head to hear her answer. "Only one!"

"What, my dearest? What?"

"Don't touch me! That he may die!"

They drew apart again, hearing each other's quick breathing through the darkness.

"You wish that too?" he said.

"I wish it always—every day, every hour, every moment!" She paused, and then let the words break from her. "You'd better know it; you'd better know the worst of me. I'm not the saint you suppose; the duty I do is poisoned by the thoughts I think. Day by day, hour by hour, I wish him dead. When he goes out I pray for something to happen; when he comes back I say to myself: 'Are you here again?' When I hear of people being killed in accidents, I think: 'Why wasn't he there?' When I read the death-notices in the paper I say: 'So-and-so was just his age.' When I see him taking such care of his health and his diet—as he does, you know, except when he gets reckless and begins to drink too much—when I see him exercising and resting, and eating only certain things, and weighing himself, and feeling his muscles, and boasting that he hasn't gained a pound, I think of the men who die from overwork, or who throw their lives away for some great object, and I say to myself: 'What can kill a man who thinks only of himself?' And night after night I keep myself from going to sleep for fear I may dream that he's dead. When I dream that, and wake and find him there it's worse than ever—"

She broke off with a sob, and the loud lapping of the water under the floor was like the beat of a rebellious heart.

"There, you know the truth!" she said.

He answered after a pause: "People do die."

"Do they?" She laughed. "Yes—in happy marriages!"

They were silent again, and Isabel turned, feeling her way toward the door. As she did so, the profound stillness was broken by the sound of a man's voice trolling out unsteadily the refrain of a music-hall song.

The two in the boat-house darted toward each other with a simultaneous movement, clutching hands as they met.

"He's coming!" Isabel said.

Wrayford disengaged his hands.

"He may only be out for a turn before he goes to bed. Wait a minute. I'll see." He felt his way to the bench, scrambled up on it, and stretching his body forward managed to bring his eyes in line with the opening above the door.

"It's as black as pitch. I can't see anything."

The refrain rang out nearer.

"Wait! I saw something twinkle. There it is again. It's his cigar. It's coming this way—down the path."

There was a long rattle of thunder through the stillness.

"It's the storm!" Isabel whispered. "He's coming to see about the launch."

Wrayford dropped noiselessly from the bench and she caught him by the arm.

"Isn't there time to get up the path and slip under the shrubbery?"

"No, he's in the path now. He'll be here in two minutes. He'll find us."

He felt her hand tighten on his arm.

"You must go in the skiff, then. It's the only way."

"And let him find you? And hear my oars? Listen—there's something I must say."

She flung her arms about him and pressed her face to his.

"Isabel, just now I didn't tell you everything. He's ruined his mother—taken everything of hers too. And he's got to tell her; it can't be kept from her."

She uttered an incredulous exclamation and drew back.

"Is this the truth? Why didn't you tell me before?"

"He forbade me. You were not to know."

Close above them, in the shrubbery, Stilling warbled:

> *"Nita, Juanita,*
> *Ask thy soul if we must part!"*

Wrayford held her by both arms. "Understand this—if he comes in, he'll find us. And if there's a row you'll lose your boy."

She seemed not to hear him. "You—you—you—he'll kill you!" she exclaimed.

Wrayford laughed impatiently and released her, and she stood shrinking against the wall, her hands pressed to her breast. Wrayford straightened himself and she felt that he was listening intently. Then he dropped to his knees and laid his hands against the boards of the sliding floor. It yielded at once, as if with a kind of evil alacrity; and at their feet they saw, under the motionless solid night, another darker night that moved and shimmered. Wrayford threw himself back against the opposite wall, behind the door.

A key rattled in the lock, and after a moment's fumbling the door swung open. Wrayford and Isabel saw a man's black bulk against the obscurity. It moved a step, lurched forward, and vanished out of sight. From the depths beneath them there came a splash and a long cry.

"Go! go!" Wrayford cried out, feeling blindly for Isabel in the blackness.

"Oh—" she cried, wrenching herself away from him.

He stood still a moment, as if dazed; then she saw him suddenly plunge from her side, and heard another splash far down, and a tumult in the beaten water.

In the darkness she cowered close to the opening, pressing her face over the edge, and crying out the name of each of the two men in turn. Suddenly she began to see: the obscurity was less opaque, as if a faint moon-pallor diluted it. Isabel vaguely discerned the two shapes struggling in the black pit below her; once she saw the gleam of a face. She glanced up desperately for some means of rescue, and caught sight of the oars ranged on brackets against the wall. She snatched down the nearest, bent over the opening, and pushed the oar down into the blackness, crying out her husband's name.

The clouds had swallowed the moon again, and she could see nothing below her; but she still heard the tumult in the beaten water.

"Cobham! Cobham!" she screamed.

As if in answer, she felt a mighty clutch on the oar, a clutch that strained her arms to the breaking-point as she tried to brace her knees against the runners of the sliding floor.

"Hold on! Hold on! Hold on!" a voice gasped out from below; and she held on, with racked muscles, with bleeding palms, with eyes straining from their sockets, and a heart that tugged at her as the weight was tugging at the oar.

Suddenly the weight relaxed, and the oar slipped up through her lacerated hands. She felt a wet body scrambling over the edge of the opening, and Stilling's voice, raucous and strange, groaned out, close to her: "God! I thought I was done for."

He staggered to his knees, coughing and sputtering, and the water dripped on her from his streaming clothes.

She flung herself down, again, straining over the pit. Not a sound came up from it.

"Austin! Austin! Quick! Another oar!" she shrieked.

Stilling gave a cry. "My God! Was it Austin? What in hell—Another oar? No, no;

untie the skiff, I tell you. But it's no use. Nothing's any use. I felt him lose hold as I came up."

After that she was conscious of nothing till, hours later, as it appeared to her, she became dimly aware of her husband's voice, high, hysterical and important, haranguing a group of scared lantern-struck faces that had sprung up mysteriously about them in the night.

"Poor Austin! Poor Wrayford . . . terrible loss to me . . . mysterious dispensation. Yes, I do feel gratitude—miraculous escape—but I wish old Austin could have known that I was saved!"

## UNCOLLECTED STORY (1919)

## WRITING A WAR STORY

As first published in Woman's Home Companion, September, 1919

MISS IVY SPANG of Cornwall-on-Hudson had published a little volume of verse before the war.

It was called "Vibrations," and was preceded by a "Foreword" in which the author stated that she had yielded to the urgent request of "friends" in exposing her first-born to the public gaze. The public had not gazed very hard or very long, but the Cornwall-on-Hudson *News-Dispatch* had a flattering notice by the wife of the rector of St. Dunstan's (signed "Asterisk"), in which, while the somewhat unconventional sentiment of the poems was gently deprecated, a graceful and lady-like tribute was paid to the "brilliant daughter of one of our most prominent and influential citizens, who has voluntarily abandoned *the primrose way of pleasure* to scale *the rugged heights of Parnassus.*"

Also, after sitting one evening next to him at a bohemian dinner in New York, Miss Spang was honored by an article by the editor of *Zigzag,* the new "Weekly Journal of Defiance," in which that gentleman hinted that there was more than she knew in Ivy Spang's poems, and that their esoteric significance showed that she was a *vers-librist* in thought as well as in technique. He added that they would "gain incommensurably in meaning" when she abandoned the superannuated habit of beginning each line with a capital letter.

The editor sent a heavily-marked copy to Miss Spang, who was immensely flattered, and felt that at last she had been understood. But nobody she knew read *Zigzag,* and nobody who read *Zigzag* seemed to care to know her. So nothing in particular resulted from this tribute to her genius.

Then the war came, and she forgot all about writing poetry.

The war was two years old, and she had been pouring tea once a week for a whole winter in a big Anglo-American hospital in Paris, when one day, as she was passing through a flower-edged court on her way to her ward, she heard one of the doctors say to a pale gentleman in civilian clothes and spectacles, "But I believe that pretty Miss Spang writes. If you want an American contributor, why not ask her?" And the next moment the pale gentleman had been introduced and, beaming anxiously at her through his spectacles, was urging her to contribute a rattling war story to *The Man-at-Arms,* a monthly publication that was to bring joy to the wounded and disabled in British hospitals.

"A good rousing story, Miss Spang; a dash of sentiment of course, but nothing to depress or discourage. I'm sure you catch my meaning? A tragedy with a happy ending—that's about the idea. But I leave it to you; with your large experience of hospital work of course you know just what hits the poor fellows' taste. Do you think you could have it ready for our first number? And have you a portrait—if possible in nurse's dress—to publish with it? The Queen of Norromania has promised us a poem, with a picture of herself giving the baby Crown Prince his morning tub. We want the first number to be an 'actuality,' as the French say; all the articles written by people who've done the thing themselves, or seen it done. You've been at the front, I suppose? As far as Rheims, once? That's capital! Give us a good stirring trench story, with a Coming-Home scene to close with . . . a Christmas scene, if you can manage it, as we hope to be out in November. Yes—that's the very thing; and I'll try to get Sargent to do us the wounded V. C. coming back to the old home on Christmas Eve—snow effect."

It was lucky that Ivy Spang's leave was due about that time, for, devoted though she was to her patients, the tea she poured for them might have suffered from her absorption in her new task.

Was it any wonder that she took it seriously?

She, Ivy Spang, of Cornwall-on-Hudson, had been asked to write a war story for the opening number of *The Man-at-Arms*, to which Queens and Archbishops and Field Marshals were to contribute poetry and photographs and patriotic sentiment in autograph! And her full-length photograph in nurse's dress was to precede her prose; and in the table of contents she was to figure as "Ivy Spang, author of *Vibrations: A Book of Verse*."

She was dizzy with triumph, and went off to hide her exultation in a quiet corner of Brittany, where she happened to have an old governess, who took her in and promised to defend at all costs the sacredness of her mornings—for Ivy knew that the morning hours of great authors were always "sacred."

She shut herself up in her room with a ream of mauve paper, and began to think.

At first the process was less exhilarating than she had expected. She knew so much about the war that she hardly knew where to begin; she found herself suffering from a plethora of impressions.

Moreover, the more she thought of the matter, the less she seemed to understand how a war story—or any story, for that matter—was written. Why did stories ever begin, and why did they ever leave off? Life didn't—it just went on and on.

This unforeseen problem troubled her exceedingly, and on the second morning she stealthily broke from her seclusion and slipped out for a walk on the beach. She had been ashamed to make known her projected escapade, and went alone, leaving her faithful governess to mount guard on her threshold while she sneaked out by a back way.

There were plenty of people on the beach, and among them some whom she knew; but she dared not join them lest they should frighten away her "Inspiration." She knew that "Inspirations" were fussy and contrarious, and she felt rather as if she were dragging along a reluctant dog on a string.

"If you wanted to stay indoors, why didn't you say so?" she grumbled to it. But the inspiration continued to sulk.

She wandered about under the cliff till she came to an empty bench, where she sat down and gazed at the sea. After a while her eyes were dazzled by the light, and she turned them toward the bench and saw lying on it a battered magazine—the midsummer "All-Story" number *of Fact and Fiction*. Ivy pounced upon it.

She had heard a good deal about not allowing one's self to be "influenced," about jealously guarding one's originality, and so forth; the editor of *Zigzag* had been particularly strong on that theme. But her story had to be written, and she didn't know how to begin it; so she decided just to glance casually at a few beginnings.

The first tale in the magazine was signed by a name great in fiction, one of the most famous names of the past generation of novelists. "The opening sentence ran: "In the month of October, 1914—" and Ivy turned the page impatiently. She may not have known much about story-writing, but she did know that *that* kind of a beginning was played out. She turned to the next.

"'My God!' roared the engineer, tightening his grasp on the lever, while the white, sneering face under the red lamp . . ."

No; that was beginning to be out of date, too.

"They sat there and stared at it in silence. Neither spoke; but the woman's heart ticked like a watch."

That was better; but best of all she liked: "Lee Lorimer leaned to him across the flowers. She had always known that this was coming . . ." Ivy could imagine tying a story on to *that*.

But she had promised to write a war story; and in a war story the flowers must be at the end and not at the beginning.

At any rate, there was one clear conclusion to be drawn from the successive study of all these opening paragraphs; and that was that you must begin in the middle, and take for granted that your reader knew what you were talking about.

Yes; but where was the middle, and how could your reader know what you were talking about when you didn't know yourself?

After some reflection, and more furtive scrutiny of *Fact and Fiction*, the puzzled authoress decided that perhaps, if you pretended hard enough that you knew what your story was about, you might end by finding out toward the last page. "After all, if the reader can pretend, the author ought to be able to," she reflected. And she decided (after a cautious glance over her shoulder) to steal the magazine and take it home with her for private dissection.

On the threshold she met her governess, who beamed on her tenderly.

"Chérie, I saw you slip off, but I didn't follow. I knew you wanted to be alone with your inspiration." Mademoiselle lowered her voice to add: "Have you found your plot?"

Ivy tapped her gently on the wrinkled cheek. "Dear old Madsy! People don't bother with plots nowadays."

"Oh, don't they, darling? Then it must be very much easier," said Mademoiselle. But Ivy was not so sure—

After a day's brooding over *Fact and Fiction*, she decided to begin on the empiric system. ("It's sure to come to me as I go along," she thought.) So she sat down before the mauve paper and wrote "A shot rang out—"

But just as she was appealing to her Inspiration to suggest the next phrase a horrible doubt assailed her, and she got up and turned to *Fact and Fiction*. Yes, it was just as she had feared, the last story in *Fact and Fiction* began: "A shot rang out—"

Its place on the list showed what the editor and his public thought of that kind of an opening, and her contempt for it was increased by reading the author's name. The story was signed "Edda Clubber Hump." Poor thing!

Ivy sat down and gazed at the page which she had polluted with that silly sentence.

And now (as they often said in *Fact and Fiction*) a strange thing happened. The sentence was there—she had written it—it *was* the first sentence on the first page of her story, it was the first sentence of her story. It was there, it had gone out of her, got away from her, and she seemed to have no further control of it. She could imagine no other way of beginning, now that she had made the effort of beginning in that way.

She supposed that was what authors meant when they talked about being "mastered by their Inspiration." She began to hate her Inspiration.

On the fifth day an abased and dejected Ivy confided to her old governess that she didn't believe she knew how to write a short story.

"If they'd only asked me for poetry!" she wailed.

She wrote to the editor of *The Man-at-Arms*, begging for permission to substitute a sonnet; but he replied firmly, if flatteringly, that they counted on a story, and had measured their space accordingly—adding that they already had rather more poetry than the first number could hold. He concluded by reminding her that he counted on receiving her contribution not later than September first; and it was now the tenth of August.

"It's all so sudden," she murmured to Mademoiselle, as if she were announcing her engagement.

"Of course, dearest—of course! I quite understand. How could the editor expect you to be tied to a date? But so few people know what the artistic temperament is; they seem to think one can dash off a story as easily as one makes an omelet."

Ivy smiled in spite of herself. "Dear Madsy, what an unlucky simile! So few people make good omelets."

"Not in France," said Mademoiselle firmly.

Her former pupil reflected. "In France a good many people have written good short stories, too—but I'm sure they were given more than three weeks to learn how. Oh, what shall I do?" she groaned.

The two pondered long and anxiously; and at last the governess modestly suggested: "Supposing you were to begin by thinking of a subject?"

"Oh, my dear, the subject's nothing!" exclaimed Ivy, remembering some contemptuous statement to that effect by the editor of *Zigzag*.

"Still—in writing a story, one has to have a subject. Of course I know it's only the treatment that really matters; but the treatment, naturally, would be yours, quite yours. . . ."

The authoress lifted a troubled gaze upon her Mentor. "What are you driving at, Madsy?"

"Only that during my year's work in the hospital here I picked up a good many stories—pathetic, thrilling, moving stories of our poor poilus; and in the evening sometimes I used to jot them down, just as the soldiers told them to me—oh, without any art at all . . . simply for myself, you understand. . . ."

Ivy was on her feet in an instant. Since even Mademoiselle admitted that "only the treatment really mattered," why should she not seize on one of these artless tales and transform it into Literature? The more she considered the idea, the more it appealed to her; she remembered Shakespeare and Moliere, and said gayly to her governess: "You darling Madsy! Do lend me your book to look over—and we'll be collaborators!"

"Oh—collaborators!" blushed the governess, overcome. But she finally yielded to her charge's affectionate insistence, and brought out her shabby copybook, which began with lecture notes on Mr. Bergson's course at the Sorbonne in 1913, and suddenly switched off to "Military Hospital No. 13. November, 1914. Long talk with the Chasseur

Alpin Emile Durand, wounded through the knee and the left lung at the Hautes Chaumes. I have decided to write down his story. . . ."

Ivy carried the little book off to bed with her, inwardly smiling at the fact that the narrative, written in a close, tremulous hand, covered each side of the page, and poured on and on without a paragraph—a good deal like life. Decidedly, poor Mademoiselle did not even know the rudiments of literature!

The story, not without effort, gradually built itself up about the adventures of Emile Durand. Notwithstanding her protests, Mademoiselle, after a day or two, found herself called upon in an advisory capacity, and finally as a collaborator. She gave the tale a certain consecutiveness, and kept Ivy to the main point when her pupil showed a tendency to wander; but she carefully revised and polished the rustic speech in which she had originally transcribed the tale, so that it finally issued forth in the language that a young lady writing a composition on the Battle of Hastings would have used in Mademoiselle's school days.

Ivy decided to add a touch of sentiment to the anecdote, which was purely military, both because she knew the reader was entitled to a certain proportion of "heart interest," and because she wished to make the subject her own by this original addition. The revisions and transpositions which these changes necessitated made the work one of uncommon difficulty; and one day, in a fit of discouragement, Ivy privately decided to notify the editor of *The Man-at-Arms* that she was ill and could not fulfill her engagement.

But that very afternoon the "artistic" photographer to whom she had posed for her portrait sent home the proofs; and she saw herself, exceedingly long, narrow and sinuous, robed in white and monastically veiled, holding out a refreshing beverage to an invisible sufferer with a gesture half way between Mélisande lowering her braid over the balcony and Florence Nightingale advancing with the lamp.

The photograph was really too charming to be wasted, and Ivy, feeling herself forced onward by an inexorable fate, sat down again to battle with the art of fiction. Her perseverance was rewarded, and after a while the fellow authors (though Mademoiselle disclaimed any right to the honors of literary partnership) arrived at what seemed to both a satisfactory result.

"You've written a very beautiful story, my dear," Mademoiselle sighed with moist eyes; and Ivy modestly agreed that she had.

The task was finished on the last day of her leave; and the next morning she traveled back to Paris, clutching the manuscript to her bosom, and forgetting to keep an eye on the bag that contained her passport and money, in her terror lest the precious pages should be stolen.

As soon as the tale was typed she did it up in a heavily-sealed envelope (she knew that only silly girls used blue ribbon for the purpose), and dispatched it to the pale gentleman in spectacles, accompanied by the Mélisande-Nightingale photograph. The receipt of both was acknowledged by a courteous note (she had secretly hoped for more enthusiasm), and thereafter life became a desert waste of suspense. The very globe seemed to cease to turn on its axis while she waited for *The Man-at-Arms* to appear.

Finally one day a thick packet bearing an English publisher's name was brought to her: she undid it with trembling fingers, and there, beautifully printed on the large rough pages, her story stood out before her.

At first, in that heavy text, on those heavy pages, it seemed to her a pitifully small thing, hopelessly insignificant and yet pitilessly conspicuous. It was as though words meant to be murmured to sympathetic friends were being megaphoned into the ear of a heedless universe.

Then she began to turn the pages of the review: she analyzed the poems, she read the Queen of Norromania's domestic confidences, and she looked at the portraits of the authors. The latter experience was peculiarly comforting. The Queen was rather good-looking—for a Queen—but her hair was drawn back from the temples as if it were wound round a windlass, and stuck out over her forehead in the good old-fashioned Royal Highness fuzz; and her prose was oddly built out of London drawing-room phrases grafted onto German genitives and datives. It was evident that neither Ivy's portrait nor her story would suffer by comparison with the royal contribution.

But most of all was she comforted by the poems. They were nearly all written on Kipling rhythms that broke down after two or three wheezy attempts to "carry on," and their knowing mixture of slang and pathos seemed oddly old-fashioned to the author of "Vibrations." Altogether, it struck her that *The Man-at-Arms* was made up in equal parts of tired compositions by people who knew how to write, and artless prattle by people who didn't. Against such a background "His Letter Home" began to loom up rather large.

At any rate, it took such a place in her consciousness for the next day or two that it was bewildering to find that no one about her seemed to have heard of it. "The Man-at-Arms" was conspicuously shown in the windows of the principal English and American book shops, but she failed to see it lying on her friends' tables, and finally, when her tea-pouring day came round, she bought a dozen copies and took them up to the English ward of her hospital, which happened to be full at the time.

It was not long before Christmas, and the men and officers were rather busy with home correspondence and the undoing and doing-up of seasonable parcels; but they all received *The Man-at-Arms* with an appreciative smile, and were most awfully pleased to know that Miss Spang had written something in it. After the distribution of her tale Miss Spang became suddenly hot and shy, and slipped away before they had begun to read her.

The intervening week seemed long; and it was marked only by the appearance of a review of *The Man-at-Arms* in the *Times*—a long and laudatory article—in which, by some odd accident, "His Letter Home" and its author were not so much as mentioned. Abridged versions of this notice appeared in the English and American newspapers published in Paris, and one anecdotic and intimate article in a French journal celebrated the maternal graces and literary art of the Queen of Norromania. It was signed "Fleur-de-Lys," and described a banquet at the Court of Norromania at which the writer hinted that she had assisted.

The following week, Ivy reentered her ward with a beating heart. On the threshold one of the nurses detained her with a smile.

"Do be a dear and make yourself specially nice to the new officer in Number 5; he's only been here two days, and he's rather down on his luck. Oh, by the way—he's the novelist, Harold Harbard; you know, the man who wrote the book they made such a fuss about."

Harold Harbard—the book they made such a fuss about! What a poor fool the woman was—not even to remember the title of *Broken Wings!* Ivy's heart stood still with the shock of the discovery; she remembered that she had left a copy of *The Man-at-Arms* in Number 5, and the blood coursed through her veins and flooded her to the forehead at the idea that Harold Harbard might at that very moment be reading "His Letter Home."

To collect herself, she decided to remain a while in the ward, serving tea to the soldiers and N. C. O.'s before venturing into Number 5, which the previous week had been occupied only by a polo-player drowsy with chloroform and uninterested in anything but his specialty. Think of Harold Harbard lying in the bed next to that man!

Ivy passed into the ward, and as she glanced down the long line of beds she saw several copies of *The Man-at-Arms* lying on them, and one special favorite of hers, a young lance-corporal, deep in its pages.

She walked down the ward, distributing tea and greetings; and she saw that her patients were all very glad to see her. They always were; but this time there was a certain unmistakable emphasis in their gladness; and she fancied they wanted her to notice it.

"Why," she cried gayly, "how uncommonly cheerful you all look!"

She was handing his tea to the young lance-corporal, who was usually the spokesman of the ward on momentous occasions. He lifted his eyes from the absorbed perusal of *The Man-at-Arms*, and as he did so she saw that it was open at the first page of her story.

"I say, you know," he said, "it's simply topping—and we're so awfully obliged to you for letting us see it."

She laughed, but would not affect incomprehension.

"That?" She laid a light finger on the review. "Oh, I'm glad—I'm awfully pleased, of course—you *do* really like it?" she stammered.

"Rather—all of us—most tremendously—!" came a chorus from the long line of beds.

Ivy tasted her highest moment of triumph. She drew a deep breath and shone on them with glowing cheeks.

"There couldn't be higher praise . . . there couldn't be better judges. . . . You think it's really like, do you?"

"Really like? Rather! It's just topping," rand out the unanimous response.

She choked with emotion. "Coming from you—from all of you—it makes me most awfully glad."

They all laughed together shyly, and then the lance-corporal spoke up.

"We admire it so much that we're going to ask you a most tremendous favor—"

"Oh, yes," came from the other beds.

"A favor—?"

"Yes; if it's not too much." The lance-corporal became eloquent. "To remember you by, and all your kindness; we want to know if you won't give one to each of us—"

("Why, of course, of course," Ivy glowed.)

"—to frame and take away with us," the lance-corporal continued sentimentally. "There's a chap here who makes rather jolly frames out of Vichy corks."

"Oh—" said Ivy, with a protracted gasp.

"You see, in your nurse's dress, it'll always be such a jolly reminder," said the lance-corporal, concluding his lesson.

"I never saw a jollier photo," spoke up a bold spirit.

"Oh, do say yes, nurse," the shyest of the patients softly whispered; and Ivy, bewildered between tears and laughter, said, "Yes."

It was evident that not one of them had read her story.

She stopped on the threshold of Number 5, her heart beating uncomfortably.

She had already recovered from her passing mortification: it was absurd to have imagined that the inmates of the ward, dear, gallant young fellows, would feel the subtle meaning of a story like "His Letter Home." But with Harold Harbard it was different. Now, indeed, she was to be face to face with a critic.

She stopped on the threshold, and as she did so she heard a burst of hearty, healthy laughter from within. It was not the voice of the polo-player; could it be that of the novelist?

She opened the door resolutely and walked in with her tray. The polo-player's bed was empty, and the face on the pillow of the adjoining cot was the brown, ugly, tumultuous-locked head of Harold Harbard, well-known to her from frequent photographs in the literary weeklies. He looked up as she came in, and said in a voice that seemed to continue his laugh: "Tea? Come, that's something like!" And he began to laugh again.

It was evident that he was still carrying on the thread of his joke, and as she approached with the tea she saw that a copy of *The Man-at-Arms* lay on the bed at his side, and that he had his hand between the open pages.

Her heart gave an apprehensive twitch, but she determined to carry off the situation with a high hand.

"How do you do, Captain Harbard? I suppose you're laughing at the way the Queen of Norromania's hair is done."

He met her glance with a humorous look, and shook his head, while the laughter still rippled the muscles of his throat.

"No—no; I've finished laughing at that. It was the next thing; what's it called? 'His Letter Home,' by—" The review dropped abruptly from his hands, his brown cheek paled, and he fixed her with a stricken stare.

"Good lord," he stammered out, "but it's *you!*"

She blushed all colors, and dropped into a seat at his side. "After all," she faltered, half-laughing too, "at least you read the story instead of looking at my photograph."

He continued to scrutinize her with a reviving eye. "Why—do you mean that everybody else—"

"All the ward over there," she assented, nodding in the direction of the door.

"They all forgot to read the story for gazing at its author?"

"Apparently." There was a painful pause. The review dropped from his lax hand.

"Your tea—?" she suggested, stiffly.

"Oh, yes; to be sure. . . . Thanks."

There was another silence, during which the act of pouring out the milk, and the dropping of the sugar into the cup, seemed to assume enormous magnitude, and make an echoing noise. At length Ivy said, with an effort at lightness, "Since I know who you are, Mr. Harbard,—would you mind telling me what you were laughing at in my story?"

He leaned back against the pillows and wrinkled his forehead anxiously.

"My dear Miss Spang, not in the least—if I *could.*"

"If you could?"

"Yes; I mean in any understandable way."

"In other words, you think it so silly that you don't dare to tell me anything more?"

He shook his head. "No; but it's queer—it's puzzling. You've got hold of a wonderfully good subject: and that's the main thing, of course—"

Ivy interrupted him eagerly. "The subject is the main thing?"

"Why, naturally; it's only the people without invention who tell you it isn't."

"Oh," she gasped, trying to readjust her carefully acquired theory of esthetics.

"You've got hold of an awfully good subject," Harbard continued; "but you've rather mauled it, haven't you?"

She sat before him with her head drooping, and the blood running back from her pale cheeks. Two tears had gathered on her lashes.

"There!" the novelist cried out irritably. "I knew that as soon as I was frank you'd resent it! What was the earthly use of asking me?"

She made no answer, and he added, lowering his voice a little, "Are you very angry with me, really?"

"No, of course not," she declared with a stony gayety.

"I'm so glad you're not; because I do want most awfully to ask you for one of these photographs," he concluded.

She rose abruptly from her seat. To save her life she could not conceal her disappointment. But she picked up the tray with feverish animation.

"A photograph? Of course—with pleasure. And now, if you've quite finished. I'm afraid I must run back to my teapot."

Harold Harbard lay on the bed and looked at her. As she reached the door he said, "Miss Spang!"

"Yes?" she rejoined, pausing reluctantly.

"You were angry just now because I didn't admire your story; and now you're angrier still because I do admire your photograph. Do you wonder that we novelists find such an inexhaustible field in Woman?"

THE END

www.ingramcontent.com/pod-product-compliance
Lightning Source LLC
Chambersburg PA
CBHW020240030726
47499CB00001B/2